"大学堂"开放给所有向往知识、崇尚科学，对宇宙和人生有所追求的人。

"大学堂"中展开一本本书，阐明各种传统和新兴的学科，导向真理和智慧。既有接引之台阶，又具深化之门径。无论何时，无论何地，请你把它翻开……

小说鉴赏

双语修订第 3 版

［美］布鲁克斯
［美］沃伦
编著

四川人民出版社

译者简介（部分）

主　万（1924—2004），资深翻译家，原名叶治，安徽桐城人。曾入复旦大学授翻译课，后转华东师范大学任教授，兼任全国美国文学研究会及上海翻译家协会理事；为上海外文学会、上海作家协会会员。主要译著有纳博科夫《洛丽塔》全译本、劳伦斯作品集、狄更斯《远大前程》、海明威《危险的夏天》、亨利·詹姆斯《阿斯彭文稿》，还有美国索尔·贝娄、德莱赛、格林等人的作品。

冯亦代（1913—2005），翻译家、著名作家、出版家和学者，原名贻德，浙江杭州人。主张以开放的态度译介当代外国文学，并在美国文学的评介研究方面做了不懈的努力。其代表译著有海明威《第五纵队》等近 20 本书，是最早把海明威引介到国内的学者。

丰子恺（1898—1975），翻译家、现代画家、文学家、艺术教育家，浙江崇德人。一生译著 30 多种，多为日本艺术作品，文学作品主要有日本紫式部《源氏物语》和俄国屠格涅夫《猎人笔记》。主张译者要准确表达原文的意思，但不必拘泥于原文的句法与结构；译出的中文要自然、流畅，为中国读者所习惯、爱读。

草　婴（1923—2015），著名翻译家，原名盛峻峰，浙江镇海人。原上海翻译家协会会长，现任中国译协副会长。从事俄语翻译，主要译著有《列夫·托尔斯泰小说全集》、肖洛霍夫《静静的顿河》、《一个人的遭遇》、《处女地》（第一部、第二部）和莱蒙托夫长篇小说《当代英雄》等。

汝　龙（1916—1991），江苏苏州人。杰出的俄罗斯文学翻译家，一名契诃夫专家。主要译著有列夫·托尔斯泰《复活》、《契诃夫全集》以及高尔基等人的作品。

郑克鲁（1939—2020），著名翻译家，广东中山人。北京大学西方语言文学系毕业，致力于引介法国文学，曾获法国政府受予的法国教育文化一级勋章。现任上海师范大学图书馆馆长。主要译著有《基督山恩仇记》、《茶花女》、《家族复仇》、《项链》、《于勒叔叔》、《蒂博一家》、《凡尔纳科幻小说》、乔治·桑《魔沼》、塞斯布隆《红衣主教》、比利时梅特林克《青鸟》和《外国现代派作品选》（合译）等。

董衡巽（1934—），浙江余姚人。中国社科院外文所研究员，全国美国文学研究会名誉会长。专攻美国文学，主要译著有海明威《老人与海》和《西班牙大地》、马克·吐温《百万英镑》（合译）和《王子与贫儿》、高尔斯华绥《苹果树》和约翰·斯坦贝克《人鼠之间》；编著有《海明威评传》、《美国文学简史》（合者）、《外国现代派作品选》（合译）等。

李文俊（1930—），著名翻译家，广东中山人。中国社科院外文所学术委员会委员、中国译协副会长，长期担任《世界文学》主编。主要译著有福克纳《喧哗与骚动》、《我弥留之际》、《去吧，摩西》和《押沙龙，押沙龙！》，《变形记》、《城堡》、《麦琪的礼物》、《伤心咖啡馆之歌》、《外国现代派作品选》（合译）等；著有《妇女画廊》、《福克纳评传》、《美国文学简史》（合著）等。

刘文荣（1952—），上海师范大学比较文学与世界文学副教授。主要译著有《人类动物园》，英国莫里斯《裸猿》；论著有《中外文化概论》、《19世纪英国小说史》等。

潘庆舲（1930—），资深翻译家，上海社科院文学所译审、教授，中国作协会员。从事英文、俄文翻译工作五十余年。作为我国波斯语言文学界有突出贡献的学者，曾获伊朗总统亲自授予的最高总统奖。主要译著有《波斯短篇小说集》、《九亭宫》、《波斯诗圣菲尔多西》、美国德莱塞《嘉莉妹妹》、《珍妮姑娘》、《美国悲剧》，辛克莱·路易斯《金融家》、《大街》、《巴比特》等。

万　紫（1915—），浙江杭州人，专业翻译家，从事英文、俄文翻译工作五十余年。主要译著有《卖牛奶的台维》、《喀尔巴阡山狂想曲》、《我们的夏天》、《大伟人华尔德传》、《欧文短篇小说选》、《新东方夜谭》、《一块牛排》（合译）、《热爱生命》（合译）等。

雨　宁（1919—1988），原名李震，翻译家，江苏丰县人。与万紫合译多部作品，主要译著有《阿尔罕伯拉》、《杰克·伦敦短篇小说选》（合译）、杰克·伦敦《热爱生命》（合译）、马克·吐温《卡拉维拉斯县驰名的跳蛙》、《一块牛排》（合译）、爱伦·坡《失窃的信》、《欧文短篇小说选》（合译）。

海　观（1908—1985），著名翻译家，全名朱海观，安徽寿县人。曾任中国作协会员、《世界文学》编委。主要译著有法捷耶夫等《苏联文学论集》、英国赖尔夫·派克《反和平的阴谋》、苏联伊林《人与自然》、陀思妥耶夫斯基《罪与罚》（合译）、美国沃克《战争风云》（合译）、海明威《老人与海》等。

屠　珍（1934—），翻译家，北京人，梅兰芳之子梅绍武之妻。对外国女作家及外国戏剧有很深的研究。多与梅绍武合译，主要译著有《福尔摩斯探案精选》、《重返呼啸山庄》、《马尔科姆》、《欧美短篇侦控小说选》、《瘦子》、尤奈斯库《阿迈迪或脱身术》、《阿尔巴尼亚短篇小说集》（与梅绍武合译），奥康纳《好人难寻》、克里斯蒂《赫尔克里的丰功伟绩》、希尔顿《鸳梦重温》、格林《炸弹宴会》；与梅绍武合编有《梅兰芳全集》。

杨岂深（1909—），翻译家，安徽怀宁人。复旦大学著名教授。主要译著有美国R·韦勒克《近代文学批评史》（合译）、福克纳《纪念爱米丽的一朵玫瑰花》；主编有《英国文学选读》、《美国文学选读》和《外国文学名著欣赏》。

郑启吟，福建人。主要译著有《动物园的故事》、《金丝雀》、《曼斯菲尔德短篇小说选》（合译）、哈代《彼特利克夫人》、《荒诞派戏剧集》（合译）、《外国现代派作品选》（合译）。

蓝仁哲（1940—），四川资阳人。四川外语学院教授，上海外国语大学博士生导师。主要译著有《加拿大短篇小说选》、《英国哲理散文选》、《托马斯·哈代诗选》、《大大方方的输家》、《八月之光》。

目　录
Contents

第七章　阅读材料 雨宁 译　　547
Stories for Reading

审阅者序

与这样一部书相遇也许是值得庆贺的。

这些年,无论是出入文学创作的圈子还是出入文学批评的圈子,时不时总有一种清冷的、空寂的孤独感莫名地从心野浮起,且由淡而浓。如此状态,倒也不是我没有朋友——我这样一个对人性抱了宽容态度的人是不可能没有朋友的;只是觉得自己对文学的领会、理解以及由此而产生的那一套文学主张,未免太有点儿单腔独调。面对那些陌生的目光,我觉得自己已是一个跟时代(时尚)严重脱节的落伍者。虽然在许多场合还是振振有辞地宣扬那些不合时宜的言论,但心中的虚弱感却是抑制不住地摇撼着自己。越是声调向高,就越是感到世界阔大无边、声音犹如被海绵吸尽一般凄清。我试图放弃自己的言说而进入那样一种趋之若鹜的话语,但总不能成功——不是我难以掌握那样一个知识系统,而是内心不肯对这样一种知识系统就范,加上性格的固执,尽管身处那样一个强大的语言场域之中,但依然还是你是你我是我,无法加入那样声势浩大、金碧辉煌的大合唱。为了避免这样的尴尬,这些年我一般也就不参加那些以文学的名义而召开的国内国外的各种学术会议了。但在 2005 年的夏天,我遭遇了美国人哈罗德·布鲁姆的《西方正典》,心中不禁感动不已。那个远在天涯的美国人对文学的认知与解释,甚至是在对观念的叙述上,都与我如出一辙,而这个人是个学界宿将、文坛大腕。那些天,我逢人必谈布鲁姆。从那个夏天开始,我的孤独感大大地缓解了。

没有想到,2006 年的秋天,我又与布鲁克斯和沃伦的《小说鉴赏》相遇。他们的出现,再度使我感到了极大的欣慰。布鲁姆、布鲁克斯和沃伦让我知道,在这一片天空下,并不只是我一个人是那样看待文学、解读文学的。环顾四周,我觉得天地间虽然苍茫四合,但天边却有熟悉而温和的人声。我再也不必去怀疑自己,只顾走下去就是了。我相信这远方的声音是实在的,是永恒的。

《小说鉴赏》将小说放置在文学而不是社会学的范畴中来加以分析——这样一种分析实在已经久违了。它感兴趣的问题是人物、叙述、结构、场景、情节、细节,在这里,小说是被当成艺术品来鉴赏而不仅仅是被当成社会学的一份材料来加以利用的。小说被看成是一种天然的、自足的形式。这种形式是小说特有的,不可替代的。优秀的小说家,必须重视形式,并处心积虑地在形式上显示自己的智慧和对形式做出别出心裁的处理。通过对作品细致入微的分析,该书将若干容易被我们忽略而又恰是小说成功的十分重要的元素向我们展示出来。它思考的问题看上去似乎都微不足道:这篇小说中为什么会设计一个旁观者?如果将这篇小说扩展成较长篇幅的小说,那么在现有的这篇作品中被省略的神秘中间部分可能是什么?为什么要通过万卡写信的方式诉说万卡的苦难处境而不是直接由作者去叙述?这种别具一格的手法是否有利于小说情节的推进？这个人物为什么会被安排在这一刻而不是那一刻出场？这段风景描写对于氛围的营造究竟有何意义？那女人为什么在说这句话时是"突然发出一阵狂叫"而不是泪流满面？为什么用这么多的笔墨去描摹那个人物的姿态？……

如此精微地解读小说，这在近20年时间的中国文学批评中，几乎已经绝迹。中国文学批评进入了有史以来最好大喜功的时期。批评家不再安于批评家的角色，而一个个争当起思想家来。没有人再有耐心去关注布鲁克斯和沃伦的问题，话题一天天地大了起来，直到与天地相当甚至与宇宙相当。"深刻"二字犹如头上悬剑，催迫着他们一路向前去追寻硕大的话题。说是评论小说，而实际上是扯不上几句，就早撇开作品撒开欢儿往前奔突了。评论小说只是一个幌子，心机全在比试所谓的文化大题上。这里没有文学，没有形式，没有艺术，而只有与文学无关的社会的、政治的、伦理的、哲学的、神话学的豪华理论。谁也不回答这样的问题：我们为什么会指认它是一篇小说？为什么确认它是一篇好小说？其结果是托尔斯泰、鲁迅就只剩下一个思想家的身影在高空中飘忽，而文学家的身影则荡然无存；殊不知这些人被认定为思想家正是在他作为一个文学家的前提下被认定的，这样的思想家与一般意义上的思想家有天壤之别，他们的思想只依附于文学而存在。关于文学的评论和关于文学的会议，雄辩滔滔、一泻千里，谈论的话题很少有文学本体的话题，而尽是政治、革命、现代性、全球化、三农、第三世界、殖民主义、独裁之类的话题。这些批评家们在布罗姆的眼中，是"业余的社会政治家、半吊子社会学家、不胜任的人类学家、平庸的哲学家以及武断的文化史家"，似乎还可加上一条：捕风捉影的巫术术士。

近二十年时间中，中国批评日益染上一个难以扳正的毛病：恋思癖。一部作品来到世间，批评家们蜂拥而上，但角度只有一个：解读它的思想或者是用思想加以解读。何以评论？惟有思想。难道仅思想一维就能判断作品高下了吗？艺术呢？形式呢？姑且抛开形式不论，一部好的作品，其维度也不当是一项，还有审美之维、情感之维等等——难道这些维度其价值就一定比思想之维低吗？就布罗姆所指认的"正典"来看，那些具有文学史意义的大师们之所以是大师，就在于他们能将各种维度均衡地结合在一起。

就我个人的创作经验以及我从同行朋友们那里感受到的是：一个小说家一旦确定基本写作意图之后，纠缠于心的就是如何干好这件活。他们思量的、盘算的、运筹的恰恰是布鲁克斯和沃伦所关心的元素。他们会为一个人物何时出场再三琢磨，会为一个词的出人意料的安排兴奋不已，会为一个绝妙细节的产生快意非常，会为一种新型结构的浮出欣喜若狂。在写作的那些日子，案前、路上、榻上乃至厕中，心头盘旋的都是这些问题，哪里有什么现代性、全球化等诸如此类的问题！因为这一切是不必费心去思考的，他身处的时代、语境，这一切都会自然而然沉淀到文字中去。此时，他们想得更多的是自己在写一篇小说，在做一件艺术品。其情形犹如木匠做活，心里总想着怎样将这件活做得好看，该塑造成怎样的形状、安排成多大的尺寸……事实上，他们一旦进入工作状态，满脑子就只剩下一件事：手艺——以及如何尽可能完美地施展自己的手艺。

对于这样的写作事实，布鲁克斯和沃伦看到了。他们现在要做的事就是带领我们这些阅读小说的人真正进入小说家的写作情景，去体察小说家们的写作心机，去观摩他们是怎样"制作"一篇小说的。相对于那些不潜心剖析文本而只顾由着性子妄谈大而无当的话题的宏文大章，我真宁愿去看布鲁克斯和沃伦那些安静的、细微的、深入的分析、提示与追问。我更愿意相信他们关于小说言论的真实性——那是可信的、可靠的。他们引领我们走上了这样一条直接走向小说之门的通途,他们的阅读方式在帮助我们逐渐培养起一种稳妥而良好的阅读姿态。看着他们的文字,我们才会切实地体会到一个词:鉴赏。而当下的阅读在那些"高屋建瓴"的批评指引下,鉴赏几乎已不复存在,剩下的就只有云山雾罩的阐释。这样一种阅读实在是太糟糕了,也太令人匪夷所思了。

鉴赏——何等美好的情景与心境?透过这个词我们回望从前先人们的阅读,可以看到他们在品评一件艺术品的优雅姿态,耳边甚至依稀能听到他们的出神入化的点评。若干世纪以来,艺术品就是这样被阅读的,也正是这样一种阅读,使文学成为了文学。说《小说鉴赏》是新批评的产物,我感到有些奇怪,因为从前的文学批评不就是一直这样一脉相承下来的吗?比如说中国古代文学批评里的《文心雕龙》《沧浪诗话》《诗品》,以及张竹坡、脂砚斋、金圣叹等人的评点,所言所论,十有八九都是关于艺术与形式的。金圣叹一句"绝妙好词",顿时使我们解悟了遣词造句的奥妙与语言的魅力究竟所在。而这样的感叹,当然只能够来自于鉴赏而不是阐释。就此一句,无论是对作者而言还是对读者而言,其作用与意义大概都不在一个关于文化的吓人的大话题之下。重读古代批评,我们会知道,所谓新批评,只不过是重捡"老枪",又出新招而已。

说布鲁克斯和沃伦只关心形式,这是不确切的,《小说鉴赏》同样关心着小说的内容,但这样的关心依然是在文学范畴的领域里展开的。它告诉我们,小说是怎样与人生经验纠缠在一起的,什么样的经验对小说而言是有意义的,什么样的经验对小说而言是无价值的,小说为什么要在意它的恒久作用而对偶然作用可以忽略不计,诸如此类。他们很清楚一个道理:如果只是到文学这里索取思想,何不直接去阅读哲学、政治学、社会学?显然,文学世界里除了思想,还有其他种种维度。

《小说鉴赏》是美国大学的教材。中国的大学也应当有这样的教材——当下的中国大学(夸夸其谈、已经没有正经的阅读姿态的大学)更需要这样的教材。而对于普通读者而言,这样的书,可能更有助于他们掌握最理想也是最有效的阅读方式,从而使他们更确切地理解小说何为,直至最终抵达小说风景最为旖旎的腹地。

这本书在当下语境中的再版,委实意味深长。

曹文轩
2006 年 11 月 5 日于北京大学蓝旗营

译者序

　　二十多年前，翻译家前辈雨宁先生找到我，要我"帮帮忙"参与一部小说集的翻译工作。我了解后，才知道这部即是闻名已久的《Understanding Fiction》。后来商定下来，让我翻译的是素以文笔细腻著称的美国女作家凯瑟琳·安·波特的《中午酒》。我译完交稿，后来也拿到了中国青年出版社1986年出版的样书，此后对这件事再没有多想。想不到不久前，后浪出版公司的吴兴元先生找到我，说他们公司要出版此书的英汉对照本，而且表示，我是本书尚健在的译者中最适合审阅并写序的人。本来，以我的文艺理论素养，是没有条件写好这样的一篇文章的。但是我面前仿佛出现了先我而去的一个个译界师友的影子，这里面有荒芜、咸荣、亦代、雨宁、乐山、绍武、主万等等。他们走得匆忙，有些事没能来得及做完，总得有人"帮忙"打点吧，于是便答应了下来。

　　美国著名作家、批评家克林斯·布鲁克斯(1906—1994)与罗伯特·潘·沃伦(1905—1989)合编的这部书最初出版于1943年，后经多次修订。这次出版的是1979年出版的第3版。在编这本书之前，他们就编过一本《诗歌鉴赏》，引起很大反响，于是便续编了这本《小说鉴赏》。这本书的体例比较特殊，它既是一部短篇小说鉴赏集，又是一本文学教科书。全书共收入作品51篇，除了英美的以外，还有欧洲、拉美等地具有代表性的作品。编者从小说鉴赏与写作的角度，把全书分为7章。每一章的开头都有编者撰写的前言，就优秀小说的一些总的原则和小说的基本要素做了深入浅出的论述。前5章所收的每一篇小说之后，还附有针对该篇小说的讨论和思考题。我们通过对这些材料的阅读与思考，不难对每一篇具体作品以及文学这一总的现象，都能有较深一步的了解。即使光从学习英语的角度来说，这些作品可以说都是值得细读的范文。作者们(包括英译者们)的语言都是既准确而又优美的。所附的中译文，据我判断，我自己译的姑且不论，也都译得严谨而又相当流畅。我相信，原来就有一定英语水平的朋友，在参照中译读过这部集子后，再阅读一般的英语小说原著，应该不会有太大的问题。

　　对于原书的两位编者我倒多少有些了解。众所周知，克林斯·布鲁克斯也是一位研究福克纳的专家，著有这方面的专著多种。我在翻译与研究福克纳的过程中曾一再学习与参考他写的书。他虽然是"新批评派"文艺理论家，但是在评论福克纳时仍然很注意联系作家的时代、地域与家族历史。他在为1985年出版的《南方文学史》所写的福克纳专论中就很明确地指出："福克纳不仅仅在出生地上沾了'地利'的光，他在降生时间上也得到了'天时'的好处。"至于罗伯特·潘·沃伦，我除译过他写的一些诗歌外，也很清楚地记得他所写的论福克纳的文章里那个警句式的结尾。他是这样写的："也许它(指考利的《便携本福克纳选集》)可以给福克纳的名声标志一个转折点。那对福克纳关系倒不大，因为他能同我们这国家这时代的任何大作家一样处之泰然。他能等待。但我们能等待吗?"我感觉到,从他们二位那里得到的知识要远远超过某些以某种怪异理论去硬套福克纳的大部头专著;而且我还觉得,"新批评派"所主张的"细读"(close reading)与具体分析,倒正好能纠正我们这里流行了多年的"时代背景——作家生平——作品思想性与艺术性"那种"三段论"式的外国文学讲授程式呢。

李文俊
2006 年深秋

原　序
Preface

　　编选一部出色的短篇小说选集并不难。这首先因为有很多作品可以说都已成为名篇——事实上，比任何一部普通集子所能收入的都要多，甚至足够为若干部特殊趣味的小说选集提供材料，如爱情小说选集、动物小说选集、儿童题材小说选集、种族关系小说选集，等等。英文 anthology（选集）一词来源于希腊文，意思是一束采集起来的鲜花，而可供采集的花朵实在是太多了。

　　一部供教学用的选集——教科书——必须考虑到许多不同的因素。本书是一册教科书。不过，就是教科书中选的小说，也应该和任何其他选集中的作品一样，除非为了教学原因而选入一些不成功的例子，它也应当给读者以乐趣。事实上，如果一册教科书达到了加深理解力和提高学生鉴赏力这一目的，那么它最终应该可以比普通选集提供更多的乐趣。一个真正懂得足球或是棒球的看客观看一场比赛，自然要比一个对比赛规则一窍不通的人更能欣赏。

　　然而，好的小说并没有一定的章法。相反的，我们只有某些总的原则，这从本书第一章至第四章的标题上就表明出来了。不过，对这些原则的理解（在本书中是通过对一篇篇小说的研读与讨论而取得的），目的在于使读者较为接近写得成功的小说的真谛——接近一种意识，知道小说与过得富有意义的生活的关系。就连所选的那类情节或是人物个性的刻

It is fairly easy to compile a very good anthology of short fiction. For one thing, there are a number of pieces that have become, as it were, classics—more, in fact, than any ordinary collection could accommodate, and enough, even, to provide for a number of anthologies of special-interest stories about, for instance, love, dogs, childhood, or ethnic affiliation. The word *anthology*, of Greek origin, means a gathering of flowers; and there are more than enough blooms to go around.

An anthology for teaching—a textbook—involves many different considerations. And this is a textbook. But even the stories in a textbook anthology should not give less pleasure than those in any other—except when a poor example is inserted for pedagogical reasons. In fact, if a textbook fulfills its purpose of deepening the comprehension and sharpening the taste of the student, it should provide, in the end, more pleasure than the ordinary anthology can. A spectator who really understands football or baseball certainly enjoys witnessing a game more than one who scarcely knows the rules of the game.

There are, however, no rules for the good story. There are, instead, certain general principles, indicated here by the headings of sections 1 to 4. But an understanding of such principles (here gained through the study of, and debate about, individual stories) is aimed at bringing the reader closer to the true center of successful fiction—to a sense of the relation of the story to life meaningfully lived. Even the type of plot or characterization chosen, though sometimes seeming to be merely

画,虽然似乎只是从技巧方面出发,却也有一个深远的心理根据,如同我们试图表明的那样。当然,这种关系的一个方面在第六章中变得很明显,第六章的标题为"小说与人生经验";在该章中,三位作家试图说明他们的小说的根源——最初出现的一个萌芽或是最初出现的一个综合因素,最终如何有了可能,成为对一次似乎偶然的经验的一种较为深刻、较为详尽的解释。

　　在这一版中,我们彻底检阅了过去几版选入的全部材料。如果先前收入的某篇作品和我们所能找到的其他任何一篇作品收到同样的效果,我们就保留下来。换言之,我们的准则绝不是单纯追求新奇。幸运的是,我们找到了一些的确为各项不同的原则提供较为出色、较为有趣的实例的作品。尽管在第一章至第四章中我们继续探讨方法与意义之间的关系,我们在第七章中却保留了(稍有改动)几篇作品,不加评论,不提出问题,这样,学生在接触那些作品时,就可以像他们在现实生活中接触到的那样——独立地、好奇地去领略其中的意义。概括起来,这次所做的改动就是:在这一版的全部51篇作品中,我们新收入了21篇。

　　第五章"新小说"是一个全新的内容。在20世纪,科学理论和社会变化自然会影响到一定数量小说的内在设想。空间与时间的崭新的科学见解,以及心理学的持续发展,使人联想到根本的差别。不论从何种来源,都重新强调了骚动不安与虐待狂式的人物——也就是有时称为哥特式①的那类作品。为此,我们选了巴塞尔姆、科塔萨尔、泰勒及其他人的作品,作为实例来说明这种变化。

　　《小说鉴赏》第2版有一篇附录,题为《小说写作中的技巧问题与原则》。显而易见,这

---

　　① 指以凄凉阴郁的背景、恐怖凶暴的事件和腐败堕落的气氛为特色的一类文学作品。

technical, has, as we try to indicate, a deep psychological basis. Of course, one aspect of this relationship becomes obvious in section 6, entitled "Fiction and Human Experience," in which three authors attempt to explain the origin of one of their stories—how a germ of early suggestion, or a complex of such early suggestions, might eventuate in a deeper and fuller interpretation of a seemingly casual experience.

In this edition there has been a thorough overhauling of all the material included in past editions. When a story previously included has served its purpose as well as any other we could find, we have kept it. That is, mere novelty has never been our criterion. We have, fortunately, found some stories that do offer better, or more interesting, examples of various principles. Though in sections 1 through 4 we have continued our discussions of the relation of method and meaning, we retain in section 7 (with some changes) stories without commentary or questions so that students may encounter stories as they would in real life—freestanding and a challenge to the interest and a sense of their meaning. To summarize the changes: We have twenty-one new stories in this edition out of a total of fifty-one.

An entirely new feature section 5, "The New Fiction." During the twentieth century changes in scientific theory and in society have naturally affected the assumptions behind a certain amount of fiction. New scientific views of space and time, and continuing developments in psychology, have suggested basic differences, and from whatever sources, there has been a new emphasis on the disturbed and the sadistic—or what is sometimes (to revive a term used in the eighteenth century for such material) called the *Gothic*. So we have offered examples from Bartnelme, Cortazar, Taylor, and others to document such changes.

The second edition of *Understanding Fiction* contained an appendix called "Technical Problems and Principles in the Composition of Fiction." Clearly, this was directed to

篇附录是针对重点放在短篇小说写作上的那些课程的(这类课程很多)。我们略去了这篇材料,把它收入《教师手册》内,因为我们认为,倘若本书用作实际写作的一种依据,那么教师作为一个对班级最了解的人,会知道特殊的问题应于何时提出并与哪些小说或章节联系起来。我们被迫多少以提纲挈领的形式处理这些原则,而教师个人对这些原则的应用和阐述,会证明对该班级是极有价值的。

最后再说一句:即便粗略地翻阅一下这一版本,也可以看出,我们在这一版中甚至比以前更严格地遵循我们的一般归纳法,认为这是给学生以置身事内之感,并使学习成为一种自然的扩张与发展的最佳方法。

我们深为感激凯瑟琳·安·波特和尤多拉·韦尔蒂,她们为《小说鉴赏》中收入的她们的作品特地写了背景情况。本书使用者的意见在修订过程中对我们很有价值,他们的人数太多,这里无法一一列举。不过我们要特别提及耶鲁大学的戴维·米尔奇、仔细校订原稿的克劳德·科尼尔斯和 Prentice Hall 公司的罗布·里维尔,谨向他们表示谢意。

克林斯·布鲁克斯
罗伯特·潘·沃伦
(主 万译)

those courses (of which there were many) in which the emphasis was on the writing of short stories. We have dropped this material, including it in the Teacher's Manual, because we believe that when the text is used as a basis for actual writing, the teacher, as the best judges of a class, will know when special questions should be raised and related to stories or sections. And the teacher's individual application and elaboration of the principles that we have been forced to treat in more or less synoptic form will prove invaluable to that class.

A final word: It should be clear from even a cursory look at this edition that here, even more than before, we have clung to our generally inductive method as the best way of giving the sense of participation to the student and of making the process of learning one of natural extension and building.

We are deeply grateful to Katherine Anne Porter and Eudora Welty for writing especially for *Understanding Fiction* their accounts of the background of their stories included. The number of users of this book whose comments have been invaluable to us in revision is too great for listing here. But we should make special reference of gratitude to David Milch, of Yale University, to Claude Conyers, for his meticulous copy editing, and to Robb Reavill, of Prentice-Hall, Inc.

C. B
R. P. W.

小说的意图与要素
Intentions and Elements of Fiction

小说是进行中的生活的生动体现，他是生活的一种富有想象力的演出；而作为演出，它是我们自我生活的一种拓展。

当夜色笼罩着外边的世界,穴居人空闲下来,围火坐定时,小说便诞生了。他因为恐惧而颤抖或者因为胜利而踌躇满志,于是用语言重现了狩猎的过程;他详细叙说了部落的历史;他讲述了英雄及机灵的人们的事迹;他说到一些令人惊奇的事物;他竭力虚构幻想,用神话来解释世界与命运;他在改编为故事的幻想中大大夸赞了自己。在高度发展的现代世界,穴居人炉边故事中的组成部分有许多都已经成为我们推论和研究的学科了——例如,历史学、文学、物理学、神学,以及心理学。我们发现在我们的小说里有许多原始的冲动在发挥作用。然而,我们发现它们并不是抽象地在发挥作用——像我们发现它们在心理学或哲学课本中那样——而是在人们现实生活的形象中发挥作用,像在小说或戏剧中那样。正如我们富于想象力地进入小说境界时那样,小说使我们扩大了经验,并使我们对于自我可能遭遇的情况增加了知识。小说是进行中的生活的生动体现——它是生活的一种富有想象力的演出,而作为演出,它是我们自我生活的一种扩展。

我们最好提醒自己,小说追溯到史前史,它体现了我们的某些最为深切的需要与利益,这是很恰当的。不过,还要提醒自己,小说经过多少年代,已经成为一种综合的艺术,正如西斯廷教堂①中米开朗琪罗②的壁画不同于史前洞穴中的动物绘画那样,它已不同于炉边故事,这也是很恰当的。

---

① 梵蒂冈宫廷中的礼拜堂。
② 米开朗琪罗(1475—1561),意大利雕刻家、画家、建筑家。

As soon as the cave man had leisure to sit around the fire while darkness covered the world beyond, fiction was born. In words, he relived, shivering with fear or gloating in victory, the events of the hunt; he recounted the past history of the tribe; he narrated the deeds of heroes and men of cunning; he told of marvels; he struggled in myths to explain the world and fate; he glorified himself in daydreams converted to narrative. In the sophisticated modern world, many of the elements involved in the cave man's fireside tales have led to branches of speculation and study—history, literature, physics, theology, and psychology, for instance—and we find in our fiction many of the original impulses at work. We find them at work, however, not in the abstract—as we find them in the textbook of psychology or philosophy—but in images of life in the process of being lived as in fiction or drama. Fiction, as we enter into it imaginatively, broadens our experience and increases our knowledge of the possibilities of the self. Fiction is a vital image of life in motion—it is an *imaginative enactment of life*—and, as such, it is an extension of our own lives.

It is well to remind ourselves that fiction goes back to prehistory and that it embodies some of our deepest needs and interests. But it is well to remind ourselves, too, that fiction has, over the ages, become a complex art, as different from the fireside tale as Michelangelo's frescoes in the Sistine Chapel are from the animal paintings in prehistoric caves.

So let us consider modern practice and the elements that go into it. We must remember that fiction changes as the world changes, that each age produces its own kind of fiction. More important, we must remember

因此，让我们来探讨一下现代的实例及其组成要素。我们必须记住，随着世道的改变，小说也改变了，每一时代产生出自己的那种小说。更为重要的是，我们必须记住，虽然在我们的技术世界中，改变一般总被认为意味着进步，艺术世界中的改变（而小说基本上是一门艺术）则未必意味着进步；谁也不会认为最近的一部畅销书就一定比荷马的或莎士比亚的作品好。更为常见的是，我们预料到起伏不定，往往还有衰退。因此，我们在本书中探讨小说时，既涉及新的，也涉及老的，既涉及它们的差异之处，也涉及它们的类似之点。我们试图在可能范围内找出一些持续不变的原则。不过本书的主要目的不是叙述短篇小说的历史，而是加深我们对各种形式的小说的鉴赏，从而加深我们对小说的兴趣。

让我们首先看看我们一般同意称之为小说的所有作品中的三个基本要素：情节、人物和主题。

主　万　译

that, though in our world of technology, change is generally taken to mean progress, change in the world of art (and fiction is primarily an art) does not *necessarily* mean progress；nobody would think that the last best seller is necessarily superior to Homer or to Shakespeare. More generally, we expect fluctuation, and sometimes decline. So in considering fiction here we are concerned with both the new *and* the old, with both their differences and their similarities. We are trying, insofar as possible, to find continuing principles. *But our main purpose here is not to give a history of the short story. It is to deepen our understanding of, and consequently our pleasure in, the various forms of fiction.*

Let us begin by looking at three basic elements found in all the compositions that we generally agree to call fiction：action, character, and theme.

001. 进攻堡垒

（美）弗朗西斯·帕克曼 著　　主 万译

001. The Attack on the Fort

by Francis Parkman

6年以前，有个名叫吉姆·贝克沃思的人 一个有着法国、美国和黑人血统的混血儿，替皮货公司在克罗人①的一个大村庄里做买卖。前一年夏天，吉姆·贝克沃思呆在圣路易斯。他是一个极其恶劣的流氓，阴险奸诈，杀人不眨眼，毫无廉耻和信义。这至少是他在大草原上的为人。然而，就他的情况而言，做人的准则并不适用，因为尽管他会在一个人的睡梦中把他刺死，可是他也会做出最奋不顾身的勇敢行为来，例如，像下面这样：他在那个克罗人村庄里时，黑脚部落②的一支作战部队，人数在三四十人之间，偷偷地穿过乡野窜来，杀死了路上孤单的行人，夺走了马匹。克罗人的战士在后面紧紧追赶，追得那么急，黑脚人逃脱不掉了，他们于是在一片悬崖绝壁下用大木头堆起了一道半圆形的胸墙，冷静地等待着克罗人到来。大木头和树枝堆了四五英尺高，在前面保护着他们。克罗人本来可以冲过胸墙，全歼敌人，但是尽管他们人数比对方多10倍，他们却做梦也没有想到直捣那个小防寨。这一行动和他们的作战概念是完全不相容的。他们呐喊、鼓噪，像魔鬼的化身那样从这边跳到那边，对着大木头发射出雨点般的枪弹和箭矢。黑脚人一个也没有受伤，可是有几个克罗人尽管又跳跃又躲闪，却被打翻了。这场战斗就以这种幼稚的方式进行了一两个小时。不时，一名克罗战士在一阵忘我的英勇自负情绪中，会尖声唱着战歌，自诩是人类最勇敢、最伟大的人，拿起战斧，冲上前去，猛劈胸墙，接着向同伴方向退下阵来，在一阵雨点般的箭下倒地阵

SIX years ago, a fellow named Jim Beckworth, a mongrel of French, American, and Negro blood, was trading for the Fur Company, in a large village of the Crows. Jim Beckworth was last summer at St. Louis. He is a ruffian of the worst stamp, bloody and treacherous, without honor or honesty; such at least is the character he bears upon the prairie. Yet in his case the standard rules of character fail, for though he will stab a man in his sleep, he will also perform most desperate acts of daring; such, for instance, as the following: While he was in the Crow village, a Blackfoot war-party, between thirty and forty in number, came stealing through the country, killing stragglers and carrying off horses. The Crow warriors got upon their trail and pressed them so closely that they could not escape, at which the Blackfeet, throwing up a semi-circular breastwork of logs at the foot of a precipice, coolly awaited their approach. The logs and sticks, piled four or five feet high, protected them in front. The Crows might have swept over the breastwork and exterminated their enemies; but though outnumbering them tenfold, they did not dream of storming the little fortification. Such a proceeding would be altogether repugnant to their notions of warfare. Whooping and yelling, and jumping from side to side like devils incarnate, they showered bullets and arrows upon the logs; not a Blackfoot was hurt, but several Crows, in spite of their leaping and dodging, were shot down. In this childish manner, the fight went on for an hour or two. Now and then a Crow warrior, in an ecstasy of valor and vainglory, would scream forth his war song, boast himself the bravest and greatest of mankind, grasp his hatchet, rush up, strike it upon the breastwork, and then, as he retreated to his companions, fall dead under a shower of arrows; yet no combined attack was made. The Blackfeet remained secure in their entrenchment. At last Jim Beckworth lost patience.

①② 北美印第安人的一个部落。

作者简介：弗朗西斯·帕克曼（Francis Parkman，1823—1893），美国历史学家。1823年9月16日生于波士顿，1893年11月8日卒于马萨诸塞州牙买加平原。哈佛大学毕业后，1846年踏上美国西部之旅，这次旅程成就了他的《加州与俄勒冈陈迹》（*The California and Oregon Trail*，1849）；《新世界》（*New World*，1865）写到了法国拓荒者；《蒙塔卡姆与沃尔夫》（*Montcalm and Wolf*，1884）展现了传记是如何透露时代精神的《半个世纪的冲突》（*A Half-Century of Conflict*，1892）是展现他的文学才华的典范之作。

亡。然而,他们始终没有发出联合攻击。黑脚人在他们的阵地内仍旧很安全。最后,吉姆·贝克沃思不耐烦起来。

"你们全都是大傻瓜和老婆子。"他对克罗人说,"有种的跟着我来,我让你们看看该怎样打仗。"

他把捕兽人穿的鹿皮上衣先脱掉,再把衣服脱个精光,像印第安人那样,又把步枪撤在地上,一手操起一柄轻便的小斧子,奔过大草原,跑向右边,利用一片洼地隐藏起来,不让黑脚人看见。接着,他攀登上岩石,到了他们后面那片悬崖的顶上。四五十名年轻的克罗战士跟随着他。凭着下面传来的呐喊、号叫,他知道黑脚人正在他的下面。他朝前跑去,跳下岩石,到了他们当中。在落地时,他一把揪住了一个人的松散的长发,把他拖翻,用战斧砍死了他。随后,他又抓住另一个人的腰带,狠狠砍了他一斧,接着站起身来,高唱着克罗人的战歌。他把斧子在自己前后左右那么飞快地挥舞着,大吃一惊的黑脚人纷纷后退,空出地方来给他。他本来可以跳过胸墙,逃出去,但是这并无必要,因为克罗战士凶神恶煞般鼓噪着连连翻过岩石,迅速跳到了他们的敌人当中。克罗人的大队人马也从正面响应了那片喊杀声,同时冲上前来。在胸墙内的那场殊死的战斗是可怕的。有一刹那,黑脚人像困住了的老虎那样喝叫,搏斗,然而屠杀工作不一会儿就结束了,血肉模糊的尸体堆陈在悬崖脚下。一个黑脚人也没有逃脱。

"You are all fools and old women," he said to the Crows; "come with me, if any of you are brave enough, and I will show you how to fight."

He threw off his trapper's frock of buckskin and stripped himself naked, like the Indians themselves. He left his rifle on the ground, took in his hand a small light hatchet, and ran over the prairie to the right, concealed by a hollow from the eyes of the Blackfeet. Then climbing up the rocks, he gained the top of the precipice behind them. Forty or fifty young Crow warriors followed him. By the cries and whoops that rose from below, he knew that the Blackfeet were just beneath him; and running forward, he leaped down the rock into the midst of them. As he fell he caught one by the long loose hair, and dragging him down, tomahawked him; then grasping another by the belt at his waist, he struck him also a stunning blow, and gaining his feet, shouted the Crow war cry. He swung his hatchet so fiercely around him that the astonished Blackfeet bore back and gave him room. He might, had he chosen, have leaped over the breastwork and escaped; but this was not necessary, for with devilish yells the Crow warriors came dropping in quick succession over the rock among their enemies. The main body of the Crows, too, answered the cry from the front, and rushed up simultaneously. The convulsive struggle within the breastwork was frightful; for an instant the Blackfeet fought and yelled like pent-up tigers; but the butchery was soon complete, and the mangled bodies lay piled together under the precipice. Not a Blackfoot made his escape.

讨　论

我们就这篇轶事(见重要词汇)先提出两个初步的看法:第一,这件事据说是真实的,并不是凭空虚构的。第二,帕克曼写下这篇故事,主要不是因为它本身生动有趣,而是因为它说明了他想要向国内人民描述的生活的一个方面。这些看法提出了两个问题:第一,倘若帕克曼不用事实,仅仅凭想象虚构出来,这篇轶事会成为一篇受人欢迎的小说吗? 第二,倘若帕克曼写下这篇故事不是为了教导读者,而是因为它本身有趣,它会成为一篇受人欢迎的小说吗?

Let us make two preliminary observations on this *anecdote* (see Glossary). First, it is allegedly true; it is not made up. Second, Parkman wrote it not primarily because it was spirited and interesting in itself but because it illustrated one aspect of the life he wanted to describe to the people back home. These observations raise two questions. First, would this anecdote be an acceptable piece of fiction if, instead of using fact, Parkman had simply made it up out of his head? Second, would it be an acceptable piece of fiction if Parkman had written it not to instruct his readers but because it was interesting in itself?

对于第一个问题,我们必须做否定的回答,因为尽管小说并不全靠事实,它却可以利用事实。许多小说都像这篇一样尽量利用历史事实。对于第二个问题,我们也必须做否定的回答,因为虽然许多小说都想教导读者,但它们并不仅仅试图用事实真相来教导读者。

如果我们并没有因为这篇轶事是真实的(而不是因为作者公开承认他的目的是教导读者),就不把它称作小说的话,那么为什么不可以把它看作一篇受人欢迎的小说呢?要回答这个问题,我们必须看看这篇轶事本身的性质。

这篇轶事本身不过是一篇情节生动的叙述。在情节上,它是前后统一的。这就是说,我们有促成战斗的局面,黑脚人的狡猾的防御措施为进攻的克罗人造成了一个问题,克罗人无法解决他们的问题,贝克沃思的大胆解决了问题。这篇轶事作为故事,情节是统一的,因为它提出了问题与解决办法,还因为它有开端、经过和结局。我们对结局的好奇心得到了满足,不过这个结局并没有充分满足我们对小说的兴趣。就其中的一点来说,这篇轶事记载的情节纯粹是外界的,它没有充分涉及人物与人类行动的动机。有关心理活动的唯一一点就是,贝克沃思"不耐烦起来"。

让我们看看另一个例子。在这个例子中,重点是放在人物上。这就是马克·吐温关于密西西比河上一个汽艇老舵手的简洁的叙述。

(主 万 译)

We must answer no to the first question because, though fiction is not tied to fact, it may use fact. Many pieces of fiction make as much use of historical fact as does this. We must answer no to the second question because, though many pieces of fiction are written with a desire to instruct the reader, they are not written with the purpose to instruct the reader merely about matters of fact.

If we are not debarred from calling this anecdote fiction because it is true and not because the author's avowed purpose was to instruct the reader, why, then, is it not to be considered a piece of acceptable fiction? To answer this question, we must look at the nature of the anecdote itself.

The anecdote proper is simply the account of a spirited piece of action that, as a piece of action, is unified. That is, we have the situation precipitating the fight, the cunning defense by the Blackfeet that creates a problem for the attacking Crows, the failure of the Crows to solve their problem, then the daring solution by Beckworth. The anecdote, as action, is unified because it presents problem and solution, because it has a beginning, a middle, and an end. Our curiosity about the outcome is satisfied. But this outcome does not satisfy fully the interest that we bring to fiction. For one thing, the action recorded in this anecdote is purely external; it does not sufficiently involve the character and motive of human action. The only item of psychological interest is that Beckworth "lost patience."

Let us look at another example, in which the emphasis is on character: Samuel Clemens' brief account of an old Mississippi River steamboat pilot.

002. 艾赛亚·塞勒斯船长

(美)马克·吐温 著　　主　万 译

002. Captain Isaiah Sellers

by *Mark Twain*

　　我们谈起了艾赛亚·塞勒斯船长,他如今已经去世多年了。他是一个善良人,一个心高气傲的人,在岸上和在河上都很受人家尊敬。他身材高大、体格结实、一表人才。就连在老年——据我记得——他的头发都仍旧像印第安人一样乌黑,眼睛和双手也跟印第安人同样坚定有力,精神和目光跟老老少少随便哪一个同行舵手同样平稳、清楚。他是这个行业里的老前辈。在汽艇时代以前,他是龙骨船上的一名舵手,后来在我提到的时期还活着的任何一个其他的汽艇舵手转动舵轮之前,就成为一名汽艇舵手了。因此,同行弟兄们十分敬畏地看待他,就像过去时代幸存下来的著名人士,总受到他们同伴的敬畏那样。他知道自己受到什么样的看待,也许,这一事实给他那生来就十分高傲的尊严增添了几分更加高傲的气度。

　　他留下了一本日记,不过日记似乎并不始于他第一次乘汽艇航行的日子。据说,那是 1811 年,也就是第一条汽艇翻搅起密西西比河河水的那一年……

　　每逢塞勒斯船长走到一群闲聊着的舵手面前时,那儿顿时就会安静下去,谈话也停止了。因为当 6 个舵手聚在一起时,他们中总有一两个新手,老资格的人于是便在这些可怜人面前"卖弄",高谈阔论地讲着从前在河上的经验,使新手们很伤心地感到自己多么没有阅历,自己的崇高身份只是前不久才取得的,以及自己的地位多么低微。那些老手总把一切事情的日期讲得尽可能早,这样好尽可能使新手们强烈地感到自身多么缺乏经验,并且同样强烈地羡慕这些老手。而那些自鸣得意的秃脑袋瓜子竟然自吹自擂,撒

WE had some talk about Captain Isaiah Sellers, now many years dead. He was a fine man, a high-minded man, and greatly respected both ashore and on the river. He was very tall, well built, and handsome; and in his old age—as I remember him—his hair was as black as an Indian's, and his eye and hand were as strong and steady and his nerve and judgment as firm and clear as anybody's, young or old, among the fraternity of pilots. He was the patriarch of the craft; he had been a keelboat pilot before the day of steamboats; and a steamboat pilot before any other steamboat pilot, still surviving at the time I speak of, had ever turned a wheel. Consequently, his brethren held him in the sort of awe in which illustrious survivors of a bygone age are always held by their associates. He knew how he was regarded, and perhaps this fact added some trifle of stiffening to his natural dignity, which had been sufficiently stiff in its original state.

He left a diary behind him; but apparently it did not date back to his first steamboat trip, which was said to be 1811, the year the first steamboat disturbed the waters of the Mississippi. . . .

Whenever Captain Sellers approached a body of gossiping pilots, a chill fell there, and talking ceased. For this reason: whenever six pilots were gathered together, there would always be one or two newly fledged ones in the lot, and the elder ones would be always "showing off" before these poor fellows; making them sorrowfully feel how callow they were, how recent their nobility, and how humble their degree, by talking largely and vaporously of old-time experiences on the river; always making it a point to date everything back as far as they could, so as to make the new men feel their newness to the sharpest degree possible,

作者简介:马克·吐温(**Mark Twain**,1835—1910),美国幽默作家,演讲家,原名塞缪尔·克莱门斯。1835 年 11 月 30 日生于密苏里州的小镇佛罗里达,1910 年 8 月 21 日卒于宾夕法尼亚州雷丁市。他曾经作过印刷学徒工、轮船水手。1863 年他开始用笔名"马克·吐温"。他的旅行颇丰,他的著作都以他的游历为主要题材。他的少年历险故事赢得全世界读者的好评,特别是《汤姆·索亚历险记》(*The Adventures of Tom Sawyer*,1876)和《哈克贝利·费恩历险记》(*The Adventures of Huckleberry Finn*,1884),后者是美国最杰出的小说作品之一。另外还有带有讽刺性的小说《亚瑟王法庭中的康涅狄格美国佬》(*A Connecticut Yan-kee in King Arthur's Court*,1889)和《傻瓜威尔逊》(*The Tragedy of Pudd'nhead Wilson*,1894)等。

谎扯淡,把日期说早——10年,15年,20年;他们多么欣赏自己的讲话对这些惊讶、羡慕的青年人所产生的影响啊!

或许,正当这类事情进行到这个快乐的当口,艾赛亚·塞勒斯船长,这位真正的、唯一地道的"古老人士"的气象堂皇的身体会很庄重地踱到他们中间来。想想看,他顿时所带来的那一大片的寂静!再想想看,当那位老船长随意而漫不经心地闲扯起一些往事时,那些秃脑袋瓜子会怎么想,方才还是他们听众的新手们心头又是如何喜悦啊!他总缅怀往事,讲到一些失踪了的岛屿和更改了的河道。这些都是在那群人中年纪最大的秃脑袋瓜子踏进操舵室30多年以前的事情!

有好多次,这位老水手都像上文所说的那样出现,在自身周围撒播下灾难与耻辱。如果我们可以相信那些舵手的话,他总把他说的那些岛屿失踪的日期定在河运史的含混不清的早期。他从来不重复提到同一个岛屿,而且也从来不提到一个还存在的岛屿或是举出在场的人有谁年纪够大、早先可能听说过的一个名称。如果你可以相信那些舵手的话,他对于细节总是一本正经地十分考究。例如,他从来不讲到"密西西比州"——不啊,他总说"当密西西比还是眼下阿肯色所在的地方的时候"。他也从来不笼统地讲到路易斯安那或是密苏里,从而在你心上留下一个不正确的印象——不啊,他总说"当路易斯安那还在河上游较远的地方时",或者"当密苏里还在伊利诺斯那面的时候"。

■ 讨　论 ■

在这篇特写中,作者幽默而深情地把艾赛亚船长写成一个熟悉那条大河掌故的人物。他讲的故事显然是浮夸的、惊人的,使其他舵手所讲的故事全部黯然失色。在马克·吐温把这篇特写一步步写来时,他并没有着重说明船长的故事就其本身而言是引人入胜的冒险故事。相反,它们是关于"河运史的含混不清的早期"的传说,而且马克·吐温还近乎明点出来,它们是荒诞无稽的,而不是真实的。

然而,不难想象,这些河上生活的故事有

and envy the old stagers in the like degree. And how these complacent baldheads *would* swell, and brag, and lie, and date back—ten, fifteen, twenty years, and how they did enjoy the effect produced upon the marveling and envying youngsters!

And perhaps just at this happy stage of the proceedings, the stately figure of Captain Isaiah Sellers, that real and only genuine Son of Antiquity, would drift solemnly into the midst. Imagine the size of the silence that would result on the instant! And imagine the feelings of those baldheads, and the exultation of their recent audience, when the ancient captain would begin to drop casual and indifferent remarks of a reminiscent nature—about islands that had disappeared, and cut-offs that had been made, a generation before the oldest baldhead in the company had ever set his foot in a pilot-house!

Many and many a time did this ancient mariner appear on the scene in the above fashion, and spread disaster and humiliation around him. If one might believe the pilots, he always dated his islands back to the misty dawn of river history; and he never used the same island twice; and never did he employ an island that still existed, or give one a name which anybody present was old enough to have heard of before. If you might believe the pilots, he was always conscientiously particular about little details; never spoke of "the state of Mississippi" for instance—no, he would say, "When the state of Mississippi was where Arkansas now is"; and would never speak of Louisiana or Missouri in a general way, and leave an incorrect impression in your mind—no, he would say, "When Louisiana was up the river farther," or "When Missouri was on the Illinois side."

In this sketch Captain Isaiah is treated humorously, though affectionately, as a repository of stories about the river. His stories are obviously marvelous and grandiose and put those told by the other pilots very much in the shade. As Clemens (Mark Twain) develops his sketch, he places little stress on the captain's stories as absorbing tales of adventure in their own right. They are rather legends about the "misty dawn of river history," and Twain more than hints that they are fabulous rather than real.

It is easy, however, to imagine that some

若干篇如果是以不同的转折变化讲述出来，可能会成为涉及到道德冲突、英雄行为或极端痛苦地做出的伦理决定的严肃小说的素材。说到头，如同马克·吐温告诉我们的，艾赛亚船长是一个心高气傲的人，具有"和随便哪一个同样坚定有力的"铁手腕，以及"同样平稳、清楚的精神和目光"。在下面的一段里，他提到艾赛亚船长是"一个如果责任需要……会坚守（在舵轮旁）直到烧成灰烬为止的人"。这位船长在河上的一篇英勇故事中可能扮演的角色就讲到这儿。不过我们也很容易看出，在一篇风貌与这篇人物特写很相似的幽默小说中，艾赛亚船长可能会扮演怎样的人物。我们可以想象，他揭穿一个大言不惭的人在密西西比河上奋不顾身的事迹，再不然也许就是他以自己的一篇高超的吹嘘胜过了那个人。我们甚至可以想象出一篇使人怜悯的小说，叙说艾赛亚船长突然发现，自己竟然被人看作一个遗民，一个从另一个早已过去的时代遗留下来的人物。

如果在《艾赛亚·塞勒斯船长》中，我们只有潜在的情节和最少限度的我们可以称为主题的东西的话，让我们现在转向记叙文的一个走向极端的例子。这个例子把情节和人物压缩到一个单一的目的：即说明一个要点，解释一个主题。《圣经》中的一篇寓言故事（见重要词汇）可以为我们提供一个绝好的例子。让我们来看一下《马可福音》第四章里撒种人的寓言故事：

> 你们听啊，有一个撒种的出去撒种。
> 撒的时候有落在路旁的，飞鸟来吃尽了。
> 有落在土浅石头地上的，土既不深，发苗最快。
> 日头出来一晒，因为没有根就枯干了。
> 有落在荆棘里的，荆棘长起来，把它挤住了，就不结实。

of these stories of life on the river, told with a different inflection, might become the material of serious fiction involving moral conflict, heroism, or ethical decisions agonizingly made. After all, as Twain tells us, Captain Isaiah was a high-minded man with an iron hand "as strong and steady and [a] nerve and judgment as firm and clear as anybody's." And in a further paragraph he refers to Captain Isaiah as "a man who... would have stayed [at the pilot wheel] till he burned to a cinder, if duty required it." So much for the possibility of the captain's figuring in a heroic tale of the river. But it is also easy to see how Captain Isaiah might figure in a humorous story whose spirit would be close to that of this character sketch. One can imagine his exposing some boaster of deeds of derring-do on the Mississippi or perhaps his outdoing him with a superior boasting of his own. We can even imagine a story of pathos, as Captain Isaiah suddenly discovers that he has come to be regarded as a relic, something left over from another, outdated time.

If in "Captain Isaiah Sellers" we have only the potential of action and a minimum of what we may call thematic emphasis, let us now turn to an extreme example of narrative that reduces action and character to the sole purpose of illustrating a point, of defining a theme. A biblical *parable* (see Glossary) will give us a perfect example. Let us look at the parable of the sower, in chapter 4 of Mark：

> Hearken; Behold, there went out a sower to sow:
> And it came to pass, as he sowed, some fell by the way side, and the fowls of the air came and devoured it up.
> And some fell on stony ground, where it had not much earth; and immediately it sprang up, because it had no depth of earth;
> But when the sun was up, it was scorched; and because it had no root, it withered away.
> And some fell among thorns, and the thorns grew up, and choked it, and it yielded no fruit.

又有落在好土里的，就发生长大，结实有 30 倍的，有 60 倍的，有 100 倍的①。

后来，耶稣向使徒们解释和阐明了这篇寓言：

撒种之人所撒的，就是道。

那撒在路旁的，就是人听了道，撒旦立刻来把撒在他心里的道夺了去。

那撒在石头地上的，就是人听了道，立刻欢喜领受。

但他心里没有根，不过是暂时的，及至为道遭了患难，或是受了逼迫，立刻就跌倒了。

还有那撒在荆棘里的，就是人听了道，后来有世上的思虑、钱财的迷惑和别样的私欲进来把道挤住了，就不能结实。

那撒在好地上的，就是人听道，又领受，并且结实，有 30 倍的，有 60 倍的，有 100 倍的②。

然而，《圣经》中的这篇寓言故事不过是我们现在讨论的这类记叙体小说中的一个例子。也许，世俗形式中这一类作品的最出名的例子就是《伊索寓言》，这些寓言是从古代传下来的。十分明显，《伊索寓言》向我们展示了一些异想天开的场面，在那些场面里动物受到人类动机的驱使，像人那样说话，并且显露出自己是某几类人的相当明白的实例。不过《伊索寓言》通常表示出对生活的一个相当明确的、可以作为教训表达出来的评论。例如，狐狸和葡萄那则寓言的一篇通俗的译文，结尾就是这么一个教训："轻视你无法获得的东西，是容易的。"

---

① 见《新约·马太福音》第 4 章第 3 节—第 8 节。

② 同上，第 14 节—第 20 节。

And other fell on good ground, and did yield fruit that sprang up and increased; and it brought forth, some thirty, and some sixty, and some an hundred.

Later, Jesus explains and interprets the parable to his disciples:

The sower soweth the word.

And these are they by the way side, where the word is sown; but when they have heard, Satan cometh immediately, and taketh away the word that was sown in their hearts.

And these are they likewise which are sown on stony ground; who, when they have heard the word, immediately receive it with gladness;

And have no root in themselves, and so endure but for a time; afterward, when affliction or persecution ariseth for the word's sake, immediately they are offended.

And these are they which are sown among thorns, such as hear the word,

And the cares of this world, and the deceitfulness of riches, and the lusts of other things entering in, choke the word, and it becometh unfruitul.

And these are they which are sown on good ground; such as hear the word, and receive *it*, and bring forth fruit, some thirty-fold, some sixty, and some an hundred.

The biblical parable is, however, only one example of the type of fictional narrative we now discuss. Perhaps the best-known examples of the type in its secular form are Aesop's fables, which have come down to us from ancient times. His fables, it is quite obvious, give us fantastic situations in which animals are actuated by human motivations, speak like human beings, and reveal themselves as rather transparent instances of certain human types. But Aesop's fables usually express a fairly explicit comment on life that can be expressed as a moral. For example, a popular translation of the fable of the fox and the grapes concludes with the moral tag "It is easy to despise what you cannot get."

寓言(见重要词汇)的形式分见于多种语言之中，有原始的形式，有高深的形式。现代有些小说明显地或巧妙地倾向于给读者一点儿"教益"。还有，某些现代小说十分复杂地，甚至冷嘲热讽地运用了寓言的意义。我们即将读到的纳撒尼尔·霍桑写的《年轻的布朗大爷》，就是一个例子。那篇作品虽然是小说，却具有一篇寓言的思想内容。不过我们应该记住，大多数现代小说，不论含义可能何等深奥，不论对人类价值可能做出何等严肃认真的评论，却倾向于通过交织在一起的人物、情节与主题来实现这一思想，以达到这一目的。

下面三篇作品，每一篇都是我们所要讨论的某种类型中相当突出的一个例子：着重情节的小说，着重人物的小说和着重主题的小说。但是，如同我们已经说过的那样，一篇小说要写得成功，必须是一个整体。让我们设法来看一下，在下面各篇作品里，最重要的部分是如何和其他部分交织在一起的。　（主　万　译）

Forms of the *fable* (see Glossary) are found in many languages, in primitive or sophisticated forms, and some modern fiction is slanted toward the "moral" in an insistent or a subtle way. Again, some modern fiction quite complexly, even ironically, uses the sense of the fable. One example we shall soon come to is "Young Goodman Brown," by Nathaniel Hawthorne, which though a piece of fiction, has the inner content of a fable. But we should remember that most modern fiction, however deeply significant it may be and however serious a comment it may make on human values, tends to do so through the realization of idea in character *and* plot *and* theme as intertwined.

Each of the three following stories is a rather extreme example of one of the types we have been discussing: the story of action, the story of personality, and the story of theme. But, as we have already remarked, a story, to be successful, must be a unity. Let us try to see how, in the stories that follow, the most emphasized element is intertwined with others.

003. 格拉米格纳的情人

(意大利)乔万尼·维尔加 著　　姚梅琪 译

003. Gramigna's Lover
by Giovanni Verga

　　亲爱的法里娜①，我现在寄给你的并不是一篇完整的小说，而是一篇小说的梗概。因此，它至少具有简洁、真实的优点——按现时的说法，它是一篇人类的记录。也许，这会引起你，以及那些想研究人心这部巨著的人的兴趣。故事是我在乡间小路上偶然听到的。我深信，与其要你从书本的字里行间，或者从作者的角度去探索它，还不如让你面对赤裸裸的事实。所以，我多少打算按照我听到的那样，用并给我听的那些人的朴实而生动的语言来叙述它。简单的充满人性的事实，总会引起我们深思，它的价值就在于它永远是真实的，真诚的眼泪，兴奋激动，真情实感。种种激情交织在一起，以它们隐蔽、曲折，有时又似乎是互相抵触的方式融合、成熟、发展。这个神秘的过程在未来很长时期内还会构成一种心理现象的诱惑力，而这种心理现象正是现代科学分析试图极为精确地注意着的，我们则称之为小说的主题。今天的这篇故事，我仅仅讲个开头和结尾；对你，这已经足够了，或许有朝一日对其他的人也会很够了。

　　如今，由于采用了不同的艺术方法，我们在艺术上取得了许许多多极其辉煌的成就。我们对细节比过去更为讲究、更为重视。为了使故事发展符合逻辑，我们情愿牺牲过去的艺术大师们凭着几乎是超人的直觉构思出来的悲剧性结局与心理危机的巨大效果。这样，我们就必然没有过去那么惊人，那么具有戏剧性，虽然也同样是劫数难逃的。我们即便不是太自卑，也是太谦虚了，不过我们在描写真实心理上的

DEAR Farina,① I'm sending you here not a story, but the outlines of a story. So it will have at least the merit of being brief, and of being true—a human document, as they say nowadays, interesting, perhaps, for you and for those who would study the great book of the heart. I'll tell it you just as I picked it up in the lanes among the fields, more or less in the same simple and picturesque words of the people who told it to me, and you, I am sure, will prefer to stand face to face with the naked, honest fact rather than have to look for it between the lines of the book, or to see it through the author's lens. The simple human fact will always set us thinking; it will always have the virtue of *having really happened*, the virtue of real tears, of fevers and sensations which have really passed through the flesh. The mysterious process by which the passions knot themselves together, interweave, ripen, develop in their own way underground, in their own tortuous windings that often seem contradictory, this will still constitute for a long time to come the attractive power of the psychological phenomenon which we call the theme of a story, and which modern analysis seeks to follow with scientific exactitude. I shall only tell you the beginning and the end of the story I am sending you to-day, but for you that will be enough, and perhaps one day it will be enough for everybody.

Nowadays we work out differently the artistic process to which we owe so many glorious works of art, we are more particular about trifles, and more intimate; we are willing to sacrifice the grand effect of the catastrophe, or of the psychological crisis, which was visioned forth with almost divine intuition by the great artists of the past, to the logical development, and hence we are necessarily less startling, less dramatic, but not less fatal; we are more modest, if not more humble; but the conquests in psychological truth made

---

① 维尔加这封信的收信人。这篇小说就是以这种形式来叙述的。——原注。

① The recipient of Verga's letter, in which form the story is cast.

作者简介：乔万尼·维尔加（Giovanni Verga，1840—1922），意大利作家。1840 年 9 月 2 日生于西西里卡塔尼亚，1922 年 1 月 27 日卒于同地。他是现实主义小说流派的最重要小说家。维尔加出生于地主家庭，后来他离开西西里去大陆，呆在那里一直到 1893 年。在那里，他形成了简明扼要和感情充沛的写作风格。他最好的作品包括短篇小说《西西里小说》(*Little Novels of Sicily*，1883)、长篇小说《马拉沃利亚一家》(*The House by the Medlar Tree*，1881)、《堂·杰苏阿多师傅》(*Mastro-Don Gesualdo*，1889)和剧本《乡村骑士》(*Rustic Chivalry*，1884)，《乡村骑士》后来被马斯卡尼改编成歌剧而名声大噪。他的作品对第二次世界大战之后的意大利新现实主义作家影响极大。

收获,将使未来的艺术同样获益匪浅。难道我们在研究感情方面,就永远不能达到这样一个尽善尽美的境界,使得进一步去考察人的内心世界成为没有必要的了吗?难道人类心灵的科学,这门新的艺术的硕果,就不能把想象力的种种源泉开发到这样的深度和广度,使得未来的小说和故事仅仅成为这种现象的各个不同事实的记载吗?

同时,我也相信,当小说的各部分圆满地联结起来,使整个创作过程同人类感情的发展过程一样神秘莫测,小说的形式完美一致,小说的内容真实可信,小说的方法与存在如此吻合,使小说具有真人真事的效果,不露一丝人工雕琢的痕迹,艺术作品似乎自行变得成熟,一点儿不必依赖作者,就像自然事件那样本能地表现出来。到那时,小说就会获得巨大的成功,就会成为所有艺术作品中最完美、最富有人性的创作。这样,在小说的各个现行形式中,我们就看不出任何构思的迹象,任何想象的幻影,任何吐出第一句话,如同造物主的命令那样的痕迹。小说像它应该也必须做到的那样,自成一种体裁。它像一尊巍然常存的铜像,经常洋溢着生活,而它的作者则以非凡的勇气把自己隐藏起来,消失在他的不朽著作之中。

几年前,人们在那儿沿着西莫内托河追捕一名强盗。如果我没记错的话,那是一个名叫格拉米格纳的家伙。这个名字和它所代表的那种莠草① 一样,受到人们的诅咒。它使全省的人一听到就恐怖万分。骑兵、步兵和民兵骑警队跟踪了他两个月,始终没有能逮住他:他孤身一人,却抵得上 10 条汉子。这棵莠草甚至扬言要扎下根来。再说,收获的季节即将来临,田野里堆满了一垛垛干草,沉甸甸的麦穗正催着人们去收割。虽然割禾的人们早已镰刀在手,但依然没有一个地主胆敢到自己的田里去一下,因为他们生怕碰上格拉米格纳蹲伏在垄沟里,两腿夹着枪,准备把第一个下田来窥探他的人的脑袋轰掉。人们因此怨声载道。省长于是把所有的警官、骑兵军官和民兵骑警队长全召集拢来,向他们训话,使他们全凝神静听。第二天,他们展开了全面行动:每条沟渠里,每堵石墙后,到处都布满了巡逻队、小股的武装人员和岗哨。他们通过电报传递消息,骑马、步行,日以继夜地追捕

by us will be not less useful to the art of the future. Shall we never arrive at such perfection in the study of the passions, that it will be useless to prosecute further that study of the inner man? The science of the human heart, which will be the fruit of the new art, will it not develop to such a degree and to such an extent all the resources of the imagination that the novels and stories of the future will merely record *the various facts* of the case?

But in the meantime I believe that the triumph of the novel, that most complete and most human of all works of art, will be reached when the affinity and the cohesion of all its parts will be so complete that the process of the creation will remain a mystery, a mystery as great as that of the development of the human passions; and that the harmony of its form will be so perfect, the sincerity of its content so evident, its method and its *raison d'être* so necessary, that the hand of the artist will remain absolutely invisible, and the novel will have the effect of real happening, and the work of art will seem *to have made itself*, to have matured and come forth spontaneously like a natural event, without preserving any point of contact with its author; so that it may not show in any of its living forms any imprint of the mind in which it was conceived, any shadow of the eye which visioned it, any trace of the lips that murmured the first words, like the *fiat* of the Creator; let it stand by itself, in the single fact that it is as it must be and has to be, palpitating with life and immutable as a bronze statue, whose creator has had the divine courage to eclipse himself and to disappear in his immortal work.

Several years ago, down there along the Simoneto, they were in pursuit of a brigand, a fellow called Gramigna, if I'm not mistaken; a name accursed as the grass① which bears it, and which had left the terror of its fame behind it from one end of the province to the other. Carabiniers, soldiers, and mounted militia followed him for two months, without ever succeeding in setting their claws in him: he was alone, but he was worth ten men, and the ill weed threatened to take root. Add to this that harvest time was approaching, the hay was already spread in the fields, the ears of wheat were already nodding yes! to the reapers who had the sickle already in their hand, yet none the less there was not a proprietor who dared poke his nose over the hedges of his own land, for fear of seeing Gramigna crouching between the furrows, his gun between his legs, ready to blow the head off the first man who came prying into his affairs. Hence thecomplaints were general. Then the Prefect summoned all the officers of the police, of the carabiniers, and of the mounted

---

① 一种蔓生的野草,贫苦的农民用作牲口的饲料。——原注。

① A root-spreading grass, used as cattle feed by poor peasants.

着他，就像去追赶一只可恶的野兽那样跑遍了全省。格拉米格纳一次次从他们手中溜掉。假如他们追赶得太近，他就用子弹回敬他们。在旷野，在村闾，在农庄上，在小酒馆的树荫下，在俱乐部和大会堂里，格拉米格纳和这次疯狂的搜捕以及他的拼死的逃窜，成了人们唯一的话题。骑兵的马精疲力竭，倒了下去；民兵疲惫不堪，横七竖八地躺在马厩里；巡逻兵站着就打盹；只有他，格拉米格纳，永不感到疲乏，从不合眼打盹，他不停地逃窜，攀登悬崖峭壁，偷偷地溜过庄稼地，匍匐着爬过满是仙人掌的丛林，像一条狼似的从干涸的河床里脱身出去。在俱乐部和村里的门阶上，交谈的主要话题就是，被追捕的人在 6 月毒日晒得焦干的广阔平原上，必定会感到口干舌燥。闲聊的人们说到这个，不由得把眼睛睁得大大的。

那时，佩帕，利科迪亚的美貌姑娘之一，正打算和绰号叫"蜡烛"的邻居菲努结婚。他自己有一小块土地，马房里还有一头栗色的骡子。"蜡烛"是个个儿高高的小伙子，像太阳那样漂亮，他不用弯腰就能像一根柱子似的把圣玛格丽特的旗子高高擎起。

佩帕的母亲因为女儿交上了好运，高兴得流下了眼泪。她花了好多时间去翻看新娘箱子里的嫁妆：全都是白色的四件一套，"可以和一个皇后媲美"，垂肩的耳环，能戴满十个手指的金戒指。她拥有的金子和圣玛格丽特一样多。婚礼就定在圣玛格丽特节举行，恰好在 6 月干草收获以后。每天晚上，"蜡烛"从田里归来，把骡子拴在佩帕家门口，然后进屋对她说，今年的收成好极了，假如格拉米格纳不来放火的话，那间打开了门正对着床的小谷仓，无论如何也放不下今年的收获。他觉得似乎还要等上一千年，才能让自己的新娘坐在骡背上他自己的身后，接回家去。

随后，在一个晴朗的日子里，佩帕对他说："那头骡子你也用不着了，我现在不想结婚了。"

可怜的"蜡烛"简直像遭了雷打似的。那个老女人听到自己的女儿回绝了村里最好的一门亲事，急得动手揪自己的头发。

"我喜欢的是格拉米格纳，"姑娘对母亲说，"除了他，我谁也不嫁。"

"啊！"母亲像一个女巫似的披散着花白头发，尖叫着满屋乱撞，"啊，这个魔鬼居然跑到这儿来迷惑我的女儿啦。"

"不，"佩帕回答说，眼神就像钢铁一般坚定，"不，他没来过这儿。"

militia, and addressed a few words to them that made them prick up their ears. The next day there was a general upheaval: patrols, small bands of armed men, outposts everywhere, in every ditch and behind every dry-stone wall; they drove him before them like an accursed beast across all the province, by day and by night, on foot, on horseback, by telegraph. Gramigna slipped through their hands, and replied with bullets if they got too close on his heels. In the open country, in the villages, in the farmsteads, under the bough-shelter of the inns, in the clubs and meeting-places, nothing was spoken of but him, Gramigna, and of that ferocious hunt, of that desperate flight; the horses of the carabiniers fell dead tired; the militiamen threw themselves down exhausted in every stable; the patrol slept standing; only he, Gramigna, was never tired, never slept, always fled, scrambled down the precipices, slid through the corn, ran on all-fours through the cactus thicket, extricated himself like a wolf down the dry beds of the streams. The principal theme of conversation in the clubs, and on the village door-steps, was the devouring thirst which the pursued man must suffer, in the immense plain dried up under the June sun. The idlers widened their eyes when they spoke of it.

Peppa, one of the handsomest girls of Licodia, was at that time going to marry Neighbour Finu, "Tallow-candle" as they called him, who had his own bit of land and a bay mule in his stable, and was a tall lad, handsome as the sun, who could carry the banner of Saint Margaret as if he were a pillar, without bending his loins.

Peppa's mother wept with satisfaction at her daughter's good fortune, and spent her time turning over the bride's trousseau in the chest, all white goods, and four of each, "good enough for a queen," and earrings that hung to her shoulders, and golden rings for all the ten fingers of her hands; she had as much gold as St. Margaret herself, and they were going to get married just on St. Margaret's day, that fell in June, after the hay-harvest. Tallow-candle left his mule at Peppa's door every evening as he returned from the fields, and went in to say to her that the crops were wonderful, if Gramigna didn't set fire to them, and that the little corn-chamber that opened its gate-door opposite the bed would never be big enough for all the grain this harvest, and that it seemed to him a thousand years, till he could take his bride home, seated behind him on the bay mule.

But one fine day Peppa said to him: "You can leave your mule out of it; I'm not going to get married."

Poor Tallow-candle was thunderstruck, and the old woman began to tear her hair as she heard her daughter turning down the best match in the village.

"It's Gramigna I care for," the girl said to her mother, "and I don't want to marry anybody but him."

"你在哪儿见到他的?"

"我没见到过他,只是听人说起过他。可是,听呀!在我被烧死之前,我可以感觉到他就在这儿。"

尽管他们试图瞒住这件事,可村里还是议论纷纷了。那些原先因为丰产的麦田、栗色的骡子,以及不用弯腰就能举起圣玛格丽特大旗的那个漂亮小伙子而忌妒佩帕的主妇们,四处散布流言蜚语,说格拉米格纳和她夜晚在厨房里幽会,说她们有人看见他躲在床底下等等。可怜的母亲给在炼狱里涤罪的灵魂点了一盏灯,甚至神父也来到佩帕的家里,用自己的圣衣去碰她的心房,好把盘踞在她心头的那个格拉米格纳魔鬼驱赶走。她始终坚持说,自己确实连看也没看见过他,只是在晚上梦见过,早上起来嘴唇干裂,似乎她自己的身体也感到了他必然经受着的那种干渴。

因此,老女人只得把她关在家里,不让她听到任何有关格拉米格纳的议论。她甚至用圣像把门上的裂缝都遮挡住。佩帕站在圣像后面偷听着外面的街谈巷议,脸上红一阵、白一阵,好像魔鬼把一切痛苦都赶到了她面前。

最后,她听说格拉米格纳已经被赶进了帕拉戈马的仙人掌丛中。"他们交火了两小时,"主妇们说,"死了一个骑兵,三个以上的民兵负了伤。但密集的子弹像阵雨一样朝他射击。这会儿,他们在他待过的地方发现了一摊血。"

于是佩帕在老女人的床头对着自己身上画了一个十字,就从窗口逃出去了。

格拉米格纳藏在帕拉戈马的霸王树丛中,尽管身负重伤,十分痛苦,他们仍旧没能把他从野兔的藏身之地赶出来。两天来,他没吃过一点儿东西,脸色苍白,发着高烧,却仍然牢牢地握着枪,当他在朦胧的晨光中看见她穿过仙人掌丛,果敢地朝他走来时,他犹豫了一下,不知是否应该开枪——"你想要什么?"他问她,"你到这儿来干吗?"

"我来和你待在一起。"她对他说,眼睛坚定地望着他,"你是不是格拉米格纳?"

"是的,我是格拉米格纳。如果你是冲着这20个沾满血污的几尼来的,你可打错了算盘。"

"不,我是来和你待在一起的。"她回答道。

"回去!"他说,"你不能和我待在一起,我不要什么人和我待在一起。如果你想来弄点钱,那你可找错了人啦!看见吗?我告诉你,我身无分文!两天来我

"Ah!" The mother rushed around the house, screaming, with her grey hair flying loose like a very witch. "Ah! that fiend has even got in here to bewitch my girl for me."

"No," replied Peppa, her eyes fixed and hard as steel. "No, he's not been here."

"Where have you seen him?"

"I've not seen him. I've heard about him. Hark, though! I can feel him here, till it burns me."

It caused a great talk in the village, though they tried to keep it dark. The goodwives who had envied Peppa the prosperous cornfields, the bay mule, and the fine lad who carried St. Margaret's banner without bending his loins, went round telling all kinds of ugly stories, that Gramigna came to her at night in the kitchen, and that they had seen him hidden under the bed. The poor mother had lit a lamp to the souls in Purgatory, and even the priest had been to Peppa's house, to touch her heart with his stole, and drive out that devil of a Gramigna who had taken possession of it. Through it all she insisted that she had not so much as set eyes on the fellow; but that she saw him at nights in her dreams, and in the morning she got up with her lips parched as if she were feeling in her own body all the thirst he must be suffering.

Then the old woman shut her up in the house, so that she should hear no more talk about Gramigna, and she covered up all the cracks in the house-door with pictures of the saints. Peppa listened behind the blessed pictures to all that was said outside in the street, and she went white and red, as if the devil were blowing all hell in her face.

At last she heard say that they had tracked down Gramigna to the cactus thickets at Palagonia. — "They've been firing for two hours!" the goodwives said. "There's one carabinier dead, and more than three of the militia wounded. But they fired such showers of bullets on him that this time they've found a pool of blood, where he was."

Then Peppa crossed herself before the old woman's bed-head, and escaped out of the window.

Gramigna was among the prickly-pear cactuses of Palagonia, nor had they been able to dislodge him from that cover for rabbits, torn, wounded though he was, pale with two days' fasting, parched with fever, and his gun levelled: as he saw her coming, resolute, through the thickets of the cactus, in the dim gleam of dawn, he hesitated a moment whether to fire or not. — "What do you want?" he asked her. "What have you come here for?"

"I've come to stay with you," she said to him, looking at him steadily. "Are you Gramigna?"

"Yes, I am Gramigna. If you've come to get those twenty guineas blood-money, you've made a mistake."

"No, I've come to stay with you," she replied.

"Go back!" he said. "You can't stay with me, and I don't want anybody staying with me. If you've come

连一片面包也没吃过！"

"可现在我没法回家去，"她说，"路上尽是兵。"

"走开！这不干我的事！人人都必须当心保护他自己。"

当她像一条被人用脚踢开的狗那样转身打算离去时，格拉米格纳又叫住了她："听着！到那边的小溪里去给我打一瓶水来。如果你真要和我待在一起，你不得不冒生命的危险。"

佩帕一声不吭地走了。格拉米格纳听到枪声，便尖刻地大笑起来，一面自言自语道："这些可都是为我准备的啊！"但是不一会儿，当他看见她脸色苍白，鲜血淋淋，腋下夹着一个瓶子跑回来时，他猛地扑上去，一把夺过瓶子，直到喝得喘不过气来后，才问她道：

"这么说，你躲开了他们？你是怎样逃脱的？"

"士兵们都在那边，这边的仙人掌又很密。"

"不过他们还是在你身上打了个窟窿？衣服底下在流血吗？"

"是的。"

"你哪儿受了伤？"

"肩上。"

"这没关系，你能走。"

就这样，他答应让她留下。她追随着他，衣服划破了，身子因为那个伤口而发着烧，还要光着双脚去给他弄一瓶水或是一片面包。每当她冒着枪林弹雨空手回来时，她的情人由于受不住饥渴的煎熬，就会揍她。后来，有一天晚上，月光照在仙人掌丛上，格拉米格纳对她说："他们过来了。"他叫她在石缝的底部躺下，随后自己就逃到另一个地方。仙人掌丛中响起了经久不息的枪声，东一点西一点的火光一闪一闪地划破了漆黑的夜空。突然，佩帕听到身旁响起了一阵脚步声，抬眼一看，格拉米格纳拖着一条断腿走了回来，正靠在仙人掌宽阔的茎叶上往枪里装子弹。"全完了！"他对她说，"现在他们要抓住我了。"然而，最使她恐惧不安的是他那闪闪发光的眼睛，就像疯了一般。接着他像一捆木柴似的倒在干枯的树枝上，许多民兵一拥而上。

第二天，他被放在一辆马车上，从村里的街上慢慢走过，浑身上下伤痕累累，血迹斑斑。围观的人们蜂拥而上。当他们看到他这样瘦小，像傀儡戏中的丑角那样苍白、难看时，他们止不住大笑起来。佩帕正是为了他才离开那个"蜡烛"的！可怜的"蜡烛"跑去

after money you've mistaken your man, I tell you, I've got nothing, see you! It's two days since I even had a bit of bread."

"I can't go back home now," she said. "The road is full of soldiers."

"Clear out! What do I care! Everybody must be looking out for their own skin."

While she was turning away from him, like a dog driven off with kicks, Gramigna called to her.—"Listen! Go and fetch me a bottle of water from the stream down there. If you want to stay with me, you've got to risk your skin."

Peppa went without a word, and when Gramigna heard the firing he began to laugh bitingly, saying to himself: "That was meant for me!"—But when he saw her coming back, a little later, with the flask under her arm, herself pale and bleeding, he first threw himself on her and snatched the bottle, and then when he had drunk till he was out of breath, he asked her:

"You got away then? How did you manage?"

"The soldiers were on the other side, and the cactuses were thick this side."

"They've made a hole in you, though. Is it bleeding under your clothes?"

"Yes."

"Where are you wounded?"

"In the shoulder."

"That doesn't matter. You can walk."

Thus he gave her permission to stay with him. She followed him, her clothes torn, her body burning with the fever of her wound, shoeless, and she went to get him a flask of water or a hunk of bread, and when she came back empty-handed, in the thick of the firing, her lover, devoured by hunger and by thirst, beat her. At last, one night when the moon was shining on the cactus grove, Gramigna said to her: "They are coming!" and he made her lie down flat, at the bottom of the cleft in the rock, and then he fled to another place. Among the cactus clumps continual firing was heard, and the darkness flushed here and there with brief flames. All at once Peppa heard a noise of feet near her and she looked up to see Gramigna returning, dragging a broken leg, and leaning against the broad stems of the cactus to load his gun. "It's all up!" he said to her. "They'll get me now"—and what froze her blood more than anything was the glitter in his eyes that made him look like a madman. Then when he fell on the dry branches like a bundle of wood, the militiamen were on him in a heap.

Next day they dragged him through the streets of the village on a cart, all torn and blood-stained. The people who pressed forward to see him began to laugh when they saw how little he was, pale and ugly like a figure in a Punch-and-Judy show. And it was for him that Peppa had left Neighbour Finu, the "Tallow-candle"! Poor Tallow-candle, he went and hid himself as if the shame was his, and Peppa was led away between

躲了起来,好像这是他的耻辱。佩帕的金子虽然和圣玛格丽特一样多,却戴着手铐,被两个士兵押走了,像是另一个强盗那样。为了使自己的孩子获释,可怜的老母亲不得不卖掉嫁妆中"所有那些洁白的什物",金耳环和十个手指上戴的戒指,去请律师,随后还得把她带回家去。佩帕这时候贫病交加,受了耻辱,简直和格拉米格纳一样丑陋,怀里还抱着格拉米格纳的孩子。等审讯结束,他们把女儿交还给那个可怜的老女人时,她在朦胧的暮色笼罩着的光秃秃兵营里,当着骑兵反复念诵着"圣母玛利亚",仿佛得到的是一件无价之宝,因为女儿就是她的一切,可怜的老东西。宽慰的泪水如同泉水似的涌了出来。与此相反,佩帕的眼泪似乎已经枯竭,她什么话也没说,也从没见她在村里走动,尽管母女俩从此不得不靠辛勤的劳动来维持生活。人们说佩帕在灌木丛中学会了晚上出去偷东西的本领。事实上,她像一只野兽一样被悄悄地关起来待在厨房里,直到她的老母亲因为操劳过度而死去,不得不把房子卖掉。这时,她才重新露面。

"你瞧!"仍在爱着她的"蜡烛"说,"每当我想到你给自己和别人带来的不幸时,我真想一头撞死在石头上。"

"是的,"佩帕回答说,"这我知道!这是上帝的旨意。"

她把房子和留下给她的几件家具卖掉,然后同上次回来时一样,在夜里离开了村庄,一次也没回头看看自己居住了那么多年的家。她遵循着上帝的旨意,带着她的男孩到城里去,在关押格拉米格纳的监狱附近住了下来。在高大死寂的监狱正面,除了窗子的铁栅,什么都看不见。倘若她目光炯炯地站在那儿寻觅着他的"家"时,看守总把她赶走。最后,他们告诉她,他已经不在那儿了。他们给他戴上手铐,脖子上套上篮子,从海上带走不少时候了。她什么也没说,也没有搬走,因为她不知道上哪儿是好,也没有人可以投奔。她似乎已经成了这幢阴暗寂静的高大建筑物的一部分,靠着给士兵和监狱的看守干一些零星活儿勉强糊口。后来,她又对那些在仙人掌丛中用子弹打断了格拉米格纳的腿、把他从她身边带走的骑兵产生了一种恭敬而体贴的心情,一种对蛮力的兽性的崇拜。每逢节日,当她看见骑兵们帽子前面插着那簇鲜红的羽毛,穿着镶有红条纹的深蓝军礼服,佩戴着耀眼的肩章,结实而挺直地站在那儿时,她总目不转睛地看

the soldiers, handcuffed, as if she were another robber, she who had as much gold as Saint Margaret herself. Peppa's poor old mother had to sell "all the white goods" of the trousseau, and the golden ear-rings, and the rings for the ten fingers, to pay the lawyers to get off her child; then she had to take her back into the house, poor, sick, disgraced, and herself as ugly now as Gramigna, and with Gramigna's child at her breast. But when they gave her back her daughter, at the end of the trial, the poor old woman repeated her *Ave Maria*, there in the darkening twilight of the naked barracks, among all the carabiniers, and it was as if they had given her a treasure, poor old thing, for this was all she had, and she wept like a fountain with relief. Peppa, on the contrary, seemed as if she had no more tears, and she said nothing, nor was she ever seen in the village, in spite of the fact that the two women had to go and earn their bread labouring. People said that Peppa had learned her trade out in the thickets, and that she went stealing at night. The truth was, she stayed lurking shut up in the kitchen like a wild beast, and she only came forth when her old woman was dead, worn out with hard work, and the house had to be sold.

"You see!" said Tallow-candle, who still cared for her. "I could knock my head against the stones when I think of all the misery you've brought on yourself and on everybody else."

"It's true," replied Peppa. "I know it! It was the will of God."

After she had sold the house and the few bits of furniture that remained to her, she left the village, in the night, as she had returned to it, without once turning back to look at the roof, under which she had slept for so many years; she went to fulfil the will of God in the city, along with her boy, settling near the prison where Gramigna was shut up. She could see nothing but the iron gratings of the windows, on the great mute façade, and the sentinels drove her off, if she stood to gaze searchingly for some sign of him. At last they told her he'd been gone from there for some time, that they'd taken him away over the sea, handcuffed and with the basket round his neck. She didn't say anything. She didn't change her quarters, because she didn't know where to go, and had nobody to go to. She eked out a living doing small jobs for the soldiers and the keepers of the prison, as if she too had been a part of that great, gloomy, silent building; and then she felt for the carabiniers who had taken Gramigna from her, in the cactus thicket, and who had broken his leg with a bullet, a sort of respectful tenderness, a sort of brute admiration of brute force. On feast days, when she saw them with their scarlet tuft of feathers sticking up in front of their hats, and with glittering epaulettes, all standing erect and square in their dress uniforms of dark-blue with the scarlet stripes, she devoured them with her eyes, and she was always about the barracks, sweeping out the big general rooms, and

着。她老是在兵营各处走动，打扫一间间公厍的大房间，给他们擦皮靴，后来他们干脆叫她"骑兵们的擦鞋布"。只有在黄昏时分，当她看到他们佩带好武器，卷起裤腿，腰间插着手枪，一对对地出发，或者看到在路灯下，他们骑着马，步枪被照得闪闪发光，听着马刀的铿锵声和马蹄声渐渐远去，只有到这时，她才会脸色惨白，哆嗦着把马厩的门关上。她的孩子和一些小顽童一起在监狱前的平地上玩，在士兵们的胯下蹿来蹿去。当那些孩子跟在他后面，叫他"格拉米格纳的小崽子，格拉米格纳的小崽子"时，她就勃然大怒，用石头把他们赶走。

讨 论 ■

这篇小说维尔加用致友人书简的形式写成。小说很短，可能是因为维尔加意识到，他的朋友能领会据他说是省略了的"中间部分"——事实上，他说，这样一种使人人都能发挥想象力的写作方法，最终有可能使"人人都感到很够了"——那就是，到了他们学会怎样去感受小说的内在动机和感情，不再依赖于作家的进一步解释和干预的时候①。

换句话说，维尔加试图让读者也卷进小说的创作中去。

回到小说本身：这里我们只把这篇作品当做一个引言，因为至少在表面上，这是一篇强调情节，剧烈的具体情节的故事——在西西里晒得焦干的乡野，对大盗格拉米格纳进行大规模的追捕。就像"在村间，在农庄上，在小酒馆的树荫下，在俱乐部和大会堂里"所叙述的那样，这是一个逐日展开的故事，不过它却从格拉米格纳被放逐的故事转向了另一个"放逐"的故事。年轻、美丽的佩帕和全村的骄傲，既有钱又"像太阳那样漂亮"的菲努订了婚，忽然声称她不爱他，爱的是人们日夜追捕着的格拉

polishing boots, till they called her "the carabinier's shoe-rag." Only when she saw them fasten on their weapons after nightfall, and set off two by two, their trousers turned up, the revolver at their stomach; or when they mounted on horseback, under the street-lamp that made their rifles glitter, and she heard the tread of horses lose itself in the distance, and the clink of sabres; then every time she turned pale, and as she shut the stable door she shuddered; and when her youngster was playing about with the other urchins on the level ground in front of the prison, running between the legs of the soldiers, and the other brats shouted after him: "Gramigna's kid! Gramigna's kid!" she got in a rage, and ran after them, throwing stones at them.

This story is in the form of a letter to a friend of Verga. It is very short, presumably because Verga sensed that his friend would seize on the "middie" that he says is missing—and he says, in fact, that presumably such an act of participatory imagination will eventually be "enough for everybody"—that is, when they have learned to sense the inner motivations and feelings of fiction and not to depend on mere explanation or intrusion by the author. ①

In other words, Verga seeks to involve the reader's own creative power in the story itself.

To return to the story: we use it here as an introduction because it is, superficially at least, a story emphasizing action, violent physical action—the massive hunt across the parched countryside of Sicily for the outlaw Gramigna. This is the story that day by day unfolds as it is told "in the villages, in the farmsteads, under the bough-shelter of the inns, in the clubs and meeting-places." But to Cramigna's tale of outlawry is grafted the tale of another kind of "outlawry." The beautiful young Peppa, engaged to the pride of the village, Finu, who is both prosperous and "handsome as the sun," announces that she is in love not with Finu but with the outlaw

---

① 这里提到了现实主义和想象力的全部问题，同时也提到了作家和他的素材的关系。——原注。

---

① The whole question of *realism* and *imagination* (see Glossary) is suggested here, as is the relation of the author to his material.

米格纳,一个她素不相识的强盗。后来,消息传来说他被包围了,受了伤,断了水,她就逃奔到他那儿去,非但得不到他的感激,反而受到粗暴的对待。当格拉米格纳被抓住,拘禁起来,终于被关进监狱时,她自己也受了伤,怀着孩子,为人们所不齿。

　　确实,小说中有不少情节,但这些情节掩盖着一个不可思议的东西,这就是作者没有讲述的故事的"中间部分"。是一种什么样的"非法行为"吸引着佩帕去寻找被追捕的格拉米格纳?为了一个素昧平生的强盗——而且据我们所知,他一点也不爱她,她竟然失去了体面、舒适、富裕和菲努对她的真诚的爱,这是一种什么性质的爱情呢?当调皮的孩子们嘲笑她的儿子,管他叫"格拉米格纳的小崽子"时,她就朝他们扔石头,是什么驱使她在孤独和贫困中以这种奇特的方式对她的强盗始终忠贞不渝呢?

　　因此,这篇着重情节的小说终究也是一篇着重人物和心理描写的小说,还是一篇有主题的小说。它让我们去思索一个关于爱情性质的神秘问题,一个涉及到爱情与舒适和冒险之间的关系,涉及到献出爱情和接受爱情之间的关系的问题。

　　不过,我们能否把小说中的情节、人物和主题这些部分截然区分出来呢?不,它们都是同一个重要事件的各个侧面,是一个整体的必不可少的组成部分。

Gramigna, who is being hunted day and night, and whom she has never seen. Finally, when word comes that he has been surrounded and wounded and is cut off from water, she flees to him, to be received not gratefully but gruffly, and in the end to be wounded, left pregnant, and outcast, when Gramigna is taken and jailed, eventually to be sent off to a prison.

There is action enough here, certainly, hut there is a mystery in the story beyond the action, the mystery that the author leaves in the untold "middle" of the story. What kind of "outlawry" draws Peppa to seek the hunted Gramigna? What is the nature of the "love" that makes her forfeit respectability, comfort, prosperity, Finu's true adoration for her, all for an outlaw she has never seen—and who, as far as we ever know, cares nothing for her? What makes her remain, through isolation and poverty, faithful to the end, in her strange way, to her outlaw, as she throws stones at the brats who tease her son, shouting at him, "Gramigna's kid"?

So the story of action is a story of character and psychology after all, and a story of theme, leaving us to ponder a mysterious question about the nature of love, a question involving the relation of love to ease and risk, to receiving and giving.

But can we sort out these elements of action, character, and theme as distinct elements in the story? No, they are all aspects of the same massive event. They are part of a vital unity.

—思考题—■

1. 显然,大多数年轻姑娘不会像佩帕那样行事,她们会按照村里的习俗和菲努一起幸福地生活。佩帕期望从这与众不同的爱情中得到什么?你是如何评价她所期望的一切?

2. 我们怎样来理解佩帕和格拉米格纳的关系?

1. Clearly, most young girls would not act as Peppa does. They would settle down happily with Finu and village conventionality. What does Peppa expect from love that is different? How do you assess the value of her expectations?

2. What are we to make of the relation of Peppa

怎样来理解他们的初遇？后来,她还生养下他的孩子,然而我们能否从某种意义上假定他"爱"她呢？

3. 如果要你用较长的篇幅来写这篇小说,你将在省略掉的神秘的"中间部分"增加些什么内容呢？现在,你是如何理解佩帕最后采取的根本立场的？它是否是一种后悔、怨恨、屈从于命运、对价值看法改变的表现呢？

（姚梅琪 译）

and Gramigna? What are we to make of their first encounter? Later on, she is to have a child by him, yet in any sense can we assume that he "loves" her?

3. If you were to write the story on a larger scale, what would you put into the mysterious and missing "middle"? What do you now make of Peppa's basic attitude at the end? Is it one of regret, bitterness, acceptance of fate, a change of values?

004. 沃尔特·米蒂①的隐秘生活　004. The Secret Life of Walter Mitty

（美）詹姆斯·瑟伯 著　　冯亦代 译　　　　　　　　　　　　*by James Thurber*

"我们一定要冲出去！"大队长的声音像块正在碎裂的薄冰。他穿着全套军礼服，一顶满镶着金线的白色军帽神气地斜压在一只冷酷的灰色眼睛上。"我们办不到，长官。飓风马上就来，要是你问我的意见。""我没有在问你！伯格少尉。"大队长说，"打开强光灯！加速到 8500！我们一定要冲出去！"汽缸的砰砰声增加了：哈—扑克嗒—扑克嗒—扑克嗒—扑克嗒。大队长盯着机舱窗上结着的冰凌。他走过去调动着一排复杂的仪表盘。"打开 8 号辅助器！"他喊着。"打开 8 号辅助器！"伯格少尉重复了一遍。"加强 3 号炮塔！"大队长喊。"加强 3 号炮塔！"这架巨大的向前冲去的八引擎海军水上飞机里的全部人员，各自操纵着自己管理的部分，这时却相互望望，而且咧开嘴笑了起来。"老头子要带我们冲出去了，"他们彼此说，"老头子是连地狱也不怕的！"……

"不要那么快！你把车开得太快了！"米蒂太太说，"你开得这么快干什么？"

"嗯？"沃尔特·米蒂说。他瞧瞧坐在身旁的妻子，吃了一惊。她看来完全是陌生的，像是人群里冲他嚷嚷的一位素不相识的女人。"你开到 55 英里了。"她说，"你明知道我不喜欢快过 40 英里。你居然开到 55。"沃尔特·米蒂默默地开向华脱勃雷镇。在 20 年的海军航空生涯中，那次 SN202 号吼叫着冲过最险恶的暴风雨的飞行，已经在他心里那条遥远而又亲切的

───────────

　① "沃尔特·米蒂"在美国已经成为一个做白日梦者的代名词。米蒂原来是个没有特长而且缺乏闯劲的人，他只能通过白日梦来逃避他所应付不了的现实。

"WE'RE going through!"The Commander's voice was like thin ice breaking. He wore his full-dress uniform, with the heavily braided white cap pulled down rakishly over one cold gray eye. "We can't make it, sir. It's spoiling for a hurricane, if you ask me.""I'm not asking you, Lieutenant Berg," said the Commander. "Throw on the power lights! Rev her up to 8,500! We're going through!" The pounding of the cylinders increased; ta-pocketa-pocketa-pocketa-*pocketa-pocketa*. The Commander stared at the ice forming on the pilot window. He walked over and twisted a row of complicated dials. "Switch on No. 8 auxiliary!" he shouted. "Switch on No. 8 auxiliary!" repeated Lieutenant Berg. "Full strength in No. 3 turret!"shouted the Commander. "Full strength in No. 3 turret!" The crew, bending to their various tasks in the huge, hurtling eight-engined Navy hydroplane, looked at each other and grinned. "The Old Man'll get us through," they said to one another. "The Old Man ain't afraid of Hell!"...

"Not so fast! You're driving too fast!"said Mrs. Mitty. "What are you driving so fast for?"

"Hmm?" said Walter Mitty. He looked at his wife, in the seat beside him, with shocked astonishment. She seemed grossly unfamiliar, like a strange woman who had yelled at him in a crowd. "You were up to fiftyfive,"she said. "You know I don't like to go more than forty. You were up to fifty-five. " Walter Mitty drove on toward Waterbury in silence, the roaring of the SN202 through the worst storm in twenty years of Navy flying fading in the remote, intimate airways of his mind. "You're tensed up again,"said Mrs. Mitty. "It's one of your days. I wish you'd let Dr. Renshaw look you over. "

作者简介：詹姆斯·瑟伯（James Thurber，1894—1961），美国作家、漫画家。1894 年 12 月 8 日生于俄亥俄州哥伦布，1961 年 11 月 2 日卒于纽约。他的第一本书《性是必要的么？》（*Is Sex Necessary*? 1929，与 E. B. 怀特合著）中的插图是他自己画的。他的漫画在美国几乎人人皆知。1940 年视力的衰减迫使他缩减图画量。1952 年他的视力几近失明，他不得不彻底地放弃画画。他的作品有《我的生活与艰苦岁月》（*My Life and Hard Times*，1933）、《我们时代的寓言》（*Fables for Our Time*，1940）和童书《13 时钟》（*The 13 Clocks*，1950）。他以描写迷惑的都市人而出名，如他的短篇小说《沃尔特·米蒂的隐密生活》（*The Secret Life of Walter Mitty*，1939）中的主人公，终日逃避在自己的幻想中。

的航线上慢慢淡薄了。"你又神经紧张了。"米蒂太太说，"今天你又有毛病了，我劝你找任肖大夫检查一下。"

沃尔特·米蒂把汽车停在他妻子要去卷头发的那座大楼前面。"我在这儿卷头发，你不要忘记去买套鞋。"她说。"我用不着套鞋。"米蒂说。她把小镜子放回手提包。"这些话用不着再提了。"她说，下了车，"你已经不再是年轻人了。"他把引擎加快了一些。"为什么你不戴手套？你把手套丢失了吧？"沃尔特·米蒂从衣袋里掏出了手套。他把手套戴在手上，但是一等她转过身走进那座大楼，而且车也开到了有红灯的地方，就又把手套除下来。"快开，伙计！"灯光一变就有一个警察叫了一声，米蒂匆匆戴上手套，吭吭两下把车开向前去。他漫无目的地在街上绕了几个圈子，然后把车开过医院一直开到停车场去。

……"是那个大财主银行家，威灵顿·麦克米伦。"漂亮的女护士说。"是吗？"沃尔特·米蒂说，慢吞吞地除了他的手套，"谁在主治？""任肖大夫和班波大夫，但是这儿还有两位专家。纽约的雷明登博士和从伦敦来的泼烈贾－密特福先生。他是飞来的。"在那条长长的阴凉的走廊里一扇门打开了，任肖大夫走了出来。他一副心神不宁和憔悴的样儿。"你好，米蒂。"他说，"麦克米伦可真叫我们费事了，这位大财主银行家，罗斯福总统的亲密好友。管道梗阻。第三期。希望你去看看他。""好吧。"米蒂说。

在手术室里低声低气地介绍了一下。"雷羽登博士，米蒂大夫。泼烈贾－密特福先生，米蒂大夫。""我读过你关于炼丝菌学的那本书。"泼烈贾－密恃福一面说话一面握手，"真是出色的成绩，先生。""谢谢你的夸奖。"沃尔特·米蒂说。"我不知道你在美国，米蒂。"雷明登咕哝着，"把我和密特福来这儿治第三期，岂不是白费工夫。""你真客气。"米蒂说。一具巨大、复杂的机器，有许多管道、线路和手术台连接在一起，这时忽然扑克嗒－扑克嗒地响了起来。"新的麻醉器出毛病了！"一个实习大夫喊了起来，"在东部地区没有人懂得修理这台机器！""安静些，朋友！"米蒂说，声音又低又镇定。他跳向机器，它的声音现在变成扑克嗒－扑克嗒－奎泼－扑克嗒－奎泼。他开始巧妙地摆弄那一排光亮的仪表盘。"给我一支自来水笔！"他急促地说。有人递给他一支。他从机器里取出一个坏了的活塞，把自来水笔塞进原来的地方。

Walter Mitty stopped the car in front of the building where his wife went to have her hair done. "Remember to get those overshoes while I'm having my hair done," she said. "I don't need overshoes," said Mitty. She put her mirror back into her bag. "We've been all through that," she said, getting out of the car. "You're not a young man any longer." He raced the engine a little. "Why don't you wear your gloves? Have you lost your gloves?" Walter Mitty reached in a pocket and brought out the gloves. He put them on, but after she had turned and gone into the building and he had driven on to a red light, he took them off again. "Pick it up brother!" snapped a cop as the light changed, and Mitty hastily pulled on his gloves and lurched ahead. He drove around the streets aimlessly for a time, and then he drove past the hospital on his way to the parking lot.

… "It's the millionaire banker. Wellington McMillan," said the pretty nurse. "Yes?" said Walter Mitty, removing his gloves slowly. "Who has the case?" "Dr. Renshaw and Dr. Benbow, but there are two specialists here, Dr. Remington from New York and Dr. Pritchard-Mitford from London. He flew over." A door opened down a long, cool corridor and Dr. Renshaw came out. He looked distraught and haggard. "Hello, Mitty," he said. "We're having the devil's own time with McMillan, the millionaire banker and close personal friend of Roosevelt. Obstreosis of the ductal tract. Tertiary. Wish you'd take a look at him." "Glad to." said Mitty.

In the operating room there were whispered introductions: "Dr. Remington, Dr. Mitty. Dr. Pritchard-Mitford, Dr. Mitty." "I've read your book on streptothricosis," said Pritchard-Mitford, shaking hands. "A brilliant performance, sir." "Thank you," said Walter Mitty. "Didn't know you were in the States, Mitty," grumbled Remington. "Coals to Newcastle, bringing Mitford and me up here for a tertiary." "You are very kind," said Mitty. A huge, complicated machine, connected to the operating table, with many tubes and wires, began at this moment to go pocketa-pocketa-pocketa. "The new anaesthetizer is giving way!" shouted an interne. "There is no one in the East who knows how to fix it!" "Quiet, man!" said Mitty, in a low, cool voice. He sprang to the machine, which was now going pocketa-pocketa-queep-pocketa-queep. He began fingering delicately a row of glistening dials. "Give me a fountain pen!" he snapped. Someone handed him a fountain pen. He pulled a faulty piston out of the machine and inserted the pen in its place. "That will hold for ten minutes," he said. "Get on with the

"这可以顶用 10 分钟。"他说,"继续动手术。"一个护士匆匆过来,轻声对任肖说了些什么,米蒂看到任肖的脸色变成煞白。"瞳孔变化。"任肖紧张地说,"你来接手怎么样,米蒂?"米蒂望望任肖,也望望那贪杯的班波的畏缩样子,还望了望那两位大专家严肃而又狐疑的脸相。"如果你要我。"他说。他们把一件白手术衣披在他的身上;他戴上了口罩,和一双薄薄的手套;护士们给他递过了发亮的……

　　"倒,倒,麦克! 当心那辆别克车!"沃尔特·米蒂忙着刹车。"不是这一列,麦克。"停车场的服务员说,紧盯住米蒂。"啊,是吗。"米蒂含糊地说了声。他开始小心翼翼地把汽车倒退出标志着"出口"二字的行列。"把车子留在那儿。"服务员说,"我会把它停好的。"米蒂跳下了车。"嗨,把钥匙留下来。""哦。"米蒂说,把油门钥匙交给了那个人。服务员钻进汽车,用一种不当一回事的熟练技术,把车倒在应该停的地方。

　　这帮家伙真是目空一切,沃尔特·米蒂忖了一下,便走向大街去;这帮人自以为对一切都是行家。有一次他在新密尔福郊外,想把车上的链子取下来,不料竟缠到车轴上去了。一个人不得不从一辆救险车里走下来,把链子卸掉,这是个年轻的、咧着嘴在笑的汽车修理工。从此,米蒂太太总是要他把车开到修理库去把链子取掉。下一次,他想,我一定把右手吊在绷带里,那样他们就不会笑话我了。我把右手吊在绷带里,他们准看到我自己不可能把链子卸下来。他踢着人行道上的泥浆块。"套鞋。"他对自己说,开始去找鞋铺了。

　　等他从铺子里再走到街上,手臂下挟着一个装套鞋的盒子,沃尔特·米蒂使劲想他妻子还告诉他要买的什么东西。她叮嘱了两次,就在他们离家到华脱勃雷镇之前。在某种程度上,他讨厌每星期到镇上来的旅行——他总得要出点什么岔子。"克林尼克斯"卫生纸,他想,"施贵玉"药丸,刮胡子刀片? 不是。牙膏,牙刷,小苏打,金刚沙,创制权还是复决权①? 他不再费力去想了。可是她会记住的哟。"那个叫什么的东西在哪里?"她会问,"不要对我说你忘掉买那个

――――――――――
　　① 此处原文是 bicarbonate, carborundum, initiative and referendum,全是多音节词,前两词是化学品名,是要买的东西,后两词是政治术语,是从前面两词的声音联想起来的,是一种文字游戏,并无实义。

operation. " A nurse hurried over and whispered to Renshaw, and Mitty saw the man turn pale. "Coreopsis has set in, "said Renshaw nervously. "If you would take over, Mitty? "Mitty looked at him and at the craven figure of Benbow, who drank, and at the grave, uncertain faces of the two great specialists. "If you wish, "he said. They slipped a white gown on him; he adjusted a mask and drew on thin gloves; nurses handed him shining. . .

　　"Back it up, Mac! Look out for that Buick!" Walter Mitty jammed on the brakes. "Wrong lane, Mac, "said the parking-lot attendant, looking at Mitty closely. "Gee. Yeh, "muttered Mitty. He began cautiously to back out of the lane marked "Exit Only. " "Leave her sit there, "said the attendant. "I'll put her away. "Mitty got out of the car. "Hey, better leave the key. ""Oh, "said Mitty, handing the man the ignition key. The attendant vaulted into the car, backed it up with insolent skill, and put it where it belonged.

　　They're so damn cocky, thought Walter Mitty, walking along Main Street; they think they know everything. Once he had tried to take his chains off, outside New Milford, and he had got them wound around the axles. A man had had to come out in a wrecking car and unwind them, a young grinning garage man. Since then Mrs. Mitty always made him drive to a garage to have the chains taken off. The next time, he thought, I'll wear my right arm in a sling; they won't grin at me then. I'll have my right arm in a sling and they'll see I couldn't possibly take the chains off myself. He kicked at the slush on the sidewalk. "Overshoes, "he said to himself, and he began looking for a shoe store.

　　When he came out into the street again, with the overshoes in a box under his arm, Walter Mitty began to wonder what the other thing was his wife had told him to get. She had told him, twice before they set out from their house for Waterbury. In a way he hated these weekly trips to town—he was always getting something wrong. Kleenex, he thought, Squibb's, razor blades? No. Toothpaste, toothbrush, bicarbonate, carborundum, initiative, and referendum? He gave it up. But she should remember it. "Where's the what's-its-name? "she would ask. "Don't tell me you forgot the what's-its-name. "A newsboy went by shouting something about the Waterbury trial.

　　. . . "Perhaps this will refresh your memory. "The District Attorney suddenly thrust a heavy automatic at the quiet figure on the witness stand. "Have you ever seen this before? "Walter Mitty took the gun and examined it expertly. " This is my Webley-Vickers

叫什么的了。"一个报童喊着有关华脱勃雷审判案的什么事情。

……"也许这个会引起你的记忆来。"区检察官突然对证人席上那个默不作声的人送过来一把重型自动手枪,"你以前曾经见过这个吗?"沃尔特·米蒂接过了枪,内行地看了一下。"这是我的魏勃莱—伐克50.80。"他镇静地说。法庭里顿时发出一阵骚动的嗡嗡声。法官敲敲木槌叫人们遵守秩序。"我相信你用任何武器都是个能手吧?"区检察官暗示说。"抗议!"米蒂的律师喊了起来。"我们已经证明被告不可能开这一枪。我们已经证明他在 7 月 14 日晚上,右手是吊在绷带里的。"沃尔特·米蒂伸出手来轻轻一挥,吵吵嚷嚷的律师便不出声了。"我能够用任何一类枪支在 300 英尺外使左手把葛利高雷·费佐斯特打死。"他平静地说。法庭里爆发了一阵大混乱,在疯子般的吵嚷声中听见一声女人的尖叫,突然有个漂亮的一头黑发的女郎投身在沃尔特·米蒂的臂圈里。区检察官狂暴地打她。没有离开他坐的椅子,米蒂就在区检察官的下颚上打了一拳。"你这个卑鄙的狗杂种!"……

"小狗饼干。"沃尔特·米蒂说。他站住脚步,华脱勃雷的高楼大厦拨开法庭的迷雾,又围在他身旁了。一个女人从他身旁走过,笑了。"他说'小狗饼干'。"她对同伴说,"那个男人自顾自说'小狗饼干'。"沃尔特·米蒂匆匆向前走去。他走进"大西洋—太平洋"商店,不是他首先经过的那一家,而是在街那面较小的一爿。"我要给小狗吃的饼干。"他对店员说。"要名牌的吗,先生?"这位世界上最伟大的枪手想了一会儿。"有种盒子上写着'小狗吠着要吃'的。"沃尔特·米蒂说。

他妻子一刻钟之内可以在理发店里完事了,米蒂瞄瞄他的表,除非他们在吹干头发时出了麻烦,有时候,他们就在烘干时出麻烦的。她不愿比他先到旅馆;她愿意他照常先在那儿等她。他在旅馆休息室里找了把大皮椅,面朝着窗,把套鞋和小狗饼干放在椅旁的地板上。他随手拿了本过期的《自由》杂志,便埋头坐在大皮椅里。《德国能够从空中征服世界吗?》,沃尔特·米蒂看着轰炸机和街上废墟的图片。

……"炮轰使小拉莱昏晕了,长官。"中士说。米蒂上尉透过乱蓬蓬的头发望望他。"把他抱到床上去,"他疲惫地说,"让他跟别人在一起。我一个人去

50.80,"he said calmly. An excited buzz ran around the courtroom. The judge rapped for order. "You are a crack shot with any sort of firearms, I believe?" said the District Attorney, insinuatingly. "Objection!" shouted Mitty's attorney. "We have shown that the defendant could not have fired the shot. We have shown that he wore his right arm in a sling on the night of the fourteenth of July." Walter Mitty raised his hand briefly and the bickering attorneys were stilled. "With any known make of gun," he said evenly, "I could have killed Gregory Fitzhurst at three hundred feet *with my left hand*." Pandemonium broke loose in the courtroom. A woman's scream rose above the bedlam and suddenly a lovely, dark-haired girl was in Walter Mitty's arms. The District Attorney struck at her savagely. Without rising from his chair, Mitty let the man have it on the point of the chin. "You miserable cur!"...

"Puppy biscuit," said Walter Mitty. He stopped walking and the buildings of Waterbury rose up out of the misty courtroom and surrounded him again. A woman who was passing laughed. "He said 'Puppy biscuit'" she said to her companion. "That man said 'Puppy biscuit' to himself." Walter Mitty hurried on. He went into an A. & P., not the first one he came to but a smaller one farther up the street. "I want some biscuit for small, young dogs," he said to the clerk. "Any special brand, sir?" The greatest pistol shot in the world thought a moment. "It says 'Puppies Bark for It' on the box," said Walter Mitty.

His wife would be through at the hairdresser's in fifteen minutes, Mitty saw in looking at his watch, unless they had trouble drying it; sometimes they had trouble drying it. She didn't like to get to the hotel first; she would want him to be there waiting for her as usual. He found a big leather chair in the lobby, facing a window, and he put the overshoes and the puppy biscuit on the floor beside it. He picked up an old copy of *Liberty* and sank down into the chair. "Can Germany Conquer the World through the Air?" Walter Mitty looked at the pictures of bombing planes and of ruined streets.

... "The cannonading has got the wind up in young Raleigh, sir," said the sergeant. Captain Mitty looked up at him through tousled hair. "Get him to bed," he said wearily, "with the others. I'll fly alone." "But you can't, sir," said the sergeant anxiously. "It takes two men to handle that bomber and the Archies are pounding hell out of the air. Von Richtman's circus is between here and Saulier." "Somebody's got to get

飞。""但是你不能去，长官。"中士急切地说，"要两个人才能驾驶轰炸机，而且高射炮火在上空又那么厉害。冯·列切曼飞行队就在这儿和骚列之间。""总得有人去炸掉那个军火库的。"米蒂说，"我去。来点儿白兰地吗?"他给中士倒了杯，给自己也倒了杯。战斗在地下掩蔽部外面雷鸣着，而且猛击着入口。屋子里横飞着炸断的木料和碎片。"差点儿打中。"米蒂上尉不经意地说。"高射炮火越来越集中了。"中士说。"我们只能活一次，中士。"米蒂说，带着淡淡的一掠而过的笑容，"我们不是这样吗?"他又倒了杯白兰地，一口吞了下去。"我从来没见过像你这样能喝白兰地的人，长官。"中士说，"对不起，长官。"米蒂上尉站起身来，用皮带束好了他那把魏勃莱—伐克自动手枪。"要飞过40公里的地狱之火，长官。"中士说。米蒂喝干了最后一杯白兰地。"说到底，"他温柔地说，"又有哪儿不是地狱?"大炮的轰击声越来越密了;还有啦一达一达的机关枪声，什么地方还有新喷火器吓人的扑克嗒—扑克嗒—扑克嗒的吼声。沃尔特·米蒂一面走向地下掩蔽室的门口，一面嘴里哼着"挨近我的金发女郎"。他转过身来向中士打个招呼。"再见!"他说……

有什么在打着他的肩头。"我在旅馆里找遍了你。"米蒂太太说，"为什么你要躲在这把破椅子里?你打算让我怎样找到你呢?""事情越来越紧了。"米蒂含糊地说了声。"什么?"米蒂太太说，"你买到了那个叫什么的吗? 小狗饼干? 盒子里是什么?""套鞋。"米蒂说。"你不能在铺子里就穿上吗?""我刚才是想……"沃尔特·米蒂说，"你明白吗，有时候我也会在想些什么的?"她盯了他一眼。"等到了家，我要给你量量体温。"她说。

他们从那扇一推就发出轻轻的像嘲弄声的旋转门走出了旅馆。到停车场要走过两排房屋。到了街角的杂货店，她说:"在这儿等我，我忘掉要买的东西了。用不了一分钟。"她花了比一分钟更多的时间。沃尔特·米蒂点燃了一支烟。天开始下雨了，雨里夹着雪。他贴着杂货店的墙边站着，吸着烟……他并着脚跟挺出胸部。"不蒙他妈的鬼手帕不行吗?"沃尔特·米蒂讥嘲地说。他狠狠地最后吸了口烟头，啪的一声扔掉了。接着，在嘴唇上带着那种淡淡的一掠而过的笑容，他面对行刑队，挺直而屹立，自傲而轻蔑，"永不战败"的沃尔特·米蒂，到了最后关头还是不可思议的。

that ammunition dump," said Mitty. "I'm going over. Spot of brandy?" He poured a drink for the sergeant and one for himself. War thundered and whined around the dugout and battered at the door. There was a rending of wood and splinters flew through the room. "A bit of a near thing," said Captain Mitty carelessly. "The box barrage is closing in," said the sergeant. "We only live once, sergeant," said Mitty, with his faint, fleeting smile. "Or do we?" He poured another brandy and tossed it off. "I never see a man could hold his brandy like you, sir," said the sergeant. "Begging your pardon, sir. Captain Mitty stood up and strapped on his huge Webley-Vickers automatic. "It's forty kilometers through hell, sir," said the sergeant. Mitty finished one last brandy. "After all," he said softly, "what isn't?" The pounding of the cannon increased; there was the rat-tat-tatting of machine guns, and from somewhere came the menacing pocketa-pocketa-pocketa of the new flame-throwers. Walter Mitty walked to the door of the dugout humming "*Auprès de Ma Blonde*." He turned and waved to the sergeant. "Cheerio!" he said. . . .

Something struck his shoulder. "I've been looking all over this hotel for you," said Mrs. Mitty. "Why do you have to hide in this old chair? How did you expect me to find you?" "Things close in," said Walter Mitty vaguely. "What?" Mrs. Mitty said. "Did you get the what's-its-name? The puppy biscuit? What's in that box?" "Overshoes," said Mitty. "Couldn't you have put them on in the store?" "I was thinking," said Walter Mitty. "Does it ever occur to you that I am sometimes thinking?" She looked at him. "I'm going to take your temperature when I get you home," she said.

They went out through the revolving doors that made a faintly derisive whistling sound when you pushed them. It was two blocks to the parking lot. At the drugstore on the corner she said, "Wait here for me. I forgot something. I won't be a minute." She was more than a minute. Walter Mitty lighted a cigarette. It began to rain, rain with sleet in it. He stood up against the wall of the drugstore, smoking. . . . He put his shoulders back and his heels together. "To hell with the handkerchief," said Walter Mitty scornfully. He took one last drag on his cigarette and snapped it away. Then, with that faint, fleeting smile playing about his lips, he faced the firing squad; erect and motionless, proud and disdainful, Walter Mitty the Undefeated, inscrutable to the last.

┌讨 论─■

这篇作品也许看来只是另一篇人物特写，而根本不是小说。诚然，某些事情的确发生了，可是这些发生的事情有意义吗？郊区居民米蒂先生驾车把妻子载进市中心去买东西。他把车开得太快，挨了一顿骂之后，在理发店门口让她下了车，把车子停放到停车场上去。他买了一双套鞋和一盒狗饼干，然后到他妻子将在那儿和他会面的旅馆休息室去。在他们回到停车场的路上，他的妻子想起了自己需要到杂货铺买的一件东西。米蒂先生在铺子外面等候她，故事就这样结束了。如果我们把这些就称作这篇作品的"情节"，那么，发生的事情的确很少。而如果我们接下去说，实际上构成这篇作品主要部分的米蒂先生的幻想，和情节根本无关，只是个性方面的一种直接表现，那么否认这篇作品是小说的这一立场，就变得相当有说服力了。看来这个简略的"情节"不过是一个方便的挂物架，上面悬挂着米蒂先生内心生活的种种不同表现。这样看待这篇故事，我们可能会不承认瑟伯的作品构成了通过情节展现个性这一点，而这一点我们说过是小说所不可缺少的。

当然，就一种意义讲，关于这篇作品的以上陈述是正确的：通篇故事的构思是为了展现人物性格的。除了这一展现之外，发生的事情的确很少。然而，证明它是一篇真正的小说毕竟并不困难。

第一，作者始终没有对沃尔特·米蒂的个性做过一次直接的评论。诚然，我们要推断出米蒂在停车场服务员的心目中，或者在他嘟哝着"小狗饼干"时经过他身旁的那个女人的心目中构成何种形象，这是并无困难的。但是作者始终没有亲自告诉我们应该怎样想法。他对于发生的事情的报导实际上是相当客观的。我们通过那些人的行动与评论——不是通过作者所做的任何评述——知道了人们对沃尔

This story may seem to be merely another character sketch, and not fiction at all. True, certain things do happen here, but are the happenings meaningful? Mr. Mitty, a suburbanite, drives his wife into the center for some shopping. After having been reproved for driving the fast, he lets her out at the hairdresser's and leaves his car at the parking lot. He buys a pair of overshoes and a box of dog biscuit, then goes to the lobby of the hotel where his wife is to meet him. On their way back to the parking lot, his wife remembers something that she needs to buy in the drugstore and the story ends as Mr. Mitty waits for her outside. If we call this the "action" of the story, then indeed precious little happens. And if we go on to say that Mr. Mitty's daydreaming, which actually makes up most of the story, is not really connected with the action at all, being a direct expression of character, then the case for denying that the story is fiction becomes rather grave. It looks as if the very sketchy "plot" is simply a convenient rack on which to hang the various manifestations of Mr. Mitty's interior life. Looking at the story in this way, we may be tempted to deny that Thurber's story constitutes that revelation of character *through* action that we have said is essential to fiction.

There is a sense, of course, in which the foregoing account of the story is true: the whole narrative *is* constructed to reveal the character of the man, and aside from that revelation, very little does happen. Yet, it will not be difficult to show that it is a genuine piece of fiction after all.

In the first place, the author never once makes a direct comment upon Walter Mitty's character. We have no difficulty, it is true, in deducing what kind of figure Mitty cuts in the eyes of the parking-lot attendant or of the woman who passes him as he mutters "puppy biscuit." But the author never tells us in his own person what we are to think. He is really quite objective in his report of what happens. We learn what people think of Walter Mitty through the actions and comments of those

特·米蒂的看法。

　　第二，到了米蒂如何看待他自己的这一问题上，那也是通过"情节"传达出来的。我们看见米蒂在幻想。我们看见米蒂太太提到家庭大夫任肖医师怎样使米蒂想入非非：他成了一家大医院手术室里的出色医务人员，再不然就是他对区检察官说的那句毁灭性的驳斥，"你这个卑鄙的狗杂种"——这本身就是他的一次幻想的一部分——怎样竟然使他一下想起，他应该记住购买的，是小狗饼干。

　　然而，最为重要的是，"情节"虽然琐细，却使米蒂的幻想有了意义。它揭示了米蒂需要从他生活在其中的世界上逃走这一事实，来表明这些胡思乱想的动机。在那个世界上，他扮演的是一个怕老婆的丈夫这一角色，他的那个凶悍的、毫无想象力的妻子显然早已把米蒂先生对于英勇大胆行为的渴望很有效地压制下去了。这篇小故事中的"情节"使这种关系强有力地戏剧化了。虽然涉及的事情本身是平凡的——米蒂每小时开 55 英里或是米蒂对于穿套鞋所表示的反对——它们却阐明了米蒂生活的核心。

　　我们对沃尔特·米蒂应该采取什么态度呢？这里描绘的场面实质上就是连环漫画中怕老婆的丈夫的那种场面。可是这里指望造成的影响，并不像一套连环漫画所造成的那么明显。虽然沃尔特·米蒂的幻想包含着惊险小说及电影中最最陈腐的题材，他却并没有被写得滑稽怪诞。他还具有某种使人同情的地方，尽管他的创造者显然被他的儒弱无能逗得乐起来了。那么我们应该相当郑重地看待他，从他的困境中看到一个注定该遭受挫折的心地高尚的人所受到的束缚吗？也绝不是这样。那些幻想的性质，以及它们很怪诞地一个堆砌在一个上面的那种方式，有效地阻止我们一本正经地看待沃尔特·米蒂的困境。不过读者并不需要特殊的帮助来决定如何"看待"这篇作品。这方面，故事的"情节"又有助于提醒我

people—not through any summary made by the author.

In the second place, when it comes to a matter of the way in which Mitty sees himself, that too is mediated through "action." We see Mitty at his business of daydreaming. We see how Mrs. Mitty' mention of the family physician, Dr. Renshaw, sends Mitty into a fantasy in which he becomes the medical hero in the operating room of a great hospital, or how his withering retort to the district attorney, "You miserable cur"—itself a part of one of his daydreams—suddenly reminds him that it is puppy biscuit that he is to remember to purchase.

Most important of all, however, the "action," trivial though it is, gives point and meaning to Mitty's daydreams. It indicates the motivation for these fantasies by revealing Mitty's need to escape from the world in which he lives. It is a world in which his own role is that of the husband henpecked by an overbearing and unimaginative wife who evidently long ago effectually suppressed Mr. Mitty's yearnings for the heroic and venturesome. The "action" in this little story effectively dramatizes this relationship, and though the events in question are in themselves commonplace—Mitty's driving at 55 miles an hour or Mitty's protest at wearing overshoes—they illuminate the very core of Mitty's life.

What attitude are we to take toward Walter Mitty? The situation portrayed is in essence that of the henpecked husband of the comic strips. Yet the effect aimed at here is not so blatant as that of a comic strip. Walter Mitty, though his daydreams embody the stalest of clichès of adventure fiction and the movies, is not made farcically grotesque. He is allowed a certain kind of pathos, even though his creator is obviously amused by his ineffectuality. Are we to take him rather seriously, then, and see in his plight the imprisonment of a high-hearted soul condemned to frustration? Scarcely that, either. The nature of the daydreams and the way that they are grotesquely piled up one upon another effectually prevent our taking the plight of Walter Mitt really seriously. But the reader will need

们,应该以那种既同情又好笑的恰当的复杂心情来看待米蒂先生。作者一点儿也没有告诉我们应该如何感受,只戏剧化地向我们展示出米蒂先生生活中的几小时,然后就留下来让我们自己去推断。

且不问我们对沃尔特·米蒂应该采取何种态度,我们不妨先提出这样一个问题,即这篇作品的语调(见重要词汇)如何。语调就是故事结构中所反映出的作者的态度——对他的素材和对他的读者的态度。一篇作品的语调可以说成是阴沉的或欢快的,含蓄的或奔放的,直率的或嘲弄的,快乐的或忧伤的,严肃的或玩笑的,拘谨的或感情用事的——我们可以继续下去,说出上百个其他的形容词来。然而,实际上,大多数故事的语调通常总过于特殊,过于复杂,无法用任何一个形容词来充分加以说明。举例而言,瑟伯作品的语调是一种玩笑游戏的语调,但是我们看到它里面丝毫没有嘲弄的意味,甚至还带有一点儿唤起人同情的痕迹。

语调作为一个用来说明文体的词,是从"嗓音的声调"上引申出来的。说出一件事的声调,修饰了所说的话,甚至可以使意义变得相反。"他真是个好人",用挖苦的声调说出来,就表示说话的人根本不认为提到的这人是一个好人。在我们的口语中,我们通过说话的声调经常对我们所说的词句做出明确无误的修饰。文学家通常不能把他的著作朗诵给我们听,但是如果他是艺术家,他可以很有力、很确切地控制我们"接受"他写在书页上的语言的方式。在往后几篇作品里,语调问题往往非常重要。我们将不得不经常问,这一节或这一整篇小说的语调是什么。(如果我们主要想到的不是故事而是作者,我们也许宁愿把我们的问题从故事的语调改换成作者的态度。)

no special help in deciding how to "take" this story. Here again the "action" of the story serves to suggest the proper blend of sympathy and amusement with which we are to view Mr. Mitty. Far from telling us what to feel, the author gives us a dramatic presentation of a few hours of Mr. Mitty's life and leaves it up to us to make our own inferences.

Instead of asking what attitude we should take toward Walter Mitty, we might put this question by asking what the *tone* (see Glossary) of the story is. The tone is the reflection in the makeup of the story of the author's attitudes—toward his material and toward his reader. The tone of a story may be characterized as grave or gay, reserved or ebullient, straightforward or mocking, merry or melancholy, solemn, playful, prim, sentimental—and one might continue through a hundred other adjectives. Actually, however, the tone of most stories will usually be too special and too complicated to be adequately described by any one adjective. The tone of Thurber's story, for example, is one of amused playfulness, but we have seen that it has nothing of scorn in it and that it even allows for a trace of pathos.

Tone as a term used to characterize style derives from "tone of the voice." The tone in which a thing is uttered modifies what is said and may even reverse the meaning. "He's a fine fellow," delivered in a sarcastic tone, means that the speaker does not think that the person in question is a fine fellow at all. In our spoken language, we are constantly giving exact qualifications to what our words literally say by the tone in which we say them. The literary artist usually cannot read us his work aloud; yet if he is an artist, he can control very powerfully and exactly the way we are to "take" what he puts on the page. In the stories that follow, the problem of tone is frequently a matter of primary importance. We shall often have to ask what the tone of a passage or of a whole story is. (If we are thinking primarily not of the story but of the author we may prefer to transpose our question from the tone of the story to the attitude of the author.)

思考题 ■

1. 沃尔特·米蒂的形象在这种夸张的描绘下，可以被看作一种讽刺漫画。在这一实例中，这种夸张像一个出色的漫画家所运用的手法那样，是否合情合理？纵然歪曲夸张，它是否让人信服这并没有脱离现实？

2. 这篇小说的最后一句话可否说是一个恰当的结论？从字面上看，这句句子当然是提到米蒂在自己全神贯注的那一特殊幻想中所采取的姿态，但是可不可以说它也适用于另一标准？有没有一种意义表明沃尔特·米蒂果真是"永不战败的，到最后关头还是不可思议的"？对谁是不可思议的呢？

3. 考虑一下下列这些项目在产生幽默效果方面所起的作用：米蒂喜欢用"扑克嗒—扑克嗒"这样的音节来表示某种声音；"长官，中士说"这类短语里所包含的头韵①（见重要词汇）；以及故事中叙说米蒂历次想入非非的那部分里使用的从惊险小说中吸取来的套话（见重要词汇）。　　　（王 万译）

1. In its distortion, the portrait of Walter Mitty may be regarded as a kind of caricature. In this instance is the distortion, like that employed by a good cartoonist, justified? Does it, even through distortion or exaggeration, make a convincing reference to actuality?

2. May the last sentence of the story be said to be an appropriate conclusion? Literally, of course, this sentence refers to the pose Mitty assumes in the particular fantasy in which he is absorbed, but can it be said to apply at another level? Is there a sense in which Walter Mitty is indeed "the Undefeated, inscrutable to the last"? and inscrutable to whom?

3. Consider the function of the following items in making for the humorous effect: Mitty' fondness for the syllables "pocketa-pocketa" as expressive of certain sounds; the *alliteration* (see Glossary) involved in such phrases as "sir, said the sergeant"; the use, in the parts of the story that recount Mitty's various fantasies, of *clichès* (see Glossary) drawn from thriller stories.

---

①　"长官，中士说"，原文是："sir, said the sergeant" sir, said 和 sergeant 三个词的第一个字母都是"s"。

005. 年轻的布朗大爷

(美)纳撒尼尔·霍桑 著　　主 万 译

005. Young Goodman Brown

by Nathaniel Hawthorne

年轻的布朗大爷①在落日时分出来走到塞勒姆村②的那条街上，他跨出门槛便又回过头，跟年轻的妻子吻别。妻子很恰当地名叫费思③，这时候把自己美丽的头伸到街上，让风吹拂着软帽上的粉红色缎带，一面向布朗大爷叫唤。

"亲爱的心肝儿，"等她的嘴唇凑近他的耳朵时，她温柔地、相当伤感地小声说，"请你把这次旅程推迟到日出以后，今儿晚上还是在自己的床上安歇吧。一个孤独的女人常受到她自己往往很害怕的那种噩梦和忧虑的烦扰。在一年里所有的夜晚中，亲爱的丈夫，今儿夜晚请你留下陪着我吧。"

"我亲爱的费思，"年轻的布朗大爷回答，"在一年里所有的夜晚中，我这一夜非得离开你不待在家中。我的往返旅程，如同你所说的，必须在现在和日出之间完成。怎么，亲爱、美丽的妻子，你已经怀疑我了吗，我们结婚才不过3个月啊？"

"那么，愿上帝降福给你！"扎着粉红色缎苔的费思说，"愿你回来时，发觉一切顺遂。"

"阿门④！"布朗大爷喊了一声，"你祈祷吧，亲爱的费思，黄昏时分就上床睡觉，不会遭什么损害的。"

这样，他们分别了。年轻人启程上路。后来在那个聚会所⑤旁边预备拐弯时，他回顾了一下，看见费

────────

① 原文为"goodman"，专用来称呼体面、富裕的公民，并不涉及家族关系。——原注。
② 现为美国马萨诸塞州东北部的一处海港。
③ 原文为 Faith，意思是："信仰"，"信义"，"忠诚"。
④ 基督教祈祷及圣歌中的结束语，意思是："心愿如此"。
⑤ 原文是 meeting-house，指基督教教友会的礼拜堂。

YOUNG Goodman Brown① came forth at sunset into the street at Salem village; but put his head back, after crossing the threshold, to exchange a parting kiss with his young wife. And Faith, as the wife was aptly named, thrust her own pretty head into the street, letting the wind play with the pink ribbons of her cap while she called to Goodman Brown.

"Dearest heart," whispered she, softly and rather sadly, when her lips were close to his ear, "prithee put off your journey until sunrise and sleep in your own bed to-night. A lone woman is troubled with such dreams and such thoughts that she's afeard of herself sometimes. Pray tarry with me this night, dear husband, of all nights in the year."

"My love and my Faith," replied young Goodman Brown, "of all nights in the year, this one night must I tarry away from thee. My journey, as thou callest it, forth and back again, must needs be done 'twixt now and sunrise. What, my sweet, pretty wife, dost thou doubt me already, and we but three months married?"

"Then God bless you!" said Faith, with the pink ribbons; "and may you find all well when you come back."

"Amen!" cried Goodman Brown. "Say thy prayers, dear Faith, and go to bed at dusk, and no harm will come to thee."

So they parted; and the young man pursued his way until, being about to turn the corner by the meeting-house, he looked back and saw the head of Faith still peeping after him with a melancholy air, in spite of her pink ribbons.

────────

① The term "Goodman" was used of a respectable and prosperous citizen without reference to blood.

作者简介：纳撒尼尔·霍桑（Nathaniel Hawthorne，1804—1864），美国小说家。1804年7月4日生于马萨诸塞州塞勒姆，1864年5月19日卒于新罕布什尔州普利茅斯。霍桑是清教徒的后裔，深受道德洗礼。他的作品包括《我的亲属，莫理斯上校》(My Kinsman, Major Molineux，1832)、《罗杰·马尔文的葬礼》(Roger Malvin's Buria，1832)和《年轻的布朗大爷》(Young Goodman Brown，1835)。他最出名的作品是《红字》(The Scarlet Letter，1850)，讲述了一个新英格兰殖民地背景下的通奸故事，被列入美国最好的小说之一。他是一位文学艺术家，也是寓言兼象征主义大师，他被列入美国最伟大的小说家行列。

思的头仍然带着一种忧郁的神气在注视着他,根本不顾那条粉红色缎带。

"可怜的小费思!"他想着,因为他心里十分难受,"我撇下她去办这样一件事,是个多么卑鄙的家伙啊!她还谈到做梦。我觉得她说着的时候,脸上有烦恼的神色,仿佛有一场梦事先已经告诉了她,今儿夜晚将干出什么事来。可是,不,不;想着它会送了她的性命的。嗨,她是世上一位幸运的天使。过了这一夜之后,我就紧紧捏着她的裙子,跟随她上天堂去。"

　　布朗大爷对未来抱着这种高超的决心以后,觉得自己有理由更为迅速地去从事眼下的邪恶勾当了。他走的是一条沉寂的道路,树林里所有最最幽暗的树木把这条路遮得一片漆黑。那些树木简直长得密密匝匝,不容这条羊肠小道穿过,而且总在后面立刻就又合拢起来。四下里一片凄凉,只有这样一片落寞中的这一特色,行路人并不知道那无数的树身和头上的粗枝可能隐藏着些什么人,所以他迈着孤单单的步伐,可能还在经过一大群隐而不现的人哩。

　　"也许每棵树后面都藏着一个凶恶的印第安人。"布朗大爷暗自这么说。他满怀恐惧地朝身后瞥了一眼,又加上一句:"要是魔鬼本人竟然就在我的身旁,那可怎么好!"

　　他回头张望着,走过了路上一处弯曲的地方,然后又朝前望去,看见一个人穿着朴实大方的服装,坐在一棵老树的脚下。布朗大爷走近时,他站起身来,和他并排朝前走去。

　　"你来晚了,布朗大爷,"他说,"我穿过波士顿前来的时候,老南方①的大钟正在敲着,已经整整过去15分钟了。"

　　"费思使我耽误了一会儿。"年轻人回答,嗓音有点儿发抖,这是因为他同伴蓦然出现的缘故,尽管那并不完全出乎意料。

　　这时候,树林里十分幽暗,特别是这两个人正在赶路的那一带地方。根据尽可能辨别出的情形来看,第二个行路人大约50岁上下,似乎和布朗大爷属于同一个阶级,和他长得很有几分相似,虽然也许主要是在神态方面而不是在容貌方面。话虽这么说,他们可以被看做父子俩。但是,尽管年长人的衣着和年轻人的一样朴实,举止也一样质朴,他却有一种形容不

---

① 酒店的字号。

"Poor little Faith!" thought he, for his heart smote him. "What a wretch am I to leave her on such an errand! She talks of dreams, too. Methought as she spoke there was trouble in her face, as if a dream had warned her what work is to be done to-night. But no, no; 't would kill her to think it. Well, she's a blessed angel on earth; and after this one night I'll cling to her skirts and follow her to heaven."

With this excellent resolve for the future, Goodman Brown felt himself justified in making more haste on his present evil purpose. He had taken a dreary road, darkened by all the gloomiest trees of the forest, which barely stood aside to let the narrow path creep through, and closed immediately behind. It was all as lonely as could be; and there is this peculiarity in such a solitude, that the traveler knows not who may be concealed by the innumerable trunks and the thick boughs overhead; so that with lonely footsteps he may yet be passing through an unseen multitude.

"There may be a devilish Indian behind every tree," said Goodman Brown to himself; and he glanced fearfully behind him as he added, "What if the devil himself should be at my very elbow!"

His head being turned back, he passed a crook of the road, and, looking forward again, beheld the figure of a man, in grave and decent attire, seated at the foot of an old tree. He arose at Goodman Brown's approach and walked onward side by side with him.

"You are late, Goodman Brown," said he. "The clock of the Old South was striking as I came through Boston, and that is full fifteen minutes agone."

"Faith kept me back a while," replied the young man, with a tremor in his voice, caused by the sudden appearance of his companion, though not wholly unexpected.

It was now deep dusk in the forest, and deepest in that part of it where these two were journeying. As nearly as could be discerned, the second traveler was about fifty years old, apparently in the same rank of life as Goodman Brown, and bearing a considerable resemblance to him, though perhaps more in expression than features. Still they might have been taken for father and son. And yet, though the elder person was as simply clad as the younger, and as simple in manner too, he had an indescribable air of one who knew the world, and who would not have felt abashed at the governor's dinner table or in King William's court, were it possible that his affairs should call him thither. But the only thing about him that could be fixed upon as remarkable was his staff, which bore the likeness

出的风度，是一个世故很深的人，纵然有可能因为自身的事务使他坐到了总督的餐桌上或者去到了威廉王①的朝廷上，他也不会感到局促不安。不过，他身边可以算作引人注目的一件东西，就是他的手杖。手杖就像一条大黑蛇，制作得那么稀奇，简直可以看见它像一条活蛇那样蜿蜒蠕动了。当然，这一定是凭借那种捉摸不定的光线在视觉方面所造成的一和错觉。

"来啊，布朗大爷，"他的同路人喊着说，"开始上路，这可是一个很沉闷的地方。拿着我的手杖吧，要是你这么快就疲乏了的话。"

"朋友，"另一个说，把原来缓慢的步伐完全停了下来，"我遵守约言在这儿和你会面，现在我打算回到来的地方去了。我对你所知道的那件事很有顾虑。"

"你这么说吗？"手握黑蛇的那人侧过脸微笑着回答，"话虽如此，让我们往前走去，边走边说理由。如果我说服不了你，你就回去。我们在树林里还不过刚走了一点儿路。"

"太远啦！太远啦！"这位大爷嚷着，一面不自觉地重新走了起来，"我父亲从没有为这样一件事跑进森林里来，他的父亲在他之前也从没这样过。从殉道者的时代以来，我们家一直就是正派人和虔诚的基督教徒。我会是第一个姓布朗的走上这条蹊，交上……"

"这样的伙伴，你会这么说，"年长的人对他的停顿这样解释说，"说得好，布朗大爷！我对你们家跟对清教徒中任何一个人同样熟悉，这说起来可不是废话。你祖父，那位警官，那么厉害地鞭打那个贵格会②女人，一路穿过塞勒姆的街道，我帮助了也。后来，在菲利普王战争③中，把在我火炉上点着的一个油松节瘤拿去给你父亲，让他放火烧了一座印第安村庄的，也是我。他们俩都是我的好朋友。我们沿着这条小路做过许多次愉快的散步，午夜之后又快快活活地回去。为了他们，我很乐意和你交朋友。"

"如果是像你说的这样，"布朗大爷回答，"那我很

---

① 指英国国王威廉三世(1689—1702)。

② 基督教教友会又称贵格会。

③ 菲利普王是印第安人万帕诺格部落的酋长。清教徒殖民地的扩张使他大为惊慌，于是在1675年出动来屠杀入侵者。经过多次粗暴冷酷的斯杀之后，菲利菩败下阵去，遭到追捕，被杀害了。——原注

of a great black snake, so curiously wrought that it might almost be seen to twist and wriggle itself like a living serpent. This, of course, must have been an ocular deception, assisted by the uncertain light.

"Come, Goodman Brown," cried his fellow-traveler, "this is a dull place for the beginning of a journey. Take my staff if you are so soon weary."

"Friend," said the other, exchanging his slow pace for a full stop, "having kept covenant by meeting thee here, it is my purpose now to return whence I came. I have scruples touching the matter thou wot'st of."

"Sayest thou so?" replied he of the serpent, smiling apart. "Let us walk on, nevertheless, reasoning as we go; and if I convince thee not thou shalt turn back. We are but a little way in the forest yet."

"Too far! too far!" exclaimed the goodman, unconsciously resuming his walk. "My father never went into the woods on such an errand, nor his father before him. We have been a race of honest men and good Christians since the days of the martyrs; and shall I be the first of the name of Brown that ever took his path and kept"—

"Such company, thou wouldst say," observed the elder person, interpreting his pause. "Well said, Goodman Brown! I have been as well acquainted with your family as with ever a one among the Puritans; and that's no trifle to say. I helped your grandfather, the constable, when he lashed the Quaker woman so smartly through the streets of Salem; and it was I that brought your father a pitch-pine knot, kindled at my own hearth, to set fire to an Indian village, in King Philip's war.①They were my good friends, both; and many a pleasant walk have we had along this path, and returned merrily after midnight. I would fain be friends with you for their sake."

"If it be as thou sayest," replied Goodman Brown, "I marvel they never spoke of these matters; or, verily, I marvel not, seeing that the least rumor of the sort would have driven them from New England. We are a people of prayer, and good works to boot, and abide no such wickedness."

"Wickedness or not," said the traveler with the twisted staff, "I have a very general acquaintance here in New England. The deacons of many a church have

---

① King Philip, chief of the Wampanoag Indians, alarmed by the expansion of Puritan colonies, set out, in 1675, to massacre the intruders. After much pitiless violence on both sides, Philip was defeated and hunted down and killed.

奇怪,他们怎么从来没有提起过这些事;再不然,说实在的,我并不觉得奇怪,因为一丁点儿这样的谣言就会把他们从新英格兰①赶出去。我们是向上帝祈祷的人,而且专做好事,不能容忍这样的坏事。"

"坏事不坏事,"挂着弯曲手杖的行路人说,"我在新英格兰这儿有不少熟人。许多教堂里的执事全跟我一块儿喝过圣餐酒,好几个镇上的行政委员都邀我去做他们的主任委员,而州议会的大多数人都坚决支持我的利益。总督和我也——不过这些全是机密大事。"

"真会是这样吗?"布朗大爷喊着,惊讶地睁大眼睛望着他那泰然自若的同伴,"然而,我跟总督和议会全然无关,他们有他们自己的作风,对于一个像我这样朴朴实实的庄稼人并不是什么典范。但是我如果跟你走下去,怎么有脸去见塞勒姆村上的那位老好人,我们的教长呢?啊,他的声音在安息日和讲道日都会使我发抖的。"

到这时候为止,年长的行路人一直严肃认真地听着,可是这当儿,他却忍俊不禁,发出了一阵欢笑,同时自己颤动得那么厉害,蛇一般的手杖当真似乎也同情地蠕动起来。

"哈!哈!哈!"他连连笑着,随后才镇静下来,"唔,往下说呀,布朗大爷,往下说呀,不过务必请你别叫我笑死。"

"好,为了马上了结这件事,"布朗大爷相当恼怒地说,"还有我的妻子费思。这样会叫她那娇小可爱的心伤透了,我宁愿自己伤心。"

"好,倘若是这情形,"另一个回答,"那么说真的,就走你的路吧,布朗大爷。我决不为了20个在我们前边蹒跚行走的那类老婆子而让费思遭到什么损害。"

他说着用手杖指指小路上的一个女人形影。布朗大爷认出来那是一位很虔诚的模范老妇人,曾经在他少年时期教过他教义问答,今天跟教长和古金执事一起,仍旧是他的道德与精神的导师。

"说真的,克洛伊斯大娘②黄昏时分竟然跑到这

---

① 指美国现在东北部的康涅狄格州、缅因州、马萨诸塞州、新罕布什尔州、罗得岛和弗蒙特州一带地区。

② 克洛伊斯,像下文出现的卡里尔一样,也在 1692 年因为行使巫术而被判罪。霍桑的一位祖先是判处她死刑的那个法庭的成员。——原注。

drunk the communion wine with me; the selectmen of divers towns make me their chairman; and a majority of the Great and General Court are firm supporters of my interest. The governor and I, too—But these are state secrets. "

"Can this be so?" cried Goodman Brown, with a stare of amazement at his undisturbed companion. "Howbeit, I have nothing to do with the governor and council; they have their own ways, and are no rule for a simple husbandman like me. But, were I to go on with thee, how should I meet the eye of that good old man, our minister, at Salem village? Oh, his voice would make me tremble both Sabbath day and lecture day. "

Thus far the elder traveler had listened with due gravity; but now burst into a fit of irrepressible mirth, shaking himself so violently that his snake-like staff actually seemed to wriggle in sympathy.

"Ha! ha! ha!" shouted he again and again; then composing himself, "Well, go on, Goodman Brown, go on; but, prithee, don't kill me with laughing. "

"Well, then, to end the matter at once," said Goodman Brown, considerably nettled, "there is my wife, Faith. It would break her dear little heart; and I'd rather break my own. "

"Nay, if that be the case," answered the other, "e'en go thy ways, Goodman Brown. I would not for twenty old women like the one hobbling before us that Faith should come to any harm. "

As he spoke he pointed his staff at a female figure on the path, in whom Goodman Brown recognized a very pious and exemplary dame, who had taught him his catechism in youth, and was still his moral and spiritual adviser, jointly with the minister and Deacon Gookin.

"A marvel, truly, that Goody Cloyse① should be so far in the wilderness at nightfall," said he. "But with your leave, friend, I shall take a cut through the woods until we have left this Christian woman behind. Being a stranger to you, she might ask whom I was consorting with and whither I was going. "

"Be it so," said his fellow-traveler. "Betake you the woods, and let me keep the path. "

Accordingly the young man turned aside, but took care to watch his companion, who advanced softly

---

① Cloyse, like Carrier, who appears later in the story, was condemned for witchcraft in 1692. One of Hawthorne's ancestors was of the court that gave the death sentence.

么遥远的荒野来,这可真怪,"他说,"不过,朋友,要是你同意,我将走一条较近的小路穿过森林,直到我们把这个基督教女人撇在身后。她对你说来是一个陌生人,也许会问我跟谁结伴同行,以及我在往哪儿去。"

"要是这样,"他的同路人说,"你就上森林里去,让我由这条路走。"

于是年轻人转向一旁,不过仍旧留神注意着他的同伴。他的同伴沿大路平稳地往前走去,直到他离开那个老妇人不到一根手杖的距离。同时,老妇人正尽力向前赶路,就这么大年龄的一个女人来说,速度是出奇的。她边走,边咕哝着一些不清不楚的话——无疑是一篇祈祷文。那个行路人伸出手杖,用看来像是蛇尾的那一头碰了一下她那枯槁的颈子。

"魔鬼!"那个虔诚的老女人尖叫起来。

"这么说,克洛伊斯大娘认识她的老朋友了?"行路人说,他拄着蠕动的手杖,面对着她。

"呀,真的,真是阁下吗?"那位善良的老妇人喊着说,"唔,果真是的,活像我的老朋友布朗大爷,就是现在那个傻小子的祖父。不过——阁下相信吗?——我的扫帚柄莫名其妙地不见了,我猜是被那个还没给绞死的巫婆科里大娘偷去了,而且还是当我浑身涂满了野芹菜汁、洋莓属和附子草……"

"跟上好的小麦和新生婴儿的脂肪搅和在一起。"那个活像老布朗大爷的人说。

"啊,阁下知道这个配方,"老女人喊起来,大声咯咯笑着,"所以像我方才所说的,完全准备停当要去参加这次集会,但是又没有马骑。我于是决定步行前往,因为他们告诉我,今儿晚上要领一个很好的青年人去参加圣餐式。可现在,阁下,请你来搀扶着我,我们转眼就可以到那儿。"

"这可办不到。"她的朋友回答,"我也许无法搀扶着你,克洛伊斯大娘,不过要是你乐意拿着的话,这是我的手杖。"

这么说着,他把手杖扔到了她的脚下,它到那儿或许就有了生命,因为它是原来的主人从前借给埃及魔术师们的一根魔杖①。不过关于这个事实,布朗大

---

① 当摩西的哥哥亚伦把他的杖丢在法老面前时,杖就变作蛇。法老的博士看到这情形,也把自己的杖丢下(根据霍桑的故事,这些杖是由撒旦提供的),那些杖也显示出了同样的魔力。见《旧约·出埃及记》第7章。——原注。

---

along the road until he had come within a staff's length of the old dame. She, meanwhile, was making the best of her way, with singular speed for so aged a woman, and mumbling some indistinct words—a prayer doubtless—as she went. The traveler put forth his staff and touched her withered neck with what seemed the serpent's tail.

"The devil!" screamed the pious old lady.

"Then Goodly Cloyse knows her old friend?" observed the traveler, confronting her and leaning on his writhing stick.

"Ah, forsooth, and is it your worship indeed?" cried the good dame. "Yea, truly it is, and in the very image of my old gossip, Goodman Brown, the grandfather of the silly fellow that now is. But—would your worship believe it? —my broomstick hath strangely disappeared, stolen, as I suspect, by that unhanged witch, Goody Cory, and that, too, when I was all anointed with the juice of smallage, and cinquefoil, and wolf's bane"—

"Mingled with fine wheat and the fat of a newborn babe," said the shape of old Goodman Brown.

"Ah, your worship knows the recipe," cried the old lady, cackling aloud. "So, as I was saying, being all ready for the meeting, and no horse to ride on, I made up my mind to foot it; for they tell me there is a nice young man to be taken into communion to-night. But now your good worship will lend me your arm, and we shall be there in a twinkling."

"That can hardly be," answered her friend. "I may not spare you my arm, Goody Cloyse; but here is my staff, if you will."

So saying, he threw it down at her feet, where, perhaps, it assumed life, being one of the rods which its owner had formerly lent to the Egyptian magi. ①Of this fact, however, Goodman Brown could not take cognizance. He had cast up his eyes in astonishment, and, looking down again, beheld neither Goody Cloyse nor the serpentine staff but this fellowtraveler alone, who waited for him as calmly as if nothing had happened.

"That old woman taught me my catechism," said the young man; and there was a world of meaning in

---

① When the staff of Aaron, brother to Moses, was cast before Pharaoh, it turned into a serpent. At this the magi of Pharaoh cast down their staves (which had been provided according to Hawthorne's story by Satan), which showed the same miraculous power. See Exodus 7.

爷却无法注意到。他惊骇地翻起了眼睛，等再往下看时，既没有看见克洛伊斯大娘，也没有看见那根蛇形手杖，只看见那个同路人独个儿镇静地等候着他，就仿佛什么也没有发生似的。

"那个老女人教过我教义问答。"年轻人说，他这句简单的话里包含有许许多多意义。

他们继续朝前走，同时年长的行路人劝告他的同伴加快步伐，沿那条路继续走下去。他话讲得那么恰当，因此他的议论似乎是从听话人的胸中涌起的，而不是由他提出来的。他们朝前走着时，他掰下一枝枫树枝做拐棍儿，动手把大小枝杈去掉，由于晚间的露水，这些枝杈全都是湿的。他手指碰到它们时，它们立刻很古怪地变得干枯下去，仿佛经过一星期的日晒似的。这样，这两个人以无拘无束的步伐往前走去，后来在大路上一处黑暗的洼地上，布朗大爷突然在一个树桩上坐下，不肯再往前走了。

"朋友，"他顽固地说，"我已经打定主意了。决不为这件事再朝前移动一步。如果一个卑鄙的老女人在我以为她会升入天堂的时候，决心去见魔鬼，那又怎样呢？那难道是我应当离开亲爱的费思，跟着她走的任何理由吗？"

"你不一会儿就会对这件事重新考虑的，"他的熟人镇定自若地说，"坐在这儿，休息一会儿。等你觉得乐意再走的时候，有我的手杖可以支撑着你。"

他没再多说，就把枫树枝扔给了他的同伴，随即迅速不见了，仿佛消失在不断加深的幽暗里似的。年轻人在路旁坐了一会儿，对自己大加夸赞，心想在清晨散步时自己可以以多么清白的良心迎上教长，也用不着在善良的老古金执事的目光下畏缩不前了。而且这一夜他会睡得多么安静啊！这一夜本来会那么邪恶地度过的，可是如今却这么纯洁、这么甜蜜地偎在费思的怀抱里！在这种愉快和值得称颂的默想中，布朗大爷听见马蹄声顺着大路传来，他认为藏到林边比较可取，因为他意识到使自己去到那里的罪恶目的，尽管他现在已经很幸运地避开了。

马蹄声和骑马人的谈话声越来越近，原来是两个庄重、苍老的人声一本正经地交谈着。这些混在一起的声音显然在年轻人藏身之处几码以外沿着大路响了过去，但无疑是由于那个地点分外幽暗，行路人和他们的马匹全都没有能看见。虽然他们的身体擦到

this simple comment.

They continued to walk onward, while the elder traveler exhorted his companion to make good speed and persevere in the path, discoursing so aptly that his arguments seemed rather to spring up in the bosom of his auditor than to be suggested by himself. As they went, he plucked a branch of maple to serve for a walking stick, and began to strip it of the twigs and little boughs, which were wet with evening dew. The moment his fingers touched them they became strangely withered and dried up as with a week's sunshine. Thus the pair proceeded, at a good free pace, until suddenly, in a gloomy hollow of the road, Goodman Brown sat himself down on the stump of a tree and refused to go any farther.

"Friend," said he, stubbornly, "my mind is made up. Not another step will I budge on this errand. What if a wretched old woman do choose to go to the devil when I thought she was going to heaven: is that any reason why I should quit my dear Faith and go after her?"

"You will think better of this by and by," said his acquaintance, composedly. "Sit here and rest yourself a while; and when you feel like moving again, there is my staff to help you along."

Without more words, he threw his companion the maple stick, and was as speedily out of sight as if he had vanished into the deepening gloom. The young man sat a few moments by the roadside, applauding himself greatly, and thinking with how clear a conscience he should meet the minister in his morning walk, nor shrink from the eye of good old Deacon Gookin. And what calm sleep would be his that very night, which was to have been spent so wickedly, but so purely and sweetly now, in the arms of Faith! Amidst these pleasant and praiseworthy meditations, Goodman Brown heard the tramp of horses along the road, and deemed it advisable to conceal himself within the verge of the forest, conscious of the guilty purpose that had brought him thither, though now so happily turned from it.

On came the hoof tramps and the voices of the riders, two grave old voices, conversing soberly as they drew near. These mingled sounds appeared to pass along the road, within a few yards of the young man's hiding-place; but, owing doubtless to the depth of the gloom at that particular spot, neither the travelers nor their steeds were visible. Though their figures brushed the small boughs by the wayside, it could not be seen that they intercepted, even for a moment, the faint

路旁的小树枝，可是布朗大爷连一刹那也没能看到他们截断他们必然横着经过的那一小片清朗的天空射下来的暗淡微光。他一会儿蹲下身子，一会儿踮着脚站起来，扳开树枝，把脑袋伸到胆敢伸的那么远，然而连一个影子也没有辨别出来。使他更为烦恼的是，他可以发誓（如果可以这么做的话），自己认出来那是教长和古金执事的声音。他们像去参加一场授予圣职典礼或教会会议时惯常做的那样，安安静静地缓步前进。在他还可以听见的距离内，有一个骑马人停下马来采折了一根细软的枝条。

"说到这两件事，尊敬的长老，"像执事的那个人的声音说，"我宁愿错过一场授职晚餐，也不愿错过今儿晚上的聚会。人家告诉我，除了几个印第安巫师外，我们教友中有些人将要从法尔默斯和法尔默斯以外的地方上这儿来，还有些人将要从康涅狄格和罗得岛来。那几个印第安巫师按着他们的方式，对于魔法知道得几乎和我们当中最高明的人不相上下。再说，还有一个标致的年轻女人要给领来参加圣餐式。"

"很好，古金执事！"教长的庄严苍老的音调这么回答，"加快速度，要不我们要迟到了。在我进入场地之前，你知道，什么事也办不了。"

马蹄声又得得地响起来，在空旷的大气中那么奇怪地交谈着的人声，穿过树林向前移去，从来没有教徒在那儿集会过，也从来没有一个基督徒在那儿祈祷过。那么这些圣职人员这么深入异教徒的乡野，会是往哪儿去呢？年轻的布朗大爷感到虚软无力，满心痛苦难受，简直要瘫倒在地上，于是连忙抓住一棵树来支撑着身体。他抬头望望天空，怀疑他上面是否真有一座天国。然而，上面却是那片苍穹，无数的星星在里面闪闪烁烁。

"上有苍天，下有费思，我还是得站稳脚跟，抵挡魔鬼！"布朗大爷喊着。

他仍旧抬脸凝视着浩瀚的天穹，正举起手来祈祷时，一片云气（虽然那时并没有风在吹动）快速地掠过天顶，把灿烂的繁星全都遮挡起来。苍茫的天空仍然可以看见，只有他头顶上面给遮挡住，因为那团云气正在他头上面迅速往北掠去。在高空里面，仿佛从云气深处，传来一片混乱、含糊的人声。有一会儿，听着的人想象自己可以辨别出自己镇上人们的口音，男男女女，有虔诚信教的，有不敬上帝的，有许多人他都在

gleam from the strip of bright sky athwart which they must have passed. Goodman Brown alternately crouched and stood on tiptoe, pulling aside the branches and thrusting forth his head as far as he durst without discerning so much as a shadow. It vexed him the more, because he could have sworn, were such a thing possible, that he recognized the voices of the minister and Deacon Gookin, jogging along quietly, as they were wont to do, when bound to some ordination or ecclesiastical council. While yet within hearing, one of the riders stopped to pluck a switch.

"Of the two, reverend sir," said the voice like the deacon's, "I had rather miss an ordination dinner than to-night's meeting. They tell me that some of our community are to be here from Falmouth and beyond, and others from Connecticut and Rhode Island, besides several of the Indian powwows, who, after their fashion, know almost as much deviltry as the best of us. Moreover, there is a goodly young woman to be taken into communion."

"Mighty well, Deacon Gookin!" replied the solemn old tones of the minister. "Spur up, or we shall be late. Nothing can be done, you know, until I get on the ground."

The hoofs clattered again; and the voices, talking so strangely in the empty air, passed on through the forest, where no church had ever been gathered or solitary Christian prayed. Whither, then, could these holy men be journeying so deep into the heathen wilderness? Young Goodman Brown caught hold of a tree for support, being ready to sink down on the ground, faint and overburdened with the heavy sickness of his heart. He looked up to the sky, doubting whether there really was a heaven above him. Yet there was the blue arch, and the stars brightening in it.

"With heaven above and Faith below, I will yet stand firm against the devil!" cried Goodman Brown.

While he still gazed upward into the deep arch of the firmament and had lifted his hands to pray, a cloud, though no wind was stirring, hurried across the zenith and hid the brightening stars. The blue sky was still visible, except directly overhead, where this black mass of cloud was sweeping swiftly northward. Aloft in the air, as if from the depths of the cloud, came a confused and doubtful sound of voices. Once the listener fancied that he could distinguish the accents of towns-people of his own, men and women, both pious and ungodly, many of whom he had met at the communion table, and had seen others rioting at the tavern. The next moment, so indistinct were the sounds,

圣餐桌上见过,有许多则看见在酒馆里喧闹过。一刹那间,声音变得那么隐隐约约,他很怀疑自己听到的是否仅仅是老树林里的飒飒声,虽然无风,却沙沙作响。接着,那些熟悉的声调变响亮了,那些声调是他在塞勒姆村的阳光下每天都可以听到的,可是直到这时还从来不曾从夜间的一团云气里传来过。声调里有一个年轻女人的嗓音纵声恸哭,却不知是为了什么事伤心,它只是恳求着某种恩惠,也许得到这种恩惠反会使她十分伤心。那群隐而不现的人,贤德的和有罪的,似乎全都鼓励她继续向前。

"费思!"布朗大爷用痛苦绝望的声音喊叫。树林里的回声仿效他,喊道:"费思! 费思!"仿佛好些惊慌可怜的人正在荒野中四处寻找她那样。

当这个愁眉不展的丈夫屏住呼吸,等候回音时,悲伤、愤怒、惊恐的喊声还在响彻夜空。那团乌云迅速远去,撇下那片清朗、寂静的天空在布朗大爷的头顶上,这时响起了一声尖叫,立即被一阵较响的喊喊喳喳的人声掩没了,人声低沉下去,变成了一阵遥远的欢笑。但是有件东西从空中轻盈地飘落下来,缠绕在一棵树的树枝上。年轻人一把抓住了它,看到是一条粉红色缎带。

"我的费思去了!"他惊呆了一刹那后这么喊着。"世上没有善良,罪恶不过是一个名称。来吧,魔鬼,这个世界是献给你的。"

布朗大爷绝望得发了疯,长时间放声大笑。然后一把抓起手杖,又出发了。他走得那么快,简直像沿着林间小路在飞,而不是在行走或奔跑。那条路变得更荒凉落寞,更不易辨别出来,最终竟然完全消失,撇下他在黑沉沉的荒野中凭着指引凡人走向邪恶的那种本能,仍然在朝前奔跑。整个树林里布满了可怕的声音——树木的吱嘎声,野兽的嗥叫声,以及印第安人的吆喝声。同时,疾风时而像远处教堂的钟声那样鸣响,时而又在这个行路人的四周发出一阵响亮的呼号,仿佛万物都在嘲笑他。不过他本人却是这个场面中最令人惊骇的人物,一点儿也不畏避其他种种可怕的事物。

"哈! 哈! 哈!"风嘲笑布朗大爷的时候,他这么喝着,"让我们来听听谁笑得最响。别想用你的恶作剧来吓唬我。来呀,巫婆;来呀,巫师;来呀,印第安巫师;来呀,魔鬼本人;你布朗大爷来啦。你们最好也像他惧怕你们那样惧怕他吧。"

he doubted whether he had heard aught but the murmur of the old forest, whispering without a wind. Then came a stronger swell of those familiar tones, heard daily in the sunshine at Salem village, but never until now from a cloud of night. There was one voice, of a young woman, uttering lamentations, yet with an uncertain sorrow, and entreating for some favor, which, perhaps, it would grieve her to obtain; and all the unseen multitude, both saints and sinners, seemed to encourage her onward.

"Faith!" shouted Goodman Brown, in a voice of agony and desperation; and the echoes of the forest mocked him, crying, "Faith! Faith!" as if bewildered wretches were seeking her all through the wilderness.

The cry of grief, rage, and terror was yet piercing the night, when the unhappy husband held his breath for a response. There was a scream, drowned immediately in a louder murmur of voices, fading into far-off laughter, as the dark cloud swept away, leaving the clear and silent sky above Goodman Brown. But something fluttered lightly down through the air and caught on the branch of a tree. The young man seized it, and beheld a pink ribbon.

"My Faith is gone!" cried he, after one stupefied moment. "There is no good on earth; and sin is but a name. Come, devil; for to thee is this world given."

And, maddened with despair, so that he laughed loud and long, did Goodman Brown grasp his staff and set forth again, at such a rate that he seemed to fly along the forest path rather than to walk or run. The road grew wilder and drearier and more faintly traced, and vanished at length, leaving him in the heart of the dark wilderness, still rushing onward with the instinct that guides mortal man to evil. The whole forest was peopled with frightful sounds—the creaking of the trees, the howling of wild beasts, and the yell of Indians; while sometimes the wind tolled like a distant church bell, and sometimes gave a broad roar around the traveler, as if all Nature were laughing him to scorn. But he was himself the chief horror of the scene, and shrank not from its other horrors.

"Ha! ha! ha!" roared Goodman Brown when the wind laughed at him. "Let us hear which will laugh loudest. Think not to frighten me with your deviltry. Come witch, come wizard, come Indian powwow, come devil himself, and here comes Goodman Brown. You may as well fear him as he fear you."

In truth, all through the haunted forest there could be nothing more frightful than the figure of Goodman Brown. On he flew among the black pines,

按实在说，在那片幽灵出没的树林四处，不可能有什么比布朗大爷的形影更可怕的事物了。他在黑松树间飞奔，挥舞着手杖做出种种疯狂的姿势，一会儿灵机一动，发出一阵可怕的亵渎神明的咒骂，一会儿又哄然大笑起来，使树林中所有的回声像他四周的恶魔那样哈哈大笑。现出原形的魔鬼，反而不及他在人类胸臆中猖獗时那么可怕。这样，这个鬼迷心窍的人飞快地向前赶路，后来到午夜时分，他看见前面有片红光在树木之间摇曳，就像林间空地上砍倒的树身和树枝燃烧起来，把熊熊的火焰衬着天空向上喷起那样。他在驱策着他朝前的那阵大风暴的一次暂息中停下，听见逐渐响亮起来的一阵好像是唱赞美诗的声音，它以许多人声的音量从远处庄严地哄然传来。他知道这个调子，它是村上聚会所唱诗班中很熟悉的一个。诗句缓缓地消失了，又由一个迭句予以廷长；它不是人类的声音，而是夜色笼罩着的荒野间各种各样的声音庄严和谐地共同鸣响。布朗大爷大声呼喊，可是他的喊声和荒野间的呼声会合起来，连他自己也听不见。

在那片短暂的寂静中，他悄悄向前走去，直到亮光正照射到他的眼睛上。在树林形成一道黑森森的大墙围绕着的一片空地的一端，耸立着一块岩石，天生粗略地有点儿像一座祭坛或是讲道坛，四周由四棵熊熊燃烧的松树围绕着，树梢全点着了，树干尚未烧到，像一个晚间聚会上的蜡烛似的。岩石顶上遍长着的那一大丛绿叶，全着了火，炫耀的火光高高地射入夜空，忽明忽暗，照亮了整个田野。每一个垂挂下的小枝和长满叶子的花环都烧成了一片。通红的火光一会儿亮一会儿暗，许多教会会众交替地显现出来，又消失在黑暗中，接着仿佛又从黑暗中长了出来，使荒凉的森林深处顿时又充满了人。

"一群严肃的、衣着阴暗的人。"布朗大爷说。

实际上，他们正是这样。在他们当中，在幽暗和光辉之间来回晃动的，有一些第二天在州行政会议上就会见到的人脸，还有些一个个休息日都从国内最神圣的讲道坛上虔诚地望着天空，并慈祥地向下望着教堂内那一排排拥挤的座位上的人脸。有些人断言，总督夫人也在那儿。至少是有几位她很熟悉的地位很高的夫人，还有可尊敬的丈夫的妻子，许许多多寡妇，年纪很大、声誉卓著的老小姐，以及唯恐母亲看见、战战兢兢的年轻美貌的姑娘。不是突然一下闪射过那

brandishing his staff with frenzied gestures, now giving vent to an inspiration of horrid blasphemy, and now shouting forth such laughter as set all the echoes of the forest laughing like demons around him. The fiend in his own shape is less hideous than when he rages in the breast of man. Thus sped the demoniac on his course, until, quivering among the trees, he saw a red light before him, as when the felled trunks and branches of a clearing have been set on fire, and throw up their lurid blaze against the sky, at the hour of midnight. He paused, in a lull of the tempest that had driven him onward, and heard the swell of what seemed a hymn, rolling solemnly from a distance with the weight of many voices. He knew the tune; it was a familiar one in the choir of the village meeting-house. The verse died heavily away, and was lengthened by a chorus, not of human voices, but of all the sounds of the benighted wilderness pealing in awful harmony together. Goodman Brown cried out, and his cry was lost to his own ear by its unison with the cry of the desert.

In the interval of silence he stole forward until the light glared full upon his eyes. At one extremity of an open space, hemmed in by the dark wall of the forest, arose a rock, bearing some rude, natural resemblance either to an altar or a pulpit, and surrounded by four blazing pines, their tops aflame, their stems untouched, like candles at an evening meeting. The mass of foliage that had overgrown the summit of the rock was all on fire, blazing high into the night and fitfully illuminating the whole field. Each pendent twig and leafy festoon was in a blaze. As the red light arose and fell, a numerous congregation alternately shone forth, then disappeared in shadow, and again grew, as it were, out of the darkness, peopling the heart of the solitary woods at once.

"A grave and dark-clad company," quoth Goodman Brown.

In truth they were such. Among them, quivering to and fro between gloom and splendor, appeared faces that would be seen next day at the council board of the province, and others which, Sabbath after Sabbath, looked devoutly heavenward, and benignantly over the crowded pews, from the holiest pulpits in the land. Some affirm that the lady of the governor was there. At least there were high dames well known to her, and wives of honored husbands, and widows, a great multitude, and ancient maidens, all of excellent repute, and fair young girls, who trembled lest their mothers should espy them. Either the sudden gleams of light flashing over the obscure field bedazzled Goodman

片黑暗旷野的亮光使布朗大爷眼花缭乱，就是他认出了20多个以身份特别神圣而知名的塞勒姆村的教会成员。善良的老古金执事到了，待在那位德高望重的圣徒、他的可尊敬的牧师身旁。然而，跟这些庄重、体面、虔诚的人，这些教会长老，这些端庄的夫人和纯洁的处女大为不敬地混杂在一起的，有生活放荡的男子，声名不好的女子，沉湎在种种卑鄙龌龊的罪恶中，甚至据信犯有可怕罪行的坏蛋。看来也真奇怪，善良的人并不躲避邪恶的人，有罪的人也不因为见到贤德的人而局促不安。散布在脸色苍白的敌人① 当中的，还有一些印第安祭司，他们常以英国巫术望尘莫及的可怕咒语，使当地的树林内大起恐慌。

"可是费思在哪儿呢？"布朗大爷想着。接下去，等他心里生出了希望时，他哆嗦起来。

赞美诗的另一句唱起来了，是一节徐缓、悲哀的旋律，就是虔诚的人喜爱的那种，不过配上一些词句，表达出了我们本性对于罪恶可能想象出的一切，而且还暗暗影射出远不止此的含义。魔鬼之道是一般人难以探测的。一行诗一行诗唱过去了；荒野的叠句在一句句之间仍然像一个强大的风琴发出最深沉的音调那样响起。随着那首可怕的颂歌的最后一阵歌声，又传来一个声音，仿佛风声怒吼，溪流奔腾，野兽咆哮，以及这片不协调的荒野中的一切其他声音，它们全混合起来，符合于有罪的人向万众之主致敬的声音。那四棵熊熊燃烧的松树喷起了一道更高的火焰，在那一大群邪恶不敬的人们头上的烟圈上面，模模糊糊地照出了一些恐怖的形状与容貌。同时，岩石上的火红通通地喷射起来，在底部之上形成了一座闪闪发光的弓形门，一个人形这时候出现在那儿。让我们恭恭敬敬地说，这个人形在衣着和态度方面丝毫不像新英格兰教堂中一位庄重的教士。

"把皈依的人带上来！"一个人声这么喊着，在那片旷野中发出了回声，轰响着传入树林里去。

布朗大爷听到这话，从树木的阴暗处走出来，朝那群会众面前走去。他凭借自己心里对一切邪恶事物的同情，感到跟这群人有一种令人恶心的同胞关系。他简直可以发誓说，自己亡父的形状正从一个烟圈中朝下望着，招手叫他走上前去，同时一个女人，一脸黯然绝望的神情，伸出一只手来告诫他，叫他退回。

----

① 指白人，这是就印第安人而言。

Brown, or he recognized a score of the church members of Salem village famous for their especial sanctity. Good old Deacon Gookin had arrived, and waited at the skirts of that venerable saint, his revered pastor. But, irreverently consorting with these grave, reputable, and pious people, these elders of the church, these chaste dames and dewy virgins, there were men of dissolute lives and women of spotted fame, wretches given over to all mean and filthy vice, and suspected even of horrid crimes. It was strange to see that the good shrank not from the wicked, nor were the sinners abashed by the saints. Scattered also among their pale-faced enemies were the Indian priests, or powwows, who had often scared their native forest with more hideous incantations than any known to English witchcraft.

"But where is Faith?" thought Goodman Brown; and, as hope came into his heart, he trembled.

Another verse of the hymn arose, a slow and mournful strain, such as the pious love, but joined to words which expressed all that our nature can conceive of sin, and darkly hinted at far more. Unfathomable to mere mortals is the lore of fiends. Verse after verse was sung; and still the chorus of the desert swelled between like the deepest tone of a mighty organ; and with the final peal of that dreadful anthem there came a sound, as if the roaring wind, the rushing streams, the howling beasts, and every other voice of the unconcerted wilderness were mingling and according with the voice of guilty man in homage to the prince of all. The four blazing pines threw up a loftier flame, and obscurely discovered shapes and visages of horror on the smoke wreaths above the impious assembly. At the same moment the fire on the rock shot redly forth and formed a glowing arch above its base, where now appeared a figure. With reverence be it spoken, the figure bore no slight similitude, both in garb and manner, to some grave divine of the New England churches.

"Bring forth the converts!" cried a voice that echoed through the field and rolled into the forest.

At the word, Goodman Brown stepped forth from the shadow of the trees and approached the congregation, with whom he felt a loathful brotherhood by the sympathy of all that was wicked in his heart. He could have well-nigh sworn that the shape of his own dead father beckoned him to advance, looking downward from a smoke wreath, while a woman, with dim features of despair, threw out her hand to warn him back. Was it his mother? But he had no power to retreat one step, nor to resist, even in thought, when the

那是他的母亲吗? 可是他没有力量后退一步,也没有力量哪怕在思想上加以抗拒,因为这时教长和善良的老古金执事一把揪住他的胳膊,把他领到那个熊熊燃烧的岩石面前。一个遮着面纱的女人的苗条身材,由那个虔诚的教义问答老师克洛伊斯大娘和得到魔鬼允诺、要当地狱王后的马撒·卡里尔领着,也来到了那儿。马撒是一个蛮横跋扈的巫婆。皈依的人全站在那儿,在那个烈火形成的华盖之下。

"欢迎,弟子们,"那个黑暗的人形说,"欢迎来参加你们同道的圣餐式。你们已经发现你们的本性和你们的命运如此年轻。弟子们,朝身后看去!"

他们回过身。这时可以看见,崇拜魔鬼的人仿佛在一片火焰中红光闪闪地走上前来,每一张脸上都阴沉沉地闪现出欢迎的微笑。

"那儿,"那个黑暗的人形说下去,"就是你们从少年时期便尊敬的所有人士。你们认为他们比自身还要神圣,于是吓得逃避开自己的罪恶,拿自己的罪恶和他们的正直的、渴望升入天国的生活进行对比。然而,他们全在这儿,在参拜我的会众里。今天夜晚,你们就可以得知他们的种种阴私:教会的白胡须的长老,如何向他们家里年轻的女佣人悄悄说了些淫荡的话;许多女人急渴渴地想成为寡妇,如何在就寝之前给丈夫喝上一杯,让他在自己的怀抱中长眠不醒;乳嗅未干的青年人如何赶紧想要继承父亲的财富;美貌的少女——别害羞,可爱的人儿——如何在花园里掘一个小坟坑,盼咐我这个独一无二的来宾去参加一个婴儿的葬礼。你们凭借你们人类对罪恶的同情心,将会找出所有犯罪的现场——不论是在教堂里、寝室内、街道上、田野间或树林中——并且将会欣喜地看到,全世界是一个有罪的斑点,一个血污的地方。还远不止此。从每一个胸腔中看穿罪恶的奥秘,看穿所有旁门左道的根源,以及永远比人力——比我的最大的力量——通过行为所能表明出来的提供更多邪恶冲动的那股势力,这就是你们的任务。现在,我的弟子们,你们彼此看看。"

他们照办了。靠了地狱点燃起的火把的熊熊火焰,这个可怜人看到了他的费思,那个妻子也看到了她的丈夫,两人都在那个邪恶的祭坛前面嗦嗦颤抖。

"看呀,你们站在那儿,弟子们,"那个人形用深沉、严肃的音调说,几乎对自己音调里绝望可怕的意味感到伤心,仿佛他从前那天使的本性还会为我们这

minister and good old Deacon Gookin seized his arms and led him to the blazing rock. Thither came also the slender form of a veiled female, led between Goody Cloyse, that pious teacher of the catechism, and Martha Carrier, who had received the devil's promise to be queen of hell. A rampant hag was she. And there stood the proselytes beneath the canopy of fire.

"Welcome, my children," said the dark figure, "to the communion of your race. Ye have found thus young your nature and your destiny. My children, look behind you!"

They turned; and flashing forth, as it were, in a sheet of flame, the fiend worshippers were seen; the smile of welcome gleamed darkly on every visage.

"There," resumed the sable form, "are all whom ye have reverenced from youth. Ye deemed them holier than yourselves, and shrank from your own sin, contrasting it with their lives of righteousness and prayerful aspirations heavenward. Yet here are they all in my worshipping assembly. This night it shall be granted you to know their secret deeds: how hoary-bearded elders of the church have whispered wanton words to the young maids of their households; how many a woman, eager for widows' weeds, has given her husband a drink at bedtime and let him sleep his last sleep in her bosom; how beardless youths have made haste to inherit their fathers' wealth; and how fair damsels—blush not, sweet ones—have dug little graves in the garden, and bidden me, the sole guest, to an infant's funeral. By the sympathy of your human hearts for sin ye shall scent out all the places—whether in church, bed-chamber, street, field, or forest—where crime has been committed, and shall exult to behold the whole earth one stain of guilt, one mighty blood spot. Far more than this. It shall be yours to penetrate, in every bosom, the deep mystery of sin, the fountain of all wicked arts, and which inexhaustibly supplies more evil impulses than human power—than my power at its utmost—can make manifest in deeds. And now, my children, look upon each other."

They did so; and, by the blaze of the hell-kindled torches, the wretched man beheld his Faith, and the wife her husband, trembling before that unhallowed altar.

"Lo, there ye stand, my children," said the figure, in a deep and solemn tone, almost sad with its despairing awfulness, as if his once angelic nature could yet mourn for our miserable race. "Depending upon one another's hearts, ye had still hoped that virtue were not all a dream. Now are ye undeceived. Evil is the

些可怜人悲悯似的，"你们信赖彼此的心肠，原来还希望德行并不完全是一场梦。现在，你们醒悟过来了。邪恶是人类的本性。邪恶必然是你们唯一的幸福。弟子们，再一次欢迎你们来参加你们同道的圣餐式。"

"欢迎。"那些崇拜魔鬼的人异口同声绝望而得意地又喊了一遍。

他们站在那儿，似乎是到了这个黑暗世界的邪恶边缘还在踟蹰的唯一一对。那块岩石上天生有一个洼下去的水盆。它里面有被火光照红的水吗？是不是血呢？再不然，也许是一种液体火焰？那个邪恶的化身就在那儿把手浸到水里，预备把洗礼的标志打在他们的额头上，从而好使他们参与罪恶的奥秘，在行为与思想两方面对别人的秘密罪行可以比现在对他们自己的更为清楚。丈夫对脸色苍白的妻子望了一眼，费思也对他望了一眼。下一眼会让他们互相看到两个品德多么败坏的可怜虫呢？他们对自己暴露出的和自己所看到的会同样发抖！

"费思！费思！"丈夫喊着，"抬头望着天，抵制这个邪恶的家伙。"

费思听从他没有，他并不知道。他刚把话说完就发觉自己待在宁静的夜晚和荒野的地方，听着穿过树林缓缓逝去的那阵风的呼啸。他步履蹒跚地靠到了岩石上，觉得它又冷又湿。同时，本来全部燃烧着的一个下垂的小树枝，在他的面颊上洒下了最最冰冷的露水。

第二天早上，年轻的布朗大爷慢吞吞地走上了塞勒姆村的那条街，像一个心醉神迷的人那样睁大眼睛四下观望。善良的老教长正在墓地里散步，想为早餐增加点儿食欲，一面默想着自己的讲道。他走过时，向着布朗大爷祝福。他躲避开这个德高望重的贤人，好像躲避开一个被诅咒的人那样。老古金执事正在家里做礼拜，他祈祷时所念的神圣词句从敞开的窗外也可以听到。"这个巫师在对什么上帝祈祷呢？"布朗大爷说。克洛伊斯大娘，那个优秀的老基督教徒，站在自己的格子窗下面清晨的阳光里，向一个把早上的一品脱①牛奶送来给她的小姑娘提问教义。布朗大爷把那孩子一把拉走，就像从魔鬼本人手里夺走她那样。他转过聚会所旁边的路转角，瞥见了费思的头，

---

① 英美制容量单位。

nature of mankind. Evil must be your only happiness. Welcome again, my children, to the communion of your race. "

"Welcome," repeated the fiend worshippers, in one cry of despair and triumph.

And there they stood, the only pair, as it seemed who were yet hesitating on the verge of wickedness in this dark world. A basin was hollowed, naturally, in the rock. Did it contain water, reddened by the lurid light? or was it blood? or, perchance, a liquid flame? Herein did the shape of evil dip his hand and prepare to lay the mark of baptism upon their foreheads, that they might be partakers of the mystery of sin, more conscious of the secret guilt of others, both in deed and thought, than they could now be of their own. The husband cast one look at his pale wife and Faith at him. What polluted wretches would the next glance show them to each other, shuddering alike at what they disclosed and what they saw!

"Faith! Faith!" cried the husband, "look up to heaven, and resist the wicked one. "

Whether Faith obeyed he knew not. Hardly had he spoken when he found himself amid calm night and solitude, listening to a roar of the wind which died heavily away through the forest. He staggered against the rock, and felt it chill and damp; while a hanging twig, that had been all on fire, besprinkled his cheek with the coldest dew.

The next morning young Goodman Brown came slowly into the street of Salem village, staring around him like a bewildered man. The good old minister was taking a walk along the graveyard to get an appetite for breakfast and meditate his sermon, and bestowed a blessing, as he passed, on Goodman Brown. He shrank from the venerable saint as if to avoid an anathema. Old Deacon Gookin was at domestic worship, and the holy words of his prayer were heard through the open window. "What God doth the wizard pray to?" quoth Goodman Brown. Goody Cloyse, that excellent old Christian, stood in the early sunshine at her own lattice, catechizing a little girl who had brought her a pint of morning's milk. Goodman Brown snatched away the child as from the grasp of the fiend himself. Turning the corner by the meeting-house, he spied the head of Faith, with the pink ribbons, gazing anxiously forth, and bursting into such joy at sight of him that she skipped along the street and almost kissed her husband before the whole village. But Goodman Brown

扎着粉红色缎带,她正焦急地向前凝视,看到他之后那样高兴起来,沿着街道连蹦带跳地跑上前,几乎要当着全村亲一下她的丈夫。可是布朗大爷严厉而伤心地盯着她的脸,没有打招呼就走过去了。

布朗大爷是不是在树林中睡着了,仅仅做了一场巫术集会的噩梦呢?

您乐意这么说就这么说吧。可是,哎呀! 就年轻的布朗大爷来说,这可是一场预兆不祥的噩梦。自从做了这场可怕的噩梦的那一夜之后,他就变成了一个严厉、伤心、阴沉沉地深思的人,一切即便不是不顾死活,也怀疑一切。到安息日,会众唱着圣歌时 他无法倾听,因为一首罪恶的颂歌很响地传进他的耳鼓,淹没了全部福音。当教长从讲道坛上一手按着打开的《圣经》,热情洋溢、雄辩有力地讲到我们宗教的神圣真理、圣徒般的生活与洋洋自得的死亡,以及未来的幸福或难以形容的苦难时,布朗大爷禁不住脸色发白,唯恐屋顶会轰隆一声塌下来,压在这个头发斑白的亵渎神明者和听众们的头上。时常,他在半夜突然醒来,畏缩地避开费思的胸膛。早晨或薄暮,全家跪下祈祷时,他总蹙起眉来,暗自嘀咕,严厉地凝视着妻子,然后把脸避开。等他活了好多年,须发皤然的尸体被抬到坟墓去时,费思——一个老女人—— 和儿女们、孙儿女们,还有为数不少的邻居,一个相当长的行列,跟随在后面。但是他们在他的墓碑上并没有刻下充满希望的诗句,因为他临终时是悲观绝望的。

▀ 讨 论 ▀

这篇小说的背景——17世纪末叶的塞勒姆村——在时间和地点方面给了读者一个坚实的基础。现代读者觉得十分古怪的巫术这件事,在那时期实际上是一种坚定的信念,而对女巫的几次审判(以及有几个牺牲者的姓名)给这篇故事的气氛提供了相当的真实性①。

---

① 霍桑在准备从事写作的岁月里,居住在塞勒姆他寡母宅子楼上的一间房内。在那些孤独寂寞的岁月中,他除了做别的事外,还潜心研究了新英格兰的殖民地历史。他自己家庭跟审判女巫案件的关系在一个脚注中已经提及。——原注。

looked sternly and sadly into her face, and passed on without a greeting.

Had Goodman Brown fallen asleep in the forest and only dreamed a wild dream of a witch-meeting?

Be it so if you will; but, alas! it was a dream of evil omen for young Goodman Brown. A stern, a sad, a darkly meditative, a distrustful, if not a desperate man did he become from the night of that fearful dream. On the Sabbath day, when the congregation were singing a holy psalm, he could not listen because an anthem of sin rushed loudly upon his ear and drowned all the blessed strain. When the minister spoke from the pulpit with power and fervid eloquence, and, with his hand on the open Bible, of the sacred truths of our religion, and of saint-like lives and triumphant deaths, and of future bliss or misery unutterable, then did Goodman Brown turn pale, dreading lest the roof should thunder down upon the gray blasphemer and his hearers. Often, awaking suddenly at midnight, he shrank from the bosom of Faith; and at morning or eventide, when the family knelt down at prayer, he scowled and muttered to himself, and gazed sternly at his wife, and turned away. And when he had lived long, and was born to his grave a hoary corpse, followed by Faith, an aged woman, and children and grandchildren, a goodly procession, besides neighbors not a few, they carved no hopeful verse upon his tombstone, for his dying hour was gloom.

The setting of this story—Salem village in the very late seventeenth century—gives the reader a firm grounding in place and time. The element of witchcraft which seems so odd to the modern reader, was actually a firm belief of the period, and the witch trials (and the names of some of the victims) provide plausibility to the atmosphere of the story①.

---

① Hawthorne, in the lonely years when he lived in an upper room in his widowed mother's house in Salem, during which he was preparing to be a writer, stepped himself, among other things, in the colonial history of New England. His own family connection with the witch trials has already been mentioned in a footnote.

不过和这种历史现实主义形成对照的是，我们很早就得到某种暗示，表明有超出那一时期种种信念的异想天开的事情。费思新婚不久之后丈夫就做的这次旅程，如同他所说的，将在"一年里所有的夜晚中的"这一夜撇下她独自一个，可是他对这件事却没有向费思说明缘由，这是很奇怪的，是不是呢？费思说："一个孤独的女人常受到她自己往往很害怕的那种噩梦和忧虑的烦扰。在一年里所有的夜晚中，亲爱的丈夫，今儿夜晚请你留下陪着我吧。"我们从这番话里发现了一个同样难以想象的暗示。这一夜有什么事那么特别呢？还有，在丈夫离开费思之后，他想道："嗨，她是世上一位幸运的天使。过了这一夜之后，我就紧紧捏着她的裙子，跟随她上天堂去。"我们记得《格拉米格纳的情人》那篇作品，想到西西里和格拉米格纳的恋爱事件也许离开我们的世界太远了，不过西西里和格拉米格纳的恋爱事件是一种不同方式的离奇古怪。

早期的清教徒认为树林是一个自然与超自然邪恶的渊薮。很清楚，当年轻的布朗大爷走进树林之后，我们就离开了寻常的现实主义境界。尽管它们是作为一个"真实的"树林和旅程而描述出来的，我们却得到一些暗示，表明它们具有哲学的或心理学的象征主义。等真正的魔鬼出现时，那是很奇怪的，但是等我们认识到他很像布朗，后来又很像布朗的父亲时，我们发现这暗示着一种血统上的邪恶"交流"——结果竟然是一种普遍性的交流。跟年轻的布朗大爷的交流后来较为亲密，因为魔鬼的议论似乎是从听话人的胸中涌起的，而不是由他提出来的。我们可不可以说，从某种意义来讲，树林就是年轻的布朗大爷的内心，一切全是在那里发生的？

走进树林，"首次"去参加那个盛大的邪恶的"同道圣餐式"，的确具有一种逐步紧张的气氛，正如一篇着重情节的故事那样，不过那片紧张是针对着一个哲理性目标的，而不是指向

But in contrast to such historical realism we are early given some hint of the fantastic beyond the beliefs of the period. It is odd, is it not, that Faith has been offered no excuse for her new husband's journey, which will leave her alone, he says, this "of all nights of the year"? And an equally fantastic suggestion has just been found in Faith's statement: "A lone woman is troubled with such dreams and such thoughts that she's afeard of herself sometimes. Pray, tarry with me this night, dear husband, of all nights in the year." What is so special about this night? Further, after the husband has left her, he thinks "Well, she's a blessed angel on earth; and after this one night, I'll cling to her skirts and follow her to heaven." Remembering the story "Gramigna's Lover", we reflect that Sicily, and the affair of Gramigna, may be far enough from our world, but they are strange in a very different way.

Clearly, we have left the realm of ordinary realism when young Goodman Brown enters the forest, which early Puritans thought to have been a haunt of natural and supernatural evil. Though they have been presented as a "real" forest and journey, we have hints that they have philosophical or psychological symbolism. When the real devil appears, that is strange enough, but when we realize his resemblance to Brown, and later to Brown's father, we find suggested a "communion" of evil in the blood—a communion that in the end turns out to be universal. The communion with young Goodman Brown is more intimate later, for the devil's arguments seemed rather to spring up in the bosom of the auditor than to be suggested by himself. Can it ever be said that, in a sense, the forest is the inwardness of young Goodman Brown, and that all takes place there?

The journey into the forest toward the great "initiation" into the evil "communion of the race" does have a growth of suspense, as does a story of action, but the suspense is directed at a philosophical point and not toward the resolution of an action. Even Goodman Brown's hesitation and hope of turning back

一个情节的。我们感到,就连布朗大爷的犹豫不决和希望折回,都不是由于一个名叫费思的女人,而是由于这个词的另一种意义①,因为费思只是一个寓言性的人物。那个"信仰"使他能让教长和古金执事骑马继续向前。

因为纵然教长和执事的出现削弱了他的决心,他却瞥见了晚间的一片苍天和星星,并且大声喊道:"上有苍天,下有费思,我还是得站稳脚跟,抵挡魔鬼!"

然而,这时刻,一片云气掠过苍天,一阵杂乱的人声响了起来,其中有许多都是很熟悉的,有一个年轻女人的嗓音纵声恸哭。布朗听出来是费思的嗓音。接下去,他叫唤她的名字,树林里发出了回声,"仿佛好些惊慌的可怜人正在荒野中四处寻找她那样。"这当然似乎是暗示,在邪恶的圣餐会上的人们毕竟全只在寻求信仰。同时,费思的粉红色缎带飘落下来,布朗抓住了它,发出疯狂的大笑,奔过树林,朝那个可怕的皈依地点奔去。这就是说,那个真实的女人费思也可能同邪恶交流——这在她担心丈夫不在家时自己会做噩梦的这件事上,就已经暗示出来了。

那儿,在那场亵渎神明的仪式上,皈依的人全被领去晋见那个黑暗的人形。他结束他的欢迎词时说:"你们信赖彼此的心肠,原来还希望德行并不完全是一场梦。现在,你们醒悟过来了。邪恶是人类的本性。弟子们,再一次欢迎你们来参加你们同道的圣餐式。"在高潮中,费思被领去准备接受洗礼的标志。

看到这幕情景,年轻的布朗大爷高声叫唤,要她抵制,但是他无法知道结局,因为突然他又独自一个,听着穿过树林缓缓逝去的那阵风的呼啸。第二天早上,他找路回到村子里,所有的人,有道德的和不道德的,诚实的和奸诈的,全像以前那样在那儿过活。

———————
① 指"信仰"而言。

is not, we sense, based on a woman named Faith, but on the other meaning of the word, on Faith as an allegorical figure. That "faith" enables him to let the minister and Deacon Gookin ride on.

For even though his resolution is weakened by the appearance of the minister and the deacon, he catches a glimpse of a patch of blue evening sky and stars, and cries out: "With heaven above and Faith below, I will stand firm against the devil!"

At this moment, however, a cloud sweeps over the blue and a sound of many voices bursts out, many familiar, among them the voice of a young woman uttering a lamentation, which Brown recognizes as that of Faith. Then he cries her name, and the forest echoes "as if bewildered wretches were seeking her all through the wilderness. "This, of course, seems to imply that all in the communion of evil seek, after all, only faith. Meanwhile, Faith's pink ribbon has come fluttering down; and grasping it, Brown bursts into maniacal laughter and rushes through the forest toward the spot of fearful initiation. That is to say, the actual woman Faith may also be of the communion of evil—which has already been hinted at in her fear of dreams during her husband's absence.

There, after the blasphemous ritual, the proselytes are presented to the dark figure, who concludes his speech of welcome: "Depending upon one another's hearts, ye had still hoped that virtue was not all a dream. Now are ye undeceived. Evil is the nature of mankind. Welcome again, my children, to the communion of your race. " At the climax, Faith is presented for the mark of baptism.

At the sight young Goodman Brown cries out for her to resist, but he cannot know the end, for suddenly he is alone, listening to the roar of wind disappearing into the forest. Next morning he has found his way back to the village, where all lead their lives as before, the virtuous and unvirtuous, those in truth and those in deception.

这篇小说最后留下了一个问题。它难道只是一场梦吗？无论如何，年轻的布朗大爷失去了对生活的信心。他继续跟费思一起生活，虽然并没有信仰，后来到老年才去世，有儿女和孙儿女，可是墓碑上却没有充满希望的题词。他的一生是一个毫无意义的字谜。

这篇寓言说的是什么呢？它在一个标准上提出问题来，但是并没有加以回答。这是一个有关人性的根本问题，一个在历史中曾经一再被提出来的问题。人类生性是邪恶的吗——例如，在"原始罪恶"的教义中所说的那样？再不然，人类生性是善良的吗，像各个不同的派别，最著名的是法国哲学家卢梭所坚持的那样？或者根据现代的一种说法，德行是优良环境的结果而邪恶是恶劣环境的结果？邪恶与善良难道只是环境决定的结果吗？无论如何，这篇小说是一则寓言，提出了一个持续多年的问题。对于这个问题，每一代人都用自己的语言做出了回答。

我们可不可以说，这篇小说把善恶问题看作绝对的而回避开了呢——即人性是一个复杂的问题，人生在世必须根据自己的信仰努力做出自己的解释？这样的话，我们可不可以大胆地说，布朗大爷完全是一个理想主义者，他不会按照生活必然的那样去生活？

（主　万　译）

The story is left as a question. Had it been merely a dream? In any case, young Goodman Brown has lost his confidence in life. He continues to live with Faith, though without faith, and dies at a ripe age, with children and grandchildren, but with no sentiment of hope on his tomb. His life has been a meaningless charade.

What is the parable saying? At one level it asks, and does not answer, a fundamental question about human nature, a question that has been asked again and again throughout history. Is man naturally evil—as, for example, in the doctrine of Original Sin? Or is he naturally good, as has been held by various sects, but most notably by the French philosopher Rousseau? Or in one modern version, is virtue the result of good environment, and evil the result of bad environment? Are evil and good merely the results of conditioning? In any case, the story is a parable asking a perennial question, in which each generation answers in its own terms.

Can we say that the story by-passes the question of vice and virtue as absolutes—that human nature is a complex thing and that man must live in the effort to make his own definition by faith? In which case, can we hazard that Goodman Brown is the total idealist who cannot live life as it necessarily is?

情 节
What Plot Reveals

生动的细节一抓住人们的想象力，就能产生一种特别鲜明的色调，即一篇小说给人们的"感受"，而"这种"感受，这种气氛，就是表明小说含义深邃隽永的一种要素。

前面谈到《进攻堡垒》时,我们提出了事实与虚构的关系问题。帕克曼的记述虽然可能是真实的,但这还不是我们不承认它是虚构的理由。当然,我们知道许多被认为虚构的作品,都包含着事实,或者实质上可能就是事实。真正的区别并不是与——我们习惯上常说的——"虚构"相对立的"事实",而是有着更为复杂的情况,要放到有关小说情节的整个问题中去加以思考。

我们可以从研究写历史的作者来探讨事实与虚构之间的区别。历史学家或传记作家笔下写的都是事实,而且可能还只写事实。但即使这样,历史学家还必须对他所写的事实加以阐述。历史是不会自己来写的,而研究历史极容易产生争论,并竞相进行阐述。不过,历史学家坚持他所着意阐述的事实都要具有真实性。他要求他的这种"真实"是和事实相符合的,而建立这样一种真实就是他的目的所在——虽然,正如我们刚才所说,他还必须对自己所写的事实加以阐述。另一方面,写小说的作者(即使他也可以非常忠实地处理了历史题材)并不觉得应该丝毫不差地同事实完全符合;他倒是觉得受到一种真实的连贯性(见重要词汇)所约束,而这里所谓"连贯性",我们就是指这部小说所有组成要素之间应具有的那种重要关系。当然就是指情节,人物,主题——但同样还有许许多多其他因素,包括他所选择的事实在内。我们一定要时刻牢记住:实际生活——或者历史记录——决不会给予小说家以他所需要的东西——他所需要的全部东西——从而形成错觉和他自己对生活的解释。只要可以想象得到的生活的本质照样还存在,那个过程的寓意(即最广义上的"寓

Earlier, in connection with "The Attack on the Fort," we raised the question of the relation of fact and fiction. Though Parkman's anecdote is presumably true, that was not the reason we found it unacceptable as fiction. We know, indeed, that much work accepted as fiction involves fact or may be substantially fact. The real distinction is not "fact" as opposed to "fiction"—as common usage has it—but something much more complex. Such a consideration lies behind the whole question of plot.

We can approach the distinction by considering the writer of history. The historian or biographer deals with facts, and presumably only with facts. But even he *must* interpret his facts. History does not write itself, and the study of history is a hotbed of controversy, of competing interpretations. But the historian insists on the authenticity of the facts that he means to interpret. He claims that his "truth" is one of *correspondence* (see Glossary) with fact, and to establish such a truth is his aim—though, as we have said, his facts must be interpreted. On the other hand, the writer of fiction (even though he may deal with historical materials very faithfully) does not feel bound to precise correspondence with fact: rather he feels bound by a truth of *coherence* (see Glossary) and by "coherence" we here mean the significant relation of all the elements in the fiction. Plot, character, theme—certainly—but a thousand other factors as well, including his selection of facts. And always we must keep in mind that real life—or historical records—never give the fiction writer what he needs—*all* he needs—to create the illusion and his own interpretation of life. The imagined *inwardness* of life being lived, and the moral ("moral" in the broadest sense) of that process must finally depend on imagination and on the significance of the

意"），最后一定要取决于想象力以及整个作品的旨趣。我们可以粗略地（因考虑到论述事实时又会出现重复的缘故）概括如下：历史学家心中所关注的，就是去发现这些事实所包含的那种模式（和旨趣）；小说家可以根据他心中想要表现的人的行动和价值的方式，去选择或者"创造出"一些事实来。

让我们根据下面将要谈到的所有问题来考察这种区别吧。

我们只要一谈到"一篇小说的动作过程"，通常就是指构成这篇小说的一系列事件。换句话说，"动作"（见重要词汇）一词，与我们通常所想象的"情节"（见重要词汇）这个字眼大体上相等。当我们用这种方式谈论时，我们只是想到一系列事件，不知怎的却和这些事件中有关人物分开了，同时也和主题思想分开了——即使我们知道，事实上我们根本不能使一个动作同完成这个动作的人物截然分开，或者使一个动作同它的意义截然分开。我们头脑里习以为常地会做出类似这样的区别、分析和抽象概念，因为这些东西我们在处理自己的和别人的日常生活时都很需要。

但是，当我们谈到小说的时候，就必须坚持要求把动作和情节明确地区分开来。

至于动作方面，我们指的不是一个单独的事件（布朗大爷走进了森林），而是一系列经过时间运行并展示出统一性和重要性的事件。这样的一系列事件，可以说要经历三个逻辑推理的阶段：开始阶段、中间阶段和结尾阶段。

一个动作的开始阶段，呈现在我们面前的，常常是处于某种不稳定因素、某种矛盾或某种对比（它们可能是明确的，或是含蓄的，甚至是暂时还不知道的）的状态之中。一个动作的中间阶段，则展示出矛盾的发展，以及各种力争达到一种新的稳定、同时又不断做出重新调整的力量。一个动作的结尾阶段表明：从某种程度上来说，已经达到了稳定（哪怕还是暂时性的）；各种起作用的力量之间的矛盾，也都

coherence of the whole work. We may summarize crudely (making allowance for the overlaps that occur in relation to fact) as follows: the historian is concerned to discover the pattern implied by the facts (and the significance); the fiction writer may choose *or* "create" facts in accordance with the pattern of human action and values that he wishes to present.

Let us ponder this distinction, as underlying all that is to follow.

Ordinarily, when we speak of "the action of a story," we mean the ring of events that constitute the story. In other words, "action" serves as a rough equivalent of what we commonly think of as "plot." When we talk in this fashion we are thinking of the string of events as somehow separable from the characters involved in the events and separable from the main theme—even though we know that, in fact, we cannot really separate an act from the person who commits it, or an act from its meaning. Our minds are in the habit of making such distinctions, abstractions, and analyses, for we need them in dealing with our daily lives and those of others.

When we come to fiction, however, it is necessary to insist on a sharp distinction between *action* and *plot* (see Glossary).

As for action, we do not mean a single event (Goodman Brown went into the forest), but a series of events moving through time and exhibiting unity and significance. Such a series can be regarded as moving through three logical stages: the beginning, the middle, and the end.

The beginning of an action always presents us with a situation in which there is some element of instability, some conflict or contrast (which may be specified or implied, or even, for the moment, ignored). The middle of an action exhibits the development of conflict and the readjustment of forces as they struggle to settle into a new kind of stability. The end of an action shows that some point of stability has been reached (however temporarily); the conflicts among forces that have been brought into play have been resolved. At dawn of the day of the Battle of

得到了解决。发生滑铁卢之战的那一天清晨，欧洲的命运还悬而未决；到了落日时分，拿破仑已是一个穷困潦倒的人了。1776 年 6 月 7 日，来自弗吉尼亚的理查德·亨利·李句大陆会议提交了一项决议案，宣称："这些北美殖民地①现在是，而且有权是自由独立的合众国"；7 月 4 日，《独立宣言》签字通过了。当富豪兼中年银行家汤姆·史密斯遇到伊夫琳·彭布罗克的时候，他立即认出了她那虚荣轻浮的本性，但那种认识却抵御不了她所施展出来的诱惑力；当史密斯这位社会名流的台柱人物因盗用公款而遭到逮捕时，整个莫里斯城都大吃一惊。在上述两个属于历史性的情节和一个纯属虚构的情节中，我们都可以看出矛盾如何经过一定时间以后终于获得解决的发展过程。

在这些情节中，我们还可以发觉统一性和旨趣：有些事情已得到了解决。但获得解决的事情的性质如何，那就得根据哪一种观点来看才能决定。滑铁卢之战可以被看成是一个完整无缺的情节，但它同样也可以被看成是意义更宽广的行动——比方说，不列颠帝国的崛起——中的一个事件。或者我们还可以把我们想象中的情节——比方说，有关这个银行家和爱好虚荣的伊夫琳·彭布罗克的叙述——不当做一个完整的情节，而仅仅看成是上述两人一生——或者甚至看成是比方说史密斯儿子的一生——中的一个插曲。

当我们一谈到情节的时候，我们心中所关注的是：作家对于从一个（真实的或想象中的）情节中引出来的一些事实如何加以选择和安排的问题——而这篇小说的统一性和旨趣，就是由这种选择和安排所决定的。所以说，情节无非就是对于动作富有意义地加以使用而已。一篇作品的讲述人，不管他是随便闲扯也好，

---

① 即北美的英国 13 个殖民地，美国独立时即由此组成 13 个州。

Waterloo, the fate of Europe hung in balance; at sunset Napoleon was a broken man. On June 7, 1776, Richard Henry Lee of Virginia presented to the Continental Congress a resolution declaring that "these United Colonies are, and of right ought to be, free and independent States"; on July 4 the Declaration of Independence was signed. When Tom Smith, a wealthy, middle-aged banker, met Evelyn Pembroke, he immediately recognized her vain and frivolous nature, but that recognition could not overcome the attraction she exerted; and all of Morristown was surprised when Smith, the very pillar of respectability, was arrested for embezzlement. In each of these actions, two historical and one fictional, we recognize the movement of conflict through time to a point of rest, or resolution.

In these actions we recognize, too, unity and significance; something is settled. But the nature of the thing settled may depend on a point of view. The Battle of Waterloo may be regarded as a completed action, but it may also be regarded as one event in a broader action, in, say, the rise of the British Empire. Or we may regard our imaginary action, say, the account of the banker and the vain Evelyn Pembroke, not as a fulfilled action, but as merely an episode in the life of one of the two persons concerned, or even in the life of, say, Smith's son.

When we come to plot we are concerned with a writer's selection and arrangement of facts drawn from an action (real or imaginary)—a selection and arrangement that determine the unity and significance of the fiction. *Plot, then, is the meaningful manipulation of action.* The teller of a story, whether in idle conversation or in the serious business of writing a novel, cannot possibly use all the thousands of facts involved in the action. He has to *select* the facts that seem to him useful for his particular purpose.

还是在一本正经地写一部小说也好,不可能把情节中所包含的许许多多事实通通都用上去。他必须选择他觉得对他特定的目的有用的那些事实。

讲故事的人认为,事实有两种用处。一个事实(不管它是真实的或想象中的)只要内容生动(那就是说,足以激发人们的想象来接受这篇小说),那它就是有用的。一个生动的事实,可以突然使我们觉得整整一段叙述都是真实可信的。一个事实只要能直接或间接地表明这篇小说中所遵循的发展线索(那就是说,只要它能表明一个事件如何导致另一个事件,或者这些事件的运动过程意味着什么的话),那它同样是有用的。生动性和旨趣——这些就是选择有用的事实时的两块试金石。但是这两种特性极容易消失。生动的细节一抓住人们的想象力,就能产生一种特别鲜明的色调,即一篇小说给人们的"感受",而这种"感受",这种氛围(见重要词汇),就是表明小说含义深邃隽永的一种要素。

所以说,我们只要一检验小说,就会不断地遇到有关事实方面的一些问题。为什么要选择这个事实呢?是什么东西使得作家采用这些事实,而拒不采用别的一些事实?而选择了别的一些现成事实,又如何会变成一篇截然不同的小说?(记住:一个事实在这里可以是想象中的。)

要回答这样一些问题是很复杂的,但这些问题却值得深思。它们可以指引我们去理解一篇小说的全部意义。

一个作家在选定了他所需要的事实之后,随之而来的是先后次序的问题。到此刻为止,我们所想到的情节,就是指它在外部世界所有错综复杂的细节,它的所有组成部分都按照它们真实的年代先后顺序排列的。然而,许多小说——实际上,严格地说,包括所有的小说——不管怎样,在这个现实世界上认为一个情节所具有的那种严格的按照年代先后排列

For the storyteller, facts have two kinds of usefulness. A fact (real or imaginary) is useful if it is vivid, that is, if it stirs the imagination to accept the story. One vivid fact may suddenly make a whole passage of narrative seem real to us. A fact is also useful if it indicates, directly or indirectly, the line of development pursued in a story, that is, if it indicates how one thing leads to another, or what the movement of events means. Vividness and significance—these are the tests of usefulness in selection. But the two tend to merge. The vivid detail that catches the imagination helps to create the special quality, the "feel" of a story, and this "feel," this *atmosphere* (see Glossary) is an element of the meanings.

So if we examine fiction we are continually faced with questions about facts. Why was a particular fact selected? What led the writer to use some facts and reject others? How might the choice of other available facts have made a very different story? (Remember that here a "fact" may be imaginary.)

Answers to such questions are always complicated, but the questions are worth pondering. They may lead us toward the full meaning of a story.

After a writer has selected his facts, there comes the question of order. Thus far we have thought of the action as existing in all of its intricate detail out in the world, with all of its components disposed in their actual chronological order. Yet many stories—indeed, in a strict sense, all stories—violate in one way or another the strict chronological sequence of an action *as thought* of in the actual world. To take an example, no writer can give simultaneously in his narrative two things that occur simultaneously in the action. His order of narration is bound to be artificial. To take another example, the beginning of a story may, or may not, happen to pick up the beginning of the action that it

的顺序,反正都被打乱了。举个例子来说,没有一个作家可以将同时发生的两件事情,同时写到他的作品中去。他在叙述时的顺序,应该是自己主观决定的。再举一个例子来说,一篇小说的开端,可以(或者是不可以)碰巧和它所表现的这个情节的开端完全吻合。这个情节也可以使我们置身于正好是事情的中间那一段,随后,再一段接一段地使我们又回到那个情节的开端部分。或者还可能将各个时期错综复杂地都交织在一起。这一概念可用下面这一篇假设中的小说的图表来加以说明。

动作顺序: a b c d e f g h i j k l m n o p q r s t u v w x y z

情节顺序: F A B H I J E R S T V Y Z

我们可以从上面图表中看到:凡是动作的所有事实,情节并没有全部采用;而且按照年代先后排列的顺序,也已经被打乱了。因此,情节就是一篇小说中所表现的那个动作的结构。它代表了讲故事人对他那个动作中的事件如何加以处理的一种方法。

在讨论一个情节的性质时,我们必定要接触到统一性和旨趣这两个问题。现在让我们回过头来(特别是在提到情节的时候)再研究这些问题。

当我们说"一部小说"、"一则故事"或"一个情节"的时候,我们就本能地包含了这样一个完整的概念。我们所指的就是,许多组成部分,亦即形形色色的个别事件,都已经结合在一起了。首先,就有因果关系这个问题。在任何一篇小说中,我们都指望能发现从一件事情引起了另一件事情。如果说我们根本发现不了它们之间所包含的任何合理的关系,如果说反正什么"逻辑推理"关系都不存在的话,那么,我们就会失掉兴趣。每一篇小说一定要指明它各个组成部分之间的关系的主要实质,因为小说本身就是某一个作家在说明你如何才

presents. The plot may plunge us into the very middle of things, and then, stage by stage, take us back to the beginning of the action. Or there may be a complicated interweaving of times. The accompanying chart of a hypothetical story indicates this notion.

Sequence of Action: a b c d e f g h i j k l m n o p q r s t u v w x y z

SEQUENCE OF PLOT: F A B H I J E R S T V Y Z

We can see, in our chart, that the plot does not use all the facts of the action, and that the chronological order has been scrambled. The plot, then, is the structure of the action *as presented* in a piece of fiction. It represents the treatment the storyteller makes of the events of his action.

In discussing the nature of an action we have necessarily touched on unity and significance. Let us now return to these topics with more special reference to plot.

When we say "*a* novel," "*a* story," or "*a* plot," we instinctively imply the idea of unity. We imply that the parts, the various individual events, hang together. To begin with, there is the matter of cause and effect. In any story we expect to find one thing bringing on another. If we can detect no reasonable connection between them, if there is no "logic" whatever, we lose interest. Every story must indicate some basis for the relation among its parts, for the story itself is a *particular writer's way of saying how you can make sense of human experience.*

Cause and effect constitute one of the ways of saying this. In works of fiction, however, we cannot think of cause as a mechanical thing—as though one event were one domino knocking over the next one in a long series. The events are human events; that is, they

能理解人的经验的一种方式。

原因和效果构成了这种表达方式之一。但是,在许多小说作品中,我们不能把原因当作一种机械刻板的东西——好像一个事件就同玩多米诺骨牌一样,会把长长的一系列事件都给推翻了。这些事件都是有关人的事件;那就是说,它们包含着人对变化中的环境所做出的种种反应,其中包括对改变现存环境而采取行动的可能性。许多不属于人的事情,可以进入一篇小说的逻辑中去——毁坏了庄稼的天气,使船只沉没的冰山,破坏矿山的爆炸,从国王使者的坐骑的马蹄铁上掉了一枚钉子——但到最后,我们心中所关注的中心逻辑,却还是人的动机形成的逻辑。人的需要和情感本身又是怎样产生的? 所以说,情节就是行动中的人物。

逻辑,其中包括动机(见重要词汇)形成的逻辑在内,把一个情节中的许多事件联结起来,成为一个整体。这个整体,当然,就是一个充满活力的整体。它是一个包含着变化的整体:没有变化,就没有小说。正如我们前面所讲过的,我们会在一篇小说的开头,发现一个包含着某种不稳定因素的环境。到了小说的结尾处,我们发现事情又一次变成稳定了。有些事情已经得到了解决:吉姆·贝克沃思攻占了黑脚人的堡垒;沃尔特·米蒂做了一个梦,我们后来才知道,他永远没有醒过来;布朗大爷发现了错综复杂的人性。从不稳定向稳定发展的这一过程,正如我们上面所说的,包含着某些自然阶段——开始,中间和结尾阶段。

当我们开始考虑到这些自然阶段怎样通过情节的方式得到处理的时候,我们发现我们还得借助于一些特殊名词来加以说明。情节的开始阶段叫做破题(见重要词汇)——即对小说将要由此得到发展的那些假设加以"阐明"。中间阶段叫做开展(见重要词汇),亦即趋于复杂的过程,因为它在通向稳定的过程中遇到了日益增多的困难。举例来说,如果一个

involve human responses to changing situations, including the possibility of action taken to change existing situations. Many nonhuman things may enter into the logic of a story—the weather that ruins a crop, the iceberg that sinks a ship, the explosion that wrecks a mine, the nail lost from the shoe of the horse of the king's messenger—but in the end the central logic we are concerned with is the logic of human motivation. How do human needs and passions work themselves out? Plot, then, is character in action.

Logic, including the logic of *motivation*, (see Glossary), binds the events of a plot together into a unity. This unity is, of course, a dynamic unity. It is a unity involving change: no change, no story. At the beginning of a story we find, as we have earlier said, a situation with some element of instability in it. At the end of the story, we find that things have become stable once more. Something has been settled: Jim Beckworth has captured the Blackfoot fort; Walter Mitty, we have come to know, will never wake up from his dream; Goodman Brown has discovered the complexity of human nature. This movement from instability toward stability involves, as we have said, certain natural stages—the beginning, the middle, and the end.

When we come to consider how these natural stages are treated in terms of plot, we find that we need some special terms. The beginning of the plot action is called the *exposition* (see Glossary)—the "setting forth" of the assumptions from which the story will develop. The middle is called the *complication* (see Glossary), for it presents the increasing difficulty encountered in the movement toward stability. If, for example, a character moves easily toward his triumph, or his ruin, there is really no story. It is no story to tell how a

人物轻而易举地走向胜利或走向灭亡,老实说,那也就没有故事可讲了。单讲一只圆木桶滚到山脚下去,也就不成其为小说了。小说之所以令人感到兴趣,就在于遇到了各种阻力,再加以克服(或者克服不了)——就在于有如下述的逻辑推理的结果,必然使阻力引起了许多反应,于是回过来又遇到了(或者又产生了)新的阻力,需要加以对付。正当某些事情不得不发生,某些事情不得不垮掉的时候,情节却愈益复杂地朝着某一时刻、某一事件移动。只要小说一转向它的解决方向发展,这一时刻就达到了最高度的紧张状态。这就叫做——高潮(见重要词汇)。因此,这篇小说就成为说明矛盾合乎逻辑地经过相当错综复杂的几个阶段不断得到发展的一篇小说了。

结尾阶段——结局(见重要词汇)——给予我们的,就是矛盾发展的结果,问题的圆满解决,以及建立了一种新的稳定的基础。当然,我们知道,刚才达到的那种稳定所赖以寄托的基础,可能只是暂时性的,某些事情还可能继续把那种来之不易的稳定又给推翻掉。例如,如果我们读一篇经过激烈追求,最后"小伙子搞到了姑娘"的小说,我们知道,除了神话故事里"从今以后他们就过着美满幸福的生活"那种老套式以外,要是所有的矛盾,所有的斗争,所有的难题都解决不了,那姑娘自然也不会开这个金口的。结局只不过给我们解决了某一个具体行动——求婚——那就是作者选定要讲述的这个故事。

但是,解决的意义常常超出了某一个具体行动范围。这种论点将使我们重新回到情节的旨趣这个问题上来。当然,一个情节的发展只要显示它合乎逻辑推理,那它早已在显示出它的旨趣来了——它正在告诉我们,或者正在向我们显示有关人的品行的某些东西。从这种逻辑推理引出来的结论,给予我们的,不仅仅是小说中叙述的某种个别经历的评估,而且还是从中概括出来的总的评估。一篇成

barrel rolls downhill. The story interest inheres in the resistances encountered and overcome, or not overcome—in the logic by which resistance evokes responses that, in their turn, encounter or create new resistances to be dealt with. The complication moves toward a moment, an event, when something has to happen, when something has to crack. This moment is the point of highest tension, the moment when the story turns toward its solution. This is called the *climax* (see Glossary). The story, then, is the story of *conflict* developing logically through the stages of the complication.

The end—the *denouement* (see Glossary)—gives us the outcome of the conflict, the solution to the problem, the basis of a new stability. We realize, of course, that the basis of stability now reached may be only provisional and temporary, that something may come along to upset the hard-won stability. If, for example, we have the story of a stormy courtship and "boy gets girl" in the end, we know that, except in the fairy-tale formula of "and they lived happily ever after," no promise is made of an end to all conflict, all struggle, all problems. The denouement simply gives us the settling of a particular action—the courtship—which is the story that the author has elected to tell.

The meaning of the settlement, however, always reaches beyond the particular action. And this idea takes us back to the question of significance in plot. Insofar, of course, as the development of a plot exhibits logic, it is already exhibiting significance—it is telling us, or showing us, something about human nature and human conduct. The conclusion that stems from this logic aims to give us not only an evaluation of the particular experience related in the story, but a *generalized*

功的小说结尾,常常把一种可取的总的人生观留给了我们。这篇小说包含着对人的价值所做出的一种评价——亦即指出了人的品行方面的优劣之处以及每个人最终可以选取的人生观。那就是说,任何一篇具体的小说,会常常以一种哪怕是模糊不清,但却具有经验的含义的形象,出现在我们的想象和感受之中。

这种含义的表达方式,可以因每一个实例而各有不同。可以有一段非常清晰的、相当完整的概述——正如我们马上就要在本章最后一篇小说《国王迷》的题词中所看到的那样。或者一篇小说也可以运用象征手法,这样,当我们将要在小说结尾处读到我们的评价时,就可以回过头来再去解释这种说法了。即使小说结局似乎只能使那些事件了结,并避免做出解释,我们将发现这篇小说(如果它是一篇成功的小说)会使我们去回顾小说本身所包含的某些基本特性;而且我们还将发现那种特性可能不知不觉地已经改变了我们的感情和态度。它可以增进我们的同情心——就像契诃夫的小说《万卡》那样——因此,我们现在对别人就可能更容易表现出宽厚谦逊的态度来。或者它还可能——如同弗兰克·奥康纳所写的小说《醉汉》那样——给予我们一种喜剧式的轻松感。或者这篇小说还可以在一种粗俗的讽刺或冷酷的嘲弄之中结束。然而,我们常常指望在小说中能得到一种关于经验方面的见解(或某些实例),而我们要是得不到的话,就会觉得不满。我们感到受骗了。换句话说,我们觉得这篇小说在逻辑上是连贯不起来的——尽管动机形成的逻辑推理等等可以一段接一段地好像自己正在产生预期的结果,但情节本身并没有起到应有的作用。我们不喜欢听人家说教,但我们十分需要得到一种意味深长的启发。

所以我们一讨论情节,就使我们回到主题上来,正如在讨论动机的时候,它早就把我们引向人物性格问题一样。那才是自然的现象,

evaluation. Always the end of a successful story leaves us with an attitude to take toward life in general. The story embodies a comment on human values—on what is good or bad in human nature and human conduct, on what attitude one may take, finally, toward life and the business of living. That is, any particular story will always appear, in our imagination and feelings, as an image, however shadowy, of the meaning of experience.

The way the meaning is presented may vary from instance to instance. There may be a perfectly explicit general statement, more or less complete—as we will soon find in the epigraph of "The Man Who Would Be King" at the end of this section. Or a story may use *symbolism* (see Glossary) that can be read back into statement as we shall do in our comment on the end of the story. Even when the denouement may seem merely to wind up events and avoid interpretation, we shall find that the story, if it is a successful one, will turn us back toward some basic quality in the story itself; and we shall find that that quality may have subtly modified our feelings and attitudes. It may have enlarged our sympathies—as does "Vanka," by Chekhov—so that we may now more readily regard other People with charity and humility. Or it may have given us a liberating sense of the comedy of experience—as "The Drunkard" by Frank O' Connor. Or the story may conclude on a note of savage satire or chilling irony. Always, however, we expect in fiction an idea about, some stance toward, experience, and if we do not get it we are dissatisfied. We feel cheated. We don't know what the shooting has been about. We feel, in other words, that the story is incoherent—the Plot has not fulfilled itself, even though stage by stage the logic of motivation, and the like, may have been seeming to work itself out. We do not like to be preached at, but we do demand a sense of meaningfulness.

So our discussion of plot brings us back to theme, just as it has already led us, in discussing motivation, to the question of character. And that is only natural, for a good story

因为一篇好的小说毕竟是一个整体。它本身是前后一致的。它所表现的想象世界——用我们早已用过的名词来说——就叫作连贯性。

我们竭力指出一个情节中各个组成部分所起的作用，以及它们内部之间的关系问题。让我们提出下面这样一个问题：我们要不要注意到各个组成部分之间会有什么特殊的比例？回答是：不。

在某些小说中——无论是长篇也好，短篇也好——破题可能要占很大篇幅。作为危急时刻的背景，过去的经历可能占很大分量，而且，如果说我们要理解这篇小说的话，那我们就一定要理解它所具有的含义。或者我们可能还需要对我们也许很不熟悉的一个特殊的世界有所了解。

有时候，一篇小说需要有一个篇幅很长，并精心设计的结局。我们将会看到，《国王迷》在某种意义上说，就是在德雷沃特满不在乎地走到了桥上，大声吼叫，"割断吧，你们这些穷光蛋"的时候才告结束。不过，在我们充分意识到那个时刻以前，就非得要有很大篇幅和很多文字叙述不可。可是，想一想《沃尔特·米蒂的隐秘生活》这篇小说，它在结尾时却根本用不着多大的篇幅。当然，这一篇小说篇幅比另一篇小说要长一些，而且内容更为复杂，但即使这样，有一点却是根本不同的，即和类似这样的长度问题毫无关系。《国王迷》是使一个人物性格得到发展的小说，当这种发展已经过去了的时候，它需要一些时间和一些洋尽的细节，以便让人们感到作品的分量很重。约翰·科利尔的《埋葬》，正如我们将要看到的，是在小说结尾处方令人震惊地给予揭露。这一震惊就是要害所在。要是我们把那个结局拖得很长的话，我们就会失去震惊感，从而感到作品索然无味了。这篇小说确实包含着分量很重的暗示，但这些暗示并不需要加以精心安排，它们的力量是由震惊所决定的。

概括成一句话来说：比例可不是机械地规

is, after all, a unity. It is consistent within it-self. The world of imagination that it presents is—to repeat a term we have already used—*coherent*.

We have tried to indicate something of the function of the parts of a plot, and something of the relation among them. Let us ask the next question: are we to be concerned with any particular *proportion* among the parts? The answer is no.

In some pieces of fiction—whether novels or stories—a great deal of exposition may be required. There may be a great weight of the past behind the moment of crisis, and if we are to understand the story, we must understand what lies behind it. Or we may need to know something of a special world that may be unfamiliar to us.

Sometimes a story needs a long and elaborate denouement. In one sense "The Man Who Would Be King," we shall see, ends when Dravot walks boldly out on the bridge and yells, "Cut, you beggars!" But a good deal of space, and a good deal of narrative, is required before we have the full implications of that moment. Think, however, how little is required to end the story of Walter Mitty. Of course, one story is longer than the other, and more complicated, but even so, there is a fundamental difference that has little to do with the question of length as such. "The Man Who Would Be King" is a story giving the development of a character, and when the development is over it requires some time and some elaboration for its full weight to be felt. John Collier's "De Mortuis," as we shall see, is concerned with a shocking revelation at the end. The shock is the point. If we were to spin out the denouement, we should lose the sense of shock, and add nothing significant. The story does have weighty implications, but they do not need to be elaborated; their force depends on the shock.

What all this amounts to is simple: proportion is not mechanically determined. It

定下来的。它取决于这一篇具体的小说的素材和作家打算利用这些素材写成哪一类小说。我们在阅读作品时,一定要想方设法了解情况的需要,领悟作家的意图。

还有一个问题,就是有关情节如何划分问题:我们是不是指望在破题和开展两阶段之间,或者在开展和结局两阶段之间找到一条泾渭分明的界线? 当然,两者之间也许可以截然划分开来,有时候界线鲜明会大大地增强作品的效果——如同小说《万卡》那样。可是,正如我们在那张有关动作与情节区分的小小图表中所指明的,有时候这一部分和那一部分之间却是相互渗透、融合在一起的(特别是在破题和开展两个阶段之间),但高潮和结局有时候也许好像已经消失了。这样一来可能也会有某些好处,例如,很早(也许是在一开头)的时候就出现了开展的因素,抓住了读者的注意力,这时读者甚至还来不及去理解呈现在他面前的那个事件的充分意义。有时候,破题可能老是迟迟不肯披露,直到读者觉得非有不可的时候,它才以富有戏剧性的活力出现了。在这里,我们的原则还是要求讲究圆熟灵活。根本没有什么严格的现成规章可循。作为读者,我们一定要力求看到:在一个情节所包含的各个部分之间截然分开,或者相互渗透、融合在一起,跟作品最后效果又有怎样的关系。

在本章中,我们并不仅仅限于阅读和讨论那些情节要素特别突出的小说——比方说,像《国王迷》那样的小说。事实上,我们还将阅读一些情节似乎不太紧凑的小说。这是一个合理的办法,因为我们在这里所关心的,是要看到:情节这个要素——不管它是特别突出,或是相当潜隐——对于小说的其他方面来说,它又是怎样起到作用的。

再说,我们这里研究的,也并不仅仅限于那些情节按照重要顺序展示出来的小说。我们将会看到一些实例,其中一些事件并不是按照重要顺序排列的,而且并没有把人的价值充

depends on the materials of the particular story and the kind of story the writer is trying to make of those materials. As we read, we must try to sense the needs of the situation, and try to understand the intention of the writer.

One more question presents itself in regard to the divisions of a plot: are we to expect to find a sharp line between the exposition and complication, or between complication and denouement? There may, of course, be sharp division, and sometimes the sharpness contributes greatly to the effect—as in "Vanka." But, as we have indicated on our little chart distinguishing between action and plot, there is sometimes considerable interpenetration between one part and another, and especially between exposition and complication, but climax and denouement may sometimes seem to merge. There may be certain advantages, for example, in presenting an element of complication very early, at the very start perhaps, to catch the reader's attention, even before he can get the full import of the event before him. And sometimes a piece of exposition may be withheld until fairly late until the reader feels the need for it and it will come with dramatic force. Our principle here, again, is one of tact, of flexibility. There is no hard and fast rule. As readers, we must try to see how sharp separations or intricate interpenetrations among the parts of a plot are related to the final effect.

In this section we shall not confine ourselves to reading and discussing stories in which the element of plot is strongly marked—stories, for example, like "The Man Who Would Be King.' We shall, in fact, read some stories whose plots seem slight. This is a reasonable procedure, for we are concerned here to see how the element of plot, whether strongly marked or recessive, works in relation to other aspects of fiction.

Furthermore, we shall not confine ourselves to stories in which the plot exhibits significant order. We shall look at some instances in which the events are not in significant order, in which they do not adequately

分体现出来——总而言之,在这些实例中,情节是连贯不起来的。我们将会就我们在本书中所读到的小说提出一些问题来。例如,情节是不是连贯的?它的意义在哪里?如具说它毫无意义的话,那它又是在哪一方面失败的?换句话说,我们一定要经常思考情节同人物和主题的关系问题。

但也不仅仅同人物和主题有关。短篇小说和长篇小说都是用语言创作的,所以我们还将不得不思考一下,情节与作家所运用的语言优劣之间究竟还有什么关系。正如我们将要看到的,这里也会出现作品的连贯性等问题。

（潘庆舲 译）

embody human values—instances, in short, in which the plot is incoherent. Of all the stories we read in this book we shall be asking questions. Is the plot coherent? Does it make sense? If it does not make sense, in what particular way does it fail? We must, in other words, constantly consider the relation of plot to character and theme.

But not only to character and theme. Stories and novels are composed in words, and so we shall have to think a little about the relation of plot to the resources of language that the writer uses well or badly. Problems of coherence, as we shall see, arise here too.

006. 带家具出租的房间

(美)欧·亨利 著　　刘文荣 译

006. The Furnished Room

by O. Henry

在西南区的红砖房街区，有那么一大批人，他们就像时间一样流动不停、晃荡不安。说他们无家可归吧，他们又四处为家。他们从一个带家具出租的房间转到另一个带家具出租的房间，永远不得安定——住处不得安定，心灵和思想也不得安定。他们怪声怪气地唱着"家呀，可爱的家"；他们把 lares et penates（法语：门神和家神）装在帽盒里随身带着；他们的葡萄藤攀结在一顶宽沿帽上；一束橡皮枝叶就是他们的无花果树①。

这地区的房屋里既然住着成千的房客，那当然就有成千的轶闻趣事可供谈谈啰，毫无疑问，绝大多数是沉闷单调的；但在所有这些流动房客身后，如果找不出一两个幽灵来，那才怪哩。

一天晚上天黑以后，有个年轻人在这些破败不堪的红砖房之间踯躅，挨家挨户地打门铃。打到第12家门口，他把瘪塌塌的手提包放在台阶上，伸手擦擦帽檐和额头上的灰尘。铃声在冷清而空洞的深处响了，显得很微弱，很遥远。

在第12家的门口他打了铃，有个女房东走了出来。这女房东的样子使他想起一条吃得太饱而懒洋洋的蛆虫。这蛆虫好像已经把一个果核吃得只剩下一只空壳，现在就等着那些可供充饥的房客来填补这个空间了。

他问是不是有房间出租。

---

① 葡萄藤和无花果树为家庭生活的象征，典出《旧约·列王纪上》："所罗门在世之日，从丹恩到比斯巴的犹太人和以色列人都在自己的葡萄藤下和无花果树下安然居住。"

RESTLESS, shifting, fugacious as time itself is a certain vast bulk of the population of the red brick district of the lower West Side. Homeless, they have a hundred homes. They flit from furnished room to furnished room, transients forever—transients in abode, transients in heart and mind. They sing "Home, Sweet Home" in ragtime; they carry their *lares et penates* in a bandbox; their vine is entwined about a picture hat; a rubber plant is their fig tree.

Hence the houses of this district, having had a thousand dwellers, should have a thousand tales to tell, mostly dull ones, no doubt; but it would be strange if there could not be found a ghost or two in the wake of all these vagrant guests.

One evening after dark a young man prowled among these crumbling red mansions, ringing their bells. At the twelfth he rested his lean hand baggage upon the step and wiped the dust from his hatband and forehead. The bell sounded faint and far away in some remote, hollow depths.

To the door of this, the twelfth house whose bell he had rung, came a housekeeper who made him think of an unwholesome, surfeited worm that had eaten its nut to a hollow shell and now sought to fill the vacancy with edible lodgers.

He asked if there was a room to let.

"Come in," said the housekeeper. Her voice came from her throat; her throat seemed lined with fur. "I have the third floor, back, vacant since a week back. Should you wish to look at it?"

The young man followed her up the stairs. A faint light from no particular source mitigated the shadows

作者简介：欧·亨利（O. Henry，1862—1910），美国短篇小说家。1862 年 9 月 11 日生于北卡罗来纳州格林斯博罗，1910 年 6 月 5 日卒于纽约。欧·亨利的短篇小说精彩纷呈，充满令人惊讶和具有讽刺意味的转折。他最有名的作品有《最后的行吟诗人》(*The Last of the Troubadours*)、《麦琪的礼物》(*The Gift of the Magi*)和《红酋长的赎金》(*The Ransom of Red Chief*)。欧·亨利善于描写美国社会尤其是纽约百姓的生活。他的著作以情节取胜，结局常常出人意外。欧·亨利的作品都刊登在全国报纸杂志上，他的作品还有《白菜与国王》(*Cabbages and Kings*，1904)、《西部之心》(*Heart of the West*，1907)和《城市之声》(*The Voice of the City*，1908)。

"进来。"女房东回答。她的声音发自喉咙,而她的喉咙里又好像长满了厚厚的绒毛。"有间三楼的后房,已经空了一个星期。你想看看吗?"

年轻人跟着她上楼。一缕不知从何而来的微光摇曳在黑洞洞的过道里。他们悄然无声地踏着楼梯和毡毯,那条毡毯简直不成样子,大概连原先织它的织机也认不出它了。它似乎已经变成植物,在腐恶阴暗的空气里,它长在这楼梯上,就像一大块滑腻腻的地衣或一大片苔藓,踩上去活像那种粘糊糊的有机物。楼梯的每个转弯处,墙上都挂着空荡荡的壁龛。也许,这里面曾经放过花草。果真这样的话,那它们准是在这混浊腐恶的空气里枯死了。也有可能,这里面曾放过圣徒的雕像,不过很容易想象,他们早已被妖魔鬼怪拖进黑暗,拖到某个带家具出租的地狱的邪恶深渊里去了。

"就是这间房。"女房东从毛茸茸的喉咙里发出声音说,"这间房挺舒适的。难得没人住。去年夏天,这里还住过几位高级客人哩——他们一点不找麻烦,总是先付后住。水就在过道那头。施普劳斯和蒙纳在这儿住过3个月。她们是演杂剧的。布蕾达·施普劳斯小姐——你也许听人说起过她——哦,那不过是她的艺名——她的结婚证就挂在那个梳妆台上面,还配了镜框哩。煤气灯在这儿,你看这壁橱有多大。这房间人人都喜欢。这儿从来不会空出很久的。"

"你这儿常有剧团的人来租房?"年轻人问。

"他们来了又去了。我的房客中有好多人是和剧院有关系的。是啊,先生,这儿有的是剧院。那些当演员的从来不在一个地方待很久。我不过有我的一份生意。是啊,他们来了又去了。"

他租下这房间,准备预付一星期房钱。他说他很累,想立刻住下来。他把钱数好。女房东说,房间里样样都有,连毛巾和洗脸水也准备好了。说完,她转身想出去,这时年轻人把他那个挂在唇边曾一千次向人打听过的问题问了出来:

"你可记得,在你的房客中是不是有过一个年轻姑娘——瓦什纳小姐——艾洛伊丝·瓦什纳小姐?她很可能就在剧院里唱歌。一个很漂亮的姑娘,身材不高不矮,很苗条,头发是棕红色的,左边眉毛旁边有一颗黑痣。"

"记不起了,我记不起那名字了。他们那些演戏的人常常换名字,就像他们常常换房间一样。他们来

of the halls. They trod noiselessly upon a stair carpet that its own loom would have foresworn. It seemed to have become vegetable; to have degenerated in that rank, sunless air to lush lichen or spreading moss that grew in patches to the staircase and was viscid under the foot like organic matter. At each turn of the stairs were vacant niches in the wall. Perhaps plants had once been set within them. If so, they had died in that foul and tainted air. It may be that statues of the saints had stood there, but it was not difficult to conceive that imps and devils had dragged them forth in the darkness and down to the unholy depths of some furnished pit below.

"This is the room," said the housekeeper, from her furry throat. "It's a nice room. It ain't often vacant. I had some most elegant people in it last summer—no trouble at all, and paid in advance to the minute. The water's at the end of the hall. Sprowls and Mooney kept it three months. They done a vaudeville sketch. Miss B'retta Sprowls—you may have heard of her—oh, that was just the stage names—right there over the dresser is where the marriage certificate hung, framed. The gas is here, and you see there is plenty of closet room. It's a room everybody likes. It never stays idle long."

"Do you have many theatrical people rooming here?" asked the young man.

"They comes and goes. A good proportion of my lodgers is connected with the theaters. Yes, sir, this is the theatrical district. Actor people never stays long anywhere. I get my share. Yes, they comes and they goes."

He engaged the room, paying for a week in advance. He was tired, he said, and would take possession at once. He counted out the money. The room had been made ready, she said, even to towels and water. As the housekeeper moved away he put, for the thousandth time, the question that he carried at the end of his tongue.

"A young girl—Miss Vashner—Miss Eloise Vashner—do you remember such a one among your lodgers? She would be singing on the stage, most likely. A fair girl, of medium height and slender, with reddish, gold hair and a dark mole near her left eyebrow."

"No, I don't remember the name. Them stage people has names they change as often as their rooms. They comes and they goes. No, I can't call that one to

了又去了。我可没能耐记着某个人的名字。"

记不起。问来问去总是记不起。5个月来不断地打听，而结果一无所获。花了那么多时间，白天在经理那儿、在代理人那儿、在剧团里和合唱团里到处打听；晚上，在观众堆里询问，不管是明星群聚的大剧院，还是那些低级得连他自己都害怕不会有希望找到她的游乐场，他都问遍了。他，曾深深地爱过她，现在他要想方设法找到她。他知道，她离家出走之后，一定流落在这个沿海大城市①的某个地方，可是这个城市却像一大片无底的流沙，每一颗沙粒都在不停地沉浮，永远也不固定，今天还浮在上面，明天又沉到污泥秽土里去了。

这个带家具出租的房间，就像一个强颜欢笑、忸怩作态的妓女，带着那种初次见面时的虚情假意欢迎着刚到的客人。那破破烂烂的家具上映着一层淡淡的虚光，给人一种诡黠难言的感觉。一张睡榻，两把椅子，上面的缎子褴褛不堪，两扇窗之间挂着一面一英尺宽的镜子，旁边是一两只涂金镜框，屋子的角落里放着一张铜床。

客人有气无力地坐在一把椅子上，而整个房间呢，则像巴比伦高塔②的一层塔面，在语无伦次地向他诉说早先在此居住过的房客们的种种情况。

一块花花绿绿的地毯就像波涛翻滚的大海上的一个长方形的、鲜花盛开的热带岛屿。糊着灰纸的墙上贴着那些无家可归的人所常带的画片——《胡格诺教教徒的情侣》《初次相争》《新婚早餐》《泉边倩影》。歪歪斜斜、不成样子的帷帘就像亚马逊舞女的饰巾半遮着轮廓分明的壁炉。壁炉台上零零落落地散放着一些东西——几个不值钱的花瓶、几张女明星的照片、一个药瓶、几张不同花头的扑克牌；曾在这房间里住过的房客们就像航船遇难后漂落到海岛上的旅客，当他们有幸被别的船所救而能去另一港口时，便扔下随身所带的东西不管了。

就像密码给慢慢地破译出来一样，早先在此居住过的房客们留下的遗痕也渐渐地清楚了。梳妆台前，那张地毯上磨破的地方说明有许多美貌女子在这上

---

① 指纽约。

② 《旧约·创世记》第11章：巴比伦人要建造一座城市和一座通天高塔，耶和华上帝变乱他们的口音，使他们彼此语言不通，因此只能停工不造。

mind. "

No. Always no. Five months of ceaseless interrogation and the inevitable negative. So much time spent by day in questioning managers, agents, schools, and choruses; by night among the audiences of theaters from all-star casts down to music halls so low that he dreaded to find what he most hoped for. He who had loved her best had tried to find her. He was sure that since her disappearance from home this great, water-girt city held her somewhere, but it was like a monstrous quicksand, shifting its particles constantly, with no foundation, its upper granules of today buried tomorrow in ooze and slime.

The furnished room received its latest guest with a first glow of pseudo-hospitality, a hectic, haggard, perfunctory welcome like the specious smile of a demi-rep. The sophistical comfort came in reflected gleams from the decayed furniture, the ragged brocade upholstery of a couch and two chairs, a foot-wide cheap pier glass between the two windows, from one or two gilt picture frames and a brass bedstead in a corner.

The guest reclined, inert, upon a chair, while the room, confused in speech as though it were an apartment in Babel, tried to discourse to him of its divers tenantry.

A polychromatic rug like some brilliant-flowered rectangular, tropical islet lay surrounded by a billowy sea of soiled matting. Upon the gray-papered wall were those pictures that pursue the homeless one from house to house—The Huguenot Lovers, The First Quarrel, The Wedding Breakfast, Psyche at the Fountain. The mantel's chastely severe outline was ingloriously veiled behind some pert drapery drawn rakishly askew like the sashes of the Amazonian ballet. Upon it was some desolate flotsam cast aside by the room's marooned when a lucky sail had borne them to a fresh port—a trifling vase or two, pictures of actresses, a medicine bottle, some stray cards out of a deck.

One by one, as the characters of a cryptograph become explicit, the little signs left by the furnished room's procession of guests developed a significance. The threadbare space in the rug in front of the dresser told that lovely women had marched in the throng. The tiny finger prints on the wall spoke of little prisoners trying to feel their way to sun and air. A splattered stain, raying like the shadow of a bursting bomb, witnessed where a hurled glass or bottle had

面踩踏过。墙上的那些小小的手指印表明年幼的囚徒曾在此摸索,想寻求阳光和新鲜空气。一块向四面八方迸散的痕迹证明曾有人把盛满东西的杯子或者瓶子扔到了墙上。挂镜上,有人曾用金刚钻歪歪斜斜地刻上了"玛丽"这样的名字。看样子,住在这个带家具出租的房间里的房客们,不论是先还是后,都是些满腹怨气的人——也许是这房间太阴森太冷漠而使他们难以忍受的缘故吧——他们于是便拿房间里的东西来出气。家具被弄得乱七八糟、伤痕累累;那张弹簧一根根露在外面的睡榻,看上去就像一头在拼命挣扎时给人杀死的可怕的怪物。由于某种更为猛烈的震动,大理石壁炉台也给刮去了一大块。地板上处处是凹痕和裂纹,而每一处都有其自身独特的痛苦由来。使人难以相信的是,对这房间所施加的种种怨恨和损害都是由那些曾一度把它称之为"家"的人所干的;然而,他们之所以这样怒火中烧,也许就是因为他们不自觉地感到了那种恶家的本能,从而激起了他们对这冒牌的家庭守护神的敌意吧。而如果这个家是属于我们自己的,那即使换成一间草棚,我们也会加以打扫、装饰和爱护的。

那年轻的房客坐在椅子上,听凭种种思想在他的心头萦绕、盘旋,这时从别的带家具出租的房间里,传来了"出租的"声音和"出租的"气味。他听到某个房间里飘出淫荡的、软绵绵的低笑声,另一些房间里,有人在自说自话地大声詈骂,有人在嘎拉嘎拉地掷骰子,有人在哼催眠曲,有人在抽泣,在他头顶上,一只五弦琴快活地丁东作响。不知哪儿,房门乒乒乓乓,高架电车时不时地隆隆而过,后院的篱笆上有只猫在悲切地号叫。他呼吸着屋子里的空气——与其说是空气,不如说是一股潮湿味——一股就像从地下室的油布和烂木头里散发出来的冷飕飕的霉气。

而就在这时,正当他这样歇息着的时候,忽然之间,房间里充满了浓烈而甜美的木樨香味。这香味似乎是随着一阵轻风飘来的,而且是那样分明,那样浓郁,那样强烈,简直就像是一个有血有肉的来客。年轻人就像被谁叫到了名字似的,一下子跳起来,左右张望着,还大声喊:"怎么啦,亲爱的?"那阵浓香围拢过来,将他裹在中央。他伸出手去摸索,这时他的一切知觉都变得混杂而紊乱了。一个人怎么会分明听到一种气味的召唤呢?不用说,那一定是声音。旦是,他刚才感觉到的,还想伸手去捉摸的,难道是声音吗?

splintered with its contents against the wall. Across the pier glass had been scrawled with a diamond in staggering letters the name "Maire." It seemed that the succession of dwellers in the furnished room had turned in fury—perhaps tempted beyond forebearance by its garish coldness—and wreaked upon it their passions. The furniture was chipped and bruised; the couch, distorted by bursting springs, seemed a horrible monster that had been slain during the stress of some grotesque convulsion. Some more potent upheaval had cloven a great slice from the marble mantel. Each plank in the floor owned its particular cant and shriek as from a separate and individual agony. It seemed incredible that all this malice and injury had been wrought upon the room by those who had called it for a time their home; and yet it may have been the cheated home instinct surviving blindly, the resentful rage at false household gods that had kindled their wrath. A hut that is our own we can sweep and adorn and cherish.

The young tenant in the chair allowed these thoughts to file, softshod, through his mind, while there drifted into the room furnished sounds and furnished scents. He heard in one room a tittering and incontinent, slack laughter; in others the monologue of a scold, the rattling of dice, a lullaby, and one crying dully; above him a banjo tinkled with spirit. Doors banged somewhere; the elevated trains roared intermittently; a cat yowled miserably upon a back fence. And he breathed the breath of the house—a dank savor rather than a smell—a cold, musty effluvium as from underground vaults mingled with the reeking exhalations of linoleum and mildewed and rotten woodwork.

Then, suddenly, as he rested there, the room was filled with the strong, sweet odor of mignonette. It came as upon a single buffet of wind with such sureness and fragrance and emphasis that it almost seemed a living visitant. And the man cried aloud: "What, dear?" as if he had been called, and sprang up and faced about. The rich odor clung to him and wrapped him around. He reached out his arms for it, all his senses for the time confused and commingled. How could one be peremptorily called by an odor? Surely it must have been a sound. But, was it not the sound that had touched, that had caressed him?

"She has been in this room," he cried, and he sprang to wrest from it a token, for he knew he would recognize the smallest thing that had belonged to her

"她在这房间里住过。"他喊起来,急切地想在房间里找到什么凭据,因为他知道,凡是属于她的或者被她触摸过的东西,哪怕是极微小的东西,他也能辨认出来。这股萦绕不散的木樨香味就是她喜爱而且是她所特有的气味——这气味是从哪儿来的呢?

房间里乱糟糟的。梳妆台薄薄的台布上散乱地放着五六只发夹——那些东西没有特点,不声不响,却是女人的随身物,但一般女人都喜欢它们,这里没有固定的人称,也没有固定的时态。他没有理会发夹,因为他知道从发夹上是找不到什么线索的。他翻着梳妆台的抽屉,发现有一块被人扔下的破烂的小手帕。他把手帕按到脸上。手帕上有一股刺鼻的金盏草气味,他狠劲儿地把手帕扔在地上。在另一只抽屉里,他发现有几颗纽扣、一份剧院节目单、一张当票、两粒没吃的软糖和一本占梦的书。最后,还有一个女人用的黑发结,这东西使他一阵火热又一阵冰冷,踌躇了好一会儿。然而,黑发结毕竟是一般女人都有的普通装饰品,并不是某人专用的,所以丝毫也不能说明什么。

他于是就像猎狗追踪嗅迹似的在房间里到处搜索;扫视墙壁,趴下身子仔细查看角落里地毯鼓起的地方,检查壁炉台、桌子、窗帘、帷布以及角落里的那只东倒西歪的柜子,一心想找到什么明显的迹象。然而,他却没有意识到,她就在他旁边,在他周围,在他前面,在他里面,在他上面,她正偎依着他,在向他诉说着爱情,在通过那微妙的感觉痛苦地呼唤他,而他那迟钝的感觉也业已听到了这种呼唤。他不止一次地大声回答:"来了,亲爱的!"同时又回过头瞪眼凝视着空中,因为他还不能从那木樨香味里分明看到人体、颜色、爱情和向他伸来的手臂。啊,上帝!那香味究竟从何而来?从何而始,那发出呼唤之声的香味?于是他依然搜寻着。

他翻掘裂罅和角落,找到了一些瓶塞和烟蒂。这些东西他不屑一顾,一点儿不加理会。只有一次,他在地毯的皱纹里找到一支抽过的雪茄烟,他把雪茄烟一脚踩烂,还恶狠狠地咒骂了几句。他把房间从这头到那头搜索了一遍。他发现了许多在此栖息过的流浪客的细微而凄惨的遗痕,然而对于他所要寻找的、可能也在此住过、仿佛灵魂还在周围萦绕的她,却丝毫也没找到痕迹。

这时,他想到了女房东。

or that she had touched. This enveloping scent of mignonette, the odor that she had loved and made her own—whence came it?

The room had been but carelessly set in order. Scattered upon the flimsy dresser scarf were half a dozen hairpins—those discreet, indistinguishable friends of womankind, feminine of gender, infinite of mood and uncommunicative of tense. These he ignored, conscious of their triumphant lack of identity. Ransacking the drawers of the dresser, he came upon a discarded, tiny, ragged handkerchief. He pressed it to his face. It was racy and insolent with heliotrope; he hurled it to the floor. In another drawer he found odd buttons, a theater program, a pawnbroker's card, two lost marshmallows, a book on the divination of dreams. In the last was a woman's black satin hair-bow, which halted him, poised between ice and fire. But the black satin hair bow also is femininity's demure, impersonal, common ornament and tells no tales.

And then he traversed the room like a hound on the scent, skimming the walls, considering the corners of the bulging matting on his hands and knees, rummaging mantel and tables, the curtains and hangings, the drunken cabinet in the corner, for a visible sign, unable to perceive that she was there beside, around, against, within, above him, clinging to him, wooing him, calling him so poignantly through the finer senses that even his grosser ones became cognizant of the call. Once again he answered loudly: "Yes, dear!" and turned, wildeyed, to gaze on vacancy, for he could not yet discern form and color and love and outstretched arms in the odor of mignonette. Oh, God! whence that odor, and since when have odors had a voice to call? Thus he groped.

He burrowed in crevices and corners, and found corks and cigarettes. These he passed in passive contempt. But once he found in a fold of the matting a half-smoked cigar, and this he ground beneath his heel with a green and trenchant oath. He sifted the room from end to end. He found dreary and ignoble small records of many a peripatetic tenant; but of her whom he sought, and who may have lodged there, and whose spirit seemed to hover there, he found no trace.

And then he thought of the housekeeper.

He ran from the haunted room downstairs and to

他从阴森森的房间跑到楼下，到了一扇微微透出灯光的门前。女房东听到他的敲门声便出来了。他尽量控制住自己的不安。

"太太，请你告诉我，"他恳求她，"在我来这儿之前，是谁租用这房间的？"

"哎，你这位先生，我再告诉你一遍吧。我已经说过，是施普劳斯和蒙纳，在剧院里她叫布蕾达·施普劳斯小姐，而她就是蒙纳太太。我这屋子人人都知道是规规矩矩的。他们的结婚证书夹在镜框里，就挂在……"

"施普劳斯小姐是怎样一个人——我的意思是，她长得怎么样？"

"唔，黑头发，先生，矮个儿，胖胖的，脸长得很滑稽。他们是上星期二走的，已经一个星期了。"

"那他们前面的房客又是谁呢？"

"唔，是个做杂货生意的单身汉。他还欠我一星期房钱哩。他前面是克劳特太太和她的两个孩子，他们住了 4 个月。再前面是陶威尔老先生，他的房钱还是他的儿子给付的。这样说来就已经有一年哩，先生，再前面我就记不清啰。"

他向她道谢，然后垂头丧气地回到自己房间。房间里死一般沉寂。那一度赋予它生命的原质已经消失。那木樨香味已经飘散。继而代之的又是那股从发霉的家具上散发出来的臭烘烘的气味，那种像来自贮藏室的腐臭味。

他的希望幻灭了，信心也随之丧失。他呆坐着，两眼直勾勾地望着那咝咝发响的煤气灯的毫光。不一会儿，他走到床边，把床单撕成一条一条的碎片。他用小刀的刀背把布条塞进窗框和门框的缝里，把它们堵得密不透风。当这一切都准备就绪之后，他吹灭了煤气灯，又把煤气开到最大，随后怀着感激的心情躺到床上。

这天晚上轮到麦柯尔太太打啤酒。她于是打了酒来，和珀蒂太太一起坐在地下室里，那儿是房东太太们聚会的地方，也是蛆虫不会死的地方①。

"今晚我总算把三楼的那间后房给租出去了，"珀蒂太太面对着一大片酒泡说，"是个年轻人租下的。

---

① 参见《新约·马可福音》第 9 章第 48 节："在那里（地狱）虫是不死的，火是不灭的。"

door that showed a crack of light. She came out to his knock. He smothered his excitement as best he could.

"Will you tell me, madam," he besought her, "who occupied the room I have before I came?"

"Yes, sir. I can tell you again. 'Twas Sprowls and Mooney, as I said. Miss B'retta Sprowls it was in the theaters, but Missis Mooney she was. My house is well known for respectability. The marriage certificate hung, framed, on a nail over—"

"What kind of a lady was Miss Sprowls—in looks, I mean?"

"Why, black-haired, sir, short, and stout, with a comical face. They left a week ago Tuesday."

"And before they occupied it?"

"Why, there was a single gentleman connected with the draying business. He left owing me a week. Before him was Missis Crowder and her two children that stayed four months; and back of them was old Mr. Doyle, whose sons paid for him. He kept the room six months. That goes back a year, sir, and further I do not remember."

He thanked her and crept back to his room. The room was dead. The essence that had vivified it was gone. The perfume of mignonette had departed. In its place was the old, stale odor of moldy house furniture, of atmosphere in storage.

The ebbing of his hope drained his faith. He sat staring at the yellow, singing gaslight. Soon he walked to the bed and began to tear the sheets into strips. With the blade of his knife he drove them tightly into every crevice around windows and door. When all was snug and taut, he turned out the light, turned the gas full on again, and laid himself gratefully upon the bed.

It was Mrs. McCool's night to go with the can for beer. So she fetched it and sat with Mrs. Purdy in one of those subterranean retreats where housekeepers foregather and the worm dieth seldom.

"I rented out my third floor, back, this evening," said Mrs. Purdy, across a fine circle of foam. "A young man took it. He went up to bed two hours ago."

"Now, did ye, Mrs. Purdy, ma'am?" said Mrs. McCool, with intense admiration. "You do be a wonder for rentin' rooms of that kind. And did ye tell him, then?" she concluded in a husky whisper laden with

他两小时前就上床睡了。"

"是吗，珀蒂太太?"麦柯尔太太说，口气里充满了羡慕，"你出租这种房间真是有办法。那么，你没有告诉他?"她最后一句话是神秘地压低了嗓子说的。

"房间嘛，"珀蒂太太用她那带着绒毛的声音回答，"本来就是带家具一起出租的。我没告诉他，麦柯尔太太。"

"你做得对啊，太太，咱们是靠房钱糊口的呀。你也真会做生意，太太。有好些人要是知道那床上有人自杀过，他们就不会租那个房间了。"

"是啊，是啊，咱们总得糊口活命吧。"珀蒂太太说。

"是啊，太太，一点儿不错。就在上星期的今天，我还帮你收拾三楼的那间后房哩。那么漂漂亮亮的一个小姑娘，真没想到会用煤气自杀——她那张小脸怪惹人爱的唄，珀蒂太太。"

"是啊，是啊，她长得倒挺漂亮，"珀蒂太太随声附和，不过又吹毛求疵地加了一句，"可惜她左眉毛旁边长了那么颗黑痣。麦柯尔太太，把你的杯子再斟斟满吧。"

┌ 讨　论 ┐

这篇小说显然可分成两个部分。第一部分以房客之死而告终，涉及到男主人公找寻情人的失败，木樨香味，女房东的谎言，以及自杀；第二部分则是真相大白，由女房东对她的知己朋友说：一个星期以前，他的情人早就在这同一个房间里自杀了。欧·亨利认为必须用这样的方式来处理这个故事，原因是什么？是什么东西把这篇小说的两个部分联成一起的？这个情节的中心思想是什么？

最饶有兴味的问题，是和一个年轻人所引起的动机有关。欧·亨利先不讲这个年轻人不知道他情人已死的消息，故意使得他的动机问题变得更加难办；事实上，他在这个房间里闻到了木樨香味，无疑又激起了一种新的希望。那么，在这样的情况下，为什么他还会自杀呢？也许可以做这样的解释：他已经找寻了5个月，还是一无所得；我们知道，现在他已是疲惫不堪——而且，我们还可以假设，他不仅

mystery.

"Rooms," said Mrs. Purdy, in her furriest tones, "are furnished for to rent. I did not tell him, Mrs. McCool."

"'Tis right ye are, ma'am; 'tis by rentin' rooms we kape alive. Ye have the rale sense for business, ma'am. There be many people will rayjict the rentin' of a room if they be tould a suicide has been after dyin' in the bed of it."

"As you say, we has our living to be making," remarked Mrs. Purdy.

"Yis, ma'am; 'tis true. 'Tis just one wake ago this day I helped ye lay out the third floor, back. A pretty slip of a colleen she was to be killin' herself wid the gas—a swate little face she had, Mrs. Purdy, ma'am."

"She'd a-been called handsome, as you say," said Mrs. Purdy, assenting but critical, "but for that mole she had a-growin' by her left eyebrow. Do fill up your glass again, Mrs. McCool."

This story is obviously divided into two parts. The first part, which ends with the death of the lodger, concerns his failure in the search for his sweetheart, the odor of mignonette, the lie of the landlady, and the suicide; the second part concerns the revelation, by the landlady to her crony, that his sweetheart had, a week earlier, committed suicide in the same room. What accounts for the fact that O. Henry felt it necessary to treat the story in this fashion? What holds the two parts of the story together? What is the central meaning of this plot?

The most interesting question has to do with the young man's motivation. In one sense, O. Henry has deliberately made the problem of his motivation more difficult by withholding the information that the young man does not know that his sweetheart is dead; indeed, in the room, he gets, with the scent of mignonette, a renewed hope. Why then, under these circumstances does he commit suicide? Presumably, the explanation is this: he has been searching fruitlessly for five

体力上时感疲乏,而且精神上也是萎靡颓唐。我们确实知道:

"他知道,她离家出走之后,一定流落在这个沿海大城市的某个地方,可是这个城市却像一大片无底的流沙,每一颗沙粒都在不停地沉浮,今天还浮在上面,明天又沉到污泥秽土里去了。"

但是即使这样,我们仍无法相信:就在这天晚上,他非得旋开煤气开关不可,除非由木樨香味引起的希望已经破灭,使他陷入绝望之中。这就是作者对自杀的动机所做出的交代。

但是,如上所说的这种动机,真的能令人信服吗?那就取决于这个人物的性格了。他算是哪一种人呢?事实上,关于这个人物,欧·亨利给我们介绍得非常之少,只不过说他是个年轻人,找寻他的情人已有5个月,如今深感疲惫不堪。特别是在他偶然间注意到木樨香味以后,这个人物的性格问题,以及心理状态,才被提出来。那么,他真的闻到了木樨香味吗?"他呼吸着屋子里的空气——与其说是空气,不如说是一股潮湿味——一股就像从地下室的油布和烂木头里散发出来的冷飕飕的霉气。而就在这时,正当他这样歇息着的时候,忽然之间,房间里充满了浓烈而甜美的木樨香味。这香味似乎是随着一阵轻风飘来的。"

根据他发现香味的突然性,事实上他又不能找到香味的来源,最后香味却又完全消失——所有这一切都暗示着:他仅仅是在心中想象木樨香味。但与这种观点相反,我们就可以让女房东出来作证,不久前他的情人确实住过这个房间。这个问题对那个年轻人陷入严重的绝望,曾经起了决定性的作用。如果说这香味是真的,那作者一定会使得他的读者相信这一阵香味确实存在过;如果说它还是在想象之中,那作者一定会使他的读者相信:正是由于这个年轻人的心理作祟的缘故,这一阵香味才得以明显存在。这些就是检验的标准,读者

months; he is, we are told, tired—and, we assume, not only momentarily tired physically, but spiritually weary. Indeed, we are told:

"He was sure that since her disappearance from home this great, water-girt city held her somewhere, but it was like a monstrous quicksand, shifting its particles constantly, with no foundation, its upper granules of today buried tomorrow in ooze and slime."

But we are not supposed to believe, even so, that he would have necessarily turned on the gas this particular evening, except in despair at the loss of hope raised by the scent of mignonette. This is the author's account of the motivation of the suicide.

But is the motivation, as presented, really convincing? That will depend on the character of the man. What sort of man is he? Actually, O. Henry tells us very little about him except that he is young, has searched for his sweetheart for five months, and is tired. Especially does the question of the man's character, and state of mind, come up in the incident in which he notices the odor of mignonette. Did he really smell it? Did he merely imagine that he smelled it? "And he breathed the breath of the house... a cold, musty effluvium... mingled with the reeking exhalations of linoleum and mildewed and rotten woodwork. Then, suddenly, as he rested there, the room was filled with the strong, sweet odor of mignonette. It came as upon a single buffet of wind."

The suddenness with which he notices the odor, the fact that he can find no source for the odor, and finally the complete disappearance of the odor, all tend to imply that he merely imagines it. But over against this view, we have the testimony of the landlady that the sweetheart had actually occupied the room. This question is crucial for the young man's lapse into acute despair. If the odor is real, the author must convince his reader that it exists; if it is imaginary, the author must convince his reader that the psychological condition of the young man will account for its apparent existence. These are the tests the

必须把它们应用于这个重要情节中去。我们早就指出,不论读者和作者,双方对这个问题都持有一些证据。当然,读者一定要由自己来决定,究竟应采纳哪一种解释为好,而且更重要的是,这种解释是不是令人信服,并使人觉得这个情节真实可信。作者也许把确有香味出现的证据分量看得太重了。如果情况确是这样的话,那么,对于找寻不到香味的来源(特别是这阵香味是那么强烈地不断袭来)这一事实,我们又如何做出解释呢? 或者,也许作者心里认为:这一阵香味就在这一对恋人之间激起了一种匪夷所思的感情交流。可是,这一点并不能免除小说作者对他的意图不必提供一些特殊的线索了(再说,如果我们把这整整一段经历看成一种幻觉的话,作者当然免不了还得给这个事件说明一些清晰的动机)。换句话说,作者正在开读者的玩笑——"故意叫他感到困惑不解"。

　　概括起来说:从对这个房间进行详尽描写来看,显而易见,欧·亨利是力图给这个年轻人对这个房间本身的性质的感受提供背景的。那就是说,从这个乱七八糟、邋里邋遢、充满陈腐霉臭和无名者留下的垃圾破烂的房间,就可以反映出那个大城市(纽约)来,因为就在这个大城市里,他的情人已告失踪,所有的人似乎都沦于堕落而又残酷无情。欧·亨利想要在主人公眼里的肮脏环境和他心目中的木樨香味之间暗示出一种鲜明的对照。既然那个女人已在这个大城市某个地方失踪了,所以这阵木樨香味也在这个房间某个角落里消失了。在这个年轻人获悉那个女人并没有住过那个房间以后,在他没法找到这阵香味的来源以后,这个房间本身就应该成为他枉然徒劳的一种最大象征。作者这种意图可能是非常正确的,但我们所看到的这种意图的实际情况,并不意味着这种意图已经实现了。这篇小说的整个效果取决于香味这件事,而我们已经看到对于这个细节的处理是混乱的。我们看后得

reader must apply to the situation. We have already pointed out that there is some evidence on both sides of the question. The reader must, of course, decide for himself which explanation must be taken, and more important, whether the explanation is convincing, and renders the action credible. The author, perhaps, weighs the evidence toward the presence of the real odor. If this is the case, how are we to account for the fact that the search reveals no source of it, especially since the odor is so overpoweringly strong? Or, perhaps the author has in mind some idea that the odor provokes a mystical communion between the two lovers. But this does not relieve the fiction writer from the necessity for furnishing some sort of specific clue to his meaning. (Moreover, if we are to take the whole experience as an hallucination, the author is certainly not relieved from providing some clear motivation for the event.)In other words, the author is playing with his reader—"mystifying him. "

To sum up: it is obvious enough, from the detailed description of the room, that O. Henry is trying to suggest a ground for the man's experience in the nature of the room itself. That is, the room in its disorder, its squalor, its musty smell, its rubbish and debris of nameless lives, reflects the great city, in which his sweetheart has been lost, and in which all humanity seems to become degraded and brutalized. O. Henry wants to suggest the contrast between what the sordid surroundings mean to the hero and what the odor of mignonette means to him. As the girl is lost somewhere in the great city, so the odor is lost somewhere in the room. After the young man is told that the girl has not been there, and after he has been unable to find the source of the odor, the room itself is supposed to become a sort of overwhelming symbol for the futility of his effort. This intention on the part of the author may be sound enough, but the fact that we see what the intention is does not mean that the intention has been carried out. The whole effect of the story depends on the incident of the odor, and we have seen

到的是一种带着淡淡的象征意味的联想,这种来源不明的香味,代表这个年轻人最后破灭了的希望,同这个肮脏不堪的房间形成对照,而且这种对照对他来说也未免太难受了。

以上这些,就是这篇小说在人物心理描写方面的弱点。但作者却以他对这个年轻人所做的相当单薄而又概括的描写为基础,要在最后一分钟出其不意地让情节来一个转折。女房东就是在小说的第二部分中,对她的知己朋友供认不讳,当那个年轻人问到那个女人时,她自己却说了谎话。

这一真相的揭示,究竟有什么效果呢?显而易见,它的意图在于强调"命运的嘲弄",阐明年轻人发现自己所在的这个城市的残酷无情,证明年轻人的最大感觉(即这个女人在这个房间住过)完全属实,而且,从各方面来说,使得这篇小说保持协调一致。在富有同情心的读者看来,这个结论应该令人联想到:越过这个混乱、肮脏的大城市,爱情结合在一起了,而且,在某种意义上来说,这个年轻人四处找寻情人,最后还是成功的,因为这一对恋人终于在九泉之下得到了团圆。事实上,这个年轻人在这个大城市里所找到的这个房间,对他来说,可谓死得其所。

但是,请问这篇小说真的保持了协调一致吗?小说的结尾取决于女房东的谎言。但这一对恋人的命运有没有因为这个谎言而有所改变呢?这个谎言是不是导致年轻人死亡的原因?可以设想,要是女房东讲了实话,这个令人震惊的消息本来也许会救了这个年轻人,不至于自寻短见,但这些只不过是一点儿猜测罢了。当女房东对他说那个女人没有住过这个房间,那个年轻人(正如小说里描写的那样)就在绝望之中自杀了;要是女房东对他说那个女人已无法挽救地失踪,以至命归西天,可能也会产生同样的后果。或者说不定还会救了他一命?

事实上,这个谎言除了欺骗读者以外还有

that the handling of this detail is confused. What we have is a faintly symbolic suggestion that the sourceless odor, standing for the young man's finally thwarted hope, is in contrast to the sordidness of the room, and the contrast is too much for him.

Such is the psychological frailty of the story. But resting upon his rather thin and sketchy characterization of the young man, the author chooses to give a turn to the plot by a last-minute surprise. In the second part of the story the landlady tells her crony that she has lied to the young man about the girl.

What is the effect of this revelation? It is intended, obviously, to underline the "irony of fate," to illustrate the hardheartedness of the city in which the young man finds himself, to justify the young man's overwhelming sense that the girl has been in the room, and, all in all, to pull the story together. For the sympathetic reader this conclusion is supposed to suggest that the bonds of love stretch across the confusion and squalor of the great city, and that, in a sense, the young man has finally succeeded in his search, for the lovers are at last united in death. The young man finds, as it were, the proper room in the great city in which to die.

But is the story really pulled together? The end of the story depends on the lie. But are the lives of the lovers altered by the lie? Does the lie cause the death of the young man? It is conceivable that, had the landlady told the truth, the shock of the information might have saved the young man from suicide, but this is the merest speculation. The character, as given in the story, commits suicide in despair when the landlady tells him that the girl has not been there; the landlady's telling him that the girl is irretrievably lost, is dead, would presumably have had the same effect. Or would that fact have saved him?

Actually, is there any point in the lie except to trick the reader—to provide the illusion

没有其他目的——让读者幻想出一个意味深长的结尾？结尾处所包含的嘲弄，是建立在牵强附会的偶然巧合之上，并不取决于女房东事实上说的是这个事情而不是那个事情（凡是认为这篇小说结尾富于意义的读者们，不妨试着把这篇小说结构改变一下，说那个年轻人在叩房间时，令人毛骨悚然地发现他的情人已在一个星期前自杀，于是他就租下了那个房间，旋开了煤气开关。那时，我们虽然照样会看到充满嘲弄意味的偶然巧合和这一对恋人在阴曹地府的团圆，但像这样的小说似乎显得极其平淡乏味了）。现在，这个消息欧·亨利先按下不表，直到小说结尾处才叫我们大吃一惊，不外乎使读者产生幻觉，认为这个消息是意味深长的。因此，那种嘲弄（正如我们在这篇小说中所看到的）无非是在捉弄读者，而不是命运在捉弄那个年轻人。

凡是觉得小说结尾属于拙劣的骗局的读者，还会指出其他一些虚伪低劣的迹象：人物性格刻画尚嫌单薄，描写显得杂乱无章，有时令人作呕，作者甚至还采取一种哄骗的语调，写出如下一些语句，显然是为了博取读者的同情："啊，上帝！那香味究竟从何而来？从何而始，那发出呼唤之声的香味？"换句话说，我们一下子就可以猜测到：惊人的结尾处的那个圈套，可能企图弥补一下小说结构本身所存在的一些缺陷。要知道，一个劲儿激动读者的情绪，以及令人作呕和哄骗的语调——所有这些手法，都是企图弥补小说本身所缺乏的逻辑性，亦即作品的连贯性。感伤情调（见重要词汇）有时来源于缺乏逻辑性——不管这个场合是不是合情合理，总是动不动诉诸感情。

光靠情节的诀窍，小说是写不出来的。惊人的结尾可能在一篇最佳小说中间出现，但只有当这种惊人的事物，对读者来说，心里早已做好充分准备，方才恰到好处。这样，继而一想，读者心里立刻明白：这个惊人的结尾，毕竟是从过去引申出来的一种合乎逻辑推理、意味

of a meaningful ending? Whatever irony lies in the ending is based on a farfetched coincidence, and does not depend on the fact that the woman said one thing rather than another. (Readers who are inclined to accept the conclusion of the story as meaningful might try reconstructing the story with the young man's calling at the door, finding with horror that his sweetheart has committed suicide there a week before, renting the room, and turning on the gas. We would then still have the ironical coincidence and a sort of union of the lovers, but the story would seem very tame and flat.) O. Henry, by withholding certain information and thus surprising us with it at the end, has simply tried to give the reader the illusion that the information was meaningful. The irony, in the story as we have it, simply resides in a trick played on the reader rather than in a trick that fate has played on the young man.

Readers who feel that the end of this story is a shabby trick will be able to point out other symptoms of cheapness: the general thinness of characterization, the cluttered and sometimes mawkish description, the wheedling tone taken by the author, and the obvious play for emotional sympathy in such writing as the following: "Oh, God! whence that odor, and since when have odors had a voice to call?" In other words, we can readily surmise that the trickery involved in the surprise ending may be an attempt to compensate for defects within the body of the story itself. The straining to stir the emotions of the reader, the mawkish and wheedling tone—all are attempts to make up for a lack of logic, a lack of coherence, in the story itself. *Sentimentality* (see Glossary) often springs from such a lack of coherence—emotionalism without reference to a reasonable occasion for it.

A trick of plot does not make a story. A surprise ending may appear in a very good story, but only if the surprise has been prepared for, so that, upon second thought, the reader realizes that it is, after all, a logical and meaningful development from what has gone before, and not merely a device employed by the author to give him an easy way out of his

深长的故事发展,而不仅仅是作者为了摆脱自己的困境而采取的一种权宜之计。这个同样的原则适用于通常所谓巧合(见重要词汇)。巧合经常会在现实生活中发生,有时甚至还是相当惊人的巧合;而且,在某种意义上说,每一篇小说都建立在巧合之上——也就是说,某些特定的事件会碰巧在一起发生,例如,这样一些人物就在这样一个时刻,这样的一种情况之下碰巧会见了。但是,由于小说同人物和行动的逻辑之间关系极大,巧合——要是它纯然不符合逻辑推理的话——在小说中也就毫无地位可言。真实比虚构更要令人不可思议,因为真实是"真的"——根据它自己的优点是可以接受的——但是,小说中的偶然发生的事件,正如我们已经看到的,一定要根据和小说中其他要素的逻辑关系,并根据意义是否深刻等等,才能证明自己真实可信。巧合要是用来解决小说中的某个问题——例如,帮助作者摆脱自己的困境,那当然是决不可取的。

你能想出一个更为简单有效的办法,并用这些基本材料写成一篇小说吗?不要写成新的改写本,但是要考虑到可能发生的事物。

(潘庆龄 译)

difficulties. The same principle applies to *coincidence* (see Glossary) in general. Coincidences do occur in real life, sometimes quite startling ones, and in one sense every story is based on a coincidence—namely, that the particular events happen to occur together, that such and such characters happen to meet, for example, at such and such a moment under such and such circumstances. But since fiction is concerned with a logic of character and action, coincidence, insofar as it is purely illogical, has little place in fiction. Truth can afford to be stranger than fiction, because truth is "true"—is acceptable on its own merits—but the happenings of fiction, as we have seen, must justify themselves in terms of logical connection with other elements in fiction and in terms of meaningfulness. Certainly coincidence is never acceptable when it is used to solve the problem of a story—to bail the author out of his difficulties.

Can you think of a more honest and effective way for these basic materials to be turned into a story? Do not write a new version; simply mull over the possibilities.

007.万 卡

(俄)安东·契诃夫 著　　汝 龙 译

007. Vanka

by Anton Chekhov

　　9 岁的男孩万卡·茹科夫 3 个月前被送到靴匠阿里亚兴的铺子里来做学徒。这时候是圣诞节的前夜，他没有上床睡觉。他等着老板夫妇和师傅们出外去做晨祷以后，从老板的立柜里取出一小瓶墨水和一支安着锈笔尖的钢笔，然后在自己面前铺平一张揉皱的白纸，写起来。他在写下第一个字以前，好几次战战兢兢地回过头去看一下门口和窗子，斜起眼睛瞟一下乌黑的圣像和那两旁摆满鞋楦头的架子，断断续续地叹一口气。那张纸铺在一条长凳上，他自己在长凳前面跪着。

　　"亲爱的爷爷，康司坦丁·玛卡雷奇！"他写道，"我在给你写信。祝你圣诞节好，求上帝保佑你万事如意。我没爹没娘，只剩下你一个亲人了。"

　　万卡抬起眼睛看着乌黑的窗子，窗上映着他的蜡烛的影子。他生动地想起他祖父康司坦丁·玛卡雷奇，地主席瓦烈夫家的守夜人的模样。那是个矮小而消瘦又异常矫健灵活的小老头，年纪约摸 65 岁，老是笑容满面，眯着醉眼。白天他在仆人的厨房里睡觉，或者跟厨娘们取笑，到了夜里就穿上肥大的羊皮袄，在庄园四周走来走去，不住地敲着梆子。他身后跟着两条狗，耷拉着脑袋，一条是老母狗卡希坦卡，一条是鳗鱼，之所以起这样的名字，是因为它的毛是黑的，而且身子细长像是黄鼠狼。这条鳗鱼倒是异常恭顺亲热的，不论见着自家人还是见着外人，一概用脉脉含情的目光瞟着，然而它是靠不住的。在它的恭顺温和的后面，隐藏着极其狡狯的险恶。任凭哪条狗也不如它那么善于抓住机会，悄悄溜到人的身旁，在腿肚子

VANKA Zhukov, a boy of nine, who had been for three months apprenticed to Alyahin the shoemaker, was sitting up on Christmas Eve. Waiting till his master and mistress and the workmen had gone to the midnight service, he took out of his master's cupboard a bottle of ink and a pen with a rusty nib, and, spreading out a crumpled sheet of paper in front of him, began writing. Before forming the first letter he several times looked round fearfully at the door and the windows, stole a glance at the dark ikon, on both sides of which stretched shelves full of lasts, and heaved a broken sigh. The paper lay on the bench while he knelt before it.

　　"Dear grandfather, Konstantin Makaritch," he wrote, "I am writing you a letter. I wish you a happy Christmas, and all blessings from God Almighty. I have neither father nor mother, you are the only one left me."

　　Vanka raised his eyes to the dark ikon on which the light of his candle was reflected, and vividly recalled his grandfather, Konstantin Makaritch, who was night watchman to a family called Zhivarev. He was a thin but extraordinarily nimble and lively little old man of sixty-five, with an everlastingly laughing face and drunken eyes. By day he slept in the servants' kitchen, or made jokes with the cooks; at night, wrapped in an ample sheepskin, he walked round the grounds and tapped with his little mallet. Old Kashtanka and Eel, so-called on account of his dark colour and his long body like a weasel's, followed him with hanging heads. This Eel was exceptionally polite and affectionate, and looked with equal kindness on strangers and his own masters, but had not a very good reputation. Under his politeness and meekness was hidden the most Jesuitical cunning. No one knew better how

作者简介：安东·契诃夫（Anton Chekhov，1860—1904），俄国剧作家、短篇小说家。1860 年 1 月 29 日生于俄国塔甘罗格。1904 年 7 月 14 日或 15 日卒于德国巴登魏勒尔。他从医时写了他的第一部长剧《伊万诺夫》（*Ivanov*，1887），但是并不受欢迎。他用短篇小说表现严肃的主题。他的第二部长剧《木魔》（*The Wood Demon*，1889）被他修改成他的名篇《凡尼亚舅舅》（*Uncle Vanya*，1897）。他的剧作《海鸥》（*The Seagull*，1896）起初受到冷落，直到 1899 年斯坦尼斯拉夫斯基才让这部剧作焕发光彩，大获成功。契诃夫的戏剧作品采用悲喜剧角度描写地区生活的陈腐之气和俄国贵族的过气生活。他的作品被翻译成英语或别的语言之后，受到国际的赞誉。他被视为无可匹敌的短篇小说家。

上咬一口，或者钻进冷藏室里去，或者偷农民的鸡吃。它的后腿已经不止一次被人打断，有两次人家索性把它吊起来，而且每个星期都把它打得半死，不过它老是养好伤，又活下来了。

眼下他祖父一定在大门口站着，眯细眼睛看乡村教堂的通红的窗子，顿着穿高统毡靴的脚，跟仆人们开玩笑。他的榔子挂在腰带上。他冻得不时拍手，缩起脖子，一会儿在女仆身上捏一把，一会儿在厨娘身上掐一下，发出苍老的笑声。

"咱们来吸点鼻烟，好不好？"他说着，把他的鼻烟盒送到那些女人跟前去。

女人们闻了点鼻烟，不住打喷嚏。祖父乐得什么似的，发出一连串快活的笑声，嚷道：

"快擦掉，冻在鼻子上了！"

他还给狗闻鼻烟。卡希坦卡打喷嚏，皱了皱鼻子，委委屈屈，走到一旁去了。鳗鱼为了表示恭顺而没打喷嚏，光是摇尾巴。天气好极了。空气纹丝不动，清澈而新鲜。夜色黑暗，可是整个村子以及村里的白房顶、烟囱里冒出来的一缕缕烟子、披着重霜而银白的树木、雪堆，都能看清楚。整个天空点缀着繁星，快活地眨眼。天河那么清楚地显出来，就好像有人在过节以前用雪把它擦洗过似的。……

万卡叹口气，用钢笔蘸一下墨水，继续写道：

"昨天我挨了一顿打。老板揪着我的头发，把我拉到院子里，拿师傅干活用的皮条狠狠地抽我，怪我摇他们摇篮里的小娃娃，一不小心睡着了。上个星期老板娘叫我收拾一条青鱼，我从尾巴上动手收拾，她就捞起那条青鱼，把鱼头直戳到我的脸上来。师傅们总是要笑我，打发我到小酒店里去打酒，怂恿我偷老板的黄瓜，老板随手捞到什么就用什么打我。吃食是什么也没有。早晨吃面包，午饭喝稀粥，晚上又是面包，至于茶啦，白菜汤啦，只有老板和老板娘才大喝而特喝。他们叫我睡在过道里，他们的小娃娃一哭，我就根本不能睡觉，一个劲儿摇摇篮。亲爱的爷爷，发发上帝那样的慈悲，带着我离开这儿，回家去，回到村子里去吧，我再也熬不下去了。我给你叩头了，我会永远为你祷告上帝，带我离开这儿吧，不然我就要死了。"

万卡嘴角撇下来，举起黑拳头揉一揉眼睛，抽抽搭搭地哭了。

"我会给你搓碎烟叶，"他接着写道，"为你祷告上

to creep up on occasion and snap at one's legs, to slip into the store-room, or steal a hen from a peasant. His hind legs had been nearly pulled off more than once, twice he had been hanged, every week he was thrashed till he was half dead, but he always revived.

At this moment grandfather was, no doubt, standing at the gate, screwing up his eyes at the red windows of the church, stamping with his high felt boots, and joking with the servants. His little mallet was hanging on his belt. He was clasping his hands, shrugging with the cold, and, with an aged chuckle, pinching first the housemaid, then the cook.

"How about a pinch of snuff?" he was saying, offering the women his snuff-box.

The women would take a sniff and sneeze. Grandfather would be indescribably delighted, go off into a merry chuckle, and cry:

"Tear it off it has frozen on!"

They give the dogs a sniff of snuff too. Kashtanka sneezes, wriggles her head, and walks away offended. Eel does not sneeze, from politeness, but wags his tail. And the weather is glorious. The air is still, fresh, and transparent. The night is dark, but one can see the whole village with its white roofs and coils of smoke coming from the chimneys, the trees silvered with hoar frost, the snowdrifts. The whole sky spangled with gay twinkling stars, and the Milky Way is as distinct as though it had been washed and rubbed with snow for a holiday. . . .

Vanka sighed, dipped his pen, and went on writing:

"And yesterday I had a wigging. The master pulled me out into the yard by my hair, and whacked me with a boot-stretcher because I accidentally fell asleep while I was rocking their brat in the cradle. And a week ago the mistress told me to clean a herring, and I began from the tail end, and she took the herring and thrust its head in my face. The workmen laugh at me and send me to the tavern for vodka, and tell me to steal the master's cucumbers for them, and the master beats me with anything that comes to hand. And there is nothing to eat. In the morning they give me bread, for dinner, porridge, and in the evening, bread again; but as for tea, or soup, the master and mistress gobble it all up themselves. And I am put to sleep in the passage, and when their wretched brat cries I get no sleep at all, but have to rock the cradle. Dear grandfather, show the divine mercy, take me away from here, home to the village. It's more than I can bear. I bow down to your feet, and will pray to God for you for ever, take me away from here or I shall die. "

Vanka's mouth worked, he rubbed his eyes with his black fist, and gave a sob.

"I will powder your snuff for you," he went on. "I

帝，要是我做了错事，就只管抽我，像抽西多尔的山羊那样。要是你认为我没有活儿干，那我就会求总管看在基督面上让我给他擦皮靴，或者替菲德卡去做牧童。亲爱的爷爷，我再也熬不下去，简直只有死路一条了。我本想跑回村子里去，可又没有皮靴，我怕冷。等我长大了，我就会为这件事养活你，不许人家欺侮你，等你死了，我就祷告你的灵魂安息，就跟为我的妈妈彼拉盖雅祷告一样。

"莫斯科是个大城。房屋全是老爷们的。马倒有很多，羊却没有，狗也不凶。这儿的孩子不举着星星走来走去①，唱诗班也不准人随便参加唱歌。有一回我在一家铺子的橱窗里看见过钓钩摆着卖，都安好了钓鱼线，能钓各式各样的鱼，很不错，有一个钓钩甚至经得起40磅重的大鲇鱼呢。我还看见几家铺子卖各式各样的枪，跟老爷的枪差不多，所以每支枪恐怕要卖一百个卢布。……肉铺里有野乌鸡，有松鸡，有兔子，这些东西都是在哪儿打的，铺子里的伙计却不肯说。

"亲爱的爷爷，等到老爷家里摆着圣诞树，上面挂着礼物，你就给我摘下一个用金纸包着的核桃来，收在那口小绿箱子里。你问奥尔迦·伊格纳捷芙娜小姐要吧，就说是给万卡的。"

万卡颤巍巍地叹一口气，又凝神瞧着窗子。他回想祖父总是到树林里去给老爷家砍圣诞树，带着孙子一路去。那种时候可真快活啊！祖父喀喀地咳嗽，严寒把树木冻得喀喀地响，万卡就学他们的样子也喀喀地叫。往往在砍树以前，祖父先吸完一袋烟，闻很久的鼻烟，讪笑冻僵的万卡。……那些做圣诞树用的小云杉披着白霜，站在那儿不动，等着看它们谁先死掉。冷不防，不知从哪儿来了一只野兔，在雪堆上像箭似的窜过去。祖父忍不住叫道：

"抓住它，抓住它……抓住它！嘿，短尾巴鬼！"

祖父把砍倒的云杉拖回老爷的家里，大家就动手装饰它。……忙得最起劲的是万卡所喜爱的奥尔迦·伊格纳捷芙娜小姐。当初万卡的母亲彼拉盖雅还活着，在老爷家里做女仆的时候，奥尔迦·伊格纳捷芙娜就常给万卡糖果吃，由于闲着没事做而教他念书，写字，从一数到一百，甚至教他跳四组舞。可是等到彼拉盖雅死后，孤儿万卡就给送到仆人的厨房里去

————————
① 指基督教的习俗，圣诞节前夜小孩们举着用箔纸糊的星星走来走去。

will pray for you, and if I do anything you can thrash me like Sidor's goat. And if you think I've no job, then I will beg the steward for Christ's sake to let me clean his boots, or I'll go for a shepherd-boy instead of Fedka. Dear grandfather, it is more than I can bear, it's simply no life at all. I wanted to run away to the village, but I have no boots, and I am afraid of the frost. When I grow up big I will take care of you for this, and not let anyone annoy you, and when you die I will pray for the rest of your soul, just as for my mammy's.

"Moscow is a big town. It's all gentlemen's houses, and there are lots of horses, but there are no sheep, and the dogs are not spiteful. The lads here don't go out with the star, and they don't let anyone go into the choir, and once I saw in a shop window fishing-hooks for sale, fitted ready with the line and for all sorts of fish, awfully good ones, there was even one hook that would hold a forty-pound sheat-fish. And I have seen shops where there are guns of all sorts, after the pattern of the master's guns at home, so that I shouldn't wonder if they are a hundred roubles each.... And in the butchers' shops there are grouse and woodcocks and fish and hares, but the shopmen don't say where they shoot them.

"Dear grandfather, when they have the Christmas tree at the big house, get me a gilt walnut, and put it away in the green trunk. Ask the young lady Olga Ignatyevna, say it's for Vanka."

Vanka gave a tremulous sigh, and again stared at the window. He remembered his grandfather always went into the forest to get the Christmas tree for his master's family, and took his grandson with him. It was a merry time! Grandfather made a noise in his throat, the forest crackled with the frost, and looking at them Vanka chortled too. Before chopping down the Christmas tree, grandfather would smoke a pipe, slowly take a pinch of snuff and laugh at frozen Vanka.... The young fir trees, covered with hoar frost, stood motionless, waiting to see which of them was to die. Wherever one looked, a hare flew like an arrow over the snowdrifts.... Grandfather could not refrain from shouting: "Hold him, hold him... hold him! Ah, the bob-tailed devil!"

When he had cut down the Christmas tree, grandfather used to drag it to the big house, and there set to work to decorate it.... The young lady, who was Vanka's favourite, Olga Ignatyevna, was the busiest of all. When Vanka's mother Pelageya was alive, and a servant in the big house, Olga Ignatyevna used to give him goodies, and having nothing better to do, taught him to read and write, to count up to a hundred, and even to dance a quadrille. When Pelageya died, Vanka had been transferred to the servants' kitchen to be

跟祖父住在一起,后来又从厨房给送到莫斯科的靴匠阿里亚兴的铺子里来了。

"你来吧,亲爱的爷爷,"万卡接着写道,"我求你看在基督和上帝面上带我离开这儿吧。你可怜我这个不幸的孤儿吧,这儿人人都打我,我饿得要命,气闷得没法说,老是哭。前几天老板用鞋楦头打我,把我打得昏倒在地,好不容易才活过来。我的生活苦透了,比狗都不如。……替我问候阿辽娜、独眼的叶果尔卡、马车夫,我的手风琴不要送给外人。孙伊凡·茹科夫草上。亲爱的爷爷,你来吧。"

万卡把这张写好的纸叠成四折,把它放在昨天晚上花一个戈比买来的信封里。……他略为想一想,用钢笔蘸一下墨水,写上地址:

寄交乡下祖父收

然后他搔一下头皮,再想一想,添了几个字:

康司坦丁·玛卡雷奇

他写完信而没有人来打扰,心里感到满意,就戴上帽子,顾不上披皮袄,只穿着衬衫就跑到街上去了。……

昨天晚上他问过肉铺的伙计,伙计告诉他说信件丢进了邮筒,就由喝醉酒的车夫驾着邮车,把信从邮筒里收走,响起铃铛,分送到世界各地去。万卡跑到就近的一个邮筒,把那封宝贵的信塞进了筒口。……

他抱着美好的希望而定下心来,过一个钟头就沉酣地睡熟了。……在梦中他看见一个炉灶。祖父坐在灶台上,耷拉着一双光脚,给厨娘们念信。……鳗鱼在炉灶旁边走来走去,摇尾巴。……

讨 论

这是一篇非常奇特的小说——当然,指它的结构而言。在开头第一段里,小万卡就开始写信了,所以写信的动作就成为这篇小说的主要情节。这封信的内容,叙述了万卡的简短生平和目前苦难的生活,几乎纯属说明性质,具体解释他写信的原因。随后是结尾:故事的突然转折,是发生在带着小万卡全部希望的这封地址不明的信一丢进邮筒的时候。在最后一段中着重写道,万卡在梦中看见那封信平安到

with his grandfather, and from the kitchen to the shoemaker's in Moscow.

"Do come, dear grandfather," Vanka went on with his letter. "For Christ's sake, I beg you, take me away. Have pity on an unhappy orphan like me; here everyone knocks me about, and I am fearfully hungry; I can't tell you what misery it is, I am always crying. And the other day the master hit me on the head with a last, so that I fell down. My life is wretched, worse than any dog's. . . . I send greetings to Alyona, one-eyed Yegorka, and the coachman, and don't give my concertina to anyone. I remain, your grandson, Ivan Zhukov. Dear grandfather, do come."

Vanka folded the sheet of writing-paper twice, and put it into an envelope he had bought the day before for a kopeck. . . . After thinking a little, he dipped the pen and wrote the address:

To grandfather in the village.

Then he scratched his head, thought a little, and added:

Konstantin Makaritch.

Glad that he had not been prevented from writing, he put on his cap and, without putting on his little greatcoat, ran into the street as he was in his shirt. . . .

The shopmen at the butcher's, whom he had questioned the day before, told him that letters were put in post-boxes, and from the boxes were carried about all over the earth in mailcarts with drunken drivers and ringing bells. Vanka ran to the nearest postbox, and thrust the precious letter in the slit. . . .

An hour later, lulled by sweet hopes, he was sound asleep. . . . He dreamed of the stove. On the stove was sitting his grandfather, swinging his bare legs, and reading the letter to the cooks. . . .

By the stove was Eel, wagging his tail.

Here is a very odd story—certainly, in its structure. In the opening paragraph little Vanka begins to write his letter, and the act of the writing is the main action of the story. The content of the letter, the story of Vanka's short history and present misery, is almost purely expository, the explanation for the occasion of the letter. Then comes the denouement: the sudden turn as the improperly addressed letter, carrying all little Vanka's hopes, is dropped into the post box. Then in the closing paragraphs,

达目的地,他的爷爷正在大声念信。

这篇小说的重点放在动人哀怜的词句上,很可能产生伤感的气氛。假定用另一种写法,只是大致按年代顺序,历叙万卡一生中的所有苦难,直到圣诞节的前夜,他独自一人待在那个阴暗寒冷的小屋里做祷告。要是这样描写,这篇小说根本就毫无小说味道了,充其量只不过是一篇充满感伤气氛的速写。或者假定这封信按照确切地址送到了爷爷手里,无奈爷爷没法违反学徒合同,以致万卡得到的境遇比过去还要糟。那该是一篇多么拙劣的小说啊!

正是由于不知道确切地址——最后这么一点儿年幼无知,确实哀婉动人——才使得这篇小说定型。而且,这是采取一种尖刻、挖苦的笑话形式,再加上突然转折,因此这种转折就不需要做任何解释,早已包含了前面的全部内容,只是通过笑话这个形式表现出来。欧·亨利的《带家具出租的房间》的突然转折,也是一个笑话。这不是写得不高明的急剧的转折;这是事实上要强调(而且是混淆不清地强调)引起读者怜悯的因素(而欧·亨利的失败的基本原因,也就在这里)。进行对比时,请注意契诃夫这篇小说里质朴无华的事实。在这里,笑话这个形式起到了减少感伤情调的作用(这种感伤情调正在使小说受到损害)。它改变了调子。它在某种程度上已使读者变成铁石心肠。

然而,在这里有一种悖论(见重要词汇),也就是自相矛盾的地方。我们姑且谈寄信地址这个笑话,我们知道这封信根本送不到万卡的爷爷手里。那么,它会送到谁的手里呢?它送到了读者——也就是你们大家的手里。它终究成为来自世界上所有小万卡寄给我们大家的一封信,所以"耍花招的结尾"毕竟远远地不止是一个花招了。我们从这里就可以对这篇小说的奇特结构,以及破题中冗长而又不太均衡的组成部分有所理解了。

你们认为欧·亨利将会怎样处理这篇小说呢? (潘庆舲 译)

which serve as a kind of accent, Vanka dreams of the letter, safe at its destination, being read aloud by his grandfather.

The emphasis of this story is on extreme pathos, with all the dangers of sentimentality. Imagine a treatment that would simply trace, in almost chronological order, all the miseries of Vanka until he sits alone on Christmas Eve, praying in his cold little hole of a room. Told thus, the story would be no story at all, merely a kind of sentimental sketch. Or suppose the letter were properly addressed and sent off to the grandfather, who cannot break the articles of apprenticeship, and so Vanka is treated worse than ever. What a poor story that would be!

It is the lack of a proper address—a last touch of pathetic ignorance—that gives the story its shape. And this is the shape of a bitterly ironical joke, with a snapper, a turn, that calls for no explanation, that implies all that lies ahead, but in the shape of a joke. The snapper of O. Henry's "The Furnished Room"is like a joke too. It is not the sharp turn that is bad; it is the fact of the insistence(and the confused insistence)on the pathos that is at the base of O. Henry's failure. In contrast, note the naive factuality of Chekhov's story. Here the shape of the joke works to mitigate the sentimentality threatening the story. It changes the tone. It hardens, in a way, the reader's heart.

There is, however, a *paradox* here (see Glossary). We have the joke of the address; we know that the letter will not reach Vanka's grandfather. But whom does it reach? It reaches the reader—you and you and you. It is, after all, a letter from all the little Vankas in the world to us all, and so the"trick ending"is something more than a trick, after all. And here we may see some explanation of the odd structure of the story, of the long, disproportionate element of exposition.

How do you think O. Henry would have told this story?

008. 埋 葬

（英）约翰·科利尔 著　　潘庆舲 译

008. De Mortuis
by John Collier

兰金大夫是个骨瘦如柴的大个子，款式最新的衣服只要一穿到他身上，立时就像 20 年前照片里过了时的旧装一样。这可要怪他的躯体干吗长得那么方方正正，不妨打个比方说，就像是货箱制造厂的老板用几块板条凑合着钉起来的。他的脸部表情也是木头木脑，显出一副粗坯相；他头上好像戴着假发，自然也最忌讳木梳了。此外，他还有一双样子怪不雅观的大手——不过有了它，小镇上的医生简直如获至宝一样，因为直到如今，小镇上的乡巴佬对畸人怪相仍然饶有兴味，他们认为：手越是像类人猿，做起切除扁桃体的细巧手术来，也就越是精确，准保出不了差错。

这个结论要是用到兰金大夫身上，倒是完全合适。比方说，这天早晨正赶上天气晴朗，他眼前的活儿也不算怎么棘手，只不过给他地窖地坪上一大块破窟窿铺一层水泥罢了。但他在运用他的那双样子怪不雅观的大手时，却显得那么从容不迫，胸有成竹，所以铺好的水泥地坪里面决不会含有一个气孔，就是外面也不会留下一个难看的瘢痕。

临了，兰金大夫就横看竖看，从各个角度来检查自己的手艺，又在这里添上一点儿，那里再抹上一点儿，来回修整，终于达到了光滑匀整，够得上地地道道的泥水师傅的水平。随后，他把最后几小块烂泥屑粒扫拢来，一块儿扔进了炉子，又把自己刚用过的铁镐和铁锹撂在一旁，就歇了一会儿。这时，他发现还可以用高超的技艺挥舞一下他手里的泥刀，让新铺砌的那块地坪闪闪发亮，和周围的地板相映生辉。就在这思想高度集中的当儿，上面走廊里门突然轰的一声响，就像一颗小型炮弹的爆炸声，使得兰金大夫如同被弹片击中一样直跳了起来。

DR. RANKIN was a large and rawboned man on whom the newest suit at once appeared outdated, like a suit in a photograph of twenty years ago. This was due to the squareness and flatness of his torso, which might have been put together by a manufacturer of packing cases. His face also had a wooden and a roughly constructed look; his hair was wiglike and resentful of the comb. He had those huge and clumsy hands which can be an asset to a doctor in a small upstate town where people still retain a rural relish for paradox, thinking that the more apelike the paw, the more precise it can be in the delicate business of a tonsillectomy.

This conclusion was perfectly justified in the case of Dr. Rankin. For example, on this particular fine morning, though his task was nothing more ticklish than the cementing over of a large patch on his cellar floor, he managed those large and clumsy hands with all the unflurried certainty of one who would never leave a sponge within or create an unsightly scar without.

The doctor surveyed his handiwork from all angles. He added a touch here and a touch there till he had achieved a smoothness altogether professional. He swept up a few last crumbs of soil and dropped them into the furnace. He paused before putting away the pick and shovel he had been using, and found occasion for yet another artistic sweep of his trowel, which made the new surface precisely flush with the surrounding floor. At this moment of supreme concentration, the porch door upstairs slammed with the report of a minor piece of artillery, which, appropriately enough, caused Dr. Rankin to jump as if he had been shot.

作者简介：约翰·科利尔（John Collier，1901—1980），英国作家，以写短篇小说出名。生于 1901 年 5 月 3 日，卒于 1980 年 4 月 6 日。他的很多短篇小说发表在 20 世纪 30 年代至 50 年代的《纽约客》上。这些作品被收入到 1951 年出版的《奇幻故事和晚安》（*Fancies and Goodnights*）一书中，这本书至今还在重印。他的单篇小说经常编选入小说选集中。他的作品得到了一些作家的赞誉，如安东尼·伯吉斯、雷·布拉德伯里和尼尔·加曼。

医生紧蹙眉头抬起脸来,竖直耳朵倾听着。他果然听到了两双沉甸甸的、特别厚的鞋底从走廊里发出回响的地板上穿过去的声音。他听到了屋子门给打开了,来客走进了只有几级台阶与地窖相通的过道。他听到了巴克和巴德先是吹口哨,接着是大声叫嚷,"大夫!嗨,大夫!他们正在钓鱼呢!"

不知那一天是大夫根本不愿去钓鱼,或是他突然受惊,如同别的大块头一样,就产生特别强烈的不爱交际的反应呢,还是他只想去做不受干扰,急于完成他手头的活儿,然后再开始去做更为重要的事情——反正他对朋友的诱人的呼喊并没有马上应答。相反,他在屏息静听那个呼喊声自然而然地由强转弱,最后消失在一种惹人发窘而又着恼的对话之中。

"我料他一定出门了。"

"我就留个便条——说我们在小溪那里,赶快来吧。"

"我们总得关照一声艾琳吧。"

"可她也不在这里。你认为她也许不会走远吗。"

"从屋里的样子来看,应该是这样。"

"你可说对啦,巴德。看这张餐桌就得了。你不妨就留下你的名字———"

"嘘——嘘——嘘!你瞧!"

显然,最后说话的那个人已经发现地窖的门虚掩着,而且从底缝里还露出一丝亮光来。那道门一下子就被踢开,巴德和巴克两眼俯视着下面。

"喂,大夫!原来你在这儿!"

"难道你没听见我们大声嚷嚷?"

大夫对刚才耳闻的那些话心里虽然不太高兴,但当他的那两个朋友走下台阶的时候,他脸上还是露出相当呆板的笑容。"我想我刚才听见有人声。"他说。

"刚才我们使劲儿在大声喊叫呢,"巴克说,"以为没有人在家。艾琳在哪儿?"

"拜客嘛。"大夫说,"她出门拜客去了。"

"嗨,出了什么事啦?"巴德说,"你这是在干啥呀?是在把你的一个病人埋掉,还是干别的什么事呀?"

"哦,因为这儿不断往上冒地下水,"大夫说,"我估计下面说不准有一股泉水开了口呢!"

"你可别胡说!"巴德立刻装出一副房地产经纪人那种公平交易、童叟无欺的腔调说,"哎哟哟,大夫,这份房地产原是我经手卖给你的。你可别说我把这个有地下水的鬼地方修修补补之后才转给你。"

"反正就是有水嘛。"大夫说。

"是呀,可是,大夫,你不妨查看一下基沃尼斯俱乐

The Doctor lifted a frowning face and an attentive ear. He heard two pairs of heavy feet clump across the resonant floor of the porch. He heard the house door opened and the visitors enter the hall, with which his cellar communicated by a short flight of steps. He heard whistling and then the voices of Buck and Bud crying, "Doc! Hi, Doc! They're biting!"

Whether the Doctor was not inclined for fishing that day, or whether, like others of his large and heavy type, he experienced an especially sharp, unsociable reaction on being suddenly startled, or whether he was merely anxious to finish undisturbed the job in hand and proceed to more important duties, he did not respond immediately to the inviting outcry of his friends. Instead, he listened while it ran its natural course, dying down at last into a puzzled and fretful dialogue.

"I guess he's out."

"I'll write a note—say we're at the creek, to come on down."

"We could tell Irene."

"But she's not here, either. You'd think *she'd* be a-round."

"Ought to be, by the look of the place."

"You said it, Bud. Just look at this table. You could write your name—"

"Sh-h-h! Look!"

Evidently the last speaker had noticed that the cellar door was ajar and that a light was shining below. Next moment the door was pushed wide open and Bud and Buck looked down.

"Why Doc! There you are!"

"Didn't you hear us yelling?"

The Doctor, not too pleased at what he had overheard, nevertheless smiled his rather wooden smile as his two friends made their way down the steps. "I thought I heard someone," he said.

"We were bawling our heads off," Buck said. "Thought nobody was home. Where's Irene?"

"Visiting," said the Doctor. "She's gone visiting."

"Hey, what goes on?" said Bud. "What are you doing? Burying one of your patients, or what?"

"Oh, there's been water seeping up through the floor," said the Doctor. "I figured it might be some spring opened up or something."

"You don't say!" said Bud, assuming instantly the high ethical standpoint of the realtor. "Gee, Doc, I sold you this property. Don't say I fixed you up with a dump

部印发的那份地质构造示意图。好的天然地基——镇上就是一块都没有。"

"看来他是在哄骗你呢。"巴克龇牙咧嘴地说。

"不，"巴德说，"你要知道，大夫刚到这里的时候还太嫩。你得承认他太嫩些。他毕竟没见过世面！"

"他还买过特德·韦伯的老爷汽车。"巴克说。

"要是我转让给他，本来他就会把杰索普的房子都买下来，"巴德说，"可是我不乐意叫他上当。"

"不就是来自波基普西的那个十分蹩脚的骗子。"巴克说。

"有人也许会这样看他的，"巴德说，"这样看他的人说不定有。可不是我。那份地产原是我经手介绍的。他和艾琳一结婚，就搬进来了。我可不是存心叫大夫住到有地下水的鬼地方呀。"

"哦，别提它，"大夫被这一番良心话弄得很窘，就说，"我猜想因为正好下过好几场大雨吧。"

"我的老天哪！"巴克朝着那弄脏了的铁镐的尖头看了一眼说，"不用说，你一定挖得很深，嘿，一下子挖到粘土层？"

"4 英尺深才挖得到粘土层。"巴德说。

"才 18 英寸呢。"大夫说。

"要 4 英尺，"巴德说，"我可以给你看示意图。"

"来呀。别抬杠，"巴克说，"你看怎么样，大夫？到小溪那里去，一两个钟头，嗯？他们正在钓鱼呢。"

"不行，小伙子们，"大夫说，"我还得去看几个病人。"

"哎哟哟，自己活可也得让别人活呀，大夫。"巴德说，"饶了他们这一回吧。难道说你要叫倒霉的镇上人丁越来越少吗？"

大夫目光俯视，就笑了笑，喃喃自语道，——只要有人给开这种特别玩笑，他总是露出这副样子来。"对不起，小伙子，"他说，"我可去不了。"

"好吧，"巴克失望地说，"我想我们还是走吧。那么艾琳怎么样？"

"艾琳？"大夫反问道，"没什么。她出门拜客去了。到阿尔巴尼去了。坐的是 11 点的火车。"

"是 11 点？"巴克说，"开往阿尔巴尼的？"

"难道刚才我是说阿尔巴尼吗？"大夫说，"我要说的是沃特汤。"

"在沃特汤有朋友吗？"巴克说。

"有斯莱特太太，"大夫说，"就是斯莱特夫妇嘛。据艾琳说，是她小时候住在赛卡莫尔大街的隔壁的邻居。"

where there's an underground spring."

"There was water,"said the Doctor.

"Yes, but, Doc, you can look on that geological map the Kiwanis Club got up. There's not a better section of subsoil in the town."

"Looks like he sold you a pup,"said Buck, grinning.

"No,"said Bud. "Look. When the Doc came here he was green. You'll admit he was green. The things he didn't know!"

"He bought Ted Webber's jalopy,"said Buck.

"He'd have bought the Jessop place if I'd let him,"said Bud. "But I wouldn't give him a bum steer."

"Not the poor, simple city slicker from Poughkeepsie,"said Buck.

"Some people would have taken him,"said Bud. "Maybe some people did. Not me. I recommended this property. He and Irene moved straight in as soon as they were married. I wouldn't have put the Doc on to a dump where there'd be a spring under the foundations."

"Oh, forget it,"said the Doctor, embarrassed by this conscientiousness. "I guess it was just the heavy rains."

"By gosh!"Buck said, glancing at the besmeared point of the pickaxe. "You certainly went deep enough. Right down into the clay, huh?"

"That's four feet down, the clay,"Bud said.

"Eighteen inches,"said the Doctor.

"Four feet,"said Bud. "I can show you on the map."

"Come on. No arguments,"said Buck. "How's about it, Doc? An hour or two at the creek, eh? They're biting."

"Can't do it boys,"said the Doctor. "I've got to see a patient or two."

"Aw, live and let live, Doc,"Bud said. "Give 'em a chance to get better. Are you going to depopulate the whole darn town?"

The Doctor looked down, smiled, and muttered, as he always did when this particular jest was trotted out. "Sorry, boys,"he said. "I can't make it."

"Well,"said Bud, disappointed, "I suppose we'd better get along. How's Irene?"

"Irene?"asked the Doctor. "Never better. She's gone visiting. Albany. Got the eleven o'clock train."

"是斯莱特吗?"巴德说,"同艾琳是隔壁邻居。可不是在这个镇上。"

"哦,是的。"大夫说,"她是在昨天夜里跟我念叨这些事的。她还接到过一封信。有一次艾琳的母亲住院,好像还亏得这位斯莱特太太照料呢。"

"不。"巴德说。

"那都是她亲口跟我说的,"大夫说,"当然啦,是在好多年以前。"

"你听着,大夫,"巴克说,"巴德和我从小就是在这个镇上土生土长的。艾琳家里老老小小——我们哪一个都认得。他们家里我们一天到晚进进出出。他们隔壁从来都没有一个邻居名叫斯莱特的。"

"也许是,"大夫说,"她这个女人后来又嫁了人。也许这是另外一个名字。"

巴德摇摇头。

"艾琳什么时候上火车站的?"巴克问。

"哦,大约在一刻钟以前。"大夫说。

"你没有开车送她?"巴克说。

"她自己走着去的。"大夫说。

"我们从大街上走来,"巴克说,"我们可没有碰见过她。"

"说不定她打牧场那边穿过去的。"大夫说。

"拎着手提包真够呛哪。"巴克说。

"她那个小包里才一两件小玩意儿。"大夫说。

巴德还是一个劲儿在摇头。

巴克先是看了一眼巴德,然后又看看那把铁镐,还有那新铺在地坪上的一层湿漉漉的水泥。"哎哟哟,我的老天呀!"

"哦,我的天呀,大夫!"巴德说,"瞧你这个家伙!"

"我的天哪,真没想到你们两个傻小子在琢磨些什么呢?"大夫问,"你们到底打算要说些什么呀?"

"是地下水!"巴德说,"我应该马上弄清楚这决不是什么地下水。"

这时,大夫两眼直瞅着他铺的水泥地坪,铁镐,以及他那两个朋友尴尬的脸孔。至于他自己的脸一下子也发青了。"难道我疯了吗?"他说,"要不然,就是你们疯了?你们话里有话,胡说我——还有那个艾琳——我的妻子——哦,看你们再胡说八道!滚出去!得了,快去报告警察局长。通知他上这儿来挖东西。你们——都给我滚出去!"

巴德和巴克面面相觑,两脚来回挪动了一下,但

"Eleven o'clock?"said Buck. "For Albany?"

"Did I say Albany?" said the Doctor. "Watertown,I meant. "

"Friends in Watertown?"Buck asked.

"Mrs. Slater," said the Doctor. "Mr. and Mrs. Slater. Lived next door to 'em when she was a kid,Irene said,over on Sycamore Street. "

"Slater?"said Bud. "Next door to Irene. Not in *this* town. "

"Oh, yes," said the Doctor. "She was telling me all about them last night. She got a letter. Seems this Mrs. Slater looked after her when her mother was in the hospital one time. "

"No,"said Bud.

"That's what she told me,"said the Doctor. "Of course,it was a good many years ago. "

"Look,Doc,"said Buck. "Bud and I were raised in this town. We've known Irene's folks all our lives. We were in and out of their house all the time. There was never anybody next door called Slater. "

"Perhaps," said the Doctor, "she married again, this woman. Perhaps it was a different name. "

Bud shook his head.

"What time did Irene go to the station?" Buck asked.

"Oh, about a quarter of an hour ago," said the Doctor.

"You didn't drive her?"said Buck.

"She walked,"said the Doctor.

"We came down Main Street," Buck said. "We didn't meet her. "

"Maybe she walked across the pasture,"said the Doctor.

"That's a tough walk with a suitcase,"said Buck.

"She just had a couple of things in a little bag," said the Doctor.

Bud was still shaking his head.

Buck looked at Bud, and then at the pick, at the new, damp cement on the floor. "Jesus Christ!" he said.

"Oh,God,Doc!"Bud said. "A guy like you!"

"What in the name of heaven are you two bloody fools thinking?"asked the Doctor. "What are you trying to say?"

"A spring!" said Bud. "I ought to have known right away it wasn't any spring. "

The Doctor looked at his cement-work, at the

仍然伫立在那里。

"看你们再胡说八道。"大夫说。

"我可不知道。"巴德说。

"看来他好像是冒火了。"巴克说。

"天知道。"巴德说。

"天知道,"巴克说,"你知道。我知道。全镇也都知道。可是要不要报告陪审团。"

大夫把自己的手搭在脑门上。"那是怎么回事?"他说,"怎么啦? 刚才你们在议论什么? 你们到底是什么意思?"

"你要是消息灵通一些就好!"巴克说,"大夫,现在你总可以知道这是怎么一回事。不过要动动脑子,思考一下。我们可是一见如故,是怪要好的朋友嘛。"

"不过我们总得好好思考一下,"巴德说,"要认真才行。不管冒火不冒火,买卖地产都得照规章办事。不然,那样的事就叫做串通一气。"

"你们在说什么冒火不冒火。"大夫说。

"你说对了,"巴克说,"你是我们的朋友嘛。要是这种说法完全名副其实的话——"

"反正我们认为是这样的。"巴德说。

"是完全名副其实吗?"大夫说。

"你早晚一定会知道的。"巴克说。

"也许我们早就告诉了你,"巴德说,"只是——到底为了什么缘故?"

"我们早就告诉了你,"巴克说,"我们差不多都说过了。是在 5 年以前。那时你还没有跟她结婚。你来这儿还不到 6 个月,但我们对你多少有点好感。是想过要给你一点儿暗示,而且还正式说过呢。巴德,你记得吗?"

巴德点点头。"真有趣,"他说,"一知道杰索普的房产,我马上就奔到那里。我可不会让你把那个买下来的,大夫。可是一结了婚,那事情就又当别论了。反正我们早就告诉过你。"

"我们俩可都是非常负责的。"巴克说。

"我 50 岁了,"大夫说,"我想艾琳会觉得我相当老了。"

"只要你像 21 岁的约翰尼·韦斯马勒,那就没有关系啦。"巴克说。

"我知道有人认为她根本不是一个好妻子,"大夫说,"也许她确实不是,她年轻,她充满了活力。""哦,别提了!"巴克突然说道,两眼望着刚铺上的那层湿漉

pick, at the large worried faces of his two friends. His own face livid. "Am I crazy?" he said. "Or are you? You suggest that I've—that Irene—my wife—oh, go on! Get out! Yes, go and get the sheriff. Tell him to come here and start digging. You—get out!"

Bud and Buck looked at each other, shifted their feet, and stood still again.

"Go on," said the Doctor.

"I don't know," said Bud.

"It's not as if he didn't have the provocation," Buck said.

"God knows," Bud said.

"God knows," Buck said. "You know. I know. The whole town knows. But try telling it to a jury."

The Doctor put his hand to his head. "What's that?" he said. "What is it? Now what are you saying? What do you mean?"

"If this ain't being on the spot!" said Buck. "Doc, you can see how it is. It takes some thinking. We've been friends right from the start. Damn good friends."

"But we've got to think," said Bud. "It's serious. Provocation or not, there's a law in the land. There's such a thing as being an accomplice."

"You were talking about provocation," said the Doctor.

"You're right," said Buck. "And you're our friend. And if ever it could be called justified—"

"We've got to fix this somehow," said Bud.

"Justified?" said the Doctor.

"You were bound to get wised up sooner or later," said Buck.

"We could have told you," said Bud. "Only—what the hell?"

"We could," said Buck. "And we nearly did. Five years ago. Before ever you married her. You hadn't been here six months, but we sort of cottoned to you. Thought of giving you a hint. Spoke about it. Remember, Bud?"

Bud nodded. "Funny," he said. "I came right out in the open about that Jessop property. I wouldn't let you buy that, Doc. But getting married, that's something else again. We could have told you."

"We're that much responsible," Buck said.

"I'm fifty," said the Doctor. "I suppose it's pretty old for Irene."

"If you was Johnny Weissmuller at the age of twenty-one, it wouldn't make any difference," said Buck.

漉的水泥。"别提了，大夫，看在上帝的面上。"

大夫用手抹了一下自己的脸孔。"各人口味不同嘛，"他说，"我这个人是冷冰冰的，平时轻易不肯说话。至于艾琳——你们就会说她放荡。"

"这是你说的。"巴克说。

"她根本不是家庭主妇，"大夫说，"这个我可知道。可那并不是一个男人所需要的唯一东西。她挺会享乐的。"

"是呀，"巴克说，"她挺会享乐的。"

"那才叫我喜欢呢，"大夫说，"因为要享乐我自己还不会。至于智力方面，她就浅薄得很。是的，不妨说，她就是愚蠢。可我并不在乎。再加上懒，做事不是井井有条。哦，反正我自己有条不紊就得了。她挺会享乐的，这可就是美。天真无邪，就像一个小孩子。"

"是呀。但愿就是这些才好。"巴克说。

"不过，"大夫目光全部移到他身上说，"你好像还知道更多的事儿。"

"那些事儿反正人人都知道。"巴克说。

"一个老实巴交、正经八百的家伙，来到了像这样的一个地方，就跟镇上的那个放荡女人结了婚，"巴德语调尖酸刻薄地说，"而谁都没有告诉他。人们只是在冷眼旁观罢了。"

"而且人们都在嘲笑他，"巴克说，"其中包括你和我，巴德，还有其他的人。"

"我们跟她说过正在观察她的一举一动。"巴德说，"我们曾经警告过她。"

"人人都警告过她，"巴克说，"但是人们都厌烦了。后来连卡车司机都觉得——"

"那决不是我们，大夫，"巴德一本正经地说，"反正不是在你来了以后。"

"全镇的人将会站在你这一边。"巴克说。

"那可并不意味着要到本县的法院去打官司。"巴德说。

"啊哟哟！"大夫突然大声嚷了起来，"这可叫我怎么办？怎么办？"

"巴德，这就得看你的了，"巴克说，"我可不会告发他的。"

"放心吧，大夫，"巴德说，"镇静下来。喂，巴克。刚才我们上这儿来的时候，街上空荡荡的，是不是？"

"我想是的，"巴克说，"反正谁都没有看见我们下地窖。"

"I know a lot of people think she's not exactly a perfect wife,"said the Doctor. "Maybe she's not. She's young. She's full of life. "

"Oh, skip it!"said Buck sharply, looking at the raw cement. "Skip it, Doc, for God's sake. "

The Doctor brushed his hand across his face. "Not everybody wants the same thing,"he said. "I'm a sort of dry fellow. I don't open up very easily. Irene—you'd call her gay. "

"You said it,"said Buck.

"She's no housekeeper,"said the Doctor. "I know it. But that's not the only thing a man wants. She's enjoyed herself. "

"Yeah,"said Buck. "She did. "

"That's what I love,"said the Doctor. "Because I'm not that way myself. She's not very deep, mentally. All right. Say she's stupid. I don't care. Lazy. No system. Well, I've got plenty of system. She's enjoyed herself. It's beautiful. It's innocent. Like a child. "

"Yes. If that was all,"Buck said.

"But,"said the Doctor, turning his eyes full on him,"You seem to know there was more. "

"Everybody knows it,"said Buck.

"A decent straightforward guy comes to a place like this and marries the town floozy,"Bud said bitterly. "And nobody'll tell him. Everybody just watches. "

"And laughs,"said Buck. "You and me, Bud, as well as the rest. "

"We told her to watch her step,"said Bud. "We warned her. "

"Everybody warned her,"said Buck,"But people get fed up. When it got to truck-drivers—"

"It was never us, Doc,"said Bud, earnestly. "Not after you came along, anyway. "

"The town'll be on your side,"said Buck.

"That won't mean much when the case comes to trial in the county seat,"said Bud.

"Oh!" cried the Doctor, suddenly. "What shall I do? What shall I do?"

"It's up to you, Bud,"said Buck. "I can't turn him in. "

"Take it easy, Doc," said Bud. "Calm down. Look, Buck. When we came in here the street was empty, wasn't it?"

"I guess so,"said Buck. "Anyway, nobody saw us come down cellar. "

"And we haven't been down,"Bud said, addressing himself forcefully to the Doctor. "Get that, Doc?

"可我们并没有往地窖走下去,"巴德很有说服力地对大夫说,"明白吗,大夫? 我们在上面大声嚷嚷,逗留了一两分钟,就离开啦。但是这个地窖我们可以从来没有走下来。"

"我巴不得你们没有走下来。"大夫说话时显得很吃力。

"现在你至多只要说艾琳出门去散步,并没有回来过就得了,"巴克说,"巴德和我可以对你发誓,我们亲眼看见她跟一个家伙坐在——哦,就是坐在一辆别克小轿车里开出了小镇。那样,不用说,每个人都会相信。我们也会牢记不忘。可是后来呢? 得了,现在我们还是走吧。"

"现在就得记住。牢记在心。就算从来没有上这儿来,今天我们并没有见过你,"巴德说,"再见啦!"

巴克和巴德走上台阶,行动十分谨慎,反而显得荒唐可笑。"你最好还是……把那件事情遮盖起来吧。"巴克俯看着他的肩膀时说。

大夫独自一人,坐在一只空箱子上,两手抱住自己的脑袋。直到走廊里的门砰的一声又关上了,他还是这个样子坐着。这一回他并没有胆战心惊。他屏息静听着。屋子的大门开了又关上了。有一个声音在喊叫着,"喂——喂! 喂——喂! 我回来了!"

大夫慢条斯理地站了起来。"我在楼下呀,艾琳!"他应声说道。

地窖门开了。一个年轻的女人站在台阶入口处。"你敢打赌吗?"她说,"我错过了那班该死的火车。"

"哦!"大夫说,"你是穿过牧场走回来的吗?"

"是的,真傻啊。"她说,"本来我只要搭乘别人的便车,就准赶得上那班火车了。可惜当时我并没有想到。如果你开车送我到车站,我也还是赶得上的。"

"也许是这样,"大夫说,"你回来的路上遇到过谁呀?"

"一个人都没有,"她说,"你手头那个零舌儿弄完了没有?"

"恐怕我还得从头再弄一遍。"大夫说,"快下来,我的宝贝,让我给你看看。"

┌─ 讨 论 ─■

这篇小说如同《带家具出租的房间》一样,包含着偶然的巧合,而且结尾也很巧妙。但是

We shouted upstairs, hung around a minute or two, and cleared out. But we never came down into this cellar."

"I wish you hadn't,"the Doctor said heavily.

"All you have to do is say Irene went out for a walk and never came back,"said Buck. "Bud and I can swear we saw her headed out of town with a fellow in a—well, say in a Buick sedan. Everybody'll believe that,all right. We'll fix it. But later. Now we'd better scram."

"And remember,now. Stick to it. We never came down here and we haven't seen you today,"said Bud. "So long!"

Buck and Bud ascended the steps, moving with a rather absurd degree of caution. "You'd better get that... that thing covered up," Buck said over his shoulder.

Left alone, the Doctor sat down on an empty box, holding his head with both hands. He was still sitting like this when the porch door slammed again. This time he did not start. He listened. The house door opened and closed. A voice cried, "Yoo-hoo! Yoo-hoo! I'm back."

The Doctor rose slowly to his feet. "I'm down here,Irene!"he called.

The cellar door opened. A young woman stood at the head of the steps. "Can you beat it?" she said. "I missed the damn train."

"Oh!"said the Doctor. "Did you come back across the field?"

"Yes,like a fool,"she said. "I could have hitched a ride and caught the train up the line. Only I didn't think. If you'd run me over to the junction,I could still make it."

"Maybe,"said the Doctor. "Did you meet anyone coming back?"

"Not a soul,"she said. "Aren't you finished with that old job yet?"

"I'm afraid I'll have to take it all up again,"said the Doctor. "Come down here,my dear,and I'll show you."

This story, like"The Furnished Room," involves coincidence and has a trick ending.

不是这两个特点要比《带家具出租的房间》更为人们所接受？研究一下这两篇小说在意图之间的差别，也许我们就可以对这个问题做出最圆满的回答。

《带家具出租的房间》立意要写成一篇严肃的小说。欧·亨利要我们感到生活中的痛苦和嘲弄，大城市的残忍和烦恼与失意者的爱情和希望之间的对照。这篇小说的目的，在于激发我们的情感，从而引起我们的同情。

另一方面，《埋葬》则是一个范围扩大了的笑话。它写的是严肃的题材，即一个不正经的妻子对一个老实巴交、正经八百的男人的不忠，以及她所受到的丈夫的折磨，可是，重点并不放在人所共有的感情和痛苦之上。它采用了笑话中常有的那种写法，一方面处于很可能是严肃的，甚至充满悲剧气氛的，富于人性的情境之中，另一方面这个笑话因已突然颠倒过来而显得很有分量，因此，从某种程度来说，小说重点放在这两者之间的对照上。它给艾琳开了一个大玩笑。就是等到她走下台阶时，她也没有突然感到吃惊！好在她真的回来了。她就是在那个时候走了进来。我们在这里看到了喜剧性效果——至于同情和严肃性等要求，也就一扫而光了。正如某些心理学家所说，一到假日，我们就会突然感到如释重负似的。

事实上，这个玩笑并不仅仅是针对艾琳的。它也是针对小说中每一个人，包括并非故意要推波助澜的巴克和巴德，连同医生本人也都在内。这篇小说的意图，在于说明生活中本来就有一些相当冷酷无情的小笑话，但最好的办法就是承认它们，并对它们加以嘲笑。甚至偶然巧合的事实——巴德和巴克刚好顺便路过来串门，艾琳恰巧又没有赶上火车，谁都没有看见她穿过牧场走了回来——也都是和喜剧性效果前后保持一致的。由于令人可笑的生活正在发生作用，这些巧合我们都是承认的——因为正是生活中的不合逻辑性，才给我

But are those two things more acceptable here than in "The Furnished Room"? Perhaps we can best answer the question by considering the difference between the pretensions of the two stories.

"The Furnished Room" aspires to be a serious story. O. Henry wants us to feel the pathos and irony of life, the brutality and anonymity of the great city in contrast with the loves and hopes of the lost individuals. The story aims to stir our emotions and evoke our sympathies.

"De Mortuis," on the other hand, is a kind of extended joke. It deals with serious materials, the betrayal of a simple, decent man by an immoral wife, and his murder of her, but the emphasis is not on the human passions and suffering. The treatment is the treatment to be found in a joke, and the point, in a way, lies in the contrast between the potentially serious, even tragic, human situation, on the one hand, and the reversal and punch of the joke, on the other. It's a great joke on Irene. Just wait till she gets downstairs! Won't she be surprised! Well, she had it coming. She stepped into it that time. We have the comic effect—the liberation from the demands of sympathy and seriousness. A suddenly justified liberation for our holiday, as some psychologists would put it.

As a matter of fact, the joke isn't merely on Irene. There is a joke on everybody, on Buck and Bud, who unwittingly get the thing worked up, and on the doctor himself. Life has some rather grim little jokes, the story implies, but the best thing to do is to recognize them as jokes and laugh at them. Even the fact of coincidence—Bud and Buck just happen to drop in at the right time, Irene just happens to miss the train and come back, unseen, across the pasture—are consistent with the comic effect. We accept the coincidences as the machinery of the joke life is playing—

们提供了喜剧的题材。可怜的艾琳,以及其他人物,都被卷进了那些未必会有的巧合和始料不及的转变之中,我们对这一事实只好报之以一笑。不过由于缺乏感染力,无法使我们产生同情。作者采用了平心静气,超然物外,冷眼旁观地报道的一种语调。我们并没有被引入人物情境之中。至于没有写出严肃和受苦过程,这一事实只不过使这个喜剧的语调略感严峻尖刻而已。

总而言之,正是那种特别富于喜剧性的语调,使我们接受了那些巧合和巧妙的结尾。所谓语调,正如我们早已论述过,就是指作者的态度对他的主题和他的读者所产生的那种效果。在这里,科利尔认为生活就是一种讥诮的笑话,充满了圈套和骗局。艾琳,小心点儿亲爱的,注意那块香蕉皮。它就在你眼前。

for the illogic of life, not the logic, is what gives us the comedy. Poor Irene, and the others, are caught in the improbable coincidences and the unexpected turn, and we laugh at the fact. No appeal has been made to our sympathies. The tone is one of calm detachment, coolly reportorial. We are not involved in the human situation. The fact of the unreported seriousness and the suffering merely gives a grim little edge to the comedy.

To sum up, it is the particular comic tone that makes us accept the coincidences and the trick ending. By tone, as we have already suggested, we mean the impression that the author gives of his attitude toward his subject and his reader. Collier here takes life as a sardonic joke, full of traps and tricks. Careful, Irene, dear, watch that banana peel. It's right there before your eyes.

■ 思考题 ■

1. 试将《埋葬》里有关破题和开展的两部分区别开来。在开展部分开始发生前,你能指出哪些是属于破题的部分?
2. 倘若科利尔在小说结尾处插入一段,描写大夫在回忆自己结婚前的孤独,细想艾琳毕竟也给过自己片刻之间的缱绻柔情,因此对此刻自己突然感到可怕的冲动不寒而栗,但到最后,他却又硬起心肠来了。这样写法将会如何改变这篇小说的效果?对整个小说的基调又会产生什么样的影响?这篇小说还能保持前后一致吗?
3. 第一段描写对全篇小说来说有什么价值?

（潘庆舲 译）

1. Try to distinguish between exposition and complication in "De Mortuis." Can you point out any elements of exposition that are withheld until complication has begun?
2. Suppose Collier had interpolated toward the end of the story a passage in which the doctor remembers his loneliness before his marriage, dwells on certain moments of tenderness of which Irene had been capable, shudders at the horror of the impulse that seizes him, then steels himself to the act. How would this change the effect of the story? What would be the effect on the tone? Would the story still be coherent?
3. What value for the story does the first paragraph have?

009. 鹰溪桥上

（美）安布鲁斯·比尔斯 著

江锡祥　纪　锋 译

009. An Occurrence at Owl Creek Bridge

by Ambrose Bierce

　　亚拉巴马州北部的一座铁路桥上站着一个人，正俯视着脚下 20 英尺处湍急的流水。这个人背着双手，手腕上绑着绳子。一根绞索紧紧地套在他的脖子上，另一端系在他头上一根坚实的枕木上，中间的一段则松松地垂到他膝前。铺着铁轨的枕木上散搁着几块木板，他，还有他的行刑队就站在上面。行刑队由一位联邦军军士和他指挥的两名士兵所组成，那军士看上去很可能是和平时期的一个代理警长。这临时搭起的平台上还伫立着一个身穿戎服、腰佩武器的上尉军官。桥两端各有一名哨兵持枪而立，他们左臂横在胸前，枪身垂靠在左肩前，机枪抵在臂上。这姿势看上去一本正经，其实很不自然，整个身体必须站得笔挺。这两个哨兵对桥中心发生的一切毫不在意，他们的职责似乎仅仅是把守横在桥上的那块平台。

　　桥的一头除了一个哨兵外，空无一人，铁路笔直地向前伸展了 100 码，进入树林，然后拐了个弯就不见了。远处一定还有哨所。河对岸是一片开阔地带，平缓的斜坡上竖着一排木栅栏，上面挖了步枪射击孔，还有一个炮口，炮筒从里面探出身子，控制着桥面。桥和碉堡间的斜坡上站着一些旁观者——一队步兵在那儿"稍息"着，枪托拄地，枪口微微后倾，靠在右肩上，他们双手交叉放在枪上。一位中尉站在队伍的右侧，他的指挥刀刀尖着地，左手按在右手上。除了桥中央的 4 个人外，其他人都纹丝不动地站着。那队步兵以僵滞的目光冷漠地注视着铁桥。那两名哨兵面对河岸，看上去就像装饰铁桥的雕像一样。上尉抱着胳膊站在那儿，一声不吭地看着下属干活，什么表示也没有。死神就像达官显贵，当他来临时，须得

A MAN stood upon a railroad bridge in northern Alabama, looking down into the swift water twenty feet below. The man's hands were behind his back, the wrists bound with a cord. A rope closely encircled his neck. It was attached to a stout cross-timber above his head and the slack fell to the level of his knees. Some loose boards laid upon the sleepers supporting the metals of the railway supplied a footing for him and his executioners—two private soldiers of the Federal army, directed by a sergeant who in civil life may have been a deputy sheriff. At a short remove upon the same temporary platform was an officer in the uniform of his rank, armed. He was a captain. A sentinel at each end of the bridge stood with his rifle in the position known as "support," that is to say, vertical in front of the left shoulder, the hammer resting on the forearm thrown straight across the chest—a formal and unnatural position, enforcing an erect carriage of the body. It did not appear to be the duty of these two men to know what was occurring at the center of the bridge; they merely blockaded the two ends of the foot planking that traversed it.

Beyond one of the sentinels nobody was in sight; the railroad ran straight away into a forest for a hundred yards, then, curving, was lost to view. Doubtless there was an outpost farther along. The other bank of the stream was open ground—a gentle acclivity topped with a stockade of vertical tree trunks, loopholed for rifies, with a single embrasure through which protruded the muzzle of a brass cannon commanding the bridge. Midway of the slope between the bridge and fort were the spectators—a single company of infantry in line, at "parade rest," the butts of the rifles on the ground, the barrels inclining slightly backward against the right shoulder, the hands crossed upon the stock. A lieutenant stood at the right of the line, the point of his sword upon the ground, his left hand resting upon his right. Excepting the group of four at the center of

作者简介：安布鲁斯·比尔斯（**Ambrose Bierce**，1842—1914），美国记者，讽刺作家、短篇小说家。1842 年 6 月 24 日生于俄亥俄州梅格斯县，1914 年卒于墨西哥。美国内战服役后，他成为旧金山一家报社的专栏作者和编辑，专门抨击各种各样的欺诈行为。他的作品包括《军民故事》（*Tales of Soldiers and Civilians*，1891；修改成为《在人生中间》；其中收录小说《鹰溪桥上》）、《这种事情可能吗？》（*Can Such Things Be?* 1893）、《魔鬼字典》（*The Devil's Dictionary*，1906；有大量讽刺的解说）。

以礼相迎,尊为上宾,就连与他过往甚密的人也不例外。按照军规,静穆和肃立就表示尊敬。

那个就要被处绞刑的人看上去35岁左右,他是个平民,从服装看,是个种植园主。他长相端正——挺直的鼻梁,坚毅的嘴巴,宽阔的前额,乌黑的头发向后梳着,顺耳朵直披到他那件裁剪合身的外套领口上。他留着硬直的短髭和山羊胡子,但不是连鬓胡子,深灰色的大眼睛露出慈祥的表情,很难想象一个脖子上套着绞索的人竟会有这般表情。他显然绝不是什么卑鄙的刺客。反正军规对各色人等的绞刑都做出明文规定,就是绅士也不例外。

一切准备就绪,那两个兵士各自抽掉脚下的木板,站到两旁。中士转身向上尉敬礼,立刻站到他身后,上尉也跟着挪开一步。桥上这会儿只剩下那个受刑的人和中士,他们分别站在横跨三根枕木的一块长木板的两端。那平民站的一头几乎要碰到第四根枕木。木板原先是靠上尉的体重保持平衡的,现在则由中士取而代之。一接上尉发出的信号,中士立刻移开,木板就会随即倾斜,那受刑人将从两根枕木间坠落下去。就那受刑人看来,这样的安排倒也干净利索。他的脸和眼睛都没有蒙住。他盯着自己站的那块"摇摇晃晃的立足点"看了一会儿,然后把视线移向脚下打着漩涡的湍流急水。突然,他发现一段木头在水里翻腾,他的视线也随着那木头顺流而下。那木头漂流得多慢啊!河水也淌得多么费劲!

他合上双眼,想最后思念一下自己的妻子儿女。晨曦中,河水闪闪发光,远处,河岸两旁雾气茫茫,那座碉堡,那些士兵,以及那段打着转的木头——所有这一切都使他的思想不能集中。这时他心里才感到了一种新的不安情绪。因为扰乱他对亲人的思念的,正是一种尖锐、清晰的金属撞击声,就仿佛铁匠的锤子敲打着铁砧,有着同样激越的音色,他既不能塞耳不听,也不能理解。他想不出那是什么声音,无比的远或是无比的近——但似乎又远又近。它的反复出现是有规律的,但缓慢的时候就像丧钟一样。他不耐烦地等着每一下敲击,一种无可名状的恐惧同他袭来。随着敲击间歇的延长,那声音越来越强烈,越来越尖锐,就像一把尖刀戳痛了他的耳膜,使他心烦意乱。他害怕自己会尖叫起来。原来他所听见的只不过是自己手表发出的滴答声。

他睁开眼睛,又瞥见脚下的河水。"假如我能挣

the bridge, not a man moved. The company faced the bridge, staring stonily, motionless. The sentinels, facing the banks of the stream, might have been statues to adorn the bridge. The captain stood with folded arms, silent, observing the work of his subordinates, but making no sign. Death is a dignitary who when he comes announced is to be received with formal manifestations of respect, even by those most familiar with him. In the code of military etiquette silence and fixity are forms of deference.

The man who was engaged in being hanged was apparently about thirty-five years of age. He was a civilian, if one might judge from his habit, which was that of a planter. His features were good—a straight nose, firm mouth, broad forehead, from which his long, dark hair was combed straight back, falling behind his ears to the collar of his wellfitting frock coat. He wore a mustache and pointed beard, but no whiskers; his eyes were large and dark gray, and had a kindly expression which one would hardly have expected in one whose neck was in the hemp. Evidently this was no vulgar assassin. The liberal military code makes provision for hanging many kinds of persons, and gentlemen are not excluded.

The preparations being complete, the two private soldiers stepped aside and each drew away the plank upon which he had been standing. The sergeant turned to the captain, saluted and placed himself immediately behind that officer, who in turn moved apart one pace. These movements left the condemned man and the sergeant standing on the two ends of the same plank, which spanned three of the crossties of the bridge. The end upon which the civilian stood almost, but not quite, reached a fourth. This plank had been held in place by the weight of the captain; it was now held by that of the sergeant. At a signal from the former the latter would step aside, the plank would tilt and the condemned man go down between two ties. The arrangement commended itself to his judgment as simple and effective. His face had not been covered nor his eyes bandaged. He looked a moment at his "unsteadfast footing," then let his gaze wander to the swirling water of the stream racing madly beneath his feet. A piece of dancing driftwood caught his attention and his eyes followed it down the current. How slowly it appeared to move! What a sluggish stream!

He closed his eyes in order to fix his last thoughts upon his wife and children. The water, touched to gold by the early sun, the brooding mists under the banks at some distance down the stream, the fort, the soldiers, the piece of drift—all had distracted him. And now he became conscious of a new disturbance. Striking through the thought of his dear ones was a sound which he could neither ignore nor understand, a sharp, distinct, metallic percussion like the stroke of a blacksmith's hammer upon the anvil; it had the same ringing quality. He wondered what it was,

脱双手，"他想道，"我就可以甩掉绞索，跳进河里。我可以潜水躲过枪弹，奋力游到对岸，奔到那片林子里，然后逃回家去。谢天谢地，我的家现在还不在他们的占领区内，我的妻子儿女离占领军还远着呢。"

这些用文字记录在这里的思想，不像是出自这个行将归天的人的脑子，倒像是从外界闪进去的。就在此刻，上尉对中士点了点头，中士退开一步。

贝顿·法夸出身于历史悠久、受人尊敬的亚拉巴马家族，本人是个殷实的种植园主，就像其他奴隶主一样，他是个搞政治的，自然也是最初主张南方应该脱离联邦，并且热心支持南方的事业。由于他那傲慢的性格（这里就不必细说了），他未能加入那支曾在各种残酷战役中殊死战斗的勇敢军队，那些战役最后以科林斯镇失陷而告终。他因无法施展才干而感到恼火。他渴望有朝一日能发挥自己的能力，像士兵那样有用武之地。他也盼望能出人头地。他觉得，这种机会自然会来临，就像战争中人人都有机会一样。与此同时，他还尽力而为；只要有助于南方，无论什么低贱的事他都愿干；只要符合他这样一个在心底深处实在是军人本色的平民性格，无论什么危险他都愿承担。他毫不含糊、无条件地笃信那条露骨的格言——爱情和战争都是不择手段的。

一天傍晚，法夸和妻子正坐在家门口一条自制的长凳上，只见一名身穿灰色军服的士兵骑马奔到门前来讨水喝。法夸太太真是太愿意能用自己白净的双手为士兵效劳了。她去取水时，她丈夫走近那个满身尘土的骑手，急切地向他打听前线的消息。

"北方佬正在抢修铁路，"那个士兵说，"准备再次进攻。他们已抵达鹰溪桥，并将桥修复了，还在河北岸筑起一道栅栏。他们的指挥官下了一道命令，宣称任何企图破坏铁路、铁路桥梁、隧道和火车的人，一经俘获，就地绞死。通告到处张贴着，我亲眼见过。"

"鹰溪桥离这儿有多远？"法夸问。

"大概30英里。"

"河这边没有军队吗？"

"桥那头有一个哨兵，半英里外在铁路线上只有一个哨所。"

"假如一个人，也就是说一个平民，一个对绞刑颇有研究的人——能躲过那个哨所，甚至还能骗过那个哨兵，"法夸笑着说，"他能干些什么呢？"

士兵想了想后回答说："一个月前我在那儿的时

and whether immeasurably distant or near by—it seemed both. Its recurrence was regular, but as slow as the tolling of a death knell. He awaited each stroke with impatience and—he knew not why—apprehension. The intervals of silence grew progressively longer; the delays became maddening. With their greater infrequency the sounds increased in strength and sharpness. They hurt his ear like the thrust of a knife; he feared he would shriek. What he heard was the ticking of his watch.

He unclosed his eyes and saw again the water below him. "If I could free my hands," he thought, "I might throw off the noose and spring into the stream. By diving I could evade the bullets and, swimming vigorously, reach the bank, take to the woods and get away home. My home, thank God, is as yet outside their lines; my wife and little ones are still beyond the invader's farthest advance."

As these thoughts, which have here to be set down in words, were flashed into the doomed man's brain rather than evolved from it the captain nodded to the sergeant. The sergeant stepped aside.

Peyton Farquhar was a well-to-do planter, of an old and highly respected Alabama family. Being a slave owner and like other slave owners a politician, he was naturally an original secessionist and ardently devoted to the Southern cause. Circumstances of an imperious nature, which is unnecessary to relate here, had prevented him from taking service with the gallant army that had fought the disastrous campaigns ending with the fall of Corinth, and he chafed under the inglorious restraint, longing for the release of his energies, the larger life of the soldier, the opportunity for distinction. That opportunity, he felt, would come, as it comes to all in war time. Meanwhile he did what he could. No service was too humble for him to perform in aid of the South, no adventure too perilous for him to undertake if consistent with the character of a civilian who was at heart a soldier, and who in good faith and without too much qualification assented to at least a part of the frankly villainous dictum that all is fair in love and war.

One evening while Farquhar and his wife were sitting on a rustic bench near the entrance to his grounds, a gray-clad soldier rode up to the gate and asked for a drink of water. Mrs. Farquhar was only too happy to serve him with her own white hands. While she was fetching the water her husband approached the dusty horseman and inquired eagerly for news from the front.

"The Yanks are repairing the railroads," said the man, "and are getting ready for another advance. They have reached the Owl Creek bridge, put it in order and built a stockade on the north bank. The commandant has issued an order, which is posted everywhere, declaring that any civilian caught interfering with the railroad, its bridges, tunnels or trains will be summarily

候,注意到去年冬天的大水把河里漂浮的木头都积在这一头的桥墩下了。如今那些木头都已干了,像麻绳一样,一点就着。"

法夸太太取来了水。士兵喝完后,彬彬有礼地向她道谢,然后对她丈夫一鞠躬,跨上马就走了。一小时后,夜幕降临,那骑兵又打种植园经过,这回是朝北,向着他来的方向奔去。原来他是北方联军的一个探子。

当贝顿·法夸从桥上笔直地坠下去时,他已失去了知觉,就像死了一般。似乎过了很长时间,他才被喉咙口的一阵剧痛从不省人事的状态中惊醒过来,随之而来的是一阵窒息感。阵阵疼痛从他颈脖开始一直向下延伸到四肢和躯体的每一个细胞,疼痛好像沿着一张精密的网络,闪电般地向全身扩散开去;疼痛又像一条条火舌,灼烧得他热不可耐。他只觉得脑袋发胀,里面像是塞满了东西一样。这些感觉都和思维毫无关系,因为他的思维功能已被摧毁。他只有感觉,而这种感觉又是如此折磨人。他仿佛觉得一切都在转动,自己好像一颗燃烧着的核心,被包含在亮闪闪的云雾之中。他犹如一个巨大的钟摆,绕着一个好大的弧圈来回晃动。刹那间,他周围的亮光突然向上冲击,随之而来的是一阵水溅声,在他耳鼓里轰轰作响,一切变得又冷又暗。思维的功能恢复了。他知道,绳子断了,自己掉进了河里。这时倒没有什么窒息感了;脖子上的那根绞索早就勒得他喘不过气来,现在又正好挡着河水灌进肺里。在河底被吊死——这种念头在他看来实在可笑。黑暗中他睁开双眼,看见头顶上有一线光亮,可这光亮显得那么遥远,那么可望而不可即。他还在下沉,因为他看见头顶上的亮光越来越淡弱,最后仅仅成了一丝微光。过了一会儿,这丝微光又越来越亮了,他知道自己开始在往上浮,因为他感觉好多了,可他还不敢相信这一点。"被吊着淹死倒也不错,"他暗自思忖着,"但我不希望被枪毙。不! 决不能被枪毙,那太不公平。"

他不知道自己在干什么,可是手腕上的剧痛告诉他,他正试图为自己的双手松绑。就像一个无所事事的人观赏杂要演员的表演而对其结果毫无兴趣一样,他观看着自己的挣扎。多么惊人的努力! 多么了不起,多么超人的力量啊! 干得真漂亮! 啊,成功了! 绳子松了,双臂分开向上浮了起来。在逐渐增强的亮

hanged. I saw the order. "

"How far is it to the Owl Creek bridge?"Farquhar asked.

"About thirty miles. "

"Is there no force on this side of the creek?"

"Only a picket post half a mile out, on the railroad, and a single sentinel at this end of the bridge. "

"Suppose a man—a civilian and student of hanging—should elude the picket post and perhaps get the better of the sentinel," said Farquhar, smiling, "what could he accomplish?"

The soldier reflected. "I was there a month ago, " he replied. "I observed that the flood of last winter had lodged a great quantity of driftwood against the wooden pier at this end of the bridge. It is now dry and would burn like tow. "

The lady had now brought the water, which the soldier drank. He thanked her ceremoniously, bowed to her husband and rode away. An hour later, after nightfall, he re-passed the plantation, going northward in the direction from which he had come. He was a Federal scout.

As Peyton Farquhar fell straight downward through the bridge he lost consciousness and was as one already dead. From this state he was awakened—ages later, it seemed to him—by the pain of a sharp pressure up his throat, followed by a sense of suffocation. Keen, Poignant agonies seemed to shoot from his neck downward through every fiber of his body and limbs. These pains appeared to flash along well-defined lines of ramification and to beat with an inconceivably rapid periodicity. They seemed like streams of pulsating fire heating him to an intolerable temperature. As to his head, he was conscious of nothing but a feeling of fullness—of congestion. These sensations were unaccompanied by thought. The intellectual part of his nature was already effaced; he had power only to feel, and feeling was torment. He was conscious of motion. Encompassed in a luminous cloud, of which he was now merely the fiery heart, without material substance, he swung through unthinkable arcs of oscillation, like a vast pendulum. Then all at once, with terrible suddenness, the light about him shot upward with the noise of a loud splash; a frightful roaring was in his ears, and all was cold and dark. The power of thought was restored; he knew that the rope had broken and he had fallen into the stream. There was no additional strangulation; the noose about his neck was already suffocating him and kept the water from his lungs. To die of hanging at the bottom of a river! —the idea seemed to him ludicrous. He opened his eyes in the darkness and saw above him a gleam of light, but how distant, how inaccessible! He was still sinking, for the light became fainter and fainter until it was a mere glimmer. Then it began to grow and brighten, and he knew that he was rising toward the surface—

光中，这两只手一边一个依稀可辨。他怀着一种新的兴趣注视着，先是一只手然后又是一只手，使劲抓住脖子上的绳子，解开后又狠狠地将它抛在一边。绳子在水里浮动起伏，犹如一条水蛇。"把绳子套上，重新套上！"他觉得自己正冲着双手喊，因为绳子解开后，随之而来的是一阵他还没尝到过的剧痛。他的脖子痛得厉害，脑袋像是着了火，那颗一直在微微悸动着的心猛地跳了一下，像是要从嘴里跳出来似的。他浑身像散了架一般疼痛难忍！可是，那两只不听使唤的手，对他的命令却无动于衷。它们用力飞快地朝下划着水，将身子托出水面。他觉得自己的头先露出了水面，两眼被太阳刺得看不见东西，胸脯急剧地起伏着，随着一阵剧烈得无以复加的疼痛，他的肺部吸进了一大口空气，但很快他又一声尖叫，把它吐了出来！

现在他已经完全控制了自己身上的各种感官。事实上，这些感官还显得特别灵敏警觉。他全身处于可怕的紊乱之中，也不知是什么东西促进了、改善了他的感官，觉察到许多过去从未觉察到的东西。他感触到脸上的水波，还听到了它们每次拍来时发出的"哗哗"声。他朝河岸上的树林望去，看见了一棵棵的树，看见了树叶和每片叶子上的脉络，也看见了树叶上的小虫子，有蝗虫，有金身苍蝇，还有褐色的蜘蛛，正忙着在树桠间织网。成千上万片草叶上，五光十色的露珠闪闪发光。蠓虫在水波上载歌载舞；蜻蜓在振动双翅；水蜘蛛划动双腿，恰似船桨推动小舟——这一切组成了一支清晰的乐曲。一条鱼从他的眼皮底下"嗖"地穿过，他听到了鱼身分水的"沙沙"声。

这时他已露出水面，脸朝下游。没多久，这个看得见的世界好像慢慢地围着他转了起来，他自己成了轴心。他看见了小桥，碉堡，看见了桥上的士兵，上尉，中士，两名哨兵——他的行刑队。蔚蓝色天空清楚地勾勒出他们的轮廓。他们冲着他大喊大叫，指手画脚。上尉已拔出手枪，但没开火，其他的人都没带武器。他们的动作古怪而可怕，他们的身影异常的高大。

蓦地，他听到一声枪响，有什么东西在离他脑袋几英寸的水面上，轰地炸开了，溅了他一脸的水。接着又是一声，他瞧见一个哨兵正举着枪，枪筒里冒出一缕青烟。水中的这个人看见，桥上的那个人正从枪准星里死死盯着自己。他注意到这是一只灰眼睛；记得曾在哪本书上读到，说灰眼睛是最厉害不过的，

knew it with reluctance, for he was now very comfortable. "To be hanged and drowned," he thought "that is not so bad; but I do not wish to be shot. No; I will not be shot; that is not fair."

He was not conscious of an effort, but a sharp pain in his wrist apprised him that he was trying to free his hands. He gave the struggle his attention, as an idler might observe the feat of a juggler, without interest in the outcome. What splendid effort! What magnificent, what superhuman strength! Ah, that was a fine endeavor! Bravo! The cord fell away; his arms parted and floated upward, the hands dimly seen on each side in the growing light. He watched them with a new interest as first one and then the other pounced upon the noose at his neck. They tore it away and thrust it fiercely aside, its undulations resembling those of a water snake. "Put it back, put it back!" He thought he shouted these words to his hands, for the undoing of the noose had been succeeded by the direst pang that he had yet experienced. His neck ached horribly; his brain was on fire; his heart, which had been fluttering faintly, gave a great leap, trying to force itself out at his mouth. His whole body was wracked and wrenched with an insupportable anguish! But his disobedient hands gave no heed to the command. They beat the water vigorously with quick, downward strokes, forcing him to the surface. He felt his head emerge; his eyes were blinded by the sunlight; his chest expanded convulsively, and with a supreme and crowning agony his lungs engulfed a great draught of air, which instantly he expelled in a shriek!

He was now in full possession of his physical senses. They were, indeed, preternaturally keen and alert. Something in the awful disturbance of his organic system had so exalted and refined them that they made record of things never before perceived. He felt the ripples upon his face and heard their separate sounds as they struck. He looked at the forest on the bank of the stream, saw the individual trees, the leaves and the veining of each leaf—saw the very insects upon them: the locusts, the brilliant-bodied flies, the gray spiders stretching their webs from twig to twig. He noted the prismatic colors in all the dew-drops upon a million blades of grass. The humming of the gnats that danced above the eddies of the stream, the beating of the dragonflies' wings, the strokes of the water spiders' legs, like oars which had lifted their boat—all these made audible music. A fish slid along beneath his eyes and he heard the rush of its body parting the water.

He had come to the surface facing down the stream; in a moment the visible world seemed to wheel slowly round, himself the pivotal point, and he saw the bridge, the fort, the soldiers upon the bridge, the captain, the sergeant, the two privates, his executioners. They were in silhouette against the blue sky. They shouted and gesticulated, pointing at him. The captain

所有著名的射手都长着灰眼睛。不过,这只灰眼睛可没击中目标。

法夸被一个回旋的浪头推着转了半圈,他又朝碉堡对面的林子望去。一个响亮尖锐的嗓音,在他身后单调而有规律地喊着,传过水面,十分清晰,透过并淹没了周围的一切声响——甚至他耳边汩汩的流水声。尽管法夸不是一个军人,可他经常出入兵营,知道这种从容不迫、慢条斯理、喉音严重的腔调具有何种可怕的意义。他知道岸上的那位中尉现在不再袖手旁观了。他的声音多么冷酷无情!平稳的语调像是要逼着士兵们保持镇静。他有板有眼地喊出了这样几个残酷的字:

"全体注意……举枪……准备……瞄准……放!"

法夸向下潜去——他尽可能地向下潜去。河水在他耳边像尼亚加拉瀑布一般轰鸣,但他还是听到了排枪沉闷的轰响。他又一次浮了上来,遇见许多闪闪发亮的小铁屑,扁平得出奇,晃晃悠悠地沉没了下去。有几片触及他的脸和手,接着又落下,继续往下沉。有一片夹在他的衣领子里,热辣辣的,很不好受,他一下子把它扔了出去。

待他露出水面,喘着粗气时,他才知道在水下已经待了很长时间。他发现自己正处在很远的下游——比起刚才的地方要安全多了。那些士兵们差不多都已上好了枪膛,从枪管里抽出来的通条在阳光下一闪一闪,在空中翻了个身,"嗖"地一声又被插进了鞘套。两名哨兵又开枪了,这一回没按什么命令,也没获得什么成功。

这一切都让这个被追捕者在回头时看见了。现在他正顺着水势奋力地游去。他的头脑同四肢一样有力,正以闪电般的速度思索着。

"这位当官的,"他心里想,"是个经过严格训练的人,他不会犯第二次错误了。齐射还不是像点射一样容易躲避嘛。也许他已经下命令让士兵随便开枪了。上帝保佑,我一下子可躲不过这么多子弹!"

离他不到两码的地方,突然可怕地溅起河水,接着一阵尖啸,然后逐渐减弱。这响声听起来似乎又从空中飞回碉堡去了,最后"轰"的一声爆炸,搅乱了河底的宁静。河水像一条掀起的被单,盖在他头顶上,把他整个裹住了。他看不见东西,也喘不过气来。大炮也插手进来了。他摇了摇头,抖掉了脸上的水,听见一颗打偏了的炮弹正"嗖嗖"地凌空而过。没多久

had drawn his pistol, but did not fire; the others were unarmed. Their movements were grotesque and horrible, their forms gigantic.

Suddenly he heard a sharp report and something struck the water smartly within a few inches of his head, spattering his face with spray. He heard a second report, and saw one of the sentinels with his rifle at his shoulder, a light cloud of blue smoke rising from the muzzle. The man in the water saw the eye of the man on the bridge gazing into his own through the sights of the rifle. He observed that it was a gray eye and remembered having read that gray eyes were keenest, and that all famous marksmen had them. Nevertheless, this one had missed.

A counter-swirl had caught Farquhar and turned him half round; he was again looking into the forest on the bank opposite the fort. The sound of a clear, high voice in a monotonous singsong now rang out behind him and came across the water with a distinctness that pierced and subdued all other sounds even the beating of the ripples in his ears. Although no soldier, he had frequented camps enough to know the dread significance of that deliberate, drawling, aspirated chant, the lieutenant on shore was taking a part in the morning's work. How coldly and pitilessly—with what an even, calm intonation, presaging, and enforcing tranquillity in the men—with what accurately measured intervals fell those cruel words:

"Attention, company!... Shoulder arms!... Ready!... Aim!... Fire!"

Farquhar dived—dived as deeply as he could. The water roared in his ears like the voice of Niagara, yet he heard the dulled thunder of the volley and, rising again toward the surface, met shining bits of metal, singularly flattened, oscillating slowly downward. Some of them touched him on the face and hands, then fell away, continuing their descent. One lodged between his collar and neck; it was uncomfortably warm and he snatched it out.

As he rose to the surface, gasping for breath, he saw that he had been a long time under water; he was perceptibly farther down stream—nearer to safety. The soldiers had almost finished reloading; the metal ramrods flashed all at once in the sunshine as they were drawn from the barrels, turned in the air, and thrust into their sockets. The two sentinels fired again, independently and ineffectually.

The hunted man saw all this over his shoulder; he was now swimming vigorously with the current. His brain was as energetic as his arms and legs; he thought with the rapidity of lightning.

"The officer," he reasoned, "will not make that martinet's error a second time. It is as easy to dodge a volley as a single shot. He has probably already given the command to fire at will. God help me, I cannot dodge them all!"

An appalling splash within two yards of him was

远处的树林里便响起了"劈里啪啦"树枝折断的声音。

"好了，他们不会再这样打了，"他猜测着，"下一回他们要用葡萄弹了。我得盯着这个炮口，硝烟会给我报信的，炮声来得太晚，老是拖在炮弹的后面。这真是门好炮哇。"

猛然，他觉得自己正急速地旋转，旋转，活像一只陀螺。河水，河岸，树林，此刻在远处的桥，碉堡和士兵都混为一体，模糊不清。所有的物体只变成各种颜色，他看见的只是一条条在水平线上旋转着的光纹。原来他刚才是陷进了一个漩涡，漩涡激烈地盘旋向前，弄得他头昏眼花。没多久他被抛在一片碎石堆上，这儿是河的右岸，也是南岸。一块隆起的地方正好把他掩蔽起来，不让敌人察觉。这突如其来的停顿，加上一只手又被碎石擦破，使他喘了一口气。他高兴得流下了眼泪。他把手指插进沙子里，一把接着一把地往身上洒，一边还轻轻地感谢它。这沙子像钻石，像红宝石，像绿宝石，像他能想象的世上一切美丽的东西。河岸上的树像是大花园里的植物，他注意到，它们排列得井然有序，他又深深地吸了一口树上的花香。一束奇异的玫瑰红的光彩透过树干的空隙闪烁着，轻风在树枝上吹出悦耳的声音，像是风琴在弹奏。他不想再逃了，只想留在这块景色迷人的地方，就是重新被捕，也心甘情愿。

葡萄弹在他头顶上的树枝间"嗖嗖"、"嘎嘎"地响个不停，把他从梦幻中惊醒。那些稀里糊涂的炮手盲目地放了一阵，算是欢送。他猛地跳了起来，冲上斜坡，一头钻进了树林。

整整一天，他一点儿没歇脚，仅仅靠着太阳的移动来定方向。这林子好像无边无际，连绵不断，就连一条樵夫的小径也看不到。他还是第一次发现自己住的地方竟是如此荒芜。眼前的一切真有点神秘。

夜幕降临了，他疲惫不堪，脚痛，肚子也饿。但一想到家里的妻子儿女，他又挣扎着向前走去。最后，他终于找到一条路，他知道顺着这条路准能走回家。这条路像城里的大街一样宽阔笔直，可好像也未见有人走过似的。路边没有农田，四处不见住家，甚至听不到一声使人想起此地还有人烟的狗叫声。漆黑的树干在路的两旁竖起一道笔直的墙，逐渐延伸在地平线上，最终汇成一点，好像透视课上画的图案一样。他抬起头，透过树缝看见金光灿烂的星星在天空中眨

followed by a loud, rushing sound, *diminuendo*, which seemed to travel back through the air to the fort and died in an explosion which stirred the very river to its deeps! A rising sheet of water curved over him, fell down upon him, blinded him, strangled him! The cannon had taken a hand in the game. As he shook his head free from the commotion of the smitten water he heard the deflected shot humming through the air ahead, and in an instant it was cracking and smashing the branches in the forest beyond.

"They will not do that again," he thought; "the next time they will use a charge of grape. I must keep my eye upon the gun; the smoke will apprise me—the report arrives too late; it lags behind the missile. That is a good gun."

Suddenly he felt himself whirled round and round—spinning like a top. The water, the banks, the forests, the now distant bridge, fort and men—all were commingled and blurred. Objects were represented by their colors only; circular horizontal streaks of color—that was all he saw. He had been caught in a vortex and was being whirled on with a velocity of advance and gyration that made him giddy and sick. In a few moments he was flung upon the gravel at the foot of the left bank of the stream—the southern bank—and behind a projecting point which concealed him from his enemies. The sudden arrest of his motion, the abrasion of one of his hands on the gravel, restored him, and he wept with delight. He dug his fingers into the sand, threw it over himself in handfuls and audibly blessed it. It looked like diamonds, rubies, emeralds; he could think of nothing beautiful which it did not resemble. The trees upon the bank were giant garden plants; he noted a definite order in their arrangement, inhaled the fragrance of their blooms. A strange, roseate light shone through the spaces among their trunks and the wind made in their branches the music of Aeolian harps. He had no wish to perfect his escape—was content to remain in that enchanting spot until retaken.

A whiz and rattle of grapeshot among the branches high above his head roused him from his dream. The baffled cannoneer had fired him a random farewell. He sprang to his feet, rushed up the sloping bank, and plunged into the forest.

All that day he traveled, laying his course by the rounding sun. The forest seemed interminable; nowhere did he discover a break in it, not even a woodman's road. He had not known that he lived in so wild a region. There was something uncanny in the revelation.

By nightfall he was fatigued, footsore, famishing. The thought of his wife and children urged him on. At last he found a road which led him in what he knew to be the right direction. It was as wide and straight as a city street, yet it seemed untraveled. No fields bordered it, no dwelling anywhere. Not so much as the barking of a dog suggested human habitation. The black bodies of the trees forced a straight wall on both

着眼睛，他觉得这些星星很陌生，而且还很奇怪地组合在一块儿。他相信它们之所以这样组合，其中一定有神秘和邪恶的意义。道路两旁的树林里充满着稀奇古怪的声响，他不止一次地在这些声响中清清楚楚地听到有人在用一种莫名其妙的语言轻声说话。

脖子痛极了，他伸手去摸了摸，发觉脖子已经肿得厉害。他知道被绞索磨破的地方留下了一圈紫色痕迹，他感到双眼充血，再也无法合上。口渴得很，连舌头也肿大了，他把舌头从牙齿间壮了出来，让凉风来解热。这条人迹罕至的大道上，覆盖着多么柔软的草皮啊！现在他脚下再也感不到有什么路了！

毫无疑问，尽管浑身疼痛难忍，他一定走着走着就睡着了，要不就是他刚从一阵谵妄中苏醒过来，因为他现在看见的是另一番景象。这时他站在自己的家门口。一切还都是他离家时的老样子，晨曦中，明亮而美丽。想必他又赶了整整一夜路。他推开门，走上宽敞的白色甬道，看见一件女人的裙衫拂地而来，他的妻子容光焕发，娴静而又甜蜜，正走下前廊来接他。她站在台阶下，微笑地等待着，欣喜万分，真有举世无双的优雅和尊严。啊，她是多么美丽啊！他展开双臂，向前奔去，正要抱住她时，只觉得脖子根上重重地挨了一下。一道刺眼的白光在他四周闪耀，随之是一声巨响，好像是大炮的轰鸣——霎时间，一切又都沉浸在黑暗与寂静中！

贝顿·法夸死了。他的尸体，连同那个折断了的脖子，在鹰溪桥的枕木下慢悠悠地晃来晃去。

┌讨　论─■

这篇小说同《带家具出租的房间》《万卡》和《埋葬》一样，其结局出乎人们意料，转折处充满了讽刺意味。这些小说都提出了一个基本问题，即：这种出人意料的结局是否合乎情理；是不是被小说正文所证实；换句话说，这种结局安排仅仅是一种技巧，还是因为它的表现力强，所起的效果好？

为了彻底弄清楚这个基本问题，最好的方法也许是再提一个许多读者无疑都会提出的问题：一个即将丧命的人，会不会有像贝顿·法夸从鹰溪桥坠落时那样的感受？读者们也

sides, terminating on the horizon in a point, like a diagram in a lesson in perspective. Overhead, as he looked up through this rift in the wood, shone great golden stars looking unfamiliar and grouped in strange constellations. He was sure they were arranged in some order which had a secret and malign significance. The wood on either side was full of singular noises, among which—once, twice, and again—he distinctly heard whispers in an unknown tongue.

His neck was in pain and lifting his hand to it he found it horribly swollen. He knew that it had a circle of black where the rope had bruised it. His eyes felt congested; he could no longer close them. His tongue was swollen with thirst; he relieved its fever by thrusting it forward from between his teeth into the cold air. How softly the turf had carpeted the untraveled avenue—he could no longer feel the roadway beneath his feet!

Doubtless, despite his suffering, he had fallen asleep while walking, for now he sees another scene—perhaps he has merely recovered from a delirium. He stands at the gate of his own home. All is as he left it, and all bright and beautiful in the morning sunshine. He must have traveled the entire night. As he pushes open the gate and passes up the wide white walk, he sees a flutter of female garments; his wife, looking fresh and cool and sweet, steps down from the veranda to meet him. At the bottom of the steps she stands waiting, with a smile of ineffable joy, an attitude of matchless grace and dignity. Ah, how beautiful she is! He springs forward with extended arms. As he is about to clasp her he feels a stunning blow upon the back of the neck; a blinding white light blazes all about him with the sound like the shock of a cannon—then all is darkness and silence!

Peyton Farquhar was dead; his body, with a broken neck, swung gently from side to side beneath the timbers of the Owl Creek bridge.

This story, like "The Furnished room", "Vanka", and "De Mortuis", involves a surprise ending, an ironical turn. The basic question that such stories raise is this: is the surprise ending justified; is it validated by the body of the story; is it, in other words, a mere trick, or is it expressive and functional?

Perhaps the best way to clear the ground for a consideration of this basic question is to raise another question, which will no doubt occur to many readers of this story: is it possible for a man in the last moment of his life to have a vision of the sort that Peyton Farquhar has as he falls from Owl Creek bridge?

许就是根据自己赞成或反对这种如实描写的心理活动来评论这篇小说的。但是就凭这一点能获得完全令人信服的例证吗？这种感受的本身能使读者自然而然地相信吗？还有一个更重要的问题要考虑到：即使我们对小说里如实地描写心理活动的手法表示完全肯定，实际上会不会决定我们对小说所做出的评价的性质？根据下面所提出的原因来看，它是决定不了我们对小说所做出的评价的。因此一味注意这个问题可能会引向岔路，很容易使我们偏离主要问题。

我们现在姑且认为这篇小说从心理描写上来说是站得住脚的，下列问题就有待于读者回答：

1. 作者为什么不让读者知道这个行将死去的人的感受只不过是一种幻觉？

2. 作者这样做，是否有助于人物性格的揭示，或是达到其他显著的效果？

3. 这种秘而不宣的手法是否有利于小说情节的发展？

4. 小说的结局含有嘲讽的成分，但它是一种意味深长的嘲讽吗？

我们从这些问题中得出的结论是：从根本上来说，小说就是与人物有关的。小说中有许多饶有兴味的东西，其中我们最感兴趣的，就是对人物及其经历所做出的富有人性的描写。不论是普通的还是特殊的人物或人物的经历，都能引起我们的兴趣。这是因为那些普通的人物及其经历会引起我们的共鸣；而那些特殊的人物及其经历，则使我们醒悟过来，对新的可能性表示惊叹。但是，将人物的描写以及人物经历的叙述，与小说的特定意义等同起来，不能不说是一个非常严重的，而且是屡见不鲜的错误。正如我们已在第一章中指出的那样，一篇小说具有主题、思想、含义，以及在小说中发展并得到体现的生

Readers may be inclined to judge this story in terms of their acceptance or rejection of the psychological realism of the incident. But is it possible to have absolutely convincing evidence on this point? Isn't the fact of the vision something that, in itself, can be accepted without too much strain on the reader's credulity? But there is a much more important consideration to be taken into account. Even if we could arrive at a completely satisfying decision about the psychological realism of the incident, would this fact actually determine the nature of our judgment concerning the story? For reasons suggested below, it would not determine our judgment, and therefore preoccupation with this question is likely to prove a red herring—is likely to distract us from the real problem.

Suppose that we assume for the moment that the incident is psychologically valid; there remain these questions to be answered:

1. Why does the author withhold from the reader the knowledge that the dying man's vision is merely a vision?

2. Is any revelation of character or other significant effect accomplished thereby?

3. Does the withholding of this information throw any light on the development of a theme for the story?

4. There is an irony generated by the end of the story, but is it a meaningful irony?

These questions lead us to observe that, basically, fiction is concerned with people. One of the interests we take in it arises from the presentation of human character and human experience as merely human. Both the common and the uncommon human character or experience interest us; the common because we share in it, and the uncommon because it wakes us to marvel at new possibilities. But it is a great—and not uncommon—error to equate the presentation of character as such, or experience as such, with the specific meaning of fiction. Fiction, as we have tried to indicate in section 1, involves a theme, an idea, an interpretation, an attitude toward life developed and embodied in the piece of fiction. Directly or indirectly, through the experience of the characters in the piece

活态度。人们通过一篇小说中人物的经历,可以直接或间接地做出一种评价,而这种评价应该说基本上是合乎情理的。

　　根据人类某种特殊心理而安排的情节——譬如《鹰溪桥上》的情节——纵然可以使人为之一惊,但它本身并不具有虚构的意义。心理上的怪癖或者说"实例研究",也应该对人做出一种有意义的评价,应该开阔和加深人们的思想,只有这样,才能被人们看做一篇小说。小说描写各种各样的人物及其个人经历(其中有普通的,也有特殊的),但它不应该仅仅是一张有关医疗或心理方面的病情报告单。这一点我们必须牢记在心。从广义上来说,小说应涉及到道德问题,它所描写的对象,不应局限于那些奇事怪人,或者那些悲欢离合的事件。　　　　　　　(江锡祥　纪锋译)

of fiction, an evaluation is made—an evaluation that is assumed to have some claim to a general validity.

The plot that depends on some peculiarity of human psychology—as does "An Occurrence at Owl Creek Bridge"—may give us a shock of surprise, but it does not carry a fictional meaning. The peculiar quirk of psychology—the "case study"—must also involve some significant human evaluation, some broadening or deepening of our human attitudes, if it is to be acceptable as fiction. Fiction involves all kinds of human characters and human experiences, common and uncommon, but it is concerned to do more than make a clinical report, medical or psychological. We must keep this firmly in mind. Fiction involves what—understood in its broadest dimension—is a moral concern. It is not concerned with mere peculiarities, quirks or happy (or unhappy) accidents as such.

010. 进入波兰

（俄）艾萨克·巴贝尔 著　　潘庆舲 译

010. Crossing into Poland

by Isaac Babel

第六师司令官报告：诺弗戈拉德－沃棱斯克于今日拂晓时被攻占。司令部已经撤离克拉比弗诺，我们的辎重车队一进入人声嘈杂的后方，就铺开在从布列斯特通往华沙的公路上，这条公路早先就是尼古拉一世用农民的累累白骨修筑起来的。

田野里花花绿绿的，被罂粟花点染得分外红艳；正是中午时分，微风在渐渐变黄的稞麦中间荡漾着；洁白无瑕的荞麦，宛如远处修道院的一堵围墙耸起在地平线上。安谧的沃棱河水，蜿蜒曲折地从我们身边流过，随后就在桦树林上空蓝灰色薄雾里消失了；在遍地花开的斜坡之间匍匐爬行，还得穿过一片又一片蛇麻草，不时扎伤了两条早已疲惫不堪的胳膊。而橘黄色太阳，却像一颗被砍掉了的脑袋，从天上徐徐下降，偶尔还从云端里透出一点柔和的光影。落日时分，军旗在我们头顶上空迎风飘扬。傍晚，凉风习习，里面还掺杂着昨天浴血殊战和被宰掉的马匹的气味。黑黝黝的兹勃鲁赫河在咆哮，河水随着一团团泡沫往下游奔腾而去。各处桥梁都已经坍塌了，于是我们就只好涉水过河。这时皓月当空，波光粼粼。许多马匹都装上了后鞦，喧嚣的湍流在数百条马腿中间汩汩作响。有人沉到了水里，还在大声诅咒圣母玛利亚。河面上漂起了从马车上掉下来的黑糊糊的方方块块的碎片，而且到处是乱糟糟的噪音，夹杂着哨声和歌声，正在微弱的闪光隐约可见的山谷里，和在月光下弯弯曲曲的小径上空回响着。

我们到达诺弗戈拉德已是深更半夜了。我在被派去投宿的那个屋子里，发现有一个怀孕的妇女和两个红头发、瘦脖子的犹太人。此外，还有一个犹太人

THE Commander of the VI Division reported: Novgorad-Volynsk was taken at dawn today. The Staff had left Krapivno, and our baggage train was spread out in a noisy rearguard over the highroad from Brest to Warsaw built by Nicholas I upon the bones of peasants.

Fields flowered around us, crimson with poppies; a noontide breeze played in the yellowing rye; on the horizon virginal buckwheat rose like the wall of a distant monastery. The Volyn's peaceful stream moved away from us in sinuous curves and was lost in the pearly haze of the birch groves; crawling between flowery slopes, it wound weary arms through a wilderness of hops. The orange sun rolled down the sky like a lopped-off head, and mild light glowed from the cloud gorges. The standards of the sunset flew above our heads. Into the cool of evening dripped the smell of yesterday's blood, of slaughtered horses. The blackened Zbruch roared, twisting itself into foamy knots at the falls. The bridges were down, and we waded across the river. On the waves rested a majestic moon. The horses were in to the cruppers, and the noisy torrent gurgled among hundreds of horses' legs. Somebody sank, loudly defaming the Mother of God. The river was dotted with the square black patches of the wagons, and was full of confused sounds, of whistling and singing, that rose above the gleaming hollows, the serpentine trails of the moon.

Far on in the night we reached Novograd. In the house where I was billeted I found a pregnant woman and two red-haired, scraggy-necked Jews. A third,

作者简介：艾萨克·巴贝尔（**Isaac Babel**，1894—1940），俄国作家，生于奥德萨。他用俄国犹太方言写的《敖德萨故事》(O-dessa Tales，1921—1923)为他赢得名声。《红色骑兵》(Red Cavalry，1926)以他的军中生活经历为素材，使用库班河哥萨克人地道的俚语写成。巴贝尔是一位杰出的文学家，他的散文文字简洁有力，结合了俄国犹太讽刺漫画的特点、略带残忍意味的抒情方式和具有阴沉特点的喜剧形式。巴贝尔的作品全集由他的女儿娜塔丽编辑，于2001年出版了英语译本。

则贴着墙边,蒙住脑袋,睡着了。我又在指定给我的那个房间里,发现好几个衣柜都被兜底翻过,地板上有从女人皮袄上扯下来的破襟襟,还有人们随地乱撒的秽物,以及犹太人一年一度只在复活节使用的那些挺玄乎的陶器碎片。

"拾掇一下吧,"我对那个女人说,"脏得真不像话!"那两个犹太人从原地站了起来,穿着他们的毡底鞋,七手八脚把地上这一堆破东西给清除掉了。他们一声不响,像猴子一般满屋子跳来跳去,又像马戏团里的日本小丑那样,鼓起他们的脖子在不断旋转着。他们给我拾掇好一张原有羽毛褥垫、现已空空洞洞的床,我就只好紧挨着蒙头大睡的那个犹太人的墙边躺了下来。笼罩在我床上的那种贫困,简直令人昏厥。

这时,沉寂压倒了一切。只有那个月亮正用她蓝幽幽的手捂住自己闪闪发亮、无忧无虑的圆脸孔,活像窗外一个流浪汉在四处漂泊一样。

我给自己麻木不仁的双腿来回按摩,躺在那个千疮百孔的褥垫上,不一会儿就睡着了。我梦见第六师司令官突然出现在我跟前;他正在追赶骑在一匹笨重的牡马上的某旅司令官,对准后者的眉心开了两枪。子弹穿过了某旅司令官的脑袋,两颗眼珠子一下都掉落在地上。第六师司令官萨维茨基正冲着那个受伤的人大声嚷道:"你干吗不把全旅人马撤回来?"——说到这里,我突然惊醒了,原来是那个怀孕的妇女正用自己的手指在我脸上乱摸一气。

"好先生,"她说,"你睡觉时还在大声呼喊,你的身子老是在翻来覆去。这会儿我要让你睡到另一个角落去,因为你总是把我父亲推开去。"

她把她的那双细腿和滚圆的大肚皮从地板上抬了起来,又从睡者身上拿走了一条毯子。原来朝天躺着的是一个早已咽了气的老头儿。他的喉管已被割断,脸孔也被劈成两半,胡子上的污血早已变蓝,凝成铅块一般。

"好先生,"那个犹太女人一面猛摇那张床,一面说道,"是波兰人把他的喉管割断了。他还在一个劲儿哀求他们,说:'拉我到院子里杀吧,别让我女儿眼看着我死去。'可他们压根儿没听他的。他在屋里断气的时候还在惦念着我。——如今我真想知道,"这个女人突然发出一阵可怕的狂叫声,"我真想知道,任凭你走遍天下,哪能再找到像我亲爹那样的父亲呢?"

huddled to the wall with his head covered up, was already asleep. In the room I was given I discovered turned-out wardrobes, scraps of women's fur coats on the floor, human filth, fragments of the occult crockery the Jews use only once a year, at Eastertime.

"Clear this up," I said to the woman. "What a filthy way to live!" The two Jews rose from their places and, hopping on their felt soles, cleared the mess from the floor. They skipped about noiselessly, monkeyfashion, like Japs in a circus act, their necks swelling and twisting. They put down for me a feather bed that had been disemboweled, and I lay down by the wall next to the third Jew, the one who was asleep. Fainthearted poverty closed in over my couch.

Silence overcame all. Only the moon, clasping in her blue hands her round, bright, carefree face, wandered like a vagrant outside the window.

I kneaded my numbed legs and, lying on the ripped-open mattress, fell asleep. And in my sleep the Commander of the VI Division appeared to me; he was pursuing the Brigade Commander on a heavy stallion, fired at him twice between the eyes. The bullets pierced the Brigade Commander's head, and both his eyes dropped to the ground. "Why did you turn back the brigade?" shouted Savitsky, the Divisional Commander, to the wounded man—and here I woke up, for the pregnant woman was groping over my face with her fingers.

"Good sir," she said, "you're calling out in your sleep and you're tossing to and fro. I'll make you a bed in another corner, for you're pushing my father about."

She raised her thin legs and rounded belly from the floor and removed the blanket from the sleeper. Lying on his back was an old man, a dead old man. His throat had been torn out and his face cleft in two; in his beard blue blood was clotted like a lump of lead.

"Good sir," said the Jewess, shaking up the feather bed, "the Poles cut his throat, and he begging them: 'Kill me in the yard so that my daughter shan't see me die.' But they did as suited them. He passed away in this room, thinking of me. —And now I should wish to know," cried the woman with sudden and terrible violence, "I should wish to know where in the whole world you would find another father like my father?"

┌讨　论─■

1. 在第二段中,描写大自然的美("被罂粟花点染得分外红艳"的田野,"渐渐变黄的稞麦","安谧的河水","桦树林上空蓝灰色薄雾")等一系列形象,和代表暴力的标志("昨天浴血殊战"的气味,咆哮的兹勃鲁赫河,以及人们大声诅咒)都相互交错在一起。你觉得这一段描写和小说其他部分有什么关系? 在这里,要注意第五段中作者对窗外的月亮的描写。

2. 在第四段中,你觉得作者对犹太人,特别是对那个女人,持什么样的态度? 试想作者持同情的语调,这么一来又会使小说发生什么样的变化?

3. 那个女人为什么觉得世界上哪个父亲都比不上她自己的父亲呢? 她为什么在说这句话时会"突然发出一阵狂叫声",而不是,比如说,热泪夺眶而出,号啕大哭呢? 要是那样的写法,又会有什么不同的效果?

4. 再说,我们看到小说是在结尾处突然来了个转折点。它合乎情理吗? 从开头描写的细节和小说语调中,甚至在"暴力"中,都可以找到充分的根据吗?

5. 试想一下,这篇小说要是用相当长的篇幅,进行细致的描写,那样会减低效果吗?

到现在为止,我们在本章中一般谈论小说时,重点显然多少放在简单的转折点上,那就是说,通过情节来点明小说的意义所在。虽然所有虚构的情节都是朝着主题思想发展下去,目的是使打乱了的平衡(这篇小说即由此而产生的)重新得到恢复,并产生一种新的意义,但是许多小说作品,却比我们正在议论的那些作品都要复杂得多,而且要概括这种新的意义和新的平衡的出现,还非得有许多转折点不可。在后面的那些小说里,我们将发现就情节来说,程度都是各有不同的,而且有时候按着戏剧性的次序,还出现不止一个,而是好几个转折点。

（潘庆舲 译）

1. In the second paragraph, images of the beauty of nature (fields "crimson with poppies," " the yellowing rye," the " peaceful stream," " the pearly haze of the birch groves") are mixed with marks of violence ("the smell of yesterday's blood,"the roaring of the river, the oaths). What relation do you sense between this paragraph and the rest of the story? Notice in this connection, the description of the moon outside the window in the fifth paragraph.

2. In the fourth paragraph, what do you make of the narrator's attitude toward the Jews, particularly the woman? Suppose the narrator took a sympathetic tone. What difference would this make for the story?

3. Why does the woman think that no other father in the world could match hers? Why does she utter this thought "with sudden and terrible violence"and not, say, with a wail and outburst of tears? What difference would that make?

4. Here, again, we find a sudden turn at the end. Is it justifiable? Is it grounded in earlier details and tone in the story? Even the "violence"?

5. Suppose this story were developed at considerable length and detail. Would that impair the effect?

So far in this section we have generally dealt with stories more or less sharply focused on a single turn, a shift of plot that makes the point of the story. Though all fiction moves toward a point at which the disturbed equilibrium (which generates the story)is reestablished and a new meaning emerges, many pieces of fiction are much more complex than those we have been considering, requiring more than a simple turn to dramatize the emergence of the new meaning, the new equilibrium. In the stories that follow we shall find varying degrees of complication in plot, and sometimes not one turn but several,occurring in dramatic order.

011. 项 链

（法）盖伊·德·莫泊桑 著　郑克鲁 译

011. The Necklace

by Guy de Maupassant

世上有一些漂亮迷人的女子，仿佛是命运安排错了，生长在职员的家庭里；她便是其中的一个。她没有陪嫁费，希望渺茫，压根儿没法让一个既有钱又有地位的男子认识她，了解她，爱上她和娶了她；她只好听之任之，嫁给了教育部的一个小科员。

她打扮不起，只得穿着从简，但感到非常不幸，就像抱怨自己阶级地位下降的女子那样；因为女子原没有一定的阶层和种族，她们的美貌、娇艳和丰韵就作为她们的出身门第。天生的敏锐、高雅的本能、脑筋的灵活，只有这些才分出她们的等级，使平民的姑娘和最烜赫的命妇并驾齐驱。

她总觉得自己生来就配享受各种精美豪华的生活，因而感到连绵不绝的痛苦。住房寒碜，四壁空空，凳椅破旧，衣衫丑陋，都叫她苦不堪言。所有这些都折磨着她，使她气愤难平，而换了她那个阶层的另一个妇人的话，甚至会一无所感。看着那个替她料理家务的小个儿布列塔尼女人，她心中便抑郁不乐，想入非非。她幻想挂着东方料子的壁衣①，被青铜高脚灯照亮了的寂静的前厅；幻想那两个穿着短裤的高大男仆，被暖气管发出的闷热催起睡意，在宽大的靠背椅里酣睡着。她幻想墙上罩着古老丝绸的大客厅，里面有陈设着奇珍古玩的精致家具；幻想香气扑鼻的、风雅的内客厅，那是专为下午5点娓娓清谈的地方，来客有最亲密的男友，还有知名之士，难得的稀客，那是所有妇女都欣羡不已，渴望得到他们青睐的。

---

① 有钱人家往往在墙上蒙上一层布或壁毯，是一种豪华的装饰。

SHE was one of those pretty and charming girls who are sometimes, as if by a mistake of destiny, born in a family of clerks. She had no dowry, no expectations, no means of being known, understood, loved, wedded by any rich and distinguished man; and she let herself be married to a little clerk at the Ministry of Public Instruction.

She dressed plainly because she could not dress well, but she was as unhappy as though she had really fallen from her proper station, since with women there is neither caste nor rank; and beauty, grace, and charm act instead of family and birth. Natural fineness, instinct for what is elegant, suppleness of wit, are the sole hierarchy, and make from women of the people the equals of the very greatest ladies.

She suffered ceaselessly, feeling herself born for all the delicacies and all the luxuries. She suffered from the poverty of her dwelling, from the wretched look of the walls, from the worn-out chairs, from the ugliness of the curtains. All those things, of which another woman of her rank would never even have been conscious, tortured her and made her angry. The sight of the little Breton peasant who did her humble housework aroused in her regrets which were despairing, and distracted dreams. She thought of the silent antechambers hung with Oriental tapestry, lit by tall bronze candelabra, and of the two great footmen in knee breeches who sleep in the big armchairs, made drowsy by the heavy warmth of the hot-air stove. She thought of the long *salons* fitted up with ancient silk, of the delicate furniture carrying priceless curiosities, and of the coquettish perfumed boudoirs made for talks at five o'clock with intimate friends, with men famous and sought after, whom all women envy and whose attention they all desire.

作者简介：盖伊·德·莫泊桑（**Guy De Maupassant**，1850—1893），法国短篇小说家。1850年8月5日生于迪埃普附近的米罗梅斯尼尔古堡，1893年7月6日卒于巴黎。普法战争打断了他的法律学业，他志愿参军，军旅生活为他的作品提供了很好的素材。后来他成了文员，师从福楼拜。他以作品《羊脂球》（*Ball of Fat*，1880）成名。在接下来的10年，他出版了约300篇短篇小说、6部小说和3部游记。从他的小说作品来看，写的最多的是1870—1890年法国人的生活。他作品涉及到战争、农民、官僚、塞纳河两岸的生活、不同阶层的情感问题，甚至是幻想。

每当她坐在那张铺着三天未洗的桌布的圆桌前去吃饭，坐在对面的丈夫揭开盆盖，欣喜地说："啊！多好的炖肉！世上哪有比这更好的东西……"那时候她便幻想那些精美的筵席，亮闪闪的银餐具，挂满四壁的壁毯，上面织着古代人物和仙境森林中的异鸟珍禽；她幻想盛在华美的盘碟里的美馔佳肴，幻想一边嚼着粉红的鲈鱼肉或者松鸡翅，一边带着深不可测的微笑倾听窃窃情话的景象。

她没有华丽衣装，没有珠宝首饰，统统没有。而她偏偏就爱这些；她觉得自己生来就应该享受这些东西。她多么希望讨人喜欢，惹人嫉羡，风流诱人，被人追求呀。

她有一个有钱的女友，那是教会学校的同学，现在她再也不愿去看她了，因为每次看望回来她总感到非常痛苦。她要伤心、懊悔、绝望、凄苦得哭好几天。

可是有一天傍晚，她的丈夫回家时满脸得意洋洋，手里拿着一个大信封。

"嗨，"他说，"这玩意儿是给你的。"

她赶快撕开信封，从里面抽出一份请柬，上面印着这几行字：

兹订于1月18日（星期一）在本府举行晚会，敬请罗瓦赛尔夫妇莅临为荷。

教育部长乔治·朗波诺先生暨夫人谨上

她不但没有欢天喜地，像她丈夫所期待的那样，反而怨气冲天地把请柬往桌上一扔，嘟囔着说：

"你不想想，我要这个干吗？"

"可是，我亲爱的，我原以为你会很高兴的。你从来也不出门儿，这可是一个机会，真是难得的机会！我费了多少周折才弄到这张请柬。人人都想要，很不易到手，给职员的不多。在那儿，大小官员你都可以看到。"

她瞪着他，眼都要冒出火来，按捺不住脱口而出：

"你可叫我穿什么上那儿去呢？"

这个，他却从未想到。他咕哝着说：

"你上剧场穿的那件袍子呢？照我看，那件好像够好的……"

他戛然而止，看见妻子哭起来了，他又是惊讶又是慌乱。两大滴眼泪从他妻子的眼角慢慢顺着嘴角流下来。他结结巴巴地问：

When she sat down to dinner, before the round table covered with a tablecloth three days old, opposite her husband, who uncovered the soup tureen and declared with an enchanted air, "Ah, the good *pot-au-feu*! I don't know anything better than that," she thought of dainty dinners, of shining silverware, of tapestry which peopled the walls with ancient personages and with strange birds flying in the midst of a fairy forest; and she thought of delicious dishes served on marvelous plates, and of the whispered gallantries which you listen to with a sphinxlike smile, while you are eating the pink flesh of a trout or the wings of a quail.

She had no dresses, no jewels, nothing. And she loved nothing but that; she felt made for that. She would so have liked to please, to be envied, to be charming, to be sought after.

She had a friend, a former schoolmate at the convent, who was rich, and whom she did not like to go and see any more, because she suffered so much when she came back.

But one evening, her husband returned home with a triumphant air, and holding a large envelope in his hand.

"There," said he. "Here is something for you. "

She tore the paper sharply, and drew out a printed card which bore these words:

"The Minister of Public Instruction and Mme. Georges Ramponneau request the honor of M. and Mme. Loisel's company at the palace of the Ministry on Monday evening, January eighteenth."

Instead of being delighted, as her husband hoped, she threw the invitation on the table with disdain, murmuring:

"What do you want me to do with that?"

"But, my dear, I thought you would be glad. You never go out, and this is such a fine opportunity. I had awful trouble to get it. Everyone wants to go; it is very select, and they are not giving many invitations to clerks. The whole official world will be there. "

She looked at him with an irritated glance, and said, impatiently:

"And what do you want me to put on my back?"

He had not thought of that; he stammered:

"Why, the dress you go to the theater in. It looks very well, to me. "

He stopped, distracted, seeing his wife was crying.

"你怎么啦？你怎么啦？"

她下了个狠劲儿，把难言的苦衷压了下云，一面拭着沾湿的双颊，一面用镇静的嗓门回答："没有什么。只是我没有衣服，这次盛会我就去不成了。你有哪位同事，他的太太的衣衫总比我强的，你就把请柬送给他吧。"

他感到不是味儿。他于是又开口说：

"玛蒂尔德，咱们来算一下。一套合适的衣服，你在别的场合还可以穿的，简简单单的，得花多少钱？"

她想了一想，算了一笔账，也考虑了一下数目，她可以提出来，而不会招致节俭的科员立即回绝和吓得叫起来。

末了，她犹犹豫豫地回答：

"我不知道准数，不过有 400 法郎，我大概也就可以办妥了。"

他的脸色有点煞白，因为他正好备下这样一笔钱，要买一支枪，来年夏天好和几个朋友一道打猎作乐，星期日到南代尔平原去打云雀。

可是他还是说：

"好吧。我就给你 400 法郎。不过得设法做一件漂亮的袍子。"

晚会那天临近了，而罗瓦赛尔太太却显得抑郁不安，忧虑重重。她的衣服可是已经做好了。她的丈夫有天晚上问她：

"你怎么啦？瞧你这三天，阴阳怪气的。"

她回答：

"我没有首饰，没有宝石，身上什么也戴不出来，真叫我心烦意乱。那样我就会显出一副十足的寒酸气。我简直宁愿不赴会了。"

他接口说：

"你可以戴几朵鲜花呀。眼下这个季节，这是很雅致的。花上 10 个法郎，你就有两三朵美丽鲜艳的玫瑰花了。"

她一点儿没有被说服。

"不行……在阔太太中显出一副穷酸相，没有什么比这更丢脸的了。"

她的丈夫嚷了起来：

"你真是糊涂！你去找你的朋友福莱斯蒂埃太太，问她借几件首饰嘛。你跟她交情够好的，准行。"

她高兴得叫了出来：

"这倒是真的。我竟一点儿也没想到。"

Two great tears descended slowly from the corners of her eyes toward the corners of her mouth. He stuttered:

"What's the matter? What's the matter?"

But by violent effort, she had conquered her grief, and she replied, with a calm voice, while she wiped her wet cheeks:

"Nothing. Only I have no dress and therefore I can't go to this ball. Give your card to some colleague whose wife is better equipped than I."

He was in despair. He resumed:

"Come, let us see, Mathilde. How much would it cost, a suitable dress, which you could use on other occasions, something very simple?"

She reflected several seconds, making her calculations and wondering also what sum she could ask without drawing on herself an immediate refusal and a frightened exclamation from the economical clerk.

Finally, she replied, hesitatingly:

"I don't know exactly, but I think I could manage it with four hundred francs."

He had grown a little pale because he was laying aside just that amount to buy a gun and treat himself to a little shooting next summer on the plain of Nanterre, with several friends who went to shoot larks down there, of a Sunday.

But he said:

"All right. I will give you four hundred francs. And try to have a pretty dress."

The day of the ball drew near, and Mme. Loisel seemed sad, uneasy, anxious. Her dress was ready, however. Her husband said to her one evening:

"What is the matter? Come, you've been so queer these last three days."

And she answered:

"It annoys me not to have a single jewel, not a single stone, nothing to put on. I shall look like distress. I should almost rather not go at all."

He resumed:

"You might wear natural flowers. It's very stylish at this time of the year. For ten francs you can get two or three magnificent roses."

She was not convinced.

"No; there's nothing more humiliating than to look poor among other women who are rich."

But her husband cried:

"How stupid you are! Go look up your friend Mme. Forestier, and ask her to lend you some jewels. You're quite thick enough with her to do that."

She uttered a cry of joy:

第二天她就上朋友家,给她诉说自己的苦恼。

福莱斯蒂埃太太起身走到镶镜大柜跟前,取出一个大首饰匣,拿到罗瓦赛尔太太面前打开,对她说:

"挑吧! 亲爱的。"

她先看见几只手镯,再便是一串珠子项链,然后是一个威尼斯出品的十字架,镶嵌着黄金宝石,工巧精致。她戴上这些首饰,对着镜子试来试去,游移不决,舍不得摘下来放回去。她一个劲儿地问:

"你再没有别的了?"

"有啊。你自个儿找吧。我不知道你喜欢什么样儿的。"

突然,她在一个黑缎子的盒里发现一长串钻石项链,光彩夺目。一种过于强烈的欲望使她怦然心跳。她的手攥着它的时候直打哆嗦。她戴在脖子上,衬在袍子外面,对着镜子自我欣赏得出了神。

然后她欲言又止地、十分胆怯地问:

"你可以借给我这个吗? 就借这一样。"

"当然可以啦。"

她扑过去搂住了朋友的脖子,激动地吻着她,随后带着宝贝一溜烟跑了。

晚会那天到了。罗瓦赛尔太太十分成功。她比所有女人都漂亮,又优雅又妩媚,笑容满面,快活得发狂。所有的男子都尽瞧着她,打听她的名字,设法能被介绍。办公厅的随员全都想跟她跳华尔兹舞。部长也注意到她。

她忘怀地、尽情地跳着,被乐趣陶醉了,什么也不想,沉浸在她的美丽的凯旋中,她的成功的荣光里,一片幸福的彩云中,那是所有这些献媚、赞美、挑起的欲望、妇女心中认为十全十美的胜利所组成的。

她在清晨将近 4 点时才离开。她的丈夫从半夜起就在一间空空落落的小客厅里睡着了,客厅里还躺着另外三位先生,他们的太太也在尽情欢乐。

他怕她出门受寒,把事先带来的衣服披在她的肩上,那是平日穿的普通便服,那种寒碜和舞装的雅致很不调和。她觉觉到了,便想溜走,不让其他裹在锦裘里的太太们注意到。

罗瓦赛尔一把拉住她:

"等一等。到外边要受凉的。我去叫一辆马车。"

可是她一点儿也不听他的,便迅速下了楼梯。等他们来到街上,却找不到马车。他们东寻西找,远远看见马车走过,就追着向车夫呼喊。

"It's true. I never thought of it."

The next day she went to her friend and told of her distress.

Mme. Forestier went to a wardrobe with a glass door, took out alarge jewel-box, brought it back, opened it, and said to Mme. Loisel:

"Choose, my dear."

She saw first of all some bracelets, then a pearl necklace, then a Venetian cross, gold and precious stones of admirable workmanship. She tried on the ornaments before the glass, hesitated, could not make up her mind to part with them, to give them back. She kept asking:

"Haven't you any more?"

"Why, yes. Look. I don't know what you like."

All of a sudden she discovered, in a black satin box, a superb necklace of diamonds, and her heart began to beat with an immoderate desire. Her hands trembled as she took it. She fastened it around her throat, outside her high-necked dress, and remained lost in ecstasy at the sight of herself.

Then she asked, hesitating, filled with anguish:

"Can you lend me that, only that?"

"Why, yes, certainly."

She sprang upon the neck of her friend kissed her passionately, then fled with her treasure.

The day of the ball arrived. Mme. Loisel made a great success. She was prettier than them all, elegant, gracious, smiling, and crazy with joy. All the men looked at her, asked her name, endeavored to be introduced. All the attachés of the Cabinet wanted to waltz with her. She was remarked by the minister himself.

She danced with intoxication, with passion, made drunk by pleasure, forgetting all, in the triumph of her beauty, in the glory of her success, in a sort of cloud of happiness composed of all this homage, of all this admiration, of all these awakened desires, and of that sense of complete victory which is so sweet to a woman's heart.

She went away about four o'clock in the morning. Her husband had been sleeping since midnight, in a little deserted anteroom, with three other gentlemen whose wives were having a very good time. He threw over her shoulders the wraps which he had brought, modest wraps of common life, whose poverty contrasted with the elegance of the ball dress. She felt this, and wanted to escape so as not to be remarked by the other women, who were enveloping themselves in costly furs.

Loisel held her back.

他们走在通向塞纳河的下坡路上，垂头丧气，冻得发抖。临了，他们在岸边找到了一辆逛夜的旧马车，这种马车在巴黎只有夜里才看得见，仿佛白天它们会耻于外表的寒碜。

马车把他们一直送到殉教者街，他们的家门口。他们没精打采地上了楼，回到家里。对她来说，一切都已经结束。而他呢，他在想着10点就该到部里去办公。

她脱下裹在肩上的衣服，站在镜前，想再一次看看自己满载光荣的情景。但她突然大叫一声。原来她颈上的项链不见了！

她的丈夫衣服已经脱了一半，他问：

"你怎么啦？"

她转身对着他，吓得发狂了似的：

"我……我……我把福莱斯蒂埃太太的项链弄丢了。"

他兀地站了起来，惊惶万分：

"什么！……怎么！……这不可能吧！"

于是他们在袍子的皱褶里，大衣的皱褶里，口袋里，到处都搜寻一遍。哪儿也找不到。

他问：

"你拿得准离开舞会时，项链还戴在身上吗？"

"没错，在部里的衣帽室里，我还摸过它呢。"

"不过，要是丢在街上，我们会听见掉下来的声音的。准是掉在车里了。"

"对，这很可能。你注意过车号吗？"

"没注意。你呢，你也没有留意吧？"

"没有。"

他们相互对视，都变得痴呆了。末了，罗瓦赛尔又把衣服穿上，他说：

"刚才我们步行的那段路，我再去走一遍，看看是否能够找到。"

于是他出去了。她仍旧穿着晚会的服装，连上床去睡的气力都没有了，颓然倒在一张椅子上，既不生火，也毫无主意。

快7点时她丈夫回来了。他什么也没找到。

他又到警察厅和各报馆，请他们悬赏寻找，他还到租小马车的各个车行，总之，凡是有一点希望的地方他都去了。

她整天都在等候着，面对这可怕的灾难，一直处在惘然若失的状态中。

"Wait a bit. You will catch cold outside. I will go and call a cab."

But she did not listen to him, and rapidly descended the stairs. When they were in the street they did not find a carriage; and they began to look for one, shouting after the cabmen whom they saw passing by at a distance.

They went down toward the Seine, in despair, shivering with cold. At last they found on the quay one of those ancient noctambulant coupés which, exactly as if they were ashamed to show their misery during the day, are never seen round Paris until after nightfall.

It took them to their door in the Rue des Martyrs, and once more, sadly, they climbed up homeward. All was ended, for her. And as to him, he reflected that he must be at the Ministry at ten o'clock.

She removed the wraps which covered her shoulders, before the glass, so as once more to see herself in all her glory. But suddenly she uttered a cry. She no longer had the necklace around her neck!

Her husband, already half undressed, demanded:

"What is the matter with you?"

She turned madly towards him:

"I have—I have—I've lost Mme. Forestier's necklace."

He stood up, distracted.

"What! —how? —impossible!"

And they looked in the folds of her dress, in the folds of her cloak, in her pockets, everywhere. They did not find it.

He asked:

"You're sure you had it on when you left the ball?"

"Yes, I felt it in the vestibule of the palace."

"But if you had lost it in the street we should have heard it fall. It must be in the cab."

"Yes. Probably. Did you take his number?"

"No. And you, didn't you notice it?"

"No."

They looked, thunderstruck, at one another. At last Loisel put on his clothes.

"I shall go back on foot," said he, "over the whole route which we have taken to see if I can find it."

And he went out. She sat waiting on a chair in her ball dress, without strength to go to bed, overwhelmed, without fire, without a thought.

Her husband came back about seven o'clock. He had found nothing.

He went to Police Headquarters, to the newspaper offices, to offer a reward; he went to the cab

罗瓦赛尔傍晚才回来,脸庞陷了进去,颜色苍白;他一无所获。他说:

"只好给你的朋友写封信,告诉她你把项链的搭扣弄断了,现在正让人修理。这样我们就可以有回旋的时间。"

在他口授下,她写了一封信。

一星期过去了,他们失去了一切希望。

罗瓦赛尔仿佛老了5岁,他最后说:

"该考虑赔偿这件首饰了。"

第二天,他们拿着装项链的那只盒子,按照里面印着的字号,到了那家珠宝店。珠宝商查过账后说:

"太太,这串项链不是本店卖出的,只有盒子是本店给配的。"

于是他们从这家珠宝店跑到那家珠宝店,凭记忆要找一串一模一样的项链,两个人连愁带急眼看就要病倒。

他们在王宫附近一家店里找到一串钻石项链,看来跟他们寻找的完全一样。项链原价40000法郎。店里答应可以36000法郎让给他们。

他们请商店三天之内先不要卖出。他们还谈妥了,要是在2月底前找到原件,店里以34000法郎折价收回首饰。

罗瓦赛尔存有他父亲留给他的18000法郎。其余的便须去借了。

他向这个借1000法郎,向那个借500,这儿借5个路易①,那儿借3个。他签署借约,同意做足以败家的抵押,和高利贷者以及形形色色放债生利的人打交道。他整个晚年要大受影响,不管能不能偿还,他就冒险签押。对未来的忧患,即将压到身上的赤贫,瞻望到各种物质上的缺乏和种种精神上的折磨,就这样,他怀着惶惶不安,把36000法郎放到那个商人的柜台上,取来了那串新项链。

等罗瓦赛尔太太把首饰送还福莱斯蒂埃太太时,这位太太满脸不高兴地对她说:

"你本该早点儿还给我,因为我说不定要用得着呢。"

福莱斯蒂埃太太没有打开盒子,她的朋友害怕的正是这个。要是她发觉调换了一件,她会怎么想?她会怎么说?不会把她看成偷窃吗?

① 1个路易值20法郎。

companies—everywhere, in fact, whither he was urged by the least suspicion of hope.

She waited all day, in the same condition of mad fear before this terrible calamity.

Loisel returned at night with a hollow, pale face; he had discovered nothing.

"You must write to your friend," said he, "that you have broken the clasp of her necklace and that you are having it mended. That will give us time to turn round."

She wrote at his dictation.

At the end of a week they had lost all hope.

And Loisel, who had aged five years, declared:

"We must consider how to replace that ornament."

The next day they took the box which had contained it, and they went to the jeweler whose name was found within. He consulted his books.

"It was not I, madame, who sold that necklace; I must simply have furnished the case."

Then they went from jeweler to jeweler, searching for a necklace like the other, consulting their memories, sick both of them with chagrin and anguish.

They found, in a shop at the Palais Royal, a string of diamonds which seemed to them exactly like the one they looked for. It was worth forty thousand francs. They could have it for thirty-six.

So they begged the jeweler not to sell it for three days yet. And they made a bargain that he should buy it back for thirty-four thousand francs, in case they found the other one before the end of February.

Loisel possessed eighteen thousand francs which his father had left him. He would borrow the rest.

He did borrow, asking a thousand francs of one, five hundred of another, five louis here, three louis there. He gave notes, took up ruinous obligations, dealt with usurers and all the race of lenders. He compromised all the rest of his life, risked his signature without even knowing if he could meet it; and, frightened by the pains yet to come, by the black misery which was about to fall upon him, by the prospect of all the physical privation and of all the moral tortures which he was to suffer, he went to get the new necklace, putting down upon the merchant's counter thirty-six thousand francs.

When Mme. Loisel took back the necklace, Mme. Forestier said to her, with a chilly manner:

"You should have returned it sooner; I might have needed it."

She did not open the case, as her friend had so

罗瓦赛尔太太尝到了穷人那种可怕的生活。然而她勇气十足地横下了一条心。必须还清这笔骇人的债。她一定要还清。家里辞退了公仆,换了房子,租了一间屋顶下面的阁楼。

家庭里的粗活,厨下腻人的活计,她都尝遍了。碗碟锅盆都得自己洗刷,她粉红的指甲在油污的盆盆盖盖和锅子底儿上磕磕碰碰磨坏了。脏衣服、衬衫、抹布,也得自己搓洗,在绳上晾干;每天清早她把垃圾搬到楼下,送到街上,还要提水上楼,每一层都得停下来喘喘气。她穿着同下层妇女一样,挎着篮子上水果店、杂货店、猪肉店,讨价还价,挨骂受气,一个铜子一个铜子地保护她那一点儿可怜巴巴的钱。

每月都要偿付几笔债券,其余的则要续期,延长时间。

丈夫每天傍晚要替一个商人誊清账目,夜里常常干5个铜子一页的抄写活儿。

这样的生活过了10年。

10年之后,他们一切都还清了,不但高利贷的利息,连利滚利的利息也全都还清了。

罗瓦赛尔太太如今看来变得苍老了。她成了穷人家健壮有力的女人,又硬直,又粗犷。头发乱糟糟,裙子歪歪斜斜,两手通红,说话粗声大气,刷地氽大冲大洗。不过有时候她丈夫还在办公,她坐到窗前,就想起从前那一次晚会,在舞会上她是那么美丽,真是出够了风头。

如果她没有丢失这串项链,那又会怎么样呢,谁知道?谁知道?生活是多么奇异,多么变化莫测啊!真是一丁点事儿就能断送你或者拯救你!

且说有一个星期天,她到香榭丽舍去溜溜,消除一星期干活的劳累。突然之间,她瞅见一个妇人带着一个孩子在散步。这是福莱斯蒂埃太太,她还是那么年轻、那么美丽、那么动人。

罗瓦赛尔太太感到很激动。要去跟她说话吗?当然要去。如今既已把债还清,她可以把一切都告诉她了。为什么不可以去说呢?

她走了过去。

"你好,让娜。"

那一个一点儿认不出她了,心里很诧异,这个小市民模样的女人怎么这样亲密地称呼她。她嘟嘟囔囔地说:

"可是……太太!……我不知道……您大概认错

much feared. If she had detected the substitution, what would she have thought, what would she have said? Would she not have taken Mme. Loisel for a thief?

Mme. Loisel now knew the horrible existence of the needy. She took her part, moreover, all of a sudden, with heroism. That dreadful debt must be paid. She would pay it. They dismissed their servant; they changed their lodgings; they rented a garret under the roof.

She came to know what heavy housework meant and the odious cares of the kitchen. She washed the dishes, using her rosy nails on the greasy pots and pans. She washed the dirty linen, the shirts, and the dish-cloths, which she dried upon a line; she carried the slops down to the street every morning, and carried up the water, stopping for breath at every landing. And, dressed like a woman of the people, she went to the fruiterer, the grocer, the butcher, her basket on her arm, bargaining, insulted, defending her miserable money sou by sou.

Each month they had to meet some notes, renew others, obtain more time.

Her husband worked in the evening making a fair copy of some tradesman's accounts, and late at night he often copied manuscript for five sous a page.

And this life lasted for ten years.

At the end of ten years, they had paid everything, everything, with the rates of usury, and the accumulations of the compound interest.

Mme. Loisel looked old now. She had become the woman of improverished households—strong and hard and rough. With frowsy hair, skirts askew, and red hands, she talked loud while washing the floor with great swishes of water. But sometimes, when her husband was at the office, she sat down near the window, and she thought of that gay evening of long ago, of that ball where she had been so beautiful and so fêted.

What would have happened if she had not lost that necklace? Who knows? Who knows? How little a thing is needed for us to be lost or to be saved!

But, one Sunday, having gone to take a walk in the Champs Elysées to refresh herself from the labor of the week, she suddenly perceived a woman who was leading a child. It was Mme. Forestier, still young, still beautiful, still charming.

Mme. Loisel felt moved. Was she going to speak to her? Yes, certainly. And now that she had paid, she was going to tell her all about it. Why not?

She went up.

"Good-day, Jeanne."

了人吧。"

"没有。我是玛蒂尔德·罗瓦赛尔。"

她的朋友喊了起来：

"哎呀！我可怜的玛蒂尔德，你可是大变样啦！"

"是呀，自从那一次和你见面之后，我过的日子可艰难啦，真是千辛万苦——而这都是因为你！"

"因为我！那是怎么回事呀？"

"你还记得你借给我赴部里晚会去的那串钻石项链吧。"

"记得。那又怎样呢？"

"那又怎样！我把它弄丢了。"

"怎么会呢！你不是已经给我送回来了嘛。"

"我给你送回的是一模一样的另一串。这件首饰我们整整还了 10 年。你知道，对我们说来这可不是容易的事，我们是什么也没有呀……现在总算了结了，我是说不出的高兴。"

福莱斯蒂埃停住了脚步。

"你是说，你曾买了一串钻石项链来赔我那一串的吗？"

"是的。你一直没有发觉吧，是不是？两串真是一式一样。"

她感到一种足以自豪的，发自本心的快乐，于是露出微笑来。

福莱斯蒂埃太太非常激动，抓住了她的两只手。

"哎呀！我可怜的玛蒂尔德！我那串可是假的呀。顶多也就值 500 法郎！"

The other, astonished to be familiarly addressed by this plain goodwife, did not recognize her at all, and stammered:

"But—madam! —I do not know—You must be mistaken."

"No. I am Mathilde Loisel."

Her friend uttered a cry.

"Oh, my poor Mathilde! How you are changed!"

"Yes, I have had days hard enough, since I have seen you, days wretched enough—and that because of you!"

"Of me! How so?"

"Do you remember that diamond necklace which you lent me to wear at the ministerial ball?"

"Yes. Well?"

"Well, I lost it."

"What do you mean? You brought it back."

"I brought you back another just like it. And for this we have been ten years paying. You can understand that it was not easy for us, us who had nothing. At last it is ended, and I am very glad."

Mme. Forestier had stopped.

"You say that you bought a necklace of diamonds to replace mine?"

"Yes. You never noticed it, then! They were very like."

And she smiled with a joy which was proud and naïve at once.

Mme. Forestier, strongly moved, took her two hands.

"Oh, my poor Mathilde! Why, my necklace was paste. It was worth at most five hundred francs!"

┌ 讨　论 ─■

这篇小说也是以突然转折而告终：女主人公在丢了那串借来的项链，因而艰苦挣扎了 10 年之后，才知道，那些珠宝首饰到头来却是一钱不值的赝品。乍一想，这一意想不到的事情可能就像一个花招，正如《带家具出租的房间》的结尾是一个花招一样。可是，继而一想，就不见得那样了。为了确定它究竟是不是花招，不妨先考察下面这些问题。

1. 莫泊桑利用钻石项链是假的这个事实，作为发展故事情节的出发点呢，还是他姑且利

This story, too, ends with a surprising turn: the heroine, after years of privation and struggle caused by the loss of the borrowed necklace, learns that the jewels had, after all, been valueless. At first thought this revelation may seem to be a trick, just as the conclusion of "The Furnished Room" is a trick. On second thought, however, it may not be. To determine whether it is or not, investigate the following questions.

1. Has Maupassant made use of the fact that the jewels are paste as a starting point

用一下,仅仅作为出现惊人的结尾时的一种花招? 换句话说,在钻石项链是假的这个基本事实和罗瓦赛尔太太最终获悉这一消息的事实之间,有一种真正的重要区别吗? 即使她一辈子都不知道钻石项链的实情,这篇小说里会不会有讽刺意味?

2.有些人丢失了一串借来的钻石项链,就会立刻和盘托出,但罗瓦赛尔太太却始终不肯供认自己失落的首饰。她之所以不肯坦白出来,有充分的动机因素吗? 她的自尊心是一种真正的令人赞赏的自尊心,或者只不过是一种虚假的自尊心? 要不然就是两者兼而有之的一种讽刺的混合物? 她在丢失了项链以后的种种行动,可能是由她的性格所决定的。从逻辑上来说,这两个因素在小说中有什么关系?

3.这篇小说的基本意义,是取决于丢失项链(不管它是假的或真的)这个事实吗? 换句话说,玛蒂尔德·罗瓦赛尔不是那样一种贪图虚荣、了此一生的女人? (在这方面,请重读小说的第一段。)莫泊桑没有利用项链丢失的事件作为一种手段,来加速和加强罗瓦赛尔太太性格中早已固有的变化的过程? 如果这种说法可以成立的话,那么,钻石项链的虚假,不就成为这篇小说基本情节的一种象征吗? 那就是说,钻石项链的"虚假",不就代表了罗瓦赛尔太太从前所认为的生活价值的"虚假"象征吗?

4.我们有什么证据,足以说明作者意欲表示女主人会获得新生? 如果这样的话,我们又该怎样解释她最后发现自己为这些"真正的"首饰付出了代价?

5.我们可以说《埋葬》的讽嘲是建立在普通的人生观上,事情都是以惊人的滑稽的方式发生的,《年轻的布朗大爷》的讽嘲是建立在普通的人性论上,即对人生表示怀疑。而《项链》的讽嘲是建立在一种更为独特的思想观点上。那你又该怎样来形容它呢?

6.福莱斯蒂埃太太关于原来的项链是假

from which to develop his story, or has he used it as merely a piece of trickery to provide a surprise ending? In other words, is there a really important difference between the fundamental fact that the jewels are paste and the fact that Mme. Loisel eventually learns this? Would there be an irony in the story even if she had never learned the true nature of the jewels?

2. Some people, having lost a borrowed diamond necklace, would have made a clean breast of the situation at once, but Mme. Loisel never even considers confessing her loss. Is her failure to do so adequately motivated? Is her pride a true and admirable pride or merely a false pride? Or is there an ironical mixture of the two? Her actions subsequent to the loss of the necklace are presumably conditioned by her character. Are these two elements logically related in the story?

3. Does the fundamental meaning of the story depend on the fact of the loss of the necklace, whether paste or real? In other words, is not Mathilde Loisel the sort of woman who, in one way or another, would have wasted her life on some sort of vanity? (In this connection reread the first paragraph of the story.) Does not Maupassant use the loss of the necklace as a means to speed up and intensify a process already inherent in Mme. Loisel's character? If this can be maintained, then does not the falsity of the jewels become a kind of symbol for the root situation of the story? That is, does not the "falsity" of the jewels stand as a symbol for the falsity of the values by which Mme. Loisel once lived?

4. Have we any evidence that the author intended to indicate a regeneration of the heroine? If so, what are we to make of the fact that she discovers in the end that she has now paid for "real" jewels?

5. We may say that the irony of "De Mortuis" is based on a general view of life, the surprising and comic way in which things happen, and that the irony of "Young Goodman Brown" is based on a general view of human nature, the doubleness of human nature. The irony of "The Necklace" is based on something more specific. How would you describe it?

6. Mme. Forestier's revelation that the

的揭示,给我们读者指出了这篇小说的意义所在。那么,它给罗瓦赛尔太太又指出了些什么呢?

这篇小说给了我们一个良好的机会,去研究小说中如何处理时间概念的问题。小说对罗瓦赛尔太太是从青少年时期一直写到中年。她的少女时代在第一段里只是一句带过了,结婚后头几年在第二段至第五段中有所描述。接着,描写舞会那一段时间所占的篇幅相当长,直接写到的场景有 5 处,即罗瓦赛尔夫妇谈论衣着,谈论首饰,登门造访福莱斯蒂埃太太,舞会本身,以及找寻失物——项链。随后是含辛茹苦地度日,并把旧债偿清的时期,前后一共 10 年,占了一页左右篇幅。最后是结尾,即在公园里同福莱斯蒂埃太太邂逅。

我们可以看到,时间比较长的可用提要方式来写,时间比较短的可用多少富于戏剧性的方式加以直接描绘,但在两者之间务必保持一种平衡。写到比较长的那段时间,除了扫视一遍全景以外,作家还必须抓住一个重要的事实,或者抓住这个时期内最主要的感受。他还必须把这篇小说中最基本的东西——比方说,年轻的玛蒂尔德·罗瓦赛尔的性格,或者她在 10 年之中历尽艰辛的生活方式——首先集中提炼出来。但是在富于戏剧性——或有场景——的描写中,必须展示这一段时间里运动的进程,又是怎样一步一步地得到发展的。比方说,罗瓦赛尔太太怎样决定要在公园里向她的老朋友说话的,她是怎样走上去和她的朋友搭讪的,她一想到她买的那串项链竟然能蒙骗过福莱斯蒂埃太太,又是怎样感到一种出乎意外的喜悦,福莱斯蒂埃太太怎样揭露了真相,给我们指出了这一意义的重点所在:罗瓦赛尔太太的"喜悦",以及她那意味深长的自尊心——哪怕是瞬息即逝的。换句话说,这个场景给时间拍下了"特写镜头",而这段提要却摄下了"远距离拍摄的镜头"。

original necklace was paste carries to us, the readers, the point of the story. What does it carry to Mme. Loisel?

This story gives us a good chance to consider the problem of the treatment of time in fiction. The story takes Mme. Loisel from youth to middle age. Her girlhood is passed over in one sentence in the first paragraph, and the early years of marriage are treated in the second to the fifth paragraphs. Then the time of the ball is treated at considerable length in five direct scenes, the conversation about the dress, the conversation about the jewels, the visit to Mme. Forestier, the ball itself, the search for the lost necklace. Then the time of deprivation and payment, ten years, occupies a page or so. Then comes the denouement, the encounter with Mme. Forestier in the park.

There is, we see, a sort of balance between the long periods of time treated by summary, and the short periods, treated more or less dramatically by direct rendering. In treating the long periods, in which the eye sweeps, as it were, over a panorama, the writer needs to hit on the important fact, or the essential feeling of the period. He needs to distill the thing fundamental to the story—the character of the young Mathilde Loisel, or the way she lived through the ten years of deprivation. In the dramatic—or scenic—treatment the need, however, is to show the process of the movement through the time involved, how there is, step by step, a development; how, for example, Mme. Loisel decides to speak to her old friend in the park, how she accosts her, how she discovers the unexpected joy in the thought that the necklace she had bought had successfully deceived Mme. Forestier, how Mme. Forestier makes the revelation that, for us, will carry the burden of meaning: the "joy" of Mme. Loisel, her pride in a profound accomplishment—however momentary. The scene, in other words, gives the "close-ups" of time, and the summary gives the "long shots."

作家有时在一段提要中所写的,必须远远地不止是一段提要。要知道作家毕竟是在写小说,而小说需要写出人生的感受,不能仅仅只有干巴巴的事实。让我们细心留意一下,莫泊桑即使在几乎不事雕饰的提要中如何表现艰苦的 10 年生活的,他只是寥寥几笔,就使得我们仿佛亲身感受到罗瓦赛尔夫妇这种可怕的生活的特性。罗瓦赛尔太太"粉红的指甲在油污的盆盆盖盖和锅子底儿上磕磕碰碰磨坏了。每天清早她还要提水上楼,每一层都得停下来喘喘气"。莫泊桑告诉我们,"她成了穷人家健壮有力的女人,又硬直,又粗犷"。接着,他又写道:她"头发乱糟糟,裙子歪歪斜斜,两手通红,说话粗声大气,刷地板大冲大洗"。仅仅用了"大冲大洗"这四个字眼,我们看到这一切情景全都跃然纸上。

有些短篇小说,甚至有些长篇小说,几乎完全通过一些场景和直接描述就可以写下去的。例如,《埋葬》只给我们展示了短短一小段时间,和仅仅从过去岁月中概括出来的篇幅最小的破题。不过,许多短篇小说和几乎所有长篇小说,一定会前后徘徊在或多或少的直接描述和概括性叙述之间,而且这种概括性叙述中或多或少还包含描绘和分析的成分。读者最好能开始注意到,这两种基本描述方法(连同许许多多细致的差异和结合)之间有什么关系。我们一定还要反问自己,某一篇小说的感受,它所讲述的故事内容的逻辑性,以及它所给予我们的影响,同作家对这个时间问题的处理手法究竟有多大关系。当然,这里也没有一定惯例可说。我们一定要想方设法尽可能仔细而又坦率地来考察我们自己的反应,并且针对每个不同的实例,想象它要是采用了一种不同方法,将会产生什么样的效果。

(潘庆舲 译)

Often in a summary a writer must give more than mere summary. After all, he is writing fiction, and fiction wants to give the feeling of life, not merely the bare facts. Let us notice how even in the relatively bare summary in which Maupassant presents the years of hardship, he manages by a few specific touches to make us sense the quality of the life of the Loisels. Madame Loisel scraped "her rosy nails on the greasy pots and pans." When she carried up her household water every morning, she had to stop "for breath at every landing." She had become, Maupassant tells us, "strong and hard and rough." Then he writes: "With frowsy hair, skirts askew, and red hands, she talked loud while washing the floor with great swishes of water." It all comes alive with the phrase "great swishes of water." We *see* that.

Some pieces of fiction, even some novels, can proceed almost entirely by scenes, by direct presentation. For instance, "De Mortuis" gives us a single little segment of time, with only a minimum of summarized exposition from the past. Many stories and almost all novels, however, must swing back and forth between more or less direct treatments and narrative summary with more or less of description and analysis thrown in. It is well to begin to notice how these two basic kinds of treatment (with the various shadings and combinations) are related. We must ask ourselves how much the feeling of a particular story, the logic of its telling, the effect it has on us, are related to the writer's handling of this question of time. Again, there is no rule. We must try to inspect our own reactions as carefully and candidly as possible, and try to imagine what would be the effect, in instance after instance, if a different method were used.

012. 战 争

(意大利)路易吉·皮兰德娄 著　　潘庆舲 译

012. War

by Luigi Pirandello

搭乘夜间特别快车离开罗马的旅客们,不得不停留在法布里亚诺小站,直到次日凌晨才改坐连接苏尔蒙纳干线的小型老式普通列车,继续他们的旅程。

天蒙蒙亮,在5位旅客刚刚过了一宿的一节令人窒息、烟雾弥漫的二等车厢里,推推搡搡地给拥上来一个身穿重丧服的大块头女人——她那模样儿看上去简直就像一件鼓鼓囊囊的行李包裹。跟在她背后气喘吁吁、唉声叹气的,是她的丈夫——一个瘦弱不堪的小男人,脸色就像死人那样惨白,他的那双亮闪闪的小眼睛,露出胆怯不安的神色。

那个小男人最后落了座,彬彬有礼地向那些给他妻子帮过忙、让过座的旅客道了谢。随后,他转过身来,朝着正在把自己的大衣领子拉下来的那个女人,彬彬有礼地问道:

"你一切都好,亲爱的?"

妻子并没有搭理他,却把大衣领子又往上拉到眼边,遮住自己的脸孔。

"这个世道可糟透了。"那个丈夫喃喃自语,苦笑了一下。

他觉得自己责无旁贷,应该向他的同行旅伴讲一讲,那个可怜的女人确实值得人们同情,因为这场战争不仅要把他们辛苦了一辈子养大的那个年方20的独子从她身边夺走,而且还拆散了他们在苏尔蒙纳的那个老家,只好跟着儿子也到罗马去。当初他不得不去罗马上学,他们答应过只要他志愿入伍,至少6个月内保证不会把他送到前线去,可是现在突然接到了一份电报,说他3天之内就要开拔了,要求爸爸妈妈

THE passengers who had left Rome by the night express had to stop until dawn at the small station of Fabriano in order to continue their journey by the small old-fashioned local joining the main line with Sulmona.

At dawn, in a stuffy and smoky second-class carriage in which five people had already spent the night, a bulky woman in deep mourning was hoisted in—almost like a shapeless bundle. Behind her, puffing and moaning, followed her husband—a tiny man, thin and weakly, his face death-white, his eyes small and bright and looking shy and uneasy.

Having at last taken a seat he politely thanked the passengers who had helped his wife and who had made room for her; then he turned round to the woman trying to pull down the collar of her coat, and politely inquired:

"Are you all right, dear?"

The wife, instead of answering, pulled up her collar again to her eyes, so as to hide her face.

"Nasty world," muttered the husband with a sad smile.

And he felt it his duty to explain to his traveling companions that the poor woman was to be pitied, for the war was taking away from her her only son, a boy of twenty to whom both had devoted their entire life, even breaking up their home at Sulmona to follow him to Rome, where he had to go as a student, then allowing him to volunteer for war with an assurance, however, that at least for six months he would not be sent

作者简介:路易吉·皮兰德娄(Luigi Pirandello,1867—1936),意大利剧作家、小说家。1867年6月28日生于西西里的阿格里琴托,1936年12月10日卒于罗马。在德国波恩大学获得文学博士学位后,他转向创作诗作、短篇小说和长篇小说,其中最成功的是《已故的帕斯卡尔》(*The Late Mattia Pascal*,1904)。他的首部重要剧作《你是正确的(要是你觉得是的话)》(*Right You Are〔if You Think You Are〕*,1917)探索了真理的相对性,这是皮兰德娄一生探索的主题。《六个寻找作者的剧中人》(*Six Characters in Search of an Author*,1921)对比生活与艺术的关系。随后他创作了悲剧《亨利四世》(*Henry Ⅳ*,1922)。他是公认的20世纪戏剧界的重要人物,1934年他被授予诺贝尔文学奖。

即速赶来给他送行。

至于那个身穿外套的女人呢,她的身子一直在歪歪扭扭地蠕动着,不时还发出野兽一般的咆哮声。她深信,尽管刚才她的丈夫对种种情况都做了说明,也是无济于事,因为从那些十之八九跟她一样身陷困境的人们那里,就连一点儿同情的影子都引不起来的。他们中间有一个人在全神贯注地听了以后,就说:"你好歹还得要感谢上帝,因为你的儿子毕竟是现在才开拔到前线去。我的那个儿子,打从战争爆发头一天,就叫他上了前线。他已经两次受了伤回来,后来又把他派到前线去了。"

"那么我呢?我有两个儿子和三个外甥都上了前线。"另一个旅客接下去说。

"你说的也许不错,可是,就我们来说,那是我们的独子哪。"那个丈夫竟然放胆地说。

"你说这话到底有什么区别呢?你尽管可以拼命地宠爱你的独子,可是,如果说你还有几个儿子的话,那么在这两者之间,你总不能只宠爱他一个吧。父爱——不像面包,可以切成好几块,然后按照同样大小分给孩子们。不管一个孩子也好,还是十个孩子也好,做父亲的就是要一视同仁,把自己全部的爱交给他的每一个孩子。如果说这会儿我正替我的两个儿子揪心,那么,我替他们每一个人揪心,绝不是一半对一半,而是相反,还要加一倍呢……"

"说得有理……有理……"那个窘态毕露的丈夫叹了口气说,"可是,不妨就这么想(当然,我们大家都希望这可绝不是针对你的情况来说的),某某父亲有两个儿子在前线,要是失掉了一个儿子,那么毕竟还留下一个儿子可以安慰他……而……"

"是啊,"另一个人怒咻咻地回答道,"留下一个儿子可以安慰他,但是他也一定还要为了儿子而活下去。要是换上独子的父亲呢,只要儿子一死,父亲也会死去,从此了结他那痛苦的一生。这两种境遇,哪一种更糟呢?你不觉得我的情况要比你糟得多吗?"

"胡扯淡。"另一个旅客插话说,他是一个红脸膛的大胖子,暗淡无光的蓝眼睛里布满血丝。

他心里一直在扑扑地跳动着。他胸中难以控制的那股狂热劲儿,仿佛从他凸出的眼睛里突然迸发出来,其猛烈的程度,几乎叫他那孱弱的身体都支撑不住了。

"胡扯淡。"他又说,一面拼命用手捂住自己的嘴

to the front and now, all of a sudden, receiving a wire saying that he was due to leave in three days' time and asking them to go and see him off.

The woman under the big coat was twisting and wriggling, at times growling like a wild animal, feeling certain that all those explanations would not have aroused even a shadow of sympathy from those people who—most likely—were in the same plight as herself. One of them, who had been listening with particular attention, said: "You should thank God that your son is only leaving now for the front. Mine has been sent there the first day of the war. He has already come back twice wounded and been sent back again to the front. "

"What about me? I have two sons and three nephews at the front," said another passenger.

"Maybe, but in our case it is our *only* son," ventured the husband.

"What difference can it make? You may spoil your only son with excessive attentions, but you cannot love him more than you would all your other children if you had any. Paternal love is not like bread that can be broken into pieces and split amongst the children in equal shares. A father gives *all* his love to each one of his children without discrimination, whether it be one or ten, and if I am suffering now for my two sons, I am not suffering half for each of them but double. . . "

"True. . . true. . . " sighed the embarrassed husband, "but suppose (of course we all hope it will never be your case) a father has two sons at the front and he loses one of them, there is still one left to console him. . . while. . . "

"Yes," answered the other, getting cross, "a son left to console him but also a son left for whom he must survive, while in the case of the father of an only son if the son dies the father can die too and put an end to his distress. Which of the two positions is the worse? Don't you see how my case would be worse than yours?"

"Nonsense," interrupted another traveler, a fat, red-faced man with bloodshot eyes of the palest gray.

He was panting. From his bulging eyes seemed to spurt inner violence of an uncontrolled vitality which his weakened body could hardly contain.

巴,别让人们发现他早就掉落了的那两颗大门牙,"胡扯淡。难道说我们生儿育女,就是给自己图好处吗?"

在座的其他旅客都十分难堪,瞪起两眼直瞅着他。那个战争一爆发、儿子就上了前线的父亲,叹了一口气说:"你这话可说对啦。原来我们的孩子不是属于我们的,他们是属于国家的……"

"胡说八道。"那个大胖子旅客立刻反驳说,"试问我们生儿育女时,可曾想到过国家没有?我们的儿子之所以生下来,是因为……哦,不用说,就是因为他们非得生下来不可呗;所以,他们一生下来,就把我们自己的生命跟他们紧紧地拴在一起了。说穿了,就是这么回事。要知道我们是属于他们的,可他们从来都不是属于我们的。他们一到了20岁,他们活脱脱就像我们当年20岁时一模一样。我们也有爹娘,但是除此之外,还有那么多的其他东西……情人,香烟,幻想,新的领带……还有国家,当然啦,国家的号召那时我们原是响应过的——当时我们正在20岁上——哪怕我们的爹娘硬是不答应。如今,到了我们这样的年纪,我们对国家的爱,当然啦,还是不减当年,可现在我们对孩子的爱却总比它更强烈。在座各位中间不是有人(只要自己办得到的话)乐于顶替儿子上前线去吗?"

这时四周围一片沉默,每个人都点头表示赞同。

"那么,我说,"那个大胖子继续说道,"我们的那些孩子一到了20岁时,为什么我们不应该好好考虑一下他们的感情呢?像他们这样的年纪,他们认为自己对国家的爱(这会儿我说的,当然啦,是指那些好小子)甚至应该超过对我们的爱,难道说这就不自然吗?就算是这样,到头来他们一定要把我们看成寸步不离、株守家园的老头,难道说这也不自然吗?如果说今天国家还存在着,如果说国家是一种天然的必需品,就像我们每人为了不饿死都得要吃的面包一样,那就非得要有人去保卫它不可。而我们的儿子,他们一到20岁,果然就去了,而且,他们并不需要眼泪,因为他们万一死了,他们也都是乐于以身殉国的(这会儿我说的,当然啦,是指那些好小子)。现在,要是有人年纪轻轻就乐于为国捐躯,一点儿没有体验过生活中的阴暗面,厌世的情绪,琐事的烦扰,以及幻灭的痛苦……那我们还能向他提出更多的要求吗?每一个人都应该停止哭泣,每一个人都应该放声大笑,就像我现在这样……或者说,至少要感谢上帝——就像我

"Nonsense," he repeated, trying to cover his mouth with his hand so as to hide the two missing front teeth. "Nonsense. Do we give life to our children for our own benefit?"

The other travelers stared at him in distress. The one who had his son at the front since the first day of the war sighed: "You are right. Our children do not belong to us, they belong to the Country...."

"Bosh," retorted the fat traveler. "Do we think of the Country when we give life to our children? Our sons are born because... well, because they must be born and when they come to life they take our own life with them. This is the truth. We belong to them but they can never belong to us. And when they reach twenty they are exactly what we were at their age. We too had a father and mother, but there were so many other things as well... girls, cigarettes, illusions, new ties... and the Country, of course, whose call we would have answered—when we were twenty—even if father and mother had said no. Now at our age, the love of our Country is still great, of course, but stronger than it is the love for our children. Is there any one of us here who wouldn't gladly take his son's place at the front if he could?"

There was a silence all round, everybody nodding as to approve.

"Why then," continued the fat man, "shouldn't we consider the feelings of our children when they are twenty? Isn't it natural that at their age they should consider the love for their Country (I am speaking of decent boys, of course) even greater than the love for us? Isn't it natural that it should be so, as after all they must look upon us as upon old boys who cannot move any more and must stay at home? If Country exists, if Country is a natural necessity, like bread, of which each of us must eat in order not to die of hunger, somebody must go to defend it. And our sons go, when they are twenty, and they don't want tears, because if they die, they die inflamed and happy (I am speaking, of course, of decent boys). Now, if one dies young and happy, without having the ugly sides of life, the boredom of it, the pettiness, the bitterness of disillusion... what more can we ask for him? Everyone should stop crying; everyone should laugh as I do... or at least thank God—as I do—because my son, before dying sent me a message saying that he

现在这样——因为我的儿子在临死以前给我发来一个电报,说他就是以自己所能祈求的最好方式,即将结束自己的生命,所以他也死得其所了。正如你们看到的,我之所以连丧服都不肯穿……原因就在这里。"

他抖一抖自己身上的浅黄色外套给众人看。这时,他那缺了两颗大门牙的上嘴唇正在颤抖着,两眼泪汪汪而又凝止不动。他的这篇宏论也就在一阵尖笑声(这本来很可能是一阵呜咽声)中马上结束了。

"确实如此……确实如此……"人们众口一词地说。

挤在角落里、用外套遮住自己的那个女人,一直都在正襟危坐地倾听着。要知道最近 3 个月来,她在深切的悲痛中千方百计地从她丈夫和朋友们的言谈里去找一些宽心话,既可以安慰她,又可以指点她,作为一个母亲,应该如何心甘情愿地把她的儿子送出去,那里说不上是死路,也许只不过是一种危险的营生罢了。不过,她从他们滔滔不绝的言谈之中,哪怕是片言只语都没有找到……于是她心中的悲痛也就越发沉重了,因为她暗自琢磨,恐怕谁都不能替她分忧解愁。

可是刚才那位旅客所说的那些话,却使她为之愕然,几欲晕倒。她突然察觉到,问题不能归咎于别人理解不了她,而是偏偏怪她自己,达不到别人家父母那么高的思想境界,他们不仅在送别自己的儿子,甚至在获悉他们不幸阵亡的时候,也都是甘之如饴,从不号啕大哭。

她抬起头来,从她那个角落里探出身子,聚精会神地听着那个大胖子絮絮叨叨地给旅伴们讲他的儿子如何激昂慷慨,乐于为国王、为国家杀身成仁的具体过程。她恍惚觉得自己磕磕绊绊地走进了一个她从来都没有梦见过的陌生世界,在那里,她满心喜悦地听到:每一个人都在向那个一谈到儿子之死时还能如此以苦为乐的父亲表示祝贺。

蓦然间,她仿佛一点儿也没有听到刚才大家的谈话,几乎就像大梦初醒似的,转过身来向那个老人问道:

"那么……你儿子是真的死了吗?"

每个人都用眼光上下打量着她。那个老人也转过身来瞅着她,他瞪起那双凸出的、令人发指的泪汪汪的浅蓝色大眼睛,讳莫如深地端详着她的脸孔。他花了好半天时间想回答,可他总是说不出话来。他一个劲儿瞅着她,简直好像是——直到此刻听到了那个愚蠢的、自相矛盾的问题——他这才突然一下子觉察

was dying satisfied at having ended his life in the best way he could have wished. That is why, as you see, I do not even wear mourning. . . . "

He shook his light fawn coat as to show it; his livid lip over his missing teeth was trembling, his eyes were watery and motionless, and soon after he ended with a shrill laugh which might well have been a sob.

"Quite so. . . quite so. . . "agreed the others.

The woman who, bundled in a corner under her coat, had been sitting and listening had—for the last three months—tried to find in the words of her husband and her friends something to console her in her deep sorrow, something that might show her how a mother should resign herself to send her son not even to death but to a probably dangerous life. Yet not a word had she found amongst the many which had been said. . . and her grief had been greater in seeing that nobody—as she thought—could share her feelings.

But now the words of the traveler amazed and almost stunned her. She suddenly realized that it wasn't the others who were wrong and could not understand her but herself who could not rise up to the same height of those fathers and mothers willing to resign themselves, without crying, not only to the departure of their sons but even to their death.

She lifted her head, she bent over from her corner trying to listen with great attention to the details which the fat man was giving to his companions about the way his son had fallen as a hero, for his King and his Country, happy and without regrets. It seemed to her that she had stumbled into a world she had never dreamt of, a world so far unknown to her and she was so pleased to hear everyone joining in congratulating that brave father who could so stoically speak of his child's death.

Then suddenly, just as if she had heard nothing of what had been said and almost as if waking up from a dream, she turned to the old man, asking him:

"Then. . . is your son really dead?"

Everybody stared at her. The old man, too, turned to look at her, fixing his great, bulging, horribly watery light gray eyes, deep in her face. For some little time he tried to answer, but words failed him. He looked at her, almost as if only then—at that silly, incongruous question—he had suddenly realized at last that his son

到：他的儿子是真的死了——永远——永远——一去不复返了。他的脸孔一下子收缩，变成怪样；随后，他连忙从口袋里抓出一块手绢来，猛地发出一阵催人泪下、心肝欲裂，而又难以抑制的啜泣声，不由得使四座为之一惊。

was really dead—gone for ever—for ever. His face contracted, became horribly distorted, then he snatched in haste a handkerchief from his pocket and, to the amazement of everyone, broke into harrowing, heart-rending, uncontrollable sobs.

讨　论 ■

看来这篇小说也许特别缺少人物的动作姿态的描写，如果我们在这里所指的是人体特征方面的动作姿态的话。在那个女人"推推搡搡地给拥上了"车厢，她的那个胆怯不安、连声道歉的丈夫尾随着她爬了上来以后，只写到：那个身穿外套的女人，身子一直在歪歪扭扭地蠕动着；那个老人在说话时用手捂住自己的嘴巴，企图掩盖他那两颗大门牙早已落掉这一事实，随后，他又抖弄了一下他那浅黄色大衣，给众人看他身上根本没有穿丧服；那个女人却探出身子去倾听那个老人说话，当她最后向老人问到他的儿子时，所有人的眼光都一齐移到她身上；那个老人尽管拼命想要回答，可他的脸形却一下子变成个怪模样了。除了以上这些以外，再也没有关于人体动作方面的描写了。上述动作姿态在这篇小说里是必不可少的，其重要性就是在于：它们只是成为一些重要线索，借以理解小说中各个有关人物的感情和态度。换句话说，事实上，它们并不能构成情节。

这篇小说就情节本身来说，是由围绕着将孩子交给国家这一主题，各种人物所持的不同态度之间的矛盾冲突所构成的。其表现形式，差不多就是采取一种辩论的方式——各种不同的观点都依次得到阐述，并进行了争论。但它绝不是为辩论而辩论、徒具形式而已。这个主题对小说中有关人物来说，都具有非常重大的现实意义；他们的儿子都参加了战争，而其中有一个人（即身穿浅黄色大衣的那个老人）还失去了自己的儿子。所以说，这一场辩论对每一个参加者来说，无不具有极其重大的意义。

This story may seem peculiarly lacking in action, if by the term we mean physical action. After the woman has been "hoisted" into the compartment and her shy, apologetic husband has climbed in after her, there is no physical movement indicated except the wriggling and twisting of the woman under her coat, the attempt of the old man to cover his mouth with his hand when he talks in order to conceal the fact that two of his teeth are missing, his shaking of his fawn-colored overcoat to show that he does not wear mourning, the woman's bending forward to listen to the old man, the turning of all eyes upon the woman when she finally asks the old man about his son, and the contortion of his face as he tries to answer. These physical actions are important in the story, but their importance lies in the fact that they are clues to the feelings and attitudes of the persons involved in the story. They do not, in other words, actually constitute the plot.

The plot itself is constituted of the conflicts among the various attitudes held by the characters toward the subject: the giving of children to the country. The form, then, is almost the form of a debate—different points of view are stated and argued, one after another. But this is not a debate for the mere sake of debate. The persons involved are persons for whom the issue is very real; they have sons in the war, and one man, the old man in the fawn-colored overcoat, has already lost his son. That is, the debate is dramatically meaningful for the participants.

在这场辩论中,那个女人和那个老人所持的态度,就是代表了两种极端的看法。那个女人虽然一言不发,但是,我们知道她的看法,正如作者所描述的:"至于那个身穿外套的女人呢,她的身子一直在歪歪扭扭地蠕动着,不时还发出野兽一般的咆哮声。她深信,尽管刚才她丈夫对种种情况都做了说明,也是无济于事,因为从那些十之八九跟她一样身陷困境的人们那里,就连一点儿同情的影子都引不起来的。"她心中的悲痛,犹如病痛一样,具有一触即发的性质,也是无法理解或无法讨论的;剧痛时,她只能歪歪扭扭地蠕动身子,或发出野兽一般的声音。另一种极端的看法,即儿子已经罹难的那个老人的观点,却得到了最充分的阐述。他坚持认为,每一个人生儿育女,首先不是给自己图好处;其次,每一个年轻有为、富有远大理想的儿子,他虽然热爱父母,但他会更加热爱国家;好儿女就是为国阵亡,也会含笑九泉;有人年纪轻轻,就乐于为国捐躯,好歹也算摆脱了生活中的阴暗面、厌世的情绪、琐事的烦扰和幻灭的痛苦;因此,做父母的一知道儿子已经壮烈牺牲——照他所说的——就应该像他现在那样感到欣慰,放声大笑,或者至少应该感谢上帝。那位老人已将伤亡和悲痛的基本意义做了极其完整,而又富有哲理的论述。两种极端的思想态度,就是包括了这些内容。

现在,我们可以看到,决定这篇小说里所谓情节模式的,就是以上这两种极端的看法之间的对立。但它并不是一种静止不变的对立——仅仅是叙述两者之间的分歧。两种看法都改变了——甚至还完全颠倒过来了。

先说那个女人,本来她从她丈夫或她朋友那里根本没法得到安慰,因为她既然觉得谁都不能替她分忧解愁,所以就开始从这个陌生人的话里寻找慰藉。正因为他确实失去了一个儿子,所以他一定懂得,一定能够替她分忧解愁。他一定也很明智,因为他的损失比她要大

The two extreme positions in the debate are held by the woman and the old man. The woman says nothing, but we know what her position is: "The woman under the big coat was twisting and wriggling, at times growling like a wild animal, feeling certain that all those explanations would not have aroused even a shadow of sympathy from those people who—most likely—were in the same plight as herself." Her grief has a kind of immediacy, like physical pain; it is beyond reasoning or discussion; she can only twist as in pain or utter meaningless animal-like sounds. The other extreme position, that of the old man whose son has been killed, is the most fully stated. He argues that one does not, in the first place, have children for one's own benefit; that, in the second place, a son, being young and idealistic, is more drawn by love of country than by love of parents; that if a son dies for his country he dies happy—if he is "decent"; that one who dies young and happy has been spared the ugly side of life, boredom, pettiness, disillusion; that, therefore, a parent whose son has died heroically should be happy and laugh, as he says he does, or should at least thank God. That is, the old man has completely argued away, philosophized away, all of the fundamental sense of loss and grief. Such are the two extremes of attitude.

Now, what may be called the plot pattern of the story depends upon the opposition between these two extreme views. But it is not a static opposition—a mere statement of difference. Both views are modified—even reversed.

First, the woman, who had been unable to take consolation from her husband or her friends, because, as she felt, nobody could share her feelings, begins to take consolation from the words of the stranger. He has actually lost a son, and therefore he must know, must be able to share, her own feelings. He must be wise, because his loss is greater than

得多,要知道她的儿子现在还活着。再说那个老人极其激进的看法。和她丈夫与朋友们的所有看法都大相径庭。他竟然用一些豪言壮语对悲痛加以绝对否定——凡此种种,都使得她感到自己"磕磕绊绊地走进了一个她从来都没有梦见过的世界"。有人尽管知道自己的儿子确已死亡,但在谈到他的伤亡时却如此慷慨激昂,在她看来这似乎是不可置信的。所以"几乎就像大梦初醒似的",她开口问他,"那么……你儿子是真的死了吗?"

要是那个老人简单地回答说,"是的,他死了。"她(至少就暂时来说)也许乐于接受他的看法。要是那个老人再一次向她保证,说他儿子"真的"死了,那么,她就可能尽量仿效他那崇高的态度。她同样也能正视死亡这一事实。

但是,她提出的使小说推向高潮、并形成小说焦点的那个问题,如今在那个老人听来却是意味深长的,正如他先前所抒发的那些宏论在她听来也是意味深长的一样。所以,就像开头我们发现他已经改变了她的看法一样,随后我们发现她也改变了他的看法。当她发出"是真的死了"的问题时,每个人都"用眼光上下打量着"她——好像她说了一些很不得体、唐突无礼和令人难堪的话,好像她一下子泄露了一些令人毛骨悚然的秘密。那个老人也是一个劲儿瞅着她,但他却始终回答不了她的问题。他突然头一次才觉察到自己的儿子是"真的死了——永远——永远——一去不复返了"。现在,他一下子陷入一种卑微的、原始的、毫无理智的痛苦之中,如同她先前亲历其境那样,于是,他也就泣不成声了。

由此可见,以那个女人基本上纯属个人的、没有客套的感情为一方,又以那个老人就制度、礼俗、理智、理想的补偿等等所做出的阐述为另一方,这两者之间产生了矛盾,所以,这篇小说就得看上面的这个矛盾如何发展而定。在这里,有一种充满讽刺意味的对照,一种不可协调的对照——或者说,这一种对照,如果

hers, for her son is yet alive. Furthermore, the very violence of the old man's position, its difference from all the views given her by husband and friends, its absolute denial of grief by its heroic terms, make her feel that she has "stumbled into a world she had never dreamt of." It seems incredible to her that a man whose son is really dead can speak thus of his loss. So "almost as if waking up from a dream" she asks him, "Then... is your son really dead?"

Presumably, if the man should say, simply, "Yes, he is dead," she would be prepared to accept, for the moment at least, his position. If the man could assure her once more that the son is "really" dead, then she could try to imitate his heroic attitude. She, too, would be able to face the fact of death.

But her question, which provides the climax, the focal point of the story, reveals something to the old man, just as his previous words have revealed something to her. So, as in the first place, we find her position modified by him, we find now, in the second place, his position modified by her. When she utters the words "really dead" everybody "stares" at her—as though she has said something out of place, something impolite and embarrassing, as though she had divulged some horrible and shocking secret. The old man stares at her too, and cannot answer. For the first time, he realizes that his son is "really dead—gone for ever—for ever." He is caught now in the abject, animal-like, unreasoning misery, in which she had previously been held, and bursts into sobs.

The story then, depends on a conflict between the basic, personal, unformulable emotion on the one hand, and systems, codes, reason, ideal compensations, and interpretations on the other. There is here an ironical contrast, an irreconcilable contrast—or a contrast, that, if reconcilable, is reconcilable only by the greatest effort. The equilibrium of the man who has made the reconciliation is upset, we see, by the slightest touch, by the

要求得到协调,那只有通过最大的努力才能获得解决。那个老人思想上原来早已达到和谐一致,但是我们看到,他的那种平衡状态,被那个女人所提出的"愚蠢的、自相矛盾"——但是带有根本性——的问题轻轻地一碰,一下子就给破坏了。所以,我们能不能假设,作者无非是说礼俗、制度、理智、义务、理想等等都不重要,唯有个人感情——这才是最最重要吗?看来不能。要是这样的话,作者为什么要列举出老人的发言对那个创巨痛深的女人所产生的那种巨大的吸引力呢?不,看来皮蓝德娄是通过戏剧性方式,将一种基本矛盾寓于人所共有的经验之中——旨在说明这对立的两个方面是始终存在的,而且哪一方面都不容忽视。

　　让我们回过头来,再谈谈这篇小说的情节模式。它先是从那个女人和那个老人的两种极端不同的看法开始,接着是两人的看法相互发生变化,最后则集中到她向他提出的那个问题上。换言之,我们认为在某种意义二说,这一篇小说包含着两个"故事"——一个是那个女人改变态度的故事,另一个则是那个老人改变态度的故事。当作者给我们介绍他们两人时,每个人似乎都是坚定不移地执著于自己的特殊看法。那么,我们该怎样来说明他们态度的变化呢?这篇小说里所安排的态度变化,都能令人接受吗?

　　我们先对那个女人的态度变化进行一些分析。开始,是那个老人的一片宽慰话,使她感到那么新奇、那么崇高,因而把她吸引住了。其次,又因为他真的失去了一个儿子这一事实,使她觉得他是会"理解"她的。但是,对那个老人的态度变化,我们就没法进行那么详细的分析了。他的态度变化是突如其来的。那么,他在小说的前半部讲到自己的事情时有没有夸大的地方呢?有没有确实的迹象,说明他正是针对自己,而不是针对别人而竭力进行辩护呢?有没有暗示出一点儿歇斯底里呢?在这方面,我们不妨考察一下,在他说了自己身

woman's "silly, incongruous"—but fundamental—question. Are we to assume, therefore, that the author is simply saying that codes, systems, reason, obligations, ideals do not matter, that the only thing that matters is the fact of personal emotion? It seems not. If so, why would he illustrate the powerful appeal the old man's words make to the woman sunk in grief? No, it seems that Pirandello is putting, in dramatic terms, a basic conflict in human experience—is saying that the two terms of the opposition are always in existence and that neither can be ignored.

　　Let us turn again to the plot pattern of the story: the movement away from the two extreme positions of the woman and the old man, the process of mutual modification focused, finally, on the question she asks him. In other words, we have, in a sense, two "stories" within a story—the story of the woman's change of attitude and the story of the old man's change of attitude. Each of the two persons seems, when introduced, to be firmly fixed in a special attitude. How are we to account for the changes? Are the changes prepared for and made acceptable in the story?

　　We have some analysis of the woman's change. It is the novelty, the heroic quality, of the consolation offered by the old man, that attracts her. Further, the fact that he has really lost a son makes her feel that he will "understand" her. But we have no such explicit analysis of the change on the part of the old man. His change of attitude comes as a surprise. But does he not overstate his case in the earlier part of the story? Is there not an inkling of the fact that he is trying to argue against himself rather than against other people? Is there not a hint of hysteria? In this connection one might investigate the following sentence, which comes just after he has said that he does not even wear mourning:

上连丧服都不穿以后,马上就来了下面这么一段话:"他抖一抖自己身上的浅黄色外套给众人看。这时,他那缺了两颗大门牙的上嘴唇正在颤抖着,两眼泪汪汪而又凝止不动。他的这篇宏论也就在尖笑声(这本来很可能是一阵呜咽声)中结束了。"因此,我们可以认为:那个女人改变自己的态度,是为那个老人的最后转变做准备的。事实上,他代表了人生经验中对立的,但是又不能否认的那一面。

前面就这篇小说所做出的分析是不完全的。下面一些问题对充分阐明和理解作者的创作方法,是至关重要的。

──思考题──■

1. 在这篇小说中对人物动作姿态的描写,有什么重要性? 它们怎样为理解各种人物的感情和态度提供线索? 比如,考虑一下这个事实:那个老人一开头竭力捂住自己嘴巴,但后来却又把它忘了。

2. 在下面句子中带着重号的词语,它们有什么重要意义? "那个老人也转过身来瞅着她,他瞪起那双凸出的、令人发指的泪汪汪的浅蓝色大眼睛,讳莫如深地端详着她的脸孔。"

3. 试想一下另写一篇小说。比如说,写那个老人有一个儿子仅仅上了前线,却跟同车厢的旅客们进行争辩,按照现在这篇小说的写法,一味劝说他们。到了某一个车站,他接到了一份电报,说他的儿子已经阵亡,于是,他立刻迸发出了一阵"心肝欲裂,而又难以抑制的啜泣声",而大家都大吃一惊地直瞅着他。为什么说这样的写法同皮兰德娄上面所写的那篇小说一比,就要大为逊色呢?

（潘庆舲 译）

"He shook his light fawn coat as to show it; his livid lip over his missing teeth was trembling, his eyes were watery and motionless, and soon after he ended with a shrill laugh which might well have been a sob." Then, we may take the attitude of the woman herself as a kind of preparation for the old man's final change. She represents, as it were, the opposite pole of experience, but an undeniable pole.

The foregoing analysis of the story is not complete. Certain other questions are important for a full interpretation and for an understanding of the author's method.

1. What is the importance of the physical actions in the story? How do they offer clues to the feelings and attitudes of the characters? Consider, for instance, the fact that the old man at first tries to cover his mouth but later forgets to do so.

2. What is the significance of the words we have italicized in the following sentence? "The old man, too, turned to look at her, fixing his great, bulging, *horribly* watery light gray eyes, *deep* in her face."

3. Imagine another version of this story. Suppose that the old man, whose son is merely at the front, argues with the other people in the compartment, and persuades them, as in the present version of the story; at a station, he receives a telegram saying that his son has been killed, whereupon he bursts into "heart-rending, uncontrollable sobs" while they stare at him in amazement. Why would such a version be inferior to the story as Pirandello tells it?

013. 国王迷

(英)路德亚德·吉卜林 著　　潘庆舲 译

013. The Man Who Would Be King

by Rudyard Kipling

　　　　凡和王孙公子称兄道弟，或与贫丐莫逆交者，则为俊杰。

上面引述的这个守则，虽可作为处世待人的圭臬，但要身体力行起来，却又谈何容易。我曾经一而再地与贫丐结交朋友，由于当时环境，我们谁都无法查明对方是不是俊杰。不过，现在我仍然还得和王孙公子称兄道弟，虽然我曾经一度接近过类似下面的这种人物：他也许可以称之为一个真正的国王，并使一个王国——军队、法院、岁入和政策全部为之逆转。但在今天，深恐我的那位国王早已命归西天，如果说我想要得到一顶王冠，那我就得给自己去寻觅了。

事情是从阿杰梅尔开往姆豪的火车上开始的。由于收支预算出现了亏空，迫不得已这才出门远行，搭坐的不是票价只及头等车票一半的二等车，而是确实令人可怕的客货混合车厢。这种客货混合车厢，里面没有软席靠垫；旅客也是五方杂处，不是欧亚混血种，就是夜间长途旅行时令人作呕的土著，或是喝得烂醉如泥、逗人直发笑的游手好闲者。客货混合车厢里旅客从不光顾小吃部。他们自带一包包、一罐罐干粮，向当地小贩买糖块吃，还随便喝路旁的生水。到了热天，为什么客货混合车厢里要抬出死人来，而且平时总是让人瞧不起，原因就在这里。

赶上我坐的那节客货混合车厢，恰好是空无一人，直到纳西拉巴德才走进来一个身躯高大、衣着随便的男人。按照客货混合车厢的惯例，我们寒暄后就攀谈起来。他同我一样是漂泊无定，浪迹天涯，但他

Brother to a Prince and fellow to a beggar if he be found worthy.

THE law, as quoted, lays down a fair conduct of life, and one not easy to follow. I have been a fellow to a beggar again and again under circumstances which prevented either of us finding out whether the other was worthy. I have still to be brother to a Prince, though I once came near to kinship with what might have been a veritable King and was promised the reversion of a Kingdom—army, law courts, revenue and policy all complete. But, today, I greatly fear that my King is dead, and if I want a crown I must go and hunt it for myself.

The beginning of everything was in a railway train upon the road to Mhow from Ajmir. There had been a Deficit in the Budget which necessitated traveling, not Second-class, which is only half as dear as First-class, but by Intermediate, which is very awful indeed. There are no cushions in the Intermediate class, and the population are either Intermediate, which is Eurasian, or native, which for a long night journey is nasty, or Loafer, which is amusing though intoxicated. Intermediates do not patronize refreshment rooms. They carry their food in bundles and pots, and buy sweets from the native sweetmeat-sellers, and drink the roadside water. That is why in the hot weather Intermediates are taken out of the carriages dead, and in

作者简介：路德亚德·吉卜林（**Rudyard Kipling**，1865—1936），英国小说家、诗人。1865 年 12 月 30 日生于印度孟买，1936 年 1 月 18 日卒于英国伦敦。他在英国长大，但是他回到印度成为一名记者。他很快以自己的短篇小说作品成名，如《山中故事》（*Plain Tales from the Hills*，1888；其中包括《国王迷》）。随后他出版诗集《营房谣》（*Barrack-Room Ballads*，1892），他的诗有很强的韵律感，多为叙事民谣。他的作品还包括《丛林之书》（*The Jungle Book*）、《勇敢的船长》（*Captains Courageous*，1897）、《基姆》（*Kim*，1901）、童书《原来如此》（*Just So Stories*，1902）和童话集《普克山的小精灵》（*Puck of Pook's Hill*，1906）。1907 年他被授予诺贝尔文学奖。

附庸风雅,爱喝威士忌。他娓娓动听地讲了许多他亲历其境的事情,他曾经深入到印度帝国的僻远角落,以及为了乞食糊口不惜冒着生命危险的惊人经历。他说:"如果说印度全国上下都像你我之辈,连第二天的口粮都还不知道上哪儿去找,那么,国家要支出的岁入就不是 7000 万——而是 7 亿整了。"我朝他嘴巴和下巴颏儿望了一眼,不用说跟他有同感。

这样,我们就议论开政治了。大凡游手好闲的人在议论政治的时候,他们总是从事物的底层,亦即生活阴暗面来观察的。接下来我们就谈到了邮政设施,因为我的朋友要从下一站给阿杰梅尔拍发一个回电,而阿杰梅尔正是西行时由孟买至姆豪的干线上的一个岔道口。我的那个朋友除了吃饭钱 8 安那[①] 以外已是身无分文,而我由于上面提到的收支预算拮据,根本不名一文。再说,此刻我要到人迹罕至的荒地去,虽然我应该继续和财政部保持联系,但是那里却没有电报局。所以说要资助他,我实在力不从心。

"我们不妨对那个站长吓唬一下,让他马上就发出一个电报,"我的朋友说道,"不过那么一来就得要盘问你和我了,可我这些天来手头正忙呢。你说你过几天再坐这趟车回来?"

"10 天之内。"我说。

"你改成 8 天不行吗?"他说,"我可有急事要办。"

"10 天以内我可以拍电报给你。如果你认为那样合适的话。"我说。

"现在我一想,他不一定能收到这个电报。事情是这样的。他在 23 日离德里去孟买。那就是说,他将在 23 日夜里经过阿杰梅尔。"

"但是此刻我要去印度沙漠。"我马上说明来意。

"好,好得很。"他说,"那你就要在马尔瓦尔枢纽站换车,才能进入乔德普尔地区——你非得那么个走法不可——而他将在 24 日凌晨乘坐孟买邮车经过马尔瓦尔站。那时你赶得到马尔瓦尔站吗? 这可不会给你增添什么麻烦的,因为我知道:从印度中部各邦可以采集的东西很少——就算你装作《巴克伍兹曼报》的记者。"

"你老是耍弄那套把戏吗?"我问。

"不止一次啦。可是,当地居民会发现你的,所以趁你还有时间用刀子捅他们以前,就得找人护送到边

_____
　① 印度货币名。

all weathers are most properly looked down upon.

My particular Intermediate happened to be empty till I reached Nasirabad, when a huge gentleman in shirt sleeves entered, and, following the custom of Intermediates, passed the time of day. He was a wanderer and a vagabond like myself, but with an educated taste for whisky. He told tales of things he had seen and done, of out-of-the-way corners of the Empire into which he had penetrated, and of adventures in which he risked his life for a few days' food. "If India was filled with men like you and me, not knowing more than the crows where they'd get their next day's rations, it isn't seventy millions of revenue the land would be paying—its seven hundred millions," said he; and as I looked at his mouth and chin I was disposed to agree with him. We talked politics—the politics of Loaferdom that sees things from the underside where the lath and plaster is not smoothed off—and we talked postal arrangements because my friend wanted to send a telegram back from the next station to Ajmir, which is the turning-off place from the Bombay to the Mhow line as you travel westward. My friend had no money beyond eight annas which he wanted for dinner, and I had no money at all, owing to the hitch in the Budget before-mentioned. Further, I was going into a wilderness where, though I should resume touch with the Treasury, there were no telegraph offices. I was, therefore, unable to help him in any way.

"We might threaten a Stationmaster, and make him send a wire on tick," said my friend, "but that'd mean inquiries for you and for me, and I've got my hands full these days. Did you say you are traveling back along this line within any days?"

"Within ten," I said.

"Can't you make it eight?" said he. "Mine is rather urgent business."

"I can send your telegram within ten days if that will serve you," I said.

"I couldn't trust the wire to fetch him now I think of it. It's this way. He leaves Delhi on the twenty-third for Bombay. That means he'll be running through Ajmir about the night of the twenty-third."

境。不过,这里说的是我的那个朋友。我一定要捎个口信给他,把我的近况告诉他,要不然他不知道该上哪儿去。我请你老兄多多帮忙,但愿你务必准时离开中部印度,赶到马尔瓦尔站跟他会面。并对他说:'他去南方已有一个星期了。'他会知道那句话里的意思的。他是个蓄红胡子的大汉,他这个人可真了不起。你将在二等车厢里找到他,他活脱脱像个绅士睡在那里,四周围都是他的行李包裹。可你用不着害怕。拉下车窗,说:'他去南方已有一个星期了。'他一听心里就明白啦。这样,你停留在那里的时间仅仅缩短两天。我,作为一个陌生人,要求你——到西邹去走走。"他加重语气地说道。

"那现在你是从哪儿来的!"我说。

"从东部来,"他说,"现在我希望你就老老实实地把这个口信捎给他——看在我母亲和你自己母亲的面上。"

虽然英国人通常不会一提到母亲就心软下来,但由于某些显而易见的原因,我几乎要表示赞同了。

"这事实在非同小可,"他说,"我为什么要你去办这件事,原因就在这里——而现在,我知道我可以放心让你去办了。马尔瓦尔车站上的一节二等车厢里,睡着一个红头发的男人。你肯定记得住的。我下一站就下车,我一定留在那里,直到他来了,或者给我送来了我所需要的东西。"

"我一定把这个口信捎给他,只要我赶得上他,"我说,"看在你和我的母亲面上,我就要给你进一言。就是现在千万不要以《巴克伍兹曼报》记者的身份在印度中部各州到处走访活动了。因为有一个真正的报社记者正在这里到处采访,这样说不定会给你招来麻烦呢。"

"谢谢你,"他直率地说,"那个蠢家伙什么时候才走呢?现在我可再也受不了啦,因为他正在把我的工作给毁了。我要把我所知道的有关他寡母的情况,向德吉姆伯王公①谈一谈,让他吓一跳。"

"那么,他对待自己的寡母又是怎样的呢?"

"当她悬在横梁上的时候,他给她灌满了红辣椒水,还用拖鞋揍得她昏死过去。那是我亲自发现的,因此,唯有我一个人,才敢到邦里去拿封住自己嘴巴的钱。可是,他们想方设法要伤害我,就像从前我在乔敦姆纳敛钱时他们所作所为一样。不过,我说你在

_____
① 王公,指旧时印度各邦的统治者。

"But I'm going into the Indian Desert," I explained.

"Well *and* good," said he. "You'll be changing at Marwar Junction to get into Jodhpore territory—you must do that—and he'll be coming through Marwar Junction in the early morning of the twenty-fourth by the Bombay Mail. Can you be at Marwar Junction on that time? 'Twon't be inconveniencing you because I know that there's precious few pickings to be got out of these Central India States—even though you pretend to be correspondent of the *Backwoodsman*."

"Have you ever tried that trick?" I asked.

"Again and again, but the Residents find you out, and then you get escorted to the Border before you've time to get your knife into them. But about my friend here. I *must* give him a word o' mouth to tell him what's come to me or else he won't know where to go. I would take it more than kind of you if you was to come out of Central India in time to catch him at Marwar Junction, and say to him, 'He has gone South for the week.' He'll know what that means. He's a big man with a red beard, and a great swell he is. You'll find him sleeping like a gentleman with all his luggage round him in a Second-class compartment. But don't you be afraid. Slip down the window, and say, 'He has gone South for the week,' and he'll tumble. It's only cutting your time of stay in those parts by two days. I ask you as a stranger—going to the West," he said, with emphasis.

"Where have *you* come from?" said I.

"From the East," said he, "and I am hoping that you will give him the message on the Square—for the sake of my Mother as well as your own."

Englishmen are not usually softened by appeals to the memory of their mothers, but for certain reasons, which will be fully apparent, I saw fit to agree.

"It's more than a little matter," said he, "and that's why I ask you to do it—and now I know that I can depend on you doing it. A Second-class carriage at Marwar Junction, and a red-haired man asleep in it. You'll be sure to remember. I get out at the next station, and I must hold on there till he comes or sends me what I want."

"I'll give him the message if I catch him," I said,

马尔瓦尔枢纽站会把我的口信捎给那个人吗?"

　　他在路旁一个小站下了车,我顿时陷入沉思之中。我不止一次地听说过:有人冒充新闻记者,向一些小的邦政府威胁说要揭发,乘此机会敲竹杠,但我过去从来没有碰到过任何一个像上面那样敛钱的人。他们过着一种苦的生活,而且常常是突如其来地死掉了。各地邦政府对可能揭发他们独特的施政方法的英国报纸都很惧怕,于是,他们竭力用香槟酒来堵住新闻记者的嘴巴,或者用四匹马拉的四轮大马车干脆把他们驱逐出境。他们根本不了解,只要压迫和罪恶还没有越过界限,不论是谁,对于各地邦政府内政都是丝毫不感兴趣的,而各地统治者一年到头不是吸毒、酗酒,就是病魔缠身,动弹不得。各个土邦由上帝创造出来,只不过增添了山川如画的景色、老虎和大量长篇累牍的文件罢了。它们是地球上暗无天日的地方,充满了难以想象的暴行,一方面有现代化的铁路和电报,另一方面还处在哈伦·拉希德①的时代。我下了火车以后,就同好几个国王打交道去了。在这8天时间里,我的生活却大起大落,几经变化。有时候我身穿华服,陪伴王孙公子和政界要人,宴饮时手执水晶酒杯和纹银盘碟。但也有的时候,我却躺在地上,用化妆盒当做盘子,随便抓到什么东西,就狼吞虎咽地吃起来,而且还得喝生水,裹上如同我仆人使用的破毯子睡觉。这是习以为常,毫不稀奇的事啦。

　　随后,根据我原先约定的合适日期,我动身前往印度大沙漠。夜间邮车把我带到马尔瓦尔枢纽站,有一条由地方当局经营,虽然狭窄得可笑,却是逍遥自在的铁路线,从那里一直通往乔德普尔。来自德里的孟买邮车在马尔瓦尔停留时间很短。我刚进站,邮车才抵达,我正好赶到站台,上了车。这趟列车通共只有一节二等车厢。我放下车窗,低头望着被车上毯子盖没了一半的火红的络腮胡子。那人正在呼呼大睡,他就是我要寻找的人,于是我轻轻地碰了一下他的胸口。他哼了一声,醒过来了。我借着灯光看见了他的脸孔。那是一个闪闪发亮的大脸盘。

　　"又是车票吧?"他说。

　　"不,"我说,"我要转告你,他到南方去已有一个星期了。他到南方去已有一个星期了!"

_____

　　① 哈伦·拉希德,是阿拔斯王朝(763—809)巴格达哈里发,其事迹详见《一千零一夜》。

"and for the sake of your Mother as well as mine I'll give you a word of advice. Don't try to run the Central India States just now as the correspondent of the *Backwoodsman*. There's a real one knocking about here, and it might lead to trouble."

"Thank you," said he, simply, "and when will the swine be gone? I can't starve because he's ruining my work. I wanted to get hold of the Degumber Rajah down here about his father's widow, and give him a jump."

"What did he do to his father's widow, then?"

"Filled her up with red pepper and slippered her to death as she hung from a beam. I found that out myself, and I'm the only man that would dare going into the State to get hush money for it. They'll try to poison me, same as they did in Chortumna when I went on the loot there. But you'll give the man at Marwar Junction my message?"

He got out at a little roadside station, and I reflected. I had heard, more than once, of men personating correspondents of newspapers and bleeding small Native States with threats of exposure, but I had never met any of the caste before. They lead a hard life, and generally die with great suddenness. The Native States have a wholesome horror of English newspapers, which may throw light on their peculiar methods of government, and do their best to choke correspondents with champagne, or drive them out of their mind with four-in-hand barouches. They do not understand that nobody cares a straw for the internal administration of Native States so long as oppression and crime are kept within decent limits, and the ruler is not drugged, drunk, or diseased from one end of the year to the other. Native States were created by Providence in order to supply picturesque scenery, tigers, and tall writing. They are the dark places of the earth, full of unimaginable cruelty, touching the Railway and the Telegraph on one side, and, on the other, the days of Harun-al-Raschid. When I left the train I did business with divers Kings, and in eight days passed through many changes of life. Sometimes I wore dress clothes and consorted with Princes and Politicals, drinking from crystal and eating from silver. Sometimes I lay out

列车开始移动了。那个红胡子的人擦擦自己的眼睛。"他到南方去已有一个星期了。"他又说了一遍,"那正是他所说的傲慢无礼的话吗?他还说过我得给你一些什么东西吗?——反正我不会乐意的。"

"他没有说过。"我说完转身就走,眼看着红灯消失在黑暗之中。天气冷得够呛,因为大风正把沙土都给刮了起来。我登上了自己的车厢——这一回可不是客货混合车厢——就睡觉去了。

那个红胡子的人要是给我一个卢比①,本来我可以把它珍藏起来,作为一件相当稀奇古怪的趣事的纪念品。但我所得到的唯一的酬偿,只是意识到我已经尽到了自己的职责。

后来,我暗自思忖:那两个人好像都是我的朋友,即使他们凑在一起,冒充新闻记者,那也干不出什么名堂来;他们要是去"抢劫"中部印度或南拉杰普塔纳濒于绝境中的一个小邦,说不定会使自己陷入严重的困境。所以说,要对那些想放逐他们的人,凭我的回忆尽可能精确地把他们描述一番,就不免有些困难了(后来,我就听说,他们终于从德古姆伯边境被押了回来)。

随后,我总算好歹又回到了编辑部,在那里除了每天出报以外,根本没有什么国王之类的事情可说。但因报社编辑部对社会上三教九流的人物似乎都有吸引力,所以也就很难保持良好的秩序。身在深闺后院的印度小姐派出代表团,前来要求主笔即刻放弃自己全部职责,不要去报道基督徒在一个穷乡僻壤的贫民窟里分发奖品的事迹;有一些上校在结束了戎马倥偬的生涯以后,就坐下来拟定了10篇、12篇或24篇有关资历与选拔的社论提纲;有些传教士想要了解一下,他们作为辱骂人们的工具,很有意见,极想离开,但为什么老是不让他们脱身而去,而且此刻还在诅咒受到编辑部同仁特别保护的某个兄弟教会;有一些走投无路的剧团向报社联合声明,他们实在付不出广告费,但从新西兰或塔希提岛②一回来,他们将连同利息把它一起付清;还有一些人发明了专利大风扇牵引器、火车挂钩,以及不易破损的刀剑和轴干,他们来访时口袋里装着说明书,一连好几个钟头向报社同仁介绍情况;一些茶叶公司办事人员走进了报社,对撰稿

---

① 印度货币名。
② 位于南太平洋一岛屿。

upon the ground and devoured what I could get, from a plate made of a flapjack, and drank the running water, and slept under the same rug as my servant. It was all in the day's work.

Then I headed for the Great Indian Desert upon the proper date, as I had promised, and the night Mail set me down at Marwar Junction, where a funny little, happy-go-lucky, native-managed railway runs to Jodhpore. The Bombay Mail from Delhi makes a short halt at Marwar. She arrived as I got in, and I had just time to hurry to her platform and go down the carriages. There was only one Second-class on the train. I slipped in the window, and looked down upon a flaming red beard, half covered by a railway rug. That was my man, fast asleep, and I dug him gently in the ribs. He woke with a grunt, and I saw his face in the light of the lamps. It was a great and shining face.

"Tickets again?" said he.

"No," said I. "I am to tell you that he is gone South for the week. He is gone South for the week!"

The train had begun to move out. The red man rubbed his eyes. "He has gone South for the week," he repeated. "Now that's just like his impidence. Did he say that I was to give you anything? —'Cause I won't."

"He didn't," I said, and dropped away, and watched the red lights die out in the dark. It was horribly cold, because the wind was blowing off the sands. I climbed into my own train—not an Intermediate Carriage this time—and went to sleep.

If the man with the beard had given me a rupee I should have kept it as a memento of a rather curious affair. But the consciousness of having done my duty was my only reward.

Later on I reflected that two gentlemen like my friends could not do any good if they foregathered and personated correspondents of newspapers, and might, if they "stuck up" one of the little rat-trap states of Central India or Southern Rajputana, get themselves into serious difficulties. I therefore took some trouble to describe them as accurately as I could remember to people who would be interested in deporting them; and succeeded, so I was later informed, in having them

人详细说明他们的计划书；化装舞会的主办人常常埋怨报社对他们的舞会报道得过于详尽了；一些陌生的贵妇人衣裙窸窣作响，走进来说："我要许许多多女士名片，请马上印出来。"显而易见，这就是主笔职责的一部分了；甚至闹荡在大马路的每一个流氓，都认为自己应该去报社求职，充当一名校对员。在编辑部里，电话铃声整天都在疯狂地响个不停，一些国王正在欧洲大陆上被杀害，一些帝国却在扬言道："你也是一个帝国。"格拉德斯通先生正在责骂英国自治领，而专替报社送稿件的黑孩子就像疲惫不堪的蜜蜂一样，正在呜呜呜地哀叫"卡阿—比，恰伊—哈—耶"（意思是：副本要吧），本子上大部分都是黑糊糊的，如同莫特雷德①的盾牌一样。

　　不过，这是一年之中兴味盎然的时节。除此以外，还有剩下来的 6 个月，那就没有人来登门求访了。寒暑表上的度数一英寸、一英寸地往上升高，一直升至玻璃管顶端。报社编辑部里，除了案头的灯光以外，一片黑暗；印刷机一直在转动，摸上去滚烫滚烫；但谁都懒于执笔，写的净是印度山中避暑胜地的趣闻，或者撰写讣告而已。那时候，电话铃声就成为一种恐怖的讯号，因为它会向你报告你所熟悉的男人、女人突如其来死去了。痱子像罩袍似的布满了全身。你还得坐下来写道："来自库德·詹塔·汗地区报道，疫病稍有增加，此次突然蔓延，纯属偶然性，现经该地区当局大力拯救，几乎已近敛迹。但我们对所述的死亡情事则深表遗憾。"

　　那时，疫病确实突然发生过，只要记事报道得越少，撰稿人心中也就越安宁。但是，帝国和国王依然如同往日一样自私地尽情玩乐；领班却认为，一张日报在 24 小时内确实应该出版一次；而所有在山中避暑的人们，在他寻欢作乐时却说："我的天哪！为什么报纸不能办得更活泼些？我敢说这儿山上发生的事就够多啦。"

　　那就是不为人们所知道的一些秘闻，正如广告上常说的，"如蒙惠顾，包君满意"了。

　　正是在那样一个极其不吉利的季节里，报社开始在星期六夜间——这就是说，按照伦敦报纸惯例，是在星期日凌晨——出版本周最后一期报纸。这是一

_____

　　①　莫特雷德，是亚瑟王传奇圆桌骑士之一，以奸逆而著称。

headed back from Degumber borders.

Then I became respectable, and returned to an Office where there were no Kings and no incidents except the daily manufacture of a newspaper. A newspaper office seems to attract every conceivable sort of person, to the prejudice of discipline. Zenana-mission ladies arrive, and beg that the Editor will instantly abandon all his duties to describe a Christian prize-giving in a back-slum of a perfectly inaccessible village; Colonels who have been overpassed for commands sit down and sketch the outline of a series of ten, twelve, or twenty-four leading articles on Seniority *versus* Selection; missionaries wish to know why they have not been permitted to escape from their regular vehicles of abuse and swear at a brother missionary under special patronage of the editorial We; stranded theatrical companies troop up to explain that they cannot pay for their advertisements, but on their return from New Zealand or Tahiti will do so with interest; inventors of patent punkah-pulling machines, carriage couplings, and unbreakable swords and axletrees call with specifications in their pockets and hours at their disposal; tea companies enter and elaborate their prospectuses with the office pens; secretaries of ball committees clamor to have the glories of their last dance more fully expounded; strange ladies rustle in and say, "I want a hundred lady's cards printed *at once*, please," which is manifestly part of an Editor's duty; and every dissolute ruffian that ever tramped the Grand Trunk Road makes it his business to ask for employment as a proofreader. And, all the time, the telephone bell is ringing madly, and Kings are being killed on the Continent, and Empires are saying—"You're another," and Mister Gladstone is calling down brimstone upon the British Dominions, and the little black copy boys are whining, "*kaa-pi chay-ha-yeh*" (copy wanted) like tired bees, and most of the paper is as blank as Modred's shield.

But that is the amusing part of the year. There are other six months wherein none ever come to call, and the thermometer walks inch by inch up to the top of the glass, and the office is darkened to just above reading light, and the press machines are red-hot of

件非常方便的事,因为当铅字排好刚放到印刷机上不久,熹微的晨光就在半个钟头以内使寒暑表上的度数从华氏96°又骤然下降至84°,在那种沁人肺腑的凉意之中——在你开始祈求这种凉意以前,你根本不会知道华氏84°在草地上该有多么凉快——一个疲惫不堪的人,就可以安然入睡,趁着炎热还没有把他惊醒。

赶上星期六夜晚,我只要把报纸编好,一放到印刷机上,就算愉快地尽到了自己的职责。不管某一个国王,或某一个朝臣,或某一个名妓,或某一个社区行将销声匿迹,或者得到一部新宪法,或者在世界另一边出现了一些重大事件,报纸为了赶上最新电讯稿,直到最后一分钟,尽可能保留出空白版面。这是一个伸手不见五指的漆黑的夜晚,而且又闷热得比6月之夜更叫人透不过气来。西边刮来的热风,正在干得像火绒似的树丛间嘤嘤作响,仿佛马上就要下雨了。不时有一颗几乎煮沸了的水点落下来,像一只青蛙似的在尘土里扑腾着,但我们这些疲乏透顶的人都知道那只不过是假象罢了。倒是印刷间比报社编辑部更阴凉些,所以我就坐在那里,听咔嚓咔嚓地排捡铅字的声响,以及夜枭在窗边的哀鸣声,而那些几乎赤身裸体的排字工人老是在擦脑门上的汗水,嘴里一个劲儿喊着要水喝。那条好像对我们一直隐瞒其内容的电讯稿,直到此刻还是迟迟未到,虽然热风渐渐停息下来了,铅字最后也已经排好了,整个大地依然处在令人窒息的酷热之中,傻等着那条重大新闻。我迷迷糊糊地在暗自纳闷:那条电讯是不是一件大喜事,这个行将死亡的人,或在苦斗中的人们,是不是知道电讯稿迟到以后将会造成的那种麻烦。虽然产生紧张的情绪,除了炎热和忧虑以外,没有其他特殊原因,但是,当座钟的时针指向3点钟,机器飞轮转上两三次,看到一切都已井井有条,就在我说可以开印之前,本来我也许还会尖声叫喊起来呢。

随后,沉寂的气氛被机器飞轮发出的嘎嘎声震碎了。我站起身来要走,但有两个身穿白大褂的人站在我面前。头一个人说:"就是他!"第二个人也说:"没错,是他!"他们两人哈哈大笑的声音,几乎就像机器声一样震耳欲聋。同时,他们都在擦脑门上的汗水。"我们看见对面马路上有一处灯光还亮着。刚才我们贪图凉快,正躲在小沟里睡觉呢。我就对我身边的朋友说,'报社编辑部里还有人在办公。让我们走去跟他说说,我们怎样从德古姆伯邦被撤回来的。'"说上

touch, and nobody writes anything but accounts of amusements in the Hill stations or obituary notices. Then the telephone becomes a tinkling terror, because it tells you of the sudden deaths of men and women that you knew intimately, and the prickly heat covers you as with a garment, and you sit down and write: "A slight increase of sickness is reported from the Khuda Janta Khan District. The outbreak is purely sporadic in its nature, and, thanks to the energetic efforts of the District authorities, is now almost at an end. It is, however, with deep regret we record the death, etc."

Then the sickness really breaks out, and the less recording and reporting the better for the peace of the subscribers. But the Empires and the Kings continue to divert themselves as selfishly as before, and the Foreman thinks that a daily paper really ought to come out once in twenty-four hours, and all the people at the Hill stations in the middle of their amusements say, "Good gracious! Why can't the paper be more sparkling? I'm sure there's plenty going on up here."

That is the dark half of the moon, and, as the advertisements say, "must be experienced to be appreciated."

It was in that season, and a remarkably evil season, that the paper began running the last issue of the week on Saturday night, which is to say, Sunday morning, after the custom of a London paper. This was a great convenience, for immediately after the paper was put to bed, the dawn would lower the thermometer from 96° to almost 84° for half an hour, and in that chill—you have no idea how cold is 84° on the grass until you begin to pray for it—a very tired man could set off to sleep ere the heat roused him.

One Saturday night it was my pleasant duty to put the paper to bed alone. A King or courtier or a courtesan or a community was going to die or get a new Constitution, or do something that was important on the other side of the world, and the paper was to be held open till the latest possible minute in order to catch the telegram. It was a pitchy black night, as stifling as a June night can be, and the *loo*, the red-hot wind from the westward, was booming among the tinder-dry trees and pretending that the rain was on its

面这些话的,是他们中间个子较小的那个人。他正是我在姆豪列车上遇到过的那个人,而他的同伴就是马尔瓦尔枢纽站上的那个红胡子。这个人的眉毛和那个人的络腮胡子,我绝没有认错。

那时我可不太高兴,因为我心里正想去睡觉,不打算跟那些游手好闲的人嚼舌根。"你们想要干什么呀?"我问。

"办公室里挺凉快,同你闲扯上半个钟头,好吗?"那个红胡子说,"我们都喜欢喝一点——反正那个合约还没有开始生效,皮奇,所以你用不着东张西望——但我们真正需要的是忠告。我们并不缺钱。现在我们只是请你赏个脸,因为我们发现是你叫我们在德古姆伯上了当。"

我从印刷间走到四壁挂满地图的令人窒息的办公室,那个红胡子来回搓着自己的双手。"妙极了,"他说,"这算是找对了地方啦。现在,先生,让我向你介绍一下,皮奇·卡内汉大哥,就是他,丹尼尔·德雷沃特二哥,就是我,关于我们的职业嘛,介绍得越少越好,因为我们活到现在,各式各样活儿都干过。什么士兵、水手、排字工人、摄影师、校对员、街头传教士,而且还当过《巴克伍兹曼报》记者,因为我们认为这个报社正需要一个记者。卡内汉并没有喝醉酒,我也是那样。乍一看,你就知道这话一点儿都不假。这就不会使你把我的话给打断了。我们每人要向你拿一支雪茄烟,你对我们就会有所了解。"

于是,我察言观色了一番。那两个人绝对没有喝醉,所以我就给了他们每人一杯不冷不热的白兰地苏打水。

"好,好极了,"卡内汉眉毛一扬说,随手抹去了大胡子旁边的白沫,"现在就让我谈吧,丹①。在整个印度大地上,都有我们的足迹。什么锅炉装配工、火车司机、小包工头等等,样样杂活儿我们都干过了,我们的结论是:在我们这样的人看来,印度这个地方还不够大呢。"

他们两个对那间办公室来说,当然是太大了。当他们坐在那张大桌子跟前的时候,德雷沃特的大胡子似乎占去了半个房间,卡内汉的两个肩膀则占去了那剩下的半个房间。卡内汉继续说下去:"这个国家的资源并没有完全得到利用,因为它毕竟是归他们所统

_____

① 丹,即丹尼尔的简称。

heels. Now and again a spot of almost boiling water would fall on the dust with the flop of a frog, but all our weary world knew that was only pretense. It was a shade cooler in the press room than the office, so I sat there, while the type clicked and clicked and the nightjars hooted at the windows, and the all but naked compositors wiped the sweat from their foreheads and called for water. The thing that was keeping us back, whatever it was, would not come off, though the *loo* dropped and the last type was set, and the whole round earth stood still in the choking heat, with its finger on its lip, to wait the event. I drowsed, and wondered whether the telegraph was a blessing, and whether this dying man, or struggling people, was aware of the inconvenience the delay was causing. There was no special reason beyond the heat and worry to make tension, but as the clock hands crept up to three o'clock and the machines spun their flywheels two or three times to see that all was in order, before I said the word that would set them off, I could have shrieked aloud.

Then the roar and rattle of the wheels shivered the quiet into little bits. I rose to go away, but two men in white clothes stood in front of me. The first one said, "It's him!" The second said, "So it is!" And they both laughed almost as loudly as the machinery roared, and mopped tneir foreheads. "We see there was a light burning across the road and we were sleeping in that ditch there for coolness, and I said to my friend here, 'The office is open. Let's come along and speak to him as turned us back from the Degumber State'," said the smaller of the two. He was the man I had met in the Mhow train, and his fellow was the red-bearded man of Marwar Junction. There was no mistaking the eyebrows of the one or the beard of the other.

I was not pleased, because I wished to go to sleep, not to squabble with loafers. "What do you want?" I asked.

"Half an hour's talk with you cool and comfortable, in the office," said the red-bearded man. "We'd *like* some drink—the Contrack doesn't begin yet, Peachey, so you needn't look—but what we really want is advice. We don't want money. We ask you as a

治的,所以就是不让你去碰它一下。他们把他妈的所有时间都花在统治上面了,你想要举起铁锹,削凿岩石,勘察石油,或者干类似那样的事情,所有地方政府必定要说,'别管它,让我们来管理。'所以说,事实上就是那样,我们只好不去管它,就到另外一个地方去,在那里,你可以独来独往,好像是自己的天下一样。我们可不是微不足道的人,我们什么东西都不害怕,就是喝酒例外,为此,我们就签订了一份合约。所以说,我们将要到外地去当国王了。"

"去当由我们亲自掌权的国王。"德雷沃特喃喃自语道。

"哦,那当然啦,"我说,"你们一直头顶烈日,到处漂泊流浪,此刻正好赶上一个暖洋洋的夜晚,不妨睡一觉,对这个怪念头再好好想一想?还是明天来吧。"

"我们既没有喝醉,也没有中暑,"德雷沃特说,"这个怪念头我们反复考虑了已有半年时间。而且还要查阅许多书籍和地图集。我们的结论还在当前世界上,可供两个铁腕人物瓜分的,只有一个地方。人们都管它叫卡菲里斯坦。照我的估计,这个地方位于阿富汗右上角顶端。离白沙瓦不超过 50 英里。在他们那里,异教徒崇拜的神就有 32 个,而我们俩就要成为第 33 个神。那是一个崇山峻岭的国家,但是那一带的女人却漂亮透顶。"

"可是话又说回来,那正是合约规定所禁忌的,"卡内汉说,"一是女人,二是美酒,丹尼尔。"

"我们知道的通共就是这些,可惜那个地方谁都没有去过。听说那里的人们爱打仗,所以,凡是人们爱打仗的地方,谁只要懂得如何训练士兵,总能当上国王的。我们打算到那个地方去,不论我们找到的是哪一个国王,我们就对他说:'你要把你的仇敌消灭掉吗?'接着,我们就会指点他如何训练士兵,因为搞那个行当,我们再精通不过啦。随后,我们就把那个国王颠覆掉,篡夺了他的王位,建立一个新王朝。"

"你越过边界还不到 50 英里,恐怕早就被人斩成肉酱了。"我说,"你必须经过阿富汗才能到达那个地区。那里极目望去,都是崇山峻岭,冰川壁立,连英国人都裹足不前,视为畏途。那里的人完全是蛮夷之邦,你们即使到了那里,也干不出什么名堂来。"

"那可差不离呢,"卡内汉说,"不过,你要是认为我们有点儿痴头痴脑,这才更叫我们高兴呢。现在我们上你这儿来,就是要了解这个国家的情况,读一本

favor, because you did us a bad turn about Degumber. "

I led from the press room to the stifling office with the maps on the walls, and the red-haired man rubbed his hands. "That's something like," said he. "This was the proper shop to come to. Now, Sir, let me introduce to you Brother Peachey Carnehan, that's him, and Brother Daniel Dravot, that is *me*, and the less said about our professions the better, for we have been most things in our time. Soldier, sailor, compositor, photographer, proofreader, street preacher, and correspondents of the *Backwoodsman* when we thought the paper wanted one. Carnehan is sober, and so am I. Look at us first and see that's sure. It will save you cutting into my talk. We'll take one of your cigars apiece, and you shall see us light. "

I watched the test. The men were absolutely sober, so I gave them each a tepid peg.

"Well *and* good," said Carnehan of the eyebrows, wiping the froth from his mustache. "Let me talk now, Dan. We have been all over India, mostly on foot. We have been boiler-fitters, engine-drivers, petty contractors, and all that, and we have decided that India isn't big enough for such as us. "

They certainly were too big for the office. Dravot's beard seemed to fill half the room and Carnehan's shoulders the other half, as they sat on the big table. Carnehan continued: "The country isn't half worked out because they that governs it won't let you touch it. They spend all their blessed time in governing it, and you can't lift a spade, nor chip a rock, nor look for oil, nor anything like that without all the Government saying, 'Leave it alone and let us govern. ' Therefore, such as it is, we will let it alone, and go away to some other place where a man isn't crowded and can come to his own. We are not little men, and there is nothing that we are afraid of except Drink, and we have signed a Contrack on that. *Therefore*, we are going away to be Kings. "

"Kings in our own right," muttered Dravot.

"Yes, of course," I said. "You've been tramping in the sun, and it's a very warm night, and hadn't you better sleep over the notion? Come tomorrow. "

有关它的书,再让我们查看一些地图。你尽管说我们都是傻瓜蛋,只要把你的那些书给我们看看就得了。"他转过身来指着那些书柜。"你们真是那么正经八百的吗?"我说。

"有一点儿呗,"德雷沃特温和地说,"你有最详细的大地图,即使卡菲里斯坦在那上面还是一大片空白,以及不管你还有哪些书,都给我们看看吧。书我们都还看得懂,尽管我们文化程度很不够。"

我把那张比例为每英寸等于32公里的印度大地图和两张篇幅较小的边境地图都打开来,还把英国大百科全书中字首为INF-KAN的那一大本书也搬下来了。于是,他们两人就查阅起来了。

"看这里哪!"德雷沃特把大拇指摁在地图上说,"往上可以通到贾格达拉克,皮奇和我都知道那条路。当年我们跟着罗伯特的军队到过那里。我们必须通过拉格曼地区,再往右拐弯,才能到达贾格达拉克。随后,我们进入山区——高度是14000英尺到15000英尺——那个地方冷得要命,但从地图上看好像还不算太远。"

我把伍德著的《乌浒水河源考》一书递给了他。卡内汉就埋头啃那部大百科全书去了。

"他们那里人种混杂,"德雷沃特若有所思地说,"这么一来,我们就没法了解他们各部落的名字了。部落越多,他们越要打仗,对我们就越有利啦。从贾格达拉克到阿吉格。嗯!"

"不过,关于这个国家的所有资料,都只是概括介绍,很难说得上十分精确。"我不以为然地说,"至于这个国家究竟怎样,老实说,谁都说不上来。这里是联合后勤研究会的档案材料。念一下贝留的意见是什么。"

"贝留净是吹牛呗!"卡内汉说,"丹,他们都是异教徒,简直多如牛毛,但这本书在这里却说:他们认为同我们英国人有血亲关系。"

我抽着烟,他们两人则在浏览雷弗泰和伍德的著作,以及地图集和大百科全书。

"你等着也白搭,"德雷沃特彬彬有礼地说,"现在大约4点钟了。你要是想去睡觉的话,我们就会在6点钟以前离开,反正我们不会把什么报纸都偷走的。你用不着在这里坐等。我们两个疯子从来不做缺德的事。明儿晚上你到旅店来一趟,我们就跟你挥手告别啦。"

"Neither drunk nor sunstruck," said Dravot. "We have slept over the notion half a year, and require to see Books and Atlases, and we have decided that there is only one place now in the world that two strong men can Sar-a-*whack*. They call it Kafiristan. By my reckoning it's the top right-hand corner of Afghanistan, not more than three hundred miles from Peshawar. They have two and thirty heathen idols there, and we'll be the thirty-third. It's a mountainous country, and the women of those parts are very beautiful."

"But that is provided against in the Contrack," said Carnehan. "Neither Women nor Liqu-or, Daniel."

"And that's all we know, except that no one has gone there, and they fight, and in any place where they fight, a man who knows how to drill men can always be a King. We shall go to those parts and say to any King we find, 'D'you want to vanquish your foes?' and we will show him how to drill men; for that we know better than anything else. Then we will subvert that King and seize his Throne and establish a Dy-nasty."

"You'll be cut to pieces before you're fifty miles across the Border," I said. "You have to travel through Afghanistan to get to that country. It's one mass of mountains and peaks and glaciers, and no Englishman has been through it. The people are utter brutes, and even if you reached them you couldn't do anything."

"That's more like," said Carnehan. "If you could think us a little more mad we would be more pleased. We have come to you to know about this country, to read a book about it, and be shown maps. We want you to tell us that we are fools and to show us your books." He turned to the bookcases.

"Are you at all in earnest?" I said.

"A little," said Dravot, sweetly. "As big a map as you have got, even if it's all blank where Kafiristan is, and any books you've got. We can read, though we aren't very educated."

I uncased the big thirty-two-miles-to-the-inch map of India, and two smaller Frontier maps, hauled down volume INF-KAN of the *Encyclopaedia Britannica*, and the men consulted them.

"See here!" said Dravot, his thumb on the map. "Up to Jagdallak, Peachey and me know the road. We

"你们真是两个傻瓜蛋呀,"我回答说,"你们一到了边境,就得碰壁而归,要不然你们一踏上阿富汗的国土,就被吃掉了。你们去那个地方需要钱呢,还是要推荐介绍一番?下个星期我可以帮助你们找个事由。"

"下个星期我们自己的活儿还忙不过来呢。谢谢你。"德雷沃特说,"看来要当一个国王,可也不是那么容易。我们一旦把我们的那个王国整治得井然有序,就会通知你。你就可以来匡助我们治理那个王国。"

"两个疯子还签订过那么一个合约呢?"卡内汉带着几分矜色说,并拿出半张油腻腻的信纸给我看。那半张信纸上写着如下条款,我照着抄录下来,堪称天下奇闻:

立约人谨遵守以下各条款,但愿上帝作证,阿门。

第一条 立约人将共同解决以下问题,即是:当上卡菲里斯坦国王。

第二条 此问题一旦获得解决,立约人应拒绝任何美酒和女人(不论是黑种、白种,或棕种),以免跟任何有害的人种发生混杂现象。

第三条 立约人举止态度应保持尊严、审慎,如果其中有一人遇到麻烦,另一人仍应留在他身边。

> 立约人
> 皮奇・托利弗・卡内汉(签名)
> 丹尼尔・德雷沃特(签名)
> (上述两人均为赋闲绅士①)

"最后那一条大可不必写上的,"卡内汉不觉有点儿脸红地说,"但看来也是一种惯例吧。至于游手好闲的人是什么样的人,你是知道的——不过,丹,我们只要一出印度国界,就不算是游手好闲的人啦——如果我们不是一本正经的话,你说我们还会签订那么一份合约吗?我们所以要禁忌美酒和女人这两个东西,就是为了使人生变得更有意义。"

"如果你们要去进行这样愚蠢透顶的冒险,你们真的活腻了,不乐意再活下去了。千万别放火烧报社编辑部,"我说,"9点钟以前,你们通通滚出去。"

---

① "赋闲绅士"为作者所杜撰,在这里意思是指"无所事事的正人君子",纯系一种自我讽刺。

---

was there with Roberts's Army. We'll have to turn off to the right at Jagdallak through Laghmann territory. Then we get among the hills—fourteen thousand feet—fifteen thousand—it will be cold work there, but it don't look very far on the map."

I handed him Wood on the *Sources of the Oxus*. Carnehan was deep in the Encyclopaedia.

"They're a mixed lot," said Dravot, reflectively; "and it won't help us to know the names of their tribes. The more tribes the more they'll fight, and the better for us. From Jagdallak to Ashang. H'mm!"

"But all the information about the country is as sketchy and inaccurate as can be," I protested. "No one knows anything about it really. Here's the file of the United Services' Institute. Read what Bellew says."

"Blow Bellew!" said Carnehan. "Dan, they're an all-fired lot of heathens, but this book here says they think they're related to us English."

I smoked while the men poured over Raverty, Wood, the maps, and the Encyclopaedia.

"There is no use your waiting," said Dravot, politely. "It's about four o'clock now. We'll go before six o'clock if you want to sleep, and we won't steal any of the papers. Don't you sit up. We're two harmless lunatics and if you come, tomorrow evening, down to the Serai we'll say good-by to you."

"You *are* two fools," I answered. "You'll be turned back at the Frontier or cut up the minute you set foot in Afghanistan. Do you want any money or a recommendation down-country? I can help you to the chance of work next week."

"Next week we shall be hard at work ourselves, thank you," said Dravot. "It isn't so easy being a King as it looks. When we've got our Kingdom in order we'll let you know, and you can come up and help us to govern it."

"Would two lunatics make a Contrack like that?" said Carnahan, with subdued pride, showing me a greasy half-sheet of note paper on which was written the following. I copied it, then and there, as a curiosity:

我离开的时候,他们还在仔细观看各种地图,并在那张"合约"背后记下一些要点。"明天务必来旅店哪,"——这就是他们的告别词。

孔哈森旅店是一座四方形的大房子,真是藏污纳垢的场所,来自北方的一群群骆驼和骡马,正在那里装卸货物。中亚细亚所有各族的人在那里可以说应有尽有,但十之八九还是来自印度大陆的人。巴尔赫人和布哈拉人在那里一碰到了孟加拉人和孟买人,总是少不了暗算对方。在孔哈森旅店你可以买到小马驹、绿松石、波斯猫、马褡裢、肥尾羊和麝香,而且还可以不费分文,搞到许多稀奇古怪的东西。第二天下午,我就往那个旅店走去,想看看我的那两个朋友是不是有意信守自己的约言,还是喝得酩酊大醉,此刻早已倒下了。

一个穿着破衣烂衫的祭司,手里一本正经地捻着一个儿童玩的纸褶旋螺,高视阔步地向我走过来。后面是他的仆人,这会儿弯着腰在装载一大篓泥塑玩具。当这两个人正在给两头骆驼装货的时候,旅店里的客人都直瞅着他们,不断发出尖厉的笑声。

"这个祭司是个疯子,"一个马贩子对我这样说,"他就要到喀布尔去,把这些玩具卖给埃米尔①。赶明儿他要么是被尊奉为座上嘉宾,要么就是脑袋落地。今儿早晨他才到这里,打这以后,他的一举一动,都是疯疯癫癫的。"

"糊涂鬼自有老天爷照应哪,"一个脸颊扁平的乌兹别克人用蹩脚的印地语在结结巴巴地说话,"他们未卜先知,能预言未来一切吉凶祸福。"

"我的商队刚进入离那个山口不远的地方,就被希恩沃里斯人搞掉了,难道他们也都能预言到吗!"一个尤苏雷扎伊商人咕哝着说,原来他是拉杰普塔纳一家商行的代理人,正在越过边界的时候,他的货物全被落入凶恶的强盗手中,现在他的不幸遭遇却成为赶集人的笑柄。"喂,祭司,你从哪儿来的,你又打算上哪儿去呢?"

"我刚从鲁姆来,"这个祭司一面挥动他的纸褶旋螺,一面大声嚷道,"是从鲁姆来的,叫许许多多的魔鬼吹一口气,我就漂洋过海给刮来了②!啊,小偷、强

---

① 埃米尔,伊斯兰国家和地区统治者的称号。

② 这位假装疯祭司的冒险家在这里说的所有话语,自然都是疯话,不知所示,因而是毫无意义的,今如实译出,仅供参考而已。

This Contract between me and you pursuing witnesseth in the name of God-Amen and so forth.

(One) That me and you will settle this matter together; i. e.; to be Kings of Kafiristan.

(Two) That you and me will not, while this matter is being settled, look at any Liquor, nor any Woman, black, white or brown, so as to get mixed up with one or the other harmful.

(Three) That we conduct ourselves with dignity and discretion and if one of us gets into trouble the other will stay by him.

Signed by you and me this day.

Peachey Taliaferro Carnehan.

Daniel Dravot.

Both Gentlemen at Large.

"There was no need for the last article," said Carnehan, blushing modestly; "but it looks regular. Now you know the sort of men that Loafers are—we are Loafers, Dan, until we get out of India—and do you think that we would sign a Contrack like that unless we was in earnest? We have kept away from the two things that make life worth having."

"You won't enjoy your lives much longer if you are going to try this idiotic adventure. Don't set the office on fire," I said, "and go away before nine o'clock."

I left them still poring over the maps and making notes on the back of the "Contrack." "Be sure to come down to the Serai tomorrow," were their parting words.

The Kumharsen Serai is the great four-square sink of humanity where the strings of camels and horses from the North load and unload. All the nationalities of Central Asia may be found there, and most of the folk of India proper. Balkh and Bokhara there meet Bengal and Bombay, and try to draw eyeteeth. You can buy ponies, turquoises, Persian pussy-cats, saddle-bags, fat-tailed sheep, and musk in the kumharsen Serai, and get many strange things for nothing. In the afternoon I went down there to see whether my friends intended to keep their word or were lying about drunk.

A priest attired in fragments of ribbons and rags stalked up to me, gravely twisting a child's paper whirligig. Behind was his servant bending under the

盗、撒谎的人,皮尔·汗为猪、狗祝福,此外还有作伪证的人!有谁带领这个叨受神恩佑护的人到北方去,把这些法力无边的神符通通卖给那个埃米尔吗?赶明儿骆驼四肢不会擦伤,儿子们不会生病,但愿让我加入商队的先生们出门远行期间,他们的妻子仍然忠于自己的丈夫。有谁助我一臂之力,让那个罗尔人的国王跤着银鞋跟金拖鞋走路呢?但愿皮尔·汗保佑他马到成功!"他扯开了他那宽大的布袷袢的下摆,踮起脚尖,在拴上了套的骡马行列中间转来转去。

"有一支商队将从白沙瓦启程,20 天以后到达喀布尔,赫兹鲁特,"这个尤苏富扎伊商人说道,"我的几头骆驼跟他们一块儿走。但愿你也一起走,这会让我们走好运呢。"

"即使此刻走我也乐意!"那个祭司大声嚷道,"我将跨上我的那些带翅膀的骆驼,一天就到白沙瓦!喂!哈利尔·米尔·汗,"他冲着他的仆人大声吆喝道,"快把骆驼牵出来,不过,让我先骑上我自己的那头骆驼。"

那头骆驼一跪在地上,他纵身一跃,骑在它的背上,就转过身来冲我大声喊道,"你也上路走一程吧,萨希布①,我就会卖给你一道符咒——凭这道符咒,你包管当上卡菲里斯坦的国王。"

那时,天刚破晓,我跟着那两头骆驼走出了旅店的大门,一直走到大路上,那个祭司这才停住不走了。

"关于那个事儿,你到底有什么高见?"这时他用英语说话了,"卡内汉不会说他们的黑话,所以我就叫他做我的仆人。他做得真是顶呱呱的。我在国内到处流浪,已有 14 个年头,可不是一无所得呀。我说起那些黑话来,不是很干净利落吗?我们将在白沙瓦搭上一支商队,直至到达贾格达拉克,以后,再看看能不能找到一些毛驴,把我们的骆驼给换下来,下一步就打进卡菲里斯坦去。把纸褶旋螺送给那个埃米尔,我的老天哪!把你的手伸进那些骆驼的鞍囊,说说你摸到了什么东西。"

我摸到了一支马提尼枪的枪托,以及其他同样的东西。"通共 20 支,"德雷沃特沉着地说,"通共 20 支,还有相应的弹药,都藏在纸褶旋螺和泥娃娃的底下。"

"万一你和这些东西都被人截获了,但愿老天爷

---

① 旧日印度、巴基斯坦对人的尊称,寓有先生、老爷之意。

load of a crate of mud toys. The two were loading up two camels, and the inhabitants of the Serai watched them with shrieks of laughter.

"The priest is mad," said a horse-dealer to me. "He is going up to Kabul to sell toys to the Amir. He will either be raised to honor or have his head cut off. He came in here this morning and has been behaving madly ever since."

"The witless are under the protection of God," stammered a flatcheeked Usbeg in broken Hindi. "They foretell future events."

"Would they could have foretold that my caravan would have been cut up by the Shinwaris almost within shadow of the Pass!" grunted the Eusufzai agent of a Rajputana trading house whose goods had been feloniously diverted into the hands of other robbers just across the Border, and whose misfortunes were the laughingstock of the bazaar. "Ohé, priest, whence come you and whither do you go?"

"From Roum have I come," shouted the priest, waving his whirligig; "from Roum, blown by the breath of a hundred devils across the sea! O thieves, robbers, liars, the blessing of Pir Khan on pigs, dogs, and perjurers! Who will take the Protected of God to the North to sell charms that are never still to the Amir? The camels shall not gall, the sons shall not fall sick, and the wives shall remain faithful while they are away, of the men who give me place in their caravan. Who will assist me to slipper the King of the Roos with a golden slipper with a silver heel? The protection of Pir Khan be upon his labors!" He spread out the skirts of his gaberdine and pirouetted between the lines of tethered horses.

"There starts a caravan from Peshawar to Kabul in twenty days, *Huzrut*," said the Eusufzai trader. "My camels go therewith. Do thou also go and bring us good luck."

"I will go even now!" shouted the priest. "I will depart upon my winged camels, and be at Peshawar in a day! Ho! Hazar Mir Khan," he yelled to his servant, "drive out the camels, but let me first mount my own."

He leaped on the back of his beast as it knelt,

会帮你的忙!"我说,"一支马提尼枪的价值,在帕坦人①那边,就等于枪支重量的白银哪。"

"本钱就有 15000 卢比——每一个卢比,我们都是通过乞讨、借贷,或者干脆偷窃才得到的——一股脑儿都押在这两头骆驼身上了,"德雷沃特说,"我们可不会被人抓住的。我们将要跟随一支定期的商队通过开伯尔山口。一个可怜巴巴的疯子祭司,谁敢碰他一碰?"

"你想要的每件东西,现在都得到了吗?"我惊骇不止地问。

"还没有呢,不过我们马上就要得到了。老兄,给我一件纪念品,表表你的心迹。昨天你帮了我的忙,还有在马尔瓦尔的那一次。俗语说得好,你准定拿到我的半个王国。"我从我的表链上摘下一只漂亮的小指南针,就递给了那个祭司。

"再见,"德雷沃特一面说,一面小心翼翼地向我伸过手来,"在最近那么几天里,这是我们最后一次同一个英国人握手。卡内汉,跟他握握手。"正当第二头骆驼从我身旁走过时,他大声嚷道。

卡内汉俯下身子来同我握手。随后,那两头骆驼沿着尘土飞扬的大路走过去了。我孤零零地站在那里,禁不住暗自纳闷。他们经过乔装打扮以后,我竟然连半点儿破绽都看不出来。在旅店的这一幕表明他们跟当地人想的完全相同。所以说,正是机会凑巧,卡内汉和德雷沃特满可以人不知鬼不觉地在阿富汗各地到处漂泊流浪了。可是,再往远处走,他们就会找到死亡,而且肯定是一种可怕的死亡。

10 天以后,我有一个老乡,从白沙瓦给我捎来了当天的新闻消息,他在信上这样写道:"最近这里发生了令人捧腹大笑的趣闻,原来有一个疯子祭司,照他的估计,就可以把那些花里胡哨的小饰物说成是法力无边的符咒,通通卖给布哈拉埃米尔殿下。他从白沙瓦出境后,就加入了前往喀布尔的第二支夏季商队。商人们都觉得喜出望外,因为他们有迷信思想,认为有了这些疯疯癫癫的家伙们结伴同行,准会使他们走好运。"

那时,他们两人早已越过了边界,我还为他们祈祷过平安,可是,就在那天夜里,有一位名副其实的国王在欧洲驾崩,需要在报上刊登一条讣告。

_____

① 印度西北境的阿富汗人。

and, turning round to me, cried, "Come thou also, Sahib, a little along the road, and I will sell thee a charm—an amulet that shall make thee King of Kafiristan. "

Then the light broke upon me, and I followed the two camels out of the Serai till we reached open road and the priest halted.

"What d'you think o' that?" said he in English. "Carnehan can't talk their patter, so I've made him my servant. He makes a handsome servant. ' Tisn't for nothing that I've been knocking about the country for fourteen years. Didn't I do that talk neat? We'll hitch on to a caravan at Peshawar till we get to Jagdallak, and then we'll see if we can get donkeys for our camels, and strike into Kafiristan. Whirligigs for the Amir, O Lor'! Put your hand under the camel bags and tell me what you feel. "

I felt the butt of a Martini, and another and another.

"Twenty of 'em," said Dravot, placidly. "Twenty of 'em, and amunition to correspond, under the whirligigs and the mud dolls. "

"Heaven help you if you are caught with those things!" I said. "A Martini is worth her weight in silver among the Pathans. "

"Fifteen hundred rupees of capital—every rupee we could beg, borrow, or steal—are invested on these two camels," said Dravot. "We won't get caught. We're going through the Khyber with a regular caravan. Who'd touch a poor mad priest?"

"Have you got everything you want?" I asked, overcome with astonishment.

"Not yet, but we shall soon. Give us a memento of your kindness, Brother. You did me a service yesterday, and that time in Marwar. Half my Kingdom shall you have, as the saying is. " I slipped a small charm compass from my watch chain and handed it up to the priest.

"Good-by," said Dravot, giving me hand cautiously. "It's the last time we'll shake hands with an Englishman these many days. Shake hands with him, Carnehan," he cried, as the second camel passed me.

Carnehan leaned down and shook hands. Then the

世界就像飞轮似的按照相同的周期在不断地旋转着。夏天去了,冬天来了,总是那样周而复始,循环不息。那份日报还在继续出版,而我也并没有离开它。到了第三个夏天,正是一个炎热的夜晚,晚上要出一期报纸,紧张地等着从世界的另一端发来的新闻电讯稿,其实,这条新闻电讯就跟从前发生过的不分轩轾。有好几个大人物已在过去的两年里与世长辞,机器转动时发出的是更多的噪音,而且报社花园里一些树木,也不见得长高了几英尺。不过要说有什么不同的地方,也就是那些罢了。

我走过那个印刷间,正如我早已描述过的那一幕情景,恰好又浮现在眼前。由于心中紧张不安,比两年以前还要强烈,我觉得天气也就更加炎热难受了。到了3点钟,我大喊一声"开印",转身要走,就在这当儿好像有一个人影儿爬到我椅子旁边。他俯下身子,好像弯成一个环儿,脑袋深陷在两个肩膀之间,而且,他一前一后正在挪动自己的两脚,那姿势简直就跟狗熊一模一样。我几乎看不清他是在走路呢,还是在爬行——这个衣衫褴褛、唉声叹气的残废人,冲着我直呼其名,大声嚷道现在他已经回来了。"你能给我一点儿喝的吗?"他呜咽着说,"看在老天爷面上,给我一点儿喝的!"

我走回编辑部办公室,那个人带着痛苦的呻吟跟在后面,于是我就把灯打开了。

"你不认得我了吗?"他气喘吁吁地说,一屁股坐在一张椅子里。于是,他的那张奇形怪状的脸,和一头乱蓬蓬的灰发,就朝着灯光转了过来。

我目不转睛地直望着他。那双一英寸宽黑带似的眉毛,记得从前我在哪里目睹过的,可是此刻反正我说不出那是在什么场合了。

"我可不认得你,"我一面说,一面把威士忌递给他,"现在你要我干什么呀?"

他咕嘟一声就一口喝干了,尽管这时天气炎热得令人窒息,但他浑身上下还是在哆嗦着。

"现在我可回来了。"他又说了一遍,"我当过卡菲里斯坦的国王——我和德雷沃特——我们俩都是正式加冕过的国王呀!这个事情从前我们就是在这个办公室里定下来的——当时你坐在那里,还给我们看了好些参考书籍。我就是皮奇——皮奇·托利弗·卡内汉,打那个时候起,你就从来没有离开过这里——我的天哪!"

camels passed away along the dusty road, and I was left alone to wonder. My eye could detect no failure in the disguises. The scene in Serai attested that they were complete to the native mind. There was just the chance, therefore, that Carnehan and Dravot would be able to wander through Afghanistan without detection. But, beyond, they would find death, certain and awful death.

Ten days later a native friend of mine, giving me the news of the day from Peshawar, wound up his letter with: "There has been much laughter here on account of a certain mad priest who is going in his estimation to sell pretty gauds and insignificant trinkets which he ascribes as great charms to H. H. The Amir of Bokhara. He passed through Peshawar and associated himself to the Second Summer caravan that goes to Kabul. The merchants are pleased, because through superstition they imagine that such mad fellows bring good fortune."

The two, then, were beyond the Border. I would have prayed for them, but, that night, a real King died in Europe, and demanded an obituary notice.

The wheel of the world swings through the same phases again and again. Summer passed and winter thereafter, and came and passed again. The daily paper continued and I with it, and upon the third summer there fell a hot night, a night issue, and a strained waiting for something to be telegraphed from the other side of the world, exactly as had happened before. A few great men had died in the past two years, the machines worked with more clatter, and some of the trees in the Office garden were few feet taller. But that was all the difference.

I passed over to the press room, and went through just such a scene as I have already described. The nervous tension was stronger than it had been two years before, and I felt the heat more acutely. At three o'clock I cried, "Print off," and turned to go, when there crept to my chair what was left of a man. He was bent into a circle, his head was sunk between his shoulders, and he moved his feet one over the other like a bear. I could hardly see whether he walked or

我不由得大为惊讶。于是，我就向他表示同情。

"这是真的，"卡内汉冷冰冰地笑着说，来回抚摩他那双缠着破布头的脚丫子，"千真万确。那时我们真的当过国王，头上都戴着王冠——我和德雷沃特——可怜的丹——哦，可怜的、可怜的丹，他从来都不肯听人家的忠告，虽然我也没有好好规劝过他！"

"喝威士忌吧，"我说，"你就慢慢来，把你尽可能记得的每一件事情，从头到尾、原原本本地讲给我听。当时你们骑着骆驼越过边界，德雷沃特假扮成一个疯疯癫癫的祭司，你就充当他的仆人。现在你还记得起来吗？"

"我还不算是疯子——不过，我马上就要发疯了。当然我都记得。你继续望着我，要不然我的话儿也许就要断断续续连不起来了。你继续望着我的眼睛，什么话都不要说。"

我俯下身子，两眼尽可能眨也不眨地直望着他的脸孔。他举起一只手，放到桌上来，我就抓住他的手腕，一看5个手指弯弯扭扭，好像一只鸟的爪子，手背上还留下一方块凹凸不平的淡红伤疤。

"不，不要看那里。朝我本人看呀。"卡内汉说。

"现在就说说后来的事情吧，可是，谢天谢地，不要再跟我打岔。当时我们跟随那支商队动身上路了，我和德雷沃特就像小丑一样，要弄各式各样滑稽的把戏，把同行的旅伴们都给逗乐了。每当傍晚时分，人们都在举炊做饭——都在举炊做饭，德雷沃特常常逗引得我们前仰后合地捧腹大笑……那时他们在干些什么呢？他们点起了一个个小火堆，火花星子嗖嗖地飞进到德雷沃特的络腮胡子里，我们大家哈哈大笑起来——差点儿要笑死呢。一个个小火堆，火花星子嗖嗖地飞进到德雷沃特的一大丛红胡子里——该是多么有意思。"他两眼不再望着我，却在暗自傻笑。

"你们点过了火堆以后，"我大胆地说，"就一直跟着那支商队到了贾格达拉克。到了那儿你们就拐弯，想法进入卡菲里斯坦。"

"不，不是这样的。你在说什么呀？当时，我们还没有到贾格达拉克就拐弯了，因为我们听说那里路好走。不过，他们对我们——我和德雷沃特——的那两头骆驼总是觉得疙疙瘩瘩，很不满意。我们一离开那支商队，德雷沃特干脆把他的和我的所有衣袍通通都脱掉，并且说从现在起我们就得扮成异教徒了，因为

crawled—this rag wrapped, whining cripple who addressed me by name, crying that he was come back. "Can you give me a drink?" he whimpered. "For the Lord's sake, give me a drink!"

I went back to the office, the man followed with groans of pain, and I turned up the lamp.

"Don't you know me?" he gasped, dropping into a chair, and he turned his drawn face, surmounted by a shock of gray hair, to the light.

I looked at him intently. Once before I had seen eyebrows that met over the nose in an inch-broad black band, but for the life of me I could not tell where.

"I don't know you," I said, handing him the whisky. "What can I do for you?"

He took a gulp of the spirit raw, and shivered in spite of the suffocating heat.

"I've come back," he repeated; "and I was the King of Kafiristan—me and Dravot—crowned Kings we was! In this office we settled it—you setting there and giving us the books. I am Peachey—Peachey Taliaferro Carnehan, and you've been setting here ever since—O Lord!"

I was more than a little astonished, and expressed my feelings accordingly.

"It's true," said Carnehan, with a dry cackle, nursing his feet, which were wrapped in rags. "True as gospel. Kings we were, with crowns upon our heads—me and Dravot—poor Dan—oh, poor, poor Dan, that would never take advice, not though I begged of him!"

"Take the whisky," I said, "and take your own time. Tell me all you can recollect of everything from beginning to end. You got across the border on your camels, Dravot dressed as a mad priest and you his servant. Do you remember that?"

"I ain't mad—yet, but I shall be that way soon. Of course I remember. Keep looking at me, or maybe my words will go all to pieces. Keep looking at me in my eyes and don't say anything."

I leaned forward and looked into his face as steadily as I could. He dropped one hand upon the table and I grasped it by the wrist. It was twisted like a bird's claw, and upon the back was a ragged, red, diamond-

卡菲尔人①历来不让穆斯林跟他们讲话的。所以,我们就把自己乔装打扮起来,装得平平常常,不好也不坏。丹尼尔·德雷沃特的那副模样儿,过去我既没有看见过,就是以后我也不想再看了。他把自己的大胡子烧去了一半,肩头上披着一块白茬儿老羊皮,并且按照他们的样式,还剃了个光头。他也给我剃了光头,叫我穿上那叫人腻味的褂子,所以看上去活像一个异教徒。因为那里到处是山连山,岭连岭,叫我们的骆驼简直寸步难行了。它们个儿又高又黑,我一回来,看见它们就像野山羊一样在打架——因为在卡菲里斯坦那里,山羊多得很。那两头骆驼一到了山里,就不再保持安静,跟山羊大不一样。它们老是爱打架,夜里也闹得你睡不成囫囵觉。"

"再喝一点儿威士忌,"我慢条斯理地说,"当骆驼因为通往卡菲里斯坦的山路崎岖,再也迈不开步子向前走的时候,那你和丹尼尔·德雷沃特又是怎么办的呢?"

"你说怎么办的?嘿,当时跟德雷沃特在一起的,就有一个人,名叫皮奇·托利弗·卡内汉。关于他的情况,我将要告诉你,好吗?他一到了那里,冷得简直受不了。有一次,皮奇老兄从桥上突然掉下来,身子一溜歪斜在空中打旋儿,活像你要卖给埃米尔约一便士一个的旋螺。不,那些旋螺一个半便士可买两个,要不然,就算我糊涂弄错了,真倒霉。……那时候,这些骆驼早已派不上用场,皮奇就对德雷沃特说,'谢天谢地,趁我们脑袋还没有搬家以前,干脆把它们干掉吧。'因为到了山里,一路上简直没有什么东西好吃的,他们就把这些骆驼给宰了,但他们事先枪支弹药箱都已卸了下来,碰巧这时有两个人正赶着4头毛驴走过来。德雷沃特站了起来,在他们面前举手投足似的比划了一阵,还拖长了调子说,'这4头毛驴就通通卖给我吧。'头一个人就回答说,'你既然有钱买得起,那就说明你有的是钱,真够我去抢呢。'但也还来不及伸手去掏自己的刀子,德雷沃特早就把他的脖子给扭断了,另一个家伙也掉头逃跑了。所以,卡内汉就把骆驼那里卸下来的枪支,都让毛驴驮着,我们就一起动身,朝着砭人肌骨的寒冷的山区进发,一路上走的净是羊肠小道。"

他沉吟了一会儿,我就问他还记不记得他一路上经过的都是一些什么样的地方。

---

① 此词是蔑称,系指不信伊斯兰教的异教徒。

shaped scar.

"No, don't look there. Look at *me*," said Carnehan.

"That comes afterwards, but for the Lord's sake don't distrack me. We left with that caravan, me and Dravot, playing all sorts of antics to amuse the people we were with. Dravot used to make us laugh in the evenings when all the people was cooking their dinners—cooking their dinners, and... what did they do then? They lit little fires with sparks that went into Dravot's beard, and we all laughed—fit to die. Little red fires they was, going into Dravot's big red beard—so funny." His eyes left mine and he smiled foolishly.

"You went as far as Jagdallak with that caravan," I said, at a venture, "after you had lit those fires. To Jagdallak, where you turned off to try to get into Kafiristan."

"No, we didn't neither. What are you talking about? We turned off before Jagdallak, because we heard the roads was good. But they wasn't good enough for our two camels—mine and Dravot's. When we left the caravan, Dravot took off all his clothes and mine too, and said we would be heathen, because the Kafirs didn't allow Mohammedans to talk to them. So we dressed betwixt and between, and such a sight as Daniel Dravot I never saw yet nor expect to see again. He burned half his beard, and slung a sheepskin over his shoulder, and shaved his head into patterns. He shaved mine too, and made me wear outrageous things to look like a heathen. That was in a most mountaineous country, and our camels couldn't go along any more because of the mountains. They were tall and black, and coming home I saw them fight like wild goats—there are lots of goats in Kafiristan. And these mountains, they never keep still, no more than goats. Always fighting they are, and don't let you sleep at night."

"Take some more whisky," I said, very slowly. "What did you and Daniel Dravot do when the camels could go no further because of the rough roads that led into Kafiristan?"

"What did which do? There was a a party called Peachey Taliaferro Carnehan that was with Dravot.

"我可尽量跟你说实话，有啥说啥，但是，我的脑瓜儿却越来越不管用了。他们后来斩钉截铁地硬逼着我听，这才听清楚德雷沃特究竟是怎样死掉的。那里群山起伏，道路崎岖，那些毛驴却偏偏故意作对，不听使唤，而且居民们又都是孤零零地分散在各处。他们翻山越岭，老是上上下下，来来往往。至于卡内汉那个家伙，却一个劲儿苦苦哀求德雷沃特不要引吭高歌，不要大声吹口哨，深恐这么一来会造成雪崩爆发。不料，德雷沃特却开导我说，一个国王要是连哼哼唱唱都不会，那也就称不上什么国王了，不仅如此，他还常常使劲儿狠揍毛驴屁股。而且，面对着严寒的日子，他从来都是满不在乎的。我们穿山越岭，来到了一大片平坦的山谷，直累得那些毛驴几乎快要咽气，所以我们干脆就把它们宰了，说实在的，是因为找不到东西来喂养它们，或者好让我们自己果腹充饥。我们就坐在弹药箱上没事干，只好玩猜单双的游戏，甚至还要弄着由于颠簸震动而逸出箱外的弹药筒。

"随后，有10个手执弓箭的人，正在追赶20个手执弓箭的人（那些弯弓——实在大得惊人），朝那个山谷直冲下来。他们都是肤色白皙的人——比你肤色还要白得多——黄头发，体格相当结实。德雷沃特一面开箱取出枪支来，一面说道，'这是头一件买卖。我们就照着那10个人打吧。'话音刚落，他朝着那20个人砰砰地开了两枪，其中有一个人被击中，倒毙在离我们歇脚的岩石200码的地方。余下来的人开始逃跑，满山谷乱窜，但卡内汉和德雷沃特端坐在弹药箱上，一看他们全都落在射程以内。便举起枪来逐个瞄准，把他们通通击毙了。随后，我们回过头来再对付山上的那10个人，这时他们也已经逃到雪地那一边，向我们射来了一支微不足道的小箭矢。德雷沃特向他们头顶上一开枪，他们就通通直挺挺地躺倒在地上。那时，德雷沃特就走过，先用脚踢踢他们，再把他们搀扶起来。同他们一一握手，向他们表示友好。他招呼他们，把那些弹药箱抬走。你看，他挥起手来，这姿势地地道道就像他早已当上了国王一样。他们抬着弹药箱，引领他穿过山谷，攀上一个小山头，走进山顶上一座松树林，那里竖立着6座巨大的石刻神像。德雷沃特向最大的那一座神像——他们管这个家伙叫英布拉——走去，把一支枪、一个弹药筒放在神像跟前，恭恭敬敬地用自己的鼻子去跟它的鼻子蹭了一下，随手又轻轻地拍拍它的头，在它的面前致

Shall I tell you about him? He died out there in the cold. Slap from the bridge fell old Peachey, turning and twisting in the air like a penny whirligig that you can sell to the Amir. No; they was two for three ha'pence, those whirligigs, or I am much mistaken and woeful sore. And then these camels were no use, and Peachey said to Dravot, 'For the Lord's sake, let's get out of this before our heads are chopped off,' and with that they killed the camels all among the mountains, not having anything in particular to eat, but first they took off the boxes with the guns and the ammunition, till two men came along driving four mules. Dravot up and dances in front of them, singing, 'Sell me four mules.' Says the first man, 'If you are rich enough to buy, you are rich enough to rob'; but before ever he could put his hand to his knife, Dravot breaks his neck over his knee, and the other party runs away. So Carnehan loaded the mules with the rifles that was taken off the camels, and together we starts forward into those bitter cold mountaineous parts, and never a road broader than the back of your hand."

He paused for a moment, while I asked him if he could remember the nature of the country through which he had journeyed.

"I am telling you as straight as I can, but my head isn't as good as it might be. They drove nails through it to make me hear better how Dravot died. The country was mountaineous and the mules were most contrary, and the inhabitants was dispersed and solitary. They went up and up, and down and down, and that other party, Carnehan, was imploring of Dravot not to sing and whistle so loud, for fear of bringing down the tremenjus avalanches. But Dravot says that if a King couldn't sing it wasn't worth being King, and whacked the mules over the rump, and never took no heed for ten cold days. We came to a big level valley all among the mountains, and the mules were near dead, so we killed them, not having anything in special for them or us to eat. We sat upon the boxes, and played odd and even with the cartridges that was jolted out.

"Then ten men with bows and arrows ran down that valley, chasing twenty men with bows and arrows and the row was tremenjus. They was fair men—fairer

敬一番。随后,德雷沃特转过身来,面对众人,频频点头,说,'对啦,对啦。个中底细我也通通知道,所有这些老怪物——都是我的朋友呀。'接着,他张开自己的嘴巴,又用手指指嘴里,于是,当第一个人给他送来食物的时候,他只说一个'不'字;当第二个人给他送来食物的时候,他又说了一个'不'字;但是,当一个年老的祭司和村里的长老给他送来食物的时候,他这才说了一声'是'。于是,他就露出不可一世的样子,慢慢地吃将起来。上面讲到的就是我们一点儿都不费劲儿,好比只是从空中翻个筋斗,来到了我们头一个村子的经过情形。不过,你要知道,我们是走在那么一座该死的绳索桥上往下翻筋斗的,你听了以后可别笑掉了牙。"

"再喝一点儿威士忌,接着往下讲吧,"我说,"刚才讲的是你到过的头一个村子。那么,你又是怎样当上了国王的?"

"我可没有当上国王,"卡内汉说,"德雷沃特他才是国王呢,他头戴金灿灿的王冠,身穿大龙袍,看上去真够潇洒飘逸的。当时,他和其他那拨人,就都待在那个村子里。每天一清早,德雷沃特端坐在英布拉老神像身边,人们都纷纷前来顶礼膜拜。原来那是德雷沃特下达的命令。后来有一些人不知怎的闯进了那个山谷,还弄不清楚自己究竟身在何处,就在这当儿,卡内汉和德雷沃特举起枪来瞄准他们,一个接一个把他们打死了,趁势往那个山谷冲下去,又登上对面那个山头,却发现了另一个村子,跟前面讲过的头一个村子完全一个样,那里的人们通通脸朝下,直挺挺地匍匐在地上。于是,德雷沃特就说,'现在你们这两个村子之间,到底有什么疙瘩解不开的?'人们用手指着一个肤色白皙犹如你、我那样的女人,就走开了。德雷沃特带着她一起回到了头一个村子,统计了一下死者——一共有8个。德雷沃特给每一个死者注地上洒下一点儿奶汁,两臂像旋螺似的来回挥动着,说,'那就算升了天吧。'说罢,他和卡内汉挽着各个村里最大的长老,一直走到山谷里,做给他们看怎样用一支矛枪沿着山坡划出一道线来,并从线的两旁各捡一块草皮泥,分别送给了他们。这时候,所有的人都走了下来,像魔鬼似的一个劲儿大声呼叫,德雷沃特就冲着他们说,'你们通通掘地去,这才会得到大丰收。'他们二话没说照着做了,虽然他们并不理解这是怎么一回事。接着,我们就问——面包、水、火和神像这

than you or more—with yellow hair and remarkable well built. Says Dravot, unpacking the guns, 'This is the beginning of the business. We'll fight for the ten men,'and with that he fires two rifles at the twenty men, and drops one of them at two hundred yards from the rock where we was sitting. The other men began to run, but Carnehan and Dravot sits on the boxes picking them off at all ranges, up and down the valley. Then we goes up to the ten men that had run across the snow too, and they fires a footy little arrow at us. Dravot he shoots above their heads and they all falls down flat. Then he walks over and kicks them, and then he lifts them up and shakes hands all around to make them friendly like. He calls them and gives them the boxes to carry, and waves his hand for all the world as though he was King already. They takes the boxes and him across the valley and up the hill into a pine wood on the top, where there was half a dozen big stone idols. Dravot he goes to the biggest—a fellow they call Imbra—and lays a rifle and a cartridge at his feet, rubbing his nose respectful with his own nose, patting him on the head, and saluting in front of it. He turns round to them men and nods his head, and says, 'That's all right. I'm in the know too, and all these old jim-jams are my friends. ' Then he opens his mouth and points down it, and when the first man brings him food, he says 'No'; and when the second man brings him food, he says 'No'; but when one of the old priests and the boss of the village brings him food, he says 'Yes'; very haughty, and eats it slow. That was how we came to our first village, without any trouble, just as though we had tumbled from the skies. But we tumbled from one of those damned rope bridges, you see, and you couldn't expect a man to laugh much after that. "

"Take some more whisky and go on," I said. "That was the first village you came into. How did you get to be King?"

"I wasn't King," said Carnehan. "Dravot he was the King, and a handsome man he looked with the gold crown on his head and all. Him and the other party stayed in that village, and every morning Dravot sat by the side of old Imbra, and the people came and

些东西在他们语言里都叫做什么名字。德雷沃特还把各村祭司领到神像跟前,叮嘱他一定要坐在那里考察谁好谁坏,要是出了乱子,那就非把他毙了不可。

"到了下星期,他们就像蜜蜂似的不声不响地把山谷里的土地都翻掘了一遍,活儿干得真是漂亮极了。就在这时,祭司们向德雷沃特如实地做了反映。'那仅仅是个开端,'德雷沃特解释道,'他们认为我们都是天上的神呢。'他会同卡内汉一起挑选了 20 名壮丁,教给他们怎样嘎啦一声扣步枪的扳机,出操时又怎样排成 4 个行列,列队前进——嘿,这些玩意儿,他们都是非常乐意去做的,而且,对于这些诀窍,他们也很聪明机灵,一看就明白了。随后,德雷沃特把他的烟斗和烟袋都掏了出来,让烟斗撂在这个村子里,烟袋则撂在那个村子里。于是,我们两人一起出发,前去了解下一个山谷里的情况。到了那里,举目四望,到处都是岩壁林立,通共只有一个小村子,卡内汉就说,'把他们干脆遣送到那个老山谷里种地去吧。'说完,果然把他们遣送到那里,并分给他们一些还没有人拿走的土地。他们都是一些可怜巴巴的人,我们不妨先用一头小山羊的鲜血,洒在他们身上①,再让他们进入这个新的王国。那就是说要给他们留下深刻的印象,这样他们才能安下心来定居。随后,卡内汉就回到了德雷沃特那里,这时德雷沃特早已进入了另一个山谷,那里群山连绵不断,遍地都是冰雪。当地居民根本一个都没有,他手下的那队人马不由得感到害怕,所以,德雷沃特就朝他们开枪,打死了一个,又继续前进,终于在一个村子里发现了一些人。于是,那队人马就前去劝说,关照他们:除非自愿前来送死,最好不要放枪,因为他们手中确实也有一些小型火绳枪。这么一来,我们同那个祭司交上了朋友,我和另外两名士兵就留在那里,教他们怎样出操练兵。这时,有一个身躯高大得惊人的酋长,带着铜鼓喇叭,正从雪地那边走过来,因为他听人说起有一个新的天神经常在各地巡游,威震四海。卡内汉一看到半英里外雪地那边黑压压一片乌合之众,就开枪把其中一个人的胳臂给打伤了。接着,他又派人去给那个酋长传话,说他如果不想白白地送死,那就还得要自己走过

---

① 古代许多国家常用小山羊献祭,作为一种宗教仪式。德雷沃特认为给当地土著洒上山羊的神圣的鲜血,更加富于宗教气氛,以便收买民心。

worshiped. That was Dravot's order. Then a lot of men came into the valley, and Carnehan and Dravot picks them off with the rifles before they knew where they was, and runs down into the valley and up again the other side, and finds another village, same as the first one, and the people all falls down flat on their faces, and Dravot says, 'Now what is the trouble between you two villages?' and the people points to a woman, as fair as you or me, that was carried off, and Dravot takes her back to the first village and counts up the dead—eight there was. For each dead man Dravot pours a little milk on the ground and waves his arms like a whirligig and 'That's all right,' says he. Then he and Carnehan takes the big boss of each village by the arm and walks them down into the valley, and shows them how to scratch a line with a spear right down the valley, and gives each a sod of turf from both sides o' the line. Then all the people comes down and shouts like the devil and all, and Dravot says, 'Go and dig the land, and be fruitful and multiply,' which they did, though they didn't understand. Then we asks the names of things in their lingo—bread and water and fire and idols and such, and Dravot leads the priest of each village up to the idol, and says he must sit there and judge the people, and if anything goes wrong he is to be shot.

"Next week they was all turning up the land in the valley as quiet as bees and much prettier, and the priests heard all the complaints and told Dravot in dumb show what it was about. 'That's just the beginning,' says Dravot. 'They think we're Gods.' He and Carnehan picks out twenty good men and shows them how to click off a rifle, and form fours, and advance in line, and they was very pleased to do so, and clever to see the hang of it. Then he takes out his pipe and his 'baccy-pouch and leaves one at one village and one at the other, and off we two goes to see what was to be done in the next valley. That was all rock, and there was a little village there, and Carnehan says, 'Send 'em to the old valley to plant,' and takes 'em there and gives 'em some land that wasn't took before. They were a poor lot, and we blooded 'em with a kid before letting 'em into the new Kingdom. That was to

来跟我握手,并且把手中武器都扔在后面。果然不出所料,那个酋长独个儿先走过来了,卡内汉就迎上去同他握手,并举起自己手中的武器——它跟德雷沃特使用过的武器完全相同——在空中旋转了一圈,不由得使那个酋长感到异常惊讶,捋了一下我的眉毛。然后,卡内汉独个儿走到酋长跟前,就像演哑剧似的问他自己有没有仇敌。'我有的,'酋长回答说。于是,卡内汉就从他部下挑选出了一些精兵,编成两个队,教他们出操练兵,过了两个星期以后,这些士兵打起仗来,就像义勇军那样神出鬼没了。因此,他就同酋长一起进军,来到了高山之巅一个大平原,酋长的部下冲进了一个村子,把它占领了。我们这3支马提尼枪的火力一个劲儿向乌合之众的敌军压过去。就是这样,我们把那个村子也拿下来了。我从我外套上撕下了一块碎布条,送给了酋长,说,'占领下来,直到我再来这里为止。'——这是引自《圣经》上的一句话。为了留下一种纪念,当我和那些士兵相隔有1800码远的时候,我曾经朝着他站在雪地附近的地方打了一发子弹,所有的人通通脸朝下匍匐在地上。随后,我给德雷沃特发出了一封信,尽管我还不知道他是在陆上,还是在海上。"

我不怕打断他的思路,插话问道:"那你又是怎样给德雷沃特那边写信的?"

"那封信吗?——哦!——那封信吗!请你盯住看我这个眉心地方。那上面就有结绳传话的字眼,这种方法我们是从旁遮普的一个瞎眼的乞丐那里学来的。"

我记得从前确实有一个盲人到编辑部办公室里来过,他手里拿着一根长着节瘤的树桠枝和一条细绳子,按照他自编的暗号把绳子缠在树桠枝上。过了好几个钟头,甚至好几天以后,他还能把那一句话倒背如流地重复讲一遍。他把所有字母都精简为11个原始语音,他竭力要把这种方法教会我,但是没有成功。

"我把那封信送给了德雷沃特,"卡内汉说,"就是通知他回来,因为这个王国现在发展得太大了,叫我实在管不过来,而且,我还要到头一个村子去,视察一下祭司们在那里的工作情况。他们把我们和酋长一起占领的那个村子叫做巴什卡伊,而把我们攻占的头一个村子叫做厄尔一赫布。在厄尔一赫布那里,祭司们的工作做得挺不错,但他们在土地方面却提出一些悬案要我来解决,而且,还说外村有一些人深更半夜

impress the people, and then they settled down quiet, and Carnehan went back to Dravot, who had got into another valley, all snow and ice and most mountaineous. There was no people there, and the Army got afraid, so Dravot shoots one of them, and goes on till he finds some people in a village, and the Army explains that unless the people wants to be killed they had better not shoot their little matchlocks; for they had matchlocks. We makes friends with the priest and I stays there alone with two of the Army, teaching the men how to drill, and a thundering big Chief comes across the snow with kettledrums and horns twanging, because he heard there was a new God kicking about. Carnehan sights for the brown of the men half a mile across the snow and wings one of them. Then he sends a message to the Chief that, less he wished to be killed, he must come and shake hands with me and leave his arms behind. The Chief comes alone first, and Carnehan shakes hands with him and whirls his arms about, same as Dravot used, and very much surprised that Chief was, and strokes my eyebrows. Then Carnehan goes alone to the Chief, and asks him in dumb show if he had an enemy he hated. 'I have,' says the Chief. So Carnehan weeds out the pick of his men, and sets the two of the Army to show them drill, and at the end of two weeks the men can maneuver about as well as Volunteers. So he marches with the Chief to a great big plain on the top of a mountain, and the Chief's men rushes into a village and takes it; we three Martinis firing into the brown of the enemy. So we took that village too, and I gives the Chief a rag from my coat and says, 'Occupy till I come'; which was scriptural. By way of a reminder, when me and the Army was eighteen hundred yeards away, I drops a bullet near him standing on the snow, and all the people falls flat on their faces. Then I sends a letter to Dravot, wherever he be by land or by sea."

At the risk of throwing the creature out of train I interrupted, "How could you write a letter up yonder?"

"The letter? —Oh! —The letter! Keep looking at me between the eyes, please. It was a string-talk letter, that we'd learned the way of it from a blind beggar

在不断地放冷箭。听了以后，我就往外走，去寻找那个村子，并从 1000 码远的地方向它打了 4 发子弹。那么一来，使我平时舍不得花的弹药全给报销了，所以，我就眼巴巴地等着外出已有两三个月之久的德雷沃特回来，同时，我还要使我的子民安分守己，不许乱来一气。

"有一天早晨，我忽然听到魔鬼似的一阵阵震天响的铜鼓喇叭声，只见丹·德雷沃特带领他的大军——后面还尾随着好几百人马——浩浩荡荡地下山来了——最最令人吃惊的，就是——一大顶金光闪闪的王冠，颤巍巍地矗起在他的头上。'我的天哪，卡内汉，'丹尼尔说，'这是一件顶顶了不起的大事，现在整个国家我们都到手了。真是太值得了。我是亚历山大①和塞米拉米斯女王②所生的儿子，你是我的老弟，也是一位天神啊！像这么惊天动地的大事业，我们破天荒头一遭才见到。6 个星期以来，我亲自率领大军出征，方圆 50 英里以内，每一个小村子都欢天喜地表示归顺。而且最最重要的是，你也会看到，现在我已成为四海之内唯我独尊的真命天子，同时，我也同样给了你一顶王冠！我已经关照过他们，在一个名叫舒的地方定做它两顶，因为在舒这一带山里有大量黄金宝藏，简直多得就像炖羊肉上的一层层板油。黄金我亲眼看见过，绿松石我从壁立千仞的悬崖那里捡到过，此外，那条大河沙滩上还有深红色石榴石，你看，这里厚厚一大块琥珀，就是某某人送给我的。把所有的祭司都叫拢来，就在这里接受你的王冠吧。'

"他们中间有一个人刚打开一只用黑色马鬃编成的口袋，我就连忙把那顶王冠戴在自己头上。尽管这顶王冠太小、太沉，但我戴上它——却觉得十分光耀。它是用大块大块黄金浇铸出来的——有 5 磅重，就像大圆桶上一道铁箍。

"'皮奇，'德雷沃特说，'我们再也不想打仗了。互济会是个法宝，可以帮我的大忙！'他当即把我留在巴什卡伊的那个酋长领了出来——后来我们管那个酋长叫做比利·菲什，因为他的长相简直就像从前在博朗河畔的马奇城开那台庞然大物的蒸汽机火车头

---

① 即亚历山大大大帝(公元前 356—公元前 323)，马其顿国王，世界征服者。

② 塞米拉米斯女王，即传说中的亚述女王，在位期间曾修筑巴比伦，征服埃及，进攻印度。

---

in the Punjab. "

I remember that there had once come to the office a blind man with a knotted twig and a piece of string which he wound round the twig according to some cipher of his own. He could, after the lapse of days or hours, repeat the sentence which he had reeled up. He had reduced the alphabet to eleven primitive sounds; and tried to teach me his method, but failed.

"I sent that letter to Dravot, "said Carnehan; "and told him to come back because this Kingdom was growing too big for me to handle, and then I struck for the first valley, to see how the priests were working. They called the village we took along with the Chief, Bashkai, and the first village we took, Er-Heb. The priests at Er-Heb was doing all right, but they had a lot of pending cases about land to show me, and some men from another village had been firing arrows at night. I went out and looked for that village and fired four rounds at it from a thousand yards. That used all the cartridges I cared to spend, and I waited for Dravot, who had been away two or three months, and I kept my people quiet.

"One morning I heard the devil's own noise of drums and horns, and Dan Dravot marches down the hill with his Army and a tail of hundreds of men, and—which was the most amazing—a great gold crown on his head. 'My Gord, Carnehan, 'says Daniel, 'this is a tremenjus business, and we've got the whole country as far as it's worth having. I am the son of Alexander by Queen Semiramis, and you're my younger brother and a God too! It's the biggest thing we've ever seen. I've been marching and fighting for six weeks with the Army, and every footy little village for fifty miles has come in rejoiceful; and more than that, I've got the key of the whole show, as you'll see, and I've got a crown for you! I told 'em to make two of 'em at a place called Shu, where the gold lies in the rock like suet in mutton. Gold I've seen, and turquoise I've kicked out of the cliffs, and there's garnets in the sands of the river, and here's a chunk of amber that a man brought me. Call up all the priests and, here, take your crown. '

"One of the men opens a black hair bag and I

的比利·菲什。'跟他握握手吧,'德雷沃特说。于是,我就去握握手,差一点缩了回来,因为比利·菲什对我使用了这个秘密会社规定的那一种特殊的握手方式①。我虽然一言不发,但用互济会伙计的握手方式跟他试了一回。这时,他回答说对啦,对啦。接着我又用互济会师傅的握手方式试了一回,不料却出了纰漏。'他是互济会里的一个伙计呀!'我对丹说,'这个名字他会知道吗?''他会知道的,'丹回答说,'所有的祭司都知道。这是一个奇迹!那些酋长和祭司可以合办一个互济会伙计分会,这个分会在某些地方跟我们英国的会社非常相似,他们常常把一些标记刻在岩壁上,但他们不知道什么叫做第三个等级,以后他们慢慢地会懂得的。老实说,这么多年来,我了解到阿富汗人是知道互济会中伙计这个等级的,这就是一个奇迹了。我是天神,我是互济会中天字第一号大师傅,我将要开设一个互济会分会,专收属于第三个等级的会友,以后我们还要提拔各个村里一些主要的祭司和酋长。'

"'没有得到任何人许可就擅自成立一个分会,'我说,'那是违反所有法律规定的。何况我们从来都没有搞过什么分会办事机构。'

"'从策略上来讲,这是最漂亮的一着,'德雷沃特说,'那就意味着:治理这个国家,好像下坡时推四轮小车一样容易呢。反正这是个好主意,因为现在他们还来不及仔细琢磨它好不好,但以后他们一发现,就会反对我们的。我有 40 个酋长,他们都跟在我脚后边转,我将根据他们的功劳大小,分别加以考评、提拔。任命这些人常驻在那些村子里,再看我们把一个互济会分会机构架子搭起来。英布拉的神庙将作为这个分会的议事会堂。那些女人必须按照你给她们看的样子缝制围裙。今天晚上我要上朝接见那些酋长,明天再接见这个分会!'

"我听了所有这些办法,简直不知所措了,但我总算还不是那么一个大傻瓜,看不见互济会这个诀窍会给我们多大的力量。我就教那些祭司的家眷怎样按照不同等级缝制围裙。可是,德雷沃特的那条围裙不是布料,而是一块白茬儿皮面子,上面蓝滚边,等级标

①　19 世纪,互济会盛行于西方各国。互济会有许多秘密仪式与会规,其成员可按伙伴、师傅、大师傅三个等级逐步晋升,并且各有各的握手方式。

slips the crown on. It was too small and too heavy, but I wore it for the glory. Hammered gold it was—five pound weight, like a hoop of a barrel.

"'Peachey,' says Dravot, 'we don't want to fight no more. The Craft's the trick, so help me!' and he brings forward that same Chief that I left at Bashkai—Billy Fish we called him afterwards, because he was so like Billy Fish that drove the big tank engine at Mach on the Bolan in the old days. 'Shake hands with him,' says Dravot, and I shook hands and nearly dropped, for Billy Fish gave me the Grip. I said nothing, but tried him with the Fellow Craft Grip. He answers, all right, and I tried the Master's know the word? 'He does,' says Dan, 'and all the priests know. It's a miracle! The Chiefs and the priests can work a Fellow Craft Lodge in a way that's very like ours, and they've cut the marks on the rocks, but they don't know the Third Degree, and they've come to find out. It's Gord's Truth. I've known these long years that the Afghans knew up to the Fellow Craft Degree, but this is a miracle. A God and a Grand Master of the Craft am I, and a Lodge in the Third Degree I will open, and we'll raise the head priests and the Chiefs of the villages. '

"'It's against all the law,' I says, 'holding a Lodge without warrant from anyone; and we never held any office in any Lodge.'

"'It's a master stroke of policy,' says Dravot. 'It means running the country as easy as a four-wheeled bogy down a down grade. We can't stop to inquire now, or they'll turn against us. I've forty Chiefs at my heel, and passed and raised according to their merit they shall be. Billet these men on the villages and see that we run up a Lodge of some kind. The temple of Imbra will do for the Lodge room. The women must make aprons as you show them. I'll hold a levee of chiefs tonight and Lodge tomorrow!'

"I was fair run off my legs, but I wasn't such a fool as not to see what a pull this Craft business gave us. I showed the priests' families how to make aprons of the degrees, but for Dravot's apron the blue border and marks was made of turquoise lumps on white hide, not cloth. We took a great square stone in the temple for the Master's chair, and little stones for the

志都镶上了一块块绿松石。我们把一块大方石放在神庙里，作为大师傅的坐椅，一些小方石就作为朝臣们的座椅，并给那条黑色甬道涂上白色方块块，我们竭尽全力把一切都布置得齐齐整整。

"那天晚上觐见朝臣仪式，是在半山腰举行的，四周围点燃了几大堆篝火，德雷沃特当众宣布他和我都是天神、亚历山大大帝的儿子，昔日互济会大师傅，现在到这里来，就是要宣告成立卡菲里斯坦国，在这个国家里，人人都应该太太平平，和睦相处，特别是要服从我们。接着，各位酋长走过来依次握手，他们是那么粗犷、耿直、大方，好像跟老朋友握手一样。我们根据他们的样子长得很像我们在印度时所认识的那些三朋四友，就分别给他们命名为——比利·菲什，霍利·迪尔沃思，以及我在姆豪时结识的市集上的老板皮基·克尔根。

"最惊人的奇迹，是第二天晚上在互济会分会那里发生的。那些年老的祭司中间，有一个人目不转睛地直盯住了我们，我不由得感到很不自在，因为我知道我们对宗教仪式一事不得不敷衍一番，我根本不了解那些人究竟知不知道。那个年老的祭司是个异乡人，从外村来到巴什卡伊的。德雷沃特一穿上女人们为他特制的那条大师傅围裙，那个祭司就呐喊怒号，一个劲儿要把德雷沃特坐着的那块大方石掀掉。'这会儿可完了，'我说，'他们竟然胆敢擅自干预互济会的事。'德雷沃特却连眼睛都没有眨巴一下，即使是在那10个祭司齐心合力，要把大师傅的座椅——那也就是说英布拉神像的基座——扳倒的时候。随后，那个祭司不知怎的开始去擦底座，为的是除掉上面的一个黑污点，不一会他就指给所有其他的祭司看那石头上刻着的大师傅的标志（它跟德雷沃特围裙上缝制的完全一模一样）。甚至连英布拉神庙里祭司们都不知道那里还有这么一个玩意儿。那个老家伙脸朝下直扑在德雷沃特跟前去吻他的脚。'又走运啦，'德雷沃特穿过互济会分会那间屋子，走来对我说道，'他们说这就是那个湮没已久的标志，其中意思谁都不明了。不过，不管怎么说，现在我们也就更加安全了。'随后，他仿佛手握议事锤似的，砰砰砰地在敲着他的那支枪的后托，说：'由于我自己最得力的助手和皮奇

"At the levee which was held that night on the hillside with big bonfires, Dravot gives out that him and me were Gods and sons of Alexander, and Past Grand Masters in the Craft, and was come to make Kafiristan a country where every man should eat in peace and drink in quiet, and specially obey us. Then the Chiefs come round to shake hands, and they was so hairy and white and fair it was just shaking hands with old friends. We gave them names according as they was like men we had known in India—Billy Fish, Holly Dilworth, Pikky Kergan that was Bazaar-master when I was at Mhow, and so on and so on.

"The most amazing miracle was at Lodge next night. One of the old priests was watching us continuous, and I felt uneasy, for I knew we'd have to fudge the Ritual, and I didn't know what the men knew. The old priest was a stranger come in from beyond the village of Bashkai. The minute Dravot puts on the Master's apron that the girls had made for him, the priest fetches a whoop and a howl, and tried to overturn the stone that Dravot was sitting on. 'It's all up now,' I says. 'That comes of meddling with the Craft without warrant!' Dravot never winked an eye, not when ten priests took and tilted over the Grand Master's chair—which was to say the stone of Imbra. The priest begins rubbing the bottom end of it to clear away the black dirt, and presently, he shows all the other priests the Master's Mark, same as was on Dravot's apron, cut into the stone. Not even the priests of the temple of Imbra knew it was there. The old chap falls flat on his face at Dravot's feet and kisses 'em. 'Luck again,' says Dravot, across the Lodge to me, 'they say it's the missing Mark that no one could understand the why of. We're more than safe now.' Then he bangs the butt of his gun for a gavel and says, 'By virtue of the authority vested in me by my own right hand and the help of Peachey, I declare myself Grand Master of all Freemasonry in Kafiristan in this the Mother Lodge o' the country, and the King of Kafiristan equally with Peachey!' At that he puts on

的鼎力匡助所授予我的权力①，我在本会总部宣布自己任卡菲里斯坦互济会全体会员的大师傅，并与皮奇同时兼任卡菲里斯坦国王！'话音刚落，德雷沃特就把他的王冠戴在头上，同样我也把我的王冠戴在头上——我还担任最高总督要职——我们就是这样举行最充分的仪式成立互济会分会的。这是一个惊人的奇迹！我们正在履行地地道道的互济会仪式的当儿，那些祭司几乎不用提示，好像全都记得清清楚楚，就按头两个等级的要求照办了。打那以后，皮奇和德雷沃特就把那些英雄好汉提升为一些边远村子的高级祭司和酋长。比利·菲什名列前茅，可我对你说，当时我们却吓得他的魂灵儿几乎出了窍。这种事情根本不是按照宗教仪式办的，但它却是为我们的目的效劳。经我们提升的大头头没有超过 10 个，因为我们根本不想使这一个等级普遍化。但是，他们却大声喧嚣，一个劲儿要求提升。

"'到下半年，'德雷沃特说，'我们再交换一下意见，看看你们是怎样工作的。'随后，他就开口问他们村子里的情况，了解到他们相互之间正在打仗，并由此而产生了相当大的厌战情绪。不过，要是他们不干那个，那不用说就是跟穆斯林打仗了。'那些穆斯林只要一进入我国，你们尽管去打好了，'德雷沃特说，'从你们部落里派出十分之一的壮士去守卫边界，另派 200 名到这个山谷去练兵。不论是谁，只要他表现得出色，再也不会被子弹击中，或者被矛枪捅死。而且我知道你们不会欺骗我的，因为你们——都是白人——亚历山大大帝的子孙——而不是像那些老百姓，黑人穆斯林。你们是我的子民，凭上帝起誓，'他讲到最后时却用英语倒背如流地说，'我一定要把你们搞成一个他妈的呱呱叫的国家，可也说不定国家还没搞成，我就上西天了！'

"在这年下半年，我们究竟干过哪些事情，我通通都说不上来，因为德雷沃特干了很多事情，我可一点儿都领会不了，何况他多少懂得一点儿他们的语言，而我却是一窍不通。我的工作就是帮助那里的人们种地，有时跟几个士兵一起外出，了解别的村子里的工作情况，指点他们在峡谷之间架设绳索桥，要知道

---

① 这是西方国家就职典礼时常用的套语，本应由上一级机构授予权力，而在这里德雷沃特自封为王，仍套用此语，颇具讽刺意味。

his crown and I puts on mine—I was doing Senior Warden—and we opens the Lodge in most ample form. It was an amazing miracle! The priests moved in Lodge through the first two degrees almost without telling, as if the memory was coming back to them. After that, Peachey and Dravot raised such as was worthy—high priests and Chiefs of far-off villages. Billy Fish was the first, and I can tell you we scared the soul out of him. It was not in any way according to Ritual, but it served our turn. We didn't raise more than ten of the biggest men, because we didn't want to make the Degree common. And they was clamoring to be raised.

"' In another six months,' says Dravot, ' we'll hold another Communication and see how you are working.' Then he asks them about their villages, and learns that they was fighting one against the other and were fair sick and tired of it. And when they wasn't doing that they was fighting with the Mohammedans. 'You can fight those when they come into our country,' says Dravot. 'Tell off every tenth man of your tribes for a Frontier guard, and send two hundred at a time to this valley to be drilled. Nobody is going to be shot or speared at any more so long as he does well, and I know that you won't cheat me because you're white people—sons of Alexander—and not like common, black Mohammedans. You are *my* people and by God,' says he, running off into English at the end, 'I'll make a damned fine Nation of you, or I'll die in the making!'

"I can't tell all we did for the next six months because Dravot did a lot I couldn't see the hang of, and he learned their lingo in a way I never could. My work was to help the people plow, and now and again go out with some of the Army and see what the other villages were doing, and make 'em throw rope bridges across the ravines which cut up the country horrid. Dravot was very kind to me, but when he walked up and down in the pine wood pulling that bloody red beard of his with both fists I knew he was thinking plans I could not advise him about, and I just waited for orders.

"But Dravot never showed me disrespect before

那些峡谷把这个国家弄得七穿八洞，鸡零狗碎的，真讨厌。德雷沃特平时待我非常和气，可是，每当他在松树林里来回踱步，并用两个拳头搅着那血红的大胡子的时候，我心里明白这会儿他正在琢磨什么计划呀方案呀，因为我没法给他出点子，所以就只好静待他下命令了。

　　"不过话又说回来，德雷沃特从来没有让我在众人面前丢丑。他们对我和我的部下虽然都很害怕，但他们却个个都敬拜丹。他是祭司和酋长的朋友中间最好的一个。但是，只要山那边有人走过来诉苦的，德雷沃特总是耐心地把来人的话听完，随后将4个祭司叫在一起，说出了自己的处理意见。他经常召见的，有来自巴什卡伊的比利·菲什，来自舒的皮基·克尔根，还有那个年老的酋长——我们管他叫卡甫泽伦姆——它好像跟他的真名发音非常接近——每当些个村子里发生了什么开火一类事件的时候，德雷沃特就要跟他们在一起商量对策。那就是他的军事会议，而来自巴什卡伊、舒、伽瓦克和马杜拉的4位祭司，就是他的枢密院了。他们根据拈阄的结果，分派我带领40名士兵和20条步枪，还有60个人携带许许多多绿松石，启程前往戈尔班购买手工制造的马提尼式步枪，那些玩意儿原是喀布尔埃米尔工厂里的产品，现在埃米尔驻赫拉特的某个团因为要绿松石，就忍痛割爱都把它们卖掉了。

　　"我在戈尔班待了一个月光景，把我随身携带的精选品交给了当地总督，以便堵住他的嘴巴，同时又行贿买通了某团上校，这么一来，我们就从总督、上校以及部落人那里，搞到了100多条手工制造的马提尼式步枪，100支可扔600码远的上好的柯哈特·杰扎尔，以及由40人背驮回来的整脚透顶的步枪弹药。我带了我搞到的那些东西回来，就一一分配给由酋长选送到我这里来练兵的那些人手里。德雷沃特政务太忙，这些事情自然都顾不上来，但是，我们开头创建的那一支旧军队却帮了我的大忙，我们毕竟已培养出了500个人能够进行操练，还有200个人懂得怎样把枪支举得笔笔直。那些手工制造的枪支，射击时哪怕像螺旋形向前推进，在他们看来也还是一个奇迹呢。那时冬天转眼就到，德雷沃特却在松树林里踱来踱去，一个劲儿吹牛说大话，侈谈什么火药制造工场和火药制造厂。

　　"'我可不想搞一个国家啦，'他说，'我想要搞

the people. They were afraid of me and the Army, but they loved Dan. He was the best of friends with the priests and the Chiefs; but anyone could come across the hills with a complaint and Dravot would hear him out fair, and call four priests together and say what was to be done. He used to call in Billy Fish from Bashkai, and Pikky Kergan from Shu, and an old Chief we called Kafuzelum—it was like enough to his real name—and hold councils with 'em when there was any fighting to be done in small villages. That was his Council of War, and the four priests of Bashkai, Shu, Khawak, and Madora was his Privy Council. Between the lot of them they sent me, with forty men and twenty rifles, and sixty men carrying turquoises, into the Ghorband country to buy those hand-made Martini rifles, that come out of the Amir's workshops at Kabul, from one of the Amir's Herati regiments that would have sold the very teeth out of their mouths for turquoises.

"I stayed in Ghorband a month, and gave the Governor there the pick of my baskets for hush money, and bribed the Colonel of the regiment some more, and, between the two and the tribespeople, we got more than a hundred hand-made Martinis, a hundred good Kohat Jezails that'll throw to six hundred yards, and forty man-loads of very bad ammunition for the rifles. I came back with what I had, and distributed 'em among the men that the Chiefs sent to me to drill. Dravot was too busy to attend to those things, but the old Army that we first made helped me, and we turned out five hundred men that could drill, and two hundred that knew how to hold arms pretty straight. Even those corkscrewed, hand-made guns was a miracle to them. Dravot talked big about powder shops and factories, walking up and down in the pine wood when the winter was coming on.

"'I won't make a nation,' says he. 'I'll make an Empire! These men aren't niggers; they're English! Look at their eyes—look at their mouths. Look at the way they stand up. They sit on chairs in their own houses. They're the Lost Tribes, or something like it, and they've grown to be English. I'll take a census in the spring if the priests don't get frightened. There must be a fair two million of 'em in these hills. The

成——一个帝国！这些人不是黑人，他们是英国人哪！看他们的眼睛——看他们的嘴巴，看他们站起身来的那姿势。他们在自己屋里，不是照样都坐在椅子上吗。他们是湮没于世的部族①，或者差不多类似那样的家伙，他们现在已经变成英国人了。到了春天我打算进行一次人口调查，只要祭司们并不感到害怕就好。这些山区想必十十足足有20万人口。那些村子里小伢子简直多得很。200万人——就有25万人好去打仗的——而且清一色都是英国人！他们只要有步枪，再经过一点儿训练就行。要是俄国企图入侵印度，这25万名兵员，一下子就把俄国的右翼给切断了！皮奇，老兄，'德雷沃特一面在大口大口地咀嚼自己的大胡子，一面说道，'赶明儿我们就要当皇帝——当威震四方的皇帝！布鲁克王公在我们看来，只不过是一个乳臭未干的小伢子，就算是印度总督，我们也将要跟他平起平坐了。我就要求他给我派来12名精选出来的英国人——即我所认识的那12员大将——来协助我们治理一下国事。有一个名叫麦克雷的，他是在西戈领取养老金的警官——他一连好多次请我吃过饭，他的老婆还送给我一条裤子。还有一个名叫唐金的，他是托恩胡监狱里的一名狱吏。要是我在印度的话，我一伸手还可以抓到好几百条汉子。像这样的事，印度总督准会替我效劳。到了春天，我将派一个人去把那些人要来，而且我还会书面请示互济会如何进行治理，以便尽到我这个大师傅的职责。不过，要是在印度，那些土著部队一拿起马提尼枪，这里所有的后膛枪通通都得给扔掉了。因为这些后膛枪早已磨损失灵，但在山区打起仗来还是管用的。要是有12个英国人，再加上10万名手握后膛枪的士兵，就可以一点一点地渗透到这个埃米尔的国家去了——在一年以内，我要是搞到2万人，也就心满意足了——那时，我们搞成了一个帝国啦。当每一件事情都弄得井然有序的时候，我就会跪下来，把这顶王冠——就是这会儿我头上戴的王冠——奉献给维多利亚女王，女王陛下她会说，"起来吧，丹尼尔·德雷沃特爵士。"哦，这可了不起！我说，真的太了不起呀！不过话又得说回来，在每一个地方——巴什卡伊、伽瓦克以及舒等地，还有那么多的事要去办呢。'

---

① 这里指犹太人离散前大约140年从北巴勒斯坦消失了的希伯来民族的那一部分。

villages are full o'little children. Two million people—two hundred and fifty thousand fighting men—and all English! They only want the rifles and a little drilling. Two hundred and fifty thousand men, ready to cut in on Russia's right flank when she tries for India! Peachey, man', he says, chewing his beard in great hunks, 'we shall be Emperors—Emperors of the Earth! Rajah Brooke will be a suckling to us. I'll treat with the Vice-roy on equal terms. I'll ask him to send me twelve picked English—twelve that I know of—to help us govern a bit. There's Mackray, Sergeant-pensioner at Segowli—many's the good dinner he's given me, and his wife a pair of trousers. There's Donkin, the Warder of Tounghoo Jail; there's hundreds that I could lay my hand on if I was in India. The Vice-roy shall do it for me. I'll send a man through in the spring for those men, and I'll write for a dispensation from the Grand Lodge for what I've done as Grand Master. That—and all the Sniders that'll be thrown out when the native troops in India take up the Martini. They'll be worn smooth, but they'll do for fighting in these hills. Twelve English, a hundred thousand Sniders run through the Amir's country in driblets—I'd be content with twenty thousand in one year—and we'd be an Empire. When everything was shipshape, I'd hand over the crown—this crown I'm wearing now—to Queen Victoria on my knees, and she'd say, "Rise up, Sir Daniel Dravot."Oh, it's big! It's big, I tell you! But there's so much to be done in every place—Bashkai, Khawak, Shu, and everywhere else.'

"'What is it?' I says. 'There are no more men coming to be drilled this autumn. Look at those fat, black clouds. They're bringing the snow.'

"'It isn't that,' says Daniel, putting his hand very hard on my shoulder; 'and I don't wish to say anything that's against you, for no other living man would have followed me and made me what I am as you have done. You're a first-class Commander-in-Chief, and the people know you; but—it's a big country, and somehow you can't help me, Peachey, in the way I want to be helped.'

"'Go to your blasted priests, then!' I said, and I was sorry when I made that remark, but it did hurt me

"'这是怎么搞的？'我说，'今年秋天再也不会有人来操练啦。看那些密密层层的乌云，眼看着快要下雪了。'

"'这可不是那样的，'丹尼尔把一只手狠狠地搁在我肩膀上说，'我根本不想说什么话来反对你，因为没有一个活人会像你那样一直紧跟我，使得我终于得到了今天的地位。你是第一流的总司令，而且老百姓都认识你。可是，这是一个大国，无论如何你也不能怪我，皮奇，因为我实在是无可奈何。'

"'那就到你的该死的祭司那里去吧。'我说。说了那句话，我却又觉得挺难受，不过话又说回来，当我已经训练好所有的兵员，并且还完成了他交给我的嘱托，现在发现丹尼尔说话时却摆出那么一副顶头上司的姿态来，这可叫我伤心透顶。

"'让我们别吵嘴，皮奇，'丹尼尔说话时并没有骂人，'你也是一个国王嘛，这个王国半拉子就归你了。可是你觉不觉得，皮奇，我们现在需要比我们俩更聪明的人——比方说，有三四个人，我们就可以把他们分派到各地去，作为我们的代表。这是一个幅员辽阔的大国，我不是常常都能发出正确的号令，而且我又没有时间亲自操办所有事情，你看，眼下冬天马上就要到了。'他让自己一半大胡子咬在嘴里，他的大胡子如同他的那顶金灿灿的王冠一样红光四射。

"'我觉得很抱歉，丹尼尔，'我说，'我已经尽力而为了。我曾经教过他们出操练兵，又指点他们怎样把燕麦堆垛得更好些。同时，我还把那些洋铁皮步枪从戈尔班给运过来了——可是我知道你现在心里到底在打什么算盘。我想到那样子做国王总觉得挺难受的。'

"'那又是另一回事。'德雷沃特踅来踅去地说，'眼下冬天就要到了，料他们不会制造太多麻烦。要是那样的话，我们就不能老是闯东走西了。现在我需要——一个老婆。'

"'谢天谢地，千万不要去管那些娘儿们！'我说，'我们俩受尽了种种磨难，也都挺过来了，虽然我是一个傻瓜蛋。记住那个合约，还是远远地躲开那些娘儿们吧。'

"'那个合约嘛，只不过是在我们当上国王以前才有效，而现在我们已是长年累月在当国王了。'德雷沃特把他的那顶王冠放在手里掂量了一下，说，'你也去搞一个老婆，皮奇——一个漂亮的、高大健壮的胖女

sore to find Daniel talking so superior when I'd drilled all the men, done all he told me.

"'Don't let's quarrel, Peachey,' says Daniel, without cursing. 'You're a King, too, and the half of this Kingdom is yours; but can't you see, Peachey, we want cleverer men than us now—three or four of 'em, that we can scatter about for our Deputies. It's a hugeous great State, and I can't always tell the right thing to do, and I haven't time for all I want to do, and here's the winter coming on and all.' He put half his beard into his mouth, and it was as red as the gold of his crown.

"'I'm sorry, Daniel,' says I. 'I've done all I could. I've drilled the men and shown the people how to stack their oats better; and I've brought in those tinware rifles from Ghorband—but I know what you're driving at. I take it Kings always feel oppressed that way.'

"'There's another thing too,' says Dravot, walking up and down. 'The winter's coming and these people won't be giving much trouble and if they do we can't move about. I want a wife.'

"'For Gord's sake leave the women alone!' I says. 'We've both got all the work we can, though I _am_ a fool. Remember the Contrack, and keep clear o' women.'

"'The Contrack only lasted till such time as we was Kings; and Kings we have been these months past,' says Dravot, weighing his crown in his hand. 'You go get a wife too, Peachey—a nice, strappin', plump girl that'll keep you warm in the winter. They're prettier than English girls, and we can take the pick of 'em. Boil 'em once or twice in hot water, and they'll come as fair as chicken and ham.'

"'Don't tempt me!' I says. 'I will not have any dealings with a woman not till we are a dam' site more settled than we are now. I've been doing the work o' two men, and you've been doing the work o' three. Let's lie off a bit, and see if we can get some better tobacco from Afghan country and run in some good liquor; but no women.'

"'Who's talking o' _women_?' says Dravot. 'I said _wife_—a Queen to breed a King's son for the King. A

人,到了冬天,她包管使你全身热乎乎的。她们长得可比英国女人还俊俏,在她们中间,我们还可以挑挑拣拣的,净挑顶顶呱呱的那种娘儿们。让她们在沸水里泡上一两回,包管出落得像童子鸡和火腿一样肥嫩。'

"'莫要引诱我啊!'我说,'我怎么也不乐意跟一个女人打交道的,哪怕是我们落到了他妈的比我们现在还要糟糕的处境。我一直在做两个人的工作,而你也在做3个人的工作。让我们不妨歇一会儿,看看我们能不能从阿富汗国内弄到一些上等香烟,再加上一些美酒,可就是不要搞女人。'

"'谁个在谈女人呀?'德雷沃特说,'我说的是老婆——是一个王后,给国王生王储,传宗接代当国王嘛。是从最强大的部落里来的一个王后,她就会使得部落人都成你的同胞兄弟,她躺在你身边,把全体老百姓对你的看法,以及他们内部的事情都讲给你听。那些就是我最最求之不得的东西。'

"'你还记得我在莫古尔·塞拉伊当铁道养路工时供养过的那个孟加拉女人吗?'我说,'她给我的好处,可说都说不完啦。她曾经教我学孟加拉语,以及这样那样的玩意儿,但是后来出了什么事呢?——她拿了我半个月饷钱,跟那个站长的仆役一起跑了。随后,她出现在达杜尔枢纽站,后面跟着一个欧亚混血儿。而且,她居然还厚颜无耻地当着圆形机车车房里众司机面前,说我就是她的丈夫!'

"'我们跟那个事可扯不上。'德雷沃特说,'这些娘儿们肤色比你我还要白净,赶明儿我就是要找一个王后过寒冬腊月。'

"'丹,我最后一次请求你,千万别找呀。'我说,'这只会给我们带来害处。《圣经》上说过,国王们不应该把自己的精力都浪费在女人身上,特别是当他们刚得到一个新的王国值得励精图治的时候。'

"'我最后一次回答你,我可一定要找呀。'德雷沃特说。他走开了,穿过松树林,远远望去好像一个红色大魔鬼。落日映照着他的王冠和大胡子侧面,它们像两块烧红了的煤块,正在发出令人耀眼的光辉。

"可是,要搞到一个老婆,并不像丹心里想的那样容易。这个问题他虽然向枢密院提出过,但一直没有得到回复,后来比利·菲什才说他最好还是先探探那些女人的口气。德雷沃特狠狠地咒骂了他们一通。'我有什么不对的地方呢?'他站在英布拉神像旁边大声嚷道,'难道说我是一个卑鄙的人,要不然,就是我

Queen out of the strongest tribe, that'll make them your blood brothers, and that'll lie by your side and tell you all the people thinks about you and their own affairs. That's what I want.'

"'Do you remember that Bengali woman I kept at Mogul Serai when I was a plate layer?' says I. 'A fat lot o' good she was to me. She taught me the lingo and one or two other things; but what happened? She ran away with the Station Master's servant and half my month's pay. Then she turned up at Dadur Junction in tow of a half-caste, and had the impidence to say I was her husband—all among the drivers in the running shed!'

"'We're done with that,' says Dravot. 'These women are whiter than you or me, and a Queen I will have for the winter months.'

"'For the last time o' asking, Dan, do not', I says. 'It'll only bring us harm. The Bible says that Kings ain't to waste their strength on women, 'specially when they've got a new raw Kingdom to work over.'

"'For the last time of answering, I will,' said Dravot, and he went away through the pine trees looking like a big red devil. The low sun hit his crown and beard on one side and the two blazed like hot coals.

"But getting a wife was not as easy as Dan thought. He put it before the Council, and there was no answer till Billy Fish said that he'd better ask the girls. Dravot damned them all round. 'What's wrong with me?' he shouts, standing by the idol Imbra. 'Am I a dog or am I not enough of a man for your wenches? Haven't I put the shadow of my hand over this country? Who stopped the last Afghan raid?' It was me really, but Dravot was too angry to remember. 'Who brought your guns? Who repaired the bridges? Who's the Grand Master of the sign cut in the stone?' and he thumped his hand on the block that he used to sit on in Lodge, and at Council, which opened like Lodge always. Billy Fish said nothing, and no more did the others. 'Keep your hair on, Dan,' said I; 'and ask the girls. That's how it's done at Home, and these people are quite English.'

这个堂堂男子汉还配不上你们乡下娘儿们？难道说还不是我举起手来保护你们这个国家吗？最近阿富汗人入侵，又是谁挡回去的？'其实应该是我，但德雷沃特在盛怒之下，一时竟回想不起来了。'再说你们的枪支，是谁带来的？那些桥梁又是谁修好的？谁是把标志刻在石头上的大师傅？'他一面用手猛击他在互济会里常坐的那块石板，一面说道。比利·菲什一言不语，至于别人自然也都不敢吭声了。'别生气，丹，'我说话了，'去征求一下那些女人的意见也好。要知道这在我们国内就是那么办的，何况这里人们已是地地道道的英国人了。'

"'国王的婚姻——就是国家大事嘛，'丹怒不可遏地说，因为他可能感觉到——我希望——他正在违背自己的初衷。他走出了枢密院房间，别人则依然坐在那里，两眼俯视着地面。

"'比利·菲什，'我对巴什卡伊酋长说，'你在这里有什么为难的地方呢？对一个忠实的朋友，实话实说吧。''你知道，'比利·菲什说，'既然你样样事情都知道，人们还肯对你说实话？有哪家子年轻闺女肯嫁给天神或魔鬼呢？这总是不太合适吧。'

"我回想起来《圣经》上确实说过类似那样的一些话。可是，只要他们还是那样看待我们，仍然相信我们都是天神，那我总犯不着叫他们拆穿西洋镜吧。

"'要知道天神是无所不能的，'我说，'要是国王喜欢一个女人，他就不会让她死去的。''可她还是非死不可的，'比利·菲什说，'在这些山区里，就有各式各样的天神和魔鬼，经常有这样的事，一个女人只要一嫁给了某一位天神或魔鬼，以后就再也看不见了。此外，你们俩都知道刻在石头上的那个标记。只有天神他们才懂得那个玩意儿。我们心里在想你们都是凡夫俗子，一直到你们出示大师傅那个标记的。'

"那时我真巴不得我们一开始就讲清楚，互济会大师傅的真正秘密实际上根本不存在的，但我还是一言不语。那天半山腰一座黑咕隆咚的小神庙里，整夜在嘟嘟嘟地吹喇叭，我听说有一个女人哭得差不多快要死了。有一个祭司告诉我们，说这个女人此刻正在准备，就要嫁给国王陛下了。

"'我可不会干那种荒唐的事，'丹说，'我可不想干预你们的风俗习惯，但是我要给自己娶媳妇。''那个女人有一点儿害怕呢，'那个祭司说，'她心里想她此刻就要去死了，山下小神庙里，人们正在竭力给她

"'The marriage of the King is a matter of State,' says Dan, in a white-hot rage, for he could feel, I hope, that he was going against his better mind. He walked out of the Council room, and the others sat still, looking at the ground.

"'Billy Fish,' says I to the Chief of Bashkai, 'what's the difficulty here? A straight answer to a true friend.' 'You know,' says Billy Fish. 'How should a man tell you who know everything? How can daughters of men marry Gods or Devils? It's not proper.'

"I remembered something like that in the Bible; but if, after seeing us as long as they had, they still believed we were Gods, it wasn't for me to undeceive them.

"'A God can do anything,' says I. 'If the King is fond of a girl he'll not let her die.' 'She'll have to,' said Billy Fish. 'There are all sorts of Gods and Devils in these mountains, and now and again a girl marries one of them and isn't seen any more. Besides, you two know the Mark cut in the stone. Only the Gods know that. We thought you were men till you showed the sign of the Master.'

"I wished then that we had explained about the loss of the genuine secrets of a Master Mason at the first go-off; but I said nothing. All that night there was a blowing of horns in a little dark temple halfway down the hill, and I heard a girl crying fit to die. One of the priests told us that she was being prepared to marry the King.

"'I'll have no nonsense of that kind,' says Dan. 'I don't want to interfere with your customs, but I'll take my own wife.' 'The girl's a little bit afraid,' says the priest. 'She thinks she's going to die, and they are aheartening of her up down in the temple.'

"'Hearten her very tender then,' says Dravot, 'or I'll hearten you with the butt of a gun so that you'll never want to be heartened again.' He licked his lips, did Dan, and stayed up walking about more than half the night, thinking of the wife that he was going to get in the morning. I wasn't any means comfortable, for I knew that dealings with a woman in foreign parts, though you was a crowned King twenty times

鼓励呢.'

"'那就鼓励得她非常柔顺、熨帖才好呢,'德雷沃特说,'要不然我就用枪托子鼓励你,叫你一辈子都不想再受到鼓励.'这时,丹尼尔听了以后,简直垂涎欲滴,整整大半夜他独个儿踱来踱去,暗自思忖着明儿一清早他就要到手的那个娇妻.可我呢,说什么都觉得很不舒坦,因为我知道同一个外国女人打交道,即使你是老八辈子加冕国王陛下,也不免要冒风险的.转天我一清早就起身了,可德雷沃特还在呼呼大睡呢,我看见祭司们聚在一起窃窃私语,酋长们也都在交头接耳,这时他们都乜斜眼角直望着我.

"'出了什么事,菲什?'我对这个巴什卡伊酋长说.他身穿一袭皮衣,看上去真是昂藏不凡.

"'我也说不准呢,'他说,'可是,如果你能说服国王陛下放弃那个荒唐透顶的结婚想法,那么,对他、对我,甚至对你自己来说,你都会记上一大功呢.'

"'那我当然会相信的,'我说.'可是——你要知道,比利,还有我,的确是为我们打天下的,至于国王和我,无非就是万能的上帝所创造的两位俊杰罢了.没有别的,你尽管放心好了.'

"'也许就是那样,'比利·菲什说,'不过,要是果真那样的话,我心里就会觉得很难过.'他一下子把自己的脑袋缩在皮大衣里,琢磨了一会儿.'国王啊,'他说,'不管你是凡人,还是天神,还是魔鬼,今天我照样效忠于你.我手下有20个人,他们都会跟我走的.我们就去巴什卡伊,躲过这一阵风暴吧.'

"那天夜里下了一点儿雪,四下里一片白茫茫,只有那阴沉沉的大块大块乌云从北边不断刮过来.德雷沃特头戴王冠走出去的时候,他挥舞手臂直跺脚的样子,看上去简直比逗趣酒①还要逗人喜爱呢.

"'最后还是悬崖勒马为好,丹,'我低声耳语地说,'比利·菲什刚才说快要出乱子了.'

"'我的子民中间会出乱子!'德雷沃特说,'那不见得吧.皮奇,你真傻,干吗不也搞一个老婆.那个女人在哪儿呀?'他说话时声音很高,就像一头公驴在干号一样.'把所有的酋长和祭司都叫来,让皇帝陛下看一看他的未来的王后是不是跟寡人配得上.'

"谁都用不着通知了.他们全都身子靠着枪支和

––––––––––––

① 由酒、牛奶、水等和砂糖、柠檬、香料一起调成的混合饮料.

over, could not but be risky. I got up very early in the morning while Dravot was asleep, and I saw the priests talking together in whispers, and the Chiefs talking together too, and they looked at me out of the corners of their eyes.

"'What's up, Fish?' I says to the Bashkai man, who was wrapped up in his furs and looking splendid to behold.

"'I can't rightly say,' says he, 'but if you can induce the King to drop all this nonsense about marriage, you'll be doing him and me and yourself a great service.'

"'That I do believe,' says I. 'But sure, you know, Billy, as well as me, having fought against and for us, that the King and me are nothing more than two of the finest men that God Almighty ever made. Nothing more, I do assure you.'

"'That may be,' says Billy Fish, 'and yet I should be sorry if it was.' He sinks his head upon his great fur cloak for a minute and thinks. 'King,' says he, 'be you man or God or Devil, I'll stick by you today. I have twenty of my men with me, and they will follow me. We'll go to Bashkai until the storm blows over.'

"A little snow had fallen in the night, and everything was white except the greasy fat clouds that blew down and down from the north. Dravot came out with his crown on his head, swinging his arms and stamping his feet, and looking more pleased than Punch.

"'For the last time, drop it, Dan,' says I in a whisper. 'Billy Fish here says that there will be a row.'

"'A row among my people!' says Dravot. 'Not much. Peachey, you're a fool not to get a wife too. Where's the girl?' says he, with a voice as loud as the braying of a jackass. 'Call up all the Chiefs and priests, and let the Emperor see if his wife suits him.'

"There was no need to call anyone. They were all there leaning on their guns and spears round the clearing in the center of the pine wood. A deputation of priests went down to the temple to bring up the girl, and the horns blew up fit to wake the dead. Billy Fish saunters round and gets as close to Daniel as he could,

长矛，站立在松树林中间一片空地周围。祭司们派出一个代表团。前往小神庙去引领那个女人。嘟嘟嘟的喇叭声吹得几乎使死人都要惊醒过来。比利·菲什漫步走了过来，尽可能挨近丹尼尔身边。而且他背后站着他手下的那20条大汉，个个手持火绳枪。他们身材高大，没有一个人低于6英尺。我站在德雷沃特身边，而在我的后面就是那20名正规军战士。这时，那个女人走了上来，一个高大健壮的乡下女人，身上挂满银饰和绿松石，但脸色却像死人一样苍白，频频回首，两眼直瞅着祭司们。

"'她这个人品嘛，行了，'丹把她上下打量了一下说，'有什么好害怕的，小妞子！过来，跟我亲亲嘴。'他伸出手来把她搂住了。她闭上眼睛，发出一声尖叫，接着，她的脸孔就低下来，凑到丹那火红的大胡子边缘。

"这个懒娘儿们咬了我一口！'他一面说，一面用手劈啪一声拍了一下自己的脖子根儿，没有错，他手上被鲜血染红了。比利·菲什和他部下手持火绳枪的两名士兵，连忙抓住丹的胳臂，把他拽到巴什卡伊人那边去了，这时，祭司们却用他们的语言狂叫着，'原来他既不是天神，也不是魔鬼，而是一个尘世俗物！'我猛地吃了一惊，因为前面已有个祭司向我猛击过来，而背后那支军队却开始向巴什卡伊弟兄们开枪。

"'老天爷呀！'丹说，'这到底是什么意思呢？'

"'往回走！快跑呀！'比利·菲什说，'毁了，叛变啦。我们要尽可能突破重围，打回巴什卡伊去。'

"我拼命向我部下——那支正规军队——下命令，但都不管用了，所以我只好举起那支英国造马提尼枪，向他们那乌合之众开火，叫一溜儿3个穷光蛋当即饮弹毙命。满坑满谷都是大声狂叫的人群，每个人都在尖叫着说，'原来他既不是天神，也不是魔鬼，只不过是一个尘世俗物。'巴什卡伊弟兄们拼命地护卫着比利·菲什，但是，他们的火绳枪毕竟赶不上喀布尔的后膛炮威力大，他们中间有4个人倒下了。这时，丹正像一头公牛在吼叫，因为他心中感到无比愤怒，要向人群冲过去，而比利·菲什则百般阻拦他，实在很费劲。'我们支持不住了，'比利·菲什说，'快往下面山谷逃！这个地方人人都在反对我们。'那些手持火绳枪的弟兄们逃跑了，我们不管德雷沃特的抗议，也往下面山谷逃。这时候，他满脸狰狞地正在

and behind him stood his twenty men with matchlocks. Not a man of them under six feet. I was next to Dravot, and behind me was twenty men of the regular Army. Up comes the girl, and a strapping wench she was, covered with silver and turquoises, but white as death, and looking back every minute at the priests.

"'She'll do,' said Dan, looking her over. 'What's to be afraid of, lass? Come and kiss me.' He puts his arm round her. She shuts her eyes, gives a bit of a squeak, and down goes her face in the side of Dan's flaming red beard."

"'The slut's bitten me!' says he, clapping his hand to his neck, and, sure enough, his hand was red with blood. Billy Fish and two of his matchlock-men catches hold of Dan by the shoulders and drags him into the Bashkai lot, while the priests howl in their lingo, 'Neither God nor Devil, but a man!' I was all taken aback, for a priest cut at me in front and the Army behind began firing into the Bashkai men.

"'God A-mighty!' says Dan. 'What is the meaning o' this?'

"'Come back! Come away!' says Billy Fish, 'Ruin and Mutiny is the matter. We'll break for Bashkai if we can.'

"I tried to give some sort of orders to my men—the men o' the regular Army—but it was no use, so I fired into the brown of 'em with an English Martini and drilled three beggars in a line. The valley was full of shouting, howling creatures, and every soul was shrieking, 'Not a God not a Devil, but only a man!' The Bashkai troops stuck to Billy Filly all they we worth, but their matchlocks wasn't half as good as the Kabul Breechloaders, and four of them dropped. Dan was bellowing like a bull, for he was very wrathy; and Billy Fish had a hard job to prevent him running out at the crowd. 'We can't stand,' says Billy Fish. 'Make a run for it down the valley! The whole place is against us.' The matchlockmen ran, and we went down the valley in spite of Dravot's protestations. He was swearing horribly and crying out that he was a King. The priests rolled great stones on us, and the regular Army fired hard, and there wasn't more than six men, not counting Dan, Billy Fish, and Me, that came down to

赌咒发誓,大声叫嚷他是一个国王。祭司们朝我们推下来大石头,正规军队猛烈地在开火。最后活着跑到山谷底下的,如果丹、比利·菲什和我都不算在内,总共没有超过 6 个人。

"后来,他们就停止开枪了,小神庙里又在嘟嘟嘟地吹喇叭。'开路——谢天谢地开路吧!'比利·菲什说,'在我们还没有赶到巴什卡伊以前,他们将会派人四出,追到各个村子去。到了巴什卡伊,我可以保护你,但是这会儿我却无能为力。'

"我自己的看法是,打从那个时刻起,丹的脑瓜儿就开始发疯了。他瞪着两眼上下打量,就像一只傻头傻脑的蠢猪。随后,他独个儿走回去,打算赤手空拳把那些祭司都给宰了。这事也许他还能办得到吧。'要知道我是一个皇帝,'丹尼尔说,'明年我将要成为英国女王陛下的一名骑士。'

"'那敢情好,丹,'我说,'可是这会儿就寻走,趁现在还有时间。'

"'你这是失职哪,'他说,'因为没有把你手下的军队看管好。那些家伙叛变了,而你还不知道——你这个他妈的火车司机、养路工、传教士的狗腿子!'那时我实在伤心透顶,什么都不在乎,虽然眼前落到这么一败涂地,全是因为他的傻主意所造成的。

"'对不起,丹,'我说,'可就是没法把那些土著干掉。难就难在我们只有口径为 0.57 英寸的那种型号的枪。不过,我们只要一到巴什卡伊,也许还是有办法的。'

"'那就让我们去巴什卡伊吧,'丹说,'我的老天哪,有朝一日我再来这里的时候,定将这个山谷来个彻底扫荡,打个比方说,就像抖搂床单一样,连一个臭虫都不让留在上面!'

"我们赶了整整一天路,而丹却拖着沉重的步伐,整整一夜在雪地上踱来踱去,嘴里乱嚼着他的大胡子,不时还在喃喃自语。

"'要摆脱掉,可没有指望了,'比利·菲什说,'祭司们会派人追到各个村子,说你们只不过是尘世俗物罢了。事态还没有稳定下来以前,你们干吗不坚持做天神?我这个无用之人啊。'比利·菲什说罢,全身扑在雪地上,就开始祈求他的天神了。

"转天我们来到了一个怪倒霉的地方——全是高高低低的,压根儿没有一块平地,当然那里也找不到食物。那 6 个巴什卡伊人肚子饿得要命,两眼直勾勾

the bottom of the valley alive.

"Then they stopped firing and the horns in the temple blew again. 'Come away—for Gord's sake come away!' says Billy Fish. 'They'll send runners out to all the villages before ever we get to Bashkai. I can protect you there, but I can't do anything now.'

"My own notion is that Dan began to go mad in his head from that hour. He stared up and down like a stuck pig. Then he was all for walking back alone and killing the priests with his bare hands; which he could have done. 'An Emperor am I,' says Daniel, 'and next year I shall be a Knight of the Queen.'

"'All right, Dan,' says I; 'but come along now while there's time.'

"'It's your fault,' says he, 'for not looking after your Army better. There was mutiny in the midst, and you didn't know—you damned engine-driving, plate-laying, missionary's-pass-hunting hound!' I was too heartsick to care, though it was all his foolishness that brought the smash.

"'I'm sorry, Dan,' says I, 'but there's no accounting for natives. This business is our Fifty-Seven. Maybe we'll make something out of it yet, when we've got to Bashkai.'

"'Let's get to Bashkai, then,' says Dan, 'and, by God, when I come back here again I'll sweep the valley so there isn't a bug in a blanket left!'

"We walked all that day, and all that night Dan was stumping up and down on the snow, chewing his beard and muttering to himself.

"'There's no hope o' getting clear,' said Billy Fish. 'The priests will have sent runners to the villages to say that you are only men. Why didn't you stick on as Gods till things was more settled? I'm a dead man,' says Billy Fish, and he throws himself down on the snow and begins to pray to his Gods.

"Next morning we was in a cruel bad country—all up and down, no level ground at all, and no food either. The six Bashkai men looked at Billy Fish hungry-wise as if they wanted to ask something, but they said never a word. At noon we came to the top of a flat mountain all covered with snow, and when we climbed

地望着比利·菲什，好像想要乞求什么东西，可是他们始终没有说出一个字来。晌午时分，我们来到了一座白雪皑皑的大山，就往上攀登，可是抬头一看，山顶中央却有一溜士兵以逸待劳摆好了阵势！

"'追兵很快就要到了，'比利·菲什说话的时候，发出了一点儿笑声来，'他们正在等我们呢。'

"敌方有三四个人开始放枪了，有一颗子弹碰巧击中了丹尼尔的腿肚子，一下子叫他失去了知觉。他望着雪地对过的那队士兵，看到了不久前我们运进来的那些步枪。

"'我这下子可算完了，'他说，'他们都是英国人，这些人——是我干出了该死的丑事，才叫你落到了眼前这样的窘境。回去吧，比利·菲什，带着你部下一块儿走。你已经克尽己责，现在就快走吧。卡内汉，'他说，'跟我拉拉手，同比利一块儿走。也许他们不会把你杀死的。我会单枪匹马去对付他们的。我说得到就做得到，要知道我毕竟是个国王啊！'

"'走吧。'我说，'见鬼去吧，丹！我可要跟你一起在这里。比利·菲什，你快逃走吧，让我们两个来对付这些家伙。'

"'我是一个酋长，'比利·菲什泰然自若地说，'我跟你待在一起。我们部下可以走。'

"巴什卡伊弟兄们二话没说，马上四处逃命，丹和我，还有比利·菲什，就信步走到对面鼓号喧天的那个地方。那时天气很冷——冷得要命。直到这会儿我还觉得自己脖子根儿上冰冰冷，好像在那儿冷得特别透骨似的。"

那些拉布风扇的印度苦力都睡觉去了。办公室里只有两盏煤油灯还在发出令人刺眼的光辉，汗水从我脸上直淌下来，而且只要我身子往前一探，汗水就飞溅在记事本上。这时，卡内汉却浑身都在发颤，我担心说不定他思想走神了。我揩了揩脸，冒冒失失地抓住了他那双皮开肉绽的手，说："打那以后又出了什么事？"

我只是用眼光闪了一下，就把他清晰的思路都打断了。

"那你还乐意说些什么呢？"卡内汉呜咽着说，"他们一声不响地就把国王他们带走了。沿着雪地走去，连一点儿窃窃私语声都没有，当时那个国王并没有把头一个伸手来抓他的人击倒在地——老皮奇也并没有向他们乌合之众射出他那最后一发弹药。这一拨

up into it, behold, there was an Army in position waiting in the middle!

"'The runners have been very quick,' says Billy Fish, with a little bit of a laugh. 'They are waiting for us.'

"Three or four men began to fire from the enemy's side, and a chance shot took Daniel in the calf of the leg. That brought him to his senses. He looks across the snow at the Army, and sees the rifles that we had brought into the country.

"'We're done for,' says he. 'They are Englishmen, these people—and it's my blasted nonsense that has brought you to this. Get back, Billy Fish, and take your men away; you've done what you could, and now cut for it. Carnehan,' says he, 'shake hands with me and go along with Billy. Maybe they won't kill you. I'll go and meet 'em alone. It's me that did it. Me, the King!'

"'Go!' says I. 'Go to Hell, Dan! I'm with you here. Billy Fish, you clear out, and we two will meet those folk.'

"'I'm a Chief,' says Billy Fish, quite quiet. 'I stay with you. My men can go.'

"The Bashkai fellows didn't wait for a second word, but ran off, and Dan and Me and Billy Fish walked across to where the drums were drumming and the horns were horning. It was cold—awful cold. I've got that cold in the back of my head now. There's a lump of it there."

The punkah coolies had gone to sleep. Two kerosene lamps were blazing in the office, and the perspiration poured down my face and splashed on the blotter as I leaned forward. Carnehan was shivering, and I feared that his mind might go. I wiped my face, took a fresh grip of the piteously mangled hands, and said, "What happened after that?"

The momentary shift in my eyes had broken the clear current.

"What was you pleased to say?" whined Carnehan. "They took them without any sound. Not a little whisper all along the snow, not though the King had knocked down the first man that set hand on him—not

猪崽子简直一点儿响声都没有弄出来。他们只是紧紧地围拢在一起,我对你说他们身上披的毛皮又粗又硬,真螫人啊。有一个人名叫比利·菲什的,是我们的好朋友,先生,那时他们就像宰猪似的把他的喉咙给割断了。那个国王乱踢着鲜血淋漓的残雪,说道,'我们虽然壮志未酬,可是干得该有多么轰轰烈烈啊。下面又出了什么事呀?'可是皮奇,皮奇·托利弗,我对你说,先生,这是我们俩朋友之间私下里说的,他掉了脑袋,先生。不,他可还没有掉脑袋呢。倒是这位国王自己掉了脑袋,千真万确的,就是在一座巧夺天工的绳索桥上。劳驾把裁纸刀给我使一使,先生。它倾斜着,就像这个样子。他们赶着他走了一英里路,穿过了那片雪地,来到了悬在峡谷高空之间、俯瞰着大河的一座绳索桥。气势这样险要的桥,可能你早就见过。他们简直把他当成一头公牛,一个劲儿往他背上乱刺。'他妈的你们不生眼睛的!'这个国王说,'难道你们就不让我像一个出身高贵的人那样死去吗?'他转过身来看皮奇——这时,皮奇就像小伢子似的,正在号啕大哭。'是我使你落到了这样的穷途末路,皮奇,'他说,'叫你抛弃了自己荣华富贵的生活,来到了卡菲里斯坦,竟然惨遭杀身之祸,尽管你在这里还是统率皇帝陛下陆海空三军的前任总司令。我说你能原谅我吗,皮奇?''我能原谅你,'皮奇说,'我一点儿都不怪你,丹。''握握手吧,皮奇,'他说,'现在我要走了。'他果然一点儿都没有左顾右盼,径直往外走出去了,当他全身垂直地站到那些令人眩晕的、在空中乱舞的绳索中央的时候,就大声嚷道,'割断吧,你们这些穷光蛋。'于是,他们把绳索一割断,老丹就掉了下去,那是从两万英里的高空,他身子不断地在翻筋斗,过了半个钟头光景,才击坠在河面上,我依稀可辨地看到他的尸体横陈在一块岩石上,附近还有一顶金灿灿的王冠。

"可是你知道他们把皮奇架到两棵松树之间去干什么呢?他们让他如同在十字架上那样受刑,先生,从皮奇的那一双手上就看得出来。他们给他的手和脚都钉上了木钉子,可是尽管这样,他并没有死去。他吊在那里一个劲儿尖叫,第二天他们就把他放了下来,说他没有死,这可真是一个奇迹。他们终于把他放了下来——可怜的老皮奇从来没有伤害过他们——从来没有伤害过他们……"

他身子来回晃动,悲恸欲绝地痛哭起来,一面用

though old Peachey fired his last cartridge into the brown of 'em. Not a single solitary sound did those swines make. They just closed up tight, and I tell you their furs stunk. There was a man called Billy Fish, a good friend of us all, and they cut his throat, Sir, then and there, like a pig; and the King kicks up the bloody snow and says, 'We've had a dashed fine run for our money. What's coming next?' But Peachey, Peachey Taliaferro, I tell you, Sir, in confidence as betwixt two friends, he lost his head, Sir. No, he didn't neither. The King lost his head, so he did, all along o' one of those cunning rope bridges. Kindly let me have the paper cutter, Sir. It tilted this way. They marched him a mile across that snow to a rope bridge over a ravine with a river at the bottom. You may have seen such. They prodded him behind like an ox. 'Damn your eyes!' says the King. 'D'you suppose I can't die like a gentleman?' He turns to Peachey—Peachey that was crying like a child. 'I've brought you to this, Peachey,' says he. 'Brought you out of your happy life to be killed in Kafiristan, where you was late Commander-in-Chief of the Emperor's forces. Say you forgive me, Peachey,' 'I do,' says Peachey, 'Fully and freely do I forgive you, Dan.' 'Shake hands, Peachey,' says he. 'I'm going now.' Out he goes, looking neither right nor left, and when he was plumb in the middle of those dizzy dancing ropes, 'Cut, you beggars,' he shouts; and they cut, and old Dan fell, turning round and round and round, twenty thousand miles, for he took half an hour to fall till he struck the water, and I could see his body caught on a rock with the gold crown close beside.

"But do you know what they did to Peachey between two pine trees? They crucified him, Sir, as Peachey's hands will show. They used wooden pegs for his hands and his feet; and he didn't die. He hung there and screamed, and they took him down next day, and said it was a miracle that he wasn't dead. They took him down—poor old Peachey that hadn't done them any harm—that hadn't done them any..."

He rocked to and fro and wept bitterly, wiping his eyes with the back of his scarred hands and moaning

他那伤痕累累的手背擦自己的眼睛，一面像孩子似的抽噎噎地哭了一阵子。

"他们狠心得很，就让小神庙来供养他了，因为他们说，跟那个尘世俗物的老丹尼尔相比，他倒是更像一个天神。但后来不久，他们就把他赶到外面雪地里，要他滚回老家去。于是，皮奇一路上倒也相安无事，逢人乞讨，大约过了一年光景才算到家了，这一切就因为丹尼尔·德雷沃特走过来说：'一块儿来吧，皮奇，我们这是在干一项了不起的大事业。'入夜，皮奇早已走得精疲力竭，仿佛觉得高山峻岭都在狂飞乱舞，就要坍塌在皮奇的头上，但他还是在匍匐行进，手里紧紧地抓住丹尼尔的首级，怎么也舍不得扔掉①。其实，他们早就在小神庙里把丹的首级馈赠给他，叫他记住千万不要再来啦。尽管那顶王冠是纯金的，皮奇整日价肚子挨饿，但皮奇照样还是舍不得把它卖掉。正直的、令人可敬的德雷沃特大哥——你是认得德雷沃特的，先生！现在你就看他一眼吧！"

他笨手笨脚地往他腰间一大堆破襟襟襟里东寻西找，终于捧出来一只用黑色马鬃编织、上面还绣着银丝的袋子，哆哆嗦嗦地放到了我桌上——原来那是丹尼尔·德雷沃特干瘪了的首级！这时候一直使煤油灯为之黯然失色的晨曦，却洒照在那火红的大胡子和深陷下去的眼窝子上，也洒照在缀满未经琢凿的绿松石的一道滚粗的金箍上，而那些绿松石都是卡内汉从砸烂了的小神庙里细心地捡起来后，再放上去的。

"现在你看，"卡内汉说，"那个皇帝还是旧习不改，就像他生前一模一样——他这个头戴王冠的卡菲里斯坦国王。可怜的老丹尼尔——他曾经做过一代君主呢！"

我一看，不由得浑身战栗，因为，尽管他的容颜几乎毁损殆尽，但马尔瓦尔枢纽站上那个人的头，我毕竟还是认得出来的。这时，卡内汉起身要走了。我竭力拦阻他。幸好他并不打算马上往外走。"让我把那威士忌带走，再给我一点儿零钱吧，"他气喘吁吁地说，"我一度也当过国王。我就去找行政长官代表，要

---

① 丹尼尔走过来说这一段文字，表示对皮奇精神上进行鼓励，要继续他那未竟的事业；又写到皮奇说话时所产生的幻觉，好像自己手里捧着丹的首级在前进。事实上，这一幻觉已与现实结合在一起，此刻皮奇手里真的捧着丹的首级和金冠。

like a child for ten minutes.

"They was cruel enough to feed him up in the temple, because they said he was more of a God than old Daniel that was a man. Then they turned him out on the snow, and told him to go home, and Peachey came home in about a year, begging along the roads quite safe; for Daniel Dravot he walked before and said, 'Come along, Peachey, It's a big thing we're doing. ' The mountains they danced at night, and the mountains they tried to fall on Peachey's head, but Dan he held up his hand, and he never let go of Dan's head. They gave it to him as a present in the temple, to remind him not to come again, and though the crown was pure gold, and Peachey was starving, never would Peachey sell the same. You knew Dravot, Sir! You knew Right Worshipful Brother Dravot! Look at him now!"

He fumbled in the mass of rags round his bent waist; brought out a black horsehair bag embroidered with silver thread; and shook therefrom on to my table—the dried, withered head of Daniel Dravot! The morning sun that had long been paling the lamps struck the red beard and blind sunken eyes; struck, too, a heavy circlet of gold studded with raw turquoises, that Carnehan placed tenderly on the battered temples.

"You behold now," said Carnehan, "The Emperor in his habit as he lived—the King of Kafiristan with his crown upon his head. Poor old Daniel that was a monarch once!"

I shuddered, for, in spite of defacements manifold, I recognized the head of the man of Marwar Junction. Carnehan rose to go. I attempted to stop him. He was not fit to walk abroad. "Let me take away the whisky, and give me a little money," he gasped. "I was a King once. I'll go to the Deputy Commissioner and ask to set in the Poorhouse till I get my health. No, thank you, I can't wait till you get a carriage for me. I've urgent private affairs—in the South—at Marwar. "

He shambled out of the office and departed in the

求进济贫院,好让我恢复一下健康。不,谢谢尔,我可等不到你给我派一辆马车啦。我私下里还有急事要办——在南方——在马尔瓦尔。"

他踉踉跄跄地走出了编辑部办公室,朝着行政长官代表府邸走去。那天中午,碰巧我走过热得令人眩晕的马尔路,看见有一个弯腰曲背的人正在路边白蒙蒙的尘雾里匍匐爬行,手里托着一顶帽子,就像英国街头卖唱的歌手一样浑身瑟瑟发抖,真叫人看了潸然泪下。眼前一个人影儿都见不到。他孑然一身,一面不断地晃动自己的脑袋,一面从鼻子里哼唱道:

> 好男儿纷纷出发,奔赴战场,
> 会得到金光闪闪的王冠一顶;
> 他那血红的战旗在远方招展,
> 有谁跟着他的队伍继续行进?

我又等了一会儿,可再也听不到什么了,就让那个可怜的人登上我的马车,把他送到最近的一个传教士那里,以便最后把他转到济贫院去。他在车上的时候,把上面这首赞歌反复地唱了两遍,因为他压根儿不认得我,所以,我就让他嘴里一直哼呀哈地唱到了传教士那里。

两天以后,我向济贫院的管理人打听他的健康情况。

"他已被确认中了暑,昨天一清早就死了,"那个管理人说,"他光着脑袋在正午炎炎烈日下待了半个钟头,是真的吗?"

"是的,"我说,"可你知不知道他临死时身上还有什么东西?"

"我可不知道。"那个管理人说。

于是这个事情也就到此结束了。

—讨 论—■

乍一看,这好像仅仅是描写在遥远的外国某地冒险经历的一篇小说。其中写到旅途见闻,神秘的陌生人,打仗场面,异教徒神庙,疯狂的想法,以及如同在十字架上受刑等情景。许多精心安排足以引起悬念的巧妙设计,使得读者对事态的每个转折处越发萌生好奇心。

direction of the Deputy Commissioner's house. That day at noon I had occasion to go down the blinding hot Mall, and I saw a crooked man crawling along the white dust of the roadside, his hat in his hand, quavering dolorously after the fashion of street-singers at Home. There was not a soul in sight, and he was out of all possible earshot of the houses. And he sang through his nose, turning his head from right to left:

> *The Son of Man goes forth to war,*
> *A golden crown to gain;*
> *His blood-red banner streams afar—*
> *Who follows in his train?*

I waited to hear no more, but put the poor wretch into my carriage and drove him off to the nearest missionary for eventual transfer to the Asylum. He repeated the hymn twice while he was with me, whom he did not in the least recognize, and I left him singing it to the missionary.

Two days later I inquired after his welfare of the Superintendent of the Asylum.

"He was admitted suffering from sunstroke. He died early yesterday morning," said the Superintendent. "Is it true that he was half an hour bareheaded in the sun at midday?"

"Yes," said I, "but do you happen to know if he had anything upon him by any chance when he died?"

"Not to my knowledge," said the Superintendent.

And there the matter rests.

At first glance, this seems to be merely a story of adventure in a far-off and exotic place. There are journeys, mysterious strangers, battles, pagan temples, madness, a crucifixion. The reader's curiosity about the turn of events is whetted by many cunning devices for provoking suspense. For instance, the first

例如,从头一个陌生人秘密的口信,引出了二等车厢里那个蓄红胡子的人。市集上那个商人和他的仆人,后来却成为准备出门远行的冒险家。或者,更进一层说,在有关石头上标记的那段片段(见重要词汇)中,每一件事情暂时还都在悬念之中,一直到这个秘密标记被泄露时为止。换句话说,吉卜林不仅玩弄着读者对故事最后结局所怀有的那种好奇心,而且还大大增强了我们对故事中每一个情节发展的结果的悬念。读者的好奇心经常被作者所利用。

此外,我们还可以看到,在这篇看来以情节占优势的小说中,一个事件如何产生又一个事件。例如,由于结婚一事出了纰漏,从而导致这两位国王的垮台。然而,尽管我们可以把各种不同的片断连接起来,成为说明因果关系的一条链子,但我们还是可以看到:这条链子实际上是由各种人物性格本身所决定的。

其次,如果单从表面上加以考虑的话,要表现动机形成的过程,似乎并没有多大困难。许多人如同皮奇和德雷沃特一样渴求财富和权力,所以在讨论动机时,我们似乎就毋须再深入研究这个问题了(当然,这是就绝大多数冒险小说在表现动机方面来说的)。然而,我们可以看到,在这篇小说里,动机显然更为复杂。比方说,正如国王们攫取他们的权力一样,那种单纯追求财富和权力的欲望,特别是对德雷沃特来说,已开始发生了变化。对于他们统治下的子民,德雷沃特等人越来越意识到有一种责任感和自豪感。德雷沃特开始谈论到有关引进熟练的行政管理人员,并以一种意想不到的谦卑态度,承认帝王统治问题远比他过去设想的更为复杂。他甚至开始幻想不如把他的王国移交给维多利亚女王——从而使他在历史上获得大不列颠帝国缔造者之一的地位。实际上,正是这个人物性格的发展,结果成了导致他覆亡的因素之一,因为要求结婚这种欲望,不仅仅是他单纯寻求伴侣那种人所共有的欲望——虽然他也正在考虑这个问

stranger's mysterious message leads to the red-bearded man in the second-class carriage. The trader and his servant in the bazaar turn out to be the adventurers ready for their journey. Or, to go further, in the *episode* (see Glossary) concerning the mark on the stone, everything hangs for a moment in the balance until the mark is disclosed. Kipling, in other words, not only plays on the reader's curiosity about the final outcome, but plays up our suspense as to the outcome of the individual steps in the story's development. Curiosity is constantly exploited.

Furthermore, we can see how, in this story in which plot seems to be so dominant in interest, one incident is caused by another. For instance, the marriage causes the discovery that brings on the ruin of the kings. But though we can link up the various episodes into a chain of cause and effect, we can see that this chain really depends upon the characters themselves.

Again, considered superficially, the matter of motivation seems to present little difficulty. Many men desire riches and power, as do Peachey and Dravot; and it may seem that we need go no further into the matter in our discussion of the motivation. (Indeed, this is as far as most adventure stories do go in presenting motivation.) But we can see that in this story, the motivation is more complicated. For example, as the kings acquire their power, the simple desire for riches and power, especially for Dravot, begins to change. There is a growing sense of responsibility for, and pride in, the people that they rule. Dravot begins to talk about bringing in skilled administrators, recognizing with an unexpected kind of humility that the business of kingship is more complicated than he had thought. He even begins to dream of turning over his kingdom to Queen Victoria—of taking his place in history as one of the Empire Builders. Actually, it is this development of character that proves to be one of the factors leading to his downfall, for the desire for

题——而且也是代表这样一种欲望,即企图建立一种皇权,以便在他死后传给自己的后裔,继续统治这个王国。所以说,这种婚礼就必须是公开的,并且要举行相当隆重的典礼和宗教仪式。

冒险事迹本身是和人物性格的发展同时并进的。那就是说,小说一开头我们遇到的那几个人,就如下文所显示的,他们如同流浪者一样,总是"从事物的底层,亦即生活阴暗面来观察事物"的。但德雷沃特并没有像一个流浪者那样死去:"他们简直把他当成一头公牛,一个劲儿往他背上乱刺。'他妈的你们不生眼睛的!'这个国王说,'难道你们就不让我像一个出身高贵的人那样死去吗?'"他要求"像一个出身高贵的人",像一个国王和像一个王人君子那样死去。甚至于皮奇其人,尽管他的地位在通篇故事中始终依附于德雷沃特的地位,但他照样分享着这种新的尊贵的高位。也出生入死地穿越荒山野岭,历尽艰难险阻,终于回来了,但他决不把装着国王的首级和王冠——亦即皇权的象征——的那个口袋扔掉。所以,说起来似乎自相矛盾的是,当这两个流浪者,"游手闲荡的人"的那种假皇权一旦被人夺去,充分说明他们原是凡夫俗子之际,他们却成为最最地道的国王了。那就是说,失掉的只是外在的皇权,得到的却是内在的皇权。

这种设想可以提示我们再回过头来仔细琢磨一下导致他们冒险失败的原因究竟在哪里。当地土著一直认为,他们是天神——而不是世俗的国王。因此,皮奇和德雷沃特的权力,乃是作为天神的国王的权力,而不是作为尘世俗物的国王的权力。可是,作为天神的国王的德雷沃特,却一心要做一个凡夫俗子——他有七情六欲,仅仅行使天神一般的权力,那显然是满足不了的。他一心要攫取权力,做一个天神(因为,要掌握统治土著的权力,那他就非得是一个天神不可,正如我们发现的那样),而他却又渴望做一个凡夫俗子。这就是他所

marriage is not merely his simple human desire for companionship—though this is present—but it is also a desire to found a royal line, to leave someone to rule the kingdom after his death. The wedding, therefore, must be public, with due ceremony and ritual.

The adventure itself has gone hand in hand with a development of character. That is, the men we meet at the beginning of the story are the kind who, as outcasts, see "things from the underside where the lath and plaster is not smoothed off." But Dravot does not die like an outcast: "They prodded him behind like an ox. 'Damn your eyes!' says the King. 'you suppose I can't die like a gentleman?'" He does die "like a gentlemen," like a king and like a man. And even Peachey, whose position is subordinate to Dravot's throughout the story, participates in this new dignity. He comes back through the wild mountains, through terrors and hardships, but he never relinquishes the bag containing the head of the King and the crown, the symbol of kingship. So, paradoxically, the two outcasts, the "loafers," become most truly kings in the moment when their false kingship is taken from them and they become fully men. That is, when external kingship is lost, internal kingship is achieved.

This idea may prompt us to look back again at the meaning of the situation that brings about the ruin of the adventure. The natives have thought of them as gods—not as human kings. The Power of Peachey and Dravot is, thus, that of the king-as-god, not that of the king-as-man. But Dravot, the king-as-god, wants to be a man—he has human instincts that the mere exercise of godlike power cannot satisfy. He wants to have power, to be a god (for, to have power over the natives, he must be a god, as we discover), and he longs to be a man. This is the dilemma he is caught in, and the dilemma that ruins him.

陷入的进退两难的困境,正是这种困境最后把他毁了。单就这一点来说,这篇小说本身即可表明,从某种意义上而言,乃是一种皇权的研究。并且联系到德雷沃特之死,还可以对这种皇权继续进行研究,因为我们已经看到,德雷沃特虽已身亡,但他却得到了另一种皇权,而对这种皇权的性质则需要再进一步加以解释了。

也许总的目的可以概括如下。驱使这些游手闲荡的人去冒险的,就是梦想得到皇权,但是,这种种皇权既不受宪法的种种限制所束缚,也不仅仅依赖于社会协调,更不是徒具空名的国家元首,或是作为国家权力的象征,而是具有绝对权力的一种"真正的"皇权。这样一种皇权就决定作为天神的他们仍然要高高在上地脱离人性,可是话又说回来,他们毕竟是凡夫俗子,而凡夫俗子即使不是为了攫取权力,也会丧失他的人性。具有讽刺意味的是,德雷沃特最后行使他的神权,只不过是为了要成为一个凡夫俗子——去满足他那基本的人所共有的七情六欲罢了。这一步骤导致了覆亡,但更加具有讽刺意味的是,事实上,德雷沃特就在他的覆亡之际,却表现出最最地道的国王风度。这对下面这些读者来说就会觉得特别富于真实感,因为他们虽然只看到在向愚昧无知的部族人炫耀神权时,德雷沃特要弄了一种庸俗的噱头和骗术,但对他那种临危不惧、视死如归的风度却大为赞赏。所以说,这篇小说里包含着在各种不同的皇权之间所形成的对照,以及在各种不同的权力(包括外在的权力和内在的权力,驾驭他人的权力和驾驭自己的权力)之间所形成的对照。

上述有关《国王迷》的介绍,当然并不等于说对这篇小说已做出了充分的阐述。各种观点和其他技巧细节方面,都应该加以考虑研究。下列问题只不过是在全面分析了这篇小说后应该提出的问题中极小的一部分。学生可以任选几题作为练习,并分别进行详细论述。

The story at this point shows itself to be in a sense, then, a study of kingship, and there is a continuation of this study of kingship in the account of Dravot's death, where, as we have seen, Dravot achieves another kind of kingship and the nature of kingship is redefined.

Perhaps the general point may be summarized as follows. The loafers are impelled by a dream of kingship, but not a kingship hedged about by constitutional limitations, not a kingship dependent upon a mere social arrangement, not a kingship with a mere figurehead or symbol for the power of the state, but a "real" kingship of absolute power. Such power depends upon their remaining aloof from humanity as gods; yet they are men, and man, not even for power, will forfeit his humanity. It is ironical that Dravot finally exercises his godlike power only in order to become a man—to satisfy his basic human desires. This step brings ruin, but there is a further irony in the fact that Dravot becomes most truly kingly at the moment of his ruin. Especially is this true for the reader who sees simply a kind of tawdry showmanship and deception in the parade of godlike power over the ignorant tribesmen, but who admires the way Dravot meets his death. Thus the story involves a contrast between kinds of kingship, between kinds of power, external and internal, power over others and power over oneself.

This account of "The Man Who Would Be King" does not, of course, provide a full interpretation of the story. Various aspects of *point* of *view* (see Glossary) and other technical matters should be considered. The questions that follow are only a few of those that should be raised in a full analysis of the story. The student should choose several of these topics as exercises and write a full discussion of one of them.

思考题 ■

1. 皮奇正在哼唱的那一支赞歌竟被作者听到了,为什么说这是恰如其分的? 唱这一支赞歌符合他的性格吗? 这一支赞歌和这篇小说的"意义"有何联系? 明确指出这一件小事中所包含的讽刺意义。

2. 不管德雷沃特是"神"还是"人",比利·菲什都效忠于他吗? 在这篇小说的其他部分中,还有哪些地方可以说明他确实是忠心耿耿的?

3. 德雷沃特和皮奇签订的这个合约,是幽默而又惹人生怜,还是大言不惭,夸夸其谈?

4. 这篇小说用第一人称讲述,对我们来确定各种人物的身份有何帮助? 其实有两个讲述者,即新闻记者和皮奇。这里面所包含的逻辑是什么?

5. 皮奇如同在十字架上一样受刑,这一情节有什么意义? （潘庆舲 译）

1. Why is it appropriate that Peachey should be heard singing the particular hymn that he sings? Is it in his character to sing this particular hymn? How is the hymn related to the "meaning" of the story? Define the ironies involved in this incident.

2. Is Billy Fish loyal to Dravot as "god" or as "man"? What light does the fact of his loyalty shed on the rest of the story?

3. Is the contract signed by Dravot and Peachey humorous, pathetic, or heroic?

4. How does the fact that this story is told by a first-person narrator help us to define the characters? As a matter of fact, there are two narrators, the newspaper man and Peachey. What is the logic behind this?

5. What is the significance of the crucifixion of Peachey?

人物性格
What Character Reveals

真正震撼人心的矛盾是人与人之间发生的冲突

本章所选作品，可说是专门着眼于小说人物性格问题的。但是在这之前，我们已有机会不止一次地观察到，小说从来不是孤立地处理人物性格的，因为怎样的人决定他有怎样的行为。作为观察者，我们也是首先根据人的行为来判断人的。

如果回顾一下前章所选的作品，我们不难发现，人物的性格是和人物的行为不可分割地交织在一起的。虽然前章里我们的注意力主要集中在作品的情节问题上，但我们知道，不涉及性格问题，是无法讨论这些作品的。所以我们曾一再地提出人物行为是否符合性格的问题，就是说，他们的行为在心理上是否真实可信？

虽然情节和性格是相互渗透的，但在某一时期强调其某一方面也未尝不可。我们在这一章里就着重考察一下有关人物性格的某些问题。我们不妨从性格的外部特征方面谈起。从某种根本意义上讲，小说中的每个人物肯定和我们自己很相像，那就是说他或者她肯定是可以认识的人，甚至是我们自己一样的人，但是有些人物又显然地与其他人物不相同，也就是说具有更强的个性。在《沃尔特·米蒂的隐秘生活》里，我们遇到的是个一眼就能辨认的性格典型。《国王迷》里的德雷沃特则是一个一般读者不常遇到的人物。如果说他显得很真实，那是因为他得到了令人信服的刻画。德雷沃特是个行动着的人，而不是个内向的人，这就使作者在刻画他时容易多了。如果人物的内心活动比他的外部表现更加复杂也更具意义的话，那么这里就会产生更为复杂特殊的性格表现问题。

作家是怎样表现他的人物的呢？是直接

The stories in this section may be considered with a special view to the problem of character in fiction. But, as we have had occasion to observe several times before this, fiction never deals with character in isolation, for what a man is determines what he does, and it is primarily through what he does that we who observe him know what he is.

The proof of the inextricable interweaving of character and action may be most readily seen by a glance back at the stories in the preceding section. Though our attention was focused there upon problems of plot, we found that we could not discuss these stories without going into the problems of character. We had constantly to ask whether the actions performed were "in character"; that is, whether they were psychologically credible.

Though plot and character interpenetrate each other, there is some justification for stressing one problem at a time: let us consider here some of the problems of characterization. We may begin with the problem of exposition. In some fundamental sense, every character in fiction must resemble ourselves; that is, he or she must be recognizably human even as we are. But some characters are obviously much more special than others, and require much fuller characterization. In "The Secret Life of Walter Mitty" we encounter an easily recognized type. Dravot in "The Man Who Would Be King" is a man quite outside the average reader's common acquaintance, and if he is to seem real, he must be convincingly presented. The fact that Dravot is a man of action, not an introspective man, makes the author's task easier. If the character's inward life is more complicated and significant than his outer, more special problems of presentation may arise.

对人物的品质和特点加以概括呢,还是间接地(即通过对话和动作)加以揭示?就小说的本质而言,后者是它的特有的手段,但直接表现也经常被运用于小说,往往还很成功。这就要看作品的基本意图如何,要看取材的规模及其范围如何了。如果作家对每个人物的性格都采取间接表现法,即坚持每个人物都得通过自身的自然的谈吐、姿态和动作来逐渐展示其性格,那么这个过程也许会使人无法忍受。小说《项链》就表明,直接表现——甚至是概括性的表现——是可以运用得恰当而有效的(见该小说的开头3段)。但是当写到主要场景时,《项链》的作者就舍弃了概括性表现,而代之以戏剧性表现手法了。

直接表现的危害在于忽略了戏剧生动性和诱发读者的想象力。所以,直接叙述的表现用于相当平庸而成类型的人物,或者作为一种手段用于迅速地交代一些辅助性材料时是再好不过的了。对人物的直接表现也就是对人物的直接评论,这时作者只想"告知"我们应该如何感受和思考,而不想"描绘"一个场景以供我们想象。例如,在小说《带家具出租的房间》里,欧·亨利每每给主人公的动机和信念"加上评语",他老是牵牵读者的衣袖,用臂肘推推读者,要读者同情主人公的命运,这样真叫人受不了,简直会使人觉得他描写的整个场景好像都是虚假的。然而,在本章所选的劳伦斯的小说《请买票》里,我们就会看到直接评论——甚至明确地解释人物的动机——是有可能被作者运用得很成功的。

把相当平庸的人物和不同一般的人物加以对照,可以提示出小说范围内两个相反的极端。平庸而成类型的人物在小说里总是次要的。我们倾向于注意"有个性"的人物,虽然他在很多方面看上去都很平常。如果没有个性的人物在作品里占着主导地位,那么这篇作品也许称之为传说或者寓言更为恰当些(极端平庸的人物,仅仅是些类型,当然有可能会使我

How shall the author present his character? Directly, with a summary of his traits and characteristics, or indirectly (that is, through dialogue and action)? The very nature of fiction suggests that the second method is its characteristic means, yet direct presentation is constantly used in fiction, often effectively. Much depends upon the underlying purpose of the story and much depends upon matters of scope and scale. If the author made every presentation of character indirectly, insisting that each character gradually unfold himself through natural talk and gesture and action, the procedure might become intolerably boring. "The Necklace" indicates how direct presentation—and even summary presentation—can be properly and effectively used. But when he comes to the significant scenes of the story, the author of "The Necklace" discards summary in favor of dramatic presentation.

The danger of direct presentation is that it tends to forfeit the vividness of drama and the reader's imaginative participation. Direct, descriptive presentation works best, therefore, with rather flat and typical characters, or as a means to get rapidly over more perfunctory materials. When direct presentation of character becomes also direct comment on a character, the author may find himself "telling" us what to feel and think rather than "rendering" a scene for our imaginative participation. In "The Furnished Room," for example, O. Henry tends to "editorialize" on the hero's motives and beliefs, and constant plucking at the reader's sleeve and nudging him to sympathize with the hero's plight may become so irritating that the whole scene seems falsified. Yet in D. H. Lawrence's "Tickets, Please," a story near the end of this section, we shall see that direct commentary—and even explicit interpretation of the characters' motives—can on occasion be effectively used by an author.

The contrast between rather ordinary characters and out-of-the-way characters can be used to suggest the opposing extremes that bound the domain of fiction. The ordinary and typical characters tend to be secondary in a story. We tend to seek the "individualized" character, even if he seems common in many ways. If the poorly individualized character tends to be prominent, then the story is

们对小说完全失去兴趣。即使每个主人公确实在一定程度上代表我们所有的人，但任何一篇认真地展开故事情节的小说，都不可能是与普遍人性几乎同样纯粹的抽象物）。

在另一个极端，我们又会发现，小说人物是那样离奇古怪，那样不合常轨，那样巧戾乖张，以至于使人无法相信他是个正常的人。小说到了这一步就不成其为小说，倒成为精神病研究方面的病例了，不过对于有能耐的艺术家来说，这一点并不是限制他的框框。假如一个作家具有足够深刻的观察力，那么任何人物都会表现出复杂和偏颇性。就是疯狂本身也不可能游离于小说关心的范围之外。在第四章的一篇小说。《纪念爱米丽的一朵玫瑰花》里，威廉·福克纳描述的就是一个反常到近于疯狂的人物，然而许多人都觉得这篇小说具有普遍的人生意义，而不是一个特殊的病例分析报告。在"疯狂"的后面潜伏着某种含义。

由此看来，小说的领域是一个可信的人类世界，一个千姿百态、瞬息万变而令人吃惊的世界。既然这是一个人类世界，它就可以得到具体的和戏剧性的表现。小说应该排斥两个极端。一个极端是纯抽象的世界，经纪人、平庸的家庭主妇、标准的美国人、普通人类；另一个极端是单纯的荒诞行为、心理变态者、精神病患者病例上的记录（不过，艺术家完全有可能根据俄狄浦斯的情绪把平庸的家庭主妇或者年轻人写进成功的作品，但他这样做时，当然比必须仅仅满足科学上的或统计学上的兴趣还要多一点东西，进行抽象概括时必须真实而可信，而且要具有某种广义的"道德"观念方面的意义）。

据前所述，不难看到，作家在表现人物性格时选择何种方法是取决于多种因素的。作家决定何时对人物的特征和事件进行概括，何时进行直接表现，何时通过人物对话和动作来表达人物的感情，这些取决于小说的基本目的，取决于小说的结构方式，这种方式使情节

probably tilted toward fable or parable. (*Completely* flat characters, mere types, would, of course, probably take us out of fiction altogether. Even if every hero does at some level represent all of us, no seriously developed story can be about as pure an abstraction as our common humanity.)

At the opposite extreme, we find the fictional character who is so eccentric, so much out of the way, so perverse, that he ceases to be humanly credible. Fiction at this point passes off imperceptibly into the psychiatric case study. This is not to put narrow limits upon what the artist can do. If one looks deep enough, any character reveals complexities and eccentricities. Even madness is not to be automatically ruled out of the subject matter of fiction. In "A Rose for Emily," a story in section 4, William Faulkner tells of a character perverted to the point of madness; yet many people will feel that the story has a large human significance, and is not merely a clinician's report. Behind the "madness" lurks a meaning.

The domain of fiction is, then, the world of credible human beings, admittedly an amazingly diverse and varied world. Since it is the world of human beings, it can be presented concretely and dramatically. What is excludes at either end is the world of pure abstraction: economic man, Mrs. Average Housewife, the typical American, *Homo sapiens*; and at the other extreme, the mere freak, the psychological monster, the report from the psychiatrist's casebook. (But of course an artist may be able to put Mrs. Average Housewife or the young man with the classic Oedipus complex into a successful story. To do so, of course, he must satisfy more than a scientific and statistical interest: the abstraction must be made credible and significant in some broad "moral" sense.

From what has been said already, it is plain that an author's selection of modes of character presentation will depend upon a number of things. His decision on when to summarize traits or events, on when to describe directly, and on when to allow the character

得以展开,经过错综复杂的中间阶段而最终促成不可避免的结局。

揭示人物性格的最重要的手段之一,当然是人物语言,人物的谈话方式。讲话简短的士兵,爱发牢骚的打杂女工,腼腆的教会学校女学生,饶舌的酒店掌柜,迂腐的教授——所有这些人物都有他们自己的语汇以及组合这些语汇的方式。要使作品可信,一个作家必须使他笔下人物的说话"符合性格",因为要表现一个异乎寻常的人物性格,作家惯用的方法就是用这个人物的口头语或者习惯用词来吸引我们的注意力。比如,皮奇和德雷沃特的富有个性的语言就是这样。

这样运用人物语言是达到戏剧性表现的一种卓有成效的方法。但是,如果运用得过于频繁,这就很可能会使一篇小说由于对话过多而不成为小说。间接的交代,就像人物的概述和性格描写一样,也是一种能够较快奏效的方法,在小说里有其非常重要的作用。比如在小说《战争》里就是这样,丈夫对妻子如何应该得到同情所做的解释就是一段非常适当的间接交代:他觉得自己责无旁贷,应该……讲一讲,那个可怜的女人确实值得人们同情,因为这场战争……要把……独子从她身边夺走。但是,那位竭力赞成应该为国家献出儿子才显其崇高的老人所说的话,则是一种直接的交代。老人的讲话对于这篇小说是很重要的,这是为了戏剧生动性的需要,是故事发展的转折点——他的话全部做了直接交代。所以我们便读到了"'胡扯淡。'另一个旅客插话说"等等的内容。

人物性格对小说来说是如此重要,所以要想了解一篇小说的基本情况,唯一的方法就是问一下"这是谁的故事?"这也就是说,要想知道小说所系的是谁的命运往往是首先提出来的重要问题。有时,回答相当明确。例如,在《沃尔特·米蒂的隐秘生活》里,显而易见的是沃尔特·米蒂的故事,而不是米蒂太太的故

to express his feelings through dialogue and action, will depend upon the general end of the story and upon the way in which the action of the story is to be developed from a beginning, through a complicating middle, to an inevitable end.

One of the most important modes for character revelation is, of course, speech—the ways that characters talk. The laconic soldier, the querulous charwoman, the shy convent-school girl, the garrulous barkeep, the pedantic professor—all have their own vocabularies and their ways of putting words together. An author, in order to be convincing, must have his characters speak "in character," and his normal way of presenting an unusual character is to give us the flavor of his dialect and idiom, for instance, notice the characteristic language of Peachey and Dravot.

This use of speech is a rich resource for dramatic presentation. But again, if used incessantly it might kill a story by making it too talky. Indirect discourse, like character summary and character description, is a quicker way of getting over the ground, and in fiction has its very important uses. Notice, for example, in "War" that the husband's explanation of why his wife is to be pitied is very properly indirect discourse: "And he felt it his duty to explain... that the poor woman was to be pitied, for the war was taking away from her her only son," But the speeches of the old man who argues for the sublimity of sacrificing one's son for one's country are given as direct discourse. The importance of the old man's speeches to the story, the need for dramatic vividness, the very pace of the story—all call for direct discourse. Thus we have "'Nonsense,' interrupted another traveler," and so on.

So important is character to fiction that one way to approach the basic pattern of a story is to ask "Whose story is this?" In other words, it usually is the first importance to see whose fortunes are at stake. Sometimes the answer is quite obvious. In "The Secret Life of Walter Mitty," for example, it is very easy to

事。米蒂太太的作用,仅仅是使她丈夫的境遇清楚地显示出来罢了。米蒂太太无疑也有自己的故事——我们中间谁没有自己的故事?——詹姆斯·瑟伯本可以有选择地讲述一点她的故事,但是,他在小说里并没有这样做。一眼就可以看出小说写的是米蒂先生的故事。但是,在《国王迷》里,要想看出这是有关谁的故事就不那么容易了。一种意见倾向于认为这是德雷沃特的故事,理由是德雷沃特是作为两个人中的强者出现的,尤其在小说结尾时,他以英雄的姿态屹然而立,而且如同一个国王一般地死去。但另一种意见至少可以争辩说,这是皮奇的故事,皮奇因为目睹了德雷沃特的英雄行为已对为王者应具的品性了解得一清二楚,再说他又是那样忠贞不渝地怀念着德雷沃特,因此他自身就起到了主人公的作用。虽然,要想确切地说出或者更为重视地判断这篇小说究竟讲的是谁的故事,并不容易,但问题的提出倒是很有价值的。探讨这个问题将有助于理清人物与人物之间的相互关系。

关于德雷沃特和皮奇之间的关系,可以进一步说:从小说表面上看,我们读到的主要是属于某个叫"皮奇"的人的故事,也就是说,主要是某个不自觉地参与了事件并对事件做了解释的观察者的故事,但肇事者却是某个叫"德雷沃特"的人。在一篇小说中,"发生"的什么事情肯定不会仅是某种表面的东西。内在的东西——譬如关系的改易,心灵的变化——才是改变一个人生活的决定因素。

我们回头看一看《年轻的布朗大爷》中那些几乎毫无个性的人物吧。那个丈夫,还有那个妻子,在小说里除了扮演一对年轻恩爱的夫妻,并相互坚信对方的"善良"之外,简直可以说是不存在的人物。从总体上说,这篇小说的基点与其说在于创造某种特色,不如说在于它叙述了在森林中发生的那些事情。这篇小说简直就像一个传说,或者一则寓言,因为它对

see that this is Mr. Mitty's story and not Mrs. Mitty's. Her only function is to throw light upon her husband's situation. Mrs. Mitty undoubtedly has a story—who of us has not? —and James Thurber might have elected to tell it. But he has not done so here. It is easy to see that this is Mr. Mitty's story, but it is not so easy to see whose story it is that is related in "The Man Who Would Be King." One is inclined to say that is it Dravot's story. He is pictured as the dominant member of the pair; it is he who rises to the heroic gesture at the end and who dies like a king. Yet one could at least argue that this is Peachey's story, since he too learns the nature of kingship through witnessing Dravot's heroic action and since, magnificently loyal to the memory of Dravot, he acts out a heroic role himself. But even when it is not easy to say— or even important to determine—precisely whose story it is, the question is usually worth putting. To entertain the question is to throw light upon the relation of character with character.

One further word about the Dravot-Peachey relationship: we shall encounter in this text stories that belong primarily to a "Peachey"—that is, to an observer of the action who unconsciously participates in and interprets the meaning that a "Dravot" initates. For what "happens" in a story is not necessarily some external thing. An internal thing—a shifted relationship, a change of heart—may decisively change someone's life.

Let us return to "Young Goodman Brown" to observe characters that have very little to individualize them. Both the husband and the wife scarcely exist beyond the roles they play as the loving young couple, each believing in the "goodness" of the other. The story depends on what happens in the forest—*in general*—rather than on a special quality. It approaches fable, or parable, with interest in character reduced to a minimum.

人物性格的兴趣几乎接近于零。

　　我们在前章讨论情节问题时,曾就小说的矛盾冲突做过大量探讨。矛盾冲突和人物性格有着极其密切的关系,因为我们不可能对无人格的抽象的矛盾冲突长久地感兴趣。虽然说动物之间的冲突也会激发起我们的兴趣,但那是因为我们很容易就会用我们自己去替代它们。确实,就是在人和自然或者其他无生命力量的冲突中,我们也会进行这样的替代。一个与大火搏斗的人,或者一个在暴风雨中奋然前进的人,或者一个竭力想置饥饿和痛苦于度外的人,他们很可能会把那些无人格的力量,当做另一个有生命的人——一个有血有肉的敌人那样来对待。

　　人类跟自然界的竞争是一种最简单的斗争形式,这种形式终究很少使人感兴趣。可以说,几乎没有什么小说是单纯地写人跟自然界的冲突的。真正震撼人心的矛盾是人与人之间发生的冲突。这是绝大多数小说所取的题材。在这里,我们看到英雄战胜恶人,真正的爱情折服纨绔子弟,业余侦探巧算狡黠的谋杀者,诸如此类的成套的故事。这些都是当今颇为流行的那些小说的标准内容。但是,就在这张开列着人与人冲突内容的一览表里,我们还看到了许多更敏感、更有深度也更动人的小说。人类,我们自己也不例外,是善与恶的混合体,所以人常常会发现自己处于各种意志的矛盾中,处于冲突中——不仅对外界事物,在自己内心也有多种因素在相互冲突着。确实,较为成熟的典范性小说曾处理过各种不同性格之间的矛盾冲突,现在更为成熟的第三阶段已经形成,在这个阶段,小说不得不处理的是人与其自身的矛盾冲突。

　　我们可以借助某些你读过的小说来证实上面最后一句话。《国王迷》是一篇"动作"小说,其主要冲突是德雷沃特跟野蛮的土人之间的冲突,德雷沃特想在他们身上实现自己的意愿。然而,就在这篇小说里,更重要也更具有

In our earlier discussion of plot we had a good deal to say about conflict in fiction. Conflict has the closest relation to character, for we cannot remain long interested in conflicts between impersonal forces. If conflicts between animals strike us as interesting, that is because we can rather easily project ourselves into them. We actually make some such projection even in the instance of a man's conflict with the elements or with some other inanimate force. A man who is fighting a fire or trying to beat his way through a great storm, or who is trying to hold out against hunger and pain is likely to treat the impersonal force as if it were another being—the Enemy.

Man's contest with external forces is the simplest kind of struggle and finally the least interesting. Few stories deal with it in purity. The great and typical human conflicts is one human being's conflict with other human beings. This is the stuff most fiction is made of. Here we find typical stories of the hero defeating the villain, of the true lover winning out over the wealthy roué, of the amateur detective outwitting the clever murderer. These are the standard contests of our more popular fiction. But in this general category of one human being against another, we also find stories of greater sensitivity and depth and penetration. For human beings, being the mixture of good and bad that we are, frequently find themselves at cross purposes and in conflict—not only with outsiders but with aspects of their own natures. Indeed, the more mature examples of conflict between character and character shade off into the third category that has to do with man's conflict with himself.

We can illustrate this last statement by referring to some of the stories that you have already read. "The Man Who Would Be King" is an "action" story, and the conflict is primarily a conflict between Dravot and the wild tribesmen upon whom he means to impose his will. But even in this story, a more important and significant conflict is an inward

意义的冲突,则发生在人物的内心。由于欲望和那与日俱增的治国意识之间的冲突,致使德雷沃特丧失了他的王国。后来,还是通过另一内心过程,即德雷沃特克服了他自己之后,他才最终获得了精神上的胜利。看一下皮兰德娄的《战争》,内心冲突的重要性同样能得到证实。从表面上看,这篇小说的冲突是那个情绪激烈的老人对自己儿子为国捐躯的看法和火车车厢里那些持怀疑态度但又通情达理的旅客的看法之间的冲突,那个老人据理力争,使其他人都心悦诚服,然而,就在说服他人的同时,老人却第一次发现他其实从未说服过自己。

在本书开头几章里我们就强调过,小说中真实的连贯性的重要意义。并强调它与事实完全符合的真实性有别。因为文学作品并不伪称自己就像记录实际事例的文件那样面面俱到,它所要表现的只是典型的、有代表性的和一般准则的要求。就小说或诗歌自身而言,我们首先关注的是真实的连贯性——各部分是如何连贯而构成一个有意义的整体的。

对于人物性格的表现来说,连贯性无论如何也不能说是无所谓的。人物必须真实可信,必须打动人,必须能驾驭我们的信心。诚然,提出来讨论的人物可以是有怪癖的人,也可以是个凶残的罪犯,甚至可以是个疯子,但他的思想和行为必须完全连贯统一。如果一篇小说的人物性格苍白而不动人,我们就会对这篇小说嗤之以鼻。但是不要忘记,小说人物所感受到的是符合他性格的感受,并不是我们读者的感受。举例说,一个比《项链》中的玛蒂尔德·罗瓦赛尔更明事理而少一点傲气的女人,如遇到同样的事情,也许就会把自己的苦衷向朋友和盘托出,从而很可能就避免了那种可怕的、不必要的后果。然而,罗瓦赛尔夫人有其自身性格的连贯统一性,这一点莫泊桑已经向

event. The conflict between his appetites and his growing sense of statesmanship costs Dravot his kingdom. And it is through another inward event, Dravot's conquest of himself, that his final spiritual victory comes. One can also illustrate the importance of inward conflict from Pirandello's story "War." Ostensibly the conflict is between the fervent old man's attitude toward sacrificing his son for his country and the attitudes of his apprehensive, all-too-human companions in the railway compartment. The old man's passionate arguments prevail over the minds of the others; but in persuading them, he discovers for the first time that he has never really persuaded himself.

Earlier in this book we argued for the importance of the truth of coherence as distinguished from the truth of correspondence. Since a work of literature does not pretend to be a factual document of actual events, but a typical and representative "action," the demands of truth of correspondence tend to be limited to correspondence to human nature and to the human norms. Within the story or poem itself we are primarily and unremittingly concerned with truth of coherence—with how the parts cohere into a total meaningful pattern.

Nowhere are the claims for coherence asserted more plainly than in the matter of character presentation. A character must be credible—must make sense, must be able to command our belief. True, the character in question may be an eccentric; he may be brutally criminal; he may even be mad. But his thoughts and actions must ultimately be coherent. If the characters in a story simply don't make sense, we have to reject the story. But we must remember that the kind of sense a character must make is his own kind, not our kind. For example, a more sensible, less proud woman than Mathilde Loisel in "The Necklace" might have made a clean breast of things to her friend and been spared the terrible and unnecessary consequences, but it is the coherence of Mme. Loisel's character that Maupassant must persuade us of. If he does not persuade us that his Mme. Loisel is really capable of accepting, and persisting

我们指明了,如果他不向我们指明,他的罗瓦赛尔夫人按其性格确实有可能承受失去项链后的那种困境,那么整篇小说就不可信了。由此可见,考察小说的一种明显办法就是问一下该小说中人物的动机和行为是否连贯统一。艺术大师们始终有能力把那么多怪诞不经而且经常显得自相矛盾的人性范例加以连贯统一的表现,这真是小说的光辉! （王秋荣 译）

through, the life of hardship that comes with the loss of the necklace, then the story itself is incredible. An obvious test of fiction then is to ask if the motives and actions of its characters are rendered coherent. It is the glory of fiction that great artists have been able to render coherent so many strange and out-of-the-way, often apparently self-contradictory, examples of human nature.

014. 田纳西的伙伴

（美）布雷特·哈特 著　　主 万 译

014. Tennessee's Partner

by Bret Harte

　　我想我们始终就不知道他的真名实姓。可是我们不知道他的姓名，的确一点儿没叫我们在交际上觉得怎么不方便，因为1854年在"沙洲"，大多数人都另取了个名字。有时候，这些名字是由于服装上的某种特色，像"粗蓝布杰克"；或是由于习惯上的一种癖好，像"发酵粉比尔"，这个人给这样叫着，因为他每天吃的面包里那种化学品数量特别多；再不然就是因为一种倒霉的错误，像"铁血海盗"，这是一个温和的老好人，他因为倒霉，把"黄铁矿"这几个字的音读错了①，因而博得了这个骇人听闻的称号。也许，这就是阀阅文章的简陋的开端，不过我不得不认为，这是因为在那种日子，一个人的真名实姓全要靠他自己空口来说。"你自己说你姓克利福德吗？"波斯顿异常轻蔑地向新来的一个怯生生的人说，"地狱里满是这种姓克利福德的！"接着，他把那个恰巧真姓克利福德的倒霉蛋介绍作"乡下佬查礼"——一时恶毒的奇想 后来竟然永远给叫下去了。

　　但是话回到田纳西的伙伴身上来，我们始终不知道他有什么别的名字，只知道他叫这个牵涉到别人的名称。后来我们才知道，他以前也是一个单独的有名有姓的人。他似乎在1853年离开了扑克滩到旧金山去，扬言要去讨个老婆。他走到斯托克屯，就此没再向前了。在斯托克屯，他在吃饭的那家旅馆里被一个年轻的女侍者迷住。一天早晨，他对她说了句话，逗得她相当亲切地笑了，不知怎么一撒娇，把一碟烤面包砸在他仰着的严肃、质朴的脸上，接着便迳进厨房

I DO not think that we ever knew his real name. Our ignorance of it certainly never gave us any social inconvenience, for at Sandy Bar in 1854 most men were christened anew. Sometimes these appellatives were derived from some distinctiveness of dress, as in the case of "Dungaree Jack"; or from some peculiarity of habit, as shown in "Saleratus Bill," so called from an undue proportion of that chemical in his daily bread; or from some unlucky slip, as exhibited in "The Iron Pirate," a mild, inoffensive man, who earned that baleful title by his unfortunate mispronunciation of the term "iron pyrites." Perhaps this may have been the beginning of a rude heraldry; but I am constrained to think that it was because a man's real name in that day rested solely upon his own unsupported statement. "Call yourself Clifford, do you?" said Boston, addressing a timid newcomer with infinite scorn; "hell is full of such Cliffords!" He then introduced the unfortunate man, whose name happened to be really Clifford, as "Jay-bird Charley"—an unhallowed inspiration of the moment that clung to him ever after.

But to return to Tennessee's Partner, whom we never knew by any other than this relative title. That he had ever existed as a separate and distinct individuality we only learned later. It seems that in 1853 he left Poker Flat to go to San Francisco, ostensibly to procure a wife. He never got any farther than Stockton. At that place he was attracted by a young person who waited upon the table at the hotel where he took his meals. One morning he said something to her which caused her to smile not unkindly, to somewhat coquettishly break a plate of toast over his upturned, serious, simple face, and to retreat to the kitchen. He followed her, and emerged a few moments later, covered with more toast and victory. That day week they were married by a justice of the peace, and returned to

---

　　① "黄铁矿"英文为 iron pyrites，"铁血海盗"为 iron pirate，读音和拼法都相近。

作者简介：布雷特·哈特（**Bret Harte**，1836—1902），美国小说家。1836年8月25日生于纽约州奥尔巴尼，1902年卒于英国伦敦。他经历加利福尼亚短暂的矿工生活后，成为报纸、期刊编辑和作家。他的作品建立了美国小说的地方色彩学派，如短篇小说《咆哮营的幸运儿》（*The Luck of Roaring Camp*，1868）和《扑克滩放逐的人们》（*The Outcasts of Poker Flat*，1869），诗作《异教徒中国佬》（*The Heathen Chinee*，1870）和与马克·吐温合著的剧作《啊，罪》（*Ah Sin*，1877），这些著作使他蜚声国际。19世纪70年代，他的作品失去了早年的光彩，之后他到欧洲担任领事，再也没回美国。

去了。他跟进去，一会儿工夫走出来，脸上沾着更多的烤面包，赢得了胜利。一星期后，他们由一个治安推事①公证结婚，回到扑克滩去。据我知道，这件事里还大有文章，不过我宁愿按照"沙洲"——产金的溪谷和酒吧间里——流传的那套话来说，因为在那里，一切看法都被一种强烈的幽默感冲淡了。

关于他们婚后的幸福，我们知道得很少。这也许是因为田纳西那会儿跟他的伙伴住在一块儿。有一天，他趁机向新娘子说了一套衷肠话儿，新娘子当时据说只相当亲切地笑笑，便规规矩矩地退避开了——这一次一直退到了马里斯维尔。田纳西跟到那儿去，他们俩没请治安推事帮忙，就在那儿成起家来了。田纳西的伙伴把老婆逃跑的这件事看得很平淡又很认真，这本来是他一贯的态度。可是，使大家惊讶的是，当田纳西有一天没带他伙伴的老婆——她已经又对别人笑笑，跟着别人走了——从马里斯维尔回来的时候，田纳西的伙伴却是第一个亲热地跟他握手来欢迎他的人。聚集到峡谷里来想看开枪火拼的小伙子，自然全大感愤慨。他们本来也许想说一些刻薄话来发泄自己的愤怒，可是看见田纳西的伙伴目光里那种严肃认真的神气，他们又止住了。其实，他是一个不苟言笑的人，一贯聚精会神在为难的情况下、令人不很愉快的那些切合实际的小事上。

同时，"沙洲"对田纳西普遍起了反感。大家都知道他是一个赌棍，又疑心他是一个小偷。田纳西的伙伴也给牵连到这片疑云里去了。他在上述那件事发生后，仍旧继续跟田纳西亲近，这只能归到他们俩可能有共同犯罪的关系上去。最后田纳西劣迹昭彰。有一天，他赶上一个到"红狗"去的陌生人。据那个陌生人后来说，田纳西讲了些有趣的掌故和旧事来消磨时间，可是谈到末了，竟然不合理地说出下面这些话来："现在，年轻人，请你把小刀、手枪和钱全交给我，你瞧，你的武器在红狗也许给你惹麻烦的，钱对心怀歹意的人的诱惑又太大。我想你说过，你住在旧金山。我设法来拜访你好了。"这儿也许可以说一下，田纳西非常风趣，这是任他怎么聚精会神地办正事时，都抑制不住的。

这一场"功绩"是他的最后一场。"红狗"和"沙

---

① 治安推事，英美两国的一种官职，其职务为处理和执行村镇上的琐细案件。

Poker Flat. I am aware that something more might be made of this episode, but I prefer to tell it as it was current at Sandy Bar—in the gulches and barrooms—where all sentiment was modified by a strong sense of humor.

Of their married felicity but little is known, perhaps for the reason that Tennessee, then living with his partner, one day took occasion to say something to the bride on his own account, at which, it is said, she smiled not unkindly and chastely retreated—this time as far as Marysville, where Tennessee followed her, and where they went to housekeeping without the aid of a justice of the peace. Tennessee's Partner took the loss of his wife simply and seriously, as was his fashion. But to everybody's surprise, when Tennessee one day returned from Marysville, without his partner's wife—she having smiled and retreated with somebody else—Tennessee's Partner was the first man to shake his hand and greet him with affection. The boys who had gathered in the cañon to see the shooting were naturally indignant. Their indignation might have found vent in sarcasm but for a certain look in Tennessee's Partner's eye that indicated a lack of humorous appreciation. In fact, he was a grave man, with a steady application to practical detail which was unpleasant in a difficulty.

Meanwhile a popular feeling against Tennessee had grown up on the Bar. He was known to be a gambler; he was suspected to be a thief. In these suspicions Tennessee's Partner was equally compromised; his continued intimacy with Tennessee after the affair above quoted could only be accounted for on the hypothesis of a copartnership of crime. At last Tennessee's guilt became flagrant. One day he overtook a stranger on his way to Red Dog. The stranger afterward related that Tennessee beguiled the time with interesting anecdote and reminiscence, but illogically concluded the interview in the following words: "And now, young man, I'll trouble you for your knife, your pistols, and your money. You see your weppings might get you into trouble at Red Dog, and your money's a temptation to the evilly disposed. I think you said your address was San Francisco. I shall endeavor to call." It may be stated here that Tennessee had a fine flow of humor, which no business preoccupation could wholly subdue.

This exploit was his last. Red Dog and Sandy Bar made common cause against the highwayman. Tennessee was hunted in very much the same fashion as his prototype, the grizzly. As the toils closed around him, he made a desperate dash through the Bar, emptying

洲"联合起来追捕这个绿林大盗。他们像搜索他的原型——灰熊——那样来追捕他。等罗网围着也越收越紧的时候。他拼死地夺路冲出"沙洲"去,朝着安凯酒吧间门前的那群人把子弹打光,一路奔到友熊谷,可是在"灰熊谷"那头,一个身材矮小的人骑着一匹灰马迎头拦住了他。他们默不作声地互相对望了一会儿。两个人都毫不畏怯,两个人都冷静、坚强,都是一种文明的典型人物,这在 17 世纪就会被称做是英勇的,而在 19 世纪就只不过是"不顾死活"。

"你手里有什么? ——我先叫①。"田纳西镇静地说。

"两张王牌②,一张一点。"那个陌生人同样镇静地说,一面拿出两把手枪和一柄猎刀来。

"我给你吃了。"田纳西回答。他说完赌徒的这句短语后,丢下那把没有用的手枪,跟着捕获他的人骑马跑回来。

那是一个温暖的夜晚。通常,当太阳落到遍长着小檞树的大山后面时,总吹起一点儿凉风,可是那一晚,凉风竟然避开了"沙洲"。小谷里闷得尽是热烘烘的树胶味;洲上腐烂的浮木也发出微弱的、难闻的霉湿气。白昼的狂热激动的情绪,依然充满了那个营地。灯光沿着河岸不定地晃动,在黄褐色的河流上射不出什么反影来。捷运公司办事处上面那个旧阁楼的窗子,衬着黑黝黝的松树,显得分外明亮。从没有窗帘遮住的窗玻璃外边,下面的闲人可以看见那时还在决定田纳西命运的那些人的身影。在这一切之上,矗立着内华达山,遥远而又冷漠,镂刻在黑暗的苍天之上,上面高悬着更遥远而又冷漠的星斗。

审讯田纳西的法官和陪审团都觉得,自己在判决方面多少应当为先前不合法的逮捕和起诉加以辩解,所以案件审讯得很公正,和他们的这种想法完全相符。"沙洲"的法律是毫不容情的,不过也不是报复性的。追捕时的紧张激动和私人情绪全都过去,田纳西现在已经安安稳稳地给抓住了,他们打算耐心听听不管什么辩护的意见,因为他们已经深信这种意见是不充足的。他们心里既然毫无疑问,自然乐意暂且假定这个犯人是无罪的。其实他们已经确信,他原则上应

---

① 我先叫,打牌术语,即要求对方摊牌。

② 原文为 bower。在 euchre 牌戏中,以 11 点为王牌,称做 bower。

his revolver at the crowd before the Arcade Saloon, and so on up Grizzly Cañon, but at its farther extremity he was stopped by a small man on a gray horse. The men looked at each other a moment in silence. Both were fearless, both self-possessed and independent; and both types of a civilization that in the seventeenth century would have been called heroic, but in the nineteenth simply "reckless."

"What have you got there? —I call," said Tennessee, quietly.

"Two bowers and an ace," said the stranger, as quietly, showing two revolvers and a bowie knife.

"That takes me," returned Tennessee; and, with this gambler's epigram, he threw away his useless pistol, and rode back with his captor.

It was a warm night. The cool breeze which usually sprang up with the going down of the sun behind the chaparral-crested mountain was that evening withheld from Sandy Bar. The little cañon was stifling with heated resinous odors, and the decaying driftwood on the Bar sent forth faint, sickening exhalations. The feverishness of the day and its fierce passions still filled the camp. Lights moved restlessly along the bank of the river, striking no answering reflection from its tawny current. Against the blackness of the pines the windows of the old loft above the express office stood out staringly bright; and through their curtainless panes the loungers below could see the forms of those who were even then deciding the fate of Tennessee. And above all this, etched on the dark firmament, rose the Sierra, remote and passionless, crowned with remoter passionless stars.

The trial of Tennessee was conducted as fairly as was consistent with a judge and jury who felt themselves to some extent obliged to justify, in their verdict, the previous irregularities of arrest and indictment. The law of Sandy Bar was implacable, but not vengeful. The excitement and personal feelings of the chase were over; with Tennessee safe in their hands, they were ready to listen patiently to any defense, which they were already satisfied was insufficient. There being no doubt in their own minds, they were willing to give the prisoner the benefit of any that might exist. Secure in the hypothesis that he ought to be hanged on general principles, they indulged him with more latitude of defense than his reckless hardihood seemed to ask. The judge appeared to be more anxious than the prisoner, who, otherwise unconcerned, evidently took a grim pleasure in the responsibility he had created. "I don't take any hand in this yer game," had been his invariable, but good-humored

当受绞刑,所以在辩护方面待他比较宽大,超出了他的不顾死活的胡作非为似乎应当享有的范围。法官显得比犯人更为急切。犯人却满不在乎,显然只对自己所惹起的责任感到一种恶毒的乐趣。不论问他什么话,他总是愉快地回答说:"我不参加这场游戏。"法官——也就是捕获他的那个人——有一会儿有点儿后悔,那天早上没有"一瞧见他"就把他打死,可是他立刻又把人性上的这个弱点排开,认为这是法官所不应有的想法。然而,当有人敲了一下门,说是田纳西的伙伴到那儿来替犯人说话的时候,他不加多问,立刻就叫田纳西的伙伴进来。陪审团里年纪较轻的人正觉得审问显得顾虑太多、令人厌烦,所以也许把田纳西的伙伴简直看做一个缓和一下气氛的人物那样来欢迎了。

说真的,他的确不是一个仪表堂堂的人,身个儿又矮又胖,生着一张四四方方的脸,给太阳晒成了异乎寻常的红色,身上穿着一件宽大的帆布工装,裤子上溅满了一道红土。不论在任何情况下,他的样子都显得很古怪,而现在则简直是可笑的。他弯身把拿着的一个沉甸甸的毡制手提包放到脚下。这时,大家全看得很清楚,根据泄露出的一部分传说和记载,他用来补裤子的料子,原来是打算作不相干的遮盖物用的。然而,他很庄重地走上前来,勉强做得很亲切地跟房里每个人握手,然后用一条大红手帕(颜色比他的肤色稍许淡点儿)把严肃、惶惑的脸揩揩,把强有力的大手放在桌上,稳住自己,向法官说道:

"我打这儿经过,"他用道歉的口气开始说,"我想顺便走进来看看田纳西——我的伙伴,看他的事儿搞得怎么样了。今儿晚上真热。我不记得洲上以前有过这样的天气。"

他停了片刻,但是没有人主动去回想气候方面的什么其他情况,于是他又求助于那条手帕,用力地擦了好半天脸。

"你有什么话要替犯人说吗?"法官终于这么问。

"对啦,"田纳西的伙伴用深感宽慰的音调说,"我是以田纳西的伙伴的身份上这儿来的——我认识他前前后后、好好歹歹、倒霉走运——将近有 4 个年头了。他的做人行事并不总跟我一样,不过这个年轻人的一切特点,他所搞的随便什么热闹事儿,我没有不知道的。你对我说,你说——推心置腹地——你说,'你知道什么对他有利的事儿吗?'我对你说,我

reply to all questions. The judge—who was also his captor—for a moment vaguely regretted that he had not shot him "on sight" that morning, but presently dismissed this human weakness as unworthy of the judicial mind. Nevertheless, when there was a tap at the door, and it was said that Tennessee's Partner was there on behalf of the prisoner, he was admitted at once without question. Perhaps the younger members of the jury, to whom the proceedings were becoming irksomely thoughtful, hailed him as a relief.

For he was not, certainly, an imposing figure. Short and stout, with a square face, sunburned into a preternatural redness, clad in a loose duck "jumper" and trousers streaked and splashed with red soil, his aspect under any circumstances would have been quaint, and was now even ridiculous. As he stooped to deposit at his feet a heavy carpetbag he was carrying, it became obvious, from partially developed legends and inscriptions, that the material with which his trousers had been patched had been originally intended for a less ambitious covering. Yet he advanced with great gravity, and after having shaken the hand of each person in the room with labored cordiality, he wiped his serious perplexed face on a red bandana handkerchief, a shade lighter than his complexion, laid his powerful hand upon the table to steady himself, and thus addressed the judge:

"I was passin' by," he began, by way of apology, "and I thought I'd just step in and see how things was gittin' on with Tennessee thar—my pardner. It's a hot night. I disremember any sich weather before on the Bar."

He paused a moment, but nobody volunteering any other meteorological recollection, he again had recourse to his pocket handkerchief, and for some moments mopped his face diligently.

"Have you anything to say on behalf of the prisoner?" said the judge finally.

"That's it," said Tennessee's Partner, in a tone of relief. "I come yar as Tennessee's pardner—knowing him nigh on four year, off and on, wet and dry, in luck and out o' luck. His ways ain't aller my ways, but thar ain't any p'ints in that young man, thar ain't any liveliness as he's been up to, as I don't know. And you sez to me, sez you—confidential-like, and between man and man—sez you, 'Do you know anything in his behalf?' and I sez to you, sez I—confidential-like, as between man and man—'What should a man know of his pardner?'"

"Is this all you have to say?" asked the judge impatiently, feeling, perhaps, that a dangerous sympathy

说——推心置腹地，'一个人对他的伙伴该知道点儿什么呢？'"

"你要说的就是这话吗？"法官不耐烦地问。他也许觉得，一种危险的诙谐同情的情绪正开始使法庭上的人软化下去了。

"是呀，"田纳西的伙伴继续说下去，"本来也不该由我来说什么反对他的话。这案子的经过是怎么回事呢？田纳西要钱花。非常需要，他又不乐意向他的老伙伴要。瞧，田纳西怎么办呢？他躲起来去等一个陌生人，他抓住了他，于是你们躲起来等他，你们抓住了他——荣誉来得是很便当的。我本人是个公正的人，想把这一点提出来，征求你们的意见，请你们各位先生以公正的人的身份看看，事情是不是这样。"

"犯人，"法官插嘴说，"你有什么话要问这个人吗？"

"慢着！慢着！"田纳西的伙伴赶忙说下去，"我是独个儿来说这番话的。开门见山地说，不过就是这样，田纳西对一个陌生人和这个营地干得太粗暴、耗费太大啦。现在，怎样才公平呢？有人会主张罚得重，有人会主张罚得轻。这儿有 1700 块钱的沙金和一只表，这差不多是我的全部财产了，咱们就两抵吧。"大家还没有来得及伸手阻拦他，他已经把手提包里的东西全部倒在桌子上了。

有一刹那，他的性命非常危险。有一两个人跳起身来，好几只手都去摸暗藏着的武器，还有人提议"把他扔出窗子去"，这完全靠了法官一摆手才拦住了。田纳西哈哈大笑。而田纳西的伙伴显然不理会这一阵紧张激动，反而利用这机会又拿手帕去揩揩脸。

等秩序恢复之后，法官用使人信服的辞令解释给这个人听，田纳西的罪行是不能用钱来赎的。这时候，田纳西的伙伴的脸色变得更严肃、更血红。那些待得靠他最近的人注意到，他的粗手在桌上微微有点儿哆嗦。他踌躇了一会儿，缓缓地把沙金放回手提包去，仿佛他还不能完全领会支配法庭的那种崇高的正义感，不知所措地以为他出的钱还不够哩。接下来，他转身朝着法官说道："这是我个人的主张，是我独个儿干的，跟我的伙伴毫不相干。"他向陪审团鞠了一躬、正打算退出去的时候，法官又把他唤回来。

"你要是有什么话要对田纳西说，最好现在就说。"

于是，犯人和他的奇怪的辩护人的眼睛，那天晚

of humor was beginning to humanize the court.

"Thet's so," continued Tennessee's Partner. "It ain't for me to say anything agin' him. And now, what's the case? Here's Tennessee wants money, wants it bad, and doesn't like to ask it of his old pardner. Well, what does Tennessee do? He lays for a stranger, and he fetches that stranger; and you lays for *him*, and you fetches *him*; and the honors is easy. And I put it to you, bein'a fa'r-minded man, and to you, gentlemen all, as fa'r-minded men, ef this isn't so."

"Prisoner," said the judge, interrupting, "have you any questions to ask this man?"

"No! no!" continued Tennessee's Partner, hastily. "I play this yer hand alone. To come down to the bedrock, it's just this: Tennessee, thar, has played it pretty rough and expensive-like on a stranger, and on this yer camp. And now, what's the fair thing? Some would say more, some would say less. Here's seventeen hundred dollars in coarse gold and a watch,—it's about all my pile,—and call it square!" And before a hand could be raised to prevent him, he had emptied the contents of the carpetbag upon the table.

For a moment his life was in jeopardy. One or two men sprang to their feet, several hands groped for hidden weapons, and a suggestion to "throw him from the window" was only overridden by a gesture from the judge. Tennessee laughed. And apparently oblivious of the excitement, Tennessee's Partner improved the opportunity to mop his face again with his handkerchief.

When order was restored, and the man was made to understand, by the use of forcible figures and rhetoric, that Tennessee's offense could not be condoned by money, his face took a more serious and sanguinary hue, and those who were nearest to him noticed that his rough hand trembled slightly on the table. He hesitated a moment as he slowly returned the gold to the carpetbag, as if he had not yet entirely caught the elevated sense of justice which swayed the tribunal, and was perplexed with the belief that he had not offered enough. Then he turned to the judge, and saying, "This yer is a lone hand, played alone, and without my pardner," he bowed to the jury and was about to withdraw, when the judge called him back:

"If you have anything to say to Tennessee, you had better say it now."

For the first time that evening the eyes of the prisoner and his strange advocate met. Tennessee smiled, showed his white teeth, and saying, "Euchred, old man!" held out his hand. Tennessee's Partner took it in his own, and saying, "I just dropped in as I was passin' to see how things was gettin' on," let the hand

上这才第一次互相对望着了。田纳西笑笑，露出洁白的牙齿，说："打输了，朋友！"一面伸出手来。田纳西的伙伴握着他的手，说："我只是经过这儿，顺便进来看看事情到底怎样。"他让那只手木然地垂了下去，又补上一句道："今儿晚上很热。"然后，他又用手帕揩揩脸，没再说一句话便退出去了。

这两个人从此就没能活着再见过面。因为不管林奇法官①是顽固、软弱还是气量狭小，他至少是清廉的——向他行贿的那个前所未闻的侮辱，在这个神秘的大人物心里把关系到田纳西命运的任何犹疑不定的判决，给确定下来了。破晓的时候，田纳西在严密的戒备下被押到马雷氏山顶上处决了。

他临刑前的情形，他的冷静，他的一言不发，以及委员会安排的周密，全由当时在场的《红狗号角报》编辑翔实地加以报道，他在后面还附加了一番告诫，警告一切往后想做坏事的人。现在，就请读者去读一下他那活泼有力的文章吧。不过，他对那个仲夏清晨的明媚风光，气宇的和谐，悠闲的树林和山冈清醒后所发出的生气，大自然的欢乐的复苏和希望，特别是贯穿在这一切里的无限的宁静，全没有加以报道，因为这跟社会教化是毫无关系的。然而，当那件懦弱、愚蠢的事干完，一条生命带着它的希望和义务从吊在空中的畸形的东西②中逝去之后，鸟儿叫着，花儿开着，阳光普照着，全和先前一样愉快。那么，也许《红狗号角报》倒是对的。

许多人围着那棵不祥之树站着，可是田纳西的伙伴却并不在内。当那群人转身散去的时候，他们才注意到，有一辆奇特的驴车一动不动地停在路边。等他们走近后，他们立刻认出那匹老"珍妮"和那辆二轮车是田纳西的伙伴的财产，是他用来从矿地上搬运烂泥的。再朝前走几步，车主本人坐在一棵七叶树下面，正从红彤彤的脸上把汗水揩去。他们问他来干吗，他回答说，是来领"死者"的尸体的，"如果委员会无所谓的话"。他并不想"催着办"，他可以"等待"。那天他不干活儿，等先生们对"死者"的手续办完以

① 林奇法官，原文为 Judge Lynch。"林奇"原为美国弗吉尼亚州一个保安官的姓氏。他在 1780 年用私刑处罚"暴徒"。因此私刑在英文中叫 Judge Lynch，有"私刑裁判"的意思，表示对田纳西的审判完全是不合法的。

② 指尸体。

passively fall, and adding that "it was a warm night," again mopped his face with his handkerchief, and without another word withdrew.

The two men never again met each other alive. For the unparalleled insult of a bribe offered to Judge Lynch—who, whether bigoted weak, or narrow, was at least incorruptible—firmly fixed in the mind of that mythical personage any wavering determination of Tennessee's fate; and at the break of day he was marched, closely guarded, to meet it at the top of Marley's Hill.

How he met it, how cool he was, how he refused to say anything, how perfect were the arrangements of the committee, were all duly reported, with the addition of a warning moral and example to all future evildoers, in the *Red Dog Clarion*, by its editor, who was present, and to whose vigorous English I cheerfully refer the reader. But the beauty of that midsummer morning, the blessed amity of earth and air and sky, the awakened life of the free woods and hills, the joyous renewal and promise of Nature, and above all, the infinite serenity that thrilled through each, was not reported, as not being a part of the social lesson. And yet, when the weak and foolish deed was done, and a life, with its possibilities and responsibilities, had passed out of the misshapen thing that dangled between earth and sky, the birds sang, the flowers bloomed, the sun shone, as cheerily as before; and possibly the *Red Dog Clarion* was right.

Tennessee's Partner was not in the group that surrounded the ominous tree. But as they turned to disperse, attention was drawn to the singular appearance of a motionless donkey cart halted at the side of the road. As they approached, they at once recognized the venerable Jenny and the two-wheeled cart as the property of Tennessee's Partner, used by him in carrying dirt from his claim; and a few paces distant the owner of the equipage himself, sitting under a buckeye tree, wiping the perspiration from his glowing face. In answer to an inquiry, he said he had come for the body of the "diseased," "if it was all the same to the committee." He didn't wish to "hurry anything"; he could "wait." He was not working that day; and when the gentlemen were done with the "diseased," he would take him. "Ef thar is any present," he added, in his simple, serious way, "as would care to jine in the fun'l, they kin come." Perhaps it was from a sense of humor, which I have already intimated as a feature of Sandy Bar—perhaps it was from something even better than that, but two thirds of the loungers accepted the invitation at once.

It was noon when the body of Tennessee was

后，他就把他领去。"在场哪位，"他以他的朴实、严肃的态度补充道，"要是乐意去参加葬礼的话，可以请过来。"也许是出于一种幽默感——我在上文已经说过，这是"沙洲"的一个特征，也许是出于什么比那还好的情绪，三分之二的闲人顿时都接受了他的邀请。

等田纳西的尸体交给他伙伴的时候，已经是晌午了。驴车走到那棵不祥之树下面就停下来。我们注意到，车上放着一口长方形的粗匣子——显然是用一段淘金槽做的——一半放着树皮和松果。车上还装饰着柳枝，又用七叶树花弄得香喷喷的。当尸体盛放进木盒以后，田纳西的伙伴把一块黑油布盖在它上面，严肃地爬上前面的窄座位，把两脚踏在车杠上，赶着小驴朝前走去。"珍妮"在平时不这么庄严的情况下一向走得规规矩矩，现在还是以规矩、端庄的步伐拖着车子缓缓朝前走去。人们——一半出于好奇心，一半爱要开玩笑——全高高兴兴地跟在车旁踱着，有些走在这辆朴实的灵车前面，有些则稍许落在后面。但是，当车子朝前走着时，不知是因为道路变得狭窄，还是因为某种一时的礼节感，人们两个两个落到了后面，各自调整步伐，依然排成了一条正式的队列。开头的时候，杰克·福斯林比哑然无声地装作用一个假想的大喇叭在吹奏一支葬礼进行曲，这会儿因为缺乏同情与欣赏，已经停止了——也许是没有真正幽默大师的能耐，不能单单欣赏自己的玩笑就感到满足了。

这个队列一路穿过灰熊谷——这时候，谷里已经披上了丧服和暮色。红杉把鹿皮靴般的树根埋藏在红土里，沿着小道一长行地排列下去，用低垂的枝条向经过的尸体一路传递着简单的祝福。一只兔子在队列经过时，吓愣住了，不知如何是好，笔直地坐在路旁的羊齿草里打颤。松鼠赶忙从较高的树枝上无忧无虑地向外探望。蓝背樫鸟张开翅膀，像仪仗似的在前面振翼翱翔。这样一路来到"沙洲"的郊外，抵达了田纳西的伙伴的孤零零的小屋。

在较好的情况下看来，这也算不了一个愉快的地方。单调呆板的地点，粗陋丑恶的外形，以及加利福尼亚矿工那窠巢般住宅所独具的那种乏味的细节，这儿都齐全了。此外。还有那种凋零凄凉的意味。离小屋没有几步路，有一片坑坑洼洼的圈地，在田纳西的伙伴婚后短短的幸福的日子里，这片地是当做花园的，但是现在，它却遍长着羊齿草。我们走近前时，惊奇地发觉，我们原先以为是新近耕作的地方，竟然是

delivered into the hands of his partner. As the cart drew up to the fatal tree, we noticed that it contained a rough oblong box,—apparently made from a section of sluicing,—and half filled with bark and the tassels of pine. The cart was further decorated with slips of willow, and made fragrant with buckeye blossoms. When the body was deposited in the box, Tennessee's Partner drew over it a piece of tarred canvas, and gravely mounting the narrow seat in front, with his feet upon the shafts, urged the little donkey forward. The equipage moved slowly on, at that decorous pace which was habitual with Jenny even under less solemn circumstances. The men—half curiously, half jesting-ly, but all good-humoredly— strolled along beside the cart, some in advance, some a little in the rear of the homely catafalque. But whether from the narrowing of the road or some present sense of decorum, as the cart passed on, the company fell to the rear in couples, keeping step, and otherwise assuming the external show of a formal procession. Jack Folinsbee, who had at the outset played a funeral march in dumb show up-on an imaginary trombone, desisted from a lack of sympathy and appreciation—not having, perhaps, your true humorist's capacity to be content with the enjoy-ment of his own fun.

The way led through Grizzly Cañon, by this time clothed in funereal drapery and shadows. The red-woods, burying their moccasined feet in the red soil, stood Indian file along the track, trailing an uncouth benediction from their bending boughs upon the pass-ing bier. A hare, surprised into helpless inactivity, sat upright and pulsating in the ferns by the roadside, as the cortege went by. Squirrels hastened to gain a se-cure outlook from higher boughs; and the bluejays, spreading their wings, fluttered before them like out-riders, until the outskirts of Sandy Bar were reached, and the solitary cabin of Tennessee's Partner.

Viewed under more favorable circumstances, it would not have been a cheerful place. The unpictur-esque site, the rude and unlovely outlines, the unsavor-y details, which distinguish the nest-building of the California miner, were all here, with the dreariness of decay superadded. A few paces from the cabin there was a rough enclosure, which, in the brief days of Tennessee's Partner's matrimonial felicity, had been used as a garden, but was now overgrown with fern. As we approached it, we were surprised to find that what we had taken for a recent attempt at cultivation was the broken soil about an open grave.

The cart was halted before the enclosure, and re-jecting the offers of assistance with the same air of simple self-reliance he had displayed throughout, Tennessee's Partner lifted the rough coffin on his

一个敞开的墓穴四周翻起的泥土。

驴车在圈地外边停下来。田纳西的伙伴以他一贯表现的质朴、自信的神气，拒绝了别人的帮助，用背背起那口粗劣的棺木，独个儿把它放到浅浅的墓穴里。他把当做盖子的木板钉好，然后站上旁边的小土墩，脱下帽子，用手帕慢吞吞地揩了揩脸。人们觉得这是要说话的先声，于是各自在树桩和圆石上坐下来等待。

"如果一个人，"田纳西的伙伴慢条斯理地开始说，"整天都在外边放荡，他应该做的是什么事儿呢？嘿，回家呀，如果他不能回家，他的好朋友怎么办？嘿，把他接回来！田纳西就老在外边放荡，我们把他从游荡中接回家来了。"他停了一会儿，拾起一小块石英，沉思地在袖口上擦着，继续说道："你们瞧见我刚才把他驮在背上。这并不是第一次。这也不是我第一次在他要人照顾的时候把他接到这所屋里来。我和'珍妮'也不是第一次在他不能说话、认不清我的时候等在那边山上，抬起他来，把他带回家。不过现在，这是最后一次了，嘻——"他停住，把那块石英轻轻地在袖口上擦着，"你们瞧，他的伙伴多少有点儿难受。现在，先生们，"他突然加上一句，一边拾起长柄铲子，"葬礼结束了。谢谢各位来参加，我也替田纳西谢谢各位。"

他拒绝了人家的帮助。把背朝着大家，开始把土填进墓穴里去。大家踌躇了一会儿，渐渐散去。在他们越过遮住"沙洲"的那座小山脊的时候，有些人回头看了一眼，他们觉得看见田纳西的伙伴干完了活儿，正把铲子放在双膝之间，坐在坟头上，把脸埋在大红手帕里。但是，有些人争辩说，从那么远的距离，你不可能辨别出他的脸和手帕来，所以这一点就成了悬而未决的疑问了。

那天的紧张兴奋，接下去发生了一个反作用。在这种作用的影响下，田纳西的伙伴并没有给人忘掉。他们进行了一场秘密的调查，结果证明他丝毫没有参与过田纳西的罪行，所以人们现在只怀疑他的精神是否健全了。"沙洲"的人们决定去看望他，给他种种粗率而善意的帮助。可是从那天起，他的壮健的身体和强大的气力似乎全很显眼地衰退下去。等雨季到来，田纳西墓上石堆里开始露出小草瓣的时候，他竟然病倒在床了。

一天夜晚，小屋旁边的松树在狂风暴雨中摆动，

back, and deposited it unaided within the shallow grave. He then nailed down the board which served as a lid, and mounting the little mound of earth beside it, took off his hat and slowly mopped his face with his handkerchief. This the crowd felt was a preliminary to speech, and they disposed themselves variously on stumps and boulders, and sat expectant.

"When a man," began Tennessee's Partner slowly, "has been running free all day, what's the natural thing for him to do? Why, to come home. And if he ain't in a condition to go home, what can his best friend do? Why, bring him home. And here's Tennessee has been running free, and we brings him home from his wandering." He paused and picked up a fragment of quartz, rubbed it thoughtfully on his sleeve and went on: "It ain't the first time I've packed him on my back, as you see'd me now. It ain't the first time that I brought him to this yer cabin when he couldn't help himself; it ain't the first time that I and Jinny have waited for him on yon hill, and picked him up and so fetched him home, when he couldn't speak and didn't know me. And now that it's the last time, why"—he paused, and rubbed the quartz gently on his sleeve—"you see it's sort of rough on his pardner. And now, gentlemen," he added abruptly, picking up his long-handled shovel, "the fun'l's over; and my thanks, and Tennessee's thanks, to you for your trouble."

Resisting any proffers of assistance, he began to fill in the grave, turning his back upon the crowd, that after a few moments' hesitation gradually withdrew. As they crossed the little ridge that hid Sandy Bar from view, some, looking back, thought they could see Tennessee's Partner, his work done, sitting upon the grave, his shovel between his knees, and his face buried in his red bandana handkerchief. But it was argued by others that you couldn't tell his face from his handkerchief at that distance, and this point remained undecided.

In the reaction that followed the feverish excitement of that day, Tennessee's Partner was not forgotten. A secret investigation had cleared him of any complicity in Tennessee's guilt, and left only a suspicion of his general sanity. Sandy Bar made a point of calling on him, and proferring various uncouth but well-meant kindnesses. But from that day his rude health and great strength seemed visibly to decline; and when the rainy season fairly set in, and the tiny grass blades were beginning to peep from the rocky mount above Tennessee's grave, he took to his bed.

One night, when the pines beside the cabin were swaying in the storm and trailing their slender fingers

纤细的松枝在屋顶上晃荡,下面,上涨的河水发出一片汹涌的呼啸。这时,田纳西的伙伴把头从枕上拾起来说:"现在,是去找田纳西的时候了,我得把'珍妮'套上车子。"他当真会从床上爬起来的,幸亏陪他的人把他拦住了。他挣扎不停,依旧不放弃他的古怪的幻想:"喂,留神,'珍妮'——留神,驴儿。多么黑呀!留神车道——还要留神着他,驴儿。有时候,你知道,他烂醉如泥,就摔倒在小路当中。一直走到山顶上那棵松树那儿去。那儿——我告诉你——他就在那儿——也朝这面来啦——独自个儿,并没有喝酒,脸上兴冲冲的。田纳西!伙伴!"

于是他们重逢了。

讨 论 ▪

这篇小说是写一个人对朋友的赤诚之心。那个叫田纳西的人其实已与他的伙伴的妻子偷情了,但是两个男人间的友谊甚至经受住了如此严峻的考验,他们言归于好,后来当田纳西因在公路上进行抢劫而被处死后,他的伙伴还领回他的尸体并尽其可能以体面的仪式埋葬了他,他自己也日益颓唐而死去。而使这种忠诚显得更为令人注目的是,田纳西的伙伴并不是我们通常说的那种多愁善感的人。然而,这一点并不影响小说,其他作家也都表彰过这种单纯而"无书卷气"的人物在感情上的至诚至善。举例来说,同时代的作家厄内斯特·海明威就时常让他的"粗鲁"而"铁石心肠"的人物一反表面的冷漠无情而流露出某种情感。

这篇小说的困难之处在于必须使田纳西的伙伴的行为令人信服。我们当真相信他会做得这样宽宏大量吗?这有赖于我们对他性格的了解,也就是说,要看布雷特·哈特对人物的心理变化是如何表现的,因为田纳西的伙伴只有在某种心理变化的情况下才有可能做出这种简直不可信的行为来。无论怎么说,妻子被引诱毕竟是件难以容忍的事情。

over the roof, and the roar and rush of the swollen river were heard below, Tennessee's Partner lifted his head from the pillow, saying, "It is time to go for Tennessee; I must put Jinny in the cart"; and would have risen from his bed but for the restraint of his attendant. Struggling, he still pursued his singular fancy: "There, now, steady, Jinny—steady, old girl. How dark it is! Look out for the ruts—and look out for him, too, old gal. Sometimes, you know, when he's blind drunk, he drops down right in the trail. Keep on straight up to the pine on the top of the hill. Thar! I told you so! —thar he is—coming this way, too—all by himself, sober, and his face a-shining. Tennessee! Pardner!"

And so they met.

This is the story of a man's intense loyalty to his friend. The man Tennessee actually steals his partner's wife, but the friendship of the men survives even this severe test: they become reconciled, and later after Tennessee has been executed for highway robbery, his partner claims the body, buries it with such rites of decency as he can contrive, and soon himself wastes away and dies. What makes this display of loyalty even more remarkable is that Tennessee's partner is not a man to whom we would ordinarily ascribe much delicacy of feeling. Not that this latter point invalidates the story. Other writers have remarked upon the intensity and rightness of the feelings of simple and "unliterary" persons. To take an instance from a contemporary writer, Ernest Hemingway frequently allows his "tough" and "hard-boiled" characters to reveal a sensitivity that belies their apparent callousness.

The difficulty with this story has to do with the credibility of the actions of Tennessee's partner. Do we really believe that he would act so magnanimously? That will depend upon our understanding of his character; and that in turn will have to do with Bret Harte's presentation of the psychological steps by which Tennessee's partner arrives at the actions in question. In any case, the episode of the wife-stealing will be the hardest to accept.

就此而言,伙伴关系肯定要遭遇麻烦。按照一般的规律,由于田纳西的伙伴蒙受了丧失名誉的耻辱,必然会导致流血事件。况且,伙伴对具体的和个人的事务并非是糊涂之至的——他出庭作证时即表明他毫无什么抽象的正义观,并且把夫妻关系看做完全是个人的和具体的。像这样一个人怎么会原谅田纳西呢?(当然,如果他把妻子仅仅看做是一件动产的话,那他的原谅行为也就失去了所有的意义,因为这样的矛盾,一方面爱朋友,另一方面又爱妻子,这种两难情况并不存在。)然而,布雷特·哈特事实上是避开了这种心理问题。虽然,他的意思很清楚,他是把葬礼而不是把妻子被引诱这件事作为小说的高潮来写的,但是我们依然有权要求妻子被诱奸这件事得到令人信服的结局。事实上,如果这件事不能使人相信,那么整篇小说也就失去了基点。

那么,布雷特·哈特为那作为高潮的葬礼这段情节又给我们做了何种铺垫呢?他给了我们那段试图行贿的情节。这段情节的目的似乎在于表明伙伴对社会习俗、法律性质甚至抽象的正义感本身都是天真无知的。显而易见,他是真的认为田纳西的处境已到了非用钱才能解决的地步。受害人应为其损失而受到赔偿并因其受扰而有所得益。这儿可能还暗示出他打算贿赂法庭。诚然,法官后来根据法律给了这个人这样的回答:"田纳西的罪行是不能用钱来赎的。"但是,这段情节的另一目的则在于加强伙伴朋友死心塌地的忠诚所给人的印象.他愿意为朋友牺牲自己的"大笔钱财"。

法庭事件终究对我们意味着什么呢,当然,并不仅仅为了后面的埋葬之事,如表面看来的那样。因为即使在粗俗的公众里,也常有人埋葬被绞死的人,甚至还真带着同情心理(就拿田纳西来说,出于伙伴关系——小说好几次生动地写到他们有感情而又冷静相待的关系——他的某些品质也应该受到特殊的尊

The community, in this instance, certainly expected trouble: according to the primitive code the loss of honor that Tennessee's partner has suffered definitely demands bloodletting. Moreover, the partner is a man who evidently sees everything in very concrete and personal terms—witness his conduct at the trial in which he shows that he has no conception of abstract justice, and the relation of a man to his wife is a very personal and concrete relation. How could this man forgive Tennessee? (If, of course, he had regarded his wife as a mere chattel, then the whole meaning of his act of forgiveness is lost, for the conflict—between affection for his friend on the one hand and affection for his wife on the other—disappears from the situation.) But Bret Harte has really dodged this psychological problem. Even though it is plain that he meant the burial scene and not the wife-stealing episode to be the climax of the story, we still have a right to ask that the wife-stealing episode be credibly developed. In fact, if it is not made credible, the whole story loses its point.

What else does Bret Harte give us in preparation for the climactic burial scene? He gives us the scene of attempted bribery. The purpose of this scene seems to be to indicate the partner's naiveté with regard to the conventions of society, to the nature of law, and even to the concept of abstract justice itself. Apparently, he honestly sees the situation Tennessee has fallen into as one that can be settled by a money payment. The stranger will be compensated for his losses and will be given something for his trouble. Perhaps there is the implication that he is attempting to bribe the court. Indeed, the judge proceeds to give the man a lecture on the nature of law: "the man was made to understand... that Tennessee's offense could not be condoned by money." But another purpose of the scene is to develop the idea of the partner's doglike devotion: he is willing to sacrifice his "pile" for his friend.

For what, after all, does this court incident intend to prepare us? It is, of course, not merely for the incident of the burial, as such. For some one among the rough citizenry would have buried the hanged man in any case, and perhaps with a kind of elemental pity. (Tennessee, has, for instance, certain qualities that would extort special admiration in this primitive community—a courage and

重）。小说设定的高潮是墓前演说，这是田纳西的伙伴对在场的人说的。就在这里，作者料想我们的悲怆之情会达到顶点。

但是，如果要使这种悲怆感达到顶点而且有意义的话，作者必须先使我们相信，第一，这个性格特殊的人物在这样的情况下发表演说是合乎逻辑的；第二，他的演说能使前述各个事件所具有的意义及其解释得到集中的表现。

然而，困难重重。首先，由于伙伴的生活受到自己对朋友的纯粹私人感情的控制，再加他根本无法理解他的朋友为何非要被绞死（就像行贿情节所表明的），他更可能是对那些置他的朋友于死地的人抱着某种阴沉的愤恨之感，因为在他看来，他们没有充分的理由（他不可能糊涂到认为那些旁人参加葬礼是出于对田纳西的爱戴）。在这样的情况下，他可能做这样的演说吗？

其次，即使伙伴要发表演说，他可能像布雷特·哈特要他讲的那样讲吗？譬如，他可能向那些旁人表示歉意并且对他们的同情表示感谢吗？请注意，布雷特·哈特并没有意思要把这次演说写得好像是一个心灵受伤者的尖刻讽刺，而是写得好像某种基督般的宽宥之心的表现。伙伴简单善良到了令人无法相信的地步。所有的目的全在于抒发感情。

再请注意，就在这点上，当伙伴因为心碎而临死之际，布雷特·哈特让他说了些什么。这里，甚至人物的语言也变得不真实了，它完全不符合伙伴的讲话习惯，难道他会说"喂，留神，'珍妮'——留神，驴儿。多么黑呀！"而如果他说"天黑得像地狱"或者说"我的老天爷啊，天黑了"，不是更合情理吗？在雷特·哈特为何要破坏伙伴的讲话习惯呢。因为他正致力于达到某种强烈的感情效果，他觉得像生活中一样的语言不够好，于是便采取"诗化"人物的方式了。同样，在临终遗言这一段里，那山顶上的松树的象征性意义也是采取这种方式的。

coolness dramatized several times in the story.) The intended high point in the story is the funeral oration, which Tennessee's partner delivers to the camp. It is here that our full sense of the pathos is supposed to emerge.

But if such pathos is to emerge to the full, and is to be meaningful, the author must have persuaded us (1) that it is logical for this particular character to deliver the oration under the circumstances and (2) that this oration brings to focus elements of interpretation and meaning implicit in previous incidents.

But there are more difficulties. First, the partner, whose life had been dominated by a merely personal attachment to his friend and who had been completely incapable of understanding why his friend had to be hanged (as indicated by the bribery scene), would more probably have felt a sullen resentment against the men who had done his friend to death for, in his eyes, no good reason. (He can be under no illusion the spectators have come to the funeral out of love for Tennessee.) Under such circumstances would he give this oration?

Second, assuming that the partner would have delivered the oration, would he have said what Bret Harte makes him say? For example, would he have apologized to the spectators and have thanked them for their trouble? Notice that Bret Harte does not intend for us to take this as the bitter irony of a hurt man, but as a manifestation of a kind of Christlike forgiveness. The partner is almost too good to be true. The whole attempt is an appeal to sentiment.

Notice further, in this connection, what Bret Harte has the partner say in his delirium as he dies of a broken heart. Here, even the language becomes unrealistic; it is entirely out of the partner's idiom. For example, would he have said "There, now, steady, Jinny—steady, old girl. How dark it is!" Isn't it more likely that he would have said "It's dark as hell"? or "God-a-mighty, it's dark!" Why does Bret Harte break out of the partner's idiom? Because he is straining for a highly emotional effect, and feeling that the realistic language is not good enough, he resorts to "poeticizing" the character. The same thing is true of the symbolic reference, in the dying speech, to the pine tree on the top of the hill.

在小说的前面部分，还可以找到好些这样的例子。譬如，当伙伴把朋友的尸体带到墓地时，小说里有这样的描述："这个队列一路穿过灰熊谷——这时候，谷里已经披上了丧服和暮色。红杉把鹿皮靴般的树根埋藏在红土里，沿着小道一长行地排列下去，用低垂的枝条向经过的尸体一路传递着简单的祝福。"显然，大自然也在与伙伴的悲哀一起叹息。像伙伴一样，大自然所给予的仅是一种"简单的祝福"，不过它也已尽其可能表达出它的挖心掏肚般的同情感了。人们承认，作家可以合理地把景物描写作为一种手段以用来渲染叙事作品中的气氛，甚至可以把景物作为某种特殊的象征物。但是，应该弄个水落石出的是，布雷特·哈特在这里并没有合理地使用。景物描写在这里是被用来制造幻觉以加强场面的悲怆性的，而这种景物描写就像伙伴的临终遗言一样是"诗化"了的。譬如，红杉树"把鹿皮靴般的树根埋藏在红土里"这样的描写，完全是多此一举，而且是一种追求虚饰的表现，这是作者致力于达到感情效果的又一例证，而作者似乎也感到，这种效果并未得到环境本身给予的支持。

这种致力于感情效果的表现是人们陷入感伤状态时最为明显的症状之一，就如我们所见的那样，感伤也许可以被解释为一种过分的——或者根本就是不合时宜的感情反应。我们说一个人为了一点小事就痛哭流涕是感伤的表现。这种人缺乏感情上的平衡感，他们从感情的自我发泄中得到某种病态的享受。而当我们把这个词运用于文学作品譬如一篇小说时，我们通常的意思是指，作者试图让读者经受强烈的感情，而这种感情却不是小说内容实际上所能给予的。

如前所述，感伤的症状之一就是作者全然不顾作品的戏剧性情节而一味地强调、美化或者诗化自己的语言。

症状之二也时常可以看到，那就是作者单方面地"发议论"——向读者指出应该感受什

But other examples of such strain are to be found earlier in the story. Take, for example, the description of nature as the partner carries the body to the place of burial: "The way led through Grizzly Cañon, by this time clothed in funeral drapery and shadows. The redwoods, burying moccasined feet in the red soil, stood in Indian file along the track, trailing an uncouth benediction from their bending boughs upon the passing bier." Nature, apparently, is sympathetic with the partner's grief. Like him, it can give only an "uncouth benediction," but it expresses its brooding sympathy as best it can. One recognizes that a writer may legitimately use description of nature as a device for defining the atmosphere of a piece of fiction, or may even use it as specific symbolism. But it should be quite clear that Bret Harte here is not using it legitimately. It is used here to give a false heightening to the pathos of the scene, and the description is as "poeticized" as is the partner's dying speech. For example, the description of the redwoods "burying their moccasined feet in the red soil" is completely irrelevant and represents an attempt at fanciful decoration; it is another instance of the author's straining for effects that, he seems to feel, are not adequately supported by the situation in itself.

The presence of this straining for an emotional effect is one of the surest symptoms that one is dealing with a case of sentimentality. In its general sense, as we have seen, sentimentality may be defined as an emotional response in excess of the occasion—or without relevance to the occasion. We speak of a person who weeps at some trivial occurrence as being sentimental. Such a person lacks a sense of proportion and gets a morbid enjoyment from an emotional debauch for its own sake. When we apply the term to a piece of literature, a story, for instance, we usually mean that the author intends for the reader to experience an intense emotion that is actually not justified by the materials of the story.

One symptom of sentimentality is, as we have said, the author's straining to heighten and prettify and poeticize his language quite apart from the dramatic issues involved in the story.

A second symptom frequently to be found is "editorializing" on the part of the author—pointing out to the reader what he

么,暗示读者做出反应——而如果作品本身能做到的话,这些手段也实属多余(譬如,布雷特·哈特对绞刑做了这样的议论:"然而,当那件懦弱、愚蠢的事干完,一条生命带着它的希望和义务从吊在空中的畸形的东西中逝去之后,鸟儿叫着,花儿开着,阳光普照着,全和先前一样愉快")。

症状之三是每每避开那些为小说最终产生效果而应该加以注意的真实问题。也就是说,一个一心想制造感情效果的作家总是不惜以任何手段来达到这个目的的。譬如,在这篇小说里,布雷特·哈特念念不忘的是制造关于伙伴忠诚行为的悲怆感,所以他根本就不顾及这种忠诚行为的基础是否合理。就如已经指出过的那样,他没有把妻子被诱这件事作为矛盾的真正焦点。由于忽略了这一点,并转而为制造悲怆感而做了最后的努力,他使整篇小说显得既无重点又无逻辑性。要不是他对事件的心理意义如此不感兴趣而不做详细的研究,他肯定会意识到,有关的问题简直复杂到了使他无法把握的程度。

这篇小说产生了一个关于人物性格的基本问题:布雷特·哈特不是没有为小说设置一个主题吗?他也许在其他小说中曾看到过,要达到动人的感情效果必须有一个主题。他试图以一种新的浪漫故事来冒充主题,虽然辅之以地方色彩(如对伙伴关系的描述和方言的使用)以及诗化的文体,却没有把小说放在与它有关的各种现实的心理问题的基础上加以表现——换言之,也就是没有着力于理解他的主要人物的性格。

should feel, nudging the reader to respond—devices that would not be necessary if the story could make its own case. (For example, Bret Harte comments on the hanging as follows: "And yet, when the weak and foolish deed was done, and a life, with its possibilities and responsibilities, had passed out of the misshapen thing that dangled between earth and sky, the birds sang, the flowers bloomed, the sun shone, as cheerily as before. ")

A third symptom is the tendency to dodge the real issues that should prepare for the final effect of a story. That is, an author who is primarily concerned with giving an e-motional effect may not be too scrupulous a-bout the means adopted to that end. For example, in this story Bret Harte is so thoroughly obsessed with the pathos of the partner's loyalty that he has devoted no thought to the precise nature of the basis of that loyalty. As has already been pointed out, he does not bring the wifestealing episode into real focus. By skimping it and moving toward the final effort at pathos, he has made the whole story seem anticlimactic and illogical. Either he was so little interested in the psychology of the situation that he did not investigate it, or he was aware that the issues involved were too complicated for him to handle.

This story raises a basic question of character: has not Bret Harte taken a theme—which, perhaps, he had seen successfully employed for pathetic effects in other fiction—and attempted to trick it out with a new romantic setting, touches of local color (such as descriptions of the community and bits of dialect), and poeticized writing, without ever grounding the story in a presentation of the real psychological issues involved—without, in other words, trying to understand his main character?

▬ 思考题 ▬■

1. 将田纳西和他的伙伴的关系同《国王迷》中德雷沃特和皮奇的关系加以比较。吉卜林是如何避免感伤的?

1. Compare the relation of Tennessee and his partner with that of Dravot and Peachey in "The Man Who Would Be King". How did Kipling avoid sentimentality?

2. 将《带家具出租的房间》里欧·亨利的"议论"与这篇小说里布雷特·哈特的"议论"加以比较。两种"议论"各自起到的作用如何？

3. 讨论《万卡》里的感伤问题。契诃夫避免感伤吗？若是，如何避免的？　　（刘文荣 译）

2. Compare the "editorializing" of O. Henry in "The Furnished Room" with that of Bret Harte in this story. What is the function of the "editorializing" in each?

3. Discuss the question of sentimentality in "Vanka." Did Chekhov avoid sentimentality? If so, how?

015. 阿拉比

（爱尔兰）詹姆斯·乔伊斯 著　宗 白 译

015. Araby

by James Joyce

　　北理查蒙德街的一头是不通的，除了基督兄弟学校的学童们放学回家那段时间外，平时很寂静。在街尽头有一幢无人住的两层楼房，跟一块方地上的其他房子隔开着。街上那些有人住的房屋沉着不动声色的褐色的脸，互相凝视。

　　我们从前的房客，一个教士，死在这屋子的后客厅里。由于长期关闭，所有的房间散发出一股霉味。厨房后面的废物间里，满地都是乱七八糟的废纸。我在其中翻到几本书页卷起而潮湿的平装书：沃尔特·司各特所著的《修道院长》，还有《虔诚的圣餐者》和《维道克回忆录》。我最喜欢末一本，因为那些书页是黄的。屋子后面有个荒芜的花园，中间一株苹果树，四周零零落落地有几株灌木。在一棵灌木下面我发现死去的房客的一个生锈的自行车打气筒。教士是个心肠很好的人，他在遗嘱中把全部存款捐给了各种慈善机构，又把家具赠给他的妹妹。

　　到了日短夜长的冬天，晚饭还没吃完，夜幕就降落了。当我们在街上玩耍时，一幢幢房屋变得阴森森的。头上的夜空是一片变幻的紫罗兰色，同街灯的微光遥遥相映。寒气刺人，我们不停地玩着，直到浑身暖和。我们的喊叫声在僻静的街心回响。我们窜到屋子后面黑暗、泥泞的巷子里，玩粗暴的野孩子玩的夹道鞭打游戏，又跑到一家家幽暗阴湿的花园后门口，那里一个个灰坑发出难闻的气味。然后再到黑黝黝的满是马粪味的马厩去。马夫在那里梳马，或用扣着的马具，摇出铿锵的声音。当我们折回街道时，灯光已经从一家家厨房的窗子里透出来，把这一带照亮

NORTH Richmond Street, being blind, was a quiet street except at the hour when the Christian Brothers' School set the boys free. An uninhabited house of two stories stood at the blind end, detached from its neighbors in a square ground. The other houses of the street, conscious of decent lives within them, gazed at one another with brown imperturbable faces.

The former tenant of our house, a priest, had died in the back drawing room. Air, musty from having been long enclosed, hung in all the rooms, and the waste room behind the kitchen was littered with old useless papers. Among these I found a few paper-covered books, the pages of which were curled and damp: *The Abbol*, by Walter Scott, *The Devout Communicant*, and *The Memoirs of Vidocq*. I liked the last best because its leaves were yellow. The wild garden behind the house contained a central apple tree and a few straggling brushes under one of which I found the late tenant's rusty bicycle pump. He had been a very charitable priest; in his will he had left all his money to institutions and the furniture of his house to his sister.

When the short days of winter came dusk fell before we had well eaten our dinners. When we met in the street the houses had grown somber. The space of sky above us was the color of ever-changing violet and towards it the lamps of the street lifted their feeble lanterns. The cold air stung us and we played till our bodies glowed. Our shouts echoed in the silent street. The career of our play brought us through the dark muddy lanes behind the houses where we ran the gauntlet of the rough tribes from the cottages, to the back doors of the dark odorous stables where a coachman smoothed and combed the horse or shook music

作者简介：詹姆斯·乔伊斯（James Joyce，1882—1941），爱尔兰小说家。1882 年 2 月 2 日生于爱尔兰都柏林，1941 年 1 月 13 日卒于瑞士苏黎世。他在都柏林接受教育，1902 年迁居巴黎。他的生活艰难，财政危机不断，慢性眼疾有时使他完全失明，作品审查经常遇到麻烦，他的女儿还患有精神病。小说集《都柏林人》（The Dubliners，1914）和自传体小说《一个年轻艺术家的肖像》（Portrait of the Artist as a Young Man，1916）和他早期的散文集体现他讲故事的天赋和他的智慧。他在朋友和赞助人的资助下，花 7 年时间完成了备受争议的作品《尤里西斯》（Ulysses，1922）（最初在美国和英国被禁），后来被认定为 20 世纪最伟大的英语小说，这篇小说是探索内心独白和意识流写作方式的代表作。

了。这时，假如我叔叔正拐过街角，我们便藏在暗处，直到他安抵家中。如果曼根的姐姐在门口石阶上呼唤弟弟回家吃茶点，我们就在暗中看着她对街道东张西望。我们等着看她待住不走呢，还是进屋去。要是她一直不进去，我们就从暗处走出来，没奈何地走到曼根家台阶前。她在等我们，灯光从半掩的门里射出来，映现出她的身形。她弟弟在顺从她以前，总要先嘲弄她一番，我则靠着栏杆望着她。她一移动身子，衣服便摇摆起来，柔软的辫子左右摆动。

　　每天早晨，我躺在前客厅的地板上，望着她家的门，百叶窗拉下来，只留一英寸不到的缝隙，那样别人就看不见我了。她一出门走到台阶上，我的心就怦怦跳。我冲到过道里，抓起书就奔，跟在她后面。我紧紧盯住她穿着棕色衣服的身形。走到岔路的地方，我便加快步子赶过她。每天早晨都是如此。除了随便招呼一下之外，我从未同她讲过话。可是，她的名字总是使我愚蠢地情绪激动。

　　她的形象甚至在最不适宜于有浪漫的想象的场合也陪伴着我。每逢周末傍晚，我都得跟姑姑上街买东西，替她拎一些包儿，我们穿行在五光十色的大街上，被醉鬼和讨价还价的婆娘们挤来挤去，周围一片喧嚣：劳工们的诅咒，站在一桶桶猪颊肉旁守望的伙计的尖声叫嚷，街头卖唱的用浓重的鼻音哼着的关于奥唐纳万·罗沙①的《大伙儿都来》，或一支关于爱尔兰动乱的歌谣。在我看来，这些噪声汇合成一片熙熙攘攘的众生相。我仿佛感到自己正端着圣餐杯，在一群对头中间穿过。有时，在莫名其妙地做祷告或唱赞美诗时，她的名字几乎从我嘴里脱口而出，我时常热泪盈眶（自己也说不清为什么）。有时，一股沸腾的激情从心底涌起，流入胸中。我很少想到前途。我不知道自己究竟会不会同她说话，要是说了，怎么向她倾诉我迷茫的爱慕。这时，我的身子好似一架竖琴，她的音容笑貌宛如拨弄琴弦的纤指。

　　有一天，薄暮时分，我踅到教士在里面死去的后客厅内。那是一个漆黑的雨夜，屋子里一片沉寂。透过破碎的玻璃窗，我听到雨密密麻麻地泻在土地上，像针似的细雨在湿透了的泥地上不断跳跃。远处，有

---

① 奥唐纳万·罗沙（1831—1915）：爱尔兰政治鼓动家与作家，青年时期曾为革命文艺团体"凤凰社"的领导者之一，1871 年后移居美国。

from the buckled harness. When we returned to the street, light from the kitchen windows had filled the areas. If my uncle was seen turning the corner we hid in the shadow until we had seen him safely housed. Or if Mangan's sister came out on the doorstep to call her brother in to his tea we watched her from our shadow peer up and down the street. We waited to see whether she would remain or go in and, if she remained, we left our shadow and walked up to Mangan's steps resignedly. She was waiting for us, her figure defined by the light from the halfopened door. Her brother always teased her before he obeyed and I stood by the railings looking at her. Her dress swung as she moved her body and the soft rope of her hair tossed from side to side.

Every morning I lay on the floor in the front parlor watching her door. The blind was pulled down to within an inch of the sash so that I could not be seen. When she came out on the doorstep my heart leaped. I ran to the hall, seized my books and followed her. I kept her brown figure always in my eye and, when we came near the point at which our ways diverged, I quickened my pace and passed her. This happened morning after morning. I had never spoken to her, except for a few casual words, and yet her name was like a summons to all my foolish blood.

Her image accompanied me even in places the most hostile to romance. On Saturday evenings when my aunt went marketing I had to go to carry some of the parcels. We walked through the flaring streets, jostled by drunken men and bargaining women, amid the curses of laborers, the shrill litanies of shop boys who stood on guard by the barrels of pigs' cheeks, the nasal chanting of street singers, who sang a *come-all-you* about O'Donovan Rossa, or a ballad about the troubles in our native land. These noises converged in a single sensation of life for me: I imagined that I bore my chalice safely through a throng of foes. Her name sprang to my lips at moments in strange prayers and praises which I myself did not understand. My eyes were often full of tears (I could not tell why) and at times a flood from my heart seemed to pour itself out into my bosom. I thought little of the future. I did not know whether I would ever speak to her or not or, if I spoke to her, how I could tell her of my confused adoration. But my body was like a harp and her words and gestures were like fingers running upon the wires.

One evening I went into the back drawing room in which the priest had died. It was a dark rainy evening and there was no sound in the house. Through one of the broken panes I heard the rain impinge upon the earth, the fine incessant needles of water playing in the

一盏街灯的光或是哪一家窗口透出来的光在下面闪烁。我庆幸自己不能看清一切。我的全部感官似乎想隐蔽起来,我觉得自己快要失去知觉了,于是把双手紧紧地合在一起,以致手颤抖了,同时喃喃自语:"啊,爱!啊,爱!"

她终于跟我说话了。她一开口,我就慌乱不堪,呆在那儿,不知道说什么好。她问我去不去阿拉比①。我记不起怎么回答的。她说那儿的集市一定丰富多彩,她很想去呐。

"为啥不去呢?"我问。

她不断转动着手腕上的银镯子说,她不能去,因为这一星期女修道院里要做静修。那时,她弟弟正在和两个男孩抢帽子。我独自站在栏杆旁。她手中握着一支熏衣草,低下头,凑近我。门对面,街灯的光照着她白嫩的脖子的曲线,照亮了披垂的头发,也照亮了搁在栏杆上的手。她从容地站着,灯光使她衣服的一边清晰可见,显出裙子的白色镶边。

"你真该去看看。"她说。

"要是我去的话,"我说,"一定给你捎点什么的。"

从那一晚起,数不清的愚蠢的怪念头充塞在我白天的幻想和夜半的梦中!但愿出发之前那段乏味的日子一下子过去。学校里的功课使我烦躁。每当夜晚在寝室里或白天在教室中读书时,她的形象便闪现在啃不进的书页之间。Araby(阿拉比)的音节在静谧中向我召唤,我的心灵沉溺在寂静中,四周弥漫着迷人的东方气氛。我要求让我星期六晚上到阿拉比的集市去。我姑姑听了吃一惊,疑心我跟共济会②有什么勾搭。在课堂里,我很少回答得出问题。我瞧着老师的脸从和蔼变得严峻。他说,希望你不要变得懒惰。我成天神思恍惚。生活中的正经事使我厌烦,它们使我的愿望不能尽快实现,所以在我看来,都像小孩子的游戏,单调乏味的小孩子游戏。

星期六早晨,我对叔叔说晚上我要到集市去。他正在前厅的衣帽架边手忙脚乱地找帽刷子,漫不经心地说:"行,孩子,我知道了。"

他待在过道里,我就没法去前客厅,躺在窗边了。

---

① 阿拉比是阿拉伯的古名。此处是指一个以"阿拉比"命名的、布置成阿拉伯集市式样的百货商场。

② 一种互助性质的秘密社团,在欧美许多地方有分支。

---

sodden beds. Some distant lamp or lighted window gleamed below me. I was thankful that I could see so little. All my senses seemed to desire to veil themselves and, feeling that I was about to slip from them, I pressed the palms of my hands together until they trembled, murmuring: "O love! O love!" many times.

At last she spoke to me. When she addressed the first words to me I was so confused that I did not know what to answer. She asked me was I going to *Araby*. I forgot whether I answered yes or no. It would be a splendid bazaar, she said; she would love to go.

"And why can't you?" I asked.

While she spoke she turned a silver bracelet round and round her wrist. She could not go, she said, because there would be a retreat that week in her convent. Her brother and two other boys were fighting for their caps and I was alone at the railings. She held one of the spikes, bowing her head towards me. The light from the lamp opposite our door caught the white curve of her neck, lit up her hair that rested there and, falling, lit up the hand upon the railing. It fell over one side of her dress and caught the white border of a petticoat, just visible as she stood at ease.

"It's well for you," she said.

"If I go," I said, "I will bring you something."

What innumerable follies laid waste my waking and sleeping thoughts after that evening! I wished to annihilate the tedious intervening days. I chafed against the work of school. At night in my bedroom and by day in the classroom her image came between me and the page I strove to read. The syllables of the word *Araby* were called to me through the silence in which my soul luxuriated and cast an Eastern enchantment over me. I asked for leave to go to the bazaar on Saturday night. My aunt was surprised and hoped it was not some Freemason affair. I answered few questions in class. I watched my master's face pass from amiability to sternness; he hoped I was not beginning to idle. I could not call my wandering thoughts together. I had hardly any patience with the serious work of life which, now that it stood between me and my desire, seemed to me child's play, ugly monotonous child's play.

On Saturday morning I reminded my uncle that I wished to go to the bazaar in the evening. He was fussing at the hall stand, looking for the hat brush, and answered me curtly:

"Yes, boy, I know."

As he was in the hall I could not go into the front parlor and lie at the window. I left the house in bad humor and walked slowly towards the school. The air was pitilessly raw and already my heart misgave me.

我悻悻地走出家门,到学校去。空气透骨的阴冷,我心里一阵阵忐忑不安。

我回家吃饭,叔叔还没回来。时光还早呢。我坐着望了一会儿钟,滴答滴答的钟声使我心烦意乱起来,便走出房间,登上楼梯,走到楼上。那些高敞的空房间,寒冷而阴沉,却使我无拘无束。我唱起歌来,从一个房间跑到另一个房间。透过正面的玻璃窗,我看见伙伴们在街上玩。他们的喊声隐隐约约传到我耳边。我把前额贴住冰冷的玻璃窗,望着她住的那幢昏暗的屋子。大约一个小时过去了,我还站在那儿,什么都没看见,只在幻想中看见她那穿着棕色衣服的身形,街灯的光朦胧地照亮呈曲线的脖子、搁在栏杆上的手以及裙子下摆的镶边。

我再下楼时,看见当铺老板的遗孀莫塞太太坐在火炉边。这个长舌妇,为了某种虔诚的目的收集用过的邮票。我陪着吃茶点,得耐着性子听她嚼舌。开晚饭的时间早已过了一个小时,叔叔还没回来。莫塞太太站起身来说对不起,不能久等,8点过了,她不愿在外面待得太晚,夜里的风她受不了。她走后,我在屋里踱来踱去,紧攥着拳头。姑姑说:

"兴许今晚去不成了,改天再去看集市吧。"

9点,我忽然听见叔叔用弹簧锁钥匙在开过道门。接着听见他在自言自语,听到衣架被他挂上去的大衣压得直晃荡。我很了解这些举动的含义。晚饭吃到一半,我向他要钱到集市去。他已把这件事给忘得一干二净了。

"人们早已上床,睡过一阵了。"他说。

我没笑。姑姑大声地说:

"还不给钱让他去?你已经叫他等得够长啦!"

他说非常抱歉,忘了这件事。然后又说他很欣赏那句老话:"只工作不去玩,任何孩子都变傻。"他又问我去哪儿,于是我再讲一遍。他便问我知不知道《阿拉伯人向骏马告别》①。我走出厨房时,他正要给姑姑背诵那故事的开场白哩。

我紧紧攥着一枚两先令银币,沿着白金汉大街向火车站迈开大步走去。街上熙熙攘攘,尽是买东西的人,煤气灯照耀如同白昼,这景象提醒我快到集市去。我在一列空荡荡的火车的三等车厢找了个座位。火车迟迟不开,叫人等得恼火,过了好久才缓慢地驶出

_____

① 可能指《一千零一夜》中《乌木马的故事》。

When I came home to dinner my uncle had not yet been home. Still it was early. I sat staring at the clock for some time and, when its ticking began to irritate me, I left the room. I mounted the staircase and gained the upper part of the house. The high cold empty gloomy rooms liberated me and I went from room to room singing. From the front window I saw my companions playing below in the street. Their cries reached me weakened and indistinct and, leaning my forehead against the cool glass, I looked over at the dark house where she lived. I may have stood there for an hour, seeing nothing but the brown-clad figure cast by my imagination, touched discreetly by the lamplight at the curved neck, at the hand upon the railings and at the border below the dress.

When I came downstairs again I found Mrs. Mercer sitting at the fire. She was an old garrulous woman, a pawnbroker's widow, who collected used stamps for some pious purpose. I had to endure the gossip of the tea table. The meal was prolonged beyond an hour and still my uncle did not come. Mrs. Mercer stood up to go: she was sorry she couldn't wait any longer, but it was after eight o'clock and she did not like to be out late, as the night air was bad for her. When she had gone I began to walk up and down the room, clenching my fists. My aunt said:

"I'm afraid you may put off your bazaar for this night of Our Lord."

At nine o'clock I heard my uncle's latchkey in the hall door. I heard him talking to himself and heard the hall stand rocking when it had received the weight of his overcoat. I could interpret these signs. When he was midway through his dinner I asked him to give me the money to go to the bazaar. He had forgotten.

"The people are in bed and after their first sleep now," he said.

I did not smile. My aunt said to him energetically:

"Can't you give him the money and let him go? You've kept him late enough as it is."

My uncle said he was very sorry he had forgotten. He said he believed in the old saying: "All work and no play makes Jack a dull boy." He asked me where I was going and, when I had told him a second time he asked me did I know *The Arab's Farewell to His Steed*. When I left the kitchen he was about to recite the opening lines of the piece to my aunt.

I held a florin tightly in my hand as I strode down Buckingham Street towards the station. The sight of the streets thronged with buyers and glaring with gas recalled to me the purpose of my journey. I took my seat in a third-class carriage of a deserted train. After

车站,爬行在沿途倾圮的房屋中间,驶过一条闪闪发亮的河流。在威斯特兰罗车站,来了一大群乘客,往车厢门直拥。列车员说,这是直达集市的专车,这才把他们挡回去。我独自坐在空车厢里。几分钟后,火车停在一个临时用木头搭起的月台旁。我下车走到街上。有一只钟被亮光照着,我瞅了一眼:9:50。我的面前矗立着一座大建筑物,上面闪亮着那魅人的名字。

我怎么也找不到花 6 便士就能进去的入口处。我生怕集市关门,便三脚两步穿过一个旋转门,把一个先令付给一位神情疲惫的看门人。我发现自己走进一所大厅,它周围环绕着只有它一半高的长廊。几乎所有的棚摊都关门了。大半个厅黑沉沉的。我有一种阒寂之感,犹如置身于做完礼拜后的教堂中。我怯生生地走到商场中间。那儿还有些人围着仍在营业的摊子。一块布帘上面用彩色电灯拼成"乐声咖啡馆"①。两个男人正在一只托盘上数钱。我倾听着铜币落盘时发出的丁当声。

我困难地想起到这儿来是为什么,便随意走到一个搭棚摊前,端详着那里陈列的瓷花瓶和印花茶具。棚摊门口有个女郎,正在同两位年轻的先生说笑,我听出他们的英国口音,模模糊糊地听着他们交谈。

"噢,我从没说过那种事。"

"哎,你肯定说过。"

"不,肯定没有!"

"难道她没说过?"

"说过的,我听见她说的。"

"啊,这是……小小的撒谎。"

那位女郎看见我,走过来问我要买什么。她的声音冷冰冰的,好像出于责任感。我诚惶诚恐地瞧着两排大坛子,它们排在棚摊门两侧,好似东方卫士,接着我低声说:"不买,谢谢。"

那女郎把一只花瓶移动了一下,然后回到两个年轻人身边去了。他们又谈起同一个话题。那女人回头瞟了我一两次。

我逗留在棚摊前,仿佛真的对那些货物恋恋不舍似的,尽管心里明白这样待着毫无意义。最后,我慢吞吞地离开那儿,沿着集市中间的小道走去。我把两

---

① 原文为法语 Café Chantant:一种有音乐伴奏或举行音乐会的咖啡馆。

an intolerable delay the train moved out of the station slowly. It crept onward among ruinous houses and o-ver the twinkling river. At Westland Row Station a crowd of people pressed to the carriage doors; but the porters moved them back, saying that it was a special train for the bazaar. I remained alone in the bare carriage. In a few minutes the train drew up beside an impro-vised wooden platform. I passed out on to the road and saw by the lighted dial of a clock that it was ten mi-nutes to ten. In front of me was a large building which displayed the magical name.

I could not find any sixpenny entrance and, fea-ring that the bazaar would be closed, I passed in quick-ly through a turnstile, handing a shilling to a weary-looking man. I found myself in a big hall girdled at half its height by a gallery. Nearly all the stalls were closed and the greater part of the hall was in darkness. I rec-ognized a silence like that which pervades a church af-ter a service. I walked into the center of the bazaar timidly. A few people were gathered about the stalls which were still open. Before a curtain, over which the words *Café Chantant* were written in colored lamps, two men were counting money on a salver. I listened to the fall of the coins.

Remembering with difficulty why I had come I went over to one of the stalls and examined porcelain vases and flowered tea sets. At the door of the stall a young lady was talking and laughing with two young gentlemen. I remarked their English accents and lis-tened vaguely to their conversation.

"O, I never said such a thing!"

"O, but you did!"

"O, but I didn't!"

"Didn't she say that?"

"Yes, I heard her."

"O, there's a...fib!"

Observing me, the young lady came over and asked me did I wish to buy anything. The tone of her voice was not encouraging; she seemed to have spoken to me out of a sense of duty. I looked humbly at the great jars that stood like eastern guards at either side of the dark entrance to the stall and murmured:

"No, thank you."

The young lady changed the position of one of the vases and went back to the two young men. They be-gan to talk of the same subject. Once or twice the young lady glanced at me over her shoulder.

I lingered before her stall, though I knew my stay was useless, to make my interest in her wares seem the more real. Then I turned away slowly and walked down the middle of the bazaar. I allowed the two pen-nies to fall against the sixpence in my pocket. I heard a

个便士丢进口袋,跟里面一枚 6 便士的硬币碰响。接着,我听见长廊尽头传来熄灯的喊声。顿时,大厅上面漆黑一片。

我抬头凝视着黑暗,感到自己是一个受到虚荣心驱使和播弄的可怜虫,于是眼睛里燃烧着痛苦和愤怒。

▬ 讨　论 ▬

就所谓最简单的标准来说,这是一篇写少年失恋的小说。但是,小说的大部分并没有写到那个少年的恋爱,而是写他周围的世界——对他住的那条街道的描写,关于那个已故教士以及教士遗下的财产的情况介绍,还有他跟叔叔和姑姑的关系。这些事情都是自然而然地出现在小说里的,也就是说,按照现实主义原理,这些事情在小说里都是合情合理的。这样的成分如果只是作为"背景"或者仅仅作为"环境"来处理的话,那么这篇小说就会被无关的材料所压垮。然而,任何读者——除非是最奇特的怪人——都很清楚,这篇小说中的各条线索都是相互联系而起作用的。我们一旦发现这些表面看来互不相干的线索在《阿拉比》里是以何种方式联系起来并都和那个少年的失恋有关的话,我们也就得出了小说的主题。

那么,像已故教士的财产啦、朋友们在抢帽子玩时那个少年却在和那个少女遥通音讯啦、茶会上的嚼舌啦、叔叔的迟迟不来啦之类的事情,究竟和少年的失恋有何关系呢?通过这些事情,间接地暗示出一件事情,那就是少年与日俱增的孤独感,也就是在他和朋友、老师及家庭之间缺乏同情心。他说:"我仿佛感到自己端着圣餐杯,在一群对头中间穿过。"举例来说,如当叔叔站在大厅里时,少年就不能走进前室躺在窗台上,或者在学校里,他的日常学习也开始显得像"单调乏味的小孩子的游戏"。但是这种孤独感也有它几乎是狂喜的时刻。火车的列车员把人群往后挡,"说这是直达集市的专车",不是为他们开的。那个少年

voice call from one end of the gallery that the light was out. The upper part of the hall was now completely dark.

Gazing up into the darkness I saw myself as a creature driven and derided by vanity; and my eyes burned with anguish and anger.

On what may be called the simplest level this is a story of a boy's disappointment. A great part of the story, however, does not directly concern itself with the boy's love affair, but with the world in which he lives—the description of his street, the information about the dead priest and the priest's abandoned belongings, the relations with the aunt and uncle. These matters seem to come very naturally into the story; that is, they may be justified individually in the story on realistic grounds. If such elements served *merely* as "setting" or *only* as atmosphere, then the story would be overloaded with nonfunctional material. Obviously, however, for any reader except the most casual, these items do have a function. If we find in what way these apparently irrelevant items in "Araby" are related to each other and to the disappointment of the boy, we shall have defined the theme of the story.

What, then, is the relation of the boy's disappointment to such matters as the belongings of the dead priest, the fact that he stands apart talking to the girl while his friends are quarreling over the cap, the gossip over the tea table, the uncle's lateness, and so on? One thing that is immediately suggested by the mention of these things is the boy's growing sense of isolation, the lack of sympathy between him and his friends, teachers, and family. He says, "I imagined that I bore my chalice safely through a throng of foes." For instance, when the uncle is standing in the hall, the boy could not go into the front parlor and lie at the window; or at school his ordinary occupations began to seem "ugly monotonous child's play." But this sense of isolation has, also, moments that are almost triumphant. The porters at the station wave the

独自待在空荡荡的车厢里,但他正在去"阿拉比"的路上,正在狂喜地奔向某个充满浪漫色彩和异国情调的目的地。圣餐杯的隐喻暗示出同样珍奇的内心喜悦。不管怎样,围绕着他的不再是普通的日常世界,在日常世界里他无论痛苦还是欣喜时都感到孤独。就是对那个少女,他也感到孤独。他和她仅谈过一次话,而当时他又是那样迷乱不堪,竟不知如何对答。但现在,他希望为她从阿拉比带点什么来,这样做总不失为他和她之间一种联络感情的方式,不失为在充满敌意的世界上他们关系的某种象征。

最后写集市的那段情节,有意识地——虽然是含蓄地——为那个少年单方面地领悟事实做了铺垫。"临时用木头搭起的月台"和出现在建筑物上方的"魅人的名字"形成了对照。在里面,大多数售货棚摊关闭着。那位"女郎"以及和她在一起谈话的那些年轻的先生是铺垫中的主要部分。他们对少年毫不留意,只有那个"女郎"因为她的职务是售货员,才勉强地问他想买什么东西。而她的声调也是"冷冰冰的"。她也属于敌意的世界,但是她又属于一个他试图进入其中的世界,她和那些向她献媚的人在一起进行着轻松而亲昵的谈话——这种亲昵的样子同他和曼根的姐姐的关系正成对照。这是一个辽远而又丰富多彩的世界,他无法进入这个世界,他只能用目光"诚惶诚恐地瞧着两排大坛子,它们排在棚摊门两侧,好似东方卫士"。具有讽刺意味的是,那个"女郎"和那些献媚者对自己正处于神圣而受到防卫的地位却毫不自知,他们纵情于嬉戏逗笑,这似乎在亵渎和贬低那个把少年隔绝在外的神秘世界。我们何以得知这种情形的呢? 小说对此并未直说,但是从那个女郎和献媚者谈话的神情与那句提到"大坛子"的话的语调的对比中,却表现出了这层意思。

类似这样的情节,有助于使小说前文中表现的那种一般意义上的孤独感得到明朗化和

crowds back, "saying that it was a special train for the bazaar" and was not for them. The boy is left alone in the bare carriage, but he is going to "Araby," moving triumphantly toward some romantic and exotic fulfillment. The metaphor of the chalice implies the same kind of precious secret triumph. It is not only the ordinary surrounding world, however, from which he is cruelly or triumphantly isolated. He is also isolated from the girl herself. He talks to her only once, and then is so confused that he does not know how to answer her. But the present he hopes to bring her from Araby would somehow serve as a means of communicating his feelings to her, a symbol for their relationship in the midst of the inimical world.

In the last scene at the bazaar, there is a systematic, though subtle, preparation for the final realization on the part of the boy. There is the "improvised wooden platform" in contrast with the "magical name" displayed above the building. Inside, most of the stalls are closed. The "young lady" and young men who talk together are important in the preparation. They pay the boy no mind, except insofar as the "young lady" is compelled by her position as clerk to ask him what he wants. But her tone is "not encouraging." She, too, belongs to the inimical world. But she, also, belongs to a world he is trying to penetrate: she and her admirers are on terms of easy intimacy—an intimacy in contrast to his relation to Mangan's sister. It is an exotic, rich world into which he cannot penetrate: he can only look "humbly at the great jars that stood like eastern guards at either side of the dark entrance to the stall." Ironically, the "young lady" and her admirers, far from realizing that they are on holy, guarded ground, indulge in trivial, easy banter, which seems to defile and cheapen the secret world from which the boy is barred. How do we know this? It is not stated, but the contrast between the conversation of the young lady and her admirers, and the tone of the sentence about the "great jars" indicates such an interpretation.

Such scenes, then, help to point up and particularize the general sense of isolation

具体化,并由此而为小说的结束做好了铺垫。在结束时,那个少年在简陋得像谷仓似的集市里突然降临的暗影下看到自己就像"一个受到虚荣心驱使和播弄的可怜虫",而同时他眼睛里却燃烧着"痛苦和愤怒"。

我们已经看到,这些表面上看来与题无关的事件和段落在小说里是有作用的,它们有助于表现那个少年难以忍受的孤独感,有助于表现他遭到那个处于神秘状态的世界排斥时的感受。但这只是这些材料所起到的部分作用。细心的读者会留意到,小说里还有那么多有关信仰和宗教礼仪的直接或间接的旁涉材料。我们看到了已故的教士,基督兄弟学校,姑姑对集市和共济会的联想。这些旁涉材料在一定程度上构成了那个易受影响的少年周围的社会组合形式,那个少年就将在这样的社会中长大。但是,还有一些其他的旁涉材料,虽然不很明确,却与少年的生活经验有着更加密切的关系。对他来说,就是那劳工们的诅咒,商店小伙计的尖声叫嚷和街头卖唱声汇合成的"众生相"。他想象他"从一群对头中间"端起一只"圣餐杯",而当他孤零零一个人时,那曼根的姐姐的名字就会像"祷告词或赞美诗"似的从他嘴里脱口而出。所以,当他讲到自己"迷茫的爱慕"时,我们便认识到对那个少女的爱情在他已具有某种宗教经验的神秘色彩。使用"迷茫"一词也即暗示出在他心里浪漫的爱和宗教的爱同时混合并存着。

那个少年孤立于一个对他的爱显得茫然无知甚至抱有敌意的世界之外。从某种程度上讲,他知道他的姑姑和叔叔是很仁慈的,但是他们却不了解他。他也曾一度从与同伴们的交往中以及在自己的学业中得到过满足,但是他对这两者都已感到不耐烦。因为他有另一种感受,由于这种感受,他容忍自己落落寡合甚至为此觉得很自豪。世界不但不了解他的内心甚至还要贬低和玷污它。在小说内容的背景上,那从一大群对头中间端起圣餐杯的

suggested by the earlier descriptive materials, and thereby to prepare for the last sentence of the story, in which, under the sudden darkness of the cheap barnlike bazaar, the boy sees himself as "a creature driven and derided by vanity," while his eyes burn with "anguish and anger."

We have seen how the apparently casual incidents and items of description do function in the story to build up the boy's sense of intolerable isolation, his sense of being isolated from the common world in so sacred a precinct. But this is only part of the function of this material. The careful reader will have noticed how many references, direct or indirect, there are to religion and the ritual of the church. We have the dead priest, the Christian Brothers' School, the aunt's hope that the bazaar is not "some Freemason affair," her mention, when the uncle has been delayed, of "this night of Our Lord." At one level, these references merely indicate the type of community in which the impressionable boy is growing up. But there are other, less obvious, references, which relate more intimately to the boy's experience. Even the cries of the shop boys for him are "shrill litanies." He imagines that he bears a "chalice safely through a throng of foes." When he is alone the name of Mangan's sister springs to his lips "in strange prayers and praises." For this reason, when he speaks of his "confused adoration," we see that the love of the girl takes on, for him, something of the nature of a mystic, religious experience. The use of the very word *confused* hints of the fact that romantic love and religious love are mixed up in his mind.

The boy is isolated from a world that seems ignorant of, and even hostile to, his love. In a sense he knows that his aunt and uncle are good and kind, but they do not understand him. He had once found satisfaction in the society of his companions and in his schoolwork, but he has become impatient with both. But there is also a sense in which he accepts his isolation and is even proud of it. The world not only does not understand his secret but would cheapen and contaminate it. The metaphor of the chalice borne through a throng of foes, supported as it is by the

隐喻即暗示出了某种类似宗教信徒式的献身精神。这些有关宗教的旁涉材料有助于解释那个少年的意愿，并且点明了他为何要在集市里漫游而流连忘返的缘由。所以，有趣的是，关于他的幻灭和绝望的最初表现，就是用了一个关于教堂的隐喻来加以表示的："几乎所有的棚摊都关门了。大半个厅里黑沉沉的。我有一种孤寂之感，犹如置身于做完礼拜后的教堂中……两个男人正在一只托盘上数钱。我倾听着铜币落盘时发出的丁当声。"当然，这个细节的出典就是《圣经》中耶路撒冷神殿里的兑钱人（《马可福音》11 章 15 节），而在这里使我们想到，尘世的污浊业已侵蚀了爱的神殿（问题也许是有人会认为这样的解释是强加给作品的。但是无论对个别的情节做出怎样的解释，有一点可以肯定，作家们在创作类似这篇小说的、经过精心设计的作品时，就是用这样的指示或者暗示来体现作品的基本含义的）。

这是不是一篇感伤小说呢？这篇小说写的是年轻人的恋爱而且是"初恋"，这样的恋爱通常是轻率的，往往是一时之兴。这篇小说里的那个少年也显然在捕风捉影，自作多情，他在小说结束时自己也承认他已陷入了自我蒙骗。那么作者又如何避免这样的指责，即认为他对待这样的事是否过于认真了？

要回答这个问题，就要看看小说是从哪个角度来写的。这篇小说是由主人公自叙的，但时间是在很久以后，也即在他成年之后。当然，这个情况在小说里并没有点明，但是这篇小说的语言风格显然不是未成年的少年人的风格。小说在风格上条理清晰而又复杂多变，含蓄的隐喻随处可见。换言之，既超然又具评判性，这是一个成年男子在回忆自己的少年时代。譬如，少年在经受痛苦时是决不会进行这样的自我暴露的："除了随便招呼一下之外，我从未同她讲过话。可是，她的名字总使我愚蠢地情绪激动。"事实上，这个成年人已经明白

body of the story, suggests a sort of consecration like that of the religious devotee. The implications of the references to religion, then, help define the boy's attitude and indicate why, for him, so much is staked upon the journey to the bazaar. It is interesting to note, therefore, that the first overt indication of his disillusionment and disappointment is expressed in a metaphor involving a church: "Nearly all the stalls were closed and the greater part of the hall was in darkness. I recognized a silence like that which pervades a church after a service…Two men were counting money on a salver. I listened to the fall of the coins." And this episode, of course, is an echo of the money-changers in the Temple at Jerusalem(Mark l 1: l5); so here we have the idea that the contamination of the world has invaded the very temple of love. (The question may arise as to whether this is not reading too much into the passage. But whatever interpretation is to be made of the particular incident, it is by just such suggestion and implication that closely wrought stories, such as this one, are controlled by their authors and embody their fundamental meaning.)

Is this a sentimental story? It is about an adolescent love affair, about "puppy love," which is usually not taken seriously and is often an occasion for amusement. The boy of the story is obviously investing casual incidents with a meaning they do not deserve; he himself admits, in the end, that he has fallen into self-deception. How does the author avoid the charge that he has taken the matter overseriously?

The answer to this question would involve a consideration of the point of view from which the story is told. It is told by the hero himself, but after a long lapse of time, after he has reached maturity. This fact, it is true, is not stated in the story, but the style itself is not that of an adolescent boy. It is a formal and complicated style, rich in subtle implications. In other words, the man is looking back upon the boy, detached and judicial. For instance, the boy, in the throes of the experience, would never have said of himself: "I had never spoken to her, except for a few casual words, and yet her name was like a summons to all my foolish blood." The man

了自己少年时的行为在某种意义上讲是愚蠢的，少年时的感情是迷茫的。他早已摆脱此种迷茫，而且已经认识到这是过去存在的情况以及它为何存在的原因。

　　既然这个成年人已经摆脱了少年时的迷茫，那么事情为何对他依然有意义呢？他仅仅是在回忆少年时所经受过的痛苦吗？看来，不仅是这样，当他回忆少年生活时他还从中领悟到对某种问题的预示，而那个问题正是他在少年期后的生活经历中遇到的。对于儿童来说，现实和理想的矛盾可以说并不存在，而对于成年人来说，这种矛盾——其说法形形色色——却是一个恒常的问题。这篇小说所写的就是一个少年初次遇到了这个问题——因为，他即将成年。成年人对这个问题也许已经做过种种调整，或许已经得到了某些暂时的解决办法，但是，当他回忆往事之际，他依然会辨认出这个问题，而且是一个重要的问题。少年时代产生的幻灭感和孤独感虽然显得有点幼稚可笑，但是它们到了成年人的生活经验之中非但不会消失，而且会变得更强烈、更彻底。由此看来，这篇小说并不是一篇关于人的成长过程的流水账，也不是想表现某种关于人的心理变化的医疗兴趣。它是一幅关于成年人生活经验中主要矛盾的象征性示意图。

knows, as it were, that the behavior of the boy was, in a sense, foolish. The emotions of the boy are confused. He has unraveled the confusion long after, knows that it existed and why it existed.

If the man has unraveled the confusions of the boy, why is the event still significant to him? Is he merely dwelling on the pathos of adolescent experience? It seems, rather, that he sees in the event, as he looks back on it, a foreshadowing of a problem that has run through later experience. The discrepancy between the real and the ideal scarcely exists for the child, but it is a constant problem, in all sorts of terms, for the adult. This story is about a boy's first confrontation of that problem—that is, about his growing up. The man may have made adjustments to this problem, and may have worked out certain provisional solutions, but, looking back, he still recognizes it as a problem, and an important one. The sense of isolation and disillusion that sprang from the boy's experience—though it may seem trivial—becomes not less but more aggravated and fundamental in the adult's experience. So, the story is not merely an account of a stage in the process of growing up; it does not merely represent a clinical interest in the psychology of growing up. It is a symbolic rendering of a central conflict in mature experience.

思考题 ■

1. 那个少年和那个已故教士有何共同之处？设想，如果那个已故的人是个店老板或者是个律师或者是其他任何不"端圣餐杯"的人的话，那么小说是否会发生变化？

2. 人们认为儿童比成人更具想象力，那么，当那个少年把自己以往的生活看做"单调乏味的小孩子游戏"时，这里意味着什么？

3. 在这篇小说里，戏剧性的生动材料相对来说比较少，你能说说这是什么原因吗？这种情况与小说的基调以及主题是否相一致？

1. What does the boy have in common with the dead priest? Suppose that the dead man had been a shopkeeper, a lawyer, or anyone else who did not "carry a chalice." Would that have made any difference in the story?

2. Children are supposed to have more imagination than adults. What has happened when, for the boy, his previous occupations seem to be "ugly monotonous child's play"?

3. There is in this story a relatively small amount of dramatically rendered material. Can you say why? Is this fact consistent with the general tone and meaning of the story?

4. 思考一下,如果要把这篇小说写成一篇感伤的、痛哭流涕的关于"初恋"失意的作品,有何难度? 就这一点谈谈由于事件发生时间和分析性语言造成的讲故事时的时间"差距感"。就这一点谈谈小说的风格。

（刘文荣 译）

4. Think how easy it would have been to make this a sentimental, tear-jerking story about the disappointment of "first love." In this connection, comment on the "distancing" of the time of the telling from the time of the event and the tone of analysis. Comment on style in this connection.

016. 县城的医生

(俄)伊凡·屠格涅夫 著　　丰子恺 译

016. The District Doctor

by Ivan Turgenev

有一次,秋天,我从远离庄园的原野打猎回来,路上受了风寒,生起病来。幸而发热的时候我已经到了一个县城里,住在旅馆里了,我就派人去请医生。半个钟头之后,县城的医生来了,这人身材不高,瘦瘦的,长着一头黑发。他替我开了一服普通的发汗剂,叫我贴上芥末膏,很敏捷地把一张五卢布钞票塞进翻袖口里——但同时干咳一声,望望旁边——已经准备回家去了,忽然不知怎的同我谈起话来,就留下来了。我正苦于发烧,预料今夜会睡不着,喜欢有个好心人同我谈谈话。茶拿来了。我的医生就开始谈话。这人很不傻,讲话流利而且富有风趣。世间往往有奇怪的事:有的人你和他长住在一起,保持亲密的关系,然而从来不同他推心置腹地讲真心话;而有的人呢,刚刚相识,就一见如故,彼此像忏悔一样把所有的秘密都泄漏出来了。不知道我凭什么博得了我的新朋友的信任,他竟无缘无故地,即所谓不管三七二十一地把一件非常特殊的事讲给我听了。现在我就把他的故事传达给我的善意的读者。我努力保留医生原来的语调。

"您可知道,"他用微弱而颤抖的声音(这是纯粹的别列索夫鼻烟的作用)开始说,"您可知道这里的法官巴维尔·卢基奇·牟洛夫吗?……不知道……嗯,没有关系。(他清清喉咙,擦擦眼睛)我告诉您,这件事发生在——让我仔细想想,哦——发生在大斋期,正是解冻的天气。我在他家里——我们的法官家里——玩朴烈费兰斯①。我们的法官是一个好人,喜

---

① 一种纸牌游戏的名称。

ONE day in autumn on my way back from a remote part of the country I caught cold and fell ill. Fortunately the fever attacked me in the district town at the inn; I sent for the doctor. In half-an-hour the district doctor appeared, a thin, dark-haired man of middle height. He prescribed me the usual sudorific, ordered a mustard plaster to be put on, very deftly slid a five-ruble note up his sleeve, coughing drily and looking away as he did so, and then was getting up to go home, but somehow fell into talk and remained. I was exhausted with feverishness; I foresaw a sleepless night, and was glad of a little chat with a pleasant companion. Tea was served. My doctor began to converse freely. He was a sensible fellow, and expressed himself with vigour and some humour. Queer things happen in the world; you may live a long while with some people, and be on friendly terms with them, and never once speak openly with them from your soul; with others you scarcely have time to get acquainted, and all at once you are pouring out to him or he to you—all your secrets, as though you were at confession. I don't know how I gained the confidence of my new friend—anyway, with nothing to lead up to it, he told me a rather curious incident; and here I will report his tale for the information of the indulgent reader. I will try to tell it in the doctor's own words.

"You don't happen to know," he began in a weak and quavering voice (the common result of the use of unmixed Berezov snuff); "you don't happen to know the judge here, Mylov, Pavel Lukich?... You don't know him?... Well, it's all the same. " (He cleared his throat and rubbed his eyes.) "Well, you see, the thing happened, to tell you exactly without mistake, in Lent, at the very time of the thaws. I was sitting at his house—our judge's, you know—playing preference. ①

---

① A card game resembling whist.

作者简介: 伊凡·屠格涅夫(**Ivan Turgenev**,1818—1883),俄国小说家、诗人和剧作家。1818 年 11 月 9 日生于俄国奥廖尔,1883 年 9 月 3 日卒于法国布吉瓦尔。他以现实、热情地描写俄国农民阶层和深入刻画希望把国家推进新时代的俄国知识分子阶层闻名。他早期最著名作品是《零余者日记》(*The Diary of a Superfluous Man*,1850)。他以短篇小说《猎人手记》名噪一时。随后他创作了名篇《村居一月》(*A Month in the Country*,1855)和小说《罗亭》(*Rudin*,1856)。受到争议的小说《父与子》(*Fathers and Sons*,1862)体现了他对变革和两代间的差异的关注,这是他最好的小说。他的作品没有夸夸其谈,具有均衡感,关注艺术价值,这让他的作品有别于同时代的其他作品。

欢玩朴烈费兰斯。突然(我的医生常常用'突然'这两个字),他们对我说:'有人找您'。我说:'有什么事?'他们说:'送一个字条来——也许是病家送来的。'我说:'把字条给我看。'果然是病家送来的。……唔,很好——这,您知道吗,就是我们的食粮。……原来是这么一回事:是一个女地主:一个寡妇——写给我的,她写着:'我的女儿病势垂危了,请您看在上帝面上劳驾出诊,我现在打发马车来接您。'嗯,这都没有什么。……可是她住在离城20俄里的地方,已经夜深了,而且路难走极了!况且她家里境况不好,两个银卢布以上是不必希望的,就连这也很难说呢,也许只能得到些粗麻布或是一些谷物罢了。可是,您知道,服务第一——人快要死了呢。我突然把纸牌交给常任委员卡利奥宾,回到家里。一看,一辆小马车停在阶前。马是农家的马——大肚子马,真是大肚子马,马毛简直像毡子,马车夫为了表示恭敬,脱了帽子坐着。我心里想,看样子,老兄,你的主人不见得是堆金积玉的。……您在笑了,可是我告诉您,我们这班穷人,凡事都要考虑考虑。……如果马车夫神气活现地坐着,不摘下帽子来,还从胡须底下露出冷笑,摇着马鞭——那么包管你可以拿到两张钞票!可是我看出今天不是这种生意。不过,我想,没有办法,服务第一。我拿了最必需的药品,就出发了。您信不信,我差点儿到不了啦。路坏透了:有小川,有雪,有泥泞,有水坑,突然堤坝有缺口了——真糟糕!可是我终于来到了。房子很小,盖着麦秆。窗子里有灯光,大概在等我。一位戴着便帽的端庄的老太太来迎接我,说:'请您救救命,病很危险了。'我说:'请不要着急。……病人在哪儿?''来,请到这边来。'我一看,一间很干净的房间,屋角里点着一盏灯,床上躺着一位年约20岁的姑娘,已经不省人事了。她的热度很高,呼吸很困难——害的是热病。房间里还有两位姑娘,是她的姊妹,她们都吓坏了,哭得满脸泪痕。她们说:'昨天还很健康,胃口很好。今天早晨嚷着头疼,到晚上突然变成这个样子了。'……我还是那句话:'请不要着急。'——您知道,这是医生的责任——我就着手医治。我替她放出点血,叫她们替她贴上芥末膏,开了一服合剂。这时候我老望着她,望着她,您可知道——咳,说实话,我从来没有见过这样漂亮的脸蛋儿……总而言之,是一个绝色美人!我心里充满了怜惜。她的面貌多么可爱,她的眼睛……好,谢天谢地,

Our judge is a good fellow, and fond of playing preference. Suddenly," (the doctor made frequent use of this word, suddenly) "they tell me, 'There's a servant asking for you.' I say 'What does he want?' They say 'He has brought a note—it must be from a patient.' 'Give me the note,' I say. So it is from a patient—well and good—you understand—it's our bread and butter.... But this is how it was: a lady, a widow, writes to me; she says, 'My daughter is dying. Come, for God's sake!' she says, 'and the horses have been sent for you!'... Well, that's all right. But she was twenty miles from town, and it was midnight out of doors, and the roads in such a state, my word! And as she was poor herself, one could not expect more than two silver rubles, and even that problematic; and perhaps it might only be a matter of a roll of linen and a sack of oatmeal in payment. However, duty, you know, before everything: a fellow-creature may be dying. I hand over my cards at once to Kalliopin, the member of the provincial commission, and return home. I look; a wretched little trap was standing at the steps, with peasant's horses, fat—too fat—and their coats as shaggy as felt; and the coachman sitting with his cap off out of respect. Well, I think to myself, 'It's clear, my friend, these patients aren't rolling in riches.'... You smile; but I tell you, a poor man like me has to take everything into consideration.... If the coachman sits like a prince, and doesn't touch his cap, and even sneers at you behind his beard, and flicks his whip—then you may bet on six rubles. But this case, I saw, had a very different air. However, I think there's no help for it; duty before everything. I snatch up the most necessary drugs, and set off. Will you believe it? I only just managed to get there at all. The road was infernal: streams, snow, watercourses, and the dyke had suddenly burst there—that was the worst of it! However, I arrived at last. It was a little thatched house. There was a light in the windows; that meant they expected me. I was met by an old lady, very venerable, in a cap. 'Save her!' she says; 'she is dying.' I say, 'Pray don't distress yourself—where is the invalid?' 'Come this way.' I see a clean little room, a lamp in the corner; on the bed a girl of twenty, unconscious. She was in a burning heat, and breathing heavily—it was fever. There were two other girls, her sisters, scared and in tears. 'Yesterday,' they tell me, 'she was perfectly well and had a good appetite; this morning she complained of her head, and this evening, suddenly, you see, like this.' I say again: 'Pray don't be uneasy.' It's a doctor's duty, you know—and I went up to her and bled her, told them to put on a mustard plaster, and prescribed a mixture. Meantime I looked at her, you know—there, by God! I had never seen such a face! —she was a beauty, in a word! I felt quite shaken by pity. Such lovely features; such

她安静些了，出了汗，好像清醒过来了，她向周围望望，微笑一下，用手摸摸脸。……她的姊妹弯下身子去看她，问她："你怎么样？""没有什么。'她说着，就把脸转过去。……我一看，她已经睡着了。我说，好啦，现在要让病人安静一下。于是我们都踮着脚走出去，留一个丫头在这里随时侍候。客厅里桌子上已经摆好茶炊，还有牙买加糖酒，在我们的业务中，这是非有不可的。她们端茶给我，要求我在这里过夜……我就同意了，现在还能到哪里去呢！老太太老是叹气。我说：'您何必这样呢？一定会好的，请您不要着急，还是自己去休息一下吧，已经 1 点多了。''如果有什么事，请您叫人喊醒我。''好的，好的。'老太太就出去了，两位姑娘也回到自己房间里去了。客厅里已经替我预备了一张床。我躺在床上了，可是睡不着——这是多么奇怪的事！似乎已经很疲倦了。我总是忘不了我的病人。我终于忍不住，突然坐起来，我想：让我去看看，病人怎么样了？她的卧室就在客厅隔壁。于是，我就起了床，悄悄地开了门，可是我的心怦怦地跳。我一看，丫头已经睡着，嘴巴张开，还打鼾呢，这家伙！病人脸朝着我躺着，伸展着两手，怪可怜的！我走近去……她突然睁开眼睛，盯住我看！……'是谁？是谁？'我不好意思起来。'别害怕，'我说，'小姐，我是医生，我来看看您现在怎么样了。''您是医生？''我是医生，我是医生……是您母亲派人到城里接我来的。我们已经替您放过血了，小姐，现在请您安心休养吧，再过两三天，上帝保佑，我们就会把您治好啦。''啊，是的，是的，医生，不要让我死啊……求求您，求求您。''您怎么了，上帝保佑您！'我心里想，她又在发烧了。我替她按脉，果然有热度。她对我望了一阵子，突然握住了我的手。我告诉您，为什么我不愿意死，我告诉您，我告诉您……现在只有我们两个人，可是请您别告诉任何人……您听我说……我俯下身子，她的嘴唇凑近我的耳朵边，她的头发碰着我的脸——说实话，那时候我的头发昏啦——她就开始低声说话。……我一点儿也听不懂。……啊，她是在那里说梦话。……她说着，说着，说得很快，而且好像不是俄国话，说完之后，她哆嗦一下，把头倒在枕头上，竖起一根手指威吓我，'记住啊，医生，别告诉任何人。……'我好容易使她安静了，给她喝了点水，叫醒了丫头，就出去了。"

医生说到这里，又猛烈地嗅了一会鼻烟，呆了一

eyes!... But, thank God! she became easier; she fell into a perspiration, seemed to come to her senses, looked round, smiled, and passed her hand over her face.... Her sisters bent over her. They ask, 'How are you?' 'All right,' she says, and turns away. I looked at her; she had fallen asleep. 'Well,' I say, 'now the patient should be left alone.' So we all went out on tiptoe; only a maid remained, in case she was wanted. In the parlour there was a samovar standing on the table, and a bottle of rum; in our profession one can't get on without it. They gave me tea; asked me to stop the night.... I consented; where could I go, indeed, at that time of night? The old lady kept groaning. 'What is it?' I say, 'she will live; don't worry yourself; you had better take a little rest yourself; it is about two o'clock.' 'But will you send to wake me if anything happens?' 'Yes, yes.' The old lady went away, and the girls too went to their own rooms; they made up a bed for me in the parlour. Well, I went to bed—but I could not get to sleep, for a wonder! for in reality I was very tired. I could not get my patient out of my head. At last I could not put up with it any longer; I got up suddenly; I think to myself, 'I will go and see how the patient is getting on.' Her bedroom was next to the parlour. Well, I got up, and gently opened the door—how my heart beat! I looked in; the servant was asleep, her mouth wide open, and even snoring, the wretch! but the patient lay with her face towards me, and her arms flung wide apart, poor girl! I went up to her... when suddenly she opened her eyes and stared at me! 'Who is it? who is it?' I was in confusion. 'Don't be alarmed, madam,' I say; 'I am the doctor; I have come to see how you feel.' 'You the doctor?' 'Yes, the doctor; your mother sent for me from the town; we have bled you, madam; now pray go to sleep, and in a day or two, please God! we will set you on your feet again.' 'Ah, yes, yes doctor, don't let me die... please, please.' 'Why do you talk like that? God bless you!' She is in a fever again, I think to myself; I felt her pulse; yes, she was feverish. She looked at me, and then took me by the hand. 'I will tell you why I don't want to die; I will tell you.... Now we are alone; and only, please don't you... not to anyone... Listen...!' I bent down; she moved her lips quite to my ear; she touched my cheek with her hair—I confess my head went round—and began to whisper.... I could make out nothing of it.... Ah, she was delirious!... She whispered and whispered, but so quickly, and as if it were not in Russian; at last she finished, and shivering dropped her head on the pillow, and threatened me with her finger: 'Remember, doctor, to no one.' I calmed her somehow, gave her something to drink, waked the servant, and went away."

At this point the doctor again took snuff with exasperated energy, and for a moment seemed stupefied

阵子。

　　"可是，"他继续说，"到了第二天，和我的期望相反，病人并没有见好。我再三考虑，突然决定留在这里，虽然有别的病人在等我。……您也知道，对病家是不可以怠慢的，这对我的业务有妨碍。但是，第一，病人的确是濒于绝望了；第二，我得说实话，我对她很有好感。况且，她们一家人我都喜欢。她们虽然是没有家产的人，但是所受的教养可说是罕有的。……她们的父亲是一个有学问的人，是著作家，当然是在贫困中死去的，可是他已经给孩子们受到了很好的教育，又遗下许多书籍。不知道是为了我热心照顾病人的缘故呢，还是另有缘故，总之，我敢说，她们都像亲人一样爱我。……这时候，道路泥泞得厉害，一切交通，可说是完全断绝了，到城里去买药也非常困难。病人没有起色。……一天又一天，一天又一天。……但是……这时候……"医生沉默了一会。"我实在不知道应该怎样对您讲。"他又嗅鼻烟，喉头咯咯作响，喝了一口茶，"对您痛快地说了吧，我的病人……怎么说好呢，可说是，爱上了我……或者，不，不是爱上了我……不过……实在，这怎么，这个……"医生低下了头，脸红了。"不，"他热烈地继续说，"怎么可以说是爱上了我呢！一个人到底应该知道自己的身价。她是一个有教养的、聪明博学的女子，而我呢，连我的拉丁文也可说是完全忘记了。至于品貌呢（医生微笑着看看自己），似乎也没有什么可以自傲。可是上帝并没有把我造成一个傻瓜，我不会把白叫作黑，我多少懂得一点。譬如说，我心里很明白，亚历山德拉·安德列叶芙娜——她名叫亚历山德拉·安德列叶芙娜——对我不是发生了爱情，而是有了一种所谓友谊的好感和尊敬。虽然她自己在这一方面也许是弄错了，可是她当时所处的地位是怎样的，请您判断吧……不过，"医生带着显著的慌张，一口气说出了这些断断续续的话之后，又补充说，"我的话似乎说得有点乱了。……这样说您一定一点儿也听不懂……那么让我把一切按照次序说给您听吧。"

　　他喝干了那杯茶，用较为平静的声调说起来。

　　"唔，是这样的。我的病人的病一天重似一天，一天重似一天。先生，您不是医生，您不能了解我们医生的心情，尤其是当他最初预料到病魔将要战胜他的时候的心情。自信力不知道哪儿去了！你突然胆小起来，简直到难以形容的地步。你似乎觉得你所知道

by its effects.

　　"However,"he continued,"the next day, contrary to my expectations, the patient was no better. I thought and thought, and suddenly decided to remain there, even though my other patients were expecting me.... And you know one can't afford to disregard that; one's practice suffers if one does. But, in the first place, the patient was really in danger; and secondly, to tell the truth, I felt strongly drawn to her. Besides, I liked the whole family. Though they were really badly off, they were singularly, I may say, cultivated people.... Their father had been a learned man, an author; he died, of course, in poverty, but he had managed before he died to give his children an excellent education; he left a lot of books too. Either because I looked after the invalid very carefully, or for some other reason; anyway, I can venture to say all the household loved me as one of the family.... Meantime the roads were in a worse state than ever; all communications, so to say, were cut off completely; even medicine could with difficulty be got from the town.... The sick girl was not getting better... Day after day, and day after day... but... here...." (The doctor made a brief pause.) "I declare I don't know how to tell you."... (He again took snuff, coughed, and swallowed a little tea.)"I will tell you without beating about the bush. My patient... how should I say?... Well she had fallen in love with me... or, no, it was not that she was in love... however... really, how should one say?" (The doctor looked down and grew red.)"No," he went on quickly, "in love, indeed! A man should not over-estimate himself. She was an educated girl, clever and well-read, and I had even forgotten my Latin, one may say, completely. As to appearance" (the doctor looked himself over with a smile) "I am nothing to boast of there either. But God Almighty did not make me a fool; I don't take black for white; I know a thing or two; I could see very clearly, for instance, that Aleksandra Andreyevna—that was her name—did not feel love for me, but had a friendly, so to say, inclination—a respect or something for me. Though she herself perhaps mistook this sentiment, anyway this was her attitude; you may form your own judgment of it. But," added the doctor, who had brought out all these disconnected sentences without taking breath, and with obvious embarrassment, "I seem to be wandering rather—you won't understand anything like this.... There with your leave, I will relate it all in order."

　　He drank a glass of tea, and began in a calmer voice.

　　"Well, then. My patient kept getting worse and worse. You are not a doctor, my good sir; you cannot understand what passes in a poor fellow's heart, especially at first, when he begins to suspect that the disease is getting the upper hand of him. What becomes

的一切都忘记了，病人不信任你了，别人已经看出你的慌张，勉强地报告你征候，用怀疑的眼光看你，交头接耳地议论……唉，真倒霉！你心里想，一定有对症的药，只要把它找出来。对啦，是这药吧？试一试看——不对，不是这药！不等到药力发生作用的时间……一会儿用这种药，一会儿用那种药。你常常拿出药书来……心里想，药在这里了，在这里了！其实有时是随便翻翻书的，想碰碰运气看。……可是在这期间病人已经快死了。别的医生也许会医好这病人的，你就说，一定要会诊，我一个人是不能负责的。这时候你竟变成了蠢材！但是后来渐渐习惯，也就没有什么了。人死了——不是你的罪过，因为你是照规矩行事的。可是还有更难受的，你眼看见别人盲目地信任你，而你自己明知道是无能为力的。亚历山德拉·安德列叶芙娜全家对我的信任正是这样，因而忘记了她们家的女儿正在危险中。而我呢，也宽慰她们，说是不要紧的，可是自己心里呢，灵魂都吓出窍了。尤其不幸的，偏又碰到道路那样泥泞的时候，马车夫去买药，常常要好几天。我常常待在病人的房间里，寸步也不能离开她，您知道，我讲各种好笑的故事给她听，跟她玩纸牌。夜里也在那里坐守。老太太流着眼泪感谢我，可是我心里想：'我是不值得您感谢的。'我坦白告诉您——现在不必隐瞒了——我爱上了我的病人。而亚历山德拉·安德列叶芙娜也对我亲昵，常常除我之外不要别人走进房间来。她跟我谈起话来，问我曾经在哪儿念书，生活过得怎样，有哪些亲人，和哪些人来往了。我觉得她不应该谈话，想禁止她，可是您知道，要坚决地禁止她，我是办不到的。我常常捧着自己的头想：'你在干什么，你这强盗？……'可是她拉住我的手不放，老是对我望着，望了很久很久，然后转过头去，叹一口气，说：'您这人真好啊！'她的手发烫，一双眼睛很大，可是没有精神。她说：'嗯，您真好，您是好人，您跟我们这里的邻居不同……不，您不是那样的人，您不是那样的人。……怎么我以前不认识您呢！'亚历山德拉·安德列叶芙娜，您安静些吧，'我说，'……实在，我觉得，我不知道有什么值得您这般看重……可是请您安静些，看上帝面上，请您安静些……就会好的，您会恢复健康的。'说到这里，我还得告诉你，"医生把身体俯向前些，挺起眉毛，继续说，"她们和邻居们不大来往，因为地位低的人跟她们不相称，而富人呢，自尊心又阻止她们跟他们交往。

of his belief in himself? You suddenly grow so timid it's indescribable. You fancy then that you have forgotten everything you knew, and that the patient has no faith in you, and that other people begin to notice how distracted you are, and tell you the symptoms with reluctance; that they are looking at you suspiciously, whispering.... Ah! it's horrid! There must be a remedy, you think, for this disease, if one could find it. Isn't this it? You try—no, that's not it! You don't allow the medicine the necessary time to do good.... You clutch at one thing, then at another. Sometimes you take up a book of medical prescriptions—here it is, you think! Sometimes, by Jove, you pick one out by chance, thinking to leave it to fate.... But meantime a fellow creature's dying, and another doctor would have saved him. 'We must have a consultation,' you say; 'I will not take the responsibility on myself.' And what a fool you look at such times! Well, in time you learn to bear it; it's nothing to you. A man has died—but it's not your fault; you treated him by the rules. But what's still more torture to you is to see blind faith in you, and to feel yourself that you are not able to be of use. Well, it was just this blind faith that the whole of Aleksandra Andreyevna's family had in me; they had forgotten to think that their daughter was in danger. I, too, on my side assure them that it is nothing, but meantime my heart sinks into my boots. To add to our troubles, the roads were in such a state that the coachman was gone for whole days together to get medicine. And I never left the patient's room; I could not tear myself away; I tell her amusing stories, you know, and play cards with her. I watch by her side at night. The old mother thanks me with tears in her eyes; but I think to myself, 'I don't deserve your gratitude.' I frankly confess to you—there is no object in concealing it now—I was in love with my patient. And Aleksandra Andreyevna had grown fond of me; she would not sometimes let any one be in her room but me. She began to talk to me, to ask me questions; where I had studied, how I lived, who are my people, whom I go to see. I feel that she ought not to talk; but to forbid her to—to forbid her resolutely, you know—I could not. Sometimes I held my head in my hands, and asked myself, 'What are you doing, villain?'... And she would take my hand and hold it, give me a long, long look, and turn away, sigh, and say, 'How good you are!' Her hands were so feverish, her eyes so large and languid.... 'Yes,' she says, 'you are a good, kind man; you are not like our neighbours.... No, you are not like that.... Why did I not know you till now!' 'Aleksandra Andreyevna, calm yourself,' I say.... 'I feel, believe me, I don't know how I have gained... but there, calm yourself.... All will be right; you will be well again.'

我告诉您，这家庭是极有教养的——所以，您知道，我觉得很光荣。她只肯在我手里服药……可怜的人，靠我搀扶坐起来，服了药，就盯住我看……我的心怦怦地乱跳。可是，她的病越来越重了，越来越重了。我想，她要死了，一定要死了。您相信吗，我恨不得自己躺在棺材里了，因为她的母亲和姊妹老是望着我，盯着我看，……对我渐渐失去信任了。'什么？怎么样了？''不要紧，不要紧！'怎么叫作不要紧，我自己也糊里糊涂。有一天夜里，我又是一个人坐在病人旁边。丫头也坐在那里，正在大声地打鼾。……这可怜的丫头也难怪，她也累坏了。亚历山德拉·安德列叶芙娜整个晚上都觉得很不好过，发烧折磨着她。她翻来覆去一直到半夜里，最后仿佛睡着了，至少躺着不动了。一盏灯点在屋角里的圣像前面。我坐着，低下头，也打瞌睡了。突然似乎有人推我的身体，我转过头来。……啊呀，我的天哪！亚历山德拉·安德列叶芙娜睁大眼睛盯住我……嘴巴张开，面颊热得通红。'您怎么了？''医生，我快死了吗？''哪有这事！''不，医生，不，求求您，求求您，请您不要说我是会好的……不要这样说……要是您知道……您听我说，看在上帝面上，请您不要隐瞒我的病状！'她的呼吸异常急促。'如果我确实知道我要死了……我要把一切都告诉您，一切！''亚历山德拉·安德列叶芙娜，别那么想吧！''您听我说，我一点也不曾睡着，我一直在看您……看在上帝面上……我相信您，您是个好人，您是个正直的人，为了世界上神圣的一切，我恳求您对我说真话吧！您要知道这对我是非常重要的。……医生，看在上帝面上请您告诉我。我的病危险了吗？''叫我对您说什么呢，亚历山德拉·安德列叶芙娜，别那么想吧！''看在上帝面上，我恳求您！''我不能瞒您，亚历山德拉·安德列叶芙娜——您的病的确危险了，但是上帝是慈悲的……''我要死了，我要死了……'她仿佛很欢喜，脸上露出非常高兴的样子，我害怕起来。'您别害怕，别害怕，死一点儿也不能威吓我。'她突然略微抬起身子来，用一条胳膊肘支撑着。'现在……唔，现在我可以告诉您，我全心全意地感谢您，您是个善良的好人，我爱您，……'我对她看，好像发痴了。您知道，我心里害怕。……'您听见吗，我爱您……''亚历山德拉·安德列叶芙娜，我怎么值得您爱呢！''不，不，您不了解我……亲爱的，你不了解我……'突然她伸出两只手，抱住我的头吻了一下。

And meanwhile I must tell you," continued the doctor, bending forward and raising his eyebrows, "that they associated very little with the neighbours, because the smaller people were not on their level, and pride hindered them from being friendly with the rich. I tell you, they were an exceptionally cultivated family, so you know it was gratifying for me. She would only take her medicine from my hands ... she would lift herself up, poor girl, with my aid, take it, and gaze at me.... My heart felt as if it were bursting. And meanwhile she was growing worse and worse, worse and worse, all the time; she will die, I think to myself; she must die. Believe me, I would sooner have gone to the grave myself; and here were her mother and sisters watching me, looking into my eyes... and their faith in me was wearing away. 'Well, how is she?' 'Oh, all right, all right!' All right, indeed! My mind was failing me. Well, I was sitting one night alone again by my patient. The maid was sitting there too, and snoring away in full swing; I can't find fault with the poor girl, though! she was worn out too. Aleksandra Andreyevna had felt very unwell all the evening; she was very feverish. Until midnight she kept tossing about; at last she seemed to fall asleep; at least, she lay still without stirring. The lamp was burning in the corner before the holy image. I sat there, you know, with my head bent; I even dozed a little. Suddenly it seemed as though someone touched me on the side; I turned round.... Good God! Aleksandra Andreyevna was gazing with intent eyes at me... her lips parted, her cheeks seemed burning. 'What is it?' 'Doctor, shall I die?' 'Merciful heavens!' 'No, doctor, no; please don't tell me I shall live... don't say so.... If you knew.... Listen! For God's sake don't conceal my real position,' and her breath came so fast. 'If I can know for certain that I must die... then I will tell you all—all!' 'Aleksandra Andreyevna, I beg!' 'Listen! I have not been asleep at all... I have been looking at you a long while.... For God's sake!... I believe in you; you are a good man, an honest man; I entreat you by all that is sacred in the world—tell me the truth! If you knew how important it is for me.... Doctor, for God's sake tell me.... Am I in danger?' 'What can I tell you, Aleksandra Andreyevna pray?' 'For God's sake, I beseech you!' 'I can't conceal from you,' I say, 'Aleksandra Andreyevna; you are certainly in danger; but God is merciful.' 'I shall die, I shall die.' And it seemed as though she were pleased; her face grew so bright; I was alarmed. 'Don't be afraid, don't be afraid! I am not frightened by death at all.' She suddenly sat up and leaned on her elbow. 'Now... yes, now I can tell you that I thank you with my whole heart... that you are kind and good—that I love you!' I stared at her, like one possessed; it was terrible for me, you know. 'Do you hear, I love you!' 'Aleksandra

……您相信吗，我几乎叫起来……我突然跪下，把头埋藏在枕窝里了。她默不作声，她的手指在我头发上发抖，我听见她哭了。我开始安慰她，宽她的心……我实在不知道对她说了些什么话。我说：'您要把丫头吵醒了，亚历山德拉·安德列叶芙娜……我感谢您……请您相信……您安静些吧。''好，别说了，别说了，'她反复地说，'什么都不要紧，嘿，醒了也好，嘿，有人进来也好，都没有关系，反正我要死了。……可是你顾虑什么呢，怕什么呢？抬起头来。……也许您不爱我吧，也许是我弄错了……如果这样，请您原谅我。''亚历山德拉·安德列叶芙娜，您说哪儿话？……我爱您，亚历山德拉·安德列叶芙娜。'她直盯着我看，张开了两只手臂。'那么你拥抱我呀……'我坦白告诉您，我不知道这一夜我怎么会不发疯的。我觉得我的病人在毁灭自己。我看得出，她的神志不很清醒。我又明白，如果她不知道自己快要死了，她就不会想到我。您想哪，活了20岁没有爱过一个人而死去，毕竟是含恨的事。正是这一点使她痛苦，因此她在绝望之余，就拉住了像我这样的一个人——现在您明白了吧？她的手抱住我不放。'请体恤我，亚历山德拉·安德列叶芙娜，也请体恤你自己。'我这样说。'为什么，'她说，'有什么可惜？反正我是要死了……'她不断地反复这句话，'如果我知道我会活着，仍旧做体面的姑娘，那我才要害羞，真要害羞……可是现在有什么关系呢？''谁对您说您要死了？''嗳，得了，别说了，你瞒不过我，你不会说谎的，你瞧瞧你自己。''您的病会好的，亚历山德拉·安德列叶芙娜，我会医好您。我们要征得您母亲的允许……我们结为夫妇，过幸福的生活。''不，不，我已经听到您的话，我一定要死了……你答应我了……你对我说过了……'我很痛苦，有种种原因使我痛苦。您想，有时候发生点小事，似乎没有什么关系，其实很痛苦。她忽然问起我的名字来，不是姓，而是名字。不幸我的名字叫做得利丰①。嗯，嗯，叫作得利丰，叫作得利丰·伊凡内奇。在她家里，大家都叫我医生。我没有办法，只得说：'我叫得利丰，小姐。'她眯着眼睛，摇摇头，用法语轻轻地说了些话——唉，大概是不好的话——后来她笑了，笑得也不妙。我就是这样跟她在一起过了差不多一整夜。早晨我走出来，就像发了疯似的。我再

----

① 得利丰是很俗气的名字。

Andreyevna, how have I deserved—"No, no, you don't—you don't understand me.'... And suddenly she stretched out her arms, and taking my head in her hands, she kissed it.... Believe me, I almost screamed aloud.... I threw myself on my knees, and buried my head in the pillow. She did not speak; her fingers trembled in my hair; I listen; she is weeping. I began to soothe her, to assure her.... I really don't know what I did say to her. 'You will wake up the girl,' I say to her; 'Aleksandra Andreyevna, I thank you... believe me... calm yourself.' 'Enough, enough!' she persisted, 'never mind all of them; let them wake, then; let them come in—it does not matter; I am dying, you see.... And what do you fear? Why are you afraid? Lift up your head.... Or, perhaps you don't love me; perhaps I am wrong.... In that case, forgive me.' 'Aleksandra Andreyevna, what are you saying!... I love you, Aleksandra Andreyevna.' She looked straight into my eyes, and opened her arms wide. 'Then take me in your arms.' I tell you frankly, I don't know how it was I did not go mad that night. I feel that my patient is killing herself; I see that she is not fully herself; I understand, too, that if she did not consider herself on the point of death she would never have thought of me, and, indeed, say what you will, it's hard to die at twenty without having known love; this was what was torturing her; this was why, in despair, she caught at me—do you understand now? But she held me in her arms, and would not let me go. 'Have pity on me, Aleksandra Andreyevna, and have pity on yourself,' I say. 'Why,' she says, 'what is there to think of? You know I must die.'... This she repeated incessantly.... 'If I knew that I should return to life, and be a proper young lady again, I should be a-shamed... of course, ashamed... but why now?' 'But who has said you will die?' 'Oh, no, leave off! you will not deceive me; you don't know how to lie—look at your face.'... 'You shall live, Aleksandra Andreyevna; I will cure you; we will ask your mother's blessing... we will be united—we will be happy.' 'No, no, I have your word; I must die... you have promised me... you have told me.'... It was cruel for me—cruel for many reasons. And see what trifling things can do sometimes; it seems nothing at all, but it's painful. It occurred to her to ask me, what is my name; not my surname, but my first name. I must needs be so unlucky as to be called Trifon. Yes, indeed; Trifon Ivanich. Every one in the house called me doctor. However, there's a help for it. I say, 'Trifon, madam.' She frowned, shook her head, and muttered something in French—ah, something unpleasant, of course! —and then she laughed—disagreeably too. Well, I spent the whole night with her in this way. Before morning I went away, feeling as though I were mad. When I went again into her room it was daytime,

走进她房间里去的时候，已经是下午，喝过茶之后了。我的天，我的天！她已经认不得了，比放进棺材里去的人还难看了。我对您发誓，我现在不懂得——完全不懂得——当时怎样忍受了这种精神上的磨难。我的病人又延续了三天三夜的残喘……多么痛苦的夜晚啊！她对我说了些什么话呀！……最后的一夜，请您想象——我坐在她旁边，只向上帝请求一件事，请早些把她收拾了，同时也把我收拾了。……突然老母亲闯进房间里来。……我昨天已经对她——对母亲——说过，我说，很少有希望了，不好了，可以去请牧师了。病人看见了母亲，就说：'嗳，很好，你来了……你看我们，我们互相恋爱，互相起了誓。'她这是怎么了，医生，她怎么了？'我面无人色了。我说：'她是说梦话，因为发烧……'可是她说：'得啦，得啦，你刚才对我说的完全不同，你还接受了我的戒指。……你为什么要装假呢？我母亲是好人，她会原谅的，她会理解的，我快要死了——我何必说谎。把手给我……'我跳起来，跑出去了。老太太当然猜测到了。"

"可是，我不想再多打扰您了，而且我自己回想起这一切来，实在也很痛苦。我的病人在第二天就去世了。祝她升入天堂！（医生用急速的语调附说这一句，又叹了一口气。）她临终前，要求她家里的人都走出去，单留我一个人陪她。'请您原谅我，'她说，'我也许对不起您……病啊……可是请您相信，我没有比爱您更深地爱过别人，请您别忘记我……保存好我的戒指……'"

医生把脸扭向一旁，我握住了他的手。

"唉！"他说，"让我们谈些别的话吧，或者玩一下小输赢的朴烈费兰斯如何？您知道，像我们这种人，不配体味这么高尚的感情。我们只希望孩子们不要啼啼哭哭，老婆不要吵吵闹闹。以后我也曾举行所谓正式的结婚。……可不是吗！……娶了一个商人的女儿，带来了 7000 卢布的嫁产。她名叫阿库丽娜，倒跟得利丰很相配呢[①]。我告诉您，这女人很凶，幸而一天到晚睡觉。……怎么，玩不玩朴烈费兰斯。"

我们就坐下来玩一戈比为单位的朴烈费兰斯。得利丰·伊凡内奇赢了我两个半卢布——到很迟的时候才离去，十分满足于自己的胜利。

[①] 阿库丽娜也是很俗气的名字。

after morning tea. Good God! I could scarcely recognise her; people are laid in their grave looking better than that. I swear to you, on my honour, I don't understand—I absolutely don't understand—now, how I lived through that experience. Three days and nights my patient still lingered on. And what nights! What things she said to me! And on the last night—only imagine to yourself—I was sitting near her, and kept praying to God for one thing only: 'Take her,' I said, 'quickly, and me with her.' Suddenly the old mother comes unexpectedly into the room. I had already the evening before told her—the mother—there was little hope, and it would be well to send for a priest. When the sick girl saw her mother she said: 'It's very well you have come; look at us, we love one another—we have given each other our word.' 'What does she say, doctor? What does she say?' I turned livid. 'She is wandering,' I say; 'the fever.' But she: 'Hush, hush; you told me something quite different just now, and have taken my ring. Why do you pretend? My mother is good—she will forgive—she will understand—and I am dying.... I have no need to tell lies; give me your hand.' I jumped up and ran out of the room. The old lady, of course, guessed how it was.

"I will not, however, weary you any longer, and to me, too, of course, it's painful to recall all this. My patient passed away the next day. God rest her soul!" the doctor added, speaking quickly and with a sigh. "Before her death she asked her family to go out and leave me alone with her."

"'Forgive me,' she said, 'I am perhaps to blame towards you... my illness... but believe me, I have loved no one more than you... do not forget me... keep my ring.'"

The doctor turned away; I took his hand.

"Ah!" he said, "let us talk of something else, or would you care to play preference for a small stake? It is not for people like me to give way to exalted emotions. There's only one thing for me to think of; how to keep the children from crying and the wife from scolding. Since then, you know, I have had time to enter into lawful wedlock, as they say.... Oh... I took a merchant's daughter—seven thousand for her dowry. Her name's Akulina; it goes well with Trifon. She is an ill-tempered woman, I must tell you, but luckily she's asleep all day.... Well, shall it be preference?"

We sat down to prference for halfpenny poins. Trifon Ivanich won two rubles and a half from me, and went home late, well pleasd with his success.

┌ 讨　论 ─■

像《阿拉比》一样,《县城的医生》也是一篇恋爱小说,而且这篇小说和乔伊斯的那篇小说有着某种独特的关系。在乔伊斯的那篇小说里,我们通过一个成年男子对自己年轻时初次产生恋情的回忆,得到了有关初恋及其失意的总印象。在屠格涅夫的这篇小说里,我们所看到的可说是乔伊斯小说在某种程度上的分解,是三个相互有联系的故事片断。第一个故事片断是关于那个年轻姑娘的,那个姑娘一方面明知自己死期已近,另一方面又感到自己决不能没有经历过爱情就如此死去,她爱上了那个单纯、正派、没有多大吸引力而且有个俗气名字的年轻医生,最后还和他订了婚。第二个故事片断是关于那个医生的,他已是个能体贴人的中年男子,但在他年轻时,他曾不顾社会上的一般观念而爱上了一个垂死的女病人——她也不顾死期临头和日常生活的种种不幸同他一样沉溺于理想爱情的梦幻中。在小说里,实际上还有第三个故事片断:关于那个医生在昙花一现的理想爱情(显然是超脱尘世的)过去之后的生活,他依然操着那单调而辛劳的职业,最后娶了一个阴郁易怒的女人为妻(可能是因为她有嫁产)。我们不妨在此设想,那个医生后来的生活倒是一种人所共有的生活,同《阿拉比》里的那个故事叙述者后来的生活比较起来(他回忆自己那次在集市里的漫游并把它作为自己往后生活和幻灭感的主要象征),虽然具体细节上有差别,但是基本上是相互一致的。

┌ 思考题 ─■

1. 讲述那个医生讲故事时的情况及其对生活的态度。讲述医生在他自己讲的故事里的那种情形。把小说里的线索整理一下并就小说的结尾找出有关的材料。

"The District Doctor,""like"Araby,"is a story of love, but it bears a peculiar relation to Joyce's story. With Joyce, we have an account of first love and its disappointment as told by a mature man looking back on his first adolescent attachment. With Turgenev, we have something that might be thought of, in a way, as a splintering of Joyce's story into three related stories. The first splinter story is that of the young girl who, knowing that she is to die and feeling that she must not die without having known love, falls in love with the simple, decent, not particularly attractive young doctor, with the funny name, and at last gives him her ring. The second splinter story is that of the doctor, now a modest, middle-aged man, who had, when young, fallen in love, against all common sense, with his dying patient—caught in the same dream of an ideal love beyond the reach of death and the accidents of common life. And there is, too, really a third splinter story: the subsequent life of the doctor, who, after having had the glimpse of an ideal love (clearly beyond the common world), has gone on with his duty to his humdrum practice and has eventually married an ill-tempered woman (presumably for her dowry). We can here assume that the doctor's later life is a common one, corresponding basically, if not in detail, with that of the narrator of "Araby," who looks back on his trip to the bazaar as a key symbol of his later life and disillusionments.

1. Describe the doctor as he now is, and his attitude toward life. Describe him as he must have been at the time of the story he tells. Draw evidence from the story. Make special reference to the ending.

2. 注意这篇小说叙述角度的复杂性——故事套故事,再套故事:第一层,是作者讲的(他被赋予了某种个性并似乎有一个故事要讲,但是中途刹住了);第二层,是那个病人讲的(所讲的故事就是我们称之为的中心故事);第三层,是医生讲的(他讲的是自己的生活经历)。你能理解使用这种方法的原因吗?

3. 那个医生为什么要把自己的事情偏偏讲给作者听,你能想出什么比较合理的原因来吗?医生会不会乐意把自己的事情讲给某个老朋友或者客栈酒吧里的某个老搭档听呢?或者会乐意讲给交际场所里的某个熟人听吗?

4. 作者(作为小说人物)听了故事之后所做出的反应给了我们怎样的提示?关于作者自己(小说里第一个病人)的生活这儿有所暗示吗?

5. 假定在作者做出反应之后,小说到此结束,这会产生怎样的效果?是有所损失呢,还是有所增益?就这一点,讨论感伤问题。

6. 试归纳《县城的医生》所含的争论点或者主题。

7. 根据小说内容发挥想象力,譬如,可以假定那个年轻姑娘根本就没有让那个医生去看病或者当那个医生一到她很快就那么死了。你是否能想象一下,这两种情况之中哪一种可能会使他改变最后娶那个女人的态度?

(刘文荣 译)

2. Observe that the point of view is complicated here—a story within a story, and within a story: first, that of the author (who is given a personality and the hint of a story, however limited); second, that of the patient(who tells what we may call the central story); and third, that of the doctor (who tells his own experience). Can you see any reason for this method?

3. Can you think of any plausible reason why the doctor should now tell the story of his youth to the author? Would he have been more likely to tell an old friend or a crony at the bar of the inn? Or some acquaintance in the community?

4. What indication do we have of the author's response (as a character) to the story? What may it suggest about the life of the author(as the first patient in the story)?

5. Suppose the story ended at the moment when the author shows his response. What would be the effect? What might be lost, or gained? Discuss the question of sentimentality in this regard.

6. Try to state the issue, or theme, behind "The District Doctor."

7. Let your imagination play over the materials of the story. For instance, suppose that the young girl had never been the doctor's patient, or that she had simply died soon after his arrival. Can you imagine that either circumstance might have made a difference in the attitude of the woman whom he eventually married?

017. 侨 民

（美）卡森·麦卡勒斯 著　　　彭嘉林 译

017. The Sojourner

by Carson McCullers

这天早晨似醒非醒之际他依稀到了罗马：飞溅的喷泉，狭窄弯曲的街道，到处是鲜花，到处是年代久远的石头建筑，好一座金色的城市。在这种迷离恍惚的时刻，他有时仿佛又在巴黎居停，有时在德国的战争废墟间栖身，或者在瑞士的滑雪旅舍小住。有时候，他还似乎置身佐治亚州的休耕地上，迎来狩猎之晨。今天早上，在没有年月的梦境里，他又神游罗马。

约翰·费里斯在纽约一家旅馆里醒来了。他有种预感，好像有什么不愉快的事情在等着他，至于是什么事，他不知道。这感觉虽然被早晨的种种需要所淹没，但直到穿好衣服下了楼，还在隐隐作祟。这是个晴空无云的秋日，苍白的阳光让淡颜色的摩天楼丛割裂成绺绺片片。费里斯走进隔壁的药店①，在尽头临街有窗口的一个小间里坐下，点了份有炒蛋和香肠的美国式早餐。

费里斯从巴黎赶回佐治亚故乡，参加了一个星期前举行的父亲的葬礼。这噩耗使他意识到自己青春已逝。他的发际正渐渐后移，光秃秃的颞颥上青筋毕现，周身的肌肉也已松弛消瘦，可肚皮却开始挺了出来。费里斯过去很爱父亲，父子间关系异常密切，可是后来流逝的光阴冲淡了他的孝心。父亲的死虽早在他意料之中，但临了还是给他留下意料之外的哀痛。他已尽可能在家里多待了一些时候，与母亲和兄弟们团聚一起。而明天，他就要乘飞机返回巴黎了。

他掏出通讯录，想查对一份地址。翻着翻着，他注意力越来越集中。这些姓名地址，有纽约的，欧洲

---

① 这种药店也经营书报、糖果和小吃等。

THE twilight border between sleep and waking was a Roman one this morning: splashing fountains and arched, narrow streets, the golden lavish city of blossoms and age-soft stone. Sometimes in this semi-consciousness he sojourned again in Paris, or German war rubble, or a Swiss skiing and a snow hotel. Sometimes, also, in a fallow Georgia field at hunting dawn. Rome it was this morning in the yearless region of dreams.

John Ferris awoke in a room in a New York hotel. He had the feeling that something unpleasant was awaiting him—what it was, he did not know. The feeling, submerged by matinal necessities, lingered even after he had dressed and gone downstairs. It was a cloudless autumn day and the pale sunlight sliced between the pastel skyscrapers. Ferris went into the next-door drugstore and sat at the end booth next to the window glass that overlooked the sidewalk. He ordered an American breakfast with scrambled eggs and sausage.

Ferris had come from Paris to his father's funeral which had taken place a week before in his home town in Georgia. The shock of death had made him aware of youth already passed. His hair was receding and the veins in his now naked temples were pulsing and prominent and his body was spare except for an incipient belly bulge. Ferris had loved his father and the bond between them had once been extraordinarily close—but the years had somehow unraveled this filial devotion; the death, expected for a long time, had left him with an unforseen dismay. He had stayed as long as possible to be near his mother and brothers at home. His plane for Paris was to leave the next morning.

Ferris pulled out his address book to verify a number. He turned the pages with growing attentiveness.

作者简介：卡森·麦卡勒斯（Carson McCullers，1917—1967），美国小说家。1917 年 2 月 19 日生于佐治亚州哥伦布，1967 年 9 月 29 日卒于纽约州奈阿克。在哥伦比亚和纽约接受大学教育，最后在格林尼治村定居下来。童年时期的疾病造成她局部瘫痪。她通常把故事放在南方小社区的背景下，描写孤独人们的内心生活。她的小说作品包括《心是孤独的猎手》（*The Heart Is Lonely Hunter*，1940）、《金色眼睛里的倒影》（*Reflections in a Golden Eye*，1941）、《婚礼的成员》（*A Member of the Wedding*，1946）和《伤心咖啡馆之歌》（*The Ballad of the Sad Cafe*，1951）等。

各都会的,还有几个字迹已模糊,还是南方故乡的呢。这些褪了色的地址,有的是规规矩矩的印刷体,有的却歪歪斜斜,醉了似的。贝蒂·威尔斯,一位水性杨花的姑娘,现在已结了婚。查里·威廉斯,在赫特根森林负了伤,以后就再也没得过他的音讯。格兰特·老威廉斯,活着还是死了?唐·沃克,电视里的大人物,已经成了阔佬。亨利·格林,战后身体垮了,据说还在疗养院里。科济·霍尔,听说她死了。大大咧咧,嘻嘻哈哈的科济,这傻丫头也会死,真叫人不可思议。费里斯合上本子,一种近乎恐惧,感慨人生无常的伤感油然而生。

　　他蓦地一震,原来他正隔窗凝望的时候,看见前妻就在窗外的人行道上。伊丽莎白离他相当近,正慢慢走着。他不懂自己的心为何震颤,也不理解随之而来的冲动和她走过后仍萦绕胸臆的柔情。

　　费里斯匆匆付款后就赶到人行道上。伊丽莎白正站在街角上等着穿过五号街。他快步朝她走去,想和她说话,但还没赶到,红绿灯变了颜色,她已经穿过了马路。他发现自己也莫名其妙地磨蹭起来。她那头金发盘成朴素的发式,费里斯目追着前妻,不禁想起有一次他父亲称赞伊丽莎白"举止优雅"。她转过了前面的街角。他仍然跟在后面,但要追上她的欲念已经烟消云散。费里斯直纳闷,为什么一见伊丽莎白,他就身心骚动,掌心潮润,心脏怦怦乱跳?

　　费里斯已经有 8 年没和前妻见面了。他知道她早已再嫁,而且还有了孩子。近几年他极少想起她来。但离婚初期,这损失却几乎把他毁了。时间慢慢抚平了创伤,他重新恋爱,再恋爱了,目前他的情人叫珍妮。毫无疑问,他对前妻的爱恋早已成为过去。那么身心的震动又如何解释呢?他只知道自己阴郁的心境与晴朗无云的秋景极不协调。他突然转过身,迈开大步,跑一般回了旅店。

　　费里斯倒了杯酒,这时还不到 11 点,他却像累乏了似的,摊开手脚靠在扶手椅上,慢慢啜饮这杯兑水威士忌。去巴黎的飞机明天上午才起飞,他还得待上一整天。他逐件清点要干的事情:运行李上法航办事处,陪老板进午餐,买鞋子、大衣。还有——没别的事啦?费里斯把酒喝光,打开了电话号码簿。

　　他一时冲动,决定给前妻打电话。号码列在她丈夫贝利的名下,他不让自己有时间犹豫就拨电话。他和伊丽莎白也曾互赠过圣诞卡,接到她宣布结婚的消

Names and addresses from New York, the capitals of Europe, a few faint ones from his home state in the South. Faded, printed names, sprawled drunken ones. Betty Wills: a random love, married now. Charlie Williams: wounded in the Hürtgen Forest, unheard of since. Grand old Williams—did he live or die? Don Walker: a B. T. O. in television, getting rich. Henry Green: hit the skids after the war, in a sanitarium now, they say. Cozie Hall: he had heard that she was dead. Heedless, laughing Cozie—it was strange to think that she too, silly girl, could die. As Ferris closed the address book, he suffered a sense of hazard, transience, almost of fear.

It was then that his body jerked suddenly. He was staring out of the window when there, on the sidewalk, passing by, was his ex-wife. Elizabeth passed quite close to him, walking slowly. He could not understand the wild quiver of his heart, nor the following sense of recklessness and grace that lingered after she was gone.

Quickly Ferris paid his check and rushed out to the sidewalk. Elizabeth stood on the corner waiting to cross Fifth Avenue. He hurried toward her meaning to speak, but the lights changed and she crossed the street before he reached her, but he found himself lagging unaccountably. Her fair hair was plainly rolled, and as he watched her Ferris recalled that once his father had remarked that Elizabeth had a "beautiful carriage. "She turned at the next corner and Ferris followed, although by now his intention to overtake her had disappeared. Ferris questioned the bodily disturbance that the sight of Elizabeth aroused in him, the dampness of his hands, the hard heartstrokes.

It was eight years since Ferris had last seen his ex-wife. He knew that long ago she had married again. And there were children. During recent years he had seldom thought of her. But at first, after the divorce, the loss had almost destroyed him. Then after the anodyne of time, he had loved again, and then again. Jeannine, she was now. Certainly his love for his ex-wife was long since past. So why the unhinged body, the shaken mind? He knew only that his clouded heart was oddly dissonant with the sunny, candid autumn day. Ferris wheeled suddenly and, walking with long strides, almost running, hurried back to the hotel.

Ferris poured himself a drink, although it was not yet eleven o'clock. He sprawled out in an armchair like a man exhausted, nursing his glass of bourbon and water. He had a full day ahead of him as he was leaving by plane the next morning for Paris. He checked over his obligations: take luggage to Air France, lunch with his boss, buy shoes and an overcoat. And something—

息,他还寄给她一套雕刻品当礼物呢。没有理由不打电话嘛。可是,他一面听着电话线另一端的响声,等着人来接,一面却又被疑虑弄得心烦意躁。正好是伊丽莎白来接电话,她熟悉的声音又使他一震。他不得不重复了两次自己的名字。但一明白过来是谁后,伊丽莎白的声音显得很高兴。他解释说他只在城里逗留一天。她说他们已定好晚上上戏院——可是她希望他能上她家吃晚餐,他们可以早些开饭。他回答说很乐意去。

在办事的间隙,他仍有种不安的感觉,好像把什么大事给忘了。快黄昏时他洗了澡,换好衣服,心里老想着珍妮,明晚就可以和她在一块啦。"珍妮,"他要告诉她,"我路过纽约的时候碰见了我的前妻,和她,当然啰,也和她丈夫吃了顿饭。真怪,隔了这么多年后又见面了。"

伊丽莎白住在东50街。在出租汽车里费里斯还能间或瞥一眼依依夕照,但到达目的地时秋夜已经降临。这是幢有大门罩的大楼,还设有门房。伊丽莎白的寓所在7楼。

"请进,费里斯先生。"

费里斯原先满以为开门的会是伊丽莎白,甚至也可能是她那位想象不出是什么样子的丈夫,但绝没料到来了位长雀斑的红发小男孩。他知道她有孩子,但不知怎的心里总不愿承认。他惊讶得笨拙地倒退了一步。

"这是我们家,"小孩彬彬有礼地说,"你就是费里斯先生吧?我叫比利。请进来吧。"

伊丽莎白的丈夫就在厅那边的起居室里,他也叫费里斯吃了一惊,费里斯在感情上也是不承认他的。贝利是位体态笨重,举止从容的红发男子。他站起来,伸出手表示欢迎。

"我就是比尔·贝利。很高兴能看到你。伊丽莎白马上就来,她在穿衣服。"

最后一句话触发了费里斯的记忆,往昔的情景一幕幕晃过他的脑海:浴前的伊丽莎白,一丝不挂,白皙的肌肤透出玫瑰色的红润;她半穿衣服,在妆台前对镜梳刷榛壳色的秀发;甜蜜随便的亲昵,软玉般可爱的肉体不容置辩地属他所有。费里斯躲闪开决堤的记忆,强迫自己去正视比尔·贝利的目光。

"比利,把厨房桌上的酒托盘拿来好吗?"

孩子很听话,立刻走了。费里斯亲热地称赞:"你

wasn't there something else? Ferris finished his drink and opened the telephone directory.

His decision to call his ex-wife was impulsive. The number was under Bailey, the husband's name, and he called before he had much time for self-debate. He and Elizabeth had exchanged cards at Christmastime, and Ferris had sent a carving set when he received the announcement of her wedding. There was no reason *not* to call. But as he waited, listening to the ring at the other end, misgiving fretted him.

Elizabeth answered; her familiar voice was a fresh shock to him. Twice he had to repeat his name, but when he was identified, she sounded glad. He explained he was only in town for that day. They had a theater engagement, she said—but she wondered if he would come by for an early dinner. Ferris said he would be delighted.

As he went from one engagement to another, he was still bothered at odd moments by the feeling that something necessary was forgotten. Ferris bathed and changed in the late afternoon, often thinking about Jeannine; he would be with her the following night. "Jeannine," he would say, "I happened to run into my ex-wife when I was in New York. Had dinner with her. And her husband, of course. It was strange seeing her after all these years."

Elizabeth lived in the East Fifties, and as Ferris taxied uptown he glimpsed at intersections the lingering sunset, but by the time he reached his destination it was already autumn dark. The place was a building with a marquee and a doorman, and the apartment was on the seventh floor.

"Come in, Mr. Ferris."

Braced for Elizabeth or even the unimagined husband, Ferris was astonished by the freckled red-haired child; he had known of the children, but his mind had failed somehow to acknowledge them. Surprise made him step back awkwardly.

"This is our apartment," the child said politely. "Aren't you Mr. Ferris? I'm Billy. Come in."

In the living room beyond the hall, the husband provided another surprise; he too had not been acknowledged emotionally. Bailey was a lumbering red-haired man with a deliberate manner. He rose and extended a welcoming hand.

"I'm Bill Bailey. Glad to see you. Elizabeth will be in, in a minute. She's finishing dressing."

The last words struck a gliding series of vibrations, memories of the other years. Fair Elizabeth, rosy and naked before her bath. Halfdressed before the mirror of her dressing table, brushing her fine, chestnut hair. Sweet, casual intimacy, the soft-fleshed

们这孩子真乖。"

"这孩子是听话。"

两人都不说话了,一直到孩子回来。他端来了杯子和一个鸡尾酒摇杯。借酒助兴,他们好不容易才聊了起来。他们谈俄国,谈纽约的人造雨,还谈曼哈顿和巴黎的住房情况。

"费里斯先生明天就要飞过大西洋,"贝利告诉乖乖地坐在椅子扶手上的小男孩,"你敢情愿意藏在他的皮箱里偷渡过去吧。"

比利把额前的头发往后拢拢。"我要坐飞机,要像费里斯先生一样当个新闻记者。"他还用突如其来的肯定态度补上一句:"我长大了就干这个。"

贝利逗他:"你过去不是要当医生的吗?"

"对呀!我两样都当。我还要当造原子弹的科学家。"

伊丽莎白抱着一个小女孩进来了。

"哟,约翰!"她招呼一声,把小女孩放到她父亲的膝上,"见到你真高兴。你能来真叫人高兴。"

小女孩一本正经地坐在父亲腿上。她穿一件粉红色的广东绉纱罩衫,沿着衣裳抵肩绣有小花朵,一根色调很协调的丝发带扎住她柔软的浅色鬈发。她的皮肤晒得黑黑的,褐色的眼珠闪烁着金色的光点与笑意。她伸手去摸弄父亲的角框眼镜,贝利就把眼镜取下,让她透过镜片看了一会儿。"我的老坎迪怎么啦?"

伊丽莎白很美,也许他过去一直都没意识到她有这么美。整洁的长发光润发亮,面部皮肤比过去还要柔嫩,她容光焕发,情态安详。这是种圣母般的贞静的美,只有生活在幸福和睦的家庭中的妇女才会有。

"你样子几乎一点儿也没变,"伊丽莎白说,"可时间却过去了好多年了。"

"8年了。"进一步交谈起当年的赏心乐事时他不自然地摸了摸自己日渐稀薄的头发。

蓦地他觉得自己是个旁观者,无端闯进贝利一家中来。干吗他要来呢?他很难过。他生活得那么孤单,犹如一根无所支撑的脆弱的柱子,孑然立在岁月的废墟中间。再在这家庭气氛十足的地方待下去,他觉得受不了。

他瞥瞥手表:"你们就要上戏院吧?"

"真是对不起,"伊丽莎白说,"一个多月以前就定好了的。不过,约翰,你肯定不久就会回来的。你不会成为一个放弃国籍的人吧,对吗?"

"放弃国籍的人,"费里斯重复道,"我不怎么喜欢

loveliness indisputably possessed. Ferris shrank from the unbidden memories and compelled himself to meet Bill Bailey's gaze.

"Billy, will you please bring that tray of drinks from the kitchen table?"

The child obeyed promptly, and when he was gone Ferris remarked conversationally, "Fine boy you have there."

"We think so."

Flat silence until the child returned with a tray of glasses and a cocktail shaker of Martinis. With the priming drinks they pumped up conversation: Russia, they spoke of, and the New York rainmaking, and the apartment situation in Manhattan and Paris.

"Mr. Ferris is flying all the way across the ocean tomorrow," Bailey said to the little boy who was perched on the arm of his chair, quiet and well behaved. "I bet you would like to be a stowaway in his suitcase."

Billy pushed back his limp bangs. "I want to fly in an airplane and be a newspaperman like Mr. Ferris." He added with sudden assurance, "That's what I would like to do when I am big."

Bailey said, "I thought you wanted to be a doctor."

"I do!" said Billy. "I would like to be both. I want to be a atom-bomb scientist too."

Elizabeth came in carrying in her arms a baby girl.

"Oh, John!" she said. She settled the baby in the father's lap. "It's grand to see you. I'm awfully glad you could come."

The little girl sat demurely on Bailey's knees. She wore a pale pink crepe de Chine frock, smocked around the yoke with rose, and a matching silk hair ribbon tying back her pale soft curls. Her skin was summer tanned and her brown eyes flecked with gold and laughing. When she reached up and fingered her father's horn-rimmed glasses, he took them off and let her look through them a moment. "How's my old Candy?"

Elizabeth was very beautiful, more beautiful perhaps than he had ever realized. Her straight clean hair was shining. Her face was softer, glowing and serene. It was a madonna loveliness, dependent on the family ambiance.

"You've hardly changed at all," Elizabeth said, "but it has been a long time."

"Eight years." His hand touched his thinning hair self-consciously while further amenities were exchanged.

Ferris felt himself suddenly a spectator—an interloper

这字眼。"

"那怎么说好呢?"她问。

他沉吟片刻。"说侨民也许比较妥当。"

费里斯又瞥了一眼手表,伊丽莎白再次道歉:"要是我们事先知道——"

"我只在这里待一天。我是突然回来的。你不知道吧,爸爸上星期去世了。"

"爸爸去世啦?"

"是的。在约翰·霍普金斯医院去世的。他在那儿医治了将近一年。葬礼在南边佐治亚老家举行。"

"啊,真叫人难过,约翰。我最喜欢爸爸啦。"

小男孩从椅子背后走出来,好看清妈妈的面部。他问:"谁去世啦?"

费里斯没注意,他还在想父亲的死。他仿佛又看见他的尸体,直挺挺躺在棺材里的垫子上,让人离奇古怪地抹上胭脂,那双熟悉的手交叉着沉重地搁在葬礼玫瑰上。记忆消失了,他听见伊丽莎白平静的声音。

"费里斯先生的父亲逝世了,比利。他是个真正了不起的人。不过你不认识他。"

"可是你为什么叫他爸爸呢?"

贝利和伊丽莎白交换了一下窘迫的眼色。结果还是贝利答复了这个好问的孩子:"很久以前,你妈和费里斯先生结过婚。那时还没有你呢——这是很久以前的事了。"

"费里斯先生?"

小男孩不相信,瞪大眼睛惊讶地望着费里斯。对着孩子疑惑的目光,费里斯的眼睛不知怎的也流露出怀疑的神情。难道这一切是真的?在床上他曾经把这位陌生人伊丽莎白叫做野鸭子,他们在一起生活了大约有 1000 个日日夜夜——最后——婚姻关系因为种种摩擦(忌妒、酒和经济纠纷)而丝丝破裂,突然承受起孤独的悲哀。

贝利告诉孩子们:"该吃饭了。去吧。"

"可是,爹!妈妈和费里斯——我——"

比利令人不可忘怀的眼睛——困惑,还闪现出一丝敌意——使费里斯想起了另一个小男孩,珍妮的儿子。他只有 7 岁,小脸蛋上罩着愁云,膝关节比腿还大。费里斯总是避免和他见面,平时也不把他放在心上。

"快步走!"贝利和蔼地把比利的身子转向门口,"说晚安吧,孩子。"

"晚安,费里斯先生。"接着又不高兴地说,"我还以为能等到上蛋糕呢。"

among these Baileys. Why had he come? He suffered. His own life seemed so solitary, a fragile column supporting nothing amidst the wreckage of the years. He felt he could not bear much longer to stay in the family room. He glanced at his watch. "You're going to the theater?"

"It's a shame," Elizabeth said, "but we've had this engagement for more than a month. But surely, John, you'll be staying home one of these days before long. You're not going to be an expatriate, are you?"

"Expatriate," Ferris repeated, "I don't much like the word."

"What's a better word?" she asked.

He thought for a moment. "Sojourner might do."

Ferris glanced again at his watch, and again Elizabeth apologized. "If only we had known ahead of time—"

"I just had this day in town. I came home unexpectedly. You see, Papa died last week."

"Papa Ferris is dead?"

"Yes, at Johns Hopkins. He had been sick there nearly a year. The funeral was down home in Georgia."

"Oh, I'm so sorry, John. Papa Ferris was always one of my favorite people."

The little boy moved from behind the chair so that he could look into his mother's face. He asked, "Who is dead?"

Ferris was oblivious to apprehension; he was thinking of his father's death. He saw again the outstretched body on the quilted silk within the coffin. The corpse flesh was bizarrely rouged and the familiar hands lay massive and joined above a spread of funeral roses. The memory closed and Ferris awakened to Elizabeth's calm voice.

"Mr. Ferris's father, Billy. A really grand person. Somebody you didn't know."

"But why did you call him *Papa* Ferris?"

Bailey and Elizabeth exchanged a trapped look. It was Bailey who answered the questioning child. "A long time ago," he said, "your mother and Mr. Ferris were once married. Before you were born—a long time ago."

"Mr. Ferris?"

The little boy stared at Ferris, amazed and unbelieving. And Ferris's eyes, as he returned the gaze, were somehow unbelieving too. Was it indeed true that at one time he had called this stranger, Elizabeth, Little Butterduck during nights of love, that they had lived together, shared perhaps a thousand days and nights and—finally—endured in the misery of a sudden solitude the fiber by fiber (jealousy, alcohol and money quarrels) destruction of the fabric of married love?

"到时你可以再来吃,"伊丽莎白说,"和爸爸一起去吃你们的饭去吧。"

房间里只剩下费里斯和伊丽莎白了。好一阵子两人都不说话,非常局促。费里斯问可不可以给自己倒杯酒,伊丽莎白就把鸡尾酒摇杯放到他旁边的桌子上。他看看房里那架大钢琴,发现架上还有乐谱。

"你现在弹得还有过去漂亮吗?"

"我还是很喜欢弹。"

"请你弹弹吧,伊丽莎白。"

伊丽莎白立即站起来。她一向爽快,只要别人请她演奏,她从不忸怩推辞。现在她更是求之不得,便如释重负地朝钢琴走去。

她弹起巴赫的一首《序奏及赋格》。序奏欢欣明快,犹如暗室里晨光透过的三棱镜一般虹彩缤纷。赋格的第一声部呈示单纯的主题,与第二声部交融重现,又按赋格复杂的结构再次重现,整个多声部乐曲平缓安详,表现出从容不迫的庄严。主旋律交织于两个声部之中,数不清的技巧使它臻于完美——时而压倒一切,时而隐没,自有种个体不怕服从整体的崇高气概。快结尾时,采用"增值"手法,最后一次强调主题,最后,主题以和弦形式再现,宣告曲子终结。费里斯闭着眼睛,头靠在椅背上。在曲终后的寂静里,从厅那边的房间里传来了清晰的童声。

"爹爹,怎么妈妈和费里斯先生——"门关上了。

钢琴又响了——什么曲子?记不起标题,却似曾相识。明澈的旋律在他心头蛰伏了好一阵子,接着向他诉说往昔的岁月和场景——这是支伊丽莎白常演奏的曲子。优美的曲调唤起狂乱的回忆。昔日的热望、冲突、互相矛盾的欲望纷乱如麻,费里斯茫然若失。真奇怪,催化剂般引起心境骚乱的音乐,本身却如此安详、透明。如歌的琴声被女仆的出现打断了。

"贝利女士,晚餐已摆好了。"

直到费里斯坐在男女主人中间进餐的时候,没完结的音乐仍在他心头蒙上一层愁云。他微带醉意了。

"L'improvisation de la vie humaine①,"他说,"再没有别的东西像没完的歌一样使我觉得人生无常。或许还有旧的通讯录吧。"

"通讯录?"贝利反问,但又有礼貌地、不置可否地打住了。

_____

① 法语,意为人生即兴曲。

Bailey said to the children, "It's somebody's suppertime. Come on now. "

"But Daddy! Mamma and Mr. Ferris—I—"Billy's everlasting eyes—perplexed and with a glimmer of hostility—reminded Ferris of the gaze of another child. It was the young son of Jeannine—a boy of seven with a shadowed little face and knobby knees whom Ferris avoided and usually forgot.

"Quick march!"Bailey gently turned Billy toward the door. "Say good night now, son. "

"Good night, Mr. Ferris. " He added resentfully, "I thought I was staying up for the cake. "

"You can come in afterward for the cake, "Elizabeth said. "Run along now with Daddy for your supper. "

Ferris and Elizabeth were alone. The weight of the situation descended on those first moments of silence. Ferris asked permission to pour himself another drink and Elizabeth set the cocktail shaker on the table at his side. He looked at the grand piano and noticed the music on the rack.

"Do you still play as beautifully as you used to?"

"I still enjoy it. "

"Please play, Elizabeth. "

Elizabeth arose immediately. Her readiness to perform when asked had always been one of her amiabilities; she never hung back, apologized. Now as she approached the piano there was the added readiness of relief.

She began with a Bach prelude and fugue. The prelude was as gaily iridescent as a prism in a morning room. The first voice of the fugue, an announcement pure and solitary, was repeated intermingling with a second voice, and again repeated within an elaborated frame, the multiple music, horizontal and serene, flowed with unhurried majesty. The principal melody was woven with two other voices, embellished with countless ingenuities—now dominant, again submerged, it had the sublimity of a single thing that does not fear surrender to the whole. Toward the end, the density of the material gathered for the last enriched insistence on the dominant first motif and with a chorded final statement the fugue ended. Ferris rested his head on the chair back and closed his eyes. In the following silence a clear, high voice came from the room down the hall.

"Daddy, how *could* Mamma and Mr. Ferris—" A door was closed.

The piano began again—what was this music? Unplaced, familiar, the limpid melody had lain a long while dormant in his heart. Now it spoke to him of another time, another place—it was the music Elizabeth used to play. The delicate air summoned a wilderness of memory. Ferris was lost in the riot of past longings,

"你跟过去一样,还是个老小孩,约翰尼。"伊丽莎白的语气夹杂着一丝往日的温存。

这餐饭是南方口味,菜肴全是他一向喜欢吃的,有炸子鸡、玉米布丁,还有味道浓厚、色泽光亮的糖煮甘薯。席间,只要一静场,伊丽莎白就设法激起大家的谈兴,引得费里斯谈起了珍妮。

"我和珍妮是在去年秋天——也是这种时候——在意大利认识的。她是个歌唱演员,那时正在罗马演出。我希望我们很快就能结婚。"

这番话显得那么真诚,那么自然而然,竟弄得费里斯开始心里还不承认是谎言。他和珍妮压根儿就没提过结婚的事,而且她实际上还没离婚——她丈夫是个白俄,在巴黎当货币兑换商,她与他已分居5年了。不过来不及更正了,伊丽莎白已经接过话头说:"这消息真叫人高兴。祝贺你,约翰尼。"

他想用实话来弥补弥补。"罗马的秋天真美。到处鲜花,到处花香。"他又加上,"珍妮有个6岁大的小男孩。小家伙真怪,说三种语言。我时常带他上退列里公园。"

又撒谎了。他只带这孩子去那里玩过一次。这面黄肌瘦的外国男孩穿着短裤,光着又细又长的腿,在池里玩了一会儿小船,还骑了一阵马。他还想去看木偶戏,可是没时间了,因为费里斯在文书饭店还有个约会。他答应改天下午再带瓦伦丁上木偶剧院。费里斯就只带瓦伦丁上了这么一次退列里公园。

发生了一场小小的骚动。女仆端来了一个涂有糖霜的蛋糕,上面还插有粉红色的蜡烛。身穿睡衣的两个小孩也进来了。费里斯闹不清是怎么回事。

"生日快乐,约翰,"伊丽莎白说,"吹蜡烛吧。"

费里斯这才记起这天是自己的生日。烛焰晃动着熄灭了,空气中飘着一股蜡味。费里斯38岁了,太阳穴上已青筋毕露。

"你们该上戏院了。"

费里斯感谢伊丽莎白为他举行生日宴会,又客气地与大家道别。贝利全家送他到门口。

弯弯的月亮在高空放着柔光,下面是黑魆魆参差不齐的摩天楼群。街上风很大,很冷。费里斯匆忙赶到3号街,叫了一辆出租汽车。怀着即将离去,甚至是告别的心情,他用心地观看城市的夜景。他觉得无比孤单,恨不得班机起飞的时刻及早来到。他焦渴地盼望明天的飞行。

第二天他从空中俯瞰,纽约城反射着阳光,宛如

conflicts, ambivalent desires. Strange that the music, catalyst for this tumultuous anarchy, was so serene and clear. The singing melody was broken off by the appearance of the maid.

"Miz Bailey, dinner is out on the table now."

Even after Ferris was seated at the table between his host and hostess, the unfinished music still overcast his mood. He was a little drunk.

"*L'improvisation de la vie humaine*," he said. "There's nothing that makes you so aware of the improvisation of human existence as a song unfinished. Or an old address book."

"Address book?" repeated Bailey. Then he stopped, noncommittal and polite.

"You're still the same old boy, Johnny," Elizabeth said with a trace of the old tenderness.

It was a Southern dinner that evening, and the dishes were his old favorites. They had fried chicken and corn pudding and rich, glazed candied sweet potatoes. During the meal, Elizabeth kept alive a conversation when the silences were overlong. And it came about that Ferris was led to speak of Jeannine.

"I first knew Jeannine last autumn—about this time of the year—in Italy. She's a singer and she had an engagement in Rome. I expect we will be married soon."

The words seemed so true, inevitable, that Ferris did not at first acknowledge to himself the lie. He and Jeannine had never in that year spoken of marriage. And indeed, she was still married—to a White Russian money-changer in Paris from whom she had been separated for five years. But it was too late to correct the lie. Already Elizabeth was saying: "This really makes me glad to know. Congratulations, Johnny."

He tried to make the amends with truth. "The Roman autumn is so beautiful. Balmy and blossoming." He added, "Jeannine has a little boy of six. A curious trilingual little fellow. We go to the Tuileries sometimes."

A lie again. He had taken the boy once to the gardens. The sallow foreign child in shorts that bared his spindly legs had sailed his boat in the concrete pond and ridden the pony. The child had wanted to go in to the puppet show. But there was not time, for Ferris had an engagement at the Scribe Hotel. He had promised they would go to the guignol another afternoon. Only once had he taken Valentin to the Tuileries.

There was a stir. The maid brought in a white-frosted cake with pink candles. The children entered in their night clothes. Ferris still did not understand.

"Happy birthday, John," Elizabeth said. "Blow out the candles."

Ferris recognized his birthday date. The candles blew out lingeringly and there was the smell of burning wax. Ferris was thirty-eight years old. The veins in his temples darkened and pulsed visibly.

精巧的玩具。接着美国留在后面了,飞机下面只有大西洋,遥远的前方是欧洲海岸。云朵下面,大海是淡乳白色的,很平静。费里斯打了大半天盹。天快黑时,他想念起伊丽莎白,回忆头天晚上的访问。怀着渴望、温柔的妒慕和无法解释的悔恨,他想象伊丽莎白在家人中间的样子。他竭力回忆那深深触动了他心灵的音乐,那支没奏完的曲子,但怎么也想不起旋律,只记起了节奏。倒是有些不相关的曲调不找自来。伊丽莎白弹奏过的那首赋格曲的第一声部在他耳内回响——而且还嘲弄似的,竟是倒转后的小调形式。高飞在大洋上空,人生无常的感慨和孤独的伤感不再作祟,他平静地想起了父亲的死。晚饭时分,班机飞临法兰西海岸上空。

半夜里费里斯乘出租汽车穿过巴黎。这是个浓云满天的夜晚,雾气环绕着协和广场上的路灯。濡湿的人行道微弱地反射出深夜咖啡馆的灯光。和平常跨越大洋的洲际飞行一样,变化太突然了。早晨还在纽约,半夜却出现在巴黎。费里斯杂沓的经历在他眼前掠过:一座座城市,一场场短暂的爱情。光阴,岁月不祥的滑音,流水般的光阴。

"Vite!Vite!"他恐惧地叫门,"Dèpêchez-vous。①"

瓦伦丁为他开了门。小家伙穿着睡衣和一件过短的红袍子。看见费里斯经过他身边走进套间,孩子带黑晕的灰眼睛亮了片刻。

"J'attends Maman。②"

珍妮还在一家夜总会里演唱,这个钟头内不会回来。瓦伦丁又去画他的画了,他手拿蜡笔蹲着,纸就铺在地板上。费里斯勾头看了看——瓦伦丁画了一个弹班卓琴的人,旁边还有用线条圈着的文字和波状线。

"咱们上退列里公园去。"

孩子抬起头,费里斯把他拉到膝前。那旋律,伊丽莎白没奏完的那首乐曲突然像在拍击他的耳膜。记忆自动抛出了它的负担——这一次他却马上认出是什么曲子,它给他带来的只是突如其来的欢乐。

"先生,"孩子问他,"你看见他了吗?"

费里斯茫然了,因为此刻他只想着另一位小孩——那位长有雀斑、备受家庭钟爱的小男孩。"看

---

① 法文,意为"快!快!快开门。"
② 法文,意为"我在等妈妈。"

"It's time you started for the theater."

Ferris thanked Elizabeth for the birthday dinner and said the appropriate good-byes. The whole family saw him to the door.

A high, thin moon shone above the jagged, dark skyscrapers. The streets were windy, cold. Ferris hurried to Third Avenue and hailed a cab. He gazed at the nocturnal city with the deliberate attentiveness of departure and perhaps farewell. He was alone. He longed for flighttime and the coming journey.

The next day he looked down on the city from the air, burnished in sunlight, toylike, precise. Then America was left behind and there was only the Atlantic and the distant European shore. The ocean was milky pale and placid beneath the clouds. Ferris dozed most of the day. Toward dark he was thinking of Elizabeth and the visit of the previous evening. He thought of Elizabeth among her family with longing, gentle envy and inexplicable regret. He sought the melody, the unfinished air, that had so moved him. The cadence, some unrelated tones, were all that remained; the melody itself evaded him. He had found instead the first voice of the fugue that Elizabeth had played—it came to him inverted mockingly and in a minor key. Suspended above the ocean the anxieties of transience and solitude no longer troubled him and he thought of his father's death with equanimity. During the dinner hour the plane reached the shore of France.

At midnight Ferris was in a taxi crossing Paris. It was a clouded night and mist wreathed the lights of the Place de la Concorde. The midnight bistros gleamed on the wet pavements. As always after a transocean flight the change of continents was too sudden. New York at morning, this midnight Paris. Ferris glimpsed the disorder of his life: the succession of cities, of transitory loves; and time, the sinister glissando of the years, time always.

"Vite! Vite!"he called in terror. "Dèpêchez-vous."

Valentin opened the door to him. The little boy wore pajamas and an outgrown red robe. His grey eyes were shadowed and, as Ferris passed into the flat, they flickered momentarily.

"J'attends Maman."

Jeannine was singing in a night club. She would not be home before another hour. Valentin returned to a drawing, squatting with his crayons over the paper on the floor. Ferris looked down at the drawing—it was a banjo player with notes and wavy lines inside a comic-strip balloon.

"We will go again to the Tuileries."

The child looked up and Ferris drew him closer to his knees. The melody, the unfinished music that Elizabeth had played, came to him suddenly. Unsought, the load of memory jettisoned—this time bringing only recognition and sudden joy.

"Monsieur Jean," the child said, "did you see him?"

见谁呀,瓦伦丁?"

"你爸爸,在佐治亚死去了的爸爸呀。"他又加上一句,"他好吗?"

费里斯急切地说:"以后咱们常上退列里去。去骑马,还要上木偶剧院。咱们一定要看木偶戏,再也不匆匆忙忙的了。"

"先生,木偶剧场现在已经关门了。"

恐惧又袭来了,他又意识到岁月已荒废,又承认死亡了。敏感的瓦伦丁仍然信赖地依偎在他怀里。他的脸贴着孩子柔嫩的腮部,他感觉得出孩子的纤柔睫毛在轻轻扫刷自己的皮肤。怀着一种内心的失望,他把孩子抱得紧紧的——仿佛一种像他的爱情一般多变的激情能控制时间的脉搏。

Confused, Ferris thought only of another child—the freckled, family-loved boy. "See who, Valentin?"

"Your dead papa in Georgia." The child added, "Was he okay?"

Ferris spoke with rapid urgency: "We will go often to the Tuileries. Ride the pony and we will go into the guignol. We will see the puppet show and never be in a hurry any more."

"Monsieur Jean," Valentin said. "The guignol is now closed."

Again, the terror, the acknowledgment of wasted years and death. Valentin, responsive and confident, still nestled in his arms. His cheek touched the soft cheek and felt the brush of the delicate eyelashes. With inner desperation he pressed the child close—as though an emotion as protean as his love could dominate the pulse of time.

思考题 ■

1. 纽约只是费里斯旅途上的一个中转点,故事的绝大部分情节都发生在这里。可是他归国回佐治亚老家这件事对这故事却具有特殊的意义,为什么?

2. 费里斯翻通讯录与偶然看见伊丽莎白这两件事之间有什么关系?可否说这一偶然发现改变了他对纽约的看法?(设想一下,如果把这事当作故事的开头,会失去些什么?)

3. 小说告诉我们,费里斯"决定"给伊丽莎白打电话是出于"一时冲动",是没经过反复考虑的。可是这"一时冲动"还有什么背景?我们是什么时候发现的?

4. "在办事的间隙,他仍有种不安的感觉……"这一段有什么特别的意义?

5. 为什么迎接他进家的红发男孩会使费里斯"惊讶"?他不知道伊丽莎白再婚后已有了孩子?

6. 费里斯看见红发男孩这件事与他突然回忆起伊丽莎白洗澡、梳妆的模样以及其他"决堤的回忆"之间有何关系?

7. 指出几处叫人油然产生岁月变迁的感触的地方。这对费里斯有什么影响?他指望从岁月的变迁中获得什么?

1. New York, where most of this story is laid, is merely one of Ferris's stopping places. But why is his return to America, and to his home in Georgia, significant for the story?

2. What is the relation between Ferris's looking over an old address book and his unexpected glimpse of Elizabeth? Can it be said that this glimpse changes his view of New York? (Think of this scene as the opening of the story. What would be lost?)

3. We are told that Ferris's "decision" to call Elizabeth was "impulsive," not inspected and debated. But what lies behind this "impulse"? When do we know this?

4. What is the significance of the paragraph beginning "As he went from one engagement to another, he was still bothered"?

5. Why is Ferris "astonished" by the red-haired boy who lets him into the Bailey apartment? Hadn't he known that Elizabeth had children by her second marriage?

6. What is the relation between the sight of the red-haired boy and Ferris's sudden images of Elizabeth at her bath and dressing table with his other "unbidden memories"?

7. Locate several points at which the idea of the passage of time emerges. What is the effect on Ferris? What does he expect from the passage of time?

8. 瓦伦丁对于这故事,特别是在故事的结尾,有什么意义?迎接费里斯的是瓦伦丁而不是珍妮,这一点是很重要的,为什么?

9. 为什么费里斯要撒谎说他和珍妮很快就要结婚?

10. 回到巴黎寓所时,费里斯发现了些什么?他是否在欺骗自己?是否这故事并没有回答这问题?

11. 这篇小说用"侨民"做标题,有什么意思?

（彭嘉林 译）

8. What is the significance of Valentin for the story? Especially in the last scene. Why is it important that Ferris is greeted by Valentin instead of Jeannine?

9. Why does Ferris lie about an impending marriage with Jeannine?

10. Upon his return to the apartment in Paris, what does Ferris discover? Or does he deceive himself? Or is the question to be left open in the story?

11. What does the title mean in relation to the story?

018. 醉 汉

（爱尔兰）弗兰克·奥康纳 著　　彭嘉林 译

018. The Drunkard

by Frank O'Connor

斜坡巷的杜利先生死了，这对我爸爸是个可怕的打击。杜利先生是位流动销货员，自己有小汽车，两个儿子上的都是多米尼克教会学校。论社会地位，他要比我们高出十万八千丈，但从来不摆臭架子。杜利先生是个知识分子，也像所有的读书人一样，他最喜欢的就是聊天；而爸爸呢，还勉强算得上读过好些书，能够欣赏知识分子的高谈阔论。杜利先生真是个了不起的聪明人。他做生意交游很广，与宗教界又常有接触，所以城里发生了什么事情，他几乎没有不清楚的。他夜夜从街那边走到我们家来，对我父亲大谈新闻背后的新闻。他嗓门低低的，很诱人，脸上常带着聪颖的笑容。爸爸总是惊讶地倾听，不时也说几句引他往下讲。爸爸还会得意洋洋地插上这么一句，满面生辉地问我母亲："你知道杜利先生要告诉我什么事吗？"直到今天，每逢有人向我传播什么小道消息，我还总是想问："是不是杜利先生告诉你的？"

直到我亲眼看见他穿着褐色的寿衣躺在那里，蜡黄的手指上缠着念珠，我还是不能把噩耗当真。我总还觉得其中有诈，说不定哪一个夏日的黄昏，杜利先生又会在我家门口出现，向我们大揭阴间黑幕。可是爸爸却很难过，这既因为杜利先生与他年龄相仿，他的死难免叫爸爸担心什么时候也轮到自己，也因为从此以后，再也没人会把市政当局肮脏的内幕新闻告诉他了。我们布拉尼巷里，像杜利先生一样读报的居民屈指可数，而且他们都不忽略这一事实，我爸爸只是个干力气活的。就连沙利文木匠，虽然他压根儿算不了老几，也自认比爸爸高出一头。因此，杜利先生的死的确非同小可。

IT was a terrible blow to Father when Mr. Dooley on the terrace died. Mr. Dooley was a commercial traveller with two sons in the Dominicans and a car of his own, so socially he was miles ahead of us, but he had no false pride. Mr. Dooley was an intellectual, and, like all intellectuals the thing he loved best was conversation, and in his own limited way Father was a well-read man and could appreciate an intelligent talker. Mr. Dooley was remarkably intelligent. Between business acquaintances and clerical contacts, there was very little he didn't know about what went on in town, and evening after evening he crossed the road to our gate to explain to Father the news behind the news. He had a low, palavering voice and a knowing smile, and Father would listen in astonishment, giving him a conversational lead now and again, and then stump triumphantly in to Mother with his face aglow and ask: "Do you know what Mr. Dooley is after telling me?" Ever since, when somebody has given me some bit of information off the record I have found myself on the point of asking: "Was it Mr. Dooley told you that?"

Till I actually saw him laid out in his brown shroud with the rosary beads entwined between his waxy fingers I did not take the report of his death seriously. Even then I felt there must be a catch and that some summer evening Mr. Dooley must reappear at our gate to give us the lowdown on the next world. But Father was very upset, partly because Mr. Dooley was about one age with himself, a thing that always gives a distinctly personal turn to another man's demise; partly because now he would have no one to tell him what dirty work was behind the latest scene at the Corporation. You could count on your fingers the number of men in Blarney Lane who read the papers as Mr. Dooley did, and none of these would have overlooked

作者简介：弗兰克·奥康纳（Frank O'Connor，1903—1966），爱尔兰作家。1903 年生于爱尔兰科克县，1966 年 3 月 10 日卒于柏林。奥康纳在贫苦中长大，后来成为图书管理员、都柏林阿比剧院院长。他的短篇小说让他闻名美国，小说中的琐碎事件刻画了爱尔兰的生活。他的作品收录在《国家的客人们》（*Guests of the Nation*，1931）、《山楂果冻》（*Crab Apple Jelly*，1944）和《纽约客》杂志中。他还对爱尔兰生活、文学和 9 世纪至 20 世纪盖尔文学作品进行评论，其中包括 17 世纪伟大的讽刺文学作品《午夜宫廷》（*The Midnight Court*，1945）。

"两点半到达克拉公墓。"爸爸若有所思地放下了报纸。

"你该不是要去参加葬礼吧?"妈妈发慌了。

"这也该料得到的。"爸爸已察觉到妈妈反对的意思,"我可不能让人说闲话。"

妈妈按捺着性子说:"我看你去不去送葬,在别人眼里,不过和你送不送他上殡仪馆一样罢了。"

(当然啰,"上殡仪馆"是另一回事,因为送尸体上殡仪馆是下工后的事,而送葬却意味着少挣半天的工钱。)

"那些人又差不多全都不认识我们。"她又补上一句。

"上帝保佑我们,"父亲庄严地回答,"要轮到我们自己,也会希望人家来的。"

平心而论,为了老邻居,爸爸从来都是舍得放弃半天的收入的。主要的原因倒不是他喜欢葬礼,而是他是个讲良心的人,他希望别人怎么待自己,也就怎么去待别人。他一想到日后自己死了,别人也一定会为他举行体面的葬礼,就感到莫大的安慰。不过,也得为妈妈说句公道话,她倒不是吝啬半天的收入,这好歹我们总还算大方得起。

你要知道,爸爸有个大毛病——酗酒。他可以强忍住,几个月甚至几年滴酒不沾。这种时候他可真像金子打成的好人。早上他总是头一个起来,烧好茶端一杯到妈妈床头,晚上也总是待在家里读报。他用省下的钱买了一套崭新的蓝哔叽衣服,还有顶圆顶呢帽。他讥笑那些酒鬼笨蛋,一星期一星期把挣来的血汗钱送进酒店老板的腰包。有时候,为了打发无聊的时光,他还拿出纸笔,精确地计算一番,看看当一个禁酒主义者每周能省下多少钱。由于天性乐观,有时他还会把可能的寿命也计算在内,得出的总数叫人兴奋得喘不过气来。到他归天之时,会有好几百镑呢!

我似乎只知道,这是个不祥之兆,说明他心里的骄傲情绪已经膨胀,他自认为要比邻居们强。迟早这种情绪会膨胀到非要发泄不可的地步,一定得庆祝一番才甘休。于是乎他就来上一杯——当然不是威士忌,不是诸如此类的烈酒——只是黑啤酒之类温和无害的饮料。可这一来就糟了。第一杯刚下肚,他就意识到自己当了傻瓜,要用第二杯来洗刷这耻辱的记忆,没用,又干上第三杯……最后回家的时候,他已经醉得踉踉跄跄的了。正如劝人为善的印刷品上所说,从此开始了"醉汉发展过程"。第二天他总是头晕得没法上工,只好让妈妈去替他请假。接下来的两个星

the fact that Father was only a laboring man. Even Sullivan, the carpenter, a mere nobody, thought he was a cut above Father. It was certainly a solemn event.

"Half past two to the Curragh, "Father said meditatively, putting down the paper.

"But you're not thinking of going to the funeral?" Mother asked in alarm.

"'T would be expected, "Father said, scenting opposition. "I wouldn't give it to say to them. "

"I think, "said Mother with suppressed emotion, "it will be as much as anyone will expect if you go to the chapel with him. "

("Going to the chapel, "of course, was one thing, because the body was removed after work, but going to a funeral meant the loss of a halfday's pay.)

"The people hardly know us, "he added.

"God between us and all harm," Father replied with dignity, "we'd be glad if it was our own turn. "

To give Father his due, he was always ready to lose a half day for the sake of an old neighbor. It wasn't so much that he liked funerals as that he was a conscientious man who did as he would be done by; and nothing could have consoled him so much for the prospect of his own death as the assurance of a worthy funeral. And, to give Mother her due, it wasn't the half-day's pay she begrudged, badly as we could afford it.

Drink, you see, was Father's great weakness. He could keep steady for months, even for years, at a stretch, and while he did he was as good as gold. He was first up in the morning and brought the mother a cup of tea in bed, stayed at home in the evenings and read the paper; saved money and bought himself a new blue serge suit and bowler hat. He laughed at the folly of men who, week in and week out, left their hard-earned money with the publicans; and sometimes, to pass an idle hour, he took pencil and paper and calculated precisely how much he saved each week through being a teetotaller. Being a natural optimist he sometimes continued his calculation through the whole span of his prospective existence and the total was breathtaking. He would die worth hundreds.

If I had only known it, this was a bad sign; a sign he was becoming stuffed up with spiritual pride and imagining himself better than his neighbors. Sooner or later, the spiritual pride grew till it called for some form of celebration. Then he took a drink—not whisky, of course; nothing like that—just a glass of some harmless drink like lager beer. That was the end of Father. By the time he had taken the first he already realized that he had made a fool of himself, took a second to forget it and a third to forget that he couldn't forget, and at last came home reeling drunk. From this on it was "The Drunkard's Progress, "as in the moral prints. Next day he stayed in from work with a sick

期里,他会又变得可怜、粗野、沮丧。他一旦喝开了头,就会一个劲儿喝下去,直到连厨房里那座时钟也喝光。妈妈和我太熟悉这一切了,所以对所有能挑逗他酗酒的危险机会都怕得要命。葬礼,也是这种机会之一。

"我得上邓菲那儿去干半天活,"妈妈忧心忡忡地说,"可谁来照管拉里呢?"

"让我来吧,"爸爸和蔼地说,"走动一下对他也有好处。"

用不着多说,大家都明白,我才用不着别人照看,要让我留在家,我还能把索尼照料得好好的呢。要我跟父亲一道,是想让我充当他的制动器。尽管我这个制动器从来不灵,但妈妈还是认定我行。

第二天,我刚放学回来,爸爸已在家里。他替我和他煮了一盅茶。他煮茶是好手,但干别的手脚都太笨,他切面包的那个样子简直叫人打颤。喝过茶,我们就走下斜坡上教堂去。爸爸穿着他最好的那套蓝哔叽,圆顶呢帽斜戴在头上,有点风流哥儿的味道。他在来送葬的人当中,发现了彼得·克劳利,真是高兴极了。彼得也是个危险信号,凭以往星期日早弥撒后的经验,我早就懂得这一点。就像妈说的,他是坏人,他参加葬礼只为了不花钱白喝酒。事实上他根本就不认识杜利先生!爸爸也有点儿瞧不起他,认为他还不如那些把血汗钱花在酒店里的笨蛋,因为他喝酒差不多从不自己掏腰包!

在爸爸看来,这葬礼够气派的。我们还没出发,还没冒着午后的阳光,跟在灵车后面朝墓地走去,他已经把一切都调查得一清二楚了。

"5辆马车!"他报道说,"5辆马车,16辆篷车!一位市府参事,两名地方议员,还有不计其数的教士。自从酒店老板威利·麦克死后,我还没见过谁的葬礼有这种排场。"

"这自然啰,他人缘好呀。"克劳利的沙哑嗓门响了。

"我的天,还用你来告诉我?"父亲尖声说,"难道他不是我最要好的老朋友?他去世前两天——仅仅两天哇——他那天晚上还到我家来过,把住宅合同的情况告诉我。市政府那些人全是强盗。不过,就连我也没料到他结交有这么广。"

爸爸快步朝前走,兴奋得像个小孩,周围的一切都叫他感兴趣:送葬者、山迪威尔路上的漂亮房屋。最危险的信号全出现了:阳光灿烂的天气,气派十足的葬礼,僧俗两方面的大人物。这一切都在挑逗、刺

head while Mother went off to make his excuses at the works, and inside a fortnight he was poor and savage and despondent again. Once he began he drank steadily through everything down to the kitchen clock. Mother and I knew all the phases and dreaded all the dangers. Funerals were one.

"I have to go to Dunphy's to do a half-day's work," said Mother in distress. "Who's to look after Larry?"

"I'll look after Larry," Father said graciously. "The little walk will do him good."

There was no more to be said, though we all knew I didn't need anyone to look after me, and that I could quite well have stayed at home and looked after Sonny, but I was being attached to the party to act as a brake on Father. As a brake I had never achieved anything, but Mother still had great faith in me.

Next day, when I got home from school, Father was there before me and made a cup of tea for both of us. He was very good at tea, but too heavy in the hand for anything else; the way he cut bread was shocking. Afterwards, we went down the hill to the church. Father wearing his best blue serge and bowler cocked to one side of his head with the least suggestion of the masher. To his great joy he discovered Peter Crowley among the mourners. Peter was another danger signal, as I knew well from certain experiences after Mass on Sunday morning: a mean man, as Mother said, who only went to funerals for the free drinks he could get at them. It turned out that he hadn't even known Mr. Dooley! But Father had a sort of contemptuous regard for him as one of the foolish people who wasted their good money in public-houses when they could be saving it. Very little of his own money Peter Crowley wasted!

It was an excellent funeral from Father's point of view. He had it all well studied before we set off after the hearse in the afternoon sunlight.

"Five carriages!" he exclaimed. "Five carriages and sixteen covered cars! There's one alderman, two councillors and 'tis unknown how many priests. I didn't see a funeral like this since Willie Mack, the publican, died."

"Ah, he was well liked," said Crowley in his husky voice.

"My goodness, don't I know that?" snapped Father. "Wasn't the man my best friend? Two nights before he died—only two nights—he was over telling me of the goings-on about the housing contract. Them fellows in the Corporation are night and day robbers. But even I never imagined he was as well connected as that."

Father was stepping out like a boy, pleased with everything: the other mourners, and the fine houses along Sunday's Well. I knew the danger signals were there in full force: a sunny day, a fine funeral, and a distinguished company of clerics and public men were

激,让父亲暴露出天性中虚荣、轻浮的一面。眼看他的老友被送进墓穴,他内心产生了一种类似欢愉的感觉,有种尽了义务的轻松感,而且也不无庆幸,不管以后在漫长的夏日黄昏,他会如何强烈怀念可怜的杜利先生,但毕竟是他想杜利,而不是杜利怀念他。

"咱们在人散前走吧。"爸爸悄悄对克劳利说,这时掘墓人才刚向穴里撒下第一锹土。父亲离开了墓地,蹦蹦跳跳的,活像头从一个草墩跳到另一个草墩的山羊。那些马车夫,虽然不像爸爸那样已经几个月没喝酒了,但瘾头似乎也不比他小,他们都满怀希望地抬头张望。

"那边快完事了吧,米克?"一位马车夫大声问道。

"快了,只剩下最后的祈祷啦!"听父亲说话那调门,活像在宣布什么特大喜讯。

离酒店还有几百码,马车队卷着尘龙超过了我们。虽然天气一热,爸爸的腿就不灵便,但他还是加快了步子,还一面紧张地回头,看看大队的送葬者是否翻过岭来了。人群一到,你就可能要等啦。

我们到达酒店时,那些马车早已排成一行停在店外。系着黑领带、神气庄严的先生们正小心安慰那些神秘的女士,她们很庄重,只从放下的马车遮帘后伸出手来。酒店里只有马车夫和两个骚婆娘。我想,是刹车的时候了,于是就扯扯爸爸的衣角。

"爹,咱们现在就回家不好吗?"

"只等两分钟,"他满脸堆笑,十分亲切地说,"喝完一瓶柠檬水就走。"

这叫收买拉拢,我明白,但我一向是个意志薄弱的孩子。爸爸要了一瓶柠檬水和两品脱啤酒。我口很渴,一下就喝光了我的那份。爸爸可不像我,他几个月没喝过酒了,眼下可要慢慢地仔细地享受这无穷无尽的乐趣。他掘出烟斗,吹气通了通,装上烟丝,劈劈啪啪地划了几声火柴来点烟,他拼命吸着.眼珠都凸出来了。然后,他不慌不忙地转过身,背朝酒柜,一只胳膊肘支在柜台上,好像根本就不知道背后还有酒,慢条斯理地刷掉手掌上的烟末。他已安心要待到天黑,从容不迫地逐一讲起他所参加过的盛大葬礼。马车全走了,那些次要的送葬者也拥进来了,店里已经半满。

"爹,"我又扯扯他的衣裳,"咱们回去吧。"

"呃,你妈还要过很久才能回家。"他说得还挺好听,"到外面马路上玩去,好不好?"

bringing out all the natural vanity and flightiness of Father's character. It was with something like genuine pleasure that he saw his old friend lowered into the grave; with the sense of having performed a duty and the pleasant awareness that however much he would miss poor Mr. Dooley in the long summer evenings, it was he and not poor Mr. Dooley who would do the missing.

"We'll be making tracks before they break up," he whispered to Crowley as the gravediggers tossed in the first shovelfuls of clay, and away he went, hopping like a goat from grassy hump to hump. The drivers, who were probably in the same state as himself, though without months of abstinence to put an edge on it, looked up hopefully.

"Are they nearly finished, Mick?" bawled one.

"All over now bar the last prayers," trumpeted Father in the tone of one who brings news of great rejoicing.

The carriages passed us in a lather of dust several hundred yards from the public-house, and Father, whose feet gave him trouble in hot weather, quickened his pace, looking nervously over his shoulder for any sign of the main body of mourners crossing the hill. In a crowd like that a man might be kept waiting.

When we did reach the pub the carriages were drawn up outside, and solemn men in black ties were cautiously bringing out consolation to mysterious females whose hands reached out modestly from behind the drawn blinds of the coaches. Inside the pub there were only the drivers and a couple of shawly women. I felt if I was to act a brake at all, this was the time, so I pulled Father by the coattails.

"Dadda, can't we go home now?" I asked.

"Two minutes now," he said, beaming affectionately. "Just a bottle of lemonade and we'll go home."

This was a bribe, and I knew it, but I was always a child of weak character. Father ordered lemonade and two pints. I was thirsty and swallowed my drink at once. But that wasn't Father's way. He had long months of abstinence behind him and an eternity of pleasure before. He took out his pipe, blew through it, filled it, and then lit it with loud pops, his eyes bulging above it. After that he deliberately turned his back on the pint, leaned one elbow on the counter in the attitude of a man who did not know there was a pint behind him, and deliberately brushed the tobacco from his palms. He had settled down for the evening. He was steadily working through all the important funerals he had ever attended. The carriages departed and the minor mourners drifted in till the pub was half full.

"Dadda," I said, pulling his coat again, "can't we go home now?"

"Oh, your mother won't be in for a long time yet," he said benevolently enough. "Run out in the

但我一听就知道是扯淡。一个人孤零零的,怎么能在陌生的街道上玩儿呢?和以往一样,我很快就厌倦了。我知道爸爸挺能挨,非到天黑他是不会走的。我明白,恐怕我得领他回家了,他会醉得一塌糊涂,布拉尼巷的老女人们会全都跑到门口看笑话,说什么,"瞧,米克·德莱尼又醉啦。"他还知道,妈会着急得半疯,生怕爸爸第二天上不了工,这星期还没过完,她就得把那钟用披肩盖住,朝当铺里跑。厨房里要没个钟,静悄悄的,我怎么也习惯不了。

我的口还是渴。我发觉只要踮起脚尖,就够得着爸爸的酒杯。一个念头在我脑里一闪:试试杯里东西是啥滋味可是怪有趣的。爸爸背朝酒杯,是不会发现的。我拿下酒杯,小心翼翼地尝了一口。真扫兴。我真不明白他怎么能喝得下这种玩意儿。看来他是从来没沾过柠檬水的吧。

我本想劝他改喝柠檬水,可他正在一本正经地高谈阔论。他说,乐队是葬礼一个重要的附加成分。他摆出一副姿势,像倒持着一支步枪,哼了几节肖邦的《葬礼进行曲》。克劳利敬佩得直点头。我又喝了一大口,马上就领略了黑啤酒的妙处。我觉得精神兴奋,心情开朗而且达观。爸爸又哼了几节《扫罗》里的《死亡进行曲》。这酒店是个好地方,这葬礼也真够排场,我相信可怜的杜利先生在天之灵一定十分满意。同时我还想,他们可能也给他一个乐队。就像爸爸说的,乐队是重要的附加成分呀。

啤酒的妙处还在后头呢。它能叫你超脱自身躯壳,或者说使你飘飘然,就像腾云驾雾的六翼天使,在一旁观看你自己的模样。瞧你,两腿交叉,斜靠酒柜,超脱了琐事的烦扰,成人般思索深邃、严肃、有关生与死的问题。看着自己的模样,想想多滑稽,你一定会突然觉得很窘,总想咯咯笑出声来。可是,等我把一杯全喝完,这种状态也完结了,我发觉要把酒杯放回原处很困难,柜台像长高了不少。我的忧郁症又复发了。

"是啊,"爸爸一面向后伸手去拿酒杯,一面虔诚地说,"不论他在天堂还是地狱,愿上帝让这可怜的灵魂安息!"他打住了,先瞧瞧杯子,又望望周围的人。"喂,"听他声音还挺和气,他还当是别人和他恶作剧呢,"谁干的好事?"

谁也没吭声,酒店掌柜和那两位老女人先看看爸爸,又望望他的酒杯。

road and play, can't you?"

It struck me as very cool, the way grown-ups assumed that you could play all by yourself on a strange road. I began to get bored as I had so often been bored before. I knew Father was quite capable of lingering there till nightfall. I knew I might have to bring him home, blind drunk, down Blarney Lane, with all the old women at their doors, saying: "Mick Delaney is on it again." I knew that my mother would be half crazy with anxiety; that next day Father wouldn't go out to work; and before the end of the week she would be running down to the pawn with the clock under her shawl. I could never get over the lonesomeness of the kitchen without a clock.

I was still thirsty. I found if I stood on tiptoe I could just reach Father's glass, and the idea occurred to me that it would be interesting to know what the contents were like. He had his back to it and wouldn't notice. I took down the glass and sipped cautiously. It was a terrible disappointment. I was astonished that he could even drink such stuff. It looked as if he had never tried lemonade.

I should have advised him about lemonade but he was holding forth himself in great style. I heard him say that bands were a great addition to a funeral. He put his arms in the position of someone holding a rifle in reverse and hummed a few bars of Chopin's Funeral March. Crowley nodded reverently. I took a longer drink and began to see that porter might have its advantages. I felt pleasantly elevated and philosophic. Father hummed a few bars of the Dead March in *Saul*. It was a nice pub and a very fine funeral, and I felt sure that poor Mr. Dooley in Heaven must be highly gratified. At the same time I thought they might have given him a band. As Father said, bands were a great addition.

But the wonderful thing about porter was the way it made you stand aside, or rather float aloft like a cherub rolling on a cloud, and watch yourself with your legs crossed, leaning against a bar counter, not worrying about trifles but thinking deep, serious, grown-up thoughts about life and death. Looking at yourself like that, you couldn't help thinking after a while how funny you looked, and suddenly you got embarrassed and wanted to giggle. But by the time I had finished the pint, that phase too had passed; I found it hard to put back the glass, the counter seemed to have grown so high. Melancholia was supervening again.

"Well," Father said reverently, reaching behind him for his drink, "God rest the poor man's soul, wherever he is!" He stopped, looked first at the glass, and then at the people round him. "Hello," he said in a fairly good-humoured tone, as if he were just prepared

"谁也没喝你的酒,我的好人。"一位女人愤愤不平地说,"你当我们是贼?"

"呃,米克,这儿是没人会干这种勾当的呀。"听口气掌柜的也很惊讶。

"哼,是有人把我的酒偷了。"爸爸脸上的笑容消散了。

"真要有人喝,也只能是你身边的人干的。"那女人阴阳怪气地说,还狠狠地扫了我一眼。爸爸马上恍然大悟。我想当时我一定是醉眼飞斜的了。爸爸弯下腰,摇着我。

"你没事吧,拉里?"他大惊失色。

彼得·克劳利低头朝我龇牙直笑。

"怎么能叫人相信这种事?"

我能,而且毫无困难。我要呕吐了。爸爸生怕弄脏他那套好衣服,吓得往后一跳,连忙打开后门。

"快跑!快!快!"他喊道。

门口对面有堵攀满青藤的墙,阳光正照在它上面。我拔腿就朝外冲。我的动机本来很好,可动作却过火了,因为我一扑,和墙壁撞了个正着,我心想,它该让我撞得够疼的了。我素来很讲礼貌,所以在和它碰第二次前,还说了声"对不起"。爸爸还是担心他那套衣服,他走我背后,在我呕吐的时候,小心翼翼地扶住我。

"好孩子!"他鼓励道,"吐了就舒服了。"

天啊,我可不舒服,怎么也谈不上舒服。我一点儿也不顾他的面子,哇哇大哭起来,他领我回到店里,让我坐在那两位骚女人旁边的一张凳子上。她们愤慨地挺直身板,还在生父亲的气,怨他错怪了她们。

"老天爷啊!"一个女人呻吟般叫道,怜悯地望着我,"这德行,配做父亲么?"

"米克,"掌柜的慌张地说,他正朝我留下的污迹撒锯屑,"这里可不是孩子待的地方。趁警察没发现,你最好赶快带他回家去吧。"

"仁慈的天父啊!"爸爸抽抽噎噎地说。他翻眼看天,无声地击掌,只有在六神无主的时候,他才有这副模样。"我倒是什么霉哟!他妈会怎么说啊……女人就该待在家里照管自己的孩子!"他咆哮着补上一句,显然是冲着那两个骚娘们说的,"马车全走了吗,比尔?"

"早走完了,米克。"酒店掌柜回答。

"那我领他回去吧。"爸爸垂头丧气地说,"我再也

to consider it a joke, even if it was in bad taste, "who was at this?"

There was silence for a moment while the publican and the old women looked first at Father and then at his glass.

"There was no one at it, my good man," one of the women said with an offended air. "Is it robbers you think we are?"

"Ah, there's no one here would do a thing like that, Mick," said the publican in a shocked tone.

"Well, someone did it," said Father, his smile beginning to wear off.

"If they did, they were them that were nearer it," said the woman darkly, giving me a dirty look, and at the same moment the truth began to dawn on Father. I suppose I must have looked a bit starry-eyed. He bent and shook me.

"Are you all right, Larry?" he asked in alarm.

Peter Crowley looked down at me and grinned.

"Could you beat that?" he exclaimed in a husky voice.

I could, and without difficulty. I started to get sick. Father jumped back in holy terror that I might spoil his good suit, and hastily opened the back door.

"Run! run! run!" he shouted.

I saw the sunlit wall outside with the ivy overhanging it, and ran. The intention was good but the performance was exaggerated, because I lurched right into the wall, hurting it badly, as it seemed to me. Being always very polite, I said "Pardon" before the second bout came on me. Father, still concerned for his suit, came up behind and cautiously held me while I got sick.

"That's a good boy!" he said encouragingly. "You'll be grand when you get that up."

Begor, I was not grand! Grand was the last thing I was. I gave one unmerciful wail out of me as he steered me back to the pub and put me sitting on the bench near the shawlies. They drew themselves up with an offended air, still sore at the suggestion that they had drunk his pint.

"God help us!" moaned one, looking pityingly at me, "isn't it the likes of them would be fathers?"

"Mick," said the publican in alarm, spraying sawdust on my tracks, "that child isn't supposed to be in here at all. You'd better take him home quick in case a bobby would see him."

"Merciful God!" whimpered Father, raising his eyes to heaven and clapping his hands silently as he only did when distraught, "what misfortune was on me? Or what will his mother say?... If women might stop at home and look after their children themselves!" he added in a snarl for the benefit of the shawlies. "Are them carriages all gone, Bill?"

不带你出来了。"他恐吓我。"给,"他从胸袋里掏出一条干净手帕,"按住你的眉棱。"

看见手帕上的血迹,我才知道自己的头破了。我的太阳穴马上怦怦直跳,我又号哭起来。

"嘘!别!别!"爸爸烦躁地说,领我出了店门,"人家还当你撞死了呢!这不要紧嘛,到家洗洗就好啦。"

"坚强些,老伙计!"走在我另一边的克劳利安慰道,"一会儿就没事啦。"

我还从来没见过这样的两个人,他们根本就不懂喝了酒会怎样。我一遇风,又被太阳一晒,酒力发作得更厉害了。我跟跟跄跄,摇摇晃晃,就像在风头浪尖上颠簸一样。爸爸又抽抽噎噎的了。

"全能的上帝啊!全街人都出来了!我怎么老是这么倒霉!你就不能走好些吗?"

我走不好。但我看得一清二楚。布拉尼巷的娘儿们,不论老少,全让阳光引出来了。她们有的靠着矮门,有的坐在门槛上,现在全都停止饶舌,张开嘴巴观看眼前的怪事,两位毫无醉态的中年人,带着一个眉棱上开了道口子的、醉醺醺的小男孩回家。爸爸左右为难,一方面羞得无地自容,恨不得快些让我藏进家里,但另一方面又觉得有必要解释一番,申明不是他的过错。后来,我们在罗奇太太的屋前停下了。街对面一家门前聚集着一群老太婆,我一看就讨厌,看样子她们对我全都太感兴趣了。我斜靠着罗奇太太家的墙壁,双手插在裤兜里,满怀伤感,怀念起可怜的杜利先生,他躺在克拉公墓冰冷的坑里,再也不能在这街道上迈步。我越想越动感情,就唱起了一首父亲最喜欢的歌。

　　墓穴冷冰冰,见不了明蒂尼亚,也回不了钦科拉。

"唉,可怜的孩子!"罗奇太太叹道,"他的嗓子可不挺好的嘛,上帝保佑他吧!"

我也自认如此,爸爸却举起一根手指威胁我:"别嚷了!"这就叫我觉得真是咄咄怪事。也许是他还没意识到现在唱这支歌是正当其时吧,于是我就唱得更响了。

"住口,我叫你住口!"他尖声嚷道,按着又朝罗奇太太挤出一笑,"我们快到家了。让我抱你走吧。"

"The carriages are finished long ago, Mick," replied the publican.

"I'll take him home," Father said despairingly.... "I'll never bring you out again," he threatened me. "Here," he added, giving me the clean handkerchief from his breast pocket, "Put that over your eyes."

The blood on the handkerchief was the first indication I got that I was cut, and instantly my temple began to throb and I set up another howl.

"Whisht, whisht, whisht!" Father said testily, steering me out the door. "One'd think you were killed. That's nothing. We'll wash it when we get home."

"Steady now, old scout!" Crowley said, taking the other side of me. "You'll be all right in a minute."

I never met two men who knew less about the effects of drink. The first breath of fresh air and the warmth of the sun made me groggier than ever and I pitched and rolled between wind and tide till Father started to whimper again.

"God Almighty, and the whole road out! What misfortune was on me didn't stop at my work! Can't you walk straight?"

I couldn't. I saw plain enough that, coaxed by the sunlight, every woman old and young in Blarney Lane was leaning over her half-door or sitting on her doorstep. They all stopped gabbling to gape at the strange spectacle of two sober, middle-aged men bringing home a drunken small boy with a cut over his eye. Father, torn between the shamefast desire to get me home as quick as he could, and the neighborly need to explain that it wasn't his fault, finally halted outside Mrs. Roche's. There was a gang of old women outside a door at the opposite side of the road. I didn't like the look of them from the first. They seemed altogether too interested in me. I leaned against the wall of Mrs. Roche's cottage with my hands in my trousers pockets, thinking mournfully of poor Mr. Dooley in his cold grave on the Curragh, who would never walk down the road again, and, with great feeling, I began to sing a favorite song of Father's.

Though lost to Minonia and cold in the grave
He returns to Kincora no more.

"Wisha, the poor child!" Mrs. Roche said. "Haven't he a lovely voice, God bless him!"

That was what I thought myself, so I was the more surprised when Father said "Whisht!" and raised a threatening finger at me. He didn't seem to realize the appropriateness of the song, so I sang louder than ever.

"Whisht, I tell you!" he snapped, and then tried to work up a smile for Mrs. Roche's benefit. "We're nearly home now. I'll carry you the rest of the way."

尽管我醉成了这样子，还不至于糊涂到这么丢脸，让人给抱回家。

"得了，"我声色俱厉，"你别打扰我好不好？我好好的，能走。只是我的头有点儿晕。只要歇一会儿就好的。"

"要歇就回家上床歇去。"他恶狠狠地说，想把我抱起来，看他满面通红，我知道他发火了。

"上帝呀，"我蛮横地说，"回家干什么？你他妈的就不能别管我？"

不知道为什么，对面街上那群老太婆觉得这很逗趣，一个个笑得前仰后合。想到你喝上一滴酒左邻右舍就全都来笑你，我气得肚皮都快炸了。

"你们笑谁？"我吆喝，朝她们攥拳头，"再不让开我就打肿你们的脸，叫你们笑笑自个儿。"

她们却觉得更好笑了，我可从来没遇见过这么没教养的人。

"滚开，你们这帮脏母狗！"我咒骂。

"住口，住口！你给我住口！"爸爸收起强装出的好脸，咆哮了。他抓住我的手臂，拖着我就走。婆娘们的尖笑气得我发狂，爸爸的威胁气得我发疯。我拼命想站定不动，但力气小，哪里拗得过他，只好扭过头来朝那帮女人瞪眼睛。

"小心些，不然回头我叫你们知道我的厉害！"我叫骂道，"我要教训教训你们，叫你们懂得给体面人让路。你们该待在家里，洗干净你们的脏脸。"

"马上全街人都传遍了，"爸爸抽抽噎噎地说，"不干了，再也不干了，哪怕能活一千岁我也不干了！"

直到今天我都还不清楚，当时他到底是发誓不再带我出门，还是说不再喝酒了。他把我拖进家里，为了显示我的英雄气概，我嚷起了《韦克斯福德少年》这首歌。克劳利知道他留下会有麻烦，便溜了。爸爸替我脱了衣服，把我弄到床上，但我却睡不着，只觉得天旋地转，难受极了。我又吐了，爸爸弄了块湿布进来替我擦地板。我浑身发烫地躺着，只听见他劈柴生火，后来又摆弄餐桌。

突然，砰的一声，大门撞开了，妈抱着索尼一阵狂风似的冲了进来，她平素和蔼温顺的样子全没有了，换上了一副暴跳如雷的凶相。显然，邻居把什么都告诉她了。

"米克·德莱尼，"她歇斯底里地叫道，"你把我的儿子怎么啦？"

But, drunk and all as I was, I knew better than to be carried home ignominiously like that.

"Now," I said severely, "can't you leave me alone? I can walk all right. 'Tis only my head. All I want is a rest."

"But you can rest at home in bed," he said viciously, trying to pick me up, and I knew by the flush on his face that he was very vexed.

"Ah, Jasus," I said crossly, "what do I want to go home for? Why the hell can't you leave me alone?"

For some reason the gang of old women at the other side of the road thought this very funny. They nearly split their sides over it. A gassy fury began to expand in me at the thought that a fellow couldn't have a drop taken without the whole neighborhood coming out to make game of him.

"Who are ye laughing at?" I shouted, clenching my fists at them. "I'll make ye laugh at the other side of yeer faces if ye don't let me pass."

They seemed to think this funnier still; I had never seen such ill-mannered people.

"Go away, ye bloody bitches!" I said.

"Whisht, whisht, whisht, I tell you!" snarled Father, abandoning all pretence of amusement and dragging me along behind him by the hand. I was maddened by the women's shrieks of laughter. I was maddened by Father's bullying. I tried to dig in my heels but he was too powerful for me, and I could only see the women by looking back over my shoulder.

"Take care or I'll come back and show ye!" I shouted. "I'll teach ye to let decent people pass. Fitter for ye to stop at home and wash yeer dirty faces."

"'Twill be all over the road," whimpered Father. "Never again, never again, not if I lived to be a thousand!"

To this day I don't know whether he was forswearing me or the drink. By way of a song suitable to my heroic mood I bawled "The Boys of Wexford," as he dragged me in home. Crowley, knowing he was not safe, made off and Father undressed me and put me to bed. I couldn't sleep because of the whirling in my head. It was very unpleasant, and I got sick again. Father came in with a wet cloth and mopped up after me. I lay in a fever, listening to him chopping sticks to start a fire. After that I heard him lay the table.

Suddenly the front door banged open and Mother stormed in with Sonny in her arms, not her usual gentle, timid self, but a wild, raging woman. It was clear that she had heard it all from the neighbors.

"Mick Delaney," she cried hysterically, "what did you do to my son?"

"Whisht, woman, whisht, whisht!" he hissed, dancing from one foot to the other. "Do you want the whole road to hear?"

"Ah," she said with a horrifying laugh, "the road

"嘘,女人,嘘!嘘!"爸爸连嘘了几声,左脚换右脚地蹦跳,"你想让全街人都听见?"

"哈,"妈发出吓人的怪笑,"街上的人早知道喽。谁还不知道?你和那头畜生为了寻开心,竟拿黄汤灌我倒霉的儿子。他好端端的犯了你们什么啦?"

"我可没给他酒呀!"他高声辩白,邻人对这倒霉事可怕的曲解叫他不胜惊骇,"趁我转过背去,他把酒喝了。天啊,妈的你把我都看成什么人啦?"

"哼,"妈尖刻地回答,"什么人,现在谁还不知道你是什么人?上帝饶恕你吧,把咱们辛辛苦苦挣来的那几个血汗钱花去喝酒还不算,还想带坏儿子,让他也变成和你一样游手好闲的酒鬼。"

说罢她走进房里,在我床边跪下。看见我眉棱上的伤口,她不禁进出呻吟。厨房里,索尼哇哇大哭了。一会儿,爸爸出现在房门口,他的帽子遮住眼睛,满脸自我怜悯的神情。

"好哇,我已经够倒霉的了,你还要这样责怪我,"他埋怨,"我一整天没沾过一滴酒。他都喝光了我还喝啥?要说可怜,该算我呢,白白花费一天,还要在满街人面前丢人现眼。"

第二天早上,他起床后就老老实实提着饭盒上工去了。他一走,妈妈就扑到我床边吻我,好像这全是我的功劳。她还要替我请假,等到我眼睛好些了才去上学。

"我的小勇士!"她的眼睛发亮,"是上帝让你去的。你是他的守护天使。"

knows all about it by this time. The road knows the way you filled your unfortunate innocent child with drink to make sport for you and that other rotten, filthy brute."

"But I gave him no drink,"he shouted,aghast at the horrifying interpretation the neighbors had chosen to give his misfortune. "He took it while my back was turned. What the hell do you think I am?"

"Ah,"she replied bitterly,"everyone knows what you are now. God forgive you,wasting our hard-earned few ha'pence on drink,and bringing up your child to be a drunken corner-boy like yourself."

Then she swept into the bedroom and threw herself on her knees by the bed. She moaned when she saw the gash over my eye. In the kitchen Sonny set up a loud bawl on his own,and a moment later Father appeared in the bedroom door with his cap over his eyes, wearing an expression of the most intense self-pity.

"That's a nice way to talk to me after all I went through,"he whined. "That's a nice accusation,that I was drinking. Not one drop of drink crossed my lips the whole day. How could it when he drank it all? I'm the one that ought to be pitied,with my day ruined on me,and I after being made a show for the whole road."

But next morning,when he got up and went out quietly to work with his dinner-basket,Mother threw herself on me in the bed and kissed me. It seemed it was all my doing,and I was being given holiday till my eye got better.

"My brave little man!"she said with her eyes shining. "It was God did it you were there. You were his guardian angel."

┌ 讨　论 ─■

在这个滑稽故事里,人物的位置颠倒了。成了家庭丑闻,引起邻居非议讥笑的事情不是父亲醉倒街头,年幼的儿子吓怕了,可怜巴巴地想把父亲领回家,不让他在众人面前丢丑;倒是小孩子醉步蹒跚,走腔走调大唱其歌,还咒骂女邻居是"脏母狗",弄得父亲六神无主,心慌意乱。如果这故事只是简单地给我们讲述这颠倒离奇的情节,而且到此为止,那么,充其量它也只能算一个博人一笑而已的笑话。它就不怎么像篇小说,甚至还算不上好笑话。因为隽永的笑话,也必须扎根于对人性的真正理解之中。

In this amusing story,there is a reversal of roles. It is not the father who comes reeling down the street,the scandal of the family and the talk of the neighbors,as the appalled little son tries to lead him home and put him mercifully out of sight. It is the little boy who is unsteady on his feet,singing off key,calling the neighbor women "bloody bitches"—to the horror of the appalled father. If the story simply presented us with this topsy-turvy situation and let it go at that,it would amount to no more than a joke that was momentarily amusing. It would not be very much of a story and it would not even wear well as a joke. For even a joke,if it is to continue to seem funny,must be rooted in a true perception of human nature.

在这个故事里,父子位置的颠倒不是一时之技。只要我们稍加追溯,就可以发现这种颠倒是贯串整个故事的。在对待父亲酗酒毛病的大事上,拉里这孩子接受了母亲的观点。他像个大人,关心家庭的利益,但同时还必须提防自己孩子气的弱点。拉里忧心忡忡,知道什么是坏"兆头"。他太熟悉父亲一开酒戒就会发生什么后果。他一直很关心父亲,直到啤酒对他起了作用,他的忧虑才头一次消失。

在故事里,倒是父亲有种孩童般的天真坦白,这种性格常常还很讨人喜欢。想想他参加葬礼时的高兴劲儿吧:"在爸爸看来这场葬礼够气派的。"他报道说有"5辆马车,16辆篷车!"后来,拉里又说他,"眼看他的老友被送进墓穴,他内心产生了一种类似欢愉的感觉,有种尽了义务的轻松感。而且也不无庆幸,不管以后在漫长的夏日黄昏,他会如何强烈怀念可怜的杜利先生,但毕竟是他想杜利,而不是杜利怀念他。"后来,他告诉那些等着上酒店的马车夫,说下葬仪式快结束了:"'快了,只剩下最后的祈祷啦!'听父亲说话那调门,活像在宣布什么特大喜讯。"而几分钟后,他进了酒店准备开酒戒、解长渴的时候,更别提他有多高兴了!

如果拉里的父亲稍有些心计,或者稍为自觉,这种幽默的韵味就会失去,因为这么一来我们对他就会采取另外一种态度了。也因为单纯天真闯了祸,也因为单纯天真获得读者谅解。与其说他有罪,还不如说他受罪——由于邻居婆娘们"可怕的曲解",说他灌醉了自己的儿子,使他受到妻子责骂的时候,这一点尤其显得突出。这位父亲的性格,不但与故事本质的意义有密切的关系,甚至还能决定我们认为这故事是不是真有趣的看法。尽管"一切情况都说明他不对",他还是有种受到伤害的无辜的感觉。

The reversal of the roles of father and son in this story is not a momentary trick. If we think back a bit, we shall see that the reversal is assumed throughout the story. On the important matter of his father's weakness for drink, Larry, the little boy, takes his mother's viewpoint. His is the adult concern for an essentially good but childishly weak character who must be protected from himself. Larry is apprehensive and worried. He knows what "signs" are ominous. He knows all too well what the consequences of the first drink will be. His consciousness continues to be suffused with this kind of concern for his father until the beer finally takes effect upon *him*, and for the first time in the story, his apprehensions melt away.

Throughout the story it is the father who has the childlike guilessness—and the charm that frequently accompanies such guilessness. Consider his delight in the funeral: "It was an excellent funeral from Father's point of view." He exclaims that there are "five carriages and sixteen covered cars!" Later, as Larry remarks, "It was with something like genuine pleasure that he saw his old friend lowered into the grave; with the sense of having performed a duty and the pleasant awareness that however much he would miss poor Mr. Dooley in the long summer evenings, it was he and not Mr. Dooley who would do the missing." Later still, he tells the waiting coachmen that the service at the grave is nearly over: "'All over now bar the last prayers,' trumpeted Father in the tone of one who brings news of great rejoicing" And how happily a few minutes later he settles down in the pub as he gets ready to break his long drought!

If Larry's father were a more calculating man, or even a more self-conscious man, the special quality of the humor would be lost, for we would have to take a different attitude toward him. If it is his simplicity and his naiveté that cause troubles, they go far toward relieving him of adult responsibility for them. He is a man more sinned against than sinning—and nowhere more so than when he has to face the "horrifying interpretations" of the neighbor women that he has got his own son drunk. The character of the father thus has everything to do with the point of the story and even with the matter of whether or not we find the story genuinely funny. Though "all occasions inform against him," he has the consciousness of outraged innocence.

人物位置大致颠倒的最逗笑的例子，就是在从酒店回家的路上，父亲并没有强迫叫叫嚷嚷、醉态蹒跚的儿子住口，而是哀求他清醒些，别嚷了——照常理推测，如果喝醉的是父亲，拉里也会这样对待父亲的。然而，这种颠倒逗笑的主要根源，却出自父亲的性格，如果他是个残酷野蛮的人，就会强迫儿子闭嘴。而这样父子就不会有什么逗人发笑的事了，一强迫，一粗暴，也就无幽默可言了。

这种颠倒最出人意料的地方，是在故事的末尾（也是故事的高潮），小孩子的淘气被曲解为神的安排，醉醺醺、摇摇晃晃在大街上出丑的小男孩，在母亲眼里却成了引导意志薄弱的父亲走正道的"守护天使"。我们觉得这位母亲可笑——她赞扬拉里的说法，简直荒唐得像马拉柏洛柏太太①一样令人吃惊——不过，从她的观点来看，她的话也有相当道理，拉里成了小"男子汉"了。他使她少跑了一次常上的当铺。

—— 思考题 ——■

1. 拉里偷喝父亲啤酒这件事写得合情合理吗？拉里是否常干这类事？拉里父亲把酒搁在背后，让儿子喝光了都还不知道，这事可信吗？

2. 作为一个孩子，拉里对他父亲的观察是否太成熟了？这故事是拉里事后不久就写的呢，还是隔了许多年，他成人后才写的？

3. 这篇小说，情况的交待安排得很有技巧。请试加评论。迟迟不点出拉里父亲好酒，这样有什么好处？

4. 拉里眉棱裂了个口子，这有什么重要意义？伤口和鲜血是否能为这意外事件增添某种反响？

5. 是什么因素使得这个故事不光是个笑话？如果你在答案中使用了"塑造人物"这个术语，请解释你的意思。　　（彭嘉林 译）

———————
① 谢立丹的喜剧《竞争者》中的人物，以误用文学著名。

The most amusing instance of the general reversal of roles occurs on the way home from the pub, when the father does not forcibly shut up the noisy, tipsy little boy, but pleads with him to be reasonable and quiet just as Larry himself might have pleaded with the drunken father—if our normal expectations about this particular expedition had been realized. But this most amusing of the reversals is also rooted in the father's character: a more cruel man, a more brutal man, would have forced the boy to hush. He would thus have eliminated the humorous exchanges, and the suppression of these—and perhaps also the harshness by which they were suppressed—would have deprived the scene of its humor.

The most startling of the reversals (the one that caps the story) is the twist at the end in which the episode of juvenile delinquency becomes Providential and the little boy drunkenly weaving down the street becomes in the mother's eyes a "guardian angel" guiding aright the steps of the weak father. We laugh at the mother—the way in which she has expressed her commendation is almost as startling as the phrasings of Mrs. Malaprop—and yet what she says is, from her point of view, quite right: Larry has been a little "man." He has saved the family one of the usual visits to the pawnbroker.

1. Is the episode in which Larry drinks his father's pint of beer made plausible? Is this the sort of thing that Larry usually does? Is it credible that the father should have neglected his hint long enough for the child to drink it?

2. Are the observations made by Larry upon his father too sophisticated for a child to make? Is this story being told by Larry soon after the events described, or long after, when Larry has become a man?

3. The exposition in this story is managed very skillfully. Comment upon it. What is gained by delaying the introduction of the father's propensity to drink?

4. What is the importance of the fact that Larry gets a little nick over his eye? Does the fact of the blood and the wound help account for certain reactions to the incident?

5. What elements in the story make it more than a joke? If your answer includes "characterization," explain what you mean.

019. 请买票

（英）D. H. 劳伦斯 著　　邢 历 译

019. Tickets, Please

by D. H Lawrence

在英国中部有一路单轨车。这条线路勇敢地告别县城，跃身冲进黑色的工业近郊，忽而冲上山峦，忽而跌入峡谷，穿过一个个长且丑陋的工人村，跨沟渠，过铁路，从那庄严耸立在茫茫烟雾之上的教堂脚下驶过。它经过死气沉沉、肮脏阴冷的小集市区，斜身从电影院和商店旁飞驰而过，一头扎进矿谷，然后又向上爬，绕过一个当地的小教堂，穿过梣木林——一个冲刺到达终点——工业区最后一个丑陋的小地方，一个倚在黑暗的荒野边不断颤抖的寒冷小镇。就在这里，那绿色与乳白色相间的有轨车像猫似的收住了脚，带着一种不寻常的满足喵呜几声。但几分钟之后——批发商合作协会楼上的大钟敲响了——于是，它出发了！再一次登上历险的旅程。它又是不顾一切地向山下俯冲，在弯弯曲曲的山谷间上下颠簸，又是山顶集市那寒冷的小站，又是教堂脚下那令人心悸的陡峭的大下坡，又是环形道口那耐心等待错车的临时停车，就这样走啊走啊，走了漫长的两个小时，一直走到城市从那庞大的煤气工厂身后隐约露出轮廓，一直走到一个个狭小的工厂扑面而来。这时，它便踏上了这座了不起的县城的污秽街道，再一次怯生生地滑进终点站。在那些红白相间、伟大的市内电车面前，它是那样局促不安。然而，它依旧生气勃勃，充满自信，多少有点像一个敢作敢为的小东西，像是一叶从黑色矿区花园里伸展出来的荷兰芹①，绿油油的充满了活力。

坐这种车总是一种历险。因为是在战争时期②，

---

① 荷兰芹，一种植物。
② 指第一次世界大战。

THERE is in the Midlands a single-line tramway system which boldly leaves the country town and plunges off into the black, industrial countryside, up hill and down dale, through the long, ugly villages of workmen's houses, over canals and railways, past churches perched high and nobly over the smoke and shadows, through stark, grimy, cold little market-places, tilting away in a rush past cinemas and shops down to the hollow where the collieries are, then up again, past a little rural church, under the ash trees, on in a rush to the terminus, the last little ugly place of industry, the cold little town that shivers on the edge of the wild, gloomy country beyond. There the green and creamy colored tram-car seems to pause and purr with curious satisfaction. But in a few minutes—the clock on the turret of the Co-operative Wholesale Society's Shops gives the time—away it starts once more on the adventure. Again there are the reckless swoops downhill, bouncing the loops: again the chilly wait in the hill-top market-place: again the breathless slithering round the precipitous drop under the church: again the patient halts at the loops, waiting for the outcoming car: so on and on, for two long hours, till at last the city looms beyond the fat gas-works, the narrow factories draw near, we are in the sordid streets of the great town, once more we sidle to a standstill at our terminus, abashed by the great crimson and cream-coloured city cars, but still perky, jaunty, somewhat dare-devil, green as a jaunty sprig of parsley out of a black colliery garden.

To ride on these cars is always an adventure. Since we are in wartime, the drivers are men unfit for active service: cripples and hunchbacks. So they have

作者简介：D. H. 劳伦斯（David Herbert Lawrence, 1885—1930），英国短篇小说家、诗人和评论家。1885 年 9 月 11 日生于英国诺丁汉郡伊斯特伍德，1930 年 3 月 2 日卒于法国旺斯。他的第一部长篇小说是《白孔雀》（*The White Peacock*, 1911）。劳伦斯经常从他自己生活或者与周围人的生活中提取素材。《儿子和情人》（*Sons and Lovers*, 1913）是一部自传体小说，描写了工人阶级的家庭生活。《彩虹》（*Rainbow*, 1915）和《恋爱中的女人》（*Women in Love*, 1920）探讨了工业化对人们精神的影响而产生的现代文明的病态。《袋鼠》（*Kangaroo*, 1923）描述战争对他带来的迫害。《羽蛇》（*The Plumed Serpent*, 1926）的灵感来源于他对阿兹特克文化的热爱。他的作品以张力和牲描写著称。他的几部作品如《查泰莱夫人的情人》（*Lady Chatterley's Lover*, 1928）曾因淫秽被禁。

司机都是些不适于做大活动量工作的男人，像跛子和驼子。因此，他们身上都具有一种魔鬼的精神。坐车变成了障碍越野赛。哦！我们利索地纵身一跳，便跃过了运河大桥——现在该向交叉路口进发了。随着一声嘶鸣和一道亮光划过，我们又过去了。说实在的，有轨车经常脱轨，可这又有什么呢？它蹲在一条沟里，一直等到其他有轨车来把它拖出去。

在难以冲破的黑夜中，一辆车，实实足足地塞满了大活人，会一下子动不了了，像这种事也是司空见惯的。在这黑沉沉的深夜，前不着村后不着店，司机和女售票员会突然大喊起来：“全下去——车着火了！”可是乘客们非但没有惊恐地冲下车，反倒无动于衷地回敬他们：“上车——上车！我们不下。就在这儿待着吧！加油！乔治！”就这样一直待到火苗真的蹿了起来。

他们之所以不愿下车，是因为在这大风呼号、冰冷漆黑的夜里，一辆车就是一个避风港。矿工们从这个村跑到那个村，就是为了换个电影院，换个姑娘，或是换个酒馆。每辆车都拼命地塞满了人，谁愿意就因为车子出了点毛病而冒险跑到外面幽黑的荒野中去等待？没准还得再等上一个小时才来下一趟车，而看到的竟是车上那倒霉的牌子：“到站才停”。谁愿意冒险去迎候那灯光辉煌却也拥挤不堪的三节厢有轨车，而听着它发出一声嘲笑的鸣叫疾驰而过呢？深夜里来往的车啊，你只能听到它的声音。

正如官方人士骄傲地宣称的那样，这种英格兰最危险的有轨车上的售票员全部由姑娘们担任。司机是些腿脚不便的愣小伙，再不就是些柔弱有病的年轻人，战战兢兢地开着车向前爬行。而女孩子却是些天不怕地不怕的野姑娘。别看她们身着难看的蓝色制服，裙子都遮不住膝盖，头顶没有模样的旧尖顶帽，可身上却都有一种老兵油子式的沉着和自信。虽然车上挤满了吵吵嚷嚷的矿工，下边一层吼着赞美诗，上边一层此起彼伏地哼着淫荡小曲儿，这些小姑娘却都安然自得。她们猛地扑向那些不买票就想混下车的小青年，而对那些到站该下车的男人却是一阵好搡。她们眼里可不揉沙子——别想找她们的便宜。她们谁也不怕——可人人都怕她们。

“喂，安妮！”

“喂，特德！”

“哦，我有鸡眼，斯通①小姐！我敢担保你的心准

_____

① 斯通（Stone），英国姓，在英文中有“石头”的意思。

the spirit of the devil in them. The ride becomes a steeple-chase. Hurray! we have leapt in a clear jump over the canal bridges—now for the four-lane corner. With a shriek and a trail of sparks we are clear again. To be sure, a tram often leaps the rails—but what matter! It sits in a ditch till other trams come to haul it out. It is quite common for a car, packed with one solid mass of living people, to come to a dead halt in the midst of unbroken blackness, the heart of nowhere on a dark night, and for the driver and the girl conductor to call, "All get off—car-'s on fire!" Instead, however, of rushing out in a panic, the passengers stolidly reply: "Get on—get on! We're not coming out. We're stopping where we are. Push on, George." So till flames actually appear.

The reason for this reluctance to dismount is that the nights are howlingly cold, black, and windswept, and a car is a haven of refuge. From village to village the miners travel, for a change of cinema, of girl, of pub. The trams are desperately packed. Who is going to risk himself in the black gulf outside, to wait perhaps an hour for another tram, then to see the forlorn notice "Depot Only," because there is something wrong! or to greet a unit of three bright cars all so tight with people that they sail past with a howl of derision. Trams that pass in the night.

This, the most dangerous tram-service in England, as the authorities themselves declare, with pride, is entirely conducted by girls, and driven by rash young men, a little crippled, or by delicate young men, who creep forward in terror. The girls are fearless young hussies. In their ugly blue uniform, skirts up to their knees, shapeless old peaked caps on their heads, they have all the sang-froid of an old non-commissioned officer. With a tram packed with howling colliers, roaring hymns downstairs and a sort of antiphony of obscenities upstairs, the lasses are perfectly at their ease. They pounce on the youths who try to evade their ticket-machine. They push off the men at the end of their distance. They are not going to be done in the eye—not they. They fear nobody—and everybody fears them.

"Hello, Annie!"

"Hello, Ted!"

"Oh, mind my corn, Miss Stone. It's my belief you've got a heart of stone, for you've trod on it again."

"You should keep it in your pocket," replies Miss Stone, and she goes sturdily upstairs in her high boots.

是石头做的,你看你又踩着我了。"

"你该把脚丫子装在兜儿里。"斯通小姐回敬了一句,抬起高筒靴迈着刚健的步伐到上层去了。

"哪位没买票?请买票啦!"

她坚毅专横,疑心很重,时刻准备主动出击。她一个人能抵挡上万人。车上的踏板就是她的塞莫波雷隘口①。

然而,在这些车上,在安妮坚实的胸膛里。有着某种热烈的罗曼蒂克气氛。上午 10 点到 1 点之间,工作相当清闲,这也就是轻松浪漫的时刻了。不过,赶集日和星期六除外。这时,安妮便有时间环顾一下四周了。司机们正在大马路上聊天,此刻她通常是跳下车,钻进一家她看好了什么东西的商店。姑娘们和司机关系融洽。他们这只历经艰险的大船——有轨车——满载货物,无休止地在陆地的风暴波涛中颠簸,那么,他们难道不是同舟共济的伙伴吗?

而且,检票员也多半在这清闲的时候出现。鉴于某种原因,这条线路上的工作人员都很年轻,没有也不会有鬓发灰白的老翁。因而检票员也都是风华正茂,而且其中有一个,就是那个检票领班,还很漂亮。那是个潮湿阴沉的早晨,只见他身裹一件长长的油布雨衣,尖顶帽低低地压在眼眉上,站在那里等车。他面色红润,棕色小胡子上沾着露水,脸上挂着一丝粗野无礼的微笑。即便是穿着雨衣,他也显得相当高大敏捷。他跳上车和安妮打招呼:

"喂,安妮!没淋湿吧?"

"还好。"

车上只有两个人。查票工作很快就结束了。随之而来的便是踏板上毫无顾忌的一路长谈,一场很好、很轻松、长达 12 英里的闲聊。

这位检票员名叫约翰·托马斯·雷诺——人们总是叫他约翰·托马斯②,除非有时出于恶意,叫他科迪③。如果有人远远地用这个简称叫他,他就会勃然大怒。有半打村子里都流传着他那为数不算少的丑闻。他早晨和女售票员调情,晚上待她们离开车场后,又缠着要同她们一起去"散步"。当然了,这就不

---

① 塞莫波雷,希腊山中的一个关隘,古希腊人和波斯人曾在此大战。

② 约翰·托马斯(John Thomas),这是诨名,意思是"风流鬼"。

③ 科迪(Coddy),意为"色鬼"。

"Tickets, please."

She is peremptory, suspicious, and ready to hit first. She can hold her own against ten thousand. The step of that tram-car is her Thermopylae.

Therefore, there is a certain wild romance aboard these cars—and in the sturdy bosom of Annie herself. The time for soft romance is in the morning, between ten o'clock and one, when things are rather slack: that is, except market-day and Saturday. Thus Annie has time to look about her. Then she often hops off her car and into a shop where she has spied something, while the driver chats in the main road. There is very good feeling between the girls and the drivers. Are they not companions in peril, shipments aboard this careering vessel of a tram-car, for ever rocking on the waves of a stormy land.

Then, also, during the easy hours, the inspectors are most in evidence. For some reason, everybody employed in this tram-service is young: there are no grey heads. It would not do. Therefore the inspectors are of the right age, and one, the chief, is also good-looking. See him stand on a wet, gloomy morning, in his long oilskin, his peaked cap well down over his eyes, waiting to board a car. His face is ruddy, his small brown moustache is weathered, he has a faint impudent smile. Fairly tall and agile, even in his waterproof, he springs aboard a car and greets Annie.

"Hello, Annie! Keeping the wet out?"

"Trying to."

There are only two people in the car. Inspecting is soon over. Then for a long and impudent chat on the footboard, a good, easy, twelve-mile chat.

The inspector's name is John Thomas Raynor—always called John Thomas, except sometimes, in malice, Coddy. His face sets in fury when he is addressed, from a distance, with this abbreviation. There is considerable scandal about John Thomas in half a dozen villages. He flirts with the girl conductors in the morning and walks out with them in the dark night, when they leave their tram-car at the depot. Of course, the girls quit the service frequently. Then he flirts and walks out with the newcomer: always providing she is sufficiently attractive, and that she will consent to walk. It is remarkable, however, that most of the girls are quite comely, they are all young, and this roving life aboard the car gives them a sailor's dash and recklessness. What matter how they behave

断导致一些姑娘离去。于是他又与新来的姑娘故伎重演，不过也总得这个姑娘相当漂亮，而且，她也是同意去"散步"的。值得一提的是，这儿的大部分姑娘都非常年轻标致，这种乘着车子四处飘荡的生活赋予她们水手般大无畏的气魄。船停泊在港口，她们在岸上举止如何又有什么关系呢？明天她们就会又回到甲板上去了。

　　然而，安妮颇有点儿鞑靼人①的味道，而且，几个月来，她那条锋利的舌头一直使约翰·托马斯不敢近前。不过，她可能为此反倒更加喜欢他了。他走来时总是面带微笑，笑容里有一股厚颜无耻的劲头。她注视着他征服一个又一个姑娘。早上，在他和安妮调情时，安妮可以根据他的嘴角和眼神，说出他在前一天晚上曾和这个或那个姑娘出去过。他真可谓是个唐璜式的人物。安妮算是把他看透了。

　　在这种微妙的对峙气氛中，他们宛若是两个老友，彼此了如指掌，而相互关系中的那种敏感狡黠则几乎像夫妻之间一样。但安妮总是与他保持一段距离。况且，她还有自己的男朋友呢。

　　斯达秋兹游艺会11月份在比斯特伍德举行。安妮正好在星期一晚上休班。那天晚上，气候恶劣，细雨霏霏，可她还是装扮一番，上游艺会去了。她只身前往，盼望能很快结交一个什么朋友。

　　游艺转台转来转去，吱吱啦啦地放出"音乐"，杂耍表演热闹非常。在打椰棚②里没有椰子，而是些战争时期的人造代用品，孩子们说那是用铁丝绑上的。可悲的是，远不如以前那样光彩夺目、华贵奢侈了。然而，那地面却仍像过去一样泥泞，仍旧是拥挤的人群和在灯火辉映下攒聚的面孔。空气中仍充斥着那种石脑油、马铃薯和电器的混合味道。

　　安妮小姐在游艺场里第一个碰到的不是别人，偏偏是约翰·托马斯。他身穿一件黑色大衣，扣子一直系到下巴，头戴一顶苏格兰呢帽，低低地压在眼眉上。帽子和大衣中间的一张脸红腻腻的，像往常一样微笑着，还是那么活泼。他的嘴角会怎么挑动，安妮是再清楚不过的了。

　　她非常高兴能有个"男孩子"陪她。到游艺场来

---

①　鞑靼人，以性情暴躁著称。
②　打椰棚，游艺场里搭的一种供游艺的棚子，可以在里面用球投掷树上的椰子，以打掉为胜。

when the ship is in port. Tomorrow they will be a-board again.

Annie, however, was something of a Tartar, and her sharp tongue had kept John Thomas at arm's length for many months. Perhaps, therefore, she liked him all the more: for he always came up smiling, with impudence. She watched him vanquish one girl, then another. She could tell by the movement of his mouth and eyes, when he flirted with her in the morning, that he had been walking out with this lass, or the other, the night before. A fine cock-of-the-walk he was. She could sum him up pretty well.

In this subtle antagonism they knew each other like old friends, they were as shrewd with one another almost as man and wife. But Annie had always kept him sufficiently at arm's length. Besides, she had a boy of her own.

The Statutes fair, however, came in November, at Bestwood. It happened that Annie had the Monday night off. It was a drizzling ugly night, yet she dressed herself up and went to the fair ground. She was alone, but she expected soon to find a pal of some sort.

The roundabouts were veering round and grinding out their music, the side shows were making as much commotion as possible. In the cocoanut shies there were no cocoanuts, but artificial war-time substitutes, which the lad declared were fastened into the irons. There was a sad decline in brilliance and luxury. None the less, the ground was muddy as ever, there was the same crush, the press of faces lighted up by the flares and the electric lights, the same smell of naphtha and a few fried potatoes, and of electricity.

Who should be the first to greet Miss Annie, on the show ground, but John Thomas. He had a black overcoat buttoned up to his chin, and a tweed cap pulled down over his brows, his face between was ruddy and smiling and handy as ever. She knew so well the way his mouth moved.

She was very glad to have a "boy." To be at the Statutes without a fellow was no fun. Instantly, like the gallant he was, he took her on the Dragons, grim-toothed, roundabout switchbacks. It was not nearly so exciting as a tram-car actually. But, then, to be seated in a shaking green dragon, uplifted above the sea of bubble faces, careering in a rickety fashion in the lower heavens, whilst John Thomas leaned over her, his cigarette in his mouth, was after all the right style. She

玩,没有个伴儿多没意思。约翰·托马斯很会讨女人的欢心,他马上就带她去乘小火车——那条龇牙咧嘴、绕来绕去的铁龙。实际上,坐这玩意儿并不像坐有轨车那样令人激动。然而,坐在摇晃的绿色铁龙里,浮游在人头攒动的海洋之上,东倒西歪地在低空中疾驰,同时,还有叼着香烟的约翰·托马斯俯在她的头上,这对她来说,是件最对口味的事。她是个丰满、灵巧、活泼的姑娘,因此,她颇为激动,心里非常高兴。

约翰·托马斯拉着她又坐了一圈。这样,当约翰·托马斯这么温柔抚爱地挽住她,把她搂得更靠近自己时,她怎么好拒人于千里之外呢?况且,他还是小心翼翼的,一切都做得尽量不太唐突。她低头看了看,看见他那只红润漂亮的手并没有露在人们的视野之中。他们相互真是太了解了。因此,他们一心兴致勃勃地逛游艺场。

乘完铁龙,他们又去骑木马。每次都是约翰·托马斯付钱,所以,她只能表现得很温顺了。约翰·托马斯当然是骑靠外侧的那匹马了——马的名字叫"黑拜斯"——而她呢,则脸朝他侧身坐在里侧的马上——马的名字叫"野火"。约翰·托马斯当然也不会抓着铜扶手、规规矩矩地骑在"黑拜斯"身上。他们在灯光下飞快地旋转着,起伏着。他一边转,一边在木马上打旋,抬起一条腿从安妮的坐骑上抢过,然后,半仰着朝她大笑,那条腿在空中可怕地踢上踹下。他兴高采烈。安妮呢,唯恐自己的帽子歪到一边去了,她感到兴奋异常。

他投套圈给她赢来了两个浅蓝色的帽卡子。这时,他们听到电影院里传来下一场电影的预报,便爬上台阶,走进影院。

当然了,放映时机器经常会出毛病,影院里不断出现伸手不见五指的黑暗。于是场里便会发出一阵狂喊,同时是一片喷喷的响亮的接吻声。此时,约翰·托马斯便把安妮搂过来。不管怎么说,他的拥抱给姑娘一种温暖舒适的感觉,仿佛总是那样自然,恰到好处。而且,这种搂抱令人心旷神怡,又惬意,又温暖,又美好。他俯下身来,安妮感觉到了他的呼吸,她明白,他是想吻她的嘴唇。他是那样的热烈,安妮又是那样娇弱地依偎着他。总而言之,安妮希望他吻她。

但灯光一下亮了,安妮像触电一样抬起身,扶正

was a plump, quick, alive little creature. So she was quite excited and happy.

John Thomas made her stay on for the next round. And therefore she could hardly for shame repulse him when he put his arm round her and drew her a little nearer to him, in a very warm and cuddly manner. Besides, he was fairly discreet, he kept his movement as hidden as possible. She looked down and saw that his red, clean hand was out of sight of the crowd. And they knew each other so well. So they warmed up to the fair.

After the dragons they went on the horses. John Thomas paid each time, so she could but be complaisant. He, of course, sat astride on the outer horse—named "Black Bess"—and she sat sideways, towards him, on the inner horse—named " Wildfire. " But of course John Thomas was not going to sit discreetly on "Black Bess,"holding the brass bar. Round they spun and heaved, in the light. And round he swung on his wooden steed, flinging one leg across her mount, and perilously tipping up and down, across the space, half lying back, laughing at her. He was perfectly happy; she was afraid her hat was on one side, but she was excited.

He threw quoits on a table and won for her two large, pale-blue hatpins. And then, hearing the noise of the cinemas, announcing another performance, they climbed the boards and went in.

Of course, during these performances pitch darkness falls from time to time, when the machine goes wrong. Then there is a wild whooping, and a loud smacking of simulated kisses. In these moments John Thomas drew Annie towards him. After all, he had a wonderfully warm, cosy way of holding a girl with his arm, he seemed to make such a nice fit. And after all, it was pleasant to be so held: so very comforting and cosy and nice. He leaned over her and she felt his breath on her hair; she knew he wanted to kiss her on the lips. And after all, he was so warm and she fitted in to him so softly. After all, she wanted him to touch her lips.

But the light sprang up; she also started electrically, and put her hat straight. He left his arm lying nonchalantly behind her. Well, it was fun, it was exciting to be at the Statutes with John Thomas.

When the cinema was over they went for a walk across the dark, damp fields. He had all the arts of

帽子。约翰·托马斯随随便便地将手臂留在了安妮身后。啊,和约翰·托马斯一起逛游艺会多么有趣,多么激动人心啊。

电影散场后,他们漫步走过黑暗潮湿的田野。他懂得全部求爱的艺术。但他最擅长的是在黑茫茫、雨濛濛的夜晚搂抱着姑娘坐在篱笆梯磴①上,他的拥抱就好像把姑娘抱在空中,四周荡漾着他的温馨和喜悦。他的吻轻柔、缓慢,带着寻觅的味道。

于是安妮跟着约翰·托马斯走了,尽管她仍和她原来的男朋友保持着若即若离的关系。有些售票姑娘喜欢表现得桀骜不驯,但是在这个世间,这个问题上,你必须面对现实。

安妮非常喜欢约翰·托马斯,这是毫无疑问的。每当他来到她的身旁,她总是从心底里感到那么充实和温暖。约翰·托马斯也是真心喜欢安妮,比往常更甚。安妮能使男人筋酥骨软,神魂颠倒,就好像她融化进了他的身体一样。这可真是罕见而又令人销魂的。他对此赞赏不已。

随着不断的接触,他们之间产生了一种亲昵的关系,这种关系日益发展着。安妮想将他作为一个人,一个男人来看待,她要从各个方面了解他,也希望约翰·托马斯同样了解她。她不想只保持一种肉体关系,可到目前为止,约翰·托马斯仅限于此。安妮为约翰·托马斯离不开她而感到骄傲。

安妮在这里犯了一个错误。约翰·托马斯意在只保持这种关系,从未想过要成为安妮面面俱到、形影不离的伴侣。当安妮开始对他的精神世界、他的生活和他的性格发生兴趣时,他断然抛弃了她。他憎恨这种东西。并且他知道制止它的唯一办法就是避开它。安妮心中的那种女性占有欲被唤醒了。因此,约翰·托马斯离开了安妮。

要说安妮不感到惊讶,那是瞎说。一开始她感到震惊,慌了手脚,因为她一直极为自信她已经抓住了他。有一段时间,她不知所措,一切事物对她都变得捉摸不定。随后,她怀着一腔怒气、怨恨、凄凉和悲痛哭了一场。接着,她感到一阵绝望。事过之后,约翰·托马斯仍那样恬不知耻地来到她的车上,与她仍旧那样熟识亲密,但一举一动都向安妮显示出,他目

---

① 篱笆梯磴,为防范牲畜,只供人上下的放在篱笆两边的小梯子。

love-making. He was especially good at holding a girl, when he sat with her on a stile in the black, drizzling darkness. He seemed to be holding her in space, against his own warmth and gratification. And his kisses were soft and slow and searching.

So Annie walked out with John Thomas, though she kept her own boy dangling in the distance. Some of the tram-girls chose to be huffy. But there, you must take things as you find them, in this life.

There was no mistake about it, Annie liked John Thomas a good deal. She felt so rich and warm in herself whenever he was near. And John Thomas really liked Annie more than usual. The soft, melting way in which she could flow into a fellow, as if she melted into his very bones, was something rare and good. He fully appreciated this.

But with a developing acquaintance there began a developing intimacy. Annie wanted to consider him a person, a man; she wanted to take an intelligent interest in him, and to have an intelligent response. She did not want a mere nocturnal presence, which was what he was so far. And she prided herself that he could not leave her.

Here she made a mistake. John Thomas intended to remain a nocturnal presence; he had no idea of becoming an all-round individual to her. When she started to take an intelligent interest in him and his life and his character, he sheered off. He hated intelligent interest. And he knew that the only way to stop it was to avoid it. The possessive female was aroused in Annie. So he left her.

It is no use saying she was not surprised. She was at first startled, thrown out of her count. For she had been so *very* sure of holding him. For a while she was staggered, and everything became uncertain to her. Then she wept with fury, indignation, desolation, and misery. Then she had a spasm of despair. And then, when he came, still impudently, on to her car, still familiar, but letting her see by the movement of his head that he had gone away to somebody else for the time being and was enjoying pastures new, then she determined to have her own back.

She had a very shrewd idea what girls John Thomas had taken out. She went to Nora Purdy. Nora was a tall, rather pale, but well-built girl, with beautiful yellow hair. She was rather secretive.

"Hey!" said Annie, accosting her, then softly,

前又找到别人了,而且正在他新的征服领地里津津有味地享乐。此时,安妮才下决心一定要报复。

安妮清楚地知道约翰·托马斯都和哪些姑娘出去过。她找到娜拉·普尔蒂。娜拉是个细高、白皙而体态匀称的姑娘,有着一头美丽的金发,对一切都守口如瓶。

"喂!"安妮和她打招呼,然后轻声说,"约翰·托马斯又和谁勾搭上了?"

"我不知道。"娜拉说。

"得了,你知道,"安妮嘲弄地改用方言说,"你知道得和我一样清楚。"

"嗯,我知道,那又怎么样?"娜拉说,"反正不是我,你就别操心了。"

"是西西·米金,对吗?"

"就我所知,就是她。"

"他真不要脸!"安妮说,"我打心眼儿里讨厌他那个厚脸皮。他要找我,我就把他踢到踏脚板底下去。"

"没准哪天他真得挨上一顿揍。"娜拉说。

"哎,一定的。不过得等到有人真下决心教训他的时候,我真想亲眼看着扫扫他的威风,你呢?"

"我不反对。"娜拉说。

"你和我都有理由关心这件事,"安妮说,"哪天咱们揍他一顿,我的姑娘。什么?你不乐意?"

"我不反对。"娜拉说。

其实,娜拉比安妮更富有报复心。

安妮一个个地串通好了约翰·托马斯那些旧日的女友。事也凑巧,西西·米金很快就离开了车队。她母亲逼她走的。这时,约翰·托马斯又变得quivive① 起来了,他的眼光又投向他旧日的猎物,最后落到了安妮身上。他想安妮现在已经学乖了,况且,他还是喜欢她的。

安妮计划星期日晚上与约翰·托马斯一起回家。那天她的车正好九点半回到车场,而末班车要到十点一刻才到。所以,约翰·托马斯就得在那儿等她。

姑娘们在车场有一间自己的小休息室。那房子很简陋,但却舒适,屋里生着火,还有一只炉灶、一面镜子、一张桌子和几把木椅。有半打对约翰·托马斯了解得非常透彻的姑娘都设法倒成了这个星期日下午的班。开始收车了,这些姑娘们都聚到休息室里。

---

① quivive,法语,意为"蠢蠢欲动"。

"Who's John Thomas on with now?"

"I don't know," said Nora.

"Why tha does," said Annie, ironically lapsing into dialect. "Tha knows as well as I do."

"Well, I do, then," said Nora. "It isn't me, so don't bother."

"It's Cissy Meakin, isn't it?"

"It is, for all I know."

"Hasn't he got a face on him!" said Annie. "I don't half like his cheek. I could knock him off the footboard when he comes round at me."

"He'll get dropped-on one of these days," said Nora.

"Ay, he will when somebody makes up their mind to drop it on him. I should like to see him taken down a peg or two, shouldn't you?"

"I shouldn't mind," said Nora.

"You've got quite as much cause to as I have," said Annie. "But we'll drop on him one of these days, my girl. What? Don't you want to?"

"I don't mind," said Nora.

But as a matter of fact, Nora was much more vindictive than Annie.

One by one Annie went the round of the old flames. It so happened that Cissy Meakin left the tramway service in quite a short time. Her mother made her leave. Then John Thomas was on the qui-vive. He cast his eyes over his old flock. And his eyes lighted on Annie. He thought she would be safe now. Besides, he liked her.

She arranged to walk home with him on Sunday night. It so happened that her car would be in the depot at half-past nine: the last car would come in at ten-fifteen. So John Thomas was to wait for her there.

At the depot the girls had a little waiting-room of their own. It was quite rough, but cosy, with a fire and an oven and a mirror, and table and wooden chairs. The half dozen girls who knew John Thomas only too well had arranged to take service this Sunday afternoon. So, as the cars began to come in, early, the girls dropped into the waiting-room. And instead of hurrying off home, they sat around the fire and had a cup of tea. Outside was the darkness and lawlessness of war-time.

John Thomas came on the car after Annie, at about a quarter to ten. He poked his head easily into the girls' waiting-room.

她们并没有急着回家,而是围着火坐下,喝起茶来。外面是一片漆黑和战争时期的混乱。

约翰·托马斯乘安妮后面的一辆车回场,时间是差一刻十点。他随随便便地把脑袋探进姑娘们的休息室。

"在做祈祷吗?"他问了一句。

"嗳,"洛拉·夏波说,"只许妇女参加。"

"可这是我呀。"约翰·托马斯说。这是他最喜欢说的一句口头禅。

"关上门,小子。"缪丽尔·拜格莱说。

"噢,让我在门里还是在门外?"约翰·托马斯说。

"随你便吧。"波丽·博金说。

他进了屋,随手关上门。姑娘们挪动了一下,在靠火的地方给他腾出一个空儿来。他脱下大衣,把帽子往后一推。

"谁掌壶?"他说。

娜拉·普尔蒂默默地给他斟了一杯茶。

"想来点面包和烤肥肉吗?"缪丽尔·拜格莱问他。

"嗳,给我们来点吧。"

他吃起那块面包来。

"哪儿也不如家里好啊,姑娘们。"他说。

他吐出这么一句无耻的话,她们全看他。而他,在这么多姑娘的目光下显得得意洋洋,仿佛是在沐浴着温暖的阳光。

"要是你不怕摸黑回家的话。"洛拉·夏波说。

"我! 一个人走,我可害怕。"

他们一直坐到听见末班车进了场。几分钟之后,艾玛·赫斯蕾进来了。

"过来,老太婆。"波丽·博金喊了一声。

"真是冻死人了。"艾玛说着把手伸向火。

"可是……我害怕,天黑,回家。"洛拉·夏波唱起来,曲子自然而然地随口而出。

"你今晚和谁一起走,约翰·托马斯?"缪丽尔·拜格莱冷冷地问。

"今晚?"约翰·托马斯说,"噢,我今晚自己回家——我自个儿走。"

"可这是我呀。"娜拉·波蒂用他那句口头禅说。

姑娘们尖声笑起来。

"我跟你一样,娜拉。"约翰·托马斯说。

"不明白你什么意思。"洛拉说。

"Prayer-meeting?"he asked.

"Ay,"said Laura Sharp. "Ladies only. "

"That's me!"said John Thomas. It was one of his favourite exclamations.

"Shut the door,boy,"said Muriel Baggaley.

"On which side of me?"said John Thomas.

"Which tha likes,"said Polly Birkin.

He had come in and closed the door behind him. The girls moved in their circle,to make a place for him near the fire. He took off his greatcoat and pushed back his hat.

"Who handles the teapot?"he said.

Nora Purdy silently poured him out a cup of tea.

"Want a bit o' my bread and drippin'?"said Muriel Baggaley to him.

"Ay,give us a bit. "

And he began to eat his piece of bread.

"There's no place like home,girls,"he said.

They all looked at him as he uttered this piece of impudence. He seemed to be sunning himself in the presence of so many damsels.

"Especially if you're not afraid to go home in the dark,"said Laura Sharp.

"Me! By myself I am. "

They sat till they heard the last tram come in. In a few minutes Emma Houselay entered.

"Come on,my old duck!"cried Polly Birkin.

"It *is* perishing,"said Emma,holding her fingers to the fire.

"But—I'm afraid to,go home in,the dark,"sang Laura Sharp,the tune having got into her mind.

"Who're you going with tonight,John Thomas?" asked Muriel Baggaley,coolly.

"Tonight?" said John Thomas. "Oh,I'm going home by myself tonight—all on my lonely-O. "

"That's me!"said Nora Purdy,using his own ejaculation.

The girls laughed shrilly.

"Me as well,Nora,"said John Thomas.

"Don't know what you mean,"said Laura.

"Yes,I'm toddling,"said he,rising and reaching for his overcoat.

"Nay,"said Polly. "We're all here waiting for you. "

"We've got to be up in good time in the morning,"he said in the benevolent official manner.

They all laughed.

"Nay,"said Muriel. "Don't leave us all lonely,

"哎,我该颠儿了。"他说着站起身,伸手去拿大衣。

"别走,"波丽说,"我们都在这儿等你呢。"

"明天早上都还得早起呢。"他以一种长官的仁慈口吻说。

她们全部大笑起来。

"别呀,"缪丽尔说,"别让我们那么孤零零的,约翰·托马斯,带一个走!"

"如果你们愿意,我全都带走。"他殷勤地回答。

"那也不成,"缪丽尔说,"两人才配对,七人可太多了。"

"别呀——带一个,"洛拉说,"公平合理,漂到桌面上说,到底带哪个?"

"哎,"安妮喊起来,这是她第一次开口,"挑啊,约翰·托马斯,看你挑谁。"

"别这样,"他说,"我要安安静静地回家。我今晚感觉良好,就这一次。"

"去哪?"安妮说,"好好乐一乐嘛。你得从我们当中带一个走。"

"不行,我怎么能只带一个呢,"他不自然地笑着说,"我可不想结仇。"

"你只会和一个人结仇。"安妮说。

"就是你选中的那个。"洛拉补上一句。

"噢,我的天哪,谁说和姑娘结仇了!"约翰·托马斯惊叹了一声,转身又要溜,"好吧……晚安。"

"别走,你必须得挑一个,"缪丽尔说,"转过去,脸朝墙,说说看拍你的是谁。快点儿——我们只拍你的后背——我们当中的一个,快点儿——脸朝墙转过去,不许偷看! 说是谁拍你的。"

约翰·托马斯忐忑不安,也不相信她们。但又没有勇气逃出去。她们把他推到墙根下,让他脸朝墙站在那儿。她们在他背后做鬼脸,吃吃地笑着。他看上去非常可笑。他不安地环顾着四周。

"快点吧!"他叫了一声。

"你偷看……你偷看!"她们大喊起来。

他把头扭过去。突然,安妮就像一只猫,飞身上前,对着他的太阳穴狠狠一击,把他的帽子打飞了,人也跟跄了几步。他疾转过身来。

随着安妮的信号,姑娘们一齐扑上来,又是抽,又是掐,又是揪头发。她们虽然满腔怨恨,但更多的却是出于好玩。然而,约翰·托马斯却怒不可遏。他的蓝眼睛里燃烧着奇异的恐惧和愤怒的火焰。他低着

John Thomas. Take one!"

"I'll take the lot, if you like," he responded gallantly.

"That you won't, either," said Muriel. "Two's company; seven's too much of a good thing."

"Nay—take one," said Laura. "Fair and square, all above board, and say which."

"Ay," cried Annie, speaking for the first time. "Pick, John Thomas; let's hear thee."

"Nay," he said. "I'm going home quiet tonight. Feeling good, for once."

"Whereabouts?" said Annie. "Take a good un, then, But tha's got to take one of us!"

"Nay, how can I take *one*," he said, laughing uneasily. "I don't want to make enemies."

"You'd only make one," said Annie.

"The chosen *one*," added Laura.

"Oh, my! Who said girls!" exclaimed John Thomas, again turning, as if to escape. "Well—good-night."

"Nay, you've got to make your pick," said Muriel. "Turn your face to the wall and say which one touches you. Go on—we shall only just touch your back—one of us. Go on—turn your face to the wall, and don't look, and say which one touches you."

He was uneasy, mistrusting them. Yet he had not the courage to break away. They pushed him to a wall and stood him there with his face to it. Behind his back they all grimaced, tittering. He looked so comical. He looked around uneasily.

"Go on!" he cried.

"You're looking—you're looking!" they shouted.

He turned his head away. And suddenly, with a movement like a swift cat, Annie went forward and fetched him a box on the side of the head that set his cap flying, and himself staggering. He started round.

But at Annie's signal they all flew at him, slapping him, pinching him, pulling his hair, though more in fun than in spite or anger. He, however, saw red. His blue eyes flamed with strange fear as well as fury, and he butted through the girls to the door. It was locked. He wrenched at it. Roused, alert, the girls stood round and looked at him. He faced them, at bay. At that moment they were rather horrifying to him, as they stood in their short uniforms. He was distinctly afraid.

"Come on, John Thomas! Come on! Choose!" said Annie.

"What are you after? Open the door," he said.

"We sha'n't—not till you've chosen!" said Muriel.

头冲出姑娘们的包围,跑到门前,但门已经锁上了。他使劲拧动门锁。姑娘们振作精神,警觉地站在周围盯着他。他面对她们,准备决一死战。此刻,这些穿短制服的姑娘使他毛骨悚然。显然,他害怕了。

"来啊,约翰·托马斯! 来啊,挑啊!"安妮说。

"你们这是要干什么? 开门。"他说。

"我们不开——直到你挑完了才开!"缪丽尔说。

"挑什么?"他说。

"挑一个你要跟她结婚的。"她回答说。

他犹豫了一下。

"开开这该死的门!"他说,"都清醒清醒。"他带着长官的口气说。

"你必须得挑。"姑娘们嚷着。

"快啊!"安妮盯着他的眼睛大叫了一声,"快啊! 快啊!"

他漫无目的地朝前走了几步,安妮解下了腰带在手里抢着。她用皮带扣在他头上狠狠一抽。他一蹿身抓住了安妮。但其他的姑娘们顿时一拥而上,又揪又撕又打。她们热血沸腾。他现在成了她们手中的玩物,她们要报仇雪恨。她们就像一群奇怪的疯狂的野兽,有的吊在他身上,有的扑将上来要把他掀倒在地。他的外衣从后背一撕两半。娜拉揪住他的后衣领,简直要把他勒死。幸运的是,扣子绷开了。他死命地挣扎,又是狂怒又是恐惧,恐惧得简直要发疯。他的外衣后片整个被撕掉了。衬衣袖子也撕掉了,只剩下裸露的手臂。姑娘们扑到他身上,攥起拳头搐他,拽他,或者是扑向他,推他,使尽全身力气用头撞他,再不就是抢开了揍他。他缩着头,吓得东躲西藏,左冲右撞。这更激怒了姑娘们。

他终于倒下了。她们扑上去,用膝盖压住他,约翰·托马斯再也没有气力动弹了。他脸上不知被谁抓了长长的一道,鲜血淋漓,眼睛也打青了。

安妮跪在他身上,其他的姑娘也都用膝盖顶着他,不离左右。她们满脸通红,披头散发,眼睛里闪着奇特的光芒。他总算躺在那儿不大动了。只有脸左右躲避着,就像一头被击中的躺在猎人脚下的动物。他有时向上瞥一眼姑娘们激动的脸庞。他的胸口剧烈地起伏着,手腕也扭伤了。

"现在,喂,伙计,"安妮终于气喘吁吁地说,"现在,喂……现在……"

听见她那冰冷可怕的、胜利者的声音,约翰·托

"Chosen what?"he said.

"Chosen the one you're going to marry,"she replied.

He hesitated a moment.

"Open the blasted door,"he said,"and get back to your senses."He spoke with official authority.

"You've got to choose!"cried the girls.

"Come on!"cried Annie,looking him in the eye. "Come on! Come on!"

He went forward,rather vaguely. She had taken off her belt,and swinging it,she fetched him a sharp blow over the head with the buckle end. He sprang and seized her. But immediately the other girls rushed upon him,pulling and tearing and beating him. Their blood was now thoroughly up. He was their sport now. They were going to have their own back,out of him. Strange,wild creatures,they hung on him and rushed at him to bear him down. His tunic was torn right up the back,Nora had hold at the back of his collar,and was actually strangling him. Luckily the button burst. He struggled in a wild frenzy of fury and terror,almost mad terror. His tunic was simply torn off his back,his shirtsleeves were torn away,his arms were naked. The girls rushed at him,clenched their hands on him and pulled at him;or they rushed at him and pushed him,butted him with all their might;or they struck him wild blows. He ducked and cringed and struck sideways. They became more intense.

At last he was down. They rushed on him,kneeling on him. He had neither breath nor strength to move. His face was bleeding with a long scratch,his brow was bruised.

Annie knelt on him,the other girls knelt and hung on to him. Their faces were flushed,their hair wild,their eyes were all glittering strangely. He lay at last quite still,with face averted,as an animal lies when it is defeated and at the mercy of the captor. Sometimes his eye glanced back at the wild faces of the girls. His breast rose heavily,his wrists were torn.

"Now,then,my fellow!"gasped Annie at length. "Now then—now—"

At the sound of her terrifying,cold triumph,he suddenly started to struggle as an animal might,but the girls threw themselves upon him with unnatural strength and power,forcing him down.

"Yes—now,then!"gasped Annie at length.

And there was a dead silence,in which the thud of heart-beating was to be heard. It was a suspense of pure silence in every soul.

马斯突然像头野兽似的，又开始挣扎，但姑娘们再次以一种非凡的力量扑上来，把他压下去。

"对……现在，喂！"安妮总算气喘吁吁地吐出几个字。

屋里死样的沉寂，静得能听见心脏的跳动。这是每个人的灵魂停滞时产生的一种真空般的静谧。

"现在你该懂了吧。"安妮说。

姑娘们看见他那白皙裸露的手臂更加疯狂了。他昏昏沉沉地躺在地上，恐惧和仇恨交织在一起。姑娘们感到自己充满了神奇的力量。

突然，波丽放声大笑——疯狂地咯咯大笑——不由自主地大笑，艾玛和缪丽尔也跟着笑起来。但是安妮、娜拉和洛拉仍保持原状，紧张、警觉，眼睛闪闪发光。他避开了她们的眼光。

"对了，"安妮悄悄地、咬牙切齿地说，声音低得出奇，"对了！这回你知道厉害了吧。你都干过什么，你心里明白，是不是？你心里明白。"

他一声不吭地躺在那里，只有两眼熠熠发光。他把血淋淋的脸扭向一边。

"早该把你杀死，那才是你应得的下场，"安妮狠狠地说，"早该把你杀死。"她的声音里有一和令人不寒而栗的渴望。

波丽慢慢恢复了平静。她停住笑，嘴里发出长长的嘘声和叹息。

"他必须挑。"她发出含含糊糊的声音。

"噢，对了，他必须挑。"洛拉不依不饶地说。

"你听见了吗……你听见了吗？"安妮说着，猛一下把他的脸转过来。他疼得抽动了一下。

"你听见没有？"她摇着他又问了一遍。

但是他木木然一言不发。她给了他一记响亮的耳光。他一惊，眼睛猛地睁大了，随即他的脸色又暗淡下来，带着一丝蔑视。

"你听见没有？"她又重复了一遍。

他只是用敌对的眼光望着她。

"说呀！"她将脸凑上去，贴近他的脸恶狠狠地说。

"什么？"他说，几乎精疲力竭了。

"你必须得挑！"她叫喊着，就好像这句话是一种什么可怕的威胁，就好像它伤害她已经到了无以复加的程度。

"什么？"他恐惧地说。

"挑你的姑娘，科迪，你必须现在就挑。你要是还

"Now you know where you are," said Annie.

The sight of his white, bare arm maddened the girls. He lay in a kind of trance of fear and antagonism. They felt themselves filled with supernatural strength.

Suddenly Polly started to laugh—to giggle wildly—helplessly—and Emma and Muriel joined in. But Annie and Nora and Laura remained the same, tense, watchful, with gleaming eyes. He winced away from these eyes.

"Yes," said Annie, in a curious low tone, secret and deadly. "Yes! You've got it now! You know what you've done, don't you? You know what you've done."

He made no sound nor sign, but lay with bright, averted eyes, and averted, bleeding face.

"You ought to be *killed* that's what you ought," said Annie tensely. "You ought to be *killed*." And there was a terrifying lust in her voice.

Polly was ceasing to laugh, and giving long-drawn oh-h-hs and sighs as she came to herself.

"He's got to choose," she said vaguely.

"Oh, yes, he has," said Laura, with vindictive decision.

"Do you hear—do you hear?" said Annie. And with a sharp movement that made him wince, she turned his face to her.

"Do you hear?" she repeated, shaking him.

But he was quite dumb. She fetched him a sharp slap on the face. He started, and his eyes widened. Then his face darkened with defiance, after all.

"Do you hear?" she repeated.

He only looked at her with hostile eyes.

"Speak!" she said, putting her face devilishly near his.

"What?" he said, almost overcome.

"You've got to *choose*!" she cried, as if it were some terrible menace, and as if it hurt her that she could not exact more.

"What?" he said in fear.

"Choose your girl, Coddy. You've got to choose her now. And you'll get your neck broken if you play any more of your tricks, my boy. You're settled now."

There was a pause. Again he averted his face. He was cunning in his overthrow. He did not give in to them really—no, not if they tore him to bits.

"All right, then," he said, "I choose Annie." His

不老实,小子,就拧断你的脖子。你已经完了。"

短时间的沉默。他又把脸掉开了。尽管他被打败了,但仍很狡猾。他并没有真的向她们屈服——不,就是她们把他撕成碎片,他也不会屈服。

"那好吧,"他说,"我挑安妮。"他冷冷的声音里满含着仇恨。安妮仿佛被烫了似的,一下子松开他。

"他挑中了安妮!"姑娘们异口同声地说。

"我!"安妮叫起来。她仍然跪着,但已经离开了他。他还是仰面朝天地躺在那儿,脸扭向一边。姑娘们不安地围拢过来。

"我!"安妮又说了一遍,声音里有一种凄惨的苦涩。

然后她站起身,带着令人感到陌生的厌恶和痛苦朝后退去。

"我才不要碰他呢。"安妮说。

她的脸由于痛苦而抽搐着,仿佛要跌倒。其他姑娘都背过脸去。他仍然躺在地上,衣服破烂不堪,脸上鲜血淋淋。

"哦,如果他已经挑好了……"波丽说。

"我不要他……他可以再挑一次。"安妮说,依然是那样痛苦、绝望。

"起来,"波丽说着,拉起他的肩膀,"起来。"

他慢慢地爬起来。一个衣衫褴褛、摇摇晃晃的怪物。姑娘们悄悄地从远处好奇而凶狠地看着他。

"谁要他?"洛拉粗暴地喊了一声。

"没人要。"她们鄙夷地回答。然而每个人又都等着他看自己,希望他能够看她。所有的人都这样盼着,只有安妮除外。她心中有某种东西破碎了。

然而,他埋着头,不看任何人。一切都结束似的寂然无声。他从地上拾起他的衣服碎片,不知如何是好。姑娘们不安地站在周围,满脸通红,喘息不定,下意识地整理着自己的头发和衣服,而眼睛却望着他。他谁也不看。他发现自己的帽子丢在一个角落里,便走过去捡起来,戴上。见到他这副模样,一个姑娘爆发出一阵歇斯底里的尖笑。可他毫不理会,径直朝挂着大衣的挂钩走去。姑娘们触电似的闪开路,免得碰到他。他穿上大衣,扣子一直扣到底。接着,他把碎布片团成一卷,呆呆地立在锁着的门前。

"谁把门开开。"洛拉说。

"安妮拿着钥匙呢。"一个姑娘说。

安妮默默地把钥匙递给姑娘们。娜拉打开了门。

voice was strange and full of malice. Annie let go of him as if he had been a hot coal.

"He's chosen Annie!"said the girls in chorus.

"Me!"cried Annie. She was still kneeling, but away from him. He was still lying prostrate, with averted face. The girls grouped uneasily around.

"Me!"repeated Annie, with a terrible bitter accent.

Then she got up, drawing away from him with strange disgust and bitterness.

"I wouldn't touch him,"she said.

But her face quivered with a kind of agony, she seemed as if she would fall. The other girls turned aside. He remained lying on the floor, with his torn clothes and bleeding, averted face.

"Oh, if he's chosen—"said Polly.

"I don't want him—he can choose again," said Annie, with the same rather bitter hopelessness.

"Get up," said Polly, lifting his shoulder. "Get up."

He rose slowly, a strange, ragged, dazed creature. The girls eyed him from a distance, curiously, furtively, dangerously.

"Who wants him?"cried Laura roughly.

"Nobody," they answered with contempt. Yet each one of them waited for him to look at her, hoped he would look at her. All except Annie, and something was broken in her.

He, however, kept his face closed and averted from them all. There was a silence of the end. He picked up the torn pieces of his tunic, without knowing what to do with them. The girls stood about uneasily, flushed, panting, tidying their hair and their dress unconsciously, and watching him. He looked at none of them. He espied his cap in a corner and went and picked it up. He put it on his head, and one of the girls burst into a shrill, hysteric laugh at the sight he presented. He, however, took no heed but went straight to where his overcoat hung on a peg. The girls moved away from contact with him as if he had been an electric wire. He put on his coat and buttoned it down. Then he rolled his tunicrags into a bundle, and stood before the locked door, dumbly.

"Open the door, somebody,"said Laura.

"Annie's got the key,"said one.

Annie silently offered the key to the girls. Nora unlocked the door.

"Tit for tat, old man,"she said. "Show yourself a

"一报还一报,老伙计,"她说,"像个男子汉,别记仇。"

但他没有任何反应,只是打开门,毫无表情地耷拉着头走了。

"这回可教训他了。"洛拉说。

"科迪!"娜拉说。

"闭嘴吧,看上帝的份儿上!"安妮恶狠狠地嚷着,仿佛正受着煎熬。

"好吧,我该走了,波丽。赶快!"缪丽尔说。

姑娘们都急于离开。她们匆忙地收拾着,脸上带着呆痴麻木的神情。

man,and don't bear a grudge."

But without a word or sign he had opened the door and gone,his face closed,his head dropped.

"That'll learn him,"said Laura.

"Coddy!"said Nora.

"Shut up,for God's sake!"cried Annie fiercely,as if in torture.

"Well,I'm about ready to go,Polly. Look sharp!" said Muriel.

The girls were all anxious to be off. They were tidying themselves hurriedly, with mute, stupefied faces.

讨　论

这篇小说的故事很简单。一个名叫约翰·托马斯的年轻电车线路监票员勾搭上了一个名叫安妮的年轻女售票员,而当他知道安妮在认真对待他的好感时,他又抛弃了她。安妮纠合了一些曾受过约翰·托马斯同样对待的姑娘一起商定给他点儿厉害瞧瞧。她们虽然揍了他几下而且还撕破了他的短上衣,但并没有伤得他很厉害。约翰·托马斯走了。姑娘们呢,却对自己的所作所为感到惶惑不解,有点儿昏昏然,甚至有点儿惧怕。

这篇小说虽然安置了许多情节,甚至有剧烈的情节,却没有什么结局。约翰·托马斯和安妮可以推知会各走各的路。小说也确是用一句悬而未决的话来结束的。粗心的读者很可能会因小说的这种结尾感到茫然,从而对它不加理会。

但是细心的读者可能会觉得,这篇小说的内在情节才是至关重要的。确实,就是这种戛然中止的结尾,暗示出某种剧烈的心理变迁。姑娘们进入了她们无法自制的境地,发现她们对约翰·托马斯的感情竟远甚于报复时那种颇为泼辣的狂热。约翰·托马斯走后,作者在小说的最后一句里告诉我们,姑娘们脸上都露出了"呆痴麻木的神情"。

The plot of this story is quite simple. One of the young inspectors of the tram line, John Thomas, begins to go out with Annie, one of the girl conductors. He drops her when he realizes that she is taking his attentions seriously. Annie arranges a meeting with the other girls whom he has treated in this fashion, and they join her in roughing him up. They do not seriously hurt him, though they get in some blows and they tear his tunic. John Thomas leaves, and the girls find themselves nonplussed at what they have done, a little dazed, and even a little frightened.

Though the story presents a good deal of action, even violent action, not very much has been resolved. Presumably John Thomas and Annie will continue to go their separate ways. Indeed, the story ends on a note of uneasy irresolution. The superficial reader may even be baffled by the ending of the story and so dismiss it.

Other readers, however, may feel that the internal action is important. Indeed, the very debacle of the ending points toward an exciting psychological development. The girls have got in over their depth and find that their emotions toward John Thomas are in excess of, and indeed widely different from, the rather tomboyish triumph of their revenge. As the author tells us in the last sentence, after John Thomas's departure, the girls wear "mute, stupified faces."

这篇小说在对那种可称之为爱情的"双重性"——即在恋爱中表现出来的那种既主动又被动、既残忍又温柔、既想占有又想背弃的奇怪而复杂的感情——进行一连串生动描写的过程中展示出丰富的内容。小说里所有的人物都或多或少经受着这些矛盾的感情,但是作者又严格地把焦点集中在安妮这个特殊人物身上。她比其他人更深地卷入其中,所以她不仅比其他人对这种经验更有感受,而且在这种经验里比其他人更加无可奈何地受着种种相互矛盾的冲动的支配。

安妮究竟想从她对约翰·托马斯的恶作剧中得到什么呢?从有意识方面讲,可以推知她只想让他当着所有姑娘的面出丑,使他受到她们的嘲笑而已。但是,在无意识当中,安妮肯定还有更多的欲求——这一点只要我们根据小说后面实际上发生的情形来加以判断即可明白。可以肯定,她极希望能和他分明对抗——包括肉体上的对抗关系。她也极希望得到机会以发泄一下自己因受伤而产生的愤恨之感,恶作剧便给了她想这样做的合适途径。而在心底里,她或许正希望着能听到他叫她的名字而选定她——如果一有这种机会她便要对他说,她对他丝毫也不感兴趣。但是,无论是安妮还是其他姑娘实际上都没有考虑过,她们这样恶作剧究竟想达到何种目的或者表示何种意思。

上面最后一点已经很清楚,所以我们也已经明白,她们之中是谁也不知道该怎样来结束这出闹剧的。她们一度这样做了,而她们的行为实际上是出于感情冲动,出于性要求,而从某种意义上说,也正是这种性要求使姑娘们感到惶惑甚至感到惧怕。她们既然使自己陷入了她们自己也不理解的疯狂迷乱之中,那么这种情形或许也只能以最剧烈的行为来加以终结。安妮打在约翰·托马斯脸颊上的那一拳很可能比她原先设想的要重。这点表明,姑娘们攻击约翰·托马斯"与其说是怨恨或者愤怒

The story derives much of its richness from the fact that it succeeds in dramatizing what may be called the "doubleness" of love— its strange mixture of aggressiveness and passivity, of cruelty and tenderness, of possessiveness and surrender. All the characters in the story experience something of these contradictory feelings, but the author has properly kept the focus upon one particular character, Annie, who is more deeply involved than the others, and who therefore not only feels the experience more intensely but is also the more intensely subject to the contradictory impulses within the experience.

What is it that Annie wants from the trick to be played on John Thomas? On the conscious level, presumably no more than the humiliation that he will suffer at facing all the girls together and the taunts that they mean to hurl at him. But unconsciously Annie must have wanted much more—if we are to judge from what actually happens in the latter part of the story. Certainly she must have wanted the specific confrontation with him— including the physical contact. She must also have wanted a chance to pour out some of her feelings of hurt and anger; the prank will afford her a kind of justification for doing so. Secretly, perhaps she wanted to hear him name her as his choice—if only to have the chance to tell him she has no interest in him. But it is plain that neither Annie nor the rest of the girls have really thought out just what they expect the prank to accomplish or to mean.

The last point comes out clearly when we see that nobody knows just how to end the joke. Once they have got into it, their actions are emotional and compulsive, sexual in fact, and sexual in a way that puzzles and even frightens the girls. They have worked themselves in a wild frenzy that they cannot understand and that might conceivably end in extreme violence. Annie gives John Thomas a box on the side of the head that is probably much harder than she had first meant to strike. At this signal the girls fly at John

不如说是戏弄"。但是她们很快就"心火上升"了,狂乱地打起来。而当约翰·托马斯停止抵抗时,姑娘们却感到自己在等待着什么,不知道接着该做什么,而是语无伦次地、"含含糊糊地"一再要求他"非表态不可"。确实,有几个姑娘还"咯咯地大笑"起来,她们显然到了歇斯底里的边缘。

　　当然,对于任何一个姑娘来说,这件事不可能有令人满意的解决办法——尤其对于这次恶作剧的领头人安妮来说,情形更是如此,因为她和约翰·托马斯的关系在感情上是那样自相矛盾。这种复杂的感情——由于肉搏更显得强烈——唯一令人满意的结局是占有对方或者结婚,但泼辣的恶作剧却使这样的解决变得不可能(对于安妮来说,情形至少会看起来是这样)。安妮的报复从表面上看似乎更有希望使约翰·托马斯做出选择,然而由于强迫他的意愿,要他在选择时非选择她不可,那就使选择本身在实际上已变得不可能。安妮搞的恶作剧也就此宣告无效,而从中她却领悟到了某些有关她自身的、她自己不曾预料到的事物。

Thomas"more in fun than in spite or anger."But soon they have their"blood…up"and are attacking in frenzy. When John Thomas stops resisting,the girls find themselves waiting for something to happen,not knowing what to do next, and repeating illogically and"vaguely"that he has"got to choose."Indeed, some of the girls, beginning"to giggle wildly,"are obviously on the verge of hysteria.

　　There is, of course, no way for the episode to end satisfactorily for any of the girls—least of all for the leader of the prank, Annie, whose relation to John Thomas is so emotionally ambiguous. The only satisfactory ending for such a mixture of feelings—and of feelings waked to such intensity by the physical struggle—is possession and marriage. But this is the solution that the tomboy prank has made impossible. (To Annie at least it will now *seem* so.) It is as if Annie's revenge has made John Thomas more desirable, and yet the forcing of his admission that, having to choose, he would indeed choose her, has made that choice in fact impossible. The very frustration of the prank she has engineered has revealed to her things about herself that she had not surmised.

■ 思考题 ■

1. 为什么安妮在说"我不要他"时,神色却是"失望至极"的?
2. 作者说到安妮"心里有什么东西在破灭"时有何示意?
3. 小说结束时安妮对约翰·托马斯的感觉如何?
4. 约翰·托马斯对安妮的感觉如何?
5. 对于约翰·托马斯的感情,尤其在小说的后半部分,作者是否写得太多了? 还是太少了?
6. 注意作者时常给予我们的关于人物心理活动和某些人物动作的含义的提示,譬如,"约翰·托马斯忐忑不安,也不相信她们。"以及"她们……每个人又都等着他看自己,希望他能够看她。"即便如此,小说还是显得生动

1. Why is it with"bitter hopelessness"that Annie says"I don't want him"?
2. What is meant by the author's saying of Annie that"something was broken in her"?
3. What are Annie's feelings toward John Thomas at the end of the story?
4. What are John Thomas's feelings toward Annie?
5. Has the author put too much emphasis upon John Thomas's emotions, particularly in the last half of the story? Or too little emphasis?
6. Note that the author is constantly telling us what the characters think and what certain of their actions mean: for example, "He was uneasy, mistrusting them"and"yet each one of them... hoped he would look at

而富有"戏剧性"。为什么作者的议论和插话没有使这篇小说丧失连续性？

7. 注意小说最初几页的语调。对电车线路的描述给人以轻率而滑稽的印象。其实，直到约翰·托马斯抛弃安妮，小说给人的总的印象一直是喜剧性的或者至少是超脱的，就是到了那算账情节开始时也还如此。这时，又突然一个转变，这里含有怎样的意味？姑娘中是否有任何一个曾想象到这次事件？这段情节是否表现出某种自我发现性质的东西，甚或某种令人惧怕的东西？

（刘文荣 译）

her. "Even so, the story is vivid in its presentation and remains "dramatic." Why don't the author's comments and interpretations kill the immediacy of this story?

7. Observe the tone of the story for the first several pages. The effect in describing the course of the tram is harum-scarum and comic. In fact, until John Thomas drops Annie, the general effect is comic, or at least detached, as is even the beginning of the get-even scene. What is implied in the sudden shift at this point? How is the shift of tone central to the meaning of the story? Is the event one that any individual girl might have imagined possible? Is there an element of self discovery, even a frightening one, that comes out of the episode?

020. 理 发

(美)林·拉德纳 著　雨 宁 译

020. Haircut

by Ring Lardner

我有了另外一位理发的伙计，他是从卡特维尔来的，每星期六帮我干活，其余的时间我一个人满可以对付了。你自个儿也看得出来，这儿不是纽约市，再说，小伙子们大半都整天工作，没有哪个闲空到这儿串串，把他们自个儿拾掇得漂漂亮亮。

你是新来的人，对不对？我觉得以前没见过你。我愿意你喜欢这儿，能够待下来。我说过，咱们这儿不是纽约市，也不是芝加哥，可是日子过得挺乐和。不过，自从吉姆·肯德尔给打死之后，就不像往常那么欢腾了。他活着的时候，他跟霍德·迈耶斯经常弄得镇上乐呵呵的。我敢打赌。在全美国这样大小的镇上，数咱们这儿的乐子最多。

吉姆挺滑稽，霍德跟他差不离儿是一搭一档。自从吉姆去世之后，霍德还打算像先前一样卖弄他那一套，可是没人跟他搭档，这事儿也难办。

经常在星期六，这儿可热闹啦。星期六旳1到4点过后，我这个地方总是挤满了人，吉姆跟霍德在晚饭之后6点左右就露面了。吉姆总是要坐在最靠近蓝痰桶的那张大椅子上。谁要原来坐在那张椅子上，嘿，吉姆一进门，他就得起来把位子让给吉姆。

你大概以为这好像戏圈子里有时候留下的包座。霍德平常总是站着，要么走来走去，要么在哪个星期六，他也会在这张椅子上坐一段时间，理理发。

喔，吉姆会在那儿坐上好一会儿，也不开口，除非是吐痰。末了，他会对我说："惠蒂呀，"——我的本名，也就是说，我实实在在的教名，叫做狄克，可是这儿人人都管我叫惠蒂——吉姆于是说："惠蒂，今儿晚上你的鼻子像个玫瑰花骨朵。你一定是喝了一点你的古龙香水吧。"

I GOT another barber that comes over from Carterville and helps me out Saturdays, but the rest of the time I can get along all right alone. You can see for yourself that this ain't no New York City and besides that, the most of the boys works all day and don't have no leisure to drop in here and get themselves prettied up.

You're a newcomer, ain't you? I thought I hadn't seen you round before. I hope you like it good enough to stay. As I say, we ain't no New York City or Chicago, but we have pretty good times. Not as good, though, since Jim Kendall got killed. When he was alive, him and Hod Meyers used to keep this town in an uproar. I bet they was more laughin' done here than any town its size in America.

Jim was comical, and Hod was pretty near a match for him. Since Jim's gone, Hod tries to hold his end up just the same as ever, but it's tough goin' when you ain't got nobody to kind of work with.

They used to be plenty fun in here Saturdays. This place is jampacked Saturdays, from four o'clock on. Jim and Hod would show up right after their supper round six o'clock. Jim would set himself down in that big chair, nearest the blue spitoon. Whoever had been settin' in that chair, why, they'd get up when Jim come in and give it to him.

You'd of thought it was a reserved seat like they have sometimes in a theaytre. Hod would generally always stand or walk up and down or some Saturdays, of course, he'd be settin' in this chair part of the time, gettin' a haircut.

Well, Jim would set there a w'ile without openin' his mouth only to spit, and then finally he'd say to me, "Whitey,"—my right name, that is, my right first name, is Dick, but everybody round here calls me Whitey—Jim would say, "Whitey, your nose looks like a rosebud tonight. You must of been drinkin' some of your aw de cologne."

作者简介：林·拉德纳（**Ring Lardner**，1885—1933），美国作家。1885 年 3 月 6 日生于密歇根州奈尔斯，1933 年 9 月 25 日卒于纽约东汉普顿。他在出版小说前做过报纸记者、体育新闻记者和专栏作家，之后他的棒球运动员的喜剧故事受到很大欢迎，有些收录到《埃尔，你知道我》(*You Know Me, Al*, 1916) 当中。随后的作品以讽刺、叙述技巧和方言闻名，如《怎样写短篇小说》(*How to Write Short Stories*, 1924) 和《爱巢》(*Love Nest*, 1926)。

于是我说："没有，吉姆，你倒像喝过了那股子水，也许什么更次的东西。"

吉姆听了大概也只好笑笑，可是他也会爽爽快快地说："没有，我什么也不喝，可这也不是说我不愿意喝点什么，哪怕是木醇，我也不在乎。"

于是霍德·迈耶斯就会说："你老婆也不在乎。"这话会引得人人都笑起来，因为吉姆跟他老婆不大合得来。她本来要跟他离婚的，可是没有机会得到赡养费，她也没有办法照顾她自个儿和孩子们。她怎么也摸不透吉姆。吉姆是有点霸道，可心眼儿里还是个好人。

他跟霍德变着法儿逗弄米尔特·谢泼德。我捉摸你大概没见过米尔特。嘿，他那个喉结瞧起来倒跟香瓜差不离儿。我给米尔特刮起脸来，一到往他脖子那儿刮下去的时候，霍德就叫唤："嘿，惠蒂，等一会儿！你先别切下去，咱们凑个局来猜有多少瓜子，瞧谁能猜得差不离儿。"

这时候吉姆就会说："米尔特要是不像猪那样贪嘴，他本来该买半个罗马甜瓜，不买一个整的，那也不会卡在他嗓子里了。"

小伙子们听到这个，都哄堂大笑，虽然大伙都拿米尔特起哄，他自个儿倒也要勉强地笑笑。吉姆真是个会逗哏的怪物！

这就是他刮脸用的肥皂缸子，就放在架子上，紧靠着查理·维尔的那个。"查尔斯·M·维尔。"这就是那个杂货店掌柜的。他经常一星期来刮三次脸。吉姆的缸子是靠着查理的那个。"詹姆士·H·肯德尔。"现在，吉姆用不着刮脸的肥皂缸子了，可我为了老交情，仍旧把它放在那儿。吉姆真是个少见的怪人！

前好几年，吉姆给卡特维尔的一家罐头公司工作，经常出门。他们卖罐头食品，吉姆管的是这个州的整个北半边，一个星期里，他有 5 天都在出差。他常在星期六到这儿串串，谈一谈他在那个星期里经过的事。他经过的事着实不少。

照我看，他的心思大半都用在开玩笑了，没注意做买卖。最后，那家公司不用他了，他于是回到这儿，他不像大多数的人那样说他辞职了，他见人就说他给开除了。

那一天是星期六，我这个店里客满，吉姆从那张椅子里站起来说："各位先生，我有一件重要的事要宣布。我已经给公司里开除了。"

好吧，他们问他是不是当真，他说这是当真的，谁

So I'd say, "No, Jim, but you look like you'd been drinkin' somethin' of that kind or somethin' worse."

Jim would have to laugh at that, but then he'd speak up and say, "No, I ain't had nothin' to drink, but that ain't sayin' I wouldn't like somethin'. I wouldn't even mind if it was wood alcohol."

Then Hod Meyers would say, "Neither would your wife." That would set everybody to laughin' because Jim and his wife wasn't on very good terms. She'd of divorced him only they wasn't no chance to get alimony and she didn't have no way to take care of herself and the kids. She couldn't never understand Jim. He *was* kind of rough, but a good fella at heart.

Him and Hod had all kinds of sport with Milt Sheppard. I don't suppose you've seen Milt. Well, he's got an Adam's apple that looks more like a mushmelon. So I'd been shavin' Milt and when I'd start to shave down here on his neck, Hod would holler, "Hey, Whitey, wait a minute! Before you cut into it, let's make up a pool and see who can guess closest to the number of seeds."

And Jim would say, "If Milt hadn't of been so hoggish, he'd of ordered a half a cantaloupe instead of a whole one and it might not of stuck in his throat."

All the boys would roar at this and Milt himself would force a smile, though the joke was on him. Jim certainly was a card!

There's his shavin' mug, setting on the shelf, right next to Charley Vail's. "Charles M. Vail." That's the druggist. He comes in regular for his shave three times a week. And Jim's is the cup next to Charley's. "James H. Kendall." Jim won't need no shavin' mug no more, but I'll leave it there just the same for old time's sake. Jim certainly was a character!

Years ago, Jim used to travel for a canned goods concern over in Carterville. They sold canned goods. Jim had the whole northern half of the State and was on the road five days out of every week. He'd drop in here Saturdays and tell his experiences for that week. It was rich.

I guess he paid more attention to playin' jokes than makin' sales. Finally the concern let him out and he come right home here and told everybody he'd been fired instead of sayin' he'd resigned like most fellas would of.

It was a Saturday and the shop was full and Jim got up out of that chair and says, "Gentlemen, I got an important announcement to make. I been fired from my job."

Well, they asked him if he was in earnest and he said he was and nobody could think of nothin' to say till Jim finally broke the ice himself. He says, "I been sellin' canned goods and now I'm canned goods myself."

也想不出有什么话可说,末了,还是吉姆自个儿打破了僵局。他说:"我一直是卖罐头食品的,现在我自个儿成了罐头食品了。"

你也知道,他工作的那家公司是一个制造罐头食品的工厂,开设在卡特维尔。可是这时候吉姆说他自个儿给装进了罐头。他真是个会逗眼的怪物。

吉姆在旅行的时候经常玩弄他的一个拿手把戏。例如,他乘上火车,火车开到了一个什么小镇,比方,噢,比方,噢,比方说本顿。吉姆于是从车窗里瞧出去,看着商店的招牌。

例如,有一家的招牌上写着"亨利·史密斯,布匹服装"。好吧,吉姆于是把商店和小镇的名称都写下来,等他到了他要去的什么地方,他会写一张明信片寄给本顿的亨利·史密斯,也不签名,不过,他会在明信片上写着,噢,比方说:"向你老婆打听打听上一个星期消磨了一下午的那个书商。"要么,"问你太太,上星期你在卡特维尔的时候,是谁使她不觉得寂寞的。"然后他在明信片上写着:"一个朋友。"

当然,他从来也不知道这些玩笑真的会同出什么事,不过他能想得出大概会发生什么事,那也就够了。

吉姆丢掉了他在卡特维尔人那儿的职位之后,也没有稳稳当当地工作过。他在镇上干了些零活儿,他赚到手的钱,嗨,差不多都花在杜松子酒上了,要是商店里没有让他们拉账,他一家人也许都要挨饿了。吉姆的老婆也做点裁缝活儿碰碰运气,可是在这个镇上,没有人会靠做裁缝发财的。

我说过,她本来要跟吉姆离婚,可是她知道她不能养活她自个儿和孩子们,她总是巴望着有一天吉姆会改掉他的习气,一个星期给她的钱不止这两三块。

有一个时期,他给谁干活,她就到谁那儿去,要他们把他的工钱给她,她这么做了一两次,可是后来,他把大部分工钱都提前借走了,比她先下了手。他在镇上到处都说他怎么干得比他老婆还狡猾。也真是个与众不同的怪人!

可是他还不称心,这不过是手段比她高明罢了。他恼火的是她做出了这种事,要抢走他的工钱。于是他下定决心要报复她一下。嘿,他一直等到伊文思马戏团贴出了要到镇上来的广告。他于是告诉他老婆和两个孩子,说他要带他们去看马戏。马戏演出的那天,他告诉他们他要去买票,在大帐篷入口的外面跟他们见面。

You see, the concern he'd been workin' for was a factory that made canned goods. Over in Carterville. And now Jim said he was canned himself. He was certainly a card!

Jim had a great trick that he used to play w'ile he was travelin'. For instance, he'd be ridin' on a train and they'd come to some little town like, well, like, well, like, we'll say, like Benton. Jim would look out the train window and read the signs on the stores.

For instance, they'd be a sign, "Henry Smith, Dry Goods." Well, Jim would write down the name and the name of the town and when he got to wherever he was goin' he'd mail back a postal card to Henry Smith at Benton and not sign no name to it, but he'd write on the card, well, somethin' like "Ask your wife about that book agent that spent the afternoon last week," or "Ask your Missus who kept her from gettin' lonesome the last time you was in Carterville." And he'd sign the card, "A Friend."

Of course, he never knew what really come of none of these jokes, but he could picture what *probably* happened and that was enough.

Jim didn't work very steady after he lost his position with the Carterville people. What he did earn, doin' odd jobs round town, why, he spent pretty near all of it on gin, and his family might of starved if the stores hadn't of carried them along. Jim's wife tried her hand at dressmakin', but they ain't nobody goin' to get rich makin' dresses in this town.

As I say, she'd of divorced Jim, only she seen that she couldn't support herself and the kids and she was always hopin' that some day Jim would cut out his habits and give her more than two or three dollars a week.

They was a time when she would go to whoever he was workin' for and ask them to give her his wages, but after she done this once or twice, he beat her to it by borrowin' most of his pay in advance. He told it all round town, how he had outfoxed his Missus. He certainly was a caution!

But he wasn't satisfied with just outwittin' her. He was sore the way she had acted, tryin' to grab off his pay. And he made up his mind he'd get even. Well, he waited till Evans's Circus was advertised to come to town. Then he told his wife and two kiddies that he was goin' to take them to the circus. The day of the circus, he told them he would get the tickets and meet them outside the entrance to the tent.

Well, he didn't have no intentions of bein' there or buyin' tickets or nothin'. He got full of gin and laid round Wright's poolroom all day. His wife and the kids waited and waited and of course he didn't show

嘿,他根本没打算到那儿去,也没打算去买票,什么都没有。他喝足了杜松子酒,在赖特的弹子房里混了一整天。他的老婆跟孩子们等了又等,他当然没有露面。我估计他老婆身上连一角钱也没有,也没有别的地方去。所以,末了,她只好对孩子们说,看不成了,他们哭哭闹闹,没完没了。

嘿,说来凑巧,正在他们哭的时候,斯太尔医生来了,他问这是怎么回事,可是肯德尔太太很倔,不肯告诉他,不过孩子们对他说了,他于是一定要请他们和他们的母亲看马戏。后来,吉姆知道了这件事,这也是他对斯太尔医生怀恨在心的一个原因。

斯太尔医生大约是在一年半以前来的。他是个非常漂亮的年轻人,他的衣服好像都是定做的。他每一年要到底特律去两三次,他一定是待在那儿的时候叫裁缝给他量了尺寸,给他定做了一套。这种衣服价钱要贵一倍,可是这比从商店里买现成的穿起来要合身得多。

有一个时期,人人都纳闷,为什么像斯太尔这样年轻的医生要到咱们这个镇上来。这儿本来有甘布尔医生和富特医生,镇上的医务一直是由这两位老医生分担的。

当时流传着的一种说法是,斯太尔医生的女朋友把他扔掉了,那是一个住在北方半岛什么地方的姑娘,他到这儿来的原因是为了躲起来,忘掉这件事。他自个儿说,他认为,要把一个人锻炼成一个全面的好医生,没有什么比到咱们这地方来当普通医生更好了。这就是他来的原因。

总之,时间不久他就赚得足够过日子了,可是据他们对我说,谁要欠了他的钱,他从来不去催账,这儿的人也的确有个欠账的习气,连我这一行也免不了。要是我能单单把刮脸的账都收回来,我就能到卡特维尔去,在默塞尔旅馆里住一个星期,每天晚上看一场新电影。譬如说,其中就有老乔治·珀迪,不过我看,我还是不应当说人家闲话。

好吧,去年,我们的验尸官死了,得流行性感冒死的。肯·贝蒂,这是他的姓名。他是验尸官。所以,大伙得选另外一个人来替换他当验尸官,他们选中了斯太尔医生。起先,他笑笑,说他不要当这个差事,可是他们还是劝他接下来了。这可不是个有人要争夺的职位,干这种事的人,一年里赚的钱只不过够买他花园里用的花籽儿。不过,医生就是那种人,如果你

up. His wife didn't have a dime with her, or nowhere else, I guess. So she finally had to tell the kids it was all off and they cried like they wasn't never goin' to stop.

Well, it seems, w'ile they was cryin', Doc Stair come along and he asked what was the matter, but Mrs. Kendall was stubborn and wouldn't tell him, but the kids told him and he insisted on takin' them and their mother in the show. Jim found this out afterwards and it was one reason why he had it in for Doc Stair.

Doc Stair come here about a year and a half ago. He's a mighty handsome young fella and his clothes always look like he has them made to order. He goes to Detroit two or three times a year and w'ile he's there must have a tailor take his measure and then make him a suit to order. They cost pretty near twice as much, but they fit a whole lot better than if you just bought them in a store.

For a w'ile everybody was wonderin' why a young doctor like Doc Stair should come to a town like this where we already got old Doc Gamble and Doc Foote that's both been here for years and all the practice in town was always divided between the two of them.

Then they was a story got round that Doc Stair's gal had throwed him over, a gal up in the Northern Peninsula somewhere, and the reason he come here was to hide himself away and forget it. He said himself that he thought they wasn't nothin' like general practice in a place like ours to fit a man to be a good all round doctor. And that's why he'd came.

Anyways, it wasn't long before he was makin' enough to live on, though they tell me that he never dunned nobody for what they owed him, and the folks here certainly has got the owin' habit, even in my business. If I had all that was comin' to me for just shaves alone, I could go to Carterville and put up at the Mercer for a week and see a different picture every night. For instance, they's old George Purdy—but I guess I shouldn't ought to be gossipin'.

Well, last year, our coroner died, died of the flu. Ken Beatty, that was his name. He was the coroner. So they had to choose another man to be coroner in his place and they picked Doc Stair. He laughed at first and said he didn't want it, but they made him take it. It ain't no job that anybody would fight for and what a man makes out of it in a year would just about buy seeds for their garden. Doc's the kind, though, that can't say no to nothin' if you keep at him long enough.

But I was goin' to tell you about a poor boy we got here in town—Paul Dickson. He fell out of a tree when he was about ten years old. Lit on his head and it

缠着他,时间一长,他对什么事都不会说个"不"字。

　　不过我要跟你说的是我们镇上一个可怜的孩子,保尔·狄克逊。大约 10 岁那年,他从树上摔下来。头先落地,他受了点影响,后来一直也没好过。没什么要紧,他不过傻里傻气罢了。吉姆·肯德尔经常管他叫布谷鸟,这是吉姆给头脑不正常的人起的名字,不过他把人的脑袋又叫做蚕豆。这是他逗乐的一种笑话,把脑袋叫作蚕豆,把疯子叫做布谷鸟。可是保尔并不疯,就是傻里傻气罢了。

　　你可以想得到,吉姆总是变着法儿来逗弄保尔。他会叫他到白门面汽车修理店去拿一个左旋活动扳手。当然,根本就没有左旋活动扳手这种东西。

　　有一回,咱们这儿有集市,胖子队和瘦子队要比赛棒球,在比赛开始之前,吉姆把保尔叫过去,让他到老远的施拉德尔五金商店去买一把打开投球手箱子的钥匙。

　　凡是逗弄人的事,只要吉姆存着这份儿心,他没有什么想不出的办法。

　　可怜的保尔老是对人有点疑心,也许这是吉姆常让他上当的缘故。保尔跟谁也不大愿意来往,除了他的亲娘,斯太尔医生和镇上的一个叫做朱莉·格雷格的姑娘。其实,她早已经不是姑娘了,都快 30 或者 30 出头了。

　　医生初来到镇上的时候,保尔似乎难得有了一位真心的朋友。大部分的时间,他都在医生诊所里待着,只有回家吃饭睡觉,或者看见朱莉到商店里买东西了,他才不在那儿。

　　他从医生的窗户里向外瞧,一看见她,他就奔下楼,跟她在一块儿,随着她到各家商店里去。这个可怜的孩子对朱莉着了迷,她也一直对他很好,让也觉得他是受欢迎的,当然,在她那一面,这不过是可怜他罢了。

　　医生尽了一切力量来提高他的智力,他有一次对我说,他真的觉得这孩子好点了,有时候,他也挺聪明,通情达理,跟别人一样。

　　可是我正要跟你说说朱莉·格雷格的事。老头子格雷格是做木材生意的,可是他喝上了酒,把大部分的钱都赔了,他死的时候,也没留下什么,只不过那栋房子和只够这个姑娘克扣着过日子的一俭保险金。

　　她母亲大概是个半残疾,从来不走出那栋房子。老头子死后,朱莉本来想把这地方卖了搬到别的地方去,可是她母亲说她生在这儿,也要死在这儿。这可

done somethin' to him and he ain't never been right. No harm in him, but just silly. Jim Kendall used to call him cuckoo; that's a name Jim had for anybody that was off their head, only he called people's head their bean. That was another of his gags, callin' head bean and callin' crazy people cuckoo. Only poor Paul ain't crazy, but just silly.

You can imagine that Jim used to have all kinds of fun with Paul. He'd send him to the White Front Garage for a left-handed monkey wrench. Of course they ain't no such thing as a left-handed monkey wrench.

And once we had a kind of a fair here and they was a baseball game between the fats and the leans and before the game started Jim called Paul over and sent him away down to Schrader's hardware store to get a key for the pitcher's box.

They wasn't nothin' in the way of gags that Jim couldn't think up, when he put his mind to it.

Poor Paul was always kind of suspicious of people, maybe on account of how Jim had kept foolin' him. Paul wouldn't have much to do with anybody only his own mother and Doc Stair and a girl here in town named Julie Gregg. That is, she ain't a girl no more, but pretty near thirty or over.

When Doc first came to town, Paul seemed to feel like here was a real friend and he hung round Doc's office most of the w'ile; the only time he wasn't there was when he'd go home to eat or sleep or when he seen Julie Gregg doin' her shoppin'.

When he looked out Doc's window and seen her, he'd run downstairs and join her and tag along with her to the different stores. The poor boy was crazy about Julie and she always treated him mighty nice and made him feel like he was welcome, though of course it wasn't nothin' but pity on her side.

Doc done all he could to improve Paul's mind and he told me once that he really thought the boy was getting better, that they was times when he was as bright and sensible as anybody else.

But I was goin' to tell you about Julie Gregg. Old man Gregg was in the lumber business, but got to drinkin' and lost the most of his money and when he died, he didn't leave nothin' but the house and just enough insurance for the girl to skimp along on.

Her mother was a kind of a half invalid and didn't hardly ever leave the house. Julie wanted to sell the place and move somewheres else after the old man died, but the mother said she was born here and would die here. It was tough on Julie as the young people round this town—well, she's too good for them.

She'd been away to school and Chicago and New

叫朱莉难办,因为镇上这一带的年轻小伙子……嗨,她比他们强得太多了。

她在外地进的学校,她到过芝加哥、纽约和别的好些地方。没有哪个题目她谈不上来的,可是你要拿这儿其余的年轻人来看,你要跟他们谈起格洛里亚·斯旺森和汤米·梅恩以外的随便什么事情,他们都会以为你在说胡话。你看过格洛里亚演的《贞操的报酬》吗?你可错过了眼福!

好吧,斯太尔医生到这儿还不过一个星期,有一天,他到这儿来刮脸,我认出了他是谁,因为有人把他指点给我瞧过,于是我跟他谈起了我的老婆子。她生病有两年了,不论是甘尔尔医生,还是富特医生,好像一个也没有把她治得好一点儿。于是他说,他愿意出诊来给她看病,可是如果她自个儿能够走出门,最好是带她到诊所里来,他可以全面地检查一下。

于是我带她到他的诊所里,我在候诊室里等她,这时候朱莉·格雷格来了。每逢有人来到斯太尔医生的诊所的时候,他里面的办公室里的那个铃就会响起来,让他知道有人来看他。

于是他把我老婆留在里面,走到外面的办公室里,这是他跟朱莉第一次见面,我估计这就是他们说的一见钟情了。不过这不是一家一半。这个年轻的小伙子是她在这个镇上见过的人里最英俊俏皮的,她不由自主地爱上了他。对他来说,她不过是一位要来看医生的小姐。

她到这儿来要商量的事跟我一样。她母亲由甘布尔医生和富特医生医治了几年,也不见好。所以,她听说镇上来了一位新医生,决定让他试一试。他答应当天就去给她母亲瞧瞧。

刚才我说,在她那一面,这是一见钟情。我不是单从她后来怎么做的来评论的。我是从她第一天到诊所里怎么瞧着他来断定的。我不是那种能猜中别人心思的人,可是她一个心眼儿地爱上了他,那是在她脸上明摆着的。

再说吉姆·肯德尔,他不但专门逗弄人,酒量也挺好,嗨,他还是个专门勾引女人的家伙。我捉摸着他在给卡特维尔的人出门办事的时候大概要乱来的,除了这些,他在本镇上也有两件勾勾搭搭的小事儿。我说过,他老婆本来要跟他离婚的,不过没有办法罢了。

可是吉姆像大多数男人一样,我看,也像大多数

York and different places and they ain't no subject she can't talk on, where you take the rest of the young folks here and you mention anything to them outside of Gloria Swanson or Tommy Meighan and they think you're delirious. Did you see Gloria in *Wages of Virtue*? You missed somethin'!

Well, Doc Stair hadn't been here more than a week when he come in one day to get shaved and I recognized who he was, as he had been pointed out to me, so I told him about my old lady. She's been ailin' for a couple years and either Doc Gamble or Doc Foote, neither one, seemed to be helpin' her. So he said he would come out and see her, but if she was able to get out herself, it would be better to bring her to his office where he could make a completer examination.

So I took her to his office and w'ile I was waitin' for her in the reception room, in come Julie Gregg. When somebody comes in Doc Stair's office, they's a bell that rings in his inside office so as he can tell they's somebody to see him.

So he left my old lady inside and come out to the front office and that's the first time him and Julie met and I guess it was what they call love at first sight. But it wasn't fifty-fifty. This young fella was the slickest lookin' fella she'd ever seen in this town and she went wild over him. To him she was just a lady that wanted to see the doctor.

She'd came on about the same business I had. Her mother had been doctorin' for years with Doc Gamble and Doc Foote and without no results. So she'd heard they was a new doc in town and decided to give him a try. He promised to call and see her mother that same day.

I said a minute ago that it was love at first sight on her part. I'm not only judgin' by how she acted afterwards but how she looked at him that first day in his office. I ain't no mind reader, but it was wrote all over her face that she was gone.

Now Jim Kendall, besides bein' a jokesmith and a pretty good drinker, well, Jim was quite a lady-killer. I guess he run pretty wild durin' the time he was on the road for them Carterville people, and besides that, he'd had a couple little affairs of the heart right here in town. As I say, his wife would have divorced him, only she couldn't.

But Jim was like the majority of men, and women, too, I guess. He wanted what he couldn't get. He wanted Julie Gregg and worked his head off tryin' to land her. Only he'd of said bean instead of head.

Well, Jim's habits and his jokes didn't appeal to Julie and of course he was a married man, so he didn't have no more chance than, well, than a rabbit. That's

女人一样。他要的是他得不到的东西。他要朱莉·格雷格,即使挖空脑袋也要把她弄到手。其实他本来该说挖空那粒蚕豆,不说脑袋的。

嗨,吉姆的习气和笑话都不讨朱莉欢喜,再说,当然,他是个结了婚的人,所以,他也没有机会,就跟,嗨,就跟兔子差不离儿。这是吉姆自个儿用的一个词儿。谁要没有机会当选,或者没有得到什么东西的机会,吉姆总是说他们没有机会,跟兔子差不离儿。

他对他想要怎么干,也不遮遮盖盖。就在这儿,不止一次,当着大伙的面,他说他看中了朱莉,谁要能帮他把朱莉弄到手,谁就可以利用他的房子,连他的老婆孩子都算上。可是朱莉不愿意跟他有一点儿牵连,甚至不愿意在街上跟他说话。最后,他知道用他寻常的那一套办法走不通,他就决定用霸道的办法试试。有一天傍晚,他干脆到她家里去,她开开门,他硬闯进去,抓住她。可是她挣开了,在他拦住她之前,她跑到隔壁的房间里,锁上门,给乔·巴恩斯打电话。乔是这儿的警长。吉姆听得出她在给谁打电话,没等到乔来,他就逃跑了。

乔是朱莉的父亲的老朋友。第二天,乔到吉姆那儿,告诉他要是再干这种事就会出什么问题。

我不知道这段小事怎么透露了消息。大概是乔·巴恩斯告诉他老婆,他老婆又告诉什么人的老婆了,她们又告诉她们的丈夫了。总之,消息传出去了,霍德·迈耶斯居然有胆量拿这件事来逗弄吉姆,就在我这个店里。吉姆什么也不否认,他笑了笑,也不在意,并且说让我们都等着瞧。好多人都打算让他出丑,可是他从来也不饶人。

这时候,镇上人人都明白朱莉在拼命追求医生。我不敢说他们俩在一块儿的时候,朱莉会知道她的脸色变成了什么样子。她当然不会知道,要不,她也会避开他了。她也不知道我们都在注意她借口到他的诊所里去了多少次,有多少次她在街对面路过诊所的时候望着他的窗户,瞧他是不是在里面。我替她难受,别的人也大半都替她难受。

霍德·迈耶斯翻来覆去地跟吉姆说医生怎么把他顶掉了,拿这些话来气他。吉姆倒不把这些逗弄放在心上,你可以看出他正在合计着要开一个玩笑。

吉姆有一个绝招,他能改变他的声音。他能使你以为他是一个姑娘在那儿说话,他能学任何人的声音。为了让你知道他有多大本事,我跟你说说有一次

an expression of Jim's himself. When somebody didn't have no chance to get elected or somethin', Jim would always say they didn't have no more chance than a rabbit.

He didn't make no bones about how he felt. Right in here, more than once, in front of the whole crowd, he said he was stuck on Julie and anybody that could get her for him was welcome to his house and his wife and kids included. But she wouldn't have nothin' to do with him; wouldn't even speak to him on the street. He finally seen he wasn't gettin' nowheres with his usual line so he decided to try the rough stuff. He went right up to her house one evenin' and when she opened the door he forced his way in and grabbed her. But she broke loose and before he could stop her, she run in the next room and locked the door and phoned to Joe Barnes. Joe's the marshal. Jim could hear who she was phonin' to and he beat it before Joe got there.

Joe was an old friend of Julie's pa. Joe went to Jim the next day and told him what would happen if he ever done it again.

I don't know how the news of this little affair leaked out. Chances is that Joe Barnes told his wife and she told somebody else's wife and they told their husband. Anyways, it did leak out and Hod Meyers had the nerve to kid Jim about it, right here in this shop. Jim didn't deny nothin' and kind of laughed it off and said for us all to wait; that lots of people had tried to make a monkey out of him, but he always got even.

Meanw'ile everybody in town was wise to Julie's bein' wild mad over the Doc. I don't suppose she had any idear how her face changed when him and her was together; of course she couldn't of, or she'd of kept away from him. And she didn't know that we was all noticin' how many times she made excuses to go up to his office or pass it on the other side of the street and look up in his window to see if he was there. I felt sorry for her and so did most other people.

Hod Meyers kept rubbin' it into Jim about how the Doc had cut him out. Jim didn't pay no attention to the kiddin' and you could see he was plannin' one of his jokes.

One trick Jim had was the knack of changin' his voice. He could make you think he was a girl talkin' and he could mimic any man's voice. To show you how good he was along this line, I'll tell you the joke he played on me once.

You know, in most towns of any size, when a man is dead and needs a shave, why, the barber that shaves him soaks him five dollars for the job; that is, he don't soak *him*, but whoever ordered the shave. I just charge three dollars because personally I don't mind much

他怎么逗弄我的。

你知道,在大多数这样大小的镇上,一个人死了都得要修面,嘿,理发的干这个活可以敲死人的竹杠,赚5块钱,这就是说,挨敲的不是死人,是那个来通知的人。我只要3块,因为我这个人并不在乎给死人修面。死人躺在那儿比活的顾客要安静得多。只有一件事,你不会去跟他们说话,觉得有点闷得慌。

好吧,两年前的那个冬天,那天冷极了,从来没遇到过,我才回家里吃午餐,电话响了,我去接电话,是一个女人的声音,她说她是约翰·司各脱太太,她丈夫死了,问我愿不愿意去给他修面。

老约翰一向是我的一位好主顾。可是他们住在乡下。有7英里路,在去斯垂特尔的路上。不过我也不好说不干。

于是我说,我愿意去,不过得乘小出租汽车,除了修面的费用可能要加三四块钱。于是她,也就是那个声音说都可以,我于是找弗兰克·阿勃特开车送我到那儿,我到了那儿,开门的不是别人,正是老约翰自个儿!他哪里死了,嗨,跟兔子差不离儿。

至于谁跟我开了这个小玩笑,那用不着找私家侦探来合计。除了吉姆·肯德尔,谁也不会想出这个点子。他真是个擅长恶作剧的怪物!

我告诉你这段小事,不过是为了让你知道他会怎么样改变嗓音,弄得你以为是别人在说话。我可以发誓,打电话给我的是斯各脱太太。总之,是个什么女的。

好吧,吉姆等到他把斯太尔医生的口音学得一点儿也不差了,然后开始报复。

有一天晚上,他知道医生到卡特维尔去了,于是给朱莉打电话。她一点儿也不疑心,那还能不是医生的口音。吉姆说,他一定要在当天晚上跟她见面,他有一件事情要告诉她,不能再等下去了。她兴奋极了,叫他到她家里去。可是他说他正在等一个重要的长途电话,请她暂且不拘礼节,到他诊所里去。他说,他们不会伤害她的,谁也不会瞧见她,他只不过一定要跟她谈一小会儿。嘿,可怜的朱莉上当了。

医生总是让诊所里晚上有灯光,所以朱莉看起来就好像诊所里有人似的。

这时候,吉姆·肯德尔已经到赖特的弹子房去了,有一大伙人正在那儿玩乐。他们大半都喝了很多杜松子酒,这伙人即使在清醒的时候也很粗野。他们

shavin' a dead person. They lay a whole lot stiller than live customers. The only thing is that you don't feel like talkin' to them and you get kind of lonesome.

Well, about the coldest day we ever had here, two years ago last winter, the phone rung at the house w'ile I was home to dinner and I answered the phone and it was a woman's voice and she said she was Mrs. John Scott and her husband was dead and would I come out and shave him.

Old John had always been a good customer of mine. But they live seven miles out in the country, on the Streeter road. Still I didn't see how I could say no.

So I said I would be there, but would have to come in a jitney and it might cost three or four dollars besides the price of the shave. So she, or the voice, it said that was all right, so I got Frank Abbott to drive me out to the place and when I got there, who should open the door but old John himself! He wasn't no more dead than, well, than a rabbit.

It didn't take no private detective to figure out who had played me this little joke. Nobody could of thought it up but Jim Kendall. He certainly was a card!

I tell you this incident just to show you how he could disguise his voice and make you believe it was somebody else talkin'. I'd of swore it was Mrs. Scott had called me. Anyways, some woman.

Well, Jim waited till he had Doc Stair's voice down pat; then he went after revenge.

He called Julie up on a night when he knew Doc was over in Carterville. She never questioned but what it was Doc's voice. Jim said he must see her that night; he couldn't wait no longer to tell her somethin'. She was all excited and told him to come to the house. But he said he was expectin' an important long distance call and wouldn't she please forget her manners for once and come to his office. He said they couldn't nothin' hurt her and nobody would see her and he just *must* talk to her a little w'ile. Well, poor Julie fell for it.

Doc always keeps a night light in his office, so it looked to Julie like they was somebody there.

Meanw'ile Jim Kendall had went to Wright's poolroom, where they was a whole gang amusin' themselves. The most of them had drank plenty of gin, and they was a rough hunch when sober. They was always strong for Jim's jokes and when he told them to come with him and see some fun they give up their card games and pool games and followed along.

Doc's office is on the second floor. Right outside his door they's a flight of stairs leadin' to the floor above. Jim and his gang hid in the dark behind these

总是起劲儿地跟着吉姆凑热闹，所以，他叫他们跟着他去瞧什么乐子的时候，他们就不玩纸牌，不打弹子，跟着去了。

医生的诊所在二楼。打门外面起，有一个扶梯通到楼上。吉姆和他那一伙都藏在扶梯后面黑乎乎的地方。

嘿，朱莉来到医生门口拉门铃，一点儿也没有动静。她又拉铃，拉了七八次。原来她推了推门发现门锁上了。这时候，吉姆弄出了一点儿响声，她听见了，等了一会儿，然后她说："是你吗？拉尔夫。"拉尔夫是医生的教名。

没有人回答，她一定是突然想到她上了当了。她几乎从扶梯上摔下去，那一伙人全跟着她。他们一路追到她家，叫唤着"是你吗？拉尔夫"，还有"哦，拉尔夫，亲爱的，是你"。吉姆说他自个儿叫唤不出来，因为他笑得太厉害了。

可怜的朱莉！后来有很久，很久，她都没在大街上露过面。

当然，吉姆和他那伙人在镇上见人就说，除了斯太尔医生以外的每一个人。他们都不敢告诉医生，要不是亏了保尔·狄克逊，他大概永远也不会知道。这个可怜的布谷鸟，吉姆是这么叫他的，有一天晚上他到我这个店里来，吉姆仍然在扬扬得意地说他对朱莉干的那件事。保尔把他能听明白的话都记在心里，连忙把这件事告诉了医生。

那还用说，医生气崩了，他发誓要让吉姆吃吃苦头。不过这种事很难办，因为如果传出去他把吉姆狠揍了一顿，朱莉一定会听到的，那么，她也会明白医生都知道了，当然，医生也知道，朱莉明白了会使她比以前更难受。他要想个办法，不过得好好合计合计。

嘿，两天之后，吉姆又到我店里来了，那个布谷鸟也来了。吉姆打算第二天去打野鸭，他来找霍德·迈耶斯跟他一块儿去。我碰巧知道霍德到卡特维尔去了，要到周末才回来。吉姆于是说他不愿意一个人去，看样子只好吹了。这时候，可怜的保尔说话了，他说，吉姆要愿意带他去，他愿意去。吉姆想了一会儿，然后说，好吧，他觉得有个傻子总比没人好点儿。

我估计他是打算把保尔弄到船里，然后戏弄他一下，譬如说把他推到水里。总之，他说保尔可以去。他问他打过野鸭没有，保尔说没有，他手里从来没拿过枪。于是吉姆说，他可以坐在小船里瞧他打，如果

stairs.

Well, Julie come up to Doc's door and rung the bell and they was nothin' doin'. She rung it again and she rung it seven or eight times. Then she tried the door and found it locked. Then Jim made some kind of a noise and she heard it and waited a minute, and then she says, "Is that you, Ralph?" Ralph is Doc's first name.

They was no answer and it must of came to her all of a sudden that she'd been bunked. She pretty near fell downstairs and the whole gang after her. They chased her all the way home, hollerin', "Is that you, Ralph?" and "Oh, Ralphie, dear, is that you?" Jim says he couldn't holler it himself, as he was laughin' too hard.

Poor Julie! She didn't show up here on Main Street for a long, long time afterward.

And of course Jim and his gang told everybody in town, everybody but Doc Stair. They was scared to tell him, and he might of never knowed only for Paul Dickson. The poor cuckoo, as Jim called him, he was here in the shop one night when Jim was still gloatin' yet over what he'd done to Julie. And Paul took in as much of it he could understand and he run to Doc with the story.

It's a cinch Doc went up in the air and swore he'd make Jim suffer. But it was a kind of a delicate thing, because if it got out that he had beat Jim up, Julie was bound to hear of it and then she'd know that Doc knew and of course knowin' that he knew would make it worse for her than ever. He was goin' to do somethin', but it took a lot of figurin'.

Well, it was a couple days later when Jim was here in the shop again, and so was the cuckoo. Jim was goin' duck-shootin' the next day and had came in lookin' for Hod Meyers to go with him. I happened to know that Hod had went over to Carterville and wouldn't be home till the end of the week. So Jim said he hated to go alone and he guessed he would call it off. Then poor Paul spoke up and said if Jim would take him he would go along. Jim thought a w'ile and then he said, well, he guessed a half-wit was better than nothin'.

I suppose he was plottin' to get Paul out in the boat and play some joke on him, like pushin' him in the water. Anyways, he said Paul could go. He asked him had he ever shot a duck and Paul said no, he'd never even had a gun in his hands. So Jim said he could set in the boat and watch him and if he behaved himself, he might lend him his gun for a couple of shots. They made a date to meet in the mornin' and that's the last I seen of Jim alive.

他还安生,他也许会把枪借给他,让他放两下。他们约好在早上见面,这是我最后一次看到吉姆还活着。

第二天早晨,我开门还不到10分钟,斯太尔医生来了。他的样子有点儿紧张。他问我瞧见保尔·狄克逊没有。我说,没有,可是我知道他在哪儿,跟吉姆·肯德尔打野鸭去了。医生说他也是这么听人说的,不过他不明白,因为保尔对他说过,只要吉姆还活着,他永远不会跟他再来往的。

他说保尔曾经告诉他吉姆对朱莉玩弄的恶作剧。他说,保尔曾经问他对这种恶作剧有什么想法,医生于是告诉他不应当让干出这种事的人活着。

我说这种事是有点儿下流,不过吉姆是忍不住要开玩笑的,不管多么下流。我说我认为他心地倒还好,就是尽搞些恶作剧。医生转身就走开了。

中午的时候,他接到老约翰·司各特的电话。吉姆跟保尔去打猎的那片湖水在约翰的地面上。几分钟之前,保尔跑到约翰家里,说出了事。吉姆打了几只野鸭之后,把枪交给保尔,要他试试运气。保尔从来没拿过枪,他十分紧张。他抖得很厉害,使不了枪。他让枪走了火,吉姆就倒在船里,死了。

斯太尔医生是验尸官,他跳上弗兰克·阿勃特的小汽车,赶到司各特的农场上。保尔和老约翰都在湖岸上。保尔已经把船划得靠岸了,可是他们把尸首留在船里,等医生来。

医生检查了尸体,说他们还不如把尸首运回镇上。放在这儿没用,也用不着召集陪审团,因为这个案子是清清楚楚的意外走火事故。

拿我自个儿来说,要是我在船上,除非我准知道他懂得点儿枪法,我绝不会让别人在同一条船上放枪的。吉姆是自讨苦吃,把他的枪交给了一个新手,而且又是一个傻子。吉姆落到这样,大概也是自作自受。不过我们这儿都还惦记着他。他真是个会恶作剧的怪物!上油还是干梳?

Next mornin', I hadn't been open more than ten minutes when Doc Stair come in. He looked kind of nervous. He asked me had I seen Paul Dickson. I said no, but I knew where he was, out duck-shootin' with Jim Kendall. So Doc says that's what he had heard, and he couldn't understand it because Paul had told him he wouldn't never have no more to do with Jim as long as he lived.

He said Paul had told him about the joke Jim had played on Julie. He said Paul had asked him what he thought of the joke and the Doc told him that anybody that would do a thing like that ought not to be let live.

I said it had been a kind of a raw thing, but Jim just couldn't resist no kind of a joke, no matter how raw. I said I thought he was all right at heart, but just bubblin' over with mischief. Doc turned and walked out.

At noon he got a phone call from old John Scott. The lake where Jim and Paul had went shootin' is on John's place. Paul had came runnin' up to the house a few minutes before and said they'd been an accident. Jim had shot a few ducks and then give the gun to Paul and told him to try his luck. Paul hadn't never handled a gun and he was nervous. He was shakin' so hard that he couldn't control the gun. He let fire and Jim sunk back in the boat, dead.

Doc Stair, bein' the coroner, jumped in Frank Abbott's flivver and rushed out to Scott's farm. Paul and old John was down on the shore of the lake. Paul had rowed the boat to shore, but they'd left the body in it, waiting for Doc to come.

Doc examined the body and said they might as well fetch it back to town. They was no use leavin' it there or callin' a jury, as it was a plain case of accidental shootin'.

Personally I wouldn't never leave a person shoot a gun in the same boat I was in unless I was sure they knew somethin' about guns. Jim was a sucker to leave a new beginner have his gun, let alone a half-wit. It probably served Jim right, what he got. But still we miss him round here. He certainly was a card! Comb it wet or dry?

┌─讨　论─■

在这篇小说里,主要情节就是那个怪人——那个恶作剧者的故事。这个人毫无人心,也毫无人情,自然,他玩的把戏也是又粗野又愚蠢,仅仅是一种狂妄自大的表现而已。到

The main action here is the story of the "card," the practical joker. He has no shred of human perception or feeling, and his Jokes are, naturally, brutal and stupid, only a way of

最后,他的把戏出了洋相,恶作剧者自食其果,这使我们为之感到精神上的满足。恶作剧者总会因自己的恶劣性,由于不可能理解他人、留神他人而自作自受的。虽然,一个怪人的个性写得很充分,对那个小镇作为背景也写得很充分,情节呢,也是经过合理而精心安排的,但就其要描绘出一幅专横跋扈场景的图画而言,我们依然会感到像小说里这样的主要情节总嫌过于简单、过于类型化,甚至过于说教、过于直露。无论如何,看来林·拉德纳肯定已经感觉到了,他感到如果把主要情节赤裸裸地表现出来,也就是作者自己来讲故事,这不会使人满意,所以他设计了一个叙述者,就是那个理发师,而通过理发师把故事转述给我们。

使用叙述者这个角色,首先是为了使小说显得不那么干巴巴,不那么单调无味——当然,如果仅仅是为了表面的复杂而复杂化,那并不解决问题——其次是,可以通过理发师的嘴使我们对小镇也有所了解,对店铺里那些食客的无聊和粗野有所了解。但是,拉德纳设计理发师这个叙述者,是否还有别的明显的用意呢?关于这个问题我们最好先问另一个问题:理发师是何许人?明确一点,也就是说他对自己讲的故事抱着怎样的态度?

我们随即看到,理发师感到小镇生活由于没有了那个怪人而变得很无味了。理发师本人是不无同意地参与那些粗野的恶作剧的,所以他和那个怪人可算是一丘之貉。这里,我们对简单的基本情节有了深入的了解,知道那伙合谋作恶者的联系还很广泛。

另外,还有一种深入了解,不是在内容方面,而是在表述方面。我们想一想,叙述者理发师告诉我们的仅仅是些和他同类人的事情,而这些人呢,也都是些和那个怪人合谋干坏事的心照不宣的同谋,而叙述者本人又认为这些人也理应受到指责。这样一来,我们就会发现自己马上就得和叙述者抱同样的态度。叙述者的态度和我们的态度就会毫无抵触了。但

inflating his own ego. In the end, one of his jokes backfires, and we have the moral satisfaction of seeing the biter bit, the joker caught in the destructive consequences of a joke whose destructive nature for other people he could never have understood or cared about. Assuming that the card is adequately characterized, that the setting of the small town is adequately rendered for us, and that the plot is logically worked out, we might still feel that this main action, taken by itself, is somewhat too simple and predictable, even too moralistic and too obviously an illustration of brutal arrogance being paid off. Anyway, it seems that Ring Lardner must have felt that a naked presentation of the main action, that is, the story told straight by the author, would be unsatisfactory, for he provides a narrator, the barber, who gives us his version of the business.

The use of the narrator does, for the first thing, make the story seem less bare and simple—though, of course, complication for the mere sake of complication scarcely justifies itself—and, for another thing, the barber does give us a sense of the town, of the blankness and brutality of the hangers-on at the shop. But what other positive values was Lardner aiming at in his use of the barber as the narrator? To answer this we may well begin by asking another question: what is the barber like: More specifically, what is his attitude toward the story he tells?

The barber, we quickly discover, thinks that life is pretty dull around town now that the card is gone. The barber has vicariously participated in the brutal jokes, and is, therefore, a kind of accomplice. So we have a deepening of the originally simple action—a sense of the spreading ripples of complicity always around the evil act.

There is, also, another kind of deepening, not in content but in presentation. Let us suppose that the narrator of the story had merely told us about people like the barber, people who had some tacit complicity with the card's jokes, and that he himself, the narrator, found such people reprehensible. Given this treatment, we would find ourselves in immediate agreement with his attitude. There

是，从实际情况来看，我们的态度和叙述者的态度是有抵触的，因为我们老是想不和他同流合污，老是想在（善良的）我们和（邪恶的）理发师之间制造某种紧张的戏剧性状态。换言之，拉德纳使用的是一种倒转的、含有讽刺意味的手法。叙述者表现的既不是作者的观点，也不是我们的观点。那个理发师讲故事时每每歪曲故事的含义，借此作者提醒我们，对小说里什么东西是加以肯定的应抱更大的警惕心，甚至刺激我们，使我们警觉到自己不能和理发师那样显得又残忍又愚钝。

这篇小说如果采取平铺直叙的方法，或者让叙述者在讲故事时采取与我们完全一样的态度的话，那么势必至于，我们会把那个怪人仅仅认作为一个畜生、一只虫豸，而他的所作所为也就是理所当然的。但由于这样做过于简单，我们便会忽略整篇小说的内容。而采取现在这样的方法，这就迫使我们或多或少地对理发师制造的麻烦加以注意，而当我们这样做时，也就不知不觉地被更深地引进了小说。

叙述者的这种运用法，可说是一种既简单又巧妙的手法，它所要达到的目的就是所谓的"读者参与"——就是使读者对自己有所知觉，使他把某种表面上的含义（在这篇小说里就是理发师的观点）倒转过来看，并进入小说内部或者扩大小说的含义而不受小说实际范围的限制。反衬、克制叙述（见重要词汇）、欲言不语——这些手法可以引起读者对事物进行反复思考，对自己的感情进行反复检讨，从而更深入地进入小说情节的发展过程。

这里考察一下视角或者叙事焦点（见重要词汇）的一般情况肯定是有益的。我们刚才看到，《理发》这篇小说就是通过理发师的主观意识来表现的，这何等重要，我们看到，也就是这种"视角"的使用，影响到整篇小说和我们对小说的看法。视角——这由小说作者加以决定——对于任何叙事作品来说，都是一个至关重要的问题。情节必须通过语言才能表现，但

would be no shock of the collision between the narrator's attitude and our own. But as things actually stand, there is a shock of collision between the narrator's attitude and our own, a growing need to repudiate his attitude, and a sense of tension and drama between the(good) us and the(bad) barber. In other words, Lardner has used an inverted and ironical method. The narrator represents neither the author's view nor our own. The barber is used to belie, as it were, the meaning of the story, and by so doing to irritate us to a fuller awareness of what is at stake in the story, even to stir our awareness of our own less obvious cruelties or obtusities.

If the story were told directly, or told by a narrator whose attitudes were congenial with our own, we should be inclined to say that the card, of course, is a brute, a louse, and that he got just what he deserved. But we might say it too easily, and be inclined to dismiss the whole business. As it is, we are compelled, in a greater or lesser degree, to take issue with the barber, and in taking issue we are drawn more deeply into the story.

The use of this kind of narrator is, then, a fairly simple device for provoking what we may call "reader participation"—for making the reader do some of the interpreting himself, for drawing him into the story by making him invert an apparent meaning(here the barber's valuations) or develop meaning beyond the point where the story actually comes to rest. Irony, *understatement* (see Glossary), withholding—these are ways to provoke the reader to reassess things, to reassess his own feelings, and thus enter more deeply into the process of the piece of fiction.

Here it might be well to consider the general problem of the *point of view* or the *focus of narration* (see Glossary). We have just seen how important it is that"Haircut"is presented through the mentality of the barber, and we have seen how the use of this point of view affects the whole story and our reception of the story. The point of view—the choice of the teller of the story—is a question of the greatest importance for any piece of fiction. The action has to come to us through

是通过谁的语言呢？这个问题必须解决，因为其他一切可以说都将由此而定。对此，我们提出以下几个辅助性问题：

1. 叙述者对故事以外的各种事情知道哪些？他能讲哪些？
2. 叙述者已经讲了他所知道的一切吗？如果不是，为什么？他保留不讲的事情或者情况有多少？如果他有保留，这样做是合情合理的呢，还是仅仅为了弄虚作假？
3. 他为什么只讲了他所讲的这些事情？作为叙述者他的动机如何？
4. 叙述者对自己讲的故事的态度如何？

围绕小说视角问题，虽然会产生许多其他的重要问题，而我们依然可以从中认定，视角同小说结构和主题之间的关系是最为重要的问题。但是，在我们考察这类关系之前，先要弄清楚，在小说中可能会出现的视角有哪几种。

显然，第一人称是一种——如在《理发》里，由一个"我"用第一人称和他自己的语言讲故事，讲的内容也仅限于他理应知道的或者感兴趣的。我们一眼就看出，这种叙述者的个人形象在各篇小说中是各不相同的。一个极端是，"我"是主要人物，他所讲的也就是他自己的故事，譬如，《阿拉比》里的叙述者就是这样；另一个极端是，"我"仅仅是旁观者或者旁听者，他看到或者听到某件事而实际上与事情关系不大，譬如《国王迷》里的那个记者，他是个传话人，只是为真正的叙述者传传话而已。他实质上只是小说"真实性背景"的一个组成部分。

在这两个极端中间，可以说包括着各种不同程度和关系的叙述者，从那种不是中心人物但又和故事关系密切的叙述者（如皮奇），到类似理发师之类的叙述者（此类叙述者不是在直接的意义上和事件有关而只是具有某种精神

words, but through whose words? On the answer to that question, all else may often hinge. So we have such subsidiary questions as these:

1. What does the narrator know of the total action lying beyond the story? What can he tell?
2. Does he tell all he knows? If not, why not? What accounts for his withholding any information or narrative? If there is withholding, is it reasonable and justifiable, or merely trickery and mystification?
3. Why does he tell what he does tell? What is his motivation as narrator?
4. What is the narrator's attitude toward what he tells?

Though there are many other important questions that may develop around the point of view of a piece of fiction, we can see from these that the point of view bears most important relations to the structure and meaning of fiction. Before we go into such relations, however, we should sort out what points of view are possible in fiction.

There is, obviously, the first person—the story told, as is "Haircut," by an "I," speaking in his own person and in his own language, telling only what he himself can be reasonably supposed to know and what he is interested in telling. We are immediately aware that the status of such a narrator varies from story to story. At one extreme, the "I" may be the main character, as in "Araby," who tells his own story, or, at the other extreme, the "I" may be a mere observer or auditor who has seen or heard about the action of a story but has taken no significant part in it, like the newspaperman in "The Man Who Would Be King," who is a sort of marginal narrator, reporting the real narrator. He is really an aspect of the "convincing background."

In between these extremes may be all sorts of shadings and relationships, from the narrator who is not central but is deeply involved, like Peachey, through the narrator

联系),直至《县城的医生》里的那个叙述者(他虽然对事件表现了某种最低限度的个人反应,但也仅仅是一种媒介,一个旁听者或者一个复述者),凡此种种,都包括其中。

用第三人称叙述故事是另一种被普遍采用的视角——作者不露面,讲故事时也不自称。一个极端是,由一个"外在的"叙述者做纯客观的叙述,也就是说,有一个叙述者,但他仅仅叙述从外部看到或听到的事物——他就像一架照相机或者一个传声筒。这是一个戏剧的方法,也即直叙的方法,不做简要的提示,没有心理描写,也没有任何想进入人物思想、感情的企图。举例来说,约翰·科利尔的《埋葬》可以说是这方面的一个几乎是完美的例子。

第三人称的另一极端是,人物的主观世界,由一个全知叙述者来加以揭示,这个叙述者对小说里出现的任何人、任何事都无所不知,无所不晓。使用这种方法,旨在于使我们深入到一个人物甚或几个人物的思想和感情中去,有时甚至会深入到那种地步,致使整篇小说变得仅像一幅人物思想、感情活动的临摹图。《沃尔特·米蒂的隐秘生活》就属这样的小说。米蒂的梦境成了小说仅有的场景,但是,我们既已获准进入其中,我们就会对它做出判断,犹如在欣赏它的表演似的。诚然,作者把我们引进了人物的意识中,但他自己往往并不抱着同情心去追随人物的思想感情变化,他对它们进行解剖、综合和分析,譬如《项链》里的那些心理描写就是如此。

视角的四种主要类型间的关系,可由下列图表给予说明。

like the barber, who is not involved in any direct sense but who has a moral connection with the action, to the narrator of "The District Doctor," who, though he does show a minimal human reaction to the story, is little more than a conduit, a listener and repeater.

The other general point of view from which a story may be told is the third person, an unidentified author speaking impersonally. At one extreme here is the purely objective record made by an "external" narrator, that is, one who tells only what can be seen and heard from the outside—as though he were a camera and sound machine. John Collier's "De Mortuis" is an almost perfect example of such *dramatic* method, the immediate reportorial method, without summary or psychological interpretation or any entering into the thoughts or feelings of characters.

At the other extreme in the third person is the subjective revelation that can be made by an omniscient narrator, who knows everything about everybody in a story. This method does let us into the thoughts and feelings of one or more characters, sometimes so intimately into them that the story is little more than the tracing of their reactions. "The Secret Life of Walter Mitty" is such a story. Mitty's dream world is the world of the story, and by being admitted into it, we make a judgment on it even as we enjoy its comedy. But an author may, of course, lead us into a character's consciousness, not to follow more or less sympathetically the flow of thought and feeling but to dissect, summarize, and analyze, as in the subjective passages of "The Necklace."

The four main kinds of point of view can be related as shown in the accompanying chart.

	事件的内部分析	事件的外部分沂
第一人称（叙述者在小说里作为一个人物）	1. 主要人物讲述自己的故事	2. 次要人物讲述主要人物的故事
第三人称（叙述者在小说里不是一个人物——仅仅是旁观者而且是不可被明确辨认的）	4. 分析的或者全知的叙述者讲述故事并且进入人物的思想感情	3. 叙述者（不可明确辨认，即作者本人）带或者不带个人判断和解释，作为旁观者讲述故事

	Internal analysis of events	*External analysis of events*
First person (*narrator as a character in story*)	1. Main character tells own story.	2. Minor character tells main character's story.
Third person (*narrator not a character in story —mere observer, but identified*)	4. Analytic or omniscient narrator tells story, entering thoughts and feelings.	3. Narrator (unidentified, i. e., author) tells story as observer, with or without personal judgment and interpretation.

现在,我们再回头看一看《国王迷》,以便回到关于视角同小说结构和意义的关系问题上来。在那篇小说里,叙述者不是一个,而是两个。那个新闻记者用第一人称以那种吉卜林式的阴郁调子给了我们总的叙述,在他的叙述里,具体的情节又有皮奇的叙述,用的也是第一人称。吉卜林选择了这种方法,其道理何在?

首先,我们知道,用第一人称叙述故事比较自然。这倒不是说读者真会那么天真,会去"相信"用第一人称叙述的故事,而是说,这样做可以将有些事情较为轻松而随便地引入小说,虽然我们知道第一人称手法本身也是一种"惯例"(见重要词汇),一种虚构方式而已。在吉卜林这篇小说里,我们需要对印度那个陌生世界有所了解,要是用第三人称来叙述,那么仅注释性的材料就会把小说充塞得笨拙不堪。而像现在这样,那个新闻记者至少可以较随便、较顺手地给予我们一个关于他那个世界的十分完整的概念,而在处理这些注释忄材料时又可以不让我们觉得这是附加的,虽然这也是他生活的一部分。

其次,用第一人称叙述可以使小说不露出"选材"(见重要词汇)的痕迹。由于第一人称叙述者讲的仅仅是自己的所见所闻,或者自己的合理推测,那些为有前提的、潜在的情节所做的大量铺叙就毫无必要了。要是叙述者明

To return to our remarks about the relation of point of view to structure and meaning, we may take a backward glance at "The Man Who Would Be King". That story has not only one narrator, but two. There is the newspaperman who gives us the general narration in his own person, a sort of shadow of Kipling, but within his narration there is the action narrated by Peachey, again in the first person. What is the logic of Kipling's choice of method?

First, we may observe that by taking a first-person narrator, a certain naturalness may be gained. This is not to say that the reader is so innocent that he more readily "believes" a story told in the first person, but it is to say that certain things can be introduced into a story more informally and casually, even though we recognize that the first-person method itself is a *convention* (see Glossary), a fiction. In this particular story we need to know something about the strange world of India, and if that information were given in the third person the burden of mere exposition would be more apparent. As it is, the newspaperman can more or less casually and incidentally give us a fairly complete notion of his world; he can feed the expository material in without making us feel that it is labeled, for it is part of his life.

Second, the presence of a first-person narrator introduces naturally into a story a device for *selectivity* (see Glossary). Since the narrator can tell only what he has observed, heard, or reasonably surmised, a considerable

确选定了某一特定事件,那么他必须做的跳跃就会显得很自然,同时又有充分的选择。我们会感到他所讲的也就是他能够讲的或者必须讲的。

譬如,在《国王迷》里,我们看到的那件事——卡菲里斯坦的被占领——就其本来来说可以写成一部长篇小说,然而吉卜林感兴趣的只是一件事——关于王权、神权和人权的观念——他处理必要的背景性材料仅仅为了使德雷沃特的发展显得生动而可信。在小说里,德雷沃特的故事通过新闻记者和皮奇的嘴讲得很生动,而有些事件则略而不谈了。按照通常的展开方式来写会铺满几页纸的情节被缩成一两句话——如山里夺驴子那件事。处理事件的程度也受到叙述者说话方式的制约——他是以自己的方式讲故事的,是他在遣词造句。准确、鲜明、简练——这些在任何小说里都自然需要,而采用第一人称叙述故事,则具备了一种可达到此类目的的内在手段。换言之,小说情节安排及剪裁尺度——即,我们实际上看到的情节结构——是视小说所选视角而定的。

不仅仅结构要视视角而定。我们再以皮奇为例。根据我们的观点,他是事件的叙述者,也就是小说结构的给予者,是有用的,但同时他又是德雷沃特发展的一面镜子,起到反映作用,也即制约作用。我们并不仅仅想知道他所知道的事情,我们还要知道他对那件事的意义知道些什么。'我们一眼就能看出,德雷沃特是他们两人中的强者,是一个有抱负、有想象力的人物,是他想出了那个洗劫王国的计划。皮奇只是满足于跟随而已。在德雷沃特从仅是一个抢劫者到最后达到成功顶点的整个精神历险中,他们两人始终保持着这种关系。德雷沃特成功的每一步都出乎皮奇的意料,皮奇这个没有想象力的家伙如果让他独自一个人的话,他仅仅作为分赃者和抢劫者就会感到心满意足。而就是通过皮奇错误百出的估计和

body of material from the hypothetical underlying action is not available to him. If for a particular story the narrator is well chosen, then the deletions he must make will seem natural, and the selections significant. We feel that *what* he has to tell is what he *can* tell and *must* tell.

For example, in "The Man Who Would Be King" we are dealing with an action that, taken in itself, is potentially a novel—the conquest of Kafiristan. Kipling is, however, interested in only one thing—the idea of kingship, godhood, and manhood—and he wants to render only so much of the general action as is needed to make vivid and credible the development of Dravot. By the time Dravot's story is filtered through Peachey and the newspaperman only vivid and telling strokes are left. A piece of action that might require pages if given any ordinary development comes down to a sentence or two—for example, the taking of the four mules in the mountains. The scale of treatment can be controlled in terms of the narrator's presence—he tells it in his way, he makes the emphasis. *Selection, foreshortening, summary*—these things are natural to all fiction, but with the first-person narrator we have, as it were, a built-in device for controlling them. In other words, the plot of a story and the scale of the episodes—that is, the structure of action as it is actually presented to us—depend on the point of view.

Not only does structure depend on point of view. Let us take Peachey again. He is useful in the way we have said, as a narrator of events, the giver of the structure, but he is also a mirror to Dravot's development, a device of interpretation as well as of control. We can ask not merely what he knows of the action, but what he knows of the meaning of the action. We sense immediately that Dravot is the powerful one of the pair, the one with ambition and imagination, the one who starts the great scheme of looting a kingdom. Peachey is content to follow at an admiring distance. This same relationship prevails as Dravot begins his spiritual journey from mere looter up to the point that he achieves in the end. Each new phase of his development is played off against Peachey, the unimaginative follower who, if left alone, would be perfectly content

一知半解的反应,我们感觉到了德雷沃特所表现出来的老谋深算。我们不妨说,正因为皮奇感觉迟钝、头脑单纯,他才起到了反衬和克制叙述作用。事实上,这篇小说主题方面的思想含义就是通过这个人反映出来的,这个人除非和德雷沃特合作,否则至今还是个分赃者和抢劫者,这就是反衬对照——虽然这里的反衬不像《理发》里的那种,它使我们把叙述者想得更好而不是更坏。德雷沃特故事的意义,通过皮奇的嘴说出是克制叙述的,没有说出全部意义。这就是说,皮奇只是个引起我们反复思考的向导,虽然是个颇蹩脚的向导。但是到最后,正是他,通过他在山里的昏乱无措的表现,烘托出了德雷沃特的神一般的形象——是他守住了山头。正是皮奇的头脑单纯,使我们接受德雷沃特这一形象成为可能。我们在接受它的主题真实性同时,因为看到这个形象是从皮奇头脑单纯的胡扯乱谈中反映出来的,所以也就会接受这个形象本身可能有的真实性。

至此,我们也许已足够说明视角对结构和主题的重要性了。根据上述情况,请考虑以下问题:

1.《埋葬》的视角同作品的基调有何联系?假如那个医生是故事的叙述者,或者叙述者是他的某个朋友,那么就可能遇到什么新问题?

2.假如,《国王迷》这篇小说的通篇故事会由新闻记者一个人讲述,连由皮奇讲述的关于他和德雷沃特的事情也由新闻记者来加以解释和概述,那么这篇小说和原来的会有什么不同?

3.如果《醉汉》这篇小说用的是第三人称叙述法,那么这篇小说会欠缺些什么?

4.在《请买票》这篇小说里,安妮是否有可能自述自己的故事?安妮是否像作者劳伦斯一样真正地理解自己的故事?她愿意理解它吗?

我们现在清楚地看到,人物性格的发展或

to be merely the self-indulgent loafer and looter. It is through Peachey's blundering account and not entirely comprehending response that we sense the depth of experience represented by Dravot. We may say that Peachey, with his blunt lack of sensitivity and his simplicity of mind, is a device of irony and understatement. The fact that the spiritual significance of the theme comes through the man who, except for his association with Dravot, would remain loafer and looter, gives an ironical contrast—though the irony here, unlike that in "Haircut," makes us think not worse, but better, of the narrator. The meaning of Dravot's story, as filtered to us through Peachey, is understated: the full significance is not offered. Peachey is, as it were, a guide for our response, though a rather limping one. But in the end it is he who, in his delirium in the mountains, presents the image of the godlike Dravot who can hold up the peaks. Peachey's simplicity of mind makes it possible for us to accept the image. We accept the thematic truth of it and at the same time, because it comes from the delirium of Peachey's simple mind, accept the plausibility of it.

We have by now perhaps said enough to indicate something of the importance of point of view for both structure and meaning. In light of that, consider these questions:

1. How is the point of view of "De Mortuis" related to the tone of the story? Suppose the doctor were the narrator, or one of his friends. What new problems would have to be faced?

2. Suppose that the whole of "The Man Who Would Be King" were narrated by the newspaperman, with only his paraphrases and summaries of Peachey's account of what happened to him and Dravot. How would the story be different?

3. What would be lost if "The Drunkard" were set in the third person?

4. Could Annie, in "Tickets, Please," have told her own story? As Lawrence, the author, tells it, does Annie really grasp the full meaning of her own story? Should she?

者揭示,是和小说的视角选择有着密切的关系的。它和小说的风格(见重要词汇)也有密切的联系。尤其是当一篇小说是用第一人称来叙述时,这种联系更为明显,因为,言即其人(皮奇不是《县城的医生》里的叙述者,但是试设想,如果他是的话,那这篇小说就会怎样地面目全非了——由他转述的人物对话就会大不相同,甚至可以说,他对这样一个故事几乎是不可能理解的)。同样,用第三人称叙述的小说,其中风格和人物的关系也很密切。我们曾指出,我们认为《带家具出租的房间》和《田纳西的伙伴》这两篇小说的风格不够严谨,作品里的那些和实际素材不相匹配的渲染成分和抒情成分使小说内容失去了含蓄的艺术魅力。恰恰相反,我们认为像《阿拉比》这样的作品则富有这种艺术魅力。这篇小说的风格在于:它使敏感的读者同时注意到,小说既写了少年人的初恋,但又显然不是以少年人的笔调或者口吻来叙述的。可以说,小说表现的是一个成年男子的痛苦经验,而这种经验则是通过他的真实的思想感情,由他自己回忆,自己取舍,自己处理,然后组织成篇的。

在此我们不能对风格上的问题一一分析,但是,在此应该加以强调的是:就以塑造人物为主的小说而言,作品风格同作品中的人物、作家的态度以及读者对他的态度都有着本质上的联系。从某种意义上讲,作品的风格就是作家的一切——同时又是他自己。

(刘文荣 译)

We have seen how closely the development or revelation of character is related to the matter of point of view. It is related with equal intimacy to the matter of *style* (see Glossary). When a story is told in the first person, this relationship is most obvious: a man's language is the man. (Peachey is not the narrator of "The District Doctor", but try to imagine how different it would be if he were—how much the dialogue would change in his language; how little, even, he could understand of such a story.) Similarly, there are intimate relations between style and character in stories told in the third person. We have already remarked what we regard as defects of style in "The Furnished Room" and "Tennessee's Partner": inflation and poeticism that do not match the material, that are inappropriate to the context of the stories. But consider, in contrast, the appropriateness of style of "Araby", for instance. It is the style that at once informs the sensitive reader that though the story is one of painful adolescent love, it was not written or spoken by any adolescent boy. Rather it presents that painful experience as recollected, assimilated, judged, and set in true perspective by a man grown to maturity.

This is not the place to analyze a number of stylistic questions, but it is the place to insist on the fact that the style of the story that a character inhabits does have an essential relation to him, and to the attitude of author and reader toward him. In one sense, the style of the story is his world—and himself.

主 题
What Theme Reveals

主题是某种观念，某种意义，某种对人物和事件的诠释，是体现在整个作品中的对生活的深刻而又融贯统一的观点。

在讨论迄今所谈到的作品时，我们始终着眼于小说的主题、思想和意义。我们不可能不注意小说的主题而能深入地了解小说的情节和人物，因为正如我们所强调的，一篇好的小说，它是一种有机的统一体，其中各种重要因素相互之间都有联系。一种因素会牵涉到其他所有的因素，而它们又是为同一个预定目的服务的。

在对小说的主题做进一步系统研究时，我们先重申一下我们对主题的看法。首先，不能把小说的主题简单地看作就是故事的题意——虽然主题这个词有时也在这个意义上被广义地使用。譬如，我们会说海明威的《杀手》和赖特的《人，差点儿》这两篇作品十分相像，因为它们有同样的题意，即都是写少年最初进入成年时期的情形。至于两篇题目一样的小说——如莫泊桑的《爱情》和斯图尔特的《爱情》——它们当然表现相同的题意，但是我们虽然会发现这两篇小说在处理上颇为相似，可我们同样也会发现，这两篇小说的含义以及作品所赋有的"感情色彩"是截然不同的。我们认为，主题是通过题意表现出来的东西。它是小说在其展开过程中所涉及到的思想性内容的集中表现。

主题就是对一篇小说的总概括。它是某种观念，某种意义，某种对人物和事件的诠释，是体现在整个作品中对生活的深刻而又融贯统一的观点。它是通过小说体现出来的某种人皆有之的人生经验——在小说中，总是直接或间接地含有某种对人性价值和人类行为价值的议论。

后面这句话可能会引起两种反对意见。有些人认为，这种说法会使小说成为一种带有

In discussing the stories we have read thus far we have continually referred to the theme, the idea, the meaning. We cannot very long consider the actions or characters of a story without coming to some concern with theme of a story, for insofar as it is a good story, it is, as we have insisted, an organic unity in which all the vital elements have interrelations. Each element implies all the other elements, and implies them in motion toward a significant end.

Now, as we turn to a more systematic treatment of theme in fiction, let us review some of our notions. For one thing, the theme of a piece of fiction is not to be thought of as merely the topic of the story—though the word is sometimes loosely used in this sense. For instance, we may say that two stories shortly to be encountered, "The Killers", by Ernest Hemingway, and "The Man Who Was Almost a Man", by Richard Wright, have the same topic: growing up, the initiation into manhood. The titles of another pair—"Love" by Guy de Maupassant, and "Love" by Jess Stuart—proclaim the same topic, but even though we shall find considerable similarity in treatment, we shall also find significant differences in meaning and differences in the very "feel" of the stories. *The theme, then, is what is made of the topic*. It is what amounts to the comment of the idea *implied* in the process of the story.

The theme is what a piece of fiction stacks up to. It is the idea, the significance, the interpretation of persons and events, the pervasive and unifying view of life embodied in the total narrative. It is what we are to make of the human experience rendered in the story—always involving, directly or indirectly, some comment on values in human nature and conduct.

This last remark may provoke two objections. Some may feel that it makes fiction a

图解的单纯说教。另一些人则认为这种说法对于那些轻松愉快的娱乐性小说来讲毫无说服力。我们姑且就取这两种反对意见来加以讨论。

对第一种意见我们从侧面来考察一下。我们在读一篇好的小说时,往往会在不同程度上对那篇小说产生各种各样的兴味。我们会发现其中某个人物具有吸引力而把他当作现实生活中的某个朋友那样来对待;或者会因其中陌生的环境或情节而感到惊异——为了满足这种好奇心我们也会继续读下去;或者会抱有疑问,急于想知道下一步的发展情况。我们甚至会对作者本人的个性、他的精神魅力、他对生活所做的生动的观察,或者他的富有诗意的语言,感到兴味无穷;或者会因小说里的事情而浮想联翩,做起白日梦来,因为在我们自己贫乏枯燥的生活里,这样的事情是从来不会发生的。说实在的,我们会被小说中任何联想所左右。

但是,谈到最后,我们总会产生这样的问题:"这篇小说总的讲些什么? 它的意义何在?"如果我们不能从那些事情中得出某种有意义的稳定性因素,我们就会有受骗上当的感觉。我们不应忘记,每个人或早或晚都会提出这样的问题,即生活的"意义何在"? 要是一篇小说不以这样或那样的方式来关心这个问题,我们就会失望之至。

产生这种失望的原因就在于一般人总期望事物是有条有理的。我们乐于看到一篇小说能自成一体,和谐有致——正像我们觉得自己的生活应该合乎情理一样。在生活中,我们要求因果联系合乎逻辑,推论合乎理性,同样,对于小说我们也有这样的要求。我们要求小说具有合乎逻辑的主题——即某种主题结构,并由这种主题结构将各种成分规划而成一个有机的整体。所以说,无主题便无小说。

以上是针对那种认为我们对主题的看法会使小说变成图解式说教的反对意见而言的。

kind of mere moralizing, with illustrations. Others may feel that it gives no accommodation to stories that are gay, lighthearted, and comic. Both objections are well taken, and deserve discussion.

Let us take an indirect approach to the first. When we read a good piece of fiction we may be caught by any number of interests, in different degrees. We may simply find a character attractive, and relish his company as we would that of a friend in real life. Or we may find our curiosity stimulated by strange backgrounds or events—the satisfaction of the same desire that leads us to travel. Or we may be held by suspense, the anxiety to know what comes next. We may even be caught by the writer's personality, his charm of spirit, his sprightliness of observation on life, or his poetic expression. Or we may enjoy daydreaming into experiences that we can never have in out humdrum lives. We may, in fact, be caught by any combination of things.

But in the end there is always the question "What does it add up to? what does it mean?" If we do not feel that things work out to some moment of significant stability, we feel defrauded. And we should not forget that the question every person, sooner or later, asks about life is "What does it mean?" If a story does not deal with this question, in some way or other, we are left dissatisfied.

One reason for such dissatisfaction is our simple human craving to have things put into order. We like to observe a story working itself out into a unity—just as we feel a need to have our own lives make sense. We demand the logic of cause and effect in fiction, and reasonable motivation, in the same way we demand it in life. We demand that there be a logic of them—a thematic structure into which the various elements are drawn into unity. Thus, *no theme, no story*.

That is one approach to the objection that out discussion of theme seems to make fiction mere moralizing with illustrations. Another approach is related, but dissimilar. Let

与此有关而又不尽相同的问题是关于"图解"这个词,我们也来考察一下。

小说不是图解,虽然有时它表面上看来仿佛是图解——譬如我们在读《国王迷》时,会觉得它仿佛在图解这样一句格言:"凡和王孙公子称兄道弟,或与贫丐莫逆交者,则为俊杰。"但是小说不是图解,因为就图解来说,我们始终认为被图解的观念才是至关重要的,图解的内容则始终是由那个被图解的东西——某种"观念"——所决定的。图解只是释义,而不是对生活的不断的发现。

但是在成功的小说里,想象力所创造的世界显然有其自身存在的权利。在那些名篇杰作里,其真实性无论从哪方面来说都不容否认,我们甚至会觉得它们往往比许多我们耳闻目睹的事实还要亲切。可以说,在我们心目中,哈姆雷特就要比乔治·华盛顿或者某某邻居来得更逼真。即使不说名篇杰作,就是那些范篇佳作也在一定程度上具有这种自在自为的迷惑力。

自在自为这个问题与主题又有什么关系?简单地说,就是在一篇成功的小说里,根据自在自为这个概念,人物既自动也被动,一个事件会导出另一个事件,与此同时我们越来越清楚地领悟到整篇作品的意义。这也就是说,我们逐渐地领悟到主题是在深化,意义在丰富。我们觉得自己正卷入在一个活生生的变化过程中,并随着这个过程进而明确了其中的意义。正由于这种感受最后会使我们对自己的生活(如果我们不是像禽兽般生活的话)也发生兴趣,感到从经验中得到了进一步的发现。所以,小说绝不是观念的简单图解。它是对人类生活的创造性模仿,借此我们感到我们自己正在赋予我们自身的生活经验以某种意义。

现在,我们转到第二种反对意见上来。这种反对意见认为我们对主题在小说中的地位的强调是忽略了小说的娱乐性或者喜剧性。要充分讨论这个问题,就得对喜剧性本身加以

us examine the word *illustration* in this connection.

Fiction is not illustration, even though it sometime's pretends to be—as we see when we read "The Man Who Would Be King", which pretends to be an illustration of its motto: "Brother to a Prince and fellow to a begger if he be found worthy."Fiction is not illustration, because with illustration we are always aware that the idea being illustrated comes first in importance, that the content of the illustration is always being dictated by the nature of the thing—the"idea"—being illustrated. The illustration is an explanation, then, not a discovery developed from life.

But with fiction, insofar as it is successful, the imagination creates a world that exists, as it were, in its own right. With great masterpieces, this reality, in all aspects, is so compelling that it often seems closer to us than things we know to be hard facts. Hamlet, let us say, is more vivid to us than George Washington or the man next door. But even fiction that is merely good, not great, carries with it some degree of this illusion of independent existence.

How does this question of independent existence bear on the question of theme? Simply, thus: in a successful piece of fiction, out of this sense of an independent world, as the characters act and are acted upon, as one event leads to another, we become more and more aware of the significance of the whole. That is, *we gradually sense the development of a theme*, *the growth of significance*. We feel ourselves caught up in a vital process in which meaning emerges from experience. It is such a sense that, in the end, makes our own lives, insofar as we live above a brute level, interesting to us: the sense of deepening discovery in experience. Fiction, then, is never the mere illustration of an idea. *It is the created image of the very life process by which we* feel *ourselves moving toward meaning in our own experience.*

Let us turn, at long last, to the second objection, the objection that our emphasis on the place of theme in fiction leaves little play for the gay or comic. A full discussion of this

深入的分析。不过,在这儿应该说清楚的是,只有和严肃的小说做一种含蓄的对照——不论这种对照怎样模糊——我们才会意识到喜剧性,而且在喜剧的笑声里总含有某种想逃避生活紧迫感——乃至痛苦——的意味。

如果我们回顾一下读过的喜剧小说——像《沃尔特·米蒂的隐秘生活》和《醉汉》——不难看出,只要略微改变一下小说的重点就会使我们陷入一个与小说中的世界完全不同的境地。喜剧,无论是辛辣的讽刺还是温和的幽默,其中都包含着失望和震惊,包含着希望的遭难和挫败,包含着表面和实质的差异,以及对适应不断变化的生活要求所感到的无能为力。那个戴着高帽子、鼻子翘到天上而踩到香蕉皮一跤滑倒的人是所有喜剧里的主要形象——然而,就是这种不正不经的乱跌跤,有时也许会跌断脊梁骨。从哈哈大笑到哇哇地叫救护车,两者之间并非相距甚远。

这里,有人也许又会发问,既然主题是关于人类价值观念的一种议论,那么我们怎么会一方面不接受某篇小说的主题,一方面又能欣赏这篇小说呢?用漂亮的空谈作为掩护以试图回避这个问题是无益的。否认这个问题的重要性或者否认真正回答这个问题的困难性也是无益的。

我们还是把有关小说的问题统统搁置一边,先来思考一下我们和他人的关系吧。我们和形形色色的人们生活在一起,我们和其中大多数人在意见上、爱好上以及价值观念上都有着这样或那样的严重分歧。在文艺方面我们和苏珊意见相背,每次和她一起看电影都要争论;在政治方面,我们和约翰·雅各布斯看法相左;关于打桥牌,我们又和吉姆·科贝克合不来。我们还对玛丽·莫赖特的智力感到很悲观。然而——问题就在这里——我们跟他们各位仍然可以成为好朋友。我们甚而会爱上其中的一位而且和他(她)结婚。换言之,我们承认他们当中任何一位都有某些特别的品

would take us far into an analysis of the comic in itself, but it should be enough to say here that we are aware of the comic only by an implied contrast, however remote, with the serious, that the laughter of comedy always has in it some element of escape from the urgency—even the pain—of life.

If we look back at the comic stories read thus far—say, "The Secret Life of Walter Mitty" and "The Drunkard"—we readily see that always a slight shift of emphasis would plunge us into a world entirely different from that of the story. Comedy, including even warm humor, as well as savage satire, has to do with disappointment and surprise, the criticism and defeat of aspirations, contrasts of pretension and actuality, inability to adjust to the changing demands of life. The top-hatted man with his nose in the air who slips on a banana peel is the image behind all comedy—but the fall that rebukes vanity may sometimes break a neck. The distance between a good laugh and the need to call an ambulance is not very great.

At this point another question may be asked. Since theme is a comment on human values, how can we appreciate a story whose theme we cannot accept? There is no use in trying to evade this question by taking refuge in nice generalities, and no use in denying its importance or the difficulty of trying to give an honest answer.

To begin, let us forget fiction altogether, and think of our relations with other people. We live with a variety of people, and with most of them, we have, at some point or another, serious differences in opinion, tastes, and values. With Susie we disagree violently on literary matters, and every time we go to a movie with her we have an argument. With John Jacobs we disagree on politics; with Jim Kobeck, on how to play a hand of bridge. And we take a very dim view of Mary Moffet's intelligence. But—and here is the point—we may be good friends with all of them. We may even fall in love with, and marry, one of them. In other words, we recognize in any one of them, some particular qualities that we value despite disagreements. More important, we

格值得我们尊重,尽管我们和他们有分歧。更为重要的是,我们承认他们都心地善良,都怀着诚意想弄懂问题,而且做得也很体面。承认了这些事实,我们自己就会觉得心平气和,能设身处地为人着想了。在这个过程中我们会认识到世界是复杂的,比实际上看到的更为丰富多彩。我们会懂得要想生活充实,就必须克服自己的武断态度和主观偏见。

这并非说人人无异,可以一视同仁。我们每人都各有各的价值尺度,而且都以此待人处世。我们向来所强调的只是这样的意思:当我们碰到不同意见时,我们要尽力了解对方的意见实质,尽力找到最基本的共同之处。只有这样,人类的相互尊重才有可能。

这种观点又怎能用来对待小说呢?是这样的,我们可以把小说的作者当作我们的朋友或熟人看待,即使在意见相左的时候,我们也努力设法去弄清楚他的思想的基本逻辑是什么,因为小说的主题也就是这种逻辑的进一步展示。

那么,所谓的共同之处又是什么呢?共同之处就在于理解这样一个事实:在一篇小说里,如果主题是合乎逻辑地加以展示的话,我们在阅读这篇小说的同时,也就目击了或者参与了人类为寻找生活意义而做的巨大努力。小说,如前所述,就是人类生活进程的一种模仿。

在此,我们也愿意做某种让步。我们不能不承认,有些作家和某些作品,他(它)们和我们是那样地格格不入,我们实在无法找到什么共同之处。我们反对一篇小说就像反对现实生活中的某个人一样,是因为他(它)触犯了我们的基本价值观念。

但是,我们有时对某篇小说表示反感倒并不是因为这篇小说的主题触犯了我们,我们所以反感,只是因为它不可信——虽然它的主题我们是赞同的。这种小说的失败在于它的意图不甚明确,人物没有代表性,或者未能从情节的发展中表现作者的思想。也许这种小说的主题只有在感伤的意义上才能被接受,而作

may recognize an underlying good will, and an honest attempt to make sense of things and to achieve decency. On recognizing such things, we may discover in ourselves some tolerance and some power of sympathetic imagination. In this process we realize that the world is complicated, and is the richer for the fact. We find that to live fruitfully we must modify our dogmatic attitudes and beliefs.

This is not to say that one thing is as good as another. Each of us has to work out his own scale of values and live by it. But what we have been saying *does* mean that when we encounter differences, we must try to understand their nature, and try to find the underlying common ground that makes human respect possible.

But how does this apply to fiction? In this way: we can think of the authors of stories as we think of friends and associates; we can make, even in disagreement, the imaginative effort to realize what underlies their logic, the logic by which a theme unfolds.

What, then, of the common ground? The common ground is the understanding of the fact that, insofar as a theme is coherently developed through a story, we are, as we read, witnessing and taking part in the great human effort to achieve meaning through experience. A story, as we have said, is an image of the life process.

We must here be prepared to make a concession. We must simply recognize that some writers, and some stories, offend us at so deep a level that we simply cannot find the common ground. We reject a story as we reject a person in real life, as an offense to our basic values.

Sometimes, however, we reject a story not because it offends us by its theme. We may reject it simply because it is unconvincing—even though we agree with the theme. The story fails in its logic of motivation, in its presentation of character, in the attempt to make the idea develop from the action. Or perhaps the story with the acceptable theme

者要求读者在感情上和逻辑上做出的反应，实际上并不是通过人物和情节得到的。关于这种情况，我们觉得作者表达思想的方法也似乎太简单，太直截了当了。我们所以对他的小说反感，因为我们知道任何有价值的思想总是和生活密切相关的，是要经过深刻的观察才能得到的。诸如此类的异议，合起来一句话，就是这种小说不能令人信服，因为它缺乏完整性。小说里的各种成分没有合成一体。

这儿我们又回到了第一章的引言，在那里我们曾讨论过同一的真实性和统一的真实性。如果我们对一篇小说表示反感，其原因是小说的主题触犯了我们，那么我们就要表明我们自己认为真实的生活原则和价值观念是什么。如果我们对一篇小说反感是出于我们提到过的其他原因——如像我们通常说的，这篇小说"不可信"——那么我们所要表明的就是统一的真实性。一篇小说，其自身的各种成分都没有能合成一体，那么它无论想表达怎样的意思，实际上都不可能出自于小说本身。而关于小说的绝大多数问题也都是由于统一性这个问题引起的。从统一性这个概念可以引申出这样一种看法：好的小说，其含义——即主题——总是全面渗透在整个作品中的。一篇小说只有显示出它是一个有机的统一体，小说的各种成分才会有助于主题的表现。诚然，我们生活在一个不完美的世界里，世上也几乎没有已经尽善尽美地利用了题材的作品。然而，我们可以先假定某一篇作品是统一的，随后再对它做全面的考察，直到得出结论为止。进行这种考察的唯一方法就是尽量找到贯串在作品里并不断发展着的是怎样的观念、怎样的感情和怎样的态度。

我们可以注意观察作品中的人物属于哪种类型以及作品中的环境属于哪种性质。这是第一步，因为这样做可以使我们对作者的兴趣、阅历和感情有所了解。我们可以追问某个人物——或者几个人物——内心所执著的是什么，或者作品最终揭示了什么。我们可以注

is merely sentimental, and the emotional and logical response demanded is not really justified by the characters and events. In such a case, the author has made the idea we believe in seem too easy to come by, too mechanical; so we reject his story because we know that any valuable idea is really related to life and demands some depth of scrutiny. To sum up such objections, the story fails to convince us because it is not *coherent*. The parts do not hang together.

This leads us back to our opening comments in section 1, where we discuss the *truth of correspondence* and the *truth of coherence*. If we reject a story because the theme offends us, we are appealing to what we take to be the truth about life and values. If we reject a story because of the other reasons given—if, as we usually put it, it is "unconvincing"—we are appealing to the truth of coherence. The story does not hang together on its own terms and therefore whatever meaning it may claim to offer does not really come out of the experience of the story. Most of our problems with fiction spring from problems of coherence.

The notion of coherence leads to the notion that the meaning—the theme—of a good story is general and pervasive. If a story shows organic unity, all parts contribute to the meaning. We live, of course, in an imperfect world, and few stories perfectly digest all their material. Nevertheless, let us assume that a story is coherent until we have given it a fair inspection. One way to give this inspection is to try to find what idea, what feeling, what attitude consistently develops in the process of the story.

We can look at what kinds of characters and what kind of world are presented. That is a starting point, for it tells us something of the interests of the writer and his range of experience and sympathy. We can ask what is at stake for a character—or characters—and

意观察情节的结构并尽量弄清楚这样的结构意味着什么，因为情节的结构如何是很重要的。我们可以看看作品的语调如何，其中又含有怎样的感情。是冷嘲热讽的？严酷无情的？冷眼旁观的？入情入理的？哀婉动人的？抑或滑稽可笑的？还是怒气冲冲的？我们可以看看人物的语言是否恰到好处，并设法判断作者的风格。然而，我们自始至终都不应忘记问一问这篇作品是否具有统一性。唯有这样，我们才有可能对主题做出最后的判断。

我们下面对小说进行的考察并不想着眼于小说的道德教益如何。甚至，我们不想着眼于为各种小说的主题做一般性的概述。虽然这样做的话，对我们的研究来说也并非毫无必要。但比做这类一般性概述更为重要的是进行下面这两种考察：

首先，要弄清楚一篇小说的主题（如果这是一篇好小说的话）是怎样势所必然地来自生活的，它只是在小说中得到表现而已。当然，我们在这里要涉及到统一性问题。

其次，要弄清楚主题是怎样独立地得到发展的。这样做就意味着我们必须设法弄清楚主题（如果我们用一般性的语言来谈理论是可能的话）在作品中被具体处理时是怎样受到限定和制约的，而由于受到限定和制约，作品最终"说出的"东西也就比原来设想的更特殊，更独立无倚。当然，这是我们讨论中的最大的难题。

本章所选的作品使用各种不同的方法表现它们的主题。有的是用概括加以表达，有的是用譬喻和象征（见重要词汇）加以暗示。有的是用写实的戏剧性场景加以展现。但是我们必须永远记住，整个作品，包括作品里总的气氛在内，都是主题的体现。我们在第二章里讨论情节时曾经说过，我们必须把整篇小说当作一种对生活的模仿来加以认识，这种模仿虽然并不完全相像，却也表现出生活的意义。我们可以把整个作品看作表现主题的具体的象征物。

（刘文荣 译）

what discoveries develop in the end. We can look at the pattern of plot and try to see what significant issues emerge, and what patterns seem important. We can ask what is the tone of the story, what is the pervasive feeling. Is it ironical, cold, reportorial, sympathetically analytic, pathetic, comic, angry? We can ask about the validity of the speech of the characters and try to judge the style of the author. And always, we are asking if the story is coherent. Only then are we really ready to pass a final judgment on the theme.

Our examination of the stories that follow is not to be taken as an exercise in moral hunting. It is not even to be taken, primarily, as an exercise in giving a general statement to the themes of the various stories—although the attempt to make such statements is a necessary part of our study. More important than framing such general statements are these two considerations:

First, to see how the theme of a story, if it is a good story, *necessarily* develops from the experience as presented in the story. Here, of course, we are dealing with problems of coherence.

Second, to see how the theme is *uniquely* developed. To do this means that we must try to see how a theme—even supposing we are able to state it in general terms—may be, in fact, qualified and modified by the actual treatment in the story, so that what the story "says" finally becomes something more special, uniquely applicable. And this, of course, is the most difficult of our problems.

The stories in this section employ various methods in the presentation of their themes. There may be general statements. There may be *allegory* and *symbolism* (see Glossary). There may be realistic dramatic situation. *But we must always remember that the total story, including its general atmosphere, is the embodiment of the theme.* As we have said in discussing plot in section 2, we must think of the whole story as an image, however shadowy, of the meaning of experience. It may be thought of as a massive symbol of the theme.

021. 爱情：某猎人笔记上的三页

021. Love: Three Pages from a Sportsman's Book
by Guy de Maupassant

（法）盖伊·德·莫泊桑 著　　刘家有 译

　　我刚从某报纸的琐事趣闻栏里读到一则爱情悲剧。一个男的杀了女的，然后自杀了，这样看来他肯定还很爱她。无论是他还是她，与我又有什么关系？我注意到的只是他们之间的爱情，而这爱情又不能使我发生兴趣，因为它使我意志消沉，使我十分惊恐，使我思绪万千，或者使我苦于冥想。然而他们的爱情却唤起了我年轻时期的一段回忆，一段关于打猎的异乎寻常的往事的回忆。在那次打猎时，爱神就像天空中的十字架向早期基督徒显圣一样，向我显现了一次。

　　我生来就具有原始人类的所有本能和知觉，但是又受过文明人多思多虑习性的熏陶。我酷爱打猎，然而一见到受伤的野物，一见到羽毛上或者沾在我手上的血迹，我的心就会悚悚地抽紧，而且会透不过气来。

　　那一年深秋时分，天气骤然转冷，我表兄卡尔·德·厄维勒邀我和他一起大清早去沼泽地打野鸭。

　　我表兄是个40来岁的快活人，红头发，身体很棒，满脸络腮胡子。他是个乡下绅士，脾气随和而又有点任性。他富有高卢人的机智，常能化平庸为神奇。他住的房子既不像农庄又不像城堡，坐落在一片谷地里，谷地很开阔，还有一条小河流经其间。左旁右近的小山上树木成荫，那是属于世袭封地的古老树林，里面留存着好些名贵树木。在那儿还可以找到在法国这一带地区已极为少见的奇禽珍鸟。偶尔还打得到老鹰，至于路过的候鸟，那些几乎不敢飞进我国人口过于密集地区的鸟类，则经常会在那些高大的橡树上停留栖息，它们似乎早已知道或者早已认得那原始森林所遗留下来的这个小小的角落还可以作为它们夜间落脚的临时庇护所。

I HAVE just read among the general news in one of the papers a drama of passion. He killed her and then he killed himself, so he must have loved her. What matters He or She? Their love alone matters to me, and it does not interest me because it moves me or astonishes me or because it softens me or makes me think, but because it recalls to my mind a remembrance of my youth, a strange recollection of a hunting adventure where Love appeared to me, as the Cross appeared to the early Christians, in the midst of the heavens.

I was born with all the instincts and the senses of primitive man, tempered by the arguments and the restraints of a civilized being. I am passionately fond of shooting, yet the sight of the wounded animal, of the blood on its feathers and on my hands, affects my heart so as almost to make it stop.

That year the cold weather set in suddenly toward the end of autumn, and I was invited by one of my cousins, Karl de Rauville, to go with him and shoot ducks on the marshes at daybreak.

My cousin Was a jolly fellow of forty with red hair, very stout and bearded, a country gentleman, an amiable semibrute of a happy disposition and endowed with that Gallic wit which makes even mediocrity agreeable. He lived in a house, half farmhouse, half château, situated in a broad valley through which a river ran. The hills right and left were covered with woods, old manorial woods where magnificent trees still remained and where the rarest feathered game in that part of France was to be found. Eagles were shot there occasionally, and birds of passage, such as rarely venture into our overpopulated part of the country, invariably lighted amid these giant oaks as if they knew or recognized some little corner of a primeval forest

作者简介：盖伊·德·莫泊桑（Guy De Maupassant，1850—1893），法国短篇小说家。1850 年 8 月 5 日生于迪埃普附近的米罗梅斯尼尔古堡，1893 年 7 月 6 日卒于巴黎。普法战争打断了他的法律学业，他志愿参军，军旅生活为他的作品提供了很好的素材。后来他成了文员，师从福楼拜。他以作品《羊脂球》（Ball of Fat，1880）成名。在接下来的 10 年，他出版了约 300 篇短篇小说、6 部小说和 3 部游记。从他的小说作品来看，写的最多的是 1870—1890 年法国人的生活。他的作品涉及战争、农民、官僚、塞纳河两岸的生活、不同阶层的情感问题，甚至是幻想。

谷地里有大片大片的草地牧场,其间有沟渠灌溉,还用树篱隔开。再朝前,那条原先一直夹在两岸间流淌的小河在那儿流散开来成了一片开阔的沼泽地。那沼泽地是我从未见过的最好的猎场。那是我表兄据之如宝的地方,他一直把它作为禁猎区保护着。那儿长满蒲草,一眼看去似波浪起伏,时而又沙沙作响,就在这蒲草中间,开掘出一条窄窄的水道,若撑竹篙驾小船悠悠地行驶在那如镜的水面上,会触动水边的蒲草而使敏捷的小鱼往来疾窜于水草之间,而那些白肚黑头的水禽也会把它们尖尖的脑袋倏地钻入水里。

我素来爱水。我爱海,虽然它是那样浩瀚,那样波翻浪涌而不能停滞;我爱河水,它是那么动人,源源不断而昼夜不息;我尤爱那沼泽里的涓涓细流,那里有许多水生的小动物在默默地度完一生,世代不息。沼泽地是我们这个星球上的一个自成一体的大千世界——一个不同的世界,它过着自己的生活.有固定的居民,有往来的过客,有自己的语言,有自己的喧嚣,尤其是,它有自己的秘密。再没有什么地方能比一大片低洼的沼泽地更令人神往,更令人不安,甚或更令人惊惧了。为什么在那片被水覆盖着的洼地里竟会笼罩着一种模糊的恐惧呢?是那蒲草在沙沙作响,是那磷火在依稀明灭?是那夜气弥漫的静谧?是那帷幕般迤逦在水面上的沉沉雾霭?还是那捉摸不定的噗噗声息?这声息是那样微细,那样温柔,然而听来却比人们的大炮甚或天上的响雷更为怕人。难道就是这些,才使那沼泽地显得仿佛是个梦境般的国度——那令人胆寒的国度,显得那样神秘莫测又危险四伏吗?

不,不仅如此——沼泽地还有它别样的神奇之处,那也许就是造物主自身的神奇之处!不就是从这泥浆混浊的水里,从这阳光煦暖的湿土的滋润中,那生命的胚芽才得以萌生,从而延绵至今的吗?

傍晚时分,我到了表兄家里。天气冷得连石头也会开裂。

晚饭是在一个大房间里吃的,房间里的柜橱上、墙壁上以及天花板上都挂满了鸟类标本,有的看来似乎展翅欲飞,有的则停枝栖息——有隼、苍鹭、猫头鹰、欧洲夜莺、鸧鹒、雄鹰、秃鹫、猎鹰——我表兄呢,穿着一件海豹皮夹克,也活像一头来自北国的稀有动

which had remained there to serve them as a shelter during these short nocturnal halts.

In the valley there were large meadows watered by trenches and separated by hedges; then, further on, the river, which up to that point had been kept between banks, expanded into a vast marsh. That marsh was the best shooting ground I ever saw. It was my cousin's chief care, and he kept it as a preserve. Through the rushes that covered it, and made it rustling and rough, narrow passages had been cut, through which the flat-bottomed boats, impelled and steered by poles, passed along silently over dead water, brushing up against the reeds and making the swift fish take refuge in the weeds and the wild fowl, with their pointed black heads, dive suddenly.

I am passionately fond of the water: of the sea, though it is too vast, too full of movement, impossible to hold; of the rivers which are so beautiful but which pass on and flee away; and above all of the marshes, where the whole unknown existence of aquatic animals palpitates. The marsh is an entire world in itself on the world of earth—a different world which has its own life, its settled inhabitants and its passing travelers, its voices, its noises and above all its mystery. Nothing is more impressive, nothing more disquieting, more terrifying occasionally, than a fen. Why should a vague terror hang over these low plains covered with water? Is it the low rustling of the rushes, the strange will-o'-the-wisp lights, the silence which prevails on calm nights, the still mists which hang over the surface like a shroud; or is it the almost inaudible splashing, so slight and so gentle, yet sometimes more terrifying than the cannons of men or the thunders of the skies, which make these marshes resemble countries one has dreamed of, terrible countries holding an unknown and dangerous secret?

No, something else belongs to it—another mystery, perhaps the mystery of the creation itself! For was it not in stagnant and muddy water, amid the heavy humidity of moist land under the heat of the sun, that the first germ of life pulsated and expanded to the day?

I arrived at my cousin's in the evening. It was freezing hard enough to split the stones.

During dinner, in the large room whose sideboards, walls and ceiling were covered with stuffed birds with wings extended or perched on branches to which they were nailed—hawks, herons, owls, nightjars, buzzards, tercels, vultures, falcons—my cousin, who, dressed in a sealskin jacket, himself resembled some strange animal from a cold country, told me what preparations he had made for that same night.

物。餐间,他告诉我,明晨打猎所需的一切都已准备就绪了。

我们将在明晨 3 点半出发,以便在 4 点半左右到达他选好的可供潜伏瞭望的地方。在那里已经用冰块砌好了一间小屋,用来抵挡黎明前令人难耐的寒风。那种风冷得像钢锯在锯人体肤,使皮肤开裂,又像刀口一样割人,像毒刺一样螫人,像钳子一样夹人,像火焰一样灼人。

表兄搓着双手。"我还从来没见过这样的大冷天,"他说,"才晚上 6 点,温度就降到零下 12 度啦。"

一吃完饭,我就钻进被窝,在壁炉的熊熊炉火发出的亮光里睡着了。

3 点钟,表兄把我叫醒。这回我也穿了一件羊皮大衣,而我看见卡尔表兄穿着一件熊皮大衣。我们每人灌下两杯滚烫的咖啡,又喝了几杯浓烈的白兰地,就出发了。和我们一起去的还有一个猎场看守人和两只狗——勃朗金和皮埃罗。

刚一迈出大门,我就觉得寒气直侵骨髓。真是一个天寒地冻的夜晚。空气似乎也已冻结,成了可以碰可以摸的东西,行路仿佛在撞墙,真叫人受罪。冷得一丝风也没有,真个凝固冻结了。寒气袭人体肤,直透心髓,使人浑身僵直,使草木虫鸟纷纷遭难,有些小鸟从枝头跌落到坚硬的地上,在凛冽严寒的掐扼下不动了。

天上的月亮将近下弦,在广漠冥冥的太空里似乎奄奄一息,微弱得似乎连隐去的力气也没有了。这肃杀的天气把她抓住,使她不能动弹,强迫她远远地耽在那里。她给大地蒙上一层哀婉的幽光,而每月到她行将隐逝的时候,她总要向人间洒下这种惨淡临终的哀光。

卡尔和我并肩走着。我们弯着腰,手插在衣袋里,枪挟在腋下。为了在结冰的河面行走而不致滑倒,我们在皮靴上包了一层毡,所以走起来没有声响。我看见我们的狗在气喘吁吁,嘴里直吐白气。

我们很快到了沼泽地边上,又踅进一条枯草覆盖的小路。这条路通向树林的下方。

我们的手肘碰触着长长的带状枯叶,留下一阵轻微的刷刷声,这时我猛地产生一种强烈而异常的感觉,这种感觉在我过去进沼泽地时是从来没有的。这地方,即使我们正在这儿踏着它枯黄的草丛行走,它却是死的,已经冻死了。

We were to start at half-past three in the morning so as to arrive at the place which he had chosen for our watching place at about half-past four. On that spot a hut had been built of lumps of ice so as to shelter us somewhat from the trying wind which precedes daybreak, a wind so cold as to tear the flesh like a saw, cut it like the blade of a knife, prick it like a poisoned sting, twist it like a pair of pincers, and burn it like fire.

My cousin rubbed his hands. "I have never known such a frost," he said; "it is already twelve degrees below zero at six o'clock in the evening."

I threw myself onto my bed immediately after we had finished our meal and went to sleep by the light of a bright fire burning in the grate.

At three o'clock he woke me. In my turn I put on a sheepskin and found my cousin Karl covered with a bearskin. After having each swallowed two cups of scalding coffee, followed by glasses of liqueur brandy, we started, accompanied by a gamekeeper and our dogs, Plongeon and Pierrot.

From the first moment that I got outside I felt chilled to the very marrow. It was one of those nights on which the earth seems dead with cold. The frozen air becomes resisting and palpable, such pain does it cause; no breath of wind moves it, it is fixed and motionless; it bites you, pierces through you, dries you, kills the trees, the plants, the insects, the small birds themselves, who fall from the branches onto the hard ground and become stiff themselves under the grip of the cold.

The moon, which was in her last quarter and was inclining all to one side, seemed fainting in the midst of space, so weak that she was unable to wane, forced to stay up yonder, seized and paralyzed by the severity of the weather. She shed a cold mournful light over the world, that dying and wan light which she gives us every month at the end of her period.

Karl and I walked side by side, our backs bent, our hands in our pockets and our guns under our arms. Our boots, which were wrapped in wool so that we might be able to walk without slipping on the frozen river, made no sound, and I looked at the white vapor which our dogs' breath made.

We were soon on the edge of the marsh and entered one of the lanes of dry rushes which ran through the low forest.

Our elbows, which touched the long ribbonlike leaves, left a slight noise behind us, and I was seized, as I had never been before, by the powerful and singular emotion which marshes cause in me. This one was dead, dead from cold, since we were walking on it in

在一条小路的拐弯处,我猛然看到了那间冰块砌成的小屋,那是用来给我们避寒的。我走了过去,因为我们还得等上个把小时那些野鸟才会醒来四处漫游,我裹着随身带来的毛毯,这样也许会暖和些。随后我又仰天躺下,望着那变了形的月亮,从这所极地冰屋的微微透明的墙壁里望出去,那月亮好像乍出了4只角。但是从冰封的沼泽地里腾起的寒气,从冰墙上逼拢来的寒气,加上从上面压下来的寒气,使我彻骨灌心地发冷,我咳嗽起来。我的卡尔表兄显得不安了。

"今天打不到多少猎物倒无所谓,"他说,'我可不能让你感冒,我们生个火吧。"说着,他便吩咐那个猎场看守人去割些草来。

我们在冰屋中央生起一堆火,屋顶中间有个洞可以出烟,当红红的火焰升起,烘烤着那些水晶般明澈的冰块时,冰块慢慢地,很难察觉地开始溶化,仿佛在出汗。卡尔一直在外面,这时只听到他大声喊我:"快出来,看!"我大吃一惊,赶忙走出冰屋。这才知道我们的冰屋已呈圆锥形,看上去就像一颗巨大约钻石,还带着一颗火红的心,这颗心是在沼泽地里的这堆冰块中间一下子点燃的。我们看到那里面还有两个奇形怪状的影子,那是我们的狗,它们正在火边取暖。

但是一阵奇特的叫声,一阵迷惘而飘忽的叫声,在我们头上回荡而过,借着那座冰炉子里的火光,我们看见了那些野禽。在这冬日凌晨,曦光尚天现于天际之时,听到生命的呼唤声,尤其是只闻其户而不见其面,听着这生命的呼声迅速地穿过昏暗的寒气然后消失在大地的尽头,这是何等美妙,又何等动人!在这五更寒彻的时刻,我仿佛觉得,那随着鸟翼渐渐远去的呼唤声就像是来自这世间的灵魂的叹息!

"把火熄了,"卡尔说,"天亮了。"

确实,天空已开始现出白色,成群的野鸭正一字儿排开,疾飞而过,随即在长空里消失了。

一道火光划破若明若暗的晨空,卡尔开了一枪,两只狗飞奔向前。

这之后,几乎每一分钟,不是他,就是我,只要一看见水草上空有一群飞禽的影子掠过,便马上举枪瞄准。至于皮埃罗和勃朗金,则气喘吁吁、欢蹦乱跳地衔回血淋淋的野禽,那些野禽的眼睛有时还朝我们瞪着哩。

太阳升起了,是个碧空万里的大晴天。我们打算离开此地。这时,有两只飞禽正展翅从我们头上飞掠

the middle of its population of dried rushes.

Suddenly, at the turn of one of the lanes, I perceived the ice hut which had been constructed to shelter us. I went in, and as we had nearly an hour to wait before the wandering birds would awake I rolled myself up in my rug in order to try and get warm. Then, lying on my back, I began to look at the misshapen moon, which had four horns through the vaguely transparent walls of this polar house. But the frost of the frozen marshes, the cold of these walls, the cold from the firmament penetrated me so terribly that I began to cough. My cousin Karl became uneasy.

"No matter if we do not kill much today," he said. "I do not want you to catch cold; we will light a fire." And he told the gamekeeper to cut some rushes.

We made a pile in the middle of our hut, which had a hole in the middle of the roof to let out the smoke, and when the red flames rose up to the clear crystal blocks, they began to melt, gently, imperceptibly, as if they were sweating. Karl, who had remained outside, called out to me: "Come and look here!" I went out of the hut and remained struck with astonishment. Our hut, in the shape of a cone, looked like an enormous diamond with a heart of fire which had been suddenly planted there in the midst of the frozen water of the marsh. And inside we saw two fantastic forms, those of our dogs, who were warming themselves at the fire.

But a peculiar cry, a lost, a wandering cry, passed over our heads, and the light from our hearth showed us the wild birds. Nothing moves one so much as the first clamor of a life which one does not see, which passes through the somber air so quickly and so far off just before the first streak of a winter's day appears on the horizon. It seems to me, at this glacial hour of dawn, as if that passing cry which is carried away by the wings of a bird is the sigh of a soul from the world!

"Put out the fire," said Karl, "it is getting daylight."

The sky was, in fact, beginning to grow pale, and the flights of ducks made long rapid streaks which were soon obliterated on the sky.

A stream of light burst out into the night; Karl had fired, and the two dogs ran forward.

And then nearly every minute now he, now I, aimed rapidly as soon as the shadow of a flying flock appeared above the rushes. And Pierrot and Plongeon, out of breath but happy, retrieved the bleeding birds whose eyes still, occasionally, looked at us.

The sun had risen, and it was a bright day with a blue sky, and we were thinking of taking our departure,

而过。我开了一枪,打落了其中的一只,它几乎就落在我的脚旁。这是一只银色胸脯的水鸭。这时,就在我们头上的蓝天里我听见一种声音,那飞禽的叫声。声音很短促,似乎哀痛欲绝,叫个不停。那只禽鸟,那只逃过枪弹的小动物,在我们头顶上空的蓝天里兜着圈子,眼睛注视着已被我抓在手里的它那死去的伴侣。

卡尔蹲下身子,把枪举到肩上,紧紧盯住那只飞禽,等它进入自己的射程。"你打下那只雌的,"他说,"这只雄的是不会飞走的。"

雄野鸭果然没有飞走。它在我们头上一圈一圈地兜着,一边不住地哀鸣。从未有过什么痛苦的呻吟能像这阵阵哀鸣,像这只空中失偶的可怜的飞禽发出的悲怨指责之声那样使我心痛。

有时,它也避开那紧盯着它的枪口的威胁,似乎准备只身继续它的长途飞行,然而它终于下不了决心,又飞回来寻觅它失去的伴侣。

"你把那只雌的扔在地上,"卡尔对我说,"雄的过一会儿就会飞进射程的。"雄鸭果真不顾危险,向我们飞近。由于那种动物的爱情,由于对它那刚被我杀死的情侣的痴情,它已经不顾一切了。

卡尔开枪了,正如一只放在空中的纸鹞被人一刀割断了放飞的牵绳,我看到一个黑糊糊的东西跌落下来,又听见跌到枯草间的声响。皮埃罗跑去把它衔来给了我。

我把它俩——它们已经冰凉——一起装进猎物袋。当天晚上我就回巴黎去了。

when two birds with extended necks and outstretched wings glided rapidly over our heads. I fired, and one of them fell almost at my feet. It was a teal with a silver breast, and then, in the blue space above me, I heard a voice, the voice of a bird. It was short, repeated heart—rending lament; and the bird, the little animal that had been spared, began to turn round in the blue sky over our heads, looking at its dead companion which I was holding in my hand.

Karl was on his knees, his gun to his shoulder, watching it eagerly until it should be within shot. "You have killed the duck," he said, "and the drake will not fly away."

He certainly did not fly away; he circled over our heads continually and continued his cries. Never have any groans of suffering pained me so much as that desolate appeal, as that lamentable reproach of this poor bird which was lost in space.

Occasionally he took flight under the menace of the gun which followed his movements and seemed ready to continue his flight alone, but as he could not make up his mind to this he returned to find his mate.

"Leave her on the ground," Karl said to me; "he will come within shot by and by." And he did indeed come near us, careless of danger, infatuated by his animal love, by his affection for his mate which I had just killed.

Karl fired, and it was as if somebody had cut the string which held the bird suspended. I saw something black descend, and I heard the noise of a fall among the rushes. And Pierrot brought it to me.

I put them—they were already cold—into the same gamebag, and I returned to Paris the same evening.

思考题 ——■

1. 试述这篇作品的主题。
2. 你对第一段有什么看法?这个故事为何引起叙述者的兴趣?
3. 第二段有什么意义?这个作品中有什么冲突?
4. 表兄这个人物的塑造和主题是否有某种联系?
5. 对沼泽地所进行的大段的环境描写有何值得一读的意义?
6. 你对小说的最后一句话作何理解?

(刘家有 译)

1. State the theme of this story.
2. What do you make of the first paragraph? Why does the story interest the narrator?
3. What is the significance of the second paragraph? What conflict is there in the story?
4. Does the characterization of the cousin serve any purpose in relation to the theme?
5. What is the value, if any, of the long atmospheric description of the marshes?
6. What do you make of the last sentence of the story?

022. 爱 情

〔美〕杰西·斯图尔特 著　　刘家有 译

022. Love

by Jesse Stuart

昨天,强烈的阳光直射在已经枯萎的玉米苗上,父亲和我绕着新买进的土地兜了一圈,想筑一道栅栏。那些奶牛老是穿过峭壁上的栗色橡树林,到玉米地上来乱跑。它们啃去玉米苗的尖梢,还把玉米秆踩倒。

父亲在一垄垄玉米间走着,我们的牧羊狗鲍勃走在他前面。我们听见一阵土松鼠发出的吱吱声从悬崖那边林间空地的枯树梢上传来。"嗨,捉住它,鲍勃。"父亲说。他拾起一株玉米苗,苗秆已经干枯了,这是土松鼠掘出来的,它吃了上面的甜籽粒,把它的根苗给丢下了。今年春天干旱,但地里的玉米还是长得很好,种子都已发芽生长起来。土松鼠就爱吃这种玉米苗。它们把玉米成排成排地挖起来,吃那甜籽粒。被掘起的玉米苗全死了。我们只得补种。

我看见父亲一直在使唤鲍勃去追咬土松鼠。鲍勃跳过一垄垄的玉米苗,开始向土松鼠跑去。我也拔腿向林中的空地奔跑,鲍勃就在那里又跳又咬。我们脚下腾起阵阵灰土。灰土在我们身后聚成一团尘雾。

"一条雄的大黑蛇!"我父亲说,"咬死它,鲍勃!咬死它,鲍勃!"

鲍勃蹦跳着向那条蛇乱吠,想惹它窜出来离开那个洞。今年春天以来,鲍勃已经咬死了 28 条铜头蛇。他①懂得怎样咬死一条蛇。他并不猛冲直撞。他总是从容不迫地把这事儿干得很漂亮。

"别打死这条蛇吧,"我说,"黑蛇是无害的,它捕杀毒蛇,捕杀铜头蛇。它在田里捉的老鼠比猫捉的还要多。"

我看得出这条蛇不愿意跟狗斗。它想逃跑。鲍勃不让它逃。我很奇怪这条蛇为什么要朝小山拐子

---

① 原文如此,本文主要写动物,故用人称代词。

YESTERDAY when the bright sun blazed down on the wilted corn my father and I walked around the edge of the new ground to plan a fence. The cows kept coming through the chestnut oaks on the cliff and running over the young corn. They bit off the tips of the corn and trampled down the stubble.

My father walked in the cornbalk. Bob, our collie, walked in front of my father. We heard a ground squirrel whistle down over the bluff among the dead treetops at the clearing's edge. "Whoop, take him, Bob," said my father. He lifted up a young stalk of corn, with wilted dried roots, where the ground squirrel had dug it up for the sweet grain of corn left on its tender roots. This has been a dry spring and the corn has kept well in the earth where the grain has sprouted. The ground squirrels love this corn. They dig up rows of it and eat the sweet grains. The young corn stalks are killed and we have to replant the corn.

I can see my father keep sicking Bob after the ground squirrel. He jumped over the corn rows. He started to run toward the ground squirrel. I, too, started running toward the clearing's edge where Bob was jumping and barking. The dust flew in tiny swirls behind our feet. There was a cloud of dust behind us.

"It's a big bull blacksnake," said my father. "Kill him, Bob! Kill him, Bob!"

Bob was jumping and snapping at the snake so as to make it strike and throw itself off guard. Bob had killed twenty-eight copperheads this spring. He knows how to kill a snake. He doesn't rush to do it. He takes his time and does the job well.

"Let's don't kill the snake," I said. "A blacksnake is a harmless snake. It kills poison snakes. It kills the copperhead. It catches more mice from the fields than a cat."

I could see the snake didn't want to fight the dog. The snake wanted to get away. Bob wouldn't let

作者简介：杰西·斯图尔特(**Jesse Stuart**,1906—1984),美国作家,以短篇小说、长篇小说和诗歌闻名。生于 1906 年 8 月 8 日,卒于 1984 年 2 月 17 日。他在肯塔基州格里纳普县长大,作品主要描写了肯塔基州东北的乡村生活。据他所说,他的大部分作品都来源于他所观察到的或者听到的真实事仵。

上一堆黑色沃土游去。我也很奇怪它刚才为什么会从悬崖上栗色橡树苗地里和那长满绿蔷薇的地方钻出来。我望着它昂起漂亮的头想招架鲍勃的一次次扑咬。"这不是一条雄黑蛇，"我说，"是条雌蛇。你看它颈下的白斑。"

"蛇总是我的敌人，"父亲厉声叫道，"我就恨蛇。咬死它，鲍勃。冲过去咬住它，别跟它弄着玩了！"

鲍勃服从了父亲的命令。我讨厌看到他咬住那蛇的喉颈。她①在阳光下优美的身段伸得笔直。鲍勃正咬在她喉部的白斑上。他像甩马鞭子一样把她长长的身体在空中甩来甩去。他总是逆风甩。血从她细致弯曲的喉部汩汩流出。有什么东西像药丸似的打在我腿上。鲍勃把蛇往地上一掼。我仔细看看究竟是什么打了我腿上。原来是蛇蛋。鲍勃把蛋从蛇肚里甩了出来。她原来是去沙堆那边下蛋的，在那里，阳光就像孵蛋的母鸡，可以使蛇蛋受热孵化。

鲍勃又在地上咬住她的身体，殷红的血流到地上，汇到了灰色的肥堆旁边。她的身体还在痛苦地扭动着。她的动作就像一根嫩草在烧荒的火苗上烧着。鲍勃恶狠狠地把她摔了好几次。他衔住她那软弱无力的身体乱甩。现在她软得像一根鞋带一样在风中摆动。鲍勃把她满是伤孔的身体扔回沙堆。她犹如一片树叶，在懒洋洋的微风里轻轻抖动，不久她满是伤痕的身体便全然不动了。血染红了蛇身周围的沃土。

"看这蛇蛋，看见了吗？"我父亲说。我们数了一下，共有 37 只。我捡起一只放在手心里。仅仅分把钟之前这蛋里还有着生命。这是一粒来不及成熟的种子。它再也孵不出生命来了。太阳妈妈再也无法使它在温暖的泥土里孵化了。我手上的蛋和鹌鹑蛋差不多大小。蛋壳又薄又韧，而透过这蛋壳那里面便是一颗水汪汪的蛋。

"啊，鲍勃，现在你该明白那蛇为什么会斗不过你了吧。"我说，"这就是生活。弱者引起了强者的贪心，就是在人类中间也是这样的。狗咬死蛇。蛇吞下鸟。鸟吃掉蝴蝶。人战胜一切。人，还以屠杀取乐呢。"

鲍勃气喘吁吁。回家路上，他走在我们前面。他的舌头拖在嘴外面。他累了。他披着一身密密的粗毛实在太热了。他的舌头几乎要碰到地上的干土，舌

---

① 原文如此，本文主要写动物，故用人称代词。

it. I wondered why it was crawling toward a heap of black loamy earth at the bend of the hill. I wondered why it had come from the chestnut oak sprouts and the matted greenbriars on the cliff. I looked as the snake lifted its pretty head in response to one of Bob's jumps. "It's not a bull blacksnake," I said. "It's a she-snake. Look at the white on her throat. "

"A snake is an enemy to me," my father snapped. "I hate a snake. Kill it, Bob. Go in there and get that snake and quit playing with it!"

Bob obeyed my father. I hated to see him take this snake by the throat. She was so beautifully poised in the sunlight. Bob grabbed the white patch on her throat. He cracked her long body like an ox whip in the wind. He cracked it against the wind only. The blood spurted from her fine-curved throat. Something hit against my legs like pellets. Bob threw the snake down. I looked to see what had struck my legs. It was snake eggs. Bob had slung them from her body. She was going to the sand heap to lay her eggs, where the sun is the setting-hen that warms them and hatches them.

Bob grabbed her body there on the earth where the red blood was running down on the gray-piled loam. Her body was still writhing in pain. She acted like a green weed held over a new-ground fire. Bob slung her viciously many times. He cracked her limp body against the wind. She was now limber as a shoe-string in the wind. Bob threw her riddled body back on the sand. She quivered like a leaf in the lazy wind, then her riddled body lay perfectly still. The blood colored the loamy earth around the snake.

"Look at the eggs, won't you?" said my father. We counted thirty-seven eggs. I picked an egg up and held it in my hand. Only a minute ago there was life in it. It was an immature seed. It would not hatch. Mother sun could not incubate it on the warm earth. The egg I held in my hand was almost the size of a quail's egg. The shell on it was thin and tough and the egg appeared under the surface to be a watery egg.

"Well, Bob, I guess you see now why this snake couldn't fight," I said. "It is life. Weaker devour the stronger even among human beings. Dog kills snake. Snake kills birds. Birds kill the butterflies. Man conquers all. Man, too, kills for sport. "

Bob was panting. He walked ahead of us back to the house. His tongue was out of his mouth. He was tired. He was hot under his shaggy coat of hair. His tongue nearly touched the dry dirt and white flecks of foam dripped from it. We walked toward the house. Neither my father nor I spoke. I still thought about the dead snake. The sun was going down over the chestnut

头上正滴下一滴一滴白色的涎沫。我们朝屋子走去。父亲和我都一声不吭。我还在想着那死去的蛇。落日在那长着栗色橡树的小山上空慢慢西沉。一只百灵鸟在欢唱。百灵欢唱的时刻已经过去了。绚丽的晚霞浮现在我家山麓牧场上松林的上空。父亲在那小路边停下。晚风吹拂着他的黑发。白天的熏风已吹红了他的面颊。他遥望着西垂的落日。

"父亲恨蛇。"我想。

我想到临产的痛苦,那种痛苦唯有妇女才知道。我想到她们会怎样地挣扎,为了保住自己的孩子。于是,我又想到那条蛇。我想,自己的脑子里老是转着这样的想法也太傻了。

今天早晨鸡一叫,父亲和我就起来了。他说,鸡一叫,人就得起身去干一天的活。我们扛着挖桩坑用的十字镐、斧头、锄头和测量杆。我们动身到那开垦地的旁边去。鲍勃没有跟去。

露珠挂在玉米苗上。父亲横扛着挖桩坑用的十字镐走在后面。我走在前面。风徐徐吹拂。这晨风沁人肺腑,它令人仿佛觉得自己能在这小山下面把整个小山举起来翻个身。

我走过那条玉米垄头,这儿就是昨天下午我们来过的地方。我望着前面。我看见有个什么东西。我看见它在动。它在动,就像一根粗大的黑绳绕着辘轳在转动。"当心,"我对父亲说,"这儿有条雄黑蛇。"他跨前一步站在我身旁。他的眼睛越睁越大。

"你怎么知道这是雄蛇?"他说。

"现在你看见了这是条雄黑蛇,"我说,"仔细看看! 他躺在已死去的伴侣身边。他已来到她身边。也许他昨天就在追寻她了。"

雄蛇已寻到雌蛇惨遭厄运的地方。他夜里就来了,就在星空底下,月亮正向那微微抖颤的绿荫上泻下缕缕青光的时候。他发现自己的爱人已经死去。他盘绕在她的身旁,而她已经死了。

当我们绕过那死蛇旁边时,雄黑蛇昂着头盯住我们。他本该和我们拼个死活。他本该和鲍勃拼个死活。"拿根棍子来,"父亲说,"把他扔到山那边去,这样鲍勃就不会找到他了。你见过什么东西能不那样呢? 我听人家说,什么东西都是那样的。不过今天我还是头一次亲眼看到。"我用一根粗枝把雄蛇扔过堤岸,扔到山崖上那接着露珠的嫩苗丛里去了。

ridge. A lark was singing. It was late for a lark to sing. The red evening clouds floated above the pine trees on our pasture hill. My father stood beside the path. His black hair was moved by the wind. His face was red in the blue wind of day. His eyes looked toward the sinking sun.

"And my father hates a snake," I thought.

I thought about the agony women know of giving birth. I thought about how they will fight to save their children. Then, I thought of the snake. I thought it was silly for me to think such thoughts.

This morning my father and I got up with the chickens. He says one has to get up with the chickens to do a day's work. We got the posthole digger, ax, spud, measuring pole and the mattock. We started for the clearing's edge. Bob didn't go along.

The dew was on the corn. My father walked behind with the posthole digger across his shoulder. I walked in front. The wind was blowing. It was a good morning wind to breathe and a wind that makes one feel like he can get under the edge of a hill and heave the whole hill upside down.

I walked out the corn row where we had come yesterday afternoon. I looked in front of me. I saw something. I saw it move. It was moving like a huge black rope winds around a windlass. "Steady," I says to my father. "Here is the bull blacksnake." He took one step up beside me and stood. His eyes grew wide apart.

"What do you know about this," he said.

"You have seen the bull blacksnake now," I said. "Take a good look at him! He is lying beside his dead mate. He has come to her. He, perhaps, was on her trail yesterday."

The male snake had trailed her to her doom. He had come in the night, under the roof of stars, as the moon shed rays of light on the quivering clouds of green. He had found his lover dead. He was coiled beside her, and she was dead.

The bull blacksnake lifted his head and followed us as we walked around the dead snake. He would have fought us to his death. He would have fought Bob to his death. "Take a stick," said my father, "and throw him over the hill so Bob won't find him. Did you ever see anything to beat that? I've heard they'd do that. But this is my first time to see it." I took a stick and threw him over the bank into the dewy sprouts on the cliff.

思考题 —■

1. 这篇小说和莫泊桑写的《爱情》显然非常类似，但在处理上给人的总的"感觉"又很不相同。你认为这种情况会不会使两篇小说在意义上产生某些差别？

2. 这篇小说的冲突表现在哪里？

3. 这篇小说是否有什么前后变化的东西？

4. 作者为什么要用第一人称来叙述这个故事？要是用第三人称来讲，在讲述方面会出现哪些现在未出现的问题。　　（刘家有 译）

1. This story is clearly very similar to "Love" by Maupassant, but the general "feel" of the treatment is different. What difference do you think this makes in the meaning?

2. Wherein does the conflict lie in this story?

3. What change, if any, comes about in the story?

4. Why did the author choose to tell this story in the first person? If the story were told in the third person what problems of exposition might arise that do not now appear?

023. 杀 手

（美）厄内斯特·海明威 著　　海 观 译

亨利的餐馆的门开了，走进来两个人。他们在柜台前面坐下。

"你们吃点儿什么吗？"乔治问他们。

"我说不来，"一个人说，"阿尔，你想吃什么？"

"我也说不来，"阿尔说，"我也说不来想吃什么。"

外面，天渐渐黑暗下去。窗外的街灯放出了亮光。坐在柜台前面的两个人正在看菜单。尼克·亚当斯从柜台的那一头望着他们。他们进来的时候，他正在跟乔治谈话。

"我要苹果酱和马铃薯糊烤猪腰。"第一个人说。

"这个菜还没有准备。"

"那么你们为什么把它放在菜单上呢？"

"那是正餐，"乔治解释说，"6 点钟你可以吃到。"

乔治望了望柜台后面墙上的钟。

"5 点啦。"

"钟上是 5:20。"第二个人说。

"快了 20 分。"

"嘻，倒霉的钟。"第一个人说，"你这有什么可吃的？"

"我给你什么夹肉面包都可以，"乔治说，"你可以吃火腿蛋，咸肉蛋，猪肝咸肉，或者牛排。"

"给我一份奶油和马铃薯糊拌鸡肉饼。"

"那是正餐。"

"我们要什么你都说是正餐，是不是？你就用这个办法来对付我们嘛。"

"我可以给你们火腿蛋，咸肉蛋，猪肝——"

"我吃火腿蛋。"叫做阿尔的那个人说。他戴一顶常礼帽，穿一件单排扣的黑大衣。他的脸又小又白，

023. The Killers

by Ernest Hemingway

THE door of Henry's lunchroom opened and two men came in. They sat down at the counter.

"What's yours?" George asked them.

"I don't know," one of the men said. "What do you want to eat, Al?"

"I don't know," said Al. "I don't know what I want to eat."

Outside it was getting dark. The street light came on outside the window. The two men at the counter read the menu. From the other end of the counter Nick Adams watched them. He had been talking to George when they came in.

"I'll have a roast pork tenderloin with apple sauce and mashed potatoes," the first man said.

"It isn't ready yet."

"What the hell do you put it on the card for?"

"That's the dinner," George explained. "You can get that at six o'clock."

George looked at the clock on the wall behind the counter.

"It's five o'clock."

"The clock says twenty minutes past five," the second man said.

"It's twenty minutes fast."

"Oh, to hell with the clock," the first man said, "What have you got to eat?"

"I can give you any kind of sandwiches," George said. "You can have ham and eggs, bacon and eggs, liver and bacon, or a steak."

"Give me chicken croquettes with green peas and cream sauce and mashed potatoes."

作者简介：**厄内斯特·海明威**（Ernest Hemingway，1899—1961），美国作家。1899 年 7 月 21 日生于伊利诺州西塞罗，1961 年 7 月 2 日卒于爱达荷州凯彻姆。中学毕业后，他开始做新闻记者。他的作品包括短篇小说集《在我们的时代里》（In Our Time，1925）、《太阳照样升起》（The Sun Also Rises，1926）、《永别了，武器》（A Farewell to Arms，1929）和《有的和没有的》（Have and Have Not，1937）。在西班牙内战期间他在西班牙担任通讯员，从而创作了《丧钟为谁而鸣》（For Whom the Bell Tolls，1940）。1940 年后他主要居住在古巴，其间著有中篇小说《老人与海》（The Old Man and the Sea，1952），获普利策奖。1954 年，他获得诺贝尔文学奖。他早期的简洁浓缩的散文体风格影响了很多英美作家。

嘴唇绷得很紧。他还围一条丝围巾,戴着手套。

"我吃咸肉蛋。"另一个人说。他的身材跟阿尔不相上下。两个人面孔不同,但是穿得像一对双生儿似的。两个人穿的大衣都很紧。他俩坐在那儿身子探在前面,胳膊支在柜台上。

"有什么喝的没有?"阿尔问。

"白啤酒,姜汁啤酒。"乔治说。

"我说的是有什么可喝的?"

"就是刚才我说的那些。"

"这是一座很热的城市,"另一个人说,"他们把它叫做什么?"

"热点。"

"听到过吗?"阿尔问他的朋友。

"没有,"他的朋友说。"你晚上在这儿做什么?"阿尔问。

"他们在这儿吃正餐,"他的朋友说,"他们都来到这儿大吃大喝。"

"对。"乔治说。

"你觉得对吗?"阿尔问乔治。

"当然。"

"你是个挺机灵的小伙子,是不是?"

"当然。"乔治说。

"不,你不是的。"另一个矮小的人说,"阿尔,他是吗?"

"他是个傻瓜。"阿尔说。他转过去问尼克:"你叫什么名字?"

"亚当斯。"

"又一个机灵的小伙子,"阿尔说,"迈克斯,他是不是一个机灵的小伙子呀?"

"这个城市里尽是机灵的小伙子。"迈克斯说。

乔治把两个大盘子放在柜台上,一盘是火腿蛋,另一盘是咸肉蛋。他又放了两小盘油炸马铃薯,然后关上了通往厨房的便门。

"哪一盘是你的?"他问阿尔。

"你忘记了吗?"

"火腿蛋。"

"真是一个机灵的小伙子,"迈克斯说。他探一探身子,把火腿蛋拿过来。两个人都戴着手套在吃。乔治望着他们在吃。

"你看什么?"迈克斯对乔治望了望。

"没看什么。"

"That's the dinner."

"Everything we want's the dinner, eh? That's the way you work it."

"I can give you ham and eggs, bacon and eggs, liver—"

"I'll take ham and eggs," the man called Al said. He wore a derby hat and a black overcoat buttoned across the chest. His face was small and white and he had tight lips. He wore a silk muffler and gloves.

"Give me bacon and eggs," said the other man. He was about the same size as Al. Their faces were different, but they were dressed like twins. Both wore overcoats too tight for them. They sat leaning forward, their elbows on the counter.

"Got anything to drink?" Al asked.

"Silver beer, bevo, ginger ale." George said.

"I mean you got anything to *drink*?"

"Just those I said."

"This is a hot town," said the other. "What do they call it?"

"Summit."

"Ever hear of it?" Al asked his friend.

"No," said the friend.

"What do you do here nights?" Al asked.

"They eat the dinner," his friend said. "They all come here and eat the big dinner."

"That's right," George said.

"So you think that's right?" Al asked George.

"Sure."

"You're a pretty bright boy, aren't you?"

"Sure," said George.

"Well, you're not," said the other little man. "Is he, Al?"

"He's dumb," said Al. He turned to Nick. "What's your name?"

"Adams."

"Another bright boy," Al said. "Ain't he a bright boy, Max?"

"The town's full of bright boys," Max said.

George put the two platters, one of ham and eggs, the other of bacon and eggs, on the counter. He set down two side dishes of fried potatoes and closed the wicket into the kitchen.

"Which is yours?" he asked Al.

"Don't you remember?"

"Ham and eggs."

"Just a bright boy," Max said. He leaned forward and took the ham and eggs. Both men ate with their gloves on. George watched them eat.

"去你的。你在看我呢。"

"迈克斯,小伙子也许是说着玩儿的。"阿尔说。

乔治笑了。

"你不必笑,"迈克斯对他说,"你丝毫也不必笑,知道吗?"

"可以。"乔治说。

"他觉得可以,"迈克斯转过来对阿尔说,"他觉得可以。这小伙子不错。"

"哦,他是一个有头脑的人。"于是两个人继续吃下去。

"柜台那一边的一个机灵的小伙子叫作什么?"阿尔问迈克斯。

"喂,机灵的小伙子,"迈克斯对尼克说,"你跟你的伙计到柜台后面去转一转吧。"

"什么事儿?"尼克问。

"什么事儿也没有。"

"你最好走开去,机灵的小伙子,"阿尔说。于是尼克走到柜台后面去了。

"什么事儿?"乔治问。

"跟你毫不相干,"阿尔说,"谁在厨房里面?"

"黑人。"

"你说的黑人是干什么的?"

"当厨子的黑人。"

"叫他进来。"

"什么事儿?"

"叫他进来。"

"你可想到你此刻是在什么地方吗?"

"我们此刻在什么地方,我们当然是很清楚的。"那个叫作迈克斯的汉子说,"是不是我们的样子傻里傻气的。"

"你说话倒有点傻里傻气,"阿尔对他说,"你跟那个家伙争论什么呢?听我说,"他对乔治说,"告诉那个黑人到这儿来一下。"

"你预备怎样对待他?"

"没什么。机灵的小伙子,你得用你的脑子想一想。咱们对一个黑人会有什么呢?"

乔治打开了通往厨房的小窗口。"山姆,"他叫道,"进来一下。"

通往厨房的门开了,那个黑人走进来。"什么事?"他问。坐在柜台前面的那两个人朝他望了望。

"行,黑伙计。你就站在那儿吧。"阿尔说。

"What are *you* looking at?" Max looked at George.

"Nothing."

"The hell you were. You were looking at me."

"Maybe the boy meant it for a joke, Max," Al said.

George laughed.

"*You* don't have to laugh,"Max said to him. "*You* don't have to laugh at all,see?"

"All right,"said George.

"So he thinks it's all right." Max turned to Al. "He thinks it's all right. That's a good one."

"Oh,he's a thinker," Al said. They went on eating.

"What's the bright boy's name down the counter?"Al asked Max.

"Hey,bright boy,"Max said to Nick. "You go around on the other side of the counter with your boy friend."

"What's the idea?"Nick asked.

"There isn't any idea."

"You better go around,bright boy,"Al said. Nick went around behind the counter.

"What's the idea?"George asked.

"None of your damn business," Al said. "Who's out in the kitchen?"

"The nigger."

"What do you mean the nigger?"

"The nigger that cooks."

"Tell him to come in."

"What's the idea?"

"Tell him to come in."

"Where do you think you are?"

"We know damn well where we are," the man called Max said,"Do we look silly?"

"You talk silly," Al said to him. "What the hell do you argue with this kid for? Listen,"he said to George,"tell the nigger to come out here."

"What are you going to do to him?"

"Nothing. Use your head,bright boy. What would we do to a nigger?"

George opened the slit that opened back into the kitchen. "Sam,"he called. "Come in here a minute."

The door to the kitchen opened and the nigger came in. "What was it?"he asked. The two men at the counter took a look at him.

"All right, nigger. You stand right there," Al said.

黑人山姆穿着围裙站在那儿,望着坐在柜台前面的两个汉子。"是,先生。"他说,阿尔从他坐的凳子上下来。

"我要跟黑人和那个机灵的小伙子一同到后面厨房里去,"他说,"黑伙计,回到厨房里去。机灵的小伙子,你跟他一道去。"于是那个矮个儿跟在尼克和厨子山姆的后面走到后面的厨房里去。他们过去以后门就关上了。叫作迈克斯的那个人跟乔治对着面坐在柜台跟前。他不看乔治一眼,只是望着挂在柜台后面墙上的一面镜子。原来的亨利的酒吧间,现在改成了便餐馆了。

"喂,机灵的小伙子,"迈克斯说,一面望着镜子,"为什么你不说话呀?"

"这都是干什么?"

"嗐,阿尔,"迈克斯叫道,"机灵的小伙子想知道这都是干什么。"

"干吗你不告诉他呢?"阿尔的声音从厨房里传出来。

"你以为这都是干什么?"

"我不晓得。"

"你怎么想法?"

迈克斯讲话的时候一直望着镜子。

"我不愿说。"

"嗐,阿尔,机灵的小伙子说,他不愿说他想这为的是什么?"

"好,我听到了。"阿尔从厨房里说。他把通厨房的那个小窗口用手撑开,盘子和番茄汁的瓶子从那里送进厨房里去。"听着,机灵的小伙子,"他从厨房里对乔治说,"站得离柜台远一点儿。你往左边挪动一步,迈克斯。"他像一个安排团体照相的摄影师似的。

"对我说,机灵的小伙子,"迈克斯说,"你以为要发生什么事情呢?"

乔治一声也不吭。

"我告诉你,"迈克斯说,"咱们要去杀死一个瑞典人。你知道叫做奥勒·安德生的一个高大的瑞典人吗?"

"是的。"

"他每晚来这儿吃饭,是不是?"

"他有时候来这儿。"

"他在 6 点钟来这儿,是不是?"

"要是他来的话。"

Sam, the nigger, standing in his apron, looked at the two men sitting at the counter. "Yes, sir," he said. Al got down from his stool.

"I'm going back to the kitchen with the nigger and bright boy," he said. "Go on back to the kitchen, nigger. You go with him, bright boy." The little man walked after Nick and Sam, the cook, back into the kitchen. The door shut after them. The man called Max sat at the counter opposite George. He didn't look at George but looked in the mirror that ran along back of the counter. Henry's had been made over from a saloon into a lunch counter.

"Well, bright boy," Max said, looking into the mirror, "why don't you say something?"

"What's it all about?"

"Hey, Al," Max called, "bright boy wants to know what it's all about."

"Why don't you tell him?" Al's voice came from the kitchen.

"What do you think it's all about?"

"I don't know."

"What do you think?"

Max looked into the mirror all the time he was talking.

"I wouldn't say."

"Hey, Al, bright boy says he wouldn't say what he thinks it's all about."

"I can hear you, all right," Al said from the kitchen. He had propped open the slit that dishes passed through into the kitchen with a catsup bottle. "Listen, bright boy," he said from the kitchen to George. "Stand a little further along the bar. You move a little to the left, Max." He was like a photographer arranging for a group picture.

"Talk to me, bright boy," Max said. "What do you think's going to happen?"

George did not say anything.

"I'll tell you," Max said. "We're going to kill a Swede. Do you know a big Swede named Ole Andreson?"

"Yes."

"He comes here to eat every night, doesn't he?"

"Sometimes he comes here."

"He comes here at six o'clock, doesn't he?"

"If he comes."

"We know all that, bright boy," Max said. "Talk about something else. Ever go to the movies?"

"Once in a while."

"这一切我们都晓得,机灵的小伙子,"迈克斯说,"讲些别的事情吧。你有时去看电影吗?"

"偶尔去看一次。"

"你应该多去看看电影。像你这样一个机灵的小伙子,看看电影是非常好的。"

"你们干吗要把奥勒·安德生杀死呢?他有过什么对不起你们的地方没有?"

"他从来也没机会对我们怎样过。他一次没见过我们。"

"他只会见到咱们一次了。"阿尔从厨房里说。

"那么,你们干吗要杀死他呢?"

"我们替一个朋友去杀他。只是受人之托,机灵的小伙子。"

"住嘴,"阿尔从厨房里说,"他妈的你讲得太多了。"

"是啊,我叫机灵的小伙子觉得有趣。是不是,机灵的小伙子?"

"他妈的你讲得太多了,"阿尔说,"那个黑人跟我这个机灵的小伙子他们自己在觉得有趣呢。我把他们两个像是修道院的一对女朋友似的绑在一起了。"

"我想你原来像是在一所修道院里吧?"

"你不知道。"

"你原来像是在一所真正的修道院里。你就是从那儿来的。"

乔治抬头望了望钟。

"要是有人来了,你告诉他们厨子不在,要是他们还在追问,你告诉他们你到后面去亲自替他们做菜。你懂得了吗,机灵的小伙子?"

"懂得了,"乔治说,"你们要怎样对待我们呢?"

"那要看情况了,"迈克斯说,"有许多事情在当时是不知道的,这件事就是。"

乔治抬头望了望钟。此刻是 6:15。临衍的大门开了,一个电车司机走进来。

"喂,乔治,"他说,"有晚饭吃吗?"

"山姆出去了,"乔治说,"大概半个钟头左右就会回来。"

"那么我倒不如到街那一头去吧。"那个司机说。乔治望了望钟。现在是 6:20。

"很好,机灵的小伙子,"迈克斯说,"你真是个十足的绅士。"

"他知道我会用枪打死他的。"阿尔从厨房里说。

"You ought to go to the movies more. The movies are fine for a bright boy like you. "

"What are you going to kill Ole Andreson for? What did he ever do to you?"

"He never had a chance to do anything to us. He never even seen us. "

"And he's only going to see us once," Al said from the kitchen.

"What are you going to kill him for, then?" George asked.

"We're killing him for a friend. Just to oblige a friend, bright boy. "

"Shut up," said Al from the kitchen. "You talk too goddamn much. "

"Well, I got to keep bright boy amused. Don't I, bright boy?"

"You talk too damn much," Al said. "The nigger and my bright boy are amused by themselves. I got them tied up like a couple of girl friends in a convent. "

"I suppose you were in a convent. "

"You never know. "

"You were in a kosher convent. That's where you were. "

George looked up at the clock.

"If anybody comes in you tell them the cook is off and if they keep after it, you tell them you'll go back and cook yourself. Do you get that, bright boy?"

"All right," George said. "What you going to do with us afterward?"

"That'll depend," Max said. "That's one of those things you never know at the time. "

George looked up at the clock. It was a quarter past six. The door from the street opened. A street-car motorman came in.

"Hello, George," he said. "Can I get supper?"

"Sam's gone out," George said. "He'll be back in about half an hour. "

"I'd better go up the street," the motorman said. George looked at the clock. It was twenty minutes past six.

"That was nice, bright boy," Max said. "You're a regular little gentleman. " At six-fifty-five George said: "He's not coming. "

Two other people had been in the lunchroom. Once George had gone out to the kitchen and made a ham-and-egg sandwich "to go" that a man wanted to

"不，"迈克斯说，"你说得不对。机灵的小伙子是不错的。他是一个很好的小伙子。我喜欢他。"

到了6:55的时候，乔治说:"他不会来了。"

餐馆里还有另外两个人。乔治到厨房去了一次，去那儿做一份给一个客人要带走的面包片夹火腿蛋，他在厨房里看见阿尔把常礼帽歪戴在脑后，坐在便门旁边的凳子上，一支锯短了的枪的枪口靠在架子上。尼克和厨子在一个墙角落里背对背给捆在一起，每人的嘴上绑了一条毛巾。乔治做了夹肉面包，用油纸把它包起来，放进一个袋子，然后拿到餐厅去，那个人付了钱便走了。

"机灵的小伙子什么事都会做，"迈克斯说，"他会做菜，什么都会做。机灵的小伙子，你可以把一个女孩子训练成一个很好的老婆。"

"怎么?"乔治说，"你的朋友，奥勒·安德生不来了吗?"

"我们再等他10分钟。"迈克斯说。

迈克斯留意着镜子和那座钟。钟上的指针是7点钟，一会儿又过了5分钟。

"来，阿尔，"迈克斯说，"咱们不如回去吧。他不会来了。"

"最好再等他5分钟。"阿尔从厨房里说。

过了5分钟，一个人走进来，乔治向他说厨子生病了。

"干吗你们不另找一个厨子呢?"那个人问，"你不是在开餐馆吗?"说罢他走出去了。

"来，阿尔。"迈克斯说。

"那两个机灵的小伙子跟那个黑人该怎么办?"

"他们是挺可靠的。"

"你这样想吗?"

"当然。咱们已经没事了。"

"这不能叫我开心，"阿尔说，"粗心大意的。你话讲得太多了。"

"啊，这又有什么要紧，"迈克斯说，"咱们只不过是开开心罢了，是不是呢?"

"不管怎样，你还是话讲得太多了。"阿尔说。他从厨房里走出来。锯短了的鸟枪枪身在他的过于窄小的大衣上身里面微微地鼓出来。他用他的戴着手套的手把衣服理了一理。

"再会了，机灵的小伙子，"他对乔治说，"你太走运了。"

take with him. Inside the kitchen he saw Al, his derby hat tipped back, sitting on a stool beside the wicket with the muzzle of a sawed-off shotgun resting on the ledge. Nick and the cook were back to back in the corner, a towel tied in each of their mouths. George had cooked the sandwich, wrapped it up in oiled paper, put it in a bag, brought it in, and the man had paid for it and gone out.

"Bright boy can do everything," Max said. "He can cook and everything. You'd make some girl a nice wife, bright boy."

"Yes?" George said. "Your friend, Ole Andreson, isn't going to come."

"We'll give him ten minutes," Max said.

Max watched the mirror and the clock. The hands of the clock marked seven o'clock, and then five minutes past seven.

"Come on, Al," said Max. "We better go. He's not coming."

"Better give him five minutes," Al said from the kitchen.

In the five minutes a man came in, and George explained that the cook was sick.

"Why the hell don't you get another cook?" the man asked. "Aren't you running a lunch counter?" He went out.

"Come on, Al," Max said.

"What about the two bright boys and the nigger?"

"They're all right."

"You think so?"

"Sure. We're through with it."

"I don't like it," said Al. "It's sloppy. You talk too much."

"Oh, what the hell," said Max. "We got to keep amused, haven't we?"

"You talk too much, all the same," Al said. He came out from the kitchen. The cut-off barrels of the shotgun made a slight bulge under the waist of his too tight-fitting overcoat. He straightened his coat with his gloved hands.

"So long, bright boy," he said to George. "You got a lot of luck."

"That's the truth," Max said. "You ought to play the races, bright boy."

The two of them went out the door. George watched them, through the window, pass under the arc light and cross the street. In their tight overcoats and derby hats they looked like a vaudeville team. George

"那倒是真的,"迈克斯说,"你应该赌一赌赛马去,机灵的小伙子。"

那两个人走出门去。乔治从窗户里面望着他们在弧光灯下经过,走到街对面去。他们的窄小的大衣和常礼帽使他们看上去像一对玩杂耍的人似的。乔治从转门走进厨房,把尼克跟厨子两个人松开了绑。

"那回事儿我再也不想碰到了,"厨子山姆说,"那回事儿我再也不想碰到了。"

尼克站起了身。他以前从来也没有被人用一条毛巾绑在嘴上过。

"告诉我,"他说,"究竟是怎么一回事儿?"他正在设法把毛巾甩掉。

"他们要杀害奥勒·安德生,"乔治说,"他们准备在他进来吃饭的时候用枪把他打死。"

"奥勒·安德生吗?"

"正是。"

那个厨子用大拇指摸着他的嘴角。

"他们都走了吗?"他问。

"是的,"乔治说,"他们都走了。"

"这件事真叫我不高兴,"厨子说,"没有一星半点儿叫我高兴的。"

"听我说,"乔治对尼克说,"你最好到奥勒·安德生那儿去看一看他。"

"好的。"

"你最好丝毫也别过问这件事情,"厨子山姆说,"你最好离远点。"

"你要是不愿去就别去吧。"乔治说。

"牵连在这件事里面对你不会有什么好结果的,"厨子说,"你还是离远点。"

"我要去看他,"尼克对乔治说,"他住在什么地方?"

厨子掉过脸去。

"小孩子们对于自己想做的事情总是自以为是知道的。"他说。

"他住在赫思奇的公寓里。"乔治对尼克说。

"我要到那儿去一趟。"

外面弧光灯的亮光透过光秃的树枝。尼克沿着电车轨道走去,到下一盏弧光灯的地方转了一个弯,朝一条小街走去。街上的第三幢房子就是赫思奇的公寓。尼克走上那两条阶石,然后去按门铃。一个女人来到了门前。

went back through the swinging door into the kitchen and untied Nick and the cook.

"I don't want any more of that," said Sam, the cook. "I don't want any more of that."

Nick stood up. He had never had a towel in his mouth before.

"Say," he said. "What the hell?" He was trying to swagger it off.

"They were going to kill Ole Andreson," George said. "They were going to shoot him when he came in to eat."

"Ole Andreson?"

"Sure."

The cook felt the corners of his mouth with his thumbs.

"They all gone?" he asked.

"Yeah," said George. "They're gone now."

"I don't like it," said the cook. "I don't like any of it at all."

"Listen," George said to Nick. "You better go see Ole Andreson."

"All right."

"You better not have anything to do with it at all," Sam, the cook, said. "You better stay way out of it."

"Don't go if you don't want to," George said.

"Mixing up in this ain't going to get you anywhere," the cook said. "You stay out of it."

"I'll go see him," Nick said to George. "Where does he live?"

The cook turned away.

"Little boys always know what they want to do," he said.

"He lives up at Hirsch's rooming house," George said to Nick.

"I'll go up there."

Outside the arc light shone through the bare branches of a tree. Nick walked up the street beside the car tracks and turned at the next arc light down a side street. Three houses up the street was Hirsch's rooming house. Nick walked up the two steps and pushed the bell. A woman came to the door.

"Is Ole Andreson here?"

"Do you want to see him?"

"Yes, if he's in."

Nick followed the woman up a flight of stairs and back to the end of a corridor. She knocked on the door.

"奥勒·安德生住在这里吗?"

"你想看他吗?"

"是的,要是他在家的话。"

尼克跟着那个女人走上一段楼梯,然后又折转来走到一条走廊的尽头处。她敲了门。

"谁呀?"

"有人来看你,安德生先生。"那个女人说。

"我是尼克·亚当斯。"

"进来。"

尼克推开了门,走进屋里去。奥勒·安德生穿着全身衣服正躺在床上。他从前是个重量级的拳击手。他的身子长得那张床容不下去。他的头靠在两个枕头上。他没有朝尼克望一眼。

"什么事儿?"

"我在亨利的餐馆里干活,"尼克说,"两个家伙进来,把我跟厨子用绳子绑上,他们说他们要杀死你。"

他说这些话的时候叫人听上去有些呆里呆气似的。奥勒·安德生一声也不吭。

"他们把咱俩赶到厨房里,"尼克说下去,"他们要趁你来咱们这儿用晚餐的时候用枪把你打死。"

奥勒·安德生望着墙,一声也不吭。

"乔治觉得,要我最好来把这件事情告诉你。"

"这件事我什么办法也没有。"奥勒·安德生说。

"我告诉你他俩是什么样儿的。"

"我不想知道他俩是什么样儿的。"奥勒·安德生说。他望着墙:"谢谢你来告诉我这件事情。"

"别客气。"

尼克望着躺在床上的那个身材魁梧的汉子。

"你要我去找警察吗?"

"不,"奥勒·安德生说,"那不会有什么用处的。"

"有什么可以让我去办的事情?"

"不。没有什么要办的事情。"

"也许这只是恐吓罢了。"

"不,这不是恐吓。"

奥勒·安德生翻了一个身朝向墙壁那边去。

"唯一的一件事情是,"他对着墙壁说,"我还拿不定主意下决心走出去。我已经待在家里一天了。"

"你不能走到城外去吗?"

"不,"奥勒·安德生说,"我再不想那样跑来跑去的了。"

他望着墙。

"Who is it?"

"It's somebody to see you, Mr. Andreson," the woman said.

"It's Nick Adams."

"Come in."

Nick opened the door and went into the room. Ole Andreson was lying on the bed with all his clothes on. He had been a heavyweight prize fighter and he was too long for the bed. He lay with his head on two pillows. He did not look at Nick.

"What was it?" he asked.

"I was up at Henry's," Nick said, "and two fellows came in and tied up me and the cook, and they said they were going to kill you."

It sounded silly when he said it. Ole Andreson said nothing.

"They put us out in the kitchen," Nick went on. "They were going to shoot you when you came in to supper."

Ole Andreson looked at the wall and did not say anything.

"George thought I better come and tell you about it."

"There isn't anything I can do about it," Ole Andreson said.

"I'll tell you what they were like."

"I don't want to know what they were like," Ole Andreson said. He looked at the wall. "Thanks for coming to tell me about it."

"That's all right."

Nick looked at the big man lying on the bed.

"Don't you want me to go and see the police?"

"No," Ole Andreson said. "That wouldn't do any good."

"Isn't there something I could do?"

"No. There ain't anything to do."

"Maybe it was just a bluff."

"No. It ain't just a bluff."

Ole Andreson rolled over toward the wall.

"The only thing is," he said, talking toward the wall, "I just can't make up my mind to go out. I been in here all day."

"Couldn't you get out of town?"

"No," Ole Andreson said. "I'm through with all that running around."

He looked at the wall.

"There ain't anything to do now."

"现在没有什么可办的事了。"

"你不能想点办法把这件事情了结掉吗?"

"不成。我得罪了人啦。"他依然用那种懒洋洋的腔调在说话,"没有什么好办法。过一会儿,我再拿定主意走出去。"

"那么我不如回去看一看乔治吧。"尼克说。

"再会了。"奥勒·安德生说。他并没有朝尼克望一眼:"谢谢你来这儿一趟。"

尼克走出门去。当他带上门的时候,他看见奥勒·安德生穿着全身的衣服躺在床上,眼睛一直望着墙。

"他已经在屋里待了一整天,"女房东在楼下说,"我想他的身体恐怕不舒服。我对他说:'安德生先生,这样好的秋天天气,你应该出去散散步才是。'但是他却不想出去。"

"他不愿出去。"

"我很替他的身体不舒服觉得不好过,"那个女人说,"他这个人真是好极了。你知道吗,他是干拳击那一行的。"

"我知道。"

"要不是看到他脸上的那个模样,你决不会知道他是干拳击的。"那个女人说。他俩紧靠在大门的里边在谈话。"他这个人真够和气的。"

"好吧,晚安,赫思奇太太。"尼克说。

"我不是赫思奇太太,"那个女人说,"这所公寓是她的。我只是个替她照管的人。我是贝尔太太。"

"好,晚安,贝尔太太。"尼克说。

"晚安。"那个女人说。

尼克从暗淡的街上走到弧光灯照着的街角。然后沿着电车轨道回到亨利的餐馆去。乔治正在柜台后面。

"你看到奥勒了吗?"

"看到了,"尼克说,"他待在屋里,不愿走出去。"

山姆刚打开厨房的那扇门,就听到尼克的声音。

"我连听也不要听。"他说,说罢就把门关上。

"你把那件事情告诉他了吗?"乔治问。

"当然。我告诉了他,但是他知道这都是怎么一回事儿。"

"那么他打算怎么办呢?"

"什么打算也没有。"

"他准是卷进什么赌博斗殴的事儿里面了。"

"Couldn't you fix it up some way?"

"No. I got in wrong." He talked in the same flat voice. "There ain't anything to do. After a while I'll make up my mind to go out."

"I better go back and see George," Nick said.

"So long," said Ole Andreson. He did not look toward Nick. "Thanks for coming around."

Nick went out. As he shut the door he saw Ole Andreson with all his clothes on, lying on the bed looking at the wall.

"He's been in his room all day," the landlady said downstairs. "I guess he don't feel well. I said to him: 'Mr. Andreson, you ought to go out and take a walk on a nice fall day like this,' but he didn't feel like it."

"He doesn't want to go out."

"I'm sorry he don't feel well," the woman said. "He's an awfully nice man. He was in the ring, you know."

"I know it."

"You'd never know it except from the way his face is," the woman said. They stood talking just inside the street door. "He's just as gentle."

"Well, good-night, Mrs. Hirsch," Nick said.

"I'm not Mrs. Hirsch," the woman said. "She owns the place. I just look after it for her. I'm Mrs. Bell."

"Well, good-night, Mrs. Bell," Nick said.

"Good-night," the woman said.

Nick walked up the dark street to the corner under the arc light, and then along the car tracks to Henry's eating house. George was inside, back of the counter.

"Did you see Ole?"

"Yes," said Nick. "He's in his room and he won't go out."

The cook opened the door from the kithen when he heard Nick's voice.

"I don't even listen to it," he said and shut the door.

"Did you tell him about it?" George asked.

"Sure. I told him but he knows what it's all about."

"What's he going to do?"

"Nothing."

"They'll kill him."

"I guess they will."

"He must have got mixed up in something in Chicago."

"我也这样想。"尼克说。

"事情真糟糕。"

"事情太可怕了。"尼克说。

他俩不再说下去。乔治伸手去拿一条毛巾,把柜台擦了擦。

"我不晓得到底他干下了什么事情。"尼克说。

"欺骗了什么人啦。他们就是为了这个缘故要把他杀害的。"

"我准备离开这个市镇。"尼克说。

"好呀,"乔治说,"那倒是一桩好事。"

"我不忍去想,他明知道要被人杀害还在屋里等待着。太可怕了。"

"得啦,"乔治说,"你最好不如别去想着这件事儿吧。"

讨 论

这篇小说在技巧上具有相当明显的特点。整个小说分为一个长景和三个短景。显而易见通篇所用的几乎全是描写,场景之间的过渡仅用三四句话就带过了。所用的角度完全是客观的,尤其是,小说内容全部由简洁而合乎生活实际的人物对话来表现。在第一个场景里,歹徒们的意图仅用几个生动的细节就暗示出来——如歹徒吃饭时不脱手套(以免留下指印),眼睛老盯着柜台后面的镜子,当尼克和厨子被捆起来后,那个拿短枪的歹徒在卖酒的柜台旁边"像一个安排团体照相的摄影师似的"向他的伙伴和乔治布置任务——所有这些,在写到他们特殊使命前就已表现得清清楚楚。

关于这篇小说的技巧,还可以做其他多方面的考察,譬如文章的灵巧多变,如第一场景写得很含蓄,歹徒们逗笑打趣,使人捉摸不透,而在第二场景则又换了一种写法,等等。但是,做这类考察虽说也未尝不可,它们却不能回答读者心中最初产生的(或者应该产生的)问题:这篇小说说明了什么?

需要及早回答这个问题的迫切性在于:对这篇小说肯定会有两种意见完全不同的读者,

"I guess so," said Nick.

"It's a hell of a thing."

"It's an awful thing," Nick said.

They did not say anything. George reached down for a towel and wiped the counter.

"I wonder what he did?" Nick said.

"Double-crossed somebody. That's what they kill them for."

"I'm going to get out of this town," Nick said.

"Yes," said George. "That's a good thing to do."

"I can't stand to think about him waiting in the room and knowing he's going to get it. It's too damned awful."

"Well," said George, "you better not think about it."

There are certain fairly obvious points to be made about the technique of this story. It breaks up into one long scene and three short scenes. Indeed, the method is so thoroughly scenic that not over three or four sentences are required to make the transitions. The focus of narration is objective throughout: practically all information is conveyed in simple realistic dialogue. In the first scene the revelation of the mission of the gangsters is accomplished through a few significant details—the fact that the gangsters eat with gloves(to avoid leaving fingerprints), the fact that they keep their eyes on the mirror behind the bar, the fact that, after Nick and the cook have been tied up, the gangster who has the shotgun at the service window stations his friend and George out front "like a photographer arranging for a group picture"—all of this before the specific nature of their mission is made clear.

Other observations concerning the technique of the story could be made—the cleverness of composition, the subtlety with which the suspense is maintained in the first scene by the banter of the gangsters, and then is transferred to another level in the second scene. But such observations, though they are worth making, do not answer the question that first comes(or should come) to the reader's mind: what is the story about?

而这两种意见又都很典型。第一种读者在开始读这篇小说时就会觉得,小说写完第一场景就已经够了,但事实上第一场景本身没有形成焦点——没有一个"重点"。第二种读者则会由于第一场景没有结局而认为第一场景实际上是用来"导出"第二场景的。他因为看到奥勒·安德生不打算躲避歹徒——不想再"那样跑来跑去"——就产生了以上的看法。这种读者觉得小说应该到此结束。他们认为小说的最后几页是画蛇添足,而且不明白作者为什么要把效果冲淡。可以说,第一种读者觉得《杀手》是一篇讲歹徒的小说——一篇没有结尾的小说。第二种读者较为老练,把小说理解为安德生的故事,虽然可能会有些奇怪,写安德生的故事又为什么不直截了当地写而要这样大兜圈子。

换言之,第二种读者是想把"小说说明了什么"这个问题换成"小说写的是谁"。而当他们这样摆出问题时,他们碰到的事实是:海明威既没有把小说的焦点落在歹徒身上,也没有落在安德生身上,而是落在饭馆里的那些小伙子身上。试看小说的最后几句话:

> "我准备离开这个市镇。"尼克说。
>
> "好呀,"乔治说,"那倒是一桩好事。"
>
> "我不忍去想,他明知道要被人杀害还在屋里等待着。太可怕了。"
>
> "得啦,"乔治说,"你最好不如别去想着这件事儿吧。"

这里可以看出,两个小伙子中间,很显然是尼克对事件印象深刻。乔治已经和环境妥协了。由此推知,小说主要是写尼克,写他如何发现了罪恶。

这样确定这篇小说的主题虽然已经能为人接受,但是,我们照例还得根据具体的情节结构对此加以验证。评定一篇小说就像了解一篇小说一样,必须把那种用来体现主题的技

The importance of giving an early answer to this question can be seen by considering two readers who have typical but different reactions to the story. One reader, upon first acquaintance with the story, is inclined to feel that it is exhausted in the first scene, and in fact that the first scene itself does not come to focus—does not have a "point." The other reader sees that the first scene, with its lack of resolution, is really being used to "charge" the second scene. He finds his point in Ole Andreson's decision not to try to escape the gangsters—to stop "all that running around." This reader feels that the story should end here. He sees no relevance in the last several pages of the story, and wonders why the author has flattened his effect. The first reader, we may say, feels that "The Killers" is the gangsters' story—a story of action that does not come off. The second and more sophisticated reader interprets it as Andreson's story, though perhaps with some wonder that Andreson's story has been approached so indirectly and is allowed to trail off so irrelevantly.

In other words, the second reader is inclined to transpose the question "What is the story about?" into the question, "Whose story is it?" When he states the question in this way, he confronts the fact that Hemingway has left the story focused not on the gangsters, nor on Andreson, but on the boys at the lunchroom. Consider the last sentences of the story:

> "I'm going to get out of this town," Nick said.
>
> "Yes," said George. "That's a good thing to do."
>
> "I can't stand to think about him waiting in the room and knowing he's going to get it. It's too damned awful."
>
> "Well," said George, "you better not think about it."

So, of the two boys, it is obviously Nick on whom the impression has been made. George has managed to come to terms with the situation. By this line of reasoning, it is Nick's story. And the story is about the discovery of evil.

This definition of the theme of the story, even if it appears acceptable, must, of course, be tested against the detailed structure. In evaluating the story, as well as in understanding it,

巧也考虑过去。例如,提一个很实在的问题:小说作者是否在小说的最后部分,向读者阐明了那些最初仅仅作为偶然的生活琐事出现的细节的含义?

如果我们把尼克发现罪恶作为主题,那么像尼克被歹徒捆绑、嘴里被塞上东西以及后来又被乔治释放等细节就有了意义。小说写道:"尼克站起了身。他以前从来也没有被人用一条毛巾绑在嘴上过。'告诉我,'他说,'究竟是怎么一回事儿?'他正在设法把毛巾甩掉。"嘴里给塞上东西,这是在惊险小说里才能读到而并非生活中所能碰到的事,它给人的最初印象是一种刺激,很像是欢快之感,因为这显然是可以表现男子气的事情(值得注意的是,海明威在这里用了毛巾这个具体名词,而不是嘴塞子这个一般性名词。用毛巾一词在感觉上造成的效果肯定要比嘴塞子一词来得强烈——因为毛巾使人想到口腔黏膜与粗糙的棉织品接触而产生的一种干燥难受的感觉。不过,这种制造感觉效果的有利之处很可能会因另一种情况而被蒙上暗影。因为在惊险小说里,毛巾作为嘴塞子被到处使用,这里也就显得有恐怖小说的陈腐气了)。"以前从来没有被人用一条毛巾绑在嘴上过"——这个明显而真实的细节作为小说结局的一种预示,又为整个事件的完成做好了铺垫。

另一个预示是歹徒对电影的打趣:"你应该多去看看电影。像你这样一个机灵的小伙子,看看电影是非常好的。"毫无疑问,一再重复地提到电影,而且是歹徒们在饭馆里安排停当之后提到,从某种意义上讲是一种间接的说明:读者是知道合伙谋杀他人的一般原因和一般过程的。而从另一个意义上讲,这些话着重指出了这样的发现,即报纸和电影里胡诌乱扯的那些离奇事现在已成现实。

乔治是听懂了关于看电影的暗示的,因为他接着就问:"你们干吗要把奥勒·安德生杀死呢?他有过什么对不起你们的地方没有?"

the skill with which the theme has been assimilated must be taken into account. For instance, to put a concrete question: does the last paragraph of the story illuminate for the reader certain details that had, at their first appearance, seemed to be merely casual, realistic items?

If we take the theme to be the boy's discovery of evil, several such details do find their meaning. Nick had been bound and gagged by the gangsters, and has been released by George. To quote: "Nick stood up. He had never had a towel in his mouth before. 'Say,' he said. 'What the hell?' He was trying to swagger it off." Being gagged was something you read about in a thriller and not something that happened to you; and the first effect is one of excitement, almost pleasurable, certainly an excuse for a manly pose. (It may be worth noting in this connection that Hemingway uses the specific word *towel* and not the general word *gag*. It is true that the word *towel* has a certain sensory advantage over the word *gag*—because it suggests the coarseness of the fabric and the unpleasant drying effect on the membranes of the mouth. But this advantage in immediacy is probably overshadowed by another: the towel is sanctified in the thriller as the gag, and here the cliché of the thriller has come true.) The way the whole incident is given—"He had *never* had a towel in his mouth *before*"—charges the apparently realistic detail as a pointer to the final discovery.

Another pointer appears in the gangster's wisecrack about the movies: "You ought to go to the movies more. The movies are fine for a bright boy like you." In one sense, of course, the iterated remarks about the movies, coming just after the gangsters have made their arrangements in the lunchroom, serve as a kind of indirect exposition: the reader knows the standard reason and procedure for gang killings. But at another level, these remarks emphasize the discovery that the unreal clichés of the newspaper and movie have become a reality.

The boy to whom the gangster speaks understands the allusion to the movies, for he immediately asks: "What are you going to kill

"他从来也没有机会对咱们怎样过。他一次也没见过我们。"那个歹徒回答。

那个歹徒甚至还有点扬扬得意地认可自己的生活地位——那种与小镇环境完全不相称的生活地位。他好像是根据某种信条来生活的,这种信条使他把个人的爱憎问题抛到九霄云外。这种虚假的信条——说它虚假是因为它与普通人的生活原则正好相反——就像插科打诨一样,在小说中猝然而现,这种虚假的而又富有戏剧性的东西表现在对歹徒们的外貌描写上,那时他们离开饭馆走到外面的弧光灯下并穿过大街:"他们的窄小的大衣和常礼帽使他们看上去像一对玩杂耍的人似的。"这种信条也反映在他们的谈话里。他们的谈话本身就有一种老一套的插科打诨和哗众取宠的低级趣味,某种一成不变的逗闹打趣,这种逗闹打趣一直是事件的一种前奏,而且淹没了事件本身。在这个意义上讲,把他们比作玩杂耍的是对各种细节的一种明确概括,而那些细节本身则表现得颇为含蓄,也颇有戏剧性。从另一个意义上讲,歹徒们心智疲乏而又强作精神,其中含有令人作呕的意味。这也就表明他们是专门受人差遣干这种行当的,这行当却使小伙子们震惊不已。这些人盛气凌人而使人厌恶,他们在那些涉世不深的小伙子面前,一下子就暴露出他们的厚颜无耻和百无聊赖。这种信条突然从惊险电影的虚诞世界里走出来,成了活生生的现实,这已经够吓人的了,然而使尼克更为震惊的是奥勒·安德生,这个被追猎的人,居然也容忍这种信条。在尼克当面向他报告了那个消息之后,他竟然拒绝了连那个小孩子也能想得出来的所有建议,他既不愿去报告警察,也不把这件事看做仅仅是一种恐吓,又不愿离开那个城镇。"你不能想点办法把这件事情了结了吗?"小伙子问他。"不成。我得罪了人啦。"

我们已经知道,这儿就是某一类读者所认为的小说高潮,根据这种读者的意见,小说应

Ole Andreson for? What did he ever do to you?" "He never had a chance to do anything to us. He never even seen us," the gangster replies.

The gangster accepts, and even glories a little in, the terms by which he lives—terms that transcend the small-town world. He lives, as it were, by a code, which lifts him above questions of personal likes or personal animosities. This unreal code—unreal because it denies the ordinary personal elements of life—has, like the gag, suddenly been discovered as real. This unreal and theatrical quality is reflected in the description of the gangsters as, after leaving the lunchroom, they go out under the arc light and cross the street: "In their tight overcoats and derby hats they looked like a vaudeville team." It even permeates their dialogue. The dialogue itself has the sleazy quality of mechanized gag and wisecrack, a kind of stereotyped banter that is always *a priori* to the situation and overrides the situation. On this level the comparison to the vaudeville team is a kind of explicit summary of details that have been presented more indirectly and dramatically. On another level, the weary and artificial quality of their wit has a grimmer implication. It is an index to the professional casualness with which they accept a situation that to the boys is shocking. They are contemptuous and even bored, with the contempt and boredom of the initiated when confronted by callow lay observers. This code, which has suddenly been transferred from the artificial world of the movie thriller into reality, is shocking enough, but even more shocking to Nick is the fact that Ole Andreson, the hunted man, accepts the code too. Confronted by the news that Nick brings, he rejects all the responses the boy would consider normal: he will not call the police; he will not regard the thing as a mere bluff; he will not leave town. "Couldn't you fix it up some way?" the boy asks. "No. I got in wrong."

As we observed earlier, for one type of reader this is the high point of the story, and the story should end here. If we are to convince such a reader that the author is right in

该到此结束。要说服这种读者,使他相信作者往下写并非是画蛇添足,我们就必须回答他们的问题:"接着往下写尼克和贝尔太太的谈话,写这种既单调乏味又显然离题万里的区区小事又有何意义?"有人或许会说,提到贝尔太太是为了稍稍推迟小说的结局,或者是为了赢得读者的同情从而使小说明朗化,因为在贝尔太太看来,安德生"这个人真是好极了",一点儿不像她心目中的拳击师。然而,这种说法并不足以使敏感的读者感到满意,而敏感的读者对此表示不满也是对的。说实在的,贝尔太太就像《麦克佩斯》中地狱门前的波特。她代表普通人世界,现在这个普通人的世界在其通常所行的轨道上由于生活的涌流泛滥而正在摇摇晃晃。在她看来,奥勒·安德生是个好人,虽则说他是个生活在拳击场上的人。在这样的好天气,他应该到外面去散散步。她指的是他日常的个人生活,这种生活与那种无人性的信条所要求的东西适成对照。即使恐怖电影中虚假而骇人的场面已成现实,即使那个被追猎的人躺在床上辗转不安,拿不定主意是走呢还是不走,贝尔太太还是贝尔太太。她不是赫思奇太太。赫思奇太太拥有房子,她呢,不过为赫思奇太太管管房子而已。她是贝尔太太,普通人世界的一员。

在公寓门口,尼克遇见了贝尔太太——普通人世界,她对这种富有讽刺意味的对照出现在她眼前毫无所知。回到饭馆,尼克恢复正常状态,但是这种正常的状态正在承受着恐惧的冲击。饭馆依然如故,乔治和厨子照例忙忙碌碌。不过他们是不同于贝尔太太的,他们知道发生过什么事。然而,即便如此,他们也几乎没有改变他们的生活常规。乔治和厨子代表着两种对事件的不同态度。厨子从一开始就不想卷进这件事。他一听见尼克回来时的讲话声,就说:"我连听也不要听。"说着就把厨房的门关上了。乔治虽然先前曾建议尼克去看一下安德生,把情况告诉他,然而还是说:

proceeding, we are obliged to answer his question "What is the significance of the rather tame, and apparently irrelevant, little incident that follows, the conversation with Mrs. Bell?" It is sometimes said that Mrs. Bell serves to give a bit of delayed exposition or even to point the story by gaining sympathy for Andreson, who is, to her, "an awfully nice man," not at all like her idea of a pugilist. But this is not enough to satisfy the keen reader, and he is right in refusing to be satisfied with this. Mrs. Bell is, really, the Porter at Hell Gate in *Macbeth*. She is the world of normality, which is shocking now from the very fact that life continues to flow on in its usual course. To her, Ole Andreson is just a nice man, despite the fact that he has been in the ring; he ought to go out and take his walk on such a nice day. She points to his ordinary individuality, which is in contrast to the demands of the mechanical code. Even if the unreal horror of the movie thriller has become real, even if the hunted man lies upstairs on his bed trying to make up his mind to go out, Mrs. Bell is still Mrs. Bell. She is not Mrs. Hirsch. Mrs. Hirsch owns the place, she just looks after it for Mrs. Hirsch. She is Mrs. Bell: normal life.

At the door of the rooming house Nick has met Mrs. Bell—normality unconscious of the ironical contrast it presents. Back at the lunchroom, Nick returns to the normal scene, but the normal scene conscious of the impingement of horror. It is the same old lunchroom, with George and the cook going about their business. But they, unlike Mrs. Bell, know what has happened. Yet even they are scarcely deflected from their ordinary routine. George and the cook represent two different levels of response to the situation. The cook, from the first, has wanted no part of it. When he hears Nick's voice, on his return, he says, "I don't even listen to it." And he shuts the door. But George had originally suggested

"你要是不愿去就别去吧。"而当尼克回来把经过告诉他后,乔治虽则说:"事情真糟糕。"但至少在某种意义上,可以说乔治也认可了那种信条。当尼克说:"我不晓得到底他干下了什么事情?"乔治也应和着杀手那种自己也吃不准的腔调,回答说:"欺骗了什么人啦。他们就是为了这个缘故要把他杀害的。"换言之,厨子是因为事件有涉于他自身的安全而在战战兢兢。乔治则意识到此事别有牵连,只能回避。他们两人都没有从那事件中看到罪恶。只有尼克看到了,因为他还不懂得应该接受乔治的那种世故的劝告:"得啦,你最好不如别去想着这件事儿吧。"

除了从结构上考察事件和人物态度方面的各种关系之外,还可以提出另外一些有趣的问题。海明威对他的题材采取何种态度?这种态度又是如何得到表现的?

接触这些问题的最简单的方法也许是先对海明威所写到的事件和人物的类型加以考虑。海明威小说里的事件总是含有强烈的成分:在《太阳照样升起》里写的是酗酒狂欢和性关系的混乱;在《永别了武器》《丧钟为谁而鸣》以及《不能走那条路》里写的是战争中的混乱和残忍;在《太阳照样升起》《午后之死》和《打不败的人》以及《五万美元》里,写的是斗牛场上或拳击场上那种危险而惊心动魄的场面;至于在《杀手》《有的和没有的》和《赌徒、修女和收音机》里,则是写种种罪行。海明威式的人物通常是些硬汉子,他们经受着周围世界的严峻考验而又显得无动于衷,如《永别了武器》中的亨利中尉,《乞力马扎罗的雪》里的猎豹人,《丧钟为谁而鸣》里的罗伯特·乔丹,就是奥勒·安德生也是如此。他们又每每是失败者。然而,他们又能从实际的失败中设法得到某种补救。在这一点上,我们捉摸到了海明威对他所写的事件和人物的基本兴趣所在。他的人物是打不败的,除非他们自己承认,他们中的有些人甚至还赞美失败,即使在实际上失

that Nick go see Andreson, telling him, however, "Don't go if you don't want to. " After Nick has told his story, George can comment, "It's a hell of a thing, " but George, in one sense at least, has accepted the code, too. When Nick says, "I wonder what he did?" George replies, with an echo of the killers' own casualness: "Double-crossed somebody. That's what they kill them for. " In other words, the situation is shocking to the cook only insofar as it involves his own safety. George is aware of other implications but can dismiss them. Neither of them makes a discovery of evil in the situation. But Nick does, for he has not yet learned to take George's adult advice: "Well, you better not think about it. "

Aside from such structural concerns as the relations among incidents and the attitudes of the characters, other interesting questions can be raised. What is Hemingway's attitude toward his material? How does this attitude find its expression?

Perhaps the simplest approach to these questions may be through a consideration of the kinds of situations and characters that Hemingway wrote about. The situations are usually violent ones: the hard-drinking and sexually promiscuous world of the The Sun Also Rises; the chaotic and brutal world of war in A Farewell to Arms, For Whom the Bell Tolls, and "A Way You'll Never Be"; the dangerous and exciting world of the bull ring or the prize ring in The Sun Also Rises, Death in the Afternoon, "The Undefeated," and "Fifty Grand"; the world of crime in "The Killers," To Have and to Have Not, and "The Gambler, the Nun, and the Radio. " Hemingway's typical characters are usually tough men, experienced in the hard worlds they inhabit, and apparently insensitive: Lieutenant Henry in A Farewell to Arms, the big-game hunter in "The Snows of Kilimanjaro," Robert Jordan in For Whom the Bell Tolls, or even Ole Andreson. They are, also, usually defeated men. Out of their practical defeat, however, they have managed to salvage something. And here we come upon Hemingway's basic interest in such situations and such characters. They are not defeated except upon their

败了,他们仍旧坚持着他们的理想,他们就是靠了这种有时清晰可辨,有时又模糊不清的理想,才得以生存下来。

从某种意义上讲,海明威对生活的态度和罗伯特·路易斯·斯蒂文森很相像,斯蒂文森在一篇题为《尘土与阴影》的文章中曾这样写道:

> 可怜的人,他来到人间如此缺少欢乐,如此备尝艰难困苦,抱的愿望如此不协调,如此前后矛盾,受到野蛮的包围和野蛮的袭击,无可救药地注定要伤害同类的生命。要是他像命中注定的那样仅仅是一个野蛮人,谁还会来责备他呢?可是我们又看到他有着不完美的道德:……一种维持体面的理想(只要有可能,他是不会抛弃这种理想的;有起码的羞耻之心,只要有可能,他本来是不会干太丢人的事情的)……人做好事的确是注定要失败的。但是在最优秀的人老是失败的情况下,大家还继续奋斗,这真是太了不起了。在一个不能成功的领域里,我们人类却不停地奋斗,我们觉得这既是动人心弦的,又是令人振奋的。……不管我们在哪里看,在什么环境中观察他,在社会发展的什么阶段,愚昧到什么程度,抱有什么样的错误观念,这些都无关紧要。在阿西尼波恩的篝火旁,大雪覆盖了他的肩膀,寒风掀掉了他的毯子,他坐在那里,按照礼节递烟袋,像位罗马元老院议员那样说出自己的严肃的主张。在大海中的航船上,一个人习惯于艰难困苦和邪恶的乐趣。他最美好的希望是在小酒馆里有把提琴,有个涂脂抹粉的妓女。她卖身与他为的是抢夺他的钱财。尽管如此,他还是显得单纯、天真、善良得像个孩子,他常年劳累,为了别人,甘冒灭顶的危险。……在窑子里,这个被社会抛弃的人,主要靠喝

own terms; some of them have even courted defeat; certainly, they have maintained, even in the practical defeat, an ideal of themselves, formulated or unformulated, by which they have lived.

Hemingway's attitude is, in a sense, like that of Robert Louis Stevenson, as Stevenson states it in one of his essays, "Pulvis et Umbra":

> Poor soul, here for so little, cast among so many hardships, filled with desires so incommensurate and so inconsistent, savagely surrounded, savagely descended, irremediably condemned to prey upon his fellow lives: who should have blamed him had he been of a piece with his destiny and a being merely barbarous? And we look and behold him instead filled with imperfect virtues:... an ideal of decency, to which he would rise if it were possible; a limit of shame, below which, if it be possible, he will not stoop.... Man is indeed marked for failure in his efforts to do right. But where the best consistently miscarry, how tenfold more remarkable that all should continue to strive; and surely we should find it both touching and inspiriting, that in a field from which success is banished, our race should not cease to labor.... It matters not where we look, under what climate we observe him, in what stage of society, in what depth of ignorance, burthened with what erroneous morality; by campfires in Assiniboia, the snow powdering his shoulders, the wind plucking his blanket, as he sits, passing the ceremonial calumet and uttering his grave opinions like a Roman senator; in ships at sea, a man inured to hardship and vile pleasures, his brightest hope a fiddle in a tavern and a bedizened trull who sells herself to rob him, and he for all that, simple, innocent, cheerful, kindly like a child, constant to toil, brave to drown, for others;... in the brothel,

烈酒生活,受尽侮辱。他是个笨蛋,是个小偷,是小偷的同伙。尽管如此,他还是讲信义,有恻隐之心,常常以效劳来回报人间对他的轻蔑,常常坚定地面对困难,并且付出应付的代价。他轻视财富,处处有某种受到珍视或喜爱的道德,处处有正确的思想和行为,处处会领悟到人类的善行是徒劳无益的!

　　在每次失败的情况下,他失去希望,失去健康,也无人对他表示感谢,他仍然在不引人注目地打一场德行的败仗。在窖子里或在绞刑架上,他仍然依恋着某种荣誉的标签——他们灵魂中的可怜的珍宝!他们可能想逃走,但是他们做不到,这不单单是他们的荣幸或光彩,而是他们命里注定的结局,人们给他们定的罪名就是某种崇高的荣誉。

　　在斯蒂文森看来,演出这幕戏剧的世界客观地来说是一个充满暴力的、无意义的世界。"我们的旋转的岛屿装载着掠夺成性的生命而且浸透了鲜血……比从前反叛的海船上的血更多,穿过广漠的太空向前飞驰。"这也就是海明威的世界。但海明威世界里的人物,至少是海明威小说里的主要人物,他们都竭尽全力地想修补这个支离破碎的、无意义的世界:他们想赋予自己漫无秩序的生活以某种方式,那种斗牛士或运动员的技艺、那种士兵的准则、那种歹徒的信条,所有这些,虽说是粗野的,违背人性的,但它们有其自身的道德标准(奥勒·安德生自愿吞下苦丸而不哼一声。又如《赌徒、修女和收音机》里的迈克西肯至死不肯告密,尽管侦探劝告他"揭发伤害自己的人并不丢脸")。他们的生活方式虽然永不会和世界协调合拍,但是对这种生活方式的忠诚都会使他们虽败犹荣。

　　我们说过,典型的海明威式的主人公是硬汉子,而在表面上,又显得感觉迟钝。但仅仅

the discard of society, living mainly on strong drink, fed with affronts, a fool, a thief, the comrade of thieves, and even here keeping the point of honor and the touch of pity, often repaying the world's scorn with service, often standing firm upon a scruple, and at a certain cost, rejecting riches;—everywhere some virtue cherished or affected, everywhere some decency of thought and carriage, everywhere the ensign of man's ineffectual goodness!

　　Under every circumstance of failure, without hope, without health, without thanks, still obscurely fighting the lost fight of virtue, still clinging, in the brothel or on the scaffold, to some rag of honor, the poor jewel of their souls! They may seek to escape, and yet they cannot; it is not alone their privilege and glory, but their doom, they are condemned to some nobility...

For Stevenson, the world in which this drama is played out is, objectively considered, a violent and meaningless world: "our rotary island loaded with predatory life and more drenched with blood... than ever mutinied ship, scuds through space." This is Hemingway's world, too. But its characters, at least those whose stories Hemingway cares to tell, make one gallant effort to redeem the incoherence and meaninglessness of this world: they attempt to impose some form upon the disorder of their lives, the technique of the bullfighter or sportsman, the discipline of the soldier, the code of the gangster, which, even though brutal and dehumanizing, has its own ethic. (Ole Andreson is willing to take his medicine without whining. Or the dying Mexican in "The Gambler, the Nun, and the Radio" refuses to squeal, despite the detective's argument: "One can, with honor, denounce one's assailant.") The form is never quite adequate to subdue the world, but the fidelity to it is part of the gallantry of defeat.

We have said that the typical Hemingway hero is tough and, apparently, insensitive. But

是表面的,因为对于某种信念和某种准则的忠诚可能表明他们是敏感的,海明威的人物就凭着这种敏感时时地正视着自己所处的困境,也就是这种硬汉子——在海明威看来,他们是守信用的人——经常地,而且经常是在厄运临头之际,真正地懂得同情或者悲怜。孤独而倔强(这作为个人的信念,也许是世界所要求的)可能会和某种更合乎自然也更深地基于人类本性的感情发生冲突,这种个人信念与这种感情相比,甚至会显得是违背人性的。然而,海明威的主人公虽然也意识到这种发自人类本性的感情要求,他们都害怕屈从于这些要求,他们懂得,面对着一个残忍而任性的世界,要保持"尊严",保持人格,保持人的气度,唯一的方法就是凭自己的信念生活。海明威的主人公就是在这种具有讽刺意味的情势下发现了自己的。他们觉得自己是新入世的高贵者,并且遵守着一种孤傲的美德。海明威的主人公也做自我表白,但并不是夸夸其谈,慷慨陈词,而是自我讽嘲,语言节度有制。从粗鲁和感伤的对比中,以及从强烈和感伤的对比中,流露出克制的态度,这是海明威在方法上的一贯表现,这种情况在好几年前就被登在《纽约客》上的一幅漫画生动地勾勒出来。漫画家画了一只毛茸茸的、粗壮的手臂,强有力的大手中抓着一朵小小的玫瑰花。这幅漫画题名是《厄内斯特·海明威的灵魂》。就如海明威的人物在失败之中还有一点儿额外的胜利一样,海明威人物的那个残酷而暴烈的世界里,也存在着一点点儿额外的温情。

我们说,奥勒·安德生正合这种模式。安德生并不唉声叹气。但是奥勒·安德生的故事又被套在一个范围更大的故事里,这个故事的焦点集中在尼克身上。尼克·亚当斯是否合乎这个模式呢?事实表明,海明威向来就习惯用两种不同程度的方法来分别处理作品的基本情节的。在一个故事里,写某个人,这个人一旦被引进了那个世界,一旦形成了自己欣

only apparently, for the fidelity to a code, to a discipline, may be an index to a sensitivity that allows his characters to see, at moments, their true plight. At times, and usually at times of stress, it is the tough man—for Hemingway, the disciplined man—who actually is aware of pathos or tragedy. The individual toughness (which may be taken to be the private discipline demanded by the world), may find itself in conflict with some more natural and spontaneous human emotion; in contrast with this, the discipline may, even, seem to be inhuman; but the Hemingway hero, though he is aware of the claims of this spontaneous human emotion, is afraid to yield to those claims because he has learned that the only way to hold on to "honor," to individuality, to the human order as against the brute chaos of the world, is to live by his code. This is the irony of the situation in which the hero finds himself. Hemingway's heroes are aristocrats in the sense that they are the initiate, and practice a lonely virtue. Hemingway's heroes utter themselves, not in rant and bombast, but in terms of ironic understatement. This understatement, stemming from the contrast between the toughness and the sensitivity, the violence and the sensitivity, is a constant aspect of Hemingway's method, an aspect that was happily caught in a cartoon in the *New Yorker* some years ago. The cartoonist showed a brawny, hairy forearm and a muscled hand clutching a little rose. The cartoon was entitled "The Soul of Ernest Hemingway". Just as there is a margin of victory in the defeat of the Hemingway characters, so there is a little margin of sensibility in their brutal and violent world.

Ole Andreson, as we have noted, fits into this pattern. Andreson won't whimper. But Ole Andreson's story is buried in the larger story, which is focused on Nick. How does Nick Adams fit into the pattern? Hemingway, as a matter of fact, is accustomed to treat his basic situation at one or the other of two levels. There is the story of the person who is already initiated, who has already adopted his appropriate code, or discipline, in

赏的信念或者准则,那么这个人就无法应付其他诸方面的事物(人们可以从《太阳照样升起》里的杰克和布列特身上和《丧钟为谁而鸣》里的乔丹和比拉身上,《打不败的人》和其他许多小说里的斗牛士身上也能看到这类例子)。另一类小说是写主人公刚刚踏进社会,发现社会的罪恶和混乱,并初步具有那种信念时的情形。这就是尼克的故事(类似的基本内容在海明威其他许多小说中也同样出现,如在《在密执安北部》《印第安人的营地》和《三天大风》里)。

除了行为倔强和外表迟钝之外,一般说来,典型的海明威式的人物还很单纯。海明威之所以要写这种单纯人物,其动机和浪漫派诗人华兹渥斯也同样写这种人物的动机是一样的。华兹渥斯觉得农夫或者儿童的感情比那些有教养的人更诚实,因而也更富有诗意,所以他许多诗篇中人物就是农夫和儿童。在海明威的作品中,替代华兹渥斯笔下的农夫的是那些斗牛士、士兵、革命者、运动员或者歹徒,而替代华兹渥斯笔下的儿童的则是像尼克这样的少年人。当然,华兹渥斯和海明威在程度上是存在着差别的,但是就过于敏感这一点而言,他们几乎没有什么区别。

产生两位作家之间的主要差别的原因在于他们属于两个不同的世界。海明威生活的时代,较之华兹渥斯生活的那个淳朴、天真的时代远为混乱,也远为残酷。因此,海明威的人物对世界本质的感受也就比华兹渥斯的人物来得更为强烈,更为隔膜。这种情况导致一种讽嘲态度,而这种态度在华兹渥斯的作品中是找不到的。海明威压制了这种敏感,把它隐藏在自己粗犷的风格中。格特鲁德·斯坦因在写到海明威时曾说:"海明威是我熟悉的作家中最含蓄、最富于自尊心、最温馨的作者。"她所说的"含蓄",显然是指他所用的讽刺和克制写法而言的。海明威式的人物很敏感,但是他们的敏感性又往往是不彻底的,他们很值得

the world that otherwise he cannot cope with. (One finds examples in Jake and Brett in *The Sun Also Rises*, Jordan and Pilar in *For Whom the Bell Tolls*, the bullfighter in "The Undefeated" and many other stories.) There is also the story of the process of the initiation, the discovery of evil and disorder, and the first step toward the mastery of the discipline. This is Nick's story. (The same basic situation occurs in many other stories by Hemingway, for example, "Up in Michigan", "Indian Camp" and "The Three-Day Blow".)

Besides being tough and apparently insensitive, the typical Hemingway character is also, usually, simple. The impulse that led Hemingway to the simple character is akin to that that led the Romantic poet Wordsworth to the same choice. Wordsworth felt that peasants or children, who are the characters of so many of his poems, were more honest in their responses than the cultivated man, and therefore more poetic. Instead of Wordsworth's typical peasant we find in Hemingway's work the bullfighter, the soldier, the revolutionist, the sportsman, and the gangster; instead of Wordsworth's children, we find young men like Nick. There are, of course, differences between the approach of Wordsworth and that of Hemingway, but there is little difference on the point of marginal sensibility.

The main difference between the two writers depends on the difference in their two worlds. Hemingway's world is a more disordered world, and more violent, than the simple and innocent world of Wordsworth. Therefore, the sensibility of Hemingway's characters is in sharper contrast to the nature of his world. This creates an irony not found in the work of Wordsworth. Hemingway plays down the sensibility as such, and sheathes it in the code of toughness. Gertrude Stein once wrote of Hemingway: "Hemingway is the shyest and proudest and sweetest-smelling storyteller of my reading. "When she refers to his "shyness" she was, apparently, thinking of his use of irony and understatement. The typical character is sensitive, but

人们同情，但是他们却往往不需要人们的同情。海明威作品中的基本态度可以这样归纳：只有经受过生活折磨的人从心底里发出来的同情才是真诚的，只有从来不需要人们同情的人，才能得到真正的同情。所以，他对不安宁的生活本身也给予珍视。

这又会产生一个问题。海明威的文体风格和他的小说中的原始意图又有何种联系呢？就《杀手》而言，这篇小说和他的其他许多作品一样，其文体风格简洁到了几乎是惜墨如金的程度。句子的特点是简单句，有时也用复合句，但即使是复合句，在短语复合中也毫无含糊之处。段落结构也很有特色，基本上是单线排列①。我们首先可以看到，这种风格和人物以及情节之间有着明显的联系，作者着意使质朴无华的人物和简单的基本情节通过一种明快的文体得到表现。

更有趣的是，关于风格问题还可以从另一方面来看，这儿不涉及人物的敏感性，而仅仅涉及作者本人的敏感性。短促的节奏，短句的并列以及很少使用从属句——这些都使人联想到一个支离破碎的世界。海明威显然是想在自己的文体中表现直接经验——各种事物就像它们当初被看到和被感觉到时一样，逐个地出现，而并不对它们刻意进行整理和分类。那种曲折多变、语意晦涩的文体，那种堆砌词句、诘屈聱牙、人为造作的文体，是通过理智处理经验的产物。海明威则显然着重于表达经验的直接印象，而不过细地对经验进行分析或评价（这里，我们可以注意到海明威在作品中

———————
① 在海明威的有些作品里，特别是长篇小说里，有好多地方比《杀手》写得更流畅，更有节奏感。但是，即使在这些地方，我们也可以看到，流畅、有节奏感这种效果主要是通过使用连接词"和"产生出来的，两个短句用"和"相连接，其中没有从属含义，而仅仅是一连串意义明确的字眼的平行排列。这种节奏感可以被视为过于敏感的一种表现，而敏感又可通过分析由这些富于节奏感的段落组成的情节来加以说明。——原注。

his sensitivity is never insisted upon; he may be worthy of pity, but he never demands it. The underlying attitude in Hemingway's work may be stated like this: pity is valid only when it is wrung from a man who has been seasoned by experience, and is only earned by a man who never demands it. Therefore, a premium is placed upon the fact of violent experience.

A further question suggests itself. How is Hemingway's style related to his basic fictional concerns? In "The Killers", as in many of his other stories, the style is simple even to the point of monotony. The characteristic sentence is simple, or compound; and if compound, there is no implied subtlety in the coordination of the clauses. The paragraph structure is, characteristically, based on simple sequence①. First, we can observe that there is an obvious relation between this style and the characters and situations with which the author is concerned: unsophisticated characters and simple, fundamental situations are rendered in an uncomplicated style.

There is another, and more interesting, aspect of the question of style, involving not the sensibility of the characters but the sensibility of the author himself. The short simple rhythms, the succession of coordinate clauses, and the general lack of subordination—all suggest a dislocated and ununified world. Hemingway was apparently trying to suggest in his style the direct experience—things as seen and felt, one after another, and not as the mind arranges and analyzes them. A style that involves subordination and complicated shadings of emphasis, a style that tends toward complex sentences with many qualifying clauses and phrases, implies an exercise of critical discrimination—the sifting of experience through the intellect. But Hemingway,

———————
① In some of Hemingway's work, especially in the novels, there are examples of a more fluent, lyrical style than us found in "The Killers." But even in such examples, one can observe that the fluency and the lyrical effect is based on the conjunction *and*—that there is no process of subordination but rather a process of sequence in terms of direct perceptions. The lyrical quality of such examples is to be taken as a manifestation of the "marginal sensibility," as can be demonstrated by an analysis of the situations in which the lyrical passages occur.

很少对人物做心理分析，也很少注意性格发展的具体过程）。他使用自己的这种文体似乎在于表明，通过理智虽然可做仔细的辨别，但会使经验的表达显得模糊不清，甚至会使经验变得虚假。就海明威对那种过于敏感的人物抱着由衷的关切这层意思而言，他的文体风格也许可以被看作在解决人类基本问题方面对理智抱不信任态度的表现。他似乎想表明，即使在解决世界性问题时发挥了人的理智，世界也还是一个漫无秩序而又凶狠残暴的庞然大物。要想找到任何明确的价值标准都几乎是不可能的。所以，最好还是记住生活中的基本事实——那些与性、爱、危难和死亡有关的事实，其中至关重要的是生的本能——并设法解决这些问题，因为这些问题一直被社会习惯势力或者空洞的理性所掩盖甚至歪曲。最好还是记住勇敢、诚实、忠贞、守信这些人类的基本德性。

但是，这样是否就等于说，海明威实际上是抱着天真、淡薄和粗俗的态度在从事写作呢？并非如此，事实上，他的风格是经过周密思考后的结果，严格地说，全然不是心血来潮或者感情用事的。他的风格是某种戏剧手法的表现，这种手法由于注意赋予作品恰如其分的整体效果而得到了发展。一个实际上没有创造力的、心血来潮的作家是绝不可能像海明威在其杰作中那样创造出充满活力而又栩栩如生的形象来的，而且就在这样的作品中，海明威的基本态度和客观事物得到了有机的统一。

在对这篇小说进行评述时，我们故意偏重于谈论小说风格和小说主题的关系，偏重于把这篇小说里的各种特点跟海明威作品的概貌以及海明威对世界的态度联系起来。在一般情况下，我们总是从某一个方面来考察小说的，但是在考察这篇小说时，我们认识到同一个优秀作家创作的各种各样的小说（虽然常常是各不相同的），其中始终贯穿着某种基本一

apparently, was primarily concerned with giving the immediate impact of experience rather than with analyzing and evaluating it in detail. (We can notice, in this connection, that in his work he rarely indulges in any psychological analysis, and is rarely concerned with the detailed development of a character.) His very style, then, seems to imply that the use of the intellect, with its careful discriminations, may blur the rendering of experience and may falsify it; and this style, in connection with his basic concern for the character of marginal sensibility, may be taken as implying a distrust of the intellect in solving man's basic problems. Despite the application of the human intellect to the problems of the world, he seems to be saying, the world is still a disorderly and brutal mess. And it is hard to find any sure scale of values. Therefore, it is well to remember the demands of fundamental situations—those involving sex, love; danger, and death, in which the instinctive life is foremost—because they are frequently glossed over or falsified by social conventions or sterile intellectuality. It is well to remember the simple virtues of courage, honesty, fidelity, discipline.

But is all of this a way of saying that Hemingway is really writing innocently, without calculation, crudely? Now, as a matter of fact, his style is a result of calculation, and is not, strictly speaking, spontaneous and naive at all. His style is, then, a dramatic device, developed because of its appropriateness to the total effect he intends to give. A writer who was in point of fact uninstructed and spontaneous would probably not be able to achieve the impression of spontaneity and immediacy found in Hemingway's best work, the work in which his basic attitude and subject matter can be functionally coordinated.

In our comment on this story we have tried, among other and more obvious concerns, to relate the style of the story to the theme and then to relate the various qualities of this story to the general body of Hemingway's work and his attitude toward his world. Ordinarily we have been studying stories taken individually, but it is time for us to realize that the various (and often quite different) stories done by a good writer always

致的态度——因为一个人毕竟只能是他自己。由此可知,只要我们把某篇小说和这篇小说作者的其他作品联系起来考察,我们就往往能够深入地考察这篇小说并对它有更充分的理解。因为优秀的作家是不会像万花筒似的向我们显示五花八门的主题的,他总是反反复复地处理非常有限的几个主题,而这几个主题是他在实际生活中以及他在对生活的观察中认为是极其重要的主题。

　　试想,如果你读了《县城的医生》或是《醉汉》,不知道作者是谁,若有人对你说那是海明威写的,你会相信吗? 要是不相信,为什么?

(刘家有 译)

have some fundamental unifying attitudes—for a man can be only himself. Since this is true,we can nearly always enter more deeply into a piece of fiction and understand it more fully when we are prepared to relate it to the writer's other work. A good writer does not offer us, for instance, a glittering variety of themes. He probably treats, over and over, those few themes that seem to him most important in his actual living and observation of life.

　　Suppose you had read"The District Doctor" or "The Drunkard" without knowing the author and had been told it was by Hemingway. Would you have believed this? If not, why not?

024. 林中之死

（美）舍伍德·安德森 著　　刘文荣 译

024. Death in the Woods

by Sherwood Anderson

一

　　她是个老妇人，住在我住的小镇附近的农庄上。乡下人和小镇居民都很熟悉这样的老妇人，然而谁都不了解她们。这样的一个老妇人，她赶着一匹病弱的老马到镇上来，要不就是挎着一只篮子徒步走来。她可能养了几只鸡，所以有些鸡蛋可以出卖。她把鸡蛋放在篮子里带到镇上交给杂货商。在那儿，她把鸡蛋廉价卖掉。她买些咸肉和蚕豆。随后她买一磅或者两磅砂糖，还有一些面粉。

　　随后，她到屠夫那儿向他要些狗肉。她也许要花10美分或者15美分，但她付钱时还要讨点东西。一般说来，如果有人要，屠夫总把牛肝随便送人。我们家就老吃这个东西。有一次，我的一个哥哥从镇火葬场附近的屠宰场里拿回来整整一只牛肝。我们吃这个东西吃腻烦了。这是不用花一分钱的。我后来一想起这东西就恼怒。

　　老农妇要了些牛肝，还有一根煮汤的骨头。她从不拜访什么人，所以拿了所要的东西便匆匆回家了。那些东西对她这样一个老弱的人来说，也可算是一种负担。没有人捎她一程。人们驾着车沿路而过，但对这样一个老妇人是谁也不会注意的。

　　那年的夏天和秋天，当时我还是个小孩子并且在生一种叫作风湿发炎症什么来着的病，那时就有这样一个老妇人，经常到镇上来。还打我们家门前走过。她要到很晚才回家，背上背着一只沉甸甸的口袋。在她身后，有两三只瘦骨嶙峋的狗跟着。

I

SHE was an old woman and lived on a farm near the town in which I lived. All country and small-town people have seen such old women, but no one knows much about them. Such an old woman comes into town driving an old worn-out horse or she comes afoot carrying a basket. She may own a few hens and have eggs to sell. She brings them in a basket and takes them to a grocer. There she trades them in. She gets some salt pork and some beans. Then she gets a pound or two of sugar and some flour.

Afterwards she goes to the butcher's and asks for some dog meat. She may spend ten or fifteen cents, but when she does she asks for something. Formerly the butchers gave liver to anyone who wanted to carry it away. In our family we were always having it. Once one of my brothers got a whole cow's liver at the slaughterhouse near the fairgrounds in our town. We had it until we were sick of it. It never cost a cent. I have hated the thought of it ever since.

The old farm woman got some liver and a soup-bone. She never visited with anyone, and as soon as she got what she wanted she lit out for home. It made quite a load for such an old body. No one gave her a lift. People drive right down a road and never notice an old woman like that.

There was such an old woman who used to come into town past our house one summer and fall when I was a young boy and was sick with what was called inflammatory rheumatism. She went home later carrying a heavy pack on her back. Two or three large gaunt-looking dogs followed at her heels.

The old woman was nothing special. She was one of the nameless ones that hardly anyone knows, but

作者简介：舍伍德·安德森（Sherwood Anderson，1876—1941），美国作家。1876 年 9 月 13 日生于俄亥俄州，1941 年 3 月 8 日卒于巴拿马科隆。他的学校教育断断续续。婚后，他离开家庭和生意去往芝加哥成为一名作家。他的首部成熟作品《俄亥俄州的温斯堡镇》（*Winesburg*，*Ohio*，1919）描写了关于小镇市民隐秘生活的一系列互不相关的故事，让他声名鹊起。他的短篇小说收录在《鸡蛋的胜利》（*The Triumph of the Egg*，1921）、《马与人》（*Horses and Men*，1923）和《林中之死》（*Death in the Woods*，1933）中。他的叙事风格立足于日常对话基础上，受到格特鲁德·斯坦作品的影响。而他的风格后来又影响了厄内斯特·海明威和威廉·福克纳等其他作家。

那老妇人没有什么令人注意的地方。她属于那种简直无人知晓的无名的人，然而，正是她，闯进了我的思想。纵然到了现在，虽然那么多年过去了，我还是会突然想到她，想到那些事情。说来成了一个故事。她姓格赖姆斯，和丈夫、儿子一起住在镇外 4 英里处的一条小河边上一所没有粉刷过的小屋里。

丈夫和儿子都很粗暴。儿子虽然只有 21 岁，却已经坐过一次牢。人们暗地里传说，说这女人的丈夫偷马，把马弄到别的县去卖掉。时常，有人家的马不见了，那男人也就找不到了。谁也没有抓住过他。有一次，我在汤姆·瓦德海的马棚里玩耍，那个男人来了，坐在一张长凳上，那儿还有两三个人坐着，不过没有一个人理他。他坐了一会儿，站起身来走了。在他离开时，还转身对那几个人瞪了一会儿。他眼睛里有一种像是挑衅的目光。"好吧，我是想客客气气的。你们不想睬我。我到这镇上来，到处都这个样子。等着瞧，要是你们的一匹好马不见了，哼，那时看你们怎么样！"实际上他什么也没说。"我真想给你们来个耳刮子。"这是他眼光里透出的意思。我记得，他的目光真叫我害怕得发抖。

这个年长的男人祖上曾经一度很有钱。他叫杰克·格赖姆斯。现在事情都已经弄清楚了。他父亲约翰·格赖姆斯在当地刚开发时曾拥有一个锯木工场，赚过钱。后来，他就酗酒、追女人。他死的时候，没留下多少钱。

杰克把留下的一点儿钱用光。没多久，这儿没有什么木料要锯了，他的地产也几乎全卖光了。

6 月里收麦子时，他给一个德国农场主打工，从德国人那儿他弄了个老婆。那时她还是个黄花闺女，吓得要死。我想，她是个养女，那农场主一定对她干过什么事，农场主的妻子在疑神疑鬼。她趁自己男人不在时从姑娘嘴里得知了事情。但是，农场主趁自己妻子不得不到镇上去看病时，又狠狠地教训她。她告诉年轻的杰克说，其实压根儿没有那回事，但是他却不知道相信好呢，还是不相信好。

他第一次和她一起出去，就叫她感到轻松愉快。要不是那个德国农场主要他滚蛋的话，他是不会娶她的。那时他在场地上打谷，一天晚上，他让她和自己一块儿坐在马车上赶车，这样，到第二个星期天晚上他又去叫她。

她想法走出了屋子，没有让主人看见，但正当她

she got into my thoughts. I have just suddenly now, after all these years, remembered her and what happened. It is a story. Her name was Grimes, and she lived with her husband and son in a small unpainted house on the bank of a small creek four miles from town.

The husband and son were a tough lot. Although the son was but twenty-one, he had already served a term in jail. It was whispered about that the woman's husband stole horses and ran them off to some other county. Now and then, when a horse turned up missing, the man had also disappeared. No one ever caught him. Once, when I was loafing at Tom Whitehead's livery barn, the man came there and sat on the bench in front. Two or three other men were there, but no one spoke to him. He sat for a few minutes and then got up and went away. When he was leaving he turned around and stared at the men. There was a look of defiance in his eyes. "Well, I have tried to be friendly. You don't want to talk to me. It has been so wherever I have gone in this town. If, some day, one of your fine horses turns up missing, well, then what?" He did not say anything actually. "I'd like to bust one of you on the jaw," was about what his eyes said. I remember how the look in his eyes made me shiver.

The old man belonged to a family that had had money once. His name was Jake Grimes. It all comes back clearly now. His father, John Grimes, had owned a sawmill when the country was new, and had made money. Then he got to drinking and running after women. When he died there wasn't much left.

Jake blew in the rest. Pretty soon there wasn't any more lumber to cut and his land was nearly all gone.

He got his wife off a German farmer, for whom he went to work one June day in the wheat harvest. She was a young thing then and scared to death. You see, the farmer was up to something with the girl—she was, I think a bound girl and his wife had her suspicions. She took it out on the girl when the man wasn't around. Then, when the wife had to go off to town for supplies, the farmer got after her. She told young Jake that nothing really ever happened, but he didn't know whether to believe it or not.

He got her pretty easy himself, the first time he was out with her. He wouldn't have married her if the German farmer hadn't tried to tell him where to get off. He got her to go riding with him in his buggy one night when he was threshing on the place, and then he came for her the next Sunday night.

She managed to get out of the house without her employer's seeing, but when she was getting into the buggy he showed up. It was almost dark, and he just popped up suddenly at the horse's head. He grabbed

爬上马车时,主人发觉了。天已经很暗,主人一下子冲到马头跟前。他一把抓住马嚼子,这时杰克抽出了赶车的鞭子。

事情一团糟!那个德国佬也是个粗人。他可能不会在乎妻子是否会知道这事情。杰克用赶车鞭子揍他的脸和肩,这时马却受惊了,走动起来,于是他又不得不跳下车来。

两个男人就这样打了起来。姑娘没有看见。马奔跑起来,沿路跑了近一英里,才被姑娘给止住。她接着设法把马拴在路旁的一棵树上(真怪,我怎么会知道这些?一定是我小时候在镇上听了些谣传又记在心上了)。杰克甩掉了德国佬,到那儿找到了她。她正蜷缩在马车坐垫上,在哭,怕得要死。她对杰克讲了许多废话,说那德国佬怎样想奸污她,有一回他怎样把她骗到牲口棚里,还有一回他们两人正巧单独在一起,他怎样把她胸前的衣服全撕开。她说,要不是那德国佬听到自己那个老婆娘的车已到了大门口,他也许会把她给奸污了。那老婆娘是到镇上看病去的。啊,她就要到牲口棚里来拴马了。德国佬想溜到田野里去,不让他的女人发现。他对姑娘说,要是她讲出去,他就杀死她。她怎么办呢?她撒了个谎,说她在牲口棚喂牲口不小心钩破了自己的衣服。我现在记起来了,她是个养女,不知道自己的父母在哪儿。说不定她根本就没有父亲。你知道我的意思是什么。

这种寄养的孩子常常受尽虐待。他们是些没爹没娘的孩子,其实是奴隶。那时还没有什么孤儿院。他们就根据法律寄养在有些家庭里。这样的处理还算是件幸运透了的事哩。

二

她嫁给杰克,生了一个儿子和一个女儿,不过,女儿死了。

她于是便安心喂养牲口。那是她的职业。在德国佬那儿,她给德国佬和他女人煮饭。德国佬的女人是个大屁股的壮女人,大多数时间和她男人一块儿在田里干活。姑娘喂养他们,又要喂养牲口棚里的母牛,喂养猪、马和鸡。每日每时,年轻的姑娘老是在喂养着什么。

她现在嫁给了杰克·格赖姆斯,也得喂养他。她

the horse by the bridle and Jake got out his buggy whip.

They had it out all right! The German was a tough one. Maybe he didn't care whether his wife knew or not. Jake hit him over the face and shoulders with the buggy whip, but the horse got to acting up and he had to get out.

Then the two men went for it. The girl didn't see it. The horse started to run away and went nearly a mile down the road before the girl got him stopped. Then she managed to tie him to a tree beside the road. (I wonder how I know all this. It must have stuck in my mind from small-town tales when I was a boy.) Jake found her there after he got through with the German. She was huddled up in the buggy seat, crying, scared to death. She told Jake a lot of stuff how the German had tried to get her, how he chased her once into the barn, how another time, when they happened to be alone in the house together, he tore her dress open clear down the front. The German, she said, might have got her that time if he hadn't heard his old woman drive in at the gate. She had been off to town for supplies. Well, she would be putting the horse in the barn. The German managed to sneak off to the fields without his wife seeing. He told the girl he would kill her if she told. What could she do? She told a lie about ripping her dress in the barn when she was feeding the stock. I remember now that she was a bound girl and did not know where her father and mother were. Maybe she did not have any father. You know what I mean.

Such bound children were often enough cruelly treated. They were children who had no parents, slaves really. There were very few orphan homes then. They were legally bound into some home. It was a matter of pure luck how it came out.

II

She married Jake and had a son and a daughter, but the daughter died.

Then she settled down to feed stock. That was her job. At the German's place she had cooked the food for the German and his wife. The wife was a strong woman with big hips and worked most of the time in the fields with her husband. She fed them and fed the cows in the barn, fed the pigs, the horses and the chickens. Every moment of every day, as a young girl, was spent feeding something.

Then she married Jake Grimes and he had to be fed. She was a slight thing, and when she had been married for three or four years, and after the two children

是个瘦弱的人,结了婚三四年,又生过两次孩子,瘦削的肩膀很佝偻了。

杰克总要在屋子旁边养许多大个的狗,那屋子呢,就盖在小河旁边那个报废了的锯木场边上。他不偷东西时就做着马匹买卖,自己也养了许多皮包骨头的瘦马。他还养了三四只猪和一头牛。这些个东西全放养在格赖姆斯家祖传下来的那小块儿地上,杰克又很少到那儿去干活。

因为歉收,他背了债,拖欠了好几年也没有还清。人家又不相信他。他们老担心他会在夜里偷谷子。他不得不到老远的地方去找活儿干,但是又没有到那儿去的路费。冬天,他打打猎,砍些个柴,到附近镇上去卖。儿子长大了,长得挺像父亲。他们俩一块儿喝酒。他们回家时,要是屋里没什么可吃的,那年老的男人就会在那年老的女人头上啪地一巴掌。她自己养了几只鸡,这时就只好匆匆忙忙地去杀一只。待到这些鸡杀光了,她也就没有鸡蛋可卖了,那时她再到镇上来还有什么事可干呢?

她费尽心机想弄些东西喂养,弄些猪养养,因为猪会长肥,到秋天就能宰了。可到猪宰了之后,她的男人拿了大部分肉到镇上去,自个儿卖了。要是他不先这样做,那儿子就会这样做。他们有时打架,在他们打架时,那老妇人就站在一边浑身哆嗦。

她对什么事都沉默惯了——那不会变了。有时,她看上去很老——她还不到 40 岁哪——有时,男人和儿子都出去了,做马匹买卖去了,或者喝酒去了,或者偷东西去了,她这时就绕着屋子和牲口棚直打转转,嘴里又咕咕哝哝。

她将怎样喂养好每种东西呢?——这是她的烦恼。狗得喂养。牲口棚里马和牛吃的干草也不多了。那些鸡要是不喂,它们怎么会下蛋呢?没有蛋卖,她在镇上又用什么去买东西,买那些维持生计所必需的东西呢?谢天谢地,丈夫总算不要她喂养了。他们婚后,尤其生了孩子以后,就没有长久待在一起过。他离家远走,上哪儿去她不知道。有时,他一出门就一个星期,到孩子长大后,爷儿俩一起外出。

他们把屋里的事全扔给她操劳,她却身无分文。她不认识一个人。镇上谁也不和她讲话。到冬天,她得去拾柴来生火,又得靠一丁点儿粮食巴结着喂牲口。

牲口在牲口棚里饥肠辘辘地对着她啼叫,狗缠着她打转。鸡在冬天很少生蛋。它们蜷缩在鸡棚角落

were born, her slender shoulders became stooped.

Jake always had a lot of big dogs around the house, that stood near the unused sawmill near the creek. He was always trading horses when he wasn't stealing something and had a lot of poor bony ones about. Also he kept three or four pigs and a cow. They were all pastured in the few acres left of the Grimes place and Jake did little enough work.

He went into debt for a threshing outfit and ran it for several years, but it did not pay. People did not trust him. They were afraid he would steal the grain at night. He had to go a long way off to get work and it cost too much to get there. In the winter he hunted and cut a little firewood, to be sold in some nearby town. When the son grew up he was just like the father. They got drunk together. If there wasn't anything to eat in the house when they came home the old man gave his old woman a cut over the head. She had a few chickens of her own and had to kill one of them in a hurry. When they were all killed she wouldn't have any eggs to sell when she went to town, and then what would she do?

She had to scheme all her life about getting things fed, getting the pigs fed so they would grow fat and could be butchered in the fall. When they were butchered her husband took most of the meat off to town and sold it. If he did not do it first, the boy did. They fought sometimes and when they fought the old woman stood aside trembling.

She had got the habit of silence anyway—that was fixed. Sometimes, when she began to look old—she wasn't forty yet—and when the husband and son were both off, trading horses or drinking or hunting or stealing, she went around the house and the barnyard muttering to herself.

How was she going to get everything fed? —that was her problem. The dogs had to be fed. There wasn't enough hay in the barn for the horses and the cow. If she didn't feed the chickens how could they lay eggs? Without eggs to sell how could she get things in town, things she had to have to keep the life of the farm going? Thank heaven, she did not have to feed her husband—in a certain way. That hadn't lasted long after their marriage and after the babies came. Where he went on his long trips she did not know. Sometimes he was gone from home for weeks, and after the boy grew up they went off together.

They left everything at home for her to manage and she had no money. She knew no one. No one ever talked to her in town. When it was winter she had to gather sticks of wood for her fire, had to try to keep the stock fed with very little grain.

The stock in the barn cried to her hungrily, the

里,她得看住它们。冬天鸡要是在棚里下蛋而你不发觉,蛋就会冻坏、碎裂。

那年冬天里有一天,老妇人带了些蛋出门上镇上去,几只狗跟着她。她是将近 3 点钟才出发的,雪下得太大。这些天来,她一直感到不舒服,所以一路上她嘴里咕咕哝哝,衣衫单薄,驼着背。她带着一只谷子袋,袋里的谷子已经吃得精光,所以她把鸡蛋放在袋里。鸡蛋不多,不过在冬天蛋的价钱很贵。她用蛋可以换回一些东西,一些咸肉啦,一点儿砂糖啦,或许还有一点儿咖啡。很可能,屠夫还会给她一块牛肝。

她到了镇上,三钱不值两钱地卖了鸡蛋,那些狗就躺在门外。还算不错,需要的东西都买好了,比她希望的还多了一些。她随后到屠夫那儿,屠夫给了她一些牛肝和一些狗肉。

这是很久以来第一次有人和她客客气气地谈话。她进去时,屠夫正一个人在铺子里,想到这么个样子的又病又老的女人在这么个天气跑到外面来,心里很纳闷。天冷得很,下午雪稍停了一阵儿,眼下又在纷纷扬扬。屠夫说到她的男人和儿子,咒骂他们,老妇人眼睁睁地看着他,一边听他说话,一边眼睛里露出微微吃惊的神情。屠夫说,要是她的男人或儿子想来拿点牛肝或者想要点像他刚才装进谷子袋里的上面还挂了些碎肉的大骨头,他宁愿先看到他们挨饿。

挨饿,嗯? 啊,牲口得喂了。人也得喂,那些马实在很糟,不过大概还能卖掉,那头可怜的瘦母牛已经 3 个多月没有出一滴奶了。

马,牛,猪,狗,人。

三

只要有可能,老妇人总是趁天没黑就回家。狗跟在她屁股后面,嗅着驮在她背上的沉甸甸的谷子袋。她走到镇口,在一道篱笆旁边停下,拿出一根绳子把谷子袋缚在自己背上,那根绳子也就是为了这个目的才放在她上衣口袋里的。

这样轻多了。她感到两条胳膊又酸又痛。她得从那道篱笆下面钻过去,这真不容易,不过她没有迟疑,趴下身子在雪地上爬着。那些狗在旁边跳来跳去。她还得跟跟跄跄站起身来,她也这样做了。爬过这道篱笆,有一条近路可以直接通到一座小山旁的一

dogs followed her about. In the winter the hens laid few enough eggs. They huddled in the corners of the barn and she kept watching them. If a hen lays an egg in the barn in the winter and you do not find it, it freezes and breaks.

One day in winter the old woman went off to town with a few eggs and the dogs followed her. She did not get started until nearly three o'clock and the snow was heavy. She hadn't been feeling very well for several days and so she went muttering along, scantily clad, her shoulders stooped. She had an old grain bag in which she carried her eggs, tucked away down in the bottom. There weren't many of them, but in winter the price of eggs is up. She would get a little meat in exchange for the eggs, some salt pork, a little sugar, and some coffee perhaps. It might be the butcher would give her a piece of liver.

When she had got to town and was trading in her eggs the dogs lay by the door outside. She did pretty well, got the things she needed, more than she had hoped. Then she went to the butcher and he gave her some liver and some dog meat.

It was the first time anyone had spoken to her in a friendly way for a long time. The butcher was alone in his shop when she came in and was annoyed by the thought of such a sick-looking old woman out on such a day. It was bitter cold and the snow, that had let up during the afternoon, was falling again. The butcher said something about her husband and her son, swore at them, and the old woman stared at him, a look of mild surprise in her eyes as he talked. He said that if either the husband or the son were going to get any of the liver or the heavy bones with scraps of meat hanging to them that he had put into the grain bag, he'd see him starve first.

Starve, eh? Well, things had to be fed. Men had to be fed, and the horses that weren't any good but maybe could be traded off, and the poor thin cow that hadn't given any milk for three months.

Horses, cows, pigs, dogs, men.

III

The old woman had to get back before darkness came if she could. The dogs followed at her heels, sniffing at the heavy grain bag she had fastened on her back. When she got to the edge of town she stopped by a fence and tied the bag on her back with a piece of rope she had carried in her dress pocket for just that purpose. That was an easier way to carry it. Her arms ached. It was hard when she had to crawl over fences and once she fell over and landed in the snow. The

片树林。要是她顺大路绕着走，得多走一英里路。她怕自己会走不动。再说，牲口也到了该喂食的时候了。剩下的干草已经不多，谷子也不多了。她男人和儿子回家时也许会带上一点儿。他们驾着格赖姆斯家唯一的那辆马车出门去了。那辆马车已经摇摇晃晃，上面套着一匹同样摇摇晃晃的马，还有两匹马也戴着笼头套在上面，也是摇摇晃晃的。他们在做马匹买卖，要是可能，想赚一点儿钱。他们会喝得醉醺醺地回家。他们回家时，屋里最好要准备好一点儿吃的东西。

儿子和一个住在 15 英里外县城里的女人有勾搭。那是个很粗鲁的女人，一个泼妇。有一回，在夏天，儿子曾把她带到家里来过。儿子和她一起喝酒。杰克·格赖姆斯不在家里。儿子和那女人就像使唤仆人一样使唤老妇人。她并不在乎，她这样惯了。无论怎样，她从来不吭一声。她就是这样过日子的。当她还是个姑娘在德国佬那儿时，她就这样过日子了。嫁给格赖姆斯以后，也还是这样。她儿子把那女人带到家里住了一整夜，两个人就像结过婚一样睡在一起。这并没有使老妇人吃惊，没有。她对生活早就不会吃惊了。

她背着口袋，踩着雪，跟跟跄跄穿过开阔的田野，进了树林。

那儿有一条小路，不过这条路很难走。一过山顶，那儿树木长得特别密，中间却有一块空地。是不是曾有人想在这儿造房子？空地的大小和镇上房子的地基大小差不多，足够造一间屋和一个院子。小路正好打空地边经过，老妇人到了那儿，便在一棵树下坐下来休息。

这是件蠢事。她把口袋抵住树干，歇下身子，这当然轻松多了，但是她还能重新站起来吗？她为此忧虑了一会儿，接着就安静地闭上了眼睛。

她很想睡一会儿。人冷到一定的时候也就不觉得冷了。下午稍微温和一点儿，雪也下得小多了。又过了一会儿，天气转晴了。月亮也出来了。

跟着这位格赖姆斯夫人一起去镇上的是 4 只格赖姆斯家的狗，都是些高大而又瘦骨嶙峋的家伙。像杰克·格赖姆斯和他儿子这号人，也只配养这样的狗。他们打它们，骂它们，而这些狗倒没有逃走。因为老是忍饥挨饿，格赖姆斯家的狗就得自己设法寻食，它们趁老妇人背靠着树干没有积雪的一面睡着了

dogs went frisking about. She had to struggle to get to her feet again, but she made it. The point of climbing over the fences was that there was a short cut over a hill and through a woods. She might have gone around by the road, but it was a mile farther that way. She was afraid she couldn't make it. And then, besides, the stock had to be fed. There was a little hay left and a little corn. Perhaps her husband and son would bring some home when they came. They had driven off in the only buggy the Grimes family had, a rickety thing, a rickety horse hitched to the buggy, two other rickety horses led by halters. They were going to trade horses, get a little money if they could. They might come home drunk. It would be well to have something in the house when they came back.

The son had an affair on with a woman at the county seat, fifteen miles away. She was a rough enough woman, a tough one. Once, in the summer, the son had brought her to the house. Both she and the son had been drinking. Jake Grimes was away and the son and his woman ordered the old woman about like a servant. She didn't mind much; she was used to it. Whatever happened she never said anything. That was her way of getting along. She had managed that way when she was a young girl at the German's and ever since she had married Jake. That time her son brought his woman to the house they stayed all night, sleeping together just as though they were married. It hadn't shocked the old woman, not much. She had got past being shocked early in life.

With the pack on her back she went painfully along across an open field, wading in the deep snow, and got into the woods.

There was a path, but it was hard to follow. Just beyond the top of the hill, where the woods was thickest, there was a small clearing. Had someone once thought of building a house there? The clearing was as large as a building lot in town, large enough for a house and a garden. The path ran along the side of the clearing, and when she got there the old woman sat down to rest at the foot of a tree.

It was a foolish thing to do. When she got herself placed, the pack against the tree's trunk, it was nice, but what about getting up again? She worried about that for a moment and then quietly closed her eyes.

She must have slept for a time. When you are about so cold you can't get any colder. The afternoon grew a little warmer and the snow came thicker than ever. Then after a time the weather cleared. The moon even came out.

There were four Grimes dogs that had followed Mrs. Grimes into town, all tall gaunt fellows. Such men as Jake Grimes and his son always keep just such dogs. They kick and abuse them, but they stay. The

的时候，便寻食去了。它们在树林里，在附近田野里追逐野兔，它们吠叫的声音又引来了另外3只乡下狗。

过了一会儿，所有的狗都回到了空地上。它们觉得有点儿兴奋。这样的时候，寒冷、明净，天上一轮明月，这正是狗的好时光。也许是某种往日旳本能吧，那种来自于当初还是狼并成群结队在冬夜旳树林里漫游时的本能，现在又在它们身上复萌了。

狗在空地上，在老妇人前面，抓到两三只野兔，急迫的饥饿感得到了解决。它们开始玩耍，在空地上团团奔跑。它们一圈又一圈地奔跑，一只狗的鼻子触到另一只狗的尾巴。在积着雪的树枝下，在冬日的月光里，空地上呈现出一幅奇妙的景象，它们这样一声不响地奔跑着，松软的雪地上被踏出了一大圈脚印。狗没有发出声响。它们绕着圈子奔跑，跑了一圈又一圈。

也许，老妇人在临死前看见了它们在这样奔跑吧。她大概醒过一两回，用朦胧而衰弱的目光注视过这种奇妙的景象。

现在，她不会再觉得冷了，因为她昏昏欲睡。生命缥缥缈缈持续了很久。也许，老妇人的灵魂已经出窍。也许，她在梦见自己的少女时代，梦见在德国佬那儿时的情景，梦见在那以前，她还是个孩子时的情景，那时她母亲还没有突然逝去，还没有将她扔下。

她的梦不可能做得很快活。她从未遇到过什么快活的事情。

时不时地，格赖姆斯家的狗中间有哪一只会离开奔跑着的圈子，走到她面前站着，那只狗会用自己的脸贴近她的脸。它红红的舌头伸到了嘴外面。

也许，狗的奔跑就是一种哀悼的仪式吧。也许是，在这夜晚，在这样的奔跑之中，那原始的狼的本能也就复萌了，这使它们总显得有点可怕。

"现在我们不再是狼了。我们是狗，人门的仆役。活着吧，人们啊！人死了我们就又变成狼了。"

有时，一只狗走到老妇人背靠树干而坐的地方，把鼻子凑到她脸上嗅着，显出满足的样子，接着又回到狗群里奔跑起来。在这天夜里，格赖姆斯家的每一只狗在她临死前都轮流用鼻子嗅过她。关于这样的事，我是后来才知道的，那时我已长大成人。有一次，也是一个冬天的夜里，我在伊利诺斯的一个对林里看到一群狗也是这样做的。那群狗等着我死去，就像这天夜里（那时我还是个小孩）它们等着老妇人死去一样。不过，我碰到这种事的时候，正当年轻力壮，什么

Grimes dogs, in order to keep from starving, had to do a lot of foraging for themselves, and they had been at it while the old woman slept with her back to the tree at the side of the clearing. They had been chasing rabbits in the woods and in adjoining fields and in their ranging had picked up three other farm dogs.

After a time all the dogs came back to the clearing. They were excited about something. Such nights, cold and clear and with a moon, do things to dogs. It may be that some old instinct, come down from the time when they were wolves and ranged the woods in packs on winter nights, comes back into them.

The dogs in the clearing, before the old woman, had caught two or three rabbits and their immediate hunger had been satisfied. They began to play, running in circles in the clearing. Round and round they ran, each dog's nose at the tail of the next dog. In the clearing, under the snow-laden trees and under the wintry moon they made a strange picture, running thus silently, in a circle their running had beaten in the soft snow. The dogs made no sound. They ran around and around in the circle.

It may have been that the old woman saw them doing that before she died. She may have awakened once or twice and looked at the strange sight with dim old eyes.

She wouldn't be very cold now, just drowsy. Life hangs on a long time. Perhaps the old woman was out of her head. She may have dreamed of her girlhood, at the German's, and before that, when she was a child and before her mother lit out and left her.

Her dreams couldn't have been very pleasant. Not many pleasant things have happened to her. Now and then one of the Grimes dogs left the running circle and came to stand before her. The dog thrust his face close to her face. His red tongue was hanging out.

The running of the dogs may have been a kind of death ceremony. It may have been that the primitive instinct of the wolf, having been aroused in the dogs by the night and the running, made them somehow afraid.

"Now we are no longer wolves. We are dogs, the servants of men. Keep alive, man! When man dies we become wolves again. "

When one of the dogs came to where the old woman sat with her back against the tree and thrust his nose close to her face he seemed satisfied and went back to run with the pack. All the Grimes dogs did it at some time during the evening, before she died. I knew all about it afterward, when I grew to be a man, because once in a woods in Illinois, on another winter night, I saw a pack of dogs act just like that. The dogs were waiting for me to die as they had waited for the old woman that night when I was a child, but when it

叫作死,我是毫不关心的。

老妇人慢慢地、平静地死了。

她死了,一只格赖姆斯家的狗走到她面前,发现她死了,这时,所有的狗停止了奔跑。

它们围在她旁边。

啊,现在她死了。她活着的时候,曾喂养过格赖姆斯家的这些狗,现在又怎样呢?

在她背上,有一只口袋,一只谷子袋,里面装着那咸肉,装着屠夫送给她的牛肝,还有狗食和煮汤的骨头。镇上的那个屠夫,因为一时动了恻隐之心,竟把她的谷子袋装得那样沉甸甸的。这曾是老妇人的一大收获。

现在,成了狗的一大收获。

四

有一只格赖姆斯家的狗突然从狗群里跳出来,去拱老妇人背上的口袋。要是狗真的成了狼,那么就有一只要成为狼群的头头。它怎么做,其他所有的狗也就怎么做。

它们一起啮咬老妇人曾用绳子缚在自己背上的谷子袋。

它们把老妇人的尸体拖到空地上。本来就破旧的衣服一下子被它们撕破,露出了双肩。当一两天后她的尸体被人发现时,她的衣服已经被全部撕去,露出了屁股。不过,那些狗并没有动她的身体。它们把谷子袋里的肉拖出来,吃得精光。人们发现她时,她的身体已经冻得硬邦邦的,两只肩膀是那样消瘦,身体是那样纤细,虽然已经死了,看上去却像一个少女迷人的身体。

这样的事情,在中西部的各个小镇上,在小镇附近的农庄上,是时常发生的。不过,那时我还是个孩子。是一个猎人在追赶野兔时发现老妇人的尸体的,他没有走近她。在那块白雪覆盖的小小空地上,有一条成圆形的不知是谁踏出来的小路,周围一片死寂,而就在这地方,那些狗曾拱着老妇人的尸体,用劲儿把谷子袋从尸体上拖下来或者把它咬破——这儿的情景使那个猎人大吃一惊,他赶紧跑回镇上。

我那时和我的一个哥哥正巧在大街上,我哥哥是镇上的报童,正在给杂货铺送晚报。那时大概已经入夜了。

那个猎人走进一家铺子,把自己看见的事情告诉

happened to me I was a young man and had no intention whatever of dying.

The old woman died softly and quietly. When she was dead and when one of the Grimes dogs had come to her and had found her dead all the dogs stopped running.

They gathered about her.

Well, she was dead now. She had fed the Grimes dogs when she was alive, what about now?

There was the pack on her back, the grain bag containing the piece of salt pork, the liver the butcher had given her, the dog meat, the soup bones. The butcher in town, having been suddenly overcome with a feeling of pity, had loaded her grain bag heavily. It had been a big haul for the old woman.

It was a big haul for the dogs now.

IV

One of the Grimes dogs sprang suddenly out from among the others and began worrying the pack on the old woman's back. Had the dogs really been wolves, that one would have been the leader of the pack. What he did, all the others did.

All of them sank their teeth into the grain bag the old woman had fastened with ropes to her back.

They dragged the old woman's body out into the open clearing. The worn-out dress was quickly torn from her shoulders. When she was found, a day or two later, the dress had been torn from her body clear to the hips, but the dogs had not touched her body. They had got the meat out of the grain bag, that was all. Her body was frozen stiff when it was found, and the shoulders were so narrow and the body so slight that in death it looked like the body of some charming young girl.

Such things happened in towns of the Middle West, on farms near town, when I was a boy. A hunter out after rabbits found the old woman's body and did not touch it. Something, the beaten round path in the little snow-covered clearing, the silence of the place, the place where the dogs had worried the body trying to pull the grain bag away or tear it open—something startled the man and he hurried off to town.

I was in Main Street with one of my brothers who was town newsboy and who was taking the afternoon papers to the stores. It was almost night.

The hunter came into a grocery and told his story. Then he went to a hardware shop and into a drugstore. Men began to gather on the sidewalks. Then they started out along the road to the place in the woods.

别人。接着,他走进一家五金店,随后又走进一家烟纸店。人们开始围集在路旁。接着,他们沿着大路向林子的那个地方走去。

我哥哥本应该继续送他的报纸的,他却扔下不做了。大伙儿都向树林走去。承办丧事的殡仪员也去了,还有镇长。有几个人驾了一辆马车,不走大路却蹚进那条通往树林的小路,因为马打着很硬的铁蹄,在滑溜溜的大路上走不快。不过,他们并不比我们步行的人走得快一点儿。

镇长是个大个子,一条腿在内战时受过伤。他挂着一根粗大的拐杖,沿着大路一拐一拐地大步走。我哥哥和我跟在他后面,一路上,又有些男人和孩子加入我们的行列。

我们走到老妇人当初离开大路的地方时,天越来越黑了,不过月亮已经升起。镇长怀疑这可能是谋杀。他一再询问那个猎人。那个猎人肩扛着枪也和我们在一起走,身后跟着一只狗。一个打野兔的猎人是不大有机会受人重视的,他滔滔不绝地讲着,一边给镇长引路。"我没看见她身上有伤。她是个好看的小姑娘。脸埋在雪里。不,我不认识她。"事实上,那个猎人并没有仔细看过尸体。他害怕了。她可能是被人暗杀的,说不定有谁还躲在树后面冷不防跳出来杀了他。那时是黄昏,树林里一片死寂,人在那里总有点心惊胆战,毛骨悚然的。再说,看到别人遇到什么不测之祸,人们考虑到的也总是拔腿逃跑而已。

大伙儿走到当初老妇人穿过田野的地方,接着又跟着镇长和那个猎人走上稍斜的坡地,进了树林。

我哥哥和我都默不作声。我哥哥肩上挂着一只口袋,里面装着一捆报纸。回到镇上他得在晚饭前把报纸送完。如果我和他一起,对这一点他毫无疑问,我们俩都会误了晚饭。母亲或姐姐会给我们热晚饭的。

我们会有话说的。小孩子不总能碰上这种事。那个猎人走进杂货铺时,我们正好在那儿。那个猎人是个乡下佬。我们俩过去谁也没有见过他。

大伙儿现在到了空地上。冬天的晚上,照例来说这儿很快就会一片漆黑,不过一轮满月又使那儿的每一样东西都清晰可辨。我哥哥和我站在那棵树旁边,老妇人就死在这棵树下。

她看上去并不很老,在月光、冰雪和宁静里躺着。有个男人把她在雪地上翻了个身,我什么都看见了。一阵奇怪而神秘的感觉向我袭来,我浑身战栗了,我

My brother should have gone on about his business of distributing papers but he didn't. Everyone was going to the woods. The undertaker went and the town marshal. Several men got on a dray and rode out to where the path left the road and went into the woods, but the horses weren't very sharply shod and slid about on the slippery roads. They made no better time than those of us who walked.

The town marshal was a large man whose leg had been injured in the Civil War. He carried a heavy cane and limped rapidly along the road. My brother and I followed at his heels, and as we went other men and boys joined the crowd.

It had grown dark by the time we got to where the old woman had left the road, but the moon had come out. The marshal was thinking there might have been a murder. He kept asking the hunter questions. The hunter went along with his gun across his shoulders, a dog following at his heels. It isn't often a rabbit hunter has a chance to be so conspicuous. He was taking full advantage of it, leading the procession with the town marshal. "I didn't see any wounds. She was a beautiful young girl. Her face was buried in the snow. No, I didn't know her." As a matter of fact, the hunter had not looked closely at the body. He had been frightened. She might have been murdered and someone might spring out from behind a tree and murder him. In a woods, in the late afternoon, when the trees are all bare and there is white snow on the ground, when all is silent, something creepy steals over the mind and body. If something strange or uncanny has happened in the neighborhood all you think about is getting away from there as fast as you can.

The crowd of men and boys had got to where the old woman had crossed the field and went, following the marshal and the hunter, up the slight incline and into the woods.

My brother and I were silent. He had his bundle of papers in a bag slung across his shoulder. When he got back to town he would have to go on distributing his papers before he went home to supper. If I went along, as he had no doubt already determined I should, we would both be late. Either Mother or our older sister would have to warm our supper.

Well, we would have something to tell. A boy did not get such a chance very often. It was lucky we just happened to go into the grocery when the hunter came in. The hunter was a country fellow. Neither of us had ever seen him before.

Now the crowd of men and boys had got to the clearing. Darkness comes quickly on such winter nights, but the full moon made everything clear. My brother and I stood near the tree beneath which the old woman had died.

哥哥也和我一样。这也许是寒冷的缘故吧。

我们俩过去从来没有看见过女人的身体。也许是因为雪粘在凉硬的肉体上，老妇人的尸体看上去是那么洁白，那样可爱，那样像鹅卵石般地光滑。和我们一起从镇上来的人中间没有一个女人，不过，有一个男人，镇上的铁匠，脱下自己的外套盖在她身上。接着，他又把她抱起来，转身向镇上走去，其他人都默默地跟在后面。那时，还没有一个人知道她是谁。

五

我什么都看见了，我看到了雪地上那个像微型跑道似的椭圆形圈子，那些狗就是沿着这个圈子奔跑的。我看到人们怎样地显出诡秘的神色，看到了那两条像少女似的洁白而光滑的肩膀，还听到了人们窃窃的议论声。

人们都显得很诡秘。他们把尸体送到殡仪员那儿去，当铁匠、猎人、镇长和另外几个人进了屋之后，他们就把门关上了。要是上帝在那儿的话，他或许可以进去，可我们是孩子，进不去。

我和我哥哥一起把剩下的报纸送完，随后回到家里，我哥哥和我谈起了那件事。

我没作声，很早就上了床。这大概是我对他讲到那些事情时的态度感到不满的缘故吧。

后来，我在镇上当然也听到了有关老妇人的其他一些零零星星的事。她是在第二天被人认出来的，于是就把通知发了出去。

人们不知在什么地方找到了她的丈夫和儿子，还把他们带到镇上并试图把老妇人的死和他们联系起来。不过这是徒劳。他们有足够的理由表明他们当时并不在场。

不过，镇上的人们对他们很反感。他们只好离开这儿。他们上哪儿去了，我一点儿也不知道。

我只记得树林里的情景，记得站在那儿的人们，记得那具赤裸裸的、像少女似的躯体，脸正埋在雪地里，还记得那条狗奔跑时踩出来的跑道和头顶上清明而寒彻的夜空。空中正飘过一朵朵浮云。云朵很快地越过那小小的林中空地的上空。

就是这林中的情景，在我不知不觉中，成了我现在正在讲给你们听的这个真实故事的原始材料。你们知道，我是在很久以后才慢慢地收集到其他一些零

She did not look old, lying there in that light, frozen and still. One of the men turned her over in the snow and I saw everything. My body trembled with some strange mystical feeling and so did my brother's. It might have been the cold.

Neither of us had ever seen a woman's body before. It may have been the snow, clinging to the frozen flesh, that made it look so white and lovely, so like marble. No woman had come with the party from town; but one of the men, he was the town blacksmith, took off his overcoat and spread it over her. Then he gathered her into his arms and started off to town, all the others following silently. At that time no one knew who she was.

V

I had seen everything, had seen the oval in the snow, like a miniature race track, where the dogs had run, had seen how the men were mystified, had seen the white bare young-looking shoulders, had heard the whispered comments of the men.

The men were simply mystified. They took the body to the undertaker's and when the blacksmith, the hunter, the marshal and several others had got inside they closed the door. If Father had been there perhaps he could have got in, but we boys couldn't.

I went with my brother to distribute the rest of his papers and when we got home it was my brother who told the story.

I kept silent and went to bed early. It may have been I was not satisfied with the way he told it.

Later, in the town, I must have heard other fragments of the old woman's story. She was recognized the next day and there was an investigation.

The husband and son were found somewhere and brought to town and there was an attempt to connect them with the woman's death, but it did not work. They had perfect enough alibis.

However, the town was against them. They had to get out. Where they went I never heard.

I remember only the picture there in the forest, the men standing about, the naked girlish-looking figure, face down in the snow, the tracks made by the running dogs and the clear cold winter sky above. White fragments of clouds were drifting across the sky. They went racing across the little open space among the trees.

The scene in the forest had become for me,

星材料的。

　　事情就是这样。我后来长大了,成了一个小伙子,我也在一个德国佬的农庄里干活。那个雇来的姑娘也很怕主人。那个农庄主的女人也恨这姑娘。

　　我在那儿明白了许多事情。后来有一次,也是一个清朗有月的冬夜,我在伊利诺斯的树林里还真有点不可思议地遇到过那些狗。在我是个学生的时候,夏日里有一天,曾和一个小伙伴一起从镇上出发,沿小河走好几英里路来到那所老妇人曾经住过的屋子前。她死后,这屋子就没人来住过。门都东倒西歪,窗棂也破败不堪。我和我的伙伴一起站在那条路旁边,这时就有两只狗,毫无疑问是无家可归的乡下野狗,正在屋子边上奔跑,团团地打转。两只狗都很高大,也很瘦,它们走到篱笆前,透过篱笆朝我们张望。那时我们站在路上。

　　后来,我长得更大了,对我来说,那件关于老妇人之死的事情变得就像从远处飘来的音乐声。每一个音符都得慢慢琢磨才听得清楚。其中有些东西还得加以理解。

　　那个死去的女人生来注定要喂养畜生。不管怎样,她所做的也仅仅如此。她未生之前就在喂养畜生,在她童年时以及在她少女时代在德国佬的农庄上干活时,还有在她嫁人之后又一天天衰老时,甚至在她临死之际,她一直在喂养着畜生。她养活牛,养活马,养活猪,养活狗,养活人。她的女儿年幼时就死了,而和她的独生子在一起,她又一点儿也没有做母亲的地位。就在她死的那个夜晚,她还在匆匆赶回家,背上还背着可以养活那些畜生的食物。

　　她死在林中的空地上,她直到死后还继续在养活畜生。

　　你们知道,那天晚上我们回家后,我哥哥和我谈起这件事,我母亲和我姐姐当时也坐在一边听着,而我似乎觉得,他并没有把事情真正讲清楚。他太年轻,我也是。有一件有头有尾的事情也够动听了。

　　我并不想强调什么。我只是想解释一下,我当时为什么会感到不满,现在我既然已经讲了,那么,你们也许已经明白我为什么要费那么大劲儿来重讲这个简单故事的原因了吧。

without my knowing it, the foundation for the real story I am now trying to tell. The fragments, you see, had to be picked up slowly, long afterward.

　　Things happened. When I was a young man I worked on the farm of a German. The hired girl was afraid of her employer. The farmer's wife hated her.

　　I saw things at that place. Once later, I had a half-uncanny, mystical adventure with dogs in an Illinois forest on a clear, moonlit winter night. When I was a schoolboy, and on a summer day, I went with a boy friend out along a creek some miles from town and came to the house where the old woman had lived. No one had lived in the house since her death. The doors were broken from the hinges; the window lights were all broken. As the boy and I stood in the road outside, two dogs, just roving farm dogs no doubt, came running around the corner of the house. The dogs were tall, gaunt fellows and came down to the fence and glared through at us, standing in the road.

　　The whole thing, the story of the old woman's death, was to me as I grew older like music heard from far off. The notes had to be picked up slowly one at a time. Something had to be understood.

　　The woman who died was one destined to feed animal life. Anyway, that is all she ever did. She was feeding animal life before she was born, as a child, as a young woman working on the farm of the German, after she married, when she grew old, and when she died. She fed animal life in cows, in chickens, in pigs, in horses, in dogs, in men. Her daughter had died in childhood and with her one son she had no articulate relations. On the night when she died she was hurrying homeward, bearing on her body food for animal life.

　　She died in the clearing in the woods and even after her death continued feeding animal life.

　　You see, it is likely that when my brother told the story that night when we got home and my mother and sister sat listening I did not think he got the point. He was too young and so was I. A thing so complete has its own beauty.

　　I shall not try to emphasize the point. I am only explaining why I was dissatisfied then and have been ever since. I speak of that only that you may understand why I have been impelled to try to tell the simple story over again.

思考题 ——■

1.《年轻的布朗大爷》中的主题较为明确呢,还是《林中之死》中的主题较为明确?

2. 同样,试比较《林中之死》和《进入波兰》及《杀手》的主题。

3. 如果从这篇小说里把关于狗的事情全部删去,那么这篇小说的意义和效果会有什么不同?

4. 在这篇小说里,作为作者感情和态度的体现的语调有何重要性?

5. 这篇小说的主题是什么?那个男孩——即叙述者——从事件中发现了什么?这个故事是在实际事件发生后很久才讲的,这有什么好处?你是否能说出,这篇小说里隐藏着的是怎样的感情?　　　　(刘文荣 译)

1. Is the theme more specific in "Young Goodman Brown" or in "Death in the Woods"?

2. On the same ground, compare "Death in the Woods" with "Crossing into Poland" and "The Killers".

3. Suppose the dogs were omitted from this story. How different would be the meaning and effect?

4. How important is tone—a prevailing emotion and attitude—in this story?

5. What is the theme of this story? What does the boy, the narrator, discover by the event? What is gained by the fact that the story is told long after the actual event? What could you say is the dominant emotion of the story?

025. 人，差点儿

(美)理查德·赖特 著　刘家有 译

　　大福一蹦一跳穿过田野，穿过灰白的微光匆匆回家。在地里跟他们黑鬼讲话管啥用？不管怎样，他母亲正在把晚饭端到桌上来。他们黑鬼啥也不懂。总有一天他会弄到一支枪，还要练习射击，这样他们就不会像对小孩一样地对他说话了。他慢下脚步，看着地面。呸！就算他们比哇(我)长得大，哇(我)也要把他们吓泡(跑)！噢，哇(我)知道哇(我)能干啥。今晚哇(我)要到老乔点(店)里弄一本西斯·罗巴枪的画片簿，样样枪都看看。妈从老霍金斯那里领到哇(我)的工钱时，大开(概)妈会浪哇(让我)买一把的。哇(我)求她给哇(我)一些钱。哇(我)这么大也盖(该)有枪了。哇(我)今年17。差点儿就大人了。他朝前走着，觉得自己长长的四肢软绵绵的。呸！一个人管(干)了一整天重活，盖(该)弄支小枪玩玩。

　　他到了乔的店铺门前。一盏昏黄的吊灯照在门廊上。他跨上台阶，撩起门帘走进去，门在他身后砰的一声响。铺子里有股浓浓的煤油味还夹着鱼腥味。他起先觉得蛮有信心，后来当他看到肥胖的乔穿过店堂后门走进来时，他的信心反而有点动摇了。

　　"好，好，大福！你药(要)迈(买)啥？"

　　"里(你)好，乔先申(生)？噢，哇(我)不买啥。哇(我)想要里浪哇(你让我)看一会儿那本画片簿。"

　　"可以！你要在这里看吗？"

　　"不是，先申(生)，哇(我)想带回家看。明儿哇(我)从田里回来哇(我)一定就带来还。"

　　"你大(打)算买东西？"

　　"是先申(生)。"

025. The Man Who Was Almost a Man
by Richard Wright

DAVE struck out across the fields, looking homeward through paling light. Whut's the use talkin wid em niggers in the field? Anyhow, his mother was putting supper on the table. Them niggers can't understan nothing. One of these days he was going to get a gun and practice shooting, then they couldn't talk to him as though he were a little boy. He slowed, looking at the ground. Shucks, Ah ain scareda them even ef they are biggern me! Aw, Ah know whut Ahma do. Ahm going to ol Joe's sto n git that Sears Roebuck catlog n look at them guns. Mebbe Ma will lemme buy one when she gits mah pay from ol man Hawkins. Ahma beg her t gimme some money. Ahm ol ernough to hava gun. Ahm seventeen. Almost a man. He strode, feeling his long loose-jointed limbs. Shucks, a man oughta hava little gun aftah he done worked hard all day.

He came in sight of Joe's store. A yellow lantern glowed on the front porch. He mounted steps and went through the screen door, hearing it bang behind him. There was a strong smell of coal oil and mackerel fish. He felt very confident until he saw fat Joe walk in through the rear door, then his courage began to ooze.

"Howdy, Dave! Whutcha want?"

"How yuh, Mistah Joe? Aw, Ah don wanna buy nothing. Ah jus wanted t see if yuhd lemme look at tha catlog erwhile."

"Sure! You wanna see it here?"

"Nawsuh. Ah wans t take it home wid me. Ah'll bring it back termorrow when Ah come in from the fiels."

作者简介：理查德·赖特(Richard Wright，1908—1960)，美国小说家。1908 年 9 月 4 日生于美国密西西比州纳切兹，1960年 11 月 28 日卒于法国巴黎。祖父是奴隶的他在贫困中长大。他的首部中篇小说《汤姆叔叔的孩子们》(Uncle Tom's Children，1938)赢得广泛关注。《土生子》(Native Son，1940)，虽然有骇人听闻和暴力的描写，但是成了一本畅销书。他的自传体小说《黑孩子》(Black Boy，1945)生动描述了他艰难困苦的童年时代和青春时期。第二次世界大战之后，他定居巴黎。他是主张黑人要和白人一样有平等待遇的作家之一。

"你妈现在浪（让）你拿着自个儿的工钱啦？"

"嗨，乔先申（生），哇（我）像别人一样是大人啰。"

乔笑笑，用一块红的印花大手帕揩揩油腻腻的白面孔。

"你想买啥？"

大福瞅着地板，用手搔搔头，又抓抓大腿，笑笑。然后怯生生地抬起头来。

"哇（我）告诉里（你），乔先申（生），里（你）要答应决不说出去。"

"我答应。"

"啊，哇（我）要买支枪。"

"买枪？你要枪干啥？"

"哇（我）要带着。"

"你不过是个孩子哪。你要枪也没用。"

"噢，乔先申（生），把那本画片簿浪（让）哇（我）看看，哇（我）一定还给你。"

乔走到店堂后门里去。大福得意洋洋，他看看四周的白糖桶和面粉桶。他听见乔出来了。他伸长脖子想看看他果真把那本簿子拿来没有。是啰，他拿来了。好家伙，他真的拿来了！

"给你，但是你一定得还来，我只有这么一本。"

"大（当）然，乔先申（生）。"

"唔，你要是真想买支枪，干吗不上我这儿来买？我有枪要卖。"

"能打吗？"

"当然能打。"

"是哪一种的？"

"噢，一种老式的……左轮枪。手枪。老大的。"

"枪里装了子弹吗？"

"装的。"

"哇（我）看看西（行）吗？"

"你有钱吗？"

"里（你）要多钱？"

"卖给你，就两块钱吧。"

"只要两块？嗬，哇（我）拿到哇（我）的工钱就能买啦。"

"你要买，什么时候都可以来。"

"号（好）的，先申（生）。哇（我）要来每（买）的。"

他走出店门，听到身后的门又砰的一声响。哇（我）要向妈要点钱，买哇（我）的枪！只要两块！他挟着厚厚的广告画册急急忙忙地走了。

"You plannin on buying something?"

"Yessuh. "

"Your ma lettin you have your own money now?"

"Shucks. Mistah Joe, Ahm gittin t be a man like anybody else!"

Joe laughed and wiped his greasy white face with a red bandanna.

"Whut you plannin on buyin?"

Dave looked at the floor, scratched his head, scratched his thigh, and smiled. Then he looked up shyly.

"Ah'll tell yuh, Mistah Joe, ef yuh promise yuh won't tell. "

"I promise. "

"Waal, Ahma buy a gun. "

"A gun? Whut you want with a gun?"

"Ah wanna keep it. "

"You ain't nothing but a boy. You don't need a gun. "

"Aw, lemme have the catlog, Mistah Joe. Ah'll bring it back. "

Joe walked through the rear door. Dave was elated. He looked around at barrels of sugar and flour. He heard Joe coming back. He craned his neck to see if he were bringing the book. Yeah, he's got it. Gawddog, he's got it!

"Here, but be sure you bring it back. It's the only one I got. "

"Sho, Mistah Joe. "

"Say, if you wanna buy a gun, why don't you buy one from me? I gotta gun to sell. "

"Will it shoot?"

"Sure it'll shoot. "

"Whut kind is it?"

"Oh, it's kinda old. . . a left-hand Wheeler. A pistol. A big one. "

"Is it got bullets in it?"

"It's loaded. "

"Kin Ah see it?"

"Where's your money?"

"Whut yuh wan fer it?"

"I'll let you have it for two dollars. "

"Just two dollahs? Shucks, Ah could buy tha when Ah git mah pay. "

"I'll have it here when you want it. "

"Awright, suh. Ah be in fer it. "

He went through the door, hearing it slam again

"孩子,你上哪去了?"他母亲端着一盘热气腾腾的黑豆。

"噢,妈,哇(我)就站在路边跟伙伴们讲话来着。"

"你知道,哇(我)晚饭早做好等你哪。"

他坐下,把广告画册放在桌子边上。

"你别坐在那儿,先到井边去洗洗干净!哇(我)不要在屋里喂小猪。"

她抓住他的肩膀,推他。他摇摇晃晃地走出屋子。一会儿又回来拿那本广告册。

"这是啥?"

"噢,妈,这是一本画片簿子。"

"你从谁那儿拿的?"

"乔呗,镇上开点(店)的。"

"啊,好啰。哇(我)用它揩屁股。"

"不西(行),妈,"他想夺回广告册,"簿子柊哇(给我),妈。"

她抓住册子不放,眼睛瞪着他。

"别嚷嚷!你出了啥个事?你个蠢东西,嗯?"

"号(好)啦,妈,给哇(我),那不是哇(我)的!是乔的!交哇(叫我)蒙(明)天还他哩。"

她放开册子。他把册子挟在腋下,摇摇摆摆走下后门的台阶。他稀里哗啦地洗了手、脸,闭着眼睛摸回厨房,笨手笨脚地在角落里摸到一条毛巾。他一屁股坐到椅子上,椅子在地板上咯咯响,广告册掉落在他脚边。他揩干眼睛,拾起册子又挟在腋下,他母亲站在那里一直看着他。

"你要是把那本破书用来干蠢事,哇(我)可就要把它烧掉。"

"不西(行),妈,不西(行)的。"

"唔,坐下,别嚷嚷!"

他坐下来,把油灯移近一点儿。他一页一页地翻着看,也不管母亲放到桌上的食物。他父亲走进来。他弟弟也来了。

"里(你)在那里看个啥,大福?"他父亲问。

"广告簿。"他回答,头也没抬。

"嗬,乖乖在这儿!"他一眼看到一支蓝黑色左轮手枪。他眨眨眼睛,心里乱慌慌的。他父亲正看着他。他合上书不看了,拿到桌子下面放在自己膝上。做过饭前祷告,他就吃起来。他狼吞虎咽,吃光了豌豆,又叉进几块肥肉,嚼也来不及嚼就喝浓牛奶把肉冲下肚里。他不想在父亲面前提起钱的事。他觉得

behind him. Ahma git some money from Ma n buy me a gun! Only two dollahs! He tucked the thick catalogue under his arm and hurried.

"Where yuh been, boy?" His mother held a steaming dish of blackeyed peas.

"Aw, Ma, Ah jus stopped down the road t talk wid the boys."

"Yuh know bettah t keep suppah waitin."

He sat down, resting the catalogue on the edge of the table.

"Yuh git up from there and git to the well n wash yoself! Ah ain feedin no hogs in mah house!"

She grabbed his shoulder and pushed him. He stumbled out of the room, then came back to get the catalogue.

"Whut this?"

"Aw, Ma, it's jusa catlog."

"Who yuh git it from?"

"From Joe, down at the sto."

"Waal thas good. We kin use it in the outhouse."

"Naw, Ma." He grabbed for it. "Gimme ma catlog, Ma."

She held onto it and glared at him.

"Quit hollerin at me! Whut's wrong wid yuh? Yuh crazy?"

"But Ma, please. It ain mine! It's Joe's! He tol me t bring it back t im termorrow."

She gave up the book. He stumbled down the back steps, hugging the thick book under his arm. When he had splashed water on his face and hands, he groped back to the kitchen and fumbled in a corner for the towel. He bumped into a chair; it clattered to the floor. The catalogue sprawled at his feet. When he had dried his eyes he snatched up the book and held it again under his arm. His mother stood watching him.

"Now, ef yuh gonna act a fool over that ol book, Ah'll take it n burn it up."

"Naw, Ma, please."

"Waal, set down n be still!"

He sat down and drew the oil lamp close. He thumbed page after page, unaware of the food his mother set on the table. His father came in. Then his small brother.

"Whutcha got there, Dave?" his father asked.

"Jusa catlog," he answered, not looking up.

"Yeah, here they is!" His eyes glowed at blue-and-black revolvers. He glanced up, feeling sudden

最好还是当母亲一个人时去缠她。他不安地斜眼瞟着父亲。

"孩子，里(你)怎么蠢乎乎的，吃饭还呆(带)着那本书？"

"唔——"

"里(你)和霍金斯老头在一起怎么样？"

"嗯？"

"里(你)听不见？为什么不听？哇(我)问里(你)和霍金斯老头在一起怎么样？"

"噢，很号(好)，爸。哇(我)在那边耕底(地)比谁都耕得朵(多)。"

"唔，里(你)做事敢(该)朵朵(多多)留神。"

"唔——"

大福给自己的汤盆里倒满糖浆，用玉米面包沾着慢慢吃。他父亲和弟弟吃罢离开厨房时，他仍然坐在那里，把广告册里的那些枪又看了一遍，想鼓起勇气去和母亲谈这件事。天呀，要是哇(我)有一把漂亮的枪该朵号(多好)！他仿佛觉得自己的手指已经摸到了那把光溜溜的武器。只要他有那样一支枪，他一定会把它擦得精光雪亮，永不生锈。哇(我)要装上子弹，老天牙(爷)！

"妈？"他的声音听来很犹豫。

"嗯？"

"霍金斯老头把哇(我)的工钱给里(你)啦？"

"给啦，可你不能用，你换(还)小，会丢掉的，钱哇(我)把你剩(存)着，今年冬天给你做衣服，浪(让)你上学。"

他站起身走到母亲身旁，手里捧着那本打开的广告册。她还忙着洗碟子，埋头在那个平底锅上。他怯生生地举起广告册，声音又急促又含糊地开始说。

"妈，老天牙(爷)知道，哇(我)想要一把这个。"

"一把啥？"她问，眼皮也没抬。

"一把这个。"他又说，连指也不敢指一下。她对那书页一瞥，马上对着他睁大了眼睛。

"鬼东西，你疯了？"

"啊，妈——"

"快光(滚)开！不准你对哇(我)提到枪！你个笨蛋！"

"妈，哇(我)支(只)要两块钱买把枪。"

"不西(行)，哇(我)说不西(行)，你不西(许)买。"

"可是里(你)答应哇(我)一次……"

guilt. His father was watching him. He eased the book under the table and rested it on his knees. After the blessing was asked, he ate. He scooped up peas and swallowed fat meat without chewing. Buttermilk helped to wash it down. He did not want to mention money before his father. He would do much better by cornering his mother when she was alone. He looked at his father uneasily out of the edge of his eye.

"Boy, how come yuh don quit foolin wid tha book n eat yo suppah?"

"Yessuh."

"How you n ol man Hawkins gitten erlong?"

"Suh?"

"Can't yuh hear? Why don yuh lissen? Ah ast yu how wuz yuh n ol man Hawkins gittin erlong?"

"Oh, swell, Pa. Ah plows mo lan than anybody over there."

"Waal, yuh oughta keep yo mind on whut yuh doin."

"Yessuh."

He poured his plate full of molasses and sopped it up slowly with a chunk of cornbread. When his father and brother had left the kitchen, he still sat and looked again at the guns in the catalogue, longing to muster courage enough to present his case to his mother. Lawd, ef Ah only had tha pretty one! He could almost feel the slickness of the weapon with his fingers. If he had a gun like that he would polish it and keep it shining so it would never rust. N Ah'd keep it loaded, by Gawd!

"Ma?" His voice was hesitant.

"Hunh?"

"Ol man Hawkins give yuh mah money yit?"

"Yeah, but ain no usa yuh thinking bout throwin nona it erway. Ahm keepin tha money sos yuh kin have cloes t go to school this winter."

He rose and went to her side with the open catalogue in his palms. She was washing dishes, her head bent low over a pan. Shyly he raised the book. When he spoke, his voice was husky, faint.

"Ma, Gawd knows Ah wans one of these."

"One of whut?" she asked, not raising her eyes.

"One of these," he said again, not daring even to point. She glanced up at the page, then at him with wide eyes.

"Nigger, is yuh gone plumb crazy?"

"Aw, Ma—"

"哇(我)答应一个啥哪! 你支(只)是个小孩子哇!"

"妈,里(你)要是浪(让)我买把枪,哇(我)就再不向里(你)要沙(啥)东西啰。"

"哇(我)说里滚(你滚)! 里(你)的钱不百里(许你)动一分去买啥个枪! 哇(我)要霍金斯先申(生)把里(你)的工钱来交给哇(我)就是支(这)个道利(理),哇(我)晓得你不通(懂)事。"

"可是,妈,哇(我)们家里要有一把枪。爸姆(没)有枪。哇(我)们屋里要有把枪。说不停(定)会发生啥个事情哪。"

"哦,不要胡哇(唤我),孩儿! 哇(我)们就是又(有)枪,你也别想要!"

他放下广告册,轻轻地抱住母亲的腰。

"噢,妈! 哇(我)卖力干活干了正正(整整)一个夏天,姆(没)有向里(你)要过啥东西,是吗,嗯?"

"这样你就想要啥个枪啦?"

"可是妈,哇(我)就是要。里(你)就浪(让)哇(我)从哇(我)的工钱里拿两块吧。求求啦,妈,哇(我)会把枪给爸……求求啦,妈! 哇(我)爱里(你)妈。"

他母亲说话的声音变得温和了。

"你要枪干啥哪,大福? 你用不着枪的。有了枪,你会闯祸的。要是爸知道是哇浪(我让)你拿钱买枪,他会法(发)脾气的。"

"哇(我)会把枪藏号(好),妈,一把枪支(只)要两块钱嘛。"

"天哪,孩子,你出了啥事情?"

"哇(我)啥事也姆(没)出。妈,哇(我)现在差不多是大人了,哇(我)想要把枪。"

"谁跟(肯)把枪卖给你?"

"那点(店)里的老乔。"

"枪支(只)要两块钱就能买?"

"支(只)要两块,妈,两块够啦,求求里(你),妈。"

他母亲把碟子摞到一边,慢慢垂下双手,默默地思索起来。大福一声不响,焦急地等着。最后,她转脸看着他。

"你要是答应哇(我)一件事,哇(我)就浪里(让你)买枪。"

"答应啥,妈?"

"你买了枪就拿回家给哇(我),你听见吗? 枪是买给爸的。"

"唔! 哇(我)现在就去吧,妈。"

"Git outta here! Don yuh talk t me bout no gun! Yuh a fool!"

"Ma, Ah kin buy one fer two dollahs."

"Not ef Ah knows it, yuh ain!"

"But yuh promised me one—"

"Ah don care whut Ah promisedl Yuh ain nothing but a boy yit!"

"Ma, ef yuh lemme buy one Ah'll *never* ast yuh fer nothing no mo."

"Ah tol yuh t git outta here! Yuh ain gonna toucha penny of tha money fer no gun! Thas how come Ah has Mistah Hawkins t pay yo wages t me, cause Ah knows yuh ain got no sense."

"But, Ma, we needa gun. Pa ain got no gun. We needa gun in the house. Yuh kin never tell whut might happen."

"Now don yuh try to maka fool outta me, boy! Ef we did hava gun, yuh wouldn't have it!"

He laid the catalogue down and slipped his arm around her waist.

"Aw, Ma, Ah done worked hard alla summer n ain ast yuh fer nothin, is Ah, now?"

"Thas whut yuh spose t do!"

"But Ma, Ah wans a gun. Yuh kin lemme have two dollahs outta mah money. Please, Ma. I kin give it to Pa. . . Please, Ma! Ah loves yuh, Ma."

When she spoke her voice came soft and low.

"What yu wan wida gun, Dave? Yuh don need no gun. Yuh'll git in trouble. N ef yo pa jus thought Ah let yuh have money t buy a gun he'd hava fit."

"Ah'll hide it, Ma. It ain but two dollahs."

"Lawd, chil, whut's wrong wid yuh?"

"Ain nothin wrong, Ma. Ahm almos a man now. Ah wans a gun."

"Who gonna sell yuh a gun?"

"Ol Joe at the sto."

"N it don cos but two dollahs?"

"Thas all, Ma. Jus two dollahs. Please, Ma."

She was stacking the plates away; her hands moved slowly, reflectively. Dave kept an anxious silence. Finally, she turned to him.

"Ah'll let yuh git tha gun ef yuh promise me one thing."

"Whut's tha, Ma?"

"Yuh bring it straight back t me, yuh hear? It be fer Pa."

"Yessum! Lemme go now, Ma."

她弯下腰，稍稍侧着身子，掀起裙子下摆，把一只长统袜往下卷一点，拿出一小叠钞票，又站直身子。

"给，"她说，"天晓得，你真的需要枪。说你爸倒真是需要的。你把枪买来就交给哇（我），你听见吗？哇（我）可就把它藏号（好）的。你要是不听哇（我）的话，哇（我）就要你爸爸红红（狠狠）揍你，浪（让）你亡（忘）不了。"

"唔。"

他拿了钱，跑下台阶，穿过院子。

"大福！你——你——大——福——"

他听见母亲在喊，但是他现在不会停步了。快去，啊！

第二天清早，他一睁眼就伸手到枕头下去摸枪。在熹微的晨光里轻轻地握着那枪，心里觉得自己很威严。有了这样一支枪他就能杀死一个人。杀死任何人，无论是黑人还是白人。再说他手里拿着一支枪，谁也就不敢欺侮他了，人们只得尊敬他。这是老大的一把枪，长长的枪筒，沉甸甸的枪柄。他拿着枪，举起来，又放下去，这把枪竟有这么重，他心里惊叹不已。

他没有听从母亲的吩咐把枪直接带回家里，而是拿着枪待在田野里，时不时地举枪瞄准某个想象中的仇敌。不过，他没有开枪，因为他一直怕父亲会听见枪声。况且，他还弄不清楚枪是怎样开的哩。

为了不交出手枪，他只能在吃准家里人都已睡觉之后才进家门。深夜里，母亲蹑手蹑脚走到他的床前，向他要枪，他起先装睡，支支吾吾，接着又说藏在门外了，早晨一定给她。现在，他把枪慢慢地从一只手里移到另一只手里。他把枪拆开，取出子弹，用手摸摸，然后又装进去。

他轻轻下床，从皮箱里找出一块长长的旧绒布，把枪裹好，然后把它贴肉紧紧缚在大腿上，枪里就那么装着子弹。他没有到厨房吃早饭。他一径出门上吉姆·霍金斯的种植园去，虽然天还未大亮。而当日头初露时，他已走进了拴着骡子、放着犁、锄的牲口棚了。

"嗨！是你，大福？"

他转过身。吉姆·霍金斯摸不着头脑了，直往他瞧。

She stooped, turned slightly to one side raised the hem of her dress, rolled down the top of her stocking, and came up with a slender wad of bills.

"Here,"she said. "Lawd knows yuh don need no gun. But yer pa does. Yuh bring it right back t me,yuh hear? Ahma put it up. Now ef yuh don, Ahma have yuh pa lick yuh so hard yuh won fergit it. "

"Yessum. "

He took the money, ran down the steps, and across the yard.

"Dave! Yuuuuuh Daaaaave!"

He heard, but he was not going to stop now. "Naw,Lawd!"

The first movement he made the following morning was to reach under his pillow for the gun. In the gray light of dawn he held it loosely,feeling a sense of power. Could kill a man with a gun like this. Kill anybody, black or white. And if he were holding his gun in his hand, nobody could run over him; they would have to respect him. It was a big gun,with a long barrel and a heavy handle. He raised and lowered it in his hand, marveling at its weight.

He had not come straight home with it as his mother had asked; instead he had stayed out in the fields, holding the weapon in his hand, aiming it now and then at some imaginary foe. But he had not fired it;he had been afraid that his father might hear. Also he was not sure he knew how to fire it.

To avoid surrendering the pistol he had not come into the house until he knew that they were all asleep. When his mother had tiptoed to his bedside late that night and demanded the gun, he had first played possum; then he had told her that the gun was hidden outdoors, that he would bring it to her in the morning. Now he lay turning it slowly in his hands. He broke it, took out the cartridges, felt them, and then put them back.

He slid out of bed,got a long strip of old flannel from a trunk wrapped the gun in it,and tied it to his naked thigh while it was still loaded. He did not go in to breakfast. Even though it was not yet daylight, he started for Jim Hawkins' plantation. Just as the sun was rising he reached the barns where the mules and plows were kept.

"Hey! That you,Dave?"

He turned. Jim Hawkins stood eying him suspiciously.

"你这么早来干什么?"

"哇(我)也不知道会起得这么早,霍金斯先申(生),哇(我)要套詹尼,拿(拉)它下地。"

"好啊,你来得这么早,看来可以一直犁到树林的那边上啰?"

"西(行)啊,霍金斯先申(生)。"

"好吧,这就去吧!"

大福给詹尼套上了犁,朝田野那边走去。好哇!这正是他求之不得的事。只要他到了树林旁边,就可以试试自己的枪了,在那里试是没人会听见枪声的。他跟在犁后面,听着缰绳嘎吱嘎吱的声音,伸手摸摸紧缚在大腿上的枪。

到了树林边上,他先犁了两畦地,随后决定把枪拿出来。终于,他站定了,向四面望了望,便解下枪,握在手里。他转过脸来看看那头骡子,笑笑。

"詹尼,里(你)知道这是个啥,里(你)不会知道的!里(你)只是头老骡子啊!不过,这是一把枪哪,还能打哩,老天牙(爷)!"

他拿着枪,手臂伸直。他妈的,哇(我)就打这东西?他又朝詹尼看看。

"听好啦,詹尼!哇(我)在扣这扳机时,哇克(我可)不要里(你)跑,不要装傻,听着!"

詹尼垂头站着,两只短耳朵竖得笔直。大福走到离它大约20英尺远的地方,伸直手臂让手里的枪远远离开自己,还把头背过去。妈的,他自言自语说,哇(我)怕着呢。他无力地握着枪,又发疯似的把枪摇了一阵子。随后他闭上眼睛,食指向后扳紧。叭!一声枪响,差点把他震昏,他觉得右手好像从手臂上断了下来。他听见詹尼在哀声叫唤,在田野上狂奔,他这才知道自己正跪在地上,手指紧夹在两腿之间。他的手已经麻木,他把它塞进嘴里,想焐焐它,止止痛。枪已掉在他脚边。他还不明白究竟发生了什么事。他站起来,眼睛呆呆地看着那把枪,好像在看一件活的东西。他咬咬牙!踢踢枪。就是里(你)差一点儿把哇(我)的手臂弄断!他回头去找詹尼,詹尼正远远地在田野那边,正晃着脑袋,还发狂地乱踢蹄子。

"占(站)住啦,老骡!"

他跑到骡子旁边,骡子浑身打颤,对着他直翻大白眼。犁子已丢得老远,缰绳也扯断了。这对大福忽然慌了,看着,简直不敢相信。詹尼正在流血。它左边的身体已一片殷红,鲜血淋漓。他走近一点。老天

"What're yuh doing here so early?"

"Ah didn't know Ah wuz gittin up so early, Mistah Hawkins. Ah wuz fixin t hitch up ol Jenny n take her t the fiels."

"Good. Since you're so early, how about plowing-that stretch down by the woods?"

"Suits me, Mistah Hawkins."

"O. K. Go to it!"

He hitched Jenny to a plow and started across the fields. Hot dog! This was just what he wanted. If he could get down by the woods, he could shoot his gun and nobody would hear. He walked behind the plow, hearing the traces creaking, feeling the gun tied tight to his thigh.

When he reached the woods, he plowed two whole rows before he decided to take out the gun. Finally, he stopped, looked in all directions, then untied the gun and held it in his hand. He turned to the mule and smiled.

"Know what this is, Jenny? Naw, yuh wouldn know! Yuhs jusa ol mule! Anyhow, this is a gin, n it kin shoot, by Gawd!"

He held the gun at arm's length. Whut t hell, Ahma shoot this thing! He looked at Jenny again.

"Lissen here, Jenny! When Ah pull this ol trigger, Ah don wan yuh t run n acka fool now!"

Jenny stood with head down, her short ears pricked straight. Dave walked off about twenty feet, held the gun far out from him at arm's length, and turned his head. Hell, he told himself, Ah ain afraid. The gun felt loose in his fingers; he waved it wildly for a moment. Then he shut his eyes and tightened his forefinger. Bloom! A report half deafened him and he thought his right hand was torn from his arm. He heard Jenny whinnying and galloping over the field, and he found himself on his knees, squeezing his fingers hard between his legs. His hand was numb; he jammed it into his mouth, trying to warm it, trying to stop the pain. The gun lay at his feet. He did not quite know what had happened. He stood up and stared at the gun as though it were a living thing. He gritted his teeth and kicked the gun. Yuh almos broke mah arm! He turned to look for Jenny; she was far over the fields, tossing her head and kicking wildly.

"Hol on there, ol mule!"

When he caught up with her she stood trembling, walling her big white eyes at him. The plow was far

牙(爷)，发发慈悲吧！支(这)是哇(我)打了这骡子？他抓住詹尼的鬃毛。骡子退缩着，哼着，挣扎着，不停地摇着脑袋。

"占(站)住啦！占(站)住！"

这时，他看见了詹尼身上的洞正在肋骨之间。洞圆圆的，血淋淋的，殷红殷红。一股暗红的血流顺着前腿直往下淌，流个不停。老天牙(爷)！哇(我)姆(没)对这头骡子打枪哪。他心慌意乱。他知道必须把血止住，否则詹尼会流血而死的。他有生以来还未见过这么多血。他跑了半英里路追赶着骡子，想把它逮住。最后，它自己停下了，气喘吁吁，短粗的尾巴稍稍翘起。他抓住鬃毛，把它拉到丢着犁子和枪的地方。随后他俯身抓起一把潮湿的黑土，设法塞住那个弹孔。詹尼浑身抖颤，哀号不止，接着又挣扎着从他身边跑开了。

"占(站)住！占(站)住哪！"

他再想把那弹孔塞住，但是血总是流个不停，他的手指头倒又热又粘了。他把干土放在手掌里搓着，想把手指头弄干。随后，他又试着去塞那个弹孔，但是詹尼闪开了，还乱蹦乱跳。他束手无策。他又不能不管。他跑到詹尼身边，它又躲开。他看见一道血流顺着詹尼的腿淌下来，在蹄子周围汇成红红的一大摊。

"詹尼……詹尼……"他有气无力地叫唤着。

他嘴唇发抖，骡子会流血死的！他望望自己家所在的方向，想回去，求别人来帮忙。但是他又看见了那把丢在湿漉漉的黑泥地上的手枪。他产生了一种古怪的感觉。要是他当初只把手枪弄着玩而不打，情况也就不会这样了，詹尼也就不会在那里流着血等死了。

他又一次走到詹尼身边时，骡子没有动。它站着，眼睛里透出矇眬而混沌的目光，他用手摸摸它，它发出一声哀切的低鸣，跪倒在地上，两只前膝支在血污里。

"詹尼……詹尼……"他低声叫着。

它撑起脖子坚持了好一会儿。接着便慢慢地垂下了脑袋。它的肋部一起一伏，呼吸艰难，一会儿就死了。

大福觉得肚里一阵虚慌，非常虚慌。他拾起枪，用大拇指和食指战兢兢地拈着。他把枪埋在一棵树底下。他用一根树枝拨着土，想把地上的那摊血用土

away; the traces had broken. Then dave stopped short, looking, not believing. Jenny was bleeding. Her left side was red and wet with blood. He went closer. Lawd, have mercy! Wondah did Ah shoot this mule? He grabbed for Jenny's mane. She flinched, snorted, whirled, tossing her head.

"Hol on now! Hol on. "

Then he saw the hole in Jenny's side, right between the ribs. It was round, wet, red. A crimson stream streaked down the front leg, flowing fast. Good Gawd! Ah wuzn't shootin at tha mule. He felt panic. He knew he had to stop that blood, or Jenny would bleed to death. He had never seen so much blood in all his life. He chased the mule for half a mile trying to catch her. Finally she stopped, breathing hard, stumpy tail half arched. He caught her mane and led her back to where the plough and gun lay. Then he stooped and grabbed handfuls of damp black earth and tried to plug the bullet hole. Jenny shuddcred, whinnied, and broke from him.

"Hol on! Hol on now!"

He tried to plug it again, but blood came anyhow. His fingers were hot and sticky. He rubbed dirt into his palms, trying to dry them. Then again he attempted to plug the bullet hole, but Jenny shied away, kicking her heels high. He stood helpless. He had to do something. He ran at Jenny; she dodged him. He watched a red stream of blood flow down Jenny's leg and form a bright pool at her feet.

"Jenny... Jenny," he called weakly.

His lips trembled. She's bleedingt death! He looked in the direction of home, wanting to go back, wanting to get help. But he saw the pistol lying in the damp black clay. He had a queer feeling that if he only did something, this would not be; Jenny would not be there bleeding to death.

When he went to her this time, she did not move. She stood with sleepy, dreamy eyes; and when he touched her she gave a low-pitched whinny and knelt to the gound, her front knees slopping in blood.

"Jenny... Jenny... "he whispered.

For a long time she held her neck erect; then her head sank, slowly. Her ribs swelled with a mighty heave and she went over.

Dave's stomach felt empty, very empty. He picked up the gun and held it gingerly between his thumb and forefinger. He buried it at the foot of a tree. He took a

盖住——但是这又有什么用呢？詹尼就躺在那里，张着嘴，眼睛失神地睁着。他不能告诉吉姆·霍金斯说自己开枪打死了詹尼。但是他又不能什么也不说呀。唔，哇（我）对大（他）们说詹尼发红（疯）了，跌倒在犁口上……仅是，骡子是不会发生这种事的。他低下头，慢慢穿过他犁过的那块地。

　　黄昏时分，吉姆·霍金斯家的两个长工就在那片树林旁边挖了一个大坑，准备埋葬詹尼。大福给一小群人围着，这些人全都低头看着地上的死骡子。

　　"我真不明白，世界上怎么会有这种事。"吉姆·霍金斯已经这样说了十遍。

　　人群分开了，大福的父亲、母亲和弟弟挤到了中央。

　　"大福在哪儿？"他母亲喊着。

　　"在这儿。"吉姆·霍金斯说。

　　他母亲一把抓住他。

　　"出了啥事，大福？你干了啥？"

　　"没啥。"

　　"过来，孩子，说吧。"他父亲说。

　　大福深深吸了一口气，编了个他自己也知道谁也不会相信的故事。

　　"嗯——"他慢吞吞地说，"哇（我）把那詹尼强（牵）到这儿，哇（我）就犁地。里（你）们看吧，哇（我）犁了又（有）两弄（垄）。"他顿了一下，指指那两垄长长的翻过的地，"后来那詹尼不知出了啥个毛病。它就是不听支欢（使唤）。它碰（喷）鼻子，特（踢）蹄子。哇（我）想拿（拉）住它，可它强（挣）开了，还碰（蹦）起来。它把犁尖子凶（掀）得老高，这时它又团团跑，身子一窝（歪）碰在犁尖上……它自个碰的，血就搂（流）出来。哇（我）啥个办法都想啦，姆（没）用的。它死啰。"

　　"有谁出生以来听说过这样的事吗？"吉姆·霍金斯问。

　　人群里有白人也有黑人。他们叽叽咕咕地咬耳朵。大福的母亲走到他身边，打量着他的面孔。"说实话，大福！"她说。

　　"骡子身上好像有个子弹洞。"有人说。

　　"大福，你弄（用）枪干啥啦？"她母亲问。

　　人群骚动起来，大伙都看着他。他把双手插进裤袋，脑袋慢慢地左右摆动，一面向后退。他的眼睛睁得老大，充满痛苦。

stick and tried to cover the pool of blood with dirt— but what was the use? There was Jenny lying with her mouth open and her eyes walled and glassy. He could not tell Jim Hawkins he had shot his mule. But he had to tell something. Yeah, Ah'll tell em Jenny started gitting wil n fell on the joint of the plow.... But that would hardly happen to a mule. He walked across the field slowly, head down.

　　It was sunset. Two of Jim Hawkins' men were o-ver near the edge of the woods digging a hole in which to bury Jenny. Dave was surrounded by a knot of peo-ple, all of whom were looking down at the dead mule.

　　"I don't see how in the world it happened," said-Jim Hawkins for the tenth time.

　　The crowd parted and Dave's mother, father, and small brother pushed into the center.

　　"Where Dave?" his mother called.

　　"There he is," said Jim Hawkins.

　　His mother grabbed him.

　　"Whut happened, Dave? Whut yuh done?"

　　"Nothin. "

　　"C mon, boy, talk," his father said.

　　Dave took a deep breath and told the story he knew nobody believed.

　　"Waal," he drawled. "Ah brung ol Jenny down here sos Ah could do mah plowin. Ah plowed bout two rows, just like yu see. "He stopped and pointed at the long rows of upturned earth. "Then somethin musta been wrong wid ol Jenny. She wouldn ack right a-tall. She started snortin n kickin her heels. Ah tried t hol her, but she pulled erway, rearin n goin in. Then when the point of the plow was stickin up in the air, she swung erroun n twisted herself back on it... She stuck herself n started t bleed. N fo Ah could do anything, she wuz dead. "

　　"Did you ever hear of anything like that in all your life?" asked Jim Hawkins.

　　There were white and black standing in the crowd. They murmured. Dave's mother came close to him and looked hard into his face. "Tell the truth, Dave," she said.

　　"Looks like a bullet hole to me," said one man.

　　"Dave, whut yuh do wid the gun?" his mother asked.

　　The crowd surged in, looking at him. He jammed his hands into his pockets, shook his head slowly from left to right, and backed away. His eyes were wide and

"他有枪?"吉姆·霍金斯问。

"老天牙(爷)在上,哇(我)对里(你)说,那是枪打的。"有人说,边说还边拍着屁股。

他父亲抓住他的双肩,拼命地摇他,摇得他牙齿咯咯响。

"说,出了啥事,里(你)这混蛋! 说啥个……"

大福望着詹尼僵直的长腿,哭了。

"你弄(用)那枪干啥啦?"他母亲又问。

"他咋会有枪的?"他父亲问。

"讲吧,老实讲,"霍金斯说,"不用怕,讲了也不要紧……"

他母亲紧挨着他。

"是你开枪打了骡子,大福?"

大福还是哭,他看到周围的那些白人和黑人的脸全都变得模糊不清了。

"哇(我),哇(我)不——是想——打它……哇(我)对——老天牙(爷)保——证,哇哇(我我)不……哇(我)支(只)试试看,那个枪——管不管打——"

"里(你)枪从拉(哪)来的?"他父亲问。

"哇(我)从乔那儿,那点(店)里弄的。"

"里(你)那钱拉(哪)来的?"

"妈给哇(我)呗。"

"他老是缠着哇(我),鲍勃。哇姆(我没)法,哇(我)交(叫)他把枪就拿回家克哇(给我)……那是克里(给你)买的,那枪。"

"可你怎么去打那头骡子了呢?"吉姆·霍金斯问。

"哇(我)不是要打骡子,霍金斯先申(生),哇(我)扣那扳机,那枪跳了……詹尼在那流血,哇(我)一点儿不吃(知)道。"

有人在人群里哈哈大笑。吉姆·霍金斯走到大福旁边,看看他的脸。

"唔,大福,看来你得赔头骡子啰。"

"哇(我)对老天牙(爷)保证,哇(我)不想打死那骡子,霍金斯先申(生)!"

"可你已经把它打死啦!"

这时人群里所有的人都咯咯地发笑起来。他们都踮着脚,从别人的肩膀上探出头来。

"得啦,小子,看来你就赔了这头死骡子吧! 哈哈!"

"不要巴休(怕羞)哪。"

painful.

"Did he hava gun?"asked Jim Hawkins.

"By Gawd, Ah tol yuh tha wuz a gun wound," said a man, slapping his thigh.

His father caught his shoulders and shook him till his teeth rattled.

"Tell whut happened, yuh rascal! Tell whut…"

Dave looked at Jenny's stiff legs and began to cry.

"Whut yuh do wid tha gun?"his mother asked.

"Whut wuz he doin wida gun?"his father asked.

"Come on and tell the truth," said Hawkins. "Ain't nobody going to hurt you…"

His mother crowded close to him.

"Did yuh shoot the mule, Dave?"

Dave cried, seeing blurred white and black faces.

"Ahh ddinn gggo tt sshooot hher… Ah ssswear ffo Gawd Ah ddin…. Ah wuz a-tryin t sssee ef the old gggun would sshoot—"

"Where yuh get the gun from?"his father asked.

"Ah got it from Joe, at the sto. "

"Where yuh git the money?"

"Ma give it t me. "

"He kept worryin me, Bob. Ah had t. Ah tol im t bring the gun right back tme… It was fer yug, the gun. "

"But how yuh happen to shoot that mule?"asked Jim Hawkins.

"Ah wuzn shootin at the mule, Mistah Hawkins. The gun jumped when Ah pulled the trigger… N fo Ah knowed anythin Jenny was there a-bleedin. "

Somebody in the crowd laughed. Jim Hawkins walked close to Dave and looked into his face.

"Well, looks like you have bought you a mule, Dave. "

"Ah swear fo Gawd, Ah didn go t kill the mule, Mistah Hawkins!"

"But you killed her!"

All the crowd was laughing now. They stood on tiptoe and poked heads over one another's shoulders.

"Well, boy, looks like yuh done bought a dead mule! Hahaha!"

"Ain tha ershame. "

"Hohohohoho. "

Dave stood, head down, twisting his feet in the dirt.

"Well, you needn't worry about it, Bob, "said Jim

"呵、呵、呵、呵。"

大福站在那儿,低着头,两只脚在泥地里碾着。

"好啦,不要为这事操什么心了,鲍勃。"吉姆·霍金斯对大福的父亲说,"让这孩子继续干活,每月付我两块钱就得了。"

"配(赔)里(你)的骡子得多少钱?霍金斯先申(先)?"

吉姆·霍金斯眯起眼睛。

"50 块钱。"

"里(你)把那枪咋个办啦?"大福父亲厉声问。

大福不作声。

"里(你)是要哇(我)去拔棵树来打得里(你)讲!"

"不、不!"

"里(你)枪咋办啦?"

"哇(我)把它扔了。"

"哪里?"

"哇(我)……哇(我)把它扔到小河里了。"

"好吧,回家去。明糟(早)天一亮去那条河里把枪糟(找)来。"

"是啰。"

"买枪花多少钱?"

"两块。"

"把枪找来,把钱弄回来,交给霍金斯先申(生),听见吗?还友(有)要是亡(忘)了,哇(我)揍你个稀烂!自各(个)儿回家去吧,记住!"

大福转过身慢慢地走了。他听见人们咯咯地笑。大福瞪瞪眼睛,眼里还噙着泪水。他怒火满腔。不过,他还是忍耐了,蹒跚地走了。

那天夜里大福没合眼。他既为自己竟能那样轻而易举就打死了骡子而感到高兴,又为此觉得伤心。但他一想起人们嘲笑他的那副样子心里就仿佛有股怒火在燃烧。他在床上翻来覆去,头搁在硬邦邦的枕头上。爸说还要打我哩……他想起过去曾遭受过的毒打,脊梁骨嗦嗦发抖。不西(行),哇(我)不要在(再)浪(让)他那样打哇(我)了。他们都开(该)死!没有人给过他什么东西。他所有的一切就是干活。他们对哇(我)就像对一支(只)骡子,还打哇(我)。他咬牙切齿。可妈会帮哇(我)说话的。

呵,他得把两块钱交给霍金斯老头,好像这是非要做不可了。但是这就意味着得把枪卖了。他却想要把枪留着。一头死骡得赔 50 块钱。

Hawkins to Dave's father. "Just let the boy keep on working and pay me two dollars a month. "

"Whut yuh wan fer yo mule, Mistah Hawkins?"

Jim Hawkins screwed up his eyes.

"Fifty dollars. "

"Whut yuh do wid tha gun?" Dave's father demanded.

Dave said nothing.

"Yuh wan me t take a tree n beat yuh till yuh talk!"

"Nawsuh!"

"Whut yuh do wid it?"

"Ah throwed it erway. "

"Where?"

"Ah. . . Ah throwed it in the creek. "

"Waal, c mon home. N firs thing in the mawnin git to tha creek n fin tha gun. "

"Yessuh. "

"Whut yuh pay fer it?"

"Two dollahs. "

"Take tha gun n git yo money back n carry it t Mistah Hawkins, yuh hear? N don fergit Ahma lam you black bottom good fer this! Now march yosef on home, suh!"

Dave turned and walked slowly. He heard people laughing. Dave glared, his eyes welling with tears. Hot anger bubbled in him. Then he swallowed and stumbled on.

That night Dave did not sleep. He was glad that he had gotten out of killing the mule so easily, but he was hurt. Something hot seemed to turn over inside him each time he remembered how they had laughed. He tossed on his bed, feeling his hard pillow. N Pa says he's gonna beat me. . . He remembered other beatings, and his back quivered. Naw, naw, Ah sho don wan im t beat me tha way no mo. Dam em all! Nobody ever gave him anything. All he did was work. They treat me like a mule, n then they beat me. He gritted his teeth. N Ma had to tell on me.

Well, if he had to, he would take old man Hawkins that two dollars. But that meant selling the gun. And he wanted to keep that gun. Fifty dollars for a dead mule.

He turned over, thinking how he had fired the gun. He had an itch to fire it again. Ef other men kin shoota gun, by Gawd, Ah kin! He was still, listening. Mebbe they all sleepin now. The house was still. He

他翻个身，想起自己白天打枪时的情景来。他多么想再打一次枪。别人克（可）以打枪，老天牙（爷）啊，哇（我）也克（可）以！他一动不动，侧耳倾听。他们大概全都睡着了吧。屋子里静悄悄的。他听见弟弟轻轻的呼吸声。是的，睡着了！他要去把枪取出来，看看自己究竟能不能打枪！他轻轻地下床，悄悄地套上了外衣。

月光很好。他一路上几乎一直在奔跑，一口气到了树林旁边。他在地上摸来摸去，找寻他埋枪的地方。嗯，枪在这儿。他像一只饿狗扑向骨头，急忙把枪刨了出来。他鼓动着黑面颊，把枪栓和枪筒上的尘土吹掉。他把枪拆开，发现里面还有 4 粒子弹。他向四周望望，枪捏在手里。然而，就在他想扣那扳机的当儿，他又闭上了眼睛，转过了头。不西（行），哇（我）不能闭着眼睛，掉转头打枪。他竭力睁开眼睛，随后扣动扳机。砰！他僵立着，屏着气。那枪依然在他手里。妈的，他会打枪啦！再打一枪。砰！他微笑。砰！砰！咔嗒，咔嗒。看吧！子弹都打完了。既然谁都能打枪，他当然也能。他把枪放进裤后的口袋里，朝田野那边走去。

他来到崖顶，在月光下，挺胸站在那儿，心里感到很自豪。他望着吉姆·霍金斯白色的大屋子，摸摸那把斜插在裤袋里的手枪。老天牙（爷），要是哇（我）在（再）有一粒子弹就号（好）啦。哇（我）要对那屋子打一枪。哇（我）要把那霍金斯老头吓一跳……哇（我）就要浪（让）他吃（知）道，哇（我）大福·桑德斯是个人啦。

在他左边，一条大路沿山盘旋，连通着伊利诺斯中部铁路线。他侧过头去，仔细倾听。只听见远远地传来一种微弱的声音：呼——夫，呼——夫，呼——夫……他毅然伫立。每个月还两块钱。浪哇（让我）看看……那是说得还上两年哪。呸！见鬼去吧！

他上了那条路，向铁路走去。唔，这儿就是，到啦！他站在轨道旁，站得笔直。这儿就是，到了，占（转）个弯……到啦！里（你）这懒猪罗！到啦！他一只手握住自己的枪，他肚子里有什么东西在翻腾。这时，火车隆隆驶来，那灰褐色的车厢辘辘而过，嚓嚓作响。他紧紧地握住枪，接着他把手抽出口袋。哇（我）不管什么狗屁账啦！哇（我）不管……车厢在一节一节闪过去，钢轮辗着铁轨。今天夜里哇（我）爬到里（你）上面啦，老天牙（爷）帮个忙！他浑身热血沸腾。

heard the soft breathing of his brother. Yes, now! He would go down and get that gun and see if he could fire it! He eased out of bed and slipped into overalls.

The moon was bright. He ran almost all the way to the edge of the woods. He stumbled over the ground, looking for the spot where he had buried the gun. Yeah, here it is. Like a hungry dog scratching for a bone, he pawed it up. He puffed his black cheeks and blew dirt from the trigger and barrel. He broke it and found four cartridges unshot. He looked around; the fields were filled with silence and moonlight. He clutched the gun stiff and hard in his fingers. But, as soon as he wanted to pull the trigger, he shut his eyes and turned his head. Naw, Ah can't shoot wid mah eyes closed n mah head turned. With effort he held his eyes open; then he squeezed. *Blooooom*! He was stiff not breathing. The gun was still in his hands. Dammit, he'd done it! He fired again. *Blooooom*! He smiled *Blooooom*! *Blooooom*! *Click, click*. There! It was empty. If anybody could shoot a gun, he could. He put the gun into his hip pocket and started across the fields.

When he reached the top of a ridge he stood straight and proud in the moonlight, looking at Jim Hawkins' big white house, feeling the gun sagging in his pocket. Lawd, ef Ah had just one mo bullet. Ah'd taka shot at tha house. Ah'd like t scare ol man Hawkins jusa little... Jusa enough t let im know Dave Saunders is a man.

To his left the road curved, running to the tracks of the Illinois Central. He jerked his head, listening. From far off came a faint *hoooof-hoooof*; *hoooof-hoooof*; *hoooof-hoooof*... He stood rigid. Two dollahs a mont. Less see now... The means it'll take bout two years. Shucks! Ah'll be dam!

He started down the road, toward the tracks. Yeah, here she comes! He stood beside the track and held himself stiffly. Here she comes, erroun the ben... C mon, yuh slow poke! C mon! He had his hand on his gun; something quivered in his stomach. Then the train thundered past, the gray and brown box cars rumbling and clinking. He gripped the gun tightly; then he jerked his hand out of his pocket. Ah betcha Bill wouldn't do it! Ah betcha... The cars slid past, steel grinding upon steel. Ahm ridin yuh ternight, so hep me Gawd! He was hot all over. He

他只迟疑了片刻,随即一纵身,攀住了一节车厢,翻上了车顶,平直地卧在上面。他摸摸手枪,枪还在那儿。抬头张望,那漫无尽头的钢轨在月光下闪闪发光,向前伸展,伸展,伸展到不知什么地方,而就在那地方,他将要成为一个人……

hesitated just a moment; then he grabbed, pulled atop of a car, and lay flat. He felt his pocket; the gun was still there. Ahead the long rails were glinting in the moonlight, stretching away, away to somewhere, somewhere where he could be a man. . .

讨　论　▪

　　像《阿拉比》《县城的医生》《杀手》和本书所选的其他一些作品一样,这篇小说所写的也是少年初熟,始涉世务时的情形。《阿拉比》和《县城的医生》着重写初恋,这篇小说则和《杀手》一样,提出了少年最初进入成年时期的某些更为普遍的问题。小说中虽然没有涉及性的问题,但是那手枪可以看作成年男子的某种标志。

　　从总的背景上看,很清楚,大福是大约50年前密西西比州一个种植园黑人佃户的儿子,完全明白自己的父亲不是一个真正的人,只是种植园主的一种工具而已。因此,从一个更为普遍意义上讲,他也为自己被别人和那些年长的雇工称为"小子"而感到屈辱。

　　他一旦有了手枪,就觉得力量倍增。他可以"杀死任何人,无论黑人还是白人"——潜在的动机就是这样表露出来的。白人是他下意识中的打击目标。小说结尾时,大福在爬上火车前,最后产生的幻想是要向种植园主霍金斯先生的白色大屋子开一枪。不,他自己对自己说,他并不想要打死他,而只是想吓他一下,"浪(让)他吃(知)道,哇(我)大福·桑德斯是个人啦。"——这样他下意识地感觉到自己已经最后找到了应该找到的生活目标。

　　As in "Araby", "The District Doctor", "The Killers" and other stories in this collection, the subject here is growing up, initiation. "Araby" and "The District Doctor" are concerned with initiation into love, but this story, like "The Killers", deals with a youth's introduction into a more general kind of maturity. But here, though sex does not explicitly enter the story, the pistol may be taken as a mark of maturity and manhood.

　　It is clear from the general situation that Dave, the son of a black plantation tenant in Mississippi some half century ago, sees even his father as less than a man and finds his father a mere instrument of the plantation owner. And more generally speaking, he feels himself victimized as a mere "boy" by the other and older field hands.

　　Once he has the pistol he feels a surge of power. He can "kill anybody, black or white"—and so the hidden motive creeps out. The white man is his subconscious target. At the end of the story, before Dave catches the freight train, his last fantasy is to fire a shot at the big white house of Mr. Hawkins, the owner. No, not to hit him, he tells himself, only to scare him "jusa enough t let im know Dave Saunders is a man"—but he subconsciously knows he has at last found his logical target.

┌─ **思考题** ─■

1. 当大福带着枪跳上货车时，他是在驶向"自由"和独立生活呢，还是在驶向一种新的奴役？

2. 在掩埋骡子时，大福成了人群中其他雇工取笑的对象，这件事有何意义？这和小说的基本主题有何联系？其他雇工取笑他是出于什么动机？

3. 为什么大福自我解释说要是他可以向那所白色屋子打枪的话，他不会把霍金斯先生打死的？这种保留态度是出于何种心理动机？

4. 你对这篇小说的主题有何见解？

（刘家有 译）

1. When Dave hops the freight train with his pistol, is he riding toward "freedom" and maturity or toward a new kind of bondage?

2. While the mule is being buried, Dave is made the butt of the jokes of other field hands in the crowd. What is the significance of this? How does this relate to the basic theme of the story? What is the motive behind the jokes of the other hands?

3. Why does Dave explain to himself that if he could fire at the white house he wouldn't really want to hit Mr. Hawkins? What is the impulse behind this reservation?

4. How do you define the theme of this story?

026. 纪念爱米丽的一朵玫瑰花

(美)威廉·福克纳 著　　杨岂深 译

026. A Rose for Emily

by William Faulkner

一

　　爱米丽·格里尔生小姐过世了,全镇的人都去送丧。男子们是出于敬慕之情,因为一个纪念碑倒下了。妇女们呢,则大多数出于好奇心,想看看她屋子的内部。除了一个花匠兼厨师的老仆人之外,至少已有 10 年光景谁也没进去看看这幢房子了。

　　那是一幢过去漆成白色的四方形大木屋,座落在当年一条最考究的街道上,还装点着 19 世纪 70 年代风味的圆形屋顶、尖塔和涡形花纹的阳台,带有浓厚的轻盈气息。可是汽车间和轧棉机之类的东西侵犯了这一带庄严的名字,把它们涂抹得一干二净。只有爱米丽小姐的屋子岿然独存,四周簇拥着棉花车和汽油泵。房子虽已破败,却还是执拗不驯,装模作样,真是丑中之丑。现在爱米丽小姐已经加入了那些名字庄严的代表人物的行列,他们沉睡在雪松环绕的墓园之中,那里尽是一排排在南北战争时期杰斐逊战役中阵亡的南方和北方的无名军人墓。

　　爱米丽小姐在世时,始终是一个传统的化身,是义务的象征,也是人们关注的对象。打 1894 年某日镇长沙多里斯上校——也就是他下了一道黑人妇女不系围裙不得上街的命令——豁免了她一切应纳的税款起,期限从她父亲去世之日开始,一直到她去世为止,这是全镇沿袭下来对她的一种义务。这也并非说爱米丽甘愿接受施舍,原来是沙多里斯上校编造了一大套无中生有的话,说是爱米丽的父亲曾经贷款给镇政府,因此,镇政府作为一种交易,宁愿以这种方式

I

　　WHEN Miss Emily Grierson died, our whole town went to her funeral: the men through a sort of respectful affection for a fallen monument, the women mostly out of curiosity to see the inside of her house, which no one save an old manservant—a combined gardener and cook—had seen in at least ten years.

　　It was a big, squarish frame house that had once been white, decorated with cupolas and spires and scrolled balconies in the heavily lightsome style of the seventies, set on what had once been our most select street. But garages and cotton gins had encroachea and obliterated even the august names of that neighborhood; only Miss Emily's house was left, lifting its stubborn and coquettish decay above the cotton wagons and the gasoline pumps—an eyesore among eyesores. And now Miss Emily had gone to join the representatives of those august names where they lay in the cedar-bemused cemetery among the ranked and anonymous graves of Union and Confederate soldiers who fell at the battle of Jefferson.

　　Alive, Miss Emily had been a tradition, a duty, and a care; a sort of hereditary obligation upon the town, dating from that day in 1894 when Colonel Sartoris, the mayor—he who fathered the edict that no Negro woman should appear on the streets without an apron—remitted her taxes, the dispensation dating from the death of her father on into perpetuity. Not that Miss Emily would have accepted charity. Colonel Sartoris invented an involved tale to the effect that Miss Emily's father had loaned money to the town, which the town, as a matter of business, preferred this

作者简介:威廉·福克纳(**William Faulkner**,1897—1962),美国作家。1897 年 9 月 25 日生于密西西比州新奥尔巴尼,1962 年 7 月 6 日卒于密西西比州拜黑利亚。他高中退学后,接受了短暂的大学教育。他以一系列以约克纳帕塔法郡为背景的作品闻名,约克纳帕塔法郡成为美国南部和其悲剧历史的象征。他的首部重要作品《喧哗与骚动》(*The Sound and the Fury*,1929)以其对写作技巧的实验性探索闻名,如意识流。《袖珍本福克纳选集》(*The Portable Faulkner*,1946)最终使他的作品广泛流行。1949 年,他获得诺贝尔文学奖。他的《短篇小说集》(*Collected Stories*,1950)获得美国国家图书奖。在本国和海外,特别是拉丁美洲,他都是 20 世纪最有影响力作家之一。

偿还。这一套话，只有沙多里斯一代的人以及像沙多里斯一样头脑的人才能编得出来，也只有妇道人家才会相信。

等到思想更为开明的第二代人当了镇长和参议员时，这项安排引起了一些小小的不满。那年元旦，他们便给她寄去了一张纳税通知单。2 月份到了，还是杳无音信。他们发去一封公函，要她方便时到司法长官办公处去一趟。一周之后，镇长亲自写信给爱米丽，表示愿意登门访问，或派车迎接她，而所得回信却是一张便条，写在古色古香的信笺上，书法流利，字迹细小，但墨水已不鲜艳，信的大意是说她已根本不外出。纳税通知附还，没有表示意见。

参议员们开了个特别会议，派出一个代表团对她进行了访问。他们敲敲门，自从 8 年或者 10 年前她停止开授瓷器彩绘课以来，谁也没有从这大门出入过。那个上了年纪的黑人男仆把他们接待进阴暗的门厅，从那里再由楼梯上去，光线就更暗了。一股尘封的气味扑鼻而来，空气阴湿而又不透气，这屋子长久没有人住过。黑人领他们到客厅里，里面摆设的笨重家具全都包着皮套子。黑人打开了一扇百叶窗，这时，便更可看出皮套子已经开裂。等他们坐了下来，大腿两边就有一阵灰尘冉冉上升，尘粒在那一缕阳光中缓缓旋转。壁炉前已经失去金色光泽的画架上面放着爱米丽父亲的炭笔画像。

她一进屋，他们全都站了起来。一个小模小样、腰圆体胖的女人，穿了一身黑衣，一条细细的金表链拖到腰部，落到腰带里去了，一根乌木拐杖支撑着她的身体，拐杖头的镶金已经失去光泽。她的身架矮小，也许正因为这个缘故，在别的女人身上显得不过是丰满，而她却给人以肥大的感觉。她看上去像长久泡在死水中的一具死尸，肿胀发白。当客人说明来意时，她那双凹陷在一脸隆起的肥肉之中，活像揉在一团生面中的两个小煤球似的眼睛不住地移动着，时而瞧瞧这张面孔，时而打量那张面孔。

她没有请他们坐下来。她只是站在门口，静静地听着，直到发言的代表结结巴巴地说完，他们这时才听到那块隐在金链子那一端的挂表嘀嗒作响。

她的声调冷酷无情。"我在杰斐逊无税可纳。沙多里斯上校早就向我交代过了。或许你们有谁可以去查一查镇政府档案，就可以把事情弄清楚。"

"我们已经查过档案，爱米丽小姐，我们就是政府

way of repaying. Only a man of Colonel Sartoris' generation and thought could have invented it, and only a woman could have believed it.

When the next generation, with its more modern ideas, became mayors and aldermen, this arrangment created some little dissatisfaction. On the first of the year they mailed her a tax notice. February came, and there was no reply. They wrote her a formal letter, asking her to call at the sheriff's office at her convenience. A week later the mayor wrote her himself, offering to call or to send his car for her, and received in reply a note on paper of all archaic shape, in a thin, flowing calligraphy in faded ink, to the effect that she no longer went out at all. The tax notice was also enclosed, without comment.

They called a special meeting of the Board of Aldermen. A deputation waited upon her, knocked at the door through which no visitor had passed since she ceased giving china-painting lessons eight or ten years earlier. They were admitted by the old Negro into a dim hall from which a stairway mounted into still more shadow. It smelled of dust and disuse—a close, dank smell. The Negro led them into the parlor. It was furnished in heavy, leather-covered furniture. When the Negro opened the blinds of one window, a faint dust rose sluggishly about their thighs, spinning with slow motes in the single sun-ray. On a tarnished gilt easel before the fireplace stood a crayon portrait of Miss Emily's father.

They rose when she entered—a small, fat woman in black, with a thin gold chain descending to her waist and vanishing into her belt, leaning on an ebony cane with a tarnished gold head. Her skeleton was small and spare; perhaps that was why what would have been merely plumpness in another was obesity in her. She looked bloated, like a body long submerged in motionless water, and of that pallid hue. Her eyes, lost in the fatty ridges of her face, looked like two small pieces of coal pressed into a lump of dough as they moved from one face to another while the visitors stated their errand.

She did not ask them to sit. She just stood in the door and listened quietly until the spokesman came to a stumbling halt. Then they could hear the invisible watch ticking at the end of the gold chain.

Her voice was dry and cold. "I have no taxes in Jefferson. Colonel Sartoris explained it to me. Perhaps one of you can gain access to the city records and satisfy yourselves."

"But we have. We are the city authorities, Miss Emily. Didn't you get a notice from the sheriff signed

当局。难道你没有收到过司法长官亲手签署的通知吗?"

"不错,我收到过一份通知,"爱米丽小姐说道,"也许他自封为司法长官……可是我在杰斐逊无税可交。"

"可是纳税册上并没有如此说明,你明白吧。我们应根据……"

"你们去找沙多里斯上校。我在杰斐逊无税可交。"

"可是,爱米丽小姐——"

"你们去找沙多里斯上校(沙多里斯上校死了将近10年了)。我在杰斐逊无税可纳。托比!"黑人应声而来。"把这些先生们请出去。"

二

她就这样把他们"连人带马"地打败了,正如30年前为了那股气味的事战胜了他们的父辈一样。那是她父亲死后两年,也就是在她的心上人——我们都相信一定会和她结婚的那个人——抛弃她不久的时候。父亲死后,她很少外出。心上人离去之后,人们简直就看不到她了。有少数几位妇女竟冒冒失失地去访问过她,但都吃了闭门羹。她居处周围唯一的生命迹象就是那个黑人男子拎着一个篮子出出进进,当年他还是个青年。

"好像只要是一个男子,随便什么样的男子,都可以把厨房收拾得井井有条似的。"妇女们都这样说。因此,那种气味越来越厉害时,她们也不感到惊异。那是芸芸众生的世界与高贵有势的格里尔生家之间的另一联系。

邻家一位妇女向年已80的法官斯蒂芬斯镇长抱怨。

"可是太太,你叫我对这件事又有什么办法呢?"他说。

"哼,通知她把气味弄掉,"那位妇女说,"法律不是有明文规定吗?"

"我认为这倒不必,"法官斯蒂芬斯说."可能是她用的那个黑鬼在院子里打死了一条蛇或一只老鼠。我去跟他说说这件事。"

第二天,他又接到两起申诉,一起来自一个男的,

by him?"

"I received a paper, yes," Miss Emily said. "Perhaps he considers himself the sheriff... I have no taxes in Jefferson."

"But there is nothing on the books to show that, you see. We must go by the—"

"See Colonel Sartoris. I have no taxes in Jefferson."

"But, Miss Emily—"

"See Colonel Sartoris." (Colonel Sartoris had been dead almost ten years.) "I have no taxes in Jefferson. Tobe!" The Negro appeared. "Show these gentlemen out."

II

So she vanquished them, horse and foot, just as she had vanquished their fathers thirty years before about the smell. That was two years after her father's death and a short time after her sweetheart—the one we believed would marry her—had deserted her. After her father's death she went out very little; after her sweetheart went away, people hardly saw her at all. A few of the ladies had the temerity to call, but were not received, and the only sign of life about the place was the Negro man—a young man then—going in and out with a market basket.

"Just as if a man—any man—could keep a kitchen properly," the ladies said; so they were not surprised when the smell developed. It was another link between the gross, teeming world and the high and mighty Griersons.

A neighbor, a woman, complained to the mayor, Judge Stevens, eighty years old.

"But what will you have me do about it, madam?" he said.

"Why, send her word to stop it," the woman said. "Isn't there a law?"

"I'm sure that won't be necessary," Judge Stevens said. "It's probably just a snake or a rat that nigger of hers killed in the yard. I'll speak to him about it."

The next day he received two more complaints, one from a man who came in diffident deprecation. "We really must do something about it, Judge. I'd be the last one in the world to bother Miss Emily, but we've got to do something." That night the Board of Aldermen met—three graybeards and one younger man, a member of the rising generation.

"It's simple enough," he said. "Send her word to

用温和的语气提出意见。"法官,我们对这件事实在不能不过问了。我是最不愿意打扰爱米丽小姐的人,可是我们总得想个办法。"那天晚上全体参议员——3位老人和1位年纪较轻的新一代成员在一起开了个会。

"这件事很简单,"年轻人说,"通知她把屋子打扫干净,限期搞好,不然的话……"

"先生,这怎么行?"法官斯蒂芬斯说,"你能当着一位贵妇人的面说她那里有难闻的气味吗?"

于是,第二天午夜之后,有4个人穿过了爱米丽小姐家的草坪,像夜盗一样绕着屋子潜行,沿着墙角一带以及在地窖通风处拼命闻嗅,而其中一个人则用手从挎在肩上的袋子中掏出什么东西,不断做着播种的动作。他们打开了地窖门,在那里和所有的外屋里都撒上了石灰。等到他们回头又穿过草坪时,原来暗黑的一扇窗户亮起了灯,爱米丽小姐坐在那里,灯在她身后,她那挺直的身躯一动不动像是一尊偶像一样。他们蹑手蹑脚地走过草坪,进入街道两旁洋槐树树荫之中。一两个星期之后,气味就闻不到了。

而这时人们才开始真正为她感到难过。镇上的人想起爱米丽小姐的姑奶奶韦亚特老太太终于变成了十足疯子的事,都相信格里尔生一家人自视过高,不了解自己所处的地位。爱米丽小姐和像她一类的女子对什么年轻男子都看不上眼。长久以来,我们把这家人一直看作一幅画中的人物。身段苗条、穿着白衣的爱米丽小姐立在背后,她父亲叉开双脚的侧影在前面,背对爱米丽,手执一根马鞭,一扇向后开的前门恰好嵌住了他们俩的身影。因此当她年近30,尚未婚配时,我们实在没有喜幸的心理,只是觉得先前的看法得到了证实。即令她家有着疯癫的血液吧,如果真有一切机会摆在她面前,她也不至于断然放过。

父亲死后,传说留给她的全部财产就是那座房子。人们倒也有点感到高兴,到头来,他们可以对爱米丽表示怜悯之情。单身独处,贫苦无告,她变得懂人情了。如今她也体会到多一便士就激动喜悦、少一便士便痛苦失望的那种人皆有之的心情了。

她父亲死后的第二天,所有的妇女们都准备到她家拜望,表示哀悼和愿意接济的心意,这是我们的习俗。爱米丽小姐在家门口接待她们,衣着和平日一样,脸上没有一丝哀愁。她告诉她们,她的父亲并未死。一连3天她都是这样,不论是教会牧师访问她也

have her place cleaned up. Give her a certain time to do it in, and if she don't . . . "

"Dammit, sir," Judge Stevens said, "will you accuse a lady to her face of smelling bad?"

So the next night, after midnight, four men crossed Miss Emily's lawn and slunk about the house like burglars, sniffing along the base of the brickwork and at the cellar openings while one of them performed a regular sowing motion with his hand out of a sack slung from his shoulder. They broke open the cellar door and sprinkled lime there, and in all the outbuildings. As they recrossed the lawn, a window that had been dark was lighted and Miss Emily sat in it, the light behind her, and her upright torso motionless as that of an idol. They crept quietly across the lawn and into the shadow of the locusts that lined the street. After a week or two the smell went away.

That was when people had begun to feel really sorry for her. People in our town, remembering how old lady Wyatt, her great-aunt, had gone completely crazy at last, believed that the Griersons held themselves a little too high for what they really were. None of the young men were quite good enough for Miss Emily and such. We had long thought of them as a tableau; Miss Emily a slender figure in white in the background, her father a spraddled silhouette in the foreground, his back to her and clutching a horsewhip, the two of them framed by the back-flung front door. So when she got to be thirty and was still single, we were not pleased exactly, but vindicated; even with insanity in the family she wouldn't have turned down all of her chances if they had really materialized.

When her father died, it got about that the house was all that was left to her; and in a way, people were glad. At last they could pity Miss Emily. Being left alone, and a pauper, she had become humanized. Now she too would know the old thrill and the old despair of a penny more or less.

The day after his death all the ladies prepared to call at the house and offer condolence and aid, as is our custom. Miss Emily met them at the door, dressed as usual and with no trace of grief on her face. She told them that her father was not dead. She did that for three days, with the ministers calling on her, and the doctors, trying to persuade her to let them dispose of the body. Just as they were about to resort to law and force, she broke down, and they buried her father quickly.

We did not say she was crazy then. We believed she had to do that. We remembered all the young men

好,还是医生想劝她让他们把尸体处理掉也好。正当他们要诉诸法律和武力时,她垮下来了,于是他们很快地埋葬了她的父亲。

当时我们还没有说她发疯,我们相信她这样做是控制不了自己。我们还记得她父亲赶走了所有的青年男子,我们也知道她现在已经一无所有,只好像人们常常所估计的一样,死死拖住抢走了她一切的那个人。

三

她病了好长一个时期。再见到她时,她的头发已经剪短,看上去像个姑娘,和教堂里彩色玻璃窗上的天使像不无相似之处——有几分悲怆肃穆。

行政当局已订好合同,要铺设人行道,就在她父亲去世的那年夏天开始动工。建筑公司带着一批黑人、骡子和机器来了,工头是个北方佬,名叫荷默·伯隆,个子高大,皮肤黝黑,精明强干,声音洪亮,双眼比脸色浅淡。一群群孩子跟在他身后听他用不堪入耳的话责骂黑人,而黑人则随着铁镐的上下起落有节奏地哼着劳动号子。没有多少时候,全镇的人他都认识了。随便什么时候人们要是在广场上的什么地方听见哈哈大笑的声音,荷默·伯隆肯定是在人群的中心。过了不久,逢到礼拜天的下午我们就看到他和爱米丽小姐一齐驾着轻便马车出游了。那辆黄轮车配上从马房中挑出的栗色辕马,十分相称。

起初我们都高兴地看到爱米丽小姐多少有了一点寄托,因为妇女们都说:"格里尔生家的人绝对不会真的看中一个北方佬,一个拿日工资的人。"不过也有别人,一些年纪大的人说就是悲伤也不会叫一个真正高贵的妇女忘记"贵人举止",尽管口头上不把它叫作"贵人举止"。他们只是说:"可怜的爱米丽,她的亲属应该来到她的身边。"她有亲属在亚拉巴马,但多年以前,她的父亲为了疯婆子韦亚特老太太的产权问题跟他们闹翻了,以后两家就没有来往。他们连丧礼也没派人参加。

老人们一说到"可怜的爱米丽",就交头接耳开了。他们彼此说:"你当真认为是那么回事吗?""当然是啰。还能是别的什么事?……"而这句话他们是用手捂住嘴轻轻地说的,轻快的马蹄得得驶去的时候,

her father had driven away, and we knew that with nothing left, she would have to cling to that which had robbed her, as people will.

III

She was sick for a long time. When we saw here again, her hair was cut short, making her look like a girl, with a vague resemblance to those angels in colored church windows—sort of tragic and serene.

The town had just let the contracts for paving the sidewalks, and in the summer after her father's death they began to work. The construction company came with niggers and mules and machinery, and a foreman named Homer Barron, a Yankee—a big, dark, ready man, with a big voice and eyes lighter than his face. The little boys would follow in groups to hear him cuss the niggers, and the niggers singing in time to the rise and fall of picks. Pretty soon he knew everybody in town. Whenever you heard a lot of laughing anywhere about the square, Homer Barron would be in the center of the group. Presently we began to see him and Miss Emily on Sunday afternoons driving in the yellowwheeled buggy and the matched team of bays from the livery stable.

At first we were glad that Miss Emily would have an interest, because the ladies all said, "Of course a Grierson would not think seriously of a Northerner, a day laborer. "But there were still others, older people, who said that even grief could not cause a real lady to forget *noblesse oblige*—without calling it *noblesse oblige*. They just said, "Poor Emily. Her kinsfolk should come to her. "She had some kin in Alabama; but years ago her father had fallen out with them over the estate of old lady Wyatt, the crazy woman, and there was no communication between the two families. They had not even been represented at the funeral.

And as soon as the old people said, "Poor Emily," the whispering began. "Do you suppose it's really so?" they said to one another. "Of course it is. What else could. . . " This behind their hands; rustling of craned silk and satin behind jalousies closed upon the sun of Sunday afternoon as the thin, swift clop-clop-clop of the matched team passed; "Poor Emily. "

She carried her head high enough—even when we believed that she was fallen. It was as if she demanded more than ever the recognition of her dignity as the last Grierson; as if it had wanted that touch of earthiness

关上了遮挡星期日午后骄阳的百叶窗，还可听出绸缎的窸窣声，"可怜的爱米丽。"

她把头抬得高高——甚至当我们深信她已经堕落下的时候也是如此，仿佛她比历来都更要求人们承认她作为格里尔生家族末代人物的尊严，仿佛她的尊严就需要同世俗的接触来重新肯定她那不受任何影响的性格。比如说，她那次买老鼠药砒霜的情况。那是在人们已开始说"可怜的爱米丽"之后一年多，她的两个堂姐妹也正在那时来看望她。

"我要买点毒药。"她跟药剂师说。她当时已30出头，依然是个削肩细腰的女人，只是比往常更加清瘦了，一双黑眼冷酷高傲，脸上的肉在两边的太阳穴和眼窝处绷得很紧，那副面部表情是想象中的灯塔守望人所应有的。"我要买点毒药。"她说道。

"知道了，爱米丽小姐。要买哪一种？是毒老鼠之类的吗？那么我介——"

"我要你们店里最有效的毒药，种类我不管。"

药剂师一口说出好几种。"它们什么都毒得死，哪怕是大象。可是你要的是——"

"砒霜，"爱米丽小姐说，"砒霜灵不灵？"

"是……砒霜？知道了，小姐。可是你要的是……"

"我要的是砒霜。"

药剂师朝下望了她一眼。她回看他一眼，身子挺直，面孔像一面拉紧了的旗子。"噢噢，当然有，"药剂师说，"如果你要的是这种毒药。不过，法律规定你得说明做什么用途。"

爱米丽小姐只是瞪着他，头向后仰了仰，以便双眼好正视他的双眼，一直看到他把目光移开了，走进去拿砒霜包好。黑人送货员把那包药送出来给她，药剂师却没有再露面。她回家打开药包，盒子上骷髅骨标记下注明："毒鼠用药"。

四

于是，第二天我们大家都说："她要自杀了。"我们也都说这是再好没有的事。我们第一次看到她和荷默·伯隆在一块儿时，我们都说："她要嫁给他了。"后来又说："她还得说服他呢。"因为荷默自己说他喜欢和男人来往，大家知道他和年轻人在麇鹿俱乐部一道儿喝酒，他本人说过，他是无意于成家的人。以后每逢礼拜天下午他们乘着漂亮的轻便马车驰过，爱米丽

to reaffirm her imperviousness. Like when she bought the rat poison, the arsenic. That was over a year after they had begun to say "Poor Emily," and while the two female cousins were visiting her.

"I want some poison," she said to the druggist. She was over thirty then, still a slight woman, though thinner than usual, with cold, haughty black eyes in a face the flesh of which was strained across the temples and about the eyesockets as you imagine a lighthouse-keeper's face ought to look. "I want some poison," she said.

"Yes, Miss Emily. What kind? For rats and such? I'd recom—"

"I want the best you have. I don't care what kind."

The druggist named several. "They'll kill anything up to an elephant. But what you want is—"

"Arsenic," Miss Emily said. "Is that a good one?"

"Is... arsenic? Yes ma'am. But what you want—"

"I want arsenic."

The druggist looked down at her. She looked back at him, erect, her face like a strained flag. "Why, of course," the druggist said. "If that's what you want. But the law requires you to tell what you are going to use it for."

Miss Emily just stared at him, her head tilted back in order to look him eye for eye, until he looked away and went and got the arsenic and wrapped it up. The Negro delivery boy brought her the package; the druggist didn't come back. When she opened the package at home there was written on the box, under the skull and bones: "For rats."

IV

So the next day we all said, "She will kill herself"; and we said it would be the best thing. When she had first begun to be seen with Homer Barron, we had said, "She will marry him." Then we said, "She will persuade him yet," because Homer himself had remarked—he liked men, and it was known that he drank with the younger men in the Elk's Club—that he was not a marrying man. Later we said, "Poor Emily," behind the jalousies as they passed on Sunday afternoon in the glittering buggy, Miss Emily with her head high and Homer Barron with his hat cocked and a cigar in his teeth, reins and whip in a yellow glove.

Then some of the ladies began to say that it was a

小姐昂着头,荷默歪戴着帽子,嘴里叼着雪茄烟,戴着黄手套的手握着马缰和马鞭。我们在百叶窗背后都不禁要说一声:"可怜的爱米丽。"

后来有些妇女开始说,这是全镇的羞辱,也是青年的坏榜样。男子汉不想干涉,但妇女们终于迫使浸礼会牧师——爱米丽小姐一家人都是属于圣公会的——去拜访她。访问经过他从未透露,但他再也不愿去第二趟了。下个礼拜天他们又驾着马车出现在街上,于是第二天牧师夫人就写信告知爱米丽住在亚拉巴马的亲属。

原来她家里还有近亲,于是我们坐待事态的发展。起先没有动静,随后我们得到确讯,他们即将结婚。我们还听说爱米丽小姐去过首饰店,订购了一套银质男人盥洗用具,每件上面都刻着"荷·伯'。两天之后人家又告诉我们她买了全套男人服装,包括睡衣在内,因此我们说:"他们已经结婚了。"我们着实高兴。我们高兴的是两位堂姐妹比起爱米丽小姐来,更有格里尔生家族的风度。

因此当荷默·伯隆离开本城——街道铺路工程已经竣工好一阵子了——时,我们一点也不感到惊异。我们倒因为缺少一番送行告别的热闹,不无失望之感。不过我们都相信他此去是为了迎接爱米丽小姐做一番准备,或者是让她有个机会打发走两个堂姐妹(这时已经形成了一个秘密小集团,我们都站在爱米丽小姐一边,帮她踢开这一对堂姐妹)。一点儿也不差,一星期后她们就走了。而且,正如我们一直所期待的那样。荷默·伯隆又回到镇上来了。一位邻居亲眼看见那个黑人在一天黄昏时分打开厨房门让他进去了。

这就是我们最后一次看到荷默·伯隆。至于爱米丽小姐呢,我们则有一段时间没有见到过她。黑人拿着购货篮进进出出,可是前门却总是关着。偶尔可以看到她的身影在窗口晃过,就像人们在撒石灰那天夜晚曾经见到过的那样,但却有整整 6 个月的时间,她没有出现在大街上。我们明白这也并非出乎意料,她父亲的性格三番五次地使她那作为女性的一生平添波折,而这种性格仿佛太恶毒,太狂暴,还不肯消失似的。

等到我们再见到爱米丽小姐时,她已经发胖了,头发也已灰白了。以后数年中,头发越变越灰,变得像胡椒盐似的铁灰色,颜色就不再变了。直到她 74 岁去世之日为止,还是保持着那旺盛的铁灰色,像是

disgrace to the town and a bad example to the young people. The men did not want to interfere, but at last the ladies forced the Baptist minister—Miss Emily's people were Episcopal—to call upon her. He would never divulge what happened during that interview, but he refused to go back again. The next Sunday they again drove about the streets, and the following day the minister's wife wrote to Miss Emily's relations in Alabama.

So she had blood-kin under her roof again and we sat back to watch developments. At first nothing happened. Then we were sure that they were to be married. We learned that Miss Emily had been to the jeweler's and ordered a man's toilet set in silver, with the letters H. B. on each piece. Two days later we learned that she had brought a complete outfit of men's clothing, including a nightshirt, and we said, "They are married." We were really glad. We were glad because the two female cousins were even more Grierson than Miss Emily had ever been.

So we were not surprised when Homer Barron— the streets had been finished some time since—was gone. We were a little disappointed that there was not a public blowing-off, but we believed that he had gone on to prepare for Miss Emily's coming, or to give her a chance to get rid of the cousins. (By that time it was a cabal, and we were all Miss Emily's allies to help circumvent the cousins.) Sure enough, after another week they departed. And, as we had expected all along, within three days Homer Barron was back in town. A neighbor saw the Negro man admit him at the kitchen door at dusk one evening.

And that was the last we saw of Homer Barron. And of Miss Emily for some time. The Negro man went in and out with the market basket, but the front door remained closed. Now and then we would see her at a window for a moment, as the men did that night when they sprinkled the lime, but for almost six months she did not appear on the streets. Then we knew that this was to be expected too; as if that quality of her father which had thwarted her woman's life so many times had been too virulent and too furious to die.

When we next saw Miss Emily, she had grown fat and her hair was turning gray. During the next few years it grew grayer and grayer until it attained an even pepper-and-salt iron-gray, when it ceased turning. Up to the day of her death at seventy-four it was still the vigorous iron-gray, like the hair of an active man.

From that time on her front door remained

一个活跃的男子的头发。打那时起,她的前门就一直关闭着,除了她 40 左右的那段约有六七年的时间之外。在那段时期,她开授瓷器彩绘课。在楼下的一间房里,她临时布置了一个画室,沙多里斯上校的同时代人全都把女儿、孙女儿送到她那里学画,那样的按时按刻,那样的认真精神,简直同礼拜天把她们送到教堂去,还给她们二角伍分钱的硬币准备放在捐献盆子里的情况一模一样。这时,她的捐税已经被豁免了。

后来,新的一代成了全镇的骨干和精神,学画的学生们也长大成人,渐次离开了,他们没有让她们自己的女孩子带着颜色盒、令人生厌的画笔和从妇女杂志上剪下来的画片到爱米丽小姐那里去学画。最后一个学生离开后,前门关上了,而且永远关上了。全镇实行免费邮递制度之后,只有爱米丽小姐一人拒绝在她门口钉上金属门牌号,附设一个邮件箱。她怎样也不理睬他们。

日复一日,月复一月,年复一年,我们眼看着那黑人的头发变白了,背也驼了,还照旧提着购货篮进进出出。每年 12 月我们都寄给她一张纳税通知单,但一星期后又由邮局退还了,无人收信。不时我们在楼底下的一个窗口——她显然是把楼上封闭起来了——见到她的身影,像神龛中的一个偶像的雕塑躯干,我们说不上她是不是在看着我们。她就这样度过了一代又一代——高贵,宁静,无法逃避,无法接近,怪僻乖张。

她就这样与世长辞了。在一栋尘埃遍地、鬼影憧憧的屋子里得了病,侍候她的只有一个老态龙钟的黑人。我们甚至连她病了也不知道,也早已不想从黑人那里去打听什么消息。他跟谁也不说话,恐怕对她也是如此,他的嗓子似乎由于长久不用变得嘶哑了。

她死在楼下一间屋子里,笨重的胡桃木床上还挂着床帷。她那长满铁灰头发的头枕着的枕头由于用了多年而又不见阳光,已经黄得发霉了。

<h2 style="text-align:center">五</h2>

黑人在前门口迎接第一批妇女,把她们请进来,她们话音低沉,发出咝咝声响,以好奇的目光迅速扫视着一切。黑人随即不见了,他穿过屋子,走出后门,从此就不见踪影了。

closed, save for a period of six or seven years, when she was about forty, during which she gave lessons in china-painting. She fitted up a studio in one of the downstairs rooms, where the daughters and grand-daughters of Colonel Sartoris' contemporaries were sent to her with the same regularity and in the same spirit that they were sent on Sundays with a twenty-five cent piece for the collection plate. Meanwhile her taxes had been remitted.

Then the newer generation became the backbone and the spirit of the town, and the painting pupils grew up and fell away and did not send their children to her with boxes of color and tedious brushes and pictures cut from the ladies' magazines. The front door closed upon the last one and remained closed for good. When the town got free postal delivery Miss Emily alone refused to let them fasten the metal numbers above her door and attach a mailbox to it. She would not listen to them.

Daily, monthly, yearly we watched the Negro grow grayer and more stooped, going in and out with the market basket. Each December we sent her a tax notice, which would be returned by the post office a week later, unclaimed. Now and then we would see her in one of the downstairs windows—she had evidently shut up the top floor of the house—like the carven torso of an idol in a niche, looking or not looking at us, we could never tell which. Thus she passed from generation to generation—dear, inescapable, impervious, tranquil, and perverse.

And so she died. Fell ill in the house filled with dust and shadows, with only a doddering Negro man to wait on her. We did not even know she was sick; we had long since given up trying to get any information from the Negro. He talked to no one, probably not even to her, for his voice had grown harsh and rusty, as if from disuse.

She died in one of the downstairs rooms, in a heavy walnut bed with a curtain, her gray head propped on a pillow yellow and moldy with age and lack of sunlight.

<h2 style="text-align:center">V</h2>

The Negro met the first of the ladies at the front door and let them in with their hushed, sibilant voices and their quick, curious glances, and then he disappeared. He walked right through the house and out the back and was not seen again.

两位堂姐妹也随即赶到，他们第二天就举行了丧礼，全镇的人都跑来看看覆盖着鲜花的爱米丽小姐的尸体。停尸架上方悬挂着她父亲的炭笔画像，一脸深刻沉思的表情，妇女们唧唧喳喳地谈论着死亡，而老年男子呢——有些人还穿上了刷得很干净的南方同盟军制服——则在走廊上，草坪上纷纷谈论着爱米丽小姐的一生，仿佛她是他们的同时代人，而且还相信和她跳过舞，甚至向她求过爱，他们把按数学级数向前推进的时间给搅乱了。这是老年人常有的情形。在他们看来，过去的岁月不是一条越来越窄的路，而是一片广袤的连冬天也对它无所影响的大草地，只是近 10 年来才像窄小的瓶口一样，把他们同过去隔断了。

我们已经知道，楼上那块地方有一个房间，40 年来从没有人见到过，要进去得把门撬开。他们等到爱米丽小姐安葬之后，才设法去开门。

门猛烈地打开，震得屋里灰尘弥漫。这间布置得像新房的屋子，仿佛到处都笼罩着墓室一般的淡淡的阴惨惨的氛围。败了色的玫瑰色窗帘，玫瑰色的灯罩，梳妆台，一排精细的水晶制品和白银作底的男人盥洗用具，但白银已毫无光泽，连刻制的姓名字母图案都已无法辨认了。杂物中有一条硬领和领带，仿佛刚从身上取下来似的，把它们拿起来时，在台面上堆积的尘埃中留下淡淡的月牙痕。椅子上放着一套衣服，折叠得好好的，椅子底下有两只寂寞无声的鞋和一双扔了不要的袜子。

那男人躺在床上。

我们在那里立了好久，俯视着那没有肉的脸上令人莫测的龇牙咧嘴的样子。那尸体躺在那里，显出一度是拥抱的姿势，但那比爱情更能持久、那战胜了爱情的煎熬的永恒的长眠已经使他驯服了。他所遗留下来的肉体已在破烂的睡衣下腐烂，跟他躺着的木床粘在一起，难分难解了。在他身上和他身旁的枕上，均匀地覆盖着一层长年累月积下来的灰尘。

后来我们才注意到旁边那只枕头上有人头压过的痕迹。我们当中有一个人从那上面拿起了什么东西，大家凑近一看——这时一股淡淡的干燥发臭的气味钻进了鼻孔——原来是一绺长长的铁灰色头发。

The two female cousins came at once. They held the funeral on the second day, with the town coming to look at Miss Emily beneath a mass of bought flowers, with the crayon face of her father musing profoundly above the bier and the ladies sibilant and macabre; and the very old men—some in their brushed Confederate uniforms—on the porch and the lawn, talking of Miss Emily as if she had been a contemporary of theirs, believing that they had danced with her and courted her perhaps, confusing time with its mathematical progression, as the old do, to whom all the past is not a diminishing road, but, instead, a huge meadow which no winter ever quite touches, divided from them now by the narrow bottleneck of the most recent decade of years.

Already we knew that there was one room in that region above stairs which no one had seen in forty years, and which would have to be forced. They waited until Miss Emily was decently in the ground before they opened it.

The violence of breaking down the door seemed to fill this room with pervading dust. A thin, acid pall as of the tomb seemed to lie everywhere upon this room decked and furnished as for a bridal: upon the valance curtains of faded rose color, upon the rose-shaded lights, upon the dressing table, upon the delicate array of crystal and the man's toilet things backed with tarnished silver, silver so tarnished that the monogram was obscured. Among them lay a collar and tie, as if they had just been removed, which, lifted, left upon the surface a pale crescent in the dust. Upon a chair hung the suit, carefully folded; beneath it the two mute shoes and the discarded socks.

The man himself lay in the bed.

For a long while we just stood there, looking down at the proffound and fleshless grin. The body had apparently once lain in the attitude of an embrace, but now the long sleep that outlasts love, that conquers even the grimace of love, had cuckolded him. What was left of him, rotted beneath what was left of the nightshirt, had become inextricable from the bed in which he lay; and upon him and upon the pillow beside him lay that even coating of the patient and biding dust.

Then we noticed that in the second pillow was the indentation of a head. One of us lifted something from it, and, leaning forward, that faint and invisible dust dry and acrid in the nostrils, we saw a long strand of iron-gray hair.

┌ 讨 论 ─■

　　这是一篇恐怖小说。我们看到,那个住在一所破败宅邸里的女主人,由于长期与世隔绝,渐渐变得又怪诞又可怕,变成了像生长在黑暗中的潮湿的墙上的霉菌一样不成人样的东西。爱米丽·格里尔生小姐(可能迫于某种内心的压抑)自甘于离群蛰居,她弃绝了人世间的一切烟火凡尘,而到头来,当人们在楼上的房间里重新发现她时,她已向人们展示了一幅可说是令人惊心动魄而又毛骨悚然的恐怖景象。

　　写这幅恐怖景象仅仅是为了制造恐怖吗?如果不是,那么作者又为什么要着意把那么多可怕的东西写进小说里去呢?这也就是说,在福克纳的小说里,恐怖对小说主题的表现是否起作用?恐怖是否有意义?

　　要回答以上问题,我们就得仔细考察一下小说开头时的某些叙述。首先,爱米丽小姐为什么会做出那样可怕的行为?她这样做有其适当的理由吗?我们知道,福克纳对自己作品的结局一向是慎重考虑,适当铺垫的。在这篇小说里,一开头就很明确地点明了,爱米丽小姐属于那种把现实和幻觉混为一谈的人。譬如,她否认自己欠税,而当镇长提出异议时,她竟不承认他是镇长。她转而提出要沙多里斯上校来代办,但读者已经知道,沙多里斯上校大约 10 年前就已经死了。显然,在爱米丽小姐看来,沙多里斯上校仍然活着。最明确的铺垫是在她父亲死后,她竟然对镇上的居民否认她父亲已死,而且否认了 3 天之久!"正当他们要诉诸法律和武力时,她垮下来了,于是他们很快地埋葬了她的父亲"。

　　爱米丽显然是病理学上的一个病例。故事叙述者也相当明确地指出,人们觉得她很古怪。所有这些解释性的铺垫使爱米丽小姐之所以会保存她的情人——那个已经死了的情人——有了合理性,因为在她看来,她的情人

This is a story of horror. We have a decaying mansion in which the protagonist, shut away from the world, grows into something monstrous, and becomes as divorced from humanity as some fungus growing in the dark on a damp wall. Miss Emily Grierson remains in voluntary isolation(or perhaps fettered by some inner compulsion) away from the bustle and dust and sunshine of the human world of normal affairs, and what in the end is found in the upstairs room gives perhaps a sense of penetrating and gruesome horror.

Has this sense of horror been conjured up for its own sake? If not, then why has the author contrived to insert so much of the monstrous into the story? In other words, does the horror contribute to the theme of Faulkner's story? Is the horror meaningful?

In order to answer this question, we shall have to examine rather carefully some of the items earlier in the story. In the first place, why does Miss Emily commit her monstrous act? Is she supplied with a proper motivation? Faulkner has, we can see, been rather careful to prepare for his denouement. Miss Emily, it becomes obvious fairly early in the story, is one of those persons for whom the distinction between reality and illusion has blurred. For example, she refuses to admit that she owes any taxes. When the mayor protests, she does not recognize him as mayor. Instead, she refers the committee to Colonel Sartoris, who, as the reader is told, has been dead for nearly ten years. For Miss Emily, apparently, Colonel Sartoris is still alive. Most specific preparation of all, when her father dies, she denies to the townspeople for three days that he is dead:"Just as they were about to resort to law and force, she broke down, and they buried her father quickly. "

Miss Emily is obviously a pathological case. The narrator indicates plainly enough that people felt that she was crazy. All of this explanation prepares us for what Miss Emily does in order to hold her lover—the dead lover is in one sense still alive for her—the realms

在某种意义上依然活着——现实的领域和幻象的领域在她是混为一体的。但是仅仅谈到这一点，还不能说我们已经对这篇小说做出了合理的判断。因为，如果福克纳的兴趣仅在于讲述一个心理变态病例的病史的话，那么这篇东西作为小说就没有什么意义，问题也就无从谈起，除非我们再回过头来谈论"临床病史"式小说，而关于这一点我们在第二章评述《鹰溪桥上》时已经谈过了。要想对这篇小说做出合理的论断，那就必须做出某种可称之为含有道德内容的论断，必须用道德方面的词语来表述它的意义——不能仅仅用心理学方面的词语来表述。

不幸的是，这篇小说很容易被人误认为仅仅是一篇怕人的病史，作者写它也仅仅为了刺激读者。人们曾常常下结论说，福克纳的作品仅此而已，别无他意。

现实与幻觉的界限的混淆，生与死界限的混淆，指出这点固然重要，它有助于对爱米丽的动机做出解释，但是仅仅指出这种混淆还不足以对小说的主题做出解释。

我们还是先从人物的性格特征出发，进而探讨人物的动机吧！爱米丽小姐是怎样一个人？她性格中的主要动力是什么？使她把幻觉与现实混为一谈的原因是什么？她显然是个有惊人意志力的女人。在收税这件事上，她虽然表现很古怪，但从未惊慌失措过。她平静自如，她制服了那些来看她的颇为咄咄逼人的官方代理人。在买毒药那件事上，她完全镇住了那个药房伙计。她毫不弄虚作假，她拒绝向他说明自己为何要买毒药。然而这种意志力和这种含有讥讽意味的傲慢态度并没有使她免于别人对她的骚扰和伤害。她父亲曾经把那些前来拜访她的年轻人一个个赶走，而镇上人想起爱米丽小姐和她父亲在一起的情景，就好像想起一幅图画："身段苗条、穿着白衣的爱米丽小姐立在背后，她父亲叉开双脚的侧影在前面，背对爱米丽，手执一根马鞭，一扇向后开

of reality and appearance merge. But having said this, we have got no nearer to justifying the story: for, if Faulkner is merely interested in relating a case history of abnormal psychology, the story lacks meaning and justification as a story and we are back to fiction as "clinical report" which we spoke of in connection with "The Occurrence at Owl Creek Bridge" in section 2. If the story is to be justified, there must be what may be called a moral significance, a meaning in moral terms—not merely psychological terms.

Incidentally, it is very easy to misread the story as merely a horrible case history, presented in order to titillate the reader. Faulkner has been frequently judged to be doing nothing more than this in his work.

The lapse of the distinction between illusion and reality, between life and death, is important, therefore, in helping to account for Miss Emily's motivation, but merely to note this lapse is not fully to account for the theme of the story.

Suppose we approach the motivation again in terms of character. What is Miss Emily like? What are the mainsprings of her character? What causes the distinction between illusion and reality to blur for her? She is obviously a woman of tremendous firmness of will. In the matter of the taxes, crazed though she is, she is never at a loss. She is utterly composed. She dominates the rather frightened committee of officers who see her. In the matter of her purchase of the poison, she completely overawes the clerk. She makes no pretense. She refuses to tell him what she wants the poison for. And yet this firmness of will and this iron pride have not kept her from being thwarted and hurt. Her father has run off the young men who came to call upon her, and the townspeople think of Miss Emily and her father as a tableau: "Miss Emily a slender figure in white in the background, her father a spraddled silhouette in the foreground, his back to her and clutching a horsewhip, the two of them framed by the backflung

的前门恰好嵌在了他们俩的身影。"无论这幅画是一种记忆中的情景或者仅仅是一种象征性的虚构,反正这是存在于故事叙述者心中的印象。

爱米丽小姐的高傲跟她对公众舆论的轻蔑态度是分不开的。诚然,这种舆论在她跟那个被人们认为和她身份不配的工头一起驾着马车在镇上到处逛的时候就已经出现了。但她拒不承认外界的那一套清规戒律和风俗习惯,也拒不接受与她本人意志(正是这种意志使她留住了想离她而去的情人)相左的他人意志,这正是她的高傲之处。当他要抛弃她时,她不仅设法压倒他的意志和人们的讨论,而且无视死亡以及死亡后要腐烂这样的自然规律本身。

但是,这样似乎仍然没有说出这篇作品的意义。因为我们至此所说的一切,仍只是在有关心理变态的范围之内谈论问题——我们仍然仅仅局限于试论一则变态心理学方面的病史。为了使一则病史成为"有意义"的小说,我们就不得不把爱米丽小姐的思想和行为跟她背后的一般的社会生活联结起来,并且在两者之间建立起某种联系。正是关于这个问题,小说中的一个恒常因素向我们提供了一条线索。这篇小说是通过一个镇上居民的口讲述的。这个人作为贯穿小说始终的一种成分,他反映出公众对爱米丽小姐的态度。在小说中不断出现的是"我们"所说的什么什么,以及"我们"所做的什么什么,或者是"我们"看来怎样怎样是真实的等等。叙述者把事情说得甚至比实际发生的更加耸人听闻。在故事发展过程中,公众对爱米丽小姐的态度,据叙述者说是"关切的、无可奈何的、无动于衷的、平静的而又反常的"。这些形容词中的每一个都很重要,都有其含义。在某种意义上说,爱米丽小姐之所以为人们关心,就因为她的孤独和怪癖,而这也是全社会所具有的弊病。公众在某种程度上还很珍视她。具有讽刺意味的是,正由于爱

front door. "Whether the picture is a remembered scene, or merely a symbolical construct, this is the picture that remains in the storyteller's mind.

Miss Emily's pride is connected with her contempt for public opinion. This comes to the fore, of course, when she rides around about the town with the foreman whom everybody believes is beneath her. And it is her proud refusal to admit an external set of codes, or conventions, or other wills in contradiction to her own, that makes her capable at the end of keeping her lover from going away. Confronted with his jilting her, she tries to override not only his will and the opinion of other people but the laws of death and decay themselves.

But this, still, hardly gives the meaning of the story. For in all that has been said thus far, we are still merely accounting for a psychological aberration—we are still merely dealing with a case history in abnormal psychology. In order to make a case for the story as "meaningful," we shall have to tie Miss Emily's thoughts and actions back into the normal life of the community, and establish some sort of relationship between them. And just here one pervasive element in the narration suggests a clue. The story is told by one of the townspeople. And in it, as a constant factor, is the reference to what the community thought of Miss Emily. Continually through the story it is what "we" said, and then what "We" did, and what seemed true to "us," and so on. The narrator puts the matter even more sharply still. It is said, in the course of the story, that to the community Miss Emily seemed "dear, inescapable, impervious, tranquil, and perverse." Each of the adjectives is important and meaningful. In a sense, Miss Emily because of her very fact of isolation and perversity belongs to the whole community. She is even something treasured by it. Ironically, because of Emily's perversion of an aristocratic independence of mores and because of her contempt for "what people say," her life is public, even communal. And

米丽对大多数人抱着某种贵族式超然的怪癖态度，正由于她对"人们所说的"表示轻蔑，她的生活反而受到公众的注意，甚至是人人关心的。叙述者用了各种不同的词语以勾勒出对她所处地位的这种看法。如她的面部表情"是你想象中的灯塔守望人所应有的"，像一个过着孤独生活的灯塔守望人的面孔，守望人朝外看出去是一片黑暗，而他的灯光却可以为公众所利用。还有，在她父亲死后。她病了很久，而当她病后重新出现时，她显得"和教堂里彩色玻璃窗上的天使像不无相似之处——有几分悲怆肃穆"。无论我们怎样看待这些描写，可以肯定的是，作者是有意要暗示出某种宁静而庄严的神态，这种神态非尘世所有的，甚至是"超凡拔俗的"，就象天使才具有的那种神态。

这就是说，在公众眼里，爱米丽小姐是一种偶像和替罪羊的结合物。一方面，公众对爱米丽表示敬仰——她代表着往昔社会里的某些东西，这些东西当前社会是引以自豪的。人们对她抱着某种敬畏感，这情形通过镇长以及代理人在她面前的言语行为也生动地表现了出来。另一方面，她又很古怪，在日常事务方面她无法与公众相比，对于现代生活她抱着绝望的隔离态度——所有这些事实都使公众在她面前抱着某种优越感，甚至对她所代表的过去也抱着优越感。这也就是说，正因为爱米丽小姐具有这两种完全矛盾的性质，所以她的行为也就具有特殊的社会意义。

尽管爱米丽小姐以贵族自居，尽管她自以为比别人"更好"，尽管她的行为超出于或者有异于社会行为准则，但同时，她又比别人更坏，而她也确实比别人更坏，简直坏得可怕。她比别人更坏，但是同时，就像叙述者暗示的那样，她又莫名其妙地受人们敬仰。这就引起了一个根本性问题，难道可以说这是真实的吗？

也许爱米丽小姐最后做出的既令人生畏又令人钦佩的行动是出于她性格中的那个同

various phrases used by the narrator underline this view of her position. For example, her face looks "as you imagine a lighthouse-keeper's face ought to look," like the face of a person who lives in the kind of isolation imposed on a lighthouse-keeper, who looks out into the blackness and whose light serves a public function. Or, again, after her father's death, she becomes very ill, and when she appears after the illness, she had "a vague resemblance to those angels in colored church windows—sort of tragic and serene." Whatever we make of these descriptions, certainly the author is trying to suggest a kind of calm and dignity that is supermundane, unearthly, or "over-earthly," such as an angel might possess.

Miss Emily, then, is a combination of idol and scapegoat for the community. On the one hand, the community feels admiration for Miss Emily—she represents something in the past of the community that the community is proud of. They feel a sort of awe of her, as is illustrated by the behavior of the mayor and the committee in her presence. On the other hand, her queerness, the fact that she cannot compete with them in their ordinary life, the fact that she is hopelessly out of touch with the modern world—all of these things make them feel superior to her, and also to the past that she represents. It is, then, Miss Emily's complete detachment that gives her actions their special meaning for the community.

Miss Emily, since she is the conscious aristocrat, since she is consciously "better" than other people, since she is above and outside their canons of behavior, can, at the same time, be worse than other people; and she *is* worse, horribly so. She is worse than other people, but at the same time, as the narrator implies, she remains somehow admirable. This raises a fundamental question: why is this true?

Perhaps the horrible and the admirable aspects of Miss Emily's final deed arise from

样的基本事实，即她坚持按照自己的想法对待社会。她从不低声下气，从不乞求同情，她拒不做一个隐忍恬静的老处女，她拒不接受公众的普遍是非标准或者价值观念。这种精神上的独立性和孤傲态度，就她的情况来说，会使她的个性扭曲而变得怪模怪样，但同时，由于拒不接受庸俗的价值标准，又使她具有一种崇高而无畏的气质。公众感觉到这一点，我们从公众撬开楼上的房门之前先举行葬礼这个事实中即可看出。在公众的心里似乎已存在着某种谅解，觉得她已经赢得了隐居的权利，而这种权利一直可以保留到她自愿离开这个世界为止。虽然有了那个事实，叙述者还要加以说明，"我们已经知道，楼上那块地方有一个房间，40 年来从没有人见到过，要进去得把门撬开"。她的葬礼也举行得颇为隆重，"而老年男子呢——有些人还穿上了刷得很干净的南方同盟军制服——则在走廊上，草坪上纷纷议论着爱米丽小姐的一生，仿佛她是他们的同时代人，而且还相信和她跳过舞，甚至向她求过爱"！换言之，社会已承认她是自己光荣历史的一部分。这一切都是对爱米丽小姐的意志已获胜利的某种默认。我们在小说的前面部分读到，当爱米丽小姐丧失钱财时，公众对她是表示同情的，这正如他们认为她已实际上成了一个堕落女人时，对她表示惋惜一样。然而，她却高傲地超然于他们的同情、惋惜甚或谴责之上，正像她高傲地超然于他们的其他意愿之上一样。

然而，人们始终会说爱米丽小姐是个疯子。这可能是真的，但在这里有两个问题要考虑。首先，必须考虑使她"发病"的特殊原因。她的发疯显然是她的孤傲和拒不服从一般行为标准的进一步发展。这里涉及到的问题就其自身而言确实很重要，因为它肯定和人对道德的自我选择有关。其次，公众把她看做"疯子"，其中意味深长。他们即使在她拒绝他们的同情而感到失望时，还是敬仰她。叙述者

the same basic fact of her character: she insists on meeting the world on her own terms. She never cringes, she never begs for sympathy, she refuses to shrink into an amiable old maid, she never accepts the community's ordinary judgments or values. This independence of spirit and pride can, and does in her case, twist the individual into a sort of monster, but, at the same time, this refusal to accept the herd values carries with it a dignity and courage. The community senses this, as we gather from the fact that the community carries out the decencies of the funeral before breaking in the door of the upper room. There is, as it were, a kind of secret understanding that she has won her right of privacy, until she herself has entered history. Furthermore, despite the fact that, as the narrator says, "already we knew that there was one room in that region above stairs which no one had seen in forty years, and which would have to be forced," her funeral is something of a state occasion, with "the very old men—some in their brushed Confederate uniforms—on the porch and the lawn, talking of Miss Emily as if she had been a contemporary of theirs, believing that they had danced with her and courted her perhaps." In other words, the community accepts her into its honored history. All of this works as a kind of tacit recognition of' Miss Emily's triumph of will. The community, we are told earlier, had wanted to pity Miss Emily when she had lost her money, just as they had wanted to commiserate over her when they believed that she had actually become a fallen woman, but she had triumphed over their pity and commiseration and condemnation, just as she had triumphed over all their other attitudes.

But, still, it may be said that Miss Emily is mad. This may be true, but there are two things to consider in this connection. First, one must consider the special terms that her "madness" takes. Her madness is simply a development of her pride and her refusal to submit to ordinary standards of behavior. So, because of this fact, her "madness" is meaningful after all. It involves issues that in themselves are really important and have to do with the world of conscious moral choice. Second, the

（作为公众的一个发言人）认识到那最后的残酷事实作为一个例子，恰恰揭示出她的道德标准实质上和公众的最后结论是符合的。她愿意和那个平常的劳动者荷默·伯隆结婚，而且不顾公众对此有何看法。她只是不愿被遗弃。她愿意把他作为爱人。但是一切得遵从她自己的主张。她实在太桀骜不驯了，与凡俗的日常世界是那样地格格不入。

许多评论家曾经说过，悲剧里时常出现某个英雄。他惯于我行我素，始终按照他自己的信念待人处世，他是那样执著于追求，或者是那样执著于生活，因此，他不可能接受任何妥协。这篇小说当然不能和任何伟大的悲剧如《哈姆雷特》或者《李尔王》相提并论，但可以指出的是，这篇小说以它自己的方式提出了某些与伟大的悲剧作品所提出的相同的基本问题。可以肯定地说，爱米丽小姐的高傲、孤独以及独立不羁会使我们想起典型的悲剧人物形象。还可以指出的便是，如果说她的行为造成的恐怖感是公众的平凡生活所不能容忍的话，那么同样，她的独立不羁的品格也是一般道德所不能容忍的。

community interprets her "madness" as meaningful. They admire her, even if they are disappointed by her refusals to let herself be pitied, and the narrator, who is a spokesman for the community, recognizes the last grim revelation as an instance of her having carried her own values to their ultimate conclusion. She would marry the common laborer, Homer Barron, let the community think what it would. She would not be jilted. And she would hold him as a lover. But it would all be on her own terms. She remains completely dominant, and contemptuous of the day-to-day world.

It has been suggested by many critics that tragedy implies a hero who is completely himself, who insists on meeting the world on his own terms, who wants something so intensely, or lives so intensely, that he cannot accept any compromise. It cannot be maintained that this story is comparable to any of the great tragedies, such as *Hamlet* or *King Lear*, but it can be pointed out that this story, in its own way, involves some of the same basic elements. Certainly, Miss Emily's pride, isolation, and independence remind us of aspects in the character of the typical tragic hero. And it can be pointed out that, just as the horror of her deed lies outside the ordinary life of the community, so the magnificence of her independence lies outside its ordinary virtues.

——思考题——■

1. 如果用第三人称的视角来写这篇小说，将会有何种难处？

2. 爱米丽小姐选中被人们轻蔑地称为"北方佬，一个拿日工资的人"作为自己的情人，为什么说这种举动是意味深长的？

3. 就其一般的象征性意义，回顾一下《年轻的布朗大爷》和《杀手》这两篇作品，能不能说现在这篇小说也像那两篇一样，具有更为普遍的意义——即对当前社会提出了一种象征性的批评？若是，你又如何对此加以论证？
（刘家有 译）

1. What difficulties would arise if you tried to tell this story from the point of view of the third person?

2. Why is it significant that Miss Emily chooses for her lover a man who is scornfully regarded by the community as a "Northerner, a day laborer"?

3. Look back at "Young Goodman Brown" and "The Killers" in the light of their general symbolic significance. Can it be argued that the present story, like them, has a more general significance—that it is a symbolic commentary on our society? If so, how would you argue this point?

027. 好人难寻

(美)弗兰纳里·奥康纳 著　　屠珍译

027. A Good Man Is Hard to Find

by Flannery O'Connor

老奶奶不愿意去佛罗里达州,而想到田纳西州东部去探望一下亲友,因此想方设法叫贝雷改变主意。贝雷是她的独生子,老奶奶如今跟着他过日子。这当儿,贝雷正坐在紧贴桌子旁边的那把椅子上,聚精会神地看报纸上橙色版面的体育消息。"贝雷,你瞧,"她说,"看看这条消息吧!"她站在那里,一只手叉在瘦小的胯骨上,另一只手冲着贝雷的秃脑袋瓜子哗啦哗啦地摇晃手里的报纸。"那个自称不合时宜的人,从联邦监狱里逃出来了,正向佛罗里达州窜逃呐。瞧这里说他对人们都干了些什么鬼名堂。有这样一个逃犯在州里窜来窜去,我可绝不带孩子还朝那个方向去凑热闹。要是那样做,良心上说不过去哟!"

贝雷依旧津津有味地看报,头连抬都没抬一下。于是,老奶奶转身冲着孩子妈。孩子妈穿一条长裤子,脸膛亮得像棵圆白菜,露出一副天真无邪的表情,头上裹着一块绿头巾,两角扎得就跟兔子的一对耳朵一样。她抱着婴儿坐在沙发上,从罐里一勺一勺地舀杏儿喂他。老奶奶说:"孩子们已经去过佛罗里达州,该换个新鲜地方带他们去玩玩,让他们四处见识见识,开阔开阔眼界嘛。他们可从来没去过田纳西州东部。"

孩子妈好像没听见她的话,戴眼镜的8岁胖儿子约翰·韦斯利却插嘴说:"您要是不愿意去佛罗里达,干吗不待在家里呢?"他的妹妹琼·斯塔正坐在地上看滑稽画报。

"就是让她在家里当一天女皇,她也不愿意待。"琼·斯塔说。长着金发的脑袋抬也没抬。

THE grandmother didn't want to go to Florida. She wanted to visit some of her connections in east Tennessee and she was seizing at every chance to change Bailey's mind. Bailey was the son she lived with, her only boy. He was sitting on the edge of his chair at the table, bent over the orange sports section of the *Journal*. "Now look here, Bailey," she said, "see here, read this," and she stood with one hand on her thin hip and the other rattling the newspaper at his bald head. "Here this fellow that calls himself The Misfit is aloose from the Federal Pen and headed toward Florida and you read what it says he did to these people. Just you read it. I wouldn't take my children in any direction with a criminal like that aloose in it. I couldn't answer to my conscience if I did."

Bailey didn't look up from his reading so she wheeled around then and faced the children's mother, a young woman in slacks, whose face was as broad and innocent as a cabbage and was tied around with a green headkerchief that had two points on the top like rabbit's ears. She was sitting on the sofa, feeding the baby his apricots out of a jar. "The children have been to Florida before," the old lady said. "You all ought to take them somewhere else for a change so they would see different parts of the world and be broad. They never have been to east Tennessee."

The children's mother didn't seem to hear her but the eight-year-old boy, John Wesley, a stocky child with glasses, said, "If you don't want to go to Florida, why dontcha stay at home?" He and the little girl, June Star, were reading the funny papers on the floor.

"She wouldn't stay at home to be queen for a day," June Star said without raising her yellow head.

"Yes, and what would you do if this fellow, The Misfit, caught you?" the grandmother asked.

作者简介:弗兰纳里·奥康纳(Flannery O'Connor,1925—1964),美国作家。1925 年 3 月 25 日生于佐治亚州萨瓦纳,1964 年 8 月 3 日卒于佐治亚州米利奇维尔。她一生的大部分时间生活在米利奇维尔她母亲的农场。她的作品经常以南部乡村为背景,把人物置于怪异和极端的处境中,来考察个体与上帝的关系。她的第一本小说《慧血》(*Wise Blood*,1952),结合了日常对话、宗教想象力和荒诞手法,这也是她的所有作品的特色。其他作品包括短篇小说集《好人难寻》(*A Good Man Is Hard to Find*,1955)、《上升的一切必将汇合》(*Everything That Rises Must Converge*,1965)和《暴力得逞》(*The Violent Bear It Away*,1960)。她被授予美国卓越短篇小说奖。

"是啊，要是那个不合时宜的人把你们俩都逮住，该怎么办？"

"我捆他嘴巴子。"约翰·韦斯利说。

"就是给她一百万块钱，她也不愿意待在家里。"琼·斯塔又说，"她呀，总怕错过点儿什么没看见。反正咱们上哪儿，她必得跟着上哪儿。"

"好咧。小姐，"老奶奶说，"等下回你再叫我给你卷头发，咱们瞧着办吧！"

琼·斯塔说自己的头发天然就是鬈曲的。

第二天清晨，老奶奶头一个上了汽车，准备出发。她带上自己那个硕大的黑旅行袋，把它放在角落里，它看起来活像一头河马的脑袋，下面还藏着一只篮子，里面放着她的老猫咪，她可舍不得把猫孤零零地留在家里待三天，它会十分想念她的，况且她担心小宝贝儿会碰开煤气炉的开关，发生意外，窒息而死。说真的，她的儿子贝雷可不愿意带一只老猫走进汽车旅馆里活现眼。

老奶奶在汽车后座正中间就座，一边是约翰·韦斯利，一边是琼·斯塔。贝雷和孩子妈带着婴儿坐在前面。他们 8:45 离开亚特兰大。启程时，车上里程表的数字是 55890，老奶奶把它记了下来，因为她觉得等旅行回来，能说出总共逛了多少英里，那才叫有意思呢。车走了 20 分钟，才来到郊区。

于是，老奶奶舒舒服服地安顿下来，脱下雪白的线手套，连同自己的手提包一起放在后车窗架子上。孩子妈照旧穿着长裤子，头上依然扎着绿头巾。老奶奶却戴一顶海军蓝的硬边草帽，帽檐上有一戋人造的白紫罗兰。她穿一身带小白点的深蓝色长衣服，镶花边的领子和袖口全是白玻璃纱做的。领口那儿还别着一枝带香囊的布做的紫罗兰。万一发生意外，过往行人看见她暴死在公路上，谁都一眼就能辨认出她是一位高贵夫人。

她说自己早就料到今天是开车出去逛逛的好日子，天气既不太热，也不太凉。她提醒贝雷，时速不得超过 55 英里，那些巡警往往躲在广告牌和树丛后面，趁你还没来得及放慢速度就冷不防一下子把你逮住。一路上，老奶奶把奇物异景一一指点出来，石山啦，公路两旁时时出现的蓝色花岗石啦，微带紫纹而闪闪发亮的黏土斜坡啦，还有地里一排排饰带般绿油油的庄稼啦。银白色的阳光普照树丛，几株长得顶不像样的树木在明晃晃地发亮。孩子们还在看连环滑稽画报，

"I'd smack his face," John Wesley said.

"She wouldn't stay at home for a million bucks," June Star said. "Afraid she'd miss something. She has to go everywhere we go,"

"All right, Miss," the grandmother said. "Just remember that the next time you want me to curl your hair."

June Star said her hair was naturally curly.

The next morning the grandmother was the first one in the car, ready to go. She had her big black valise that looked like the head of a hippopotamus in one corner, and underneath it she was hiding a basket with Pitty Sing, the cat, in it. She didn't intend for the cat to be left alone in the house for three days because he would miss her too much and she was afraid he might brush against one of the gas burners and accidentally asphyxiate himself. Her son, Bailey, didn't like to arrive at a motel with a cat.

She sat in the middle of the back seat with John Wesley and June Star on either side of her. Bailey and the children's mother and the baby sat in front and they left Atlanta at eight forty-five with the mileage on the car at 55890. The grandmother wrote this down because she thought it would be interesting to say how many miles they had been when they got back. It took them twenty minutes to reach the outskirts of the city.

The old lady settled herself comfortably, removing her white cotton gloves and putting them up with her purse on the shelf in front of the back window. The children's mother still had on slacks and still had her head tied up in a green kerchief, but the grandmother had on a navy blue straw sailor hat with a bunch of white violets on the brim and a navy blue dress with a small white dot in the print. Her collars and cuffs were white organdy trimmed with lace and at her neckline she had pinned a purple spray of cloth violets containing a sachet. In case of an accident, anyone seeing her dead on the highway would know at once that she was a lady.

She said she thought it was going to be a good day for driving, neither too hot nor too cold, and she cautioned Bailey that the speed limit was fifty-five miles an hour and that the patrolmen hid themselves behind billboards and small clumps of trees and sped out after you before you had a chance to slow down. She pointed out interesting details of the scenery: Stone Mountain; the blue granite that in some places came up to both sides of the highway; the brilliant red clay banks slightly streaked with purple; and the various crops that made rows of green lace-work on the ground. The trees were full of silver-white sunlight

妈妈打盹儿了。

"咱们快点儿穿过佐治亚州吧,省得没完没了地尽看它。"约翰·韦斯利说。

"我要是个小孩儿,"老奶奶说,"决不用这种口气数落自己的家乡。田纳西有高山,佐治亚有小山,各有各的特点嘛!"

"田纳西不过是一块垃圾堆似的高低不平的山地罢了,"约翰·韦斯利说,"佐治亚也是个不起眼的地方。"

"说得完全对。"琼·斯塔帮腔道。

"我小时候,"老奶奶交叉着满带青筋的十指,说道,"孩子对自己的家乡啦,自己的父母啦,还有别的一切一切,都比现在更尊重。那当儿,大伙儿都规规矩矩。嗨,快瞧那个怪可爱的黑崽子!"她指着一个站在一间棚屋门口的黑孩子说。"这不是一幅画吗?"她问道,大家都转过头来,从后车窗往外瞧。黑孩子冲他们招了招手。

"他光着屁股呐。"琼·斯塔说。

"没准儿他根本没有裤子可穿,"老奶奶解释道,"乡下的黑崽子可不像咱们那样样样都有。我要是会画画儿,一定画这样一幅画。"

两个孩子交换连环画报看。

老奶奶要帮着抱抱婴儿,孩子妈就从前座靠背上把他递过来。她把孩子放在膝上轻轻颠着,给他讲沿途看见的东西。她转动眼珠,努起嘴唇,还把干瘪的老脸贴到婴儿光溜溜的脸蛋儿上。孩子偶尔恍恍惚惚地冲她微微一笑。这当儿,他们正路过一大块棉花地,当中用篱笆围着五六个坟头,好似一个小岛。"快瞧那块坟地!"老奶奶指着坟圈子说,"那是个老宅的茔地,属于这个种植园的。"

"种植园在哪儿呢?"约翰·韦斯利问。

"飘走喽①!"老奶奶说,"哈哈!"

孩子们看完了他们带的每一本连环画报,就打开饭盒吃起来。老奶奶吃了一份花生酱夹心的三明治和一枚橄榄。她不准孩子们把纸盒和揩嘴的纸巾随便往车窗外头乱扔。他们没什么事可干,于是,就玩起游戏来。每人选定天上一块云彩,让另外两个人猜它像什么。约翰·韦斯利挑了一块宛如一头牛似的

_____

① 这里借用了美国畅销小说《飘》的书名,指已不存在了。

and the meanest of them sparkled. The children were reading comic magazines and their mother had gone back to sleep.

"Let's go through Georgia fast so we won't have to look at it much,"John Wesley said.

"If I were a little boy,"said the grandmother,"I wouldn't talk about my native state that way. Tennessee has the mountains and Georgia has the hills. "

"Tennessee is just a hillbilly dumping ground," John Wesley said,"and Georgia is a lousy state too. "

"You said it,"June Star said.

"In my time,"said the grandmother, folding her thin veined fingers,"children were more respectful of their native states and their parents and everything else. People did right then. Oh look at the cute little pickaninny!"she said and pointed to a Negro child standing in the door of a shack. "Wouldn't that make a picture, now?" she asked and they all turned and looked at the little Negro out of the back window. He waved.

"He didn't have any britches on,"June Star said.

"He probably didn't have any,"the grandmother explained. "Little niggers in the country don't have things like we do. If I could paint, I'd paint that picture,"she said.

The children exchanged comic books.

The grandmother offered to hold the baby and the children's mother passed him over the front seat to her. She set him on her knee and bounced him and told him about the things they were passing. She rolled her eyes and screwed up her mouth and stuck her leathery thin face into his smooth bland one. Occasionally he gave her a faraway smile. They passed a large cotton field with five or six graves fenced in the middle of it, like a small island. "Look at the graveyard!" the grandmother said, pointing it out. "That was the old family burying ground. That belonged to the plantation. "

"Where's the plantation?"John Wesley asked.

"Gone With the Wind," said the grandmother. "Ha. Ha. "

When the children finished all the comic books they had brought, they opened the lunch and ate it. The grandmother ate a peanut butter sandwich and an olive and would not let the children throw the box and the paper napkins out the window. When there was nothing else to do they played a game by choosing a cloud and making the other two guess what shape it suggested. John Wesley took one the shape of a cow and June Star guessed a cow and John Wesley said,no, an automobile,and June Star said he didn't play fair,and they began to slap each other over the grandmother.

云彩,琼·斯塔猜它像牛,可是约翰·韦斯利说不对,是辆汽车。琼·斯塔说他不公平,两人就隔着老奶奶,劈里啪啦对打起来。

老奶奶说要是他俩肯消停下来,就给他们讲个故事。她一讲故事,眼珠就翻来翻去,晃头晃脑,活像在做戏。她说啊,在她还是少女的时候,有一位先生来自佐治亚州贾斯珀,名叫埃德加·阿特金斯·蒂加登,一个劲儿追求她。她说他长得别提有多俊啦,是个绅士。每星期六下午都来看她,还必定给她带来一个西瓜,上面刻着他的姓名缩写字母——“E·A·T”①。嗯,她说有一个星期六,蒂加登先生又夹着西瓜来了,可巧没人在家,他就把西瓜留在屋前门廊上,乘坐他那辆晃里晃荡的旧汽车回贾斯珀了。她可从来没收到那个西瓜,因为有个过路的黑崽子看到西瓜上刻的3个字母是“吃”,就把它给吃掉了!这个故事好像挠了约翰·韦斯利胳肢窝下的痒痒肉,使他格格地笑个没完,琼·斯塔却觉得没多大意思。她说她绝不会嫁给一个每逢星期六就给她带一个西瓜来的男人。老奶奶说当初她要是嫁给蒂加登先生,那才叫嫁对了,因为他是一位地地道道的绅士,“可口可乐”汽水刚一创牌子,他就买下它的不少股票。前几年他才归西,死的时候是个大阔佬。

他们在宝塔餐厅门前停下车来,过去吃烤肉三明治。这家餐厅坐落在蒂莫西郊外的一块旷地上,是用水泥和木料盖的,兼作加油站,里面还有一间舞厅。老板名叫红萨米·巴茨,是个大块头。房子这儿那儿到处张贴着招徕顾客的广告,连好几英里以外的公路上都看得见这样的广告:

> 尝尝红萨米的名牌烤肉!红萨米的烤肉美味可口,名不虚传!红萨米!那个笑眯眯的胖小子!
>
> 名副其实的烤肉专家!红萨米为您致劳!

红萨米这时正躺在餐厅外面光秃秃的平地上,头钻在一辆卡车下面修车呐,旁边有只一英尺来高的小灰猴子做伴,它被铁链拴在一棵楝树上,叽叽咕咕地叫个不停。小猴子看见孩子跳下汽车,冲它跑来,立

----

① 即“埃德加·阿特金斯·蒂加登”,这个姓名每个字的头一个字母合起来,恰是“吃”的意思。

The grandmother said she would tell them a story if they would keep quiet. When she told a story, she rolled her eyes and waved her head and was very dramatic. She said once when she was a maiden lady she had been courted by a Mr. Edgar Atkins Teagarden from Jasper, Georgia. She said he was a very good-looking man and a gentleman and that he brought her a watermelon every Saturday afternoon with his initials cut in it, E. A. T. Well, one Saturday, she said, Mr. Teagarden brought the watermelon and there was nobody at home and he left it on the front porch and returned in his buggy to Jasper, but she never got the watermelon, she said, because a nigger boy ate it when he saw the initials, E. A. T. ! This story tickled John Wesley's funny bone and he giggled and giggled but June Star didn't think it was any good. She said she wouldn't marry a man that just brought her a watermelon on Saturday. The grandmother said she would have done well to marry Mr. Teagarden because he was a gentleman and had bought Coca-Cola stock when it first came out and that he had died only a few years ago, a very wealthy man.

They stopped at the Tower for barbecued sandwiches. The Tower was a part stucco and part wood filling station and dance hall set in a clearing outside of Timothy. A fat man named Red Sammy Butts ran it and there were signs stuck here and there on the building and for miles up and down the highway saying:

> *Try red sammy's famous barbecue. None like famous red sammy's! Red sam! The fat boy with the happy laugh.*
> *A veteran! Red sammy's your man!*

Red Sammy was lying on the bare ground outside The Tower with his head under a truck while a gray monkey about a foot high, chained to a small chinaberry tree, chattered nearby. The monkey sprang back into the tree and got on the highest limb as soon as he saw the children jump out of the car and run toward him.

Inside, The Tower was a long dark room with a counter at one end and tables at the other and dancing space in the middle. They all sat down at a board table next to the nickelodeon and Red Sam's wife, a tall burnt-brown woman with hair and eyes lighter than her skin, came and took their order. The children's mother put a dime in the machine and played "The Tennessee Waltz," and the grandmother said that tune always made her want to dance. She asked Bailey if he would like to dance but he only glared at her. He

刻往回一蹿上了树,爬到最高的树梢上去了。

　　宝塔餐厅里面是间长条的屋子,黑咕隆咚,一端有个柜台,另一端放着几张桌子,中间空当权当舞池。贝雷一家人拣了自动电唱机旁边的一张桌子,坐了下来,红萨米的老婆,一个肤色晒得通红的高个儿女人,眼睛和头发的颜色比肤色还要浅,走过来招呼,问他们想吃点儿什么。孩子妈往电唱机的小洞口投进一枚硬币,顿时奏出《田纳西圆舞曲》,老奶奶说不知怎的,这支曲子总叫她想站起来跳舞。她问贝雷愿不愿意跳个舞,他只冷冷地回瞪了一眼。他可不像她那样性情开朗,旅行使他感到厌烦。老奶奶棕色的眼睛炯炯发光,脑袋瓜子摆来摆去,做出一副坐在椅子上跳舞的姿态。琼·斯塔要听另外的曲子,好跟着拍子跳跳,孩子妈又往电唱机的小洞口投进一枚硬币,于是放出一支节拍快的曲子,琼·斯塔便走进舞池,跳起踢踏舞。

　　"多么可爱的小姑娘啊!"红萨米的老婆站在柜台后面探身说,"你愿不愿意做我的小女儿?"

　　"不,当然不愿意,"琼·斯塔说,"就是给我一百万块钱,我也不愿待在这样一个破烂的鬼地方!"她跑回自己的座位上去了。

　　"多么可爱的小姑娘!"那女人又重复一句,彬彬有礼地做了个窘相。

　　"你不觉得丢脸吗?"老奶奶轻声责备道。

　　红萨米进来了,叫他的老婆少在柜台那儿磨蹭,赶紧招待顾客。他穿的那条卡其裤子,只齐到胯骨那儿,大肚子像袋粮食似的,耷拉在裤腰上,在衬衫里头颠来颠去。他走过来,在附近一张桌子旁坐下,一连声叹了好几口气,嘴里嘟囔道:"简直没法办! 没法办!"他用一块灰不拉几的手帕擦了擦红彤彤的脸膛上的汗珠子。"这年头,您真不知道该相信谁才好,"他说,"是不是这么回事?"

　　"人确实没有从前那样好啦。"老奶奶说。

　　"上星期有两个家伙闯进来,"红萨米说,"他们开一辆克莱斯勒牌汽车,一辆撞得稀里哗啦的破车,不过没有多大毛病。这两个小伙子,依我看,也还规规矩矩,说是在工厂里干活的。于是,我就让他们灌满了要买的汽油。唉,我干吗要那样做呢?"

　　"因为你是个好心肠的人!"老奶奶当即答道。

　　"是啊,夫人,我想就是这么回事。"红萨米说,仿佛深受感动似的。

didn't have a naturally sunny disposition like she did and trips made him nervous. The grandmother's brown eyes were very bright. She swayed her head from side to side and pretended she was dancing in her chair. June Star said play something she could tap to so the children's mother put in another dime and played a fast number and June Star stepped out onto the dance floor and did her tap routine.

"Ain't she cute?" Red Sam's wife said, leaning over the counter. "Would you like to come be my little girl?"

"No I certainly wouldn't," June Star said. "I wouldn't live in a broken-down place like this for a million bucks!" and she ran back to the table.

"Ain't she cute?" the woman repeated, stretching her mouth politely.

"Aren't you ashamed?" hissed the grandmother.

Red Sam came in and told his wife to quit lounging on the counter and hurry up with these people's order. His khaki trousers reached just to his hip bones and his stomach hung over them like a sack of meal swaying under his shirt. He came over and sat down at a table nearby and let out a combination sigh and yodel. "You can't win," he said. "You can't win," and he wiped his sweating red face off with a gray handkerchief. "These days you don't know who to trust," he said. "Ain't that the truth?"

"People are certainly not nice like they used to be," said the grandmother.

"Two fellers come in here last week," Red Sammy said, "driving a Chrysler. It was a old beat-up car but it was a good one and these boys looked all right to me. Said they worked at the mill and you know I let them fellers charge the gas they bought? Now why did I do that?"

"Because you're a good man!" the grandmother said at once.

"Yes'm, I suppose so," Red Sam said as if he were struck with this answer.

His wife brought the orders, carrying the five plates all at once without a tray, two in each hand and one balanced on her arm. "It isn't a soul in this green world of God's that you can trust," she said. "And I don't count nobody out of that, not nobody," she repeated, looking at Red Sammy.

"Did you read about that criminal, The Misfit, that's escaped?" asked the grandmother.

"I wouldn't be a bit surprised if he didn't attack this place right here," said the woman. "If he hears about it being here, I wouldn't be none surprised to see him. If he hears it's two cent in the cash register, I

他的老婆端来吃食,没有托盘,居然一下子把五盘全都端来了,一手拿两盘,胳膊肘上还悬乎乎地托着另一盘。"在上帝的这个花花绿绿的世界里,没有一个人能让你信得过,"她说,"没有一个人例外,没有一个人哟!"她瞧着红萨米,又重复了一句。

"报上提到那个越狱的、不合时宜的人的消息,你们看到了吗?"老奶奶问。

"他没有马上到这儿来抢劫,我一丁点儿也不感到奇怪,"红萨米的老婆说,"他要是听说有这么个地方,准保会来的。他要是听说钱柜里只有两分钱,必定会……"

"得啦,得啦,"红萨米说,"快去把'可口可乐'给客人拿来吧。"那女人走开了,去端别的东西。

"好人难寻哟,"红萨米说,"样样事情都变得糟糕透顶。我记得当年出外,大门都可以不锁。再没那种好日子喽。"

他跟老奶奶谈论往昔美好的年月。老奶奶说,依她看来,如今出现这种情况,欧洲该负全部责任。她说欧洲那种做法,叫人以为我们全是钱做的呢。红萨米认为谈这些也都白搭,不过老奶奶的话还是千真万确的。孩子跑到大太阳底下看条纹累累的楝树顶端那只猴子去了。它正忙着抓身上的跳蚤,用牙小心嗑着,好像在吃什么珍馐美味。

酷热的午后,他们继续驱车前进。老奶奶打瞌睡了,每隔几分钟就让自己的呼噜声扰醒一次。到达图姆斯博罗郊外时,她醒过来了,想起当年她还是少女的时候参观过附近的一个古老的种植园。她说那栋房子前廊矗立着六根又大又白的柱子,一条幽静的林荫道,两旁种着成排的楝树,直通到大门前。两边各有一个木格子的小凉亭,你跟情人在花园里散步累了,可以在那里歇歇脚。她记得清清楚楚从什么地方转弯就可以通到那里。她明明知道贝雷不愿意浪费一点儿时间去看一所老宅子,可是她越说越想去看看,瞧瞧那对小凉亭有没有坍掉。"那栋房子里还有一堵秘密的夹板墙呢!"她狡黠地说,说的并非实话,却希望人人相信,"传说当年谢尔曼将军①带兵过来的时候,这家人把银器全部藏在里面了,可是后来再

---

① 威廉·谢尔曼(1820—1891):美国南北战争时期的北军将领,1864年9月率军攻占佐治亚州亚特兰大,使这一地区遭到浩劫。他的名字在南方一直受人诅咒。

wouldn't be at all surprised if he. . . "

"That'll do,"Red Sam said. "Go bring these people their Co'-Colas,"and the woman went off to get the rest of the order.

"A good man is hard to find,"Red Sammy said. "Everything is getting terrible. I remember the day you could go off and leave your screen door unlatched. Not no more. "

He and the grandmother discussed better times. The old lady said that in her opinion Europe was entirely to blame for the way things were now. She said the way Europe acted you would think we were made of money and Red Sam said it was no use talking about it, she was exactly right. The children ran outside into the white sunlight and looked at the monkey in the lacy chinaberry tree. He was busy catching fleas on himself and biting each one carefully between his teeth as if it were a delicacy.

They drove off again into the hot afternoon. The grandmother took cat naps and woke up every few minutes with her own snoring. Outside of Toombsboro she woke up and recalled an old plantation that she had visited in this neighborhood once when she was a young lady. She said the house had six white columns across the front and that there was an avenue of oaks leading up to it and two little wooden trellis arbors on either side in front where you sat down with your suitor after a stroll in the garden. She recalled exactly which road to turn off to get to it. She knew that Bailey would not be willing to lose any time looking at an old house, but the more she talked about it, the more she wanted to see it once again and find out if the little twin arbors were still standing. "There was a secret panel in this house," she said craftily, not telling the truth but wishing that she were, "and the story went that all the family silver was hidden in it when Sherman came through but it was never found. . . "

"Hey!"John Wesley said. "Let's go see it! We'll find it! We'll poke all the woodwork and find it! Who lives there? Where do you turn off at? Hey Pop, can't we turn off there?"

"We never have seen a house with a secret panel!"June Star shrieked. "Let's go to the house with the secret panel! Hey Pop, can't we go see the house with the secret panel!"

"It's not far from here, I know,"the grandmother said. "It wouldn't take over twenty minutes. "

Bailey was looking straight ahead. His jaw was as rigid as a horseshoe. "No,"he said.

The children began to yell and scream that they wanted to see the house with the secret panel. John Wesley kicked the back of the front seat and June Star

也没有找到。"

"嘿!"约翰·韦斯利说,"咱们去瞧瞧!准能找到!咱们把木板全都捅穿,准能找到!现在谁住在那儿?该从哪儿转弯?嘿,爹,咱们能到那儿去转一下吗?"

"我们从来没见过带秘密夹板墙的房子!"琼·斯塔尖声喊道,"咱们到那栋带秘密夹板墙的房子去吧!嘿,爹,咱们干吗不去看看那栋带夹板墙的房子呀?"

"反正离这儿也不太远,我知道,"老奶奶说,"用不了20分钟。"贝雷直盯着前方,下巴颏儿板得像马蹄铁一般硬。"不去。"他说。

两个孩子叽叽喳喳乱叫起来,非要去看看那栋带夹板墙的房子不可。约翰·韦斯利使劲儿踹汽车前座的后背,琼·斯塔趴在妈妈的肩膀上,哼哼唧唧地诉说他们连假期都过得不开心,从来不能称心如意地干他们想做的事。婴儿也哇哇地哭起来。约翰·韦斯利猛踢椅背,劲头之足,他爹连腰眼那儿都感到了冲力。

"好,好,好!"他喊道,在路旁刹住车,"你们都给我住嘴,行不行?住嘴一秒钟,好不好?你们要是不消停下来,哪儿也不去啦。"

"去看一看,对孩子也很有教育意义嘛!"老奶奶喃喃地说。

"好啦,"贝雷说,"可是记住,只为这种劳什子停留一次。就此一次,下不为例。"

"车子倒回去差不多一英里,就到了那条该转弯的土道,"老奶奶指挥道,"刚才路过那儿,我记了一下。"

"一条土道!"贝雷嘟囔了一句。

于是,他们掉头朝那条土道驶去。老奶奶又想起那栋房子别的特征,像前厅漂亮的玻璃门啦,大厅的烛灯啦,等等。约翰·韦斯利说秘密夹板墙没准儿藏在壁炉里头吧。

"那栋房子,你们根本进不去,"贝雷说,"你们不认识房主。"

"你们在前面跟主人谈话,我就绕到屋后,跳窗户进去。"约翰·韦斯利建议道。

"我们宁愿在汽车里。"妈妈说。

他们转到那条土道,汽车颠簸地驶了进去,顿时扬起一阵阵粉红色尘土。老奶奶想起当年没有石子路。一天至多能走30英里路。"这条土道,一会儿上

hung over her mother's shoulder and whined desperately into her ear that they never had any fun even on their vacation, that they could never do what THEY wanted to do. The baby began to scream and John Wesley kicked the back of the seat so hard that his father could feel the blows in his kidney.

"All right!"he shouted and drew the car to a stop at the side of the road. "Will you all shut up? Will you all just shut up for one second? If you don't shut up, we won't go anywhere. "

"It would be very educational for them," the grandmother murmured.

"All right," Bailey said, "but get this: this is the only time we're going to stop for anything like this. This is the one and only time. "

"The dirt road that you have to turn down is about a mile back," the grandmother directed. " I marked it when we passed. "

"A dirt road,"Bailey groaned.

After they had turned around and were headed toward the dirt road, the grandmother recalled other points about the house, the beautiful glass over the front doorway and the candle-lamp in the hall. John Wesley said that the secret panel was probably in the fireplace.

"You can't go inside this house," Bailey said. "You don't know who lives there. "

"While you all talk to the people in front, I'll run around behind and get in a window,"John Wesley suggested.

"We'll all stay in the car,"his mother said.

They turned onto the dirt road and the car raced roughly along in a swirl of pink dust. The grandmother recalled the times when there were no paved roads and thirty miles was a day's journey. The dirt road was hilly and there were sudden washes in it and sharp curves on dangerous embankments. All at once they would be on a hill, looking down over the blue tops of trees for miles around, then the next minute, they would be in a red depression with the dust-coated trees looking down on them.

"This place had better turn up in a minute,"Bailey said, "or I'm going to turn around. "

The road looked as if no one had traveled on it in months.

"It's not much farther,"the grandmother said and just as she said it,a horrible thought came to her. The thought was so embarrassing that she turned red in the face and her eyes dilated and her feet jumped up, upsetting her valise in the corner. The instant the valise moved,the newspaper top she had over the basket under it rose with a snarl and Pitty Sing, the cat,

坡,一会儿下坡,不少地方还有积水。有时还得在险峻的路堤上来个急转弯。霎时间,他们的车子行驶在山坡,眺望得见几英里以外茫茫一片青里透灰的树梢。转瞬间,他们又陷入个红土坑洼里,四处满布尘土的树木都在俯视他们。

"那个鬼地方最好马上出现。"贝雷说,"要不然我就要折回去了。"

这条土道像是一条成年累月没人走过的路。

"没多远了。"老奶奶说。话刚一脱口,脑子里蓦地闪现一个糟糕的念头,窘得她满面通红,两眼发直,两条腿一抬,把那个放在角落里的旅行袋碰翻了。旅行袋一倒,老猫咪喵地一声从那个盖着报纸的篮子里蹿出来,蹦到贝雷的肩膀上去了。

孩子们摔倒在车厢里,孩子妈紧抱着婴儿被甩出车外,跌倒在路上,老奶奶也给甩到前座上去了。汽车翻了个斤斗,掉进路旁的沟壑。贝雷仍然坐在驾驶座上。那只猫——一只宽白脸,红鼻头,灰条纹的花狸猫——像条肉虫子似的紧盘在他的脖子上。

孩子们一发现脚还能动弹,便从车厢里爬出来,嘴里嚷道:"出车祸喽!"老奶奶蜷缩在前车厢的踏板上,但愿她自己受了点儿伤,免得贝雷的火气全冲她一人发来。车祸发生前,她脑子里猛地闪现的那个糟糕的念头,原来是她方才记得一清二楚的那栋房子并不在佐治亚州,而是在田纳西州。

贝雷用两只手把猫从脖子上揪下来,向窗外面一棵松树那边狠狠扔过去。接着,他下了汽车,先找孩子妈。她抱着哇哇哭的婴儿,呆坐在红黏土的沟沿上,幸好只是脸上划破一个口子,肩膀有点儿扭伤。"出车祸喽!"孩子们狂热地吱哇乱叫。

老奶奶瘸着腿从车厢里钻出来,琼·斯塔失望地说:"真可惜谁也没死!"老奶奶的帽子依然扣在脑袋上,可是前檐断裂了,往上翘起,形成一个挺时髦的角度,一边上还耷拉着那朵紫罗兰的花蕊。除了两个孩子,他们三个人都在沟里坐下来,从惊吓中慢慢苏醒过来,浑身在打颤。

"也许会有辆汽车路过吧。"孩子奶沙哑地说。

"我的内脏不定哪儿受了伤。"老奶奶说,手在揉肋骨,可是没人搭理她。贝雷气得上下牙直打磕碰。他穿一件黄运动衫,上面印着蓝鹦鹉,脸色跟运动衫一般蜡黄。老奶奶决定不提那栋房子是在田纳西州了。

sprang onto Bailey's shoulder.

The children were thrown to the floor and their mother, clutching the baby, was thrown out the door onto the ground; the old lady was thrown into the front seat. The car turned over once and landed right-side-up in a gulch off the side of the road. Bailey remained in the driver's seat with the cat—gray-striped with a broad white face and an orange nose—clinging to his neck like a caterpillar.

As soon as the children saw they could move their arms and legs, they scrambled out of the car, shouting, "We've had an ACCIDENT!" The grandmother was curled up under the dashboard, hoping she was injured so that Bailey's wrath would not come down on her all at once. The horrible thought she had had before the accident was that the house she had remembered so vividly was not in Georgia but in Tennessee.

Bailey removed the cat from his neck with both hands and flung it out the window against the side of a pine tree. Then he got out of the car and started looking for the children's mother. She was sitting against the side of the red gutted ditch, holding the screaming baby, but she only had a cut down her face and a broken shoulder. "We've had an ACCIDENT!" the children screamed in a frenzy of delight.

"But nobody's killed," June Star said with disappointment as the grandmother limped out of the car, her hat still pinned to her head but the broken front brim standing up at a jaunty angle and the violet spray hanging off the side. They all sat down in the ditch, except the children, to recover from the shock. They were all shaking.

"Maybe a car will come along," said the children's mother hoarsely.

"I believe I have an injured organ," said the grandmother, pressing her side, but no one answered her. Bailey's teeth were clattering. He had on a yellow sport shirt with bright blue parrots designed on it and his face was as yellow as the shirt. The grandmother decided that she would not mention that the house was in Tennessee.

The road was about ten feet above and they could see only the tops of the trees on the other side of it. Behind the ditch they were sitting in there were more woods, tall and dark and deep. In a few minutes they saw a car some distance away on top of a hill, coming slowly as if the occupants were watching them. The grandmother stood up and waved both arms dramatically to attract their attention. The car continued to come on slowly, disappeared around a bend and appeared again, moving even slower, on top of the hill

路面要比他们坐的地方高出 10 英尺，她们只能望见路那边的树梢。还有更多的树木，在他们陷进去的那个沟壑后面，苍郁而挺拔。几分钟过后，他们看见远方山坡上有辆汽车朝他们这个方向慢慢驶来。车里的人好像在注视他们。老奶奶站起来，使劲儿挥动两只胳臂，好让人家注意。汽车继续慢吞吞地开过来，时而在转角处隐没，时而又冒出来，驶到他们刚才路过的那个山坡时，蠕动得越发慢了。它就像一辆又黑又大、破旧不堪的枢车，里面坐着三个男人。

车在他们头顶上方的土道上停下来。司机毫无表情地凝视着他们所坐的地方，不发一语。接着，他回头跟另外两个人嘀咕了几句，三人便一块儿从汽车里下来。一个是胖胖的小伙子，穿一条黑裤子，上身是件红运动衫，胸前印着一匹飞驰的银色骏马。他蹓跶到这家人的右边，站在那里，半咧着嘴，狞笑地盯视着他们。另一个小伙子，穿一条卡其裤子和一件蓝条的外衣，头戴一顶灰礼帽，帽檐拉得很低，几乎遮住了大半个脸。他慢吞吞地踱到这家人的左边。两个人一句话也没说。

司机下了车，站在车旁低头瞧着他们。他比另外两个人年纪大，头发有点儿灰白了，戴一副银丝边眼镜，显出一副堂堂学者的派头。他生就一张马脸，皱纹挺多，没穿衬衫，也没穿背心，下身是条绷得很紧的蓝色劳动布裤子，手里拿一顶黑帽子和一把手枪。两个小伙子手里也有枪。

"我们出车祸啦！"孩子们扯起尖嗓门喊道。

老奶奶有股奇特的感觉，好像认识那个戴眼镜的人，面熟得很，仿佛已经跟他认识一辈子了，可就是想不起他到底是谁。那人离开汽车，朝沟下走来，小心翼翼地迈着步子，免得滑倒。他穿一双棕白两色的皮鞋，没穿袜子，脚脖子又红又瘦。"你们好，"他说，"我瞧见你们翻了一个滚。"

"翻了两个滚。"老奶奶答道。

"不，一个滚。"他纠正道，"我们看得一清二楚。海勒姆，你去试试他们的车子还能开动不。"他悄声对戴灰帽子的小伙子说。

"你干吗拿把手枪？"约翰·韦斯利问，"干吗拿枪啊？"

"太太，"那人对孩子妈说，"你能不能叫两个孩子挨着你坐下来？我一见孩子就心烦。我要你们一块儿坐在原地不动。"

they had gone over. It was a big black battered hearse-like automobile. There were three men in it.

It came to a stop just over them and for some minutes, the driver looked down with a steady expressionless gaze to where they were sitting, and didn't speak. Then he turned his head and muttered something to the other two and they got out. One was a fat boy in black trousers and a red sweat shirt with a silver stallion embossed on the front of it. He moved around on the right side of them and stood staring, his mouth partly open in a kind of loose grin. The other had on khaki pants and a blue striped coat and a gray hat pulled down very low, hiding most of his face. He came around slowly on the left side. Neither spoke.

The driver got out of the car and stood by the side of it, looking down at them. He was an older man than the other two. His hair was just beginning to gray and he wore silver-rimmed spectacles that gave him a scholarly look. He had a long creased face and didn't have on any shirt or undershirt. He had on blue jeans that were too tight for him and was holding a black hat and a gun. The two boys also had guns.

"We've had an ACCIDENT!" the children screamed.

The grandmother had the peculiar feeling that the bespectacled man was someone she knew. His face was as familiar to her as if she had known him all her life but she could not recall who he was. He moved away from the car and began to come down the embankment, placing his feet carefully so that he wouldn't slip. He had on tan and white shoes and no socks, and his ankles were red and thin. "Good afternoon," he said. "I see you all had you a little spill."

"We turned over twice!" said the grandmother.

"Oncet," he corrected. "We seen it happen. Try their car and see will it run, Hiram," he said quietly to the boy with the gray hat.

"What you got that gun for?" John Wesley asked. "Whatcha gonna do with that gun?"

"Lady," the man said to the children's mother, "would you mind calling them children to sit down by you? Children make me nervous. I want all you to sit down right together there where you're at."

"What are you telling US what to do for?" June Star asked.

Behind them the line of woods gaped like a dark open mouth. "Come here," said their mother.

"Look here now," Bailey began suddenly, "we're in a predicament! We're in. . ."

The grandmother shrieked. She scrambled to her feet and stood staring. "You're The Misfit!" she said. "I recognized you at once!"

"你凭什么支使我们?"琼·斯塔问。

他们身后的树林像一张咧开的大黑嘴。"过来。"孩子妈说。

"你瞧,"贝雷突然开口了,"我们现在处境十分尴尬。我们……"

老奶奶啊地尖叫一声,猛地爬起来,瞪着两只大眼。"你敢情是那个不合时宜的人!"她说,"我一眼就把你认出来了!"

"老太太,"那人说,微微一笑,仿佛被人认出来不由得自鸣得意似的,"不过,老太太,要是您没认出我是谁,也许对您全家倒会更有利些。"

贝雷很快掉过头来,跟他妈嘟哝了几句,车孩子们听见都吓了一大跳。老奶奶呜咽起来。那个不合时宜的人脸涨得通红。

"老太太,"他说,"别难过。有时一个人说话并非出自本意。我想他原来没打算跟您这样说话。'

"你不会杀害一个妇道人家吧?"老奶奶一边说,一边从袖口里掏出一块干净手绢使劲儿擦了擦眼睛。

不合时宜的人用脚尖在地上踱了个洞,又用脚把它填平。"除非万不得已,我是不愿意下毒手的。"他说。

"听我说,"老奶奶几乎像是在尖叫,"我知道你是个好人。你看上去一点儿也不像匪徒之辈。我知道你准是好人家出身!"

"对了,老太太,"他说,"世界上最好的人家。"他笑了,露出一排整齐而结实的白牙齿。"上帝再也没造出比我妈更好的女人了,我爹心地也跟赤金一样纯洁。"他说。那个穿红运动衫的家伙绕到这家人的背后站住,手枪别在胯骨那儿。不合时宜的人蹲了下来。"博比·李,看住这两个孩子,"他说,"你晓得他俩搅得我心神不定。"他瞧着身前挤作一堆的六口人,似乎有点儿发窘,仿佛不知道该说什么才好。"咦,天上一点儿云彩也没有,"他抬头看了一眼说,"不见太阳,可也没有云彩。"

"是啊,今儿天多好,"老奶奶说,"听我说,你不该管自己叫不合时宜的人,因为我知道你是个好心眼儿的人。我一眼就看出来了。"

"别说话!"贝雷嚷道,"全都闭上嘴,让我一个人来应付这局面!"他像运动员那样蹲伏在地上,仿佛要起跑,可是并没动窝。

"谢谢您的恭维,老太太。"不合时宜的人用枪托

"Yes'm,"the man said, smiling slightly as if he were pleased in spite of himself to be known,"but it would have been better for all of you, lady, if you hadn't of reckernized me."

Bailey turned his head sharply and said something to his mother that shocked even the children. The old lady began to cry and The Misfit reddened.

"Lady,"he said,"don't you get upset. Sometimes a man says things he don't mean. I don't reckon he meant to talk to you thataway."

"You wouldn't shoot a lady, would you?" the grandmother said and removed the clean handkerchief from her cuff and began to slap at her eves with it.

The Misfit pointed the toe of his shoe into the ground and made a little hole and then covered it up again. "I would hate to have to,"he said.

"Listen," the grandmother almost screamed, "I know you're a good man. You don't look a bit like you have common blood. I know you must come from nice people!"

"Yes mam,"he said,"finest people in the world." When he smiled he showed a row of strong white teeth. "God never made a finer woman than my mother and my daddy's heart was pure gold,"he said. The boy with the red sweat shirt had come around behind them and was standing with his gun at his hip. The Misfit squatted down on the ground. "Watch them children, Bobby Lee,"he said. "You know they make me nervous."He looked at the six of them huddled together in front of him and he seemed to be embarrassed as if he couldn't think of anything to say. "Ain't a cloud in the sky,"he remarked, looking up at it. "Don't see no sun but don't see no cloud neither."

"Yes, it's a beautiful day,"said the grandmother. "Listen," she said, "you shouldn't call yourself The Misfit because I know you're a good man at heart. I can just look at you and tell."

"Hush!" Bailey yelled. "Hush! Everybody shut up and let me handle this!" He was squatting in the position of a runner about to sprint forward but he didn't move.

"I pre-chate that, lady,"The Misfit said and drew a little circle in the ground with the butt of his gun.

"It'll take a half a hour to fix this here car,"Hiram called, looking over the raised hood of it.

"Well, first you and Bobby Lee get him and that little boy to step over yonder with you," The Misfit said, pointing to Bailey and John Wesley. "The boys want to ask you something,"he said to Bailey. "Would you mind stepping back in them woods there with them?"

"Listen," Bailey began, "we're in a terrible

在地上画个小圆圈。

"这辆车修好，起码得花半个小时。"海勒姆望着汽车凸起来的顶篷，提醒了一句。

"那你和博比·李先把他跟那个男孩带到那边去吧！"不合时宜的人指着贝雷和约翰·韦斯利说。"这两个小伙子要问你点儿事，"他又对贝雷说，"请跟他们到那边树林里走一趟吧。"

"您瞧，"贝雷说，"我们现在处境非常尴尬，稀里糊涂得还闹不清怎么回事呐！"他的声音嘶哑，两眼跟他衬衫上的蓝鹦鹉一般蓝而殷切。他一动也没动。

老奶奶抬手整理整理帽檐，好像也要跟儿子一块儿进入树林，可是帽檐不幸脱落在手中，她愣在那里，瞪着手里拎着的帽檐，过了半晌才松手让它落在地上。海勒姆揪住贝雷的胳膊，像搀老头儿那样把他搀扶起来。约翰·韦斯利紧拉着爸爸的手，博比·李跟在后头，他们朝树林走去。刚要进入阴森森的树林，贝雷一转身，靠在一棵光秃秃、灰暗的松树干上，喊道：娘，我一会儿就回来，等着我！"

"眼下就回来吧！"老奶奶尖声喊道，但是他们还是消逝在树林里了。

"贝雷，我的儿啊！"老奶奶凄惨地嚷道，可是她发现自己正在瞧着蹲在她面前的不合时宜的人，便绝望地对他说，"我知道您是个好人，您可一点儿也不像坏人！"

"不，我不是一个好人。"不合时宜的人好像仔细掂量了一下她的话，然后说道，"可我也不是世界上最坏的人。我多说我跟我的兄弟姐妹不一样，是另一个品种的狗崽子。'你知道，'我爹说，'有人一辈子也没问过一个为什么，可是另有一些人总爱刨根问底。这孩子就属于后一种人。他将来准会到处惹是生非！'"他戴上黑帽子，突然仰视天空，又朝树林深处张望一下，仿佛又有点发窘。"很抱歉，我在你们两位太太面前光着上身，"他说，耸耸肩膀，"我们一逃出来，就把囚犯衣服埋掉了。没有更好的改善之前，只好凑合有什么穿什么。这几件衣服也是向几位遇到的人借来的呢。"他解释道。

"没什么关系，"老奶奶说，"贝雷的箱子里也许还有件替换的衬衫。"

"我这就去看看。"不合时宜的人说。

"他们把他带到哪儿去啦？"孩子妈嚷道。

"我爹是个了不起的人，"不合时宜的人说，"你怎

predicament! Nobody realizes what this is," and his voice cracked. His eyes were as blue and intense as the parrots on his shirt and he remained perfectly still.

The grandmother reached up to adjust her hat brim as if she were going to the woods with him but it came off in her hand. She stood staring at it and after a second she let it fall on the ground. Hiram pulled Bailey up by the arm as if he were assisting an old man. John Wesley caught hold of his father's hand and Bobby Lee followed. They went off toward the woods and just as they reached the dark edge, Bailey turned and supported himself against a gray naked pine trunk, he shouted, "I'll be back in a minute, Mamma, wait on me!"

"Come back this instant!" his mother shrilled but they all disappeared into the woods.

"Bailey Boy!" the grandmother called in a tragic voice but she found she was looking at The Misfit squatting on the ground in front of her. "I just know you're a good man," she said desperately. "You're not a bit common!"

"Nome, I ain't a good man," The Misfit said after a second as if he had considered her statement carefully, "but I ain't the worst in the world neither. My daddy said I was a different breed of dog from my brothers and sisters. 'You know,' Daddy said, 'it's some that can live their whole life out without asking about it and it's others has to know why it is, and this boy is one of the latters. He's going to be into everything!'" He put on his black hat and looked up suddenly and then away deep into the woods as if he were embarrassed again. "I'm sorry I don't have on a shirt before you ladies," he said, hunching his shoulders slightly. "We buried our clothes that we had on when we escaped and we're just making do until we can get better. We borrowed these from some folks we met," he explained.

"That's perfectly all right," the grandmother said. "Maybe Bailey has an extra shirt in his suitcase."

"I'll look and see terrectly," The Misfit said.

"Where are they taking him?" the children's mother screamed.

"Daddy was a card himself," The Misfit said. "You couldn't put anything over on him. He never got in trouble with the Authorities though. Just had the knack of handling them."

"You could be honest too if you'd only try," said the grandmother. "Think how wonderful it would be to settle down and live a comfortable life and not have to think about somebody chasing you all the time."

The Misfit kept scratching in the ground with the

么也抓不着他的把柄,尽管他从来没跟官方发生过什么麻烦。他就是有办法对付他们。"

"你要是肯试着那样办,也可以成为一个堂堂的正人君子,"老奶奶说,"想想看,要是能安顿下来,舒舒服服过日子,不用成天想着有人在追捕你,那该多好啊!"

不合时宜的人一个劲儿用枪托在地上刮土。仿佛在考虑这个问题。"是啊,老太太,总是有人在追捕你。"他喃喃地说。

老奶奶发现他帽子下面的肩胛骨挺瘦,因为她正站在那里瞧着他。"你祷告吗?"她问。

他摇摇头。老奶奶只看见那顶黑帽子在他的两块肩胛骨之间晃来晃去。"不祷告。"他说。

树林里传来一声枪响,紧跟着又是一响。随后一片静寂。老奶奶猛地扭过头去。她听得见风从树梢吹来,像是心满意足地抽了口长气似的。"贝雷儿啊!"她叫唤道。

"我在唱诗班里唱过一阵子,"不合时宜的人说,"我什么都干。服过兵役,陆军啦,海军啦,国内国外都驻扎过,结过两次婚,在殡仪馆里当过差,铁路上干过一阵子。此外,种过庄稼,遇到过龙卷风,还见过一个男人活活给烧死。"他抬头瞧着孩子妈和小姑娘,她俩紧紧偎在一起,脸色惨白,目光发呆。"我还见过一个女人让人鞭打呢!"他说,"祈祷吧。"老奶奶说:"祈祷吧……"

"我记得自己从来也不是个坏孩子,"不合时宜的人用一种近乎轻柔的声调说,"可不知在哪里做了点儿错事,就被送进教养院,活活给埋没了。"他抬头注视着她,好让她注意听。

"那正是你该祷告的时候,"她说,"头一次你被送进教养院,是为了什么呀?"

"你向右转是堵墙,"不合时宜的人又仰起头来,凝视万里无云的天空,说道,"你向左转,还是堵墙。抬头是天花板,低头是地板。我忘了自己干了什么,老太太。我坐在那儿,冥思苦想,想想自己到底做了什么错事,可是直到今天也没想起来。有时觉得快想起来了,可是总没有个结果。"

"他们可能错判了吧?"老奶奶含含糊糊地问。

"没有,"他说,"没弄错。他们有白纸黑字的证据。"

"你别是偷了什么东西吧?"她问道。

butt of his gun as if he were thinking about it. "Yes'm, somebody is always after you," he murmured.

The grandmother noticed how thin his shoulder blades were just behind his hat because she was standing up looking down on him. "Do you ever pray?" she asked.

He shook his head. All she saw was the black hat wiggle between his shoulder blades. "Nome," he said.

There was a pistol shot from the woods, followed closely by another. Then silence. The old lady's head jerked around. She could hear the wind move through the tree tops like a long satisfied insuck of breath. "Bailey Boy!" she called.

"I was a gospel singer for a while," The Misfit said. "I been most everything. Been in the arm service, both land and sea, at home and abroad, been twict married, been an undertaker, been with the railroads, plowed Mother Earth, been in a tornado, seen a man burnt alive on017t," and he looked up at the children's mother and the little girl who were sitting close together, their faces white and their eyes glassy; "I even seen a woman Hogged," he said.

"Pray, pray," the grandmother began, "pray, pray..."

"I never was a bad boy that I remember of," The Misfit said in an almost dreamy voice, "but somewheres along the line I done something wrong and got sent to the penitentiary. I was buried alive," and he looked up and held her attention to him by a steady stare.

"That's when you should have started to pray," she said. "What did you do to get sent to the penitentiary that first time?"

"Turn to the right, it was a wall," The Misfit said, looking up again at the cloudless sky. "Turn to the left, it was a wall. Look up it was a ceiling, look down it was a floor. I forget what I done, lady. I set there and set there, trying to remember what it was I done and I ain't recalled it to this day. Oncet in a while, I would think it was coming to me, but it never come."

"Maybe they put you in by mistake," the old lady said vaguely.

"Nome," he said. "it wasn't no mistake. They had the papers on me."

"You must heve stolen something," she said.

The Misfit sneered slightly. "Nobody had nothing I wanted," he said. "It was a head-doctor at the penitentiary said what I had done was kill my daddy but I known that for a lie. My daddy died in nineteen ought nineteen of the epidemic flu and I never had a thing to

不合时宜的人冷笑一声。"谁也没有什么我想要的东西，"他说，"教养院的主任医师说我犯的罪是杀死了亲生父亲，可我知道那是胡说八道。我爹是1919年闹流行性感冒时死的，跟我一点儿关系也没有。他葬在霍普韦尔山浸礼会教堂的墓地，你不信可以自己去看看。"

"你要是祈祷，"老奶奶说，"耶稣会帮助你的。"

"说的是。"不合时宜的人说。

"那你干吗不祈祷啊？"她问道，突然高兴得浑身颤抖。

"我什么帮助也不要，"他说，"我自己干得蛮好。"

博比·李和海勒姆从树林里从容地走出来。博比·李手里还拎着一件印着蓝鹦鹉的黄衬衫。

"博比·李，把那件衬衫扔过来。"不合时宜的人说。衬衫嗖地飞过来，落在他的肩膀上，他就把它穿上了。老奶奶说不出这件衬衫给她带来了什么回忆。"不，老太太，"不合时宜的人一边说，一边扣扣子，"我发现犯罪没什么了不起。可以干这件事，也可以干另一件事，杀人啦，从他的车上拆下一个轮胎啦，都一个样儿，因为迟早你总会忘掉自己干了些什么，而且要为这受到惩罚。"

孩子妈呼哧呼哧地喘气，好像上气不接下气似的。

"太太，"他问道，"你和小姑娘愿不愿意跟随博比·李和海勒姆到那边去同你丈夫会合？"

"行，谢谢。"孩子妈有气无力地说。她的左胳膊不听使唤地来回晃悠，另一只胳膊抱着睡熟了的婴儿。她吃力地往沟坡上爬，不合时宜的人说："海勒姆，搀一把那个女人。博比·李，你拉着小姑娘的手。"

"我不要他拉着，"琼·斯塔说，"他那副模样让我想起一头猪。"

胖小子脸涨红了，笑了笑，抓住小姑娘的胳臂，紧跟在她妈妈和海勒姆身后，把她抱进树林。

老奶奶发现如今只剩下她和不合时宜的人单独在一起，反倒说不出话来了。天空既没有一块云彩，也没有太阳。她周围除了树林，什么也没有。她想告诉他应该祷告，张了张嘴，又闭上了，没吭一声。最后，她发现自己在念叨"耶稣啊！耶稣啊！"意思是说耶稣会帮助你，可是从她那种口气听来，倒像是在埋怨耶稣。

do with it. He was buried in the Mount Hopewell Baptist churchyard and you can go there and see for yourself. "

"If you would pray," the old lady said," Jesus would help you. "

"That's right," The Misfit said.

"Well then, why don't you pray?" she asked trembling with delight suddenly.

"I don't want no hep,' he said. "I'm doing all right by myself. "

Bobby Lee and Hiram came ambling back from the woods. Bobby Lee was dragging a yellow shirt with bright blue parrots in it.

"Throw me that shirt, Bobby Lee," The Misfit said. The shirt came flying at him and landed on his shoulder and he put it on. The grandmother couldn't name what the shirt reminded her of. "No, lady," The Misfit said while he was buttoning it up, "I found out the crime don't matter. You can do one thing or you can do another, kill a man or take a tire off his car, because sooner or later you're going to forget what it was you done and just be punished for it. "

The children's mother had begun to make heaving noises as if she couldn't get her breath. "Lady," he asked, "would you and that little girl like to step off yonder with Bobby Lee and Hiram and join your husband?"

"Yes, thank you," the mother said faintly. Her left arm dangled helplessly and she was holding the baby, who had gone to sleep, in the other. "Hep that lady up, Hiram," The Misfit said as she struggled to climb out of the ditch," And Bobby Lee, you hold onto that little girl's hand. "

"I don't want to hold hands with him," June Star said. "He reminds me of a pig. "

The fat boy blushed and laughed and caught her by the arm and pulled her off into the woods after Hiram and her mother.

Alone with The Misfit, the grandmother found that she had lost her voice. There was not a cloud in the sky nor any sun. There was nothing around her but woods. She wanted to tell him that he must pray. She opened and closed her mouth several times before anything came out. Finally she found herself saying, "Jesus, Jesus," meaning, Jesus will help you, but the way she was saying it, it sounded as if she might be cursing.

"Yes'm," The Misfit said as if he agreed. "Jesus thown everything off balance. It was the same case with Him as with me except He hadn't committed any

"是啊,老太太,"不合时宜的人仿佛同意似的说,"耶稣把一切都搅得乱七八糟。他的处境跟我差不离儿,只不过没犯什么罪罢了,而他们却能证明我犯过罪,因为他们有我犯罪的白纸黑字的证据。当然啰,"他说,"他们从来也没有给我看过我的罪证。这就是干吗现在我干脆自己签字。我老早就说过自己签字,好汉做事好汉当,然后自己保存一份原件。这样你就知道自己到底干过啥,可以衡量一下所受的惩罚跟所犯的罪是否合情合理,最后你可以拿出点儿凭据证明自己被惩罚得一点儿也不公平。我管自己叫不合时宜的人,"他说,"因为我没法认为自己被处罚得合情合理,罪有应得。"

树林里传来一声尖叫,紧跟着是声枪响。"老太太,有人没完没了地受惩罚,而别人却从来也没挨过罚,您认为这合乎情理吗?"

"耶稣啊!"老奶奶喊道,"你出身高贵,我知道你不会枪杀一个妇道人家的!我知道你是好人家抚养大的!耶稣啊!你不该枪杀一个妇道人家,我可以把我带的钱都给你!"

"老太太,"不合时宜的人说,望着树林深处,"从来也没听说过死尸赏小费给抬棺材的人的。"

又传来两声枪响,老奶奶像一只讨水喝的喉咙干燥的老火鸡那样扬起头来啼叫,"贝雷儿啊,贝雷宝贝儿啊!"心似乎都快碎了。

"只有耶稣能叫人起死回生,"不会时宜的人接着说,"他不该那么做。他把一切都搅得乱七八糟。如果他照他所说的那样做,那你最好抛弃一切,追随他去吧。如果他没有那么做,那你最好尽情享受一下生命的最后几分钟吧——杀个把人啦,放把火烧掉那人的住房啦,要不然对他干些丧尽天良的事。除了伤天害理,别无其他乐趣。"他说着,嗓音几乎变得像是在号叫。

"也许耶稣没有叫人起死回生过。"老奶奶喃喃地说,连自己也不知道在说什么。她头晕眼花,扑通一下坐倒在沟里,两腿歪扭着。

"我没在场,所以不敢说他没干过,"不合时宜的人说,"我真希望当时在场就好了。"他一边说,一边用拳头捶地。"我没在场,确实不对,因为要是在场,就会知道是怎么回事啦。听着,老太太,"他提高嗓门说,"我要是在场,就会知道怎么回事啦,我也不会变成如今这个样儿了。"他的嗓音好像要炸裂了,老奶奶

crime and they could prove I had committed one because they had the papers on me. Of course," he said, "they never shown me my papers. That's why I sign myself now. I said long ago, you get you a signature and sign everything you do and keep a copy of it. Then you'll know what you done and you can hold up the crime to the punishment and see do they match and in the end you'll have something to prove you ain't been treated right. I call myself The Misfit," he said, "because I can't make what all I done wrong fit what all I gone through in punishment."

There was a piercing scream from the woods, followed closely by a pistol report. "Does it seem right to you, lady, that one is punished a heap and another ain't punished at all?"

"Jesus!" the old lady cried. "You've got good blood! I know you wouldn't shoot a lady! I know you come from nice people! Pray! Jesus, you ought not to shoot a lady. I'll give you all the money I've got!"

"Lady," The Misfit said, looking beyond her far into the woods, "there never was a body that give the undertaker a tip."

There were two more pistol reports and the grandmother raised her head like a parched old turkey hen crying for water and called, "Bailey Boy, Bailey Boy!" as if her heart would break.

"Jesus was the only One that ever raised the dead," The Misfit continued, "and He shouldn't have done it. He thown everything off balance. If He did what He said, then it's nothing for you to do but throw away everything and follow Him, and if He didn't, then it's nothing for you to do but enjoy the few minutes you got left the best way you can—by killing somebody or burning down his house or doing some other meanness to him. No pleasure but meanness," he said and his voice had become almost a snarl.

"Maybe He didn't raise the dead," the old lady mumbled, not knowing what she was saying and feeling so dizzy that she sank down in the ditch with her legs twisted under her.

"I wasn't there so I can't say He didn't," The Misfit said. "I wisht I had of been there," he said, hitting the ground with his fist. "It ain't right I wasn't there because if I had of been there I would of known. Listen lady," he said in a high voice, "if I had of been there I would of known and I wouldn't be like I am now." His voice seemed about to crack and the grandmother's head cleared for an instant. She saw the

头脑突然清醒了一下。她看见那家伙的脸歪扭着，离她自己的脑袋不太远，仿佛要哭似的，她便小声说道："唉，你也是我的一个孩子，我的一个亲生儿哟！"她伸出两手，抚摸他的肩膀。不合时宜的人猛地闪开，好像让毒蛇咬了一口似的，朝她胸口砰砰砰连开三枪。然后，他把枪放在地上，摘下眼镜擦擦灰。

海勒姆和博比·李从树林里走出来，站在沟渠上面俯视着老奶奶，她半躺半坐在一摊鲜血里，像孩子那样盘着腿，脸上还挂着一丝微笑，仰视着万里无云的晴空。

不合时宜的人不戴眼镜，两眼显得暗淡无神，现出一圈通红的眼窝。"把她弄走，跟其他几个人扔到一块儿去！"他一边说，一边把那只在他脚边磨蹭的猫拎起来。

"这位老太太真够贫嘴的，是不是？"博比·李说，一边哼着小调从沟渠上滑下来。

"要是一辈子每分钟都有人没完没了地冲她开枪射击，"不合时宜的人说，"她也会成为一个好女人的。"

"挺有趣！"博比·李说。

"住嘴，博比·李，"不合时宜的人说，"人生根本没有真正的乐趣。"

man's face twisted close to her own as if he were going to cry and she murmured, "Why you're one of my babies. You're one of my own children!" She reached out and touched him on the shoulder. The Misfit sprang back as if a snake had bitten him and shot her three times through the chest. Then he put his gun down on the ground and took off his glasses and began to clean them.

Hiram and Bobby Lee returned from the woods and stood over the ditch, looking down at the grandmother who half sat and half lay in a puddle of blood with her legs crossed under her like a child's and her face smiling up at the cloudless sky.

Without his glasses, The Misfit's eyes were red-rimmed and pale and defenseless-looking. "Take her off and thow her where you thown the others," he said, picking up the cat that was rubbing itself against his leg.

"She was a talker, wasn't she?" Bobby Lee said, sliding down the ditch with a yodel.

"She would of been a good woman," The Misfit said, "if it had been somebody there to shoot her every minute of her life."

"Some fun!" Bobby tee said.

"Shut up, Bobby Lee," The Misfit said. "It's no real pleasure in life."

┌ 讨　论 ─■

1. 就像《纪念爱米丽的一朵玫瑰花》一样，这篇小说也写了一则关于心理变态的骇人听闻的故事。从表面上看，这篇小说所写的是一个杀人狂在路上偶尔遇到一家人，这家人既平常又善良，后来他又把他们杀了。但作者是如何通过这件具体事件对人类普遍的价值标准发表意见的？（诚然，由于这篇小说合乎统一性，其中每种成份都能用来回答这个问题，但是关键性的答案则包含在老奶奶和那个"不合时宜的人"的那段对话里。请仔细分析这段对话，然后谈谈这篇小说的主题。）

2. 老奶奶的性格如何？她是个讨人欢喜的人呢，还是个人人讨厌的人？她是值得尊敬呢，还是只配唾弃？她是自私的呢，还是不自私的？她的性格对于理解这篇小说有何意义？

1. This story, like "A Rose for Emily," presents us with a shocking piece of pathology. Viewed objectively, the story is an account of how a homicidal maniac slaughters a family of ordinary, innocent people whom he happens to encounter on the road. How does the author interpret this special situation as a comment on general human values? (Of course, insofar as the story is coherent, everything in it will bear on the answer to this question, but especially important for an answer is the dialogue between the old lady and The Misfit. Study very carefully this dialogue and then try to make a statement about the theme of the story.)

2. What is the character of the old lady? Pleasant or unpleasant? Admirable or unadmirable? Selfish or unselfish? How does her character bear on the interpretation of the story?

3. 这篇小说可以分成两部分——第一部分篇幅较长,写旅行的情况;遇到那个"不合时宜的人"以后,是小说的第二部分。请思考一下,这两个部分是通过什么东西合或一体的? 这样的结合与小说的主题有何关系? 我们或许会说,这样的结合纯属巧合——一家人遇到了意外的事,而偏偏在这时,那个"不合时宜的人"正好路过。我们曾经说过,在一般情况下,依靠巧合构成的小说是失败之作。这篇小说的情况又如何呢? 这篇小说里确实有巧合,但这种巧合是否和主题有联系?

4. 请思考一下,公路旁餐室里的那些描写具有何种意义?

5. 老奶奶对全家遭难有何责任? 这里,我们是否能发现某种模式? 若是,这又意味着什么?

6. 假如说,老奶奶是个绝顶聪明的人,同时又是个非常虔诚的基督徒,那么这对小说结束时的讽刺意味又会产生怎样的影响? 思考这个问题并回顾一下老奶奶和那个"不合时宜的人"之间的对话。这两个人,一个是理智正常的女人,另一个是杀人狂,他们之中谁比谁更深地陷入了宗教问题?

7. 老奶奶感到自己的社会地位已不如往昔,这对于整篇小说来讲,又有何种意义?

8. 你对这一家人的总的印象如何?

9. 简述老奶奶的性格特征,并谈谈你是怎样把她和小说主题联系起来的?

10. 老奶奶对那个"不合时宜的人"所讲的最后一句话有何意义? 对情节发展有何意义? 对主题表现又有何意义? （刘家有 译）

3. The story can be said to be in two parts—the long first part dealing with the trip, and the second part after the encounter with The Misfit. What, if anything, holds these two parts together? How does this connection between the parts relate to the theme of the story? In connection with this we may say that the encounter is pure coincidence—The Misfit just happens to come along at the moment when the family has the accident. We have said that, in general, dependence on coincidence is a fault in fiction. What about this instance? Does the fact of the coincidence bear on the theme?

4. What is the significance, if any, of the scene at the highway restaurant?

5. What responsibility does the old lady have for the family's disaster? Can we detect a pattern here? If so, what does it mean?

6. Let us suppose that the old lady were of unusual intelligence and were a completely devout Christian. What effect would this change have on the irony of the conclusion? In thinking of this question go back to the dialogue between the old lady and The Misfit. Which of the two, the sane woman or the maniac, is the more deeply involved in the religious question?

7. What significance for the story lies in the fact that the old lady feels that she has come down socially?

8. What impression do you have of the family in general?

9. Write a brief character sketch of the old lady. How do you relate her to the theme of the story?

10. What is the significance of the old lady's last words to The Misfit? For plot? For theme?

新小说
The New Fiction

新小说采用了远为复杂的方法，同时又探索那些新近观察到的人类动机和行为之间的复杂关系，其中包括恐惧本能、心理创伤、性欲以及肆虐狂。

如前所述，小说的目的在于创造一种想象中的现实。我们知道，小说里的"约翰"并不是某人在某保险公司保过险、住在某条街上并在大选期里老是投共和党人票的约翰。小说里的"约翰"仅仅在作家的想象中才是真实的，或者，如果那篇小说写得相当好的话，他在读者的想象中也是真实的。

我们现在读到的绝大多数小说都把其中的"约翰"——那想象中的人物——尽可能地写得像真正的约翰一样——驾驶的是福特牌或者凯迪拉克牌汽车，穿着像别人一样与其经济地位及社会地位相配的衣服，以及讲着在他的时代和阶层中流行的语言。那就是说，当今流行的绝大多数小说是现实主义的。我们对这样的事实已习以为常，我们常常忘记有任何其他种类小说的存在。

但是，让我们为此回顾一下本书的序。原始的穴居人在火堆边所讲的故事，以及他们的古代后裔如荷马时代的希腊人所讲的故事，其中经常含有现实的成分，但这些故事又屡屡是此种或那种奇思幻想，故事里每每出现的是神祇、半神半人或者怪物，要不就是力量超人的英雄——所有这一切，都是人处于蒙昧无知状态中，由于恐惧和对个人力量的向往而想象出来的事物。那是一个诸神与诸女神不仅参与人类纷争甚至对人抱着具体爱憎的世界——在那个世界里，诸神会使凡俗女子怀孕而诸女神会因凡俗男子而受孕。此外，许多世纪以来，各种传说、神话和民间故事也一直是不受日常的现实生活所限制的。当然，其中也含有现实主义成分——如对宫殿或茅舍的描绘，对航海生活的记述，对各种生活用具的临摹等等。

As we have remarked earlier, fiction seeks to create an imagined reality. The "John" in the story is not, we know, a John who has a certain Social Security number, lives on a certain street, and usually votes Republican at election time. "John" is real only in the imagination of the writer and, provided the story is sufficiently well written, real in the imagination of the reader.

Most fiction we now encounter makes its "John"—the imagined fellow—as much like the real Johns as possible—driving a Ford or a Cadillac, dressing like other men of his economic and social level, and speaking the current language of his age and class. That is, most current fiction is realistic. We are so accustomed to this fact that we often forget that any other kind exists.

At this point, however, let us go back to our introduction. The tales told by the cave man at his fire, and by his ancient descendants, such as the Greeks of Homer's time, often had elements of realism in them, but they were frequently fantasies of one kind or another, populated by gods, demigods, or monsters, or by heroes of superhuman strength—all of them images drawn from dreams of personal power or terror in a world that was not very clearly understood. It was a world in which gods and goddesses took part in human quarrels, or even loved or hated human beings—a world in which gods might beget children of mortal women or goddesses bear children to mortal men. Furthermore, for centuries fables, fairy tales, and folk tales continued to deny the limitations of the day-to-day world. Of course, elements of realism might be included also—descriptions of palaces and hovels, accounts of seamanship, references to all the paraphernalia of daily living.

就其内容而言,早期的叙事作品仅此而已。在语言和形式方面,它们与现代的现实主义小说也大不相同,那就是说,它们通常是以诗歌形式写作而成的。荷马的叙事作品(即被称之为史诗的《伊利亚特》和《奥德赛》)就是用严格的有韵诗体写的,而由于韵律的感情作用,使一种"情感的"现实主义得以存在,这种现实主义允许读者的想象力超越严格写实的现实主义的限制。在阅读富有高度想象力的诗体史诗如《奥德赛》或《罗兰之歌》这样的作品时,读者的反应和在阅读现代小说时所做出的反应也是大不相同的。在现代小说里,福特牌汽车或者凯迪拉克牌汽车的出现只是使现代社会生活得到惟妙惟肖的表现。

我们现在的大多数剧本虽然都是用散文写的,但在过去,剧本则毫无例外地用韵文来写——不仅古希腊悲剧如此,伊丽莎白时代的剧本也如此——譬如,莎士比亚的剧本就是这样。直到 17 世纪为止,诗体始终是严肃的戏剧的独特形式。虽然伊丽莎白时代的某些散文作品被留下来,它们却称不上是现实主义的。至于长篇小说,在当时简直可以说还不存在。

事实上,一直要到现代社会逐渐形成,由于城市生活繁荣、现代科学产生、工业革命到来,致使富裕的中产阶级兴起,因而使较多的人具有阅读能力,被我们称之为小说的那种长篇散文叙事作品才真正得到发展。小说是为了那些受到新的现代社会熏陶的读者而写的,其内容也就或多或少地取诸现代社会生活。尽管个人的或者地方的特性尽可以用来为加强作品的喜剧效果或者真实效果服务,小说仍以现代标准散文写成。

这里,要涉及一个受多方面影响的重要事实:18 至 19 世纪是机械论科学得到发展并被普遍接受的时代。世界像一部巨大无比、有条不紊的机器(可能由上帝操纵,虽然是远距离操纵的)。科学激发了人们想理解这部巨大机

So much for the content of this earlier fiction. It differed from our realistic fiction also in language, in style, and in the fact that it was usually written in verse. The fictive stories of Homer (*The Iliad* and *The Odyssey*, as his epics are called) were written in strictly metered verse; the emotional effect of the rhythm worked to sustain an "emotional" realism and to allow the reader's imagination to transcend the limitations of a down-to-earth realism. The response of the reader to highly imaginative verse epics such as *The Odyssey* or *The Song of Roland* was very different from that elicited by present-day fiction, in which the presence of a Ford or a Cadillac in the story is there to substantiate the actuality of the world presented.

Though most plays of our own time are written in prose, in earlier times they were, as a matter of course, written in verse—not only the tragedies of the ancient Greeks, but also those of the Elizabethan age—Shakespeare's plays, for example. As late as the seventeenth century verse was the characteristic mode of serious drama. Though some prose narratives date from the Elizabethan period, they were not notably realistic. As for the novel, in this period it can scarcely be said to have existed.

In fact, the long prose narrative, which we call the novel, did not really develop until the modern world began to take shape, with the growth of urban life; the beginnings of modern science; the coming of the Industrial Revolution; and the rise of a prosperous middle class, which generated a wider literacy. The novel, written for an audience nurtured by this new, modern world, took its content, more or less, from the nature of that world. The novel was written in the standard prose of the time, even though personal and regional peculiarities might be employed to provide realistic or comic effect.

Now, for one additional important fact underlying many others: In the eighteenth and nineteenth centuries the age of mechanical science had developed and was generally accepted. The world was a big, tidy machine (perhaps operated by God, though at a distance). Science constituted the attempt to understand this big machine, and the novel

器的愿望，小说呢，其愿望则在于试图理解——或者至少能报道——社会生活中的人，因为社会生活即是那部世界大机器在人类中的表现。

这里不宜谈论作为 20 世纪标志的全球性科学革命——譬如，量子物理学的产生、对能量所做的新解释、相对论、新的时空概念以及由大型电子望远镜观察到的宇宙问题和由电子显微镜发现的物质内部不可思议的各种现象等等。还有心理学的发展，由精神分析法以及有关研究揭示出来的关于人的动机和行为关系的复杂情况。凡此种种新的发现和新的理论都已获得高速度的发展。

换句话说，20 世纪的世界如用前几个世纪人们的眼光来看，就像是一个充塞着种种生疏、古怪而神奇的现象的世界。基于这种巨大变动以及由于人们面对着一个荒原般不确定的世界，那种被称为"科幻小说"的叙事体文学样式在本世纪初——可能还要早一些——便应运而生。但是，我们受到对世界的新观点的影响并不仅仅表现在"科幻小说"这一个方面。一般的小说也受其影响，小说对心理现实和客观现实在程度上的差别，表示越来越多的关心。小说家不再像以往写简单的故事那样，以钟表为尺度直线式处理时间，而是采用了远为复杂的方法，同时又探索那些新近观察到的人类动机和行为之间的复杂关系，其中包括恐惧本能、心理创伤、性欲以及肆虐狂——凡此种种，即是所谓"新哥特体小说"[①]的特征。

通过本章所选作品，读者将看到这种新的实验性小说的范例。当然，新形式不可能完全取代更具特色的旧形式，但是，鉴于它在作家和读者中间已初具影响，以及在其本身的样式方面已取得某些进展，这种新形式可被视为某

was an attempt to understand, or report, at least, on man in society, society being the human aspect of the big machine that was the world.

This is not the place to discuss the world-shattering revolution in science that marks the twentieth century—matters such as the rise of quantum physics, the new definitions of matter and energy, the theory of relativity, the new conceptions of time and space, the probing of the universe by powerful telescopes, and the unimaginable inwardness laid bare by the electronic microscope. One should add to these events developments in psychology—the complication of motive and behavior revealed by psychoanalysis and related studies. Such new discoveries and theories have developed at great speed.

In other words, the twentieth century would seem to the eyes of people of earlier centuries a world crammed with strange, uncanny, and fantastic events. Out of this shocking and wildly improbable world, the form of narrative which we call "science fiction" arose early in this century—perhaps earlier still. Yet not only science fiction was marked by the influence of the new view of our world. Fiction in general was affected. Fiction began to concern itself more and more with different levels of psychological and objective reality. Writers of fiction began to treat time in far more complex ways than they had in previous simple narratives, where time is linear as measured by the clock, and to explore the newly discerned complexity of human motives and actions, including the nature of shock and trauma, sexuality, and cruelty—all of which are features of the so-called neo-Gothic fiction[①].

In the stories of this section, we see some examples of the new experimental fiction. This new type has certainly not supplanted the more characteristic older type, but it is a force to be reckoned with, has already made itself felt among writers and readers, and has scored some triumphs in its mode. It may turn out to be, of course, a peripheral development,

---

① "哥特体"一词使用于 19 世纪后期，后被用来称呼一般惊险、恐怖而带感伤情绪的小说。在美国，爱伦·坡的作品可算其最好的后期模式。——原注。

---

① The term *Gothic* was applied in the late eighteenth century and for a time after to a shocking, terror-ridden, and sadistic fiction then popular. The work of Poe, for example, would be a fairly late example, in America.

一方面的力量。诚然,这种新形式也许充其量只是表面上的发展,而现代科学和哲学的深刻影响可能会导致某种全新的小说形式的出现。但不管怎样,我们在这里所要指出的仅仅是这样的事实:科学和哲学方面哪怕是极小的思想进展也会给小说在方法和内容方面的发展带来影响。

（刘文荣 译）

and the deeper effects of modern science and philosophy may take a quite different form. In any case, our main point here is to illustrate the fact that even the remote intellectual developments in science and philosophy are never without their effects on the development of fictional method and content.

028. 花园余影

（阿根廷）胡里奥·科塔萨尔 著　　刘文荣 译

028. Continuity of Parks

by Julio Cortázar

几天前，他开始读那本小说。因为有些紧急的事务性会谈，他把书搁下了，在坐火车回自己庄园的途中，他又打开了书，他不由得慢慢对那些情节、人物性格发生了兴趣。那天下午，他给庄园代理人写了一封授权信并和他讨论了庄园的共同所有权问题之后，便坐在静悄悄的、面对着种种有橡树的花园的书房里，重新回到了书本上。他懒洋洋地倚在舒适的扶手椅里。椅子背朝着房门——只要他一想到这门，想到有可能会受人骚扰就使他恼怒——用左手来回地无摸着椅子扶手上绿色天鹅绒装饰布，开始读最后的几章。他毫不费力就记起了人名，脑中浮现出人物，小说几乎一下子就迷住了他。他感受到一种简直是不同寻常的欢愉，因为他正在从缠绕心头的各种事务中一一解脱。同时，他又感到自己的头正舒坦地靠在绿色天鹅绒的高椅背上，意识到烟卷呆呆地被夹在自己伸出的手里。而越过窗门，那下午的微风正在花园的橡树底下跳舞。一字一行地，他被那男女主人公的困境窘态吸引了，情不自禁地陷入了幻景之中，他变成了那山间小屋里的最后一幕的目击者。那女的先来，神情忧虑不安，接着，她的情人进来了，他脸上被树枝划了一道口子。她万分敬慕，想用亲吻去止住那血。但他却断然拒绝她的爱抚，在周围一片枯枝残叶和条条林中诡秘小路的庇护之中，他没有重演那套隐蔽的情欲冲动。那把短剑靠在他胸口变得温暖了，在胸腔里，自由的意志愤然涌起而又隐而不露。一段激动的、充满情欲的对话像一条条蛇似的从纸面上一溜而过，使人觉得这一切都像来自永恒的天意。就是那缠住情人身体的爱抚，表面上似乎想挽留他、制止他，它们却令人生厌地勾勒出那另一个人的必须去经受毁灭的身

HE had begun to read the novel a few days before. He had put it down because of some urgent business conferences, opened it again on his way back to the estate by train; he permitted himself a slowly growing interest in the plot, in the characterization. That afternoon, after writing a letter giving his power of attorney and discussing a matter of joint ownership with the manager of his estate, he returned to the book in the tranquillity of his study which looked out upon the park with its oaks. Sprawled in his favorite armchair, its back toward the door—even the possibility of an intrusion would have irritated him, had he thought of it—he let his left hand caress repeatedly the green velvet upholstery and set to reading the final chapters. He remembered effortlessly the names and his mental image of the characters; the novel spread its glamour over him almost at once. He tasted the almost perverse pleasure of disengaging himself line by line from the things around him, and at the same time feeling his head rest comfortably on the green velvet of the chair with its high back, sensing that the cigarettes rested within reach of his hand, that beyond the great windows the air of afternoon danced under the oak trees in the park. Word by word, licked up by the sordid dilemma of the hero and heroine, letting himself be absorbed to the point where the images settled down and took on color and movement, he was witness to the final encounter in the mountain cabin. The woman arrived first, apprehensive; now the lover came in, his face cut by the backlash of a branch. Admirably, she stanched the blood with her kisses, but he rebuffed her caresses, he had not come to perform again the ceremonies of a secret passion, protected by a world of dry leaves and furtive paths through the forest. The dagger warmed itself against his chest, and underneath liberty pounded, hidden close. A lustful, panting dialogue raced down the pages like a rivulet of snakes and one felt it had all been decided from eternity. Even to

作者简介：胡里奥·科塔萨尔（**Julio Cortázar**，1914—1984），阿根廷籍法国小说家。1914 年 8 月 26 日生于比利时布鲁塞尔，1984 年 2 月 12 日卒于法国巴黎。他的父母都是阿根廷人，他在阿根廷接受教育。第一部小说集《动物寓言》（*Bestiary*，1951）是在他迁居到巴黎同一年出版的。他在巴黎度过他一生大部分时间。《跳房子》（*Hopscotch*，1963）给了读者开放式的结局，这是一部非传统的小说，读者可以自己重组各个章节。

躯。什么也没有忘记：托词借口、意外的机遇、可能的错误。从此时起，每一瞬间都有其精心设计好的妙用。那不通人情的、对细节的再次检查突然中断，致使一只手可以抚摸一张脸颊。这时天色开始暗下来。

现在，两人没有相对而视，由于一心执意于那等待着他们的艰巨任务，他们在小屋门前分手了。她沿着伸向北的小径走去。他呢，站在相反方向的小路上。侧身望了好一会儿，望着她远去，她的头发松蓬蓬的，在风里吹拂，随后他也走了，屈着身体穿过树林和篱笆。在昏黄的尘雾里，他一直走，直到能辨认出那条通向大屋子的林荫道。料想狗是不会叫的，它们果真没有叫。庄园管家在这时分是不会在庄园里的，他果真不在。他走上门廊前的三级台阶，进了屋子。血管里的血在他的耳朵里突突地响着，那女人的话音传到了他的耳朵里。先经过一间蓝色的前厅，接着是大厅，再接着便是一条铺着地毯的长长的楼梯。楼梯顶端，两扇门。第一个房间空无一人，第二个房间也空无一人。接着，就是会客室的门，他手握刀子，看到那从大窗户里射出的灯光，那饰着绿色天鹅绒的扶手椅高背和那高背上露出的人头，那人正在阅读一本小说。

those caresses which writhed about the lover's body, as though wishing to keep him there, to dissuade him from it; they sketched abominably the frame of that other body it was necessary to destroy. Nothing had been forgotten: alibis, unforeseen hazards, possible mistakes. From this hour on, each instant had its use minutely assigned. The cold-blooded, twice-gone-over reexamination of the details was barely broken off so that a hand could caress a cheek. It was beginning to get dark.

Not looking at one another now, rigidly fixed upon the task which awaited them, they separated at the cabin door. She was to follow the trail that led north. On the path leading in the opposite direction, he turned for a moment to watch her running, her hair loosened and flying. He ran in turn, crouching among the trees and hedges until, in the yellowish fog of dusk, he could distinguish the avenue of trees which led up to the house. The dogs were not supposed to bark, they did not bark. The estate manager would not be there at this hour, and he was not there. He went up the three porch steps and entered. The woman's words reached him over the thudding of blood in his ears: first a blue chamber, then a hall, then a carpeted stairway. At the top, two doors. No one in the first room, no one in the second. The door of the salon, and then, the knife in hand, the light from the great windows, the high back of an armchair covered in green velvet, the head of the man in the chair reading a novel.

讨 论

这篇小说里，情节的突然转变提出了关于现实的性质问题。那个在自己书房里读小说的人竟受到他所读的小说里的人物的威胁，这样的情节转变打破了现实主义的规律，在实际生活里，我们当然不能指望小说里的人物会这样从书页上走下来。小说世界不必服从日常生活的"法则"，但是就如我们曾指出过的，如果这是一篇首尾一贯的小说的话，它必须服从"自己的"法则。我们来看看，在这篇小说里究竟建立了怎样的法则。

《花园余影》总的背景描写使用的手法是现实主义的细节描写。那个正在阅读的人坐在自己书房的椅子上，从书房里他可以看到自己庄园里的花园，还"用左手来回地抚摸着椅子扶手上的绿色天鹅绒装饰布"。人物描写使

In this story a sudden turn of plot calls into question the nature of reality. This sudden turn, when the world of the man in the study is invaded by the characters in the novel he is reading, depends upon a rejection of realistic conventions: in real life, of course, we do not expect the characters in a novel literally to come off the page. Although the world of a story need not obey the "rules" of the everyday world, it must, as we have remarked, obey its *own* rules if the story is to be coherent. Let us see what rules are established here.

"Continuity of Parks" employs realistic detail to establish its setting. The man who is reading lets "his left hand caress repeatedly the green velvet upholstery" of the chair in his study, from which he can see the park on the grounds of his estate. Such realistic detail is also used to characterize the man, who has

用的也是这种现实主义的细节描写,他刚刚写完一封授权信,还跟庄园代理人进行了讨论,讨论的可能就是关于地产问题。在这篇小说里,背景和人物描写的真实性表现了情节的真实性,就是小说里关于天气的描写也如此。在这篇小说的故事发展中,丝毫没有不寻常的东西,这篇小说可以这样加以概括:"一个有钱人坐着读一本小说,小说讲述的是两个情侣计划谋杀他人的事情。"这里除了现实主义的情节,别无他物。

毫无疑问,就是在最充满幻想的小说里也会含有某些现实的成分,但同样毫无疑问的是,一篇使用幻想手法处理故事结局的小说,不仅在天气描写方面要真实,在比天气描写更加重要的其他某些方面也要真实,此外,它还必须遵守一般的准则以保持想象的连贯性。这就是说,在小说中,幻想的故事必须是一种可以想象的现实,必须和小说中其他要素保持有机的联系。在一篇小说里,如果所有要素都是现实的,那么按理说,它是不可能使用幻想的手法来处理小说的故事结局的。这篇小说由于它除了现实事件之外没有为读者准备任何其他东西,那情节的转变——那对情人走出书本去谋杀那个读书的人——从逻辑上讲就显得不可信。但是,这篇小说令人震惊的地方也就是那书里的现实竟和读书人的现实发生了直接的联系。由此看来,这篇小说所显示的是扩展了的现实,或者说是现实的多栏化,它所提出的就是多样化现实——所谓"真实的"现实和幻想的现实——之间的关系问题。

just written a letter conveying power of attorney to his correspondent, and has had a discussion with the caretaker of his estate, presumably concerning the maintenance of the grounds. What is true of setting and characterization in the story is also true, until its climatic moment, of plot. There is nothing unusual in a story line that can be summarized as "Wealthy man sits down to read novel; novel follows two lovers planning murder." Nothing here suggests anything other than a realistic plot.

While it is clear that even the most fantastic of fictive worlds will have certain realistic elements, it is also clear that a story that invokes the fantastic to resolve its action must invoke conventions other than the realistic at some point *prior* to the climatic moment in order to get an imaginative coherence. That is, the fantastic must become an imaginative reality within the story's world, and its functional relationship to the other elements in this world must be established. A story in which all elements are realistic inferentially excludes and cannot credibly invoke the fantastic to resolve its action. Since this story does not prepare the reader for any but realistic events, the turn of plot in which the lovers come out of the novel to kill the reader of the novel does not, in the terms laid clown, seem credible. In other words, the shock here is that the reality of the novel and that of the reader of the novel literally coincide. The story, then, is about the margins of reality, or the varieties of reality, and it asks what is the relation between varieties—the so-called "real" and the fantastic.

思考题 ■

1. 在这篇小说的现实主义背景描写里有一个细节写到那个人所坐的椅子上的绿色天鹅绒装饰布,这个细节后来又一次出现,这对小说的不同凡响的结局起了怎样的作用?

1. Among the details used to establish a realistic setting is the green velvet upholstery of the man's chair. How does the repetition of this detail contribute to the shock effect of the surprise ending?

2. 你对这篇小说的基调有何想法？这篇小说写的是不是关于现实和幻觉的关系？若是，这关系如何？或者说，这种关系的表现是不是仅仅依靠某种技巧？若是，这种技巧和《鹰溪桥上》那篇作品中所使用的技巧又有何区别？

（刘文荣 译）

2. Do you have an idea of the basic impulse of this story? Does it concern reality and illusion? If so, how? Or does it merely depend on a trick? If so, how does the trick differ from that of "Occurrence at Owl Creek Bridge"?

029. 相　遇

(阿根廷)乔治·路易斯·博尔赫斯 著

刘文荣 译

029. The Meeting

by Jorge Luis Borges

人们在早晨漫不经心地翻阅当天的报纸,不是为了逃避旁人的纠缠,就是为了给白天寻找一点儿谈话的资料。所以,毫不为奇,现在无人再会记得——甚或在梦里也不会记起——那一度曾被人纷纷议论而赫然有名的关于马尼科·尤利阿特和邓肯的事件了。况且,那事件发生在大约 1910 年,就是彗星出现和纪念独立 100 周年的那一年,而从那一年以后,我们经历了许许多多事情,也遗忘了许许多多事情。两个传奇人物现在都已死了,那些目击事件的旁观者则立誓要守口如瓶。我呢,也曾举手发誓,保证在 9 至 10 岁之间只字不提那事件的任何细枝末节。我不知道,那些人是否曾听到我说过一个字,我也不知道,他们自己是否遵守了自己的诺言。总之,那事情还是传开了,而且越传越变样,那些好好坏坏的文章呢,又不可避免地要给事情添枝加叶。

事情是这样的。那天晚上,我表兄拉菲纳邀我到一个烧烤派对去,那烧烤派对设在一所叫做禾乐尔的乡间别墅里,是他的几个朋友开设的。至于烧烤派对的确切位置,我讲不清楚,就算它是在城北郊外的任何一个小镇上吧。那些小镇都斜卧在河边,又阴凉又安宁,和伸手摊脚的布宜诺斯艾利斯城以及城周围的大草原比较起来,它们倒别具风味。路上坐了很长时间的火车,对我来说简直像漫无尽头,因为人人知道,孩子总是觉得时间过得很慢。我们走进那别墅大门时,天色已经暗了。我感觉到,这地方尽是些古里古气、原始粗糙的东西:烤得焦黄的肉散出的香味、那些树、那些狗、那些点火木,还有诱人团团围坐的火。

大约有十几个来客,全是大人。我后来才知道,

ANYONE leafing his way through the morning paper does so either to escape his surroundings or to provide himself with small talk for later in the day, so it is not to be wondered at that no one any longer remembers—or else remembers as in a dream—the famous and once widely discussed case of Maneco Uriarte and of Duncan. The event took place, furthermore, back around 1910, the year of the comet and the Centennial, and since then we have had and have lost so many things. Both protagonists are now dead; those who witnessed the episode solemnly swore silence. I, too, raised my hand for the oath, feeling the importance of the ritual with all the romantic seriousness of my nine or ten years. I do not know whether the others noticed that I had given my word; I do not know whether they kept theirs. Anyway, here is the story, with all the inevitable variations brought about by time and by good or bad writing.

My cousin Lafinur took me to a barbecue that evening at a country house called The Laurels, which belonged to some friends of his. I cannot fix its exact location; let us take any of those suburban towns lying just to the north, shaded and quiet, that slope down to the river and that have nothing in common with sprawling Buenos Aires and its surrounding prairie. The journey by train lasted long enough to seem endless to me, but time for children—as is well known—flows slowly. It was already dark when we passed through the villa's main gate. Here, I felt, were all the ancient, elemental things: the smell of meat cooking golden brown, the trees, the dogs, the kindling wood, and the fire that brings men together.

The guests numbered about a dozen; all were grown-ups. The eldest, I learned later, was not yet thirty.

作者简介:乔治·路易斯·博尔赫斯(**Jorge Luis Borges**,1899—1986),阿根廷诗人、随笔作家和短篇小说家。1899 年 8 月 24 日生于阿根廷布宜诺斯艾利斯,1986 年 7 月 14 日卒于瑞士日内瓦。从 1920 年开始,他被遗传的失明症所折磨。20 世纪 50 年代中期,他完全失明,迫使他放弃长文写作而采用口述作品。1955 年任阿根廷图书馆荣誉馆长。他的大部分作品充满幻想和隐喻寓言,如小说集《伪装》(*Ficciones*,1944)。《阿莱夫》(*The Aleph*,1949)让他赢得国际名声。《梦中的虎》(*Dreamtigers*,1960)和《想象的动物》(*The Book of Imaginary Beings*,1967)几乎抹掉散文和诗的区别。

那当中最大的也不过 30 岁。我很快就发现，他们谈起有些事来很起劲儿，什么名种马啦，好裁缝啦，摩托车啦，还有臭名昭著的华贵女人，这些我当时还都懵然无知。谁也不来抚慰一下我的尴尬相，也没有人对我稍加注意。有个雇来的侍者慢吞吞地、讲究地准备好了羊肉，这使我们在大餐厅里待了很久。关于佳酿酒的陈度，人们来来回回地争个不休。还有一只吉他，要是我没记错，我表兄唱了两首埃利亚·罗杰斯作的关于乌拉圭僻乡牧人生活的民歌，还朗诵了几首方言诗，诗中写的是乔因街窑子里的一场白刃战。咖啡和哈瓦那雪茄烟送了进来。谁也没有想到回家。我感到那种（用诗人路格尼斯的话来说）失落于惶乱中的恐惧。我不敢看那只挂钟。为了掩饰一下在大人中间自己孩子气的孤独感，我灌下了——并非真喜欢——一两杯酒。尤利阿特大声邀请邓肯打双人扑克牌。有人反对，说那种打法太没劲儿，建议四个人打一盘。邓肯同意，但尤利阿特态度固执，坚持要两个人打。他为什么要这样固执，我不理解，也不想理解。不要说 truco①——这种其实是用恶作剧和口角来消磨时间的游戏——就是温文尔雅的单人扑克，我也从来不玩。我溜了出去，谁也没注意。一所古老而又杂乱无章的屋子，既陌生又黑暗（只有大餐厅里亮着灯光），这对一个孩子，就好比异国他乡对一个旅行者一样神奇。我一步步地窥探那些房间。记得有一间弹子房，一条装着长方形和菱形玻璃橱窗的长走廊，一对摇摇欲坠的扶手椅，还有一扇窗，一看就知道，这是一幢避暑别墅。在黑暗中我迷了路，不知怎么一来，别墅的主人后来走到了我面前。已过那么多年，他的名字我记不大清了，大概叫阿塞维多，或者就是叫阿塞倍尔。不知出于好心呢还是出于收藏家的虚荣心，他把我领到一个陈列柜前。借着灯光，我看见有钢铁在闪闪发光。这里收藏着的净是些勇士武将使用过的刀剑。他对我说，在帕格秘诺省北面一带的某个地方，他有一些地产，这些东西就是他在那里费了很大劲儿收集来的。他打开陈列柜，也不看标签上的字，就一一地向我介绍陈列品。除了出产日期和产地名称不同，这些东西或多或少有点相像。我问他，这些武器中是否有胡安·莫雷拉的短剑，其人和后来的马丁·费洛及堂·塞耿多·森伯拉一样，生前

---

① 一种多人扑克游戏。

They were also—this I was soon to find out—well versed in matters about which I am still somewhat backward: race horses, the right tailors, motorcars, and notoriously expensive women. No one ruffled my shyness, no one paid any attention to me. The lamb, slowly and skillfully prepared by one of the hired men, kept us a long time in the big dining room. The dates of vintages were argued back and forth. There was a guitar; my cousin, if I remember correctly, sang a couple of Elias Regules' ballads about gauchos in the back country of Uruguay and some verses in dialect, in the incipient *lunfardo* of those days, about a knife fight in a brothel on Junin Street. Coffee and Havana cigars were brought in. Not a word about getting back. I felt (in the words of the poet Lugones) the fear of what is suddenly too late. I dared not look at the clock. In order to disguise my boyish loneliness among grown-ups, I put away—not really liking it—a glass or two of wine. Uriarte, in a loud voice, proposed to Duncan a two-handed game of poker. Someone objected that that kind of play made for a poor game and suggested a hand of four. Duncan agreed, but Uriarte, with a stubbornness that I did not understand and that I did not try to understand, insisted on the first scheme. Outside of *truco*—a game whose real aim is to pass time with mischief and verses—and of the modest mazes of solitaire, I never enjoyed cards. I slipped away without anyone's noticing. A rambling old house, unfamiliar and dark (only in the dining room was there light), means more to a boy than a new country means to a traveler. Step by step, I explored the rooms; I recall a billiard room, a long gallery with rectangular and diamond-shaped panes, a couple of rocking chairs, and a window from which you could just make out a summerhouse. In the darkness I lost my way; the owner of the house, whose name, as I recall after all these years, may have been Acevedo or Acebal, finally came across me somehow. Out of kindness or perhaps out of a collector's vanity, he led me to a display cabinet. On lighting a lamp, I saw the glint of steel. It was a collection of knives that had once been in the hands of famous fighters. He told me that he had a bit of land somewhere to the north around Pergamino, and that he had been picking up these things on his travels back and forth across the province. He opened the cabinet and, without looking at what was written on the tags, he began giving me accounts of each item; they were more or less the same except for dates and place names. I asked him whether among the weapons he might have the dagger of Juan Moreira, who was in

可算是南方牧人中的佼佼者。他抱憾地说没有,不过他倒可以给我看一把和莫雷拉的很相像的短剑。剑柄上也有U形护手。一阵愤怒的叫喊声打断了他的话。他赶紧关好陈列柜。转身走了,我跟在他后面。

尤利阿特在大声叫喊,说他的对手企图欺骗他。其他的人都站在周围观看。我记得,这群人口间身材最高的要数邓肯,他肩膀虽有点耷,体格却很魁梧,脸部没有表情,发色很淡,看上去几乎是白色的。马尼科·尤利阿特则是个暴躁易怒的人,肤色黝黑,说不定有点印第安人的血统,还蓄着乱七八糟的小胡子,样子很任性。显然,每个人都喝醉了。我弄不清楚地板上放着的空酒瓶是两只呢还是三只,也不知道这种乱哄哄的场面对我来说是否像一种错觉。尤利阿特辱骂不停,起先骂得很刺耳,后来越骂越下流。邓肯看上去似乎没有在听,但后来,他好像是听腻了似的站起身,对准尤利阿特就是一拳。尤利阿特倒在地上,咆哮着说他受不了这样的侮辱,要和邓肯决斗。

邓肯说不行,还像解释似的说:"真可惜,我有点儿怕你。"

大家都狂笑起来。

尤利阿特爬起身回答说:"我和你拼个死活,现在就拼。"

有人——希望此人为此能得到宽恕——说决斗用的武器倒很现成。

我不知道是谁去开了那只玻璃陈列柜。尤利阿特捡了一把最长也最惹人注目的短剑,就是那把有U形护手的。邓肯呢,似乎心不在焉,随手捡了一把刀背上刻着一棵小树的木柄腰刀。有人还说,尤利阿特选中一把短剑来使是再合适不过的了。他的手开始颤抖,但谁也不觉得惊奇,使人惊奇的却是邓肯,他的手也竟和尤利阿特一样,也在颤抖着。

按照惯例,决斗者要到他们不熟悉的地方去进行决斗,于是他们走了出去。我们呢,半是为了纵乐,半是出于认真,也都走到了潮湿的夜雾里。我没有喝酒——至少没有喝烈酒——但我也浑身来劲儿,我衷心希望有一个人被杀,因为这样我就可以事后和人谈论这件事而且可以一辈子不忘记。或许,当时在场的其他人也并不比我想得更多一些。我还有一种感觉,觉得有一股强大无比的洪流在冲击着我们,而且把我们给淹没了。没有一个人相信马尼科有丝毫的过错,每一个人都酒性发作了,都把这事看做传统的竞技。

that day the archetype of the gaucho, as later Martin Fierro and Don Segundo Sombra would be. He had to confess that he hadn't but that he could show me one like it, with a U-shaped crosspiece in the hilt. He was interrupted by the sound of angry voices. At once he shut the cabinet and turned to leave; I followed him.

Uriarte was shouting that his opponent had tried to cheat him. All the others stood around the two players. Duncan, I remember, was a taller man than the rest of the company, and was well built, though somewhat round-shouldered; his face was expressionless, and his hair was so light it was almost white. Maneco Uriarte was nervous, dark, with perhaps a touch of Indian blood, and wore a skimpy, petulant moustache. It was obvious that everybody was drunk; I do not know whether there were two or three emptied bottles on the floor or whether an excess of movies suggests this false memory to me. Uriarte's insults did not let up; at first sharp, they now grew obscene. Duncan appeared not to hear, but finally, as though weary, he got up and threw a punch. From the floor, Uriarte snarled that he was not going to take this outrage, and he challenged Duncan to fight.

Duncan said no, and added, as though to explain, "The trouble is I'm afraid of you."

Everybody howled with laughter.

Uriarte, picking himself up, answered, "I'm going to have it out with you, and right now."

Someone—may he be forgiven for it—remarked that weapons were not lacking.

I do not know who went and opened the glass cabinet. Maneco Uriarte picked out the showiest and longest dagger, the one with the U-shaped crosspiece; Duncan, almost absentmindedly, picked a wooden—handled knife with the stamp of a tiny tree on the blade. Someone else said it was just like Maneco to play it safe, to choose a sword. It astonished no one that his hand began shaking; what was astonishing is that the same thing happened with Duncan.

Tradition demands that men about to fight should respect the house in which they are guests, and step outside. Half on a spree, half seriously, we all went out into the damp night. I was not drunk—at least, not on wine—but I was reeling with adventure; I wished very hard that someone would be killed, so that later I could tell about it and always remember it. Maybe at that moment the others were no more adult than I was. I also had the feeling that an overpowering current was dragging us on and would drown us. Nobody

我们熙熙攘攘地拥过一片小树林，那幢避暑别墅落到了身后。尤利阿特和邓肯走在前面，相互提防着。其他人围在一片开阔的草地边上。到了那儿，邓肯在月光下站定了。用温和而威严的口气说："这地方看来挺合适。"

两个人站在中央，一下子竟忘了动手。一个声音传来："把武器扔下，用手打吧！"

但是两个人已经打起来了。他们起先打得笨手笨脚，简直怕伤害了对方似的；他们起先只看着自己的刀背，但后来两双眼睛相互对视了。尤利阿特的愤怒已消失，邓肯呢，也不再现出那种不以为然的神情来了。危险的威胁多少使他们变了样儿，现在进行的是两个男子的决斗，不是男孩的儿戏。我想象得到，这场决斗将是一种真枪实剑的混战。尽管如此，我能看下去，或者尽可能看下去，虽然这和下一盘棋没有什么两样。当时我看到的情景，由于时隔多年，现在回忆起来当然会有点变样儿，有点模糊。我不知道决斗进行了多久，有些事情是不能用普通的时间尺度来衡量的。

他们没有穿披风，穿着倒可以当做盾牌。他们用手肘抵挡对方的每一次宰劈。他们的衣袖很快变成筋筋条条，又被血渐渐地染成殷红。我想，大家肯定是想错了，还以为他们根本不懂自卫法哩。我一下子就注意到他们各有各的路数。他们的武器各不相同。为了克服自己武器上的短处，邓肯试图贴近对方；尤利阿特则步步后退，以保持距离，再从下面给对方以打击。这时，刚才那个要大家去开陈列柜的人用了同样的声音喊起来："他们要相互残杀啦！快制止他们！"

然而谁也不敢上前劝阻。尤利阿特已乱了方寸，邓肯又步步紧逼。现在，他们几乎是身贴身了。尤利阿特的短剑对准了邓肯的脸。突然，剑身好像短了一截，原来剑已刺进了高个子的胸膛。邓肯瘫倒在草地上，与此同时，嘴里又喃喃地在说："多么奇怪啊，简直像在梦中。"

他没有闭眼，但也没有动，而我已经看见了，一个人杀了另一个人。

马尼科·尤利阿特屈身俯在那具尸体上，大声抽泣，乞求宽恕。他刚才做的事并非他有意做的。我这时才明白，他并不承认自己有罪，而只承认他身不由己地失了手。

我不想再看下去了。我希望看到的一切，现在全都发生了，但却使我浑身颤抖。拉菲纳后来告诉我，

believed the least bit in Maneco's accusation; everyone saw it as the fruit of an old rivalry, exacerbated by the wine.

We pushed our way through a clump of trees, leaving behind the summerhouse. Uriarte and Duncan led the way, wary of each other. The rest of us strung ourselves out around the edge of an opening of lawn. Duncan had stopped there in the moonlight and said, with mild authority, "This looks like the right place."

The two men stood in the center, not quite knowing what to do. A voice rang out: "Let go of all that hardware and use your hands!"

But the men were already fighting. They began clumsily, almost as if they were afraid of hurting each other; they began by watching the blades, but later their eyes were on one another. Uriarte had laid aside his anger, Duncan his contempt or aloofness. Danger, in some way, had transfigured them; these were now two men fighting, not boys. I had imagined the fight as a chaos of steel; instead, I was able to follow it, or almost follow it, as though it were a game of chess. The intervening years may, of course, have exaggerated or blurred what I saw. I do not know how long it lasted; there are events that fall outside the common measure of time.

Without ponchos to act as shields, they used their forearms to block each lunge of the knife. Their sleeves, soon hanging in shreds, grew black with blood. I thought that we had gone wrong in supposing that they knew nothing about this kind of fencing. I noticed right off that they handled themselves in different ways. Their weapons were unequal. Duncan, in order to make up for his disadvantage, tried to stay in close to the other man; Uriarte kept stepping back to be able to lunge out with long, low thrusts. The same voice that had called attention to the display cabinet shouted out now: "They're killing each other! Stop them!"

But no one dared break it up. Uriarte had lost ground; Duncan charged him. They were almost body to body now. Uriarte's weapon sought Duncan's face. Suddenly the blade seemed shorter, for it was piercing the taller man's chest. Duncan lay stretched out on the grass. It was at this point that he said, his voice very low, "How strange. All this is like a dream."

He did not shut his eyes, he did not move, and I had seen a man kill another man.

Maneco Uriarte bent over the body, sobbing openly, and begged to be forgiven. The thing he had just done was beyond him. I know now that he regretted less having committed a crime than having carried out a senseless act.

他们花了很大劲儿才把那短剑拔出来。还成立了一个临时会议。他们决定尽可能少说谎,只把这场用佩刀进行的决斗宣扬为是用长剑进行的。有 4 个人还自愿充当第二手材料的听说者,阿塞倍尔也是其中之一。在布宜诺斯艾利斯,什么事情都会惹人注意,而无论何人,也总能找到朋友。

在两个决斗者打过牌的那张餐桌上,一副英国扑克牌和一堆账单乱七八糟地放在那儿,谁也不想瞧它一眼,谁也不想去碰它一碰。

到了第二年,我时常想把这事情披露给某个朋友,但我始终觉得,与其把它说出去,倒不如作为秘密留在心里来得有趣。然而,到了 1929 年前后,有一天,在一次偶尔的谈话中,我突然改变了主意,打破了为时已久的沉默。退休警长堂·约塞·奥莱弗在向人讲述关于来自雷特洛附近沿河的荒野地区的人们的事情,那些人很会使腰刀。他说,要是他们出来是为了杀死自己人的话,这些原始部落的残剩者是毫不遵守比武规则的,他又说,现在人们在舞台上看到的短剑表演全然是想象出来的,因为短剑格斗老早就绝迹了。我说,我就亲眼见到过一次,于是我便把那将近 20 年前发生的事一五一十地告诉了他。

他带着那种职业性的注意力听我讲,随后问:"你能肯定,尤利阿特和那个叫什么名字来着的人过去从来没有碰过腰刀短剑之类的武器吗?说不定他们在父亲的牧场附近捡到过这类东西。"

"我想不可能,"我回答,"那天夜里在场的人相互都非常熟悉,而我可以对你说,当大家看到他们两人决斗的各种动作时,每个人都惊呆了。"

奥莱弗保持他那种不露声色的样子,似乎在竭力思索:"一种柄上有 U 形护手的武器。这类武器中有两种是非常出名的——就是莫雷拉使用的那种和胡安·阿尔马德使用的那种。阿尔马德出生于东南部,在塔帕昆。"

有什么东西仿佛在我记忆中觉醒了。奥莱弗接着说:"你又说到那种木柄腰刀,上面还有小树标记。这类武器有成千上万种,但有一种……"

他沉默了一会儿,随后说:"阿塞维多先生在帕格密诺省一带有地产,另一个有名的坏蛋在那儿也有地产——他的名字叫胡安·阿曼扎。这大概是 100 年前的事情了。当时他 14 岁,他杀死的第一个人使用的就是这种腰刀。打那以后,真是天意,他一直使用

I did not want to look anymore. What I had wished for so much had happened, and it left me shaken. Lafinur told me later that they had had to struggle hard to pull out the weapon. A makeshift council was formed. They decided to lie as little as possible and to elevate this duel with knives to a duel with swords. Four of them volunteered as seconds, among them Acebal. In Buenos Aires anything can be fixed; someone always has a friend.

On top of the mahogany table where the men had been playing, a pack of English cards and a pile of bills lay in a jumble that nobody wanted to look at or to touch.

In the years that followed, I often considered revealing the story to some friend, but always I felt that there was a greater pleasure in being the keeper of a secret than in telling it. However, around 1929, a chance conversation suddenly moved me one day to break my long silence. The retired police captain, Don José Olave, was recalling stories about men from the tough riverside neigborhood of the Retiro who had been handy with their knives; he remarked that when they were out to kill their man, scum of this kind had no use for the rules of the game, and that before all the fancy playing with daggers that you saw now on the stage, knife fights were few and far between. I said I had witnessed one, and gave him an account of what had happened nearly twenty years earlier.

He listened to me with professional attention, then said, "Are you sure Uriarte and What's-His-Name never handled a knife before? Maybe they had picked up a thing or two around their fathers' ranches."

"I don't think so," I said. "Everybody there that night knew one another pretty well, and I can tell you they were all amazed at the way the two men fought."

Olave went on in his quiet manner, as if thinking aloud. "One of the weapons had a U-shaped crosspiece in the handle. There were two daggers of that kind which became quite famous—Moreira's and Juan Almada's. Almada was from down south, in Tapalquén."

Something seemed to come awake in my memory. Olave continued. "You also mentioned a knife with a wooden handle, one with the Little Tree brand. There are thousands of them, but there was one—"

He broke off for a moment, then said, "Señor Acevedo had a big property up around Pergamino. There was another of these famous toughs from up that way—Juan Almanza was his name. This was along about the turn of the century. When he was

着那把腰刀。胡安·阿曼扎和胡安·阿尔马德相互仇视，原因是人们往往会把他们认错，所以两人相互嫉恨。他们都到处奔走，相互寻找了很长时间，但始终没有相遇。胡安·阿曼扎后来不知在哪次比武会上被人趁乱用手枪暗杀了。阿尔马德呢，我想，大概是死在拉斯弗洛利斯的医院病床上的吧。"

他不再说下去了。我们每个人都带着自己的结论走散了。

那次决斗时，在场的大约有9个人，或者是10个人，这些人现在全都死了，而那些迅猛的刺杀和那具躺在夜空下的尸体，是我亲眼目睹的，然而很可能，我们当时亲眼看到的是另一个故事，一个古老得多的故事的结局。我疑惑了，这到底是尤利阿特杀死了邓肯呢，还是那两件武器通过某种不可思议的途径在相互格斗，而与人无关。我记起来了，当时尤利阿特一握住那把短剑，手就颤抖得那么厉害，邓肯的手也一样颤抖，看来，那刀和剑在陈列柜里并排沉睡了多年之后开始苏醒。使用过它们的那两个草原牧人业已化成灰烬，但刀和剑——是刀和剑，不是人，人只是刀剑的工具而已——却依然懂得如何进行格斗。那天夜里它们打得真精彩啊！

人去物留。谁也不知道，这刀剑是否还会相遇。谁也不知道，这故事是否到此结束。

fourteen, he killed his first man with one of these knives. From then on, for luck, he stuck to the same one. Juan Almanza and Juan Almada had it in for each other, jealous of the fact that many people confused the two. For a long time they searched high and low for one another, but they never met. Juan Almanza was killed by a stray bullet during some election brawl or other. The other man, I think, died a natural death in a hospital bed in Las Flores."

Nothing more was said. Each of us was left with his own conclusions.

Nine or ten men, none of whom is any longer living, saw what my eyes saw—that sudden stab and the body under the night sky—but perhaps what we were really seeing was the end of another story, an older story. I began to wonder whether it was Maneco Uriarte who killed Duncan or whether in some uncanny way it could have been the weapons, not the men, which fought. I still remember how Uriarte's hand shook when he first gripped his knife, and the same with Duncan, as though the knives were coming awake after a long sleep side by side in the cabinet. Even after their gauchos were dust, the knives—the knives, not their tools, the men—knew how to fight. And that night they fought well.

Things last longer than people; who knows whether these knives will meet again, who knows whether the story ends here.

思考题

1. 在这篇小说里，情节的突然转变——两个决斗者所使用的刀剑有它们自己的意志——同样提出了关于现实的性质问题。在《花园余影》里，由于想象的事物和实际生活突然发生了直接联系而前面又毫无铺垫，所以可能会遭到某种异议，这篇小说是如何避免遭受这种异议的？

2. 如果在叙述那次酒会事件之前，作者再使用一些材料来更加明确地点明两个决斗者之间的敌意，那么整篇小说是否会更令人信服？

1. In this story the sudden turn that questions the nature of reality is the suggestion that the knives used by the duelists had wills of their own. How does this story avoid the possible objection raised to "Continuity of Parks" that there is no preparation for the shock when the novel and actuality coincide?

2. Would this story be more credible if the anecdote about the enmity between the fighters were more strongly suggested before the events at the party?

3. 你是否发现,在这篇小说里,对刀剑的描述和《花园余影》里对椅子的描述,在技巧上何等相似?

4. 这篇小说体现的是一种现代观念,那就是,在当前这个技术至上的时代,人正在日益成为机器的奴隶,读完这篇小说,你是否能有所体会?要是你读过柯勒律治的《昔日船工谣》这首诗的话,你能否看出它和这篇小说有某种共同的东西?诗中的船工为何要射杀那只信天翁?不就是因为弓箭在手,岂能不射吗?船工的行为和当前技术至上的时代又有何种联系呢?　　　　　(刘文荣 译)

3. What similarity of technique do you find in the use made here of the description of the knives with that of the chair in "Continuity of Parks"?

4. Behind this story can you sense the very modern idea that in this age of technology man becomes more and more the creature of his machines? If you have read Coleridge's poem "The Rime of the Ancient Mariner" can you see a similarity here? Why does the mariner shoot the albatross? Can it be that he does so merely because the crossbow is in his hand? How does his act relate to the age of technology?

030. 密 室

(法)阿兰·罗布—格里耶 著　　刘文荣 译

030. The Secret Room

by Alain Robbe-Grillet

献给古斯塔夫·莫洛

首先看到的是一摊红色斑迹，一种深暗的、泛泛有光的红色，带着几乎是漆黑的暗影。它形成不规则的玫瑰花形状，边沿分明，以不同的长度向四面八方漫流开去，分散、变细而成为一条条波状曲线。从整体看，它在灰白色的平面上分明突出，成圆周形，既阴暗而又珍珠似的粼粼发光，圆周的半边，柔和的曲线与一大片同样灰白的颜色相连接，在若明若暗的气氛中，光晕漫射而炯然有色。这是个阴影笼罩的地方，白色已成灰色——一所牢房，一处地下室，或者就是一座大教堂。

进深处，那儿站满一根根圆形立柱，一道道重复而单调的影子一直排到宽阔的石板楼梯前，楼梯向上而稍稍转弯，越接近那高高的穹顶就显得越狭窄，到了穹顶处就终止了。

除了这楼梯和圆柱，整个背影上空然无物。然而，在显眼的前景上，一具摊开着四肢的躯体绰然可见，衬着红色的斑迹，又显得色调分明——这是一具白色的躯体，那丰腴而柔软的肌肉简直可以触摸，毫无疑问，它是虚弱不堪的。从相仿的角度看去，那血色的半圆边上又有一个同样的圆形，这个圆形完整无缺，而且，由于它周围的光晕部分颜色较深，因此可以一览无余，而旁边的那个却是溃不成形，至少是残缺不全的。

在背景上，靠近楼梯顶端的地方，可看到一个黑色的侧面人影飘然欲行，一个身披长斗篷的男子正要踏上最后一级楼梯，他毫不耽搁，因为事情已经告成。在银光闪烁的白铁高台上，放着一只香炉，一缕轻烟

To Gustave Moreau

THE first thing to be seen is a red stain, of a deep, dark, shiny red, with almost black shadows. It is in the form of an irregular rosette, sharply outlined, extending in several directions in wide outflows of un-equal length, dividing and dwindling afterward into single sinuous streaks. The whole stands out against a smooth, pale surface, round in shape, at once dull and pearly, a hemisphere joined by gentle curves to an ex-panse of the same pale color—white darkened by the shadowy quality of the place: a dungeon, a sunken room, or a cathedral—glowing with a diffused bril-liance in the semidarkness.

Farther back, the space is filled with the cylindri-cal trunks of columns, repeated with progressive vagueness in their retreat toward the beginning of a vast stone stairway, turning slightly as it rises, grow-ing narrower and narrower as it approaches the high vaults where it disappears.

The whole setting is empty, stairway and colon-nades. Alone, in the foreground, the stretched-out body gleams feebly, marked with the red stain—a white body whose full, supple flesh can be sensed, fragile, no doubt, and vulnerable. Alongside the bloody hemisphere another identical round form, this one in-tact, is seen at almost the same angle of view; but the haloed point at its summit, of darker tint, is in this case quite recognizable, whereas the other one is en-tirely destroyed, or at least covered by the wound.

In the background, near the top of the stairway, a black silhouette is seen fleeing, a man wrapped in a long, floating cape, ascending the last steps without turning around, his deed accomplished. A thin smoke rises in twisting scrolls from a sort of incense burner placed on a high stand of ironwork with a silvery glint. Nearby lies the milkwhite body, with wide streaks of blood running from the left breast, along the flank and on the hip.

作者简介：阿兰·罗布—格里耶(**Alain Robbe-Grillet**,1922—)，法国作家。1922 年 8 月 18 日生于法国布列斯特。虽然接受了统计员和农艺师的培训，但是他却成为作家和新小说派的理论家。他的叙述没有传统的写作元素，如按照时间顺序发展的情节，他的叙述由重复出现的形象和重复的对话片断组成。他的作品包括小说《橡皮》(*The Erasers*,1953)、《嫉妒》(*Jealousy*, 1957)、《精》(*Djinn*,1981)、散文集《新小说方向》(*Towards a New Novel*,1963)和论文集《镜中的幽灵》(*Ghosts in the Mirror*, 1984)。他还是编剧家和导演，他最著名的电影剧本是《去年在马里昂巴德》(*Last Year at Marienbad*,1961)。

从中袅袅升起。那具乳白色的躯体就躺在香炉附近，血正从左边胸房里涌流而出，沿着肋部流向臀部。

这是一具体态丰满圆润的女子躯体，并不肥胖，浑身一丝不挂。她仰天而卧，胸部由于背压着扔到了地板上的厚软垫而微微抬起，地板上铺着东方地毯。她身腰细挑，颀长的脖颈扭向一边，头歪着，遮蔽在暗影里，但那面部表情依然不辨，嘴半张半闭，双目圆睁，目光明寒而凝滞，一大蓬黑色长发散乱而错杂地堆积在一件揉得乱糟糟的睡衣上，睡衣看上去是天鹅绒的，手臂和肩膀也压在这睡衣上。

这是一种寻常可见的紫红色天鹅绒，也可能是由于光线的缘故才显得这样。不过，那软垫的颜色里也总含有紫色、棕色或蓝色的意味，就像地毯上的东方式花纹颜色一样——软垫只有很小一部分遮蔽在睡衣下面，由于那胸和肩压在上面，很显眼地翘了起来。朝前一点，同样的颜色点缀在铺地石上、圆石柱上、拱形门廊上、楼梯上，以及那隐匿于房间深处的模糊难辨的底色上。

这房间的大小很难确定，一眼看去，那个年轻被害者的躯体似乎已占据了房间里很大一块儿地方，但是那与房间相接的宽阔楼梯似乎给人以这样的暗示，这儿并不是房间的全部，在它的左右四周实际上还存在着相当大的面积，因为在它边沿上依次排列着的圆柱间正透露着模糊不清的深棕色和蓝色，说不定，在那儿还另有沙发，另有厚地毯和成堆的软垫及衣料，另有被害者和香炉。

同样，很难说清楚那亮光是从哪儿照进来的。无论是圆柱上还是地板上，都没有迹象表明光线的方向。没有一扇窗，也没有任何其他光源。整个场面似乎是由这具乳白色的躯体照亮的——那鼓起的胸部，那曲线柔和的大腿，那圆润的前腹，那丰满的臀部，那八字叉开的双腿，还有那表示性的、令人刺激、曾供人取乐而业已无用的黑色毛丛。

那个男子往回走了好几步。现在，他站在楼梯的第一级上，又准备走上去。楼梯的台基又宽又深，就像高楼大厦前，或者神庙和剧院前的台基那样，它越到上面就越狭窄，同时又慢慢地形成螺旋形，弧圈很大，到了接近穹顶时还没有形成半个圆周，上面又有一段没有扶手的又陡又窄的梯级，梯级的线条模模糊糊，甚至可以说完全隐没在浅黑的颜色中。

然而，那个男子并没有看着这个方向，虽然他的

It is a fully rounded woman's body, but not heavy, completely nude, lying on its back, the bust raised up somewhat by thick cushions thrown down on the floor, which is covered with Oriental rugs. The waist is very narrow, the neck long and thin, curved to one side, the head thrown back into a darker area where, even so, the facial features may be discerned, the partly opened mouth, the wide-staring eyes, shining with a fixed brilliance, and the mass of long, black hair spread out in a complicated wavy disorder over a heavily folded cloth, of velvet perhaps, on which also rest the arm and shoulder.

It is a uniformly colored velvet of dark purple, or which seems so in this lighting. But purple, brown, blue also seem to dominate in the colors of the cushions—only a small portion of which is hidden beneath the velvet cloth, and which protrude noticeably, lower down, beneath the bust and waist—as well as in the Oriental patterns of the rugs on the floor. Farther on, these same colors are picked up again in the stone of the paving and the columns, the vaulted archways, the stairs, and the less discernible surfaces that disappear into the farthest reaches of the room.

The dimensions of this room are difficult to determine exactly; the body of the young sacrificial victim seems at first glance to occupy a substantial portion of it, but the vast size of the stairway leading down to it would imply rather that this is not the whole room, whose considerable space must in reality extend all around, right and left, as it does toward the faraway browns and blues among the columns standing in line, in every direction, perhaps toward other sofas, thick carpets, piles of cushions and fabrics, other tortured bodies. other incense burners.

It is also difficult to say where the light comes from. No clue, on the columns or on the floor, suggests the direction of the rays. Nor is any window or torch visible. The milkwhite body itself seems to light the scene, with its full breasts, the curve of its thighs, the rounded belly, the full buttocks, the stretched-out legs, widely spread, and the black tuft of the exposed sex, provocative, proffered, useless now.

The man has already moved several steps back. He is now on the first steps of the stairs, ready to go up. The bottom steps are wide and deep, like the steps leading up to some great building, a temple or theater; they grow smaller as they ascend, and at the same time describe a wide, helical curve, so gradually that the stairway has not yet made a half-turn by the time it disappears near the top of the vaults, reduced then to a steep, narrow flight of steps without handrail, vaguely outlined, moreover, in the thickening darkness beyond.

But the man does not look in this direction, where his movement nonetheless carries him; his left foot on the second step and his right foot already touching the third, with his knee bent, he has turned around to look

脚步依然在移动,他的左脚跨上第二节楼梯,右脚已碰到第三级,他提着脚,一面在回头最后看一看那情景。他把一只手叉在腰里,那披挂在肩上的飘动着的长斗篷由于这种迅速的圆周运动而卷了起来——他回头转身的动作也同样敏捷。斗篷的一角停留在空中,仿佛是被一阵风吹似的,这斗篷角扭曲而成一个歪斜的S形,斗篷看上去是红丝织成而且绣有金色绲边。

那个男子面无表情,不过有点紧张,好像正在期待——也许是害怕——什么突如其来的事情,或者是在用最后的一瞥审视一下眼前的一片死寂。他回头张望,整个身体呢,又微微前倾,看上去他没有停止登楼。他左手握着斗篷边,右手臂正竭力弯向左边,伸向立有扶手的地方,好像这楼梯上有一道栏杆似的,这个不协调的动作几乎叫人不可思议,除非从这种显然想抓握并不存在的支撑物的动作里,突然冒出一道真的栏杆来。

至于他视线的方向,毫无疑问是投向那具躺在软垫上的被害者躯体的。那具躯体正摊成大字,什么都显露无遗,胸脯抬起,头部后倾。但是,由于站在楼梯的底部,那男子的视线被圆柱挡着,也许看不到她的脸。那年轻女子的右手正好触到圆柱的底部。消瘦的手腕上戴着一只铁制的腕箍。手臂几乎全部隐蔽在暗影里,只有手掌部分才有足够的光线,使人辨出那些抵住立柱下面圆形突出物的纤细的手指。圆柱上系着一根黑色金属链条,链条紧接腕箍,把那手腕牢牢地缚在圆柱上。

手臂的顶端,那压在软垫上的圆圆的肩膀也明晰而注目,脖颈、喉咙同样如此,而另一个肩膀、腋窝和腋下的细毛,还有同样被拉直、手腕被缚于另一根圆柱底部的左手臂,则占据着非常突出的地位。这一边的金属腕箍和链条暴露得无遮无蔽,就是最微小的细部也都一目了然。

同样清楚也同样占据突出地位的是在另一边,一条同样的链条,不过要粗一些,正直接缚在脚踝上,绕圆柱两周,一头系住安装在地板上的一个大铁环。离开左脚大约一码远,是右脚——看来两腿叉得不很开——毫无疑问,右脚也是缚着的,不过,左脚以及左脚上的链条则描绘得细致入微。

脚很小,细嫩而雅致。在好几个地方,链条弄破了皮肤,不过可以看到,肌肉上并没有很深的伤痕。

at the spectacle for one last time. The long, floating cape thrown hastily over his shoulders, clasped in one hand at his waist, has been whirled around by the rapid circular motion that has just caused his head and chest to turn in the opposite direction, and a corner of the cloth remains suspended in the air as if blown by a gust of wind; this corner, twisting around upon itself in the form of a loose S, reveals the red silk lining with its gold embroidery.

The man's features are impassive, but tense, as if in expectation—or perhaps fear—of some sudden event, or surveying with one last glance the total immobility of the scene. Though he is looking backward, his whole body is turned slightly forward, as if he were continuing up the stairs. His right arm—not the one holding the edge of the cape—is bent sharply toward the left, toward a point in space where the balustrade should be, if this stairway had one, an interrupted gesture, almost incomprehensible, unless it arose from an instinctive movement to grasp the absent support.

As to the direction of his glance, it is certainly aimed at the body of the victim lying on the cushions, its extended members stretched out in the form of a cross, its bust raised up, its head thrown back. But the face is perhaps hidden from the man's eyes by one of the columns, standing at the foot of the stairs. The young woman's right hand touches the floor just at the foot of this column. The fragile wrist is encircled by an iron bracelet. The arm is almost in darkness, only the hand receiving enough light to make the thin, outspread fingers clearly visible against the circular protrusion at the base of the stone column. A black metal chain running around the column passes through a ring affixed to the bracelet, binding the wrist tightly to the column.

At the top of the arm a rounded shoulder, raised up by the cushions, also stands out well lighted, as well as the neck, the throat, and the other shoulder, the armpit with its soft hair, the left arm likewise pulled back with its wrist bound in the same manner to the base of another column, in the extreme foreground; here the iron bracelet and the chain are fully displayed, represented with perfect clarity down to the slightest details.

The same is true, still in the foreground but at the other side, for a similar chain, but not quite as thick, wound directly around the ankle, running twice around the column and terminating in a heavy iron ring embedded in the floor. About a yard farther back, or perhaps slightly farther, the right foot is identically chained. But it is the left foot, and its chain, that are the most minutely depicted.

The foot is small, delicate, finely modeled. In several places the chain has broken the skin, causing noticeable if not extensive depressions in the flesh. The chain links are oval, thick, the size of an eye. The ring

链环是椭圆形的,很细,样子像一只只眼睛。与此相比,那地板上的铁环简直可用来拴马,它钉装在一根笨重的铁桩上,紧贴地面。离此几英寸远,是一张小地毯的边沿。地毯揉得很皱,显然,这是被害者试图挣扎而又肯定受到强制时,由于手脚扭动而留下的痕迹。

那个男子依然站在大约一码远的地方,身体稍稍前倾,看着那具躯体。他看看她的脸,目光游移不定。她的黑眼睛由于眼旁的黑晕而显得更大了,嘴像嘶叫似的张开。那个男子由于站立的姿势,只能看到他的模糊的侧面,他的脸色虽然严峻,又冷静又呆滞,但从中还是可以体会到某种强烈的兴奋。他的背微微弯曲。那只仅能看到的左手离躯体不很远,正提着一件衣服,衣服是深色料子的,拖曳到地板上,这肯定是一件绣有金丝的长披风。

那男子的巨大黑影大部分被那具赤裸裸的躯体遮蔽着,那躯体上又满是血迹,血从乳房里流出来,分叉成一条条细流,流到胸部和肋部苍白的表皮上,越流越细。有一条流到了腋窝处,又沿手臂径直流成一条细细的线;有的细流经过腰部,又沿腹侧流到臀部,在大腿上分成更细的网络并开始凝结;三四条很细的血流伸展到两腿间的那个洞穴旁边,相互交叉混合,流到两条大腿叉开而成的 V 字的尖端处,在黑色的毛丛里消失了。

看,那具躯体现在依然完整无缺:黑色的毛丛和洁白的大腿,线条柔和的臀部,纤细的腰肢,还有,向上一点,那珍珠般圆润的胸脯这时正上下起伏着,急速地呼吸,节奏越来越快。那个站在她身旁的男子跪下一条腿,把身体凑近一点。唯一可稍稍动弹的那颗披着长卷发的头正左右晃动着,挣扎着。终于,女子的嘴呲开了,身上的伤口洞开着,大量的血在涌流,密密地分布在柔软的皮肤上,那双有意被蒙上阴影的眼睛令人可怕地越张越大,同时嘴也越张越大,头在剧烈扭动。这样持续一段时间后,渐渐地显得无力了,头只是慢慢地左右摇动,最后颓然后倾,在一大篷散乱在天鹅绒上的乌黑头发中间兀然不动了。

在楼梯的顶端,那扇小门现在已经打开,一道微黄的、持续不变的光线射进来,衬着这光线,分明可见的是那个身披长斗篷的男子的黑色身影。也又跨上几级阶梯便到了门槛边。

接着,整个背景变得一片空白,巨大的旁间连同

in the floor resembles those used to attach horses; it lies almost touching the stone pavement to which it is riveted by a massive iron peg. A few inches away is the edge of a rug; it is grossly wrinkled at this point, doubtless as a result of the convulsive, but necessarily very restricted, movements of the victim attempting to struggle.

The man is still standing about a yard away, half leaning over her. He looks at her face, seen upside down, her dark eyes made larger by their surrounding eyeshadow, her mouth wide open as if screaming. The man's posture allows his face to be seen only in a vague profile, but one senses in it a violent exaltation, despite the rigid attitude, the silence, the immobility. His back is slightly arched. His left hand, the only one visible, holds up at some distance from the body a piece of cloth, some dark-colored piece of clothing, which drags on the carpet, and which must be the long cape with its gold-embroidered lining.

This immense silhouette hides most of the bare flesh over which the red stain, spreading from the globe of the breast, runs in long rivulets that branch out, growing narrower, upon the pale background of the bust and the flank. One thread has reached the armpit and runs in an almost straight, thin line along the arm; others have run down toward the waist and traced out, along one side of the belly, the hip, the top of the thigh, a more random network already starting to congeal. Three or four tiny veins have reached the hollow between the legs, meeting in a sinuous line, touching the point of the V formed by the outspread legs, and disappearing into the black tuft.

Look, now the flesh is still intact: the black tuft and the white belly, the soft curve of the hips, the narrow waist, and, higher up, the pearly breasts rising and falling in time with the rapid breathing, whose rhythm grows more accelerated. The man, close to her, one knee on the floor, leans farther over. The head, with its long, curly hair, which alone is free to move somewhat, turns from side to side, struggling; finally the woman's mouth twists open, while the flesh is torn open, the blood spurts out over the tender skin, stretched tight, the carefully shadowed eyes grow abnormally larger, the mouth opens wider, the head twists violently, one last time, from right to left, then more gently, to fall back finally and become still, amid the mass of black hair spread out on the velvet.

At the very top of the stone stairway, the little door has opened, allowing a yellowish but sustained shaft of light to enter, against which stands out the dark silhouette of the man wrapped in his long cloak. He has but to climb a few more steps to reach the threshold.

Afterward, the whole setting is empty, the enormous room with its purple shadows and its stone columns

其中的紫色阴影及石头圆柱也已向四面八方消散而隐匿，那旋形的、令人难忘的无扶手楼梯一面上升而进入黑暗之中，一面变得越来越狭窄，越来越模糊，最后升到拱顶的上端，在那儿消失不见了。

那具躯体上的伤口已经凝合，它的光晕也开始渐渐暗淡。旁边的那只香炉里，一缕轻烟透过静止的空气袅袅升起，起先是一个烟圈，向左飘动，随后轻快地直接上升，又转回香炉的正上方，继续向右越过香炉，又转弯回到原来的方位，这样，形成一条明确无误的曲线，而且弧度越来越大，笔直上升，升向画面的顶端。

proliferating in all directions, the monumental staircase with no handrail that twists upward, growing narrower and vaguer as it rises into the darkness, toward the top of the vaults where it disappears.

Near the body, whose wound has stiffened, whose brilliance is already growing dim, the thin smoke from the incense burner traces complicated scrolls in the still air: first a coil turned horizontally to the left, which then straightens out and rises slightly, then returns to the axis of its point of origin, which it crosses as it moves to the right, then turns back in the first direction, only to wind back again, thus forming an irregular sinusoidal curve, more and more flattened out, and rising, vertically, toward the top of the canvas.

┌讨　论─■

这篇小说在时间安排方面完全背离了现实主义传统。在小说的单一场景中，短暂的时间顺序往往是倒叙的：残杀后的瞬间出现在小说的中间部分，而谋杀前的瞬间及谋杀本身则出现在后面；所有这些，又要在对遇害者躯体和谋杀场所进行大段描述，并点明谋杀者已登上通往那间地牢外面的楼梯准备逃之夭夭之后，才加以叙述。

当然，根据日常生活经验，小说场景中的动作应该按照时间顺序发展，这有助于加强被描写场面的现实感。在《密室》里，由于短暂的时间顺序明显地被颠倒，作者有意想赋予这单一场景以某种与众不同的现实感，就会被读者认为是人为的，只有在推论上才显得"真实"，或者在描写的各个不同时刻之间才显出有意义的联系。就读者来说，在场景描写中，与其让时间起组合作用还不如让过渡性的叙述语来发挥这种作用，这就像叙述语在各个不同场景间发挥连接或过渡作用一样，就像不同作品要由不同的编者按语来简介作品内容一样。

现在，我们必须问，《密室》既然在时间安排上表现出对现实主义传统的背离，那它是否起到了作用呢？也就是说，把时间切断然后重

This story most strikingly departs from realistic convention in its handling of time. The temporal movement in the story's single scene is, as often as not, backward: the moment immediately following the slaughter is presented in the middle of the story, while the moment just before the murder and the murder itself are presented later; and all of these moments are described after the long introductory description of the victim's body and of the torture chamber, at which point the murderer is seen already in flight, ascending the stairs that lead out of the dungeon.

That the action within a scene in a story moves forward in time borrows, of course, from experience, and contributes to the realism of the rendered scene. The predominant reversal of temporal movement in "The Secret Room" establishes a different sort of reality for its single scene, a reality that the reader recognizes as artificial but that presumably conveys the "true" or significant relation among the scene's various moments. The reader thus looks to the narrative voice rather than to time as the organizing force *within* the scene, just as he looks to the narrative voice to organize transitions *between* scenes, and to make other editorial decisions in the presentation of action in other stories.

We must now ask whether "The Secret Room" fulfills the commitment implied by its rejection of realistic convention in its handling of time; whether, in fact, the significant relation among the various moments of the

新加以组合,是否明确地显示出小说单一场景中的不同时刻之间所具有的有意义的联系呢?对于这个问题,回答也许是否定的。譬如说,我们并不明确那个谋杀者的动机是什么——是某种祭祀仪式,抑或是荒唐的报复,或者干脆是性虐狂的反常行为。我们也不明确,是谁站在楼梯顶上开门放杀人者出去的——小说在此结束了,内容则回转到小说开始的时候。换言之,这篇小说没有通常所认为的情节。它基本上是绘画性的,其中没有合乎时间逻辑的动作。这篇小说所揭示的,只是动作的多种含义,而小说中的动作则借之于同名绘画作品。从某种意义上讲,这篇小说要求读者对绘画的含义尽量发挥想象力——赋予绘画中所表现的各种时间可能性以某种意义。同时,通过小说所叙述的内容,介绍了19世纪后期法国艺术家莫洛的一幅绘画。莫洛的作品经常以死亡为主题,情绪颓废,就如《密室》所表现的那样,而这篇小说也正是献给莫洛的。

由于这篇小说描述的是一幅绘画,所以它并没有解决一般意义上的连贯性问题。由于小说自始至终拘泥于它的原始材料,所以它所表示的想操纵时间的意图也就没有实现,也就是说,小说玩弄短暂时间这种把戏,想激发读者去探究小说发展中各个时刻之间的有意义的联系,但这种联系实际上并不存在。进一步说,读者最后得知的倒是,小说的叙述者就像一个醉醺醺的说大话者一样,对自己所说的话是否成篇很不负责。由此观之,这篇小说和《花园余影》一样,不过是一种扩展现实的玩意儿。

story's single scene comes clear as a result of their temporal reorganization. The answer to this question seems to be no. For example, we do not discover what were the motivations of the woman's killer—whether the murder was some form of ritual sacrifice or a grotesque retribution or simply an act of sadistic perversion. Neither do we discover who opens the door at the top of the stairs to let the killer out—this at the story's conclusion, when action had returned to the point of time at which it had begun. In other words, the story does not have a plot in the ordinary sense. It is basically pictorial, not action in a logical time sequence. What the story does offer is suggestive variations of action based on the same pictorial material. In a sense, the story asks the reader to explore imaginatively the pictorial suggestions—to turn into significant time the possibilities of time in the picture. By the way, the narrative is revealed to be a description of a painting by Gustave Moreau, a French artist of the late nineteenth century, whose work was often just a macabre and decadent as that of "The Secret Room", which is dedicated to Moreau. The story may be taken as an exploration of narrative and the emotional suggestions of the painting.

That the story describes a painting does not resolve its problems of ordinary coherence. By withholding this information until literally the last moment, the story implies an intention for its manipulation of time that it does not fulfill: this juggling of temporal moments, that is, encourages the reader to pursue a significant relation among the moments of the story's action, and this relation does not appear. Rather, the reader is finally told that the narrator, like a man who says he has found a manuscript in a bottle, is not responsible for the organization of the story he tells. Such an ending is, like that of "Continuity of Parks", a toying with the margins of reality.

┌ 思考题 ─■

1. 如你所知,这篇小说描述的是一幅绘画,读后你对画家的创作意图产生过哪些问题?

2. 类似"很难说清楚那亮光是从哪儿照进来

1. Had you known that a painting was being described, what sort of questions would you have raised about the painter's motivations as you read the story?

的"这样的陈述句有何言外之意？这篇小说毫无疑问是描述一幅绘画吗？小说在出人意外的结尾前所做的预示是否有助于这种结尾？

3. 有两种结尾出人意外的作品，一种如《带家具出租的房间》和《鹰溪桥上》，另一种如《花园余影》和《密室》，它们之间有何区别？

（刘文荣 译）

2. What retroactive meaning is given to narrative remarks such as "It is . . . difficult to say where the light comes from"? By the revelation that the story describes a painting? Does this foreshadowing of the story's surprise ending help to validate the ending?

3. What is the difference between the kinds of surprise ending in "The Furnished Room" and "An Occurrence at Owl Creek Bridge" on the other?

031. 二十九条臆想

(美)乔伊斯·卡罗尔·欧茨 著

蓝仁哲 译

031. 29 Inventions

by Joyce Carol Oates

一

"我快死了。我正在消逝。我老想到死。一睡着我就像死了似的……快死了……我能听见心跳离我而去。在我身体里,却渐渐离去。这是事实。我突然醒来,它又回到我体内,跳得很厉害。我以起床来驱除这宝贝,这心跳。我试着轻手轻脚下床,不致让他听见我醒了——他要是听见,就会坐起来说,你到哪儿去?你要干什么?像雪崩一样,他会从床的另一边扑到我身上。"

1

"I am dying. I am disappearing. I think about death all the time. Falling asleep I seem to be falling into death. . . dying. . . . I can hear my heartbeat moving away from me. It is inside me and yet moving away. This is a fact. I wake up suddenly and it comes back to me, beating hard. I get out of bed to take away this prize, this beating. I try to get away very quietly so that *he* won't hear me wake up—if he hears me he sits up and says, *Where are you going? What do you want?* It is like an avalanche, the way he falls on me from his side of the bed. "

二

我没杜撰她,没杜撰她的一切。大多数的话都是她说的。她老是前倾着坐在那张椅子上——一张藤背椅,很旧了——窗户在她的右边,玻璃上明显地覆了一层灰,脏得几乎不透明了。她总是身子朝前,和我的朋友精神病医生谈话。在她看来,我是一个速记员,护士,另一个女人,因此并不重要。她不屑看我一眼。她老在诊疗所里,在底特律中心地区一座5层楼的遗址,两旁的楼房已是一片瓦砾场。我快死了。我正在消逝。

2

I have not invented her, not all of her. Most of the words are hers. She is forever sitting forward in that chair—a canebacked chair, very old—with the window to her right, all that glaring filmed-over glass, almost opaque with dirt. She is forever leaning forward to talk to my friend, a psychiatrist. To her I am a stenographer, a nurse, I am another woman and therefore not important. She doesn't bother to look at me. She is forever there in the clinic, deep in Detroit, buildings lying in rubble on either side of that five-story relic. *I am dying. I am disappearing.*

三

我必须凭空臆想她的面庞,因为大半已经忘记。

3

I have to invent her face because most of it is gone.

作者简介:乔伊斯·卡罗尔·欧茨(Joyce Carol Oates,1938—),美国作家。1938年6月16日生于纽约州洛克波特。她执教于温莎大学(1967—1978)和普林斯顿大学(1978年始)。她描写最多的是死于血泊的经历丰富的人和由于自己无法控制的力量导致自我毁灭的人。她的主要作品包括《他们》(Them,1969)、《狐火》(Fox fire,1993)和《野兽》(Beasts,2002),还有《贝尔弗勒》(Belle fleur,1980)、《布勒兹摩传奇》(A Bloodsmoor Romance,1982)和《温特瑟恩的神秘故事》(Mysteries of Winter-thurn,1984)。

她的激动——她对我朋友的亲密——这使我难以克制自己的感情。我认为在精神病医生与他的病人之间,距离应当更大。我以一个工作人员的面目出现,为杰第思大夫做记录。她的面庞年轻但没有朝气。她经常愁眉不展,过于害怕心跳会过去,这就在她的额头上过早地烙下了皱纹。她确实有轻盈可爱的金黄头发。这我记得。她一点儿不注意她的美发,只是梳到耳根后了事。一个神经质的习惯动作,迅速举手去拂额上的几绺短发。想象中的几绺发。有一个时候——或许在读高中时——她留有一头浓发,蓬松的金发波浪式地披在肩上。我在做记录。我假装做记录,其实在本子上描绘不同的面孔。杰第思大夫几天前对我说过:你是想面对真实的人生呢?或是害怕它?

四

害怕。

五

她一开始谈话,我就不能记录了。口若悬河——不害臊——我认为她说得太直率了。她的心跳开始在屋里发出声响。我感觉得出它的振动。房间为什么这么小?我们挨得太近了,我们三个人。我注视着她那又黑又大发愣的眼睛,她的眼睛没看我,我还是不能记录。这或许是种背叛——一个女人背叛另一个女人。

六

所以,我要臆想她的大部分:纤细;肩胛骨隆现在黄色紧身毛线衣下边;头发往后梳,用发夹束住(色彩不调——棕色而不是金黄的发夹);光着的两腿红红的,满是针刺的样子;脚趾露在凉鞋外面,脏兮兮的,毫不在乎;钱包脏得发黄(某种合成品,看来像皮的);口红……不,她没抹口红,嘴小而无血色,它使我惊异,那么凶狠地张着,吐出那些我忘不了的字句:我老想到死,一睡着我就像死了似的。

The shock of her—the closeness of her to my friend—this unnerved me. I thought there was more distance between a psychiatrist and his patient. I was in disguise as a technician, taking notes for Dr. Geddes. Her face: young and yet not youthful. Premature lines on the forehead from too much frowning, too much fear for her departing heartbeat. She did have very light, fine blond hair. I remember that. She did nothing with it, just brushed it back behind her ears. A nervous habit: her hand darting to her forehead to brush away strands of hair. Imaginary strands. At one time—when she was in high school, maybe—she had a big mane of hair, a head of thick blond hair that cascaded down over her shoulders. I was taking notes. I pretended to take notes but really I was drawing faces on a pad. Dr. Geddes had said to me a few days before. *Do you want to encounter real life? Or are you afraid of it?*

4

Afraid.

5

When she began talking I couldn't take notes. Her words rushed out—no shame—it was too direct for me. Her heartbeat began to sound in the room. I could feel its vibrations. Why is that room so small? We were too close together, the three of us. I stared at her large, stunned, black eyes, that were unseeing on me, and I couldn't take notes. It would have been a betrayal—one woman betraying another.

6

So I will invent most of her: her thinness, her shoulder bones showing through a tight yellow sweater, her hair combed back and fastened with bobby pins (the wrong color—brown and not blond bobby pins), her bare legs and their prickly, flushed look, her toes in open sandals grimy and careless, her purse a soiled yellow (some synthetic material, fake leather), lipstick.... No, she wasn't wearing lipstick. Her mouth was small and colorless and it surprised me, opening so desperately, letting out those words I can't forget: *I think about death all the time. Falling asleep I seem to be falling into death.*

七

她热切地朝前靠着,嘴角边挂一丝口水。凝视着我朋友的面孔,医生的面孔。她完全不理会我。她是那种认为别的女人都无足轻重的女子,所以连瞧也不瞧我一眼。我只是一个护士,或者一位秘书 为医生做做记录而已。她永远看不见我,只看得见他——她贪婪而又焦急地注视着他。她比我年轻,有一副娇弱美丽的容貌,但眉毛太黄太浅,嘴唇也没有血色。那是一张虚弱的面孔,不是双眉深锁就是眉开眼笑讨好医生:要是我能看清离开他的路子……他会杀害我……

八

“他老是缠着我。几乎每天都想和我做爱。我累死了,想要离开那儿。他压在我身上,我头脑发空,脖子像要折断似的,我想叫喊,叫喊……可是,啊,我经常想到……想到他也要死了……在他干那事的时候……他的面孔拧成个怪相。我想到他快要死了,而我将因此获得自由……我想跑掉,那样我们两人或许都不会死。但夜里醒来,我的心在疯狂地跳动。我满身是汗,非常怕死,医生。也怕发病——要是我的心脏停止跳动怎么办? 一会儿跳得很快,一会儿不动,慢慢地消失到我的肋下。像一个广播电台,播送出去,又要把它收回来……”

九

杰第思大夫:35 岁,一张有疙瘩的长形脸;浓眉,黑发,黑眼珠,机灵,精明,总是倾听的眼神。

十

我在格雷锡俄的停车场停了车。停车场告示牌上写着:此处停车 75 美分。下边用很小的字体写着:

7

She is leaning forward earnestly. A trickle of saliva in the corner of her mouth. Staring at my friend's face, the doctor's face, paying no attention to me. She is the kind of woman who thinks other women don't matter; so she won't look at me, I am just a nurse, or a secretary, taking notes for the doctor. She never sees me. She only sees him—she stares at him hungrily, anxiously. She is younger than I am. She has a delicate, beautiful face, but the eyebrows are too blond, too faint, and the mouth colorless. It is a weak face, it is either shut tight in a frown or opened in a plea, pleading with the doctor: *If I could see my way clear to leave him.... He would like to kill me....*

8

“He is always after me. He wants to make love every day, almost. I feel so tired. I want to get out of there. He lies on top of me and my head goes empty, my neck is ready to snap, I want to scream and scream.... And, oh, I always think of ... I think of him dying too.... When he does that.... His face gets all twisted and I think of him dying and how I would be free then.... I think about running away and then maybe neither one of us would have to die. But I wake up at night and my heart is going like crazy. I'm all sweat and I'm so scared of dying, doctor, I'm scared of going crazy too—what if my heart stopped? It races fast and then it gets faint and goes away inside my ribs, it's like a radio station that is going away and you try to get it back again... ”

9

Dr. Geddes: thirty-five years old, a knobby, oblong face, thick eyebrows, dark hair, dark, clever, shrewd, listening eyes.

10

I park my car in a parking lot on Gratiot. The

"头半个小时"。我从服务员手里领了张票,他是一个大个子黑人。街上很拥挤——人行道上也拥挤——到处是人,还有小汽车、卡车、公共汽车,城市的气息闭塞而舒适。这一切都是意料中的事。我停了车,钥匙留在车里,慌忙朝那幢他在等我的大楼走去。大楼在一片需要铲平重建的街区。一个新的诊所将要在那一片瓦砾上修建起来,要有许许多多的玻璃、混凝土、镶嵌图饰、塑料躺椅、电视机……在这一切的中央,杰第思大夫交臂而立,一个圣人。

十一

我能看见他的面孔,但不是我已经描述的那样。它没那样清楚。他的个子相当高,走起路来迈着长而急速的步子。他的肌肉发达么? 我不知道。不错。他的眼珠是黑色的,阴郁而暗淡。他 35 岁,我想,尽管有时看上去老些。那女人比他年轻 10 岁,至少。然而,她如此贪婪地注视着他。

十二

"要是我能看清离开他的路子……"

她的形象模糊,纤细,带着哀求的神气。眼皮奇怪地呈粉红色,上面有些小斑片,与她的金黄睫毛混杂在一起。

沉默。

"夜里,他沉重得很,在床上。我睡不着觉。想到死,想到陷入烂泥什么的……我能感到我的心离去……要是他醒来,就火得很。"

杰第思大夫坐在桌前,一直在吸烟。我在他背后,身子靠着里墙,她看不见。尽管我们三人隔得很近。房间的天花板很高,有条裂缝。墙上挂着日历,但没人相信未来。谁也不屑去翻页。上月的最末一天是上星期五,时间在这儿打呵欠。窗外什么也没有。那女人的头动了一下,看样子睡思昏昏,不知所措。她从脸上掠掉一绺头发。我的朋友杰第思大夫往一个黑色的塑料烟缸里抖掉烟头上的灰。

他说:"后来呢?"

"你是说,要是他醒来?"

---

sign for the lot says, PARK HERE 75¢. And then in very small letters it says "first half hour." I take the ticket from the attendant, a big black man. The street is busy—the sidewalks busy—people everywhere, cars, trucks, city buses, the smell of the city confining and cozy. It is all so predictable. I park my car and leave the keys inside, and hurry across to the building where he is waiting for me. It is in a block that will be razed for urban renewal. A new clinic will be built on top of all that rubble, lots of glass and concrete and mosaic decorations and plastic lounge chairs and television sets . . . in the center of it Dr. Geddes will stand with his arms folded, a saint.

11

I can see his face, but it is not the face I have described. It is not so clear. He is a fairly tall man and he walks in long, urgent strides. Has he any muscles? I don't know. His eyes are dark, yes. Shadowed and dark. He is thirty-five, I think, though sometimes he looks older. The girl must be ten years younger than he is, at least. Yet she stares at him so hungrily.

12

"If I could see my way clear to leave him. . ."

She is vague, wispy, imploring. Her eyelids are strangely pink, there are small flakes on them, mixed in with her blond eyelashes.

Silence.

"He is so heavy at night, in bed. I can't sleep. I think about dying, about sinking into mud or something. . . I can feel my heart going away. . . If he wakes up he gets mad."

Dr. Geddes at his desk. Smoking through all this. I am behind him, against the inner wall, out of sight. The three of us are very close together though. The room has a high ceiling and it is cracked. A calendar on the wall, but no one believes in the future. No one has bothered to turn the page over; the end of the month was last Friday. Time yawns here. Outside the window there is nothing. The girl's head moves sleepy and confused. She brushes a strand of hair back from her face. Dr. Geddes, my friend, shakes ashes from his cigarette into a black plastic ashtray.

He says, "And then what?"

" If he wakes up, you mean?"

"是的,后来呢?"

"啊,后来……后来我们可能争辩……我不知道……我装着必须上厕所,躲在那儿直到他又睡去。但是,如果他睡不着,他就起来,而且……我恨他,希望他不来找我的麻烦……"

"为什么?"

她朝他眨巴着眼,眼睫毛上有些皮肤屑。她一定有什么皮肤病。"为什么个啥?"

"为什么你不要他找你的麻烦?"

"因为……"

十三

有一次,我看见她在街上,走得很快。颀长的腿,金黄的头发在她脸旁边跳动,涂了口红,带着手镯,很匆忙的样子。看起来她像个陌生人,一个大约 25 岁的女子。她没注意我,我是一个人,她也是一个人。杰第思大夫不在城里——那不是他的义务工作日,慈善活动日。他在自己的私人诊所,在几英里夕的格罗斯·坡因特。这女子没注意到我,即使注意到了,也不会记得起我。因为一个女人不重视另一个女人。她紧皱眉头,绷着脸,面色苍白。她脑子里充满胡思乱想,像野草。颀长叉开的腿。短裙——我想是白色的,但不很干净——凉鞋,脚趾很脏——头发洗过烫过,弯弯曲曲,在脸旁边跳跃。这是那种女人,某个男人——她的丈夫——夜里发现了她的隐秘,想杀死她。

"医生,他想杀害我。他说,如果我离开他,他会找到我,把我杀了。"

"为什么?"

"为什么个啥?"

"为什么你认为他要杀害你?"

"因为……"

十四

她在街角停下,转过头来看我。正面讥讽的一瞥。我刚好从赫德森商店后边出来,提着一个暗灰绿色的袋子。她注视着我,眯起眼睛来辨认我。那张小

"Yes, then what?"

"Oh, then. . . then we maybe argue. . . I don't know. . . I pretend I have to go to the bathroom and hide in there until he falls asleep again. But if he doesn't fall asleep he gets up and. . . I hate him, I wish he would let me alone. . . "

"Why?"

She blinks at him. There are tiny flakes of skin on her eyelashes; she must have a skin infection of some kind. "Why what?"

"Why do you want him to leave you alone?"

"Because. . . "

13

I saw her out on the street once, walking fast. Long legs, blond hair bobbing about her face, lipstick, bracelets. In a hurry. She looked like a stranger, a girl of about twenty-five. She didn't notice me, I was alone, she was alone. Dr. Geddes was not in the city—this wasn't his day for volunteer work, charity work. He was in his own private office in Grosse Pointe, miles away. The girl didn't notice me, but if she had she would not have remembered me, because a woman does not matter to another woman. Her face was tight with frowning, very pale. Her head was filled with wild ideas, like weeds. Her long flaring legs. Her short skirt—I think it was white, and not very clean—her sandals, dirty toes—hair washed and curled and bouncing about her face. This is the girl some man, a husband, burrows into at night and would like to kill.

"Doctor, he wants to kill me. He said if I left him he would find me and kill me. "

"Why?"

"Why what?"

"Why do you think he wants to kill you?"

"Because. . . "

14

At the street corner she paused and turned to look at me. A full, ironic stare. I had just come out the back way from Hudson's, carrying one of their dark gray-green packages. She stared at me and her eyes narrowed a little in recognition. That small careful mouth. The slight arching of her back, one woman showing off her body to another. She stared at me. I

而留心的嘴。背略为有点驼，一个女人向另一个女人显示她的身段。她瞪着我。交通灯变绿，人们在她周围走动，我却踌躇不前，她也站在那儿不动……我不能转身走开，不能装作我是别的什么人。我必须靠近她走。她张开嘴唇，慢慢启齿，露出一丝嘲弄的微笑。她小声地说："他不爱你！他爱我！"

她伸出手来，攥住我的手腕，小而硬的指甲往里掐。

十五

我跟随她回家。她不是我记得的样子。不，她没那样年轻——她或许和我的年纪相仿，30 或者出头一点儿。她的头发染过，发根是暗棕色。不，不，不对——那样的话她就不会有金黄色眉毛，而她的眉毛确实是金黄色的，我记得。很深的金黄色。纤弱、贫血的那种金黄。因此，头发没染过。刚才说的不算，改个说法。整洁、瘦长的小个子，细手腕、细脚踝，长而不干净的脖子。高贵的脖子，我看见她在街头。我隔着一段距离跟随她……她没看见我，即使看见了，也不会认出我。她在热恋杰第思大夫，永远不会看见我，一个护士。我现在跟她到家，同她走得一样快，和着她的步子，一二三，一二三。她摆动着手臂，我的手臂不能自由摆动，但是我的腿和她的一样长，一样急切，急于走出这街区，穿过约翰路，再走几条街，进入一幢公寓。

我跟她走上楼梯。飘在她身后。在她脑瓜里，在她那双细小愚笨的眼睛后边！我把钥匙插进锁孔，慢慢地、偷偷地开了门。我环视了那间杂乱的厨房，看看是否有人在那儿……这个街区发生过破门而入，小青年寻找零钱。吸毒的小青年。她进了厨房，但还未关门。如果另一间房里有人躲藏，她必须迅速跑出去……我把厨房油漆成白色，后来让油脂喷溅到天花板和四壁。油腻与灰尘。肮脏的图案很像星座。我把有圣母玛丽亚彩色蜡笔画的日历贴在墙上，玛丽亚裸露出胸口，举起一只手在祝福。我为那女人梳刷头发，直到头发像通了电似的根根竖立。尽管额上有皱纹，她是一个漂亮的年轻女子。我领她到洗澡间，那里有一面镜子，照出一张脸，她的脸。她凝视自己。她摸摸自己的脸颊。我正在消逝，她说出声来。

hesitated, but she stood there, unmoving, while the light turned green and people moved out around her... I couldn't turn away, couldn't pretend I was someone else. I had to walk near her. Her lips moved away from her teeth in a small ironic smile. She whispered, "He doesn't love you! He loves me!"

She reached out and took hold of my wrist and dug her hard little nails into it.

15

I follow her home. She is not the way I remembered her. No, she is not that young—she is probably my age, she is thirty or more. Her hair is bleached. Dark brown at the roots. No, no, that can't be right—she wouldn't have blond eyebrows then, and she does have blond eyebrows; I remember that. Too blond. Flimsy and anemic, that kind of blond. So the hair isn't bleached. Erase that. Change that. A trim, wiry little body, thin wrists and ankles, a long unclean neck. A noble neck. I saw her on the street. I followed her home at a distance... She didn't see me. If she saw me she would not have recognized me. She is in love with Dr. Geddes and never sees me, the nurse. I follow her home now, walking fast as she, keeping in time with her steps, one two three, one two three, swinging her arms, my arms are not free to swing, but my legs are as long and as eager as hers to take her out of this neighborhood, across John R. and a few blocks over, and into an apartment building.

I follow her up the stairs. I float up behind her. I am inside her skull: behind those flaky little moronic eyes! I put the key in the lock, open the door slowly, stealthily, I look around the cluttered kitchen to see if anyone is there.... Break-ins in this neighborhood, kids looking for loose change. Kids on dope. She enters the kitchen but does not yet close the door. If someone is hiding in the other room she'll have to get out fast... I paint the kitchen white and then splatter the ceiling and walls with grease. Grease and dust. Designs of dirt like constellations. I tack that calendar on the wall with the pastel Virgin Mary on it, heart exposed, hand lifted in a blessing. I brush the girl's hair for her until it is bristling with electricity. She is a pretty young woman in spite of the frown lines. I walk her into the bathroom where there is a mirror and show her this face, her face. She stares at herself. She touches her face. *I am disappearing*, she says aloud.

十六

我没跟她回家。

我在街上瞧见她，但没跟随她。我放过了她。一看见她，我的心就感到仇恨的戳痛。她比他小 10 多岁，年轻得太不相称。她注视着他，面部的神情像一幅水彩画，招引他去抚摩她，吻她，用手指头去弄脏她。"我一定得离开他。我一定要离婚。"她上一次说，星期二那天。恳求帮助。医生抽着烟，蹙着眉，思考这个问题。不，还没有。决不要破坏你的家庭。决不要改变你的生活。太快了。现在别这样做，以后要懊悔的。去和他谈谈，陈述利害。是的，可是他推开我——推开桌子——和他谈谈，解释解释。你很痛苦，你说，你的身体因为他感到疼痛，解释解释。多花点儿时间洗个澡。坐在浴盆里。热水。温和的香皂水。休息。全身放松。是的，可是他发那栏大的脾气——和他谈谈，解释清楚。不能离婚。诊疗期间不要改变生活。还有孩子们将怎么办呢？

十七

我没提到孩子们——

我是那样臆想她的：那一天，她戴着手镯，甚至金耳环，穿着凉鞋、短白裙、红色的套头绒衫，头发新洗过。好吧。但是她带着两个孩子。两个男孩，都很瘦，胸扁肩窄。她催他们快走——为什么那样快？——黄色钱包紧贴她的肋骨，一只手牵着小的一个孩子的胳膊，领着他。他显得惊慌，那个孩子。为什么他的妈让他走那样快？另一个孩子在前边一点儿跑着，绕过或钻进人群，在街沿的一堆瓦砾前转圈，跳下街沿避开一群黑人孩子，在一根停车计时柱前转一圈，重新跳回人行道。她为什么让他们快走？我跟他们三人走了一条街，不再跟了。让她走吧。让她回家，爬楼梯，开门。在里面看管喘气的孩子，匆匆进入洗澡间。在那里她可以不被人打扰，手按在心口。我正在消逝！她看见镜子里的身影时这样叫喊。

16

I don't follow her home.

I saw her on the street but I didn't follow her. I released her. My heart gave a lunge of hatred, seeing her. She is more than ten years younger than he is, too young for him. She stares at him with her face like a water color, asking him to touch her, to kiss her, to smear her with his fingers. "I've got to leave him. I've got to get a divorce," she said last time, on Tuesday. A plea for help. The doctor smoked, frowned, thought about it. No. Not yet. Mustn't break up your family. Mustn't change your life. Too fast. Not now. Regret it later. Talk it over with him. Explain. *Yes, but he shoves me-shoves the table-* Talk to him. Explain. You are sore, you say, your body is sore from him; explain. Take a long bath. Sit in the tub. Warm water. Warm soapy water. Rest. Relax. *Yes, but he gets so mad—* Talk to him. Explain. No divorce. No change of life during counseling. And what about the children?

17

I didn't mention the children—

I invented her with bracelets, even loops of gold in her ears on that day, sandals, a short white skirt, a red pullover blouse, clean hair. All right. But she had two kids with her. Two boys. They looked very thin, thin chests, narrow shoulders. She was walking them fast—why so fast? —the yellow purse pressed against her ribs and her hand on the smaller boy's upper arm, guiding him. He looked panicked, that boy. Why was his mother making him walk so fast? The other boy ran a little ahead of them, in and around people, around a pile of debris at the curb, jumping out onto the curb to avoid a group of black kids, looping out around a parking meter and jumping back onto the sidewalk. Why was she hurrying them? I followed the three of them for a block, then gave up. Let her go. Let her go home and climb the stairs and unlock the door and herd the panting kids inside and rush into the bathroom where she can be alone, pressing her hand to her heart. *I am disappearing*! she cries out at her reflection in the mirror.

十八

"他们将跟我一起过来。我想和他们在一起。"

"你如何供养他们?"

"继续当助手。"

"恐怕你不够资格。"

"那么,继续领救济。"

"马上离开你的丈夫有什么好处?"

她注视着杰第思大夫。思索,思索。

"你为什么要在这时候彻底改变你的生活? 在我这儿,你不正在逐渐好转吗?"

凝视着他。思索着。由于惶恐,她的双眼有点朦胧。今天,杰第思大夫穿一件细蓝条白衬衣,结一条深蓝色领带。在这幢大楼里,他仪态庄重,和我一道儿上楼梯——我们从不使用电梯。

"我不知道——我不知道——"女人结结巴巴地说,惊骇极了。

如果我们一齐进电梯,一关上门,就只剩我们两人,单独在一起,在一个吱吱上移的箱子里,一直到 4 楼市立诊疗所。单独在一起。不,最好走楼梯,它也发出吱吱的声音。

在我这儿,你不正在逐渐好转吗?

十九

她不是他唯一的病人。我在她周围臆想出一个真空,把她描绘成唯一的病人。不,还有其他许多病人。每星期二大约 10 点钟,我开车去市区,爬上他的办公室,我已被邀请进入他的生活领域。他在这个诊所的办公室里只有一张办公桌,只有一张办公桌的一间屋。走廊里人们川流不息,大多数是黑人。他在这里的大多数病人是黑人,不错,但我并不对黑人感兴趣。我把兴趣放在那个白种女人身上。我坐着听完他给一个黑人看病,黑人约 40 岁,黑紫色的脸,大鼻子,水汪汪的眼睛,难看的牙齿。杰第思坐在办公桌后边,对人严格但很和善。办公桌小而破旧。其他医生也用它。星期二那天归杰第思大夫用,一直用到下午很晚。据我所知,有别的人夜里进来,用这张桌子。

18

"They'll come with me. I want them with me."

"How will you support them?"

"Go on ADC."

"You wouldn't qualify."

"Go on welfare then."

"What is the advantage of leaving your husband right now?"

She stares at Dr. Geddes. Thinking. Thinking.

"Why should you change your life so radically at this time? Aren't you making progress with me here?"

Staring at him. Thinking. Her eyes film over with panic. Dr. Geddes is wearing a white shirt with narrow blue stripes today, and a dark blue tie. He carries himself cautiously in this building, up the stairs with me—we never take the elevator.

"I don't know—I don't know—" the girl stammers, terrified.

If we got into the elevator together, the door would close upon us and we would be alone, alone together, in a box moving creakily up to the fourth floor of the Metropolitan Clinic. Alone together. No, it is better to take the stairs, which creak too.

Aren't you making progress with me here?

19

She isn't his only patient. I invented a vacuum around her, describing her as if she were his only patient. No. There are many more. I drive downtown on Tuesdays around ten, I go up to his office, I have been invited into his life. This office of his at the clinic is just a desk, a room with a desk, and in the corridor people are always milling around, most of them blacks. Most of his patients here are blacks, yes, but I wasn't intercsted in them. I picked the white woman to be interested in. I sat through an interview with a black of about forty, a black-purplish face, big nose, watery eyes, bad teeth. Dr. Geddes, fastidious and kind, behind his desk. The desk is small and hattered. Other doctors use it. It is Dr. Geddes's on Tuesdays, until late afternoon; for all I know someone else comes in at night and uses it. The calendar isn't his—now someone has turned the page over. It is June. The black man with the bad teeth talked slowly, maddeningly,

日历不是他的——现在有人翻过了。6 月。那个牙齿难看的黑人在讲话,缓慢地、疯疯癫癫地,讲到 4 月里的一天早晨。我坐在那儿听。记录簿,用圆珠笔。我盯住自己的脚。黑人谈到他的房东,谈到他买的一辆车。他翻来覆去地唠叨。我不再听,光看自己的脚,同时又怕杰第思大夫发现我没在听。你想面对真实的人生吗?他曾经说过。杰第思(这不是他的真名)带有这周围医生的嘲讽、倦怠的眼神——他们什么病也治不好,只是消耗掉自己的生命而已。到了 40 岁,他们就变得酸腐。但是,我对那黑人不感兴趣。下一个进来的是一个女人,浅黑皮肤,30 多岁——身材矮胖,喷了香水,善于交际。她也不是我感兴趣的人。我想要别的人。下一个是一位金发女人,面容苍白,头发好像褪了色,带着两个骨瘦如柴的小孩,她的手指甲下积满了污垢,一脸惊慌的神色……

二十

"在我这儿,你不正在逐渐好转吗?"

"我不知道——"

"你说的什么意思?"

"我本来以为情况会——不同——我是说,我需要一些法律上的帮助,如果我离了婚,就不知道怎么办好——有时我溜下床,走进洗澡间去藏起来。我止不住哭。我怕会发疯。孩子在前一间屋里睡觉,所以我不能到那儿去。有时他们醒来。杰菲开始大喊大叫,接着他醒来,大发脾气。我想死,我认为。我不想和他同居。"

"可是,我们这儿的情形在进展,对不对?'

这儿在进展。进展。杰第思大夫怀疑地望着她。他不想让她离开丈夫。他要她在那儿和他一起,在床上,在洗澡间,早上 4 点钟赤着脚,用拳头揉她伤心发红的眼睛……

二十一

一天,在她到来之后 10 分钟,她的丈夫露面了。

他笨重的身体向我们挺进。不知怎么的,他在楼下遇见了她。他的面孔雍肿,涨得通红,怒不可遏,

one morning back in April. I sat and listened. The note pad, the ball-point pen. I stared at my own feet. The man talked about his landlord and about a car he had bought. He kept repeating himself. I stopped listening and stared at my feet, afraid that Dr. Geddes would sense I wasn't listening. *Do you want to encounter real life*? he had said. Dr. Geddes (which is not his real name) has the sardonic, weary look of doctors around here—they can't cure anything, they can only wear themselves out; they turn sour at the age of forty. But the black man did not interest me. A woman came in next, a lightskinned black woman in her thirties—heavyset, perfumy, sociable. She wasn't right either. I wanted someone else. Next came the blond girl, washed-out face and hair, two kids, scrawny kids she'd brought along with her, dirt lodged beneath her nails, the odor of panic about her...

20

"Aren't you making progress with me here?"

"I don't know—"

"What do you mean?"

"I thought it would be—different—I mean, I need some help with the law, if I get a divorce, I don't know what to do—Sometimes I slide out of bed and go into the bathroom to hide. I can't stop crying. I'm afraid I'll go crazy. The kids sleep in the front room so I can't go in there. Sometimes they wake up. Jeffy starts bawling and then *he* wakes up and gets mad as hell. I want to die, I guess. I don't want to live with him. "

"But we're making progress here, aren't we?"

Progress here. Progress. Dr. Geddes eyes her suspiciously. He doesn't want her to leave that husband. He wants her *there* with him, in the bed, in the bathroom, barefoot at four in the morning, rubbing her fists into her sore pinkened eyes...

21

Her husband showed up one day, ten minutes after she arrived.

His body was clumsy, propelled toward us. Somehow he had gotten by the girl downstairs. His face was clumsy, flushed, furious. "You the doctor?" he yelled.

Danger.

Real life.

"你就是那个医生?"他号叫。

危险。

真实的人生。

杰第思大夫立即站起身来:"你是——?"

她开始惊叫。

"你跟我闭嘴!不许叫!"男的对她说。

"你不应该到这儿来!你跟踪我!啊,你——你——"女人叫起来。

一切都乱套了。

我避开。靠墙立着。她跳起来,想跑过丈夫跟前。他一把抓住她。杰第思立即说,情绪紧张地:"等一等,请,请等一下。"

"滚开些,你!"女人叫道。

"你住嘴!"

他开始拉她出去,但不知怎的又放开她。或许她的尖叫吓住了他。楼下的守卫,一个警察,跑上楼来。

"我想事情已经平息了,警官。"杰第思迅速说。

警察是个年轻人。他仔细打量了当丈夫的。那丈夫一身酸臭气味——一件绿黑两色的运动衫,像热带植物的图案——深色的裤子在腹部的地方往外鼓着。有好几天没刮脸了。

这个人和她做爱?

"我认为一切都过去了,警官。帕立特尔夫人将和我完成她的一小时诊疗……帕立特尔先生可以在楼下等候她……"

她的丈夫气呼呼的。

"帕立特尔先生?……"杰第思大夫说。

他四下里望了望,不知所措。他不习惯那样的称呼。两眼睁得大大的。他的头有些秃了,可是他的妻子还这样年轻。这使我沮丧。他们有两个小孩。她掉进了陷阱。她永远不可能摆脱他,绝不可能。

二十二

杰第思大夫和我站在一块儿,在别人家里。星期六晚上。我们像是偶然地站在一起,离开参加聚会的其他人。

"那个女人……我不断想起那个女人……"他喃喃地说。

"帕立特尔夫人?"

Dr. Geddes got to his feet at once. "You're—?"

The girl began to scream.

"You shut up! Shut it!"the man said to her.

"You're not supposed to be here! You followed me! Oh, you—you —"the girl screamed.

Everything came undone.

I got out of the way, pressed back against the wall. The girl jumped up, tried to run past her husband. He grabbed her. Dr. Geddes said quickly, nervously,"Wait a minute, please. Please. Wait a minute."

"Get the hell out of here, you!"cried the girl.

"You shut up!"

He started to drag her out but then, for some reason, released her. Maybe her screaming frightened him. The guard from downstairs, a policeman, came running up the stairs.

"I think everything is all right now, officer,"Dr. Geddes said quickly.

The policeman was a young man. He stared at the husband. A sour smell to that husband—a sports shirt of green and black, designs like tropical vegetation—dark trousers bulging at the stomach. He hadn't shaved for a few days.

This man makes love to her?...

"I think it's all right now. Mrs. Pelletier will finish her hour with me... Mr. Pelletier can wait for her downstairs..."

The husband was breathing hard.

"Mr. Pelletier?... "said Dr. Geddes.

He looked around, baffled. He was not accustomed to that name. Big bulging eyes. He is partly bald and yet his wife is so young; this dismays me. They have two children. She is trapped. She will never get free of him, never.

22

Dr. Geddes and I, standing together, in someone's home. A Saturday evening. We are standing together as if by accident, drawn away from the rest of the party.

"That girl... I keep thinking about that girl... "he whispers.

"Mrs. Pelletier?"

"I think about her all the time. I wonder... "

I stare at him, surprised. I am leaning forward, eager and vacant.

"我时时刻刻想到她。我奇怪……"

我凝视着他,大为惊异。我前倾着,急切而又茫然。

"我奇怪,她怎么能和他一起生活?像那样一副鬼样子……"

我想划掉这句,抹去这些字。

"这种事从前发生过,好几次了,"他说,避免我的目光,"和她们之中的人产生爱情。她们老出现在你的脑际,她们的面庞,于是你无法忘记她们……"

那你为什么告诉她继续和她丈夫在一起。

二十三

杰第思和他妻子,她的年龄同他相仿,但看上去比他老。星期六的晚上。我们像偶然地碰在一起。她神经质地转动她的手表,转了一圈又一圈。她看着我,打量我。杰第思大夫今晚有些紧张——不惯于出席聚会。他带着嘲讽的神情。他的妻子穿一件金闪闪的东西——一件伪装。金色的布将光辉映在她的脸上。一个标致的女子,金光闪闪,但掩不住年轮。她瞪着我。一下午她不住地喝酒。我用不着臆想她的嘲弄的目光,松松戴着的手表。她知不知道她的丈夫和我的关系?

她收拢手掌,捏成一个拳头,打在我肩上!

我喊了出来。屋子里的人都看着我们。

二十四

我停了车,从服务员手里接过票,横过街上诊疗所去。男人们在邻近做工。7月,大热天。尘土在翻腾。热!热!星期二。穿着短装的女孩子从身旁走过,看着我:一个白种女人,或许她的钱包里有钱?我急忙上了台阶,进入休息室,由于气味难闻屏住呼吸——阴沟的臭气?问事台的女孩认识我,警察认识我,每个人都很热情,带着倦意。上楼梯。走到楼梯平台,外边又有一股尘土在翻腾。我为什么在这儿,在这炎热而又令人困惑的地方?

人们走来走去。一个婴儿在哭泣。

那天晚上,他的妻子没打我,绝对没有。什么事也没发生。

"I wonder how she can live with him? A son of a bitch like that. . . "

I want to cross this out; erase these words.

"It's happened before, a few times," he says, avoiding my look. "Falling in love with one of them. They get stuck in your head, their faces, and you can't forget them. . . "

Then why do you tell her to stay with her husband?

23

Dr. Geddes and his wife, who is his age but looks older. Saturday evening. We are drawn together as if by accident. She moves her wrist watch nervously around her wrist, around and around. She eyes me, assessing me. Dr. Geddes is strained tonight—uneasy at parties. His sardonic look has taken over. His wife is wearing something golden—a disguise. The gold cloth casts its light up on her face. A handsome woman glowing, gold, but aging. She stares at me. She has been drinking all afternoon. I don't have to invent her ironic glare, her loose wrist watch. Does she know about her husband and me?

She brings her hand around, balled into a fist, and strikes me on the shoulder!

I cry out. Everyone in the room is looking at us.

24

I park the car, take the ticket from the attendant, cross over to the clinic. Men are working next door. It is July, it is very hot. Dust explodes. Heat! Heat! It is a Tuesday. Girls in short dresses walk by slowly, looking at me: a white woman, maybe she has money in that purse? I hurry up the steps and into the foyer, holding my breath because of the smell—is it sewage? The girl at the desk recognizes me, the policeman recognizes me, everyone is very warm and tired. Up the stairs. To the landing: outside, another explosion of dust. Why am I here in this heat and confusion?

People are milling around. A baby is crying.

His wife didn't strike me that night, no. Nothing happened.

二十五

如果你爱她,你为什么告诉她继续和她丈夫在一起?

二十六

可是,他并不爱她。那是我的臆想。如果你想象人们在恋爱,那会是一串好情节——爱,挫折,注视,伤心泪,缓缓地交织在一起。不,没有的事。没有爱。人们相遇,相互注视对方的面庞,摇头摒弃杂念,往前走,忘记。没有爱情。

二十七

昨天,他来了个电话。"上星期二你哪儿去了?"

一个男人的注意,一个男人的严肃注视的目光。一件细蓝条白衬衣。我带着两个小孩沿街跑,急欲获得自由,尽快地摆脱任何人……我要办到离婚。离婚。所有那一切"离婚"的谈论,都是我的臆想,那女人自己从未说过那个词。他们不说那个词。对他们来说,太有法律意味了,那意味着律师、市法院、费用、文件、出生证、警察、麻烦。她想摆脱那鬼日子,但是不想离婚。我给了她那主意,那个词。我坐在那儿。金黄色头发,混乱的心情,身子前倾,但不是去看杰第思大夫(他是一个普普通通的人),而是看坐在他身后做记录的那个女人。她是一个护士? 秘书? 那是屋里最好的一把椅子,在后边那儿。外面有一把汽锤。它在你头颅里面敲。像是心跳。可那是谁的心——她的还是我的? 她先抱怨她的心跳太微弱,继而又说太大声。究竟是怎么回事? 是我捏造的,还是我忘掉了她中间说的什么话?

他昨天来了个电话,问:"明天你来吗?"

我停车,横过街,上了楼梯。已经10点了。门半开着,他在里边,坐在办公桌边……我站在走廊里,观察他。是的,一个普普通通的人。面孔像虚弱的国

25

If you love her why do you tell her to stay with her husband?

26

But he doesn't love her. I invented that. It is a plot if you imagine people in love—the lazy looping crisscrosses of love, blows, stares, tears. No. It doesn't happen. No love. People meet, touch stare into one another's faces, shake their heads clear, move on, forget. It doesn't happen.

27

Yesterday he telephoned me. "Where were you on Tuesday?"

A man's attention, a man's stern staring eyes. A white shirt with narrow blue stripes. I run along the street with the two children, eager to be free, to get the hell away from everyone. . . I will get a divorce. A divorce. All that talk about "divorce" was my own invention; the girl never said the word herself. They don't say that word. It is too legal for them, it means lawyers and the city courthouse and fees and papers, birth certificates, police, trouble. She wants to get the hell out but she doesn't want a divorce. I gave her the idea, the word. I was sitting there, blond and panicked, leaning forward but not staring at Dr. Geddes (who is an ordinary man) but at the woman sitting behind him taking notes. Was she a nurse? A secretary? That is the best chair in the room, back there. Outside there is an air hammer. It hammers inside your skull. It is like a heartbeat. But which heart is it—hers or mine? At first she complained about her heart beating too faintly, then too loudly. Which is which? Did I make it up, or did I forget something she said in between?

He telephoned me yesterday and said, "Are you coming tomorrow?" I park the car, cross the street, go up the stairs. It is already after ten. The door is ajar and he is inside, at the desk. . . I stand out in the corridor, watching him. Yes, an ordinary man. The face of a weak king. Sallow skin. Or is it the light? A baby is

王。肤色病黄。是灯光的关系吗? 一个婴儿在啼哭,一个年轻白种女人在厉声对婴儿说话,一边抱在怀里摇晃他。我爱那个人吗?我想要爱他吗?我站在外面走廊里,听着婴儿的啼哭和邻近建筑工地上的喧哗。一种像闹钟鸣响的声音,我的心里烦死了。那只是电话铃响,奇怪地响个不停……我爱他还是忌妒他?我希望他死去来了结这一切吗?我站在走廊里。臆想他,抹掉一个男人,臆想出另一个男人。我想要摆脱他、摆脱那女人和她的丈夫,她丈夫任意摆布着她。

杰第思大夫抬头看见我。吃了一惊。"怎么?……进来呀!"他说着。站起来。

我走进这间小办公室。

"她今天没来。"他说,向椅子示意一下。

一张空椅对着他。

"她没来电话。上次你不在这儿,她讲话疯疯癫癫……我不明白是怎么回事……"

"她讲了些什么?"

"很难弄清楚意思。她的一个孩子被卡车撞了,他径直朝车走去——她说是吸毒的影响,他在吸海洛因。他们送他去医院的接诊室——"

"吸海洛因?"

"她是那样说的。他们把小孩带去缝线,回家路上,她丈夫和她打起架来。她走到这儿时,精疲力竭了,我想她自己也在吸什么……她几乎睁不开眼睛……"

"她的儿子吸海洛因?那样小的年纪。"

我眼前像掠过一团薄雾。杰第思叨叨不绝地谈,我却听不见他说的什么。

"可是,你将怎么办呢?"我问他。

"唔——"

"你要不要找一个警察去一趟或者什么的?"

"呃,不。先等等。"

"等多久?她已经迟了20分钟了。"

"我是说等到下星期。"

"你不认为很危险吗?"

"为什么?"

"我的意思是,对于她——"

"她或许会受伤?或者伤害自己?不会的。"

"可是,你有什么把握吗?"

"有相当的把握。"

crying, a young white woman is talking sharply to the baby, rocking it in her arms. Do I love that man? Do I want to love him? I stand out in the corridor and my mind is wild with the noise from the baby and the construction next door and what sounds like an alarm clock ringing. It is only a telephone ringing, with a strange persistent ring. . . . Do I love him, am I jealous of him? Do I want him to die so that all this will be over? I am inventing him as I stand in the corridor, erasing one man and inventing another. I want to be free of him and of the girl and of her husband, who shoves her around.

Dr. Geddes glances up at me. He is startled. "What?. . . Come in!" he says, standing.

I enter the little office.

"She didn't show up today," he says, indicating the chair.

An empty chair facing him.

"She didn't telephone. Last time, you weren't here, she was talking pretty wild. . . I wonder what's going on. . ."

"What did she say?"

"It was hard to make sense of it. One of her children got hit by a truck, he walked right into it—she said he was drugged, he was taking heroin. They took him to "Receiving and—"

"Taking heroin?"

"That's what she said. They took the boy to get stitched up, then on the way home her husband started fighting with her. She came in here looking worn out, I think she's taking something herself. . . she could hardly keep her eyes open. . ."

"Her son is taking heroin? At that age?"

A haze seems to pass before my eyes. Dr. Geddes keeps on talking but I can't hear him.

"But what are you going to do?" I ask him.

"Wel. . ."

"Should you send a policeman over or something?"

"Well, no. I'll wait. "

"How long? She's twenty minutes late. "

"I mean I'll wait until next week. "

"You don't think it's dangerous?"

"Why?"

"I mean with her—"

" That she might get hurt? Or hurt herself? No. "

"But how can you be sure?"

"I'm reasonably sure. "

"Don't they ever kill themselves, your patients?"

"他们有过自杀的情形没有,你的病人?"

他没好气地耸了耸肩膀。

"如果你的病人自杀了,会对你产生什么影响?"我问他。

"他们有过。偶尔发生。"

"产生过什么影响?"

"我照样活过来了。"

他苦笑了一下。

有人走进来——可是一定是走错了。一个黑女人和一个老头儿,他们睁大眼睛看着我们,道声歉,退了回去。

"你为什么不坐下?"我的朋友说,"外面很热,对吗?"

我坐在病人的椅子上。

我的目光越过那张小破桌子,望着杰第思大夫。从这个角度,他显得有些不同——他的面庞更成长方形,鼻子有点粗大。

我快死了。我正在消逝。救命,劳驾!

二十八

丈夫因谋杀被抓了。妻子被杀害了,菜刀捅的。杰第思大夫告诉我这一切,几个月之后,当我们偶然相遇。那是 9 月。杰第思讲得很快,医生的口吻,像在口授我做记录。她再没回来,他说。我们睁着眼从彼此的肩膀上望过去。我们之间出现了可怕的紧张,像汗水紧贴在身上,但是我们拒绝承认,互不相视。他接下去讲他的繁忙而困难的日程安排,谈他的诊所。"真糟,一件事接一件事……你读到电器技师罢工的消息了吗?工作会无限期停顿下去,因为那些混蛋工会。"

二十九

9 月永不到来。

还是 7 月。

我坐在病人的藤背椅里,梦萦在外面的汽锤上。椅子的一条腿短些,起码是几条脚不一般高。椅子摇摇晃晃的。我和杰第思大夫默默相对凝视。我,我,

He shrugs his shoulders irritably.

"How would it affect you, if a patient killed himself?" I ask him.

"They do. Occasionally."

"How did it affect you?"

"I survived."

He smiles bitterly.

Someone is coming in—but it must be a mistake, it is a black woman with a very old man. They gape at us, apologize, back out.

"Why don't you sit down?" says my friend. "It's very hot outside, isn't it?"

I sit in the patient's chair.

I look across the battered little desk at Dr. Geddes. From here he looks different—his face more oblong, his nose a little lumpy.

I am dying. I am disappearing. Help me, please!

28

The husband was picked up for murder. The wife was killed, stabbed with a kitchen knife. Dr. Geddes tells me all this when we meet by accident, months later. It is September. Dr. Geddes speaks quickly and professionally, as if he were dictating notes to me. *She never did come back*, he says. We stare over each other's shoulders. A terrible tension rises between us, stinging as sweat, but we do not acknowledge it. We do not look at each other. He goes on to talk about his busy, difficult schedule, and about the clinic. "Christ, it's one thing after another . . . Did you read about the electricians' strike? The work will be held up indefinitely because of those goddamn unions."

29

September never came.

It is still July.

I sit in the patient's cane-backed chair and dream above the air hammer outside. One of the chair's legs is shorter than the others, or uneven somehow. The chair wobbles. Dr. Geddes and I stare at each other in silence. *I, I, I could make you happy! I am the only woman who could make you happy!* But it is not true. It is a lie I dream to myself, sitting here, alone with a man... I will add five years to Dr. Geddes's

我能使你幸福！我是能使你幸福的唯一的女人！可是，这不真实。那是我自己梦呓的谎言，坐在这儿，单独和一个男人在一起……我要给他的面孔增添5岁。是的，他真快40了，他的青春完蛋了。耗尽了。我要把他深色的头发臆想得更稀疏些，尤其是头顶上那一部分。我将想象他的耳边长着短髭，像牧神，很粗俗。好，瞧！他把手按住胸膛，胃的上部。他有溃疡，这位成功的医生。精神病医生的自杀率高过一般人10倍。他们死去，合上他们的硬纸夹，把他们的医道传给年轻人。他们死去，他们死去，他们停止听，他们把手指头塞进耳朵，变成聋子，灯光熄了，汽锤停了，电器技师冲进楼来，解开一切，卡断电线，连根拔掉电话。

那女人没露面。

我坐在她的椅子里，感到四周都热。我思索着。

对啦，我也要抹掉杰第思大夫。一次失败，我们的爱情。没发生过。没有电梯。我们经常使用楼梯，规规矩矩地。我也要抹掉他，那天早上我晚到10分钟，他不在那儿。他的办公室的门关着，上了锁。我站在那儿发愣。为什么他还没来？我在走廊里徘徊，感到窘，感情受了伤害。我从窗口外望底特律的天空——不是天空，只是一幢幢楼房，紧缩在一起，空虚乏味。他为什么不来？我站在那儿，孤零零地，手足无措，有一点作呕的感觉……

是的，他没来。

那女人也没来。

我等了一会儿。走廊里很不安静。一个未穿外衣的年轻人——一个医生——问我等谁。我穿得太讲究，这儿不配，可是我的举动却像一个受害者。

十点三十分。

差一刻十一点。

好了，完结了。这就是终点。我的脸由于失望和委屈涨得通红。我是一个受了委屈的女人。我下楼到了外面。横过街到停车场，付了钱给管理员——他白白向我索取一块半美元——我进了车。我在车里坐了一分钟，注视着那边的诊疗所。或许杰第思大夫会出现，慌慌忙忙地？……

或许那女人会出现？……

一个也没有。什么也没有。只我独自一人。

于是，我抹掉他们两人，宰了他们。他们一去不返了。他们从未存在过。下次我开车进入这个地区，

face. Yes. He is really about forty; his youth is finished. Drained away. I will make his dark hair thinner, especially on the top. I will imagine small stiff whiskers in his ears, faunlike and coarse. Good. Look at that! He puts his hand against his chest, the upper part of his stomach. He has ulcers, this successful doctor. Psychiatrists' suicide rate is ten times that of the normal population. They die, they close their folders, they relinquish their practice to younger men, they die, they die, they stop listening, they stick their fingers in their ears and go deaf, the lights go out, the air hammer is disconnected, the electricians rush into the building and unhook everything, cut the wires, tear the telephone out by the roots.

The girl doesn't show up.

I sit in her chair and feel the heat all about me. I think.

Yes, I will erase Dr. Geddes too. It is a failure, our love. It didn't happen. No elevator; we always took the stairs, chastely. I will erase him too. He wasn't there that morning when I arrived, ten minutes late. The door to his office was closed and locked. I stood there, stunned. Why hadn't he come? He had just telephoned me the day before, to make sure I would meet him. What was wrong?... But he wasn't there. I wandered along the corridor, bewildered, hurt. I looked out the window at the skyline of Detroit, which is not a skyline but just buildings, gaseous and plain, pressed in close. Why hadn't he come? I stand there, alone, bewildered, feeling a little sick...

No, he doesn't show up.

And the girl doesn't show up.

I wait a while. The corridor is noisy. A young man in shirt sleeves—one of the doctors—asks me whom I am waiting for. I am dressed too well for this place, but my manner is that of a victim.

Ten-thirty.

Quarter to eleven.

Well, it is finished. The end. My face is flushed with disappointment, humiliation. I am a woman who has been humiliated. I go downstairs and outside. I cross over to the parking lot and pay the attendant—he charges me $1.50, for nothing! —I get in my car. I sit there for a minute, staring over at the clinic. Maybe Dr. Geddes will appear, hurrying?...

Maybe the girl will appear?...

No one. Nothing. I am alone.

And so I erase them both, I kill them off. They are gone. They never existed. The next time I drive through this neighborhood the clinic itself will have

诊疗所本身也将被拆掉——痛快的大扫除！在阳光下，城市本身微光闪烁，看上去模糊不清。瓦砾在震动，人行道在震动。那是不是街道的一条裂缝？停车场管理员的小木屋突然倾倒，朝一边倒下一码左右。这个城市的末日到了，城市在陷落。世界的末日到了。我在抹掉这一切——抹去底特律——尘土翻腾飞扬，抹去一切。我自己，快死了。我正在消逝。我能够听见心跳离我而去。我就是一个正在死去、正在消逝、正在离去的过程。

在我们之中，只有你留下。

been torn down：good riddance! In the sunlight the city itself is shimmering and unclear. The rubble vibrates, the pavement vibrates. Is that a crack in the street? The parking lot attendant's little cabin tilts suddenly, about a yard on one side. It is the end of this city. The city is caving in. The end of the world. I am erasing them all—erasing Detroit—the dust rises in puffing explosions to erase everything. Myself, I am dying. I am disappearing. I can hear my heartbeat moving away from me. I am a process that is dying, disappearing, moving away.

Of all of us, only you remain.

讨　论 ▪

这篇小说对现实生活中产生的虚幻感表示关切。小说最引人注目的是结构形式上的人为性。这篇小说中的故事讲述者毫无艺术修饰能力。她对自己讲述的现实生活片断的处理，与其说是出于美学目的，不如说是基于心理需要。小说结尾时的那句断语——"在我们之中，只有你留下"——旨在于"伤害"读者，它断言：讲述者本人已经从自己描述的那个世界的束缚中解脱出来，而读者，由于阅读这篇小说本身已经成为他不可变更的经验，所以无法解脱。

当然，这个断言是虚假的，讲述者并未从自身经验中得到解脱。尽管她打乱了小说的情节，某些事实依然包含其中，人物感情上的痛苦，以及他们之间的冷漠状态。讲述者利用"跳跃"这种方法"删去"了有关自己的情节，而这种巧妙的手法并未减轻经验对她的影响，就像经验会对读者产生影响一样。尽管说她在小说中充当了角色是成问题的，但作为讲述者她实际上已经不可避免地卷入了这些经验之中。

This story exhibits a concern with what is illusory in the reality it creates. It calls attention to what is artificial in its organization. The narrator of this story has no artistic pretensions. Her manipulation of the categories of her narrative's reality is dependent on her psychological need rather than an aesthetic concern. The assertion that concludes the story—"Of all of us, only you remain"—is an effort to "hurt" the reader, to assert that while the narrator can free herself from the bounds of the world she has rendered, the reader, for whom the experience of reading the story has become an unalterable fact of his past, cannot.

The assertion, of course, is disingenuous; the narrator is not freed from the experience. Even as she changes the plot of the story she tells, certain factors are constants: the characters' emotional pain, and their isolation from each other. The sleight of hand, the "erasure" by which the narrator "cancels" her involvement, no more diminishes for her than for the reader the impact of experiences in which, however problematic her role as actor, the narrator *as* narrator has undeniably been a participant.

思考题

1. 那个病人把指甲戳进讲述者的手腕,这个细节不正是为了使读者对讲述者的第一次"跳跃"有所准备吗? 不正是为了使读者能容易地接受这种"跳跃"吗?

2. 在何种意义上,人物实际上的命运是怎样和小说的中心主旨不相干的? 这是讲述者之所以不解决这个问题的原因所在吗? 她是否会承认问题并没有解决? 此类问题不正是为了表明,必须牢牢记住重要的是讲述者的意图和作者本人的意图是大不一样的。

3. 小说中关于城市的情况不是正好和人们的精神状态相一致吗? 小说讲述者处于畸形的精神状态中,这是否使城市的外貌也变得奇形怪状了? 要回答这个问题并不简单,而这说明小说在创作意图上的复杂性。

（刘文荣 译）

1. How does the patient's digging her nails into the narrator's wrist serve to prepare the reader for the initial "erasure" by the narrator? How does it predispose the reader to accept this "erasure"?

2. In what sense is the physical fate of the characters irrelevant to the story's concerns? Is this why the narrator leaves the question unresolved? Would she say it was unresolved? How do such questions point to the importance of keeping in mind the distinction between narrative and authorial intention?

3. How does the condition of the city correspond to the emotional states of the people in the story? Is this picture of the city a distortion owing to the distorted consciousness of this narrator? The answer to this question is not simple and it illustrates the complexity of the story's intentions.

032. 爱玛琴的手

(美)彼得·泰勒 著　　刘文荣 译

032. The Hand of Emmagene

by Peter Taylor

高中毕业后,她就离开霍腾斯堡
到纳什维尔寻找工作。
她寄住在我们家里。
她随即进了一所秘书学校,
学习好几门功课。
说实在的,她并未真正高中毕业。
她曾在家里待了两年,我想是两年,
照料她年老的祖母,
祖母无病无痛而卧床不起。
所以她根本不是那种轻飘飘的年轻乡下姑娘,
满脑子胡思乱想,
想到纳什维尔的夜场所去兜兜风,
或者想结婚,
她甚至对自己该做什么工作也一无所知。

从一开始起,我们就留意
——我妻子和我——
她应该认识一些小伙子,
和她一样年纪的。那是我们最初的想法。
她是我们的亲戚,你知道——或者说是南希的亲戚。
她出生在霍腾斯堡,
那是个僻远的小地方,
在纳什维尔北面 30 英里,
南希和我都在那儿长大。
那就是为何我们觉得有义务
操心她的社交生活,
就像操心她的日常物质生活一样。
每有亲戚到城里来,

　　After highschool, she had come down
from Hortonsburg
To find work in Nashville.
She stayed at our house.
And she began at once to take classes
In a secretarial school.
As a matter of fact, she wasn't *right* out of high-
school.
She had remained at home two years, I think
it was,
To nurse her old grandmother
Who was dying of Bright's disease.
So she was not just some giddy young
country girl
With her head full of nonsense
About running around to Nashville nightspots
Or even about getting married
And who knew nothing about what it was to work.

　　From the very beginning, we had in mind
—My wife and I did—
That she ought to know some boys
Her own age. That was one of our first thoughts.
She was a cousin of ours, you see—or of Nancy's.
And she was from Hortonsburg
Which is the little country place
Thirty miles north of Nashville
Where Nancy and I grew up.
That's why we felt responsible
For her social life
As much as for her general welfare.
We always do what we can of course
For our kin when they come to town—
Especially when they're living under our roof.
But instead of trying to entertain Emmagene
At the Club

作者简介:彼得·泰勒(Peter Taylor,1917—1994),美国小说家、剧作家。1917 年 1 月 8 日生于新泽西州特伦顿,1994 年 11 月 2 日卒于弗吉尼亚州夏洛特维尔。泰勒在 20 世纪 30 年代研究几位关于南方文学复兴的诗人。他到过各色各样的学校任教,包括弗吉尼亚大学。他以短篇小说闻名,他的小说常常以田纳西州为背景,展现乡村社会和工业化的"新南部"间的冲突。小说《有办法的女人》(A Woman of Means,1950)是他最好的作品。他随后的作品包括《老森林和其他的故事》(The Old Forest and Other Stories,1985)和《孟斐斯的召唤》(A Summons to Memphis,1986),后者获得普利策奖。

我们确实总是尽力而为——
尤其当他们住在我们屋里的时候。
但是我们没有在夜总会里
款待爱玛琴，
也没有把熟人介绍给她认识，
南希觉得
我们首先要知道姑娘的兴趣何在。
我们应该根据她的兴趣行事。

　　呵，看来世界上使她最感兴趣的
是工作。我从来没见过什么事可与此相比。
从某些方面看，这在她似乎是件古怪透顶的事情。
她刚来时，每天一清早就起床，
当她的"南表姐"或者我还没醒时，
她已经在打扫屋子——有几天我们没有开房门
也闻到了地板蜡的气味——
或者已经在做零星的缝补活，
补台布或者补床单，
或者补我的衬衫甚至补南希的内衣。
时常，我们还不曾下楼，
她已经做好了她自己承担的
擦洗活。不过她常走到起居室里
或者阳台上或者书房里或者餐室里，
把那里的东西细细观看一面赞不绝口，
甚至抚摸不停——南希收集的镜子
或者壁橱里的广东瓷器。
一天早晨我们发现她拿着纸和笔
正从一张东方小地毡上
把小小的动物图案一一描了下来。

　　还有几天早晨，佣人们还没到来
她就下楼到厨房里烹煮。
（当然，在厨娘来准备早餐前
她已经把弄脏的盘碟都洗干净
放回了原处。）她天不亮就下来
在那儿忙忙碌碌，
为的是给南希和我做一块糕或者一块饼。
（她自己呢，不吃甜食，）
我们还不曾下床时或者正准备下楼时，
烹煮的香味已经传到我们鼻子里。
但是在那些早晨，无论她在洗涤还是在烹煮，

Or by having people in to meet her
Nancy felt
We should first find out what the girl's interests were.
We would take our cue from that.

　　Well, what seemed to interest her most in the world
Was work. I've never seen anything quite like it.
In some ways, this seemed the oddest thing about her.
When she first arrived, she would be up at dawn,
Before her "Cousin Nan" or I had stirred,
Cleaning the house - We would smell floor wax
Before we opened our bedroom door some mornings—
Or doing little repair jobs
On the table linen or bed linen
Or on my shirts or even Nancy's underwear.
Often as not she would have finished
The polishing or cleaning she had taken upon herself to do
Before we came down. But she would be in the living room
Or sun parlor or den or dining room
Examining the objects of her exertions, admiring them,
Caressing them even - Nancy's glass collection
Or the Canton china on the sideboard.
One morning we found her with pencil and paper
Copying the little geometrical animals
From one of the oriental rugs.

　　Or some mornings she would be down in the kitchen cooking
Before the servants arrived.
(And of course she'd have the dishes she'd dirtied
All washed and put away again before the cook
Came in to fix breakfast.) What she was making
Down there in the pre-dawn hours,
Would be a cake or a pie for Nancy and me.
(She didn't eat sweets, herself)
Its aroma would reach us
Before we were out of bed or just as we started down the stairs.
But whether cleaning or cooking,
She was silent as a mouse those mornings.
We heard nothing. There were only the smells
Before we came down. And after we came down there'd be
Just the sense of her contentment.

　　It was different at night. The washing machine

她总像老鼠一样悄然无声。
我们听不到声音。只闻到气味，
那是我们下楼之前。而我们下了楼一眼看到的
是她满足的神色。

晚上则不同。洗衣机
在地下室里会一直开到深夜一两点钟，
或者有时候，真空吸尘器
没等我们上楼就扫到楼上去，
或者等我们都以为全屋子都已入睡时，
又会从楼上扫到楼下。
（我们时常互问，甚至问她
按她的意思厨娘和佣人
还应该干什么。有时我们还自问
爱玛琴待在这里的时日这些人在干什么。）
她知道我们很喜欢在起居室或者书房里
生个火，她就在一清早
生好了火，而脏盘碟这时也都洗完。
到了晚上我们就听到她走到后院
把一大段木头，劈成小木块，
或者就是把一些旧木箱和乱七八糟的破木头用
斧头劈成引火柴。
我不止一次看到她在月光下走到那里，
斧头高高地举过头，
对着一段直竖着的树干或者一块二至四英寸见
方的木头
准确无误地劈下去。

晚上除了这些声音，
我们有时还听到电话铃响。
我或者我妻子便在床上拿起电话筒，
但电话里并没有人讲话。
要不只听到咔嗒一声响，
而这时我们听到楼下的电话机
也同样地咔嗒一声响。
一天夜里我对着话筒喊了她的名字——"爱玛
琴吗？"——
那时第二响咔嗒还没响，我想知道她是否在楼下。
但是爱玛琴什么也没说。
简简单单又是咔嗒一声响。

又有几回，电话铃同样响了，

Would be going in the basement till the wee hours,
Or sometimes the vacuum cleaner
Would be running upstairs before we came up
Or running downstairs after we thought
We'd put the house to bed.
(We used to ask each other and even ask her
What she thought the cook and houseman
Were meant to do. Sometimes now we ask ourselves
What did they do during the time that Emmagene
was here.)
And when she learned how much we liked to have fires
In the living room and den, she would lay them
In the morning, after cleaning out the old ashes.
But at night we'd hear her out in the back yard
Splitting a fireplace log, trying to get lightwood
Or wielding the ax to make kindling
Out of old crates or odd pieces of lumber.
More than once I saw her out there in the moonlight
Raising the ax high above her head
And coming down with perfect accuracy
Upon an up-ended log or a balanced two-by-four.

There would be those noises at night
And then we noticed sometimes the phone would ring.
One of us would answer it from bed,
And there would be no one there.
Or there would be a click
And then another click which we knew in all likelihood
Was on the downstairs extension.
One night I called her name into the phone -
"Emmagene?" -
Before the second click came, just to see if she were there.
But Emmagene said nothing.

There simply came the second click.
There were other times, too, when the phone rang
And there would be dead silence when we answered.
"Who is it" I would say. "Who are you calling?"
Or Nancy would say, "To whom do you wish to speak?"
Each of us, meanwhile, looking across the room at Emmagene.
For we already had ideas then, about it. We had already
Noticed cars that crept by the house
When we three sat on the porch in the late spring.

我们拿起电话筒,电话筒里寂然无声。

"谁啊?"我会问,"你找谁啊?"

或者南希会问:"你要请谁说话?"

这时,我们俩的目光都穿过房间望着爱玛琴。

因为我们已经有了思想准备,关于这种事。我们已经

注意到有轿车正在屋边慢驶,

这时正值暮春,我们仨人都坐在走廊里。

一辆轿车慢慢驶过,驶得那么慢我们当真会认为它要停下。

但是如果我或者南希站起身,

目光越过灌木丛朝街上张望时,

轿车会突然加速。

我们大声呼喊,驾车者便会来个急转弯。

       不止一次,我们正吃晚饭电话铃又响了,

那是星期天晚上。爱玛琴总把食物准备好,

在佣人们离开后做好饭菜,

每到星期天晚上。当然,她和我们一起吃。

每当她和我们同桌吃饭,

我就料到整个晚餐总会沉默无言。

她倒总想找个话头谈谈,

不过我们从来不这么想,

因为有点格格不入。

你知道,远在霍腾斯堡,

她的家和我妻子家是亲戚,这没问题,

但是实际上两家人隔膜很深,

她家里人属于好斗的原教旨教派,

而南希家里人则倾向于孔伯兰长老会,

或者公理会教派或者卫理会教派,糟糕透顶,

(甚至倾向于圣公会,我想我应该说,"美妙透顶"。)

事实是,南希她家——我自己家也一样——

通常到最近的教堂会做礼拜,根本不管何宗何派。

然而爱玛琴家每星期天上午总要走13英里路到某教派的某教堂去做礼拜,这教派

好像经常在改变名称,时不时在名称上加些个限定词。

一会儿退出某个组织一会儿又加入另一个。

A car would mosey by, going so slow we thought surely it would stop.

But if Nancy or I stood up

And looked out over the shrubbery toward the street,

Suddenly there would be a burst of speed.

The driver would even turn on a cut-out as he roared away.

      More than once the phone rang while we were at the supper table

On Sunday night. Emmagene always prepared that meal

And did up the dishes afterward since the servants were off

On Sunday night. And ate with us too, of course.

I suppose it goes without saying

She always ate at the table with us.

She rather made a point of that from the start,

Though it never would have occurred to us

For it to be otherwise.

You see, up in Hortonsburg

Her family and my wife's had been kin of course

But quite different sorts of people really.

Her folks had belonged to a hard bitten, fundamentalist sect

And Nancy's tended to be Cumberland Presbyterians

Or Congregationalists or Methodists, at worst

(Or Episcopalians, I suppose I might say, "at best.")

The fact was, Nancy's family-like my own—

Went usually to the nearest church, whatever it was.

Whereas Emmagene's travelled thirteen miles each Sunday morning

To a church of a denomination that seemed always

To be *chaning* its name by the addition of some qualifying adjective.

Either that or seceding from one synod or joining another.

Or deciding just to go it alone

Because of some disputed point of scripture.

      Religion aside, however, there were differences of style.

And Emmagene - very clearly - had resolved

Or been instructed before leaving home

To brook no condescension on our part.

"We're putting you in the guest room," Nancy said

Upon her arrival. And quick as a flash Emmagene added:

要不就会因为圣经教义上发生了什么争论
自顾自地独断独行。

　　　　然而,撇开宗教不谈,气质也不同。
爱玛琴——毫无疑问——在离家前
就已经抱定主意或者已受人教诲
到了我家决不低声下气。
"我们想让你住在客人房间里。"南希说,
那时她刚到。而像闪电一样快。爱玛琴回答:
"那我们在一桌子上吃饭吗?"
"噢,当然,当然。"南希说,
还用一只手臂抱住爱玛琴的肩膀。
"在餐桌上你坐贵宾席。"

　　　　呵,每星期天晚上我们就更像
贵宾临门了,
佣人们都驱开,这是当然的,
由爱玛琴为我们配制我们心爱的
乡间美味,而贮藏室里的任何东西
都任其选用,我们经常就在那儿吃这顿饭。
这真像我们大家又都回到了霍腾斯堡老家。
但是每当电话铃响,
爱玛琴会毫不犹像地从桌边站起身,
(好像这是她的屋子,我们在做客。)
到厨房墙上的电话机旁边听电话。
这时我们能看到她,也听得见她的声音,
她说"喂",然后就站在那里,听着,
听筒紧接在耳朵上,就是什么话也没说。
起先,我们甚至问也不问是谁打的电话。
我们只是相互望望,
又埋头吃饭——
我已经说过,在星期天晚上我们更像客人
在她家里做客。所以我们一直到饭后
才相互谈论这件事。
我们俩一下子想到了一块儿,
这是她的某个男朋友打的而在我们面前
她和他谈话不方便。你知道,我们一直担心她没
有男朋友,
或者连女朋友也没有。
我们一再自问
我们周围有谁可以介绍给她呢,

"And we'll take meals together?"
"Why of course,why of course,"Nancy said
Placing an arm about Emmagene's shoulder.
"You'll have place of honored guest at our ta-
ble. "

　　　Well,on Sunday nights it was more like we
Were the honored guests,
With the servants off,of course,
And with Emmagene electing to prepare our fa-
vorite
Country dishes for us,and serving everything up
Out in the pantry, where we always take that
meal.
It was as though we were all back home in Hor-
tonsburg.
But if the phone rang,
Emmagene was up from the table in a split sec-
ond,
(It might have been her own house we were in.)
And answered the call on the wall phone in the
kitchen.
I can see her now,and hear her,too.
She would say"Hello,"and then just stand there,
listening,
The receiver pressed to her ear,and saying noth-
ing more at all.
At first,we didn't even ask her who it was.
We would only look at each other
And go back to our food—
As I've said, we were more like guests at
her house
On Sunday night. And so we'd wait till later
To speak about it to each other.
We both supposed from the start
It was some boy friend of hers she was too timid
to talk with
Before us. You see,we kept worrying
About her not having any boy friends
Or any girl friends,either.
We asked ourselves again and again
Who in our acquaintance we could introduce
her to,
What nice Nashville boy we knew who would not
mind
Her plainness or her obvious puritanical nature—
She didn't wear make-up, not even lipstick or
powder,
And didn't do anything with her hair.
She wore dresses that were like maids'
uniforms except
Without any white collars and cuffs.
Nancy and I got so we hesitated to take a drink

我们认识的哪个纳什维尔的好小伙子,他会不在乎

她的相貌平常或者她明显的宗教怪癖呢——
她穿着并不引人,甚至不涂口红也不抹粉,
也不做头发。
她穿的衣服就像女仆的制服,
除了没有白围兜和袖筒。
南希和我就这样犹犹豫豫没喝完一杯酒,
甚至没抽一支烟,
这时她走过来了。
我赶紧闭口不再说话。

　　　　不知有多少回我们看到她
这样听电话或者在楼上的电话机里
听到咔嗒一声响。最后我对南希说,
她得和姑娘们谈谈话,她可以随便
把她的朋友请到家里来玩玩,
南希说等有机会就和她说。
你千万别把这意思先走漏
给爱玛琴。

　　　　有个星期天晚上厨房里的电话铃又
响了。
爱玛琴当然去接,站在那儿听了一会儿。
最后,像往常一样,她不慌不忙
把话筒放回墙上的机架上。
我感到她在直眼看我们
就像她往常放下话筒时一样。
这时南希不再装得
好像在忙于吃饭了。
"爱玛琴,那是谁?"她问,
语气很礼貌也很亲切。
"噢,我会告诉你们。"姑娘开口,
好像她一直在等着回答似的。
"是某个小伙子或者是在乡下认识的什么人,
或者是根本不认识的。"她样子难看地扭扭嘴,耸
耸肩。
"打电话的就是他们,"她又说,"你们好像老关心
着想知道。"
她说"老关心着想知道"时
那语调显然带着讽意,

Or even smoke a cigarette
When she was present.
I soon began watching my language.

　　　I don't know how many times we saw her
Answer the phone like that or heard the clickings
On the phone upstairs. At last l told Nancy
She ought to tell the girls she was free
To invite whatever friends she had to come to the house.
Nancy said she would have to wait for the opportunity;
You didn't just come out with suggestions like that
To Emmagene.

　　　One Sunday night the phone rang in the kitchen.
Emmagene answered it of course and stood listening for a time.
Finally, very deliberately, as always,
She returned the little wall phone to its hook.
I felt her looking at us very directly
As she always did when she put down the phone.
This time Nancy didn't pretend
To be busy with her food.
"Who *was* that, Emmagene?" she asked
In a very polite, indifferent tone.
"Well, I'll tell you," the girl began
As though she had been waiting forever to be asked.
"It's some boy or other I knew up home.
Or *didn't* know." She made an ugly mouth and shrugged.
"That's who it always is," she added, "in case you *care* to know."
There was a too obvious irony
In the way she said "*care* to know."
As though we ought to have asked her long before this.
"That's who it is in the cars, too," she informed us—
Again, as though she had been waiting only too long for us to ask.
"When they're off work and have nothing better to do
They ring up or drive by
Just to make a nuisance of themselves."
"How many of them are there?" Nancy asked.
"There's quite some few of them," Emmagene said with emphasis.
"Well, Emmagene," I suddenly joined in,
"You ought to make your choice

尽管我们早就应该问她了。

"也就是他们常开轿车，"她对我们说——

又是，好像她一直在等着我们问而且已经等得不耐烦了。

"他们下了班，没什么事干，

就打打电话或者开开车，

只是自己寻寻开心。"

"他们有多少人?"南希问。

"就那么几个人。"爱玛琴口气强调地说。

"噢，爱玛琴，"我突然插话，

"你应该有所选择，

也许可以邀请他们中的一两个人到家里来看看你。"

她好像有点发怒似的看看我。

"他们全不是好货，"她说，"他们全是坏料。

你是不会要他们把脚放在你的门槛上的。

更不要说你的走廊和你的屋子了。"

我很高兴事情都摊上了台面，说：

"他们不可能全是坏料。一个姑娘必须有所选择。"

她朝我看了一会儿，

那种沉默的样子也只有她做得出来。

随后她走进厨房又回来，

第二次劝我们尝尝锅里的蔬菜。

而没等我重新开口，

她已转过话题谈起布道的事来，

她上午刚听过布道，说话时带着福音派的热情，

还引用布道者的话和《圣经》的话。

那样子好像她把每天上午在纳什维尔东面

不知哪个远角落里的某个她那教派的某教堂里听来的东西

现在又重温一遍。而当她开始上教堂

听布道起，我就开始担心

爱玛琴还会和我们在一起住多久。

我不由得沉入深思：

她还没找到工作而且也没找到情人哪。

我不像南希那样对爱玛琴有点讨厌，

还希望她早点离开我们家。

我们常有乡下来的亲戚

And maybe ask one or two of them to come to the house to see you. "

She looked at me with something like rage.

"They are not a good sort, "she said. "They're a bad lot.

You wouldn't want them to set foot on your front steps.

Much less your front porch or in your house. "

I was glad it was all coming out in the open and said,

"They can't all be all bad. A girl has to be selective. "

She stood looking at me for a moment

In a kind of silence only she could keep.

Then she went into the kitchen and came back

Offering us second helpings from the pot of greens.

And before I could say more,

She had changed the subject and was talking about the sermon

She had heard that morning, quoting with evangelistic fervor,

Quoting the preacher and quoting the Bible.

It was as if she were herself hearing all over again

All she had heard that very morning

At that church of hers somewhere way over on the far side

of East Nashville. It was while she was going on

About the sermon that I began to wonder for the first time

How long Emmagene was going to stay here with us.

I found myself reflecting:

She hasn't got a job yet and she hasn't got a beau.

It wasn't that I hadn't welcomed Emmagene as much as Nancy

And hadn't really liked having her in the house.

We're always having relatives from the country

Stay with us this way. If we had children

It might be different. This big house wouldn't

Seem so empty then. (I often think we keep the servants

We have, at a time when so few people have any servants at all,

Just because the servants help fill the house.)

Sometimes it's the old folks from Hortonsburg we have

When they're taking treatments

At the Hospital or at one of the clinics.

Or it may be a wife

像这样和我们住在一起。如果我们有孩子
那情形就大不一样了。因为这大屋子就不会
像现在这样冷清清的。（我时常想我们之所以
留下
我们的佣人，也就是佣人们可以使这屋子热闹
一点，
而当时已经没有人家再雇佣什么佣人了。）
有时我们有那么几个老乡从霍腾斯堡来，
到那医院或者某个诊疗所
看病就医。
或者有个什么人的妻子
到此地来躲避一下情意不专的丈夫。
（通常是夫妻俩双双回霍腾斯堡。）
时不时的也有哪个关系很近的亲戚
或者我们在学校时的朋友或者哪个参加过我们
婚礼的人。
我们留下爱玛琴
是南希听说她很孤单，
因为她祖母死了，
又因为爱玛琴的母亲
在生前
曾是一个很勤勉的护士并在南希母亲临死前
照料过南希的母亲。就那么回事。
再没有其他什么原因。
但是我们一开始就看出她那么喜欢
待在我们这屋子里而且很喜欢南希养的小动物，
看着那些小东西像我们一样住在一个屋子里
舒舒服服地过上一阵子，
这也真使我们称心满意。但是我没有料到
那些小动物全都不及爱玛琴那样喜欢这屋子
或者全都不及她那样想讨南希和我的欢心，甚至
讨佣人们的欢心。我经常看到她
从这个房间走到那个房间，
房间对她来说是那么大而她用手轻轻地
抚摸她身边的每一件家具，
就是在我们家已住了几个月之后还是这样。
这使人感到她在霍腾斯堡住过的屋子里
——她母亲的屋子和她祖母的屋子——
那儿没有漂亮的家具——没有她喜欢抚摸的
东西。
那情形真叫人心碎。那天她打破了

Who has to leave some trifling husband for a while.
(Usually the couples in Hortonsburg go back together.)
More often than not it's one of the really close kin
Or a friend we were in school with or who was in our wedding.
We got Emmagene
Because Nancy heard she was all alone
Since her Grandma died
And because Emmagene's mother
Before *she* died
Had been a practical nurse and had looked after Nancy's mother
In her last days. It was that sort of thing.
And it was no more than that.
But we could see from the first how much she loved
Being here in this house and loved Nancy's nice things.
That's what's so satisfying about having them here,
Seeing how they appreciate living for a while
In a house like ours. But I don't guess
Any of them ever liked it better than Emmagene
Or tried harder to please both Nancy and me
And the servants, too. Often we would notice her
Even after she had been here for months
Just wandering from room to room
Allowing her rather large but delicately made hands
To move lightly over every piece of furniture she passed.
One felt that in the houses she knew around Hortonsburg
—In her mother's and grandmother's houses—
There had not been pretty things - not things she loved to fondle.
It was heartbreaking to see her the day she broke
A pretty pink china vase that Nancy had set out in a new place
In the sun parlor. The girl hadn't seen it before.
She took it up in her strong right hand
To examine it. Something startled her—
A noise outside, I think. Maybe it was a car going by,
Maybe one of those boys. - Suddenly the vase crashed to the floor.
Emmagene looked down at the pieces, literally wringing her hands
As if she would wring them off, like chicken's necks, if she could.
I was not there. Nancy told me about it later.

一只漂亮的瓷器,这瓷器南希换了地方
放在阳台上的。姑娘以前没见过这瓷器,
她用自己那只有力的右手拿着
正仔细地端详。忽然有什么事情惊动了她——
外面有一阵声响,我想。也许是一辆轿车经过,
也许是某个小伙子。——那瓷器一下子砸到地
板上。

爱玛琴低头看着碎片,直绞着双手,
像绞鸡脖子,要是可能她简直会把它们绞断。
我没有在场。这是南希后来告诉我的。
她说她虽然没有看见姑娘眼睛里有一滴眼泪,
但她从来没见过有人脸上表现出
那样抱憾而内疚的神色。而姑娘所说的话
更叫人震惊。南希和我
后来相互传达了好几次她说的话。
"多么叫人绝望。这是我的手做的,"她痛哭
流涕,
"但愿——但愿我为它受到惩罚。
我知道这只手在一个星期里做不出有用的事
情啦。"

　　　　一天晚上我们在走廊里,
那时有个小伙子驾着车到了屋前,
车像蜗牛爬,
他轻轻地按喇叭,
我对爱玛琴说:"怎么不站起来向他挥挥手,
寻个开心也好,看看怎么样。我想
他们不会伤害你的。"
"喔,你不知道!"她说,
"他们坏透了。
他们不像你和南表姐认识的
那些纳什维尔的温良小伙子。"
听了她的话南希和我一声不响地坐着,
好像我们遇到了令人难堪的事情。
当然不是她不想认识
那些纳什尔的小伙子
她想认识纳什维尔的小伙子
那些我们本可以介绍给她的靠得住的小伙子。
我开始意识到——南希也是,与此同时——
爱玛琴对自己有自己的看法
这看法就是那样的事情在她是不实际的。

She said that though there was not a sign of a
tear in the girl's eye
She had never before seen such a look of regret
and guilt
In a human face. And what the girl said
　　Was even stranger. Nancy and I
Have mentioned it to each other many times
since.
"I despise my hand for doing that,"she wailed.
"I wish - I do wish I could punish it in some way.
I ought to see it don't do anything useful for a
week."

　　　　One night on the porch
When one of those boys went by in his car
At a snail's pace
And kept tapping lightly on his horn,
I said to Emmagene, "Why don't you stand up
and wave to him,
Just for fun,just to see what happens. I don't i-
magine
They mean any harm."
"Oh, you don't know!"she said.
"They're a mean lot.
They're not like some nice Nashville boy
That you and Cousin Nan might know."
Nancy and I sat quiet after that,
As if some home truth had been served up to us.
It wasn't just that she didn't want to know
Those Hortonsburg boys.
She *wanted* to know Nashville boys
Of a kind we might introduce her to and
approve of.
I began to see - and so did Nancy, the same mo-
ment—
That Emmagene had got ideas about herself
Which it wouldn't be possible for her to realize.
She not only liked our things. She liked our life.
She meant somehow to stay. And of course
It would never do. The differences were too deep.
That is to say, she had no notion of changing her-
self.
She was just as sure now
About what one did and didn't do
As she had been when she came.
She still dressed herself without any ornamenta-
tion
Or any taste at all. And would have called it a sin
to do so.
Levity of any kind seemed an offence to her.
There was only one Book anyone need read.
Dancing and drinking and all that
Was beyond even thinking about.

她不仅喜欢我们的东西。她也喜欢我们的生活

她有意要留在这儿。而肯定的是

这绝无可能。差异太大了。

这就是说,她没有打算改变她自己。

关于行为举止

她现在所知道的

和她初来时知道的依然一个样。

她的穿着依然如故,毫不华丽

也毫无气派。而那样又简直会被她称为罪过。

任何轻佻的行为都和她无缘。

她认为任何人要读的书就是一本《圣经》。

跳舞和吃喝之类的事

那简直是不可思议的。

然而我们家里悠闲舒适的生活

已经触动了她。这种生活她已感到

无害而有益。这样的情形真糟

我们总觉得是我们犯了过失。

但除了帮助她建立自己的生活

我们还能做什么呢?

这就是我们一开始就抱着的良好意愿。

　　我调查了那些打电话的

按轿车喇叭的小伙子。在纳什维尔有办法

找到那些从你家乡到这城里来的任何人。

这就像在巴黎或者罗马

要想找到从美国来的人一样容易。

你只要在那些讲你家乡话的人中间询问就是了。

所以我询问了关于那些小伙子的情形。

很遗憾,我最后得知他们是些粗野的人,

然而,我还是对南希说:"谁可以制服他们呢,

除非像爱玛琴这样的人。在霍腾县那种地方

世世代代下来毫无例外都是这样。"

　　我不知道这对我们意味着什么,南希

和我。

我说话时的神情很严肃很认真,

竭力想使她对那些小伙子有所了解。

我不明白这对我们意味着什么。也许意味着看

到爱玛琴

干活干断了手指

——无缘无故。这毫无必要。——

And yet the kind of luxury we had in our house

Had touched her. She felt perfectly safe, perfectly good

With it. It was a bad situation

And we felt ourselves somewhat to blame.

Yet what else could we do

But help her try to find a life of her own?

That had been our good intention from the outset.

　　I investigated those boys who did the ringing up

And the horn blowing. In Nashville you have ways

Of finding out who's in town from your home town.

It's about like being in Paris or Rome

And wanting to know who's there from the U. S. A.

You ask around among those who speak the home tongue.

And so I asked about those boys.

They were, I had to acknowledge, an untamed breed.

But, still, I said to Nancy, "Who's to tame 'em

If not someone like Emmagene. It's been going on

Up there in Horton County for, I'd say - Well,

For a good many generations anyway. "

　　I don't know what got into us, Nancy and me.

We set about it more seriously, more in earnest

Trying to get her to see something of those boys.

I'm not sure what got into us. Maybe it was seeing Emmagene

Working her fingers to the bone

—For no reason at all. There was no necessity. —

And loving everything about it so.

Heading out to secretarial school each morning,

Beating the pavements in search of a job all afternoon,

Then coming home here and setting jobs for herself

That kept her up half the night.

Suddenly our house seemed crowded with her in it.

Not just to us, but to the servants, too.

I heard the cook talking to her one night in the kitchen.

" You ought to see some young folks your own age.

You ought to have yourself a nice fellow. "

"What nice young fellow would I know?"

她也许对什么事都那样热忱。

每天早晨赶到秘书学校去，

整个下午到处奔走寻找工作，

然后回到我们家里又要承担许多活儿，

这使她一直折腾到半夜。

我们的屋子似乎由于她而一下子变热闹了。

不仅我们觉得，佣人们也觉得。

我听到厨娘一天夜里在厨房里和她谈话。

"你应该认识一些和你一样年纪的年轻同乡。

你应该给自己找个好小伙子。"

"我应该认识哪个年轻的好小伙子呢？"爱玛琴低声问。

"听她说的！"厨娘说，"你以为我们没看见

那些开车打这儿过的小伙子吗？"

"可他们是些废物！"爱玛琴说，"他们中间没有一个

懂得正派姑娘喜欢的是什么！"

"听她说的！"厨娘说。

"我听了，"看屋人说，"你也听了。

但她没听我们的。除了她自己她谁也不听。"

"难道没有一个人配得上你吗？"厨娘说。

"我喜欢认识那种

住在这儿附近的小伙子。"可怜的姑娘说。

听了她的话厨娘责备说：

"不要老想着高攀，亲爱的。"

爱玛琴不再说什么。而对于这件事

我们中间无论谁听到她所说的也就这么些。

她随即离开厨房

上了后楼梯到自己的房间里。

然而就在这期间她和我们在一起

似乎比以往都要快活。她甚至还唱唱歌，

一面烹煮啦洗涤啦。我们听到

那熟悉的古老的歌谣在洗衣机和吸尘器上飘荡。

而当星期天晚餐时也同样如此！

呵，她买来了土产火腿和热香肠，

这是南希常去光顾的那些铺子里没有的。

她已经找到工作啦！

她已经完成秘书工作的训练，

现在她已经有了工作，

工作的地方就在那幢大楼里，

Emmagene asked softly.

"I'm not sure there is such a fellow - not that I would know. "

"Listen to her!"said the cook. "Do you think we don't see

Those fellows that go riding past here?"

"They're trash!" Emmagene said. "And not one of them

That knows what a decent girl is like!"

"Listen to her!"said the cook.

"I hear her," said the houseman, " and you hear her.

But she don't hear us. She don't hear nobody but herself. "

"Ain't nobody good enough for you?" the cook said.

"I'd like to meet some boy

Who lives around here,"the poor girl said.

And to this the cook said indignantly,

"Don't git above your raisin',honey. "

Emmagene said no more. It was the most

Any of us would ever hear her say on that subject.

Presently she left the kitchen

And went up the back stairs to her room.

Yet during this time she seemed happier than ever

To be with us. She even took to singing

While she dusted and cleaned. We'd hear

Familiar old hymns above the washer and the vacuum cleaner.

And such suppers as we got on Sunday night!

Why,she came up with country ham and hot sausage

That was simply not to be had in stores where Nancy traded.

And then she *did* find a job!

She finished her secretarial training

And she came up with a job

Nowhere else but in the very building

Where my own office is.

There was nothing for it

But for me to take her to work in my car in the morning

And bring her home at night.

But there was a stranger coincidence than where her job was.

One of those boys from Hortonsburg turned out to run the elevator

In our building. Another of them brought up my car each night

我的办公室也在那儿。

现在我没什么可操心的了，

除了每天早上用我的汽车送她上班，

晚上再带她回家。

但是巧中之巧还有更怪的巧遇。

那些来自霍腾斯堡的小伙子中有一个不知怎么

就在我们那大楼里开电梯。另一个每天晚上帮我

从汽车库里把我的汽车开来。我以前未加注意

那些对我直呼其名的小伙子是些什么人。

而现在我注意到他们也和她讲话，

还叫她"爱玛琴"。对此我稍稍逗弄过她，

不过没有太过分，我想。我知道适可而止，

所以没有把事情弄糟。

后来有一天晚上，在汽车库里，

那个小伙子一面给爱玛琴开车门一面对她说：

"乔治正等在那儿想让他送你回家。"

这乔治当然是另外一个也是来自霍腾斯堡的小伙子，

（不是那个在大楼里开电梯的也不是这个看汽车库的）

他正在斜道那边向我致意。

"你为什么不和他一起坐车回家呢，爱玛琴？"我说。

我想，我的语调有点催逼的意味。

这时，没等我说第二句话，也没等爱玛琴钻进我对面的车门，

那车库的小伙子就砰地一下关上了车门。

我便发动汽车，沿斜道而下——

加大油门发出咕咕的声响。

到了家，南希说我应该感到害臊。

不过她说这话的时候已经过了一小时，

那时爱玛琴还没有回家。

最后她回来了，虽然，

这时我们刚刚吃好晚饭。

我们听到外面汽车门砰的一声响。

我们相互望望，等着。

最后爱玛琴出现在餐室的过道上，

In the parking garage. I hadn't noticed before

Who those young fellows were that always called me by name.

But then I noticed them speaking to her too

And calling her "Emmagene." I teased her about them a little

But not too much, I think. I knew to take it easy

And not spoil everything.

Then one night the boy in the garage

When he was opening the car door for Emmagene, said,

"George over there wants you to let him carry you home."

This George was still another boy from Hortonsburg,

(Not one that worked in my building or in the garage)

And he saluted me across the ramp.

"Why don't you ride with him, Emmagene?" I said.

I said it rather urgently, I suppose.

Then without another word, before Emmagene could climb in beside

Me, the garage boy had slammed my car door.

And I pulled off, down the ramp —

With my tires screeching.

At home, Nancy said I ought to have been ashamed.

But she only said it after an hour had passed

And Emmagene had not come in.

At last she did arrive, though,

Just as we were finishing dinner.

We heard a car door slam outside.

We looked at each other and waited.

Finally Emmagene appeared in the dining room doorway.

She looked at us questioningly,

First at Nancy's face, then at mine.

When she saw how pleased we were

She came right on in to her place at the table.

And she sat down, said her blessing.

And proceeded to eat her supper as though nothing unusual had happened.

She never rode to or from work with me again.

There was always somebody out there

In the side driveway, blowing for her in the morning

And somebody letting her out in the driveway at night.

她疑惑地看看我们，
先看看南希的脸，又看看我的脸。
她见我们那么高兴，
于是径直走进来到了餐桌旁她自己的位置上。
她坐下，做饭前祈祷。
随后开始吃晚饭，好像什么事都未发生。

　　　她再也不和我一起坐车上下班。
每天早晨总有人在外面等着，
就在马路旁边，一面按汽车喇叭招呼她，
而到了晚上也有人在路边把她叫出去。
不知何故，她总要他们到后门边
来叫她，好像到前门去叫她
是件错事似的。
再说她回屋时也总是走后门。

　　　有时在傍晚时分她也出去，
看来一般是为了应付屋前车道上的汽车喇叭声，
好像并未有约在先。
她总走到起居室门边
对我们说她想出去兜兜风。
当我们向她报以微笑的脸色时，
她总要踌躇一阵子，好像为了弄明白
我们投给她的目光究竟意味着什么，
或者已经心里明白，也许为了领略一下其中的
滋味，
随后她走了，
一两个小时后她便回家。

　　　从表面看，她现在和我们在一起似乎
比以往还要快活。但有些事情发生了变化。
我们俩都注意到了。那歌声业已消失。
还有——这在我们简直不敢相信——
她变得越来越笨手笨脚，在屋里走动时
也开始绊绊跌跌，在厨房干活
时不时会出些小乱子。厨娘抱怨说
她把摇肉机从桌上拆下来时
老是会失手把摇肉机摔坏。
她在磨刀石上磨劈柴刀——或者是想试试吧，
但把刀磨得使管家坚持说
我们不得不再去买一把新刀。

For some reason she always made them let
her out
Near the back door, as though it would be wrong
For them to let her out at the front.
And then she would come on inside the house the
back way.

　　She went out evenings sometimes, too,
Though always in answer to a horn's blowing in
the driveway
And never, it seemed, by appointment.
She would come to the living room door
And say to us she was going out for a little ride.
When we answered with our smiling counte-
nances
She would linger a moment, as if to be sure
About what she read in our eyes
Or perhaps to relish what she could so clearly
read.
Then she would be off
And she would be home again within an hour
or two.

　　It actually seemed as if she were still happier
with us now
Than before. And yet something was
different too.
We both noticed it. The hymn singing stopped.
And - almost incredible as it seemed to us —
She developed a clumsiness, began tripping
over things
About the house, doing a little damage here
and there
In the kitchen. The cook complained
That she'd all but ruined the meat grinder
Dropping it twice when she was unfastening it
from the table.
She sharpened the wood ax on the knife sharpen-
er - or tried to,
And bent the thing so the houseman insisted
We'd have to have another.
What seemed more carelessness than clumsiness
Was that she accidentally threw away
One of Nancy's good spoons, which the cook re-
trieved
From the garbage can. Nancy got so she would
glance at me
As if to ask, "What will it be next? - poor child."
We noticed how nervous she was at the table
How she would drop her fork on her plate —
As if she intended to smash the Haviland —
Or spill something on a clean place mat.
Her hands would tremble, and she would look at

除了做事笨手笨脚她还心不在焉，
竟然把南希的一只精致的调羹
随手扔掉了。还是厨娘把它从废罐头里
找了回来。南希知道后对我望望，
好像在问："下次又会怎么样呢？——可怜的
孩子。"

在餐桌边我们注意到她是那样心神不宁，
经常把刀叉掉落到汤盘里——
好像有意要打破那哈维兰瓷器——
或者有意用汤溅污干净的草垫似的。
她的手老是颤抖，她老是对着我们看，
好像她以为我们正在打算惩罚她，
或者好像她希望我们这样做。
一天，打扫屋子时她把一座小塑像的头
打掉了，她走到南希那儿，
一只手拿着头另一只手拿着身体。
她那双手看上去那么紧张，
那么紧紧地握着那些陶瓷碎片，
手上平时看上去是乳白色的地方
青筋一根根暴出来。南希的心怦怦乱跳。
她用自己的手抓住那双手，
马上给它们按摩，
好像这是一双刚从雪地里拔出来的孩子的手。
她对姑娘说打碎那座牧人塑像
一点也没关系，
因为我们并不拥有
关系重大的东西。

　　　　这天晚上，姑娘依然
打电话。现在她对着话筒所说的
总是些暗语。一般说来
我们都听不懂她到底在说些什么。
而我们也不想听。完全出于偶然
我听到她说的——尽管我不想听——
是"闭嘴，乔治"或者"别提这件事"之类的话。
后来一天晚上南希听到她说：
"我没有合适的衣服穿着去参加这样的事情。"

　　　　那正是南希想听到的话。她完全明白
姑娘究竟已遇到了什么事。第二天上午
挨到商店开门的时候南希上街去

us
　　As though she thought we were going to repri-
mand her
　　Or as if she hoped we would.
　　One day when she broke off the head of a
little figurine
　　While dusting, she came to Nancy with the head
　　In one hand and the body in the other.
　　Her two hands were held so tense,
　　Clasping so tightly the ceramic pieces,
　　That blue veins stood out where they were usual-
ly
　　All creamy whiteness. Nancy's heart went out
to her.
　　She seized the two hands in her own
　　And commenced massaging them
　　As if they were a child's, in from the snow.
　　She told the girl that the broken shepherd
　　Didn't matter at all,
　　That there was nothing we owned
　　That mattered *that* much.

　　　　Meanwhile, the girl continued to get calls
at night
　　On the telephone. She would speak a few sylla-
bles
　　Into the telephone now. Usually
　　We couldn't make out what it was she was she
was saying.
　　And we tried not to hear. All I ever managed
　　To hear her say — despite my wish not to
hear —
　　Were things like "Hush, George" or "Don't say
such things."
　　　　Finally one night Nancy heard her say:
　　"I haven't got the kind of dress to wear to such a
thing."

　　That was all Nancy needed. She got it out of
the girl
　　What the event was to be. And next morning
　　Nancy was downtown by the time the stores
opened,
　　Buying Emmagene a sleeveless, backless evening
gown.
　　It seemed for a time Nancy had wasted her mon-
ey.
　　The girl said she wasn't going to go out anywhere
　　Dressed like that. "You don't think I'd put you in
a dress
　　That wasn't proper to wear," said Nancy,
　　Giving it to her very straight.
　　"It isn't a matter of what you think

给爱玛琴买了一件无袖裸背的晚会舞衣。

看来南希这回是白白浪费了钱。

姑娘说她并不打算到什么地方去

需要穿这样的衣服。"你不会认为这衣服

不合适吧?"南希说,

一面把衣服递到她面前。

"你认为合适的,"爱玛琴回答,

"可他们——乔治,也许还有其他人——

却会认为不合适。"

她们俩当时在客人房间里,爱玛琴所住的房间,

南希这时坐在一张双人床上,

双人床和爱玛琴所坐的床相对,所以南希正面对

着她。

"这小伙子并没有对你做什么不好的事

是吗,爱玛琴?"南希问她,"因为要是这样,

那么你也就不会和他——

和他,还有其他人,一起出去了。"

"你知道我会让他那么做的,南表姐,"她说,

"并不这样。事情不是这样,南表姐。"

"什么意思?"南希真有点摸不着头脑,问。

姑娘低头看看自己的双手,这双手正拳握在她的

膝盖上。

"我是说,他喜欢的就是我的这双手。"她说。

她迅速地把双手放到身后,不让人看见。

"这也是他们都喜欢的,好像他们没有旁的东西

可喜欢了。"

接着她看看南希,那目光就像

我们最后问她那打电话的人是谁时她的目光

一样,

就像她对问题早已有所准备似的。

随后,像过去一样,她又开口说话,

没问的也说了:

"本来嘛,这真是件叫人恶心的事情,

他们在电话里讲的也就是这件事。那些话,那

些词,

你们是不会听得懂的,南表姐。"

说完,姑娘站起身,

好像对南希说现在得让她安静一下。

南希也几乎没再说什么就回到我们自己房里。

她惶惑不解,用姑娘告诉她的那些事情

或者是姑娘竭力想告诉她的事情

Is proper,"Emmagene replied.

"It's what he would think it meant —

George,and maybe some of the others,too. "

They were in the guest room, where Emmagene was staying

And now Nancy sat down on the twin bed opposite

The one where Emmagene was sitting, and facing her.

"This boy George doesn't really misbehave with you

Does he, Emmagene?" Nancy asked her. "Because if he does,

Then you mustn't, after all, go out with him —

With him or with the others. "

"You know I wouldn't let him do that, Cousin Nan,"she said.

"Not really. Not the real thing, Cousin Nan. "

"What do you mean?"Nancy asked in genuine bewilderment.

The girl looked down at her hands, which were folded in her lap.

"I mean, it's my hands he likes," she said.

And she quickly put both her hands behind her, out of sight.

"It's what they all like if they can't have it any other way. "

And then she looked at Nancy the way she had looked

At both of us when we finally asked her who it was on the telephone,

As though she'd only been waiting for such questions.

And then, as before, she gave more

Than she had been asked for.

"Right from the start, it was the most disgusting kind of things

They all said to me on the telephone. And the language, the words.

You wouldn't have known the meaning, Cousin Nan. "

When she had said this the girl stood up

As if to tell Nancy it was time she leave her alone.

And with hardly another word, Nancy came on to our room.

She was so stunned she was half the night

Putting it across to me just what the girl had told her

Or had tried to tell her.

Naturally, we thought we'd hear no more about the dress.

打扰了我整整半夜。

　　　　　　我们自然以为不会再听到谈衣服的
事了。

　　但是，并不，就在第二天晚上，吃过晚饭，
她走进起居室来到我们面前，
给我们看她正穿着南希买给她的那件衣服。
严格地说她并未穿着那件衣服，
而是像穿舞衣那样，套在身上，
而那舞衣下面好像什么也没穿。
她脚上穿着一双黑色皮船鞋——
明显地不相称的，是她的头发像往常一样只是朝
后打了个结。
她站在那儿，虽然看上去相像，
脸擦得挺干净，头发也刚刚梳洗过，
但那样的打扮对她来说却很古怪也很别扭，
尽管人们一眼看去会觉得她具有
某种魅力。不知何故，她接着要说什么我们总
知道。

　　　　　　"我想出去。"她说，一面观察我们的
脸色，
就像她平时和我们讲话时常做的那样。
南希站起身随手把针线活扔在椅子扶手上，
针线活落到了地板上她也没理会。
显然，看到姑娘打扮得这样美貌她感到很突然，
她马上走上去对她说：
"爱玛琴，不要再和乔治一起出去了，
这很蠢。"她们走进客厅，
南希的手挽住姑娘的腰。
"我不能不去。"爱玛琴说。
正当她这么说，屋前车道上响起一阵汽车喇
叭声。
"乔治一点儿也不比别人更坏，"她说，
"也许更好。我现在已经喜欢上他了。"
汽车喇叭嘟嘟地响得更急促，
不很响但很长。
"他不是我乐意喜欢的那种人。
但是我自己也没办法。再说这衣服也是你买给
我的。"

But, no, it was the very next night, after dinner,
That she came down to us in the living room
And showed herself to us in that dress Nancy had
bought.
It can't properly be said she was wearing it,
But she had it on her like a night gown,
As if she didn't have anything on under it.
And her feet in a pair of black leather pumps —
No make-up of course, her hair pulled back as u-
sual into a knot.
There was something about her, though, as she
stood there
With her clean scrubbed face and her freshly
washed hair
And in that attire so strange and unfamiliar to her
That made one see the kind of beauty she had,
For the first time. And somehow one knew what
she was going to say.

　　　　　"I'll be going out," she said, searching
our faces
As she had got so she was always doing when she
spoke to us.
Nancy rose and threw her needle work on the
chair arm
And didn't try to stop it when it fell on to the
floor.
Clearly, she too had perceived suddenly a certain
beauty about the girl.
She went over to her at once and said,
"Emmagene, don't go out with George again.
It isn't wise." They stepped into the hall
With Nancy's arm about the girl's waist.
"I've got to go," Emmagene said.
And as she spoke a horn sounded in the drive-
way.
"George is no worse than the rest," she said.
"He's *better*. I've come to like things about
him now."
There was more tapping on the horn,
Not loud but insistent.
"He's not the kind of fellow I'd have liked to
like.
But I can't stop now. And you've gone and
bought this dress."

　　　　　Nancy didn't seem to hear her. "You mustn't
go," she said.
"I couldn't live through this evening.
I'd never forgive myself." The horn kept it up
outside,
And the girl drew herself away from Nancy.
Planting herself in the middle of the hall

南希好像没有在听她说。"你决不能去。"她说。

"今天晚上我忍受不下去了。

我决不再宽恕自己。"外面的喇叭声响个不停。

姑娘猛地抽身从南希身边走开。

到了客厅中央她又站住,

她向我们说出布道时的第一句话,这话我们过去从未听她说过。

"宽恕我们的不是我们自己。上帝宽恕我们。"

南希转身向我求助。我站起身时,

姑娘便挑衅似的说:"噢,我走了!"

她在对我们俩说话:"你们现在不能阻止我!"

汽车喇叭声变成那种嗒—嗒—嗒的声音。

"那是他喜欢。"她说,一面朝屋外车道方向

不住地点头,他正在那儿按着喇叭。

"你们现在不能阻止我!

我不是黑奴而且21岁了。

那是他对我说的。"

喇叭声依然不断。

我们无话可说也无能为力。

南希说:"喔,你得穿件外套啊。

这样的天气你不能这样出去。"

她叫厨娘,厨娘跑过来,

(她肯定一直就等在从客厅通往厨房的门那边。)

南希叫她到楼梯平台旁边的壁橱里

把她的天鹅绒披风拿来。

当姑娘穿过厨房奔出去时,

客厅里一阵忙乱,

她肩上拖着的披风在身后飘动,

几乎飘到放雨伞的钢架那样的高度,

我觉得自己所能做的最好的事情就是重新坐下来。

南希和厨娘在相互耳语,

在客厅里。我看见她们的嘴在动,

这时我突然听到一声惨叫,

声音来自厨房,整幢屋子都能听见。

我穿过起居室和贮藏室走过去,

但厨娘从客厅后门出去已先到了那里,

厨娘说她听见后门砰的一声响。

我没有听见这砰的一声响。南希说她后来听

She gave us the first line of preaching we'd ever heard from her:

"It is not for us to forgive ourselves. God forgives us."

Nancy turned and appealed to me. When I stood up

The girl said defiantly, "Oh, I'm going!"

She was speaking to both of us. "You can't stop me now!"

The car horn had begun a sort of rat-a-tat-tat.

"That's what he's like," she said, nodding her head

Toward the driveway where he was tapping the horn.

"You can't stop me now!

I'm free white and twenty-one.

That's what *he* says about me."

Still the horn kept on.

And there was nothing we could think to say or do.

Nancy did say, "Well, you'll have to have a wrap.

You can't go out like that in this weather."

She called to the cook, who came running

(She must have been waiting just beyond the hall door to the kitchen.)

And Nancy sent her to the closet on the landing

To fetch her velvet evening cape.

There was such a commotion

With the girl running out through the kitchen,

The cape about her shoulders and billowing out behind

Almost knocking over the brass umbrella stand,

I felt the best thing I could do was to sit down again.

Nancy and the cook were whispering to each other

In the hall. I could see their lips moving

And then suddenly I heard the groan or scream

That came from the kitchen and could be heard all over the house.

I went out through the dining room and the pantry

But the cook got there first by way of the back hall door.

The cook said she heard the back door slam.

I didn't hear it. Nancy said afterward she heard

The car door slam. We all heard the car roar down the driveway

In reverse gear. We heard the tires whining

As the car backed into the street and swung around

Into forward motion. None of that matters,

到的

是汽车门砰地一声响。我们大家都听到汽车在屋外车道上咕咕作响

在倒车。我们听到加油门的吱吱声,

汽车倒进大街拐了个弯,

径直开去了。这不是什么大不了的事,

而这种事到事后回忆也很困难。

我们看到厨房里到处是血。

斧头抛到了铺着亚麻油毡的地板中央,

一行斑斑点点的血迹,

这是她抛出斧头时留下的,正当厨娘和我

在那里时,看屋人

从地下室里的佣人浴室上来。

他穿过后走廊走进厨房。

当然,我们看到的他也看到了

不过他看到的更多。我跟随着他的眼光,

而他低头探寻进了长台尽头的废物间,

这正好在门廊里边。但是他又转身

眼也没抬就直奔到后走廊去。

我们听见他在那儿一声叹息。

厨娘和我你看我我看你,不知道谁应该先去。

当然,我知道这只能由我去。

我说:"你不要让南希小姐到这儿来。"

而且看着她转身进客厅。

我径直朝废物间走去,

脚踏着了那把斧头也没顾上,

只想到我必须去看看。我看到了,

脑子里首先想到的是:"呵,那是一只人手哪。"

我想大约过了 10 秒钟我才想到

这是爱玛琴的手,

是她自己用劈柴刀砍下来的。

我所能做的事可想而知。

我跑到屋外的车道上,看了看每一个血脚印,

然后回屋,从还在那里对着血污恶心的看屋人身边走过,

用厨房里的电话机给警察局挂了电话。

他们随即就赶到了。

那个待在车里等爱玛琴的

But that's the kind of thing you tend to recall later.

What we saw in the kitchen was the blood everywhere.

And the ax lying in the middle of the linoleum floor

With the smeary trail of blood it left

When she sent it flying. The houseman

Came up from the servants' bathroom in the basement

Just when the cook and I got there.

He came in through the back porch.

He saw what we saw of course

Except he saw more. I followed his eyes

As he looked down into that trash can at the end of the counter

And just inside the porch door. But he turned away

And ran out onto the back porch without lifting his eyes again.

And I could hear him being sick out there.

The cook and I looked at each other, to see who would go first.

I knew I had to do it, of course.

I said, "You keep Miss Nancy out of here,"

And saw her go back into the hall.

I went over to the trash can,

Stepping over the ax and with no thought in my head

But that I must look. When I did look,

My first thought was, "Why, that's a human hand."

I suppose it was ten seconds or so before I was enough myself

To own it was Emmagene's hand

She had cut off with the wood ax.

I did just what you would expect.

I ran out into the driveway, seeing the blood every step,

And then back inside, past the houseman still retching over the bannister rail.

And telephoned the police on the kitchen telephone.

They were there in no time.

The boy who had been waiting for Emmagene

In the car, and making the racket with his horn

Used better judgment than a lot of people might have.

When she drew back the velvet cape and showed him

并用汽车喇叭制造噪音的小伙子
比许多人都要来得头脑清醒。
当她摔开天鹅绒披风并给他看
她对自己做了什么事
并在座位上昏过去之后，
他没有犹豫，也没想到把她拖回屋。
他发动汽车直向医院急诊室。
他把她送那儿时她已经死了，
这样做无疑是再好不过了，
你想想看吧。
而每个人都对那个小伙子表示庆贺，
——警察，医生也如此，
警察在急诊室候诊处逮捕了他，
不过当天夜里我就赶到警察局，
第二天上午9点钟我们便让他得到了释放。
他实在是个傻乎乎的乡下小伙子，
对自己为何要进警察局还一无所知。
当然啰，我们得为爱玛琴料理后事，
并且通知霍腾斯堡的人来参加葬礼。
牧师从她常去的教堂来到本城公墓，
并为她举行墓边祷告。
牧师，还有大家，都向我们说了许多安慰话。
他们向我们重提我们曾对从乡下来的亲戚
总是那样好客那样殷勤，
还说爱玛琴生来是
那种性情古怪的姑娘，就是在离家前也这样，
从乡下人的角度看，
他们倒也不失为是些好心人。
连那个小伙子的父母也参加了祷告。
南希和我竭力想使他们明白
乔治并没有什么大的过错。
最后，大家从他父母的表情可以看出
他父母过去待他并不很好。
他是个乡下小伙子，无疑生性粗野，
他来到纳什维尔寻找工作，
而在这儿却没有一个有责任感的亲戚朋友
来管束他，
或者给他某些他所需要的忠告，
当然，这情况对乔治的父母
是不能说的———
无论如何，在爱玛琴的葬礼上是不能说的。

What she had done to herself
And then passed out on the seat,
He didn't hesitate, didn't think of bringing her back inside the house.
He lit out for the emergency room at the Hospital.
She was dead when he got her there,
Which no doubt was for the best
When you think about it.
But everybody congratulated the boy
— The police, and the doctors as well.
The police arrested him in the emergency waiting room,
But I went down to the Station that night
And we had him free by nine o'clock next morning.
He was just a big country boy really
Without any notion of what he was into.
We looked after arrangements for Emmagene of course
And accompanied the body up to Hortonsburg for burial.
The pastor from her church came to the, town cemetery
And held a graveside service for her.
He and everybody else said a lot of consoling things to us.
They were kind in a way that only country people
Of their sort can be,
Reminding us of how hospitable we'd always been
To our kinfolks from up there
And saying Emmagene had always been
A queer sort of a girl, even before she left home.
Even that boy George's parents were at the service.
Nancy and I did our best to make them see
George wasn't to be blamed too much.
After all, you could tell from looking at his parents
He hadn't had many advantages.
He was a country boy who grew up kind of wild no doubt.
He had come down to Nashville looking for a job
And didn't have any responsible relatives here
To put restraints upon him
Or to give him the kind of advice he needed.
That might have made all the difference for such a boy,
Though of course it wasn't something you could say
To George's parents —
Not there at Emmagene's funeral, anyway.

┌─ 讨　论 ─■

这篇小说中的故事叙述者和《二十九条臆想》中的一样,是个业余文学爱好者。但又和那篇小说里的叙述者不同,这个讲述爱玛琴故事的人丝毫没有兴趣用心理内容把故事弄得断断续续,或者至少他自己并不认为这样。所以,他致力于"平铺直叙"地讲故事,但他极其大胆地采用散文诗形式,这种技巧上的创新旨在使故事明晰易懂,而并非为了晦涩含糊或者想把故事弄得模棱两可。

《爱玛琴的手》在很大程度上代表了许多当代小说,这类小说都采用现实主义传统方法,而同时又提出关于各种不同生存环境的现实问题,小说中的人物也各自活动在不同的环境中。可以肯定,爱玛琴所接受到的现实,如宗教狂热、性犯罪的暴力活动以及她的关于性满足的观念,这些并不是一般读者所接受到的现实,更确切一点说,甚至也不是故事的叙述者和他妻子,还有那些和爱玛琴幽会的小伙子所接受到的现实。这篇小说主要叙述的是叙述者对爱玛琴生活于其中的那个不同世界的一连串发现,或者毋宁说,一连串关于差异的反复强调,因为叙述者和他妻子一直感觉到(或者制造着)他们自己和爱玛琴之间的差异。仔细分析小说,读者理应看到,在多大程度上故事叙述者本人和他妻子对爱玛琴最后遭受到的可怕后果是负有责任的,因为这种后果之所以产生就是由于他们处在两种不同的生存环境里。

这篇小说引入了许多所谓"新"小说所特有的要素,这些要素有时被认为是这一流派的某种标志,即某种"哥特式"的恐怖感或者性虐待成分。

Like the narrator in "29 Inventions", the narrator in this story is a literary amateur. But unlike the narrator in that story, the man who tells Emmagene's story has no psychological investment in distorting it, or at least he does not believe he has. His effort, then, is to tell the story "straight," and such innovative techniques as he employs, most strikingly the rendering of the story in a free-verse form, are intended to clarify rather than obscure or make ambiguous.

"The Hand of Emmagene" is thus representative of many contemporary stories that employ the conventions of realism but that raise questions about the reality of the worlds in which their characters move. Certainly the realities that Emmagene accepts—the religious fanaticism, the violence of sexual guilt, the notion of her sexual satisfaction—are not those accepted by the average reader, any more than they are, more relevantly, those accepted by the narrator and his wife, or by the boys whom Emmagene dates. The action of the story describes the process of the narrator's discovery of the different world in which Emmagene lives, or rather the process of this difference's redefinition, for the narrator and his wife have all along felt (and made) differences between themselves and Emmagene. In analyzing this story, the reader should consider the extent to which the narrator and his wife are responsible for the terrible consequences of Emmagene's final acceptance of the differences between their worlds.

This story introduces an element so characteristic of much of the "new" fiction that it is sometimes considered a mark of the genre: a "Gothic" violence or sadistic element.

── **思考题** ──■

1. 在小说的什么地方,读者最初开始怀疑爱玛琴有心理怪癖?

2. 在故事前面部分,叙述者看见爱玛琴在劈柴,这种戏剧化场面有助于作者的何种意图? 作者对爱玛琴和那些来自霍腾斯堡的小伙子之间的古怪关系,曾预先做过一系列的"例证",这个戏剧化场面不是出人意外地起到了某种无声的过渡作用吗?

3. 叙述者的妻子所讲的第一句话就使读者对她的个性有了很好的了解。注意小说中作为刻画人物性格手段的对话所起的作用。

4. 在小说结尾时,叙述者使用了"管束"这个词,其中含有何种无意识的讽刺意味?

（刘文荣 译）

1. At what point in the story does the reader first begin to suspect that Emmagene may have psychotic tendencies?

2. What authorial intention may be served by dramatizing the moment early in the action at which the narrator sees Emmagene chopping firewood? How does this dramatization accomplish what is otherwise an unannounced transition to a list of foreshadowing "proofs" of Emmagene's strange relations with the boys from Hortonsburg?

3. The first words spoken by the narrator's wife tell the reader a good deal about her personality. Consider the use of dialogue in the story as a characterizing device.

4. What unintentional irony sounds in the narrator's use of the word *restraints* at the story's conclusion?

033. 气 球

（美）唐纳德·巴塞尔姆 著　　刘文荣 译

033. The Balloon

by Donald Barthelme

从 14 号街的某个地方，确切的地点我不能透露，那只气球一整夜在向北膨胀，当时人们正在睡觉，气球一直膨胀到了公园。在那儿，我制止了膨胀。黎明时，最北面的边沿横在广场上，漫无节制的运动轻飘而和缓。但是，虽然我制止气球时感到有点儿恼怒，甚至要去保护树木，却发现毫无理由指望气球不在已被它覆盖的那部分城市上面，向上膨胀到那儿所属的"领空"中去，因此，我要求工程师加以注意。这样的膨胀进行了整整一个上午，气门里有轻度的、难以察觉的漏气现象。气球已经覆盖了大街南北两边某些地区的 45 个街区。当时的形势就是这样。

不过，称之为"形势"，也即意味到了其种解决或某种紧张状态的弛缓，那是错的，无所谓什么形势，不过是只气球悬荡在那里罢了——在周围一片胡桃色和淡黄色的衬托下，气球的绝大部分呈稍浅的深灰棕色。由于缺乏最后的润色，加上装置精巧，使表面具有一种粗糙的、易被遗忘的特征，内部正在变化的重量，在好多部位上谨慎地调整并固定了这个巨大而形状变异的球体。如今我们已对所有的工具，包括非常优美的工艺品和膨胀史上具有重大意义的产品，都有了大量独创性的见解，但当时却只有这种有形有体的气球，悬荡在那儿。

气球引起了反应。有些人发现气球"很有趣"。作为一种反应，这态度对于气球的庞大无比以及它在城市上空的突然出现，似乎很不合适。另一方面，那些没有患歇斯底里症或者其他社会性人为忧郁症的人则毅然断言，这种反应是冷静的、"成熟的"。关于

THE balloon, beginning at a point on Fourteenth Street, the exact location of which I cannot reveal, expanded northward all one night, while people were sleeping, until it reached the Park. There, I stopped it; at dawn the northernmost edges lay over the Plaza; the freehanging motion was frivolous and gentle. But experiencing a faint irritation at stopping, even to protect the trees, and seeing no reason the balloon should not be allowed to expand upward, over the parts of the city it was already covering, into the "air space" to be found there, I asked the engineers to see to it. This expansion took place throughout the morning, soft imperceptible sighing of gas through the valves. The balloon then covered forty-five blocks north-south on either side of the Avenue in some places. That was the situation, then.

But it is wrong to speak of "situations," implying sets of circumstances leading to some resolution, some escape of tension; there were no situations, simply the balloon hanging there—muted heavy grays and browns for the most part, contrasting with walnut and soft yellows. A deliberate lack of finish, enhanced by skillful installation, gave the surface a rough, forgotten quality; sliding weights on the inside, carefully adjusted, anchored the great, vari-shaped mass at a number of points. Now we have had a flood of original ideas in all media, works of singular beauty as well as significant milestones in the history of inflation, but at that moment there was only *this balloon*, concrete particular, hanging there.

There were reactions. Some people found the balloon "interesting." As a response this seemed inadequate to the immensity of the balloon, the suddenness of its appearance over the city; on the other hand, in the absence of hysteria or other societally induced anxiety,

作者简介：唐纳德·巴塞尔姆（**Donald Barthelme**，1931—1989），美国作家。1931 年 4 月 7 日生于宾夕法尼亚州费城，1989 年 7 月 23 日卒于德克萨斯州休斯敦。在出版小说之前，他做过新闻记者、杂志编辑和博物馆馆长。他以现代主义的"抽象拼贴画"闻名，以技术实验和忧郁的欢乐气氛为标志。他的短篇小说集包括《回来吧，卡里加利博士》（Come Back，Dr. Caligari，1964）、《城市生活》（City Life，1970）、《故事六十篇》（Sixty Stories，1981）和《一夜之间的许多遥远城市》（Overnight to Many Distant Cities，1983），长篇小说包括《白雪公主》（Snow White，1967）、《死去的父亲》（The Dead Father，1975）、《天堂》（Paradise，1986）和《国王》（The King，1990）。

气球的"意义"最初引起了相当规模的论争,论争又销声匿迹,因为我们懂得了不要坚持搞清意义,现在,除了讨论最简单、最无关紧要的事情以外,甚至很少有人顾及什么意义了。人们一致同意,既然关于气球的意义是绝对不可知的,那么扩大讨论是无益的,或者至少和其他人的行为比起来,譬如在某街道上的铁灰色布条下挂些绿的和蓝的纸吊灯啦,或者不失时机写些吹捧文章宣传某人适宜于表演怪诞戏剧啦,或者认识一下也很好啦等等,这样的讨论是盲目的。

大胆的孩子们欣喜欢跳,尤其当他们看见气球紧靠着某幢大楼盘旋,靠得那么近,气球和大楼之间的缝隙只有几英寸,或者当他们看见气球实际上已经和大楼的一边相碰,轻飘飘地贴着大楼,贴得那么紧,气球和大楼似乎连成一体了。气球的表面设计得真像一幅"风景画",有一条条小小的山谷,还有一垛垛的小丘,或者一堆堆的土墩。一旦登上气球,尽可以蹓跶一阵子,甚至来一次旅行,从一个地方跑到另一个地方。还可以从斜面上滑下来,然后从另一面再爬上去,两面的坡度都很平坦,或者从这一边跳到那一边去,这些真叫人感到快活。弹跳也可以,因为表面的伸缩性很好,要是你乐意,就是从上面跳下来也没关系。所有此类的各种运动和其他运动,都是人们力所能及的,在气球的"上"面游览,这使习惯于城市公寓硬邦邦表面的孩子们兴奋之极。不过,气球的目的并不是为了娱乐孩子。

还有一些人,孩子和成年人都有,他们没有充分利用上面描述的那些机会,他们显得有些胆怯,对气球缺乏信任。更有甚者,有人还抱着敌意。由于我们把那往气球内部打氢气的气泵藏了起来,又由于气球表面那么大,当局无法断定进口处——也就是气体注入处——的位置,那些市政官员显得有些灰心丧气,这种表现常常属于他们的本分。气球显而易见的无目的性使人恼火(这像气球偏偏要在"那儿"停留一样使人恼火)。如果我们在气球的侧面,用大写字母写上"实验室试验证明"或者"有效性大于 18%",那么这样的困境本来可以防止发生。但这样做我不能容忍。总的看来,这些官员考虑破格范围时特别能容忍,他们的容忍导致的结果是:首先,夜间进行的秘密试验使他们相信没有办法移动或者毁掉气球;其次,在普通市民中,某种对气球的普遍热情高涨起来(并不因为前面说过的那种敌意而有所减弱)。

it must be judged a calm, "mature" one. There was a certain amount of initial argumentation about the "meaning" of the balloon; this subsided, because we have learned not to insist on meanings, and they are rarely even looked for now, except in cases involving the simplest, safest phenomena. It was agreed that since the meaning of the balloon could never be known absolutely, extended discussion was pointless, or at least less purposeful than the activities of those who, for example, hung green and blue paper lanterns from the warm gray underside, in certain streets, or seized the occasion to write messages on the surface, announcing their availability for the performance of unnatural acts, or the availability of acquaintances.

Daring children jumped, especially at those points where the balloon hovered close to a building, so that the gap between balloon and building was a matter of a few inches, or points where the balloon actually made contact, exerting an ever-so-slight pressure against the side of a building, so that balloon and building seemed a unity. The upper surface was so structured that a "landscape" was presented, small valleys as well as slight knolls, or mounds; once atop the balloon, a stroll was possible, or even a trip, from one place to another. There was pleasure in being able to run down an incline, then up the opposing slope, both gently graded, or in making a leap from one side to the other. Bouncing was possible, because of the pneumaticity of the surface, and even falling, if that was your wish. That all these varied motions, as well as others, were within one's possibilities, in experiencing the "up" side of the balloon, was extremely exciting for children, accustomed to the city's flat, hard skin. But the purpose of the balloon was not to amuse children.

Too, the number of people, children and adults, who took advantage of the opportunities described was not so large as it might have been: a certain timidity, lack of trust in the balloon, was seen. There was, furthermore, some hostility. Because we had hidden the pumps, which fed helium to the interior, and because the surface was so vast that the authorities could not determine the point of entry—that is, the point at which the gas was injected—a degree of frustration was evidenced by those city officers into whose province such manifestations normally fell. The apparent purposelessness of the balloon was vexing (as was the fact that it was "there" at all). Had we painted, in great letters, "LABORATORY TESTS PROVE" or "18% MORE EFFECTIVE!" on the sides of the balloon, this difficulty would have been circumvented. But I could not bear to do so. On the whole, these officers were remarkably tolerant, considering the dimensions of the anomaly, this tolerance being the result of, first, secret tests conducted by night that convinced them that little or nothing could be done in the way of

就像单个的气球必须始终考虑到气球大众一样，每个市民也从自己的角度提出了一大套意见。有人甚或认为，对付气球必须使用污染这个概念，也就是说"巨大气球污染了曼哈顿明净而绚丽的天空"。根据此人的意见，气球也就是某种欺诈行为，对过去一直存在于那儿的天空有所损害，对人民和他们的天空的关系有所干扰。但是实际上，当时正值1月份，天空阴暗而丑陋，那简直不是你仰卧在街上乐意看到的天空，除非在这以前你一直受到威胁和虐待才会感到快乐。在气球下面往上看看倒令人有点愉快，我们那样看过，绝大部分呈稍浅的深灰棕色，周围是一片胡桃色以及柔和的、易被遗忘的黄色。所以，此人想到污染一词时，心底里依然有种乐滋滋的念头，这念头还正在和最初的概念发生冲突。

另一方面，又有人甚或把气球看做似乎是某种信用制度的表现，好像某人的雇主走进来说道："亨利，来，请收下我给你包好的这个钱包，因为我们的生意至今一直很兴隆，我赞赏你这种敢于冒险的精神，如果不这样做，你那个部门就不可能大获成功，或者至少不能获得这样的成功。"对于此人来说，气球也许像一种光华耀人的英雄般"敢作敢为而出奇制胜"的经历，像一种简直不可思议的经历。

又有人甚或说："史无前例——甚是可疑——不期竟会如此这般。"而且还发现有许多人同意他，或者和他争论。"膨胀"和"游动"两个词被引用，梦幻和责任两个概念也被引用了。另一些人加入进来，满脑子想入非非的小算盘，抱着某种希望，想达到的目的是既要让自己迷失在气球里，又要能吞食它。这种希望的个性特征，就它们的本源而言，深深地隐埋着而不为人知，所以对此是无话可说的，不过，显而易见的是它们分布很广。还有一个争论的问题是，当你站在气球下面，最重要的是你感觉如何。有些人宣称他们有安全感、温暖感，好像过去从未有过这种感觉，与此同时，气球的仇人则感到，或者是据报道他们感到紧张，有某种"沉重的"感觉。

评判又发生了分歧：

"胡说八道"

"废话"

××××××××"一些见不得人的勾当"

"暗欢喜"

removing or destroying the balloon, and, secondly, a public warmth that arose(not uncolored by touches of the aforementioned hostility) toward the balloon, from ordinary citizens.

As a single balloon must stand for a lifetime of thinking about balloons, so each citizen expressed, in the attitude he chose, a complex of attitudes. One man might consider that the balloon had to do with the notion *sullied*, as in the sentence *The big balloon sullied the otherwise clear and radiant Manhattan sky*. That is, the balloon was, in this man's view, an imposture, something inferior to the sky that had formerly been there, something interposed between the people and their "sky." But in fact it was January, the sky was dark and ugly; it was not a sky you could look up into, lying on your back in the street, with pleasure, unless pleasure, for you, proceeded from having been threatened, from having been misused. And the underside of the balloon was a pleasure to look up into, we had seen to that, muted grays and browns for the most part, contrasted with walnut and soft, forgotten yellows. And so, while this man was thinking *sullied*, still there was an admixture of pleasurable cognition in his thinking, struggling with the original perception.

Another man, on the other hand, might view the balloon as if it were part of a system of unanticipated rewards, as when one's employer walks in and says, "Here, Henry, take this package of money I have wrapped for you, because we have been doing so well in the business here, and I admire the way you bruise the tulips, without which bruising your department would not be a success, or at least not the success that it is." For this man the balloon might be a brilliantly heroic "muscle and pluck" experience, even if an experience poorly understood.

Another man might say, "Without the example of—, it is doubtful that—would exist today in its present form," and find many to agree with him, or to argue with him. Ideas of "bloat" and "float" were introduced, as well as concepts of dream and responsibility. Others engaged in remarkably detailed fantasies having to do with a wish either to lose themselves in the balloon, or to engorge it. The private character of these wishes, of their origins, deeply buried and unknown, was such that they were not much spoken of; yet there is evidence that they were widespread. It was also argued that what was important was what you felt when you stood under the balloon; some people claimed that they felt sheltered, warmed, as never before, while enemies of the balloon felt, or reported feeling, constrained, a "heavy" feeling.

Critical opinion was divided:

"*monstrous pourings*"

"*harp*"

"笨头笨脑的大傻瓜"

"迄今为止,保守的折中主义掌握了现代气球设计"

……"精力过剩"

"温暖的、软性的、懒洋洋的交流"

"难道统一就为了某种自由散漫而遭到牺牲吗?"

"消除祸患!"

"啪嗒"

人们开始用某种古怪的方式来确定自己与气球在方位上的关系:"气球降落点在 47 号街人行道旁,就在阿拉莫·蔡尔大厦附近,那儿正是我将要去的地方",或者,"为什么我们不站到顶上去,呼吸空气,也许散散步呢? 在那儿气球形成一条紧凑的曲线正和现代艺术画廊的正面相接——"边际交叉提供了一段时间以待进入,还有那"温暖的、软性的、懒洋洋的交流",在这里……但是说到"边际交叉",这不对,每个交叉都关系重大,一个也不能疏忽(就好像,你正在那儿走,也许会觉得无人会转移你的注意力,但突然间,从旧习惯到新习惯,很危险,然而在步步上升)。每一个交叉都关系重大,是大楼和气球的相交,气球和人的相交,气球和气球的相交。

这意味着,关于气球的赞美最后成了这样,气球是不受限制的,或者是可以下定义的。有时,一次膨胀,一次起疱,或者一个部分就能主动把所有的路都朝东引向河边,就像从远离战场的司令部所见到的那样,一支军队凭着地图在行动。过后战斗部队似乎被打退回来,或者撤回,投入新的战斗部署。第二天早晨,战斗部队会再次出击,或者全部消失。气球的这种自我变形、自我变态的能力非常受人喜爱,对于那些生活方式颇为刻板的人尤其如此,虽然他们希望变化,但是却得不到变化。气球存在了 22 天,它随意地提供了自我迷失的可能,它与我们脚下精确无误、排成方格的线路图截然不同。由于各类操作需要的复杂机器变得日益重要,当今需要的所有专业训练,以及随之而来的长期契约的可能性,都得以产生。随着这种倾向的不断加强,越来越多的人由于茫然无措而不能适应,对此,气球也许可以作为一种典范,或者"毛坯"。

我在气球下,趁你从挪威返回之际和你相会。你

× × × × × × × "certain contrasts with darker portions"

"inner joy"

"large, square corners"

" *conservative eclecticism that has so far governed*

modern balloon design"

……"*abnormal vigor*"

"*warm, soft, lazy passages*"

" *Has unity been sacrificed for a sprawling quality?*"

"*Quelle catastrophe!*"

"*munching*"

People began, in a curious way, to locate themselves in relation to aspects of the balloon: "I'll be at that place where it dips down into Forty-seventh Street almost to the sidewalk, near the Alamo Chile House," or, "Why don't we go stand on top, and take the air, and maybe walk about a bit, where it forms a tight, curving line with the facade of the Gallery of Modern Art—" Marginal intersections offered entrances with a given time duration, as well as "warm, soft, lazy passages" in which... But it is wrong to speak of "marginal intersections," each intersection was crucial, none could be ignored (as if, walking there, you might not find someone capable of turning your attention, in a flash, from old exercises to new exercises, risks and escalations). Each intersection was crucial, meeting of balloon and building, meeting of balloon and man, meeting of balloon and balloon.

It was suggested that what was admired about the balloon was finally this: that it was not limited, or defined. Sometimes a bulge, blister, or sub-section would carry all the way east to the river on its own initiative, in the manner of an army's movements on a map, as seen in a headquarters remote from the fighting. Then that part would be, as it were, thrown back again, or would withdraw into new dispositions; the next morning, that part would have made another sortie, or disappeared altogether. This ability of the balloon to shift its shape, to change, was very pleasing, especially to people whose lives were rather rigidly patterned, persons to whom change, although desired, was not available. The balloon, for the twenty-two days of its existence, offered the possibility, in its randomness, of mislocation of the self, in contradistinction to the grid of precise, rectangular pathways under our feet. The amount of specialized training currently needed, and the consequent desirability of long-term commitments, has been occasioned by the steadily growing importance of complex machinery, in virtually all kinds of operations; as this tendency increases, more and more people will turn, in bewildered inadequacy, to solutions for which the balloon may stand as a prototype, or "rough draft."

I met you under the balloon, on the occasion of

问气球是不是我的,我说是的。我说,那气球就是某种自发的自我暴露,这和你不在时我感到的不安以及性生活的丧失有关,而现在你去贝尔根的旅行既然已告结束,那么这也就不再需要和适用了。移动气球很容易,牵引车已把泄了气的气球拖走,现在它被贮放在弗吉尼亚州西部,等待着另一次不幸时刻的到来,或许,有时,我们相互发火的时候。

your return from Norway; you asked if it was mine; I said it was. The balloon, I said, is a spontaneous autobiographical disclosure, having to do with the unease I felt at your absence, and with sexual deprivation, but now that your visit to Bergen has been terminated, it is no longer necessary or appropriate. Removal of the balloon was easy; trailer trucks carried away the depleted fabric, which is now stored in West Virginia, awaiting some other time of unhappiness, sometime, perhaps, when we are angry with one another.

┌─ 讨　论 ─■

　　我们在讨论本章其他作品时,曾一再提问,那些背离现实主义传统的作品,是否使读者的想象力易于了解那些可能支配着作品内容的取舍原则。对于《气球》所写的内容,我们现在提出同样的问题。

　　小说的第一句,叙述者就说他"不能透露"纽约14号街上气球膨胀的确切地点。这种说法自会激发读者的好奇心。叙述者究竟出于何种考虑而不把地点交代清楚呢?从心理上的无能为力到国家安全都有可能,而读者总很自信,只要他知道叙述者为何保守秘密,他就有办法知道叙述者所讲述的究竟是怎样的世界,贯穿在作品中的究竟有哪几种意图,简言之,就是这篇小说究竟是什么意思。

　　叙述者始终没有给读者以任何真正令人满意的回答。他讲了关于气球出现时城市公众反应的各种情况,但是直到小说最后一段,叙述者依然没有回答(除了在小说中间部分他开玩笑似的、无关紧要地提出"气球的目的并不为娱乐孩子")他和气球的关系,他使气球膨胀的原因,或者他为什么要讲这件事的原因。小说最后一段解释说,气球是"某种自发的自我暴露,这和你不在时我感到的不安以及性生活的丧失有关"。这算是回答,但这不是读者所能理解的。即便可以理解,这也不能算是及时所做的解释,可以让读者按此而对叙述者本人和他讲的故事之间的关系形成某种概念。

　　读这篇小说,读者会渐渐感到,最好还是

In our discussions of other stories in this section we have repeatedly asked whether those stories that reject the conventions of realism make accessible to the reader's imagination the alternative principles that may govern their fictive worlds. We now ask this same question of the world created in "The Balloon".

In the story's first sentence the narrator asserts that he "cannot reveal" exactly where on Fourteenth Street in New York City the balloon was inflated. This assertion naturally stimulates the reader's curiosity. What considerations prevent the narrator from giving this information? The possibilities range from psychological incapacity to national security, and it is the reader's conviction that once he knows why the narrator withholds this information he will be on his way to knowing what the world of the narrator is like, what sorts of concerns will govern his presentation; in short, what the story is about.

The narrator never gives the reader a truly satisfactory answer. He offers all manner of information about the response of the city's populace to the presence of the balloon, but not until the last paragraph of the story (except teasingly and inconclusively, when observing in the middle of the story that "the purpose of the balloon was not to amuse children") does the narrator return to his own relation to the balloon, to his reasons for having it inflated, or for writing about it. The last paragraph of the story explains that the balloon is "a spontaneous autobiographical disclosure, having to do with the unease I felt at your absence, and with sexual deprivation." This is an answer, but it is not one the reader can understand. Neither is the explanation offered at a time when, even if it were

把一切关于叙述者贯穿于故事的主旨为何之类的问题——实际上也就是有关小说意义何在的问题——统统搁置一边。叙述者早就说过："称之为'形势',也即意味得到了某种解决或某种紧张状态的弛缓,那是错的,无所谓什么形势,不过是只气球……有形有体的东西,悬荡在那儿。"在小说的后面,叙述者又就意义问题点明:"气球……它随意地提供了自我迷失的可能,它与我们脚下精确无误、排成方格的线路图截然不同。"

关于小说《气球》的评论,都竭力想弄清楚小说所含有的预言性,这就像竭力想弄清楚气球本身一样,是徒劳无功的,而对于读者来说,合适的办法就是简简单单地也让自己暂时"迷失"一下,参与到公民们的纷争中去而不带任何先入的概念,也就是说不过问自己"迷失"的原因,也不过问自己为何要读这篇小说。人们曾一再就这篇小说争论说,这篇小说中的叙述者讲故事的动机很成问题。而如果叙述者的动机一旦弄清楚,读者就有了概念,就不仅能认识叙述者为何要讲这个故事的原因而且还能进而明了他(读者)为何要读这篇小说的目的,至少在叙述者看来他是应该读的。读者也不会感到自己随意地卷入故事中去了。

一篇小说也就是一个严密的体系,在小说严密的体系中,任何要素都不可避免地要和其他所有的要素发生联系。这种联系或许是无意义的,或许是变幻不定的,但它总是存在,而且在某种情况下对整体平衡起到作用。我们现在讨论的这篇作品,叙述者讲故事的原因不清楚。弄得清楚的是他和他所讲的故事没有一点儿有意义的联系。他使气球膨胀,其原因呢,最后表明为和他所讲的那些事件毫无关系,而当那个因其离开而引起气球膨胀的"你"从一次去挪威的莫名其妙的旅行中回来时,叙述者接着的行动是使气球泄了气(接着又运到弗吉尼亚西部去了)。叙述者本人虽是气球的所有者,但与小说所叙述的情节丝毫没有关

comprehensible, the reader could make use of it in developing a sense of the narrator's relation to the story he tells.

Rather, as he reads, the reader gradually comes to feel that all questions about the principles of narrative governing the story, in fact all questions about the story's meaning, are best put to one side. The narrator has said as much early on: "It is wrong to speak of 'situations,' implying sets of circumstances leading to some resolution, some escape of tension; there were no situations, simply the balloon... concrete particular, hanging there." Later in the story the narrator returns to the question of meaning, remarking that "the balloon... offered the possibility, in its randomness, of mislocation of the self, in contradistinction to the grid of precise, rectangular pathways under our feet."

The argument of "The Balloon" is thus that all efforts to understand the story's predication, like all efforts to understand the balloon itself, are wrongheaded, and that the proper course for the reader is simply to "mislocate" his self for a while, to enter into the experience of the story merely for what it is, participating in the differing reactions of the citizenry, without any overarching sense of the reason for this "mislocation," that is, of why he is reading the story. It is consistent with the story's argument that the narrator's motivations in telling the story be problematic. Were these to be clear, the reader would have a sense not only of why the narrator is telling the story but inferentially of why he (the reader), at least from the narrator's point of view, should be reading it. The reader would lose his sense of the "randomness" of his involvement in the story.

In a closed system, which every fiction is, all elements are inevitably related to all other elements. The relation may be insignificant, or shifting, but it exists, and in some fashion contributes to the dynamic of the whole. In the present instance, the narrator's reasons for telling the story are unclear. What does become clear is that he has no significant relation to the story he tells. He has the balloon inflated for reasons that, when finally revealed, are seen to have nothing to do with the events he describes, and his next action is

系,因为小说中的情节所表现的根本不是所有权的问题,只是讲公民们在气球出现时的种种反应。叙述者讲故事的原因既不明确,而他与所述情节又只有间接关系,这两种情况致使读者把注意力移开,不再注意讲故事的原因,而着眼于故事本身的内容。

可以说,《气球》所记述的是关于纽约市民对发生在他们周围的令人费解而又无可置疑的事实——气球的出现——所做出的种种反应。他们的反应如何又取决于气球给他们的满足如何、对他们来说意义如何以及和他们的关系如何,而这一切都是任意的和个人的。确切地说,读者对这篇小说的反应也是如此。他一节一节往下看,从中感到满足,或发现意义,或者在小说的各个不同时刻之间找到某种联系,而这些在小说中又是任意给予的,也正为此,叙述者令人莫名其妙地决定使用第一人称讲述故事。

我们似乎看到,这篇小说在创作意图上有某种前后矛盾。叙述者说,那气球——它在小说中也许始终保持在同一水平上——应该仅仅被看做是某种令人愉快的和时间短暂的"自我迷失"的机遇,但这种说法和最后一节里的议论以及那种旨在让读者了解他讲故事的动机的说明自相矛盾。他称自己的故事是"某种自发的自我暴露",还有他后来对故事中的"你"所讲的话,这些给了读者更多的表示异议的权利。读者也许会这样说:"这篇小说没有给我关于叙述者、关于他的人格和意愿、关于他所活动其间的世界以及与他共处的人们的充分材料。此外,故事从头到尾又是和叙述者本人毫不相干的。"

没有一个带有现实主义倾向的读者会感到我们的评论具有吸引力。他倒会觉得,这篇小说是通过扰乱读者关于形式和内容的概念才得以荒谬地凑合成篇的,而关于叙述者讲故

to have the balloon deflated(and subsequently trucked to West Virginia) when the "you" whose absence prompted the balloon's inflation returns from an unexplained trip to Norway. The narrator, although he is the owner of the balloon, has nothing to do with the reported action of the story, which is concerned not with the balloon's ownership but with the reactions of the citizenry to the balloon's presence. This combination of the narrator's problematic reasons for telling the story and his peripheral relation to the actions described causes the reader to shift his attention from why the story is being told to what the story is telling.

It can be argued that "The Balloon" is a chronicle of how New Yorkers respond to an inexplicable but unquestionable fact of their environment, the presence of the balloon. How they respond is to find in the balloon gratifications and meanings and relations that are arbitrary and personal. The reader responds to the story in exactly the same fashion. He moves from paragraph to paragraph, finding gratifications and meanings in and relations among the story's individual moments, all of this within the story's arbitrary given, which is the narrator's inexplicable resolve to tell the story in the first place.

This seems to bring us to an inconsistency in the story's intentions. The narrator's assertion that the balloon, which may be taken at one level to represent the story, should be seen as nothing more than a pleasant and temporary opportunity for "mislocation of the self" is contradicted by the remarks of the last paragraph and by the introductory invitation to the reader to consider the question of the narrator's motivations. His calling the story "a spontaneous autobiographical disclosure" and his subsequent remarks to the story's "you" give further legitimacy to the reader's raising objections. These might be phrased as follows: "This story gives me inadequate information about the narrator, about his personality and concerns, about the world in which he moves and the people who share it with him. Besides, between the first and last paragraphs the story has nothing to do with the narrator."

No reader with a realistic bias would find this argument persuasive. He would, rather, feel that it is the story's erosion of the reader's sense of relation between form and content that, paradoxically, gives the story unity,

事时的个人原因的牵强附会的提示是不合理的,是蒙骗读者,旨在使读者对小说的性质产生虚幻的期待感。但是一个不带有这种倾向的读者也许会承认这样的联系,虽然从心理上讲,要承认这一点是玄乎的或者是困难的。这样的读者在接受蒙骗时——当然,是暂时的——会因为能玩弄"现实"而感到满足。

然而,就是带有现实主义倾向的读者也会渐渐认可,结构松散的叙事法并未使小说的功效大大降低。譬如,我们可以指出,这篇小说反映了群众心理(叙述者指明,如果在气球上标明"实验室试验证明",那么气球的出现决不会引起骚动),同时,小说还生动地挪揄了城市知识阶层对气球所做出的一系列反应中的所谓"评判"的陈腐和晦涩。我们还可以就此指出,就是这种对自以为是而沾沾自喜态度的描写,作为小说固有的外在目的,它也可以使我们有可能认识到小说所含有的模仿讽刺性的成分。

简言之,这篇小说的意义就在于它无意义。它徒有其表而貌似有义。按照我们通常要求小说(生活也如此)应当合乎逻辑和道德的观点来看,这篇小说似乎开了一个严肃的玩笑。

and that the teasingly obscure suggestions about the narrator's private reasons for telling the story unjustifiably mislead the reader, creating a false expectation about the nature of the story. But a reader without such a bias might accept the relationships, however fantastic or difficult to locate on a psychological ground. Such a reader gets satisfaction in toying with "reality" in accepting deceptions—provisionally, of course.

Nevertheless, even a reader with a realistic bias might be led to admit that this incoherence of narrative does not diminish many of the story's virtues. We can point, for example, to the story's telling perceptions about mass psychology (had the balloon been labeled "laboratory tests prove," the narrator remarks, its presence would have caused no disturbance) as well as to the accurate parody of the clichés and jargon of "critical opinion" in its list of reactions to the balloon by the city's intelligentsia. We can point, that is, to just such individual congruences within a pleasurable randomness as the story's proper formal intention lead us to expect at the same time realizing the element of satiric parody.

To state the whole matter more succinctly, we may say that the meaning of the story is that it has no meaning. It has only the shape and pretense of meaning. It is a serious joke, as it were, on our normal demand that fiction (and life) be logically and ethically fulfilled.

思考题 ▪

1. 除了气球本身之外,《气球》中的世界和日常世界非常相似,为什么说这对于达到小说的目的是必需的? 试将《气球》和《鹰溪桥上》加以比较。
2. 在对气球的所谓"评判"的那些引文里,叙述者引出了"啪嗒"。这样做可信吗?这能不能看做滑稽演员敲板的声音而叙述者在这里做了绝妙的讽刺?如果是这样,那么这种技巧的更换起了什么作用?请注意评判引文中各行出现时的位置。

1. With the exception of the balloon itself, the world of "The Balloon" seems very much like the everyday world. Why is this necessary for the purposes of the story? Contrast "The Balloon" with "An Occurrence at Owl Creek Bridge".
2. Among the quotations of "critical opinion" of the balloon, the narrator lists "munching." Is this listing credible? Can it be seen as a sort of slapstick treatment of reactions that to this point the narrator has satirized more subtly? If so, what function is served by this change in technique? Keep in mind where in the list of opinions the word appears.

3. 当人们利用气球作为议题在一起进行探讨时,他们说的话都有点儿"故作风雅",这种对话为什么可信?

4. 能不能说,类似这样的小说——就是别出心裁地用某种貌似在讲有意义事物的方法讲述无意义事物——其实是要写多少篇就有多少篇? 若是,这样的小说你又乐意读几篇呢?

（刘文荣 译）

3. When people use the balloon as a reference point in making plans to meet, their speech sounds rather "arty." What makes this dialogue credible?

4. Can it be argued that there is no end to the number, and case, of such stories as this — stories that proclaim meaninglessness through an ingenuity of seeming to proclaim meaningfulness? If so, how many such stories do you yearn to read?

小说与人生经验
Fiction and Human Experience

真正的读者最后所得到的就是小说中的某种幻象，要得到幻象还有赖于心灵的自由活动，有赖于放松心灵的束缚，这样才能由此及彼地进行自由联想。

三篇小说的成因

当我们阅读一篇小说时,我们便从日常现实生活领域转入一个想象的生活领域。但是,那个想象的生活领域又是由某个作家根据他个人的现实生活领域创造出来的。因此,这里就涉及到了三个生活领域:我们的实际生活领域、作家的实际生活领域和作家为我们创造的那个生活领域。作家创造的那个生活领域,就是我们打算加以欣赏并从中得到享受的领域。但是,有时,我们并不能对作家创造的那个领域加以充分的领会,除非我们考虑到和它有关的另外两个领域,即作家自身的生活领域以及我们自己的生活领域。

一篇小说,只要是好的小说,就不仅仅是由词句和事件组合而成的小玩意儿,也不仅仅是一种作家所惯用的,为取乐他人、从而赚取一点稿费的漂亮诡计。它是一种尝试。不论这种尝试多么谨慎而有节制,但它力图寻求生活经历的意义,力图理解各种事物是怎样意味深长地相互联系在一起的。因此,看一看下面三位作家就他们的作品的成因所谈到的种种情况,对我们更充分地了解小说和进一步地鉴赏小说是很有裨益的。如果说,他们所谈到的情况向我们表明,每一篇单独的作品都无例外地来自于作家本人的生活领域,那么,我们也将会进一步地了解,小说中的想象的生活领域总是和实际生活领域联系着的,其中也包括我们个人的独特的生活领域——不管这种生活是什么样子。因为说到底,我们的想象力所勾勒出来的东西并不是凭空杜撰出来的东西,而是现实生活的一种投影,一种重新组合的图景。

How Three Stories Came to Be Written

When we read a piece of fiction, we move from the world where we, as people, live, into a world of imagination. But that world of imagination has been created by a writer out of the actual world in which he, as a person, lives. So there are three worlds involved here, our actual world, the writer's actual world, and the world he has created for us. The world that the writer has created is what we want to savor and enjoy, but sometimes we cannot properly appreciate it unless we comprehend its relevance to the other two worlds, the writers' world and our world.

A story, if it is a good story, is more than a little mechanical contrivance of words and events, more than a clever trick the writer has learned to do to amuse others or make an honest penny. It is an attempt, however modest and limited, to make sense of experience, to understand how things hang meaningfully together. Therefore, in our attempt to read fiction more fully and enjoy it more deeply, it may be of use to see what three writers have to say of the origins of their stories. If what they have to say can suggest to us how the individual story grew out of the personal world of the writer, then we can see more clearly how the created world of fiction relates to the world of actuality, including our own particular personal one, whatever that may be. For in the end, what our imagination craves is not a flight from actuality, but an illumination of it, a new vision of it.

诚如三位作家自己所指明的那样,他们想要告诉我们的无非是这样一件事,就是怎样写作一篇短篇小说。作家,即使是比较优秀的作家也不例外,都对章法或者模式一概不感兴趣,这就如尤多拉·韦尔蒂所说:"每一篇小说都应该开拓新的境界,提出新的课题。"由此看来,重要的问题永远是:"这篇小说是怎样写成的?"——或者,为适合本书读者需要,改一下问题:"这篇小说该怎样欣赏?"

凡严肃的作家,都把自己的每一篇作品看作是一种探索过程,即某种或明或暗地植根于作家自身生活的重要经验,而这种经验又不可能不表现出来并赋有某种意义。这也就是说,每一篇作品都表现为作家在寻求生活意义时所做出的一种努力。弄清楚这一点,我们就能进一步充分发挥自己的想象力,从而更深入到小说所创造的生活领域中去,因为很明显的是,作家在创作小说时所做的努力和我们在日常生活中为寻求生活意义而做的努力是并行不悖的。由此言之,只要我们带着这样的认识进入小说的领域,我们就会明确地看到,小说所创造的生活领域本质上是和我们每个人自身的日常生活领域密切相关的。

我们虽然在下文里并不过多地涉及技巧问题,但是我们要认识到,所有作家都认为小说的技巧问题是存在的,也就是说,存在着诸如阐述和结局是否是情节的组成部分之类的问题。大多数作家肯定会承认,对小说进行分析性研究是一项有价值的工作,可以导致对小说的充分理解。他们也会进一步承认,在分析过程中使用某些多少具有固定含义的术语是完全必要的。但是,所有的作家同时都会强调,分析过程和创作过程是截然不同的——关于这一点,我们在本书里是时常给予充分注意的。

在分析过程中,我们的工作在于把小说分解成几个组成部分——情节、主题、人物、阐述及气氛环境等等。在创作过程中,作家的工作

As their comments indicate, the last thing any of our three writers had in mind to tell us is "How to Write a Short Story." Writers, even moderately good writers anyway, are not concerned with rules and formulas as such. As Eudora Welty says, "Each story is going to open up a different prospect and pose a new problem," and the important question is always "How do I write *this* story?"—or to adjust the question to the needs of the reader of this book: "How do I read *this* story?"

Every serious writer regards each of his stories as a process of discovery: there is a vital experience with roots, more or less obscure, in his own experience that has to be brought into clarity and full meaning. Thus every story represents the author's effort to make sense of his world. By realizing this, we free our own imaginations to enter more fully the created world of fiction. For it becomes plain that the writer's effort to write his story is closely parallel to our effort to make sense of our own process of daily living. And if we enter the world of fiction with this realization, we can also see how the created world of fiction fundamentally relates to our own personal, day-to-day worlds.

Although none of the following accounts makes much reference to technical questions, all writers, we may be sure, would admit the fact that there are technical problems, that such things as exposition and denouement are parts of plot, and so on. Most of them would probably concede that the analytic study of fiction is a worthwhile endeavor and may lead to a fuller understanding of fiction, and would concede further that for such a process we need to use certain technical terms, with more or less fixed meanings. But all of them would emphasize the difference between the analytic process, with which we have been so often concerned in this book, and the creative process.

The analytic process is concerned with breaking fiction down into the component parts—plot, theme, character, exposition, atmosphere, and so on. The creative process is

在于同时表现多种事物。不过,我们可以补充说,在一般情况下,同时表现出来的东西并不就是批评分析所区分出来的同类要素。作家显然不会说:"我要用这个情节来表现这种主题",或者,"用那种环境来表现那种人物",或者诸如此类的话。因为说到底,他并不仅仅把各种事物"同时"表现出来就算了,他还要致力于得到像尤多拉·韦尔蒂所说的那种"幻象"——一种在某个生活领域里的人们以有意义的方式生活和行动的幻象,而这种幻象,由于小说的有血有肉的、具体形象的描绘,又被我们认为是真实可信的。不过,这种幻象最终还得具有实体性,也就是说,别人是否能分享这种幻象,而这一点事实上也就决定了一篇小说的成败。

为了分享作家的幻象,读者就得进行分析,就得把小说分解成几个组成部分。当然,真正的读者是会把分解开来的东西重新组合起来的,甚至会尽量忘记自己曾经对小说进行过分析,因为分析的目的是为了更好地理解小说,而当各部分重新组合在一起时,它们又形成为"幻象"。真正的读者最后所得到的也就是某种"幻象"。

要得到幻象还有赖于心灵的自由活动,有赖于放松心灵的束缚,这样才能由此及彼地进行自由联想。这种联想从表面上看似乎毫无规律可循,但归根结底,它是一种无规律运动中的规律活动。这里有其逻辑性,而意义也由此展现出来,或者,用另一种方式来说就是,当逻辑性和意义在小说的发展过程中越显明确,同时,幻象由于其不断的呈现,也就越有助于表现它们并加强它们。

在小说的五个组成部分中——即使有一千个也不妨——来到作家头脑里并起作用的可能只有一种——只有一种才帮助他勾勒出逻辑性和意义的大致轮廓。因此,当小说的初步设想出现在他头脑里时,不管这种设想起源于什么原因,是回忆、想象或者外界的暗示都

concerned with bringing things together; but we may add that, in general, *what it brings together is not even the same kind of elements that critical analysis distinguishes*. The writer does not say, "I shall put this plot with that theme," or this character with that atmosphere, or anything of the sort. He is not, in the end, trying to put things "together" at all. He is trying to attain to what Eudora Welty calls a "vision"—a vision of people alive and moving in a meaningful way in a certain world that we recognize as real and yet a world dominated by a certain feeling characteristic of the story. It is, too, a vision that must find its substance, finally, in words if it is to be shared with others and be, in fact, a story.

To share the writer's vision, the reader concerns himself with analysis, with breaking fiction into its component parts; but the good reader, of course, puts them back together again, reassembles them and even tries to forget that he ever thought analytically about them. For the analysis is for the sake of better understanding, so that when the parts once more come together, they form the "vision." The good reader ultimately attains to a sort of "vision" too.

Attaining to the vision depends on some free movement of mind, on letting the mind go loose, so that one thing leads to another, at random as it were. But this kind of association has, in the end, to be a responsible kind of irresponsibility. Logic has to develop in it, and meaning from it; or, to state the matter another way, as logic and meaning come clearer in the process, the vision will, in its subsequent stages, more and more manifest them and develop them.

Of five things, or a thousand, that come into the writer's head, only one may be useful—only one may ratch on to the emerging line of logic and meaning. Therefore, as the items come into his head, from whatever source, memory or imagination or outside suggestion, the writer's power of veto is constantly being exercised. In exercising his veto

不妨,作家始终具有否决的能力。作家在使用其否决权时,很可能他是理智的、清醒的,他会充分发挥理智作用以抵制某一部分,或者他会从骨子里感觉到某一部分不对头,于是就加以抛弃。一般说来,当逻辑性和意义在小说展开时显得越来越明确之际,作家也就越来越清楚地意识到自己的否决权。但是,他有时也可能会自己愚弄了自己。他会认为自己已经把握了逻辑性和意义,但到后来,他又时时发现,另一种逻辑性和另一种意义在另一种程度上发展着。譬如说吧,我们知道在某些名篇小说里,作家就曾中途改变了他对某个人物的基本看法,他甚至把一段对话从这个人物嘴里移到了另一个人物的嘴里,或者插进了一段情节。照例说来,作者为了小说的"感情",需要做什么事情或者需要在什么地方说到这件事情,应该是完全意识到的,但是,他很可能直到小说临近结束时,还不知道该由哪个人物来做或者说这件事情。

以上的简短讨论,如果说是对创作过程的适当的说明的话。那么当谈到小说的技巧问题以及我们在分析小说的种种意图时,又会遇到些什么麻烦呢?什么也不会遇到。对于小说本身来说,它自己才是至关重要的。小说存在于自身之中,有它自己的结构。至于作家是否把这种结构有意识地"勾画"出来,那是无关紧要的。正是因为意识到了技巧问题,一个作家在他的创作过程中才希望能把种种技巧上的考虑全盘地包容在他的整个思想和感情过程中。在足球场上,一个运动员接过队友传来的球,同时他又看到对方三个后卫冲过来,这时他是不会停下来思考自己是否会越位的。如果他停下来左右望一下的话,那么他很可能会被送进医院而比分也将糟糕透顶。运动员就是需要不停地运动,至于规则,应该是整个儿地渗透在他的中枢神经中并在那儿起作用的。对于作家来说,同样如此,他需要把技巧融合在自身之中并和小说的其他方面有机地

the writer may be very critical and conscious, and may argue out with himself the reasons for rejecting a thing; or he may simply feel in his bones that something is wrong, and chuck it. Usually, as the logic and meaning in the developing story are discovered the writer grows surer and surer in his veto. Sometimes, however, he may have fooled himself. He may think he knows the logic and knows the meaning, and then finds that all the time, at another level, there has been developing another logic and another meaning. We know, for instance, that in certain famous pieces of fiction, the writer had, in the very middle of the process, changed his whole conception of, say, a character, even switching a piece of dialogue from one person to another, or transferring an action. The writer might, for example, be aware that the "feel" of the story demanded such a thing to be done or said at a certain point, and yet might not know until late in the process of composition just which character should say or do the thing.

If this discussion, for all its brevity, is a fair account of the creative process, then what becomes of our worry about technical matters and our attempts at analysis? Nothing becomes of them. They remain important for the story itself. The story exists in itself and has its own architecture, no matter whether the author was consciously "working" it out or not. As for the awareness of technical matters, a writer may hope in his business of composition that the technical considerations will be completely absorbed into his whole way of thinking and feeling. When on the football field a man takes a pass and sees three tacklers coming, he doesn't stop and review the fundamentals of broken field running. If he does stop to make the review, he is very apt to be in the hospital and the score is apt to look very bad. The player wants to be in motion, with the fundamentals safely stowed away in his nerve centers, where they belong. So with the writer; he wants the technique absorbed into himself, and deeply related to all the other considerations of his

联系在一起。技巧服从了总的原则就能全部彻底地融合在作家的个性里，所以我们时常看到，优秀的作家无论在遣词造句还是在谋篇布局方面都很少显露出技巧的痕迹或者某种特殊的方式。我们认为，个人的气质倾向就是风格的"标记"。

那么，一个作家又是如何融合他的技巧的呢？有人可能是从训练和错误中本能地学会的。有人可能是在训练和错误中有意识地想到的。有人可能是通过琢磨其他作家的作品并希望从这种探讨中受到影响以改变自己无意识创作过程时逐渐培养而成的。舍此，没有任何其他可能性了。

毫无疑问，能彻底地将技巧问题融合在创作过程中，这对于作家来说是一种理想的境界。但是，一个作家不可能一成不变，即使在某种理想境界中也是如此，因为，当情况不妙时，他很可能不得不停下来并完全有意识地思考技巧问题。他可能不得不这样自问："现在我是不是要把这段阐述放进作品里去呢？"或者："我是不是要把这段关于房间的描写重新改写一遍，因为在我的小说里环境总不能老是不变呀？"或者："这样的对比是不是有效果？"他不知道自己为什么要这样想。他甚至不会想到自己为什么要这样想。但是，他不得不有意识地去做出某种决定。而如果他在此闭上眼睛或者莽撞的话，那他很快就会领悟到，他实际上是在冒险。

这里撰文的三位作家中有一位，凯瑟琳·安·波特。她是作为一个娴于技巧的作家而成名的，但她一点儿也没有谈及技巧问题。反之，她却以极其诚挚的语调谈论着一篇小说的来源——那幽远而不可忘怀的童年时代的生活。另外两位作家，尤多拉·韦尔蒂和罗伯特·沃伦，虽然谈到了技巧问题，但这些也不是孤立地谈论的。

尤多拉·韦尔蒂告诉我们，她是怎样在心里长期酝酿着一篇小说，但她始终没能把它写

story. By the same general principle, technique can be so thoroughly absorbed into the personal manner of a writer that we so often find among good writers little individualities of technique, their special way of doing things, from the way of putting sentences together to the handling of exposition. We recognize the personal touch, the "signature" of style.

But how does a writer get his technique absorbed? One may learn instinctively from trial and error. One may think consciously about one's own process of trial and error. One may think about the work of other writers in the hope that this study will enter into one's own unconscious processes of creation and modify them. There is no other possible way.

No doubt the total absorption of technical considerations into the process of composition is the ideal situation for a writer. But a writer never lives very long, if ever, in an ideal situation, and so when the going gets rough he may very well have to stop and reflect quite consciously on technical questions. He may have to ask himself such questions as "Shall I put this piece of exposition in now?"—or "Shall I rewrite this passage describing the room because the atmosphere is not in keeping with my story?"—or "Will the very contrast be effective?" He may not argue the reasons. He may not even put the question into words. But he has to make a conscious decision. If it is merely shutting his eyes and taking a plunge, he has to be aware even of that and of the risk he is taking.

One of the writers presented here, Katherine Anne Porter does not speak of technical questions at all—yet she is famed as an accomplished technician. Instead, she is thinking, in a peculiarly fascinating way, of the deep, far-off origins in the world of childhood of a particular story. But the other two, Eudora Welty and Robert Penn Warren, do touch on technical questions—though not on such questions taken in isolation.

Eudora Welty tells us how she had a story in her head for a long time but couldn't

出来，直到她后来到了某个地方，那个地方，她思考着自己的小说，好像小说里的事情就发生在当地，环境也和当地一模一样，这样，小说才逐渐形成，最后自然成篇了。她的讨论给我们提供了一个很好的例证，说明我们技术性地称之为环境的那种东西，是和实际生活联系着的——因为这至少使一篇小说问世了。

在尤多拉·韦尔蒂对自己小说的讨论中，环境问题又使她考虑到另一个技巧问题：视角问题。她告诉我们，由于小说发生的地点变了，这就使她对自己应该如何讲述小说内容产生了新的想法。首先，她在小说里设置了一个旁观者，并通过这个旁观者对女主人公的注意，像一面镜子一样向我们反映女主人公的情况。其次，她还对整个作品应该具有怎样的格调有了新的想法——不过，这最好还是等我们读她的文章时看看她自己是怎么说的吧。

至于《春寒》，作者告诉我们，当他由于某种偶然的回忆，心中形成了小说的原型之后，他是怎样在形式问题上犹豫不决的，因为形式可以发展，可以作为某种提纲式的东西促使作者想及其他事物并进而使它们受到作者的有意识控制。他还说到，在他实际写小说结局之前很久，他心里就有了某种结局的格式，甚至已经明确了在结尾处应该发生哪些事情。这也就是说，当时还没有确定小说的具体内容之前，他已经有了某种小说结构的设想以及某种与此结构相符合的情感。

小说可以从任何事物得到启发，可以像凯瑟琳·安·波特那样从小时候在得克萨斯州的某个夏日里远远地听到死亡的惨叫而得到启发，可以从观察或者想象某个人物得到启发，可以从看到某种小事或者听到某种传说而得到启发，可以从某种好像是莫名其妙的不知来自何处但又时时想在具体事物上找到寄托的情感得到启发，可以从某个似乎会使人联想到这儿曾经发生过不寻常事情的地方得到启发，可以从某个历史事件得到启发，可以从家

get it to work until she happened to go to a certain place; then, when she thought of the story as happening in this place, with its strange atmosphere, the story came clear and could get itself written. Her discussion provides a very nice instance of how that quality that we technically call atmosphere is related to the way in which at least one story came into being.

In Miss Welty's discussion of her story, the question of atmosphere leads her to another technical consideration: point of view. The change of scene for the story leads, she tells us, to a new conception of how the story should be told. First, it led to putting a stranger into the story to look at the heroine, to give a kind of mirror for our knowledge of her. Second, it led to a new conception of how the whole story should be looked at—but that had best be left to the author's own words when we come to her discussion.

As for "Blackberry Winter", the writer tells us how, after the story had begun in certain casual recollections, he stumbled on a pattern that could be developed, that could be used as a kind of guideline in thinking about the other things that subsequently came into consciousness. He also says that he had a kind of pattern for the denouement long before he got to the actual writing of the end, or even knew what would happen there. That is, he had some sense of the structure of the story at that point, and a feeling associated with the structure, before he had a precise content.

A story may start from anything, from the death cry heard distantly by Katherine Anne Porter on a summer day, when she was a child in Texas, from a character observed or imagined, from an episode seen or an anecdote heard, from a feeling that seems to come from nowhere and is seeking an objective mooring in actuality, from the atmosphere of a place that seems to yearn for some special thing to happen there, from a historical event, from a

庭生活中的爱憎得到启发,可以从某个观念得到启发,或者可以从某种道德信念得到启发。小说可以从任何事物发源,只要这些事物能激发人的想象力从而去完成小说的特殊使命,即把事物有机地联系起来并从中生发出某种意义来——不,不仅仅是联系起来就够了,而是要创造一个世界,在这个世界里,各种事物相互自然依存而其中又富有意义。(刘文荣 译)

family affection or hatred, from an idea, or from a moral conviction. It may stem from anything that will start the imagination on its characteristic job of putting things concretely together in a movement toward meaning—no, not putting them together, but creating a world in which they can grow naturally together in a movement toward meaning.

034. 没有你的位置，我的爱

（美）尤多拉·韦尔蒂 著　　刘文荣 译

034. No Place for You, My Love

by Eudora Welty

他们俩彼此是陌生人，对这个地方，两人也颇为陌生，现在他们却肩并肩地坐在午餐会上——一种随随便便凑合起来的聚会，男女与会者就在会上凭一面之缘相互认识并成为朋友。时间是夏日里的某个星期天——午后的几小时，这在新奥尔良正是逍遥的好时光。

他看着她那毫无表情但又很漂亮的小脸蛋，心想，这是个跟人胡来的女人。这是个荒唐古怪的聚会，总使人有种压抑感，转而又叫人疑神疑鬼。

十有八九，是和一个有妇之夫，他猜想，闪电般地勾搭上了——他自己早已结了婚——然后又觉得无聊了。这样想着，他看见她坐在那儿，头上戴着那顶帽子，手托着面颊，呆望着餐桌上的近在眼前的花束，觉得很好奇。

他不喜欢她那顶帽子，甚至不及他喜欢热带的花。这顶帽子对她很不合适，这个来自东部的生意人想，虽然他对女人的衣饰从来不感兴趣，没法鉴赏它们，因为他一想到不合传统的东西就火冒三丈。

一切都是冲着我的，她想，人们就这样认为，只要他们看着我，就可以爱我或者恨我了。人们相互了解感情总习惯于用那种陈腐的、稳妥的、慢吞吞的方式，这种阴阳怪气的方式就算是最好的吧，也应该知趣而滚蛋——它和我们有什么关系？我想，像我这样在恋爱中的人，就应该直截了当地了解每个人的秘密。

从她的神情看来，他断定，她那困惑迷惘肯定是有缘由的——不管怎么说，至少现在是这样。毫无疑问，她的这种心情只有参加各种聚会才能得到排遣。然而，也只有她那困惑的神情才使他觉得是这聚会上

THEY were strangers to each other, both fairly well strangers to the place, now seated side by side at luncheon—a party combined in a free-and-easy way when the friends he and she were with recognized each other across Galatoire's. The time was a Sunday in summer—those hours of afternoon that seem Time Out in New Orleans.

The moment he saw her little blunt, fair face, he thought that here was a woman who was having an affair. It was one of those odd meetings when such an impact is felt that it has to be translated at once into some sort of speculation.

With a married man, most likely, he supposed, slipping quickly into a groove—he was long married—and feeling more conventional, then, in his curiosity as she sat there, leaning her cheek on her hand, looking no further before her than the flowers on the table, and wearing that hat.

He did not like her hat, any more than he liked tropical flowers. It was the wrong hat for her, thought this Eastern businessman who had no interest whatever in women's clothes and no eye for them; he thought the unaccustomed thing crossly.

It must stick out all over me, she thought, so people think they can love me or hate me just by looking at me. How did it leave us—the old, safe, slow way people used to know of learning how one another feels, and the privilege that went with it of shying away if it seemed best? People in love like me, I suppose, give away the short cuts to everybody's secrets.

Something, though, he decided, had been settled about her predicament—for the time being, anyway;

作者简介：尤多拉·韦尔蒂（Eudora Welty，1909—2001），美国小说家。1909 年 4 月 13 日生于密西西比州杰克逊，2001 年 7 月 23 日卒于同地。她的作品主要关注与她的出生地以及德尔塔乡村类似的小城镇。她的主要题材是人们关系的复杂性。短篇小说集《绿窗帘》（*A Curtain of Green*，1941）让她一举成名。其他短篇小说作品包括《大网》（*The Wide Net*，1943）、《金苹果》（*The Golden Apples*，1949）和《英尼斯法伦的新娘》（*The Bride of the Innisfallen*，1955）。她的长篇小说包括《德尔塔婚礼》（*Delta Wedding*，1946）、《庞德的心》（*The Ponder Heart*，1954）和《乐观者的女儿》（*The Optimist's Daughter*，1972）等。她的作品集幽默和心理敏锐于一身，使用的是地方色彩的语言。

最明确可辨的东西,是这餐厅里唯一可看到的暗影,因为周围的镜子和风扇是那样令人眼花缭乱,本地人的叽叽喳喳的谈话声是那样使人不得安宁。那暗影就在她的手指间,就在她张开的手和她的面颊之间,仿佛在赋予她的身体以永恒的魅力。过了一会儿,她忽然把手放了下来,但那秘密依然留在那儿——它已经照亮了她。从她那顶帽子底下,仿佛有一道强烈而刺眼的光照射出来,而且像餐桌中央的花束一样紧挨在人堆里。

他是不是把她想象得毫无廉耻,甚至确认她此刻也正急于想勾引谁呢?他很明白,他并没有这样想。他们俩同时想到的只是,他们,两个北方人,已经相互认识了。她朝墙上巨大的金钟瞟了一眼,微微一笑。他并未对她报以一笑。她的脸就如他在中西部人中间看熟的那种脸,有一种淳朴的意味,但又没有理由这样想,也许是这张脸好像老是在说"要讲实话"的缘故吧。这是一张端庄的、时时在留意别人的脸。她在这一大帮南方佬中间之所以能这样不同一般,也就是因为她有这张脸。他虽然对别人的年龄从不加以猜测,但他猜测了她的年龄:32 岁。他自己的年龄要比这大多了。

在人的种种感情中,故作姿态的冷淡大概是最容易吸引人的——大概是一切情感中最成功、最不可抗拒的暗示信号。冷淡也像其他情感一样,也能使两个人陶醉。"你好像不很饿。"他说。

风扇的扇翼在他们头上投下影子,他无意间朝镜子瞥了一眼,发现自己正像个恶棍似的在对着她微笑。他的嗓音又粗又响,足以使每个人惊异地扭过头来。听起来,他好像是在回答她刚向他提出的什么问题似的。别的女人都朝他看看。她们那种南方的表情——南方的假面具——仿佛在冷冰冰地宣称"人生嘛,就如梦",而就是这种貌似大彻大悟的表情会因为一顶帽子落在地上而转眼变成愤世嫉俗的不平之色,他真想离开这儿。他宁愿看到天真朴实的脸。

"我觉得这儿闷得逼人。"她说,声音里有那种俄亥俄人的率直。

"哦——我也觉得像在蒸笼里。"他回答。

他们俩互换了一个超脱而自尊的眼色。

"我有车,就停在路边。"当参加午餐会的人都站起来准备离开而人人都带着倦意想回家睡觉时,他对她说,"如果可能的话——你是不是愿意开车到南方

the parties to it were all still alive, no doubt. Nevertheless, her predicament was the only one he felt so sure of here, like the only recognizable shadow in that restaurant, where mirrors and fans were busy agitating the light, as the very local talk drawled across and agitated the peace. The shadow lay between her fingers, between her little square hand and her cheek, like something always best carried about the person. Then suddenly, as she took her hand down, the secret fact was still there—it lighted her. It was a bold and full light, shot up under the brim of that hat, as close to them all as the flowers in the center of the table.

Did he dream of making her disloyal to that hopelessness that he saw very well she'd been cultivating down here? He knew very well that he did not. What they amounted to was two Northerners keeping each other company. She glanced up at the big gold clock on the wall and smiled. He didn't smile back. She had that naïve face that he associated, for no good reason, with the Middle West—because it said "Show me," perhaps. It was a serious, now-watch-out-everybody face, which orphaned her entirely in the company of these Southerners. He guessed her age, as he could not guess theirs: thirty-two. He himself was further along.

Of all human moods, deliberate imperviousness may be the most quickly communicated—it may be the most successful, most fatal signal of all. And two people can indulge in imperviousness as well as in anything else. "You're not very hungry either," he said.

The blades of fan shadows came down over their two heads, as he saw inadvertently in the mirror, with himself smiling at her now like a villain. His remark sounded dominant and rude enough for everybody present to listen back a moment; it even sounded like an answer to a question she might have just asked him. The other women glanced at him. The Southern look—Southern mask—of life-is-a-dream irony, which could turn to pure challenge at the drop of a hat, he could wish well away. He liked naïveté better.

"I find the heat down here depressing," she said, with the heart of Ohio in her voice.

"Well—I'm in somewhat of a temper about it, too," he said.

They looked with grateful dignity at each other.

"I have a car here, just down the street," he said to her as the luncheon party was rising to leave, all the others wanting to get back to their houses and sleep. "If it's all right with—Have you ever driven down south of here?"

去兜兜？"

　　到了波蓬街上，在 7 月的烈日里，她仰起头问他：
"从新奥尔良再朝南？我不知道比这儿再南面的还有
什么地方。是不是可以一直朝南，朝南，没个底？"她
笑了，伸手整整那顶惹人讨厌的帽子，把它戴得很古
怪。那顶帽子样子既轻佻又引人注目，帽檐上有一圈
带子，带子垂下来，上面还有什么东西在闪闪发光或
者飘飘扬扬。

　　"我就是想让你知道知道。"

　　"哦——你去过那儿？"

　　"没有！"

　　他的声音传过歪斜的、狭窄的人行道又从对面墙
上反射回来。斑斑驳驳的、五颜六色的房子像野兽皮
似的满是花纹，又邋遢又猥琐，但又是热烘烘的，好像
一堵平地升起的墙在受到某种花一般的勃勃生气地
吹拂，而这时他们走到了停在那里的轿车旁边。

　　"那里总不至于怎么糟糕——我们去看看。"

　　"是啊，是啊，"她说，"应该去看看。"

　　这样，他们的举止显得亲切友好起来，他们钻进
轿车——一辆暗红色的福特牌，相当破旧的帆布车篷
可以折起，这时由于炎热的太阳而正撑开着。

　　"这是租来的，"他解释说，"我曾要求把车篷放
下。但他们说我疯了。"

　　"真不像话。"她说，又接着说，"不过，已经不那么
热了，没关系。"

　　住在新奥尔良的外地人都要离开当地而到远处
去兜兜，就像有什么魔力在支配他们似的。现在，他
们俩正急速地驶过狭窄的街道，驶过盛开着灰蒙蒙的
紫罗兰的懒洋洋的广场，驶过深棕色的尖塔和大雕
像，还有平台，平台上有抓着笼子栏杆就像在舞池里
一样能自在蹦跳的活泼的黑猴子——它们甚至还很
有名哩，他们驶过烘烤房，那些平房外面的台阶上挂
满了色彩鲜艳的硬邦邦的天鹅①。

　　他开着车，一面打开他新买的地图把手指按在上
面。那交叉路口标着"Arabi"，从这里起，他们的路就从
一团乱糟糟中间直伸出去。他把车驶上那条路，路口，
有个小黑人在一把黑阳伞下跨腿骑在一只箱子上，还
举起棕黑色的手懒洋洋地向他们告别，那箱子上用粉
笔写着："去晒太阳"。她看见他，也向他挥挥手。

---

　　① 指烤鸭。

Out on Bourbon Street, in the bath of July, she
asked at his shoulder, "South of New Orleans? I
didn't know there was any south to *here*. Does it just
go on and on?"She laughed, and adjusted the exasperating
hat to her head in a different way. It was more than frivolous, it was conspicuous, with some sort of glitter or flit-
ter tied in a band around the straw and hanging down.

　　"That's what I'm going to show you. "

　　"Oh—you've been there?"

　　"No!"

　　His voice rang out over the uneven, narrow sidewalk and dropped back from the walls. The flaked-off,
colored houses were spotted like the hides of beasts
faded and shy, and were hot as a wall of growth that
seemed to breathe flower-like down onto them as they
walked to the car parked there.

　　"It's just that it couldn't be any worse—
we'll see. "

　　"All right, then, "she said. "We will. "

　　So, their actions reduced to amiability, they settled into the car—a faded-red Ford convertible with a
rather threadbare canvas top, which had been standing
in the sun for all those lunch hours.

　　"It's rented, "he explained. "I asked to have the
top put down, and was told I'd lost my mind. "

　　"It's out of this world. *Degrading* heat, "she said
and added, "Doesn't matter. "

　　The stranger in New Orleans always sets out to
leave it as though following the clue in a maze. They
were threading through the narrow and one-way
streets, past the pale-violet bloom of tired squares, the
brown steeples and statues, the balcony with the live
and probably famous black monkey dipping along the
railing as over a ballroom floor, past the grillwork and
the lattice-work to all the iron swans painted flesh col-
or on the front steps of bungalows outlying.

　　Driving, he spread his new map and put his finger
down on it. At the intersection marked Arabi, where
their road led out of the tangle and he took it, a small
Negro seated beneath a black umbrella astride a box
chalked "Shou Shine" lifted his pink-and-black hand
and waved them languidly good-by. She didn't miss it,
and waved back.

　　Below New Orleans there was a raging of insects
from both sides of the concrete highway, not quite together, like the playing of separated marching bands.
The river and the levee were still on her side, waste
and jungle and some occasional settlements on his—
poor houses. Families bigger than housefuls thronged
the yards. His nodding, driving head would veer from

新奥尔良再朝南,沿着水泥公路的两侧,有许许多多多的小昆虫,它们并不是聚在一起的,而是像散兵线一样零乱地分散着。河流和港埠在她这一边,荒地和丛林以及一切不引人注意的居民点在他这一边——那些可怜巴巴的房子。家里人多得房子里住不下,都群居在外面的空地上。他开着车,头一点一点,又时不时地这边望望,那边望望,样子像是朝前看又像是朝下看。时间在过去,他们离新奥尔良越来越远,而沿路所见的姑娘也越来越黑,越来越年轻,她们点缀在屋边的棚廊里,乌黑发亮的头发高高地盘在头顶上,边沿参差不齐的芭蕉扇像蝴蝶一样地上下飞舞着。向他们车边飞奔而来的孩子几乎全是光屁股的。

她注视着路面。小龙虾时常从车轮前横穿过去,样子难看,鬼鬼祟祟的。

"真像老太婆回家。"她自言自语。

他指路边邮筒顶盖上放的一只长柄锅子,锅子里满是剪短的百日草,锅柄上缚着一块八小的牌子——它从车窗边掠了过去。

他们一路上几乎不说什么话。太阳西沉了。他们看见渔夫和别的什么人在忙着干一些本地特有的活,有些人脸色蜡黄,气喘吁吁,有的在步行,有的在驾车。他们看见马车、货车、用汽艇改装的货车、汽车、用汽艇改装的汽车——形形色色,迎面而过。虽然,当他们的车驶过时,总有什么东西吸引他们,但无论是他还是她都好像什么也没看见。几乎时常有人摊手摊脚躺在车兜里,两只脚伸到车外面——样子粗鲁的红脸汉子白天睡大觉,一边睡一边还晃晃。他们接着又看见一块公墓似的场地——死人的国度,没有一个活人。他解开领带和领口。车在烈日下急驶,迎面而来的风就像风扇里打出来似的吹在他脸上。荒地上长满草木和藤丛,好像是什么东西在受难,一再地受难。石铺的小路向两边伸展。时不时地,一条木板铺的路在青黄色的草丛里蜿蜒而消失。

"那儿就像舞池。"她指着说。

他回答她说:"你过奖了,我想。"

那儿有成千上万甚至成百万的蚊子和小虫——什么虫都有,而且还在不断增加。

一家人,大约八九个,正在那条路上摇摇摆摆地走着,方向和他们的车一致,身体擦在野棕榈的枝叶上。脚跟、肩膀、膝盖、胸脯、后脑勺、手肘、手,不是这儿就是那儿被绊住——像在玩什么游戏,各人有各人的动作。

side to side, looking and almost lowering. As time passed and the distance from New Orleans grew, girls ever darker and younger were disposing themselves over the porches and the porch steps, with jet-black hair pulled high, and ragged palm-leaf fans rising and falling like rafts of butterflies. The children running forth were nearly always naked ones.

She watched the road. Crayfish constantly crossed in front of the wheels, looking grim and bonneted, in a great hurry.

"How the Old Woman Got Home," she murmured to herself.

He pointed, as it flew by, at a saucepan full of cut zinnias which stood waiting on the open lid of a mailbox at the roadside, with a little note tied onto the handle.

They rode mostly in silence. The sun bore down. They met fishermen and other men bent on some local pursuits, some in sulphurcolored pants, walking and riding; met wagons, trucks, boats in trucks, autos, boats on top of autos——all coming to meet them, as though something of high moment were doing back where the car came from, and he and she were determined to miss it. There was nearly always a man lying with his shoes off in the bed of any truck otherwise empty——with the raw, red look of a man sleeping in the daytime, being jolted about as he slept. Then there was a sort of dead man's land, where nobody came. He loosened his collar and tie. By rushing through the heat at high speed, they brought themselves the effect of fans turned onto their cheeks. Clearing alternated with jungle and canebrake like something tried, tried again. Little shell roads led off on both sides; now and then a road of planks led into the yellow-green.

"Like a dance floor in there." She pointed.

He informed her, "In there's your oil, I think."

There were thousands, millions of mosquitoes and gnats——a universe of them, and on the increase.

A family of eight or nine people on foot strung along the road in the same direction the car was going, beating themselves with the wild palmettos. Heels, shoulders, knees, breasts, back of the heads, elbows, hands, were touched in turn——like some game, each playing it with himself.

He struck himself on the forehead, and increased their speed. (His wife would not be at her most charitable if he came bringing malaria home to the family.)

More and more crayfish and other shell creatures littered their path, scuttling or dragging. These little samples, little jokes of creation, persisted and sometimes

他拍拍自己的额头，加快了车速（要是他把疟疾带回家，他妻子是决不会大发慈悲的）。

越来越多的小龙虾和其他甲壳虫蜂拥在他们车前，熙熙攘攘，乱窜乱爬。这些小小的标本，造物主开的小小的玩笑，在挣扎求生，它们时时死去，而路越往前伸入，这些东西却越多。乌龟和甲鱼从沟壑边慢吞吞地爬上来。

那后面一带更加糟糕透顶——地面上藤蔓缠结，即使用子弹或者有超人的毅力也难以穿过，原始的泥淖里发出噗噗噗的阴森森的声响。

"醒醒。"她的北方朋友时不时用手肘轻轻推她。他们把车转到靠路边一点。车依然在快速行驶，他摊开了地图。

好像是太阳升错了地方，那河水正在泛泛发光。他们把车驶上河堤，在一条卵石路上开着。

"我们要不要从这儿穿过去？"他彬彬有礼地问。

他可能多年来一直在开车，所以还有多少路他们即能赶到码头，他算得很准。现在，他们滑下堤坝，正好赶在最后一分钟，也是可以挤上去的最后一辆车。在稀疏的柳树荫下，那艘小小的、看上去不像专门摆渡的船正在发动，哗啦啦地卷动着水波，就在这时，他把车熟练地开上了甲板。

"告诉他，要他开到舱盖上去！"几个橄榄色皮肤、黑眼睛的小伙子中的有一个大声喊。这些小伙子全穿着洁白的衬衫站在栏杆旁边，正相互拉拉扯扯在打趣——这是甲板上唯一可做的乐事。另一个小伙子开始注意她坐的那边的肮脏的车门。

他打开车门跨下车，在舷桥边站了一会儿，随即便爬上了狭窄的扶梯。她高高地站在他们的轿车的上方，在那道横桥上，这地方正好在船长房间的窗口和汽笛下面。

这时，船还没开动，只是摇摇晃晃——好像是载重过多开不动似的——她站在那里，看见下面像碟子似的甲板，看见满是铁锈的船身把微微起波的河面隔成了两半。

摆渡的人在船上走来走去，推推攘攘，一副少见多怪的样子，简直——简直是些没见过世面的蹩脚旅行者。他们在欢度假日。他们相互之间全都认识。啤酒从罐子里哗哗地倒出，打赌声震天价响，关于本地那些叫他们摸不着头脑的怪事也被他们用来打赌。

perished, the more of them the deeper down the road went. Terrapins and turtles came up steadily over the horizons of the ditches.

Back there in the margins were worse—crawling hides you could not penetrate with bullets or quite believe, grins that had come down from the primeval mud.

"Wake up." Her Northern nudge was very timely on his arm. They had veered toward the side of the road. Still driving fast, he spread his map.

Like a misplaced sunrise, the light of the river flowed up; they were mounting the levee on a little shell road.

"Shall we cross here?" he asked politely.

He might have been keeping track over years and miles of how long they could keep that tiny ferry waiting. Now skidding down the levee's flank, they were the last-minute car, the last possible car that could squeeze on. Under the sparse shade of one willow tree, the small, amateurish-looking boat slapped the water, as, expertly, he wedged on board.

"Tell him we put him on hub cap!" shouted one of the numerous olive-skinned, dark-eyed young boys standing dressed up in bright shirts at the railing, hugging each other with delight that that last straw was on board. Another boy drew his affectionate initials in the dust of the door on her side.

She opened the door and stepped out, and, after only a moment's standing at bay, started up a little iron stairway. She appeared above the car, on the tiny bridge beneath the captain's window and the whistle.

From there, while the boat still delayed in what seemed a trance—as if it were too full to attempt the start—she could see the panlike deck below, separated by its rusty rim from the tilting, polished water.

The passengers walking and jostling about there appeared oddly amateurish, too—too amateur travelers. They were having such a good time. They all knew each other. Beer was being passed around in cans, bets were being loudly settled and new bets made, about local and special subjects on which they all doted. One red-haired man in a burst of wildness even tried to give away his truckload of shrimp to a man on the other side of the boat—nearly all the trucks were full of shrimp—causing taunts and then protests of "They good! They good!" from the giver. The young boys leaned on each other thinking of what next, rolling their eyes absently.

A radio pricked the air behind her. Looking like a great tomcat just above her head, the captain was

有个红头发男子甚至心血来潮发疯似的想把自己车上的虾袋扔给船那边的人——几乎所有的车上都装满了虾——一边还辱骂着,而那边的人却还在"好哇、好哇"地大喊大叫。那些勾肩搭背的小伙子百无聊赖,在想什么新玩意儿,一个个骨碌碌地转着眼珠子。

一架收音机在她身后凑热闹。船长看上去就像一只大公猫,盘踞在她头的上方,此时正在思考着一则漂亮的窃车新闻。

最后,一声巨响腾空而起——汽笛响了。随着汽笛声,每一件东西都明显地晃动起来,每个人都在说着什么——真不止每个人。

人们开始没头没脑地走动,而她的帽子被风吹跑了。帽子旋转着落到了下面的甲板上,那儿,谢天谢地,他正好从轿车里钻出来,于是便拾了起来。而这时,每个人都仰起头来粗鲁地盯着她看,从手一直看到头。

那棵小柳树向后退去,树的影子也消失了。炎热的阳光像什么东西压在她头上。她握着面前发烫的栏杆。简直像乘在一台锅炉上。她双肩下垂,头发飞扬,一阵突然的强风把她的裙子掀了起来,她站在那儿,心想,下面这些人一定看得清清楚楚,不过她也希望这样。她放下手,让那背包荡在腰间,前前后后地一晃一晃——两只手,一只背包,三者同样苍白,好像不属于任何人,她脸上的皮肤已经麻木,也许.她在大喊大叫,但一点儿也不自知。她往下看去,只见他正站在自己下面,她看见他的黑影子,看见自己的帽子和他的黑头发。他的头发被风吹着显得特别长,飘扬着。他大概并不知道,在这儿有一种动物般强烈的炙热的欲望。她举目远眺,一股光的漩涡盘转而过,在那暗色的水波上它看上去就如一颗明亮的星星。

他终于拿着那顶失而复得的帽子上了扶梯。她接过帽子——无用的东西——把它按住自己的裙子。下面的人在议论,不过要比他们那种像探照灯光似的表情文雅一点。

"你猜得出那人是打哪儿来的,那个男的。"

"我打赌,是从拉斐特来的。"

"拉斐特? 你赌什么,嗯?"——人们都蜷缩在卡车的阴影里,蹲着,坐着,嘻嘻哈哈。

这时,他的影子盖住了她的半边身体。一股激流涌来,渡船一阵晃动。她的半边的手和臂不再感到阳光的直射,但她暗暗地希望能有更多的暗影遮住她的头。看来,爬到这高处并站在太阳底下是完全合乎自

digesting the news of a fine stolen automobile.

At last a tremendous explosion burst—the whistle. Everything shuddered in outline from the sound, everybody said something—everybody else.

They started with no perceptible motion, but her hat blew off. It went spiraling to the deck below, where he, thank heaven, sprang out of the car and picked it up. Everybody looked frankly up at her now, holding her hands to her head.

The little willow tree receded as its shade was taken away. The heat was like something falling on her head. She held the hot rail before her. It was like riding a stove. Her shoulders dropping, her hair flying, her skirt buffeted by the sudden strong wind, she stood there, thinking they all must see that with her entire self all she did was wait. Her set hands, with the bag that hung from her wrist and rocked back and forth—all three seemed objects bleaching there, belonging to no one; she could not feel a thing in the skin of her face; perhaps she was crying, and not knowing it. She could look down and see him just below her, his black shadow, her hat, and his black hair. His hair in the wind looked unreasonably long and rippling. Little did he know that from here it had a red undergleam like an animal's. When she looked up and outward, a vortex of light drove through and over the brown waves like a star in the water.

He did after all bring the retrieved hat up the stairs to her. She took it back—useless—and held it to her skirt. What they were saying below was more polite than their searchlight faces.

"Where you think he come from, that man?"

"I bet he come from Lafitte. "

"Lafitte? What you bet, eh?"—all crouched in the shade of trucks, squatting and laughing.

Now his shadow fell partly across her; the boat had jolted into some other strand of current. Her shaded arm and shaded hand felt pulled out from the blaze of light and water, and she hoped humbly for more shade for her head. It had seemed so natural to climb up and stand in the sun.

The boys had a surprise—an alligator on board. One of them pulled it by a chain around the deck, between the cars and trucks, like a toy—a hide that could walk. He thought, Well they had to catch one sometime. It's Sunday afternoon. So they have him on board now, riding him across the Mississippi River.... The playfulness of it beset everybody on the ferry. The hoarseness of the boat whistle, commenting briefly,

然的。

那群小伙子有了新鲜事——一只鳄鱼爬到了甲板上。其中一个小伙子用链条把它套住，在甲板上，在轿车和卡车之间，像拖什么玩具似的团团打转——像拖一张会走路的兽皮。他想，嗨！咱们有时还老想抓一只哩。现在是星期天下午。现在他们在甲板上遇到了鳄鱼，可以骑着它渡过密西西比河……这事挺有趣，摆渡的人都围了上去。渡船的汽笛呜呜呜呜叫，声音短促，好像在为这伙作乐的人助兴。

"谁想收养这鳄鱼？谁想要，啊？"两个小伙子仰着头大喊大叫。一个手臂晒得暗红的小伙子在左右闪避，以防鳄鱼咬他。

张口咬人，那该是多么惬意的乐事？禁止这样做，那又会带来怎样的恶果？结果不就是使向来威风凛凛的英雄在乡巴佬面前受屈辱吗？

他看见她正看着那鳄鱼，一点儿也不害怕。她和鳄鱼的距离远着呢，足有几英尺几英寸远。

也许，当他们这样在河上紧挨着站在一起，恍惚处身于海上，而觉得整个世界——那暗红色的世界，正陷落在他们脚下时，她对投在她身上的他的影子也抱着同样冷静的态度。船头在水面上冲出一条条大理石花纹似的波痕，而河水就在这大地的弯弯曲曲的裂缝中涨涌。太阳好像就在河水下面滚动。万物都变得只有在记忆中的那般大小，树木已连根拔起。而且在空中上下翻动，相互碰撞。

到达对岸时，他们觉得好像是乘着战车在竞技场上狮子的包围中兜了一圈。汽笛声震动了扶梯，他们走了下来。那些小伙子，看上去都很高大，一个个拿出五颜六色的梳子，把头发向后梳起，露出油光光的前额。他们刚在河水里洗过澡。

轿车和卡车，步行的摆渡者和鳄鱼——它像一个上学的孩子似的摇摇摆摆地走着——全都上了岸，鱼贯地走过杂草丛生的河堤。

可能是出于敬意，也可能是出于怜悯，她总觉得那鳄鱼的皮老使她情不自禁地回过头去看它。在我们心里，一切都是赤裸裸的（她听人这样说过）。

他们驶完那段石子路后，他听见她轻轻地叹了口气，看见她再次掉过草黄色的头去张望。现在，她坐在车上，草帽放在膝上。她的耳环很惹人注意。一种小小的金属圆圈，上面安块小小的灰钻石，在两块小小的空地——那微微有毛的面颊两边一摆一摆。

seemed part of the general appreciation.

"Who want to rassle him? Who want to, eh?"two boys cried, looking up. A boy with shrimp-colored arms capered from side to side, pretending to have been bitten.

What was there so hilarious about jaws that could bite? And what danger was there once in this repulsiveness—so that the last wordly evidence of some old heroic horror of the dragon had to be paraded in capture before the eyes of country clowns?

He noticed that she looked at the alligator without flinching at all. Her distance was set—the number of feet and inches between herself and it mattered to her.

Perhaps her measuring coolness was to him what his bodily shade was to her, while they stood pat up there riding the river, which felt like the sea and looked like the earth under them—full of the redbrown earth, charged with it. Ahead of the boat it was like an exposed vein of ore. The river seemed to swell in the vast middle with the curve of the earth. The sun rolled under them. As if in memory of the size of things, uprooted trees were drawn across their path, sawing at the air and tumbling one over the other.

When they reached the other side, they felt that they had been racing around an arena in their chariot, among lions. The whistle took and shook the stairs as they went down. The young boys, looking taller, had taken out colored combs and were combing their wet hair back in solemn pompadour above their radiant foreheads. They had been bathing in the river themselves not long before.

The cars and trucks, then the foot passengers and the alligator, waddling like a child to school, all disembarked and wound up the weed-sprung levee.

Both respectable and merciful, their hides, she thought, forcing herself to dwell on the alligator as she looked back. Deliver us all from the naked in heart. (As she had been told.)

When they regained their paved road, he heard her give a little sigh and saw her turn her straw-colored head to look back once more. Now that she rode with her hat in her lap, her earrings were conspicuous too. A little metal ball set with small pale stones danced beside each square, faintly downy cheek.

Had she felt a wish for someone else to be riding with them? He thought it was more likely that she would wish for her husband if she had one(his wife's voice) than for the lover in whom he believed. Whatever

她是不是希望另外有人和他们同车呢？他想，如果她有丈夫（他听见自己妻子的声音），那十有八九她是希望丈夫在身边的，而如果她有情人（他对此很相信），那就不一定希望在身边。无论人们怎样想，情况（如果不是舞台布景的话）总可以分为三个方面——总有另外一个人存在着。不了解或者不能了解那两者的人就是可怕的第三者。

他低头看看放在他们中间的地图，给手表上了发条，便把车开上了大路。下午4点，天空明亮得使人不敢相信。

在河的这边，大路和堤坝平行，就在堤坝的下方。大路上比其他地方更热，更逼人，也更呛人——这是运动的神经。虽然，旁边就是一条看不见的河，路面依然滚烫。死蛇横卧在混凝土上，好像路标——蜷起的，晒干的，就像马赛克镶嵌的图案，他们的轮胎掠过如同发条般的空隙。

不，热气正迎面而来——它就在前头。他们意识到热气在鼓动他们，它在白蒙蒙的大路上空波动，始终在他们前面不远的地方，像一件闪闪发亮的衣裙，青色和金色的、火红和蔚蓝的滚边就在风中飘动。

"撒拉可斯决不会有这种天气。"他说。

"多伦多也不会。"她回答，只觉得唇干舌燥。

他们这时已驶过一大片荒原，几乎没有发现什么稍能引人注意的城镇。什么东西下面都是水汪汪的。即使眼前出现一片丛林，那树木下面也只听见咕咕的水声。开阔地里，还有一些小船时而像爬行似的在漫无边际的田野和橡皮似的花木间一英寸一英寸地蠕动。

阳光使她头昏目眩，心里一阵惶恐，直想呕吐。这样下去，那问题及其问题的答案，那心里隐藏着的东西以及这些东西的表露，何时才能得到解决——那新的问题，以它自身的力量，始终在要求回答。这样坐在车里，能得到些什么——要付出些什么？

"我看，你走的这条路是不通的，"她轻松地说，"算了吧，到处是水。"

"好，暂停。"他说，一边把车蹅进一条小路，小路是用白色卵石铺的，很窄，向右伸展。

他们总算看见了一个牛栏，那儿，沟壑里盘生着藤蔓，藤蔓顶上开着紫红色的花，曲曲弯弯，伸进一块狭长的、绿油油的空地——一个庭院。两排像坟墓似的矮房子，中间有一条铺过的小路，房子粉刷得雪白，正趾高气扬地仰视着瀚漠无涯的天际。

people liked to think, situations(if not scenes) were u-sually threeway—there was somebody else always. The one who didn't—couldn't—understand the two made the formidable third.

He glanced down at the map flapping on the seat between them, up at his wristwatch, out at the road. Out there was the incredible brightness of four o'clock.

On this side of the river, the road ran beneath the brow of the levee and followed it. Here was a heat that ran deeper and brighter and more intense than all the rest—its nerve. The road grew one with the heat as it was one with the unseen river. Dead snakes stretched across the concrete like markers—inlaid mosaic bands, dry as feathers, which their tires licked at intervals that began to seem clocklike.

No, the heat faced them—it was ahead. They could see it waving at them, shaken in the air above the white of the road, always at a certain distance ahead, shimmering finely as a cloth, with running edges of green and gold, fire and azure.

"It's never anything like this in Syracuse," he said.

"Or in Toledo, either," she replied with dry lips.

They were driving through greater waste down here, through fewer and even more insignificant towns. There was water under everything. Even where a screen of jungle had been left to stand, splashes could be heard from under the trees. In the vast open, sometimes boats moved inch by inch through what appeared endless meadows of rubbery flowers.

Her eyes overcome with brightness and size, she felt a panic rise, as sudden as nausea. Just how far below questions and answers, concealment and revelation, they were running now—that was still a new question, with a power of its own, waiting. How dear—how costly—could this ride be?

"It looks to me like your road can't go much further," she remarked cheerfully. "Just over there, it's all water."

"Time out," he said, and with that he turned the car into a sudden road of white shells that rushed at them narrowly out of the left.

They bolted over a cattle guard, where some rayed and crested purple flowers burst out of the vines in the ditch, and rolled onto a long, narrow, green, mowed clearing: a churchyard. A paved track ran between two short rows of raised tombs, all neatly white-washed and now brilliant as faces against the

小路比车身宽不了几英寸。他慢慢地把车开到这两排坟墓中间，样子像在从事什么伟大的事业。墙上，在齐眼高的地方，懒洋洋地写着几个名字，简直像某个倦于谈话的人的眼睛。他们一阵喜欢又一阵失望，因为情形就像在西班牙似的令人摸不着头脑。在一些空地里，那儿开着一束束花，有百日草、夹竹桃，还有一种紫红色的花，全都生趣盎然，硕大无比，仿佛在对客人的光临表示欢迎。

他们到了另一边的一块空地上，那儿长满青草，眼前是一座青白色的教堂模样的屋子，周围有人工花坛，无花的猩猩木一直长到窗棂边上。不远处还有一所屋子，台阶上放着一条刚捕获的像婴儿一般大小的鮰鱼——一条浑身是须、是血的鱼。院子里的一根晒衣绳上，一件教士穿的黑大褂瘪塌塌地在齐人高的地方一飘一飘，就像晚上昏睡时发出的那种有节奏的，像女人一样柔和的呼吸，它使人隐约地想起一条无形的，但可以感觉到的河流。

他们熄了引擎，在虫豸的嗡嗡声里，靠在车窗上观望外面纷乱的景色——绿的、白的、黑的、红的，还有粉红的。

"你的夫人长得好看吗？"她问。他抬起右手，摊开手掌——像铁做的、木头的，不过是修剪过的。她抬起眼睛看看他的脸。他也看看她，那表情就像他的手一样。

他点燃一支烟。那半身像，那抬着右手的姿势，在烟雾中消失了。她笑笑，看着这种舞台动作，她倒认真起来。在这片墓地里，他感到痛苦。他们两人都没有冒险去提及她的丈夫——如果她有丈夫的话。

在教堂的立柱下面，有一只小船，那儿坚实的土地到了尽头，矮棕榈，那映入眼帘的水蓝色。忽然，从他们车后，阳光低低地照射过来。照在花草上。教士出来了，穿着睡衣，站在平台上对着轿车凝视了好一阵，好像很惊奇，现在是什么时候。他收起绳上的大褂，拎起台阶上的鱼，又退了过去。他接着要做的，是晚祈祷。

从两排坟墓间把车退出来后，他开着车在落日的晚霞里继续向南。他们追上一个老头，这老头正精神抖擞地和他们同向走着，孤零零一个人，穿着一件干净整洁的衬衫，衬衫上印着两棵棕榈树，树枝在他胸前伸展着。这件衬衫最好给一个大块头黑种女人穿，

vast flushed sky.

The track was the width of the car with a few inches to spare. He passed between the tombs slowly but in the manner of a feat. Names took their places on the walls slowly at a level with the eye, names as near as the eyes of a person stopping in conversation, and as far away in origin, and in all their music and dead longing, as Spain. At intervals were set packed bouquets of zinnias, oleanders, and some kind of purple flowers, all quite flesh, in fruit jars; like nice welcomes on bureaus.

They moved on into an open plot beyond, of violent-green grass, spread before the green-and-white flame church with worked flower beds around it, flowerless poinsettias growing up to the windowsills. Beyond was a house, and left on the doorstep of the house a freshcaught catfish the size of a baby—a fish wearing whiskers and bleeding. On a clothesline in the yard, a priest's black gown on a hanger hung airing, swaying at man's height, in a vague, trainlike, lady-like sweep along an evening breath that might otherwise have seemed imaginary from the unseen, felt river.

With the motor cut off, with the raging of the insects about them, they sat looking out at the green and white and black and red and pink as they leaned against the sides of the car.

"What is your wife like?" she asked. His right hand came up and spread—iron, wooden, manicured. She lifted her eyes to his face. He looked at her like that hand.

Then he lit a cigarette, and the portrait, and the righthand testimonial it made, were blown away. She smiled, herself as unaffected as by some stage performance; and he was annoyed in the cemetery. They did not risk going on to her husband—if she had one.

Under the supporting posts of the priest's house, where a boat was, solid ground ended and palmettos and water hyacinths could not wait to begin; suddenly the rays of the sun, from behind the car, reached that lowness and struck the flowers. The priest came out onto the porch in his underwear, stared at the car a moment as if he wondered what time it was, then collected his robe off the line and his fish off the doorstep and returned inside. Vespers was next, for him.

After backing out between the tombs he drove on still south, in the sunset. They caught up with an old man walking in a sprightly way in their direction, all by himself, wearing a clean bright shirt printed with a pair of palm trees fanning green over his chest. It

但她穿不着。老人对着轿车比划着手势，像在空中画圈圈，招呼他们停下。

"你们就要走上绝路了。"老头对他们说。也指指前面，对着车上的女的轻轻拍拍自己的帽子，又指了指。"绝路，"他们不理解他的意思，"骗人。"

他们继续往前开。"只要我们一再朝前，肯定会到海边——是不是？"他问她，又对自己的这种稀奇古怪的看法把握不定。

"你比我知道得更清楚。"她很有礼貌地回答。

路的好几处正在铺设，铺路用的是鹅卵石。路通向一个小小的、人口稀疏的居民区，这个居民区和前面几英里处的那些差不多，只是周围搭了更多的帐篷。在空地的进口处，一棵青葱的柳树正背着夕阳站立着，树的前面是一排房子和一些木棚，正面对着一片浩瀚的、五颜六色而又波澜起伏的大水，大水一直延伸到天边，看上去就像一个海湾。那些房子是拼拼凑凑搭起来的，柱木都腐朽不堪，有的就用铁路枕木充当门前的台阶——房子都摇摇欲坠，而大小还不及系在岸边的小船。

"威尼斯①到了。"她听见他这么说，还把地图卷起来扔在她膝上。

他们沿着水边驶完最后一小段路。路的尽头——她记不得自己是否曾见过路的尽头——成调羹状，调羹的中央直挺挺地站着一棵树。

绕树一周之后，他停下车。他们下了车，仿佛跌进了陷阱似的，感到困顿和晕厥。他们向水边走去，那儿，在一块空荡荡的平地上，人们正三三两两地站着，背朝着他们。

正在临近的黑夜、呆立不动的残木、闪闪发光而将一整块一整块花圃浸沉的大水、棚屋、静寂、系在缆绳上的小船的阴影、从那陋墙里最初传出的人声——这一切都仿佛是逼在他们眼前。一堆堆的鹅卵石就像长年不化的积雪，微微发红，围在一间挂着啤酒招牌的木棚旁边。一个老头爬到平台上，在那儿坐下，摊开一张报纸读起来，在他对面，一只肥大的鹅蹲在地上。下面，在没有暗影也没有阳光的地方，另一个老头，帽檐下插一支花花绿绿的铅笔，正在慢吞吞地补一张船帆。

她看清了周围的一切，当她想到这些人正濒临着

___

① 意大利有名的水城，此处为暗喻。

might better be a big colored woman's shirt, but she didn't have it. He flagged the car with gestures like hoops.

"You're coming to the end of the road," the old man told them. He pointed ahead, tipped his hat to the lady, and pointed again. "End of the road." They didn't understand that he meant, "Take me."

They drove on. "If we do go any further, it'll have to be by water—is that it?" he asked her, hesitating at this odd point.

"You know better than I do," she replied politely.

The road had for some time ceased to be paved; it was made of shells. It was leading into a small, sparse settlement like the others a few miles back, but with even more of the camp about it. On the lip of the clearing, directly before a green willow blaze with the sunset gone behind it, the row of houses and shacks faced out on broad, colored, moving water that stretched to reach the horizon and looked like an arm of the sea. The houses on their shaggy posts, patchily built, some with plank runways instead of steps, were flimsy and alike, and not much bigger than the boats tied up at the landing.

"Venice," she heard him announce, and he dropped the crackling map in her lap.

They coasted down the brief remainder. The end of the road—she could not remember ever seeing a road simply end—was a spoon shape, with a tree stump in the bowl to turn around by.

Around it, he stopped the car, and they stepped out, feeling put down in the midst of a sudden vast pause or subduement that was like a yawn. They made their way on foot toward the water, where at an idle-looking landing men in twos and threes stood with their backs to them.

The nearness of darkness, the still uncut trees, bright water partly under a sheet of flowers, shacks, silence, dark shapes of boats tied up, then the first sounds of people just on the other side of thin walls—all this reached them. Mounds of shells like day-old snow, pink-tinted, lay around a central shack with a beer sign on it. An old man up on the porch there sat holding an open newspaper, with a fat white goose sitting opposite him on the floor. Below, in the now shadowless and sunless open, another old man, with a colored pencil bright under his hat brim, was late mending a sail.

When she looked clear around thinking they had a

灾难时，一轮满月从热烘烘的空气中升起来。升到树的那边，又圆又大，橘红色的，又徐徐地上升。这时，另一种光又闪入眼眶，看来比较远，像苔藓似的浮在空中，又像划火柴似的在水面上一亮一暗，而水正在侵占他们脚下的地面。

她觉得手臂被人碰了一下——是他，无意的。

"我们还刚刚开始。"他说。

她咯咯地笑，想到他的手就像棒球棍，她的目光又一下子投向一个巨大而灰白的在紫蓝色水面上漂动的东西——那东西半开半闭，摇摇晃晃的，反照着月光，高度和她的脚差不多——从那儿小船可以开辟出一条水上通道。她抽起手蒙住帽檐下的脸，她觉得自己的脸颊也好像成了紫蓝色，全身的皮肤在反照着过多的光和天，赤裸裸的。刺耳的晚祷钟声当当地响了。

"我相信，我一定是疯了，竟然来做这样的旅行。"她说，好像他早已说过同样的话，她此刻只是希望、愿意或者盲从他的话而已。

他握住她的手臂说："哦，不要泄气——我想，我们至少能在这儿搞到一些喝的东西。"

但是，从那黑魆魆的水面上传来的只是一阵沉闷的碰撞声。又一只小船驶来，粗看起来像是火炬似的摇曳不定的亮光下，它小心翼翼地避开那些由纯洁的、韧性的花朵设下的陷阱。他和她等着那小船，好像两方面都有万分耐心似的。大概是由于幽暗的微光或者是由于有人的气息的缘故吧，一大群蚊子和小虫嗡嗡地飞来袭击他们。小船砰的一声响，人们哈哈一阵笑。某个人愿意向某个人出售某些虾米。

这时，他把自己黑黑的、平庸的脸俯向她，她却没有仰起头来看他，而是转过身去。现在，那些鹅卵石堆也像木棚和树木一样呈现出单调的紫红色。那些仿佛像幻影似的窗框里也透出了亮光。一条狭长的霓虹灯招牌在啤酒棚的棚架上像害羞时的红晕似的泛现出来："巴巴酒店"。平台上，一盏灯亮了。

谷仓似的店堂里灯光通明，墙壁没有整修过，看上去很不整齐，一道板壁把整个屋子一分为二，板壁后面不知放着什么东西。四个牌友拥挤在桌子前，地板中央坐着读报人，报纸放在他的裤袋里。从门到那板壁，中间有一个柜台，看上去就像通往另一个房间的关卡，柜台上挂着一块陈旧的、上过清漆的浮雕横匾。他们穿过店堂，在一个幽静的角落里坐在木头

fire burning somewhere now, out of the heat had risen the full moon. Just beyond the trees, enormous, tangerine-colored, it was going solidly up. Other lights just striking into view, looking farther distant, showed moss shapes hanging, or slipped and broke matchlike on the water that so encroached upon the rim of ground they were standing on.

There was a touch at her arm—his, accidental.

"We're at the jumping-off place," he said.

She laughed, having thought his hand was a bat, while her eyes rushed downward toward a great pale drift of water hyacinths—still partly open, flushed and yet moonlit, level with her feet—through which paths of water for the boats had been hacked. She drew her hands up to her face under the brim of her hat; her own cheeks felt like the hyacinths to her, all her skin still full of too much light and sky, exposed. The harsh vesper bell was ringing.

"I believe there must be something wrong with me, that I came on this excursion to begin with," she said, as if he had already said this and she were merely in hopeful, willing, maddening agreement with him.

He took hold of her arm, and said, "Oh, come on—I see we can get something to drink here, at least."

But there was a beating, muffled sound from over the darkening water. One more boat was coming in, making its way through the tenacious, tough, dark flower traps, by the shaken light of what first appeared to be torches. He and she waited for the boat, as if on each other's patience. As if borne in on a mist of twilight or a breath, a horde of mosquitoes and gnats came singing and striking at them first. The boat bumped, men laughed. Somebody was offering somebody else some shrimp.

Then he might have cocked his dark city head down at her: she did not look up at him, only turned when he did. Now the shell mounds, like the shacks and trees, were solid purple. Lights had appeared in the not-quite-true window squares. A narrow neon sign, the lone sign, had come out in bright blush on the beer shack's roof: "Baba's Place." A light was on on the porch.

The barnlike interior was brightly lit and unpainted, looking not quite finished, with a partition dividing this room from what lay behind. One of the four cardplayers at a table in the middle of the floor was the newspaper reader; the paper was in his pants pocket. Midway along the partition was a bar, in the form

高凳上。一连串滑稽有趣的镜头,报纸剪贴和动画片,剃须刀商标,带给店老板巴巴的或者来帮亡修横匾的朋友的郑重其事的私人口信,说巴巴应该到那里去而他没去。

不知从哪里飘来一股咖喱、丁香和红胡椒的气味,还有一股滚烫的白雾正从一只大锅里冒出来,现在他们看清了,板壁另一边的房间后墙边有一只炉子。一个邋里邋遢的、大概是女性的人,头顶上一大蓬灰头发,手里握一只长柄勺,双手叉腰站在那儿。一个小伙子走到她旁边,用手指从锅里拈出什么东西来吃。在巴巴酒店里,人们正在煮虾米。

他打算等他们,而这时巴巴从柜台里蹓跶出来。巴巴很年轻,一头黑发,脾气也相当好。

"供应冰镇啤酒。吃的——你们想吃点什么?"

"我什么也不想吃,谢谢,"她说,"我不知道我能吃些什么。"

"哦,我想吃。"他说,一面伸着下巴。巴巴笑了。"我要一份上好的火腿三明治。"

巴巴走了。"我应该向他要点水。"她说。

他们等着,店堂里好像很安静。虾米在沸滚,巴巴在那儿笑,扑克牌在劈啪劈啪地响,就像飞蛾撞墙,声音听起来朦朦胧胧,时断时续。他们听见墙角里的一只又大又脏的狗在发出均匀的鼾声。但是店堂里很亮。屋椽上有一张像蜘蛛网一样的旧电线网,网上装着电灯,正发疯般地发亮,把屋子照得通明。一张手写的通讯稿用木头钉钉在他们前面的墙壁上,写着:"乔! 揍那个赤佬!!"稿纸看上去很黄,比巴巴酒店还要古旧。屋外,整个世界一团漆黑。

两个小男孩,几乎一般大小,穿得很整洁 偷偷地溜进来,但门却砰砰地响了两下。他们绕着牌桌团团乱转,还把手伸进那些牌友的口袋。

"大洋五块拿过来!"

"大洋五块拿过来!"

"滚你的蛋,我来坐庄!"

两个男孩团团乱转,对着狗尖声叫,又从柜台下的空当里钻进去,穿过厨房又回来,站在长凳上攀住栅栏。一个男孩的衬衫上有一只活蜥蜴,像一枚胸针别在那里——像一块天青石。

这时,又有一些人进来,带来一股天竺葵滑石粉味道——全都穿着洁白的衬衫。他们走近柜台,有的站着,有的在看赌牌。

of a pass-through to the other room, with a varnished, second-hand fretwork overhang. They crossed the floor and sat, alone there, on wooden stools. An eruption of humorous signs, newspaper cutouts and cartoons, razor-blade cards, and personal messages of significance to the owner or his friends decorated the overhang, framing where Baba should have been but wasn't.

Through there came a smell of garlic and cloves and red pepper, a blast of hot cloud escaped from a cauldron they could see now on a stove at the back of the other room. A massive back, presumably female, with a twist of gray hair on top, stood with a ladle akimbo. A young man joined her and with his fingers stole something out of the pot and ate it. At Baba's they were boiling shrimp.

When he got ready to wait on them, Baba strolled out to the counter, young, black-headed, and in very good humor.

"Coldest beer you've got. And food—What will you have?"

"Nothing for me, thank you," she said. "I'm not sure I could eat, after all. "

"Well, I could, "he said, shoving his jaw out. Baba smiled. "I want a good solid ham sandwich. "

"I could have asked him for some water, " she said, after he had gone.

While they sat waiting, it seemed very quiet. The bubbling of the shrimp, the distant laughing of Baba, and the slap of cards, like the beating of moths on the screens, seemed to come in fits and starts. The steady breathing they heard came from a big rough dog asleep in the corner. But it was bright. Electric lights were strung riotously over the room from a kind of spider web of old wires in the rafters. One of the written messages tacked before them read, "Joe! At the boyy!!" It looked very yellow, older than Baba's Place. Outside, the world was pure dark.

Two little boys, almost the same size, and just cleaned up, dived into the room with a double bang of the screen door, and circled around the card game. They ran their hands into the men's pockets.

"Nickel for some pop!"

"Nickel for some pop!"

"Go 'way and let me play, you!"

They circled around and shrieked at the dog, ran under the lid of the counter and raced through the kitchen and back, and hung over the stools at the bar. One child had a live lizard on his shirt, clinging like a

看见巴巴端着啤酒和三明治出来，她招呼起来：
"能给我点水吗？"

巴巴对每个人都咯咯地笑。她断定，那个靠墙站着的女人是巴巴的母亲。

他坐在她旁边，喝着啤酒，吃着三明治——火腿、奶酪、番茄、泡菜，还有芥末。没等他吃完，有个人进来，穿过店堂时还向他点点头。这个人就是那个穿棕榈树衬衫的老头。

她抬起头看着他走过去，而全店堂里的人又看着她。一分钟里，一张牌也没出。就像从遥远的星辰射来的光，她模糊地意识到自己很美，可能比他们每天生活中看到的女人更加娇弱。而他们呢，每当这种时候，所看惯的也就是女人脸上表现出来的这种意识。

巴巴在微笑。他把一只打开的、冰冻过的咖啡色瓶子放在她面前，还有一块厚厚的三明治，接着又站在那儿看着她。由于受到巴巴的这种待遇，她吃了一点儿东西。

"那老头想对一位朋友表示歉意，"他最后走过来说，"大概是教堂弄不下去了。大概是他的朋友说过他现在就在这儿。他的伙伴告诉他说这儿来了一位女士。"

"我看你就给他一杯啤酒得了。"她说。

"哦，看上去那老头是想吃点什么。"

只听见自动留声机从后面的角落里一下子响起来，播放着一首任何地方都听得到的谁都听腻了的歌。五六只沿墙而站的自动机器突然间像跳五朔节花柱舞似的全动了起来，一阵大发作——一队小男孩在那里操纵。

每架机器由三个小男孩操纵。看来，当地的习惯是一个人拉操纵杆，另一个同伙负责收拢硬币，而第三个人则在硬币投入后用手掌把硬币上的图案遮住，好像对它们落到这地方感到很惊讶，对事情竟会这样感到很惊讶。

那只狗在大喊大叫的自动留声机面前安然而睡，肋骨像六角手风琴似的一张一合。店堂的另一边，一个在蓬乱的白头发上戴着一顶帽子的男人竭力打开一扇边门，但门死死地关着。就是这个人，他刚才进来说了一通话被大家认为是下流玩笑。现在，他想从另一扇门出去。像门缝一样细的飞蛾试图从门缝里钻进来。几个牌友忽然间大声喊叫起来，相互嘲笑着，接着又一阵乐，然后又对这种自我嘲笑厌倦了。

breast pin—like lapis lazuli.

Bringing in a strong odor of geranium talcum, some men had come in now—all in bright shirts. They drew near the counter, or stood and watched the game.

When Baba came out bringing the beer and sandwich, "Could I have some water?" she greeted him.

Baba laughed at everybody. She decided the woman back there must be Baba's mother.

Beside her, he was drinking his beer and eating his sandwich—ham, cheese, tomato, pickle, and mustard. Before he finished, one of the men who had come in beckoncd from across the room. It was the old man in the palmtree shirt.

She lifted her head to watch him leave her, and was looked at, from all over the room. As a minute passed, no cards were laid down. In a far-off way, like accepting the light from Arcturus, she accepted it that she was more beautifui or perhaps more fragile than the women they saw every day of their lives. It was just this thought coming into a womman's face, and at this hour, that seemed familiar to them.

Baba was smiling. He had set an opened, frosted brown bottle before her on the counter, and a thick sandwich, and stood looking at her. Baba made her eat some supper, for what she was.

"What the old fellow wanted," said he when he came back at last, "was to have a friend of his apologize. Seems church is just out. Seems the friend made a remark coming in just now. His pals told him there was a lady present."

"I see you bought him a beer," she said.

"Well, the old man looked like he wanted *something*."

All at once the juke box interrupted from back in the corner, with the same old song as anywhere. The half-dozen slot machines along the wall were suddenly all run to like Maypoles, and thrown into action—taken over by further battalions of little boys.

There were three little boys to each slot machine. The local custom appeared to be that one pulled the lever for the friend he was holding up to put the nickel in, while the third covered the pictures with the flat of his hand as they fell into place, so as to surprise them all if fell into place, so as to surprise them all if anything happened.

The dog lay sleeping on in front of the raging juke box, his ribs working fast as a concertina's. At the side of the room a man with a cap on his white

他们可能在这儿已经待了一个下午了——只有他们几个,穿着既不整洁,又没刮过胡子。最初进来又出去的那对小男孩又跑了进来,发出一连串嗵嗵嗵嗵的脚步声。他们这时拿了硬币,转身从桌边像蚊子似的嗡一下窜开,窜到柜台底下,钻到后面的厨房里,飞快地到巴巴的母亲那儿去了。夜色已经逼到门口。

他们俩现在一点也不引人注意了。他在吃另一块三明治,她呢,吃过自己的那份后,正在用帽子扇自己的脸。巴巴翻开柜台台板走到店堂里。在他的脑袋后面,有一块广告牌,上面用橘黄色粉笔写着:"星期天下午举行虾米舞会。"就是今天,现在已经是晚上,舞会还在继续。

她忽然从高凳上往下一滑,大概是想到门口平台上去吹一会儿凉风。但他拉住了她的手。他也从高凳上下来,小心翼翼地把她的手翻过来,握在自己手里——她觉得晕眩,只做出听凭他摆布的样子——他开始带她旋转。他们跳起舞来。

"我在想,这就是我们得到的——你我应该得到的,"她从他肩膀上望着那店堂,喃喃而语,"自始至终,一切都是真实的。这儿是一个真实的地方——离开这儿……"

他们伴随着一首显然是用本地土语演唱的歌曲欢乐地但很规矩地跳着舞。他们俩在一起时,一直没有人注意他们,那些孩子在从容地把养家的硬币收进自动机器,一面又把操纵杆推拉得叽嘎叽嘎乱响,但没有一个人听到这种声音而感到厌烦。

她说得很慢,而同时他们正搂在一起飞快地舞着。"那些剪报中有一篇说这儿发生过一次枪杀。我猜想,他们对此还很得意。巴巴身边的那把刀真可怕……那个人招呼我时的样子真叫我心神不安。"她在他耳边低声说。

"谁?"

"就是那个向你道歉的人。"

如果他们打算就这样跳下去的话,那么当他把她搂得更紧并转动身体时,她想他一定会看到他太阳穴上的伤疤。伤疤离他的眼睛还不到6英寸。她觉得这伤疤就像一颗复仇之星(谁叫他在她一度鼓起勇气问他夫人情况时冲着她伸出右手来,这就是给他的报复)。唱片已经换过,在换唱片的间歇,他们默默无言一动不动,就那样手搭手站在店堂中央,而当新唱片开始播放时,他们又继续跳下去。

thatch was trying his best to open a side screen door, but it was stuck fast. It was he who had come in with the remark considered ribald; now he was trying to get out the other way. Moths as thick as ingots were trying to get in. The card players broke into shouts of derision, then joy, then tired derision among themselves; they might have been here all afternoon—they were the only ones not cleaned up and shaved. The original pair of little boys ran in once more, with the hyphenated bang. They got nickels this time, then were brushed away from the table like mosquitoes, and they rushed under the counter and on to the cauldron behind, clinging to Baba's mother there. The evening was at the threshold.

They were quite unnoticed now. He was eating another sandwich, and she, having finished part of hers, was fanning her face with her hat. Baba had lifted the flap of the counter and come out into the room. Behind his head there was a sign lettered in orange crayon: "Shrimp Dance Sun. PM." That was tonight, still to be.

And suddenly she made a move to slide down from her stool, maybe wishing to walk out into that nowhere down the front steps to be cool a moment. But he had hold of her hand. He got down from his stool, and, patiently, reversing her hand in his own—just as she had had the look of being about to give up, faint—began moving her, leading her. They were dancing.

"I get to thinking this is what we get—what you and I deserve," she whispered, looking past his shoulder into the room. "And all the time, it's real. It's a real place—away off down here. . ."

They danced gratefully, formally, to some song carried on in what must be the local patois, while no one paid any attention as long as they were together, and the children poured the family nickels steadily into the slot machines, walloping the handles down with regular crashes and troubling nobody with winning.

She said rapidly, as they began moving together too well, "One of those clippings was an account of a shooting right here. I guess they're proud of it. And that awful knife Baba was carrying. . . I wonder what he called me," she whispered in his ear.

"Who?"

"The one who apologized to you. "

If they had ever been going to overstep themselves, it would be now as he held her closer and turned her, when she became aware that he could not

在慢吞吞的音乐声里，他们就像两个参加比赛的对手——就像两个受过训练的、戴着假面具的西班牙舞蹈员。

显然，就是那些感情上的免疫者，有时也需要相互接触，否则一切都会变得空虚。他们两人手臂勾着手臂，身上散发出来的热气混合在一起，像两根钉子似的钉在地板上，但是两人之间归根结底又是相互隔膜的。他们自己也意识到这一点，但他们似乎并不在乎，他们身不由己地跳着舞。这种情形，也是他们两颗分离的心在这一天里所衷心希望的，无论对于他们两人来说还是对于他们各自来说，都如此。

他们就这样搂在一起，她一度抬起头淡淡地笑了笑。"我们这样究竟是为了谁的好处？"

像所有陷入恋爱的人一样，他们几乎在一踏到地板时心里就产生了一种迷信，他们不敢想到"幸福"和"不幸"这两个词，因为这两个词，无论是前者还是后者，同样会像闪电一样使他们为之晕厥。

在白雾腾腾的热气中，他们不停地舞着，这时巴巴和着唱片里的蚊子般嗡嗡刺耳的歌声唱了起来，和声在唱"Moi pas l'aimez ça①"，他手指间夹着一只煮得滚烫的虾，嘴里反复喊着"ça, ça②"。他把那老太婆放在柜台上的唱片数了一遍，在每张唱片上放一堆外壳煮成彩虹色的虾米，看上去就像一堆堆忍冬花。

一只鹅钻过柜台翻板从后面房间一摇一摆地走进来，又在桌腿和人腿之间态度傲慢地绕场一周，对两个慌忙让道的舞蹈者则连眼睛都不斜一下——虽然如此，两个舞蹈者还是模糊地感到这是一只满腹学问的鹅，他们从小就听过有位老先生朗诵这只鹅的作品。那些孩子叫这只鹅咪咪，并把它勾引出去。那个头发蓬乱的老头又在醉醺醺地想撞开那扇边门，他时而用脚踢，但是门岿然不动。那只睡着的狗抖抖毛，哼哼鼻子。

现在就等舞蹈者为自动留声机捐献硬币，巴巴为各种用途保留了一大箱。他们对当前的各种选择也渐渐产生了好感。这是一种音乐，人们可以在夜间远远地听见——可以从偶尔路过的街头小酒店里听见，不论人们是睡眼惺忪地在大城市里穿巷过街，还是在小山上纵情狂欢，人们总可以听到一种古里古怪的小

①　法文：我喜欢和这个跳舞。
②　法文：这个，这个。

help but see the bruise at her temple. It would not be six inches from his eycs. She felt it come out like an evil star. (Let it pay him back, then, for the hand he had stuck in her face when she'd tried once to be sympathetic, when she'd asked about his wife.) They danced on still as the record changed, after standing wordless and motionless, linked together in the middle of the room, for the moment between.

Then, they were like a matched team—like professional, Spanish dancers wearing masks—while the slow piece was playing.

Surely even those immune from the world, for the time being, need the touch of one another, or all is lost. Their arms encircling each other, their bodies circling the odorous, just-nailed-down floor, they were, at last, imperviousness in motion. They had found it, and had almost missed it; they had had to dance. They were what their separate hearts desired that day, for themselves and each other.

They were so good together that once she looked up and half smiled. "For whose benefit did we have to show off?"

Like people in love, they had a superstition about themselves almost as soon as they came out on the floor, and dared not think the words "happy" or "unhappy," which might strike them, one or the other, like lightning.

In the thickening heat they danced on while Baba himself sang with the mosquito-voiced singer in the chorus of "*Moi pas l'aimez ça*," enumerating the ça's with a hot shrimp between his fingers. He was counting over the platters the old woman now set on the counter, each heaped with shrimp in their shells boiled to iridescence, like mounds of honeysuckle flowers.

The goose wandered in from the back room under the lid of the counter and hitched itself around the floor among the table legs and people's legs, never seeing that it was neatly avoided by two dancers—who nevertheless vaguely thought of this goose as learned, having earlier heard an old man read to it. The children called it Mimi, and lured it away. The old thatched man was again drunkenly trying to get out by the stuck side door; now he gave it a kick, but was prevailed on to remain. The sleeping dog shuddered and snored.

It was left up to the dancers to provide nickels for the juke box; Baba kept a drawerful for every use. They had grown fond of all the selections by now. This was the music you heard out of the distance at

调在喋喋不休地唱着。这是个甜美之乡。

他们浑身大汗,心里充填着梦幻般的宁静,最后在湿润的夜雾里站在平台上,准备离去。最初来到的一群姑娘正在灯光下走上平台的台阶——她们胸前插着花,高高耸起的黑发髻里散发出一种纯粹而浓郁的气味。爽身粉在她们毛茸茸的手臂上像云母片似的一闪一闪,这是她们在教堂里时洒在自己身上的。她们一闻到天竺葵的香味,就踏着碎步手牵着手急匆匆地穿过平台走进店堂,身后留下一阵笑声。他为她们打开门。

"准备走吗?"他问她。

归途中,他们默默地开着车赶路,除了引擎的声音和树枝擦到车身发出的沙沙声,周围一片沉寂。挡风玻璃很快就模糊了。前灯光变成两道纺锤似的白团,两条朦朦胧胧的东西,好像再过一分钟就要熄灭了。他停住车,满腹怨恨地下车去擦挡风玻璃。厚厚的灰尘覆盖在路边的灌木林上。现在,月光是灰蒙蒙的,整个世界正穿行在扑朔迷离的群星之间——无数颗慢慢移动着的星辰,看上去非常远也非常近。

这是个古怪的地方,水陆两栖的——无论是水覆盖着的部分,还是林莽丛生的部分,或者,像现在这样,既没有真正的水也没有真正的树,它总是同样的凄寂。他感到沉重的睡意——像茫茫的平原,像黏糊的沼泽,像不毛的荒野(一切都像在幻觉中);但是,不管像什么都无法形容它,这是南方。浩大的、淡薄的、扩展的、灰暗的、毫无光点的星空,戴着一层电光闪闪的浮动面纱,正俯瞰着这片土地,就像俯瞰着空荡荡的大海一样。他孤零零地站在黑夜里,因为深深地看清了周围的一切而浑身颤抖,好像东南西北也业已消失——好像一场大雪骤然降下。

他爬进汽车,操着方向盘。当他恼怒地拍着自己的袖口时,她却因为闷热而在哆嗦,还把头伸到由于车速而形成的夜风里。偶尔,车灯照出了两个人影——一对黑人男女,在孤零零的小屋前的空地上,正坐在两只面对面的椅子上——两个人都因为这炎热的夜晚而喘息不止,身上半裸半衣,只有腰间裹着一条长得没有头的、像绶带似的破白布。

在空荡无人的荒野里,混浊肮脏的湖沼中央燃着昏昏蒙蒙的火光。奶牛孤寂地待在牛栏里,在这黑夜,在这炎热下,它们站在那儿一动不动——车灯闪

night—out of the roadside taverns you fled past, around the late corners in cities half asleep, drifting up from the carnival over the hill, with one odd little strain always managing to repeat itself. This seemed a homey place.

Bathed in sweat, and feeling the false coolness that it brings, they stood finally on the porch in the lapping night air for a moment before leaving. The first arrivals of the girls were coming up the steps under the porch light—all flowered fronts, their black pompadours giving out breathlike feelers from sheer abundance. Where they'd resprinkled it since church, the talcum shone like mica on their downy arms. Smelling solidly of geranium, they filed across the porch with short steps and fingers joined, just timed to turn their smiles loose inside the room. He held the door open for them.

"Ready to go?" he asked her.

Going back, the ride was wordless, quiet except for the motor and the insects driving themselves against the car. The windshield was soon blinded. The headlights pulled in two other spinning storms, cones of flying things that, it seemed, might ignite at the last minute. He stopped the car and got out to clean the windshield thoroughly with his brisk, angry motions of driving. Dust lay thick and cratered on the roadside scrub. Under the now ash-white moon, the world traveled through very faint stars—very many slow stars, very high, very low.

It was a strange land, amphibious—and whether water-covered or grown with jungle or robbed entirely of water and trees, as now, it had the same loneliness. He regarded the great sweep—like steppes, like moors, like deserts (all of which were imaginary to him); but more than it was like any likeness, it was South. The vast, thin, wide-thrown, pale, unfocused star-sky, with its veil of lightning adrift, hung over this land as it hung over the open sea. Standing out in the night alone, he was struck as powerfully with recognition of the extremity of this place as if all other bearings had vanished—as if snow had suddenly started to fall.

He climbed back inside and drove. When he moved to slap furiously at his shirtsleeves, she shivered in the hot, licking night wind that their speed was making. Once the car lights picked out two people—a Negro couple, sitting on two facing chairs in the yard outside their lonely cabin—half undressed, each battling for self against the hot night, with long white rags

过,它们只是惊恐地耸起耳朵。

终于,他再次停住了车,并在这时用一只手臂挽住她一边的肩膀吻她的嘴——他不知道这吻是温柔的呢,还是炽热的。他当时所感觉到的也就是这样的浑然无辨。这之后,他们脸贴着脸,没有接吻,也不动弹,在黑暗中持续了一段时间。炎热的空气钻进汽车团团地裹住他们,蚊子开始叮咬他们的手臂,甚至眼皮。

后来,当他开车穿过一大片开阔地时,他同时看见两堆火光。他仿佛觉得,他们一直在开着车长时间地穿越一张面孔——一张又大又宽而且不会转动的面孔。在这张面孔的眼睛和嘴巴里,就燃着那映入他们眼帘的火光,就在那儿,牛群相互挤在一起。一张面孔,一颗头颅,从这里一直伸向南方——南方的南方,从南方再朝南。接着是一个完整的躯体,摊开四肢平卧着,永恒不变,像一个星座,也像一位天使。这躯体也许在燃烧,也许在堕落,他想。

她好像睡熟了,像孩子似的仰着身体,帽子放在膝上。他依然开着车,在他身边,在他后边——他正弯着腰驾驶,想尽量开得快些——是她的侧影。她耳朵上的耳环好像很奇特地在一摇一摇。它们可能像舌头一样会说话。他直视前方继续开着车,速度快得像发疯,引擎也发烫了,不过,这对于一辆新的福特牌轿车来说是无所谓的,更何况车是租来的。

时而,有座谷仓似的建筑物从车边掠过,它的顶上和周围都装着霓虹灯——交叉路口有家电影院。他们一直沿那条长长的、白色的、平坦的大路行驶,现在这条路已到尽头,它转个弯,引着他们回家——或者毋宁说,拉着他们回家。

一件事,如果说这件事是不能使人相信的话,那也只有当这件事被人讲述了之后才有可能——他们走出世界,现在又回来了。由于他们各自的原因,他想,他们两人都不会向人谈起这件事(除非有什么东西非讲不可):他们,两个陌生人,曾一起驱车进入一个陌生的地方,又安然无恙地回来了——或许,这不过是兜了个小小的圈子而已,但这样兜上一圈也已经够了。现在,那道河堤看上去就像是灿烂夺目的北极光,而那新奥尔良的天穹,正横跨在河上,若隐若现,似有似无。现在,他们还穿过大桥,正高高地俯瞰着一切,接着便消失在一股长长的向城里涌去的由汽车灯光组成的洪流里。

in endless, scarflike motions.

In peopleless open places there were lakes of dust, smudge fires burning at their hearts. Cows stood in untended rings around them, motionless in the heat, in the night—their horns standing up sharp against that glow.

At length, he stopped the car again, and this time he put his arm under her shoulder and kissed her—not knowing ever whether gently or harshly. It was the loss of that distinction that told him this was now. Then their faces touched unkissing, unmoving, dark, for a length of time. The heat came inside the car and wrapped them still, and the mosquitoes had begun to coat their arms and even their eyelids.

Later, crossing a large open distance, he saw at the same time two fires. He had the feeling that they had been riding for a long time across a face—great, wide, and upturned. In its eyes and open mouth were those fires they had had glimpses of, where the cattle had drawn together: a face, a head, far down here in the South—south of South, below it. A whole giant body sprawled downward then, on and on, always, constant as a constellation or an angel. Flaming and perhaps falling, he thought.

She appeared to be sound asleep, lying back flat as a child, with her hat in her lap. He drove on with her profile beside his, behind his, for he bent forward to drive faster. The earrings she wore twinkled with their rushing motion in an almost regular beat. They might have spoken like tongues. He looked straight before him and drove on, at a speed that, for the rented, overheated, not at all new Ford car, was demoniac.

It seemed often now that a barnlike shape flashed by, roof and all outlined in lonely neon—a movie house at a cross roads. The long white flat road itself, since they had followed it to the end and turned around to come back, seemed able, this far up, to pull them home.

A thing is incredible, if ever, only after it is told—returned to the world it came out of. For their different reasons, he thought, neither of them would tell this (unless something was dragged out of them): that, strangers, they had ridden down into a strange land together and were getting safely back—by a slight margin, perhaps, but margin enough. Over the levee wall now, like an aurora borealis, the sky of New Orleans, across the river, was flickering gently. This time they crossed by bridge, high above everything, merging into

进城后,他一度在街上迷了路,简直在喧嚣吵闹的各种车辆间瞎闯,直到后来方才弄清方向。当他把车开到下一块路牌旁边并探出身体蹙着眉想看清楚路牌上的字时,她正在他身边端坐着。这里是 Arabi,他把车往右转。

"好,一切都结束了。"他喃喃而语,给自己点了一支烟。

在整个旅途中,他们之间似乎势必会突然发生什么事情,然而这件事终究没有发生。在每个时刻,它曾勃然崛起过,并像恐怖感一样强烈,像人本身一样发出呼喊,但又颓然平息了。

"我还一直没洗过澡哩。"她说。

她把自己所住的旅馆名字告诉他,他把车开到了那儿。站在人行道上,他说了声晚安。他们握握手。

"请原谅……"他说,因为他及时看出了她希望他这么说。

她所能做的,也就是原谅他。确实,如果她从一场昏睡中及时惊醒过来的话,那她已经把自己的事情告诉他了。她用手捋着自己的头发,就这样消失在一扇转门里。他想,这时很可能在里面的走道上有个人在来回踱着,在等着她。他回到车上,在那儿坐着。

他直到第二天黎明才离开那儿驱车回撒拉可斯。终于,他回想起了昨天为何要外出旅行的缘由。他妻子曾对他说,这一天他可以随便上哪儿,只是不要回家,因为她要接待几个大学里的尚未结婚的老朋友,免得他在家碍事。

他发动了引擎。这时,他仿佛闻到街上正弥漫着人体的暖烘烘的令人疲乏的气味,他这才领悟到,新奥尔良的夜现在刚刚开始。他驶过狄凯·咯劳根酒吧,听到著名的约瑟芬娜正用她的歌喉在跌宕有致地唱着"Clair de lune①"。当他把轿车缓缓地驶进车库时,这些年来第一次,他回忆起自己在纽约的年轻而鲁莽的学生时代,回忆起喧嚣的、可怕的、猥亵的和令人窒息的地下铁道,而就是这地下铁道里的一切,像爱情的希冀和爱情的圆舞曲一样,对他具有决定性的意义。

---

① 法文:明月光。

a long light-stream of cars turned cityward.

For a time afterward he was lost in the streets, turning almost at random with the noisy traffic until he found his bearings. When he stopped the car at the next sign and leaned forward frowning to make it out, she sat up stright on her side. It was Arabi. He turned the car right around.

"We're all right now,"he muttered,allowing himself a cigarette. Something that must have been with them all along suddenly, then, was not. In a moment, tall as panic, it rose, cried like a human, and dropped back.

"I never got my water,"she said.

She gave him the name of her hotel, he drove her there, and he said good night on the sidewalk. They shook hands.

"Forgive. . ."For, just in time, he saw she expected it of him.

And that was just what she did, forgive him. Indeed, had she waked in time from a deep sleep, she would have told him her story. She disappeared through the revolving door, with a gesture of smoothing her hair, and he thought a figure in the lobby, strolled to meet her. He got back in the car and sat there.

He was not leaving for Syracuse until early in the morning. At length, he recalled the reason; his wife had recommended that he stay where he was this extra day so that she could entertain some old, unmarried college friends without him underfoot.

As he started up the car, he recognized in the smell of exhausted, body-warm air in the streets, in which the flow of drink was an inextricable part, the signal that the New Orleans evening was just beginning. In Dickie Grogan's, as he passed, the well-known Josefina at her organ was charging up and down with "*Clair de lune.*" As he drove the little Ford safely to its garage, he remembered for the first time in years when he was young and brash, a student in New York, and the shriek and horror and unholy smother of the subway had its original meaning for him as the lilt and expectation of love.

035. 我怎样写作?

(美)尤多拉·韦尔蒂 著　　刘文荣 译

一

"我怎样写小说?"——这实在是个很难回答清楚的问题。就作家而言,他所要做的事情只是在一系列的探索过程中不停地写,写了再写。他不会花很多时间去进行自我反省,因为这样做很可能会使他的思想变得僵化。他只知道自己的每一篇作品都出自内心不断涌起的热情,他只知道自己曾经对每篇作品都做过细致入微的加工(使它尽量接近自己的愿望),除此之外,他就很难对自己的作品从总体上加以确切的评判了。对于作家来说,只要就他所知,一篇作品足以称得上完整了,他就会及时地停笔、脱稿,对这篇作品的创作热情也就随之而消失,这时他所关心的是一篇新的小说。"我曾经怎样进行写作的?"——这样一个笼统的、过去时态的问题或许可以在小说完成之后得到回答,但是当回答这个问题时,我的心情也许已经和当初写作时的心情相距甚远,因为写作时的那种心情已经随着小说的完成而消失或者改变了。事后的回顾和当时的心情总不能同日而语——在进行写作时,作家是集中精力捕捉每一种感受,尽量地发挥对事物的热忱、理解力以及好奇心,专心致志于完成自己的作品,而当小说完成之后,这一切都会随之而变。"我是怎样写作这篇小说的?"——这确实是一个值得回答的问题。不过,在回答这个问题时,也必须根据小说自身的内容而言,也就是说,要从作品本身出发(至少,一般说来是这样)。小说创作和某种对小说的外在的分析评论工作迥然不同,这就像读长笛谱和吹奏长笛一样,一个演奏者当然需要对这两件事都

I

"HOW do I write my stories?"is a blessedly open question. For the writer it is forever in the course of being studied through doing and new doing, and wouldn't last very long as a matter of self-observation, which could very well turn him to stone. Apart from what he's learned about his separate stories, out of passion, the renewable passion, of doing each in the smallest part better(at least nearer the way he wants it), he may or may not be a good judge of his work in the altogether. To him if a story is good enough to be called finished, as far as he can see, it is detached on the dot from the hand that wrote it, and the luster goes with it; what *is* attached is the new story. "How I wrote,"past tense, may be seen into from this detachment, but not with the same insight—that too is gone, displaced. Looking backward can't compete with looking forward with the story in progress—that invites and absorbs and uses every grain of his insight, and his love and wits and curiosity and strength of purpose. "How do I write *this* story?"is really the question, the vital question;but its findings can be set down only in terms of the story's own—terms of fiction. (At least, ordinarily. Story writing and an independently operating power of critical analysis are separate gifts, like spelling and playing the flute, and one person proficient in both has been doubly endowed. But even he can't rise and do both at the same time.)

作者简介:**尤多拉·韦尔蒂(Eudora Welty**,1909—2001),美国小说家。1909 年 4 月 13 日生于密西西比州杰克逊,2001 年 7 月 23 日卒于同地。她的作品主要关注与她的出生地以及德尔塔乡村类似的小城镇。她的主要题材是人们关系的复杂性。短篇小说集《绿窗帘》(*A Curtain of Green*,1941)让她一举成名。其他短篇小说作品包括《大网》(*The Wide Net*,1943)、《金苹果》(*The Golden Apples*,1949)和《英尼斯法伦的新娘》(*The Bride of the Innisfallen*,1955)。她的长篇小说包括《德尔塔婚礼》(*Delta Wedding*,1946)、《庞德的心》(*The Ponder Heart*,1954)和《乐观者的女儿》(*The Optimist's Daughter*,1972)等。她的作品集幽默和心理敏锐于一身,使用的是地方色彩的语言。

很熟练，但即使是他也不可能同时兼顾两个方面）。

我总感到，无论哪一种一般性的写作理论，和我切身掌握的写作知识都有很大的距离。我柜信对于理论性的东西，别人虽则总想把它们加以明确的定论，而我却可以把它们一个个地撂开不管，只要我在成功地写出作品之前对它们保持沉默就够了。我觉得，我唯一清楚的事情是集中精力写小说，把它当做有生命的东西来对待，所以我从工作中得到的重要的经验也就十分简单，那就是：每一篇小说都应该开拓新的境界，提出新的问题。没有一篇小说可以从另一篇小说而来，或者是对另一篇小说的补充。补充只会带来损害。我甚至可以进而说，我不相信某一作家的各种作品是经过某种外在的统一规划而写成的，如果说这些作品中有某种相同的韵味，这或许还可以。我不相信它们是根据某种典范的、可以事先制定的、合乎逻辑发展的，甚或是按年代编排的方法写出来的（因为，对于读者来说，一个优秀作家的作品也就是这位作家本人，两者没有什么区别）——我不相信有什么方法可以让作家在经过足够严格的训练之后便能使他得到某种卓越的、可靠的（废话！），或者轻松的写作手段。

我总觉得，一个作家的作品都无一例外地出自作家的内心。不管这些作品在题材上或者在感情上有多么不同，不管这些作品在影响读者的思想、情绪或者改变读者的信念方面是成功的还是失败的，它们肯定有自己的共同之处，肯定带有同样的特征，因为它们都出于同一作家的有个性的、有节奏的内心冲动——想赞美什么、眷恋什么、提示什么或者想预报什么的冲动。成千上万的作品都出自这同一的源头！所有的作家都由于那几种感情的冲动在从事写作，这几种感情为数不多但却是永恒的，那就是爱情、怜悯和不可改变的恐惧感。

追寻小说的源头并不困难，只是，也许不应该在小说本身的情感中寻找，而应该通过与小说情感关系最直接、最密切和最特殊的外部世界去寻找。最明确无误的方法是顺藤摸瓜，就是找到所谓的"灵感"，找到诱发或者刺激作家的创作欲望致使他去构思并完成小说的外来信号，即那种不可抗拒的、神奇的、使人震动的（不管是欢乐还是痛苦）力量——那不同凡响的人物、地点或者事件。

确实，对于作家而言，在小说得以产生的领域里，

I feel myself that any *generalization* about writing is remote from anything I have managed to learn about it. I believe I can make one wide one, and others must have often nailed it down, but I shall have to hold my blow till I get there. The only things I feel I really know well are stuck to the stories, part of the animal. The main lesson I've learned from work so far is the simple one that each story is going to open up a different prospect and pose a new problem; no story bears on another or helps another, even if the writing mind had room for help and the wish that it would come. Help would be a blight. I could add that it's hard for me to think that a writer's stories are a unified whole in any respect except perhaps their lyric quality. I don't believe they are written in any typical, predictable, logically developing, or even chronological way(for all that a good writer's stories are, to the reader, so immediately identifiable as his)—or in any way that after enough solid tries guarantees him a certain measure of excellence, safety(spare the word!), or delight.

I do have the feeling that all stories by one writer tend to spring from the same source within him. However they differ in subject or approach, however they vary in excellence or fluctuate in their power to alter the mind or mood or move the heart, all of one writer's stories must take on their quality, carry their signature, because of one characteristic, lyrical impulse of his mind—the impulse to praise, to love, to call up, to prophesy. But then what countless stories share a common source! All writers write out of the same few, few and eternal—love, pity, terror do not change.

Sources of stories could be examined with less confusion, perhaps, not in the subjective terms of emotion, but through finding what in the outside world leads back to those emotions most directly and tautly and specifically. The surest clue is the pull on the line, the"inspiration," the outside signal that has startled or moved the creative mind to complicity and brought the story to active being: the irresistible, the magnetic, the alarming(pleasurable or disturbing), the overwhelming person, place, or thing.

Surely, for the writer this is the world where stories come from, and where their origins are living reference plain to his eyes. The dark changes of the mind

那里的一切都作为原始的参照物活生生地展现在他眼前。在那儿，世上的一切都不停地在转变成什么东西——诗的、道德的、感情的以及由此而产生的并不断成形的观念——在那儿，思想和心灵在黑暗中摸索，没有地图也没有向导，唯一可以作为补救的方法就是像精神病医生那样对思想和心灵不断地给予治疗或者调整，唯有这样，思想和心灵才不至于在探索过程中在某种境遇中或者在生死关头显得畏畏缩缩（因为在那儿世界的变形程度甚至比墙上挂的地图还要大）。作家的思想和心灵，或许像一张一览表，或许像一个分类架，或许像一个分配者，或许像一个代理人，或许像一个预言家，各种各样无形中的事物从中匆匆流过，而在另一端诞生出来的就是一件艺术品。艺术家只会履行自身的职能，他不理会别人把他说成怎样（否则，他就会失败）——不管怎样，谁也没有能力阻止艺术家，也没有能人指导艺术家，或者给艺术家看病——虽然有人大叫大嚷说，文学是社会病害的产物，应该像拍苍蝇一样将其扑灭。我还听说有个批评家认为文学创作不过是追求死亡而已（我真不明白，这些说法究竟根据何在）。

　　诚然，进行创作只是虚构一个故事而已，但是，不管这种活动自身多么卑微，它却拥有至上的荣誉和荣耀——因为每写一篇小说都需提出新的问题，都需作家经过百般努力，所以它总能使人有所得益而作家自己也有所得——创作需要一丝不苟的精神，需要大胆质疑的胆略，不是人云亦云，不是空发议论，不是按图索骥，它是作家自身的表现。千变万化的外在世界和人可学会的创作活动当然是不尽相同的，但是我相信，虽然作家与作家、作品与作品永远都不会相同，从本质上说，它们却是相互有联系的。

　　和许许多多其他作家一样，我也受到周围环境的启示。我居住的环境，我所到之处的环境、还有其他我熟悉和喜爱的使我产生好奇心并感到亲切的各种环境，就是促使我进行小说写作的原因。我想，就有些作家而言，为他们打开心灵窗扉的也就是环境，有的是自觉的，有的则是被迫的，磨磨蹭蹭的。环境向人揭示的东西使人留下不可磨灭的印象——当然，这里含有很大程度的个人因素甚至可以说是歪曲了的。这些印象，通过作家的想象力、当时的心情、不断涌起的情感、重新勾起的回忆以及逐渐成形的观念影响下，又得到提炼和组合，随后，只要作家有幸能控制和

and heart, where all in the world is constantly *becoming* something—the poetic, the moral, the passionate, hence the *shaping* idea—are not mapped and plotted yet, except as psychiatry has applied the healing or tidying hand, and their being so would make no change in their processes, or their climates, or their way of life and death (any more than a map hung on the wall changes the world); or schedule or pigeonhole or allot or substitute or predict the mysteries rushing unsubmissively through them by the minute; or explain a single work of art that came out the other side. The artist at work functions, while whoever likes to may explain how he does it (or failing that, why)—without, however, the least power of prevention or prophecy or even cure—for some alarmists say that literature has come out of a disease of society, as if stamping out the housefly would stop it, and I've heard there's another critic who says writing is nothing but the death wish. (Exactly where in all this *standards* come in I don't know.)

It is of course the *way* of writing that gives a story, however humble, its whole distinction and glory—something learned, and learned each writer for himself, by dint of each story's unique challenge and his work that rises to meet it—work scrupulous, questioning, unprecedented, ungeneralized, uncharted, and his own. It is the changeable outside world and the learnable way of writing that are the different quotients. Always different, always differing, from writer to writer and story to story, they are—or so I believe—most intimately connected with each other.

Like a good many other writers, I am myself touched off by place. The place where I am and the place I know, and other places that familiarity with and love for my own make strange and lovely and enlightening to look into, are what set me to writing my stories. To such writers I suppose place opens a door in the mind; either spontaneously or through beating it down, attrition. The impression of place as revealing something is an indelible one—which of course is not to say it isn't highly personal and very likely distorted. The imagination further and further informs and populates the impression according to present mood, intensification of feeling, beat of memory, accretion of idea, and by the blessing of being located—contained—a story so changed

处理这些材料的话,那么在这一系列的改造之后,一篇小说也就可以开始动笔了。

创作过程和作品中的地方色彩的联系是显而易见的,只是人们总不注意这一点罢了。可以说,许许多多的作家就是用这种方法进行写作的。地方色彩是有其内在根源的,不过它表现得并不明显。环境无疑是短篇小说的最单一、最明确、最直接的来源,也是最古老的来源——行吟歌谣就来源于此——如果我可以在这里随便谈论其他作家的话,我敢说,小说和环境的联系是永恒的,不管作家本人是否意识到,事情总是如此,因为作家一动笔,这种联系就自然而然会产生。显然,地方性作家的创作构思来自于他所生长的家乡的土壤,这就像他童年时玩耍的泥饼来自于家乡的土壤一样,所不同的只是现在再经由想象力的加工,将其摆成丰盛的宴席而已。在任何艺术领域里,宴席上的酒菜都是真实的,想象力的作用只是让构思落到实处,安排就绪。

当我看到环境和作品的这种联系之后,对于我们作家来说,事情是不是有点不妙了呢?人们不是曾告诫过我们,说我们的工作本来就不值得骄傲的吗?真是这样吗?是的,对我们作家来说,有些事情确实有点不妙,我们明白这一点。但是,我对自己属于地方性作家行列依然感到很自豪,因为,在我进行写作时,虽然环境和作品的联系在深处发生作用,在占据时间,但它对我的要求却是十分严格的。这两者——环境和作品——就像我们自己内心的责任感一样,都需要我们认清。做一个地方性作家并不像加入一个俱乐部或者加入一个党派那样容易,这里没有什么东西可供你崇拜,这是一种自身的需要,而且还不是一般的需要。当你进行写作时,环境就像点金石,而在你尚未动手之前,它就已经为你指明了真理和谬误。从某种程度上说,环境就是你的荣誉,就像它是你的智慧一样,它要求你对它忠诚不渝,要求你真实地写下一切。

无论读者拿起什么小说,如果他不想动脑筋的话,他就会觉得,小说里的路一开始就是很不平坦的。有时,读者会觉得自己好像在"猜"一篇小说(从读者给我的信判断,他们在我的作品中并没有发现这种现象),在小说里好像有某种植物似的东西在不停地生长,最后长得像一棵圣诞树,枝叶交错,使人眼花缭乱,而作家为了美观起见,还要在树顶上按上一颗星星。至于乐意发挥自己想象力的读者呢,他们事先总

is now capable of being written.

The connection of this to what's called regional writing is clear but not much more informing; it does mean a lot of writers behave the same way. Regional writing itself has old deep roots; it is not the big root itself. Place is surely one of the most simple and obvious and direct sources of the short story, and one of the most ancient—as it is of lyric poetry—and, if I may presume to speak freely here for other regional writers too, the connection of story to place can go forever so long not even conscious in the mind, because taken for granted. The regional writer's vision is as surely made of the local clay as any mud pie of his childhood was, and it's still the act of the imagination that makes the feast; only in the case of any art the feast is real, for the act of the imagination gives vision the substance and makes it last.

After we see the connection between our place and our writing, has anything changed for us? We aren't admonished in any way we weren't admonished already by pride of work, surely? Yes, something *has* changed for us; we learn that. I am the proud partisan I am of regional writing because this connection between place and story *is* deep, *does* take time, and its claims on us are deep; they, like our own mind's responsibilities, are for us to find out. To be a regional writer is not like belonging to a club or a political party; it is nothing you can take credit for—it's an endowment, but more than that. It's a touchstone when you write, and shows up, before anything else does, truth and mistakes. In a way place is your honor as it is your wisdom, and would make you responsible to it for what you put down for the truth.

Whatever the story a reader takes up, the road from origin on isn't any the plainer for the simplicity of the start. Sometimes a reader thinks he is "supposed" to see in a story (I judge from letters from readers when they can't find it in mine) a sort of plant-from-seed development, rising in the end to a perfect Christmas tree of symmetry, branch, and ornament, with a star at the top for neatness. The reader of more willing imagination, who has specified for something else, may find the branchings not what he's expecting either, and the fulfillment not a perfect match, not at all to the letter of the promise—rather to a degree—

是已经有某种设想，因此很可能他们会觉得某些枝节出乎他们意料或者结尾不合他们心愿，总之，作品不能令人满意，在某种程度上（使人快活的程度）有点虚假。短篇小说就是这么回事，不过如此。至于分析家呢，小说一到他眼皮底下，也许他不会去注意那些小小的纷乱，也不会顾及什么快意，他所做的是一把抓住小说的脚跟，把小说倒拎起来（好像它肚皮里有一颗纽扣似的），然后就这样颠倒地从小说的脚后跟开始对小说进行检查，好像这样把一篇小说（或者任何一种感情过程）首足倒置地挂起来之后，就能容易地了解它的内部情况似的。"温柔可爱的分析，就是你使我把命丧！"

　　分析家，一般说来，总是逆向而行。他一路上东张西望，而脚下的路越走越窄，眼前的目标消隐在远方，唯一可见的是模模糊糊的所谓"形势"留在那儿。殊不知，作品所取的正好是和他相反的道路，作品的路总是越走越宽，它的选择也总是越来越自由，而且一路上赋予每一件事物以生命和情感。"这篇小说将要表现我的恐惧和欢乐，所以我要写它。"作家当初就是这样自信地动笔的，而我们的浮士德博士——批评家，则是从作家走过来的路上往回走，他沿途也许会因为发现某个惊险之处而大喊大叫，殊不知作家早已知道这些地方意味着什么——他早就跳着避开了。作家想自杀的话，这些地方就是很好的场所。我想，作家无拘无束所做出的选择有时在批评家眼里确实很简单，因为作家所选择的路如果不那么平坦，批评家也就到不了那儿，而作家选择这条平坦的路则是天经地义的。批评家是按原路摸索上去的，并非开辟新路，而他身上还带了一支箭。他们实际上所走的不过是小说已经开辟好了的路，一条像命运一样不可改变的路，这就是艺术的所在，感情的流露，它最初虽则出于微不足道的奇思幻想，但它却是极其真实的，它不仅合乎理性（就小说所表现的观念而言），而且每次面对着景色诱人的自杀场所时，虽然时时会因为受感而踌躇不决，但它决不会上当受骗，也决不会忘乎所以。

　　确实，一篇小说和对这篇小说所做的分析并非是相辅相成的两面镜子，两者是背道而驰的。不过，批评本身也能成为一种艺术，可以比批评的对象更加富有深意，也可以有更多的余地进行迂回，它可以拉住一篇小说并带着这篇小说一起跳华尔兹舞，对此它是用不着害羞的。但无论怎么说，批评绝不是作品的影

(and to a degree of pleasure) mysterious. This is one of the short story's finest attributes. The analyst, should the story come under his eye, may miss this gentle shock and this pleasure too, for he's picked up the story at once by its heels (as if it had swallowed a button) and is examining the writing as his own process in reverse, as though a story (or any system of feeling) could be the more accessible to understanding for being hung upside down. "Sweet Analytics, 'tis thou hast ravish'd me!"

Analysis, to speak generally, has to travel backwards; the path it goes, while paved with good intentions, is an ever-narrowing one, whose goal is the vanishing point, beyond which only "influences" lie. But writing, bound in the opposite direction, works further and further always into the open. The choices get freer and wider, apparently, as with everything else that has a life and moves. "This story promises me fear and joy and so I write it" has been the writer's honest beginning. Dr. Faustus, the critic, coming to the end of his trail, may call out the starting point he's found, but the writer long ago knew the starting point for what it was to him—the jumping off place. If they coincide, it's a coincidence. I think the writer's out-bound choices seem obstructive sometimes to analysts simply because they wouldn't be there if they weren't plain evidence that they were to the writer inevitable choices, not arguable; impelled, not manipulated; that they came with an arrow inside them. Indeed they have been *fiction's* choices: one-way and fateful; strict as art, obliged as feeling, powerful in their authenticity though for slightest illusion's sake; and reasonable (in the out-of-fiction sense) only last, and by the grace of, again, coincidence—always to be welcomed and shown consideration, but never to be courted or flattered.

Certainly a story and its analysis are not the mirror opposites of each other, for all their running off in opposite directions. Criticism can be an art too and may go deeper than its object, and more times around; it may pick up a story and waltz with it, so that it's never the same. In any case it's not a reflection. But I think that's exactly why it cannot be *used* as one, whoever holds it up, even the curious author; why it's a mistake to think you can stalk back a story by

子。我想,说到底批评也不妨作为一种手段,任何人都可以利用,就是好奇的作家也可一试。如果你觉得自己能够套住一篇小说并有能耐将它沿着分析的路往回拉,甚至认为这样做才是穿过迷途的捷径,那也未尝不可。创作和批评不仅所取的方向不同,它们的速度也不一样,所以势必有一方会发怒。不过两者的主要不同点还在于相貌各异,一个的外貌是某种构思,而另一个呢,则是以一种表率的面庞出现(天知道! ——表率自己的面庞也许也有点扭歪了),它教训人什么是好的构思,或者教训人说应该怎样小心翼翼地爬好文稿纸上的格子,使僵死的格子透出活人的气息来。创作和批评,它们各自都可以成为宏构杰作,只是,这两者的性质是切不可混淆的。

小说是一种构思。进行小说创作时,一切选择都必须由小说自身来决定,而选择自身又要做出选择,这样推而广之,小说的领域也就无限地扩大。确实,在一个不断扩大的、由各种各样可能性组成的迷宫中穿行,必须及时做出选择的决定,作家就置身于这样的陌生的土地上(它也许像批评家一样可怕)而丝毫也不能沮丧,他要懂得怎样保持尊严,怎样获取勇气。小说作家懂得(我在这里也许要发点抽象的议论)这就是生活,其中充满欲望、喧嚣、恐怖和种种可能性的诱惑——就是这些可能性给予他的小说以最大的暗示,而当他在进行工作时,他所要得到的就是各种各样的可能性。在创作过程中,作家会发现,除了小说本身,他丝毫也没有必要对自己的所作所为进行什么额外的解释,他所做的一切丝毫也没有什么神秘之处。他所想到的只是让词句滚滚地流出,越多越好——有时,为了达到精确无误的程度,他就是对表面显得简单无奇的事情也要进行一番危险的尝试(在这种时候,事情并没有失败),他不愿意用模糊的安全感来麻痹自己。只要他还没有达到目的,他就会不顾一切地在危险区里进行探索——他就是这样写一篇新的小说的。

二

我在前面说过,我相信千变万化的外在世界和人可学会的创作活动是相互有联系的。我觉得在任何小说作品里都能通过特殊的方式找到这种联系,而在地方色彩很浓的作品里,这种联系也许是最明显不过

analysis's footprints and even dream that's the original coming through the woods. Besides the difference in the direction of the two, there's the difference in speeds, when one has fury; but the main difference is in world-surround. One surround is a vision and the other is a pattern for good visions (which—who knows! —fashion may have tweaked a little) or the nicest, carefullest black-and-white tracing that a breath of life would do for. Each, either, or neither may be a masterpiece of construction; but the products are not to be confused.

The story is a vision; while it's being written, all choices must be its choices, and as these multiply upon one another, their field is growing too. The choices remain inevitable, in fact, through moving in a growing maze of possibilities that the writer, far from being dismayed at his presence on unknown ground (which might frighten him as a critic) has learned to be grateful for, and excited by. The fiction writer has learned (and here is my generalization) that it is the very existence, the very multitude and clamor and threat and lure of *possibility*—all possibilities his work calls up for itself as it goes—that guide his story most delicately. In the act of writing he finds, if no explanation outside fiction for what he is doing, or the need of it, no mystery about it either. What he does know is the word comes surest out of too much, not too little—just as the most exacting and sometimes the simplest-appearing work is brought off (when it does not fail) on the sharp edge of experiment, not in dim, reneging safety. He is not at the end yet, but it was for this he left all he knew behind, at the jumping off place, when he started this new story.

II

I made the remark above that I believed the changeable outside world and the learnable way of writing are connected with each other. I think it is this connection that can be specifically looked at in any story, but maybe a regional story could give us the easiest time. I offer here the clearest example I could find among my own stories of the working point I am

了。在此，我要用自己作品中最明显的例子来说明以上的论点，说明环境不仅启发我怎样写小说，而且还使我改变了自己业已习惯的写作方法。

事情是这样的。夏日里有一天，我受一个朋友的邀请，两人一起驾车从新奥尔良出发到南方去，我是第一次（也是仅有的一次）光顾那个地方，回来之后，我发现自己一路上不自觉地酝酿成熟了一篇我当时正在构思的小说，而且在心里形成了一个完整的新形式。我于是就动笔写，从零开始重新写了一稿，其结果是我完全抛开了第一稿而独立完成了第二稿。虽然我得声明，小说的两稿中所写到的都与我个人毫无关涉，我也从未打算要在一次愉快的假日旅行中"收集素材"，但是就是从那次旅行中，我得到了这篇小说的全部具体细节。

在小说的第一稿里，讲到一个陷入幽闭恐怖的少女，她孤独地在一个小镇上生活，很快就觉得腻烦了，加上一种无望的、朦朦胧胧而不得不将其隐匿于心间的爱情，她的生活就更显得沉滞而灰暗。这样的事情并不稀奇。经过那次旅行之后，我就把这些东西从小说里抽掉了。不过，由于性格和环境的影响，她依然被封闭在自己的小天地里，而且由于我对这个人物理解得太清楚、太透彻（小说也拖得太长），她甚至被封闭得比以前更加严实了。为了表现这个人物，我首先要做的是把她从内心的封闭状态中释放出来。我把她写成一个来自中西部的姑娘——一个南方人，这种人我过去很熟悉。我又通过一个陌生人的目光简洁地描述了她的外貌。第一稿里有五六个这样的陌生人（这些人我也同样熟悉），现在我把这些人改成单独的一个——一个男人，我把他作为陌生人引入小说。事情已经被我做绝了——你无论到哪篇小说里都不可能找到这样简单的人物安排。

然而，当我动笔之后，小说里生动的东西就从笔下源源而来。我最初想到的是要回顾一下那次旅行中的所见所闻（那一度湮没的荒僻的原野，"南方的南方"，它在我心中留下了那样深刻的印象），对于我来说，我所得到的印象仿佛就是小说里写到的困境的活生生写照，就像我后来在小说里所做的那样，它们为我指出了真实的观察角度。我外出兜了一圈，我领悟到这就是外在世界——它存在于两个人之间，高悬在空中，背衬着景色而显得像有生命似的，当小说写到这个世界时，我希望把它写得比人物或者任何其他东

hoping to make, since place not only suggested how to write the story but repudiated a way I had already tried it.

What happened was that I was invited to drive with a friend down south of New Orleans one summer day, to see that country for the first (and only) time, and when I got back home I realized that without being aware of it at the time I had treated a story, which I was working on then, to my ride, and it had come into my head in an altogether new form. I set to work and wrote the new version from scratch, which resulted in my throwing away the first and using the second. I learned all the specific detail of this story from the ride, though I should add that the story in neither version had any personal connection with myself and there was no conscious "gathering of material" on a pleasant holiday.

As first written, the story told, from the inside, of a girl in a claustrophobic predicament: she was caught fast in the over-familiar, monotonous life of her small town, and immobilized further by a hopeless and inarticulate love, which she had to pretend was something else. This happens all the time. As a result of my ride I extracted her. But she had been well sealed inside her world, by nature and circumstance both, and even more closely by my knowing her too well (the story had gone on too long) and too confidently. Before I could prize her loose, I had to take a primary step of getting outside her mind. I made her a girl from the Middle West—she'd been what I knew best, a Southerner, before. I kept outside her by taking glimpses of her through the curious eyes of a stranger: instead of the half-dozen characters (I knew them too well too) from the first version, I put in one single new one—a man whom I brought into the story *to be* a stranger. I had double-locked the doors behind me—you never dream the essentials can be simple again, within one story.

But the vital thing that happened to the story came from writing, as I began the work. My first realization of what it was came when I looked back and recognized that country (the once-submerged, strange land of "south from South" that had so stamped itself upon my imagination) as the image to me of the story's predicament come to life. This pointed out to me, as I

西都更为真实,更为有意义,因为就在这里仿佛存在着第三个人物——某种永恒的东西,那就是存在于两个人之间以及存在于两个人与世界之间的关系。就是这种关系当他们两个人作为陌生人而相遇对在他们中间不断加强,一路伴随着他们,时而和他打招呼,时而向她点点头——聆听他们的谈话,端详他们的脸色,一会儿催促他们,一会儿又拖延他们,一会儿使他们兴奋,一会儿又令他们气馁,它使他们仿佛到了忘我境界,同时忘记了自己的所作所为,一路上它既帮助他们又背弃他们。这个角色的意义就在于起着催眠作用——这就是某种关系在作祟,然而这种关系却是短暂的、试探性的、朦胧含糊的,它既幸运又不祥,既普通又不寻常。我所要暗示的是,正是这种关系促成了那次既陌生又兴奋的旅行,也正是这种关系使小说里的关于天气和情绪的描写,即那种炎热,变得十分容易理解了——这是小说的灵魂,一个惊恐不安的灵魂——我们看到,就是那种在两个携手奔跑而又互相神经过敏的人之间出没的东西。为此,我在小说里好几个地方既不说"她感到……"也不说"他觉得……"而是说"他们觉得……"这种情况其实永远也不会发生。它只能在小说里那样写写,或者大体上这样。

可以说,我先是借助于第一稿里的那个少女进行发挥,随后就抛开了那个少女。然而我却挽救了这篇小说,原因是第二稿完全不同于第一稿,对此我得加以说明。我的任务明摆在我面前,同时连环境也给我准备好了,讲述故事的方法也有了,我所要做的仅仅是心中有数地干就是了,于是我没有多加迟疑就动手了。

任何人,只要体验过这篇小说里写到的那种具体环境,那么他在阅读到这些东西的时候就一定会重新辨认出来,因为小说是有形象的,小说里的环境来自于日常生活环境。小说和产生小说的背景之间的联系可能并不十分显而易见。读者在读到某篇小说里根据作者个人的观点写出的环境时,也许丝毫也不折服。虽然有很多机会可能使他认出小说里的环境,但也可能他始终无动于衷,而且大约百分之百地他会觉得自己也一定能写出不同此类的东西来。当然,小说有自身的目的,它并不在乎读者是否看到它里面的东西和现实的东西是否"相像",至于环境,虽然对于作者来说那是一度曾进入他内心的东西,但在创作过程

wrote into the story, where the real point of view belonged. Once I was outside, I saw *it* was outside—suspended, hung in the air between the two people, fished alive from the surrounding scene, where as it carried the story along it revealed itself(I hoped)as more real, more essential, than the characters were or had any cause to be. In effect there'd come to be a sort of third character present—an Identity, rather: the relationship between the two and between the two and the world. It was what grew up between them meeting as strangers, went on the trip with them, nodded back and forth from one to the other—listening, watching, persuading or denying them, enlarging or diminishing them, forgetful sometimes of who they were or what they were doing here, helping or betraying them along. Its role was that of hypnosis—it was what a relationship *does*, be it however brief, tentative, potential, happy or sinister, ordinary or extraordinary. I wanted to suggest that its being took shape as the strange, compulsive journey itself, was palpable as its climate and mood, the heat of the day—but was its spirit too, a spirit that held territory—what's seen fleeting past by two vulnerable people who might seize hands on the run. There are times in the story when I say neither"she felt"nor"he felt"but"they felt." All this is something that *doesn't* happen all the time. It merely could, or almost could, as here.

This is to grant that I rode out of the old story on the back of the girl and then threw away the girl; but I saved the story, for entirely different as the second version was, it was what I wanted to say. My subject was out in the open, provided at the same time with a place to happen and a way to say it was happening. All I had had to do was recognize it, which I did a little late.

Anyone who has visited the actual scene of this story has a chance of recognizing it when he meets it here, for the story is visual and the place is out of the ordinary. The connection between a story and its setting may not always be so plain. A reader may not see the slightest excuse for a given story after a personal inspection of the scene that called it up; the chances are good that he may not recognize it at all, and about 100 percent that he will feel he would certainly have

中,它也不过是起到一些官能上的作用而已。

我所要做的是使其看到并相信在我的小说里什么东西对我来说是明显的有意义的——在这篇小说里,由于无情的光亮大显神威,由于写到就像暴露在地面上的矿井通道似的河流以及那越往前就越炎热的道路,南方的那种神秘而朦胧的气氛就被大大地冲淡了——然而这些却是南方的神经(这个词在小说里一再用到),那种炎热也就是一种可以感觉到的幻影,它在无边无际的视野里闪烁而晃动。我所写的是一个真实的环境,但我使它服从于自己的目的。我所写的是外在的有形的东西,写到世界的可惊的一面,但我真正的目的是想揭示出小说的内在的东西,那层外壳倒是可以抛开不管的。

对外在的表面事物进行冷静的描写构成了这篇小说的情节。但这篇小说所要揭示的却是赤裸裸的内心世界,那个姑娘的心理活动(这是我保留给她的东西)。"冷漠是那样轻轻地把我们的心肠磨硬。"我今天读了理查德·威尔伯的一首诗。两个人一起驾车到一个陌生的地方去是一件很危险的事情,是一种很危险的游戏,但其中却内含着诗意,因为两个人都把这件事当做一席盛宴来享用,而除了那可恶的炎热和它的喜剧性的干扰之外,他们相互之间并没有允诺什么,他们所做的让步或者说相互所进行的接触,不过是混在人群里跳了一阵子舞,虽然人群对于他们来说是富有喜剧性地不相协调(即绝缘的、无导性的),再有,就是他们不择时宜地接了一次吻。不管事情怎样,他们一路上却无时无刻都仿佛感觉到某种东西的存在,那东西就像我这篇小说里的第三个人物,它正睁大着眼睛、伸长着耳朵,神经过敏地介于他们两人之间。暴露开始于直觉,而在那既期待又害怕这种暴露的内心揭示中得到终结。我曾经在一篇写得很含蓄的小说里写到过这种情况,所用的言词既深奥又平常,因为那样做就能把我要说的意思隐蔽起来而不显得很直露。

(在此提一下也挺有趣,可以说,这篇小说第一稿里的基本形象是来自于某种外在对象的——一个巨大的、肮脏的、空荡荡的、放混合饮料的大钵,大钵里只放了些剪短的草,周围放一圈杯子,这种大钵在穷乡僻壤的小城镇的那些可怜巴巴的商店橱窗里经常可以见到,它们老是放在犁锄和土里土气的铁皮邮筒以及猎枪之间,根本就无人问津。即使到了今天,当

written something of a different sort himself. The point is, of course, that no matter whether the "likeness" is there for all to see or not, the place, once entered into the writer's mind in a story, is, in the course of writing the story, *functional*.

I wanted to make it seen and believed what was to me, in my story's grip, literally apparent—that secret and shadow are taken away in this country by the merciless light that prevails there, by the river that is like an exposed vein of ore, the road that descends as one with the heat—its nerve (these are all terms in the story), and that the heat is also a visual illusion, shimmering and dancing over the waste that stretches ahead. I was writing of a real place; but doing so in order to write about my subject. I was writing of exposure, and the shock of the world; in the end I tried to make the story's inside outside and then throw away the shell.

The vain courting of imperviousness in the face of exposure is this little story's plot. Deliver us all from the naked in heart, the girl thinks (this is what I kept of her). "So strangeness gently steels us," I read today in a poem of Richard Wilbur's. Riding down together into strange country is danger, a play at danger, secretly poetic, and the characters, in attempting it as a mutual feat, admit nothing to each other except the wicked heat and its comical inconvenience; the only time they will yield or touch is while they are dancing in the crowd that to them is comically unlikely (hence insulating, non-conducting) or taking a kiss outside time. Nevertheless it happens that they go along aware, from moment to moment, as one: as my third character, the straining, hallucinatory eyes and ears, the roused up sentiment being of that place. Exposure begins in intuition and has its end in showing the heart that has expected, while it dreads, that exposure. Writing it as I'd done before as a story of concealment, in terms of the hermetic and the familiar, had somehow resulted in my effective concealment of what I meant to say.

(I might say, for what interest it has here, that the original image of the story's first version came from an object—a grandiose, dusty, empty punch bowl

我在写到它们时,我对它们的印象依然很深刻——很可能,它们依然搁在那橱窗里,依然标着 13.75 美元的售价。)

在第二稿里,我竭力想使小说的情节得到展开,而这时环境已经向我指明了某种富有魅力的东西并要我加以注意——随着汽车的行驶速度,迎面而来的是那种危险,即出于疏忽或者出于鲁莽或者出于诱惑而至的危险,而在一个处处表现出敌意的世界里,感情又显得那么沉重,那么敏锐,加之炎热又时对在怂恿着两个坐在汽车里的人。在他们之间,存在着某种比一般陌生人之间的那种不冷不热状态更富有野性的东西,即除了冷漠和敬畏之外,还存在着某种更残忍同时又更温柔的东西。我觉得,而且是那样经常地觉得,就是这种东西在拼命抵抗着一个像小说里出现的那种外在世界。

我想尽我所能把抽象的观念和具体的形象比较一致地表现出来,有幸的是在这篇小说里有这种可能性——尽管这种可能性或许在实际上并没有完全达到,但在这篇小说里,背景、人物、情绪以及表现手法都是作为跟基本法则和基本情境有联系的同一事物或同一主题的各个有机部分而出现在小说里的。我删除了一些在第一稿里写上的古怪的句子,这倒并不是仅仅因为它们古怪——老实说这篇小说就很古怪——而是因为如果让这些句子留在那儿,就会导致某种纯出于理智的冷静的解释。小说要有自己的独立性以及保持自己的运动速度——这一点我觉得就和赛马一样,虽然就读者而言事情也许并不如此。至为重要的是,我虽不希望把小说写得神乎其神,但我总指望在自己可能的程度上随时地赋予小说以某种神秘的意味:一篇以现实为背景的小说,但现实在小说里又显得有点神秘。在这篇小说的结尾部分,出现了一种呼喊声,要求生存的呼喊,对于这种声音,小说里的两个人物最初还能听见(或者侧着头还能听见),但到后来却只能置若罔闻了——这种呼声来自于那种日益衰退的人类关系,即个人的、有个性的、心灵相通的关系。这种呼声就是我的小说得以存在的原因所在,所以我对这篇小说写得是否有点古怪是一点也不在乎的。一次旅行到头来竟用一种呼声来结束,而为了唤起人们的同情和爱心又不惜借助于幽灵,这未免失之浅薄。即使是某种转眼即逝的关系,也像某种天赋的才能一样有权利要求得到淋漓尽致的表现——

of cut glass surrounded by its ring of cups, standing typically in the poor, small-town hardware store window where such things go unsold for ever, surrounded by the axes and halters, and tin mailboxes and shotguns of the country trade. Even as I write it's still provocative to me—as it is probably, also, still there in the window, still $13.75.)

In my second effort to show the story happen, the place had suggested to me that something demoniac was called for—the speed of the ride pitted against the danger of an easy or ignorant or tempting sympathy, too pressing, too acute, in the face of an inimical world, the heat that in itself drives on the driver. Something wilder than ordinary communication between well-disposed strangers, and more ruthless and more tender than their automatic, saving ironies and graces, I felt, and do so often feel, has to come up against a world like that.

I did my best to merge, rather to identify, the abstract with the concrete, it being so happily possible in this story—however the possibilities may have been realized—where setting, characters, mood, and method of writing all appeared parts of the same thing and subject to related laws and conditionings. I cut out some odd sentences that occurred, not because they were odd—for the story is that—but because they would tantalize some cooling explanations out of the mind if they stayed in. The story had to be self-evident and hold its speed—which I think of as racing, though it may not seem so to the reader. Above all I had no wish to sound mystical, but I did expect to sound mysterious now and then, if I could: this was a circumstantial, realistic story in which the reality *was* mystery. The cry that rose up at the story's end was, I hope unmistakably, the cry of the fading relationship—personal, individual, psychic admitted in order to be denied, a cry that the characters were first able (and prone) to listen to, and then able in part to ignore. The cry was authentic to my story and so I didn't care if it did seem a little odd: the end of a journey *can* set up a cry, the shallowest provocation to sympathy and loves does hate to give up the ghost. A relationship of the most fleeting kind has the power inherent to loom like a

当这种关系像小说里所表现的那样达到了某种程度并取得了自身的地位时，当它虽则还是虚幻的但业已展现为某种目标时，尤其是当它那样朦胧、那样稀疏地在昏暗灰色的外在世界中一闪而过时，它最终是可以指出来的。关系实在是一种无处不在而又无时不变的神秘物，它在生活中，往往是可以意会而不可言传；但在一篇小说里，就非得把这种关系诉诸言语。这种神秘物，不管是冷酷无情的还是脉脉温情的，凡是人迹所到之处，不管是天涯还是海角，它总是存在于人们之间。在这篇我新近写的小说里，看来我在结尾的地方重新回到了我过去写过的另一篇小说的开始的地方，然而毫无疑问，我认为这篇小说更接近于我自己的目标。

　　这样对作家的荣誉并不会产生什么了不起的影响，这不过说明了对有些作家来说，小说必须有某个自救之法。情形也许是这样，但我又觉得，这正表明了在实际写作过程中，有些东西，除了作家之外对其他人也是有兴趣的，那就是主题、方法、形式、风格，诸如此类纷至沓来的东西——它们确实使人为之神昏——它们就像一阵阵充满疑问的响雷在作家耳边轰鸣。那是生活的世界所发出的爆裂声在他灵魂深处震荡，而当他精神高涨的时候，他的反应冲动就会把力量和想象熔于一炉，将它们化为一体。诚然，作家在创作时是默默无言的，但是随时都可以感觉到一种力量，这种力量为作家的情感和感觉打开大门，而当那发放出来的冲动达到一定程度时，它就会使作家和读者都不由自主地感到欣喜。生活的世界将像以往一样经久如故，然而小说，若与其他东西相比，将是足够幸运的，因为它可以每日每时地编造并讲述自己的故事。

genie—to become vocative at the last, as it has already become present and taken up room; as it has spread out as a destination however makeshift; as it has, more faintly, more sparsely, glimmered and rushed by in the dark and dust outside. Relationship *is* pervading and changing mystery; it is not words that make it so in life, but words have to make it so in a story. Brutal or lovely, the mystery waits for people wherever they go, whatever extreme they run to. I had got back at the end of the new story to suggesting what I had started with at the beginning of the old, but there was no question in my mind which story was nearer the mark.

　　This may not reflect very well on the brightness of the author; it may only serve to prove that for some writers a story has to rescue itself. This may be so, but I think it might show too what alone in the actual writing process may have interest for others besides the writer: that subject, method, form, style, all wait upon—indeed hang upon—a sort of double thunderclap at the author's ears: the break of the living world upon what is stirring inside the mind, and the answering impulse that in a moment of high consciousness fuses impact and image and fires them off together. There really never was a sound, but the impact is always recognizable, granting the author's sensitivity and sense, and if the impulse so projected is to some degree fulfilled it may give some pleasure out of reason to writer and reader. The living world remains just the same as it always was, and luckily enough for the story, among other things, for it can test and talk back to the story any day in the week.

036. 中午酒

（美）凯瑟琳·安·波特 著　　李文俊 译

036. Noon Wine

by Katherine Anne Porter

时间：1896—1905 年

地点：得克萨斯州南部一个小农场

　　两个肮里肮脏的长着亚麻色头发的小男孩正在前院的豚草丛里挖什么东西，这时候，一个黄头发的又瘦又高的男人走进门来。孩子们蹲着直起了腰对他喊了一声"喂"，但是，这人没有在大门口停下步子。很久以来，为了方便起见，大门就一直是半开着的，铰链已经断了，门坠了下来，再也不能转动，人们也不打算再把它关上了。这人对这两个孩子连看都不看一眼，更不要说打招呼了。他只是沉重地踏着他那双沾满尘土的大头皮鞋，一步步坚定地走进来，那姿势就像是一个人在扶犁，仿佛他很熟悉这个地方，知道能走到哪儿，又会找到什么似的。他在那排棟树底下绕过屋子右角，走近侧廊，汤普生先生正在那儿来回摇着一只悬在廊上的搅乳器。

　　汤普生先生是个饱经风霜的壮实汉子，头发又硬又黑，黑上髭一个星期没有刮了。他是个咋咋嚷嚷的、骄傲的人，脖子老是绷得那么直，因而他的喉结和脸往往一般高，他的黑上髭垂到颈部，和敞开的领子里那片黑压压的茸毛混成一片。搅乳器发出轰隆隆沙拉拉的声音，响得像一匹小跑着的马的肚子，因此汤普生先生也有点儿像用一只手在赶着马。有时勒住缰绳，有时又驱策它快走。他不时还转过半个身子，朝台阶上吐出一大口烟草汁。阶沿石被新吐的烟草汁染得又黄又亮。汤普生先生搅了好一阵子牛奶已经腻烦了。他积了一大口烟草汁正准备吐，这时，陌生人绕过屋角停住了脚步。汤普生先生看见站在

Time：1896—1905

Place：Small South Texas Farm

THE two grubby small boys with tow-colored hair who were digging among the ragweed in the front yard sat back on their heels and said, "Hello," when the tall bony man with straw-colored hair turned in at their gate. He did not pause at the gate; it had swung back, conveniently half open, long ago, and was now sunk so firmly on its broken hinges no one thought of trying to close it. He did not even glance at the small boys, much less give them good-day. He just clumped down his big square dusty shoes one after the other steadily, like a man following a plow, as if he knew the place well and knew where he was going and what he would find there. Rounding the right-hand corner of the house under the row of chinaberry trees, he walked up to the side porch where Mr. Thompson was pushing a big swing churn back and forth.

Mr. Thompson was a tough weather-beaten man with stiff black hair and a week's growth of black whiskers. He was a noisy proud man who held his neck so straight his whole face stood level with his Adam's apple, and the whiskers continued down his neck and disappeared into a black thatch under his open collar. The churn rumbled and swished like the belly of a trotting horse, and Mr. Thompson seemed somehow to be driving a horse with one hand, reining it in and urging it forward; and every now and then he turned halfway around and squirted a tremendous spit of tobacco juice out over the steps. The door stones were brown and gleaming with fresh tobacco juice. Mr. Thompson had been churning quite a while and he was tired of it. He was just fetching a mouthful of juice to squirt again when the stranger came around

作者简介：凯瑟琳·安·波特（**Katherine Anne Porter**，1890—1980），美国作家。1890 年 5 月 15 日生于德克萨斯州印第安克里克，1980 年 9 月 18 日卒于马里兰州银泉。她在芝加哥和丹佛做过记者，1920 年去往墨西哥。墨西哥成为她的几部小说的背景。《开花的紫荆花》（*Flowering Judas*，1930）是她的首部文集，也是最出名的。《苍白的马，苍白的骑士》（*Pale Horse，Pale Rider*，1939）中包括 3 部中篇小说。《短篇小说集》（*Collected Short Stories*，1965）获得普利策奖和美国国家图书奖。她的小说富有质感，人物叙述复杂。《愚人船》（*Ship of Fools*，1962）是她唯一的长篇小说。

他面前的是个胸部狭窄的人,蓝眼珠的颜色淡得快成了白色。那人视而不见地望着汤普生先生。汤普生先生见他人中长长的,估计他又是一个爱尔兰人。

"你好,先生。"汤普生先生客气地说道,继续摇他的搅乳器。

"我要找活儿干。"那人说,口齿很清楚,但是带着某种汤普生先生认不出来是什么地方的口音。不是卡琼人①的,不是黑人的,也不是荷兰人的,这就把他难住了。"你这儿要雇长工吗?"

汤普生先生使劲儿推了搅乳器一下,让它趁势来回晃动。他坐在台阶上,把嘴里那团烟草唾在草丛里,接着说:"坐下来。没准咱们可以谈成买卖。我也有点意思要找个人帮忙。我原来使唤着两个黑鬼,可是上星期他们在小溪那边惹出了大祸,现在一个上了西天,另一个在冷泉的大牢里蹲着。说实在的,这两个废物连弄死他们都不值得。看来我还得另外找人。你以前在哪儿干活?"

"北达科他州。"那人说,在台阶的那头坐了下来,倒不像是因为累了。他蜷起身子,舒舒服服地坐好,仿佛打算要坐很久似的。他没正眼看过汤普生先生,不过他眼光中倒也没有鬼鬼祟祟的神色。他似乎哪儿也不看。他的眼睛在脑袋上,什么东西来到他面前他就看什么。这双眼睛仿佛也不指望能看到什么有趣的东西。汤普生先生等了很久,想让他再说几句话,可是这个人陷入了沉思。

"北达科他州,"汤普生先生说,心里记不起那一州究竟在什么地方,"离这儿挺远的吧,我捉摸。"

"农场上的活儿我都会,"那人说,"工资便宜。我要找活儿。"

汤普生先生开始正式谈生意。"我姓汤普生。洛义·艾尔·汤普生。"他说。

"我姓希尔顿。奥拉夫·希尔顿。"他连身子都没有欠一欠。

"那好吧,"汤普生先生用他最动人的声音说,"我看咱们还是开门见山的好。"

每当汤普生先生想使一笔买卖成交时,他总是变得又热诚又快活。他这人别的毛病没有,只有一个缺点:最恨付给人家工资。他的道理是这样的:"你供他们吃,供他们住,"他说,"完了还要付给他们钱。这太

---

① 原来居住在路易斯安那州的法国移民的后裔。

---

the corner and stopped. Mr. Thompson saw a narrow-chested man with blue eyes so pale they were almost white, looking and not looking at him from a long gaunt face, under white eyebrows. Mr. Thompson judged him to be another of these Irishmen, by his long upper lip.

"Howdy do, sir," said Mr. Thompson politely, swinging his churn.

"I need work," said the man, clearly enough but with some kind of foreign accent Mr. Thompson couldn't place. It wasn't Cajun and it wasn't Nigger and it wasn't Dutch, so it had him stumped. "You need a man here?"

Mr. Thompson gave the churn a great shove and it swung back and forth several times on its own momentum. He sat on the steps, shot his quid into the grass, and said, "Set down. Maybe we can make a deal. I been kinda lookin' round for somebody. I had two niggers but they got into a cutting scrape up the creek last week, one of 'em dead now and the other in the hoosegow at Cold Springs. Neither one of 'em worth killing, come right down to it. So it looks like I'd better get somebody. Where'd you work last?"

"North Dakota," said the man, folding himself down on the other end of the steps, but not as if he were tired. He folded up and settled down as if it would be a long time before he got up again. He never had looked at Mr. Thompson, but there wasn't anything sneaking in his eye, either. He didn't seem to be looking anywhere else. His eyes sat in his head and let things pass by them. They didn't seem to be expecting to see anything worth looking at. Mr. Thompson waited a long time for the man to say something more, but he had gone into a brown study.

"North Dakota," said Mr. Thompson, trying to remember where that was. "That's a right smart distance off, seems to me."

"I can do everything on farm," said the man; "cheap. I need work."

Mr. Thompson settled himself to get down to business. "My name's Thompson, Mr. Royal Earle Thompson," he said.

"I'm Mr. Helton," said the man, "Mr. Olaf Helton." He did not move.

"Well, now," said Mr. Thompson in his most carrying voice, "I guess we'd better talk turkey."

When Mr. Thompson expected to drive a bargain he always grew very hearty and jovial. There was nothing wrong with him except that he hated like the devil to pay wages. He said so himself. "You furnish grub and a shack," he said, "and then you got to pay 'em besides. It ain't right. Besides the wear and

没道理了。再说，你的工具也会用旧，损坏，"他说，"他们光把事情弄得乱七八糟。"他就这样一边又是笑又是叫，一边谈他的买卖。

"现在，我要知道，你想敲我多大的竹杠?"他一边拍自己的膝头，一边叫嚷。直等到他叫累了，他才安静下来，这时他倒也觉得有点不好意思了，就切了一片烟草来嚼。希尔顿先生远远地瞪着谷仓和果园之间的某一块地方，就像眯着眼睛在睡觉似的。

"我是个好工人。"希尔顿先生说，像是从坟墓里回答，"人家给我一天一块钱。"

汤普生先生大吃一惊，都忘了纵声大笑，等他再想起来，已经错过了时机。"呵，呵，"他大叫道，"什么，一天拿一块钱，这样我自己都愿意去当工人了。你拿一块钱干的是什么活儿?"

"麦田里的活儿，在北达科他州。"希尔顿先生说，连一点点笑容都没有。

汤普生先生也敛住笑容。"哦，我这儿可绝不是麦田。我这儿基本上是一个牛奶场。"他说，感到有点抱歉，"我的老婆，她一心想办牛奶场，她像是喜欢在母牛和小牛犊堆里干活，于是我迁就了她。不过这件事做错了，"他说，"结果什么都得由我来干。我老婆身体不太好。今天她又病了，这不是吗? 这些天来她太操心了。我们种了一些饲料，一小块玉米地，另外还有一片果树，我们喂了一些猪、一些鸡，不过我们主要的出息还是奶牛。我跟你说老实话吧，这旦头根本没什么钱可赚。我真的没法给你一天一块钱，因为实际上我自己也赚不了那么多。不行，先生，如果把所有的开支都算在内，这块地一天的出息还不到一块钱呢。瞧我本来给那两个黑鬼七块钱一个月，一个人三块五，管饭。不过我总认为任何时候，一个口不溜的白人都能抵得上一大帮黑人。所以我可以给你七块钱，你跟我们一块儿吃饭，我们不把你当下人，就像人家说的——"

"行，"希尔顿先生说，"我干。"

"那么，咱们这笔交易就算做成了，是不是?"汤普生先生跳了起来，好像他记起了什么重要事情似的，"你现在拽住搅乳器晃它几下成不成? 我要骑马到镇上去办几件小事。我都有一星期走不开了。我想黄油撇出来后你知道该怎么办的，是不是?"

"我知道，"希尔顿先生说，连头也不回过来，"我会炼黄油。"他有一种奇怪的拖腔，即使他只说两个字，他

tear on your implements,"he said,"they just let everything go to rack and ruin."So he began to laugh and shout his way through the deal.

"Now, what I want to know is, how much you fixing to gouge outa me?" he brayed, slapping his knee. After he had kept it up as long as he could, he quieted down, feeling a little sheepish, and cut himself a chew. Mr. Helton was staring out somewhere between the barn and the orchard, and seemed to be sleeping with his eyes open.

"I'm good worker,"said Mr. Helton as from the tomb. "I get dollar a day. "

Mr. Thompson was so shocked he forgot to start laughing again at the top of his voice until it was nearly too late to do any good. "Haw, haw," he bawled. "Why, for a dollar a day I'd hire out myself What kinda work is it where they pay you a dollar a day?"

"Wheatfields, North Dakota," said Mr. Helton, not even smiling.

Mr. Thompson stopped laughing. "Well, this ain't any wheatfield by a long shot. This is more of a dairy farm,"he said, feeling apologetic. "My wife, she was set on a dairy, she seemed to like working around with cows and calves, so I humored her. But it was a mistake,"he said. "I got nearly everything to do, anyhow. My wife ain't very strong. She's sick today, that's a fact. She's been porely for the last few days. We plant a little feed, and a corn patch, and there's the orchard, and a few pigs and chickens, but our main hold is the cows. Now just speakin' as one man to another, there ain't any money in it. Now I can't give you no dollar a day because ackshally I don't make that much out of it. No, sir, we get along on a lot less than a dollar a day, I'd say, if we figger up everything in the long run. Now, I paid seven dollars a month to the two niggers, threefifty each, and grub, but what I say is, one middlin'-good white man ekals a whole passel of niggers any day in the week, so I'll give you seven dollars and you eat at the table with us, and you'll be treated like a white man, as the feller says—"

"That's all right,"said Mr. Helton. "I take it. "

"Well, now I guess we'll call it a deal, hey?"Mr. Thompson jumped up as if he had remembered important business. "Now, you just take hold of that churn and give it a few swings, will you, while I ride to town on a coupla little errands. I ain't been able to leave the place all week. I guess you know what to do with butter after you get it, don't you?"

"I know," said Mr. Helton without turning his head. "I know butter business. " He had a strange drawling voice, and even when he spoke only two words his voice waved slowly up and down and the

的声调也要逐渐升高，逐渐降低，重音也念得不在点上。汤普生先生纳闷，希尔顿先生究竟是哪国人。

"你刚才说你在哪儿干活来着？"他问，好像指望希尔顿先生会做出不同的回答似的。

"北达科他州。"希尔顿先生说。

"反正你在一个地方待惯了，就不觉得它跟别处有什么两样了，"汤普生先生不着边际地说，"你是个外国人吧，是不是？"

"我是瑞典人。"希尔顿先生说，他开始摇晃搅乳器了。

汤普生先生迸发出洪亮的笑声，仿佛这是他有生以来听到挖苦某人的最妙不过的笑话："哦，真有你的，我看你在这儿准会闷得慌。这一带林区里，我一个瑞典人也没见到过。"

"那没什么。"希尔顿说。他继续摇搅乳器，仿佛他在这里已经干了好多年了。

"老实说，我告诉你，你实际上是我这辈子第一次看到的瑞典人。"

"那没什么。"希尔顿先生说。

汤普生先生走进前房，绿窗帘拉着，汤普生太太躺在床上。她身边桌子上有一碗水，她眼睛上覆盖着一块湿布。听到汤普生先生的皮鞋声，她把湿布掀开，问道："外面什么事这么吵？那是谁？"

"外面来了一个人，说他是个瑞典人，艾丽，"汤普生先生说，"他说他会炼黄油。"

"但愿他不是在说瞎话，"汤普生太太说，"看来我的头疼再也不会好了。"

"你别担心。"汤普生先生说，"你脾气太急了。我现在要到镇上去订购些食品和杂货。"

"你别待得太久了，知道吗，汤普生先生。"汤普生太太说，"别上旅馆去。"她指的是酒店，老板在楼上也有空房间出租。

汤普生先生大声地笑着说："就喝几杯甜酒，对任何人都没什么害处。"

"我一辈子一滴酒也没喝过，"汤普生太太说，"而且我永远也不想沾它。"

"我没说你们女人家。"汤普生先生说。

搅乳器晃动的声音先是使得汤普生太太微微打盹，接着又催她昏昏沉沉睡去，后来她突然醒来，知道搅乳器已经停了很久。她坐起来，用手挡住怕见光的眼睛，以免让从帘底和窗台之间平射进来的夏末的阳

emphasis was in the wrong place. Mr. Thompson wondered what kind of foreigner Mr. Helton could be.

"Now just where did you say you worked last?" he asked, as if he expected Mr. Helton to contradict himself.

"North Dakota," said Mr. Helton.

"Well, one place is good as another once you get used to it," said Mr. Thompson, amply. "You're a for-riner, ain't you?"

"I'm a Swede," said Mr. Helton, beginning to swing the churn.

Mr. Thompson let forth a booming laugh, as if this was the best joke on somebody he'd ever heard. "Well, I'll be damned," he said at the top of his voice. "A Swede: well, now I'm afraid you'll get pretty lonesome around here. I never seen any Swedes in this neck of the woods. "

"That's all right," said Mr. Helton. He went on swinging the churn as if he had been working on the place for years.

"In fact, I might as well tell you, you're practically the first Swede I ever laid eyes on. "

"That's all right," said Mr. Helton.

Mr. Thompson went into the front room where Mrs. Thompson was lying down, with the green shades drawn. She had a bowl of water by her on the table and a wet cloth over her eyes. She took the cloth off at the sound of Mr. Thompson's boots and said, "What's all the noise out there? Who is it?"

"Got a feller out there says he's a Swede, Ellie," said Mr. Thompson; "says he knows how to make butter. "

"I hope it turns out to be the truth," said Mrs. Thompson. "Looks like my head never will get any better. "

"Don't you worry," said Mr. Thompson. "You fret too much. Now I'm gointa ride into town and get a little order of groceries. "

"Don't you linger, now, Mr. Thompson," said Mrs. Thompson. "Don't go to the hotel. " She meant the saloon; the proprietor also had rooms for rent upstairs.

"Just a coupla little toddies," said Mr. Thompson, laughing loudly, "never hurt anybody. "

"I never took a dram in my life," said Mrs. Thompson, "and what's more I never will. "

"I wasn't talking about the womenfolks," said Mr. Thompson.

The sound of the swinging churn rocked Mrs. Thompson first into a gentle doze, then a deep drowse from which she waked suddenly knowing that the swinging had stopped a good while ago. She sat up shading her weak eyes from the flat strips of late summer sunlight between the sill and the lowered shades.

光照得难受。感谢上帝，她还活着，虽然得准备晚饭，却不搅牛奶了，虽然还有点头晕，却也松快多了。慢慢地她理会到，即使她睡着时，她也听到了一种新的声音。有人在用口琴吹奏一支曲子呢，不是那种刺耳的忽高忽低的噪音，而是真正在奏着一支既愉快又哀伤的可爱动听的曲调。

她穿过厨房来到廊子上，面朝东站着，用手遮住眼睛。等她眼睛能看清东西时，她看见有个高高的、花白头发、穿蓝工裤的男人，在雇工小屋的门口，闭上眼睛在自我陶醉地吹他的口琴，他坐的那把硬板椅往后翘着。汤普生太太的心晃荡了几下，往下一沉。天哪，他看上去又懒惰又无能，没错儿，就是这样。先是一些成事不足败事有余的黑人，接着又来了一个没有用的白人。就好像汤普生先生专门要找这种人似的。她真希望汤普生多替别人考虑考虑，在活计上多花些工夫。她是想信任自己的丈夫的，可有很多时候就是做不到。她愿意相信明天，至迟是后天，生活会好起来的。生活充其量不过是一场战斗罢了。

她走过小屋，看也不朝旁边看，她步子跨得很小心，偃着身子，因为她胁部老是发痛，不让她安生。她朝盖在泉水上的冷藏室走去，一面使自己心肠硬下来，如果她发现这个新来的雇工活儿没有做好，她就要直率地跟他说个明白。

牛奶棚只不过是另一间破屋子而已，几年前他们急于要有个牛奶棚，匆匆忙忙用旧木板钉了一间。它本来是临时性质的，事实上也的确是临时的，现在已经走了形，东倒西歪地架在一个个水坑上，冰凉的泉水不断地从一个小泉眼里流出来，泉眼快给病恹恹的蕨草遮没了。这一带别人地里都没有泉水。汤普生夫妇觉得，如果好好加以利用，这口泉水是能给他们带来好处的。

歪歪斜斜的木架乱七八糟地围在小水池的四周，水池里放着几大桶牛奶和黄油，它们在冰凉的水里镇着，新鲜、喷香。汤普生太太一只手按着她那扁平、发痛的胁部，另一只手遮在眼睛上，探出身子朝桶里看了看。奶油已经给撇出来单放在一起，黄油厚厚的有一大块，水模子与浅锅不知多少时候以来第一次给刮擦、烫洗得干干净净，木桶里盛满了脱脂牛奶，准备喂猪和刚断奶的牛犊，夯实的泥地也给扫得光溜溜的。汤普生太太站直身子，脸上漾出了温和的笑容。她方才还打算去责备他呢，这个来找活干的穷人，他刚来

There she was, thank God, still alive, with supper to cook but no churning on hand, and her head still bewildered, but easy. Slowly she realized she had been hearing a new sound even in her sleep. Somebody was playing a tune on the harmonica, not merely shrilling up and down making a sickening noise, but really playing a pretty tune, merry and sad.

She went out through the kitchen, stepped off the porch, and stood facing the east, shading her eyes. When her vision cleared and settled, she saw a long, pale-haired man in blue jeans sitting in the doorway of the hired man's shack, tilted back in a kitchen chair, blowing away at the harmonica with his eyes shut. Mrs. Thompson's heart fluttered and sank. Heavens, he looked lazy and worthless, he did, now. First a lot of no-count fiddling darkies and then a no-count white man. It was just like Mr. Thompson to take on that kind. She did wish he would be more considerate, and take a little trouble with his business. She wanted to believe in her husband, and there were too many times when she couldn't. She wanted to believe that tomorrow, or at least the day after, life, such a battle at best, was going to be better.

She walked past the shack without glancing aside, stepping carefully, bent at the waist because of the nagging pain in her side, and went to the springhouse, trying to harden her mind to speak very plainly to that new hired man if he had not done his work.

The milk house was only another shack of weather-beaten boards nailed together hastily years before because they needed a milk house; it was meant to be temporary, and it was; already shapeless, leaning this way and that over a perpetual cool trickle of water that fell from a little grot, almost choked with pallid ferns. No one else in the whole countryside had such a spring on his land. Mr. and Mrs. Thompson felt they had a fortune in that spring, if ever they got around to doing anything with it.

Rickety wooden shelves clung at hazard in the square around the small pool where the larger pails of milk and butter stood, fresh and sweet in the cold water. One hand supporting her flat, pained side, the other shading her eyes, Mrs. Thompson leaned over and peered into the pails. The cream had been skimmed and set aside, there was a rich roll of butter, the wooden molds and shallow pans had been scrubbed and scalded for the first time in who knows when, the barrel was full of buttermilk ready for the pigs and the weanling calves, the hard packed-dirt floor had been swept smooth. Mrs. Thompson straightened up again, smiling tenderly. She had been ready to scold him, a poor man who needed a job, who had just come there and who might not have been expected to do things

到一个陌生的地方,本来就不该指望他一开始就能把事情干好。她没有别的办法补偿自己思想里对他的不公平的判断,只有去告诉他,他活儿干得这么漂亮,这么麻利,她真是高兴。她踩着小心翼翼的步子,鼓起勇气来到小屋门口。希尔顿先生睁开眼睛,停止了吹奏,把板椅放平,但他既没有瞧着她,也没有站起来。她是个弱小的女子,又厚又长的棕发拢成一根辫子,她有一张受苦的病人的嘴和一双有病的易哭的眼睛。她两只手的大拇指按在太阳穴上,其他手指交叉,遮在眼睛上方,眨着含泪的眼睑,用客气而又亲切的口气说道:"你好,先生。我是汤普生太太,我想告诉你,我认为你牛奶棚里的活儿干得很好。那个地方是不容易拾掇干净的。"

他说:"那没什么。"声音徐缓,人一动也不动。

汤普生太太等了一会儿。"你方才吹的曲子真好听。一般人用口琴往往吹不出好听的音乐来。"

希尔顿先生弓着背坐着,伸出两条长腿,脊背弯曲着,大拇指在口琴木格上滑来滑去,要不是他的手在动,你真要以为他睡着了呢。那只口琴很大,闪闪发亮,还很新。汤普生太太眼光四下里扫了扫,看见他床边架子上一溜儿放着五只口琴,也都是很好很贵的。"他准是塞在外套口袋里带来的。"她想,注意到屋子里没有一点儿别的行李的痕迹。"我看到你很喜欢音乐,"她说,"我们从前也有一只手风琴,汤普生先生拉得不错,可是给小男孩拆坏了。"

希尔顿先生颇为突然地站起来,以致椅子在他起身时发出格拉拉的声音。他伸直了膝盖,肩膀却仍然佝着,他瞪着地板,仿佛在专心致志地倾听什么。"你最好把这些口琴放在高架子上,否则小孩会来拿的,他们毛手毛脚的什么都要动。我常常教训他们,可是没用。"

希尔顿先生两只长胳膊做了个大动作,把口琴都揽到自己的胸前,然后把它们整齐地放在屋顶下墙犄角的旮旯里。他把它们往尽里面推,几乎都看不见了。

"这样大概不要紧了。"汤普生太太说。"我奇怪,"她说,转过身,在西边强烈的光线下无可奈何地眯起眼睛,"我奇怪这些小家伙跑到哪儿去了。真是看不住他们。"她讲起自己的孩子时,用的是一种特别的口气,仿佛他们是什么做客过久讨人嫌的外甥似的。

"在小溪边上。"希尔顿先生瓮声瓮气地说。汤普生太太不知所措地停住了话头,断定方才他是在回答

properly at first. There was nothing she could do to make up for the injustice she had done him in her thoughts but to tell him how she appreciated his good clean work, finished already, in no time at all. She ventured near the door of the shack with her careful steps; Mr. Helton opened his eyes, stopped playing, and brought his chair down straight, but did not look at her, or get up. She was a little frail woman with long thick brown hair in a braid, a suffering patient mouth and diseased eyes which cried easily. She wove her fingers into an eyeshade, thumbs on temples, and, winking her tearful lids, said with a polite little manner, "Howdy do, sir. I'm Miz Thompson, and I wanted to tell you I think you did real well in the milk house. It's always been a hard place to keep."

He said, "That's all right," in a slow voice, without moving.

Mrs. Thompson waited a moment. "That's a pretty tune you're playing. Most folks don't seem to get much music out of a harmonica."

Mr. Helton sat humped over, long legs sprawling, his spine in a bow, running this thumb over the square mouth-stops; except for his moving hand he might have been asleep. The harmonica was a big shiny new one, and Mrs. Thompson, her gaze wandering about, counted five others, all good and expensive, standing in a row on the shelf beside his cot. "He must carry them around in his jumper pocket," she thought, and noted there was not a sign of any other possession lying about. "I see you're mighty fond of music," she said. "We used to have an old accordion, and Mr. Thompson could play it right smart, but the little boys broke it up."

Mr. Helton stood up rather suddenly, the chair clattered under him, his knees straightened though his shoulders did not, and he looked at the floor as if he were listening carefully. "You'd better set them harmonicas on a high shelf or they'll be after them. They're great hands for getting into things. I try to learn 'em, but it don't do much good."

Mr. Helton, in one wide gesture of his long arms, swept his harmonicas up against his chest, and from there transferred them in a row to the ledge where the roof joined to the wall. He pushed them back almost out of sight.

"That'll do, maybe," said Mrs. Thompson. "Now I wonder," she said, turning and closing her eyes helplessly against the stronger western light, "I wonder what became of them little tads. I can't keep up with them." She had a way of speaking about her children as if they were rather troublesome nephews on a prolonged visit.

"Down by the creek," said Mr. Helton, in his hollow

自己的问题。他默默不语耐心地站着,也许不一定在等她快点走,但明显地也不是等着别的什么。汤普生太太知道世界上有各种各样的人,他们身上有各种各样的怪僻,她早就习以为常了。要紧的是弄明白希尔顿先生的怪僻和别人的有什么不同,然后迁就这些怪僻,让他感到自由自在。她自己的父亲就是怪人,她的兄弟和叔叔伯伯也都有自己的怪脾气,而且每一个人都不一样,此外她遇到过的每一个雇工也都有自己古怪的行为和想法。现在又来了这个希尔顿先生,他是个瑞典人,他不爱讲话,另外他还喜欢吹口琴。

"他们马上就要肚子饿了,"汤普生太太带点友好地说,"很快就要饿了,我真不知道晚饭该做什么好?你喜欢吃什么,希尔顿先生?我们新鲜黄油、牛奶、奶油倒是从来不缺,谢天谢地。汤普生先生老说应该一点儿不留全部卖掉,可我说还是自己家里吃第一要紧。"她闭上眼睛微笑着,显得怪可怜的,那张瘦小的脸完全变了形。

"我什么都吃。"希尔顿先生说,他的声调升高降低得完全不对头。

他英语说得不好,这是头一桩,汤普生太太思忖道。当他英语还不熟练时硬要拉住他说话,这是不应该的。她慢吞吞地迈着步子从小屋门口走开,还扭过头来添了一句。"除开礼拜天,我们一股都吃玉米面包。"她告诉他,"我想你在以前待的地方不大吃到好的玉米面包吧。"

希尔顿先生一声没吭。她从眼角里看到他又坐了下来,瞧着他的口琴,椅子又翘了起来。她希望他不至于忘记挤牛奶的时间快到了。她走开云时,他又吹起口琴来,还是那个曲调。

挤牛奶的时间到了又过去了。汤普生太太看见希尔顿先生在牛棚和牛奶房之间来来去去。他跨着大步,肩膀前伛,脑袋耷拉着,两只大桶像天平秤盘一样垂在他那两只瘦胳膊的末端。汤普生先生从镇上回来了,他坐在马上,身子比平时挺得更直,下巴颏儿贴在胸前,买来的满满一麻袋东西在马鞍后面晃来晃去。他先上马厩去,接着兴高采烈地来到厨房,他用自己那把又粗又硬的胡髭在汤普生太太脸颊上蹭了蹭,然后又和她亲亲热热地接了个响吻。他到旅馆去过了,这是明摆着的。"我到院子里看过了,艾丽。"他嚷嚷道,"那个瑞典人干活真不含糊。不过像他这样

voice. Mrs. Thompson, pausing confusedly, decided he had answered her question. He stood in silent patience, not exactly waiting for her to go, perhaps, but pretty plainly not waiting for anything else. Mrs. Thompson was perfectly accustomed to all kinds of men full of all kinds of cranky ways. The point was, to find out just how Mr. Helton's crankiness was different from any other man's, and then get used to it, and let him feel at home. Her father had been cranky, her brothers, and uncles had all been set in their ways and none of them alike; and every hired man she'd ever seen had quirks and crotchets of his own. Now here was Mr. Helton, who was a Swede, who wouldn't talk, and who played the harmonica besides.

"They'll be needing something to eat," said Mrs. Thompson in a vague friendly way, "pretty soon. Now I wonder what I ought to be thinking about for supper? Now what do you like to eat, Mr. Helton? We always have plenty of good butter and milk and cream, that's a blessing. Mr. Thompson says we ought to sell all of it, but I say my family comes first." Her little face went all out of shape in a pained blind smile.

"I eat anything," said Mr. Helton, his words wandering up and down.

He *can't* talk, for one thing, thought Mrs. Thompson, it's a shame to keep at him when he don't know the language good. She took a slow step away from the shack, looking back over her shoulder. "We usually have cornbread except on Sundays," she told him. "I suppose in your part of the country you don't get much good cornbread."

Not a word from Mr. Helton. She saw from her eye-corner that he had sat down again, looking at his harmonica, chair tilted. She hoped he would remember it was getting near milking time. As she moved away, he started playing again, the same tune.

Milking time came and went. Mrs. Thompson saw Mr. Helton going back and forth between the cow barn and the milk house. He swung along in an easy lope, shoulders bent, head hanging, the big buckets balancing like a pair of scales at the ends of his bony arms. Mr. Thompson rode in from town sitting straighter than usual, chin in, a tow-sack full of supplies swung behind the saddle. After a trip to the barn, he came into the kitchen full of good will, and gave Mrs. Thompson a hearty smack on the cheek after dusting her face off with his tough whiskers. He had been to the hotel, that was plain. "Took a look around the premises, Ellie," he shouted. "That Swede sure is grinding out the labor. But he is the closest mouthed feller I ever met up with in all my days. Looks like he's scared he'll crack his jaw if he opens his front teeth."

嘴紧的人，我这辈子还没见到过。他好像是担心一张嘴，下巴就会掉下来似的。"

汤普生太太在搅一大盆用脱脂牛奶和的玉米面。"你臭得像个酒鬼，汤普生先生。"她威严十足地说，"我希望你让哪个孩子给我再抱一捆柴火来。我想明天烤一炉小点心。"

汤普生先生立刻闻出自己呼吸里果真有酒气，觉得骂得有理，就乖乖地蹑手蹑脚地走出去，自己抱回来一捆柴火。阿瑟和赫伯特这两个小鬼，从乱蓬蓬的头发直到脚跟，身上也好衣服上也好，无处不是烂泥，他们踩着重重的脚步走进屋来，嚷着要吃晚饭。"先去洗洗脸，梳梳头发。"汤普生太太本能地说。他们就退到廊子上去，轮流把手伸到水泵下去冲一冲，把额上的头发沾沾湿，用手指把头发往前顺了顺，马上又回进厨房来了，生活中一切美好的东西都集中在这儿呢。汤普生太太另外摆上一个盘子，命令大孩子，8岁的阿瑟，去叫希尔顿先生来吃晚饭。

阿瑟不动窝，坐在原处像只小公牛般地吼道："喂——希——尔——顿，吃——晚——饭——了！"接着又低声加上一句："你这大个儿瑞典佬！"

"听着，"汤普生太太说，"不能这样没有礼貌。上那边好好地请他来，不然我让你多使劲儿揍你一顿。"

希尔顿先生又高又阴沉的身影出现在门口。"就坐在那儿吧。"汤普生先生大声说道，挥了一下胳膊。希尔顿先生甩开大皮鞋，两步就穿过厨房，沉重地往凳子上坐下去。汤普生先生坐的是桌子的上首，两个男孩爬上希尔顿先生对面的座位，汤普生太太坐在下首，靠近火炉。汤普生太太对握双手，垂下了头，匆匆地大声说道："主啊，为了这一切以及您其他的恩赐，我们以耶稣的名义感谢您，阿门。"她想在赫伯特的小脏手碰到最靠近他的碟子之前把祷告念完。不然的话，她就有责任把他从饭桌上撵下来，可是正在成长的孩子是需要吃东西的呀。汤普生先生和阿瑟总等她把祈祷念完，可是赫伯特才6岁，要他接受训练还早了一点。

汤普生夫妇想吸引希尔顿先生参加谈话，可是毫无结果。他们先是谈天气，接着谈收成，最后又谈奶牛，可是希尔顿先生就是不搭碴儿。汤普生先生便讲起他在镇上看到的趣事来。讲的是旅馆里几个老农民，都是他的朋友，怎样给一只山羊灌啤酒，它喝下去以后又是如何丑态百出。希尔顿先生好像没有在听。

Mrs. Thompson was stirring up a big bowl of buttermilk cornbread. "You smell like a toper, Mr. Thompson," she said with perfect dignity. "I wish you'd get one of the little boys to bring me in an extra load of firewood. I'm thinking about baking a batch of cookies tomorrow."

Mr. Thompson, all at once smelling the liquor on his own breath, sneaked out, justly rebuked, and brought in the firewood himself. Arthur and Herbert, grubby from thatched head to toes, from skin to shirt, came stamping in yelling for supper. "Go wash your faces and comb your hair," said Mrs. Thompson, automatically. They retired to the porch. Each one put his hand under the pump and wet his forelock, combed it down with his fingers, and returned at once to the kitchen, where all the fair prospects of life were centered. Mrs. Thompson set an extra plate and commanded Arthur, the eldest, eight years old, to call Mr. Helton for supper.

Arthur, without moving from the spot, bawled like a bull calf, "Say, Helton, supper's ready!" and added in a lower voice, "You big Swede!"

"Listen to me," said Mrs. Thompson, "that's no way to act. Now you go out there and ask him decent, or I'll get your daddy to give you a good licking."

Mr. Helton loomed, long and gloomy, in the doorway. "Sit right there," boomed Mr. Thompson, waving his arm. Mr. Helton swung his square shoes across the kitchen in two steps, slumped onto the bench and sat. Mr. Thompson occupied his chair at the head of the table, the two boys scrambled into place opposite Mr. Helton, and Mrs. Thompson sat at the end nearest the stove. Mrs. Thompson clasped her hands, bowed her head and said aloud hastily, "Lord, for all these and Thy other blessings we thank Thee in Jesus' name, amen," trying to finish before Herbert's dusty little paw reached the nearest dish. Othetwise she would be dutybound to send him away from the table, and growing children need their meals. Mr. Thompson and Arthur always waited, but Herbert, aged six, was too young to take training yet.

Mr. and Mrs. Thompson tried to engage Mr. Helton in conversation, but it was a failure. They tried first the weather, and then the crops, and then the cows, but Mr. Helton simply did not reply. Mr. Thompson then told something funny he had seen in town. It was about some of the other old grangers at the hotel, friends of his, giving beer to a goat, and the goat's subsequent behavior. Mr. Helton did not seem to hear. Mrs. Thompson laughed dutifully, but she didn't think it was very funny. She had heard it often before, though Mr. Thompson, each time he told it,

汤普生太太尽义务似的笑了笑,其实她并不觉得有什么可乐。这故事她以前已经听过好多遍了,虽然汤普生先生每次讲的时候都假装这件事就发生在当天。这件事如果真有,也是发生在好多年前了。汤普生太太总觉得男女同座时,讲这个故事是不得体的。问题就出在汤普生先生有个弱点:过一阵子就要喝醉一次,虽然他每逢选举都是投票赞成禁酒由本地自决。汤普生太太把菜传给希尔顿先生,他每样都拨一点儿,但都不多,要是他打算一直像方才那样卖力气,这点儿饭食是不够维持他的体力的。

最后他拿了挺大的一块玉米面包,把盘子擦得仿佛是给狗舔过那样一干二净,然后把面包满满地塞了一嘴巴,一边还嚼着就离开凳子朝门口走去。

“晚安,希尔顿先生。”汤普生太太说,家里另外那几口子也跟着零零落落地说:“晚安,希尔顿先生!”

“晚安。”希尔顿先生音调不准的回答从黑暗里传来,显得不太愿意似的。

“望昂。”阿瑟说,是在学希尔顿先生的腔调。

“望昂。”赫伯特说,他是阿瑟的应声虫。

“你学得不对。”阿瑟说,“你听我的。望——昂。”他因为学得像,大为得意,就唱了一个低音八度。赫伯特高兴得简直要发疯。

“你们不许那样,”汤普生太太说,“他那样说话是没法子。你们应该感到害臊,两个人都不好,竟这样拿一个可怜的陌生人来开玩笑。你们自己愿意在陌生的地方做陌生人吗?”

“我愿意,”阿瑟说,“我想那一定很好玩.’

“他们是一对无法无天的野孩子,艾丽,”汤普生先生说,“简直毫无教养。”他把他那副严父的可怕面孔转向他的孩子,“明年把你们俩都送进学校去,到时候你们的骨头就要收一收了。”

“我再大一点就该进教养院啦。”赫伯特尖声叫道,“那是我该去的地方。”

“噢,进教养院,你?”汤普生先生莫名其妙,“谁说的?”

“主日学校的校长。”赫伯特说,显出一副聪明孩子炫耀自己的神气。

“你听见没有?”汤普生先生说,瞪着他的太太,“我不是早就告诉过你了吗,”他勃然大怒起来,“都给我上床去!”他吼得连喉结都打颤了,“快滚,别等我来扒你们的皮!”他们走了,过不了一会儿,阁楼卧室里

pretended it had happened that self-same day. It must have happened years ago if it ever happened at all, and it had never been a story that Mrs. Thompson thought suitable for mixed company. The whole thing came of Mr. Thompson's weakness for a dram too much now and then, though he voted for local option at every e-lection. She passed the food to Mr. Helton, who took a helping of everything, but not much, not enough to keep him up to his full powers if he expected to go on working the way he had started.

At last he took a fair-sized piece of cornbread, wiped his plate up as clean as if it had been licked by a hound dog, stuffed his mouth full, and, still chewing, slid off the bench and started for the door.

"Good night, Mr. Helton," said Mrs. Thompson, and the other Thompsons took it up in a scattered chorus. "Good night, Mr. Helton!"

"Good night," said Mr. Helton's wavering voice grudgingly from the darkness.

"Gude not," said Arthur, imitating Mr. Helton.

"Gude not," said Herbert, the copy-cat.

"You don't do it right," said Arthur. "Now listen to me. Gude naht," and he ran a hollow scale in a luxury of successful impersonation. Herbert almost went into a fit with joy.

"Now you *stop* that," said Mrs. Thompson. "He can't help the way he talks. You ought to be ashamed of yourselves, both of you, making fun of a poor stranger like that. How'd you like to be a stranger in a strange land?"

"I'd like it," said Arthur. "I think it would be fun."

"They're both regular heathens, Ellie," said Mr. Thompson. "Just plain ignoramuses." He turned the face of awful fatherhood upon his young. "You're both going to get sent to school next year, and that'll knock some sense into you."

"I'm going to get sent to the'formatory when I'm old enough," piped up Herbert. "That's where I'm goin'."

"Oh, you are, are you?" asked Mr. Thompson. "Who says so?"

"The Sunday School Superintendant," said Herbert, a bright boy showing off.

"You see?" said Mr. Thompson, staring at his wife. "What did I tell you?" He became a hurricane of wrath. "Get to bed, you two," he roared until his Adam's apple shuddered. "Get now before I take the hide off you!" They got, and shortly from their attic bedroom the sounds of scuffling and snorting and giggling and growling filled the house and shook the kitchen ceiling.

传来了扭打、哼叫、格格的笑声和吼叱的声音,整座房子里都听得见,厨房的天花板直抖。

汤普生太太抱住脑袋,用游移不定的声音轻轻地说:"他们这么年轻幼稚,老训他们有什么用。我真受不了。"

"我的天哪,艾丽。"汤普生先生说,"我们必须管教他们,不能让他们长大了像野猪那样野。"

她换了一种口气说道:"那个希尔顿先生看来不错,虽然没法子引他说话。不知道他怎么会跑得这么远的。"

"我早说过,他不是一个爱嚼舌根的人。"汤普生先生说,"不过他干活的确很内行。在咱们农场上这才是第一要紧的。这一带转来转去想找活干的流浪汉有的是。"

汤普生太太正在收拾碗碟,他从汤普生先生下巴底下把他的盘子收走。"跟你说句实话,"她说,"家里有个会干活儿又不爱多嘴的人,这可是件大好事。这就是说,他不会来管咱们的事。倒不是说有什么见不得人的事,不过到底方便得多。"

"这倒不假,"汤普生先生说。"嗬,嗬,"他突然叫了起来,"这就是说,以后话都让你一个人来说,是吗?"

"只有一件事不大对头,"汤普生太太接着往下说,"那就是,他饭量不大,这一点我不太喜欢。我总爱看见一个汉子坐下来吃得津津有味。我奶奶常说,吃饭不香的男人靠不住。我希望这一回不至于这样。"

"告诉你一句老实话吧,艾丽,"汤普生先生说,身子往后靠着,用一把叉子在剔牙,他这时的心情再愉快不过了,"我一直觉得你奶奶是个奇蠢无比的老傻瓜。她有了什么想法,就随随便便地讲出来,还说什么这是上帝的真理。"

"我奶奶根本不是什么傻瓜。十有九回她的话都是很对的。我常说,一个人最初的想法往往是最有道理的。"

"哦,"汤普生先生说,又叫嚷起来了,"我一说到那个山羊的故事,你倒变得文明起来了,你什么时候在有男有女的人群前讲讲看,你倒试试看。莫非你以为在你面前的是一只母鸡跟一只公鸡吗?你的想法浸礼会牧师知道了准会吓一大跳!"他在她那瘦小的屁股上拧了一把。"连兔子都比你肉多一点,"他怜爱

Mrs. Thompson held her head and said in a small uncertain voice, "It's no use picking on them when they're so young and tender. I can't stand it."

"My goodness, Ellie," said Mr. Thompson, "we've got to raise 'em. We can't just let 'em grow up hog wild."

She went on in another tone. "That Mr. Helton seems all right, even if he can't be made to talk. Wonder how he comes to be so far from home."

"Like I said, he isn't no whamper-jaw," said Mr. Thompson, "but he sure knows how to lay out the work. I guess that's the main thing around here. Country's full of fellers trampin'round looking for work."

Mrs. Thompson was gathering up the dishes. She now gathered up Mr. Thompson's plate from under his chin. "To tell you the honest truth," she remarked, "I think it's a mighty good change to have a man round the place who knows how to work and keep his mouth shut. Means he'll keep out of our business. Not that we've got anything to hide, but it's convenient."

"That's a fact," said Mr. Thompson. "Haw, haw," he shouted suddenly. "Means you can do all the talking, huh?"

"The only thing," went on Mrs. Thompson, "is this: he don't eat hearty enough to suit me. I like to see a man set down and relish a good meal. My granma used to say it was no use putting dependence on a man who won't set down and make out his dinner. I hope it won't be that way this time."

"Tell *you* the truth, Ellie," said Mr. Thompson, picking his teeth with a fork and leaning back in the best of good humors, "I always thought your granma was a ter'ble ole fool. She'd just say the first thing that popped into her head and call it God's wisdom."

"My granma wasn't anybody's fool. Nine times out of ten she knew what she was talking about. I always say, the first thing you think is the best thing you can say."

"Well," said Mr. Thompson, going into another shout, "you're so *reefined* about that goat story, you just try speaking out in mixed comp'ny sometime! You just try it. S'pose you happened to be thinking about a hen and a rooster, hey? I reckon you'd shock the Babtist preacher!" He gave her a good pinch on her thin little rump. "No more meat on you than a rabbit," he said, fondly. "Now I like 'em cornfed."

Mrs. Thompson looked at him opened-eyed and blushed. She could see better by lamplight. "Why, Mr. Thompson, sometimes I think you're the evilest-minded man that ever lived." She took a handful of hair on the crown of his head and gave it a good, slow pull.

地说，"我爱看到这屁股让老玉米喂得肥肥的。"

汤普生太太睁大了眼瞧着他，脸上红红的。她在灯光底下眼力倒好一些。"哼，汤普生先生，我有时候觉得你是世界上思想最下流的男人。"她攥住一把他头顶心的头发，使劲儿地、慢慢地拉了一下。"也让你尝尝滋味，把人拧得这么疼，还以为是在开玩笑呢。"她温柔地说。

不管他经济情况如何，汤普生先生永远也不能消除自己顽固的信念，他认为侍候母牛和轰小鸡都是娘们儿的事。他爱吹牛说，别的男人干的活儿，者如犁地、割高粱、剥玉米、赶马、围玉米囤，他没什么拿不起来的。当然，做买卖也是男人的事。一星期两次，他赶着轻马车，拉着新鲜黄油、少量鸡蛋、时鲜水果，到市场上去卖。他把零钱揣在兜里，想怎么花就怎么花，就有一条，绝对不去动用汤普生太太的零花钱。

可是打一开始起，那些奶牛就让他心烦。它们一天两次等着挤奶，站在那儿用女性得意洋洋的脸色来责怪他。小牛犊也让他心烦，它们为了够到母牛的奶头，死命要挣脱绳子，常常把自己勒得连眼珠都鼓了出来。跟一头小牛犊斗使他显得有失身份，就像一个大男人在给娃娃换尿片。牛奶也使他心烦，一会儿变苦了，一会儿不出奶了，一会儿又变酸了。母鸡也使他心烦，整天咯咯打叽叽喳喳个没完，你料也没料到，它们就把小鸡孵出来了，还领着小鸡到马房前面的空地上去，弄得不好马儿就把小鸡踩死几只。鸡群会因为鸡瘟、歪颈症或鸡虱传染的时疫死去。尽管汤普生太太在饲养房里为它们准备了一排鸡窝，它们还是在你想都想不到的地方下蛋，因此多半不等你找到。鸡蛋已经给糟蹋了。母鸡真是该死的讨厌东西。

在汤普兰先生看来，喂猪是应该由长工来干的。宰猪倒是东家的活儿，可是刮毛切肉又是长工的事了。而娘们天生是应该洗肉、熏肉、腌肉、熬油、做香肠的。汤普生先生认为什么事都得有个规矩，他在上帝与外人的面前应该维持体面，这就使他对工作范围做了极细致的规定。"那样看起来不合适。"他不想干什么事的时候总拿这句话来搪塞。

他最操心的事自己的尊严和名声，只有极少数几种活儿算得上是爷们儿的事，值得他汤普生先生亲自干的。汤普生太太呢，虽说汤普生先生认为好多种活儿由她来干最合适不过，可是她总在他面前显示出自己不行。汤普生先生如今发现了自己对汤普生太太

"That's to show you how it feels, pinching so hard when you're supposed to be playing," she said, gently.

In spite of his situation in life, Mr. Thompson had never been able to outgrow his deep conviction that running a dairy and chasing after chickens was woman's work. He was fond of saying that he could plow a furrow, cut sorghum, shuck corn, handle a team, build a corn crib, as well as any man. Buying and selling, too, were man's work. Twice a week he drove the spring wagon to market with the fresh butter, a few eggs, fruits in their proper season, sold them, pocketed the change, and spent it as seemed best, being careful not to dig into Mrs. Thompson's pin money.

But from the first the cows worried him, coming up regularly twice a day to be milked, standing there reproaching him with their smug female faces. Calves worried him, fighting the rope and strangling themselves until their eyes bulged, trying to get at the teat. Wrestling with a calf unmanned him, like having to change a baby's diaper. Milk worried him, coming bitter sometimes, drying up, turning sour. Hens worried him, cackling, clucking, hatching out when you least expected it and leading their broods into the barnyard where the horses could step on them; dying of roup and wryneck and getting plagues of chicken lice; laying eggs all over God's creation so that half of them were spoiled before a man could find them, in spite of a rack of nests Mrs. Thompson had set out for them in the feed room. Hens were a blasted nuisance.

Slopping hogs was hired man's work, in Mr. Thompson's opinion. Killing hogs was a job for the boss, but scraping them and cutting them up was for the hired man again; and again woman's proper work was dressing meat, smoking, pickling, and making lard and sausage. All his carefully limited fields of activity were related somehow to Mr. Thompson's feeling for the appearance of things, his own appearance in the sight of God and man. "It don't *look* right," was his final reason for not doing anything he did not wish to do.

It was his dignity and his reputation that he cared about, and there were only a few kinds of work manly enough for Mr. Thompson to undertake with his own hands. Mrs. Thompson, to whom so many forms of work would have been becoming, had simply gone down on him early. He saw, after a while, how short-sighted it had been of him to expect much from Mrs. Thompson; he had fallen in love with her delicate waist and lace-trimmed petticoats and big blue eyes, and, though all those charms had disappeared, she had in the meantime become Ellie to him, not at all the

抱以太多的期望是何等的没眼光。他爱上了她的纤纤细腰、蕾丝裙边和蓝色的大眼睛。当这些魅人之处统统消失，她就成了他的艾丽，不过这可不是艾伦·布里奇斯小姐，那位蒙顿市第一浸礼会主日学校备受欢迎的老师，而是他亲爱的太太艾丽——羸弱的艾丽。但是，男人们指望靠婚姻来维持生活，对他来说却无法实现，而他对此却几乎毫无意识，只是自认失败。抬头挺胸，按时缴税，每年为教师捐赠工资，虽然是个有产业的人——一家之主、雇有长工的东家和人缘很好的快活人，可是汤普生先生不明说也知道，自己是在不断地走下坡路。天哪，他马房门前厨房阶下的垃圾积成了堆，让人看着难受，过一阵就忍不住想拿上家伙来替他打扫一番。大车棚里堆满了使坏的农械、破烂的马具、旧车轴辘、散架的牛奶桶和朽烂的木头，你简直没法把大车赶过去。家里没有人愿意去收拾。至于他呢，每天必须干的活儿就够他忙的了。到了淡季，他又一坐好几个小时为这事发愁，一面把烟汁吐在柴禾堆旁密密的豚草丛上，一面苦思冥想：像他这样条件不好的人该怎么办。他盼望两个男孩快快长大也要让他们多多经受磨炼，就像他小时候他父亲对待他那样。他要让他们学会怎样守住这份产业，管理这份产业。他不想做得太过分，可是这两个男孩以后得自食其力，否则天下的事情太没道理了。两个只会坐在那儿削木棍的傻大个儿！汤普生先生有时想象他们的前途，一想到他们没准会成为坐在那儿削木根或是盘算去不去钓鱼的大傻瓜，他就火冒三丈。哼，他得防患于未然，而且决不能拖延。

　　季节不断替换，希尔顿先生接过去的活儿越来越多，汤普生先生的心也放宽了一些。这汉子似乎没有什么活儿拿不起来的，他把一天应该干的活儿全都利利索索地干掉，而且像是理所当然似的。他一清早5点钟就起床，煮自己的咖啡，煎自己的咸肉，然后就到母牛群里去了，这时，汤普生先生还在打呵欠，伸懒腰，又吼又闹地到处找他的工裤。希尔顿先生挤奶、清理牛奶棚、炼黄油。他把母鸡圈了起来，居然做到了让它们在窝里下蛋，而不下在屋子底下①和草堆边上，他定时喂食，使它们孵出的小鸡多得让人无法落脚。一点儿一点儿的，马厩和房子周围的垃圾堆不见

---

① 美国有些农舍为了防潮，用木柱架高屋子，与地面之间有一些空隙。

same person as Miss Ellen Bridges, popular Sunday School teacher in the Mountain City First Baptist Church, but his dear wife, Ellie, who was not strong. Deprived as he was, however, of the main support in life which a man might expect in marriage, he had almost without knowing it resigned himself to failure. Head erect, a prompt payer of taxes, yearly subscriber to the preacher's salary, land owner and father of a family, employer, a hearty good fellow among men, Mr. Thompson knew, without putting it into words, that he had been going steadily down hill. God amighty, it did look like somebody around the place might take a rake in hand now and then and clear up the clutter around the barn and the kitchen steps. The wagon shed was so full of brokendown machinery and ragged harness and old wagon wheels and battered milk pails and rotting lumber you could hardly drive in there any more. Not a soul on the place would raise a hand to it, and as for him, he had all he could do with his regular work. He would sometimes in the slack season sit for hours worrying about it, squrting tobacco on the ragweeds growing in a thicket against the wood pile, wondering what a fellow could do, handicapped as he was. He looked forward to the boys growing up soon; he was going to put them through the mill just as his own father had done with him when he was a boy; they were going to learn how to take hold and run the place right. He wasn't going to overdo it, but those two boys were going to earn their salt, or he'd know why. Great big lubbers sitting around whittling! Mr. Thompson sometimes grew quite enraged with them, when imagining their possible future, big lubbers sitting around whittling or thinking about fishing trips. Well, he'd put a stop to that, mighty damn quick.

As the seasons passed, and Mr. Helton took hold more and more, Mr. Thompson began to relax in his mind a little. There seemed to be nothing the fellow couldn't do, all in the day's work and as a matter of course. He got up at five o'clock in the morning, boiled his own coffee and fried his own bacon and was out in the cow lot before Mr. Thompson had even begun to yawn, stretch, groan, roar and thump around looking for his jeans. He milked the cows, kept the milk house, and churned the butter; rounded the hens up and somehow persuaded them to lay in the nests, not under the house and behind the haystacks; he fed them regularly and they hatched out until you couldn't set a foot down for them. Little by little the piles of trash around the barns and house disappeared. He carried buttermilk and corn to the hogs, and curried cockleburs out of the horses' manes. He was gentle with the

了。他提了脱脂牛奶和老玉米去喂猪，他洗刷掉马鬃毛上的草刺。他对小牛犊很温柔，对母牛与母鸡却有点严厉。从希尔顿先生的行为来看，他从来没听说过在农场上还分什么爷们的活儿和娘们的活儿。

第二年，他把邮购定货单上的一架压酪机的图样指给汤普生先生看，说："这东西不错。你去买来，我来做干酪。"压酪机买来了，希尔顿先生真的做出了干酪，它们和产量越来越多的黄油以及一篓一篓鸡蛋一起卖了出去。有时候，汤普生先生有点瞧不起希尔顿先生的作风。一个大男子，四处去捡马车从地里回来时掉下来的几个玉米棒子，把落在地上的烂水果抬回来喂猪，把旧钉子和机器零件收在一起，花不少时间在准备送到市场上去出售的黄油上压花——这可太小里小气了。汤普生先生高高地坐在弹簧马车的座位上，车子里压了花的黄油装在五加仑的油桶里，外面裹着湿麻袋。汤普生先生吆喝着马儿，用缰绳在马背上抽得啪啪响，把车子赶到镇上去。有时候他想，希尔顿先生是个有点儿鬼鬼祟祟的人，可是他绝对不让自己的感情影响自己，他是个识货的人。事实是，他的猪喂得更像样，能卖大价钱了。事实是，希尔顿先生把庄稼安排得那么妥善，汤普生先生从此不用再买饲料了。杀牛宰猪的时节，希尔顿先生把他扔掉的下水捡回来，不厌其烦地把它们刮洗干净，月自己的方法把它们制成香肠。总之，汤普生先生是没有什么好抱怨的。在第三年上，他提高了希尔顿先生的工资，虽然希尔顿先生没有要求加薪。到第四年，汤普生先生不但还清了债，而且在银行里有了点存款，他再次给希尔顿先生长了工资。每次都是提高两块五角一个月。

"这个人值得给这么些钱，艾丽。"汤普生先生脸红红的，在为自己的慷慨行为辩护，"他使这个农场有了盈余，我要让他明白我是知道好歹的。"

汤普生一家已经完全习惯了希尔顿先生的沉默习惯了，他那灰白的眉毛与头发，他那长长的阴郁的下巴，以及他那拒绝看一切，甚至是他手里的活儿的眼睛。起初，汤普生太太不无怨言。"就像跟一个没有肉身的幽灵在一张餐桌上吃饭似的，"她说，"你总以为他迟早会找出句话来说的吧。""别去管他，"汤普生先生说，"他想说的时候自会说的。"

好几年过去了，希尔顿先生却一直没打算开口。一天的工作做完以后，他便从马厩、牛奶棚或鸡舍里

calves, if a little grim with the cows and hens; judging by his conduct, Mr. Helton had never heard of the difference between man's and woman's work on a farm.

In the second year, he showed Mr. Thompson the picture of a cheese press in a mail order catalogue, and said, "This is a good thing. You buy this, I make cheese." The press was bought and Mr. Helton did make cheese, and it was sold, along with the increased butter and the crates of eggs. Sometimes Mr. Thompson felt a little contemptuous of Mr. Helton's ways. It did seem kind of picayune for a man to go around picking up half a dozen ears of corn that had fallen off the wagon on the way from the field, gathering up fallen fruit to feed to the pigs, storing up old nails and stray parts of machinery, spending good time stamping a fancy pattern on the butter before it went to market. Mr. Thompson, sitting up high on the spring-wagon seat, with the decorated butter in a five-gallon lard can wrapped in wet towsack, driving to town, chirruping to the horses and snapping the reins over their backs, sometimes thought that Mr. Helton was a pretty meeching sort of fellow; but he never gave way to these feelings, he knew a good thing when he had it. It was a fact the hogs were in better shape and sold for more money. It was a fact that Mr. Thompson stopped buying feed, Mr. Helton managed the crops so well. When beef- and hog-slaughtering time came, Mr. Helton knew how to save the scraps that Mr. Thompson had thrown away, and wasn't above scraping guts and filling them with sausages that he made by his own methods. In all, Mr. Thompson had no grounds for complaint. In the third year, he raised Mr. Helton's wages, though Mr. Helton had not asked for a raise. The fourth year, when Mr. Thompson was not only out of debt but had a little cash in the bank, he raised Mr. Helton's wages again, two dollars and a half a month each time.

"The man's worth it, Ellie," said Mr. Thompson, in a glow of selfjustification for his extravagance. "He's made this place pay, and I want him to know I appreciate it."

Mr. Helton's silence, the pallor of his eyebrows and hair, his long, glum jaw and eyes that refused to see anything, even the work under his hands, had grown perfectly familiar to the Thompsons. At first, Mrs. Thompson complained a little. "It's like sitting down at the table with a disembodied spirit," she said. "You'd think he'd find something to say, sooner or later."

"Let him alone," said Mr. Thompson. "When he gets ready to talk, he'll talk."

出来,摇晃着他的灯笼,那双大皮鞋像马蹄一样在硬泥地上踩得蹬蹬响。汤普生一家不管是冬天坐在厨房里,还是夏天坐在后廊上,都可以听到他把木板椅拖出来,听到椅子往后翘的吱嘎声,再过一会儿,他就会用他那些口琴中的某一只吹起他唯一的曲调。每一只口琴的调性都不一样,有的音调低些,更甜美些,可是每天晚上吹的总是那支重复不变的曲子,那是一支古怪的曲子,某个地方有个突然的转折,有时候连下午坐下来歇口气的那阵子他也吹。起先汤普生一家非常喜欢它,总是停下来听,后来有一个时期他们腻烦透了,每一个都希望他能学会一支新的曲子。最后,他们根本不去听它了,那成了一种自然而然的声音,就像晚上起风的声音,牛的哞叫声,或是他们自己的声音。

汤普生太太时时为希尔顿先生的灵魂担心。看来他不是一个上教堂的人,连星期天也照样干活。"我想咱们应该邀他去听马丁博士布道,"她对汤普生先生说,"如果我们不请他,就不大像基督徒了。他不是一个很主动的人。他要等人去请的。"

"随他去吧,"汤普生先生说,"在我看来,宗教信仰是每个人自己的事。而且,他也没有星期天穿的衣服。他穿了工裤和工作服是不会去教堂的。我不知道他的钱花到哪儿去了。他肯定是没有乱花。"

可是,汤普生太太既然起了这个念头,她不邀请希尔顿先生星期天一起去教堂是不会甘心的。希尔顿先生正在果园后面的地里用叉子把干草堆成一个个挺整齐的小垛。汤普生太太戴上玻璃眼镜与遮阳布帽,一直走到地里去和他谈这件事。他停下活儿,倚在叉子上听她讲,有一阵子,汤普生太太几乎被他的脸吓着了。那双灰白的眼睛仿佛看穿了她的身子,眉头皱着,长下巴发僵。"我得干活。"他直愣愣地说,接着便举起叉子转过身子去堆草。汤普生太太感情上受到伤害,一边往回走一边寻思,虽然照说到这时候她也应该摸透希尔顿先生的脾气了,可是一个男人,即便是外国人,似乎也应该讲点礼貌,特别是人家来请你去做礼拜的时候。"他没有礼貌,这是我唯一不喜欢他的地方。"她对汤普生先生说。"他好像是不会像别人一样为人处世。仿佛这个世界亏待了他似的,"她说,"有时候我真不明白这是怎么一回事。"

在第二年上出了一件事,使汤普生太太感到不安,这种事情她用言语表达不清楚,连想也不容易想

The years passed, and Mr. Helton never got ready to talk. After his work was finished for the day, he would come up from the barn or the milk house or the chicken house, swinging his lantern, his big shoes clumping like pony hoofs on the hard path. They, sitting in the kitchen in the winter, or on the back porch in the summer, would hear him drag out his wooden chair, hear the creak of it tilted back, and then for a little while he would play his single tune on one or another of his harmonicas. The harmonicas were in different keys, some lower and sweeter than the others, but the same changeless tune went on, a strange tune, with sudden turns in it, night after night, and sometimes even in the afternoons when Mr. Helton sat down to catch his breath. At first the Thompsons liked it very much, and always stopped to listen. Later there came a time when they were fairly sick of it, and began to wish to each other that he would learn a new one. At last they did not hear it any more, it was as natural as the sound of the wind rising in the evenings, or the cows lowing, or their own voices.

Mrs. Thompson pondered now and then over Mr. Helton's soul. He didn't seem to be a church-goer, and worked straight through Sunday as if it were any common day of the week. "I think we ought to invite him to go to hear Dr. Martin," she told Mr. Thompson. "It isn't very Christian of us not to ask him. He's not a forward kind of man. He'd wait to be asked. "

"Let him alone," said Mr. Thompson. "The way I look at it, his religion is every man's own business. Besides, he ain't got any Sunday clothes. He wouldn't want to go to church in them jeans and jumpers of his. I don't know what he does with his money. He certainly don't spend it foolishly. "

Still, once the notion got into her head, Mrs. Thompson could not rest until she invited Mr. Helton to go to church with the family next Sunday. He was pitching hay into neat little piles in the field back of the orchard. Mrs. Thompson put on smoked glasses and a sunbonnet and walked all the way down there to speak to him. He stopped and leaned on his pitchfork, listening, and for a moment Mrs. Thompson was almost frightened at his face. The pale eyes seemed to glare past her, the eyebrows frowned, the long jaw hardened. "I got work," he said bluntly, and lifting his pitchfork he turned from her and began to toss the hay. Mrs. Thompson, her feelings hurt, walked back thinking that by now she should be used to Mr. Helton's ways, but it did seem like a man, even a foreigner, could be just a little polite when you gave him a Christian invitation. "He's not polite, that's the only thing I've got against him," she said to Mr. Thompson.

清楚,若是她试着去向汤普生先生解释,那就会不是说得太过分就是显得太轻描淡写。这种怪事像是快出什么灾祸之前的一种恶兆,可是往往又什么事也没有发生。那是一个炎热、宁静的春日,汤普生太太到菜园子去收点新鲜的胡萝卜、洋葱和菜豆,好做晚饭。她采摘时,遮阳帽低压在眼睛上。她把各种蔬菜分开码在篮子里,她注意到希尔顿先生除草除得多么干净,土地又是多么肥沃。他把厩肥在地里铺得匀匀的,在秋天让肥力渗进土里,蔬菜当然长得又肥又大。她打多瘤的小无花果树底下走回去,在那里,未经修剪的树枝几乎挨到地上,浓密的树叶织成了一道阴凉的帷幕。汤普生太太总是找幽暗的地方,以保护自己的眼睛。就在她懒洋洋地四处张望时,她穿过树荫看到一幅很奇怪的图景,使她大吃一惊。倘若是吵吵嚷嚷的,那倒不足为奇。正是那种寂然无声下住了她。希尔顿先生去抓住阿瑟的肩膀,正在猛烈地摇晃着,他脸色铁青,一副凶相。阿瑟的脑袋一前一后地摆荡着,没有像汤普生太太摇他的时候那样梗着脖子表示反抗,他的眼睛里显得很害怕,却又有惊异,也许更多的是惊异,而不是别的。赫伯特老老实实地站在一边瞧着。希尔顿先生放开阿瑟,又抓住了赫伯特,同样一本正经地恶狠狠地摇晃他,脸上也是那么充满了恨。赫伯特的嘴角耷拉着像是快要哭了,可是他并没有出声。希尔顿先生放开了他,转过身子迈进小屋。两个小男孩拔腿就跑,仿佛是在逃命,一声也不吭。他们在屋前拐角处消失了。

汤普生太太慢吞吞地把篮子放在厨房桌子上,她把遮阳帽推后去又拉回来,她又去瞧瞧炉子里的火是不是还燃着,然后,才去找她的孩子。他们缩着身子坐在从她卧室窗口可以看得清清楚楚的一丛楝树下,仿佛是他们发现那里最最安全。

“你们在干吗?”汤普生太太问。

他们头也不抬,眼睛斜瞥过来,一副倒霉相。阿瑟嘟哝道:“没干什么。”

“你是说,现在没干什么,”汤普生太太声色俱厉地说,“好,我正有好多活儿给你们干呢。马上进屋来,帮我摘菜。快来。”

他们巴不得似的急忙爬起来,紧紧地跟在她后面。汤普生太太竭力猜想他们刚才干了什么错事。她不喜欢希尔顿先生擅自教训她的小孩,可是她又不好问到底是怎么回事。他们可能向她撒谎,她还得揭

"He just can't seem to behave like other people. You'd think he had a grudge against the world," she said. "I sometimes don't know what to make of it."

In the second year something had happened that made Mrs. Thompson uneasy, the kind of thing she could not put into words, hardly into thoughts, and if she had tried to explain to Mr. Thompson it would have sounded worse than it was, or not bad enough. It was that kind of queer thing that seems to be giving a warning, and yet, nearly always nothing comes of it. It was on a hot, still spring day, and Mrs. Thompson had been down to the garden patch to pull some new carrots and green onions and string beans for dinner. As she worked, sunbonnet low over her eyes, putting each kind of vegetable in a pile by itself in her basket, she noticed how neatly Mr. Helton weeded, and how rich the soil was. He had spread it all over with manure from the barns, and worked it in, in the fall, and the vegetables were coming up fine and full. She walked back under the nubby little fig trees where the unpruned branches leaned almost to the ground, and the thick leaves made a cool screen. Mrs. Thompson was always looking for shade to save her eyes. So she, looking idly about, saw through the screen a sight that struck her as very strange. If it had been a noisy spectacle, it would have been quite natural. It was the silence that struck her. Mr. Helton was shaking Arthur by the shoulders, ferociously, his face most terribly fixed and pale. Arthur's head snapped back and forth and he had not stiffened in resistance, as he did when Mrs. Thompson tried to shake him. His eyes were rather frightened, but surprised, too, probably more surprised than anything else. Herbert stood by meekly, watching. Mr. Helton dropped Arthur, and seized Herbert, and shook him with the same methodical ferocity, the same face of hatred. Herbert's mouth crumpled as if he would cry, but he made no sound. Mr. Helton let him go, turned and strode into the shack, and the little boys ran, as if for their lives, without a word. They disappeared around the corner to the front of the house.

Mrs. Thompson took time to set her basket on the kitchen table, to push her sunbonnet back on her head and draw it forward again, to look in the stove and make certain the fire was going, before she followed the boys. They were sitting huddled together under a clump of chinaberry trees in plain sight of her bedroom window, as if it were a safe place they had discovered.

"What are you doing?"asked Mrs. Thompson.

They looked hang-dog from under their foreheads and Arthur mumbled, "Nothin'."

穿他们,把他们打上一顿。或者是她只得假装相信,这样就会养成他们撒谎的习惯。也许他们会向她说实话,那可能是一件使她必须揍他们一顿的错事。一想到这里她就头疼。她想也许她可以去问希尔顿先生,可是由她去问也不合适。她还是等一等,以后告诉汤普生先生,让他来查个水落石出吧。她在心里盘算着,同时嘴里不断地差遣那两个孩子。"胡萝卜的头别削得那么多,赫伯特,你给我留点儿神。阿瑟,豆角别掰得那么细,它们本来就够小了。赫伯特你去抱一把柴火来。阿瑟,你把洋葱头拿到水泵底下去洗一洗。赫伯特,你这里的事做完。就拿把扫帚,把厨房扫扫干净。阿瑟,你去拿把铁锨来把炉灰清一清。别抠鼻眼,赫伯特。我得跟你说多少回?阿瑟,你去看看我的五斗柜最上面一只抽屉,左手的,找到凡士林就拿来,我要给赫伯特鼻子抹一点儿。赫伯特,上我这儿来……"

他们给差遣得跑过来跑过去。一活动,他们的动物般的元气又恢复了。过不了多久,他们又在前院里扭打起来。他们趴在地上,对打,匍匐前进,扯来扯去,爬起来又嗥叫着倒下去,像两只小狗一样毫无目的,吵吵闹闹单调无聊。他们学各种动物的吼叫,就是不发出人的声音,他们又小又脏的脸上淌着一行汗水。汤普生太太坐在窗前,怀着硬压制下去的骄傲与怜爱,望着他们。他们这样的苗壮、健康,长得这样快。可是她心里也有点不安,她的微笑是哀愁的,她眼角里滚动着两颗泪珠,全靠阳光支撑着才不致坠落下来。这两个孩子太懒了,大浑了,仿佛他们根本不用操心未来,无需关切自己的灵魂是否能得救,啊,对了,他们到底干了什么,使希尔顿先生摇晃他们,脸上是那样的杀气腾腾?

傍晚,吃晚饭前,她只告诉汤普生先生,希尔顿先生不知为了什么事摇晃过两个孩子。她一句没提那情景使她产生了古怪的恐惧感。他上小屋去问希尔顿先生,5分钟以后他回来了,眼睛直愣愣地瞪着他的孩子。"艾丽,他说这两个小混蛋弄坏他的口琴,把它们搞得一塌糊涂,满是口水,都吹不出好声音来了。"

"他是这么说的吗?"汤普生太太问道,"不大可能吧。"

"哼,反正他的话就是这个意思。不过一提这事他就恼火。"

"真不像话,"汤普生太太说,"太不像话了。我们

"Nothing *now*, you mean," said Mrs. Thompson, severely. "Well, I have plenty for you to do. Come right in here this minute and help me fix vegetables. This minute."

They scrambled up very eagerly and followed her close. Mrs. Thompson tried to imagine what they had been up to; she did not like the notion of Mr. Helton taking it on himself to correct her little boys, but she was afraid to ask them for reasons. They might tell her a lie, and she would have to overtake them in it, and whip them. Or she would have to pretend to believe them, and they would get in the habit of lying. Or they might tell her the truth, and it would be something she would have to whip them for. The very thought of it gave her a headache. She supposed she might ask Mr. Helton, but it was not her place to ask. She would wait and tell Mr. Thompson, and let him get at the bottom of it. While her mind ran on, she kept the little boys hopping. "Cut those carrot tops closer, Herbert, you're just being careless. Arthur, stop breaking up the beans so little. They're little enough already. Herbert, you go get an armload of wood. Arthur, you take these onions and wash them under the pump. Herbert, as soon as you're done here, you get a broom and sweep out this kitchen. Arthur, you get a shovel and take up the ashes. Stop picking your nose, Herbert. How often must I tell you? Arthur, you go look in the top drawer of my bureau, lefthand side, and bring me the vaseline for Herbert's nose. Herbert, come here to me. . . ."

They galloped through their chores, their animal spirits rose with activity, and shortly they were out in the front yard again, engaged in a wrestling match. They sprawled and fought, scrambled, clutched, rose and fell shouting, as aimlessly, noisily, monotonously as two puppies. They imitated various animals, not a human sound from them, and their dirty faces were streaked with sweat. Mrs. Thompson, sitting at her window, watched them with baffled pride and tenderness, they were so sturdy and healthy and growing so fast; but uneasily, too, with her pained little smile and the tears rolling from her eyelids that clinched themselves against the sunlight. They were so idle and careless, as if they had no future in this world, and no immortal souls to save, and oh, what had they been up to that Mr. Helton had shaken them, with his face positively dangerous?

In the evening before supper, without a word to Mr. Thompson of the curious fear the sight had caused her, she told him that Mr. Helton had shaken the little boys for some reason. He stepped out to the shack and spoke to Mr. Helton. In five minutes he was back,

得惩罚他们,让他们记住以后千万不能动希尔顿先生的东西。"

"我要给他们一顿好揍,"汤普生先生说,"他们再不留点儿神,我就去拿牛绳来揍他们。"

"我看还是去让我来打吧,"汤普生太太说,"你打小孩子手太重。"

"问题就出在这里,"汤普生先生嚷道,"等到惯得没法再管时,他们就总有一天会进监牢。你根本不是在打他们,只是心疼地拍几下。我爹从前火头一上来,随手操起劈柴什么的,打得我都起不来。"

"哼,那样也不见得就对,"汤普生太太说,"我不赞成这样管教孩子。那会逼得他们从家里逃出去。这种事我也见得多了。"

"我要把他们每一根骨头都打断,"汤普生先生说,气一点点消了下来,"假如他们还是一点儿也不怕你,仍旧犟头倔脑的话。"

"快下饭桌,去洗洗脸和手。"汤普生太太突然命令起孩子来。他们悄没声息地走出去,在水泵底下沾了沾水,又悄没声息地走进来,尽量把自己蜷缩得更小些。他们很早以前就知道,每逢要有麻烦事,母亲总叫他们先去洗洗干净。他们的眼睛盯住自己的盘子。汤普生先生向他们开火了。

"好,现在你们说,干吗跑到希尔顿先生的屋子里去弄坏他的口琴?"

两个孩子马上蔫儿了,他们哭丧着脸,显出一副儿童被押上成人的无情法庭时那种绝望的神情,他们惊恐地用眼光交流思想:"这下子真的要挨揍了。"在绝望中,他们把抹了黄油的玉米面包放回到盘子里,双手无力地靠在桌子边上。

"我应该打断你们的筋骨,"汤普生先生说,"我真想这么干。"

"是的,爸爸。"阿瑟低声说,轻得几乎听不见。

"是的,爸爸。"赫伯特说,他的嘴唇在颤抖。

"好了,爸爸。"汤普生太太用一种警告的口气说。孩子们没去看她。他们对她的好意不抱幻想。她从一开始就把他们出卖了。对她是不能信任的。现在,她也可能救他们,也可能不救。指望她是没有用的。

"哼,你们该好好给揍一顿。你们罪有应得,对不对,阿瑟?"

阿瑟耷拉着脑袋。"对,爸爸。"

"下一次我看到谁还往希尔顿先生屋子那儿跑,

glaring at his young. "He says them brats been fooling with his harmonicas, Ellie, blowing in them and getting them all dirty and full of spit and they don't play good. "

"Did he say all that?" asked Mrs. Thompson. "It doesn't seem possible. "

"Well, that's what he meant, anyhow," said Mr. Thompson. "He didn't say it just that way. But he acted pretty worked up about it. "

"That's a shame," said Mrs. Thompson, "a perfect shame. Now we've got to do something so they'll remember they mustn't go into Mr. Helton's things. "

"I'll tan their hides for them," said Mr. Thompson. "I'll take a calf rope to them if they don't look out. "

"Maybe you'd better leave the whipping to me," said Mrs. Thompson. "You haven't got a light enough hand for children. "

"That's just what's the matter with them now," shouted Mr. Thompson, "rotten spoiled and they'll wind up in the penitentiary. You don't half whip 'em. Just little love taps. My pa used to knock me down with a stick of stove wood or anything else that came handy. "

"Well, that's not saying it's right," said Mrs. Thompson. "I don't hold with that way of raising children. It makes them run away from home. I've seen too much of it. "

"I'll break every bone in 'em," said Mr. Thompson, simmering down, "if they don't mind you better and stop being so bull-headed. "

"Leave the table and wash your face and hands," Mrs. Thompson commanded the boys, suddenly. They slunk out and dabbled at the pump and slunk in again, trying to make themselves small. They had learned long ago that their mother always made them wash when there was trouble ahead. They looked at their plates. Mr. Thompson opened up on them.

"Well, now, what you got to say for yourselves about going into Mr. Helton's shack and ruining his harmonicas?"

The two little boys wilted, their faces drooped into the grieved hopeless lines of children's faces when they are brought to the terrible bar of blind adult justice; their eyes telegraphed each other in panic, "Now we're really going to catch a licking"; in despair, they dropped their buttered cornbread on their plates, their hands lagged on the edge of the table.

"I ought to break your ribs," said Mr. Thompson, "and I'm a good mind to do it. "

"Yes, sir," whispered Arthur, faintly.

"Yes, sir," said Herbert, his lip trembling.

我就要把他的皮都扒掉,听见没有,赫伯特?"

赫伯特哼哼着,哽咽着,把他那块玉米面包掰得粉碎。"听见了,爸。"

"好,现在给我坐直了好好吃饭,不许再出点儿声音。"汤普生先生说,他也开始吃饭。两个孩子稍稍振作了些,咀嚼起食物来。可是每回他们抬起眼睛,总碰到父母的眼光牢牢地盯住他们。说不上大人什么时候才会想起别的新事情。孩子们小心翼翼地吃着,尽量不让人家看见他们,听见他们,可是玉米面包粘在嗓子眼里不肯下去,脱脂牛奶灌下咽喉时也会发出咕噜咕噜的声音。

"还有一件事,汤普生先生,"汤普生太太半晌之后说道,"告诉希尔顿先生,以后孩子们跟他捣乱,直接来找我们好了,不必烦扰他自己摇晃孩子。告诉他我们会处理的。"

"他们太不像样了,"汤普生先生答道,眼睛瞪着他们,"他没把他们杀死,一了百了,这倒是件怪事。"可是从他语气里阿瑟与赫伯特可以听出,现在不必再担心会有什么事了。他们深深地舒了一口气,坐直身子,伸手去拿离他们最近的食物。

"我说,"汤普生先生突然开口道,孩子们停止了吃东西,"希尔顿先生没来吃晚饭嘛。阿瑟,去告诉希尔顿先生他晚了。好好地跟他说,快去。"

阿瑟垂头丧气地滑下座位,一声不吭地朝门口走去。

发财这样的奇迹是不会降临在一个小牛奶场上的。汤普生一家没有变富,可是,正像汤普生先生老爱挂在口头的,他们也没有进贫民院,意思是尽管艾丽身体不好,天气反常,市场上莫名其妙的滞销,以及拖累他的他自己也不明白的不利条件,他总算是站稳了脚跟。希尔顿先生成了一家的希望和支柱,家里每个人都喜欢他了,至少他们不再觉得他有什么不正常,而认为他是一个好人,一个好朋友,虽然彼此之间始终有一个他们不知如何弥合的距离。希尔顿先生还是照老样子干他的活儿,吹他的曲子。9年过去了。孩子们长大了,学会干活了。他们记不得老希尔顿没来时家里是怎样的了。这倔老头,瘦骨头,挤牛奶的女人希尔顿,大个儿瑞典佬,这是他们给他起的绰号。若是让他听见了,有一些他怕是不喜欢的。可是他没有听见,再说,人家也没有恶意——字面上不大好听

"Now, papa," said Mrs. Thompson in a warning tone. The children did not glance at her. They had no faith in her good will. She had betrayed them in the first place. There was no trusting her. Now she might save them and she might not. No use depending on her.

"Well, you ought to get a good thrashing. You deserve it, don't you, Arthur?"

Arthur hung his head. "Yes, sir."

"And the next time I catch either of you hanging around Mr. Helton's shack, I'm going to take the side off *both* of you, you hear me, Herbert?"

Herbert mumbled and choked, scattering his cornbread. "Yes, sir."

"Well, now sit up and eat your supper and not another word out of you," said Mr. Thompson, beginning on his own food. The little boys perked up somewhat and started chewing, but every time they looked around they met their parents' eyes, regarding them steadily. There was no telling when they would think of something new. The boys ate warily, trying not to be seen or heard, the cornbread sticking, the buttermilk gurgling, as it went down their gullets.

"And something else, Mr. Thompson," said Mrs. Thompson after a pause. "Tell Mr. Helton he's to come straight to us when they bother him, and not to trouble shaking them himself. Tell him we'll look after that."

"They're so mean," answered Mr. Thompson, staring at them. "It's a wonder he don't just kill' em off and be done with it." But there was something in the tone that told Arthur and Herbert that nothing more worth worrying about was going to happen this time. Heaving deep sighs, they sat up, reaching for the food nearest them.

"Listen," said Mrs. Thompson, suddenly. The little boys stopped eating. "Mr. Helton hasn't come for his supper. Arthur, go and tell Mr. Helton he's late for supper. Tell him nice, now."

Arthur, miserably depressed, slid out of his place and made for the door, without a word.

There were no miracles of fortune to be brought to pass on a small dairy farm. The Thompsons did not grow rich, but they kept out of the poor house, as Mr. Thompson was fond of saying, meaning he had got a little foothold in spite of Ellie's poor health, and unexpected weather, and strange declines in market prices, and his own mysterious handicaps which weighed him down. Mr. Helton was the hope and the prop of the family, and all the Thompsons became fond of him, or at any rate they ceased to regard him as in any way peculiar, and looked upon him, from a distance they did

就是了。孩子们管他们的爸爸叫"老头儿"、"老顽固",自然是不当他的面。他们全靠体质好,走完了长大成人的那一段污秽、神秘、迂回曲折的过程,平平安安地度过了可能有的危机。他们的父母知道他们是可靠的好小伙子,尽管举止粗鲁,心地却像金子一样。汤普生先生感到很宽慰,他培养成了一对不是光会削木头的好青年,虽然他自己也不知道是怎样培养的。他们真不错,汤普兰先生开始相信他们生来就是这样的呢,就仿佛自己从没向他们说过一句重话,更不要说打他们了。赫伯特与阿瑟倒也不和他争辩。

希尔顿正在劈几根柴火,他的头发被汗弄湿了,粘在湿淋淋的脑门上,他的蓝工作服深一条浅一条的,紧贴在他的肋骨上。他慢慢地劈,斧子一直劈到木砧上,他把柴火码得整整齐齐。接着他绕过屋角,进了他的小屋,屋子和柴堆都遮在一排桑树的浓荫里。汤普生先生懒洋洋地靠在前廊上一张摇椅里,他从来就没有喜欢过这个地方。这张椅子是新的,汤普生太太要放在前廊上,虽然侧廊是该放的地方,那儿凉快些。汤普生先生要坐这把椅子,所以只好来到这儿。一等椅子用旧,艾丽不稀罕它时,他就要把它搬到侧廊上去。这会儿,8月的暑热几乎使人受不了,空气滞留得你都可以给它捅一个洞了。所有的东西上,尘土都有几英寸厚,虽然希尔顿先生每天晚上都要给整个院子洒上水。他甚至还把水管朝天,去冲树顶和屋顶。他们已经把水管接到厨房里,在院子里也安了一只水龙头。汤普生先生准是打了个盹,因为一个陌生人赶着马车来到大门口时,他刚来得及睁开眼睛闭上嘴巴,总算没出丑。汤普生先生站起身来,戴上帽子,把工裤往上提了提,看着陌生人把拉着一辆轻货车的几匹马系在拴柱上。汤普生先生认得这些马和这辆车,它们是从布达的一家马车行里租来的。那个陌生人在打开大门,那是一扇结实的门,是几年前希尔顿先生做成并且牢牢地安在合页上的,这时汤普生先生慢慢沿着小路走过去迎接他,想弄清楚到底有什么了不起的事,使这个人风尘仆仆,不怕颠簸,在这个时候上这儿来。

这人不能算是真正的胖子,更像是一个不久以前胖过的人。他的皮肤松弛下垂,衣服显得过于肥大。他照说应该是胖的,可是大概刚刚害过一场病。汤普生先生一点也不喜欢他的模样,可是也说不出为

not know how to bridge, as a good man and a good friend. Mr. Helton went his way, worked, played his tune. Nine years passed. The boys grew up and learned to work. They could not remember the time when Ole Helton hadn't been there: a grouchy cuss, Brother Bones; Mr. Helton, the dairymaid; that Big Swede. If he had heard them, he might have been annoyed at some of the names they called him. But he did not hear them and besides they meant no harm—or at least such harm as existed was all there, in the names; the boys referred to their father as the Old Man, or the Old Geezer, but not to his face. They lived through by main strength all the grimy, secret, oblique phases of growing up and got past the crisis safely if anyone does. Their parents could see they were good solid boys with hearts of gold in spite of their rough ways. Mr. Thompson was relieved to find that, without knowing how he had done it, he had succeeded in raising a set of boys who were not trifling whittlers. They were such good boys Mr. Thompson began to believe they were born that way, and that he had never spoken a harsh word to them in their lives, much less thrashed them. Herbert and Arthur never disputed his word.

Mr. Helton, his hair wet with sweat, plastered to his dripping forehead, his jumper streaked dark and light blue and clinging to his ribs, was chopping a little firewood. He chopped slowly, struck the ax into the end of the chopping log, and piled the wood up neatly. He then disappeared round the house into his shack, which shared with the woodpile a good shade from a row of mulberry trees. Mr. Thompson was lolling in a swing chair on the front porch, a place he had never liked. The chair was new, and Mrs. Thompson had wanted it on the front porch, though the side porch was the place for it, being cooler; and Mr. Thompson wanted to sit in the chair, so there he was. As soon as the new wore off of it, and Ellie's pride in it was exhausted, he would move it round to the side porch. Meantime the August heat was almost unbearable, the air so thick you could poke a hole in it. The dust was inches thick on everything, though Mr. Helton sprinkled the whole yard regularly every night. He even shot the hose upward and washed the tree tops and the roof of the house. They had laid waterpipes to the kitchen and an outside faucet. Mr. Thompson must have dozed, for he opened his eyes and shut his mouth just in time to save his face before a stranger who had driven up to the front gate. Mr. Thompson stood up, put on his hat, pulled up his jeans, and watched while the stranger tied his team, attached to a light spring wagon, to the hitching post. Mr. Thompson recognized

什么。

陌生人脱下帽子，用响亮、亲热的声音说："你是汤普生先生，洛义·艾尔·汤普生先生吗？"

"正是。"汤普生先生不动声色地说，那个陌生人过于随随便便的态度使他感到意外。

"我叫哈奇，"陌生人说，"霍默·T·哈奇，我来看你是为了想买一匹马。"

"我想你大概是弄错了，"汤普生先生说，"我没有马要卖。在一般的情况下，如果我有什么要卖，我就告诉乡邻们，并且在大门上贴上一个小小的告示。"

那个胖子张开嘴，呵呵大笑，露出了颜色像棕黄皮子的兔牙。汤普生先生头一遭觉得这件事根本没有什么好笑的。那个陌生人嚷道："那只不过是我的一个老玩笑罢了。"他伸出一只手去握住自己的另一只手，热烈地对握起来。"我去拜访陌生人时总说些这样的笑话，因为我注意到，如果一个人说他是来买什么东西的，人家就不会怀疑他是坏人，你懂吗？哈，哈，哈。"

他的快活使汤普生先生不安，因为这个人眼睛里的神情与他声音里的感情并不一致。"嘿，嘿。"汤普生先生尽义务似的轻轻笑了两声，仍然没觉得有什么好笑。"哦，这一套用在我身上是白费精力，因为我从来不怀疑，除非他自己露出了马脚，说了可疑的话或是干了可疑的事，"他解释道，"除非有这样的事。否则，对我来说，谁都是好人。"

"嗯，"那个陌生人说，突然变得非常严肃，非常通情达理，"我来这儿既不是为了买也不是为了卖。老实说，我来见你是为了一件对我们两人都有好处的事。是的，先生，我要跟你好好地谈一谈，这件事不会让你花一分钱。"

"我看谈谈也没什么坏处，"汤普生先生不太情愿地说，"到屋子边上来，这儿有点树荫。"

他们走过去，在一棵楝树树荫下两只树桩上坐了下来。

"不错，先生，霍默·T·哈奇是在下的名字，故人的国籍就是美国，"陌生人说，"我想你一定听说过这个姓吧？我从前有个本家兄弟叫詹姆生·哈奇，就住在北边不远。"

"不记得听说过这个姓，"汤普生先生说，"倒是有几个姓哈丘的住在芒坦城附近。"

"没听说过历史悠久的哈奇家？"那人非常忧虑地

the team and wagon. They were from a livery stable in Buda. While the stranger was opening the gate, a strong gate that Mr. Helton had built and set firmly on its hinges several years back, Mr. Thompson strolled down the path to greet him and find out what in God's world a man's business might be that would bring him out at this time of day, in all this dust and welter.

He wasn't exactly a fat man. He was more like a man who had been fat recently. His skin was baggy and his clothes were too big for him, and he somehow looked like a man who should be fat, ordinarily, but who might have just got over a spell of sickness. Mr. Thompson didn't take to his looks at all, he couldn't say why.

The stranger took off his hat. He said in a loud hearty voice, "Is this Mr. Thompson, Mr. Royal Earle Thompson?"

"That's my name," said Mr. Thompson, almost quietly, he was so taken back by the free manner of the stranger.

"My name is Hatch," said the stranger. "Mr. Homer T. Hatch, and I've come to see you about buying a horse."

"I reckon you've been misdirected," said Mr. Thompson. "I haven't got a horse for sale. Usually if I've got anything like that to sell," he said, "I tell the neighbors and tack up a little sign on the gate."

The fat man opened his mouth and roared with joy, showing rabbit teeth brown as shoeleather. Mr. Thompson saw nothing to laugh at, for once. The stranger shouted, "That's just an old joke of mine." He caught one of his hands in the other and shook hands with himself heartily. "I always say something like that when I'm calling on a stranger, because I've noticed that when a feller says he's come to buy something nobody takes him for a suspicious character. You see? Haw, haw, haw."

His joviality made Mr. Thompson nervous, because the expression in the man's eyes didn't match the sounds he was making. "Haw, haw," laughed Mr. Thompson obligingly, still not seing the joke. "Well, that's all wasted on me because I never take any man for a suspicious character 'til he shows hisself to be one. Says or does something," he explained. "Until that happens, one man's as good as another, so far's I'm concerned."

"Well," said the stranger, suddenly very sober and sensible, "I ain't come neither to buy nor sell. Fact is, I want to see you about something that's of interest to us both. Yes, sir, I'd like to have a little talk with you, and it won't cost you a cent."

喊道,他似乎很怜悯汤普生先生的无知,"哦,我们家是 50 年以前从佐治亚州迁来的。你在这儿住了多久啦?"

"可以说住了整整一辈子,"汤普生先生说,开始有点不高兴了,"在我之前还有我爹、我爷爷。是的,先生,我们一直住在这儿。谁都知道可以在哪儿找到汤普生家。我爷爷是 1836 年迁移来的。"

"从爱尔兰,我想?"陌生人说。

"从宾夕法尼亚州。"汤普生先生说,"你凭什么认为我们是从爱尔兰来的?"

那陌生人张开嘴巴,高兴地叫嚷起来,他又和自己握手,仿佛好久没见似的。"哦,正如我经常说的那样,一个人总得从某个地方迁移来,是不是?"

他们讲话时,汤普生先生不停地向他身边的那张脸瞥去。这人的确使汤普生先生想起了谁,没准他真的在什么地方见到过这个人,可就是记不起面目特征了。最后,汤普生先生断定,所有长着兔子牙齿的人外貌都是相像的。

"那是不错的,"汤普生先生承认,但是有点生气,"不过我总说,汤普生一家在这儿住了这么久,他们到底从哪儿来已经无关紧要了。对了,当然啦,现在是淡季,我们大家都利用这个机会喘喘气儿,不过谁手头都有点杂事要做。我倒不是要催你,不过既然你是来谈买卖的,我看咱们最好还是开始谈吧。"

"正如我所说的,不完全是买卖,但是也可以说是买卖,"那胖子说,"我眼下正在找一个叫希尔顿的人,奥拉夫·艾立克·希尔顿先生,从北达科他州来的。北边不远有人告诉我,我可以在这里找到他。我倒是愿意和他谈几句话。是的,老兄,如果你不反对的话,我想和他谈上几句。"

"我从来没听说过他还有中间名字。"汤普生先生说,"不过希尔顿先生的确在这儿,来这儿快 9 年了。他是一个十分稳妥的人,你可以告诉任何人说这是我讲的。"

"听到你这么说我真是高兴。"霍默·T·哈奇先生说,"我愿意听说有人改过自新,安定下来。不过我认识希尔顿先生时,他相当野,是的,先生,相当野,一点儿不假。他头脑一点儿也不清楚。嗯,很好,能和朋友重新相逢,发现他安定下来,努力向上,真是件无上乐事。"

"我们谁都是从青年时代过来的,"汤普生先生说,

"I guess that's fair enough,"said Mr. Thompson, reluctantly. "Come on around the house where there's a little shade. "

They went round and seated themselves on two stumps under a chinaberry tree.

"Yes, sir, Homer T. Hatch is my name and America is my nation,"said the stranger. "I reckon you must know the name? I used to have a cousin named Jameson Hatch lived up the country a ways. "

"Don't think I know the name,"said Mr. Thompson. "There's some Hatchers settled somewhere around Mountain City. "

"Don't know the old Hatch family,"cried the man in deep concern. He seemed to be pitying Mr. Thompson's ignorance "Why, we came over from Georgia fifty years ago. Been here long yourself?"

"Just all my whole life,"said Mr. Thompson, beginning to feel peevish. "And my pa and my grampap before me. Yes, sir, we've been right here all along. Anybody wants to find a Thompson knows where to look for him. My grampap immigrated in 1836. "

"From Ireland, I reckon?"said the stranger.

"From Pennsylvania,"said Mr. Thompson. "Now what makes you think we came from Ireland?"

The stranger opened his mouth and began to shout with merriment, and he shook hands with himself as if he hadn't met himself for a long time. "Well, what I always says is, a feller's got to come from *somewhere*, ain't he?"

While they were talking, Mr. Thompson kept glancing at the face near him. He certainly did remind Mr. Thompson of somebody, or maybe he really had seen the man himself somewhere. He couldn't just place the features. Mr. Thompson finally decided it was just that all rabbit-teethed men looked alike.

"That's right," acknowledged Mr. Thompson, rather sourly, "but what I always say is, Thompsons have been settled here for so long it don't make much difference any more *where* they come from. Now a course, this is the slack season, and we're all just laying round a little, but nevertheless we've all got our chores to do, and I don't want to hurry you, and so if you've come to see me on business maybe we'd better get down to it. "

"As I said, it's not in a way, and again in a way it is,"said the fat man. "Now I'm looking for a man named Helton, Mr. Olaf Eric Helton, from North Dakota, and I was told up around the country a ways that I might find him here, and I wouldn't mind having a little talk with him. No, siree, I sure wouldn't mind, if it's all the same to you. "

"I never knew his middle name," said Mr.

"这跟出麻疹一样。你突然全身都发了出来，自己讨厌自己，也给人空添麻烦，可是这事不会长，而且通常也不会留下后遗症。"他很为自己的这个比喻得意，忘乎所以地大笑起来。陌生人双手交叉搁在肚子上也情不自禁地哈哈大笑，连眼泪都流出来。汤普生先生收住笑声，不安地瞅了瞅陌生人。他跟任何人一样，也喜欢有时痛痛快快地笑一笑，可是总得有点节制呀。现在这家伙笑得都像个疯子了，一点儿不假。而且他不是因为觉得事情好玩才笑，而是别有原委。汤普生先生不快地保持着沉默，等哈奇先生安静下来。

哈奇先生掏出一块极其肮脏的蓝布印花手帕，擦擦眼睛。"这个笑话正好触到我痒处，让我憋不住要笑，"他说，几乎是在道歉了，"我真希望我也能想出这样的如珠妙语。这是一种天才，这是……"

"要是你想和希尔顿先生谈谈，我就去把他找来。"汤普生先生说，动了一下仿佛要站起身来，"现在这个时候他不是在牛奶棚便是在他自己的小屋里。"时间快近5点了，"就在拐角那边。"

"噢，这事倒也不特别急，"哈奇先生说，"我想跟他谈已有很久了，再等上几分钟我想也无所谓。我只不过想知道他在哪儿，情况怎样，如此而已。"

汤普生先生不再做出打算站起来的姿态，他又解开一个衬衫纽扣，说："嗯，他就在这儿，他这个人，要是跟你有什么账没了的话，是决不会赖掉的。他很勤快，这一点你可以放心。"

听了这些话，哈奇先生显得有点不高兴。他用手帕擦了擦脸，张开嘴正要说话，这时屋角那边传来了希尔顿先生的口琴声。汤普生先生举起一只手指。"那就是他，"汤普生先生说，"现在你可以和他去谈了。"

哈奇先生朝屋子东边侧耳听了一会儿，脸上泛出了一种挺古怪的表情。

"这个曲子我再熟悉不过了，"汤普生先生说，"可是我从未听希尔顿先生提起这是什么歌。"

"那是一首斯堪的纳维亚的什么曲子，"哈奇先生说，"在我的家乡，人们常常唱它。在北达科他州，人们也爱唱，歌词的大意是，你一清早起来，心情好极了，你欣喜若狂，因此不到中午就把酒全都喝光了。那酒是你准备中午休息时候喝的，明白吗？歌词没多大意思，可是曲调很美。那是一支劝酒歌。"他坐在那儿，稍稍有点伤感，汤普生先生不喜欢他的表情。那

Thompson, "but Mr. Helton is right here, and been here now for going on nine years. He's a mighty steady man, and you can tell anybody I said so."

"I'm glad to hear that," said Mr. Homer T. Hatch. "I like to hear of a feller mending his ways and settling down. Now when I knew Mr. Helton he was pretty wild, yes, sir, wild is what he was, he didn't know his own mind at all. Well, now, it's going to be a great pleasure to me to meet up with an old friend and find him all settled down and doing well by hisself."

"We've all got to be young once," said Mr. Thompson. "It's like the measles, it breaks out all over you, and you're a nuisance to yourself and everybody else, but it don't last, and it usually don't leave no ill effects." He was so pleased with this notion he forgot and broke into a guffaw. The stranger folded his arms over his stomach and went into a kind of fit, roaring until he had tears in his eyes. Mr. Thompson stopped shouting and eyed the stranger uneasily. Now he liked a good laugh as well as any man, but there ought to be a little moderation. Now this feller laughed like a perfect lunatic, that was a fact. And he wasn't laughing because he really thought things were funny, either. He was laughing for reasons of his own. Mr. Thompson fell into a moody silence, and waited until Mr. Hatch settled down a little.

Mr. Hatch got out a very dirty blue cotton bandanna and wiped his eyes. "That joke just about caught me where I live," he said, almost apologetically. "Now I wish I could think up things as funny as that to say. It's a gift. It's. . . ."

"If you want to speak to Mr. Helton, I'll go and round him up," said Mr. Thompson, making motions as if he might get up. "He may be in the milk house and he may be setting in his shack this time of day." It was drawing towards five o'clock. "It's right around the corner," he said.

"Oh, well, there ain't no special hurry," said Mr. Hatch. "I've been wanting to speak to him for a good long spell now and I guess a few minutes more won't make no difference. I just more wanted to locate him, like. That's all."

Mr. Thompson stopped beginning to stand up, and unbuttoned one more button of his shirt, and said, "Well, he's here, and he's this kind of man, that if he had any business with you he'd like to get it over. He don't dawdle, that's one thing you can say for him."

Mr. Hatch appeared to sulk a little at these words. He wiped his face with the bandanna and opened his mouth to speak, when round the house there came the music of Mr. Helton's harmonica. Mr. Thompson raised a finger. "There he is," said Mr.

是一种心满意足的神情,颇像一只猫刚刚吃下去一只金丝雀。

"就我所知,"汤普生先生说,"他来这儿以后没沾过一滴酒,到今年9月,就满9年了。是的,先生,就我所知,9年来,他连嗓子都没用酒润过一回。我自己都不敢说能做到这一点。"他既得意,又故作谦虚。

"是的,那是支饮酒歌,"哈奇先生说,"我年轻那阵儿,也常用小提琴拉这支《棕色的小酒杯》。"他继续说,"可是这个希尔顿,他居然念念不忘。他就那么坐着,独自吹奏。"

"9年来他就在这里不断吹奏这支曲子。"汤普生先生说,好像这事是他主办似的。

"这个歌他唱起来很好听,15年前,在北达科他,"哈奇先生说,"他实际上老是给裹在紧身衣里.直挺挺地坐着,那会儿他在疯人院——"

"你说什么?"汤普生先生说,"怎么回事?"

"糟糕,我本不想告诉你的。"哈奇先生说。下垂的眼睑里露出一丝后悔的神情,"糟糕,这完全是说漏了嘴。真怪,我早就决定一个字儿也不提的,因为这只能引起轩然大波。我的想法是,如果一个人安安静静、老老实实地过了9年,他是不是疯子已经没多大关系了,是吗? 只要他安安静静、从不伤人,这就行了。"

"你是说他们让他穿过紧身衣?"汤普生先生不安地问道,"在疯人院里?"

"常让他穿。"哈奇先生说,"他们把他关在那儿的时候,过不了一阵儿就得穿。"

"在州立疯人院里人们也给我的艾达姨妈穿那样的东西。"汤普生先生说,"她撒野的时候,他们用长袖紧身衣裹住她,把她拴在墙上的铁环上,她乱蹦乱跳,一根血管破裂了,等他们去看她,她已经死了。我想那种衣服是很危险的。"

"希尔顿先生裹在紧身衣里的时候,总是唱他的饮酒歌,"哈奇先生说,"别的他都无所谓,他就怕你逗他说话。他最受不了这个,于是就撒野,像你的艾达姨妈那样。他一撒野,人家就让他穿紧身衣,走开去不管他。他也就心满意足地躺在那儿,像你们知道的那样,唱他的饮酒歌。有一天晚上,他干脆不见了。离开了,你可以说,无影无踪,以后再也没有人见过他的任何踪迹。后来,我一路找来,发现他在这里,"哈奇先生说,"完全安定下来了,却还吹着同一支曲子。"

Thompson. "Now's your time."

Mr. Hatch cocked an ear towards the east side of the house and listened for a few seconds, a very strange expression on his face.

"I know that tune like I know the palm of my own hand," said Mr. Thompson, "but I never heard Mr. Helton say what it was."

"That's a kind of Scandahoovian song," said Mr. Hatch. "Where I come from they sing it a lot. In North Dakota, they sing it. It says something about starting out in the morning feeling so good you can't hardly stand it, so you drink up all your likker before noon. All the likker, y' understand, that you was saving for the noon lay-off. The words ain't much, but it's a pretty tune. It's a kind of drinking song," He sat there drooping a little, and Mr. Thompson didn't like his expression. It was a satisfied expression, but it was more like the cat that et the canary.

"So far as I know," said Mr. Thompson, "he ain't touched a drop since he's been on the place, and that's nine years this coming September. Yes, sir, nine years, so far as I know, he ain't wetted his whistle once. And that's more than I can say for myself," he said, meekly proud.

"Yes, that's a drinking song," said Mr. Hatch. "I used to play 'Little Brown Jug' on the fiddle when I was younger than I am now," he went on, "but this Helton, he just keeps it up. He just sits and plays it by himself."

"He's been playing it off and on for nine years right here on the place," said Mr. Thompson, feeling a little proprietary.

"And he was certainly singing it as well, fifteen years before that, in North Dakota," said Mr. Hatch. "He used to sit up in a straitjacket, practically, when he was in the asylum—"

"What's that you say?" said Mr. Thompson. "What's that?"

"Shucks, I didn't mean to tell you," said Mr. Hatch, a faint leer of regret in his drooping eyelids. "Shucks, that just slipped out. Funny, now I'd made up my mind I wouldn't say a word, because it would just make a lot of excitement, and what I say is, if a man has lived harmless and quiet for nine years it don't matter if he *is* loony, does it? So long's he keeps quiet and don't do nobody harm."

"You mean they had him in a straitjacket?" asked Mr. Thompson, uneasily. "In a lunatic asylum?"

"They sure did," said Mr. Hatch. "That's right where they had him, from time to time."

"They put my Aunt Ida in one of them things in the State asylum," said Mr. Thompson. "She got

"他对我从来没有发过狂，"汤普生先生说，"他在我这儿行动都是很有理性的。首先他根本不结婚。再说他非常勤快，像一匹马一样。而且我敢打赌他到这儿以后我给他的每一分钱他都存着。他不喝酒，不说一句话，更不要说骂人了。星期六夜晚他也不到处瞎晃悠，浪费时间。"汤普生先生说，"哼，如果那叫发疯，我倒也愿意换换口味，做个疯子。"

"嚯嚯，哈哈，"哈奇先生开口了，"嘿嘿，妙极了！哈，哈，哈，我从来没想到这一点。对了，一点儿不错！让咱们全都变成疯子，甩掉老婆，把钱省下来。怎么样？"他惹人憎厌地笑着，露出了他那些小兔牙。

汤普生先生觉得人家曲解了他的意思。他转过身子，向忍冬棚架后面打开的窗子那边指了指。"咱们走开一点，"他说，"我早该想到的。"这个客人使汤普生先生感到心烦。他有一种本事，能把汤普生先生的话头接过来，稍为转一下意思，把内容全弄拧，使得汤普生先生都搞不清自己原来说的是什么了。"我老婆身体不太结实，"汤普生先生说，"14年来她一直病病歪歪的。穷人家里有人生病，日子真不好过。她动过4次手术，"他骄傲地说，"一次紧接一次，可是一点儿也不见效。5年来连着不断，我挣的每一分钱全都献给大夫了。结果呢，她身体还是弱不禁风。"

"我的那个老太婆，"霍默·T·哈奇先生说，"倒结实得像匹骡子，是的，先生。她要是真想，连马棚都搬得动。我总说，幸好她不知道自己气力有多大。不过，她已经不在人世了。这样的体质比起病弱的，倒是消耗得更快些。这样的女人对我没有什么用，因为她老是嘀咕个没完。我很快就把她甩掉了，是的，先生，够快的。正如你所说的，养活一个女人确是所费不赀。"

这又完全违反了汤普生先生的初衷，他方才不过是想说明，能养活这么能花钱的老婆，对一个男人来说是件多光彩的事。"我太太是个通情达理的女人，"汤普生先生说，感到自己受了屈辱，"不过要是她知道了这么多年来农场上雇了一个疯子，我真不知道她会怎么说，会怎么干。"他们从窗口那儿走了开去，汤普生先生领着哈奇先生从屋子前面走，因为如果打后面走他们就得经过希尔顿先生的小屋了。为了某种原因，他不想让陌生人和希尔顿先生见面或谈话。这事说来奇怪，不过汤普生先生就是这样想的。

汤普生先生在木砧上重新坐下来，他让客人坐在

vi'lent, and they put her in one of these jackets with long sleeves and tied her to an iron ring in the wall, and Aunt Ida got so wild she broke a blood vessel and when they went to look after her she was dead. I'd think one of them things was dangerous."

"Mr. Helton used to sing his drinking song when he was in a straitjacket," said Mr. Hatch. "Nothing ever bothered him, except if you tried to make him talk. That bothered him, and he'd get vi'lent, like your Aunt Ida. He'd get vi'lent and then they'd put him in the jacket and go off and leave him, and he'd lay there perfickly contented, so far's you could see, singing his song. Then one night he just disappeared. Left, you might say, just went, and nobody ever saw hide or hair of him again. And then I come along and find him here," said Mr. Hatch, "all settled down and playing the same song."

"He never acted crazy to me," said Mr. Thompson. "He always acted like a sensible man, to me. He never got married, for one thing, and he works like a horse, and I bet he's got the first cent I paid him when he landed here, and he don't drink, and he never says a word, much less swear, and he don't waste time runnin' around Saturday nights, and if he's crazy," said Mr. Thompson, "why, I think I'll go crazy myself for a change."

"Haw, ha," said Mr. Hatch, "heh, he, that's good! Ha, ha, ha, I hadn't thought of it jes like that. Yeah, that's right! Let's all go crazy and get rid of our wives and save our money, hey?" He smiled unpleasantly, showing his little rabbit teeth.

Mr. Thompson felt he was being misunderstood. He turned around and motioned toward the open window back of the honeysuckle trellis. "Let's move off down here a little," he said. "I oughta thought of that before." His visitor bothered Mr. Thompson. He had a way of taking the words out of Mr. Thompson's mouth, turning them around and mixing them up until Mr. Thompson didn't know himself what he had said. "My wife's not very strong," said Mr. Thompson. "She's been kind of invalid now goin' on fourteen years. It's mighty tough on a poor man, havin' sickness in the family. She had four operations," he said proudly, "one right after the other, but they didn't do any good. For five years handrunnin', I just turned every nickel I made over to the doctors. Upshot is, she's a mightly delicate woman."

"My old woman," said Mr. Homer T. Hatch, "had a back like a mule, yes, sir. That woman could have moved the barn with her bare hands if she'd ever took the notion. I used to say, it was a good thing she didn't know her own stren'th. She's dead now, though.

另一个树墩上。"哼，要是在以前，这样一件事也许会使我心烦意乱，"汤普生先生说，"可是，如今，我偏偏不让任何事情使我激动。"他用他那把牛角柄小刀切了一大块烟草，请哈奇先生用，而哈奇先生也拿出了自己的烟草，打开一把刀刃很长磨得很锋利的大猎刀，切下一大块，放进自己嘴里。接着两个人便互相比较烟草，发现彼此对烟草好坏的看法竟如此悬殊，感到很惊异。

"喏，比方说，"哈奇先生说，"我的颜色淡一些。这是因为，第一，我的烟草没有加糖。我不喜欢甜的，我要天然叶子，不浓不淡。"

"就我来说，加一点糖倒关系不大，"汤普生先生说，"但是只能真正一点点。我现在的口味是，要稍为浓一点儿，要……人们怎么说来看，对了，精工制作。这儿附近有一个人，叫威廉斯，约翰·莫尔根·威廉斯，他嚼的烟叶，我的天哪，黑得像你的帽子一样，软得像熔化的柏油。他的烟叶简直往下滴糖浆，就是滴糖浆，嚼起来味道跟甘草一样。不过，我觉得味道不纯。"

"一人之苦药，他人之美酒①。"哈奇先生说，"哼，这样的烟叶我闻着都要作呕，实在不敢领教。"

"噢，"汤普生先生说，语气里有一丝歉意，"我也只不过尝尝是啥味道。仅仅往嘴里放了一小块，马上就吐出来了。"

"我连尝都不要尝，"哈奇先生说，"我喜欢不加糖的天然烟草，什么人工香味都不要。"

汤普生先生开始觉得哈奇先生是在炫耀自己是嚼烟草的大行家，而且一直会说下去，不到别人认输决不罢休。他真的讨厌起这个胖子来了。真的，这到底是个什么人？打什么地方来？他居然到处乱转，教训人家该用什么样的烟草。

"人工香味，"哈奇先生顽固地接下去说，"只不过是用来掩盖烟草的低劣质量，让人自己骗自己，像是捞到了什么便宜货。有点甜味也是烟草差劲的一个标志，你记住我的话好了。"

"我在买烟草上从不小气，"汤普生先生执拗地说，"我不是财主，我也不四处招摇撞骗充阔，可是这

─────────

① 作者这里用的是一句英谚："One man's meat is another man's poison"。或可译为："于汝甘脆肥脓，于彼腐肠之药也。"化用枚乘《七发》中吴客之语。

That kind wear out quicker than the puny ones. I never had much use for a woman always complainin'. I'd get rid of her mighty quick, yes, sir, mighty quick. It's just as you say: a dead loss, keepin' one of 'em up. "

This was not at all what Mr. Thompson had heard himself say; he had been trying to explain that a wife as expensive as his was a credit to a man. "She's a mighty reasonable woman," said Mr. Thompson, feeling baffled, "but I wouldn't answer for what she'd say or do if she found out we'd had a lunatic on the place all this time. " They moved away from the window; Mr. Thompson took Mr. Hatch the front way, because if he went the back way they would have to pass Mr. Helton's shack. For some reason he didn't want the stranger to see or talk to Mr. Helton. It was strange, but that was the way Mr. Thompson felt.

Mr. Thompson sat down again, on the chopping log, offering his guest another tree stump. "Now, I mighta got upset myself at such a thing, once," said Mr. Thompson, "but now I *deefy* anything to get me lathered up. "He cut himself an enormous plug of tobacco with his horn-handled pocketknife, and offered it to Mr. Hatch, who then produced his own plug and, opening a huge bowie knife with a long blade sharply whetted, cut off a large wad and put it in his mouth. They then compared plugs and both of them were astonished to see how different men's ideas of good chewing tobacco were.

"Now, for instance," said Mr. Hatch, "mine is lighter colored. That's because, for one thing, there ain't any sweetenin' in this plug. I like it dry, natural leaf, medium strong. "

"A little sweetenin' don't do no harm so far as I'm concerned," said Mr. Thompson, "but it's got to be mighty little. But with me, now, I want a strong leaf, I want it heavy-cured, as the feller says. There's a man near here, named Williams, Mr. John Morgan Williams, who chews a plug—well, sir, it's black as your hat and soft as melted tar. It fairly drips with molasses, jus' plain molasses, and it chews like licorice. Now, I don't call that a good chew. "

"One man's meat," said Mr. Hatch, "is another man's poison. Now, such a chew would simply gag me. I couldn't begin to put it in my mouth. "

"Well," said Mr. Thompson, a tinge of apology in his voice, "I jus' barely tasted it myself, you might say. Just took a little piece in my mouth and spit it out again. "

"I'm dead sure I couldn't even get that far," said Mr. Hatch. "I like a dry natural chew without any artificial flavorin' of any kind. "

一点上我是不含糊的,像烟草这样的东西,我只买最上等的货色。"

"加甜味,即使只加一点点,"哈奇先生又开始了,把嘴里那团烟草挪了一下位置,啪的一口,把烟草汁吐在一株干枯矮小的玫瑰丛上,这株玫瑰日子本来就不好过,它的根牢牢地抓住干裂的泥土,在毒太阳下已经站了整整一天,"也是一个标志,说明——"

"说到这位希尔顿先生,"汤普生先生说,态度非常坚决,"我看,仅仅因为一个人一生中发过一两次疯就难为他,这是没有道理的,因此我也不想采取什么措施。任何措施也不想采取。我没有理由要反对他,他一直对我不错。"他接着说,"世界上有些事情,有些人,真能活活把谁都逼疯。在这样的世道里,居然没有更多的人变成疯子,这倒是一个奇迹。"

"不错,"哈奇先生马上接下去说,他接得也太快了,仿佛是存心要把汤普生先生的意思接过来反对汤普生先生,"你恰好说出了我要说的话。并不是每一个套上紧身衣的人都是应该关在疯人院里的。哈哈,你说得对极了。真是一语中的。"

汤普生先生默不作声地坐着,不停地咀嚼烟草,呆呆地瞪着地上 6 英尺开外的地方,只觉得有一股无名怒火从内心深处慢慢升上来,一点点升上来,扩展到全身各个部位。这个家伙用意何在?他想说些什么? 问题不在于他的话本身,而在于他的神情,他的语气,那种躲躲闪闪的眼神,那种声调,仿佛他有意要让汤普生先生难堪。汤普生先生很不喜欢,可是又抓不住把柄。他想转过身去,把这家伙从树墩上推下去,可是这样做也不太聪明,万一这家伙跌下去时出了什么事呢,比方说,他跌在斧子上,碰破了,别人就会问汤普生先生为什么要推他,到时候又该怎么回答呢?倘若告诉人家,自己和他为了一块烟草的事吵了起来,这岂不是显得可笑,让人觉得莫名其妙吗?倒不如就把他推下去,然后告诉别人,这人是个胖子,天气太热他受不了,说说话头一晕就摔倒了,反正是诸如此类的话。不过那也不是实话,因为事情既不是因为天热,也不是因为烟草。汤普生先生决定尽快把这家伙从自己院子里撵走,不露声色,但眼睛要紧盯着他,直到他滚蛋为止。犯不着对一个从远地来的人热情。他们总是有所企图才来的,没事他们不会好好的在自己家里待着吗?

"有那么一些人,"哈奇先生说,"还很乐于雇一个

Mr. Thompson began to feel that Mr. Hatch was trying to make out he had the best judgment in tobacco, and was going to keep up the argument until he proved it. He began to feel seriously annoyed with the fat man. After all, who was he and where did he come from? Who was he to go around telling other people what kind of tobacco to chew?

"Artificial flavorin'," Mr. Hatch went on, doggedly, "is jes put in to cover up a cheap leaf and make a man think he's gettin' somethin' more than he *is* gettin'. Even a little sweetenin' is a sign of a cheap leaf, you can mark my words."

"I've always paid a fair price for my plug," said Mr. Thompson, stiffly. "I'm not a rich man and I don't go round settin' myself up for one, but I'll say this, when it comes to such things as tobacco, I buy the best on the market."

"Sweetenin', even a little," began Mr. Hatch, shifting his plug and squirting tobacco juice at a dry-looking little rose bush that was having a hard enough time as it was, standing all day in the blazing sun, its roots clenched in the baked earth, "is the sign of—"

"About this Mr. Helton, now," said Mr. Thompson, determinedly, "I don't see no reason to hold it against a man because he went loony once or twice in his lifetime and so I don't expect to take no steps about it. Not a step. I've got nothin' against the man, he's always treated me fair.

They's things and people," he went on, "'nough to drive any man loony. The wonder to me is, more men don't wind up in straitjackets, the way things are going these days and times."

"That's right," said Mr. Hatch, promptly, entirely too promptly, as if he were turning Mr. Thompson's meaning back on him. "You took the words right out of my mouth. There ain't every man in a straitjacket that ought to be there. Ha, ha, you're right all right. You got the idea."

Mr. Thompson sat silent and chewed steadily and stared at a spot on the ground about six feet away and felt a slow muffled resentment climbing from somewhere deep down in him, climbing and spreading all through him. What was this fellow driving at? What was he trying to say? It wasn't so much his words, but his looks and his way of talking; that droopy look in the eye, that tone of voice, as if he was trying to mortify Mr. Thompson about something. Mr. Thompson didn't like it, but he couldn't get hold of it either. He wanted to turn around and shove the fellow off the stump, but it wouldn't look reasonable. Suppose something happened to the fellow when he fell off the stump, just for instance, if he fell on the ax and cut

疯子在家里干活，他们觉得疯不疯也没多大区别。我总是说，如果人家喜欢那样，他不在乎和谁在一起，那，那，那是他的事，咱们管不着。我完全不想干涉。不过在北达科他州老家，我们的看法不是这样的。我倒想看看那儿有谁要雇一个疯子，特别是在他干出了那样的事以后。"

"我不明白你老家怎么是在北达科他了呢，"汤普生先生说，"我好像听你说是佐治亚。"

"我有一个姐妹嫁在北达科他，"哈奇先生说，"嫁给一个瑞典人，不过那倒是一个地地道道的白种人。我刚才说我们，是因为我跟他在那儿经营一点儿小买卖。因此，说家乡也不算错。"

"他干出了什么事？"汤普生先生问，他又重新感到非常不安了。

"噢，没有什么了不起的，"哈奇先生兴致勃勃地说，"只不过是有一天晒干草的时候，他用叉子在他兄弟身上刺通了一个窟窿。他们本想处死他，可是他们发现，像人们所说的那样，是天气太热使他发了狂，因此他们就把他关进了疯人院。他就不过干了这么点儿事。没什么好大惊小怪的，哈，哈，哈！"他说着，又拿出了那把锋利的刀子，像切蛋糕那样小心翼翼地切下了一块烟草。

"嗯，"汤普生先生说，"我承认这倒是一条新闻。是的，先生，一条新闻。可是我仍然要说，总有什么原因驱使他这样做。有些人仅仅是他们瞧着你的那种眼光，就使你觉得非宰掉他不可。他的兄弟没准就是那样一个胡搅蛮缠的下流家伙。"

"他兄弟那时候快要结婚了，"哈奇先生说，"晚上总去向他的姑娘求爱。有一天晚上，他借了希尔顿先生的口琴去给她奏小夜曲，把口琴弄丢了。那是一只崭新的口琴。"

"他很珍惜他的口琴。"汤普生先生说，"他只舍得在这上面花钱，他过不了一阵就给自己买一只新的。他小屋里准有成打的口琴，各种各样大大小小的都有。"

"他兄弟不肯赔他一个新的，"哈奇先生说，"希尔顿先生火了，我不是说了吗，就用他的叉子在他的兄弟身上刺了个大窟窿。现在你明白他准是早就疯了，所以才会为了鸡毛蒜皮的事气得七窍生烟。"

"敢情。"汤普生先生说，要他同意这个讨人厌的不速之客的任何看法，他实在是从心底里不情愿。他

himself, and then someone should ask Mr. Thompson why he shoved him, and what could a man say? It would look mighty funny, it would sound mighty strange to say, Well, him and me fell out over a plug of tobacco. He might just shove him anyhow and then tell people he was a fat man not used to the heat and while he was talking he got dizzy and fell off by himself, or something like that, and it wouldn't be the truth either, because it wasn't the heat and it wasn't the tobacco. Mr. Thompson made up his mind to get the fellow off the place pretty quick, without seeming to be anxious, and watch him sharp till he was out of sight. It doesn't pay to be friendly with strangers from another part of the country. They're always up to something, or they'd stay at home where they belong.

"And they's some people," said Mr. Hatch, "would jus' as soon have a loonatic around their house as not, they can't see no difference between them and anybody else. I always say, if that's the way a man feels, don't care who he associates with, why, why, that's his business, not mine. I don't wanta have a thing to do with it. Now back home in North Dakota, we don't feel that way. I'd like to a seen anybody hiring a loonatic there, aspecially after what he done. "

"I didn't understand your home was North Dakota," said Mr. Thompson. "I thought you said Georgia. "

"I've got a married sister in North Dakota," said Mr. Hatch, "married a Swede, but a white man if ever I saw one. So I say *we* because we got into a little business together out that way. And it seems like home, kind of. "

"What did he do?" asked Mr. Thompson, feeling very uneasy again.

"Oh, nothin' to speak of," said Mr. Hatch, jovially, "jus' went loony one day in the hayfield and shoved a pitchfork right square through his brother, when they was makin' hay. They was goin' to execute him, but they found out he had went crazy with the heat, as the feller says, and so they put him in the asylum. That's all he done. Nothin' to get lathered up about, ha, ha, ha!" he said, and taking out his sharp knife he began to slice off a chew as carefully as if he were cutting cake.

"Well," said Mr. Thompson, "I don't deny that's news. Yes, sir, news. But I still say somethin' must have drove him to it. Some men make you feel like giving 'em a good killing just by lookin' at you. His brother may a been a mean ornery cuss. "

"Brother was going to get married," said Mr. Hatch; "used to go courtin' his girl nights. Borrowed Mr. Helton's harmonica to give her a serenade one

一直在想,初次见到一个人就使自己这么憎厌,这样的事他还没有遇到过。

"我觉得你年复一年听他吹同一个老调子,准是腻味透了。"

"嗯,有时候我想,他若是能学支新曲子,那该多好。"汤普生先生说,"可是他不学,那也没有什么办法。好在这支曲子还不难听。"

"有一个斯堪的纳维亚人告诉过我那支歌的意思,所以我才知道,"哈奇先生说,"那一段特别有意思,就是,你太痛快了,没到中午就忍不住把手边的酒全都喝完了。看来在北欧佬的国家里,每个人照例都随身带一瓶酒,至少我是这么理解的。这些家伙什么都告诉你,虽然——"他忽然停住了,吐了一口烟汁。

一想起在这样热的天气里喝任何一种烈酒,汤普生先生就觉得昏昏然。正如一想起在这样的日子里竟有人觉得好过,他也会感到厌烦。他觉得热得实在受不了。而那个胖子仿佛已经和树墩生在一块儿了,胖子坐得挺舒服,肚子在裤子里显得松松的,他那顶宽边平顶礼帽往后推去,露出长满红痱子的窄脑门。现在来一瓶冰镇好的啤酒,倒是不赖,汤普生先生心想。他记起在冷藏室的泉水里还浸着4瓶啤酒呢。他那干涩的舌头在嘴巴里难受地蠕动起来。不过,他可不打算请这个人喝任何东西,连一滴水也不请。他甚至都不愿再和他一起嚼烟草了。他突然地把嘴里的烟草团吐掉,用手背擦了擦嘴,用心地端详起他身边的那颗脑袋来。这个人不是个好东西,他坐在那里也没安什么好心,可是他到底是来干什么的呢?汤普生先生决定再给他一点时间,让他了结他与希尔顿先生之间的纠纷——不管那是什么纠纷,这以后,要是他还不滚蛋,汤普生先生就要撵了。

哈奇先生仿佛猜到了汤普生先生的内心活动,他把他那双邪恶的、猪一般的小眼转向汤普生先生。"跟你说实话吧,"他说,好像他已经对什么事情做了决定,"我现在要办的这件小事情,说不定还需要你的帮助呢,不过决不会费你多少事。呃,你这里的这个希尔顿先生,像我所说的,是个危险的外逃疯子,就是这么回事。事实上,过去12年左右,由我抓回的外逃疯子,肯定要在20个以上,另外,还有两个逃犯居然撞上了我,老子当然顺带也把他们拿下。办这些事当然发不了财,可是如果有悬赏——往往是有的——我就能得到赏金。积少也会成多,不过主要的问题还不

evenin', and lost it. Brand new harmonica. "

"He thinks a heap of his harmonicas," said Mr. Thompson. "Only money he ever spends, now and then he buys hisself a new one. Must have a dozen in that shack, all kinds and sizes. "

"Brother wouldn't buy him a new one," said Mr. Hatch, "so Mr. Helton just ups, and I says, and runs his pitchfork through his brother. Now you know he musta been crazy to get all worked up over a little thing like that. "

"Sounds like it," said Mr. Thompson, reluctant to agree in anything with this intrusive and disagreeable fellow. He kept thinking he couldn't remember when he had taken such a dislike to a man on first sight.

"Seems to me you'd get pretty sick of hearin' the same tune year in, year out," said Mr. Hatch.

"Well, sometimes I think it wouldn't do no harm if he learned a new one," said Mr. Thompson, "but he don't, so there's nothin' to be done about it. It's a pretty good tune, though. "

"One of the Scandahoovians told me what it meant, that's how I come to know," said Mr. Hatch. "Especially that part about getting so gay you jus' go ahead and drink up all the likker you got on hand before noon. It seems like up in them Swede countries a man carries a bottle of wine around with him as a matter of course, at least that's the way I understood it. Those fellers will tell you anything, though—" He broke off and spat.

The idea of drinking any kind of liquor in this heat made Mr. Thompson dizzy. The idea of anybody feeling good on a day like this, for instance, made him tired. He felt he was really suffering from the heat. The fat man looked as if he had grown to the stump; he slumped there in his damp, dark clothes too big for him, his belly slack in his pants, his wide black felt hat pushed off his narrow forehead red with prickly heat. A bottle of good cold beer, now, would be a help, thought Mr. Thompson, remembering the four bottles sitting deep in the pool at the springhouse, and his dry tongue squirmed in his mouth. He wasn't going to offer this man anything, though, not even a drop of water. He wasn't even going to chew any more tobacco with him. He shot out his quid suddenly, and wiped his mouth on the back of his hand, and studied the head near him attentively. The man was no good, and he was there for no good, but what was he up to? Mr. Thompson made up his mind he'd give him a little more time to get his business, whatever it was, with Mr. Helton over, and then if he didn't get off the place he'd kick him off.

Mr. Hatch, as if he suspected Mr. Thompson's

在这里。事实是,我是在维护法律与秩序。我不喜欢看到犯罪者和疯子逍遥法外。他们不应该在外面乱窜。现在我想你总同意我的看法了吧,是不是?"

汤普生先生说:"噢,人们常说,具体情况还得具体对待。嗯,就我所知,希尔顿先生并不危险,这我已经告诉你了。"汤普生先生看得出,某种严重的事情快要发生了。他再也不动脑子去思考了。他干脆是让这家伙把脑子里的想法一五一十全说出来,然后再看有什么法子对付。他未加思索,就拿出刀子和烟草,想切一块来嚼,随后又记起了自己的决定,便把东西放回口袋。

哈奇先生说:"法律是完全支持我的。至于这个希尔顿先生,他成了我最棘手的一个案子。他使我不能得到满分。他变疯以前我就认得他,我也认得他一家人,所以我把搜捕他的事接了过来。哼,先生,他已变得像泥鳅一样滑了,因为我们只知道他肯定是早已死了。我们本来是无论如何也不会发现他的踪迹的,可是你知道他干了什么?哼,先生,大约两星期以前,他的老母亲收到了他的一封信,你猜她在信里发现了什么?哼,一张镇上小银行的 850 元的支票,居然是一张支票。信上没有多少话,光说他把自己的一小笔积蓄寄给她,也许她需要买点什么,可是名字、邮戳、日期,都是齐全的,老太婆简直乐得忘乎所以。她变得像个孩子,好像已经忘了她唯一活着的孩子杀过自己的兄弟,变成了疯子。希尔顿先生说他日子过得很好,还叫她千万别告诉任何人。哼,她当然保守不了秘密,还要去兑现支票什么的。因为这样,我才知道的,"他变得情不自禁了,"我简直是又惊又喜。"他又用自己的两只手对握了握,又是摇头又是晃脑,嗓子眼里不断发出"呵,呵"的声音。汤普生先生只觉得自己的嘴角在往下耷拉。好一只卑鄙下流的猎狗,竟如此鬼鬼祟祟地刺探别人的隐私,然后去领取血腥的犒赏,真是卑鄙透了,让他再讲下去。

"不错,是的,真叫人喜出望外啊,"他说,尽量想使他的声音显得平静些,"我得说这是件意外的事。"

"哈,老兄,"哈奇先生说,"我越琢磨这档子事,越觉得有必要深入调查一番,于是我去找那老太婆谈了谈。她已经老态龙钟,眼睛也半瞎了,不行了,可是她还想立刻搭火车来看她的儿子。我老老实实告诉她——她身体太弱,没法出门,如此等等。我还说,算是做好事,我愿花钱到南边去看望希尔顿先生,把他

thoughts, turned his eyes, wicked and pig-like, on Mr. Thompson. "Fact is, " he said, as if he had made up his mind about something, "I might need your help in the little matter I've got on hand, but it won't cost you any trouble. Now, this Mr. Helton here, like I tell you, he's a dangerous escaped loonatic, you might say. Now fact is, in the last twelve years or so I musta rounded up twenty-odd escaped loonatics, besides a couple of escaped convicts that I just run into by accident, like I don't make a business of it, but if there's a reward, and there usually is a reward, of course, I get it. It amounts to a tidy little sum in the long run, but that ain't the main question. Fact is, I'm for law and order, I don't like to see lawbreakers and loonatics at large. It ain't the place for them. Now I reckon you're bound to agree with me on that, aren't you?"

Mr. Thompson said, "Well, circumstances alters cases, as the feller says. Now, what I know of Mr. Helton, he ain't dangerous, as I told you. " Something serious was going to happen, Mr. Thompson could see that. He stopped thinking about it. He'd just let this fellow shoot off his head and then see what could be done about it. Without thinking he got out his knife and plug and started to cut a chew, then remembered himself and put them back in his pocket.

"The law, " said Mr. Hatch, "is solidly behind me. Now this Mr. Helton, he's been one of my toughest cases. He's kept my record from being practically one hundred per cent. I knew him before he went loony, and I know the fam'ly, so I undertook to help out rounding him up. Well, sir, he was gone slick as a whistle, for all we knew the man was as good as dead long while ago. Now we never might have caught up with him, but do you know what he did? Well, sir, about two weeks ago his old mother gets a letter from him, and in that letter, what do you reckon she found? Well, it was a check on that little bank in town for eight hundred and fifty dollars, just like that; the letter wasn't nothing much, just said he was sending her a few little savings, she might need something, but there it was, name, postmark, date, everything. The old woman practically lost her mind with joy. She's gettin' childish, and it looked like she kinda forgot that her only living son killed his brother and went loony. Mr. Helton said he was getting along all right, and for her not to tell nobody. Well, natchally, she couldn't keep it to herself, with that check to cash and everything. So that's how I come to know. " His feelings got the better of him. "You coulda knocked me down with a feather. " He shook hands with himself and rocked, wagging his head, going "Heh, heh, " in his throat. Mr. Thompson felt the corners of his mouth turning

的情况带回来一五一十告诉她。她交给我一件她亲手缝制的新衬衣，还有一块瑞典式的大糕饼，让我带给她儿子，可是我不知在路上什么地方弄丢了。其实这也没多大关系，他哪有心思来欣赏这些礼物呢。"

汤普生先生坐直了，在树墩上转过身子，望着哈奇先生，尽可能平静地问道："那么，你现在打算怎么办呢？这是个实际问题。"

哈奇先生懒洋洋地站起来，抖了抖身子。"嗯，我是做好跟他扭打一场的准备的，"他说，"我带来了手铐，不过只要能够不动武，我就尽可能不动。我没有声张，就是不想弄得沸沸扬扬的。我估计咱们两人能对付得了他。"他把手伸进衣服里面的大兜，把它们拿了出来。手铐，天哪，汤普生先生想。在一个平静的下午上人家家里来，惹是生非把人弄得心绪不宁，还在正派人院子里从兜里掏出一副手铐，好像在干极平常的农活似的。

汤普生先生脑袋里嗡嗡作响，他也站了起来。"好吧。"他严厉地说，"我要告诉你，我认为你在干的是一件很糟糕的事，你准是穷极无聊了，才干这种事。现在我想好好地奉劝你几句。你趁早死了这条心，别以为可以在这儿难为希尔顿先生，另外，你越早赶了你那辆租来的马车离开我的大门，我就越是称心。"

哈奇先生把一只手铐塞进衣兜，让另一只吊在外面。他把帽子拉得低低的，盖在眼睛上，使汤普生先生不知怎的想起他像一个警长。他好像一点儿也不紧张，也一点儿不在乎汤普生先生的话。他说："现在你听我说几句，像你这样一个人，居然想拦住不让我把一个外逃的疯子弄回他该待的地方去，那真是异想天开。你突然有这样的表现，我知道只消把你甩开就行了，可是我仍然把你看作一个正派人，希望你能帮我一起执行法律。当然，倘若你不肯干，我只得另外去找别人了。你窝藏一个杀死亲兄弟的外逃疯子在先，继而又拒绝把他交出来，这在你的乡邻看来不见得光彩吧。他们会觉得你这人十分古怪。"

汤普生先生不用他说自己也觉得挺怪。这会使他处境非常尴尬。他说："可是我没告诉你吗，这个人已经不疯了。9年来他一直老老实实。他是——他是——"

汤普生先生也想不出用什么词来说明希尔顿现在的情况。"哼，他就跟我们家里人一样，"他说，"比他更可靠的长工我还没见到过。"汤普生先生想找到

down. Why, the dirty low-down hound, sneaking around spying into other people's business like that. Collecting blood money, that's what it was! Let him talk!

"Yea, well, that musta been a surprise all right," he said, trying to hold his voice even. "I'd say a surprise."

"Well, siree," said Mr. Hatch, "the more I got to thinking about it, the more I just come to the conclusion that I'd better look into the matter a little, and so I talked to the old woman. She's pretty decrepit, now, half blind and all, but she was all for taking the first train out and going to see her son. I put it up to her square—how she was too feeble for the trip, and all. So, just as a favor to her, I told her for my expenses I'd come down and see Mr. Helton and bring her back all the news about him. She gave me a new shirt she made herself by hand, and a big Swedish kind of cake to bring to him, but I musta mislaid them along the road somewhere. It don't reely matter, though, he prob'ly ain't in any state of mind to, appreciate 'em."

Mr. Thompson sat up and turning round on the log looked at Mr. Hatch and asked as quietly as he could, "And now what are you aiming to do? That's the question."

Mr. Hatch slouched up to his feet and shook himself. "Well, I come all prepared for a little scuffle," he said. "I got the handcuffs," he said, "but I don't want no violence if I can help it. I didn't want to say nothing around the countryside, making an uproar. I figured the two of us could overpower him." He reached into his big inside pocket and pulled them out. Handcuffs, for God's sake, thought Mr. Thompson. Coming round on a peaceable afternoon worrying a man, making trouble, and fishing handcuffs out of his pocket on a decent family homestead, as if it was all in the day's work.

Mr. Thompson, his head buzzing, got up too. "Well," he said, roundly, "I want to tell you I think you've got a mighty sorry job on hand, you sure must be hard up for something to do, and now I want to give you a good piece of advice. You just drop the idea that you're going to come here and make trouble for Mr. Helton, and the quicker you drive that hired rig away from my front gate the better I'll be satisfied."

Mr. Hatch put one handcuff in his outside pocket, the other dangling down. He pulled his hat down over his eyes, and reminded Mr. Thompson of a sheriff, somehow. He didn't seem in the least nervous, and didn't take up Mr. Thompson's words. He said, "Now listen just a minute, it ain't reasonable to suppose that a man like yourself is going to stand in the way of

一条出路。的确,希尔顿先生随时可以重新变疯,而现在这个家伙倘若在村子里到处乱讲,也会使汤普生先生陷入困境。这种情况真是可怕。他想不出有什么解决的办法。"你才是疯子哩。"汤普生先生突然吼叫起来,"在我们当中,疯的是你,你比他疯得还厉害!你快滚,否则我把你的手铐上,扭送法院。你犯了非法入侵私人住宅的罪,"汤普生先生大嚷大叫道,"快滚,小心我揍扁你!"

他向那胖子跨过一步,胖子畏缩地后退了一步,一边说:"你倒试试看,你倒试试看,来呀!"紧接着事情发生了。事后,汤普生先生虽然竭力想把事情经过重新拼凑起来,却怎么也没法回忆清楚。他只记得看见那胖子手里拿着那把长猎刀,看见希尔顿先生拐过屋角急急忙忙地跑过来,长下巴耷拉着,胳膊挥动着,眼睛里充满了狂暴的神情。希尔顿先生插到他们的中间,紧握着双拳,可是他突然停住了,呆呆地瞪着胖子,巨大的身躯瘫了似的,浑身打颤,像一匹受惊的马。接着那胖子向他冲过去,一只手攥着刀,另一只手里拿着手铐。汤普生先生看见事情发生了,他看见那把刀子捅进了希尔顿先生的肚子,他知道他自己把树墩上的斧子拔出拿到自己手里,他只觉得他双手高举过头,把斧子砸在哈奇先生脑袋上,就像在敲晕一只要宰的牛。

汤普生太太不安地听着窗外的说话声,已经听了好一阵,其中一个人的声音是陌生的。起初,她因为太累,不想起床出去看看发生了什么事。但是突如其来的惊叫声使她站起身来,连拖鞋也没穿,头发松松地拢着,就穿过前廊跑了出来。她把手挡在眼睛上方,先是看见希尔顿先生猫着腰跑着穿过了果园,慌慌张张,仿佛后面有一群狗在追他,又看见汤普生先生用斧子把支撑着自己,弯下腰去摇一个陌生人的肩膀,那人对折着身体瘫坐在地上,头顶心被砸得稀烂,血不断地涌流出来,汇成了一摊黏稠的血潭。汤普生先生的手一直没有从那人的肩膀上松开,他用含混不清的声音在说:"他杀了希尔顿先生,他杀死了他,我看见的。我只好把他打晕,"他大声地嚷道,'可是他醒不过来了。"

汤普生太太有气无力地尖叫道:"可是,希尔顿先生在那边跑呢。"她指着。汤普生太太顺着屋子的墙壁慢慢地软瘫下来,脸一点点地俯向地面,她只觉得自己好像沉溺在水里,怎么也升不到水面上来,她唯

getting an escaped loonatic back to the asylum where he belongs. Now I know it's enough to throw you off, coming sudden like this, but fact is I counted on your being a respectable man and helping me out to see that justice is done. Now a course, if you won't help, I'll have to look around for help somewhere else. It won't look very good to your neighbors that you was harboring an escaped loonatic who killed his own brother, and then you refused to give him up. It will look mighty funny."

Mr. Thompson knew almost before he heard the words that it would look funny. It would put him in a mighty awkward position. He said, "But I've been trying to tell you all along that the man ain't loony now. He's been perfectly harmless for nine years. He's—he's—"

Mr. Thompson couldn't think how to describe how it was with Mr. Helton. "Why, he's been like one of the family," he said, "the best standby a man ever had." Mr. Thompson tried to see his way out. It was a fact Mr. Helton might go loony again any minute, and now this fellow talking around the country would put Mr. Thompson in a fix. It was a terrible position. He couldn't think of any way out. "You're crazy," Mr. Thompson roared suddenly, "you're the crazy one around here, you're crazier than he ever was! You get off this place or I'll handcuff you and turn you over to the law. You're trespassing," shouted Mr. Thompson. "Get out of here before I knock you down!"

He took a step towards the fat man, who backed off, shrinking, "Try it, try it, go ahead!" and then something happened that Mr. Thompson tried hard afterwards to piece together in his mind, and in fact it never did come straight. He saw the fat man with his long bowie knife in his hand, he saw Mr. Helton come round the corner on the run, his long jaw dropped, his arms swinging, his eyes wild. Mr. Helton came in between them, fists doubled up, then stopped short, glaring at the fat man, his big frame seemed to collapse, he trembled like a shied horse; and then the fat man drove at him, knife in one hand, handcuffs in the other. Mr. Thompson saw it coming, he saw the blade going into Mr. Helton's stomach, he knew he had the ax out of the log in his own hands, felt his arms go up over his head and bring the ax down on Mr. Hatch's head as if he were stunning a beef.

Mrs. Thompson had been listening uneasily for some time to the voices going on, one of them strange to her, but she was too tired at first to get up and come out to see what was going on. The confused shouting that rose so suddenly brought her up to her feet and out across the front porch without her

一的想法是:亏得孩子都不在家,他们出去了,到哈里法钓鱼去了,噢,上帝,她真高兴孩子们不在家。

太阳快落山的时分,汤普生夫妇驱赶着马车来到他们的马房前。汤普生先生把缰绳交给老伴,自己下去开那扇大门,汤普生太太吆喝老吉姆进了马房。那辆马车因为尘土与破旧,显得灰蒙蒙的,汤普生太太的脸因为尘土与疲累也显得灰蒙蒙的,汤普生先生这会儿正站在马脑袋旁边解马套,他的脸除了刚剃过的下巴与腮帮是铁青的以外,也是灰蒙蒙的,灰中带青,凹陷了下来,但是显得很沉毅,像一张死人的脸。

汤普生太太从马车上走下来,站在马房地上那片压得很瓷实的马粪堆上,抖了抖她那条印着浅色花枝的裙子。她戴着烟玻璃的眼镜,她那顶围着枯萎的红、蓝两色勿忘我花圈的宽边遮阳帽拉得低低的,遮住了前额,帽子是用一个难解的结系住的。

那匹马垂倒了头,深深地出了一口气,弯了弯僵的腿。汤普生先生的话传了进来,显得声音发闷,瓮声瓮气的。"可怜的老吉姆,"他说,清了清嗓子,"它的肋部陷下去了好些。我看这个星期它也够受罪的。"他把连成一片的马套举起来,从马身上卸开,吉姆迟疑不决地从车辕中间走出来。"好了,这是最后一回了,"汤普生先生说,还在跟吉姆聊天,"这下子你可以好好歇息了。"

汤普生太太闭上黑眼镜后面的眼睛。最后的一次,最重要的一次,他们以后再也不用去了。现在,安乐的黑暗再度降临,她不用再戴黑眼镜了,如今她的眼睛老是泪汪汪的,虽然她并没有哭,戴上眼镜,她觉得好过些,躲在黑眼镜后面似乎更安全些。她双手颤抖地取出手帕,擤擤鼻子,打从那一天起,她的手就一直是颤抖的。她说:"我看到孩子们已经点上灯了。我希望他们把炉子也生好了。"

她沿着不平坦的小路慢慢地走回去,把薄衣裙和浆得发硬的衬裙拉在身边,一步步在尖利的小石块之间找好路走。她之所以要离开马房是因为待在汤普生先生身边简直受不了,她走得这么慢又是因为她怕回到屋子里去。生活本身就是一种大恐惧,乡邻的脸、孩子的脸、丈夫的脸、全世界的脸、她自己的房子的憧憧黑影,连草的气息和树的气息,这些都使她感到害怕。没有地方可以一走了之,可以做的只有一件事,那就是好歹忍受下去——可是怎么忍受呢?她常

slippers, hair half-braided. Shading her eyes, she saw first Mr. Helton, running all stooped over through the orchard, running like a man with dogs after him; and Mr. Thompson supporting himself on the ax handle was leaning over shaking by the shoulder a man Mrs. Thompson had never seen, who lay doubled up with the top of his head smashed and the blood running away in a greasy-looking puddle. Mr. Thompson without taking his hand from the man's shoulder, said in a thick voice, "He killed Mr. Helton, he killed him, I saw him do it. I had to knock him out," he called loudly, "but he won't come to."

Mrs. Thompson said in a faint scream, "Why, yonder goes Mr. Helton," and she pointed. Mrs. Thompson sat down slowly against the side of the house and began to slide forward on her face; she felt as if she were drowning, she couldn't rise to the top somehow, and her only thought was she was glad the boys were not there, they were out, fishing at Halifax, oh, God, she was glad the boys were not there.

Mr. and Mrs. Thompson drove up to their barn about sunset. Mr. Thompson handed the reins to his wife, got out to open the big door, and Mrs. Thompson guided old Jim in under the roof. The buggy was gray with dust and age, Mrs. Thompson's face was gray with dust and weariness, and Mr. Thompson's face, as he stood at the horse's head and began unhitching, was gray except for the dark blue of his freshly shaven jaws and chin, gray and blue and caved in, but patient, like a dead man's face.

Mrs. Thompson stepped down to the hard packed manure of the barn floor, and shook out her light flower-sprigged dress. She wore her smoked glasses, and her wide shady leghorn hat with the wreath of exhausted pink and blue forget-me-nots hid her forehead, fixed in a knot of distress.

The horse hung his head, raised a huge sigh and flexed his stiffened legs. Mr. Thompson's words came up muffled and hollow. "Poor ole Jim," he said, clearing his throat, "he looks pretty sunk in the ribs. I guess he's had a hard week." He lifted the harness up in one piece, slid it off and Jim walked out of the shafts halting a little. "Well, this is the last time," Mr. Thompson said, still talking to Jim. "Now you can get a good rest."

Mrs. Thompson closed her eyes behind her smoked glasses. The last time, and high time, and they should never have gone at all. She did not need her glasses any more, now the good darkness was coming down again, but her eyes ran full of tears steadily, though she was not crying, and she felt better with the glasses, safer, hidden away behind them. She took out

常这样问自己。现在她该怎么生活下去呢？她究竟
干吗要活在人世呢？她如今希望前几回生重病的时
候干脆死掉就好了，现在这样活着真是活受罪。

孩子们在厨房里，赫伯特在看上星期天报上的连
环画，看《苦孩子》和《快乐的小瘪三》①。他双手托着
下巴，胳膊肘支在桌子上，一本正经地在看解说，在看
图画，可是他脸上却不显得快乐。阿瑟在生炉子，过
上一阵便添一根木柴，他望着那根柴怎样点燃起来，
怎样熊熊燃烧。从他脸上看，他比赫伯特显得更加心
事重重、郁郁寡欢，不过他生性本来就比较忧郁。汤
普生太太想，他总爱把事情看得太严重一些。阿瑟
说："你好，妈妈。"接着又去干他的活儿了。赫伯特把
报纸收在一起，搬到长凳上去看。他们都是大孩子
了——一个15岁，一个17岁，阿瑟都跟爸爸一般高
了。汤普生太太在赫伯特身边坐下来，开始脱帽子。
她说："我想你们都饿了吧。我们今天回来得晚了。
今天我们走的是洛克谷路，这条路越来越不好走了。"
她那苍白的嘴唇往下耷拉，两边露出两条深深的
皱纹。

"我猜你们去过曼宁家了吧？"赫伯特问。

"是的，还有弗古生家、奥尔布赖特家，以及新搬
来的麦克列伦家。"

"他们说什么了吗？"赫伯特问。

"没说什么，你知道无非就那些话，有几个人总是
说，是啊，他们知道这个案子清清楚楚，判得匕公平，
他们还说你们的爸爸总算被判无罪，他们感到很高
兴，如此等等。有几个人也的确显得挺高兴。可是看
起来人们也并不真正完全支持他。我都快累坏了。"
她说，泪珠儿重新从黑眼镜后面滴落下来。"我不明
白这样干有什么好处，可是你们的爸爸不到处去说事
情的经过，便好像不得安生。我真是不明白。"

"我觉得这没有用，一点点用处也没有。"阿瑟说，
从炉子旁边走过来，"那只能让人家没完没了地注意
这个问题，使得每一个人到处去说他听到的是怎么回
事，结果是越弄越乱。这样反而更糟。我希望你能
劝爸爸别再跟人家谈这件事了。"

"你们的爸爸知道怎样做最最合适，"汤普生太太
说，"你不应该指责他。他的烦恼已经够多了。"

---

① 都是当时报上连载的连环漫画，相当于我国的
《三毛流浪记》。

her handkerchief with her hands shaking as they had
been shaking ever since *that day*, and blew her nose.
She said, "I see the boys have lighted the lamps. I hope
they've started the stove going. "

She stepped along the rough path holding her thin
dress and starched petticoats around her, feeling her
way between the sharp small stones, leaving the barn
because she could hardly bear to be near Mr. Thompson, advancing slowly towards the house because she
dreaded going there. Life was all one dread, the faces
of her neighbors, of her boys, of her husband, the face
of the whole world, the shape of her own house in the
darkness, the very smell of the grass and the trees
were horrible to her. There was no place to go, only
one thing to do, bear it somehow—but how? She
asked herself that question often. How was she going
to keep on living now? Why had she lived at all? She
wished now she had died one of those times when she
had been so sick, instead of living on for this.

The boys were in the kitchen; Herbert was looking at the funny pictures from last Sunday's newspapers, the Katzenjammer Kids and Happy Hooligan.
His chin was in his hands and his elbows on the table,
and he was really reading and looking at the pictures,
but his face was unhappy. Arthur was building the
fire, adding kindling a stick at a time, watching it catch
and blaze. His face was heavier and darker than
Herbert's, but he was a little sullen by nature; Mrs.
Thompson thought, he takes things harder, too. Arthur said, "Hello, Momma," and went on with his
work. Herbert swept the papers together and moved
over on the bench. They were big boys—fifteen and
seventeen, and Arthur as tall as his father. Mrs.
Thompson sat down beside Herbert, taking off her
hat. She said, "I guess you're hungry. We were late today. We went the Log Hollow road, it's rougher than
ever. "Her pale mouth drooped with a sad fold on either side.

"I guess you saw the Mannings, then," said Herbert.

"Yes, and the Fergusons, and the Allbrights, and
that new family McClellan. "

"Anybody say anything?"asked Herbert.

"Nothing much, you know how it's been all a-
long, some of them keeps saying, yes, they know it
was a clear case and a fair trial and they say how glad
they are your papa came out so well, and all that, some
of 'em do, anyhow, but it looks like they don't really
take sides with him. I'm about wore out, "she said, the
tears rolling again from under her dark glasses. "I
don't know what good it does, but your papa can't
seem to rest unless he's telling how it happened. I

阿瑟不再说什么,可是他的下巴僵着。汤普生先生进来了,眼睛凹陷无神,像死人的一样,他粗厚的双手是灰白色的,皱纹很清晰,因为他每天早上都要把手洗得干干净净,好出门去拜访乡邻,讲他这方面的情况和道理。他穿着星期天穿的好衣服,那是一套米色的西装,打着一条黑领带。

汤普生太太站起身来,脑袋里晕晕乎乎的。"你们都到厨房外面去,这儿太热了,我嫌挤得慌。我要给大家弄点简单的晚饭,请你们出去给我腾个地方。"

他们出去了,显得很乐意似的,孩子们到外面院子里,汤普生先生进他的卧室里去。她听见他脱鞋时发出的呻吟声,又听见他躺下去时床的吱吱嘎嘎声。汤普生太太打开冰箱,感觉到宜人的凉气从里面流出来,她从来不敢指望能有冰箱,更不要说有钱能让里面的冰老是装得满满的了。在有了冰箱两三年之后,这件事她仍然觉得不可思议。食物贮藏在里面,又凉爽又清洁,热一热马上可以吃。要不是千巧万巧希尔顿先生有一天恰巧来到他们家,她是无论如何也购置不起这只冰箱的。希尔顿先生多么俭省,多么能干,多么善良,汤普生太太想,她胸臆间越来越发胀,她都担心自己又要晕过去了。她站在打开的门边,把头靠在门上。她一想起希尔顿先生就难过得不能自持,他那张长长的脸那么忧郁,干什么都不出声,他一直是那么安静,那么善良,那么勤快,帮了汤普生先生那么大的忙。可是那天他急急忙忙奔过灼热的田野与树林时,却像条疯狗似的被追逐,所有的人都带了绳索、枪支和棍子来抓他,要捆住他。哦,天哪,汤普生太太无泪地长长地叹息了一声,跪在冰箱前面摸索着取里面的菜。即使他们在牢房的地板和墙壁上都铺上垫子,还有五个人按住他不让他进一步伤害自己,可是他已经伤势太重,无论如何活不成了。这些都是警长巴比先生告诉她的。他说,是的,他们并不想伤害他,可是他们必须得抓住他,他疯得像个疯子,他捡起一些石块,谁走近他就要用石块砸烂谁的脑袋。他工作服里还揣着两只口琴,警长说,可是扭打时口琴掉了出来,希尔顿先生想再去捡起来,这样他们才终于按倒了他。"他们不得不动武,汤普生太太,他乱打一气,像只野猫一样。"是啊,汤普生太太想,又是一阵辛酸,当然啰,他们不得不动武。他们永远是不得不动武的。汤普生先生也不能做到和一个人争吵之后,让他太太平平地离开自己的家。没有办法的,她想,一

don't know. "

"I don't think it does any good, not a speck, "said Arthur, moving away from the stove. "It just keeps the whole question stirred up in people's minds. Everybody will go round telling what he heard, and the whole thing is going to get worse mixed up than ever. It just makes matters worse. I wish you could get Papa to stop driving round the country talking like that. "

"Your papa knows best, "said Mrs. Thompson. "You oughtn't to criticize him. He's got enough to put up with without that. "

Arthur said nothing, his jaw stubborn. Mr. Thompson came in, his eyes hollowed out and dead-looking, his thick hands gray white and seamed from washing them clean every day before he started out to see the neighbors to tell them his side of the story. He was wearing his Sunday clothes, a thick pepper-and-salt-colored suit with a black string tie.

Mrs. Thompson stood up, her head swimming. "Now you-all get out of the kitchen, it's too hot in here and I need room. I'll get us a little bite of supper, if you'll just get out and give me some room. "

They went as if they were glad to go, the boys outside, Mr. Thompson into his bedroom. She heard him groaning to himself as he took off his shoes, and heard the bed creak as he lay down. Mrs. Thompson opened the icebox and felt the sweet coldness flow out of it; she had never expected to have an icebox, much less did she hope to afford to keep it filled with ice. It still seemed like a miracle, after two or three years. There was the food, cold and clean, all ready to be warmed over. She would never have had that icebox if Mr. Helton hadn't happened along one day, just by the strangest luck; so saving, and so managing, so good, thought Mrs. Thompson, her heart swelling until she feared she would faint again, standing there with the door open and leaning her head upon it. She simply could not bear to remember Mr. Helton, with his long sad face and silent ways, who had always been so quiet and harmless, who had worked so hard and helped Mr. Thompson so much, running through the hot fields and woods, being hunted like a mad dog, everybody turning out with ropes and guns and sticks to catch and tie him. Oh, God, said Mrs. Thompson in a long dry moan, kneeling before the icebox and fumbling inside for the dishes, even if they did pile mattresses all over the jail floor and against the walls, and five men there to hold him to keep him from hurting himself any more, he was already hurt too badly, he couldn't have lived anyway. Mr. Barbee, the sheriff, told her about it. He said, well, they didn't aim to harm him but they had to catch him, he was crazy as a

边站起来,关上冰箱的门,他非得把人杀死,他非得变成杀人者,从而毁掉两个儿子的一生,还使希尔顿先生像只疯狗似的被人打死。

她的思路以一个小小的无声的爆炸而中断,然后再度变得清晰,重新开始。希尔顿先生其他的口琴仍然放在小屋里,每天到了一定的时候,他的曲调就会在汤普生太太的头脑里响起。每天黄昏,她听不到这调子还觉得有所失呢。奇怪的是,以前她始终不知道歌名,也不知道歌的内容,希尔顿走了以后才知道。汤普生太太膝头有点发软,她在水槽那儿倒了一杯水喝,把赤豆倒在烤盘里,开始让鸡块裹上面粉,准备炸面拖鸡块。有那么一个时期,她对自己说,我以为我有邻居和朋友可以依靠,有那么一个时期,我们可以抬起头来做人,那时候我的丈夫没有杀人。对任何人在任何事情上我都可以讲实话。

汤普生先生躺在床上辗转反侧,他盘算,该做的事他都做了,从现在起他要想法子撂下这件事了。他的律师柏莱先生从一开头起就跟他说:"现在你要镇定下来,振作精神。你的案子对你很有利,即使你没有见证人。你太太必须出庭,她将是影响陪审团的一个有力的因素。你只消声称自己无罪就行了,别的事都有我呢。审判只不过是一个形式,你丝毫不用发愁。要不了多久你就可以从这件事中解脱出来了。"为了有话好说,柏莱先生只好把他所知道的附近一带为了某种原因不得不杀人——反正是为了自卫呗——的案例告诉他,后来这些人都没事。他甚至还告诉汤普生先生,从前,他自己的爸爸也曾开枪打死一个人,仅仅因为那人不听劝告,非要跨进他父亲的院子。"当然啰,"柏莱先生的老太爷说,"我是为了自卫才打死那个流氓的。我告诉过他,如果他把脚踩到我院子里来,我就要向他开枪,他还往里走,于是我就开枪了。"柏莱先生说,这两个人结成冤家已有多年,老太爷为了抓住那人的把柄等了好久,他抓到后当然不肯放过机会。

"可是我跟你说过了,"汤普生先生说,"是哈奇先生拿了猎刀向希尔顿先生刺去的。正是为了这个,我才动手的。"

"那就更好了,"柏莱先生说,"那个陌生人没有任何权利到你家里去干这样的事。哼,说真的,"柏莱先生说,"你连误杀都不能算。你现在千万不要轻举妄

loon; he picked up rocks and tried to brain every man that got near him. He had two harmonicas in his jumper pocket, said the sheriff, but they fell out in the scuffle, and Mr. Helton tried to pick 'em up again, and that's when they finally got him. "They *had* to be rough, Miz Thompson, he fought like a wildcat." Yes, thought Mrs. Thompson, again with the same bitterness, of course, they had to be rough. They always have to be rough. Mr. Thompson can't argue with a man and get him off the place peaceably, she thought, standing up and shutting the icebox, he has to kill somebody, he has to be a murderer and ruin his boys' lives and cause Mr. Helton to be killed like a mad dog.

Her thoughts stopped with a little soundless explosion, cleared and began again. The rest of Mr. Helton's harmonicas were still in the shack, his tune ran in Mrs. Thompson's head at certain times of the day. She missed it in the evenings. It seemed so strange she had never known the name of that song, nor what it meant, until after Mr. Helton was gone. Mrs. Thompson, trembling in the knees, took a drink of water at the sink and poured the red beans into the baking dish, and began to roll the pieces of chicken in flour to fry them. There was a time, she said to herself, when I thought I had neighbors and friends, there was a time when we could hold up our heads, there was a time when my husband hadn't killed a man and I could tell the truth to anybody about anything.

Mr. Thompson, turning on his bed, figured that he had done all he could, he'd just try to let the matter rest from now on. His lawyer, Mr. Burleigh, had told him right at the beginning, "Now you keep calm and collected. You've got a fine case, even if you haven't got witnesses. Your wife must sit in court, she'll be a powerful argument with the jury. You just plead not guilty and I'll do the rest. The trial is going to be a mere formality, you haven't got a thing to worry about. You'll be clean out of this before you know it." And to make talk Mr. Burleigh had got to telling about all the men he knew around the country who for one reason or another had been forced to kill somebody, always in self-defense, and there just wasn't anything to it at all. He even told about how his own father in the old days had shot and killed a man just for setting foot inside his gate when he told him not to. "Sure, I shot the scoundrel," said Mr. Burleigh's father, "in self-defense; I *told* him I'd shoot him if he set his foot in my yard, and he did, and I did." There had been bad blood between them for years, Mr. Burleigh said, and his father had waited a long time to catch the other fellow in the wrong, and when he did he certainly made the most of his opportunity.

动,只管稳坐钓鱼台好了。我不关照你,你什么话也不要说。"

连误杀都不能算。那时候,汤普生先生不得不先用一块马车帆布把哈奇先生盖起来,自己骑马到镇上去报告警长。这件事使艾丽大为震惊。当他和警长、验尸官以及警长的两个副手一起回来时,他们发现她坐在路边一座架在小沟上的矮桥上,离家约有半英里路远。他让她坐在马鞍后面,带她回家。他已经告诉警长,他太太亲眼目睹了事情的全部经过,这会儿他要把她送回房去让她躺下,他就有机会告诉她,倘若他们问起来她该怎样回答。他没有说出希尔顿先生一直是疯的这件事,可是审判时露了出来。汤普生先生按柏莱先生的指导,假装对此事毫无所知,哈奇先生连一个字也没有提起。汤普生先生假装以为哈奇先生是来找希尔顿先生报旧仇的。哈奇先生家里来了两个人,他们想让汤普生先生吃官司,可是毫无结果。在柏莱先生的用心照拂下,这次审判草草了事。他开的诉讼费极为公道,汤普生先生照付了,而且心中非常感激,可是事情过后汤普生先生进城有时拐到柏莱先生办公室去,柏莱先生好像不太乐意看见他。汤普生先生总想和律师谈谈,想把当初没想起来的一些事告诉律师,目的无非是要说明哈奇先生是一条何等下流、难以对付的猎狗。柏莱先生似乎已经失去了兴趣,他一看见汤普生先生出现在门口便显得厌恶与不耐烦。汤普生先生老是对自己说,没错,他没有受到处罚,正如柏莱先生所预言的那样,可是,可是——正是在这儿,汤普生先生脑子里想不清楚,他像一只戳在鱼钩上的蚯蚓那样蠕动不已,杀死哈奇先生的是他,他是一个杀人者。正是发生在他身上的这件事的真相他不能理会,尽管他嘴里可以对自己这样或那样说。本来嘛,杀人的事,他连想都没有想过,更不要说蓄意杀哈奇先生了。要是希尔顿先生没有因为听见了吵架声出人意外地跑了过来,那么,就——不过,希尔顿先生一路跑来是为了帮他忙的呀。他弄不明白的是紧接着发生的事。他明明看见哈奇先生拿了刀扑向希尔顿先生的,他看见刀刃朝上,刀尖刺进了希尔顿先生的肚子,然后向上切,就像宰猪那样,可是他们终于逮住希尔顿先生时,他身上连一点儿刀伤也没有。汤普生先生知道自己双手握住了斧子把,也记得自己曾把斧子举起来,可是他不记得他是把斧子往哈奇先生脑袋上砸下去了。他不记得有这回事。他回

"But Mr. Hatch, as I told you," Mr. Thompson had said, "made a pass at Mr. Helton with his bowie knife. That's why I took a hand."

"All the better," said Mr. Burleigh. "That stranger hadn't any right coming to your house on such an errand. Why, hell," said Mr. Burleigh, "that wasn't even manslaughter you committed. So now you just hold your horses and keep your shirt on. And don't say one word without I tell you."

Wasn't even manslaughter. Mr. Thompson had to cover Mr. Hatch with a piece of wagon canvas and ride to town to tell the sheriff. It had been hard on Ellie. When they got back, the sheriff and the coroner and two deputies, they found her sitting beside the road, on a low bridge over a gulley, about half a mile from the place. He had taken her up behind his saddle and got her back to the house. He had already told the sheriff that his wife had witnessed the whole business, and now he had time, getting her to her room and in bed, to tell her what to say if they asked anything. He had left out the part about Mr. Helton being crazy all along, but it came out at the trial. By Mr. Burleigh's advice Mr. Thompson had pretended to be perfectly ignorant; Mr. Hatch hadn't said a word about that. Mr. Thompson pretended to believe that Mr. Hatch had just come looking for Mr. Helton to settle old scores, and the two members of Mr. Hatch's family who had come down to try to get Mr. Thompson convicted didn't get anywhere at all. It hadn't been much of a trial, Mr. Burleigh saw to that. He had charged a reasonable fee, and Mr. Thompson had paid him and felt grateful, but after it was over Mr. Burleigh didn't seem pleased to see him when he got to dropping into the office to talk it over, telling him things that had slipped his mind at first: trying to explain what an ornery low hound Mr. Hatch had been, anyhow. Mr. Burleigh seemed to have lost his interest; he looked sour and upset when he saw Mr. Thompson at the door. Mr. Thompson kept saying to himself that he'd got off, all right, just as Mr. Burleigh had predicted, but, but—and it was right there that Mr. Thompson's mind stuck, squirming like an angleworm on a fishhook: he had killed Mr. Hatch, and he was a murderer. That was the truth about himself that Mr. Thompson couldn't grasp, even when he said the word to himself. Why, he had not even once *thought* of killing anybody, much less Mr. Hatch, and if Mr. Helton hadn't come out so unexpectedly, hearing the row, why, then—but then, Mr. Helton had come on the run that way to help him. What he couldn't understand was what happened next. He had seen Mr. Hatch go after Mr. Helton with the knife, he had seen the point, blade up, go into Mr.

忆不起来。他只记得他当时决心不让哈奇先生杀死希尔顿先生。如果给他一个机会他是可以把事情全部经过解释清楚的。可是过堂的时候他们不让他说话。他们光是向他提问,让他回答"是"或"不是",他们根本不去寻根究底。审判过后,到现在,有一个星期了,他每天都梳洗干净,刮了脸,穿上最好的衣服,带了艾丽去拜访所有的乡邻,告诉他们他并非蓄意要杀死哈奇先生,可是那又有什么用呢?谁也不相信他。甚至,当他转过脸来对艾丽说:"你当时在场,你看见的,是吗?"艾丽就开口说:"是的,的确这样。汤普生先生是想救希尔顿先生的命。"当他又接着说:"如果你们不相信我,你可以相信我的太太。她是不会说假话的。"甚至这种时候汤普生先生也看出他们不相信他,他们所有的人脸上有一种神情,使他沮丧,使他心里发虚,感到毫无气力了。他们根本不相信他不是一个谋杀犯。

　　甚至艾丽也从不说一句话来安慰他。他希望她终于会这样说:"我现在记起来了,汤普生先生,我的确是刚好赶到屋子拐角,看到了所发生的一切,那不是谎话,汤普生先生。你不要担心了。"可是他们一天天默默地赶着马车在崎岖的道路上颠簸,她仍然什么话也不说。天气虽然仍然炎热又干燥,但一天比一天短了,因为秋天近了。他们变得怕见另一幢房子,怕见屋子里的人了。所有的屋子现在看起来模样都差不多,所有的人也都一样——不管是街坊还是新邻居——当汤普生先生告诉他们自己的来意,开始叙述自己所知的事实经过时,他们的表情都变得一模一样。他们的眼睛看起来好像有人从后面把眼珠子钳住似的,它们萎缩了,光彩消失了。有些人坐下来想显得友善些,露着呆板、紧张的笑容。"是的,汤普生先生,我们知道你一定觉得很难过。汤普生太太,这事对你来说真是太可怕了。是的,你知道吗,我开始有点明白,确实是有自卫杀人这一种情况的。啊,当然啦,我们相信你的话,汤普生先生,我们干吗不相信你呢?你那次审判不是既公平又很正大光明吗?呃,这个,当然啦,汤普生先生,我们觉得你的行为是无可非议的。"

　　汤普生先生很满意他们没有怀疑他。有时候,他周围责怪他的气氛是那么浓,他简直要用拳头来反击,把它们推回去,他浑身流汗,用被尘土弄得浑浊不清的嗓音嚷嚷地说出他的道理,最后他总要这样大声

Helton's stomach and slice up like you slice a hog, but when they finally caught Mr. Helton there wasn't a knife scratch on him. Mr. Thompson knew he had the ax in his own hands and felt himself lifting it, but he couldn't remember hitting Mr. Hatch. He couldn't remember it. He couldn't. He remembered only that he had been determined to stop Mr. Hatch from cutting Mr. Helton. If he was given a chance he could explain the whole matter. At the trial they hadn't let him talk. They just asked questions and he answered yes or no, and they never did get to the core of the matter. Since the trial, now, every day for a week he had washed and shaved and put on his best clothes and had taken Ellie with him to tell every neighbor he had that he never killed Mr. Hatch on purpose, and what good did it do? Nobody believed him. Even when he turned to Ellie and said, "You was there, you saw it, didn't you?" and Ellie spoke up, saying, "Yes, that's the truth. Mr. Thompson was trying to save Mr. Helton's life," and he added, "If you don't believe me, you can believe my wife. She won't lie," Mr. Thompson saw something in all their faces that disheartened him, made him feel empty and tired out. They didn't believe he was not a murderer.

Even Ellie never said anything to comfort him. He hoped she would say finally, "I remember now, Mr. Thompson, I really did come round the corner in time to see everything. It's not a lie, Mr. Thompson. Don't you worry." But as they drove together in silence, With the days still hot and dry, shortening for fall, day after day, the buggy jolting in the ruts, she said nothing; they grew to dread the sight of another house, and the people in it; all houses looked alike now, and the people—old neighbors or new—had the same expression when Mr. Thompson told them why he had come and began his story. Their eyes looked as if someone had pinched the eyeball at the back; they shriveled and the light went out of them. Some of them sat with fixed tight smiles trying to be friendly. "Yes, Mr. Thompson, we know how you must feel. It must be terrible for you, Mrs. Thompson. Yes, you know, I've about come to the point where I believe in such a thing as killing in self-defense. Why, certainly, we believe you, Mr. Thompson, why shouldn't we believe you? Didn't you have a perfectly fair and above-board trial? Well, now, natchally, Mr. Thompson, we think you done right."

Mr. Thompson was satisfied they didn't think so. Sometimes the air around him was so thick with their blame he fought and pushed with his fists, and the sweat broke out all over him, he shouted his story in a

吼叫：“你们是知道我太太的，她当时在场，她看见和听见了一切，如果你们不相信我，问她好了，她是不会说谎的！”而汤普生太太则双手紧握，直握得发痛，她下巴打着颤，总是这么说：“是的，没错，这是真的——”

　　使汤普生先生最后认清一切都无望了的是今天这一趟。汤姆·奥尔布赖特，那是艾丽以前的男朋友，哼，他曾经围着艾丽转了整整一个夏天，可是今天，他们赶着车子经过他家门口时，汤姆走出来会见他们。他没戴帽子，站在路边，明摆着是不想让他们下马。他发窘地皱着眉头，不直接看他们，而是朝他们后面望去。他说他的小姨子带了一大帮小家伙来做客，家里闹哄哄的不成模样，不然的话，他一定请他们进去坐坐。“我们正打算去看你们呢，”奥尔布赖特先生又说，挪动着脚，装出一副很忙的样子，“可是这几天正好忙得够呛。”于是他们只好说：“哦，我们只不过是路过。”说完就继续赶路了。汤普生太太说：“奥尔布赖特家从来就是势利眼。”“他们眼睛里只看到自己，就是这么回事。”汤普生先生也说。可是，这样的话连自我安慰的效果也不能达到。

　　最后，汤普生太太感到绝望了。“咱们回家吧，”她说，“老吉姆又累又渴了，咱们也走得太远了。”

　　汤普生先生说：“呃，咱们既然到了这儿，就不妨到麦克列伦家停一停吧。”他们赶了车子顺着小路朝他们屋子走去，见到一个头发乱蓬蓬的小男孩，便问他妈妈、爸爸可在家，说汤普生先生想见他们。那小男孩先是张大嘴傻愣愣地瞪着，接着一边跑进去一边喊道：“俺娘，俺爹，快出来。杀死哈奇先生的那个人瞧你们来了！”

　　那个男人穿了短袜就跑了出来，一根背带吊着，另一根断了耷拉着，他说：“下来吧，汤普生先生，进屋来坐，我老伴正在洗衣服，一会儿就会来的。”汤普生太太扶着车子走下来，在前廊的一张破摇椅上坐下，廊子的地板在她脚底下颤悠悠地陷了下去。这一家的女主人出来了，光着脚，穿着一件印花布的晨衣，她坐在廊沿上，那张病黄色的胖脸上充满了好奇的神情。汤普生先生又开始了：“呃，我想你们大概也知道了，我最近遇到了一些奇怪的麻烦事儿，啊，正像人们说的，这可不是一年之中每一天都能碰到的小问题，有些事我希望不至于在乡邻的头脑里引起误解，因此——”他停顿了下来，又磕磕巴巴地接着往下说，那

dust-choked voice, he would fairly bellow at last: "My wife, here, you know her, she was there, she saw and heard it all, if you don't believe me, ask her, she won't lie!" and Mrs. Thompson, with her hands knotted together, aching, her chin trembling, would never fail to say: "Yes, that's right, that's the truth—"

　　The last straw had been laid on today, Mr. Thompson decided. Tom Allbright, an old beau of Ellie's, why, he had squired Ellie around a whole summer, had come out to meet them when they drove up, and standing there bareheaded had stopped them from getting out. He had looked past them with an embarrassed frown on his face, telling them his wife's sister was there with a raft of young ones, and the house was pretty full and everything upset, or he'd ask them to come in. "We've been thinking of trying to get up to your place one of these days," said Mr. Allbright, moving away trying to look busy, "we've been mighty occupied up here of late." So they had to say, "Well, we just happened to be driving this way," and go on. "The Allbrights," said Mrs. Thompson, "always was fair-weather friends." "They look out for number one, that's a fact," said Mr. Thompson. But it was cold comfort to them both.

　　Finally Mrs. Thompson had given up. "Let's go home," she said. "Old Jim's tired and thirsty, and we've gone far enough."

　　Mr. Thompson said, "Well, while we're out this way, we might as well stop at the McClellans'." They drove in, and asked a little cotton-haired boy if his mamma and papa were at home. Mr. Thompson wanted to see them. The little boy stood gazing with his mouth open, then galloped into the house shouting, "Mommer, Popper, come out hyah. That man that kilt Mr. Hatch has come ter see yer!"

　　The man came out in his sock feet, with one gallus up, the other broken and dangling, and said, "Light down, Mr. Thompson, and come in. The ole woman's washing, but she'll git here." Mrs. Thompson, feeling her way, stepped down and sat in a broken rocking-chair on the porch that sagged under her feet. The woman of the house, barefooted, in a calico wrapper, sat on the edge of the porch, her fat sallow face full of curiosity. Mr. Thompson began, "Well, as I reckon you happen to know, I've had some strange troubles lately, and, as the feller says, it's not the kind of trouble that happens to a man every day in the year, and there's some things I don't want no misunderstanding about in the neighbors' minds, so—" He halted and stumbled forward, and the two listening faces took on a mean look, a greedy, despising look, a look that said

两个听着的人的脸上浮现出一种鄙夷的表情，一种贪婪的，瞧不起人的表情，那副表情再明显不过地表露出他们的思想："天哪，你也真是走投无路了，才会上我们这儿来，关心我们是怎么想的，我们知道，要是有别人可以求，你哪儿会上这儿来呢——我的天，要是我的话，是绝对不会堕落到这一步的。"汤普生先生也替自己感到惭愧起来，突然之间他怒火中烧，真想揪住这对狗男女的脏脑袋对撞，这些下贱的穷白人——可是他压住了怒火，还是把话说完。"我太太可以告诉你们，"他说，这是最难启齿的部分，因为艾丽总是一点表情也没有，好像有谁在威胁说要揍她，把她吓僵了似的，"问我太太好了，她是不会说瞎话的。"

"这是真的，我看见的——"

"哦，那么，"那人毫无表情地说，把手伸到衬衣里去挠痒痒，"这可真是太糟糕了。不过，嗯，我瞧不出这档子事跟咱有什么相干。我瞧不出跟这桩谋杀案搞在一块儿有什么好处。不管从哪个方面看，反正这事跟咱不相干。不过，你们绕这么远道来给我们叙说真情，这真是太好了。因为咱也听说了各式各样稀奇古怪的说法，离奇得没个准谱儿，我担保你听了根本摸不着头脑。"

"这年头儿，人们动不动就把别人打开瓢，"那个女的说，"咱可不喜欢杀人，《圣经》上说——"

"给我闭上你那张臭嘴，"那男的说，"牢牢地闭着，要不我来给你闭。嗯，依我看——"

"咱们不能再耽搁了，"汤普生太太说，松开了她紧握着的手，"咱们已经待得太久了。时间不早了，咱们还有好多路要赶呢。"汤普生先生懂得她的意思，站起来跟她走了。那一对夫妻懒洋洋地靠在前廊歪歪斜斜的柱子上，目送他们离开。

如今，汤普生先生躺在床上，心里明白他已经是穷途末路了。如今，在这个时刻，躺在他和艾丽一起睡了十九年的床上，待在他结婚前亲自铺瓦的屋顶下面，他用手指摸摸自己瘦削的下巴，自从早上修剪以来他的髭须又长出来了，汤普生先生觉得自己已经是个死人了。对于他从前的生活来说，他已经死了，他还不知道是怎么搞的，便已经走到事情的结局了，他必须重新起头才行，可是他不知道该怎么起头。某件不一样的事情即将开始，可是他不明白那是什么事。他不觉得他将会与它有什么关系。他爬下床来，只觉得浑身酸痛，心中空虚，他走到厨房去，汤普生太太还

plain as day, "My, you must be a purty sorry feller to come round worrying about what *we* think, *we* know you wouldn't be here if you had anybody else to turn to—my, I wouldn't lower myself that much, myself." Mr. Thompson was ashamed of himself, he was suddenly in a rage, he'd like to knock their dirty skunk heads together, the low-down white trash—but he held himself down and went on to the end. "My wife will tell you," he said, and this was the hardest place, because Ellie always without moving a muscle seemed to stiffen as if somebody had threatened to hit her; "ask my wife, she won't lie."

"It's true, I saw it—"

"Well, now," said the man, drily, scratching his ribs inside his shirt, "that sholy is too bad. Well, now, I kaint see what we've got to do with all this here, however. I kaint see no good reason for us to git mixed up in these murder matters, I shore kaint. Which ever way you look at it, it ain't none of my business. However, it's mighty nice of you-all to come around and give us the straight of it, fur we've heerd some mighty queer yarns about it, mighty queer, I golly you couldn't haridly make head ner tail of it."

"Evevbody goin' round shootin' they heads off," said the woman. "Now we don't hold with killin'; the Bible says—"

"Shet yer trap," said the man, "and keep it shet'r I'll shet it fer yer. Now it shore looks like to me—"

"We mustn't linger," said Mrs. Thompson, unclasping her hands. "We've lingered too long now. It's getting late, and we've far to go." Mr. Thompson took the hint and followed her. The man and the woman lolled against their rickety porch poles and watched them go.

Now lying on his bed, Mr. Thompson knew the end had come. Now, this minute, lying in the bed where he had slept with Ellie for eighteen years; under this roof where he had laid the shingles when he was waiting to get married; there as he was with his whiskers already sprouting since his shave that morning; with his fingers feeling his bony chin, Mr. Thompson felt he was a dead man. He was dead to his other life, he had got to the end of something without knowing why, and he had to make a fresh start, he did not know how. Something different was going to begin, he didn't know what. It was in some way not his business. He didn't feel he was going to have much to do with it. He got up, aching, hollow, and went out to the kitchen where Mrs. Thompson was just taking up the supper.

"Call the boys," said Mrs. Thompson. They had

在那儿做晚饭。

"把孩子们叫来吧。"汤普生太太说。孩子们到马房里去了，阿瑟进去前先吹灭灯，然后把它挂在门边的钉子上。汤普生先生不喜欢他们的沉默。打从那一天起，他们不管什么事情上都几乎没和他说过一句话。他们似乎在躲着他，他们俩自己把农场管了起来，好像他人不在这儿，他们干什么事都不来问他一声。"你们哥儿俩在干吗？"他问道，想显得亲切一些，"活儿干完了吗？"

"没干吗，爸爸，"阿瑟说，"没什么活儿好干的。只不过给车轴加了点油。"赫伯特什么也没说。汤普生太太低下了头："为了这些以及您所有的恩赐……阿门。"她无力地细声说道。汤普生一家坐在那里低垂着眼睛，满面忧伤，仿佛他们在参加一次丧礼。

每回汤普生先生闭上眼睛，打算睡去，他的脑子里就活动起来，就像有一只兔子在乱跑。他的思想从一处跳到另一处，想从这里或那里找到一些蛛丝马迹，把他杀死哈奇先生那天的事理出个头绪来。不管他怎么努力，除了想到过的事情以外，他再也想不出什么来，除了看到过的东西以外，他再也看不见什么，他知道这样是不行的。如果那一次他眼睛成问题，那么他杀死哈奇先生的事从头到尾就是错的，再使劲儿也没什么意思，他大可死心了。他仍然觉得，那一天他做了唯一应该做的事，也许不能算是唯一正确的事，可是究竟是不是这样呢？他是不是一定要杀死哈奇先生呢？他第一眼看见哈奇先生，就觉得再没有比这人更加可憎的人了。他本能地知道这人是来找麻烦的。他现在觉得不能理解的是他干吗不一开始就让哈奇先生滚蛋？

汤普生太太躺在他身边，双手交叉放在胸前一动不动，可是她似乎是醒着的。"睡着了吗，艾丽？"

毕竟，他是可以安安静静地叫哈奇先生滚的。他也可以揍哈奇一顿，用那副手铐铐住他，把他扭送到警长那里去，告他一个扰乱治安。他们至多把哈奇关上几天，让他冷静下来，或是罚他几个钱。他也愿意设想一下当时可以对哈奇先生说些什么话。对了，比方说，这样说就挺合适：喂，我说，哈奇先生，我想跟你像男子汉对男子汉那样说几句话。可是他的脑袋里又空空如也了。他还能说些什么，干些什么呢？不过只要他当时采取的是任何别的行动，而不是杀死哈奇

been down to the barn, and Arthur put out the lantern before hanging it on a nail near the door. Mr. Thompson didn't like their silence. They had hardly said a word about anything to him since that day. They seemed to avoid him, they ran the place together as if he wasn't there, and attended to everything without asking him for any advice. "What you boys been up to?" he asked, trying to be hearty. "Finishing your chores?"

"No, sir," said Arthur, "there ain't much to do. Just greasing some axles." Herbert said nothing. Mrs. Thompson bowed her head: "For these and all Thy blessings. . . . Amen," she whispered weakly, and the Thompsons sat there with their eyes down and their faces sorrowful, as if they were at a funeral.

Every time he shut his eyes, trying to sleep, Mr. Thompson's mind started up and began to run like a rabbit. It jumped from one thing to another, trying to pick up a trail here or there that would straighten out what had happened that day he killed Mr. Hatch. Try as he might, Mr. Thompson's mind would not go anywhere that it had not already been, he could not see anything but what he had seen once, and he knew that was not right. If he had not seen straight that first time, then everything about his killing Mr. Hatch was wrong from start to finish, and there was nothing more to be done about it, he might just as well give up. It still seemed to him that he had done, maybe not the right thing, but the only thing he could do, that day, but had he? *Did he have to kill Mr. Hatch?* He had never seen a man he hated more, the minute he laid eyes on him. He knew in his bones the fellow was there for trouble. What seemed so funny now was this: Why hadn't he just told Mr. Hatch to get out before he ever even got in?

Mrs. Thompson, her arms crossed on her breast, was lying beside him, perfectly still, but she seemed awake, somehow. "Asleep, Ellie?"

After all, he might have got rid of him peaceably, or maybe he might have had to overpower him and put those handcuffs on him and turn him over to the sheriff for disturbing the peace. The most they could have done was to lock Mr. Hatch up while he cooled off for a few days, or fine him a little something. He would try to think of things he might have said to Mr. Hatch. Why, let's see, I could just have said, Now look here, Mr. Hatch, I want to talk to you as man to man. But his brain would go empty. What could he have said or done? But if he *could* have done anything else almost except kill Mr. Hatch, then nothing would have happened to Mr. Helton. Mr. Thompson hardly ever thought of Mr. Helton. His mind just skipped over

先生,那么希尔顿先生是什么事也不会有的。汤普生先生几乎没有想到过希尔顿先生。他的思想压根儿跳过了希尔顿,想到别的事情上去了。如果他停下来想想希尔顿先生,他也就不知道会得出什么结论了。他试着想象一下,如果就是在今天晚上,希尔顿先生仍然是安然无恙的,还在院子里他的小屋里吹他的口琴,情形会是怎样? 他吹的依旧是那支歌:一早起来多么快活,一快活便把酒统统喝光,酒喝完心情也就更加痛快。而哈奇先生呢,也一定是好好地给关在监狱里,没准气得七窍生烟,可是伤害不了别人,只得听从劝告,反省自己的卑鄙行为。这条下流卑鄙的狗,竟来追踪迫害一个善良的人,把与他素来无冤无仇的家庭活活给毁了! 汤普生先生觉得他额上的血管在扩张,他的双拳紧握,仿佛在攥住斧把,他周身冒汗,从床上猛地坐起来,喉咙里透不过气地喊了一声。艾丽吓得也醒了过来,喊道:"哦,哦,别这样! 别这样!"好像她刚做了一个噩梦。他浑身打颤地站着,斗得骨头嘎嘎作响啊,他嘎声喊道:

"点灯呀,点灯呀,艾丽。"

可是,汤普生太太却无力地尖叫了一声,几乎跟那天他拿着斧子时她拐过屋角出来喊的那声一模一样。在黑暗中,他看不清她,可是她是在床上乱翻乱滚。他害怕地摸索着,摸到她的胳膊,再往上,摸到她的手,她在自己扯自己的头发呢,她脖子往后仰着,她的尖叫使她透不过气来。他叫阿瑟,叫赫伯特。"你们的妈妈!"他大声吼道,嗓子都嘶哑了。正当他紧握汤普生太太的双臂时,孩子们跌跌撞撞地冲了进来,阿瑟把灯举在头上。汤普生先生借助灯光看见汤普生太太眼睛睁得大大的,怪怕人地瞪着他,泪水汩汩地涌流出来。一看见孩子们,她便坐了起来,向他们伸去一只胳膊,那只手狂乱地扭动着,接着她又倒了下去,突然瘫了似的。阿瑟把灯往桌子上一放,转过身来看着汤普生太太。"她吓坏了,"他说,"她都快吓死了。"他满面怒容,拳头紧握,瞪着父亲,简直像要揍他。汤普生先生下巴耷拉着,大吃一惊,从床边退后去。赫伯特跑到床的那边。他们一人站在汤普生太太的一边,瞪着汤普生先生,仿佛他是一头危险的猛兽。"你把她怎么了?"阿瑟嚷道,那声音完全是成人的。"你敢再碰她一下,我把你的心都掏出来!'赫伯特脸色苍白,脸颊在抽搐,可他是站在阿瑟一边的,为了帮助阿瑟他什么都可以干得出来。

him and went on. If he stopped to think about Mr. Helton he'd never in God's world get anywhere. He tried to imagine how it might all have been, this very night even, if Mr. Helton were still safe and sound out in his shack playing his tune about feeling so good in the morning, drinking up all the wine so you'd feel even better; and Mr. Hatch safe in jail somewhere, mad as hops, maybe, but out of harm's way and ready to listen to reason and to repent of his meanness, the dirty, yellow-livered hound coming around persecuting an innocent man and ruining a whole family that never harmed him! Mr. Thompson felt the veins of his forehead start up, his fists clutched as if they seized an ax handle, the sweat broke out on him, he bounded up from the bed with a yell smothered in his throat, and Ellie started up after him, crying out, "Oh, oh, don't! Don't! Don't!"as if she were having a nightmare. He stood shaking until his bones rattled in him, crying hoarsely, "Light the lamp, light the lamp, Ellie."

Instead, Mrs. Thompson gave a shrill weak scream, almost the same scream he had heard on that day she came around the house when he was standing there with the ax in his hand. He could not see her in the dark, but she was on the bed, rolling violently. He felt for her in horror, and his groping hands found her arms, up, and her own hands pulling her hair straight out from her head, her neck strained back, and the tight screams strangling her. He shouted out for Arthur, for Herbert. "Your mother!"he bawled, his voice cracking. As he held Mrs. Thompson's arms, the boys came tumbling in, Arthur with the lamp above his head. By this light Mr. Thompson saw Mrs. Thompson's eyes, wide open, staring dreadfully at him, the tears pouring. She sat up at sight of the boys, and held out one arm towards them, the hand wagging in a crazy circle, then dropped on her back again, and suddenly went limp. Arthur set the lamp on the table and turned on Mrs. Thompson. "She's scared," he said, "she's scared to death."His face was in a knot of rage, his fists were doubled up, he faced his father as if he meant to strike him. Mr. Thompson's jaw fell, he was so surprised he stepped back from the bed. Herbert went to the other side. They stood on each side of Mrs. Thompson and watched Mr. Thompson as if he were a dangerous wild beast. "What did you do to her?"shouted Arthur, in a grown man's voice. "You touch her again and I'll blow your heart out!"Herbert was pale and his cheek twitched, but he was on Arthur's side; he would do what he could to help Arthur.

Mr. Thompson had no fight left in him. His knees bent as he stood, his chest collapsed. "Why, Arthur,"

汤普生先生再也无心与他们争斗。他膝盖发软，胸部塌陷。"唉，阿瑟，"他说，说话断断续续地，在气喘吁吁。"她又晕过去了。快去拿阿摩尼亚来。"阿瑟一动也不动，倒是赫伯特把药瓶拿了来，身子往后缩，远远地递给父亲。

汤普生先生把药水放在汤普生太太鼻子底下。他倒了一点儿在手掌里，揉她的额头。她长长地出了口气，睁开眼睛，却把脑袋转了过去，不看她丈夫。赫伯特开始悲伤，绝望地哭起鼻子来。"妈妈，"他不停地说，"妈妈你可不能死呀。"

"我没事，"汤普生太太说，"好，你们不要担心。喂，赫伯特，你千万别那样。我没事。"她闭上眼睛。汤普生先生开始穿他那条最讲究的裤子，又穿上短袜和皮鞋。两个孩子坐在床的两边，望着汤普生太太的脸。汤普生先生接着又穿上衬衣和外衣。他说："我看我得骑马去请大夫来。这样晕过去可不是什么好现象，你们看着点儿，我一会儿就回来。"他们仅仅听着，什么也不说。他又说："你们可别胡思乱想。有意伤害你们的妈妈的事，我这辈子从来没有做过。"他走了出去，又回过头看看，只见赫伯特侧着头，一双眼睛从眉毛下面直愣愣地瞪着他，真是如同陌路了。"你们是知道怎么照顾你们妈妈的吧。"汤普生先生说。

汤普生先生走进厨房。在这里他点亮了灯笼。从孩子们放课本的架子上取下一本薄薄的拍纸簿和一个铅笔头。他把灯笼挎在胳膊上，伸手到他放枪的柜子里去。那支猎枪就在手边，装上火药准备得好好的，因为一个人是说不准什么时候需要用枪的。他走出屋子，不向旁边看一眼，他往前走，也没回过头来看看，经过马房时他也是视而不见，他径直朝他田地的最远的一头走去，那是在东边半英里路以外。那么多打击，又是从四面八方向汤普生先生袭来的，他都无法停下来捉摸一下自己哪儿挨打了。他往前走，越过耕地，穿过草场，小心翼翼地从带刺的铁丝网洞里爬出去，他把枪先放过去，现在他的眼睛已经习惯了，在黑暗里也看得清了。最后，他来到最靠外面的一道篱笆，在这里，他坐了下来，后背靠着一根柱子，灯笼放在一边，拍纸簿放在膝上，他用舌头舔湿铅笔头，开始写道：

"全能的上帝，芸芸众生的审判者，当我即将趋前听候发落之际，请先听我庄严起誓：我杀死霍默·T·哈奇先生，实非出于蓄意，纯由保护希尔顿先生所致。

he said, his words crumbling and his breath coming short. "She's fainted again. Get the ammonia." Arthur did not move. Herbert brought the bottle, and handed it, shrinking, to his father.

Mr. Thompson held it under Mrs. Thompson's nose. He poured a little in the palm of his hand and rubbed it on her forehead. She gasped and opened her eyes and turned her head away from him. Herbert began a doleful hopeless sniffling. "Mamma," he kept saying, "Mamma, don't die."

"I'm all right," Mrs. Thompson said. "Now don't you worry around. Now Herbert, you mustn't do that. I'm all right." She closed her eyes. Mr. Thompson began pulling on his best pants; he put on his socks and shoes. The boys sat on each side of the bed, watching Mrs. Thompson's face. Mr. Thompson put on his shirt and coat. He said, "I reckon I'll ride over and get the doctor. Don't look like all this fainting is a good sign. Now you just keep watch until I get back." They listened, but said nothing. He said, "Don't you get any notions in your head. I never did your mother any harm in my life, on purpose." He went out, and, looking back, saw Herbert staring at him from under his brows, like a stranger. "You'll know how to look after her," said Mr. Thompson.

Mr. Thompson went through the kitchen. There he lighted the lantern, took a thin pad of scratch paper and a stub pencil from the shelf where the boys kept their schoolbooks. He swung the lantern on his arm and reached into the cupboard where he kept the guns. The shotgun was there to his hand, primed and ready, a man never knows when he may need a shotgun. He went out of the house without looking around, or looking back when he had left it, passed his barn without seeing it, and struck out to the farthest end of his fields, which ran for half a mile to the east. So many blows had been struck at Mr. Thompson and from so many directions he couldn't stop any more to find out where he was hit. He walked on, over plowed ground and over meadow, going through barbed wire fences cautiously, putting his gun through first; he could almost see in the dark, now his eyes were used to it. Finally he came to the last fence; here he sat down, back against a post, lantern at his side, and, with the pad on his knee, moistened the stub pencil and began to write:

"Before Almighty God, the great judge of all before who I am about to appear, I do hereby solemnly swear that I did not take the life of Mr. Homer T. Hatch on purpose. It was done in defense of Mr. Helton. I did not aim to hit him with the ax but only to keep him off Mr. Helton. He aimed a blow at Mr. Helton

我并非故意以斧击哈奇,仅为防其加害于希尔顿而已。当时哈奇向希尔顿袭击,希尔顿毫无戒备,倘我不加阻拦,希尔顿必定丧命无疑。详细经过我已一一向法官及陪审团面陈。法庭判我无罪,然众人不信。我出于无奈,只得用此手段证明,我绝非众人心目中的残忍凶犯。倘若当时受袭者是我,希尔顿先生亦必为我采取同样行动。我至今仍坚信:舍我当时所作所为,别无他策。我妻——"

　　写到这里,汤普生先生停下来想了一会儿。他又用舌尖舔舔笔尖,把最后两个字划掉。他坐在那里,花了不少时间涂字,一直涂到有字的地方成为一个规整的黑长方块,然后他又接着往下写:

　　"霍默·T·哈奇先生前来加害于一个忠厚善良的人。种种灾难,均由哈奇引起。哈奇固死有余辜,然结束其生命者竟为我,实为我一大憾事。"

　　他又舔舔笔尖,然后一丝不苟地签下他的全名,他把纸叠起,放在衣服外面的口袋里。接着,他把右脚的鞋、袜脱掉,让枪托支在地上,把双管枪身对着自己的头部。这样非常不得劲儿。他把脑袋支在枪口上想了片刻。他全身打颤,脑袋里轰隆隆直响,到来连什么也听不见,什么也看不见了。可是他还是侧着身子在地上躺了下来,拉过枪管对着自己的下巴,用大脚趾去探索扳机。只有这样他才能够击发。

who was not looking for it. It was my belief at that time that Mr. Hatch would of taken the life of Mr. Helton if I did not interfere. I have told all this to the judge and the jury and they let me off but nobody believes it. This is the only way I can prove I am not a cold blooded murderer like everybody seems to think. If l had been in Mr. Helton's place he would of done the same for me. I still think I done the only thing there was to do. My wife—"

Mr. Thompson stopped here to think a while. He wet the pencil point with the tip of his tongue and marked out the last two words. He sat a while blacking out the words until he had made a neat oblong patch where they had been, and started again:

"It was Mr. Homer T. Hatch who came to do wrong to a harmless man. He caused all this trouble and he deserved to die but I am sorry it was me who had to kill him."

He licked the point of his pencil again, and signed his full name carefully, folded the paper and put it in his outside pocket. Taking off his right shoe and sock, he set the butt of the shotgun along the ground with the twin barrels pointed towards his head. It was very awkward. He thought about this a little, leaning his head against the gun mouth. He was trembling and his head was drumming until he was deaf and blind, but he lay down flat on the earth on his side, drew the barrel under his chin and fumbled for the trigger with his great toe. That way he could work it.

037.《中午酒》的源流

（美）凯瑟琳·安·波特 著　　刘文荣 译

　　《中午酒》这个中篇小说以其自身的质量那样充实而完整地存在于我的心中，所以当我想要从头来谈它的形成过程或者想要顺着各种线索重新追寻它在我记忆中的源头时，我就给难住了，因为我得面对我自己的生活，面对我生于其中又长于其中的整个社会及其种种现实。我的目的在于发现社会的真谛，为此我的想象力一再地追忆往事并不断地寻求其意义。这种漫无止境的回忆虽说是作家应该做的主要工作，但在回忆中，事物会发生变化，会变形，而且会一再地受到来自不同方面的解释。这很正常也很自然，因为说到底，作家的意图在于创作小说——真实的小说，不是写一个 roman à clef①，也不是做某种稍加掩饰的自我招供——这种东西最好还是让给心理分析学家去玩弄。当我一写完《中午酒》，我就觉得这篇作品已成为某种"现实"，简直像是有血有肉的，我不仅觉得其中的故事是我自己对真人真事的记忆和想象的产物，而且完全就像我在简单地复述自己听到或者看到的某件事情一样。当然，说故事就是小说，这是不对的，但小说是从成千上万种事情中提炼出来的，这些事情曾经在我生活中的某时某地发生过，而且作为各个单一事件，它们也为其他人所铭记。只是，他们记着这些事情不像我那样记法，在我的记忆中，这些事情不仅有其自身的生存力和真实性，而且是浮动着的，它们相互交叉、相互分离、又相互混合，直到它们建立起自己的联系。我自己很清楚地看到或者感觉到，就是这些事情、片断——有时连片断也谈不上，只是一些随处闪烁的生活的星火，但又使我动心，使我

---

　　① 法语：玄妙的传奇故事。

037. "Noon Wine": The Sources

by Katherine Anne Porter

　　THIS short novel, "Noon Wine," exists so fully and wholly in its own right in my mind, that when I attempt to trace its growth from the beginning, to follow all the clues to their sources in my memory, I am dismayed; because I am confronted with my own life, the whole society in which I was born and brought up, and the facts of it. My aim is to find the truth in it, and to this end my imagination works and re-works its recollections in a constant search for meanings. Yet in this endless remembering which surely must be the main occupation of the writer, events are changed, reshaped, interpreted again and again in different ways, and this is right and natural because it is the intention of the writer to write fiction, after all—real fiction, not a *roman à clef*, or a thinly disguised personal confession which better belongs to the psychoanalyst's seance. By the time I wrote "Noon Wine" it had become "real" to me almost in the sense that I felt not as if I had made that story out of my own memory of real events and imagined consequences, but as if I were quite simply reporting events I had heard or witnessed. This is not in the least true: the story is fiction; but it is made up of thousands of things that did happen to living human beings in a certain part of the country, at a certain time of my life, things that are still remembered by others as single incidents; not as I remembered them, floating and moving with their separate life and reality, meeting and parting and mingling in my thoughts until they established their relationship. I could see and feel very clearly that all these events, episodes—hardly that, sometimes, but just mere glimpses and flashes here and there of lives strange or moving or astonishing to me—were forming a story, almost of

作者简介：凯瑟琳·安·波特（**Katherine Anne Porter**，1890—1980），美国作家。1890 年 5 月 15 日生于德克萨斯州印第安克里克，1980 年 9 月 18 日卒于马里兰州银泉。她在芝加哥和丹佛做过记者，1920 年去往墨西哥。墨西哥成为她的几部小说的背景。《开花的紫荆花》（*Flowering Judas*，1930）是她的首部文集，也是最出名的。《苍白的马，苍白的骑士》（*Pale Horse, Pale Rider*，1939）中包括 3 部中篇小说。《短篇小说集》（*Collected Short Stories*，1965）获得普利策奖和美国国家图书奖。她的小说富有质感，人物叙述复杂。《愚人船》（*Ship of Fools*，1962）是她唯一的长篇小说。

好奇,使我惊异——它们简直可以说是自动地在构成一篇小说。不管它们从表面上看是不连贯的、无联系的,反正它们群集并存在我心里,而且构成了某种具有整体意义的形式,这种整体意义,就各个独立部分而言,又并不具备。所以,我觉得这篇小说就小说所应具备的真实而言是"真实的",因为我已掌握了来自生活的各种独立的元素,只要我进行同化和纟合,一种新的有生命的存在物即能构成。

但是,记忆里的特殊事物以及早期印象为什么恰恰以这种方式组合成了这样一篇特殊的小说呢?我丝毫也不知道。不错,我是有意识地在写小说,然而这篇小说却在我立意写它之前,就已经在我心里自动地酝酿着了。与此同时,还有许多其他小说雏形在我心中不断形成,其中有的得到发展而且写了出来,有的则根本就没有写。这为什么?我觉得这个问题最有趣不过了,因为我知道,这个问题有其答案,然而又没有一个人答得出来。

至于什么时候开始动笔写这篇小说的,这我知道。当时我不惜中断了其他工作,还进行了各种具体安排,为写这篇小说挤出了时间。从 1936 年 11 月 7 日的傍晚开始,到同月的 14 日,我住在宾夕法尼亚的一所偏僻小旅馆的一间小屋里,用了似乎是胡乱拼凑起来的 7 天时间,一口气写完了这篇小说,其间只做了少量的润色。不过,早在 1932 年夏天,我在瑞士的巴塞尔就已经写好了这篇小说的中心部分,也就是哈奇先生和汤普生先生之间的那场戏,这场戏后来就引出了凶杀事件。

我从欧洲回来后 15 天便住进了那所旅馆,其间除了重返巴黎、布列塔尼、罗马和比利时做短暂的旅行之外,我好像是命中注定要将这地方作为生活的终点站似的。不过,我生活中有一段时间精神特别好,精力也特别充沛,那时我曾在国外度过了将近 14 年,在墨西哥、百慕大群岛,还有欧洲的许多地方,其中绝大部分是在巴黎。至于我在这些地方的生活,我当时就感到,现在也依然感到,是完全正常的,是适时的、合理的,严格地说是我应该到这些地方去而且在每个地方做我应做的事情。在那里我并不觉得像在家里一样,我知道我的家在哪里,然而,只要有机会周游世界,我都会,这对我是很自然的,可以说就像候鸟要不断迁移以换上新翼毛一样自然。在欧洲,所见所闻并不怎样新奇。我时常有一种愉快的感觉,觉得随处都有老家的味儿。我虽然离乡背井,但时常有朋友和我

themselves, it seemed; out of their apparent incoherence, unrelatedness, they grouped and clung in my mind in a form that gave a meaning to the whole that the individual parts had lacked. So I feel that this story is "true" in the way that a work of fiction should be true, created out of all the scattered particles of life I was able to absorb and combine and to shape into a living new being.

But why did this particular set of memories and early impressions combine in just this way to make this particular story? I do not in the least know. And though it is quite true that I intended to write fiction, this story wove itself in my mind for years before I ever intended to write it; there were many other stories going on in my head at once, some of them evolved and were written, more were not. Why? This to me is the most interesting question, because I am sure there is an answer, but nobody knows it yet.

When the moment came to write this story, I knew it; and I had to make quite a number of practical arrangements to get the time free for it, without fear of interruptions. I wrote it as it stands except for a few pen corrections in just seven days of trance-like absorption in a small room in an inn in rural Pennsylvania, from the early evening of November 7 to November 14, 1936. Yet I had written the central part, the scene between Mr. Hatch and Mr. Thompson, which leads up to the murder, in Basel, Switzerland, in the summer of 1932.

I had returned from Europe only fifteen days before I went to the inn in Pennsylvania: this was the end, as it turned out, of my living abroad, except for short visits back to Paris, Brittany, Rome, Belgium: but meantime I had, at a time of great awareness and active energy, spent nearly fourteen years of my life out of this country: in Mexico, Bermuda, various parts of Europe, but mostly by choice, Paris. Of my life in these places I felt then, and feel now, that it was all entirely right, timely, appropriate, exactly where I should have been and what doing at that very time. I did not feel exactly at home; I knew where home was; but the time had come for me to see the world for myself, and so I did, almost as naturally as a bird taking off on his new wingfeathers. In Europe, things were not so strange; sometimes I had a pleasant sense of having here and there touched home-base; if I was not at home, I was sometimes with friends. And all the time, I was making notes on stories—stories of my own place, my South—for my part of Texas was peopled

在一起。在国外的整个时间里,我一直在做些笔记,准备写小说——写关于我自己的那个地方的小说,写我的南方的小说——我出生在得克萨斯州,而那里业已充斥着从弗吉尼亚州、田纳西州、卡罗莱纳州以及肯塔基州来的南方佬——很明显,我生活在一个由各种不同心理、不同感情混合起来的州里,所以我平静地、暗暗地将各种事物加以比较,总是回忆了再回忆。这样,各种各样的事物都得到了应有的地位,得到了自然的形态和尺度,而且一再清晰地反照出它们的正确影像——简而言之,我做了一个艺术家所应该做的,这就像呼吸一样不由自己——我并未有意识地怂恿自己这样做。由于这样,我在欧洲所感觉到的情况也就不像在梦中那样生疏了,虽然欧洲肯定有其自身的魅力和优点。就是欧洲,使我回想起自己的过去、自己的家、自己的同胞——我心中的故乡。

在我童年时代的夏日的乡间,在这空间里以及在对它的回忆里,处处是迷人的景色,它们在光和色中闪烁,在声和形里浮动,即使我说上千言万语,也难以描绘出来,把它们放进我的小说。就是这样的景色构成了我所讲述的故事的生动背景,而这一切我的主人公们是那样熟悉,以致于他们几乎不再加以注意了,那些在碧绿的橡树上呢喃的鸽子,那些在镇上的每家每户后廊上点缀着的孩子般学语的鹦鹉,那些在蓝天里高高飞翔的兀鹰——那土地肥沃而富饶的乡间处处焕发着生命,处处是鸟语花香,野物待人去猎取,鱼鳗待人去垂钓,还有潺潺的流水,无数大河小溪。我至今还记得并能讲出一些河的名字——圣安东尼河、圣玛尔科斯河、特琳尼蒂河、诺埃塞斯河、格兰德河、科罗拉多河以及科罗拉多河的那条窄窄的、明净的支流——布满彩色卵石的印第安小溪,我就出生在那里。色与味都散发出各自的气息,就像声音有回响一样:兀鹰飞走之后,一阵厉风从一具摊开着的动物遗骸上吹拂而过;玫瑰花和桃花芬芳扑鼻,甜瓜和熟透了的桃子甘美润口,那篱笆边盛开着的茉莉花丛就像爆玉米一样蓬松洁白,还有楝树花刺鼻的甜滋滋的香味;枝叶繁茂的忍冬植物排排成行;沉甸甸的西红柿红透红透,在中午的烈日下晒得热烘烘的,要吃,从藤上摘下就是;青里带白的玉蜀黍诱人垂涎,刚出炉的玉米面包和着温热的牛奶一起吃美味可口;混浊的小池塘里发出咸滋滋的气味,在那儿我们抓小龙虾,还用一只小洋铁罐煮来吃;我们这些孩子,不论走到哪

almost entirely by Southerners from Virginia, Tennessee, the Carolinas, Kentucky—and I was almost instinctively living in a sustained state of mind and feeling, quietly and secretly, comparing one thing with another, always remembering and remembering; and all sorts of things were falling into their proper places, taking on their natural shapes and sizes, and going back and back clearly into right perspective—right for me as artist, I simply mean to say; and it was like breathing—I did not have consciously to urge myself to think about it. So my time in Europe served me in a way I had not dreamed of, even, besides its own charm and goodness; it gave me back my past and my own house and my own people—the native land of my heart.

This summer country of my childhood, this space and memory is filled with landscapes shimmering in light and color, moving with sounds and shapes I hardly ever describe or put in my stories in so many words; they form only the living background of what I am trying to tell, so familiar to my characters they would hardly notice them; the sound of mourning doves in the live-oaks, the childish voices of parrots chattering on every back porch in the little town, the hoverings of buzzards in the high blue air—all the life of that soft blackland farming country, full of fruits and flowers and birds, with good hunting and good fishing; with plenty of water, many little and big rivers. I shall name just a few of the rivers I remember—the San Antonio, the San Marcos, the Trinity, the Neuces, the Rio Grande, the Colorado, and the small clear branch of the Colorado—full of colored pebbles—Indian Creek, the place where I was born. The colors and tastes all had their smells, as the sounds have now their echoes: the bitter whiff of air over a sprawl of animal skeleton after the buzzards were gone; the smells and flavors of roses and melons, and peach bloom and ripe peaches, of cape jessamine in hedges blooming like popcorn, and the sickly sweetness of chinaberry florets; of honeysuckle in great swags on a trellised gallery; heavy tomatoes dead ripe and warm with the midday sun, eaten there, at the vine; the delicious milky green corn, and savory hot corn bread eaten with still-warm sweet milk; and the clinging brackish smell of the muddy little ponds where we caught, and boiled crawfish—in a discarded lard can—and ate them, then and there, we children, in

里,总有一个老黑人跟随着;关于这个老黑人,我曾在另一篇小说里写到过,他过去是我祖父的家奴,到我们出世之后,他也不过是一个仆人,一个脾气古怪但在家里又很知道安分守己的老头儿。

他的名字就叫吉姆别利大叔,他不仅是个明知自己地位的人,而且也是一个在尽职之后又能確保自身权利、权益和尊严的人。关于这一点,我想得出某种比较带普遍性的看法,因为对于那时、那个地方的社会情况我还记忆在心,而通过与那些比我年长者的交谈,更使我确信了自己的看法(不久前,我打算访问一位很有趣的老妇人,她是我母亲幼年时的伙伴。我写信给我姐姐,说我不想给那位科拉小姐多添麻烦,所以想逗留在镇上的小旅馆里,在那儿给她打电话。我姐姐当天就给我回了航空信,信中说:"天哪! 你可千万不能对科拉小姐说你住在旅馆里——她会觉得你有失端庄的!")。年长者的言语行为都遵循括号里的最后一句话,然而,无论在仪表上、在品性上、在宗教上抑或在政治上,那都早已过时了。他们说,世界不会变。而就在他们说这话的同时,一切都在改变,在分化,在消失。这种情况其实在他们刚成年的时候就已经发生了。那种巨变、那种在全国范围内发生的致命的分化瓦解、那次南北之间的战争,就是在我父亲那一辈人来到世上时发生的。不过,当时的日常生活还是由祖父那一辈人在管理着。他们的行为、言语,乃至外貌都显得很直爽——在我的记忆里,他们似乎始终是人数众多而俊美潇洒的一代人——那些轮廓分明、美妙而挺直的鼻子架起了历史的桥梁! ——当时高雅的社会风尚,就是建筑在传统的基督教信念上的。这些信念主要是新教的,但又不是代表中下阶层的清教的。在这些信念里,始终存在着某种对生活的享乐主义因素,对个人的行为也不甚拘泥。代表中下阶层的原教主义者把饮酒、跳舞、打扑克和通奸都看得同样邪恶,而他们始终没能占上风——事实上,就是某些局部地区也始终没有接受过他们,他们又仅在做某种勇敢的尝试而已。实际上,当时也不是一种民主的社会。好像每个人都有其固定的生活范围,道德和宗教的权威就这样得到了确定。好像一个人冒犯了别人,或者对别人犯了罪,他本人是自知的,他的邻人是自知的,好像他们能把什么事都看得清清楚楚似的。

这种僵化的观点同样被应用于人的社会地位。

the company of an old Negro who had once been my grandparents' slave, as I have told in another story. He was by our time only a servant, and a cantankerous old cuss very sure of his place in the household.

Uncle Jimbilly, for that was his name, was not the only one who knew exactly where he stood, and just about how far he could go in maintaining the right, privileges, exemptions of his status so long as he performed its duties. At this point, I want to give a rather generalized view of the society of that time and place as I remember it, and as talks with my elders since confirm it. (Not long ago I planned to visit a very wonderful old lady who was a girlhood friend of my mother. I wrote to my sister that I could not think of being a burden to Miss Cora, and would therefore stop at the little hotel in town and call on her. And my sister wrote back air-mail on the very day saying: "For God's sake, don't mention the word hotel to Miss Cora—she'll think you've lost your raising!") The elders all talked and behaved as if the final word had gone out long ago on manners, morality, religion, even politics: nothing was ever to change, they said, and even as they spoke, everything was changing, sliding, disappearing. This had been happening in fact ever since they were born; the greatest change, the fatal dividing change in this country, the war between the states, was taking place even as most of my father's generation were coming into the world. But it was the grandparents who still ruled in daily life; and they showed plainly in acts, words, and even looks—an enormously handsome generation they seemed to have been I remember—all those wonderful high noses with a diamond shaped bony structure in the bridge! —the presence of good society, very well based on traditional Christian beliefs. These beliefs were mainly Protestant but not yet petty middle-class puritanism: there remained still an element fairly high stepping and wide gestured in its personal conduct. The petty middle class of fundamentalists who saw no difference between winedrinking, dancing, card-playing, and adultery, had not yet got altogether the upper hand—in fact, never did except in certain limited areas; but it was making a brave try. It was not really a democratic society; if everybody had his place, sometimes very narrowly defined , at least he knew where it was, and so did everybody else. So too, the higher laws of morality and religion were defined; if a man offended

一个人如果出身卑贱，那他就很难摆脱自己的出身，他在生活中也很难有前途。如果这个人一旦发迹，过上了豪华生活，那也不过是"交了好运"。如果他和某个古老的世家联姻，那也不过是"交了桃花运"。如果他离开本地，在外面某个地方发了财，随后衣锦还乡了，那他也不过是个"来路不正的混小子"。在南方社会——我尽可以说——那里存在着一种无所不包的准则，在那里这种准则妇孺皆知，至少，他们知道自己母亲家的门户远高于父亲家的门户之类的东西。这种门户高低的看法很可能是毫无根据的，仅仅是因为母亲家来自利奇蒙或者乔治顿，而父亲家则来自宾夕法尼亚的某地或者在某个时期在阿肯色州家道曾衰落过。如果这样的一对夫妇最终还算不错的话，那他们的子女就会把这种情形归功于自己的母亲，因为好门户是决不容否定的，而他们的父亲呢，说到底也不过是个平庸之辈。只要说某人门第高贵，保证不会受到冷遇，因为一个家族的过去被认为比现在更重要，不管这个人眼下的处境多么糟糕，也不管他为自己的家系提出的证据多么无力。对于任何人来说，一心想高攀已经成为天性，而对真正的血统和出身的合理尊重只是一句空话而已。自傲和希求是决不会有人加以否定的。

在我童年时代的那种社会里，情感和思想的蛛丝马迹是存在的，在举行宗教仪式或者婚丧仪式时，人与人之间也有某种微妙的理解。我觉得，就大体而言，还算是个文明的社会，但其内部却始终存在着某种邪恶的暴虐性。这种潜在的暴虐性冲破平静的生活表面时几乎毫无预感，至少对于儿童来说是毫无预感的，他们要到后来才学会认识这种迹象。那里存在着古老而残忍的习俗，但是譬如家族世仇之类的习俗却已经在各大世家间逐渐消失了。事实上，这种仇恨从未在它们之间盛行过——属于那种等级的人们已抵制了世族间的仇恨，相互容忍了——至少在理论上是这样——也就是说，就其最后结果而言是这样。然而，乡村生活，牧场生活，终究是粗野的，至少在得克萨斯州是这样。我记得，那些蓄着胡子、穿着皮靴的彪形大汉踏着铿锵作响的马刺到处横行，他们腰间的衬衫里兜着上了子弹的枪支，就是去教堂时也带着。千真万确，要是你打开房间里的橱门，一眼看到的是黑洞洞的枪口，长枪短枪，这些武器就堆在那里，因为放枪的暗室已经堆满了。夏天，在那鸟语花香的乡

against the one, or sinned against the other, he knew it, and so did his neighbors, and they called everything by its right name.

This firm view applied also to social standing. A man who had humble ancestors had a hard time getting away from them and rising in the world. If he prospered and took to leisurely ways of living, he was merely "getting above his raising." If he managed to marry into one of the good old families, he had simply "outmarried himself." If he went away and made a success somewhere else, when he returned for a visit he was still only "that Jimmerson boy who went No'th." There is—was, perhaps I should say—a whole level of society of the South where it was common knowledge that the mother's family outranked the father's by half, at least. This might be based on nothing more tangible than that the mother's family came from Richmond or Charleston, while the father's may have started out somewhere from Pennsylvania, or to have got bogged down one time or another in Arkansas. If they turned out well, the children of these matches were allowed their mother's status, for good family must never be denied, but father remained a member of the Plain People to the end. Yet there was nothing against any one hinting at better lineage, and a family past more dignified than the present, no matter how humble his present circumstances, nor how little proof he could offer for his claim. Aspiration to higher and better things was natural to all men, and a sign of proper respect for true blood and birth. Pride and hope may be denied to no one.

In this society of my childhood there were all sorts of tender ways of feeling and thinking, subtle understanding between people in matters of ritual and ceremony; I think in the main a civilized society, and yet, with the underlying, perpetual ominous presence of violence; violence potential that broke through the smooth surface almost without warning, or maybe just without warning to children one learned later to know the signs. There were old cruel customs, the feud, for one, gradually dying out among the good families, never in fact prevalent among them—the men of that class fought duels, and abided—in theory at least—on the outcome; and country life, ranch life, was rough, in Texas, at least. I remember tall bearded booted men striding about with clanking spurs; and carrying loaded pistols inside their shirts next to their ribs, even to

间,我们这些孩子由父亲或者其他成年人照看着,在下午漫长的时间里练习射击固定靶子或者用绳子牵着鸽子,使用的是家家户户都有的武器,短枪·七发来复枪、单筒枪或者双筒枪。我从来没有打过枪,但我很熟悉枪声,只要我听见枪响,无论在哪一边,无论有多远,我都能辨出这是什么枪的声音。

有人曾问我,《中午酒》里两个男人谈论嚼烟草的那场对话,我是从哪儿听来的——显然,哈奇先生和汤普生先生的谈话是毫无目的的,他们不过是以此掩饰自己的仇恨罢了,而后来又一步一步地引向一场凶杀。很可能,我在某时某地曾听到过这类谈话,至于究竟是何时或何地,那我已经一点儿也记不得了。然而,在乡间,到处可以看见那些口嚼烟草的男人、吹着口哨的男人、干笨重的农活的男人,他们栖在栅栏上,或者是用厚厚的靴跟踩着横档,或者是用脚尖顶在栅栏里,趴在那里一连几小时漫无边际而又心安理得地闲聊天。由于我始终没有勇气走近他们去听个究竟,我常常心里纳闷,他们彼此间到底有什么可谈呢,那样一天又一天、一年又一年地谈个没完。然而,那年夏天在瑞士的巴塞尔,情况也像我小时候那样,那次我才偶尔有了一些确切的了解,而当时我还自以为在专心致志地研究埃拉斯摩的生平和宗教改革哩。有许多次,我看见那些男人拿出像剃刀一样的又长又尖的刀,把"嚼烟"切成一片一片,切上去是那样娴,那样准,就像切蛋糕似的。那些刀都磨得非常快,我曾多次看着我父亲给我撬核桃,他慢慢地把刀就这么一刬,核桃的一端就给撬开了,于是他就把核桃劈成四瓣,把里面的核仁全挖出来。这使我很好奇,不过我并没有为此而去接近那把刀,也没有想去摸摸它。在我们的乡间生活里,尤其在夏天,我们被许许多多锋利的刀刃包围着——小斧、大斧、犁铧、切肉刀、长猎刀、长剃刀。我们从小就懂得怎样躲避这些东西,至于我是否有过念头想抓一把在自己手里,那我三不记得了。我们就是这样生活在上了子弹的枪和危险的刀刃之间,4个野性的、天不怕地不怕的孩子经常会莫名其妙地碰伤,不过我们之中谁也没有严重地受过伤。发生过最糟糕的事情,那是我姐姐,有一次她把自己的一根锁骨给跌断了,这倒不是因为我们几乎是在马背上长大的,如你想象是从马上跌下来跌伤的,她是从栅栏上一滑脚跌下来的,她趴在那儿是为了看清楚两只公牛打架。然而,那些削烟草的利刀——我

church. It was quite matter of course that you opened a closet door in a bedroom and stared down into the cold eyes of shotguns and rifles, stacked there because there was no more room in the gun closet. In the summer, in that sweet smelling flowery country, we children with our father or some grown-up in charge, spent long afternoons on a range, shooting at fixed targets or clay pigeons with the ordinary domestic firearms, pistols, rifles of seven calibers, shotguns single and double. I never fired a shotgun, but I knew the sounds and could name any round of fire I heard, even at great distances.

Some one asked me once where I had ever heard that conversation in "Noon Wine" between two men about chewing tobacco—that apparently aimless talk between Mr. Hatch and Mr. Thompson which barely masks hatred and is leading towards a murder. It seems that I *must* have heard something of the sort somewhere, some time or another; I do not in the least remember it. But that whole countryside was full of tobaccochewing men, whittling men, hard-working farming men perched on fences with their high heels caught on a rail, or squatting on their toes, gossiping idly and comfortably for hours at a time. I often wondered what they found to say to each other, day in day out year after year; but I should never have dared go near enough to listen profitably; yet I surely picked up something that came back whole and free as air that summer in Basel, Switzerland, when I thought I was studying only the life of Erasmus and the Reformation. And I have seen them, many a time, take out their razor-sharp long-bladed knives and slice a "chew" as delicately and precisely as if they were cutting a cake. These knives were so keen, often I have watched my father, shelling pecans for me, cut off the ends of the hard shells in a slow circular single gesture; then split them down the sides in four strips and bring out the nut meat whole. This fascinated me, but it did not occur to me to come near the knife, or offer to touch it. In our country life, in summers, we were surrounded by sharpened blades—hatchets, axes, ploughshares, carving knives, bowie knives, straight razors. We were taught so early to avoid all these, I do not remember ever being tempted to take one in my hand. Living as we did among loaded guns and dangerous cutting edges, four wild, adventurous children always getting hurt in odd ways, we none of us were ever injured

记着它们是因为它们样子不寻常吗？我想不是。我见过这些东西，就像我常想起它们一样，肯定不下十次——但是有一天，我才真正地看到了这东西。就是这东西，在汤普生先生杀了哈奇先生，后来又觉得自己不受惩罚就无法活下去时，成了他恍恍惚惚的幻觉中的一部分。

和《中午酒》这篇小说始终联系在一起的是一种早年的回忆，虽不是最初的，但肯定在我 3 岁之前。倘若可以说有什么唯一源泉的话，那记忆就是这篇小说的最初源头。我那时还是个很小的孩子。我知道这一点是因为我还记得当时周围的一切都那样庞大，成年人在我眼里就如巨人，椅子之类的东西就像山峰那么大小，要够到桌面也得踮起脚尖。那是在夏末的黄昏时分，蝙蝠上下飞扑，空气里充满了它们的哀鸣。我独自孤零零地在一片草地里——那片草地位于屋子的东边——当时我处在那种唯有小孩才能感觉得到的本能的欣喜状态中，而就在这时，犹如一阵晴天霹雳，从不远处传来一声枪响，空气也为之震动。紧接着，传来一阵尖厉而拖长的号叫，一种我从未听到过的声音，但我知道，这是什么声音——这是死亡通过一个男人的咽喉发出来的呼喊声。我怎么会知道那是枪响呢？我怎么在那时就已经知道了呢？我又怎么会知道那是死亡呢？人是生来就知道死亡的。

让我再稍稍回想一下。那件事虽然是真实地发生的，但它却像一个记忆中的梦。而我的童年时代就是那样的一个梦。如果说，我在这个将要讲给你听的故事里有许多地方用了诗歌的语言的话，那是因为我是用那种语言记下许多事情的，而其中的感情也都出之有因，它不可能被撇开，也不可能被遗忘。

首先是，当这件事发生时，我怎么会是孤零零一个人呢？这是最不能叫人相信的。我们家有 4 个孩子，全由一屋子的大人带大的：一个祖母、一个父亲，还有好几个黑佣人，其中两个年纪很大，过去是家奴，还有来访的亲戚、叔父、姨母、表兄妹，祖母的另一些年纪比我大的外甥、孙子、孙女，也常有一两个老态龙钟的人，或男的或女的，带着到我们家来，他们好像是客人，但也帮着做家务杂事。那屋子在我眼里是那么宽大，毫无疑问足以容纳所有的人。但有一件事我完全可以肯定——没有一个人会孤单单的，除非他需要单独住一间房，而孩子当然没有这种需要，任何时候

seriously. The worst thing that happened was, my elder sister got a broken collar bone from a fall, not as you might expect from a horse, for we almost lived on horseback, but from a three-foot fall off a fence where she had climbed to get a better view of a battle between two bulls. But these sharp blades slicing tobacco—did I remember it because it was an unusual sight? I think not. I must have seen it, as I remember it, dozens of times—but one day I really *saw* it; and it became part of Mr. Thompson's hallucinated vision when he killed Mr. Hatch, and afterward could not live without justifying himself.

There is an early memory, not the first, but certainly before my third year, always connected with this story, "Noon Wine"; it is the source, if there could be only one. I was a very small child. I know this by the remembered vastness of the world around me, the giant heights of grown-up people; a chair something to be scaled like a mountain; a table top to be peered over on tiptoe. It was late summer and near sunset, for the sky was a clear green-blue with long streaks of burning rose in it, and the air was full of the mournful sound of swooping bats. I was all alone in a wide grassy plain—it was the lawn on the east side of the house—and I was in that state of instinctive bliss which children only know, when there came like a blow of thunder echoing and rolling in that green sky, the explosion of a shotgun, not very far away; for it shook the air. There followed at once a high, thin, long-drawn scream, a sound I had never heard, but I knew what it was—it was the sound of death in the voice of a man. How did I know it was a shotgun? How should I not have known? How did I know it was death? We are born knowing death.

Let me examine this memory a little, which though it is of an actual event, is like a remembered dream; but then all my childhood is that; and if in parts of this story I am trying to tell you, I use poetic terms, it is because in such terms do I remember many things, and the feeling is valid, it cannot be left out, or denied.

In the first place, could I have been alone when this happened? It is most unlikely. I was one of four children, brought up in a houseful of adults of ripening age; a grandmother, a father, several Negro servants, among them two aged, former slaves; visiting relatives,

都不需要。孩子是不必单独住一间房的。孩子们总是有人看着、有人管着、有人盯着、有人领着、有人教着、有人骂着(有人吻着,天哪,让我们就这样温柔地爱吧),童年时代的无穷无尽的岁月,整天如此,天天如此——无穷无尽,但他们那些人又到哪儿去了呢?看来很显然,在当时,当我听到那杀人的枪声的一瞬间,我是不可能一个人待在那里的,就具有外形的人而言,不可能没有别人。那又是谁和我在一起呢?一定是那个在屋子周围看管孩子的女人,而她对我说过什么吗?我是不是凭着本能知道的呢?是的,我现在可以肯定。若否,那是有人曾对我讲过什么话,告诉我发生了什么事,而这个人又被我给忘记了?对比不必多啰唆,任何猜测都是徒劳的,因为这种记忆犹如一道闪光、一抹色彩、一阵声响,而就是它在一片香黑的地平线上分明地勾画出情感的宏伟而神秘的轮廓。

然而——那是在第二天呢,还是第二年?——反正在同一个地方,就是在那片野草丛生的空地里,在光天化日之下,我又看到一支零零落落的、可令巴巴的送葬队伍,这支队伍慢慢地走过那座几乎远在天边的石桥,又走上了那条通向城外的泥泞的道路——这条路通往墓地。一辆轻便马车充当枢车,车上覆盖着黑色的油布,真是凄惨,我们家的一些佣人挤在院子门前看着枢车过去,说着:"可怜的平克·霍奇斯——是A老头——是他干的,他说他会这样干的。"这么说,我当时在充满喜悦的黄昏里听到的那声死亡的惨叫就是平克·霍奇斯发出来的?那么A老头是谁呢?他的名字我已经记不得了。使我纳闷的是,他将会怎么样呢?我什么也不知道。我只记得,我们家处处充满了对平克·霍奇斯的同情,因为他是无辜死的,因为他是个举目无亲的人,"多么可怜,可怜的人啊。"他们说。"世道真不公平。"他们又说。然而,他们做了些什么呢?是不是把A老头带来审判或者至少谴责他有罪了呢?恐怕他们什么也不会做。我于是便问了各种各样的问题,但又每每地被几个大人喝住了嘴,他们对我说,我人太小,不懂这种事情。

然而,我当时已经对有些事情渐渐地理解了,这我很有把握。事情是发生在我9岁时,同样是夏天,也是在农场附近的小镇上的那所屋子旁边,院子里正种着玫瑰花、蝴蝶花、忍冬植物和核桃树,菜园和牛栏就在屋后。那时,周围的一切在我眼里已经开始显得不那么宏大了,我的年龄在一年年增长,它们在一年

uncles, aunts, cousins; grandmother's other grandchildren older than we, with always an ill-identified old soul or two, male or female, who seemed to be guests but helped out with stray chores. The house, which seemed so huge to me, was probably barely adequate to the population it accommodated; but of one thing I am certain—nobody was ever alone except for the most necessary privacies, and certainly no child at any time. Children had no necessary privacies. We were watched and herded and monitored and followed and spied upon and corrected and lectured and scolded (and kissed, let's be just, loved tenderly, and prayed over!) all day, every day, through the endless years of childhood—endless, but where did they go? So the evidence all points to the fact that I was not, could not have been, bodily speaking, alone in that few seconds when for the first time I heard the sound of murder. Who was with me? What did she say—for it was certainly one of the care-taking women around the house. Could I have known by instinct, of which I am so certain now, or did some one speak words I cannot remember which nonetheless told me what had happened? There is nothing more to tell, all speculations are useless; this memory is a spot of clear light and color and sound, of immense, mysterious illumination of feeling against a horizon of total darkness.

Yet, was it the next day? next summer? In that same place, that grassy shady yard, in broad daylight I watched a poor little funeral procession creeping over the stony ridge of the near horizon, the dusty road out of town which led also to the cemetery. The hearse was just a spring wagon decently roofed and curtained with black oil cloth, poverty indeed, and some members of our household gathered on the front gallery to watch it pass, said, "Poor Pink Hodges—old man A—got him just like he said he would." Had it been Pink Hodges, then, I had heard screaming death in the blissful sunset? And who was old man A, whose name I do not remember, and what became of him, I wonder? I'll never know. I remember only that the air of our house was full of pity for Pink Hodges, for his harmlessness, his helplessness, "so pitiful, poor thing," they said; and, "It's just not right," they said. But what did they do to bring old man A to justice, or at least a sense of his evil? Nothing, I am afraid. I began to ask all sorts of questions, and was silenced invariably by some elder who told me I was too young to

年缩小。

那天闷热而潮湿，下起一场暴雨，雷电之后瓢泼大雨持续了很久，雨停了，我看见一辆陌生的单匹马车停在大门前。在乡下，邻居们或者亲戚们相互之间对各自的车马都很熟悉，就像熟悉自己的马车一样，而这辆马车，不仅陌生，而且看上去很不对劲。不要问我为什么。那匹马不对劲，那辆车也不对劲。无论马还是车好像都出了什么毛病。我很诧异，跑去看看，想弄明白这陌生人为什么要用这样的马拉着这样的车，而他还算是来拜访我祖母的哩（关于这点，无论说什么，只要说孩子是势利的或者狗是势利的，你就会满意。是的，是这样，就像孩子的父母是势利的，狗的主人是势利的一样，只不过，孩子和狗的势利要来得更刻薄、更露骨）。

我站在起居室门外，我祖母一时也没注意到我，她直挺挺地坐在那儿，脸上有一种古怪的表情：一丝困惑的微笑露在嘴边，额头上也由于疑虑而起了皱。她是个有决断的女人，每天要做许多决定，对她的漫无秩序的家庭施行权力。她一旦做了决定，无论是错是对，都一概不再收回——整个家庭的重荷真压得她喘不过气来。家里人虽不要求事事公正，但很会报复，而且各有各的路数。然而这事对她的家庭来说并没有什么了不起呀，而她坐在那里，忧心忡忡，疑虑不决。我过去从未见过她这样子，所以很惊愕。

这时，我一眼看到一个面色焦黄、形容憔悴的女人。她穿着一件褪了色的印花布衣服，戴着一顶破烂的小草帽，草帽上有一个花环，这花环真叫我伤心不止。她好像从未吃过一顿饱饭，也从未睡过一次好觉，浑身上下都显露出寒酸和饥饿。她双手绞着衣服下摆，两眼低垂，羞怯地望着那双手。她的眼神昏蒙蒙的。正当我那样望着她时，只听见坐在她旁边的一个男人粗声粗气地、简直像吼叫似的大声说："我发誓，这是为了自卫！我不打死他，他就会打死我！要是你不相信我，问我女人，她就在这儿。她知道这事。我女人从来不撒谎！"他反反复复地说着这些话，他的女人呢，没有抬头，也没有动一下，只是低声低气地说："是的，他说的是真话。我知道这事。"

当时，也可能在后来的什么时候，在我的感情和思想里就深深地铭记了对这件事的记忆，当时的情景在我头脑里是那样清晰，似乎从一开始起直到现在始终是清晰的。我分明看到，那男人希望他女人撒谎，

understand such things.

Yet here I am coming to something quite clear, of which I am entirely certain. It happened in my ninth year, and again in that summer house in the little town near the farm, with the yard full of roses and irises and honeysuckle and hackberry trees, and the vegetable garden and the cow barn in back. It was already beginning to seem not so spacious to me; it went on dwindling year by year to the measure of my growing up.

One hot moist day after a great thunderstorm and heavy long rain, I saw a strange horse and buggy standing at the front gate. Neighbors and kin in the whole countryside knew each other's equipages as well as they did their own, and this outfit was not only strange, but not right; don't ask me why. It was not a good horse, and the buggy was not good, either. There was something wrong with the whole thing, and I went full of curiosity to see why such strangers as would drive such a horse and buggy would be calling on my grandmother. (At this point say anything you please about the snobbism of children and dogs. It is real. As real as the snobbism of their parents and owners, and much more keen and direct.)

I stood just outside the living room door, unnoticed for a moment by my grandmother, who was sitting rather stiffly, with an odd expression on her face: a doubtful smiling mouth, brows knitted in painful inquiry. She was a woman called upon for decisions, many decisions every day, wielding justice among her unruly family. Once she struck, justly or unjustly, she dared not retract—the whole pack would have torn her in pieces. They did not want justice in any case, but revenge, each in his own favor. But this situation had nothing to do with her family, and there she sat, worried, undecided. I had never seen her so, and it dismayed me.

Then I saw first a poor sad pale beaten-looking woman in a faded cotton print dress and a wretched little straw hat with a wreath of wilted forget-me-nots. She looked as if she had never eaten a good dinner, or slept in a comfortable bed, the mark of life-starvation was all over her. Her hands were twisted tight in her lap and she was looking down at them in shame. Her eyes were covered with dark glasses. While I stared at her, I heard the man sitting near her almost shouting in a coarse, roughened voice: "I swear, it was in self-defense! His life or mine! If you

至于她呢，虽然不情愿，不乐意，但迫不得已最后还是撒了谎，这样就以她丈夫的罪愆和她自己的邪恶双倍地亵渎了神明。至于他，愚蠢，无耻，卑鄙，表面上好像是一心一意在恳求她，实质上却是要她为自己圆谎。

我在《中午酒》里用了这个场景。不过，现实生活里的那个男人并不像小说里的汤普生先生那样，是个瘦瘦的、有点驼背的、傻里傻气而又自以为是的人。不是的，他是个横肉满面、信口胡言的人，内心又邪恶又怯懦，他眼睛水汪汪的，充满醉醺醺的红丝，在我祖母面前大喊大叫："夫人，要是你不相信我，问女人！她从来不撒谎！"我祖母这时发现我在门口，就给了我一个眼色示意我走开，对于她的眼色我们做孩子的都能领会而且是从来不敢违抗的。然而，我后来还是听到了有关这件事的一些内容，那时我祖母把这件事告诉了我父亲。她说的时候声音不寻常地冷漠，她说她已经就这件事做了决定，接着又说："过去从来没有人来求我宽恕凶杀罪。真是新鲜事。"我父亲说："是啊，过去发生的倒是些真正冷酷的凶杀。"

这么说来，可怕的暴力事件真不止一次啰，而这次，凶手得到了保释，他带着可怜的妻子在乡下到处游说，为自己辩护——事情后来究竟如何，我就不得而知了。还有一次，可以肯定，是在我 11 岁之前，大概也是某个夏天吧，那年我们离开乡下搬到城里去住，当时我又有过两次难忘的见闻。我父亲和我一起驾车从农场到城里去，路上我们遇到了一个留着黑胡子的彪形大汉，他骑在马背上，坐得笔直，面颊骨和喉结可说成了一直线，身上呢，穿着干净的但又打过补丁的斜纹粗棉布衣服，领口敞开着，一顶鬼见了也要发愁的又黑又糙的大帽子歪戴在头上。他大列咧地向我们打了个招呼，把胯下的那匹强壮的黑马稍稍一勒，打一个回旋，随后又神气地放马奔驰起来。我问父亲这人是干什么的，他说，"是拉尔夫·托马斯，7 个县里最了不起的人。"我说："他凭什么这样了不起？"我父亲便说："大概是凭那匹马嘛。那匹马倒是匹好马。"听上去，他说话的语调很滑稽，好像在开玩笑，在嘲笑那个可怜的家伙荒谬之极，然而他的话又一点儿也没趣味，因为在他的话语里有一种当时我不理解的悲哀。

还有一次，也是在这样的途中，我看见一个骨瘦如柴、样子丑陋、神情疲惫的男子，他斜倚在一张椅子

don't believe me, ask my wife here. She saw it. My wife won't lie!" Every time he repeated these words, without lifting her head or moving, she would say in a low voice, "Yes, that's right. I saw it."

In that moment, or in another moment later as this memory sank in and worked in my feelings and understanding, it was quite clear to me, and seems now to have been clear from the first, that he expected her to lie, was indeed forcing her to tell a lie; that she did it unwillingly and unlovingly in bitter resignation to the double disgrace of her husband's crime and her own sin; and that he, stupid, dishonest, soiled as he was, was imploring her as his only hope, somehow to make his lie a truth.

I used this scene in "Noon Wine," but the man in real life was not lean and gaunt and blindly, foolishly proud, like Mr. Thompson; no, he was just a great loose-faced, blabbing man full of guilt and fear, and he was bawling at my grandmother, his eyes bloodshot with drink and tears, "Lady, if you don't believe me, ask my wife! She won't lie!" At this point my grandmother noticed my presence and sent me away with a look we children knew well and never dreamed of disobeying. But I heard part of the story later, when my grandmother said to my father, with an unfamiliar coldness in her voice, for she had made her decision about this affair, too: "I was never asked to condone a murder before. Something new." My father said, "Yes, and a cold-blooded murder too if ever there was one."

So, there was the dreary tale of violence again, this time with the killer out on bail, going the rounds of the countryside with his wretched wife, telling his side of it—whatever it was; I never knew the end. In the meantime, in one summer or another, certainly before my eleventh year, for that year we left that country for good, I had two other memorable glimpses. My father and I were driving from the farm to town, when we met with a tall black-whiskered man on horseback, sitting so straight his chin was level with his Adam's apple, dressed in clean mended blue denims, shirt open at the throat, a big devil-may-care black felt hat on the side of his head. He gave us a lordly gesture of greeting, caused his fine black horse to curvet and prance a little, and rode on, grandly. I asked my father who that could be, and he said, "That's Ralph Thomas, the proudest man in seven counties." I said, "What is he

上，背靠着他那间摇摇欲坠的小屋的后墙。那小屋的后墙正面对着大路，笼罩在核桃树的稀疏的树荫里。那男子的眉宇间垂挂着一缕看上去已褪了色的头发，在炎热得连蟋蟀也叫个不停的夏日里，他吹着一支口琴，曲调悲凉而忧伤，真是孤独者的活生生的写照。我对这个陌生人不由得产生了一丝同情——面对着异国的景色，他闭上了眼睛，就用那哀切的音乐安慰着自己。有人告诉我，他是瑞典人，在某人家做雇工。

就在这时——什么时候？怎么了？——那个我除了听到他死前的惨叫之外一无所知的平克·霍奇斯，却由于我看到了这个瑞典雇工而浮现在我眼前，而且是一个天生注定的受害者的形象。而我在祖母起居室里看到过的那个像牛一样粗鲁的男人就成了杀人者。然而，事情并非如此简单，这不过是个开头而已。在我的小说里，希尔顿既是受害者，同时又是个谋害者，勉强说他无罪当然也可以，因为他是个疯子。但他所起的作用并不下于实际行凶的人。在我的这篇小说里，每个人，不管他用的是这种方式或者那种方式，不管他是直接参与的还是间接参与的，都是对那次凶杀或者暴力死亡事件起过作用的。就是汤普生先生的两个年幼的儿子也如此，他们由于怯懦和无知而反对汤普生先生并站在他们的母亲一边，所以汤普生先生不需要他们。事实上，出于他们的天真无知，他们不仅相信自己所做的事是对的，而且在他们对情况的理解范围内，他们也只能这样做，他们必须保护自己的母亲……

这儿我得停一下，因为好像不知为何，我已经写到了我这篇小说里的那些人物，而当我讲到他们时，他们似乎是些实实在在存在着的人。至于作为这篇小说的基础的那些零零星星的记忆现在反而显得很纷乱。不过，它们不知在何处自行地组合起来，时而是总体，时而是个体，而我就是根据它们才最后写出这篇小说的，这是一篇包含着最痛苦的道德和感情的混乱的小说，其中所牵涉到的每个人，都自以为在尽力做正直的事情，是的，就是哈奇先生也如此。

只有在个人本性的品质高下这点上，我们才能或多或少地衡量出一个人身上的道德程度。汤普生先生的动机是极其混乱的，但是并不卑鄙。有人帮助他，他也就帮助这个人。当他用行动保护他认为对自己的生活有益的东西时，那东西就值得用任何代价来

proud of?" And my father said, "I suppose the horse. It's a very fine horse," in a goodhumored, joking tone, which made the poor man quite ridiculous, and yet not funny, but sad in some way I could not understand.

On another of these journeys I saw a bony, awkward, tired-looking man, tilted in a kitchen chair against the wall of his comfortless shack, set back from the road under the thin shade of hackberry trees, a thatch of bleached-looking hair between his eyebrows, blowing away at a doleful tune on his harmonica, in the hot dull cricket-whirring summer day: the very living image of loneliness. I was struck with pity for this stranger, his eyes closed against the alien scene, consoling himself with such poor music. I was told he was someone's Swedish hired man.

In time—when? how? Pink Hodges, whom I never knew except in the sound of his death-cry, merged with my glimpse of the Swedish hired man to become the eternal Victim; the fat bullying whining man in my grandmother's living room became the Killer. But nothing can remain so simple as that, this was only a beginning. Helton too, the Victim in my story, is also a murderer, with the dubious innocence of the madman; but no less a shedder of blood. Everyone in this story contributes, one way or another directly, or indirectly, to murder, or death by violence; even the two young sons of Mr. Thompson who turn on him in their fright and ignorance and side with their mother, who does not need them; they are guiltless, for they meant no harm, and they do not know what they have contributed to; indeed in their innocence they believe they are doing, not only right, but the only thing they could possibly do in the situation as they understand it: they must defend their mother. . . .

And here I am brought to a pause, for almost without knowing it, I have begun to write about these characters in a story of mine as though they were real persons exactly as I have shown them. And these fragments of memory on which the story is based now seem to have a random look; they nowhere contain in themselves, together or separately, the story I finally wrote out of them; a story of the most painful moral and emotional confusions, in which every one concerned, yes, in his crooked way, even Mr. Hatch, is trying to do right.

It is only in the varying levels of quality in the

加以保护,同时他又尽力要保护另一个人的生命——希尔顿先生的生命,因为希尔顿先生已证明自己是个能带来好处的人,是现存的好帮手,是真正的朋友。汤普生先生说,希尔顿先生会给我做许多事情,他这样说是对的。然而,他一看到哈奇先生就恨他,还没找到什么理由,就想揍他——是不是可以说这是因为汤普生先生本人是个有道德的人,所以他一看见哈奇先生就发现了他身上的邪恶?那一带乡村里的人——请记住,这是最重要的,因为这里表示一个人和社会的联系——他们都同意律师柏莱先生的看法,认为汤普生先生的行为是有正当理由的杀人。但是杀人毕竟是杀人,并不因为有正当理由就不是杀人了——他的邻居们就这样认为。汤普生先生不是个恶人,他不过是个单凭自己的思想一意孤行的可怜的罪人,而他的思想则由于傲慢和懒惰这样一些自然倾向,总有点昏懂懂。他仍是个有道德的人,虽然他对道德为何物并不全然明了,而正因为这样,他才有了一点儿本不该有的自信心。

　　至于哈奇呢,他是个天生的坏蛋,本性邪恶,喜欢邪恶,行为也邪恶,他对任何人——乃至于他自己——从来不做一点儿好事。他这种邪恶是最可怕、最不可救药的,因为一个人如在法律范围内安全行事,那么他就会有理由自信,他的动机虽谈不上是善良的,但也不会比别人更坏一点儿。他很简单、很自然地就会相信,别人的动机并不见得比他自己的动机更好一点儿,所以他就可以把一切有关善行的废话统统抛在一边,而且又总能在习俗、舆论和法律的边沿上站住脚。如果有人指责他,他总是有办法笃悠悠地为自己辩护,而他说的话又总不会毫无道理——唯独没有人所应有的道义,道义之类的东西他是当做耳边风,根本不放在心里的。希尔顿先生是个疯子,也由于这一点,他是超越于善恶之上的,他是受害者,同时又是害人者。至于汤普生太太,她是那个时代、那个地方、根据那种行为准则造就出来的无数女人中的一个,她所受到的教育是要求她按照业已规定好了的妇德的标准去做人,并以此为天职。这种妇德的标准是明摆着的,是不能回避的,是需要做出牺牲的,也是使人头晕眼花的,为此,她几乎丧尽了人之为人的各种品质以及精神上的勇气和见解。对她来说,撒谎是一种不可饶恕的邪恶,更何况,她撒谎是为了掩饰某种罪行,虽然这种罪行是她丈夫所犯的。她撒了谎,她

individual nature that we are able finally more or less to measure the degree of virtue in each man. Mr. Thompson's motives are most certainly mixed, yet not ignoble; he helps some one who helps him in turn; while acting in defense of what he sees as the good in his own life, the thing worth trying to save at almost any cost, he is trying at the same time to defend another life—the life of Mr. Helton, who has proved himself the bringer of good, the present help, the true friend. Mr. Helton would have done as much for me, Mr. Thompson says, and he is right. Yet he hated Mr. Hatch on sight, wished to injure him before he had a reason: could it not be a sign of virtue in Mr. Thompson that he surmised and resisted at first glance the evil in Mr. Hatch? The whole countryside, let us remember, for this is most important, the relations of a man to his society, agrees with Mr. Burleigh the lawyer, and the jury and the judge that Mr. Thompson's deed was justifiable homicide: but this did not, as his neighbors confirmed, make it any less a murder. Mr. Thompson was not an evil man, he was only a poor sinner doing his best according to his lights, lights somewhat dimmed by his natural aptitude for Pride and Sloth. He still had his virtues, even if he did not quite know what they were, and so gave himself credit for some few that he had not.

But Hatch was the doomed man, evil by nature, a lover and do-er of evil, who did no good thing for any one, not even, in the long run, himself. He was evil in the most dangerous, irremediable way: one who works safely within the law, and has reasoned himself into believing that his motives, if not good, are at least no worse than any one else's: for he believes quite simply and naturally that the motives of others are no better than his own; and putting aside all nonsense about good, he will always be found on the side of custom and common sense and the letter of the law. When challenged he has his defense pat and ready, and there is nothing much wrong with it—it only lacks human decency, of which he has no conception beyond a faint hearsay. Mr. Helton is, by his madness, beyond good and evil, his own victim as well as the victim of others. Mrs. Thompson is a woman of the sort produced in numbers in that time, that place, that code: so trained to the practice of her prescribed womanly vocation of virtue as such—manifest, unrelenting, sacrificial, stupifying—she has almost lost her human qualities,

自己也很明白，这对她的灵魂来说是件非同小可的事情（对她的自信心也同样如此，因为她的自信是建立在纯洁无瑕的感情上的），但她缺乏勇气和爱心去面对自己的邪恶并使它最终得出好的结果，也就是说，她未能全心全意地把谎撒到底，将自己的邪恶干净彻底地隐藏起来，去替丈夫说几句话，如果这样，他们倒也许能得救，无论是灵魂还是肉体——也许能，我只是说也许能。究竟能不能，我本不知道，也永远不会知道。汤普生太太不是那种心智健全的人，而这篇小说，不管怎么样，也总得有个结束……像她这类人，其中是没有一个会有足够的决断力、能在自己身上创造出救赎的奇迹的。

　　假设，我现在想象自己在某个时候真的看到了这些人，有血有肉的，那会怎么样呢？我知道我告诉你的是什么，是一些从这里或者那里、从这时或者那时得到的零零星星的见闻，但是，我知道我为什么会记住它们，为什么它们会在我的记忆里渐渐地活动起来并构成了一篇小说。那是因为，在这些有关陌生人的见闻里，每一处都释放出某种要素，某种性质，就是这些要素或性质，在我成长过程中某个有生气的时期吸引了我的注意力，并使我——一个孩子——结束了幼稚期，开始观察我本来不熟悉的外在世界。我用那样的注意力，那样的好奇心，那样的思索癖好来观察其他人，想来也是正常的、自然的，因为任何孩子都难免会滥用自己的能力。这难道不就是各种文明教育的唯一后果吗？这样的教育不是要我们对客观现实，对存在的本质以及对我们周围的那些既与我们极其相似又那样玄妙叵测地有别于我们的人，抱着越来越敏感的高度警觉吗？我不知道自己的印象是直接得来的呢——我现在相信是这样的——抑或是，由于长期不断形成的经验而逐渐地从中产生出来的？那个挺着腰、竖着颈、胡子拉碴地骑着骏马像骑兵队头头似的扬鞭催马的汉子，那"7个县里最了不起的人……"我对他的看法无疑是和我父亲一样的，认为他荒唐、愚昧，只不过考虑到凡人都想出风头这一点，我才没有嘲笑他，因为这不过是虚荣心的表现而已。

　　我称之为汤普生太太的那个女人——她的名字我始终不知道——使我第一次确信无疑地看到了那种真正羞惭的脸色。即使她匍匐在地，也不及她那种几乎到了极点的耻辱感，也不会令人更觉惊恐。我知道像她这样的情况无论出于何种原因都会置人于死

and her spiritual courage and insight, to boot. She commits the, to her, dreadful unforgivable sin of lying; moreover, lying to shield a criminal, even if that criminal is her own husband. Having done this, to the infinite damage, as she sees it, of her own soul (as well as her self-respect which is founded on her feeling of irreproachability) she lacks the courage and the love to see her sin through to its final good purpose; to commit it with her whole heart and with perfect acceptance of her guilt; to say to her husband the words that might have saved them both, soul and body—might have, I say only. I do not know and shall never know. Mrs. Thompson was not that robust a character, and this story, given all, must end as it does end. . . there is nothing in any of these beings tough enough to work the miracle of redemption in them.

　　Suppose I imagine now that I really saw all of these persons in the flesh at one time or another? I saw what I have told you, a few mere flashes of a glimpse here and there, one time or another; but I do know why I remembered them, and why in my memory they slowly took on their separate lives in a story. It is because there radiated from each one of those glimpses of strangers some element, some quality that arrested my attention at a vital moment of my own growth, and caused me, a child, to stop short and look outward, away from myself; to look at another human being with that attention and wonder and speculation which ordinarily, and very naturally, I think, a child lavishes only on himself. Is it not almost the sole end of civilized education of all sorts to teach us to be more and more highly, sensitively conscious of the reality of the existence, the essential being, of others, those around us so very like us and yet so bafflingly, so mysteriously different? I do not know whether my impressions were on the instant, as I now believe, or did they draw to their magnet gradually with time and confirming experience? That man on the fine horse, with his straight back, straight neck, shabby and unshaven, riding like a cavalry officer, "the proudest man in seven counties—"I saw him no doubt as my father saw him, absurd, fatuous, but with some human claim on respect and not to be laughed at, for all his simple vanity.

　　The woman I have called Mrs. Thompson—I never knew her name—showed me for the first time I am certain the face of pure shame; humiliation so nearly absolute it could not have been more frightening if she had grovelled in the floor; and I knew that whatever the cause, it was mortal and beyond help. In that bawling

地而且是无可奈何的。至于那个咧嘴瞪眼、汗流浃背地哇哇乱叫的男人，我从他身上看到的则是恐惧，那种由于内心虚弱而产生的恐惧，因为我知道他在撒谎。在那个黄发长腿、吹着口琴的男人身上，我好像第一次突然感觉到了自己对非肉体受害者的理解和同情。指天为誓，我应该做的我业已做了，我已为昔日的好梦洒下了一掬伤心之泪，为我珍爱而病重的人们，为我自己的痛苦和忧患。然而，这是内心的启迪，它带来温情，带来曙光，为我自私的心灵带来了上帝的慈爱。我在这里说了几句老式的文雅话，这些话虽然是按它们的本义写上的，但它们对我来说又完全是新鲜的、现实的，是"现实"的不可替换的名称。我很理解它们的含义，在此使用，只是为了尽我所能将一个孩子的感受描述出来，因为在那时，人情、人生以及博爱之心正在展现，而当灵魂正欲接受它们之际，它第一次也仅有的一次受到了触动。当然我也知道，在我还没找到词句来描述它们之前，在很久很久之前，所有重要的事情早已在那里发生过了。

sweating man with the loose mouth and staring eyes, I saw the fear that is moral cowardice and I knew he was lying. In that yellow-haired, long-legged man playing his harmonica I felt almost the first glimmer of understanding and sympathy for any suffering not physical. Most certainly I had already done my share of weeping over lost or dying pets, or beside some one I loved who was very sick, or my own pains and accidents; but *this* was a spiritual enlightenment, some tenderness, some first wakening of charity in my self-centered heart. I am using here some very old fashioned noble words in their prime sense. They have perfect freshness and reality to me, they are the irreplaceable names of Realities. I know well what they mean, and I need them here to describe as well as I am able what happens to a child when the human feelings and the moral sense and the sense of charity are unfolding, and are touched once and for all in that first time when the soul is prepared for them; and I know that the all-important things in that way have all taken place long and long before we know the words for them.

038. 春 寒^①

（美）罗伯特·潘·沃伦 著　　郑启吟 译

038. Blackberry Winter
by Robert Penn Warren

已经是 6 月了，早上过了 8 点，但是起居室的石砌大壁炉的炉底上还生着火——虽然火堆不大，只是几块木头。我站在壁炉口，躬身向火，人几乎快到烟囱那儿了。我的光脚趾在暖洋洋的石头上慢慢来回蹭着，热气使我光腿上的皮肤皱了起来，直痒痒，还扎得慌，我觉得有意思极了。我跟我妈妈喊着的时候，也还是这么蹭着玩。我妈妈大概在后面的饭厅或者厨房里。我对她叫道："可这是 6 月了，我不用穿鞋！"

"要出去就得穿上！"她喊道。

我想估估她口气里的权威性和说服力到什么程度，但是隔这么老远，实在很难判断。我打算捉摸捉摸她的语气，又想到自己刚才多傻，竟从后门出去，结果让她瞅见了我光着脚。要是我从前门或者边门走，那她根本就不会知道，不管怎么说，反正吃中饭前不会知道，到那时候，半天过去了，我早已走遍农庄，看过暴风雨造成了什么后果，也到小河那儿看过洪水了。但是我从来没想到过他们会不准你在 6 月里光脚，就算下过倾盆大雨和来过寒流又算得了什么！

从我记事起，还没有人在 6 月里阻拦过我。当你到了 9 岁，你记得的东西就好像都是一辈子忘不了的。因为你记得每一件事，每一件事都又粗又大，填满了时间，扎扎实实的，你简直可以把它当棵树，绕着它走了又走，还可以对着它看。你明白，时光流逝，时间里有种运动，但这不是时间本身。时间不是一种运动，不是流动，或者说不是风，而是指事物所处的一种

IT was getting into June and past eight o'clock in the morning, but there was a fire—even if it wasn't a big fire, just a fire of chunks—on the hearth of the big stone fireplace in the living room. I was standing on the hearth, almost into the chimney, hunched over the fire, working my bare toes slowly on the warm stone. I relished the heat which made the skin of my bare legs warp and creep and tingle, even as I called to my mother, who was somewhere back in the dining room or kitchen and said: "But it's June, I don't have to put them on!"

"You put them on if you are going out," she called.

I tried to assess the degree of authority and conviction in the tone, but at that distance it was hard to decide. I tried to analyze the tone, and then I thought what a fool I had been to start out the back door and let her see that I was barefoot. If I had gone out the front door or the side door she would never have known, not till dinner time anyway, and by then the day would have been half gone and I would have been all over the farm to see what the storm had done and down to the creek to see the flood. But it had never crossed my mind that they would try to stop you from going barefoot in June, no matter if there had been a gully-washer and a cold spell.

Nobody had ever tried to stop me in June as long as I could remember, and when you are nine years old, what you remember seems forever; for you remember everything and everything is important and stands big and full and fills up Time and is so solid that you can walk around and around it like a tree and look at it. You are aware that time passes, that there is a movement in time, but that is not what Time is. Time is not a movement, a flowing, a wind then, but is, rather, a kind of climate in which things are, and when a thing

---

① 春寒(Blackberry Winter)：直译为"乌莓之冬"，指美国南部和中部地区，每年春末乌莓花盛开时的一段低温的时期。

作者简介： 罗伯特·潘·沃伦(Robert Penn Warren，1905—1989)，美国小说家、诗人和评论家。1905 年 4 月 24 日生于肯塔基州格思里，1989 年 9 月 15 日卒于佛蒙特州斯特拉顿。他曾在几所大学任教，之后协助创办和编辑《南方评论》(Southern Review，1935～1942)，在当时美国文学杂志界最有影响力的杂志。他的作品经常针对南方传统乡村价值腐蚀下的道德困惑。他最著名的长篇小说是《国王的人马》(All the King's Men，1946)，获得普利策奖。短篇小说集《阁楼马戏团》(The Circus in the Attic，1948)包括著名的《春寒》(Blackberry Winter)。1958 年和 1979 年两次获得普利策诗歌奖，1986 年成为美国第一位桂冠诗人。

气候。一件事发生了,这件事就开始了生命,并继续生活下去,在时间里实实在在地存在着,就像一棵你可以绕着它走的树似的。如果这里面有运动,这运动也不是时间本身,就跟一阵微风并不是气候本身一样。微风所做的全部事情只是轻轻地摇摇树上的树叶,而树是活着的,实实在在的。你到了 9 岁,你就明白有些事你是不知道的;你就明白,如果你一旦知道了某些事,那就是真知道了,你懂得一件事怎么会是这样的,你懂得你可以在 6 月里光着脚。你不懂后面厨房的那个声音为什么说你不能光着脚到外面去,不能跑去看看发生了什么事,不可以在潮湿的、颤动着的青草上面蹭蹭脚,在光滑的、奶油般的红色泥土上留下完整的脚印,然后对着它沉思,仿佛你突然在世界的黎明的闪烁发光的海滩上遇到了那个单独的足迹。你从来没见过海滩,但是你读过那本书①知道那个脚印是怎么来的。

那个声音总算说完了话。我火冒三丈,看着黑袜和那双结实的、磨损了的棕色鞋子,这是我从衣橱里一直拿到炉前地毯上来的。我又一次叫道:"这可是 6 月了。"说完我就等着。

"是 6 月不错,"声音从远处回答,"可这是春寒啊!"

我已经抬起头来要答话了,好再测验一次语调里的含意,就在这时候。我看到了那个男人。

壁炉砌在起居室的尽头,因为烟囱是安在山墙那边的,就像田纳西州的许多农舍那样。烟囱两边各有一扇窗,我从北边的那扇窗户望出去,可以看到那个人。我被眼前的奇怪景象吸引住了,本来要说的话没有喊出口。我盯住他看,他还离得很远,正顺着林子边上的小路走过来。

这事怪就怪在那儿居然会有人。那条路顺着院子栅栏过来,在栅栏和林子之间穿过,通到院子里,然后从后院的鸡场出去,又顺着林子伸到一块挡住了后面农田的突出地方,接着就消失在林子里了。我知道这条路是通到后面去的,它穿过林子到沼泽地,又绕过沼泽地通到河边。沼泽没有大树,尽是些美国梧桐、水橡树、柳树、爬藤之类的植物。除了到沼泽地叉青蛙、上河边钓鱼或者去林子里打猎,人们从来不到那后面去的,而如果没有我爸爸给予的长期有效的许

---

① 那本书:指英国作家丹尼尔·笛福所著的小说《鲁滨逊漂流记》。

---

happens it begins to live and keeps on living and stands solid in Time like the tree that you can walk around. And if there is a movement, the movement is not Time itself, no more than a breeze is climate, for all the breeze does is to shake a little the leaves on the tree which is alive and solid. When you are nine, you know that there are things that you don't know, but you know that when you know something you know it. You know how a thing has been and you know that you can go barefoot in June. You do not understand that voice from back in the kitchen which says that you cannot go barefoot outdoors and run to see what has happened and rub your feet over the wet shivery grass and make the perfect mark of your foot in the smooth, creamy, red mud and then muse upon it as though you had suddenly come upon that single mark on the glistening auroral beach of the world. You have never seen a beach, but you have read the book and how the footprint was there.

The voice had said what it had said, and I looked savagely at the black stockings and the strong, scuffed brown shoes which I had brought from my closet as far as the hearth rug. I called once more, "But it's June," and waited.

"It's June," the voice replied from far away, "but it's blackberry winter."

I had lifted my head to reply to that, to make one more test of what was in that tone, when I happened to see the man.

The fireplace in the living room was at the end; for the stone chimney was built, as in so many of the farmhouses in Tennessee, at the end of a gable, and there was a window on each side of the chimney. Out of the window on the north side of the fireplace I could see the man. When I saw the man I did not call out what I had intended, but, engrossed by the strangeness of the sight, watched him, still far off, come along the path by the edge of the woods.

What was strange was that there should be a man there at all. That path went along the yard fence, between the fence and the woods which came right down to the yard, and then on back past the chicken runs and on by the woods until it was lost to sight where the woods bulged out and cut off the back field. There the path disappeared into the woods. It led on back, I knew, through the woods and to the swamp, skirted the swamp where the big trees gave way to sycamores and water oaks and willows and tangled cane, and then led on to the river. Nobody ever went back there except people who wanted to gig frogs in the swamp or to fish in the river or to hunt in the woods, and those people, if they didn't have a standing permission from my father, always stopped to ask permission to cross

可,要去渔猎的人总要在这儿停步,得到准许了再穿过院子。但是我现在看见的这个人不是猎人,虽然隔那么远,我也敢这么断定。一场暴风雨过后,一个猎人在那儿有什么可干的呢?再说,他是从河那边来的。那天早上并没有人上河边去过。我确实知道这点。因为如果有人走过,肯定地说,如果有任何陌生人走过,那些狗早就狂吠乱叫,追出去咬他了。但是这个人却正是从河边那方向来的,而且是穿过林子走来的。我的脑子里突然出现了这个人走在林子里的情景:在绿色的曙光中,在大树下,他悄然无声地在长满青草的小路上走着。不时有一大滴水像屋檐的滴水似的从树叶上或枝丫上落下,水滴落在一片硬邦邦的橡树叶上,发出轻轻的重浊的声音,像是打在铅皮上。在静悄悄的树林里,这种声响就很有意义了。

当你是个孩子时,你站在沉寂的树林里,周围是那么安静,你的心几乎要停止跳动,你简直就想在绿色的曙光里这么站下去,一直站到你感到自己的脚丫像树根那样扎进土里,紧紧抓住了泥土,你的躯体也像树叶那样通过微孔在慢慢地呼吸——你站在那儿,等着下一滴水滴到下面的树叶上,发出轻轻的单调的声音。这个声音在筹划某一件事,在结束某一件事,在开始某一种事。你迫不及待地等着它的发生,担心它不会发生,然而一旦发生,你又开始等待了,几乎害怕了。

但是,这个我认为是穿过林子走来的人并没有停下来等待,没有脚下生根长到地底下去,没有用树叶呼吸的方式大量进行悄无声息的呼吸。相反,就在他沿着林子边上小路朝房子走来的这会儿工夫,我看到了他在我想象中的绿色曙光里移动。他一步步走得很稳,却并不快,他肩膀有点拱,脑袋往前探,就像是个已经走了好多路,还有好多路要赶的人那样。我把眼睛闭上两秒钟,心想再睁开来时,这个人就根本不会在那儿了。没有什么地方可让他从那儿来,他也没有什么理由要上这儿来——他正在朝我们屋子走来。但是我睁眼睛一看,他还在,正不慌不忙地沿着林子边上走来,甚至都还没走到后院养鸡场上。

“妈妈。”我喊道。

“你把鞋穿上。”那个声音说。

“有个人走过来了,”我喊道,“在屋子后面。”

她没有回答。我猜她是到厨房的窗子那儿看去了。她会在那儿看着那个人,捉摸着他是想干什么。

the farm. But the man whom I now saw wasn't, I could tell even at that distance, a sportsman. And what would a sportsman have been doing down there after a storm? Besides, he was coming from the river, and nobody had gone down there that morning. I knew that for a fact, because if anybody had passed, certainly if a stranger had passed, the dogs would have made a racket and would have been out on him. But this man was coming up from the river and had come up through the woods. I suddenly had a vision of him moving up the grassy path in the woods, in the green twilight under the big trees, not making any sound on the path, while now and then, like drops off the eaves, a big drop of water would fall from a leaf or bough and strike a stiff oak leaf lower down with a small, hollow sound like a drop of water hitting tin. That sound, in the silence of the woods, would be very significant.

When you are a boy and stand in the stillness of woods, which can be so still that your heart almost stops beating and makes you want to stand there in the green twilight until you feel your very feet sinking into and clutching the earth like roots and your body breathing slow through its pores like the leaves—when you stand there and wait for the next drop to drop with its small, flat sound to a lower leaf, that sound seems to measure out something, to put an end to something, to begin something, and you cannot wait for it to happen and are afraid it will not happen, and then when it has happened, you are waiting again, almost afraid.

But the man whom I saw coming through the woods in my mind's eye did not pause and wait, growing into the ground and breathing with the enormous, soundless breathing of the leaves. Instead, I saw him moving in the green twilight inside my head as he was moving at that very moment along the path by the edge of the woods, coming toward the house. He was moving steadily, but not fast, with his shoulders hunched a little and his head thrust forward, like a man who has come a long way and has a long way to go. I shut my eyes for a couple of seconds, thinking that when I opened them he would not be there at all. There was no place for him to have come from, and there was no reason for him to come where he was coming, toward our house. But I opened my eyes, and there he was, and he was coming steadily along the side of the woods. He was not yet even with the back chicken yard.

"Mama," I called.

"You put them on," the voice said.

"There's a man coming," I called, "out back. "

She did not reply to that, and I guessed that she had gone to the kitchen window to look. She would be looking at the man and wondering who he was and

在乡下,人们总是那样的。如果我现在回厨房去,她不会马上注意到我是不是光着脚的。所以我就上那儿去了。

她在窗边站着。"我不认识他。"她说,没有回头看我。

"他能是从哪儿来的呢?"我问。

"我不知道。"她说。

"他在河边好干什么呢? 在夜里,在暴风雨里好干什么呢?"

她细细打量窗外那个人,然后说道:"喔,我估计他是从丹巴的地里穿过来的。"

我明白这个说法完全合乎情理。在昨晚那场暴风雨里,他并没在河边待着。他是今天早上才过来的。如果你不在乎从一大片接骨木、橡树和乌莓树丛里穿过,你是可以从丹巴那儿过来的。这些树丛把原来的通路差不多全给遮没了,再没人从那儿过了。我对这个解释暂时满意了,但也只有一小会儿。"妈妈",我问,"他昨晚在丹巴那边干什么呢?"

这时她看着我了,于是我知道自己犯了个错误了,因为她现在在看我的光脚丫了。"你还没把鞋穿上。"她说道。

但是狗救了我。正在这个时候,狗吠叫了一声,我认出是山姆,那只长毛牧羊犬的声音。然后又是一声吠叫,声音粗厉些,非常激动,那是另一只狗巴里的声音。只见一道白光一闪,巴里从后廊的拐角上出来,朝那人直冲了过去。巴里是条高大的银灰色的斗牛犬①,就是人们通常叫做农家看羊狗的那种,这种狗现在看不到了。它们胸部厚,脑袋大,但是长着漂亮的长腿,能像猎狗那样轻松地跳过栅栏。巴里刚跳过对着树林的那道白色的木栅栏,我妈妈就跑到后廊上喊起来了:"嘿,回来,巴里,回来。"

巴里在路上站住,等那个人过来,但是又吠叫了几声,声音低沉、恶狠狠的,喉咙里咯咯直响,像是从石砌水井里出来的声音。它那白色的胸膛溅上了红红的黏土,鲜血似的,令人看了情绪激动。

不管怎么说,那个人没有停步,甚至在巴里跳过栅栏,朝他冲去时也没站住。他还在继续往前走,他所做的全部事情只是把右手拿的那个小纸包很快换到左手,再把手伸到裤袋里去拿什么东西。接着我看到了一样闪闪发亮的东西,就知道他手里有把刀,也

---

① bull-dog,一种颈粗性猛的狗。

what he wanted, the way you always do in the country, and if I went back there now she would not notice right off whether or not I was barefoot. So I went back to the kitchen.

She was standing by the window. "I don't recognize him," she said, not looking around at me.

"Where could he be coming from?" I asked.

"I don't know," she said.

"What would he be doing down at the river? At night? In the storm?"

She studied the figure out the window, then said, "Oh, I reckon maybe he cut across from the Dunbar place."

That was, I realized, a perfectly rational explanation. He had not been down at the river in the storm, at night. He had come over this morning. You could cut across from the Dunbar place if you didn't mind breaking through a lot of elder and sassafras and blackberry bushes which had about taken over the old cross path, which nobody ever used any more. That satisfied me for a moment, but only for a moment. "Mama," I asked, "What would he be doing over at the Dunbar place last night?"

Then she looked at me, and I knew I had made a mistake, for she was looking at my bare feet. "You haven't got your shoes on," she said.

But I was saved by the dogs. That instant there was a bark which I recognized as Sam, the collie, and then a heavier, churning kind of bark which was Bully, and I saw a streak of white as Bully tore round the corner of the back porch and headed out for the man. Bully was a big, bone-white bull dog, the kind of dog that they used to call a farm bull dog but that you don't see any more, heavy chested and heavy headed, but with pretty long legs. He could take a fence as light as a hound. He had just cleared the white paling fence toward the woods when my mother ran out to the back porch and began calling, "Here you, Bully! Here you!"

Bully stopped in the path, waiting for the man, but he gave a few more of those deep, gargling, savage barks that reminded you of something down a stone-lined well. The red clay mud, I saw, was splashed up over his white chest and looked exciting, like blood.

The man, however, had not stopped walking even when Bully took the fence and started at him. He had kept right on coming. All he had done was to switch a little paper parcel which he carried from the right hand to the left, and then reach into his pants pocket to get something. Then I saw the glitter and knew that he had a knife in his hand, probably the kind of mean knife just made for devilment and nothing else, with a blade as long as the blade of a frog-sticker, which will

许是那种专干坏事,不派其他用场的凶器,刀身足有宰青蛙的尖刀那么长,这种尖刀只消按一下刀把上的按钮,刀身就会啪的一声立刻伸了出来。这把刀的刀把上一定也有个按钮,不然他怎么会那么快就亮出刀身,而且只用一只手就行了呢?

拿了刀去对付那些狗是怪荒唐的,因为巴里高大强壮,凶极了,跑得又快,山姆也挺行。如果这些狗认了真,它们可能没等他刺一刀,就已经把他扑翻在地,撕成碎片了。他本来该捡一根粗木棍,捡一件可以抢打狗的东西,一件狗冲过来时看得见,而且看了害怕的东西。但是这个人显然对狗不够了解,他只是低低地拿着刀,让刀身紧挨着右腿,继续往前走着。

那时我妈妈叫过了,巴里也停下来了,那个人就把刀身按回刀把,把刀放进口袋。要是知道那个陌生人口袋里有刀,许多女人准会害怕。就是说,如果是就只她们自个儿在屋里,身边除了一个9岁的男孩没有旁人。当时就我妈妈一个人在家,因为我爸爸出去了,厨娘黛里病了,在她自己的小屋里待着。但是我妈妈不害怕。她个子不大,做什么事都干脆利落,晒黑的脸上的蓝眼睛正视着每件事和每个人。她是县里第一个用跨式骑马的女人(这是在我出生之前很久,她还是个姑娘的时候)。我曾见到过她一把抓起气枪跑到外面,朝一只飞到她鸡场上空的小鹰打去,小鹰像只爆炸的飞靶似的从半空中摔下来。她是个稳重沉着、不依赖别人的女人。现在,在她死了那么多年之后,我一想起她,就会想起她那双棕色的手。手不大,比一般妇女的手宽,指甲老剪得平平整整的,不像是成年妇女的手,倒是更像小男孩的手。在那个时候,我从来没想到过她是会死的。

她在后廊上站着,看着那个人走过后门。那两只狗(巴里已经跳回院子里了)在院子里蹦来蹦去,嘴里呜噜呜噜的,不时斜眼瞟瞟我妈妈,想知道她刚才说的是否当真。那个人紧挨着狗走过来,身子几乎擦着它们,却根本不理会它们。现在我看得清他穿着旧咔叽裤和深色的毛料条纹外套,戴一顶灰色毡帽。他穿一件灰底蓝条衬衫,没结领带。但是我看见他口袋里塞了一条红蓝色相间的领带。他的穿戴哪儿都不对头。他本该穿蓝色工裤或工作服,戴顶草帽或者旧的黑毡帽。外衣呢,既然可能是毛料的,不是一件工作服,那上面就不该有这么些道道。尽管这些衣服又脏又旧,够得上是流浪汉的服装,但是显然和我们这个

snap out ready when you press a button in the handle. That knife must have had a button in the handle, or else how could he have had the blade out glittering so quick and with just one hand?

Pulling his knife against the dogs was a funny thing to do, for Bully was a big, powerful brute and fast, and Sam was all right. If those dogs had meant business, they might have knocked him down and ripped him before he got a stroke in. He ought to have picked up a heavy stick, something to take a swipe at them with and something which they could see and respect when they came at him. But he apparently did not know much about dogs. He just held the knife blade close against the right leg, low down, and kept on moving down the path.

Then my mother had called, and Bully had stopped. So the man let the blade of the knife snap back into the handle, and dropped it into his pocket, and kept on coming. Many women would have been afraid with the strange man who they knew had that knife in his pocket. That is, if they were alone in the house with nobody but a nine-year-old boy. And my mother was alone, for my father had gone off, and Dellie, the cook, was down at her cabin because she wasn't feeling well. But my mother wasn't afraid. She wasn't a big woman, but she was clear and brisk about everything she did and looked everybody and everything right in the eye from her own blue eyes in her tanned face. She had been the first woman in the country to ride a horse astride(that was back when she was a girl and long before I was born), and I have seen her snatch up a pump gun and go out and knock a chicken hawk out of the air like a busted skeet when he came over her chicken yard. She was a steady and self-reliant woman, and when I think of her now after all the years she has been dead, I think of her brown hands, not big, but somewhat square for a woman's hands, with square-cut nails. They looked, as a matter of fact, more like a young boy's hands than a grown woman's. But back then it never crossed my mind that she would ever be dead.

She stood on the back porch and watched the man enter the back gate, where the dogs(Bully had leaped back into the yard) were dancing and muttering and giving sidelong glances back to my mother to see if she meant what she had said. The man walked right by the dogs, almost brushing them, and didn't pay them any attention. I could see now that he wore old khaki pants, and a dark wool coat with stripes in it, and a gray felt hat. He had on a gray shirt with blue stripes in it, and no tie. But I could see a tie, blue and reddish, sticking in his side coat-pocket. Everything was wrong

地方不协调。这儿是后院,在小路尽头,田纳西州中部,离任何大城市都那么远,甚至离大道也还有一英里路。

他快走到台阶跟前时,还没开口,我妈妈就若无其事地说了声:"早上好。"

"早上好。"他说道,站住了,把她从上到下打量一番。他没脱帽。你可以在帽檐下看到一张毫无特征的脸,既不老也不年轻,既不胖也不瘦,脸色发灰,大约3天没刮胡子了。眼睛是难以形容的那一种,土褐色的,或者类似土褐色的,充血得厉害。他张开嘴时,参差不齐的黄牙露了出来。有两颗牙被打掉了。你知道是给打掉的,因为在下唇上,正对着缺口的地方,有道新伤疤。

"你在找活儿干吗?"我妈妈问他。

"是的,"他说——而不是说"是的,太太"——而且还不摘帽。

"我不知道我丈夫要不要人,因为他现在不在。"她说道,一点不在乎告诉这个口袋里有刀的流浪汉,或者不管他是什么人,近处没男人。"但是我可以给你找点活儿干干。我有不少鸡在暴风雨里淹死了。整整三笼呢。你可以把它们收拾出来埋了。要埋得深些,免得狗扒到。埋在林子里。再把鸡笼修好,让它们通风。在那头,在林子边上的家畜栏再过去的地方,还有一些被淹死的家禽。当时它们跑出来,我赶不回去,甚至在雨开始下大以后,它们都不肯进笼。小家禽就是没脑子。"

"是些什么东西——小家禽?"他问,往砖砌的小道上吐痰,再用脚去擦。这时,我看到他穿的是一双黑色的尖头低帮鞋,破得不像样了。在乡下穿这种鞋真是活见鬼。

"噢,是些小火鸡,"我妈妈说,"它们真傻透了。不管怎么说,我不该把它们放在这儿和那么多鸡一块儿养的。挨近鸡它们长不好,甚至分开笼养也不成。可我不愿放弃我的鸡。"说到这儿,她自己停下来,很快恢复了谈正事的口气。"你做完了这些事,可以再修整一下花圃。好多垃圾、稀泥块和石子都冲下来了。如果你小心点儿,也许能救活我的一些花儿。"

"花儿。"那人说,声音低低的,不带个人感情,似乎意味深长,却不是我理解得了的。我今天回想起来,这声音里也许并不完全是轻蔑,还不如说是对自己居然快要去花圃干力气活这件事,冷冷地表示一种与

about what he wore. He ought to have been wearing blue jeans or overalls, and a straw hat or an old black felt hat, and the coat, granting that he might have been wearing a wool coat and not a jumper, ought not to have had those stripes. Those clothes, despite the fact that they were old enough and dirty enough for any tramp, didn't belong there in our back yard, coming down the path, in Middle Tennessee, miles away from any big town, and even a mile off the pike.

When he got almost to the steps, without having said anything, my mother, very matter-of-factly, said, "Good morning."

"Good morning," he said, and stopped and looked her over. He did not take off his hat, and under the brim you could see the perfectly unmemorable face, which wasn't old and wasn't young, or thick or thin. It was grayish and covered with about three days of stubble. The eyes were a kind of nondescript, muddy hazel, or something like that, rather bloodshot. His teeth, when he opened his mouth, showed yellow and uneven. A couple of them had been knocked out. You knew that they had been knocked out, because there was a scar, not very old, there on the lower lip just beneath the gap.

"Are you hunting work?" my mother asked him.

"Yes," he said—not "yes, mam"—and still did not take off his hat.

"I don't know about my husband, for he isn't here," she said, and didn't mind a bit telling the tramp, or whoever he was, with the mean knife in his pocket, that no man was around, "but I can give you a few things to do. The storm has drowned a lot of my chicks. Three coops of them. You can gather them up and bury them. Bury them deep so the dogs won't get at them. In the woods. And fix the coops the wind blew over. And down yonder beyond that pen by the edge of the woods are some drowned poults. They got out and I couldn't get them in. Even after it started to rain hard. Poults haven't got any sense."

"What are them things—poults?" he demanded, and spat on the brick walk. He rubbed his foot over the spot, and I saw that he wore a black, pointed-toe low shoe, all cracked and broken. It was a crazy kind of shoe to be wearing in the country.

"Oh, they're young turkeys," my mother was saying. "And they haven't got any sense. I oughtn't to try to raise them around here with so many chickens, anyway. They don't thrive near chickens, even in separate pens. And I won't give up my chickens." Then she stopped herself and resumed briskly on the note of business. "When you finish that, you can fix my flower beds. A lot of trash and mud and gravel has washed

个人无关的惊讶。当时,他说完这个词后,就转过视线,朝院子对面望过去。

"是的,花儿。"我妈妈回答,声音有点严厉,似乎她不许人家说——或者暗示——反对花儿的话,"这些花儿今年本来长得很好。"她停下来,看着那个人,"你饿吗?"她问。

"是的。"他说。

她说:"我给你弄点吃的,你吃了再干。"她转过身来,命令我说,"给他带路,上那儿洗洗。"说完就进屋了。

我把那个人带到后廊尽头。那儿有个水泵,一个矮矮的木架上放着两只盆,让人好在进屋前洗洗。我站在那儿,他把他那裹着报纸的小包放下,摘下帽子,四处张望,找一个可以挂帽子的钉子。他倒上水,把手伸进去。他的手很大,看上去很有劲儿,却没有在户外干活的男人的手上通常有的那种皱褶和泥土色。但是手是很脏的,脏灰一直渗到皮肤和指甲里了。他洗完手,再倒一盆水洗脸,擦干了脸,手里还抓着毛巾就跨过去,到了墙上挂的镜子跟前。他用一只手摸摸脸上的胡子茬儿,然后细细端详自己的脸,先照这一边,再转过去照另一边,然后向后退一步,把条纹外衣披在肩上。你瞧他披上外衣,抚抚平,对着镜子细细端详自己的那副样子,就像是刚打扮好要上教堂或者去参加晚会似的。

他发现我在看他,就用那对充血的眼睛瞪了我一下,用一种低沉的粗暴的声音问:"你在看什么?"

"没什么。"我好容易才说出话来,从他面前后退了一步。

他把揉成一团的毛巾扔在架上,朝厨房门口走去,也没敲门就进去了。

我妈妈对他说了些什么,但是我听不见,我也开始往里走,随即想起了自己的光脚丫,就决定回到后院鸡场上去,那个人会上那儿收拾死鸡的。我在鸡舍后面晃来晃去,一直等到他出来。他走过鸡场时,动作里有种过分挑剔的神气,但还不完全是娇气。他朝下看着结成一块块的烂泥,上面斑斑点点沾了鸡屎,他那双黑鞋的鞋底也沾上了烂泥。我在他后面约摸 6 英尺远的地方站着,看着他捡起第一只被淹死的小鸡。他抓住鸡爪把鸡提起来,仔细观察。

再没比淹死的小鸡更难看的了。在我还是个小孩子的时候,像一般农村孩子那样,对杀猪、叉青蛙这

down. Maybe you can save some of my flowers if you are careful."

"Flowers," the man said, in a low, impersonal voice which seemed to have a wealth of meaning, but a meaning which I could not fathom. As I think back on it, it probably was not pure contempt. Rather, it was a kind of impersonal and distant marveling that he should be on the verge of grubbing in a flower bed. He said the word, and then looked off across the yard.

"Yes, flowers," my mother replied with some asperity, as though she would have nothing said or implied against flowers. "And they were very fine this year," Then she stopped and looked at the man. "Are you hungry?" she demanded.

"Yeah," he said.

"I'll fix you something," she said, "before you get started." She turned to me. "Show him where he can wash up," she commanded, and went into the house.

I took the man to the end of the porch where a pump was and where a couple of wash pans sat on a low shelf for people to use before they went into the house. I stood there while he laid down his little parcel wrapped in newspaper and took off his hat and looked around for a nail to hang it on. He poured the water and plunged his hands into it. They were big hands, and strong looking, but they did not have the creases and the earth-color of the hands of men who work outdoors. But they were dirty, with black dirt ground into the skin and under the nails. After he had washed his hands, he poured another basin of water and washed his face. He dried his face, and with the towel still dangling in his grasp, stepped over to the mirror on the house wall. He rubbed one hand over the stubble on his face. Then he carefully inspected his face, turning first one side and then the other, and stepped back and settled his striped coat down on his shoulders. He had the movements of a man who had just dressed up to go to church or a party—the way he settled his coat and smoothed it and scanned himself in the mirror.

Then he caught my glance on him. He glared at me for an instant out of the bloodshot eyes, then demanded in a low, harsh voice, "What you looking at?"

"Nothing," I managed to say, and stepped back a step from him. He flung the towel down, crumpled, on the shelf, and went toward the kitchen door and entered without knocking.

My mother said something to him which I could not catch. I started to go in again, then thought about my bare feet, and decided to go back of the chicken yard, where the man would have to come to pick up the dead chicks. I hung around behind the chicken house until he came out.

类事满不在乎,可是死鸡的鸡爪那种有气无力地、白白地蜷成一团的样子,我看了心里总不是味儿。小鸡的躯体不是胖乎乎,毛茸茸的,而全是一条条筋,毫无生气,绒毛全贴在上面,鸡脖子长长的,软软的,像一条破布条,眼睛上有层浅蓝色的薄膜,使你联想起一个病得奄奄一息的很老的老人。

那个人站在那儿细细查看小鸡,再朝四面看看,似乎不知道拿它怎么办好。

"小披屋那头有只很大很大的旧筐。"我指着和鸡舍连在一起的小屋说道。

他打量我一番,好像才发现我在场似的,然后朝小披屋走去。

"那儿还有一把铁锹。"我加上一句。他拿了筐,开始把其余的死鸡捡起来,每次慢慢地拎起一只鸡爪,然后用一种别扭的动作啪地朝筐里一扔。他不时用那双充血的眼睛瞟我一眼,每次看的时候都像是想说些什么,却又没有说出口。也许他是正想找点话来对我说说,但是我可不想等这么久。他看着我的那副神气使我那么不舒服,我离开了鸡场。

再说,我刚刚想起来,小河发大水了,把桥淹了,人们都上那儿看去了,所以,我就穿过农场朝小河走去。我走过烟草地时,看到庄稼损失不大,地里还是好好的,被水冲掉的烟草苗不算多,但是我知道我们附近一带有许多烟草苗给冲走了。吃早饭时,我爸爸这么说的。

我爸爸在桥边。我走出长满野桑树丛的那道沟上了大路时,看到他坐在马背上,突出在一群人的脑袋上面。他们站在他四周,正在观赏洪水。这一段的河面很宽,即使在水位不高的时候也是那样。小河在两英里路之外的地方汇入大河。真正的洪水来到的时候,红色的河水上了大路,再落到这座铁桥上,水远远高出桥面,甚至高出桥两边的栏杆,只有上半截铁架露出来,水在四周翻滚,冒着红色和白色的泡沫。这条小河涨起水来会这么快这么猛,因为它是从离这儿只有几英里路的山涧流下来的。每次一下雨,峡谷里马上灌满了水,小河在深深的河谷里奔流,河床两边全是石灰石的峭壁,一直到离铁桥 3/4 英里的地方才进入开阔地带。发洪水的时候,河水就像是从救火龙头里喷出来似的,从峭壁间冲出,奔腾翻滚,嘶嘶直响,还冒着汽。

每次一发大水,半个县的人都会赶来观看。不管

He moved across the chicken yard with a fastidious, not quite finicking motion, looking down at the curdled mud flecked with bits of chicken-droppings. The mud curled up over the soles of his black shoes. I stood back from him some six feet and watched him pick up the first of the drowned chicks. He held it up by one foot and inspected it.

There is nothing deader looking than a drowned chick. The feet curl in that feeble, empty way which back when I was a boy, even if I was a country boy who did not mind hog-killing or frog-gigging, made me feel hollow in the stomach. Instead of looking plump and fluffy, the body is stringy and limp with the fluff plastered to it, and the neck is long and loose like a little string of rag. And the eyes have that bluish membrane over them which makes you think of a very old man who is sick about to die.

The man stood there and inspected the chick. Then he looked all around as though he didn't know what to do with it.

"There's a great big old basket in the shed," I said, and pointed to the shed attached to the chicken house.

He inspected me as though he had just discovered my presence, and moved toward the shed.

"There's a spade there, too," I added.

He got the basket and began to pick up the other chicks, picking each one up slowly by a foot and then flinging it into the basket with a nasty, snapping motion. Now and then he would look at me out of the bloodshot eyes. Every time he seemed on the verge of saying something, but he did not. Perhaps he was building up to say something to me, but I did not wait that long. His way of looking at me made me so uncomfortable that I left the chicken yard.

Besides, I had just remembered that the creek was in flood, over the bridge, and that people were down there watching it. So I cut across the farm toward the creek. When I got to the big tobacco field I saw that it had not suffered much. The land lay right and not many tobacco plants had washed out of the ground. But I knew that a lot of tobacco round the country had been washed right out. My father had said so at breakfast.

My father was down at the bridge. When I came out of the gap in the osage hedge into the road, I saw him sitting on his mare over the heads of the other men who were standing around, admiring the flood. The creek was big here, even in low water; for only a couple of miles away it ran into the river, and when a real flood came, the red water got over the pike where it dipped down to the bridge, which was an iron bridge, and high over the floor and even the side railings

怎么说,下过一场倾盆大雨后,就什么活儿也没有了。如果大水没毁了你的庄稼,你不能耕地,就会很想休息一天庆贺一下。如果庄稼毁了,你更什么也干不了,只有压制自己不去想抵押的问题,就是说,如果你还有东西可以抵押的话。而如果你没法抵押,那你就需要有点东西来分分心,不去想到了圣诞节你的肚子该有多饿。所以,人们这时就会上桥边观看洪水。这使生活显得与平时有些不同。

大家在最初几分钟里估估这次水涨得多高,以后就没很多话好讲了。男人和孩子们光是四下站站,有的骑在马背和驴背上,或者站在大车底座上。他们看着洪水的奇异景象,看上一两个钟头,然后有个人会说该回家吃饭了,就动身走下颜色发灰的、全是水坑、泥潭的石灰石大路,或者用脚踢踢他的坐骑,就离开了。其实人人知道到了桥那儿会看到什么样的景象,可每次还总是要来,就像是上教堂或者参加葬礼似的。他们总要来的,就是说,如果这是在夏天而且水又来得出乎意外。从来没有人在冬天上河边看涨水的。我从长着柑橘树丛的土沟里走出来时,看见了这群人。大约有 15 至 20 个男人,还有许多孩子。我看见我爸爸骑在他的母马耐里·格雷的身上。爸爸是个高个儿,动作灵活,举止潇洒。看到他骑在马上,我总是感到骄傲,他在马上是那么安详,那么挺直。那天早上我跨出矮树丛里的土沟后,我记得我首先感到的就是心头涌上了一股暖流。每当见到他在马上,光这么坐着,我就总产生这种暖洋洋的感觉。我没朝他走过去,而是从人群的另一头绕过去看小河。因为首先,我拿不准他对我光着脚这件事会怎么说。可是,我马上听到他在喊我了:"赛斯!"

我朝他走去,带歉意地穿进人群。他们低下头来看我,他们的脸有的又红又胖,有的又黄又瘦。我认识其中一些人,知道他们的名字,但是我认得的人在人群中和一些陌生人混在一起,就显得和我也是素不相识的,而且不友好。我一直走到快到我爸爸的脚跟碰得着的地方才抬头看。我往上看,想观察一下爸爸的脸色,看看他是不是因为我光着脚在生气了。我还没从这张颧骨高高的、没有表情的脸上看出究竟来,爸爸已经弯下腰来,把一只手伸给我了。"抓住。"他命令道。

我抓住了,稍稍跳了一下,他说:"上来——上来——来!"他轻轻一提,就把我放到了他那副马克兰

of the bridge. Only the upper iron work would show, with the water boiling and frothing red and white around it. That creek rose so fast and so heavy because a few miles back it came down out of the hills, where the gorges filled up with water in no time when a rain came. The creek ran in a deep bed with limestone bluffs along both sides until I got within three quarters of a mile of the bridge, and when it came out from between those bluffs in flood it was boiling and hissing and steaming like water from a fire house.

Whenever there was a flood, people from half the county would come down to see the sight. After a gully-washer there would not be any work to do anyway. If it didn't ruin your crop, you couldn't plow and you felt like taking a holiday to celebrate it. If it did ruin your crop, there wasn't anything to do except to try to take your mind off the mortgage, if you were rich enough to have a mortgage, and if you couldn't afford a mortgage you needed something to take your mind off how hungry you would be by Christmas. So people would come down to the bridge and look at the flood. It made something different from the run of days.

There would not be much talking after the first few minutes of trying to guess how high the water was this time. The men and kids just stood around, or sat their horses or mules, as the case might be, or stood up in the wagon beds. They looked at the strangeness of the flood for an hour or two, and then somebody would say that he had better be getting on home to dinner and would start walking down the gray, puddled limestone pike, or would touch heel to his mount and start off. Everybody always knew what it would be like when he got down to the bridge, but people always came. It was like church or a funeral. They always came, that is, if it was summer and the flood unexpected. Nobody ever came down in winter to see high water.

When I came out of the gap in the bowdock hedge, I saw the crowd, perhaps fifteen or twenty men and a lot of kids, and saw my father sitting his mare, Nellie Gray. He was a tall, limber man and carried himself well. I was always proud to see him sit a horse, he was so quiet and straight, and when I stepped through the gap of the hedge that morning, the first thing that happened was, I remember, the warm feeling I always had when I saw him up on a horse, just sitting. I did not go toward him, but skirted the crowd on the far side, to get a look at the creek. For one thing, I was not sure what he would say about the fact that I was barefoot. But the first thing I knew, I heard his voice calling, "Seth!"

伦式马鞍的前桥上，好像我只有一根羽毛的分量。

"你在这儿可以看得清楚些。"爸爸在马鞍的弓形部分上往后挪了一点儿，好让我坐得舒服些，然后从我头顶上望出去，看着汹涌澎湃的河水，好像把我全忘了。但是他的右手放在我身子右侧，就在大腿上边一点儿的地方，好让我坐稳了。

我坐在那儿尽量不动，感到爸爸的胸膛挨着我的肩膀，随着他呼吸的一起一伏，在微微动弹。就在这个时候我看见了那只母牛。起初我朝小河上游看去，还以为这又是一大块浮木，正顺翻滚的河水冲下来。但是，一个身材高大的男孩为了看清楚些，已爬上大路边上一根电话线杆的半腰，这时喊起来了："我的妈，快看那只母牛！"

大家都去看。没问题，这是只母牛，但是也可以把它看做浮木，因为它已僵死得成了一块硬邦邦的东西，正顺着河水流下来，忽沉忽浮，一会儿脚朝上，一会儿头朝上，反正是什么朝上都无所谓了。

母牛使大家重新谈开了。有人在猜测这只牛会不会正好流进铁桥顶梁下面的一个空当儿里，通了过去，或者会缠在已经堆积在直梁和支柱边上的垃圾和漂浮物里。有个人记起来，大约在 10 年前，有一次桥上堆上那么多浮木，结果弄得桥身和桥墩都脱开了。这时，牛撞到桥了，它撞在堆在一根直梁一旁的漂浮物堆边上，就挂住了。有那么几秒钟，它好像快扯开去了。但是我们很快就看到它真给卡住了。它用一种缓慢不安的、让人看了难受的方式，上下浮动着，脖子上套了一个牛轭，这是有分杈的粗树枝做的牛轭，用来套住爱跳的牛，好让它们待在栅栏里。

"它肯定是跳过栅栏出来的。"有个人说。

"嗯，它倒真是最后一次跳了栅栏了。"

接着，他们开始猜测这可能是谁的牛。他们判定这是米尔特·阿莱的牛，他们说他有一头爱跳越障碍物的牛，养在小河上游一块四周有栅栏围住的地方。我从来没见过米尔特·阿莱，但是我知道这个人。他是个私占公地的人，住在远处山上，他的小屋盖在能引起纠纷的土地上，那块地皮只有衬衫后摆那么大。他是个穷白人，有许许多多儿女。他们去上学时我在学校见过。他们的脸瘦瘦的，头发又直又硬，跟棍儿似的，颜色就像生面团，身上有股发馊的酸奶的味儿，这并不是因为他们喝了好多酸牛奶，住在那种小屋的孩子身上都有这种味儿。阿莱家的大男孩总画些

I went toward him, moving apologetically past the men, who bent their large, red or thin, sallow faces above me. I knew some of the men, and knew their names, but because those I knew were there in a crowd, mixed with the strange faces, they seemed foreign to me, and not friendly. I did not look up at my father until I was almost within touching distance of his heel. Then I looked up and tried to read his face, to see if he was angry about my being barefoot. Before I could decide anything from that impassive, high-boned face, he had leaned over and reached a hand to me. "Grab on," he commanded.

I grabbed on and gave a little jump, and he said, "Up-see-daisy!" and whisked me, light as a feather, up to the pommel of his McClellan saddle.

"You can see better up here," he said, slid back on the cantle a little to make me more comfortable, and then, looking over my head at the swollen, tumbling water, seemed to forget all about me. But his right hand was laid on my side, just above my thigh, to steady me.

I was sitting there as quiet as I could, feeling the faint stir of my father's chest against my shoulders as it rose and fell with his breath, when I saw the cow. At first, looking up the creek, I thought it was just another big piece of driftwood steaming down the creek in the ruck of water, but all at once a pretty good-size boy who had climbed part way up a telephone pole by the pike so that he could see better yelled out, "Golly-damn, look at that-air cow!"

Everybody looked. It was a cow all right, but it might just as well have been driftwood; for it was dead as a chunk, rolling and rolling down the creek, appearing and disappearing, feet up or head up, it didn't matter which.

The cow started up the talk again. Somebody wondered whether it would hit one of the clear places under the top girder of the bridge and get through or whether it would get tangled in the drift and trash that had piled against the upright girders and braces. Somebody remembered how about ten years before so much driftwood had piled up on the bridge that it was knocked off its foundations. Then the cow hit. It hit the edge of the drift against one of the girders, and hung there. For a few seconds it seemed as though it might tear loose, but then we saw that it was really caught. It bobbed and heaved on its side there in a slow, grinding, uneasy fashion. It had a yoke around its neck, the kind made out of a forked limb to keep a jumper behind fence.

"She shore jumped one fence," one of the men said.

下流画儿给学校里的小男孩看。

这是米尔特·阿莱家的母牛。他家的牛想来也就是这样的：干瘦、衰老，背部凹了过去，脖子上套了牛轭。米尔特·阿莱是否还有第二头母牛，我很怀疑。

"爸爸，"我问，"你说米尔特·阿莱还有另外一头母牛吗？"

"你应该说'米尔特·阿莱先生'。"我爸爸静静地说道。

"你认为他有没有？"

"说不上。"我爸爸说。

那儿有一个高高的、瘦得难看的男孩，15岁光景，骑在一头矮小的皮包骨的老毛驴上，驴背上铺了一块麻袋片，驴脊梁骨像锯齿似的一节节突了出来。他一直瞪着眼看着那条母牛，这时突然也不是专对哪一个就说话了："不知道有没有人吃过淹死了的牛的肉？"

他虽然不是米尔特·阿莱的儿子，但和阿莱的孩子完全是一个类型的。褪色的工装裤打了补丁，裤子屁股后面全破了，一双沾上泥后发硬的大皮靴齐着牲口腹部耷拉着，露出了赤裸着的瘦骨嶙峋的脚踝。他说了上面的话，人们的眼光都转向他，他感到不好意思，很不高兴。他本来是不想说出来的，这点我现在很肯定。他太骄傲了，不肯说的，米尔特·阿莱也是这么骄傲的。他只是不知不觉地把自己想的话脱口说了出来。

大路上站着一个白胡子老头。"孩子，"他对骑在驴背上的那个又窘又不高兴的男孩说道，"如果你活得时间长些，你就会发现一个人到时候什么都会吃。"

"今年就有些人会碰到这种时候。"另一个人说道。

"孩子，"老人说，"我那个时候吃过的东西，人们连想都不愿意去想。我当过兵，我跟着福历斯特①骑马打仗。我们吃的那些东西呢，我来告诉你吧。我吃的那些肉，你拔出刀割一片放在火上烤后，它们还能站起来跑！它们还是欢蹦乱跳的，你得用枪托把它打倒。那些肉会像牛蛙那样蹦起来，因为肉里的蛆太多了。"

但是没人在听老头讲话。驴背上的男孩把他那

---

① 福历斯特(N. B. Forrest, 1821—1877)，美国内战时期南方军队的将领。

And another: "Well, she done jumped her last one, fer a fack."

Then they began to wonder about whose cow it might be. They decided it must belong to Milt Alley. They said that he had a cow that was a jumper, and kept her in a fenced-in piece of ground up the creek. I had never seen Milt Alley, but I knew who he was. He was a squatter and lived up the hills a way, on a shirt-tail patch of set-on-edge land, in a cabin. He was pore white trash. He had lots of children. I had seen the children at school, when they came. They were thin-faced, with straight, sticky-looking, dough-colored hair, and they smelled something like old sour butter-milk, not because they drank so much buttermilk but because that is the sort of smell which children out of those cabins tend to have. The big Alley boy drew dirty pictures and showed them to the little boys at school.

That was Milt Alley's cow. It looked like the kind of cow he would have, a scrawny, old, sway-backed cow, with a yoke around her neck. I wondered if Milt Alley had another cow.

"Poppa," I said, "do you think Milt Alley has got another cow?"

"You say 'Mr. Alley,'" my father said quietly.

"Do you think he has?"

"No telling," my father said.

Then a big gangly boy, about fifteen, who was sitting on a scraggly little old mule with a piece of croker sack thrown across the saw-tooth spine, and who had been staring at the cow, suddenly said to nobody in particular, "Reckin anybody ever et drownt cow?"

He was the kind of boy who might just as well as not have been the son of Milt Alley, with his faded and patched overalls ragged at the bottom of the pants and the mud-stiff brogans hanging off his skinny, bare ankles at the level of the mule's. belly. He had said what he did, and then looked embarrassed and sullen when all the eyes swung at him. He hadn't meant to say it, I am pretty sure now. He would have been too proud to say it, just as Milt Alley would have been too proud. He had just been thinking out loud, and the words had popped out.

There was an old man standing there on the pike, an old man with a white beard. "Son," he said to the embarrassed and sullen boy on the mule, "you live long enough and you'll find a man will eat anything when the time comes."

"Time gonna come fer some folks this year," another man said.

"Son," the old man said, "in my time I et things a man don't like to think on. I was a sojer and I rode

张怒气冲冲的脸转开，一只脚跟往驴身上一踢，走开到大路上去了。那种动作使你想到，你立刻就要听到驴骨头在那张干枯的、满是癞疥的外皮里面互相碰撞的声音了。

"这是西·丹地的儿子。"一个男人说，朝骑着驴正在上尖峰的那个身影点点头。

"我看西·丹地的孩子也得经历那种有淹死的牛吃就很满意的时候了。"另一个人说道。

长胡子的老头用他那双视力衰退、目光迟钝的眼睛瞪着他们，先看看这一个，再看看那一个。"活得时间一久，一个人就不管吃什么都能对付了。"

又是一片沉默，人们只是望着发红的，好多处起泡沫的河水。

我爸爸提起左手里的缰绳，母马转过身来，绕过人群，上了尖峰。我们往前走去，一直走到我们家大门口。我爸爸下马把门打开，让我一个人骑着耐里·格雷进去。到了那条从大车道分岔出来的小路上，离我们房子约200码的地方，我爸爸说了声："抓好了。"我抓好了，他就让我下地。"我要骑马上那边看着庄稼，"他说，"你自己走吧。"他顺小路走了，我站在车道上，看着他骑着马走开。他穿着牛皮靴和一件旧猎装，我认为这身打扮和他的骑姿使他显得富有军人气派，就像画上的军人似的。

我没朝屋子走，而是顺菜园边上走，穿过马厩后面，朝黛里的小屋走去。我想上那儿和小约伯玩。他是黛里的儿子，比我大2岁左右。再说，我也感到冷。我一面走一面打哆嗦，浑身起鸡皮疙瘩。我每走一步，冷得像冰碴儿的稀泥就往脚趾缝里钻。黛里那儿会生火，她也不会强迫我穿上鞋袜。

黛里的小屋是木头造的，因为盖在山坡上，小屋有一边搭在石灰岩石上面，小屋连着一个小走廊，周围有漆成白色的栅栏，一扇门上系了一条带有几片犁铧的细绳，有人进门，绳上就会丁当作响。院子里有两棵大白橡树，种了一些花，屋后有个挺像样的厕所，上面还爬满了忍冬花，黛里和约伯的爸爸老约伯已经在一起过了25年，虽然他们没正式结过婚。这两个人精心照料，把他们房前屋外所有一切都搞得整洁美观。他们是这一带居民中有名的利索聪明的黑人。黛里和约伯是人们常说的那种"白人的黑人"。他们的小屋和再往远去的另外两间租给其他黑人的小屋有很大不同，我爸爸把这些房子修整得风雨不透，但

with Gin'l Forrest, and them things we et when the time come. I tell you. I et meat what got up and run when you taken out yore knife to cut a slice to put on the fire. You had to knock it down with a carbeen butt, it was so active. That-air meat would jump like a bullfrog, it was so full of skippers. "

But nobody was listening to the old man. The boy on the mule turned his sullen sharp face from him, dug a heel into the side of the mule and went off up the pike with a motion which made you think that any second you would hear mule bones clashing inside that lank and scrofulous hide.

"Cy Dundee's boy," a man said, and nodded toward the figure going up the pike on the mule.

"Reckin Cy Dundee's young-uns seen times they'd settle fer drownt cow," another man said.

The old man with the beard peered at them both from his weak, slow eyes, first at one and then at the other. "Live long enough," he said, "and a man will settle fer what he kin git. "

Then there was silence again, with the people looking at the red, foam-flecked water.

My father lifted the bridle rein in his left hand, and the mare turned and walked around the group and up the pike. We rode on up to our big gate, where my father dismounted to open it and let me myself ride Nellie Gray through. When he got to the lane that led off from the drive about two hundred yards from our house, my father said, "Grab on. " I grabbed on, and he let me down to the ground. "I'm going to ride down and look at my corn," he said. "You go on. " He took the lane, and I stood there on the drive and watched him ride off. He was wearing cowhide boots and an old hunting coat, and I thought that that made him look very military, like a picture. That and the way he rode.

I did not go the house. Instead, I went by the vegetable garden and crossed behind the stables, and headed down for Dellie's cabin. I wanted to go down and play with Jebb, who was Dellie's little boy about two years older than I was. Besides, I was cold. I shivered as I walked, and I had goose-flesh. The mud which crawled up between my toes with every step I took was like ice. Dellie would have a fire, but she wouldn't make me put on shoes and stockings.

Dellie's cabin was of logs, with one side, because it was on a slope, set on limestone chunks, with a little porch attached to it, and had a little whitewashed fence around it and a gate with plow-points on a wire to clink when somebody came in, and had two big white oaks in the yard and some flowers and a nice privy in the back with some honeysuckle growing over it. Dellie and Old Jebb, who was Jebb's father and who lived

是他总不能上那儿去跟在后面收拾他们扔得哪儿都是的垃圾。他们不像黛里和约伯那样搞个菜园,像黛里那样把野梅制成果酱,把酸苹果做成果子冻,他们不肯费这个工夫。他们得过且过。我爸爸老是威胁着要把他们赶出小屋,但是他从来没赶过。当他们最后终于离开了,他们就是这么自己拔起脚来走了,什么原因也没有,又上别的地方混去了。于是,就有另外一些黑人来了。眼下住在那儿的有曼特·罗逊和他的一家,以及锡德·透纳一家。他们的孩子不干活儿的时候,我和他们在农场上到处玩。但是我不在眼前的时候,他们有时就欺负小约伯,因为那儿的房客全都妒忌黛里和约伯。

我感到这么冷,到黛里大门口那最后50码是跑着去的。我一进门就发现这场暴风雨对黛里可真不留情。我说过了,她那院子是在一个坡度很小的山坡上的。涌过院子的水把花圃给毁了,把黛里弄来的肥沃的森林黑土也给冲掉了。院子里那一点点青草现在稀稀拉拉地紧贴在地面上,就像是阴沟水流过以后那样。这使我想起了那个陌生人在我妈妈的养鸡场上捡起来的那些淹死的小鸡,它们的绒毛也是这么贴在皮肤上的。

我在通往屋子的小路上走了几步,就看到阴沟水已经把黛里屋子下面的许多垃圾和脏东西冲出来了,朝平台方向的地面再也不干净了。破布片、两三个生锈的空罐头盒、一截截烂绳子、几大块干狗屎、碎玻璃、废纸和种种这一类的东西从黛里房子下面给冲了出来,把她那干干净净的院子搞得臭气冲天。院子看上去就和另外两间小屋的院子一样糟,或者更糟。实际上是更糟,因为事出意料之外。我从来没想到过黛里屋子下会有这些脏东西。其实这一点儿不能怪她。什么屋子下面都会进去垃圾的。但是在那个时候,在我看到那些被水冲出来的脏东西堆在院子里的时候,我并没那么想。黛里有时爱用一把细树枝捆的扫把把那个院子打扫得又干净又漂亮。

我从垃圾里找路走,小心不让光脚踩在脏东西上。我向上走,来到黛里家门口,敲了敲门,听到她叫我进去的声音。

大白天从外面进去,屋里显得很黑,但是我看得出黛里斜倚在床上,身上盖了一条被子。小约伯缩着身子蹲在壁炉前,那里有一堆火在慢吞吞地燃烧着。"你好,"我对黛里说,"你觉得怎么样了?"

with Dellie and had lived with her for twenty-five years even if they never had got married, were careful to keep everything nice around their cabin. They had the name all over the community for being clean and clever Negroes. Dellie and Jebb were what they used to call "whitefolks' niggers." There was a big difference between their cabin and the other two cabins farther down where the other tenants lived. My father kept the other cabins weatherproof, but he couldn't undertake to go down and pick up after the litter they strewed. They didn't take the trouble to have a vegetable patch like Dellie and Jebb or to make preserves from wild plum, and jelly from crab apple the way Dellie did. They were shiftless, and my father was always threatening to get shed of them. But he never did. When they finally left, they just up and left on their own, for no reason, to go and be shiftless somewhere else. Then some more came. But meanwhile they lived down there, Matt Rawson and his family, and Sid Turner and his, and I played with their children all over the farm when they weren't working. But when I wasn't around they were mean sometimes to Little Jebb. That was because the other tenants down there were jealous of Dellie and Jebb.

I was so cold that I ran the last fifty yards to Dellie's gate. As soon as I had entered the yard, I saw that the storm had been hard on Dellie's flowers. The yard was, as I have said, on a slight slope, and the water running across had gutted the flower beds and washed out all the good black woods-earth which Dellie had brought in. What little grass there was in the yard was plastered sparsely down on the ground, the way the drainage water had left it. It reminded me of the way the fluff was plastered down on the skin of the drowned chicks that the strange man had been picking up, up in my mother's chicken yard.

I took a few steps up the path to the cabin, and then I saw that the drainage water had washed a lot of trash and filth out from under Dellie's house. Up toward the porch, the ground was not clean any more. Old pieces of rag, two or three rusted cans, pieces of rotten rope, some hunks of old dog dung, broken glass, old paper, and all sorts of things like that had washed out from under Dellie's house to foul her clean yard. It looked just as bad as the yards of the other cabins, or worse. It was worse, as a matter of fact, because it was a surprise. I had never thought of all that filth being under Dellie's house. It was not anything against Dellie that the stuff had been under the cabin. Trash will get under any house. But I did not think of that when I saw the foulness which had washed out on the ground which Dellie sometimes used to sweep

我站在那儿，但是她不答话，她那双大眼睛盯住我，眼白在黑脸上闪闪发亮，显得令人吃惊。模样和举止一点儿都不像黛里。黛里总是在厨房里忙得团团转，嘴里叽里咕噜的，或是自言自语，或是训斥我和小约伯，她把锅碗瓢盆弄得丁当乱响，发出各种不必要的噪音和嘟嘟囔囔的声音，就像一部老式的黑色蒸汽机头有了一个额外的蒸汽压力，不断砰砰噗嗵地冲撞调节器，轮子也震得轰隆隆直响。但是现在黛里只是那么躺在床上，盖着一条用各种颜色的布头拼起来的被子，她把那张我几乎认不出来了的黑脸转过来，那双眼白白得发亮的眼睛对着我。

"你感到怎么样了？"我又问了一遍。

"我病了。"那张陌生的黑脸发出了嘶哑的声音，这张脸不是长在黛里那个又短又粗的躯体上的，而是从一堆乱七八糟的被窝里面伸出来的。这个声音又添了一句："病得很厉害。"

"我很难过。"我好容易挤出一句话来。

那双眼睛一动也不动地盯了我一会儿，从我身上挪开，她的脑袋又滚回到枕头上去。"难过。"那个声音说，声调呆板，既不是在提问也不在说明任何事情。这只是一个空空洞洞的字眼，既没有意义也不带表情地放到空气中，让它像一口烟雾或是一根羽毛那样飘浮过去，与此同时，一双大眼睛直愣愣地瞪着天花板，眼白就像剥了壳的煮老的鸡蛋的蛋白。

"黛里，"我过了一会儿说，"我们房子那儿也有个流浪汉，他有一把刀。"

她没在听，她闭上了眼睛。

我踮着脚尖走到炉火前，在小约伯身边蹲下。我们开始低声交谈。我要他把火车拿出来玩。老约伯把一些空的线轴钉在三个雪茄烟盒下面，盒子之间用线接上，给小约伯做了一列火车。充当火车头的那个烟盒的盒盖是盖上的，插了一截扫帚把当烟囱。约伯不肯把火车拿出来，但是我对他说，如果他不拿，我就回家。所以他就把火车拿出来了，还拿了彩色石子、海百合肢体的化石和其他一些破烂，这都是他经常用来当做运载的货物的。我们开始推着火车转，用一种我们自认为是铁路工作人员的谈话方式来交谈，压低嗓门发出"咔嚓"、"咔嚓"的声音来表示火车头的响声，还不时小心翼翼、轻轻地叫着"突——突——突"代表鸣汽笛。我们玩得那么起劲儿，"突突"声越来越响了。在小火车过交叉路口时，小约伯忘乎所以，又

with a twig broom to make nice and clean.

I picked my way past the filth, being careful not to get my bare feet on it, and mounted to Dellie's door. When I knocked, I heard her voice telling me to come in.

It was dark inside the cabin, after the daylight, but I could make out Dellie piled up in bed under a quilt, and Little Jebb crouched by the hearth, where a low fire simmered. "Howdy," I said to Dellie, "how you feeling?"

Her big eyes, the whites surprising and glaring in the black face, fixed on me as I stood there, but she did not reply. It did not look like Dellie, or act like Dellie, who would grumble and bustle around our kitchen, talking to herself, scolding me or Little Jebb, clanking pans, making all sorts of unnecessary noises and mutterings like an oldfashioned black steam thrasher engine when it has got up an extra head of steam and keeps popping the governor and rumbling and shaking on its wheels. But now Dellie just lay there on the bed, under the patchwork quilt, and turned the black face, which I scarcely recognized, and the glaring white eyes to me.

"How you feeling?" I repeated.

"I'se sick," the voice said croakingly out of the strange black face which was not attached to Dellie's big, squat body, but stuck out from under a pile of tangled bedclothes. Then the voice added: "Mighty sick."

"I'm sorry," I managed to say.

The eyes remained fixed on me for a moment, then they left me and the head rolled back on the pillow. "Sorry," the voice said, in a flat way which wasn't question or statement of anything. It was just the empty word put into the air with no meaning or expression, to float off like a feather or a puff of smoke, while the big eyes, with the whites like the peeled white of hard-boiled eggs, stared at the ceiling.

"Dellie," I said after a minute, "there's a tramp up at the house. He's got a knife."

She was not listening. She closed her eyes.

I tiptoed over to the hearth where Jebb was and crouched beside him. We began to talk in low voices. I was asking him to get out his train and play train. Old Jebb had put spool wheels on three cigar boxes and put wire links between the boxes to make a train for Jebb. The box that was the locomotive had the top closed and a length of broom stick for a smoke stack. Jebb didn't want to get the train out, but I told him I would go home if he didn't. So he got out the train, and the colored rocks, and fossils of crinoid stems, and other junk he used for the load, and we began to push it around, talking the way we thought trainmen

响又亮地大叫了一声,"突——突。"

"到这儿来。"床上的声音说道。

小约伯慢慢地从地上抬起他的两手和双膝,突然给我一个明显的充满敌意的眼色。

"到这儿来!"声音说道。

约伯向床边走去。黛里有气无力地用一只胳臂支起身子,咕哝道:"走近点。"

约伯站近了些。

"这是我最不愿意做的事,可是我要做了,"黛里说,"对你说了要安静。"

她掴他嘴巴。这是可怕的一巴掌,由于出自这种软弱的状态而集中了全部力气,因此就显得更为可怕。我以前见过她打约伯,但是只是随便打打,容易忍受,你可以料到,像黛里这样一个心地善良,爱发牢骚的黑女人就会这么打的。但是这次可不一样了。这次是可怕的,约伯连一声都没吭,只是眼泪直冒。泪水顺着脸流下,呼吸也变得急促了,像在喘气。

黛里倒回床上。"连生病都不行,"她对天花板说,"你病了,他们连躺都不让你躺。他们在你身上践踏。连生病都做不到。"她说完,就闭上了眼睛。

我走出房间。我几乎是跑到房门口的。我真是跑着穿过平台,冲下台阶,出了院子的,根本不在乎是不是踩着那些从小屋下面冲出来的垃圾了。我几乎是一路跑回家的。我随即想到了我妈妈要逮住我光着脚,就向走廊走去了。

我听见小屋里有响动,就把门打开。老约伯坐在一只旧铁桶上,把玉米剥在一只容量一蒲式耳的大筐里。我走进去,把门在我身后带上,挨着他蹲在地上。我蹲在那儿有一两分钟,我们两人都没开口,我看着他剥玉米。

他的一双手很大,骨节突出,颜色发灰,手掌上全是茧子,看上去好像被铁锈分成一条条似的,铁锈还顺手指缝向上延伸,让人在手背上也可以看见。他的双手非常有劲儿且粗糙,他可以拿住一只大玉米棒子,用手掌把玉米粒从壳上搓下来,只要一个动作就行了,简直跟机器一个样。"像我干了这么久的活儿,"他会说,"慈悲的上帝就会给你一双铁铸的手,没有任何东西可以伤害它。"而他的双手确实像铁铸的,像有一条条铁锈的旧铸铁。

他是个老头,70开外了,比黛里大30岁,甚至还不止,但是壮得像头牛。他是那种矮墩子,肩膀宽厚,

talked, making a chuck-chucking sound under the breath for the noise of the locomotive and now and then uttering low, cautious toots for the whistle. We got so interested in playing train that the toots got louder. Then, before he thought, Jebb gave a good, loud *toot-toot*, blowing for a crossing.

"Come here," the voice said from the bed.

Jebb got up slow from his hands and knees, giving me a sudden, naked, inimical look.

"Come here!" the voice said.

Jebb went to the bed. Dellie propped herself weakly up on one arm, muttering, "Come closer."

Jebb stood closer.

"Last thing I do, I'm gonna do it," Dellie said. "Done tole you to be quiet."

Then she slapped him. It was an awful slap, more awful for the kind of weakness which it came from and brought to focus. I had seen her slap Jebb before, but the slapping had always been the kind of easy slap you would expect from a good-natured, grumbling Negro woman like Dellie. But this was different. It was awful. It was so awful that Jebb didn't make a sound. The tears just popped out and ran down his face, and his breath came sharp, like gasps.

Dellie fell back. "Cain't even be sick," she said to the ceiling. "Git sick and they won't even let you lay. They tromp all over you. Cain't even be sick." Then she closed her eyes.

I went out of the room. I almost ran getting to the door, and I did run across the porch and down the steps and across the yard, not caring whether or not I stepped on the filth which had washed out from under the cabin. I ran almost all the way home. Then I thought about my mother catching me with the bare feet. So I went down to the stables.

I heard a noise in the crib, and opened the door. There was Big Jebb, sitting on an old nail keg, shelling corn into a bushel basket. I went in, pulling the door shut behind me, and crouched on the floor near him. I crouched there for a couple of minutes before either of us spoke, and watched him shelling the corn.

He had very big hands, knotted and grayish at the joints, with callused palms which seemed to be streaked with rust with the rust coming up between the fingers to show from the back. His hands were so strong and tough that he could take a big ear of corn and rip the grains right off the cob with the palm of his hand, all in one motion, like a machine. "Work long as me," he would say, "and the good Lawd'll give you a hand lak cass-ion won't nuthin' hurt." And his hands did look like cast iron, old cast iron streaked with rust.

He was an old man, up in his seventies, thirty

两臂长得出奇。人们说刚果沿河土著因为老在船上划桨,就长成了这种身材。他的脑袋像枚子弹,圆乎乎的,安在强有力的肩膀上。他的皮肤黑极了,头上那层稀薄的头发现在鬈曲着,像一条旧棉花胎。眼睛很小,鼻子扁平,但不大,有一张世界上最善良最聪明的老脸,这是一张老动物的坦率、聪明而又悲为的脸,它在宽容地注视着他面前芸芸众生的活动。他是个好人,除了我爸爸妈妈,我最爱的就是他了。我在小屋的地上蹲着,看他用生锈的铸铁般的双手剥玉米,他那坦率的脸上的一双小眼睛朝下望着我。

"黛里说她病得很厉害。"我说。

"是的。"他说。

"她生什么病?"

"妇女病。"他说。

"什么是妇女病?"

"这种病找上她们,"他说,"一到时候她们就生这种病。"

"是什么病?"

"这是一种变化,"他说,"这是生命和时间的变化。"

"什么变化?"

"你太小了,不会懂。"

"告诉我。"

"到时候你就会明白一切的。"

我知道再问也没用了。当我问他一些事,他这么回答了,我就总是明白他不肯告诉我了,所以我还是缩着身子坐在那儿看他。现在我坐了有一会儿了,又感到冷了。

"你怎么打哆嗦了?"他问我。

"我冷。我冷,因为这是春寒。"

"也许是也许不是。"

"妈妈说是的。"

"我没说莎莉小姐不知道,也没说她知道。但是一个人不会样样事情都知道。"

"为什么这不是春寒?"

"季节太晚了,乌莓早就开过花了。"

"她说是春寒。"

"春寒是时间很短的一段小寒潮,它来了又去了,于是夏天就像打了一炮那样突然来到了。我说不上这次寒流会不会离开。"

"是 6 月了。"我说。

years or more older than Dellie, but he was strong as a bull. He was a squat sort of man, heavy in the shoulders, with remarkably long arms the kind of build they say the river natives have on the Congo from paddling so much in their boats. He had a round bullet-head, set on powerful shoulders. His skin was very black, and the thin hair on his head was now grizzled like tufts of old cotton batting. He had small eyes and a flat nose, not big, and the kindest and wisest old face in the world, the blunt, sad, wise face of an old animal peering tolerantly out on the goings-on of the merely human creatures before him. He was a good man, and I loved him next to my mother and father. I crouched there on the floor of the crib and watched him shell corn with the rusty cast-iron hands, while he looked down at me out of the little eyes set in the blunt face.

"Dellie says she's mighty sick," I said.

"Yeah," he said.

"What's she sick from?"

"Woman-mizry," he said.

"What's woman-mizry?"

"Hit comes on 'em," he said. "Hit just comes on 'em when the time comes. "

"What is it?"

"Hit is the change," he said. "Hit is the change of life and time. "

"What changes?"

"You too young to know. "

"Tell me. "

"Time come and you find out everything. "

I knew that there was no use in asking him any more. When I asked him things and he said that, I always knew that he would not tell me. So I continued to crouch there and watch him. Now that I had sat there a little while, I was cold again.

"What you shiver fer?" he asked me.

"I'm cold. I'm cold because it's blackberry winter," I said.

"Maybe 'tis and maybe 'tain't," he said.

"My mother says it is. "

"Ain't sayen Miss Sallie doan know and ain't sayen she do. But folks doan know everything. "

"Why isn't it blackberry winter?"

"Too late fer blackberry winter. Blackberries done bloomed. "

"She said it was. "

"Blackberry winter just a leetle cold spell. Hit come and then hit go away, and hit is growed summer of a sudden lak a gunshot. Ain't no tellen hit will go way this time. "

"It's June," I said.

"June," he replied with great contempt. "That

"6 月,"他十分不屑地说,"人们那么说罢了。6月算什么?也许会一直冷下去了。"

"为什么?"

"因为这里的大地非常累了。它累了,不肯再生产了。有一次上帝让老天下了 40 昼夜的雨,因为他对罪孽深重的人感到厌烦了。也许今年大地对上帝说了,上帝,我非常累了。上帝,让我休息吧。上帝说,大地,你尽了自己的力量了。你给他们玉米,你给他们土豆,而他们所想的只是要收获。大地,你可以休息一下了。"

"会发生什么情况呢?"

"人们会把一切都吃了。大地不再出产东西。人们因为冷,会把树全部砍下来烧了,大地不再长树了。我一直这么说的,我一直对人们这么说的。也许就是今年,正是这时候。我告诉他们大地是多么累了。但是他们不听我的话。也许他们今年会明白的。"

"什么都要死光吗?"

"所有的人和东西都死光,会是这样的。"

"就在今年?"

"我说不上。也许是今年。"

"我妈妈说这是春寒。"我蛮有把握地说,站了起来。

"我没说莎莉小姐不对。"他说道。

我朝小屋门口走去。我真的很冷。我刚才跑出了一身汗,现在就更冷了。

我赖在门边不走,看着约伯,他又在剥玉米了。

"有个流浪汉上咱们家来了。"我说。我刚才几乎把流浪汉给忘了。

"喔。"

"他从农庄后面那条路来的。暴风雨里他在那儿干些什么呢?"

"这些人来来去去,"他说,"我也说不上。"

"他有一把样子凶险的刀。"

"好人和坏人,他们来来去去,不管是有暴风雨还是出太阳,不管是白天还是晚上。他们是人,人就是那样地来来去去。"

我靠在门上直打哆嗦。

他仔细端详了我一会儿,然后说道:"你回屋子里去。不然你会伤风,你妈妈又会怎么说?"

我犹豫不定。

"你得走。"他说。

what folks say. What June mean? Maybe hit is come cold to stay. "

"Why?"

"Cause this-here old yearth is tahrd. Hit is tahrd and ain't gonna perduce. Lawd let hit come rain one time forty days and forty nights, 'cause He was tahrd of sinful folks. Maybe this-here old yearth say to the Lawd, Lawd, I done plum tahrd. Lawd, lemme rest. And Lawd say, Yearth, you done yore best, you give 'em cawn and you give 'em taters, and all they think on is they gut, and, Yearth, you kin take a rest. "

"What will happen?"

"Folks will eat up everything. The yearth won't perduce no more. Folks cut down all the trees and burn 'em cause they cold, and the yearth won't grow no more. I been tellen 'em. I been tellen folks. Sayen, maybe this year, hit is the time. But they doan listen to me, how the yearth is tahrd. Maybe this year they find out. "

"Will everything die?"

"Everything and everybody, hit will be so. "

"This year?"

"Ain't no tellen. Maybe this year. "

"My mother said it is blackberry winter," I said confidently, and got up.

"Ain't sayen nuthin' agin Miss Sallie," he said.

I went to the door of the crib. I was really cold. Running, I had got up a sweat and now I was worse.

I hung on the door, looking at Jebb, who was shelling corn again.

"There's a tramp came to the house," I said. I had almost forgotten the tramp.

"Yeah. "

"He came by the back way. What was he doing down there in the storm?"

"They comes and they goes," he said, "ain't no tellen. "

"He had a mean knife. "

"The good ones and the bad ones, they comes and they goes. Storm or sun, light or dark. They is folks and they comes and they goes lak folks. "

I hung on the door, shivering.

He studied me a moment, then said, "You git on to the house. You ketch yore death. Then what yore mammy say?"

I hesitated.

"You git," he said.

When I came to the back yard, I saw that my father was standing by the back porch and the tramp was walking toward him. They began talking before I reached them, but I got there just as my father was saying, "I'm sorry, but I haven't got any work. I got all

我走到后院,看到我爸爸挨着后廊站在院子里,流浪汉正在朝他走过去。我还没到他们跟前,他们就已经开始交谈起来了。我走到那儿时,我爸爸正在说:"对不起,但是我这儿没活儿干。我需要帮手的地方都有人了。麦收之前不需要再添工人了。"

陌生人没有回答,只是看着我爸爸。

我爸爸掏出一只皮制的放角币的钱包,拿出一枚伍毛的角子,朝那人递过去。"这是半天的工钱。"他说。那个人先看看那枚硬币,再看看我爸爸,没有伸手接钱。但是这价钱是公平的。在 1910 年邦会儿,你付给他们这些人是一天一元钱,而那个人干的活儿连半天还不到呢。

那个人伸出手来接钱了,他把角子放进外衣右面的边袋里,然后他慢吞吞地、不动声色地说道:"我本来就不想在你的——小农庄上干活儿。"

他用的那个字眼,要是我说了,他们准会把我活活打死。

我看我爸爸的脸,他那晒得黑黑的脸刷地变白了。他说道:"从这儿滚开。你要不滚开,我就要对你不住了。"

那人把右手伸进裤袋。这是他放刀的口袋。我正要对我爸爸喊出来说那儿有刀,那只手又拿出来了,手里空空的。那个人狞笑了一下,露出了在新伤痕上面那个被打掉两颗牙的地方。这时我马上想到,也许他以前正是在拔刀向别人砍去的时候,让人把牙给打掉了的。

现在他那张毫无特征的发灰的脸龇牙咧嘴地笑了一下,笑得叫人恶心,然后他往砖砌的小道上啐了一口。那一小团黏液落在离我爸爸右靴尖 6 英寸远的地方。我爸爸朝下看,我也朝下着。我想,如果这口痰落在我爸爸的靴子上,那就会出事了。我朝下看,看见了那发亮的痰。痰的这一边,是我爸爸结实的牛皮靴,上面有铜扣眼和皮带子,沉重的皮靴溅上了好看的红泥巴,稳稳地站在砖地上。痰的另一边是那双破烂不堪的尖头黑鞋,上面的泥看上去那幺可怜巴巴,那么不是地方。然后我看到一只黑鞋挪了一点儿,开始只是动了一下,后来就真正后退一步了。那个人绕了个 1/4 的圆圈走到后廊的那头去。这时候我爸爸的眼睛眨也不眨,一直牢牢盯着他走。在后廊的尽头,那人伸手到脸盆架上去取他的小报纸包。他拐过屋角消失了。我爸爸跨上走廊,一言不发走进

the hands on the place I need now. I won't need any extra until wheat thrashing."

The stranger made no reply, just looked at my father.

My father took out his leather coin purse, and got out a half-dollar. He held it toward the man. "This is for half a day," he said.

The man looked at the coin, and then at my father, making no motion to take the money. But that was the right amount. A dollar a day was what you paid them back in 1910. And the man hadn't even worked half a day.

Then the man reached out and took the coin. He dropped it into the right side pocket of his coat. Then he said, very slowly and without feeling: "I didn't want to work on your—farm."

He used the word which they would have frailed me to death for using.

I looked at my father's face and it was streaked white under the sunburn. Then he said, "Get off this place. Get off this place or I won't be responsible."

The man dropped his right hand into his pants pocket. It was the pocket where he kept the knife. I was just about to yell to my father about the knife when the hand came back out with nothing in it. The man gave a kind of twisted grin, showing where the teeth had been knocked out above the new scar. I thought that instant how maybe he had tried before to pull a knife on somebody else and had got his teeth knocked out.

So now he just gave that twisted, sickish grin out of the unmemorable, grayish face, and then spat on the brick path. The glob landed just about six inches from the toe of my father's right boot. My father looked down at it, and so did I. I thought that if that glob had hit my father's boot something would have happened. I looked down and saw the bright glob, and on one side of it my father's strong cowhide boots, with the brass eyelets and the leather thongs, heavy boots splashed with good red mud and set solid on the bricks, and on the other side the pointed-toe, broken, black shoes, on which the mud looked so sad and out of place. Then I saw one of the black shoes move a little, just a twitch first, then a real step backward.

The man moved in a quarter circle to the end of the porch, with my father's steady gaze upon him all the while. At the end of the porch, the man reached up to the shelf where the wash pans were to get his little newspaper-wrapped parcel. Then he disappeared around the corner of the house and my father mounted the porch and went into the kitchen without a word.

I followed around the house to see what the man would do. I wasn't afraid of him now, no matter if he did have the knife. When I got around in front, I saw

厨房。

我跟着也拐过屋角去看那个人要干什么。我现在不怕他了，不管他是不是有把刀。我绕过去到了前面，看见他出了院子的门，走上通往大路的大车道。于是我跑步去追他。我追上他的时候，他已在车道上走了有60码远了。

起初，我离他有七八英尺远，没有和他并排走，而是跟在后面，小孩子总是那样的。我不时跑两三步，赶上他的大步子，好保持一定距离。当我刚刚跑到他后面时，他回头看了我一眼，没有任何意义的一眼，就又把眼睛盯在路上，继续往前走。

我们在路角拐了弯，就看不到屋子了。我们又沿着树林边上往前走时，我决定上前和他并排走。我跑了几步，到了他身边，或者说几乎到了他身边，因为实际上是到了他右边几英尺远的地方。我就这样走了一会儿，但是他始终没注意我。我一直走到可以看到通向大路的那扇大门的地方，这时候我就问："你是从哪儿来的？"

他看了我那么一眼，好像对我在那儿几乎感到惊奇。他说："这不干你的事。"

我们又走了50英尺。

我又问："你上哪儿去？"

他停下来，冷冷地打量了我一会儿，突然朝我走了一步，脸朝下向我挨过来。嘴唇往两边一咧，但根本不是在笑，牙齿被打掉的地方露了出来，下唇上的那块伤疤因为绷紧了变成白色的了。

他说："不许跟着我。你再跟，我就宰了你，你这个小王八蛋。"

他又继续往大门走，上了大路。

这是35年以前的事了。后来，我父母都死了。我父亲让一架收割机的刀片切伤了，死于破伤风，那时我还是个孩子，不过是个大孩子了。我妈妈卖掉那个地方，搬到城里和她姊姊一起住。但是在我父亲死后，她始终没有振作起来，不到3年就死了，正当壮年。我姨母总是说："莎莉是心碎而死的。她是这么个忠实的妻子。"黛里也死了，但我听说她是在我们卖掉农场很久以后才死的。

至于小约伯，他长大后成了一个下流粗野的人，他在打架时杀死另外一个黑人，被关进监狱，我最后听到的消息是他还在那儿。

老约伯一直活着。我在10年前看见他，那时他

him going out the yard gate and starting up the drive toward the pike. So I ran to catch up with him. He was sixty yards or so up the drive before I caught up.

I did not walk right up even with him at first, but trailed him, the way a kid will, about seven or eight feet behind, now and then running two or three steps in order to hold my place against his longer stride. When I first came up behind him, he turned to give me a look, just a meaningless look, and then fixed his eyes up the drive and kept on walking.

When we had got around the bend in the drive which cut the house from sight, and were going along by the edge of the woods, I decided to come up even with him. I ran a few steps, and was by his side, or almost, but some feet off to the right. I walked along in this position for a while, and he never noticed me. I walked along until we got within sight of the big gate that let on the pike.

Then I said: "Where did you come from?"

He looked at me then with a look which seemed almost surprised that I was there. Then he said, "It ain't none of yore business."

We went on another fifty feet.

Then I said, "Where are you going?"

He stopped, studied me dispassionately for a moment, then suddenly took a step toward me and leaned his face down at me. The lips jerked back, but not in any grin, to show where the teeth were knocked out and to make the scar on the lower lip come white with the tension.

He said: "Stop following me. You don't stop following me and I cut yore throat, you little son-of-a-bitch."

Then he went on to the gate, and up the pike.

That was thirty-five years ago. Since that time my father and mother have died. I was still a boy; but a big boy, when my father got cut on the blade of a mowing machine and died of lockjaw. My mother sold the place and went to town to live with her sister. But she never took hold after my father's death, and she died within three years, right in middle life. My aunt always said, "Sallie just died of a broken heart, she was so devoted." Dellie is dead, too, but she died, I heard, quite a long time after we sold the farm.

As for Little Jebb, he grew up to be a mean and ficey Negro. He killed another Negro in a fight and got sent to the penitentiary, where he is yet, the last I heard tell. He probably grew up to be mean and ficey from just being picked on so much by the children of the other tenants, who were jealous of Jebb and Dellie for being thrifty and clever and being white-folks' niggers.

Old Jebb lived forever. I saw him ten years ago and he was about a hundred then, and not looking

差不多100岁了,样子没多大变化。我去看他约时候,他住在城里靠救济金生活——那是在大萧条时期。他对我说:"我太结实了,死不了。当我还是个年轻人,到处跑跑,见见世面的时候,我向上帝祷告说:噢,上帝,给我力量,使我强壮,能做事,能忍耐。上帝听到了我的祷告,他给了我力量。我过去真为自己这么强壮,是个十足的男子汉而感到骄傲。上帝祝福我,给了我力量。但是现在他走开了。把我忘了,却给我留下了力量。一个人不知道为什么祷告才好,反正他总是要死的。"就我所知,约伯也许还活着。

这就是那天早上以后发生的事。那天早上那个流浪汉脸朝下朝我挨过来,露出他的牙,说道:"不许跟着我。你再跟,我就宰了你,你这个小王八蛋。"这是他的话,叫我别跟着他,但是这些年我一直在跟着他。

much different. He was living in town then, on relief—that was back in the Depression—when I went to see him. He said to me: "Too strong to die. When I was a young feller just comen on and seen how things wuz, I prayed the Lawd. I said, Oh, Lawd, gimme strength and make me strong fer to do and in-dure. The Lawd hearkened to my prayer. He give me strength. I was in-duren proud fer being strong and me much man. The Lawd give me my prayer and my strength. But now He done gone off and fergot me and left me alone with my strength. A man doan know what to pray fer, and him mortal."

Jebb is probably living yet, as far as I know.

That is what has happened since the morning when the tramp leaned his face down at me and showed his teeth and said: "Stop following me. You don't stop following me and I cut yore throat, you little son-of-a-bitch." That was what he said, for me not to follow him. But I did follow him, all the years.

039.《春寒》:一段回忆

(美)罗伯特·潘·沃伦 著　　刘文荣 译

039. "Blackberry Winter": A Recollection
by Robert Penn Warren

　　这篇小说写作时的情形我记忆犹新,记得特别清楚的是当时有一种被动感,似乎觉得小说自己在写自己,还有这种被动感和不断闪现的自我意识、自我批判之间的平衡、牵连以及相互作用——或者不管你叫它什么。我认为无论谁在写作时,都需要做某种类似的平衡或者摆动,只是在写这篇小说时,这同一过程的两个侧面,即顺利和困难、得意和痛苦——我不妨这么说——两者之间的界限特别明显罢了。说来很奇怪,痛苦好像总是和被动联系在一起的,好像我并不愿意进入那个记忆中的世界似的,反之,得意之感则总是和独立的判断联系在一起的,因为我对那些纷至沓来进入我头脑的东西总设法加以驾驭。如果说创作过程要比我刚才所说的更错综复杂而且是事实的话。那么纵然就这方面而言有限地、局部地了解事实是可能的,我却一点儿也不了解这样的事实。

　　出现在我脑中并牢牢铭记在我心中的只是活生生的事物,这篇小说的写作也许就是出于这种情况,就是说,我想要写下什么东西。当时是 1945—1946 年的秋天,也可能是冬天,大战刚结束,那时即使没有参与过血腥活动的人也都有一种感觉,觉得整个世界连同他本人的生活都不可能再是老样子了。那时我正在读赫尔曼·麦尔维尔的诗,记得对那首《信念之战》印象特别深,那是一首大约写于美国南北战争前夕的诗。麦尔维尔说,不管怎么样,战争所揭示的不外乎是世界的"腐朽根基"。1945 年也有这种感觉,战争尽管打赢了,但我们也看见了那个腐朽根基,而即使是现在,当我写下这些时,在我脑子里出现的也就

　　I REMEMBER with peculiar distinctness the writing of this story, especially the balance, tension, interplay—or what you will—between a sense of compulsion, a sense that the story was writing itself, and the flashes of self-consciousness and self-criticism. I suppose that in all attempts at writing there is some such balance, or oscillation, but here the distinction between the two aspects of the process was peculiarly marked, between the ease and the difficulty, between the elation and, I am tempted to say, the pain. But the pain, strangely enough, seemed to be attached to the compulsion, as though in some way I did not want to go into that remembered world, and the elation attached to the critical effort I had to make to ride herd on the wrangle of things that came milling into my head. Or perhaps the truth is that the process was more complicated than that and I shall never know the truth, even in the limited, provisional way the knowing of truth is possible in such matters.

　　It crosses my mind that the vividness with which I have always remembered the writing of this story may have something to do with the situation in which it was written. It was the fall or winter of 1945—1946 just after the war, and even if one had had no hand in the blood-letting, there was the sense that the world, and one's own life, would never be the same again. I was then reading Herman Melville' poetry, and remember being profoundly impressed by "The Conflict of Convictions," a poem about the coming of the American Civil War. Whatever the rights and wrongs of the matter, the war, Melville said, would show "the

---

作者简介:罗伯特·潘·沃伦(Robert Penn Warren,1905—1989),美国小说家、诗人和评论家。1905 年 4 月 24 日生于肯塔基州格思里,1989 年 9 月 15 日卒于佛蒙特州斯特拉顿。他曾在几所大学任教,之后协助创立和编辑《南方评论》(Southern Review,1935～1942),在当时美国文学杂志界最有影响力的杂志。他的作品经常针对南方传统乡村价值腐蚀下的道德困惑。他最著名的长篇小说是《国王的人马》(All the King's Men,1946),获得普利策奖。短篇小说集《阁楼马戏团》(The Circus in the Attic,1948)包括著名的《春寒》(Blackberry Winter)。1958 年和 1979 年两次获得普利策诗歌奖,1986 年成为美国第一位桂冠诗人。

是来自于我的小说的那件极为普通的事情——暴风雨把黛里小屋下面的垃圾冲出来,老实不客气地把本来干干净净的院子弄得一塌糊涂。如果说这篇小说的根子是我过去童年时代在乡下一百次目睹过的事实,同时它的根子又在麦尔维尔的诗句里,那我是不会感到惊异的。因为 1945 年战争胜利之际,我的感受是那样复杂,不仅是麦尔维尔的诗句和黛里小屋给我留下的印象,而且还有某种可以包容我这篇短短的小说的全部意义的东西,似乎全部混杂在一起。

我当时就在类似的情形下完成了两部篇幅很大的作品,就是长篇小说《国王的人马》和一篇关于柯勒律治诗歌《古代船工》的研究文章,它们在我心里已酝酿了多年。这两部作品都不属于我个人,就像任何仆人的工作不属于他个人一样。在这两部作品中虽然渗透着许多我个人的感情,但是它们却属于和我相隔甚远的不同的世界。再说,我当时住在北方的一个多雪的现代化大城市里,挤在汽车间上面的一套狭小的房间里,这种地方和我小说里的那个世界是不能同日而语的。

在我的日常生活里,我当然不会想到也记不起那个世界。想来我当时大概正在为那两部即将出版的作品而颇觉忧心忡忡吧,因为我在它们上面押了很大的注,所以心里暗暗地确信——虽然时常又自我否定——在我的生活和经历中将要发生某种巨大的变化。当时的感觉就是这样,如果还有别的什么的话,那就要数不久后的 40 岁生日或者长期紧张工作后的那种疲乏感了。

这篇小说就是在这样的情况下开始创作的,而动笔之际还是出于某种偶然的因素。几年前,我曾写过一篇有关一个田纳西交租佃户的小说,一篇写得很糟的小说,所以一直没有发表。当时,我觉得自己有办法把这篇小说修改好。我于是真的坐下来修改这篇小说,至于这件事的结果是导致了《打开的门和贫困的汉堡人》的诞生呢,还是导致了我岔开去写了这篇《春寒》,那我就讲不清楚了。不管怎样,我当时沉溺在对童年生活的回忆之中。如果你愿意,可以说我想逃避现实。如果你愿意,可以说我想追寻往日的思绪和抱负。如果你愿意,可以说我竭力想找到新的生活起点。不管怎么说,就是人们常有的那种现在和过去融合在一起的双重生活。

我还记得那条引导我回忆往事的分明无误的途

slimed foundations" of the world. There was the sense in 1945, even with victory, that we had seen the slimed foundations, and as I now write this, the image that comes into my mind is the homely one from my story—the trash washed by the storm from under Dellie's cabin to foul her pridefully clean yard. And I should not be surprised if the picture in the story had its roots in the line from Melville as well as in such a fact, seen a hundred times in my rural boyhood. So the mixed feelings I had in our moment of victory in 1945, Melville's poem, and not only the image of Dellie's cabin, but something of the whole import of my little story, belong, it seems, in the same package.

For a less remote background, I had just finished two long pieces of work, a novel called *All the King's Men* and a critical study of Coleridge's poem *The Ancient Mariner*, both of which had been on my mind for years. Both those things were impersonal, about as impersonal as the work of any man's hand can be said to be. Even though much of my personal feeling had been drawn into both projects, they belonged to worlds very different from my own. At that time, too, I was living in a very cramped apartment over a garage, in a big, modern, blizzard-bit northern city, again a place very different from the world of my story.

In my daily life, I certainly was not thinking about and remembering that world. I suppose I was living in some anxiety about the fate of the two forthcoming pieces of work, on which I had staked much, and in the unspoken, even denied, conviction that some sort of watershed of life and experience was being approached. For one thing, the fortieth birthday, lately passed, and the sense of let-down after the long period of intense work, could account, in part at least, for that feeling.

Out of this situation the story began, but it began by a kind of accident. Some years earlier, I had written a story about a Tennessee sharecropper, a bad story that had never been published. Now I thought I saw a way to improve it. I don't know whether I actually sat down to rewrite the story that was to have the new avatar of "The Patented Gate and the Mean Hamburger" or whether I got sidetracked into "Blackberry Winter" first. In any case, I was going back into a primal world of recollection. I was fleeing, if you wish. Hunting old bearings and benchmarks, if you wish. Trying to make a fresh start, if you wish. Whatever

径，就是那种你也有过的学校放假后可以赤着脚到处奔跑的感觉。这倒不是我偏爱赤脚，我的脚长得瘦骨嶙峋。不过，就是赤脚这件事本身是重要的，这是一篇独立宣言，表明你已经从冬天和学校甚至你的家庭的权威束缚下得到了解放。就像人类学家所说，这是每个人必经的过程。然而，它还有另一层意义。它引导你返回大自然的梦境，现在你居栖在树林里而不再住在房屋里，你涉足其间的是河流而不再是街道了。当时，我望着自己所住的寒冷地带的那条冰雪四封的小巷，一种朦胧的思乡之情便油然而生，我简直怀疑春天是否还会重临这个地方（春天到底还是来了——那是 5 月 5 日，冰雪依然未消，但大朵大朵的丁香花却开了，蒙着白雪，挂着冰凌，显得分外艳丽）。

至于我对赤着脚到处奔跑的回忆，那已经是多年来常有的事了。每当短暂的夏天转眼即逝，夏意在潮湿和阴冷中消失殆尽之际，童年时代的那种叛逆感就会勃然而起。这篇小说就是在这两种回忆的共同作用下开始动笔的。如果说小说总有个样子的话，这篇小说将写成什么样子我当时一点儿也没有数。我只是坐在打字机前面为那不息的思乡之情找到一条出路而已。但是，如果我不想仅仅写一篇貌似小说而实际上只是一首阴郁的使人读之乏味的抒情诗，也不想写一篇多愁善感的散文的话，那么，要想写一篇小说，里面总得发生一些事情。总要有些事情发生，而要想有事情发生是再简单不过了，只要说：进来吧，神秘的陌生人。于是乎他就进来了。

那个流浪汉就是这样走进这篇小说的，只是他等了很长时间。等着我的想象力放他进来——毫无疑问，这是一个来自我童年生活中的、现在已记不大清楚的好些事情中的形象。城市游民成了乡间流浪汉，满腹狐疑，愤愤不平，孤僻而又沉闷，他带着自己的那种愤激之情走进一个世界，在这个世界里他几乎不指望得到他人的好意。他对自己也够厌恶的了，所以他侧着头从肩膀上漠视着笼罩在暮色里的空荡荡的小巷——一个又迷惘又可怜的人，从某种意义上说，这也是人类处境的一个阴郁的形象。不过，在当时，我所想到的仅仅是他漫无目的地闯了进来，对着一个孩子的平静而充满爱的世界感到困惑不解。

由于我在那流浪汉实际出现之前就已预感到他将会出现，所以我没有做什么计划就动手写了这篇小说的第四部分，写到我们成年之后和我在小说里很幼

people do in their doubleness of living in a present and a past.

I recollect the particular thread that led me back into that past: the feeling you have when, after vacation begins, you are allowed to go barefoot. Not that I ever liked to go barefoot, not with my bony feet. But the privilege itself was important, a declaration of independence from the tyranny of winter and school and, even, your own family. It was like what the anthropologists call a rite of passage. But it had another meaning, too. It carried you back into a dream of nature, the woods not the house was now your natural habitat, the stream not the street. Looking out into the snow-banked alley of that iron latitude where I now lived, I had a vague, nostalgic feeling and wondered if spring would ever come. (It finally came—and then on May 5 there was again snow, and the heavy-headed blooms of lilac were beautiful with their hoods of snow and beards of ice.)

With the recollection of going barefoot came another, which had been recurrent over the years: the childhood feeling of betrayal when early summer gets turned upside-down, and all its promises are revoked by the cold-spell, the gully-washer. So by putting those two recollections together, the story got started. I had no idea where it was going, if anywhere. Sitting at the typewriter was merely a way of indulging nostalgia. But something has to happen in a story, if there is to be more than a dreary lyric poem posing as a story to promote the cause of universal boredom and deliquescent prose. Something had to happen, and the simplest thing ever to have happen is to say: *Enter, mysterious stranger*. And so he did.

The tramp who thus walked into the story had been waiting a long time in the wings of my imagination—an image drawn, no doubt, from a dozen unremembered episodes of childhood, the city bum turned country tramp, suspicious, resentful, contemptuous of hick dumbness, bringing his own brand of violence into a world where he half-expected to find another kind, enough unlike his own to make him look over his shoulder down the empty lane as dusk came on, a creature altogether lost and pitiful, a dim image of what, in one perspective, our human condition is. But then, at that moment, I was merely thinking of the impingement of his loose-footedness and lostness on a stable and love-defined world of childhood.

稚地称之为立足在世界金光闪闪的海滩上的那个时期之间的差别——顺便提一下，这种比喻也只有一个生长在内地从未见过海却又老是梦见海的孩子才想得出来。后来那流浪汉来了，他不仅是从树林里走出来的，而且是从阴沉沉的成人世界里走出来的。

显然，那流浪汉是穿过河边的树林走来的，所以在男孩的表面意识上，他是一个来自树林的流浪汉。由于现在与时代发生联系的自然主题总会落入一种格局，使一种陈旧的观念披着新的伪装在小说里反复出现，所以当一个男孩看到一个流浪汉的精神形象穿过树林而出现时，一般总写到，一个成年人，尤其像这样一个成年人，他穿过树林时的情形和一个男孩在树林里的情形有何明显的区别，因为那男孩会独自静静地待在树林里，在那儿他似乎浑身长满苔藓而且生了根，他好像在那儿竭力想听清植物生长的节奏，竭力想使自己呼吸到那种生存方式的气息似的。

但是，这种树林里的与人类不同的植物世界的生活是否能用人类的语言说出来呢？——也就是说，用小说的语言该怎么说呢？我可以承认自己写那一章节是出于冲动，但是这冲动却基于某种想法，就是说，想把树林里的男孩和树林里的流浪汉两者本身的区别加以明确的阐述，因为那流浪汉不会明白一只禽鸟究竟意味着什么，说到底他也只会把它看作花云边上的一顿饭菜而已。所以，我们在这儿又看到了某种对比，就是那流浪汉的世界和孩子的纯洁的世界之间的对比，而孩子的纯洁则是通过他与大自然之间的那种亲密感表现出来的，是通过他对自己能进入大自然那样的生活的想象而得到体现的。

这一章节一写完，我就意识到它的重要性。我不由得自我确信，不管我的组织能力有何价值，我可以希望结构出一种格局，若能这样，就会有一连串的对比被表现出来。所以，很自然的，当我对那流浪汉做了一些描写，写到他的古怪和那种像鱼出了水似的呆滞，写到譬如他对狗的不熟悉等等之后，流浪汉的这种笨头笨脑而又愤愤不平的样子就和母亲的那种自以为是而自信心十足的样子形成了鲜明的对照，随后又使母亲在故事里的那种样子和她将来临死时的样子形成了对照，不过这种对照仅仅存在于记忆中——母亲现在确实已经在那永恒不变的宁静世界里安息了，然而回想起来，当时在那男孩的心里丝毫也没有想到过"她竟然会死"。

Before the tramp actually appeared, I had, however, known he was coming, and without planning I began to write the fourth paragraph of the story, about the difference between what time is when we have grown up and what it was when we stood on what, in my fancy phrase in the story, I called the glistening auroral beach of the world—a phrase which belonged, by the way, to an inland boy who had never seen a beach but whose dreams were all of the sea. Now the tramp came up, not merely out of the woods, but out of the darkening grown-up world of time.

The tramp had, literally, come up through the river woods, and so in the boy's literal speculations he sees the tramp coming through the woods. By now, however, the natural thematic distinction touched on in relation to time is moving into a pattern, the repetition in fiction of the established notion in a new guise. So when the boy sees the mental image of the tramp coming through the woods, there is the distinction set up between the way a man, particularly such a man as this, would go through woods, and the way a boy can stand in the woods in absolute quiet, almost taking root and growing moss on himself, trying to catch the rhythm, as it were, of that vegetative life, trying to breathe himself into that mode of being.

But what would this other, woodland, vegetative world of being carry with it in human terms—in terms, that is, of what a story must be about? I can promise that the passage was written on impulse, but an impulse conditioned by the idea that there had to be an expressed difference between boy-in-woods and tramp-in-woods, the tramp who doesn't know what a poult is and thinks the final degradation is to mess with a flower bed. And so here we are back to the contrast between the tramp's world and that of childhood innocence appearing in some sense of a rapport between the child and nature, his feeling that he himself might enter that very life of nature.

As soon as the passage was written I knew its import; I was following my nose, trusting, for what they were worth, my powers of association, hoping that those powers would work in relation to a pattern that had begun to emerge as a series of contrasts. And it was natural, therefore, after a few paragraphs about the strangeness and fish-out-of-waterness of the tramp, his not knowing about dogs for example, to have the mother's self-sufficiency set against the

当我写这句话时，我是完全自觉的，我不管小说将如何结束，因为我始终是凭借着推想和上帝在写，但是不管从何种感情角度出发，小说终究要有个结束。我知道这篇小说将会以某种严峻而独立的概括形式或者说以某种成年人的对事实的执拗态度作为小说的结束。所以，那些基于回忆的自然冲击而产生的东西不仅带给我思乡的情愫，而且带给我万事瞬息变幻的重荷感——那在男孩眼里不过是一种有趣景象而对别人来说却是意味着饥饿的洪水，那男孩对像米尔特·阿莱这样的白种穷光蛋的不自觉的同情，那曾跟随福历斯特打过仗的老人对饥饿的回忆，还有那患着"妇女病"的黛里。不过，在我想到黛里之前，我心里已经牢牢地记着老约伯了，一提起他的名字就会使人——至少使我——产生一种朦胧而具有讽刺意味的感觉，使人回想起那个在耶洛台文被杀死的支持南方联邦的勇敢的骑士。

也许，我在黛里这个人物身上最后所做的，实际上是从那个我称之为老约伯的人身上抽取出来的。那男孩既然在J·E·B·斯图亚特的大名回响中看不到什么具有讽刺意味的东西，那么当黛里捆她心爱的儿子时，他是有所震动的，他会感到那一巴掌从某种深刻的意义上而言就像打在他的脸颊上一样。我对此很清楚，因为我了解那所充满自豪的小屋的内情，而且由于对此早有认识而感到震惊，我在那种彼此相爱的气氛中看到了某种暗淡的、悲剧性的、悬而未决的东西。基于黛里的这种处境，我觉得我预感到了小说中的那个流浪汉。由于换了角度，这篇小说的重点就从思乡的伤感情绪移到了对人类关系的残缺和不公正这方面来了。早先无意识地和报道式地写进去的有关米尔特·阿莱的那些东西，现在也得到了有意识地系统阐述。

我说过，按照这样的设想，这篇小说的结尾就是对人类关系所做的某种严峻的概括。但是，不能仅仅认为是一种概括就完了，我所要的，是使人对突露在小说平面上的那个男孩的家庭以及约伯的家庭有所感受。我于是想到，我可以把这种有关约伯的概括当做一种引子，从而进一步使人得到我所致力于取得的那种感受，也就是说，我们一旦接受或者至少得到暗示，了解了约伯对于他自己的生活感受时，我们也就能对人类社会状况有所领悟了。我要赋予小说以某种含义，那就是：不管变易或者沉沦，人的尊严可以重

tramp's rude, resentful uncertainty, and then have her portrait at the time of the episode set against the time when she would be dead, and only a memory—though back then, of course, in the secure world of changelessness and timelessness, it had never crossed the boy's mind that "she would ever be dead."

The instant I wrote that clause I knew, not how the story would end, for I was still writing by guess and by God, but on what perspective of feeling it would end. I knew that it would end with a kind of detached summary of the work of time, some hint of the adult's grim orientation toward that fact. From now on, the items that came on the natural wash of recollection came not only with their, to me, nostalgic quality, but also with the freighting of the grimmer possibilities of change—the flood, which to the boy is only an exciting spectacle but which will mean hunger to others, the boy's unconscious contempt for poor whitetrash like Milt Alley, the recollection of hunger by the old man who had ridden with Forrest, Dellie suffering in her "woman mizry." But before I had got to Dellie, I already had Old Jebb firmly in mind, with some faint sense of the irony of having his name remind one—or at least me—of the dashing Confederate cavalryman killed at Yellow Tavern.

Perhaps what I finally did with Dellie stemmed, in fact, from the name I gave Old Jebb. Even if the boy would see no irony in that echo of J. E. B. Stuart's fame, he would get a shock when Dellie slapped her beloved son, and would sense that that blow was, in some deep way, a blow at him. I knew this, for I knew the inside of that prideful cabin, and the shock of early recognition that beneath mutual kindliness and regard some dark, tragic, unresolved something lurked. And with that scene with Dellie, I felt I was forecasting the role of the tramp in the story. The story, to put it in another way, was now shifting emphasis from the lyricism of nostalgia to a concern with the jags and injustices of human relationships. What had earlier come in unconsciously, reportorially, in regard to Milt Alley now got a conscious formulation.

I have said that the end was by now envisaged as a kind of summary of the work of time on the human relationships. But it could not afford to be a mere summary: I wanted some feeling for the boy's family and Jebb's family to shine through the flat surface. Now it struck me that I might build this summary with Jebb

新获得,而这对于业已丧失纯正的人来说则是更为可贵的。为此,我还是写下了那段概括性的话。

直到我进而写完了最后一个段落,我还不明白自己写那个流浪汉是为了什么目的。他对那个男孩粗声吼叫了一阵,随后就走了。但是我觉得,在小说结构的范围内,他的意义和我想对人物所做的概述的意义是一致的。所以,不管怎么样,小说就这样结束了。那流浪汉怀着他最后的愤怒和失望对男孩说道:"不许跟着我。你再跟,我就宰了你,你这个小王八蛋。"

那么,男孩是否停下了呢?诚然,从小说的表面看,在那条泥泞小道上,他是停下了。但是在另一层意思上——他没有停下。因为到后来,当他长大之后,当他对生活的意义真正有所了解之后,他的整个生活——如用形象的话来说——都在步那个流浪汉的后尘,而且像一个法定继承人一样尽责,因为不管他成为怎样一个人或者他的生活比那流浪汉好一点儿,但他总是和那流浪汉一样迷惘,一样自卑,一样颓唐,一样怯懦,也一样毫无价值。

可能,我这么做看上去有点像是一种逃避现实的行为,想在童年时代的天真生活中找到退身之处,然而,我们一旦理解了生活的逻辑之后,事情每每都会这样,我们总会转过一个念头,想从天真无瑕的往昔借得一点儿有意义的东西,然后又把它带到现实生活的阴影中来。我所做的看上去好像是一种个人癖好,但是目的却在于想竭力使它成为一种非个人的人类普遍经验,而一篇能遵循小说逻辑的小说作品,其所要达到的目的也仅此而已。直至今日,虽已时过境迁,但我仍然知道,这篇小说,连同不久之后完成的那部长篇和那篇关于柯勒律治的研究文章,它们所要达到的目的都是一样的。

如果我想暗示说,我上面的这些话可以当做小说创作的唯一途径或者可以看做我自己创作小说的唯一途径的话,那当然是愚不可及的胡说八道。实际上,我自己的大部分短篇小说和全部长篇小说(除了两篇尚未发表的),它们的创作动机都大不相同。对于某种客观的事物或者某些现存的情节,我加以观察或者阅读,而只有当什么东西抓住了我的视线或者想象力时,我的感情或者联想才开始活动。有时我觉得事情很奇怪,当我写完一篇小说时我总觉得这是我的最后一篇小说,而事情又很清楚,那最后一篇小说还有待于我去写(因为诗意对小说是贪得无厌的),而这

as a kind of pilot for the feeling I wanted to get; that is, by accepting, in implication at least, something of Jebb's feeling about his own life, we might become aware of our human communion. I wanted the story to give some notion that out of change and loss a human recognition may be redeemed, more precious for being no longer innocent. So I wrote the summary.

When I had finished the next to the last paragraph I still did not know what to do with my tramp. He had already snarled at the boy, and gone, but I sensed that in the pattern of things his meaning would have to coalesce with the meaning I hoped to convey in the summary about the characters. Then, for better or worse, there it was. In his last anger and frustration, the tramp had said to the boy: "You don't stop following me and I cut yore throat, you little son-of-a-bitch."

Had the boy then stopped or not? Yes, of course, literally, in the muddy lane. But at another level—no. Insofar as later he had grown up, had really learned something of the meaning of life, he had been bound to follow the tramp all his life, in the imaginative recognition, with all the responsibility which such a recognition entails, of this lost, mean, defeated, cowardly, worthless, bitter being as somehow a man.

So what had started out for me as, perhaps, an act of escape, of fleeing back into the simplicities of childhood, had turned, as it always must if we accept the logic of our lives, into an attempt to bring something meaningfully out of that simple past into the complication of the present. And what had started out as a personal indulgence had tried to be, in the end, an impersonal generalization about experience, as a story must always try to be if it accepts the logic of fiction. And now, much later, I see that the story and the novel which I had then only lately finished, as well as the study of Coleridge, all bore on the same end.

I would give a false and foolish impression if I were to imply that I think this to be the only way a story should be written, or that this is the only way I myself have ever written stories. As a matter of fact, most of my stories and all of my novels (except two unpublished ones) have started very differently, from some objective situation or episode, observed or read about, something that caught my eye and imagination so that feeling and interpretation began to flow in. And I sometimes think it strange that the last story I ever wrote and presumably the last I shall ever write (for

最后一篇小说是那样明显地理应来自于一个纯正的、回忆中的世界——那不会再是春寒之时，而应该像在印度那样的盛夏之日。

不过，如果我想暗示说，这篇《春寒》是自传性的，那也是愚不可及的。这篇小说不是自传。小说中的每个具体的人物我都不认识，不过我认识和他们相似的人，也了解和他们的世界相似的世界。我生来没有遇到过哪个流浪汉冲着我说不要跟着他否则他就要扭断我的脖子。然而，如果真有这样一个流浪汉的话，我很可能也会像小说里的那个男孩一样，跟着他走的。

poems are great devourers of stories) should have sprung so instinctively from the world of simple recollection—not a blackberry winter at all, but a kind of Indian summer.

I would give a false impression, too, if I were to imply that this story is autobiographical. It is not. I never knew these particular people, only that world and people like them. And no tramp ever leaned down at me and said for me to stop following him or he would cut my throat. But if one had, I hope that I might have been able to follow him anyway, in the way the boy in the story does.

阅读材料
Stories for Reading

阅读小说就像生活一样，需要发挥才智和想象力，才能激起乐趣。

这些短篇小说主要是供读者欣赏的，也是为了向读者再举一些例子，说明短篇小说品类繁多，几乎无穷无尽。但是，如果要尽可能领会其中的情趣，读者必须明确，阅读小说也跟生活中大部分的事情一样，例如打网球，经营管理银行，或者养育子女，都要发挥你的才智，让它参与其事，而不采取消极被动的态度，才能激起乐趣。

　　说得更明白一些，读者在阅读时，要尽可能了解得透彻些，这是尽可能发挥想象力来体会小说内容的一个必要方面。理解得不透彻就不可能设想体会。读者应当向自己提出一些诱导性的问题，并力求认真地回答这些问题。这些问题不应当只涉及小说的要旨，而且要涉及到它所采用的方法，因为，我们早已了解，这两方面是密切相关的，事实上，它们往往都是对同一事物，也就是对小说本身要看到的一些方面。不过，除此之外，对于人物和情节，也有必要力求运用想象力来感受。你在阅读一篇短篇小说的时候，就在扮演一个角色，也许还要扮演几个角色呢。　　　（雨　宁　译）

These stories are here primarily to be enjoyed—and to give to the reader additional examples of the almost infinite variety of short fiction. But if enjoyment is to be had at its fullest, the reader must first grasp that in reading fiction, as in most things in life—for instance, playing tennis or running a bank or raising a family—intelligent participation, not passivity, stimulates enjoyment.

Specifically, here the reader should try to arrive at the fullest possible understanding as an aspect of the fullest possible imaginative participation in the stories. One is not possible without the other. You should ask yourself leading questions and try seriously to answer them. And these questions should involve not only meaning but *method*; for, as we have long since seen, these two things are intimately related—are, in fact, often aspects of the same thing, the story itself. But beyond this, the effort to exercise imaginative feeling in dealing with character and action is necessary. When you read a story, you are playing a role—or several roles.

040. 芙 恩

(美)吉恩·图默 著　雨 宁 译

040. Fern

by Jean Toomer

她脸上的表情都汇合在那双眼睛里,柔和似奶油泡沫,哀怨像微波泛起,以那么一种方式汇合,所以,无论你的眼光一时落在什么地方,都会立时转移到她眼睛的那个方向。依稀的汗毛可能像鸟翼的影子那样,使她那奶油般的棕色上唇显得颜色稍稍深一点儿。嗨,你看到以后就会去搜寻她的眼光,我也没有办法跟你说清。她的鼻子是鹰钩形的,闪米特人的①。如果你听见过犹太教唱诗班领唱人唱诗的声音,如果他感动了你,使你觉得跟他的悲愁相比,你自己的悲愁算不了什么,你就会明白,当我顺着她侧面形象的曲线,像各条河流都要汇合到它们归宿的三角洲那样望上去的时候,我会有什么感触了。那是一双奇怪的眼睛。在这一点上,那双眼睛并没有追求什么东西,这就是说,不是什么明显的、看得见的东西,不是人人可以看得见的东西,它们给你一种百依百顺的印象。在一个女人追求的时候,你大概见过,她的眼睛要不承认的。芙恩的眼睛并不想要你能给她的任何东西,所以没有理由认为她的眼睛应当不露神色。男人们看到她的眼睛,都欺骗他们自己。芙恩的眼睛告诉他们她是容易到手的。她年轻的时候,有几个男人把她弄到了手,可是得不到乐趣。而且,一旦到了手,他们就觉得离不开她(跟他们对其他女人那种到了手就扔掉的情形很不一样),他们觉得仿佛要用一辈子的时间来尽到他们说不出什么名堂的一种义务。他们变得对她依依不舍,而且如饥似渴地想发现她会有什么一丝一毫的愿望。后来她长大了,从城里新来

---

① 闪米特人原来包括巴比伦人、亚述人、希伯来人和腓尼基人,现在主要指阿拉伯人和犹太人。这里是说她有犹太血统。

FACE flowed into her eyes. Flowed in soft cream foam and plaintive ripples, in such a way that wherever your glance may momentarily have rested, it immediately thereafter wavered in the direction of her eyes. The soft suggestion of down slightly darkened, like the shadow of a bird's wing might, the creamy brown color of her upper lip. Why, after noticing it, you sought her eyes, I cannot tell you. Her nose was aquiline, Semitic. If you have heard a Jewish cantor sing, if he has touched you and made your own sorrow seem trivial when compared with his, you will know my feeling when I follow the curves of her profile, like mobile rivers, to their common delta. They were strange eyes. In this, that they sought nothing—that is, nothing that was obvious and tangible and that one could see, and they gave the impression that nothing was to be denied. When a woman seeks, you will have observed, her eyes deny. Fern's eyes desired nothing that you could give her; there was no reason why they should withhold. Men saw her eyes and fooled themselves. Fern's eyes said to them that she was easy. When she was young, a few men took her, but got no joy from it. And then, once done, they felt bound to her(quite unlike their hit and run with other girls), felt as though it would take them a lifetime to fulfill an obligation which they could find no name for. They became attached to her, and hungered after finding the barest trace of what she might desire. As she grew up, new men who came to town felt as almost everyone did who ever saw her; that they would not be denied.

作者简介:吉恩·图默(Jean Toomer,1894—1967),美国诗人、小说家。1894 年 12 月 26 日生于华盛顿,1967 年 3 月 30 日卒于宾夕法尼亚州多伊尔斯顿。他从事写作之前曾经教过书。《甘蔗》(Cane,1923)被公认为是他最好的作品,描述在美国的黑人的经历,此书深深影响了年轻一代的黑人作家。他为《日晷》(The Dial)和其他小杂志撰稿。由于为复杂的种族背景和精神问题所困扰,他在随后的作品中回避了种族问题。

的男人的感觉也跟以前见过的每一个人一样，认为他们不会遭到拒绝。男人给她带来的永远是他们的身体。我估计她心里有点儿对他们感到厌倦，她把他们赶走了，可是无论怎样她也说不出为什么要这样做以及她是怎样开始这么做的。把一个兴奋得发狂的男人赶走可不是一件小事。他们开始离开了她，既感到难以理解，又觉得羞愧，可是他们却暗自发誓，将来总有一天他们都要做点儿什么对得起她的好事，每星期都送糖果给她，而且不让她知道是谁送来的，注意她结婚的日子，到时候送给她一件不署名的精美礼物，买一幢房子并且立下契约让给她。万一有什么卑鄙的家伙骗得她跟他结婚，那就要把她救出来。你也知道，男人对于他们不能理解的东西，尤其是女人，往往会把它或她看成偶像，或者怕她。她并没有拒绝他们，可是事实上他们都被拒绝了。他们的意识里渐渐产生了一种迷信，以为她是高出他们一等的。所谓高出他们一等的意思就是说，她是他们任何人都不能接近的。她变成了一个处女。在南方的城市里，一个处女可绝不是一件寻常的事情，也许你不相信我这句话。按照南方的风俗习惯，有性别之差就是为了要交配。尤其是黑人，生来就是为了交配。我刚才说了好些，讲的都是黑人。至于白人对芙恩怎么想的，我只有用类推法才说得出。他们不惹她。

当然，任何人都能看见她，都能看到她的眼睛。一天里的大多半时间，如果你在狄克西大道①上散步，多半会看到她懒洋洋地倚着门廊的栏杆，背靠着一根柱子，头微微向前倾，因为门廊柱子上有个钉子靠近她的头，不知为什么她从来没有费神去把它拔掉。如果是日落的时候，她的眼睛会悠闲地望着阳光，瞧着那好似熔化了的金子似的阳光倾泻到林子边缘的松树之间。也许，她的眼睛会凝视着小山坡上的灰色木屋，从那里会传来傍晚时唱民歌的声音。也许，她的眼光会望着一头放开了的母牛，瞧着它一边随便走动，一边吃着棉花秆和玉米叶。她的眼光也很可能落在地平线上哪个隐隐约约的地方，可是她眼睛里却不曾露出一点儿忧思的痕迹。如果暮色昏暗，她会在那儿等夜班火车的车头灯光，在灯光照射到靠近

---

① 狄克西大道是作者给这个南方城镇黑人区的一条街道起的名称，狄克西是南北美战争后南方的总称，这条路是用混凝土铺路面的，但不是税道或者偏僻地区的铁路。

Men were everlastingly bringing her their bodies. Something inside of her got tired of them, I guess, for I am certain that for the life of her she could not tell why or how she began to turn them off. A man in fever is no trifling thing to send away. They began to leave her, baffled and ashamed, yet vowing to themselves that some day they would do some fins thing for her: send her candy every week and not let her know whom it came from, watch out for her wedding-day and give her a magnificent something with no name on it, buy a house and deed it to her, rescue her from some unworthy fellow who had tricked her into marrying him. As you know, men are apt to idolize or fear that which they cannot understand, especially if it be a woman. She did not deny them, yet the fact was that they were denied. A sort of superstition crept into their consciousness of her being somehow above them. Being above them meant that she was not to be approached by anyone. She became a virgin. Now a virgin in a small southern town is by no means the usual thing, if you will believe me. That the sexes were made to mate is the practice of the South. Particularly, black folks were made to mate. And it is black folks whom I have been talking about thus far. What white men thought of Fern I can arrive at only by analogy. They let her alone.

Anyone, of course, could see her, could see her eyes. If you walked up the Dixie Pike most any time of day, you'd be most like to see her resting listless-like on the railing of her porch, back propped against a post, head tilted a little forward because there was a nail in the porch post just where her head came which for some reason or other she never took the trouble to pull out. Her eyes, if it were sunset, rested idly where the sun, molten and glorious, was pouring down between the fringe of pines. Or maybe they gazed at the gray cabin on the knoll from which an evening folk-song was coming. Perhaps they followed a cow that had been turned loose to roam and feed on cotton-stalks and corn leaves. Like as not they'd settle on some vague spot above the horizon, though hardly a trace of wistfulness would come to them. If it were dusk, then they'd wait for the search-light of the evening

她家的狄克西大道之前，你可以隔几英里都看得见。无论她的眼光在瞧什么地方，你都会随着她望去，然后又折回来。跟她的脸一样，整个农村的风光似乎都汇合到她那双眼睛里。以佐治亚州南部的柔和悠闲的节奏汇合到她眼睛里。有一次，一个年轻的黑人从路上望着她，入了迷。一个白人驾着一辆马车过来，他只好用鞭子抽他，否则车子过去，就会压死他的。我第一次看见她的时候，我正在跟一个家伙从这里走过(我是北方人，不免有人怀疑我带有偏见，气势凌人)，当他发现我的热情的时候，他那种别扭得麻木不仁的劲头也消释了。我问他她是谁。"那是芙恩。"这就是我从他那里得到的全部答案。有些人已经认为我是个爱到处打听的人，从提问题这个角度来说，我只好随他们自便。不过在我第一次看见她的时候，我觉得好像我听见一位犹太教唱诗班领唱人在唱诗。好像他的歌声是从我不曾听见的民歌合唱声中升起来的。于是我觉得对她依依不舍，我也有我的梦想，我愿意为她做点儿什么事情。我从这个城市到那个城市跑过的地方太多了，怎么会不知道仅仅换个地方没有用呢。再者，你要能画画，不妨试一试，这个肤色如奶油的孤独少女，坐在一幢公共房屋的窗户旁边，望着下面哈莱姆黑人区①神色冷漠的熙熙攘攘的人群。你也许会说，最好让她在佐治亚州黄昏的时候听民歌，我也是这么想的。要不然，假定她来到北方，结了婚，甚至嫁给了一位医生或者律师，嗨，一个过日子有把握的人，也就是说，能赚钱的人。你和我都知道，我们都是在这种事情上有过经验的人，爱情可不是像偏见那样换个地方就能变得好一点儿的。住在华盛顿、芝加哥或者纽约的男人，会不会比佐治亚州的人更胜一筹，给她带来什么在他们把肉体给她之后还空缺的东西呢？你和我都知道，住在那些城市里的人只好说，他们办不到。只会看到她在芝加哥的斯太特街上变成十足的妓女。只会看到她搬进一个南方城镇，而那里的白人更为所欲为。只会看到她变成白人的小老婆……我一定要为她做点儿什么事情。拿我自己来说吧。我能为她做什么呢？说闲话，当然。把松树林的边缘向后挪到新的地平线上。这是要达到什

---

① 哈莱姆黑人区在纽约，因为作者是从那里来的，但这段遭遇发生在南方的佐治亚州梅肯市。所以下文又说以南方的农村风光为背景较好。

train which you could see miles up the track before it flared across the Dixie Pike, close to her home. Wherever they looked you'd follow them and then waver back. Like her face, the whole countryside seemed to flow into her eyes. Flowed into them with the soft listless cadence of Georgia's South. A young Negro, once, was looking at her, spellbound, from the road. A white man passing in a buggy had to flick him with his whip if he was to get by without running him over. I first saw her on her porch. I was passing with a fellow whose crusty numbness (I was from the North and suspected of being prejudiced and stuck-up) was melting as he found me warm. I asked him who she was. "That's Fern," was all that I could get from him. Some folks already thought that I was given to nosing around; I let it go at that, so far as questions were concerned. But at first sight of her I felt as if I heard a Jewish cantor sing. As if his singing rose above the unheard chorus of a folk-song. And I felt bound to her. I too had my dreams: something I would do for her. I have knocked about from town to town too much not to know the futility of mere change of place. Besides, picture if you can, this cream-colored solitary girl sitting at a tenement window looking down on the indifferent throngs of Harlem. Better that she listen to folk-songs at dusk in Georgia, you would say, and so would I. Or, suppose she came up North and married. Even a doctor or a lawyer, say, one who would be sure to get along—that is, make money. You and I know who have had experience in such things, that love is not a thing like prejudice which can be bettered by change of town. Could men in Washington, Chicago, or New York, more than the men of Georgia, bring her something left vacant by the bestowal of their bodies? You and I know men in these cities will have to say, they could not. See her out and out a prostitute along State Street in Chicago. See her move into a southern town where white men are more aggressive. See her become a white man's concubine. . . Something I must do for her. There was myself. What could I do for her? Talk, of course. Push back the fringe of pines upon new horizons. To what purpose? and what for? Her? Myself? Men in her case seem to lose their selfishness. I lost mine before I touched her. I ask you, friend

么目的呢？为什么呢？她吗？我自己吗？碰到她这种情形的男人都失去了他们的自私心。我在没碰她一下之前就失去了我的自私心。我来问你，朋友（不论你在穿过她那条路的火车里坐的是软席卧铺还是黑人专用车，那都没有关系），你会有什么想法呢？这就是说，在你看见一个漂亮女人，脑子里一下子出现了各种念头，而她又不会拒绝你的念头，在这些事情完全过去之后，你会有什么想法呢？假定你坐在火车上，在火车轰隆轰隆飞快地开过去的一刹那间，你的眼光敏锐，出于直觉看到她坐在门廊上一晃而过吧。你会不会在下一站下车，返回去找她，把她带到什么地方去吗？在你的车到了梅肯，亚特兰大，奥古斯塔，帕萨丁纳，麦迪逊，芝加哥，波士顿，或者新奥尔良①的时候，你会一到站就把她完全忘了吗？你会告诉你的妻子或爱人，跟她讲起你看到的一个女人吗？你的想法能够帮助我，我很想知道，我愿意为她做一点儿什么事情。

有一天傍晚，我故意走到那条街上，停下来跟她打招呼。她家里的几个人都在场，可是他们走开了，让位给我。真糟糕，我不知道怎么起个话头。你知道吗？某某先生，某某小姐，人哪，天气哪，庄稼收成哪，新来的牧师哪，欢乐的聚会哪，教堂的善举哪，打兔子和鼹鼠哪，"老爷子"店里的新式冷饮哪，火车时刻表哪，梅肯是个什么样的城市哪，黑人移居北方哪，棉子象鼻虫哪，糖浆哪，《圣经》哪，说了这些，她都用"是呀，先生"或者"不是呀，先生"来支吾，没有进一步的意见。我不由开始猜想，是不是我自己情绪上敏锐，反而施展一个招数捉弄起我来了呢？"我们散步去吧。"我终于壮起胆子说。在唱了这么久的独角戏之后出来这么一条意见，这也够新鲜的，我捉摸，要叫她吃一惊。不过，也没有那么回事。有些地方使我觉得，我以前的那些男人，正是用这句话作为奉献他们的身体的序曲的。我想办法用我的眼色告诉她。我想她会明白的。她那种使我张口结舌的东西消失了。这种东西一经消失，她就以我曾经想过但从来没见过的方式变成可以看得见的了。我们沿着狄克西大道走下去，家家户户门廊上的人都张开嘴望着我们。"多叫人生气呀？"她指的是那一溜说长道短的人。她指的是这个世界。我们穿过一丛成熟得可以砍下来

---

① 这些都是美国从北到南一些城市的名称，并不都在美国东部。

(it makes no difference if you sit in the Pullman or the Jim Crow as the train crosses her road), what thoughts would come to you—that is, after you'd finished all the thoughts that leap into men's minds at the sight of a pretty woman who will not deny them; what thoughts would come to you, had you seen her in a quick flash, keen and intuitively, as she sat there on her porch when your train thundered by? Would you have got off at the next station and come back for her to take her where? Would you have completely forgotten her as soon as you reached Macon, Atlanta, Augusta, Pasadena, Madison, Chicago, Boston, or New Orleans? Would you tell your wife or sweetheart about a girl you saw? Your thoughts can help me, and I would like to know. Something I would do for her.

One evening I walked up the Pike on purpose, and stopped to say hello. Some of her family were about, but they moved away to make room for me. Damn if I knew how to begin. Would you? Mr. and Miss So-and-So, people, the weather, the crops, the new preacher, the frolic, the church benefit, rabbit and possum hunting, the new soft drink they had at Old Pap's store, the schedule of the trains, what kind of town Macon was, Negro's migration North, bollweevils, syrup, the Bible—to all these things she gave a yassur or nassur, without further comment. I began to wonder if perhaps me own emotional sensibility had played one of its tricks on me. "Let's take a walk," I at last ventured. The suggestion, coming after so long an isoltion, was novel enough, I guess, to surprise. But it wasn't that. Something told me that men before me had said just that as a prelude to the offering of their bodies. I tried to tell her with my eyes. I think she understood. The thing from her that made my throat catch, vanished. Its passing left her visible in a way I'd thought, but never seen. We walked down the Pike with people on all the porches gaping at us. "Doesnt it make you mad?"She meant the row of petty gossiping people. She meant the world. Through a canebrake that was ripe for cutting, the branch was reached. Under a sweet-gum tree, and where reddish leaves had dammed the creek a little, we sat down. Dusk, suggesting the almost imperceptible procession of giant

的甘蔗，来到一条河边，我们坐在一株香枫树下面，红色的枫叶都有点儿把小河堵住了。薄暮，它引起了一种几乎觉察不到的巨树成林的印象，在甘蔗丛周围投下了一片紫色的薄雾。我觉得怪不自在，我在佐治亚州一直有这种感觉，尤其是在黄昏时分。我觉得人们看不见的那些东西立刻变成可以捉摸的了。即使我看到了幻象，我也不会觉得惊奇。佐治亚州的人经常遇到这种事，多得你想象不到。有一次一个黑女人看见了基督的母亲，用木炭把她画在法院的墙上……一个人踏上了祖先的故土，差不多什么事都会碰上……出于习惯势力，我估计是这样。我把芙恩抱在怀里，这就是说，起先我也没有留意。后来我的思想又回到了她身上。她那双眼睛，古怪得出奇，眼睁睁地，盯住我。盯住了上帝。上帝也流到了她眼里，就像我看到一片农村风光汇合到她眼里那样。人也是那样。我一定做出了什么事情，什么，我不知道，我的感情很混乱。她跳起来，冲到离我有一段距离的地方。她跪下来，开始摇摆，摇摇摆摆。她的身体受了什么折磨，摆脱不了。仿佛沸腾的液汁涌进了她的两臂和手指，她摇动着手臂和手指，好像给烫疼了。它涌到了她嗓子里，溅出来，发出含糊不清、痛楚抽搐的声音，夹杂着对耶稣基督的呼号。于是她唱起歌来，断断续续的。像一个犹太教唱诗班领唱人在用破嗓子唱诗。像个小孩子的声音，那也不一定，也许像个老头子的。薄暮把她掩蔽起来了。我只听得见她的歌声。我觉得好像她痛苦得在用头来撞地。我向她奔过去。她晕倒在我怀里。

关于她在甘蔗地里晕倒在我怀里的事，有些闲话。镇上有些以她的保护者自命的人还恶狠狠地瞪了我一两眼。事实上，还有一些要我离开这个镇市的话。不过他们并没有这样做。可是他们派人来看着我。不久之后，我就回北方去了。火车穿过她那条街的时候，我从车窗里看到了她。看到她在门廊上，头稍稍倾向那根钉子，两只眼睛模模糊糊地注视着日落。我看到她脸上的表情汇合到她眼睛里。农村的风光和我称作上帝的什么东西也都汇合在她眼睛里……其实，从来也没有发生过什么事。芙恩从来没遇到什么事情，甚至连我也没有遇到什么事。我要为她做点儿什么事情。什么不具名的好事……朋友，你呢？她还活着。我有理由知道她还活着。她的姓名，假定你碰巧有个到那里去的机会，她的姓名是芙尔妮·梅·罗森。

trees, settled with a purple haze about the cane. I felt strange, as I always do in Georgia, particularly at dusk. I felt that things unseen to men were tangibly immediate. It would not have surprised me had I had vision. People have them in Georgia more often than you would suppose. A black woman once saw the mother of Christ and drew her in charcoal on the courthouse wall... When one is on the soil of one's ancestors, most anything can come to one... From force of habit, I suppose, I held Fern in my arms—that is, without at first noticing it. Then my mind came back to her. Her eyes, unusually weird and open, held me. Held God. He flowed in as I've seen the country-side flow in. Seen men. I must have done something—what, I dont know, in the confusion of my emotion. She sprang up. Rushed some distance from me. Fell to her knees, and began swaying, swaying. Her body was tortured with something it could not let out. Like boiling sap it flooded arms and fingers till she shook them as if they burned her. It found her throat, and spattered inarticulately in plaintive, convulsive sounds, mingled with calls to Christ Jesus. And then she sang, brokenly. A Jewish cantor singing with a broken voice. A child's voice, uncertain, or an old man's. Dusk hid her; I could hear only her song. It seemed to me as though she were pounding her head in anguish upon the ground. I rushed to her. She fainted in my arms.

There was talk about her fainting with me in the canefield. And I got one or two ugly looks from town men who'd set themselves up to protect her. In fact, there was talk of making me leave town. But they never did. They kept a watch-out for me, though. Shortly after, I came back North. From the train window I saw her as I crossed her road. Saw her on her porch, head tilted a little forward where the nail was, eyes vaguely focused on the sunset. Saw her face flow into them, the countryside and something that I call God, flowing into them... Nothing ever really happened. Nothing ever came to Fern, not even I. Something I would do for her. Some fine unnamed thing... And, friend, you? She is still living, I have reason to know. Her name, against the chance that you might happen down that way, is Fernie May Rosen.

041. 拳击大赛①

(美)拉尔夫·艾利森 著　　雨 宁 译

041. **The Battle Royal**

by Ralph Ellison

那是很久以前的事,已经 20 来年了。我这一辈子一直在寻找什么东西,我每到一个地方,总有人来告诉那是什么东西。我也接受了他们的答案,不过,这些答案往往相互矛盾,甚至自相矛盾。我很幼稚,我是在寻找我自己,那些问题都是我能够回答的,而且只有我能够回答,我却逢人便问,偏偏不问我自己。我指望能实现的那些东西都是别的每一个人似乎生来就有的,我却耗费了很长的时间,还有许多次遭到自食其果的痛苦。我是个无足轻重的人,无非就是我自己。可是首先我不得不透露一下身份,我是个隐身人。

我并非本质上有什么玄虚,我的家世也不玄虚。我是大家意料之中的人,85 年前,大家对别的事情也一视同仁(也许有些轩轾)。我的祖父母原先是奴隶,这并没有使我感到惭愧。我只为我自己感到惭愧,因为我曾经一度感到羞耻。大约在 85 年前,有人告诉他们,他们得到自由了,在与公益有关的一切事情上,他们与全国其他的人是结合在一起的,但在与群居交往有关的一切事情上,他们是像手指头一样分开的。他们相信了这种话。他们为此而感到欢欣鼓舞。他们安分守己,勤勉地工作,并且把我父亲培养起来继承家风。不过我祖父却是个独一无二的人。他是个怪老头,我的祖父,大家都说我接了他的班。是他惹出麻烦来的。他在临终的时候把我父亲叫到他眼前,他说:"儿啊,我去世之后,我要你把那场硬仗继续打下去,我从来没对你说过这件事,可是我们的生活是一场战争,我活了这一辈子,时时都在做叛徒,自从我

IT goes a long way back, some twenty years. All my life I had been looking for something, and everywhere I turned someone tried to tell me what it was. I accepted their answers too, though they were often in contradiction and even self-contradictory. I was naive. I was looking for myself and asking everyone except myself questions which I, and only I, could answer. It took me a long time and much painful boomeranging of my expectations to achieve a realization everyone else appears to have been born with: That I am nobody but myself. But first I had to discover that I am an invisible man!

And yet I am no freak of nature, nor of history. I was in the cards, other things having been equal (or unequal) eighty-five years ago. I am not ashamed of my grandparents for having been slaves. I am only ashamed of myself for having at one time been ashamed. About eighty-five years ago they were told that they were free, united with others of our country in everything pertaining to the common good, and, in everything social, separate like the fingers of the hand. And they believed it. They exulted in it. They stayed in their place, worked hard, and brought up my father to do the same. But my grandfather is the one. He was an odd old guy, my grandfather, and I am told I take after him. It was he who caused the trouble. On his deathbed he called my father to him and said, "Son, after I'm gone I want you to keep up the good fight. I never told you, but our life is a war and I have been a traitor all my born days, a spy in the enemy's country ever since I give up my gun back in the Reconstruction. Live with your head in the lion's mouth. I want you to overcome 'em with yeses, undermine 'em with grins, agree 'em to death and destruction, let 'em

---

① 这是艾利森的长篇小说《隐身人》的第一章。美国的许多选本都选用了这一章。

作者简介:拉尔夫·艾利森(Ralph Ellison,1914—1994),美国作家。1914 年 3 月 1 日生于俄克拉荷马州俄克拉荷马城,1994 年 4 月 16 日卒于纽约。他因作品《隐形人》(*Invisible Man*,1952)受到关注,作品描写了一位无名的美国黑人,引起了美国种族间的强烈反应。这部作品被认为是自从第二次世界大战后美国最杰出的作品之一。后来他又出版了《影子与行动》(*Shadow and Act*,1964)和《步入文学界》(*Going to the Territory*,1986)两部散文集。

把我的枪交还给重建南方运动之后，我就成了敌人国土里的一名间谍。把你的头放在狮子口里过日子吧，我要你用满口'是、是、是'来克服他们，要咧开嘴笑来破坏他们，要对他们表示同意来使他们死亡和毁灭，让他们把你吞下去直到他们呕吐起来或者撑破了肚子。"他们都认为老头子头脑不中用了。他一向是这里最驯良的人。于是年幼的孩子们都被赶出了房间，窗帘都拉拢了，灯里的火苗也调得很低，仿佛老头子的呼吸一样，在灯芯上扑腾。"让小一辈也学会这一招。"他拼死拼活用微弱的气息说完这句话就死了。

祖父的死倒不如他临终的一席话更使我父母感到惊慌。有人认为他根本没有死，他的话引起了重重焦虑。有人郑重其事地告诉我，要我把他说过的话完全忘掉，的确，这也是在我们家庭之外第一次有人提起了这件事。不过，这番话对我所起的作用极大，我从来也没有摸准他话里的意思。祖父是一位默不作声、从不惹事的老人，可是到了临终，他把他自己说成是叛徒和间谍，把他的驯良说成是危险的活动。这番话变成了隐藏在我头脑里无法回答的一个经常存在的谜。每逢我事事顺利，我就想起了我的祖父，感到内疚和不安。那就仿佛我身不由己地在遵循他的告诫。更糟的是，人人都因此而喜欢我。我受到了本城血统极纯的白人的称赞。他们认为我是言行有方的表率，跟我祖父生前一样。我觉得我都给闹糊涂了，老爷子偏偏把这种行为解释成阴谋。大家称赞我的品行，我却感到负疚，仿佛我的所作所为有几分实在跟白人的意愿相反，如果他们明白了。他们会指望我做得完全相反。我感到负疚的是，我居然会变得阴沉卑鄙，那种事又正是他们要我做的，即使他们受了骗，以为他们是要我这样做的，反正也都是这么回事。我生怕有那么一天，他们会把我看成叛徒，那我可完了。可是我更加不敢采取其他任何办法，因为他们根本不喜欢那一套。老爷子的话好像一种诅咒。毕业的那天，我发表了一篇演讲，说明谦卑是进步的秘诀，实在是须臾不可少的要素（并不是因为我相信这种话，想起我的祖父，我怎么能相信这种话呢？我相信的不过是这样的话行得通罢了）。这篇演说十分见效。人人都称赞我，我还承蒙邀请，要到城里出类拔萃的白人公民的一次集会上去讲讲。这是我们整个居民区的胜利。

会场是首屈一指的旅馆的主舞厅。我走到旅馆

swoller you till they vomit or bust wide open." They thought the old man had gone out of his mind. He had been the meekest of men. The younger children were rushed from the room, the shades drawn and the flame of the lamp turned so low that it sputtered on the wick like the old man's breathing. "Learn it to the young-uns," he whispered fiercely; then he died.

But my folks were more alarmed over his last words than over his dying. It was as though he had not died at all, his words caused so much anxiety. I was warned emphatically to forget what he had said and, indeed, this is the first time it has been mentioned outside the family circle. It had a tremendous effect upon me, however. I could never be sure of what he meant. Grandfather had been a quiet old man who never made any trouble, yet on his deathbed he had called himself a traitor and a spy, and he had spoken of his meekness as a dangerous activity. It became a constant puzzle which lay unanswered in the back of my mind. And whenever things went well for me I remembered my grandfather and felt guilty and uncomfortable. It was as though I was carrying out his advice in spite of myself. And to make it worse, everyone loved me for it. I was praised by the most lily-white men of the town. I was considered an example of desirable conduct—just as my grandfather had been. And what puzzled me was that the old man had defined it as *treachery*. When I was praised for my conduct I felt a guilt that in some way I was doing something that was really against the wishes of the white folks, that if they had understood they would have desired me to act just the opposite, that I should have been sulky and mean, and that that really would have been what they wanted, even though they were fooled and thought they wanted me to act as I did. It made me afraid that some day they would look upon me as a traitor and I would be lost. Still I was more afraid to act any other way because they didn't like that at all. The old man's words were like a curse. On my graduation day I delivered an oration in which I showed that humility was the secret, indeed, the very essence of progress. (Not that I believed this—how could I, remembering my grandfather? —I only believed that it worked.) It was a great success. Everyone praised me and I was invited to give the speech at a gathering of the town's leading white citizens. It was a triumph for our whole community.

It was in the main ballroom of the leading hotel.

里,发现我正好赶上一次非正式的男宾社交活动,有人对我说,既然我反正是要到这里来的,那就也来参加这场拳击大赛①吧,这是余兴节目之一,参加的人还有我的几个同学。这场拳击大赛是第一个节目。

城里所有的大人物都在场,他们身穿无尾晚礼服,狼吞虎咽地饱食自助餐的食品,喝啤酒和威士忌酒,抽黑色的雪茄烟。那是一间天花板很高的大房间。椅子整整齐齐安排在临时搭起的拳击场三面。第四面空出来,看得见发光的打蜡地板。顺便说一句,我觉得这场拳击大赛有点儿不妙。不是因为我不喜欢拳击,而是因为我不喜欢那些参加比赛的人。他们都是粗野的家伙,仿佛都没有什么祖父的诅咒使他们烦心。他们那种粗野脾气是谁也不会看错的。此外,我还捉摸着打一场拳击大赛可能使我的演讲有失尊严。在我未成为隐身人之前的那些日子里,我自视为未来的布克尔·特·华盛顿②。可是他们也不大喜欢我,他们有9个人。我觉得,在我这一行里,我比他们高明,我不喜欢那种让我们都拥挤在仆人用的电梯里的做法。他们也不喜欢我来插一脚。事实上,在一层一层明亮有暖意的地板从电梯门前闪过的时候,我们还争了几句,为的是我参加这次拳击大赛,挤掉了他们的一位朋友一夜的工作。

我们由人带领,从电梯里出来,穿过一间洛可可式③的华丽大厅,来到正厅外面的小房间里,于是有人吩咐我们换上拳击打扮。在发给我们每人一副拳击手套之后,他领着我们出去,走进那个装了些大镜子的厅堂里。我们在走进去的时候,一面小心谨慎地张望四周,一面小声交谈,生怕我们的声音会在这嘈杂的厅堂里给别人听见。雪茄烟使室内烟雾腾腾。威士忌酒业已发生作用。我看到有些当地极重要的人物醉态毕露,十分吃惊。他们全都在场,银行家,律师,法官,医生,救火会头脑,教师,商人。甚至还有一位比较时髦的牧师。前面正在发生什么事情,我们看不见。一只单簧管吹奏得抑扬悦耳,许多人站起来,急忙拥向前去。我们这一小群人处境很困难,都挤在一起,赤裸的上身相互挨着,发出预期的汗水亮光。

----

① 拳击大赛是一种拳击比赛,同时出场比赛的至少为3人,以经过一场混战最后仍站得住的那个人为胜利者。

② 布克尔·特·华盛顿(1856—1915),美国教育家。

③ 18世纪的一种纤巧、浮华的欧洲建筑风格,由于装饰得过分繁琐而显得俗气。

When I got there I discovered that it was on the occasion of a smoker, and I was told that since I was to be there anyway I might as well take part in the battle royal to be fought by some of my schoolmates as part of the entertainment. The battle royal came first.

All of the town's big shots were there in their tuxedoes, wolfing down the buffet foods, drinking beer and whiskey and smoking black cigars. It was a large room with a high ceiling. Chairs were arranged in neat rows around three sides of a portable boxing ring. The fourth side was clear, revealing a gleaming space of polished floor. I had some misgivings over the battle royal, by the way. Not from a distaste for fighting, but because I didn't care too much for the other fellows who were to take part. They were tough guys who seemed to have no grandfather's curse worrying their minds. No one could mistake their toughness. And besides, I suspected that fighting a battle royal might detract from the dignity of my speech. In those pre-invisible days I visualized myself as a potential Booker T. Washington. But the other fellows didn't care too much for me either, and there were nine of them. I felt superior to them in my way, and I didn't like the manner in which we were all crowded together into the servants' elevator. Nor did they like my being there. In fact, as the warmly lighted floors flashed past the elevator we had words over the fact that I, by taking part in the fight, had knocked one of their friends out of a night's work.

We were led out of the elevator through a rococo hall into an anteroom and told to get into our fighting togs. Each of us was issued a pair of boxing gloves and ushered out into the big mirrored hall, which we entered looking cautiously about us and whispering, lest we might accidentally be heard above the noise of the room. It was foggy with cigar smoke. And already the whiskey was taking effect. I was shocked to see some of the most important men of the town quite tipsy. They were all there—bankers, lawyers, judges, doctors, fire chiefs, teachers, merchants. Even one of the more fashionable pastors. Something we could not see was going on up front. A clarinet was vibrating sensuously and the men were standing up and moving eagerly forward. We were a small tight group, clustered together, our bare upper bodies touching and shining with anticipatory sweat; while up front the big shots were becoming increasingly excited over something we

前面的大人物正在为什么事变得越来越激动,我们仍旧看不出来。突然间,我听到先前吩咐我到这里来的那位督学吆喝道:"各位先生,把那些小黑鬼带上来!把那些小黑鬼带上来!"

我们于是被驱赶到舞厅正面,那里的烟草和酒的气味甚至更强烈。我们在推攘之下各就各位,我几乎尿湿了短裤。在我们周围只看得见无数的面孔,有的带有敌意,有的露出感到有趣的笑容。大厅中央,面对着我们,站着一位美艳的金发女郎,赤裸裸一丝不挂。顿时声息全无。我觉得一股冷风吹得我寒飕飕的。我想退出局外,可是我身后和左右都是他们的人。有些小伙子低下头站着发抖。我觉得心里有一阵毫无道理的内疚和恐惧的波动。我的牙齿打颤,起了一身鸡皮疙瘩,两只膝盖向内翻。可是我受到强烈的吸引,不由自主地望着。即使望的代价是让我变成瞎子,我也会望下去的。她的头发黄得像一个塑料的马戏班舞女,脸上的粉和胭脂太美了,仿佛要化成一只抽象的面具,两只眼睛凹进去,一抹淡蓝色,跟狒狒屁股的颜色相仿。我的眼光慢慢掠过她的身体,我真想朝她吐一口唾沫。她的乳房很饱满,很圆,像东印度庙宇的圆顶。我站得离她这么近,都看得出她那细皮肤的纹理,汗水在她那挺立的粉红色乳头周围像露珠一样闪烁着。我恨不得马上跑到室外,钻到地板下面,同时又想走到她跟前,用我的身体遮住她,让我和其他人的眼睛都看不到她,抚摸她那柔软的大腿,拥抱她,而且毁掉她,同她相爱然后弄死她,可是隐瞒着不让她知道,不过摸到她肚子上刺有小美国国旗花纹以下的地方,她的臀部形成了一个大写的 V 字,我有了一种想法,以为在室内所有的人里面,她那双纯客观的眼睛只看见了我。

于是她开始跳舞,动作缓慢优美,那一百支雪茄的烟贴附着她的身体,好似极薄的纱衣。她好像在纱幕包围之中的一位漂亮的饲鸟女郎,正在从灰蒙蒙、气势汹汹的大海表面上来呼唤我。我心驰神怡。这时,我又觉察到了单簧管吹奏的声音和那些大人物向我们吆喝的声音。我看到我右面的一个小伙子晕倒了。这时候,有一个人抓起桌上的一个银水罐,凑近他,把冰水泼在他身上,拉他起来并且硬要我们之中的两个人扶着他,他低着头,从发青的厚嘴唇里吐出了呻吟的声音。另外一个小伙子开始要求让他回家。他是我们这一伙里个子最大的,那条深红色的短裤太

still could not see. Suddenly I heard the school superintendent, who had told me to come, yell, "Bring up the shines, gentlemen! Bring up the little shines!"

We were rushed up to the front of the ballroom, where it smelled even more strongly of tobacco and whiskey. Then we were pushed into place. I almost wet my pants. A sea of faces, some hostile, some amused, ringed around us, and in the center, facing us, stood a magnificent blonde—stark naked. There was a dead silence. I felt a blast of cold air chill me. I tried to back away, but they were behind me and around me. Some of the boys stood with lowered heads trembling. I felt a wave of irrational guilt and fear. My teeth chattered, my skin turned to goose flesh, my knees knocked. Yet I was strongly attracted and looked in spite of myself. Had the price of looking been blindness, I would have looked. The hair was yellow like that of a circus kewpie doll, the face heavily powdered and rouged, as though to form an abstract mask, the eyes hollow and smeared a cool blue, the color of a baboon's butt. I felt a desire to spit upon her as my eyes brushed slowly over her body. Her breasts were firm and round as the domes of East Indian temples, and I stood so close as to see the fine skin texture and beads of pearly perspiration glistening like dew around the pink and erected buds of her nipples. I wanted at one and the same time to run from the room, to sink through the floor, or go to her and cover her from my eyes and the eyes of the others with my body; to feel the soft thighs, to caress her and destroy her, to love her and murder her, to hide from her, and yet to stroke where below the small American flag tattooed upon her belly her thighs formed a capital V. I had a notion that of all in the room she saw only me with her impersonal eyes.

And then she began to dance, a slow sensuous movement; the smoke of a hundred cigars clinging to her like the thinnest of veils. She seemed like a fair bird-girl girdled in veils calling to me from the angry surface of some gray and threatening sea. I was transported. Then I became aware of the clarinet playing and the big shots yelling at us. Some threatened us if we looked and others if we did not. On my right I saw one boy faint. And now a man grabbed a silver pitcher from a table and stepped close as he dashed ice water upon him and stood him up and forced two of us to support him as his head hung and moans issued from his thick bluish lips. Another boy began to plead to go

小,遮不住下体,露出那个直挺挺的东西,仿佛这是对单簧管在低音域呻吟的靡靡之音的答复。

　　在这一大段时间里,那个金发女人不停地跳舞。一面对那些看得入迷的大人物淡淡地微笑,一面对我们这些神色慌张的人略示哂意。我看到有一个商人像饿鬼似的尾随着她,他的嘴唇松弛地流出口水。他是一个大块头,胸前的衬衣上有一颗钻石扣子,下面的大肚子撑得衬衣圆鼓鼓的,每逢那个金发女人摆动她那起伏的臀部,他的手就会伸到他那个秃头上的稀疏头发里,在他举起双臂的时候,他的姿势笨得像个醉醺醺的熊猫,下流地慢慢扭动肚皮。这个家伙完全入了迷。音乐的节拍加快了。这个舞女一脸超然的表情,突然猛烈地转动臀部,这时候,那些人都要来伸手摸她一下。我可以看到他们粗壮的手指在戳那柔软的皮肉。有些人想制止他们,于是她开始在地板上优美地转圈子,他们就追她,滑倒在打过蜡的地板上。真是发疯。椅子撞倒了,酒泼了,他们嘻嘻哈哈,号叫着来追赶她。她刚跑到一扇门口,他们就抓住了她,拉住她四肢使她身体离地,像大学生捉弄新生那样把她抛上抛下。我看见在她那笑容凝滞的红唇之上,她眼睛里露出恐怖和厌恶的神色,差不多跟我自身感到的恐怖一样,我看出其他几个小伙子也感到同样的恐怖。我继续望下去,他们又抛了她一次,她的柔软乳房似乎在半空中给拉得扁平了,在她荡来荡去的时候,她的两腿像发狂似的挣扎。有些比较清醒的人帮助她逃走了。我也开始离开这里,跟其他小伙子向外面那间房走去。

　　有些人仍然在流泪,哭笑无常。正当我们要走出去,却被拦住了,他们命令我们走到拳击场里。没有法子,我们只好照办。我们10个人都从绳子下面钻进去,让他们用宽白布条把我们的眼睛蒙起来。他们之中有一个人似乎有一点儿同情心,在我们背靠着绳子站着的时候,他设法来使我们打起精神。我们之中有的人咧着嘴想笑。“瞧见那边的那个小子没有?”他们之中的一个说,“我要你铃声一响立刻跑过去揍他的肚子。如果你揍不倒他,我可要揍你啦。我不喜欢他那个样子。”于是我们都给蒙住了眼睛。即使在这种当口儿,我还在默诵一遍我的演说。在我头脑里,每一个字都像火焰一样灿烂发光。我感到蒙眼布绑扎得端正了,我皱起眉头,使它能在我不皱眉的时候变得松一点儿。

home. He was the largest of the group, wearing dark red fighting trunks much too small to conceal the erection which projected from him as though in answer to the insinuating low-registered moaning of the clarinet. He tried to hide himself with his boxing gloves.

　　And all the while the blonde continued dancing, smiling faintly at the big shots who watched her with fascination, and faintly smiling at our fear. I noticed a certain merchant who followed her hungrily, his lips loose and drooling. He was a large man who wore diamond studs in a shirtfront which swelled with the ample paunch underneath, and each time the blonde swayed her undulating hips he ran his hand through the thin hair of his bald head and, with his arms upheld, his posture clumsy like that of an intoxicated panda, wound his belly in a slow and obscene grind. This creature was completely hypnotized. The music had quickened. As the dancer flung herself about with a detached expression on her face, the men began reaching out to touch her. I could see their beefy fingers sink into the soft flesh. Some of the others tried to stop them and she began to move around the floor in graceful circles, as they gave chase, slipping and sliding over the polished floor. It was mad. Chairs went crashing, drinks were spilt, as they ran laughing and howling after her. They caught her just as she reached a door, raised her from the floor, and tossed her as college boys are tossed at a hazing, and above her red, fixed-smiling lips I saw the terror and disgust in her eyes, almost like my own terror and that which I saw in some of the other boys. As I watched, they tossed her twice and her soft breasts seemed to flatten against the air and her legs flung wildly as she spun. Some of the more sober ones helped her to escape. And I started off the floor, heading for the anteroom with the rest of the boys.

　　Some were still crying and in hysteria. But as we tried to leave we were stopped and ordered to get into the ring. There was nothing to do but what we were told. All ten of us climbed under the ropes and allowed ourselves to be blindfolded with broad bands of white cloth. One of the men seemed to feel a bit sympathetic and tried to cheer us up as we stood with our backs against the ropes. Some of us tried to grin. "See that boy over there?" one of the men said. "I want you to run across at the bell and give it to him right in the belly. If you don't get him, I'm going to get you. I don't like his looks." Each of us was told the same.

可是这时我突然感到一阵盲目的恐怖。我不习惯于摸黑。这就仿佛我突然发现自己是在一间充满了有毒的噬鱼蛇的黑屋子里，我听得出那些模糊的声音在叫喊着，一定要马上开始进行拳击大赛。

"到场子里面去！"

"让我来收拾那个大个子黑鬼！"

我使劲儿想听听有没有督学的声音，仿佛从这个稍微熟悉一点儿的声音里可以挤出什么安全保证。

"让我来收拾那些黑婊子养的！"有一个人叫喊道。

"不行，杰克逊，不行！"另外一个声音喊道，"这儿来个人，帮我制住杰克。"

"我要收拾那个姜黄色的黑鬼。把他的胳膊腿都拧下来。"原先的那个声音喊道。

我靠绳子站着，身上发抖。因为我正是他们当时叫做姜黄色的那种人，他的话听起来好像会把我当做一块松脆的姜汁饼放在牙齿中间嚼碎似的。

一场不小的你争我夺已在进行。椅子踢来踢去。我听得出有些十分吃力的呼噜呼噜的声音。我想瞧一瞧，我从来没有这样不顾一切地想瞧一瞧。可是那块蒙眼布紧得好像皮肤上结了一块厚瘢疤，我举起戴着手套的手要把那几层白布推开，这时候，一个声音喝道："哼，办不到，你休想，你这个黑杂种。不许碰那块布。"

"敲铃，要不，杰克逊就会弄死一个黑浣熊①了。"有人在突然的寂静中吼道。于是我听到了铿锵的铃声和脚步拖拖拉拉向前移动的声音。

一只手套打中了我的头。我就势转过身，有人从我旁边走过，我狠狠地打出一拳，震颤的感觉传遍我的手臂直到肩头。接着，好像9个小伙子全来对付我了。拳头从四面八方打到我身上，我也使出最大的本领还击。我挨打的次数太多了，不由怀疑到在这个拳击场里是不是只有我给蒙上了眼睛，要不然，也许那个叫杰克逊的人在收拾我的时候毕竟没有完全得逞。

由于蒙住了眼睛，我再也不能控制我的动作，我也无体面可言。我像一个小娃娃或者一个醉汉那样跌跌绊绊。烟雾更浓了，我每挨一次打，烟雾都似乎

---

① 浣熊是生长在美国南部沼泽地区的动物，亦称为树狸，也是美国南方白人对黑人的侮辱性称呼。

The blindfolds were put on. Yet even then I had been going over my speech. In my mind each word was as bright as flame. I felt the cloth pressed into place, and frowned so that it would be loosened when I relaxed.

But now I felt a sudden fit of blind terror. I was unused to darkness. It was as though I had suddenly found myself in a dark room filled with poisonous cottonmouths. I could hear the bleary voices yelling insistently for the battle royal to begin.

"Get going in there!"

"Let me at the big nigger!"

I strained to pick up the school superintendent's voice, as though to squeeze some security out of that slightly more familiar sound.

"Let me at those black sonsabitches!" someone yelled.

"No, Jackson, no!" another voice yelled. "Here somebody, help me hold Jack."

"I want to get at that ginger-colored nigger. Tear him limb from limb," the first voice yelled.

I stood against the ropes trembling. For in those days I was what they called ginger-colored, and he sounded as though he might crunch me between his teeth like a crisp ginger cookie.

Quite a struggle was going on. Chairs were being kicked about and I could hear voices grunting as with a terrific effort. I wanted to see, to see more desperately than ever before. But the blindfold was as tight as a thick skin-puckering scab and when I raised my gloved hands to push the layers of white aside a voice yelled, "Oh, no you don't, black bastard! Leave that alone!"

"Ring the bell before Jackson kills him a coon!" someone boomed in the sudden silence. And I heard the bell clang and the sound of feet scuffling forward.

A glove smacked against my head. I pivoted, striking out stiffy as someone went past, and felt the jar ripple along the length of my arm to my shoulder. Then it seemed as though all nine of the boys had turned upon me at once. Blows pounded me from all sides while I struck out as best I could. So many blows landed upon me that I wondered if I were not the only blindfolded fighter in the ring, or if the man called Jackson hadn't succeeded in getting me after all.

Blindfolded, I could no longer control my motions. I had no dignity. I stumbled about like a baby or a drunken man. The smoke had become thicker and with each new blow it seemed to sear and further

在把我的肺烘干,更加透不过气来。我的唾液变得像苦味的热胶水。一只手套击中我的头,使我嘴里充满了热血。到处都是拳头。我说不清我流的是汗还是血,只觉得身上潮乎乎的。有一拳狠狠打中了我的颈背,我觉得我在重温我的头碰到地板上的情形。蒙眼布后面的黑暗世界充满了一缕一缕蓝色的光线。我趴着,假装我被打晕过去了,但是觉得有人抓住我的手,猛然把我拖了起来。"赶紧一点儿,黑小子!进去混战一场!"我的胳膊好像灌了铅,我的头挨了许多拳,疼得厉害,我勉强摸到绳子旁边撑住,想喘喘气。一只手套打中我的中段,我又倒下了,觉得烟雾变成了一把刀子,插进我的内脏。他们的腿在我周围乱转,把我推来推去,我终于站直了,而且发现我能看出那些黑糊糊、汗流浃背的身形在烟蓝色空气中穿梭般地来往,好像喝醉酒跳舞的人随着像拳击声般的急骤鼓点在来回穿梭似的。

人人都在发狂似的殴斗。完全乱了套。你打我、我打他。凑合在一起去打人的事都维持不了多久。有时,两个,三个,甚至四个人一起去打一个人,接着就相互打起来,后来他们自己又受到攻击。裤带下面,肾脏,都会挨打,拳击手套有时是张开的,有时是攥紧了的,现在我的眼睛可以睁开一点儿,这种情形也不显得十分可怕了。我小心地行动,免得挨打,但避开的次数也不能太多,以免引起他们注意,我从这一群里打到那一群里。小伙子们都像瞎子一样摸索着试探,有些小心谨慎、脾气别扭的就哈着腰来保护他们的中段,他们都是缩头拱肩、神经紧张地伸出手臂,用拳头在烟雾里试探,好像过敏的蜗牛的圆头触角。我瞥见在一个角落里,有一个小伙子用拳头猛烈地向空气里戳来戳去,还听到他痛得叫喊的声音,原来他的拳头打中了拳击场的柱子。霎时间,我看到他弯下腰捂着他的手,接着,因为没护住头,挨了一拳,他就倒下了。我挑逗这群人来打那一群人,我溜过去,打一拳立刻退出来,把别人推到那场混战里去替我挨那些瞎打的拳头。烟呛得人很难受,这种拳击又不分轮次,不每隔三分钟敲一次铃,使我们从精疲力竭之中得到片刻休息。这间屋子在我周围转起来了,乱纷纷的灯、烟和流汗的身体,都在紧张的白人面孔包围之下。我的鼻子和嘴都在流血,血溅在我的胸膛上。

那些人仍然吆喝着:"狠狠揍他,黑小子!揍得他肠子流出来!"

restrict my lungs. My saliva became like a hot bitter glue. A glove connected with my head, filling my mouth with warm blood. It was everywhere. I could not tell if the moisture I felt upon my body was sweat or blood. A blow landed hard against the nape of my neck. I felt myself going over my head hitting the floor. Streaks of blue light filled the black world behind the blindfold. I lay prone, pretending that I was knocked out, but felt myself seized by hands and yanked to my feet. "Get going, black boy! Mix it up!" My arms were like lead, my head smarting from blows. I managed to feel my way to the ropes and held on, trying to catch my breath. A glove landed in my midsection and I went over again, feeling as though the smoke had become a knife jabbed into my guts. Pushed this way and that by the legs milling around me, I finally pulled erect and discovered that I could see the black, sweat-washed forms weaving in the smoky-blue atmosphere like drunken dancers weaving to the rapid drum-like thuds of blows.

Everone fought hysterically. It was complete anarchy. Everybody fought everybody else. No group fought together for long. Two, three, four, fought one, then turned to fight each other, were themselves attacked. Blows landed below the belt and in the kidney, with the gloves open as well as closed, and with my eye partly open now there was not so much terror. I moved carefully, avoiding blows, although not too many to attract attention, fighting from group to group. The boys groped about like blind, cautious crabs crouching to protect their mid-sections, their heads pulled in short against their shoulders, their arms stretched nervously before them, with their fists testing the smoke-filled air like the knobbed feelers of hypersensitive snails. In one corner I glimpsed a boy violently punching the air and heard him scream in pain as he smashed his hand against a ring post. For a second I saw him bent over holding his hand, then going down as a blow caught his unprotected head. I played one group against the other, slipping in and throwing a punch then stepping out of range while pushing the others into the melee to take the blows blindly aimed at me. The smoke was agonizing and there were no rounds, no bells at three minute intervals to relieve our exhaustion. The room spun round me, a swirl of lights, smoke, sweating bodies surrounded by tense white faces. I bled from both nose and

"向上揍他的下巴！揍死他。揍死那个大个儿的小子！"

我假装摔倒了，还看见另外一个小伙子沉重地摔倒在我旁边，仿佛我们是一拳打倒的两个人，我还看见一只穿胶底运动鞋的脚迅速踹到他的腹股沟里，那两个打倒他的人也给绊倒在他身上。我就势一滚，避开了，感到一阵恶心。

我们殴斗得越狠，那些人也变得更声势逼人。可是，我又在为我的演说担心。讲完了会有什么效果呢？他们会承认我的能力吗？他们会给我什么呢？

我正在无意识地，不由自主地搏斗，突然间，我注意到小伙子们一个接一个都在离开拳击场。我感到诧异，十分恐慌，仿佛只留下我一个人来对付什么未可知的危险。然后我明白了。那些小伙子们早已安排好了。按照习惯，留在拳击场里的那两个人要决一胜负来夺取奖品。我发现得太晚了。铃声响了，两个穿夜礼服的人跳到拳击场里，摘下了我们的蒙眼布。我看出我面前的人是塔特洛克，这一帮里个子最大的。我觉得胃里恶心。我耳朵里的铃声还没有停止，第二遍铃又响了，我看到他迅速地向我扑过来。我想不出别的办法，一拳打中了他的鼻子。他不断地过来，还带来了馊汗的强烈刺鼻的腥臭。他的脸黑糊糊地没有表情，只有两只眼睛是生动的，含着对我的憎恨，又闪露出从我们大家的共同遭遇中感到的极度恐怖。我变得焦急起来，我要发表我那篇演说，可是他又向我扑过来，好像他存心要揍得我脑子里没有这篇演说。我一次又一次地打败他，同时任凭他来打我。我突然一时心血来潮，轻轻地打他，在我们扭到一起的时候，我悄悄地说："假装我打倒了你，你可以拿走奖品。"

"我要把你的屁股打成两半。"他粗声粗气地悄悄说。

"为他们吗？"

"为我，婊子养的。"

他们叫喊着要我们分开，塔特洛克一拳打得我转了半个圆圈，我好像一架给推了一下的照相机正在拍摄一个摇晃得炫目的场景，只看见那些嗥嗥叫的红面孔都紧张地蜷缩在蓝灰色烟云之中。一时间，天摇地动，世界散开了，流动起来，接着，我头脑清醒了，塔特洛克正在我面前跳上跳下。在我眼前闪动的那个影子正是他那只猛击过来的左手。然后，我的头向前

mouth, the blood spattering upon my chest.

The men kept yelling, "Slug him, black boy! Knock his guts out!"

"Uppercut him! Kill him! Kill that big boy!"

Taking a fake fall, I saw a boy going down heavily beside me as though we were felled by a single blow, saw a sneaker-clad foot shoot into his groin as the two who had knocked him down stumbled upon him. I rolled out of range, feeling a twinge of nausea.

The harder we fought the more threatening the men became. And yet, I had begun to worry about my speech again. How would it go? Would they recognize my ability? What would they give me?

I was fighting automatically when suddenly I noticed that one after another of the boys was leaving the ring. I was surprised, filled with panic, as though I had been left alone with an unknown danger. Then I understood. The boys had arranged it among themselves. It was the custom for the two men left in the ring to slug it out for the winner's prize. I discovered this too late. When the bell sounded two men in tuxedoes leaped into the ring and removed the blindfold. I found myself facing Tatlock, the biggest of the gang. I felt sick at my stomach. Hardly had the bell stopped ringing in my ears than it clanged again and I saw him moving swiftly toward me. Thinking of nothing else to do I hit him smash on the nose. He kept coming, bringing the rank sharp violence of stale sweat. His face was a black blank of a face, only his eyes alive—with hate of me and aglow with a feverish terror from what had happened to us all. I became anxious. I wanted to deliver my speech and he came at me as though he meant to beat it out of me. I smashed him again and again, taking his blows as they came. Then on a sudden impulse I struck him lightly and as we clinched, I whispered, "Fake like I knocked you out, you can have the prize."

"I'll break your behind," he whispered hoarsely.

"For *them*?"

"For *me*, sonofabitch."

They were yelling for us to break it up and Tatlock spun me half around with a blow, and as a joggled camera sweeps in a reeling scene, I saw the howling red faces crouching tense beneath the cloud of blue-gray smoke. For a moment the world wavered, unraveled, flowed, then my head cleared and Tatlock bounced before me. That fluttering shadow before my

倾,靠在他潮湿的肩头,我悄悄地说:

"我再添 5 块钱。"

"见鬼去吧!"

他的肌肉在我的压力下松弛了,我又说:"7 块呢?"

"给你妈去。"他说着,在我心脏下面狠狠打了我一下。

在我还跟他扭在一起的时候,我用头撞他,然后闪开。我觉得拳头像连珠炮一样打来,我在绝望中拼命回击。我要发表我的演说,这比别的任何事情都要紧,因为我觉得只有这些人才能真正判断我的能力,可是现在这个蠢货正在毁掉我的机会。这时,我开始打得比较用心了,我的速度比较快,我可以逼近他给他一拳,然后又闪开。碰巧一拳打中他的下巴,我把他也打晕了——直到我听见有人高声喊道,"我在大个子身上押的赌注到手了。"

听到这种话,我放松了警惕。我拿不定主意了,我要不要针对着这句话努力打赢这一场呢?这样做会不会跟我演说里讲的相反呢?现在是不是一个可以谦卑一下,采取不抵抗态度的机会呢?正在我跳来跳去的时候,一拳打中了我的头,使我的右眼凸出得像个打开盒子跳出来的小玩具人一样,解决了我进退两难的处境。我倒下去的时候,房间变成红的了。这仿佛是在梦中摔倒的,我的身体懒洋洋的,却十分挑剔,要找到中意的地方才肯倒下去,可是后来地板变得不耐烦了,反而撞上来凑合我。过了一会儿,我醒过来了。有人用催眠术的声音着重地说:"5"。我躺在那里,迷迷糊糊望着我自己的血里有一块殷红色的变成了一只蝴蝶,闪烁着向上飞到污秽的灰帆布世界里去。

等到这个声音慢吞吞说完"10"的时候,我被他们扶起来,拖到一把椅子上。我直愣愣地坐着。我的心扑通扑通每跳一下,我的眼睛都觉得疼和肿胀,我想知道这时候他们会不会让我讲一通。我身上湿漉漉的,我的嘴还在流血。这时候,我们都靠墙站在一起。其他的小伙子都不理睬我,他们向塔特洛克祝贺,都在猜测他们能得到多少酬劳。有一个小伙子因为打伤了手还在呜呜地哭。我眼望前方,看到许多穿白上衣的侍者正在把临时搭起的拳击场搬走,在椅子围起来的空地上铺上一小块方形的地毯。我想,也许我要站在这块地毯上来发表我的演说。

eyes was his jabbing left hand. Then falling forward, my head against his damp shoulder, I whispered,

"I'll make it five dollars more."

"Go to hell!"

But his muscles relaxed a trifle beneath my pressure and I breathed, "Seven?"

"Give it to your ma," he said, ripping me beneath the heart.

And while I still held him I butted him and moved away. I felt myself bombarded with punches. I fought back with hopeless desperation. I wanted to deliver my speech more than anything else in the world, because I felt only these men could judge truly my ability, and now this stupid clown was ruining my chances. I began fighting carefully now, moving in to punch him and out again with my greater speed. A lucky blow to his chin and I had him going too—until I heard a loud voice yell, "I got my money on the big boy."

Hearing this, I almost dropped my guard. I was confused: Should I try to win against the voice out there? Would not this go against my speech, and was not this a moment for humility, for nonresistance? A blow to my head as I danced about sent my right eye popping like jackin-the-box and settled my dilemma. The room went red as I fell. It was a dream fall, my body languid and fastidious as to where to land, until the floor became impatient and smashed up to meet me. A moment later I came to. An hypnotic voice said FIVE emphatically. And I lay there, hazily watching a dark red spot of my own blood shaping itself into a butterfly, glistening and soaking into the soiled gray world of the canvas.

When the voice drawled TEN I was lifted up and dragged to a chair. I sat dazed. My eye pained and swelled with each throb of my pounding heart and I wondered if now I would be allowed to speak. I was wringing wet, my mouth still bleeding. We were grouped along the wall now. The other boys ignored me as they congratulated Tatlock and speculated as to how much they would be paid. One boy whimpered over his smashed hand. Looking up front, I saw attendants in white jackets rolling the portable ring away and placing a small square rug in the vacant space surrounded by chairs. Perhaps, I thought, I will stand on the rug to deliver my speech.

Then the M. C. called to us, "Come on up here boys and get your money."

于是司仪招呼我们："到这儿来,小伙子们,来拿给你们的钱。"

那些人一面大笑,一面坐在椅子上谈话,我们跑到他们面前等着。现在,人人都似乎变得友好了。

"钱就在地毯上。"那个人说。我看到地毯上散布着各种大小的硬币,还有几张捏皱了的纸币。可是使我感到激动的是那些零零落落散布在各处的金币。

"小伙子们,全都是你们的,"那个人说,"谁拿到的都归谁。"

"说得对,萨姆波①。"一个黄头发的人说,同时像透露机密似的对我挤了挤眼。

我激动得发抖,忘记了我的疼痛。我想,我要拿金币和纸币。我要用两只手。我要用身体挡住离我最近的小伙子,不让他拿到金币。

"现在都在地毯周围跪下来,"那个人下命令了,"在我发出信号之前,谁也不许去碰一碰那些钱。"

我们按照他的吩咐,都走到地毯周围跪下来。那个人慢慢举起了他那只长满雀斑的手,我们的眼光都随着他的手向上移动。

我听到有人说:"这些黑鬼的样子好像在做祷告似的。"

然后,"准备,"那个人说,"拿吧!"

我向地毯的蓝色图案上一枚黄澄澄的硬币伸出手去,摸到了它,大吃一惊地尖叫了一声,我周围的那些立起来的人也都在尖叫。我像发狂一样竭力来挪开我的手,可是我松不开手。一股强烈的热力冲进我全身,摇撼着我,仿佛我是一只湿淋淋的耗子。地毯通了电。在我挣开的时候,我的头发都从头上竖起来了。我的肌肉跳动,我的神经受的刺激使我受不了,疼得使我抽搐。可是我看出这并没有使其他的小伙子就此罢休。有几个又害怕又为难的,笑而不前,却把别人在痛苦的抽搐中碰掉的钱抢先抓走。我们这样倾轧,高高在上的那些人都哄堂大笑起来。

"拣起来,真该死,拣起来!"有人用鹦鹉的低哑声音叫道,"接着干,拿吧!"

我迅速地在地板上爬来爬去,拾取硬币,想办法避开铜币,拿到纸币和金币。我迅速地搜刮那些钱,乐得也不顾触电了。我发现我能够克制电——这可

---

① 萨姆波:美国黑人与印第安人或欧洲人所产的混血儿,有贬义。

We ran forward to where the men laughed and talked in their chairs, waiting. Everyone seemed friendly now.

"There it is on the rug," the man said. I saw the rug covered with coins of all dimensions and a few crumpled bills. But what excited me, scattered here and there, were the gold pieces.

"Boys, it's all yours," the man said. "You get all you grab."

"That's right, Sambo," a blond man said, winking at me confidentially.

I trembled with excitement, forgetting my pain. I would get the gold and the bills, I thought. I would use both hands. I would throw my body against the boys nearest me to block them from the gold.

"Get down around the rug now," the man commanded, "and don't anyone touch it until I give the signal."

"This ought to be good," I heard.

As told, we got around the square rug on our knees. Slowly the man raised his freckled hand as we followed it upward with our eyes.

I heard, "These niggers look like they're about to pray!"

Then, "Ready," the man said. "Go!"

I lunged for a yellow coin lying on the blue design of the carpet, touching it and sending a surprised shriek to join those rising around me. I tried frantically to remove my hand but could not let go. A hot, violent force tore through my body, shaking me like a wet rat. The rug was electrified. The hair bristled up on my head as I shook myself free. My muscles jumped, my nerves jangled, writhed. But I saw that this was not stopping the other boys. Laughing in fear and embarrassment, some were holding back and scooping up the coins knocked off by the painful contortions of the others. The men roared above us as we struggled.

"Pick it up, goddamnit, pick it up!" someone called like a bass-voiced parrot. "Go on, get it!"

I crawled rapidly around the floor, picking up the coins, trying to avoid the coppers and to get greenbacks and the gold. Ignoring the shock by laughing, as I brushed the coins off quickly, I discovered that I could contain the electricity—a contradiction, but it works. Then the men began to push us onto the rug. Laughing embarrassedly, we struggled out of their hands and kept after the coins. We were all wet and

是自相矛盾，不过倒也行之有效。这时，有些人开始把我们向地毯上推。我们一面为难地笑着，一面挣脱了他们的手，继续搂钱。我们身上都湿透了，滑溜溜，抓不住。突然间，我看到一个小伙子腾空而起，汗湿的身体发光，像一只马戏班的海豹，他摔下来的时候，潮湿的背脊严严实实紧贴带电的地毯，我听到他呼喊，看见他真个是用脊梁跳舞，他的胳膊肘得得地敲打地板，他的肌肉扭动着，像一匹马的皮肉给许多蝇子叮咬那样。最后他翻滚到地毯外面，脸色灰白，他从地板上起来奔出去的时候，满堂哄笑声，谁也不去拦住他。

"抓钱吧，"司仪说，"那可都是真正的美国现钱。"

于是我们又抓又抢，连抓带抢。这时候，我很小心，不到离地毯太近的地方去，我觉得有一股强烈的威士忌酒的气味喷到我身上，仿佛降下了一团臭气，我伸出手，抓住了一把椅子的一条腿。这把椅子上有人，我还是不顾一切地抓着。

"放手，黑鬼！放手！"

他摇晃着一张大脸，向下瞧着我的脸，想把我推开。可是我的身体滑溜溜的，他又醉得太厉害。原来是科尔考德先生，他拥有一连串电影院和"娱乐院"。他一次又一次地来抓我，我都从他手里溜了出去。这件事变成了一场真正的斗争。我最怕那张地毯，倒不太怕这个醉汉，于是我抓住椅子不放，我一时感到诧异，我居然想把他摔到地毯上去。这个主意实在恶毒极了，我觉得我真的要这么做。我想做得不太明显，可是我抓住他的腿，想让他从椅子上滚出来的时候，他却哈哈大笑地站起来了，眼光清醒沉着地看着我，恶毒地向我胸膛踢了一脚。椅子腿从我手里飞出来了，我觉得身不由己地滚动起来。仿佛我是在一堆热煤上滚动。仿佛要整整过 100 年我才会滚到煤堆外面，而在这 100 年里，我身体里最深的一层都要被烧焦，连我那战战兢兢的一口气也要被烧得干枯，甚至干枯炽热到了要爆炸的程度。在我滚开了的时候，我想，只要一刹那间，一切都会结束的。这件事也就在一刹那间结束了。

不过，还没有结束。对面的那些人正在等着，他们的身体从椅子上向前倾，红彤彤的脸都肿胀得好像中了风。我看到他们的指头向我伸过来，我就滚开了，好像一只没有接住的足球从接球人的脚尖上滚开了，又回到那个煤堆上。这一次，我碰巧把地毯推

slippery and hard to hold. Suddenly I saw a boy lifted into the air, glistening with sweat like a circus seal, and dropped, his wet back landing flush upon the charged rug, heard him yell and saw him literally dance upon his back, his elbows beating a frenzied tattoo upon the floor, his muscles twitching like the flesh of a horse stung by many flies. When he finally rolled off, his face was gray and no one stopped him when he ran from the floor amid booming laughter.

"Get the money," the M. C. called. "That's good hard American cash!"

And we snatched and grabbed, snatched and grabbed. I was careful not to come too close to the rug now, and when I felt the hot whiskey breath descend upon me like a cloud of foul air I reached out and grabbed the leg of a chair. It was occupied and I held on desperately.

"Leggo nigger! Leggo!"

The huge face wavered down to mine as he tried to push me free. But my body was slippery and he was too drunk. It was Mr. Colcord, who owned a chain of movie houses and "entertainment palaces." Each time he grabbed me I slipped out of his hands. It became a real struggle. I feared the rug more than I did the drunk, so I held on, surprising myself for a moment by trying to topple *him* upon the rug. It was such an enormous idea that I found myself actually carrying it out. I tried not to be obvious, yet when I grabbed his leg, trying to tumble him out of the chair, he raised up roaring with laughter, and looking at me with soberness dead in the eye, kicked me viciously in the chest. The chair leg flew out of my hand and I felt myself going and rolled. It was as though I had rolled through a bed of hot coals. It seemed a whole century would pass before I would roll free, a century in which I was seared through the deepest levels of my body to the fearful breath within me and the breath seared and heated to the point of explosion. It'll all be over in a flash, I thought as I rolled clear. It'll all be over in a flash.

But not yet, the men on the other side were waiting, red faces swollen as though from apoplexy as they bent forward in their chairs. Seeing their fingers coming toward me I rolled away as a fumbled football rolls off the receiver's fingertips, back into the coals. That time I luckily sent the rug sliding out of place and heard the coins ringing against the floor and the

开了,还听到那些硬币叮叮当当落在地板上的声音,小伙子们都你争我夺地来把钱拣到手,于是司仪喊道:"好了,小伙子们,到此为止。去穿上衣服再来领钱。"

我一瘸一拐,十分难堪。我的背脊觉得好像挨过钢丝抽打一样。

我们穿好了衣服,司仪进来,给我们每人5元钱,只有塔特洛克是例外,他得到了10元,因为他是拳击场里剩下的最后一个人。于是司仪叫我们都离开这里。我没有机会来发表我的演说了,我想。正在我大失所望,走出去要走进一条昏暗的小巷子里的时候,有人拦住了我,叫我回去。我于是回到了舞厅,那些人正在把椅子向后挪,一群一群地聚在一起谈话。

司仪敲打着桌面要他们安静下来。"各位先生,"他说,"我们几乎忘掉了一个重要的节目。这是一个极其重要的节目,各位先生。我们把这个小伙子带到这里来,让他讲一讲昨天他在毕业典礼上发表过的一篇演说。"

"好!"

"据说他是我们在格林伍德一带找到的最聪敏的小伙子。据说他认识的神气字眼比一本袖珍字典里印的还多呢。"

许多人都鼓掌,发出笑声。

"因此,各位先生,请大家注意听他演讲吧。"

我面向着他们,他们仍然嘻嘻哈哈,我口干,眼跳。我慢慢地开始讲。我的嗓子显然很紧张,因为他们都在叫喊:"声音大一点儿! 声音大一点儿!"

"我们年轻的一代都赞美那位伟大领袖和教育家的智慧,"我大声喊叫,"是他首先讲出了这些光辉灿烂的语言:'一艘在海上迷航多日的船突然望到一艘友好的船。从这艘不幸的船的桅杆上可以看到"水,水,我们都要渴死了!"的信号。那艘友好的船答复的信号是,"用你们的桶就地取水。"这艘陷入困境的船的船长终于听从指示,放下他的水桶,吊起了满满一桶来自亚马逊河口的晶莹淡水。'我要像他那样说,并且引用他的话来讲:'我们这个种族里有些人把改善生活条件寄托在到外国去,还有些人低估了同我们隔壁的邻居,也就是同南方白人培植友好关系的重要意义,我愿意对这些人说"用你们的水桶就地取水吧"——把桶吊下去,以各族人民的种种丈夫气概来交朋友吧,我们的周围全是各族的人民……'"

boys scuffling to pick them up and the M. C. calling, "All right, boys, that's all. Go get dressed and get your money."

I was limp as a dish rag. My back felt as though it had been beaten with wires.

When we had dressed the M. C. came in and gave us each five dollars, except Tatlock, who got ten for being last in the ring. Then he told us to leave. I was not to get a chance to deliver my speech, I thought. I was going out into the dim alley in despair when I was stopped and told to go back. I returned to the ballroom, where the men were pushing back their chairs and gathering in groups to talk.

The M. C. knocked on a table for quiet. "Gentlemen," he said, "we almost forgot an important part of the program. A most serious part, gentlemen. This boy was brought here to deliver a speech which he made at his graduation yesterday. . ."

"Bravo!"

"I'm told that he is the smartest boy we've got out there in Greenwood. I'm told that he knows more big words than a pocket-sized dictionary."

Much applause and laughter.

"So now, gentlemen, I want you to give him your attention."

There was still laughter as I faced them, my mouth dry, my eye throbbing. I began slowly, but evidently my throat was tense, because they began shouting, "Louder! Louder!"

"We of the younger generation extol the wisdom of that great leader and educator," I shouted, "who first spoke these flaming words of wisdom: 'A ship lost at sea for many days suddenly sighted a friendly vessel. From the mast of the unfortunate vessel was seen a signal: "Water, water; we die of thirst!" The answer from the friendly vessel came back: "Cast down your bucket where you are." The captain of the distressed vessel, at last heeding the injunction, cast down his bucket, and it came up full of fresh sparkling water from the mouth of the Amazon River.' And like him I say, and in his words, "To those of my race who depend upon bettering their condition in a foreign land, or who underestimate the importance of cultivating friendly relations with Southern white man, who is his next-door neighbor, I would say: "Cast down your bucket where you are"—cast it down in making friends in every manly way of the people of all races

我讲话是自动的,抱着满腔热情,所以我并没有注意到那些人仍然在谈话,仍然嘻嘻哈哈。后来,我的嘴干了,却含着一嘴从伤口里流出的血,几乎要把我憋死。我咳嗽了一下,想停一会儿,走到一只装有黄沙的高铜痰盂旁边去吐出来。可是有几个人,尤其是那位督学,都在听我讲,我不敢去。于是我把血、唾液和其他种种都咽了下去,继续演讲(在那些日子里①我的耐力多强啊!多么热心啊!我对事物的公正方面的信念多么深啊!)。我不顾痛苦说得声音更高了。可是他们仍然谈话,仍然嘻嘻哈哈,仿佛耳朵里塞了棉花,听不见。于是我加强了能感动人的那部分的语气。我充耳不闻,吞下血,直到我恶心得要呕出来。这次演讲的时间似乎比以前长一百倍,可是我不能漏掉一个字眼。全部要说出来,我背下来的每一个细枝末节都经过考虑和斟酌。这还没有都说到。每逢我说出一个三音节以上的词儿,总有一群声音嚷嚷,要我再说一遍。我用过"社会责任心"这个短语,当时他们就吆喝起来:

"你说的是个什么词儿,小伙子?"

"社会责任心。"我说。

"什么?"

"社会……"

"声音大一点儿。"

"……责任心。"

"再来一次!"

"责……"

"重说一遍!"

"……任心。"

房间里充满了闹哄哄的笑声,后来,毫无疑问,因为要吞下我的一口血,注意力分散,我出了一个错,嚷出了我常见的在报纸社论里受到谴责的一个词儿,虽则是背着他们说的,还是给听到了。

"社会……"

"什么?"他们吆喝道。

"……平等——"

笑声在突然静下来的气氛中像烟一样飘浮着。我睁开眼睛,莫名其妙。房间里充满了不愉快的声音。司仪连忙跑到前面。他们向我吆喝着含有敌意的话。可是我不懂。

---

① 指小说的主角未变成隐身人之前的时期。

by whom we are surrounded. . . . "

I spoke automatically and with such fervor that I did not realize that the men were still talking and laughing until my dry mouth, filling up with blood from the cut, almost strangled me. I coughed, wanting to stop and go to one of the tall brass, sand-filled spittoons to relieve myself, but a few of the men, especially the superintendent, were listening and I was afraid. So I gulped it down, blood, saliva and all, and continued. (What powers of endurance I had during those days! What enthusiasm! What a belief in the rightness of things!) I spoke even louder in spite of the pain. But still they talked and still they laughed, as though deaf with cotton in dirty ears. So I spoke with greater emotional emphasis. I closed my ears and swallowed blood until I was nauseated. The speech seemed a hundred times as long as before, but I could not leave out a single word. All had to be said, each memorized nuance considered, rendered. Nor was that all. Whenever I uttered a word of three or more syllables a group of voices would yell for me to repeat it. I used the phrase "social responsibility" and they yelled:

"What's that word you say, boy?"

"Social responsibility," I said.

"What?"

"Social. . ."

"Louder."

". . . responsibility."

"More!"

"Respon—"

"Repeat!"

"—sibility."

The room filled with the uproar of laughter until, no doubt, distracted by having to gulp down my blood, I made a mistake and yelled a phrase I had often seen denounced in newspaper editorials, heard debated in private.

"Social. . ."

"What?" they yelled.

". . . equality—"

The laughter hung smokelike in the sudden stillness. I opened my eyes, puzzled. Sounds of displeasure filled the room. The M. C. rushed forward. They shouted hostile phrases at me. But I did not understand.

A small dry mustached man in the front row blared out, "Say that slowly, son!"

一个坐在前排椅子上，身材矮小、胡子干巴巴的人大喝一声："慢慢地说出来，小子！"

"说什么，先生？"

"你刚才说过的话！"

"社会责任心，先生。"我说。

"你并不聪明，是不是，小伙子？"他说话的口气不算不客气。

"不聪明。先生！"

"你能肯定那个什么'平等'是误会吗？"

"啊，是的，先生，"我说，"我当时正在咽血。"

"唔，你最好说得再慢一点儿，让我们都能听明白。我们是存心对你讲公道，可是无论什么时候你都一定要知道你的地位。好吧，算了，接着讲你那篇演说吧。"

我害怕。我想离开这里，可是我又想讲，我恐怕他们会把我拉下来。

"谢谢你，先生。"我说，于是从我没讲完的地方开始讲下去，他们跟先前一样，还是不理睬我。

然而等到我讲完了的时候，鼓掌的声音如同雷鸣。我看到那位督学拿着一个用白纤维纸包的包裹走过来，感到很诧异，他做了个手势让大家安静，然后对那些人讲话。

"各位先生，大家都看得出我对这个小伙子并没有过奖。他发表了一篇很好的演说，将来总有一天他会领导他那个民族走上正确的道路的。如今在这种时代，他的演说很重要，这是不用我来说的。这个小伙子很好，又聪敏，为了鼓励他沿着正确的方向走下去，我愿意以学校董事会的名义，赠送他一件奖品，奖给他的东西是……"

他停顿了一下，拆开纤维纸，露出一个亮闪闪的小牛皮公事包。

"……奖给他的东西是夏德·惠特曼商店里的第一流商品。"

"小伙子，"他说，这是对我讲的，"把这个奖品拿去好好保存起来。要把它当作承担职责的一种标志。要珍视它。要像你现在这样发展成材，将来总有一天这里面会装满有助于确定你那个民族的命运的重要文件。"

我感动极了，简直没有办法来表示我的感谢。一串血红的口水淌到皮包面子上，构成的形状像一块未发现的大陆，我赶快把它擦干净。我有一种做梦也从未有过的了不起的感觉。

"What sir?"

"What you just said！"

"Social responsibility, sir," I said.

"You weren't being smart, were you boy?" he said, not unkindly.

"No, sir！"

"You sure that about 'equality' was a mistake?"

"Oh, yes, sir," I said. "I was swallowing blood. "

"Well, you had better speak more slowly so we can understand. We mean to do right by you, but you've got to know your place at all times. All right, now, go on with your speech. "

I was afraid. I wanted to leave but I wanted also to speak and I was afraid they'd snatch me down.

"Thank you sir," I said, beginning where I had left off, and having them ignore me as before.

Yet when I finished there was a thunderous applause. I was surprised to see the superintendent come forth with a package wrapped in white tissue paper, and, gesturing for quiet, address the men.

"Gentlemen, you see that I did not overpraise this boy. He makes a good speech and some day he'll lead his people in the proper paths. And I don't have to tell you that this is important in these days and times. This is a good, smart boy, and so to encourage him in the right direction, in the name of the Board of Education I wish to present him a prize in the form of this... "

He paused, removing the tissue paper and revealing a gleaming calfskin brief case.

"... in the form of this first-class article from Shad Whitmore's shop. "

"Boy," he said, addressing me, "take this prize and keep it well. Consider it a badge of office. Prize it. Keep developing as you are and some day it will be filled with important papers that will help shape the destiny of your people. "

I was so moved that I could hardly express my thanks. A rope of bloody saliva forming a shape like an undiscovered continent drooled upon the leather and I wiped it quickly away. I felt an importance that I had never dreamed.

"Open it and see what's inside," I was told.

My fingers a-tremble, I complied, smelling the fresh leather and finding an official-looking document inside. It was a scholarship to the state college for

"打开皮包,看看里面有什么东西。"他对我说。

我的手指发抖。我遵命,闻到了新皮革的气味,发现里面有一份公文模样的文件。原来那是一份进州立黑人大学的奖学金证书。我眼睛里充满泪水,笨手笨脚地跑开了。

我太高兴了。甚至在我发现我拣来的那些金币都是为一种牌子的汽车做广告的圆铜片的时候,我也不放在心上。

我回到家里,人人都感到激动。第二天,邻居们都来向我祝贺。我甚至觉得不会受到祖父的干扰了,他临终时的诅咒常常会使我空欢喜一场。我手持小牛皮公事包站在他的照片下面,扬扬得意,笑嘻嘻地瞧着他那张呆板的庄稼人的黑面孔,这是一张对我有强烈吸引力的脸。无论我到哪里去,他那双眼睛好像都在盯着我。

那天晚上,我梦见我跟着他去看马戏,无论那些小丑做什么他都不肯笑。后来,他叫我打开公事包,把包里的东西念给他听,我打开了,找到一个盖有州政府大印的公事信封,在信封里面装着一个又一个信封,没完没了,我想,这可麻烦死人了。"那可要不少年哩,"他说,"现在把这个拆开。"我拆开信封,发现一份用凹凸版印的文件,上面有一小段用金色字体印的文字。"念给我听,"他说,"念得声音大一点儿。'

"致有关负责人,"我拿腔拿调念起来,"让这个黑小子忙得不得闲吧。"

我醒来之后,老爷子的笑声仍然在我耳朵里回荡。

(这是我后来还记得的一场梦,而且在多年之后又梦见了一次。不过当时我并没有深知这场梦的意义。首先我得进大学。)

Negroes. My eyes filled with tears and I ran awkward-ly off the floor.

I was overjoyed; I did not even mind when I discovered that the gold pieces I had scrambled for were brass pocket tokens advertising a certain make of automobile.

When I reached home everyone was excited. Next day the neighbors came to congratulate me. I even felt safe from grandfather, whose death-bed curse usually spoiled my triumphs. I stood beneath his photograph with my brief case in hand and smiled triumphantly into his stolid black peasant's face. It was a face that fascinated me. The eyes seemed to follow everywhere I went.

That night I dreamed I was at a circus with him and that he refused to laugh at the clowns no matter what they did. Then later he told me to open my brief case and read what was inside and I did, finding an official envelope stamped with the state seal; and inside the envelope I found another and another, endlessly, and I thought I would fall of weariness. "Them's years," he said. "Now open that one." And I did and in it I found an engraved document containing a short message in letters of gold. "Read it," my grandfather said. "Out loud."

"To Whom it May Concern," I intoned. "Keep This Nigger-Boy Running."

I awoke with the old man's laughter ringing in my ears.

(It was a dream I was to remember and dream again for many years after. But at that time I had no insight into its meaning. First I had to attend college.)

042. 远和近

(美)托马斯·沃尔夫 著　　万　紫 译

042. The Far and the Near

by *Thomas Wolfe*

一个小镇,坐落在一个从铁路线连绵而来的高地上。它的郊外,有一座明净整洁装有绿色百页窗的小屋。小屋一边,有一个园子,整齐地划成一块一块,种着蔬菜。还有一架葡萄棚,到了 8 月底,葡萄就会成熟。屋前有三棵大橡树,每到夏天,大片整齐的树荫,就会遮蔽这座小屋。另一边则是一个鲜花盛开的花坛。这一切,充满着整洁、繁盛、朴素的舒适气氛。

每天下午两点过几分,两个城市间的特快列车驶过这里。那时候,长长的列车要在镇上附近暂停一下,然后又平稳地起步前进,但是它的速度还没有开足时那么惊人。在机车有力的掣动下,眼看它不慌不忙地从容驶去,沉重的车厢压在铁轨上,发出低沉和谐的隆隆声,然后消失在弯道中。在一段时间里,在草原的边缘上,每隔一定间距,汽笛吼叫,喷出一圈圈浓烟,可以感觉到列车行驶的痕迹。最后,什么也听不见了,只剩那车轮的坚实的轧轧声,在午后的寂静中悄然隐去。

20 多年来,每天,当列车驶近小屋时,司机总要拉响汽笛。每天,一个妇人一听到鸣笛,便从小屋的后门出来向他挥手致意。当初她有一个小孩缠着她的裙子,现在这孩子已长成大姑娘,也每天和她母亲一起出来挥手致意。

司机多年操劳,已经白发苍苍,渐渐变老了。他驾驶长长的列车载着旅客横贯大地已上万次。他自己的子女都已长大了,结婚了。他曾四次在他面前的铁轨上看到了可怕的悲剧所凝聚的小点,像颗炮弹似的射向火车头前的恐怖的阴影——一辆满载小孩的轻便马车和密密一排惊惶失措的小脸;一辆廉价汽车

ON the outskirts of a little town upon a rise of land that swept back from the railway there was a tidy little cottage of white boards, trimmed vividly with green blinds. To one side of the house there was a garden neatly patterned with plots of growing vegetables, and an arbor for the grapes which ripened late in August. Before the house there were three mighty oaks which sheltered it in their clean and massive shade in summer, and to the other side there was a border of gay flowers. The whole place had an air of tidiness, thrift, and modest comfort.

Every day, a few minutes after two o'clock in the afternoon, the limited express between two cities passed this spot. At that moment the great train, having halted for a breathing-space at the town near by, was beginning to lengthen evenly into its stroke, but it had not yet reached the full drive of its terrific speed. It swung into view deliberately, swept past with a powerful swaying motion of the engine, a low smooth rumble of its heavy cars upon pressed steel, and then it vanished in the cut. For a moment the progress of the engine could be marked by heavy bellowing puffs of smoke that burst at spaced intervals above the edges of the meadow grass, and finally nothing could be heard but the solid clacking tempo of the wheels receding into the drowsy stillness of the afternoon.

Every day for more than twenty years, as the train had approached this house, the engineer had blown on the whistle, and every day, as soon as she heard this signal, a woman had appeared on the back porch of the little house and waved to him. At first she had a small child clinging to her skirts, and now this child had grown to full womanhood, and every day she, too, came with her mother to the porch and waved.

The engineer had grown old and gray in service. He had driven his great train, loaded with its weight of lives, across the land ten thousand times. His own children had grown up and married, and four times he had seen before him on the tracks the ghastly dot of

作者简介:托马斯·沃尔夫(**Thomas Wolfe**,1900—1938),美国作家。1900 年 10 月 3 日生于北卡罗莱纳州阿什维尔,1938 年 9 月 15 日卒于马里兰州巴尔的摩。沃尔夫就读于北卡罗来纳大学,1923 年迁居到纽约,他在纽约大学教书期间也创作剧本。《天使,望故乡》(*Look Homeward,Angel*,1929)是他的第一部长篇小说,也是最出名的一部。《时间与河流》(*Of Time and the River*,1935)是一部略带自传风格的作品。他的短篇小说收录在《从死亡到早晨》(*From Death to Morning*,1935)中。另外两部作品《蛛网与岩石》(*The Web and the Rock*,1939)和《不能再回家》(*You Can't Go Home Again*,1940)两部作品在他过世后发表。

停在铁轨上，里面坐着吓得目瞪口呆状若木鸡的人们；一个又老又聋的憔悴的流浪汉，沿着铁路走着，听不到汽笛鸣声；一个带着惊呼的人影掠过他的窗口——所有这些，司机都历历在目，记忆犹新。他懂得一个人所能懂得的种种悲哀、欢乐、危险和辛劳。他那可敬的工作，仿佛风刀霜剑，在他脸上刻下了皱纹。现在，他虽已年老，但在长期工作中养成了忠诚、勇敢和谦逊的品质，并获得了司机们应有的崇高和智慧。

但不管他见识过多少危险和悲剧，那座小屋，那两个妇女用勇敢从容的动作向他挥手致意的景象，始终印在他的心里，看作美丽、不朽、万劫不变和始终如一的象征，纵使灾难、悲哀和邪恶，可能打破他的铁的生活规律。

他一看到小屋和两个妇女，就使他感到从未有过的非凡幸福。一千次的阴晴明晦，一百次的风雷雨雪，他总是看到她们。通过冬天严峻单调的灰蒙蒙的光线，穿过褐色冰封的荒地，他看见她们。在沃艳诱人的绿色的4月里，他又看见她们。

他感到她们和她们所住的小屋无限亲切，好像父母对于自己的子女一样。终于，他觉得她们生活的图画已深深地印在他的心中，因而他完全了解她们一天中每时每刻的生活。他决定，一旦他退休了，他一定要去找她们，最后要和她们畅谈生平，因为她们的生活已经和他自己的生活深深交融在一起了。

这一天终于来到了。最后，司机在她们居住的小镇的车站下了车，走到月台上。他在铁路上工作的年限已经到了。他目前是公司领取养老金的人，没有工作要做了。司机慢慢地走出车站，来到小镇的街上。但所有的东西对他来说都是陌生的，好像他从未看到过这小镇似的。他走着走着，渐渐感到迷惑与慌乱。这就是他经过千万次的小镇么？这些是他从高高的车厢窗口老是看见的房子么，一切是那么陌生，使他那么不安，好像梦中的城市似的。他越向前行，他的心里越是疑虑重重。

现在，房屋渐渐变成小镇外疏疏落落的村舍，大街也渐渐冷落，变成一条乡村的小路——两个妇女就住在其中一所村舍里。司机在闷热和尘埃中沉重地慢慢走着，最后他站在他要找寻的房屋前面。他立刻知道他已经找对了。他看到了那屋前

tragedy converging like a cannon ball to its eclipse of horror at the boiler head—a light spring wagon filled with children, with its clustered row of small stunned faces; a cheap automobile stalled upon the tracks, set with the wooden figures of people paralyzed with fear; a battered hobo walking by the rail, too deaf and old to hear the whistle's warning; and a form flung past his window with a scream—all this the man had seen and known. He had known all the grief, the joy, the peril and the labor such a man could know; he had grown seamed and weathered in his loyal service, and now, schooled by the qualities of faith and courage and humbleness that attended his labor, he had grown old, and had the grandeur and the wisdom these men have.

But no matter what peril or tragedy he had known, the vision of the little house and the women waving to him with a brave free motion of the arm had become fixed in the mind of the engineer as something beautiful and enduring, something beyond all change and ruin, and something that would always be the same, no matter what mishap, grief or error might break the iron schedule of his days.

The sight of the little house and of these two women gave him the most extraordinary happiness he had ever known. He had seen them in a thousand lights, a hundred weathers. He had seen them through the harsh bare light of wintry gray across the brown and frosted stubble of the earth, and he had seen them again in the green luring sorcery of April.

He felt for them and for the little house in which they lived such tenderness as a man might feel for his own children, and at length the picture of their lives was carved so sharply in his heart that he felt that he knew their lives completely, to every hour and moment of the day, and he resolved that one day, when his years of service should be ended, he would go and find these people and speak at last with them whose lives had been so wrought into his own.

That day came. At last the engineer stepped from a train onto the station platform of the town where these two women lived. His years upon the rail had ended. He was a pensioned servant of his company, with no more work to do. The engineer walked slowly through the station and out into the streets of the town. Everything was as strange to him as if he had never seen this town before. As he walked on, his sense of bewilderment and confusion grew. Could this be the town he had passed ten thousand times? Were these the same houses he had seen so often from the high windows of his cab? It was all as unfamiliar, as disquieting as a city in a dream, and the perplexity of his spirit increased as he went on.

Presently the houses thinned into the straggling outposts of the town, and the street faded into a country road—the one on which the women lived. And the man plodded on slowly in the heat and dust. At length he stood before the house he sought. He knew at once that he had found the proper place. He saw the lordly

高大的橡树,那花坛,那菜园和葡萄棚,再远,那铁轨的闪光。

不错,这是他要找寻的房子,这地方他经过了不知有多少次,这是他梦寐以求的幸福的目的地。现在,他找到了,他到了这里。但他的手为什么在门前却抖了起来?为什么这小镇、这小路、这田地,以及他所眷恋的小屋的门口,变得如此陌生,好像噩梦中的景物?为什么他会感到惆怅、疑虑和失望?

他终于进了大门,慢慢沿着小径走去。不一会儿,他踏上通向门廊的三步石级,敲了敲门。一会儿,他听到客厅的脚步声,门开了,一个妇女站在他面前。

霎时,他感到很大的失望和懊丧,深悔来此一行。他立刻认出站在他面前用怀疑的眼光瞧他的妇人,正是那个向他千万次挥手致意的人。但是她的脸严峻、枯萎、消瘦,她的皮肤憔悴、灰黄,松弛地打成褶皱,她那双小眼睛,惊疑不定地盯着他。原先,他从她那挥手的姿态所想象的勇敢、坦率、深情,在看到她和听到她冷冷的声音后,刹那间一股脑儿消失了。

而现在,当他向她解释他是谁和他的来意时,他自己的声音听来却变得虚伪、勉强了。但他还是结结巴巴地说下去,拼命把他心中涌出来的悔恨、迷惑和怀疑抑制下去,忘却他过去的一切欢乐,把他的希望和爱慕的行为视同一种耻辱。

最后,那妇人十分勉强地请他进了屋子,尖声粗气地喊着她的女儿。在一段短短的痛苦的时间里,司机坐在一间难看的小客厅里,打算和她们攀谈,而那两个女人却带着迷茫的敌意和阴沉、畏怯、抑郁、迟钝的眼光瞪着他。

最后他结结巴巴生硬地和她们道别。他从小径出来沿着大路朝小镇走去。他忽然意识到他是一个老人了。他的心,过去望着熟悉的铁路远景时,何等勇敢和自信。现在,当他看到这块陌生的、不可意料的、永远近在咫尺、从未见过、从不知悉的土地,他的心因疑惧而衰竭了。他知道一切有关迷途获得光明的神话,闪光的铁路的远景,希望的美好小天地中的幻想之地,都已一去不复返、永不再来了。

oaks before the house, the flower beds, the garden and the arbor, and farther off, the glint of rails.

Yes, this was the house he sought, the place he had passed so many times, the destination he had longed for with such happiness. But now that he had found it, now that he was here, why did his hand falter on the gate; why had the town, the road, the earth, the very entrance to this place he loved turned unfamiliar as the landscape of some ugly dreams? Why did he now feel this sense of confusion, doubt, and hopelessness?

At length he entered by the gate, walked slowly up the path and in a moment more had mounted three short steps that led up to the porch, and was knocking at the door. Presently he heard steps in the hall, the door was opened, and a woman stood facing him.

And instantly, with a sense of bitter loss and grief, he was sorry he had come. He knew at once that the woman who stood there looking at him with a mistrustful eye was the same woman who had waved to him so many thousand times. But her face was harsh and pinched and meager; the flesh sagged wearily in sallow folds, and the small eyes peered at him with timid suspicion and uneasy doubt. All the brave freedom, the warmth and the affection that he had read into her gesture, vanished in the moment that he saw her and heard her unfriendly tongue.

And now his own voice sounded unreal and ghastly to him as he tried to explain his presence, to tell her who he was and the reason he had come. But he faltered on, fighting subbornly against the horror of regret, confusion, disbelief that surged up in his spirit, drowning all his former joy and making his act of hope and tenderness seem shameful to him.

At length the woman invited him almost unwillingly into the house, and called her daughter in a harsh shrill voice. Then, for a brief agony of time, the man sat in an ugly little parlor, and he tried to talk while the two women stared at him with a dull, bewildered hostility, a sullen, timorous restraint.

And finally, stammering a crude farewell, he departed. He walked away down the path and then along the road toward town, and suddenly he knew that he was an old man. His heart, which had been brave and confident when it looked along the familiar vista of the rails, was now sick with doubt and horror as it saw the strange and unsuspected visage of an earth which had always been within a stone's throw of him, and which he had never seen or known. And he knew that all the magic of that bright lost way, the vista of that shining line, the imagined corner of that small good universe of hope's desire, was gone forever, could never be got back again.

043. 狗

（法）科莱特 著　　万 紫 译

043. The Bitch

by Colette

中士休假回到巴黎，发现他的夫人不在家。不过他还是受到了因惊喜而声音颤抖的欢迎，受到了拥抱和湿润的亲吻——那是他留给自己年轻的心上人的牧羊犬沃莱斯，它像一团火似的绕着他打转，激动得脸苍白，用舌头舔着他。同时，女佣人也弄出与狗一样多的声响来，唠叨个没完：

"真不凑巧！夫人才去玛洛特两天，去那儿锁她的房子去了。夫人的房客刚离开，她是去盘点家具的。还好，离这儿不远！先生是不是给夫人拍个电报？如果电报马上发出，夫人明天午饭前就能赶回来。请先生一定睡在这儿吧！我去把浴室里的热水龙头打开好不好！"

"我的好露西，我在基地洗过澡了。士兵休假都喜欢好好洗个澡！"

他看着镜子里的身影，他的肤色就像布列苍尼的花岗岩，红里透青。那条布里阿特的牧羊犬，肃静地蹲在他的身边，浑身的毛都在颤抖。他笑了起来，因为那条粗毛蓬松的灰蓝色牧羊犬看上去与他十分相像。

"沃莱斯！"

它抬头亲昵地望着主人，中士突然想起了他的夫人珍妮来。她多么年轻，多么轻佻——实在太年轻，太轻佻了。中士的心中不由得思绪万端。

晚餐时，牧羊犬忠实地遵循他们以往生活中的一切习惯，接住主人扔给它的面包片，对他讲的一些话汪汪地吠着。它如此执著地热烈崇拜它的主人，主人一回家，与主人分离几个月来的思念就顿时消失了。

"我多么想念你啊，"他低声对它说，"是的，你也想念我！"

他半躺在长沙发上，吸着烟。狗假装打瞌睡，耳

WHEN the sergeant arrived in Paris on leave, he found his mistress not at home. He was nevertheless greeted with tremulous cries of surprise and joy, embraced and covered with wet kisses. His bitch, Vorace, the sheep-dog whom he had left with his young sweetheart, enveloped him like a flame and licked him with a tongue pale with emotion. Meanwhile, the char-woman was making as much noise as the dog and kept exclaiming:

"Of all the bad luck! Madame's just gone to Marlotte for a couple of days to shut up her house there. Madame's tenants have just left and she's going through the inventory of the furniture. Fortunately, it isn't all that far away! Will Monsieur write out a telegram for Madame? If it goes immediately, Madame will be here tomorrow morning before lunch. Monsieur must sleep here. Shall I turn on the geyser?"

"My good Lucie, I had a bath at home. Soldiers on leave are pretty good at washing!"

He eyed his reflection in the glass; he was both bluish and ruddy, like the granite rocks of Brittany. The Briard sheep-dog, standing close to him in a reverent silence, was trembling in every hair. He laughed because she looked so like him, gray and blue and shaggy.

"Vorace!"

She raised her head and looked lovingly at her master, and the sergeant's heart turned over as he suddenly thought of his mistress Jeannine, so young and so gay—a little too young and often too gay.

During dinner the dog faithfully observed all the ritual of their former life, catching the pieces of bread he tossed for her and barking at certain words. So ardent was the worship in which she was rooted that the moment of return abolished for her the months of absence.

"I've missed you a lot," he told her in a low voice. "Yes, you too!"

作者简介：科莱特（Colette，1873—1954），法国作家。1873 年 1 月 28 日生于圣索沃尔昂皮赛，1954 年 8 月 3 日卒于巴黎。她最早的 4 部克劳丁小说是对一个天真无邪的少女的回忆，由她丈夫整理出版，她的丈夫笔名叫维利，是一位评论家。她的成熟作品包括《钟爱之人》（*Chéri*，1920）、《我妈的房子》（*My Mother's House*，1922）、《成熟的种子》（*The Ripening Seed*，1923）、《爱情的终结》（*Last of Chéri*，1926）、《西朵》（*Sido*，1930）和《吉吉》（*Gigi*，1944）等。她小说中展现的爱的快乐与痛苦，因其听觉、嗅觉、味觉、触觉的详细描写而生动非凡。她蔑视传统，多次挑战法国公众的道德观念，但是她在晚年却成为国家标志人物。

朵一动不动地竖着，像一只蹲在墓碑上的灵猩。但是只要有轻微的响动，它的眉毛便会牵动一下，表明它十分警觉。

他十分疲乏，渐渐安静地入睡了，夹着香烟的手垂在沙发坐垫上，把绸面烧焦了。他醒来，打开一本书，玩弄着一些新的小摆设和一张珍妮的照片，这张照片他以前没有见到过，是珍妮穿着短裙，裸着双臂，在乡下拍的。

"业余摄影者的快照……她的模样儿真漂亮！"

在这张未装镜框的照片后面，他读到一行字：

"'1916 年 6 月 5 日。'6 月 5 日我在哪里？……呵，想起来了，我正往阿拉斯去。6 月 5 日。这个笔迹我不认识。"

他重又坐下来，随即为瞌睡所控制，而把所有的思绪都驱走了。10 点钟，钟响起来。他醒来了，听着小钟浓重而庄严的声音他笑了；珍妮常说，小钟看起来小，声音却大。但是当钟打到十下时，狗跳了起来。

"安静！"中士睡意朦胧地说道，"躺下！"

沃莱斯没有躺下。它喷喷鼻子，伸伸爪子，这个样子就等于人戴上帽子准备要出去了。它走到主人跟前，那黄黄的眼珠清楚地表示：

"好不好？"

"嗯，"中士回答道，"你怎么啦？"

主人说话时狗出于敬意而垂下的双耳，马上又竖了起来。

"啊，你真讨厌！"中士叹了一口气，"你渴啦，想出去？"

听到"出去"两字，沃莱斯咧开嘴笑了，轻轻地喘着气，露出好看的牙齿和厚厚的舌头。

"好吧，我们就出去走走。但不能逛得太久，我实在困。"

路上，沃莱斯十分兴奋，像一头狼一样地狺狺叫着，直跳到主人脖子那么高，袭击了一只猫，又追着自己的尾巴打着圈儿。主人亲切地训斥它，它便为主人玩出各种把戏。最后安稳了下来，静悄悄地走着。中士跟在它后面，享受着温暖的夜气，唱了两三只胡思乱想编成的小调。

"明天早晨我要见到珍妮了……我要睡在舒适的床榻上……在这里还有 7 天可以消遣……"

他发觉狗已快步跑到前头去了，正在煤气灯下似乎露出不耐烦的样子在等着他。它的眼神，它摆动的

He was smoking now, half lying on the divan. Crouching like a greyhound on a tombstone, the dog was pretending to be asleep, her ears quite still. Only her eyebrows, twitching at the slightest noise, revealed that she was on the alert.

Worn out as he was, the silence gradually lulled the man, until his hand which held the cigarette slid down the cushion, scorching the silk. He roused himself, opened a book, fingered a few new knick-knacks and a photograph, which he had not seen before, of Jeannine in a short skirt, with bare arms, in the country.

"An amateur snapshot... How charming she looks!"

On the back of the unmounted print he read:

"'June the fifth 1916. 'Where was I on June the fifth?... Oh, I know, over in the direction of Arras. June the fifth. I don't know the writing. "

He sat down again and was overcome by a sleep which drove all thought away. Ten o'clock struck; he was still just sufficiently awake to smile at the rich and solemn sound of the little clock whose voice, Jeannine used to say, was bigger than its stomach. But as it struck ten the dog got up.

"Quiet!"said the sleepy sergeant. "Lie down!"

But Vorace did not lie down. She snorted and stretched her paws which, for a dog, is the same as putting on a hat to go out. She went up to her master and her yellow eyes asked plainly:

"Well?"

" Well," he answered, " What's the matter with you?"

Out of respect she dropped her ears while he was speaking, raising them again immediately.

"Oh, what a bore you are!"sighed the sergeant. "You're thirsty. D'you want to go out?"

At the words"go out, "Vorace grinned and began to pant gently, showing her beautiful teeth and the fleshy petal of her tongue.

"All right, then, we'll go out. But not for long, because I'm absolutely dropping with sleep. "

In the road Vorace was so excited that she barked like a wolf, jumped right up to her master's neck, charged a cat and spun round playing "inner circle" with her tail. Her master scolded her tenderly and she did all her tricks for him. Finally, she sobered down again and walked along sedately. The sergeant suited his pace to hers, enjoying the warm night and making a little song out of two or three idle thoughts:

"I'll see Jeannine tomorrow morning... I'm going to sleep in a comfy bed... I've got seven more days to spend here... "

He became aware that his dog, who had trotted ahead, was waiting for him under a gas lamp with the same look of impatience. Her eyes, her wagging tail

尾巴和它的全身,似乎都在问他:

"怎么了? 你来吗?"

他一赶上来,牧羊犬就断然地快步拐了弯。这时候他才意识到它是要去某个地方。

"或许,"他暗自思忖,"那女佣人经常……或许珍妮……"

他站定一会儿,又跟着狗走去,甚至没有意识到,他身上的倦意、睡意以及幸福的感觉一下子全消失了。他加快步子,狗欢快地跑在前面,像个好向导。

"走吧,走吧!"中士时时下命令。

他看了看路名,又继续往前走。他们经过许多在大门口有小屋的花园,路灯昏暗,路上空无一人。牧羊犬兴奋极了,直想咬它主人垂在一边的手。主人要制止这种兽性的冲动,无法说明,不得不打它。

它终于在一个花园的破旧颓败的围栏外面停下来。里面是一间攀满葡萄藤和紫葳的低矮的小屋,这是一间掩蔽在深处的小屋。它似乎在说:"好了,我们到啦!"

狗在木栅门前摆好一个姿势,仿佛在说:"喂,你为什么不推门啊?"

中士举手去推门,但又把手放了下来。他俯身指着从关闭的百叶窗里漏出来的一缕灯光,低声问牧羊犬:

"谁在那里? ……珍妮?"

狗发出一声尖厉的"唏",吠叫起来。

中士低低地一声"嘘——"用手拍拍它又凉又湿的嘴巴。

中士又一次犹豫不决地朝着门伸出手臂,狗也向前跳奔。但是他抓住狗的颈圈把它拉了回来,带着它走到对面的人行道上,他从那里凝视着陌生的小屋和那一缕玫瑰色的灯光。他坐在人行道上,在狗旁边。他还未把浮现在脑际的,有关他妻子可能负心的种种联想集中起来,就已经感到十分孤独和虚弱了。

"你爱我吗?"他在狗的耳边喃喃地说。

狗舔舔主人的脸颊。

"走吧,我们回去吧。"

他们离开了,这回主人走在头里。他们又回到了小小的起居室里,狗看到主人正在把内衣和拖鞋塞进一只它十分熟悉的布袋里。它失望而崇敬地注视着主人的一举一动,在它黄黄的眼睛里闪动着金色的泪珠。中士把手按在它的脖子上安抚它:

and her whole body asked:

"Well? Are you coming?"

As soon as he caught up with her, she turned the corner at a determined trot. It was then that he realized she was going somewhere.

"Perhaps," he thought to himself, "the charwoman usually. . . Or Jeannine. . ."

He stood still for a moment, then went on again, following the dog, without even noticing that he had, all at once, stopped feeling tired, and sleepy, and happy. He quickened his pace and the delighted dog went before, like a good guide.

"Go on, go on!" ordered the sergeant from time to time.

He looked at the name of a road, then went on again. They passed gardens with lodges at the gates; the road was dimly lit and they met no one. On her excitement, the dog pretended to bite the hand that hung at his side, and he had to restrain a brutal impulse, which he could not explain, in order not to beat her.

At last she stopped, as though saying: "Well, here we are!" before an old, broken-down railing protecting the garden of a little low house smothered in vines and bignonia, a timid shrouded little house.

"Well, why don't you open it?" said the dog, who had taken up a position before the wooden wicket-gate.

The sergeant lifted his hand to the latch and let it fall again. He bent down to the dog, pointed with his finger to a thread of light along the closed shutters, and asked her in a low voice:

"Who's there?. . . Jeannine?"

The dog gave a shrill "Hi!" and barked.

"Shhh!" breathed the sergeant, clapping his hands over her cool wet mouth.

Once more he stretched out a hesitant arm towards the door and the dog bounded forward. But he held her back by her collar and led her to the opposite pavement, whence he gazed at the unknown house and the thread of rosy light. He sat down on the pavement beside the dog. He had not yet gathered together all those images and thoughts which spring up round a possible betrayal, but he felt singularly alone, and weak.

"Do you love me?" he murmured in the dog's ear.

She licked his cheek.

"Come on; let's go away."

They set off, he in front this time. And when they were once more in the little sitting-room, she saw that he was putting his linen and slippers in a sack that she knew well. Desperate but respectful, she followed all his movements, while tears, the color of gold, trembled in her yellow eyes. He laid his hand on her neck to reassure her:

"You're coming too. You're not going to leave me

"你也一起走吧。你不会再离开我了。下次你不会告诉我'此后'发生的事了。也许是我错了，也许我没有完全了解你。但是你一定不要留在这里了。除了我的秘密外，你的心灵上守不住任何秘密。"

狗颤抖着，仍然不很明白，他便用手抱住它的头，低声对它说道：

"你的心灵……一条狗的心灵……美丽的心灵……"

any more. Next time you won't be able to tell me what happened 'after.' Perhaps I'm mistaken. Perhaps I haven't understood you properly. But you mustn't stay here. Your soul wasn't meant to guard any secrets but mine."

And while the dog shivered, still uncertain, he held her head in his hands, saying to her in a low voice：

"Your soul... Your doggy soul... Your beautiful soul..."

044. 魔 桶

(美)伯纳德·马拉默德 著　　董衡巽 译

044. The Magic Barrel

by Bernard Malamud

　　前些日子,纽约居民区住着一个在雅西哇大学攻读犹太教法典的学生,名叫列奥·芬克尔。他住的房间很小,有点简陋,书倒是挤得满满的。芬克尔学了6年,眼看6月份就要当上拉比(指犹太的法学博士和犹太教士。——译注),有个熟人给他出了个主意,劝他最好先结婚,这样就能赢得更多的信徒。可是结婚,眼下一点儿眉目也没有,他心里闹腾了两天,终于把宾尼·沙兹曼请到家里来。沙兹曼是个做媒的,芬克尔在犹太人的《前锋日报》①上见过他登的两行广告。

　　一天晚上,那位媒人在芬克尔住的灰砖公寓黑洞洞的四楼过道里出现,手里拿着黑色公事包,上面束着皮带,公事包用的年代久了,已经磨损。沙兹曼替人撮合亲事已有多年,他身材瘦小,仪表不俗,帽子很旧,上衣穿在身上又紧又短。他喜欢吃鱼,嘴里一股腥味儿。他和蔼的态度,奇妙地配上一副伤惑的眼神,虽掉了几颗牙,样子倒不讨人厌。他的声音、嘴唇、稀疏的胡子、瘦削的指头,动起来蛮有生气,但一静下来,他那温柔、蓝色的眼睛里便流露出一丝深深的悲哀。列奥原觉得处境尴尬,心里紧张,不过见了沙兹曼这一特征,心里略觉自在些。

　　他开门见山地告诉沙兹曼为什么请他来,说他家乡是克利夫兰,父母亲结婚较晚,幸尚健在,除父母以外,他在这世上就孑然一身了。他6年来几乎一心扑在学习上,结果可以想见,顾不上参加社交活动,也没有时间同年轻妇女交往。因此,他想与其自讨苦吃,弄出差错——瞎闯、丢丑,不如请一位见过世面的人

NOT long ago there lived in uptown New York, in a small, almost meager room, though crowded with books, Leo Finkle, a rabbinical student in the Yeshivah University. Finkle, after six years of study, was to be ordained in June and had been advised by an acquaintance that he might find it easier to win himself a congregation if he were married. Since he had no present prospects of marriage, after two tormented days of turning it over in his mind, he called in Pinye Salzman, a marriage broker whose two-line advertisement he had read in the *Forward*. ①

The matchmaker appeared one night out of the dark fourth-floor hallway of the graystone rooming house where Finkle lived, grasping a black, strapped portfolio that had been worn thin with use. Salzman, who had been long in the business, was of slight but dignified build, wearing an old hat, and an overcoat too short and tight for him. He smelled frankly of fish, which he loved to eat, and although he was missing a few teeth, his presence was not displeasing, because of an amiable manner curiously contrasted with mournful eyes. His voice, his lips, his wisp of beard, his bony fingers were animated, but give him a moment of repose and his mild blue eyes revealed a depth of sadness, a characteristic that put Leo a little at ease although the situation, for him, was inherently tense.

He at once informed Salzman why he had asked him to come, explaining that his home was in Cleveland, and that but for his parents, who had married comparatively late in life, he was alone in the world. He had for six years devoted himself almost entirely to his studies, as a result of which, understandably, he had found himself without time for a social life and the company of young women. Therefore he thought it the

---

　　① 《犹太前锋日报》,是一份有影响力的意第绪吾报纸,带有一个著名的建议专栏(浪漫的或其他的)——Brintel Brief。——原注。

---

① *Jewish Daily Forward*, influential Yiddish-language newspaper with a famous advice column(romantic and otherwise)—"Brintel Brief."

作者简介: 伯纳德·马拉默德(**Bernard Malamud**,1914—1986),美国小说家。1914年4月26日生于纽约布鲁克林,1986年3月18日卒于纽约。写有长篇小说6部,其中《修配工》获1967年普利策奖。因为出生于俄国犹太移民家庭。他的小说经常展现犹太移民的生活,如以棒球运动员为主人公的《天生运动员》(*The Natural*,1952),关于犹太食品商和非犹太强盗的《店员》(*The Assistant*,1957))和获得普利策奖的《基辅怨》(*The Fixer*,1966)。他的短篇小说也充分体现了他的天赋。

在这方面给他出出点子。他顺便提到，说媒是一项古老而又体面的职业，在犹太人中间极受推崇，它既办了必需办的事，又不碍着幸福。再说，他自己的双亲也是经人介绍成的亲。他们双方都没有什么家私，结了婚在经济上虽然谁也沾不上谁的光，两口子却始终相亲相爱，结果总算美满。沙兹曼听这话里带点歉意，感到窘迫而惊异。可是，后来他心里觉着有一种消失了多年的、对自己职业的荣誉感，他衷心赞同芬克尔的看法。

他俩着手办事。列奥请沙兹曼坐在屋里唯一一处敞亮的地方，临窗一张桌子旁边，下面是灯火通明的街市。他自己坐在媒人身旁，面朝着他，使劲儿地抑制着痒得难受的嗓子。沙兹曼急切地打开公事包，取出一叠薄薄的、用久了的卡片，拿下一根宽松的橡皮圈。他翻卡片的动作和声音，叫列奥感到肉体上的痛苦，因此，他假装没看见，只顾定神眺望窗外。虽然还是2月天气，冬天倒快过去了，这类事他多年来还是头一回注意到。他看着银白色的、圆圆的月亮在空中穿过各种动物形状的云层，他半张着嘴望着月儿钻进一只大母鸡，又穿出来，像从母鸡身上自动生下的蛋。沙兹曼装着仔细看卡片上的字，却透过刚戴上的眼镜，不时偷看年轻人那副仪表堂堂的仪容，心里挺满意那个又长又威严的学者鼻子，棕色的眼睛里深藏着学问，两片嘴唇长得灵巧而又严峻，还有那凹陷下去的黑黝黝的腮帮子。他看了看四周一架又一架的书，轻轻地满意地嘘出一口气。

列奥看了看卡片，只见沙兹曼手上摊的是6张。

他失望地问道："就这么几张？"

"我办公室有多少卡片，我说了你也不会相信，"沙兹曼回答，"抽屉都塞到顶了，我只好放在一个桶里。可每个姑娘都配得上新毕业的拉比吗？"

列奥听了脸上一红，悔不该在寄给沙兹曼的履历表上将自己什么都填写上了。他原想最好填上他严格的标准与特长，好让做媒的明了，现在又后悔填过了头，没有限制在绝对必需的几项以内。

他支支吾吾地问道："你顾客材料里有相片吗？"

"先是家庭，陪嫁多少，还有前景如何，"沙兹曼边回答边解开他太紧身的上衣扣子，往椅子背上一靠，"末了才是相片，拉比。"

"管我叫芬克尔先生吧，我还没当上拉比呢。"

沙兹曼说好吧，却叫他博士，待列奥听话不太专

better part of trial and error—of embarrassing fumbling—to call in an experienced person to advise him on these matters. He remarked in passing that the function of the marriage broker was ancient and honorable, highly approved in the Jewish community, because it made practical the necessary without hindering joy. Moreover, his own parents had been brought together by a matchmaker. They had made, if not a financially profitable marriage—since neither had possessed any worldly goods to speak of—at least a successful one in the sense of their everlasting devotion to each other. Salzman listened in embarrassed surprise, sensing a sort of apology. Later, however, he experienced a glow of pride in his work, an emotion that had left him years ago, and he heartily approved of Finkle.

The two went to their business. Leo had led Salzman to the only clear place in the room, a table near a window that overlooked the lamplit city. He seated himself at the matchmaker's side but facing him, attempting by an act of will to suppress the unpleasant tickle in his throat. Salzman eagerly unstrapped his portfolio and removed a loose rubber band from a thin packet of much-handled cards. As he flipped through them, a gesture and sound that physically hurt Leo, the student pretended not to see and gazed steadfastly out the window. Although it was still February, winter was on its last legs, signs of which he had for the first time in years begun to notice. He now observed the round white moon, moving high in the sky through a cloud menagerie, and watched with half-open mouth as it penetrated a huge hen, and dropped out of her like an egg laying itself. Salzman, though pretending through eyeglasses he had just slipped on, to be engaged in scanning the writing on the cards, stole occasional glances at the young man's distinguished face, noting with pleasure the long, severe scholar's nose, brown eyes heavy with learning, sensitive yet ascetic lips, and a certain, almost hollow quality of the dark cheeks. He gazed around at shelves upon shelves of books and let out a soft, contented sigh.

When Leo's eyes fell upon the cards, he counted six spread out in Salzman's hand.

"So few?" he asked in disappointment.

"You wouldn't believe me how much cards I got in my office," Salzman replied. "The drawers are already filled to the top, so I keep them now in a barrel, but is every girl good for a new rabbi?"

Leo blushed at this, regretting all he had revealed of himself in a curriculum vitae he had sent to Salzman. He had thought it best to acquaint him with his strict standards and specifications, but in having done so, felt he had told the marriage broker more than was absolutely necessary.

He hesitantly inquired, "Do you keep photographs of your clients on file?"

"First comes family, amount of dowry, also what

心的时候又改称拉比。

沙兹曼整了整角质架的眼镜,轻轻地清了清嗓子,用讨好的音调念头一张卡片。

"莎菲·P,24 岁。守寡一年。无儿女。中学毕业,上过两年大学。父亲愿出 8000 元陪嫁资。经营批发业,生意兴隆。还有房产。母系亲属都兰教师,有一个演员。二号街上有点声望。"

列奥惊异地抬起头来。"你说是寡妇?"

"寡妇不等于坏了女儿身啊,拉比。她可能跟她丈夫才同居了 4 个月。男的有病,她原不该嫁给他的。"

"我从来没想到要娶个寡妇。"

"这是因为你没有经验。寡妇,尤其像这立又年轻又健壮的姑娘,可真是你想娶的称心的人儿。她这一辈子都会对你感激不尽。你信我的话,我要是想讨新娘子,就找个寡妇。"

列奥想了一想,摇摇头。

沙兹曼耸了耸肩,做了一个极其轻微的失望姿势。他把这张卡片放在木头桌子上,开始念下一张:

"莉莉·H,中学教师。正规教师,非代课。有存款和新道奇车一辆。在巴黎住过一年。父亲是有成就的牙科医生,有 35 年经验。愿找有专长的男子。相当美国化的家庭。机不可失。"

"这人我认识,"沙兹曼说,"我真希望你能见见这位姑娘,是个宝贝儿,还非常聪明。你可以成天同她谈书,谈戏,她什么都懂。还懂时事。"

"我没听你提到她的年龄吧?"

"她的年龄?"沙兹曼把眉毛一扬,"她的年龄是 32。"

列奥过了一会儿说:"恐怕太大了一点儿。"

沙兹曼笑了一声。"你多大了,拉比?"

"27。"

"你说 27 跟 32 有什么不同?我自己老婆就大我 7 岁。我吃什么亏了?一点儿没吃亏。要是罗思柴尔德①的女儿想嫁给你,你会在乎她的年龄,说个'不'字?"

"是的。"列奥干巴巴地说。

沙兹曼不去理会"是的"后面"不"的意思。"大 5 岁算得了什么。我担保,你跟她过上一个礼拜,包管你忘了她多大了。大 5 岁是什么意思?难道不是比

_____

① 罗思柴尔德:有名的犹太银行家。

kind promises," Salzman replied, unbuttoning his tight coat and settling himself in the chair. "After comes pictures, rabbi."

"Call me Mr. Finkle. I'm not yet a rabbi."

Salzman said he would, but instead called him doctor, which he changed to rabbi when Leo was not listening too attentively.

Salzman adjusted his horn-rimmed spectacles, gently cleared his throat and read in an eager voice the contents of the top card:

"Sophie P. Twenty-four years. Widow one year. No children. Educated high school and two years college. Father promises eight thousand dollars. Has wonderful wholesale business. Also real estate. On the mother's side comes teachers, also one actor. Well known on Second Avenue."

Leo gazed up in surprise. "Did you say a widow?"

"A widow don't mean spoiled, rabbi. She lived with her husband maybe four months. He was a sick boy she made a mistake to marry him."

"Marrying a widow has never entered my mind."

"This is because you have no experience. A widow, especially if she is young and healthy like this girl, is a wonderful person to marry. She will be thankful to you the rest of her life. Believe me, if I was looking now for a bride, I would marry a widow."

Leo reflected, then shook his head.

Salzman hunched his shoulders in an almost imperceptible gesture of disappointment. He placed the card down on the wooden table and began to read another:

"Lily H. High school teacher. Regular. Not a substitute. Has savings and new Dodge car. Lived in Paris one year. Father is successful dentist thirty-five years. Interested in professional man. Well Americanized family. Wonderful opportunity."

"I knew her personally," said Salzman. "I wish you could see this girl. She is a doll. Also very intelligent. All day you could talk to her about books and theyater and what not. She also knows current events."

"I don't believe you mentioned her age?"

"Her age?" Salzman said, raising his brows. "Her age is thirty-two years."

Leo said after a while, "I'm afraid that seems a little too old."

Salzman let out a laugh. "So how old are you, rabbi?"

"Twenty-seven."

"So what is the difference, tell me, between twenty-seven and thirty-two? My own wife is seven years older than me. So what did I suffer? —Nothing. If Rothschild's daughter wants to marry you, would you say on account her age, no?"

"Yes," Leo said dryly.

年轻的多活了几年,多懂点事? 上帝保佑,这姑娘啊,这 5 年可没有白过。她长一岁,身价高一等。"

"她在中学教什么?"

"语文。你要听她讲法国话呀,准以为是在听音乐。我干这行买卖 25 年了,我全心全意推荐她。请相信我,我不说瞎话,拉比。"

"下一张是谁?"列奥突然问。

沙兹曼勉强地拿起第三张卡片:

"鲁丝·K,19 岁。好学生。如有合适对象,父亲愿出 13000 元现金。她父亲是医学博士,胃病专家。生意兴隆。内兄开服装铺。上等人家。"

瞧沙兹曼那副神气,像是打出了一张王牌。

"你说 19 岁?"列奥颇有兴致地问道。

"一天不多,19 岁。"

"她长得好吗?"列奥红了红脸,"漂亮吗?"

沙兹曼吻了吻手指尖。"一个小宝贝儿。这点我敢担保。我今儿晚上打电话通知她爸爸,你就会知道什么叫美人儿。"

列奥不放心:"你能肯定她这么年轻?"

"准没错儿。她爸爸可以拿出生证给你看。"

"你肯定她没有问题?"列奥还是不放心。

"谁说有什么问题?"

"我不明白像她这么年轻的美国姑娘,干吗还委托媒人。"

沙兹曼脸上掠过一丝微笑。

"跟你一样啊,你怎么去,她怎么来。"

列奥脸红了:"我是因为时间紧顾不上。"

沙兹曼自知这话说得唐突,忙解释道:"是她爸爸来托我的,不是她。他希望女儿找到最中意的丈夫,所以亲自出马挑选。我们找到合适的人了,他就介绍给他女儿,鼓励他们成全好事。这样办的亲事,要比年轻、没经验的女儿家自己去闯好得多。这个,我不说,你也知道。"

"可是,你说这位年轻姑娘不相信谈恋爱吗?"列奥心里不踏实。

沙兹曼正想大笑,但抑制住了,冷静地回答说:"碰上意中人才爱得起来,碰不上没法爱。"

列奥张着干燥的嘴唇,没有言语。沙兹曼朝下一张卡片瞥了一眼,列奥看在眼里,就提出一个聪明的问题:"她健康情况怎么样?"

"非常好,"沙兹曼回答说,呼吸有些困难,"当然

Salzman shook off the no in the eyes. "Five years don't mean a thing. I give you my word that when you will live with her for one week you will forget her age. What does it mean five years—that she lived more and knows more than somebody who is younger? On this girl, God bless her, years are not wasted. Each one that it comes makes better the bargain."

"What subject does she teach in high school?"

"Languages. If you heard the way she speaks French, you will think it is music. I am in the business twenty-five years, and I recommend her with my whole heart. Believe me, I know what I'm talking, rabbi."

"What's on the next card?" Leo said abruptly.

Salzman reluctantly turned up the third card:

"Ruth K. Nineteen years. Honor student. Father offers thirteen thousand cash to the right bridegroom. He is a medical doctor. Stomach specialist with marvelous practice. Brother in law owns own garment business. Particular people."

Salzman looked as if he had read his trump card.

"Did you say nineteen?" Leo asked with interest.

"On the dot."

"Is she attractive?" He blushed. "Pretty?"

Salzman kissed his finger tips. "A little doll. On this I give you my word. Let me call the father tonight and you will see what means pretty."

But Leo was troubled. "You're sure she's that young?"

"This I am positive. The father will show you the birth certificate."

"Are you positive there isn't something wrong with her?" Leo insisted.

"Who says there is wrong?"

"I don't understand why an American girl her age should go to a marriage broker."

A smile spread over Salzman's face.

"So for the same reason you went, she comes."

Leo flushed. "I am pressed for time."

Salzman, realizing he had been tactless, quickly explained. "The father came, not her. He wants she should have the best, so he looks around himself. When we will locate the right boy he will introduce him and encourage. This makes a better marriage than if a young girl without experience takes for herself. I don't have to tell you this."

"But don't you think this young girl believes in love?" Leo spoke uneasily.

Salzman was about to guffaw but caught himself and said soberly, "Love comes with the right person, not before."

Leo parted dry lips but did not speak. Noticing that Salzman had snatched a glance at the next card, he cleverly asked, "How is her health?"

"Perfect," Salzman said, breathing with difficulty. "Of course, she is a little lame on her right foot

啰,她右腿有点儿瘸,是她 12 岁那年让车给撞的,可
是她又聪明又漂亮,谁也不会注意她腿瘸。"

列奥心事重重地站了起来,走到窗前。他分外痛
苦,责备自己不该请媒人上门。末了,他摇了摇头。

"为什么不考虑?"沙兹曼提高了嗓门追问。

"我讨厌胃病专家。"

"她爸爸干什么跟你有什么相干? 你跟她结了
婚,还要她爸爸干什么? 谁说他每个星期五晚上非得
上你家来?"

这样的谈话,列奥听不下去,就把沙兹曼打发走
了。沙兹曼满眼忧虑,返回家去。

媒人一走,列奥心里虽松快些,第二天却精神不
振。他想这是由于沙兹曼没能给他推荐一位称心的
姑娘而引起的。沙兹曼才不在乎列奥那号顾客呢。
后来列奥发现自己迟疑不决,拿不定主意要不要找一
个比沙兹曼更有修养的媒人,这时他忽然怀疑起来:
尽管他嘴上是这么说,尽管他尊重自己的双亲,其实
他根本不相信托媒这种做法。这个念头,他即刻打发
掉了,可心里还是不安。他成天徘徊在林间——错过
了一次重要的约会,忘了把衣服送出去洗,在百老汇
一家馆子吃了饭忘了付钱,只好拿着账单跑回去。女
房东和她一个朋友在街上见了他,挺有礼貌地跟他打
招呼:"晚上好,芬克尔博士。"他居然认不出来。天黑
了他才平静下来看书,心里得到些安宁。

他刚坐下来,就有人敲门。列奥还没来得及说请
进来,爱情商人沙兹曼早已站在他房间里了。他脸色
灰白、瘦削,一副饥饿相,好像站着就要断气似的。可
是这个做媒的不知怎么抽动一下肌肉,就露出一脸
笑容。

"晚安,我受欢迎吧?"

列奥点了点头,见了他心烦,却又不愿打发他走。

沙兹曼还是满脸笑容,将公事包放在桌上。"拉
比,今儿晚上我给你带来了好消息。"

"我早告诉你别叫我拉比。我还在读书呢。"

"你不用操心啦。我替你找到一个第一流的
新娘。"

"这事你别提了吧。"列奥装出毫无兴趣的样子。

"到你举行婚礼那一天,整个世界都会纵情
欢乐。"

"沙兹曼先生,请你别说了。"

"可是先得让我恢复恢复体力。"沙兹曼有气无力

from an auto accident that it happened to her when she
was twelve years, but nobody notices on account she is
so brilliant and also beautiful. "

Leo got up heavily and went to the window. He
felt curiously bitter and upbraided himself for having
called in the marriage broker. Finally, he shook his
head.

"Why not?" Salzman persisted, the pitch of his
voice rising.

"Because I detest stomach specialists. "

"So what do you care what is his business? After
you marry her do you need him? Who says he must
come every Friday night in your house?"

Ashamed of the way the talk was going, Leo dismissed Salzman, who went home with heavy, melancholy eyes.

Though he had felt only relief at the marriage
broker's departure, Leo was in low spirits the next
day. He explained it as arising from Salzman's failure
to produce a suitable bride for him. He did not care for
his type of clientele. But when Leo found himself hesitating whether to seek out another matchmaker, one
more polished than Pinye, he wondered if it could be—
protestations to the contrary, and although he honored
his father and mother—that he did not, in essence, care
for the matchmaking institution? This thought he
quickly put out of mind yet found himself still upset.
All day he ran around in the woods—missed an important appointment, forgot to give out his laundry,
walked out of a Broadway cafeteria without paying and
had to run back with the ticket in his hand; had even
not recognized his landlady in the street when she passed with a friend and courteously called out, "A good
evening to you, Doctor Finkle. " By nightfall, however,
he had regained sufficient calm to sink his nose into a
book and there found peace from his thoughts.

Almost at once there came a knock on the door.
Before Leo could say enter, Salzman, commercial cu-
pid, was standing in the room. His face was gray and
meager, his expression hungry, and he looked as if he
would expire on his feet. Yet the marriage broker
managed, by some trick of the muscles to display a
broad smile.

"So good evening. I am invited?"

Leo nodded, disturbed to see him again, yet un-
willing to ask the man to leave.

Beaming still, Salzman laid his portfolio on the table. "Rabbi, I got for you tonight good news. "

"I've asked you not to call me rabbi. I'm still a
student. "

"Your worries are finished. I have for you a first-
class bride. "

"Leave me in peace concerning this subject. "Leo
pretended lack of interest.

地说道。他笨手笨脚地解开皮带，从皮包里拿出一个油光光的纸口袋，打里面拿出一只带果仁的面包圈儿，又取出一条熏白鱼。他用手很快地一下撕掉了鱼皮，就狼吞虎咽地嚼了起来，边吃边咕哝说："整整忙了一天。"

列奥看着他吃。

"也许你有切片的西红柿？"沙兹曼犹豫地问。

"没有。"

媒人闭上眼睛嚼着。吃完以后，他仔细清理掉碎屑，将吃剩下来的鱼放回纸袋，卷起来。他的目光透过眼镜向房间四周扫了一圈，只见书堆里有一只单炉心煤气灶，就低声下气地问道："能给杯茶喝吗，拉比？"

列奥心里过意不去，站起来冲茶。他放了一块柠檬，两块方糖，沙兹曼见了乐不可支。

沙兹曼喝了茶，体力和精神都恢复了。

"你说说，拉比，"他亲切地问道，"我昨天提到的那三位，考虑过了没有？"

"没什么好考虑的。"

"怎么啦？"

"一个也不称心。"

"什么样的才称心呢？"

列奥反正说不清，便没言语。

沙兹曼没等他答话就说："你还记得我同你说的那个姑娘，那位中学老师吗？"

"就是 32 岁的那个？"

没想到沙兹曼笑了起来："29 岁。"

列奥瞟了他一眼："从 32 岁降下来了？"

"弄错了，"沙兹曼认了错，"我今天问了牙科医生。他领我到保险柜面前，让我看了出生证。去年 8 月，她正好 29 岁。那阵子她在山上度假期，家里人就在山上给她过的生日。她爸爸头一次跟我说的时候，我忘了记下年龄，跟你说了个'32'。现在想起来了，那是另外一个顾客，是个寡妇。"

"就是你说的那个寡妇吗？我记得她是 24 吧？"

"那又是一个。这世界上寡妇多，能怨我吗？"

"不怨你。反正我对寡妇没有兴趣，中学老师呢，也没有兴趣。"

沙兹曼握紧拳头，抱在胸前，两眼瞧着天花板，虔诚地叫道："犹太孩子啊，对中学教师没有兴趣的人，我有什么好说的呢？那你对什么有兴趣呢？"

"The world will dance at your wedding."

"Please, Mr. Salzman, no more."

"But first must come back my strength," Salzman said weakly. He fumbled with the portfolio straps and took out of the leather case an oily paper bag, from which he extracted a hard, seeded roll and a small, smoked white fish. With a quick motion of his hand he stripped the fish out of its skin and began ravenously to chew. "All day in a rush," he muttered.

Leo watched him eat.

"A sliced tomato you have maybe?" Salzman hesitantly inquired.

"No."

The marriage broker shut his eyes and ate. When he had finished he carefully cleaned up the crumbs and rolled up the remains of the fish, in the paper bag. His spectacled eyes roamed the room until he discovered, amid some piles of books, a one-burner gas stove. Lifting his hat he humbly asked, "A glass of tea you got, rabbi?"

Conscience-stricken, Leo rose and brewed the tea. He served it with a chunk of lemon and two cubes of lump sugar, delighting Salzman.

After he had drunk his tea, Salzman's strength and good spirits were restored.

"So tell me rabbi," he said amiably, "you considered some more the three clients I mentioned yesterday?"

"There was no need to consider."

"Why not?"

"None of them suits me."

"What then suits you?"

Leo let it pass because he could give only a confused answer.

Without waiting for a reply, Salzman asked, "You remember this girl I talked to you—the high school teacher?"

"Age thirty-two?"

But surprisingly, Salzman's face lit in a smile. "Age twenty-nine."

Leo shot him a look. "Reduced from thirty-two?"

"A mistake," Salzman avowed. "I talked today with the dentist. He took me to his safety deposit box and showed me the birth certificate. She was twenty-nine years last August. They made her a party in the mountains where she went for her vacation. When her father spoke to me the first time I forgot to write the age and I told you thirty-two, but now I remember this was a different client, a widow."

"The same one you told me about? I thought she was twenty-four?"

"A different. Am I responsible that the world is filled with widows?"

"No, but I'm not interested in them, nor for that

列奥红了脸,但是克制了自己。

沙兹曼说:"她能说四种语言,自己在银行里还存了 10000 元钱,你对这么个好姑娘没兴趣,还对什么有兴趣呢?她爸爸保证再给 12000。她还有一辆新汽车,漂亮的衣服,谈什么都头头是道,她可以给你成立最美满的家庭,给你生孩子。你这不是快进了人间天堂了吗?"

"她要有这么好,干吗不早 10 年结婚呢?"

"干吗?"沙兹曼哈哈大笑。"干吗?因为她挑剔。就是这缘故。她要挑最好的。"

列奥一声不响,心里觉得有趣,他竟陷进去了。可是,沙兹曼已经引起了他对莉莉·H 的兴趣,他认真考虑起来,想去拜访她。媒人看出自己这番话说动了列奥,心里就有数,他俩一会儿准能达成协议。

一个星期六傍晚之前,列奥·芬克尔同莉莉·海斯康恩沿着河滨道散步,列奥心里嘀咕,沙兹曼是不是躲在近处什么地方。列奥姿态挺直,步子轻快,头戴一顶黑色软呢帽,好不醒目,帽子还是他早晨匆匆忙忙从橱顶上扬满灰尘的盒子里取出来的,一件访客穿的、庄重的黑上装掸得干干净净。列奥还有一根手杖,是他一个远亲送给他的,可是列奥马上放弃这份诱惑,没有用它。莉莉长得小巧,不算难看,一身装束透露出春意。她兴致勃勃,什么都谈,无所不晓。列奥掂量掂量莉莉说的话,发现她特别有头脑——又可以给沙兹曼记上一分。他总疑心沙兹曼躲在什么地方,说不定爬在沿街一棵大树上,用一面小镜子给莉莉姑娘发什么信号,也说不定有个羊腿潘神①,隐起身子,在他们前面边跳舞边吹着成亲的小曲儿,一面将野花的蓓蕾和紫葡萄撒了一路,象征着他俩早生贵子,其实呢,连结婚的影儿都没有哩。

莉莉开口说话,列奥才清醒过来。"我刚才正想着沙兹曼先生,这人真怪,您说呢?"

列奥不知说什么好,只点点头。

她鼓起勇气红着脸往下说:"我倒是挺感射他介绍我们认识。您呢?"

他很有礼貌地回答:"我也感谢他。"

"我是说,"她笑了一声,仪态还算大方,起码给人印象不俗,"我们这样认识,您不在乎吧?"

---

① 潘神:古希腊神话中的畜牧神,人身羊足。——译注。

---

matter, in school teachers. "

Salzman pulled his clasped hand to his breast. Looking at the ceiling he devoutly exclaimed, "Yiddishe kinder, ①what can I say to somebody that he is not interested in high school teachers? So what then you are interested?"

Leo flushed but controlled himself.

"In what else will you be interested," Salzman went on, "if you not interested in this fine girl that she speaks four languages and has personally in the bank ten thousand dollars? Also her father guarantees further twelve thousand. Also she has a new car, wonderful clothes, talks on all subjects, and she will give you a first-class home and children. How near do we come in our life to paradise?"

"If she's so wonderful, why wasn't she married ten years ago?"

"Why?" said Salzman with a heavy laugh. "—Why? Because she is *partikiler*. This is why. She wants the *best*."

Leo was silent, amused at how he had entangled himself. But Salzman had aroused his interest in Lily H., and he began seriously to consider calling on her. When the marriage broker observed how intently Leo's mind was at work on the facts he had supplied, he felt certain they would soon come to an agreement.

Late Saturday afternoon, conscious of Salzman, Leo Finkle walked with Lily Hirschorn along Riverside Drive. He walked briskly and erectly, wearing with distinction the black fedora he had that morning taken with trepidation out of the dusty hat box on his closet shelf, and the heavy black Saturday coat he had throughly whisked clean. Leo also owned a walking stick, a present from a distant relative, but quickly put temptation aside and did not use it. Lily, petite and not unpretty, had on something signifing the approach of spring. She was au courant, animatedly, with all sorts of subjects, and he weighed her words and found her surprisingly sound—score another for Salzman, whom he uneasily sensed to be somewhere around, hiding perhaps high in a tree along the street, flashing the lady signals with a pocket mirror; or perhaps a cloven-hoofed Pan, piping nuptial ditties as he danced his invisible way before them, strewing wild buds on the walk and purple grapes in their path, symbolizing fruit of a union, though there was of course still none.

Lily startled Leo by remarking, "I was thinking of Mr. Salzman, a curious figure, wouldn't you say?"

Not certain what to answer, he nodded.

She bravely went on, blushing, "I for one am grateful for his introducing us. Aren't you?"

---

① "Jewish children!"

列奥倒是喜欢她这么直来直去，明白她是想把关系弄好，有点儿生活经验又有胆量的人才敢这么做。没见过世面的不敢这样子提出话头。

他问答说他不在乎，沙兹曼这种职业古老而又体面，说不定有所收获，有其价值，不过，他又说，弄不好常常白费工夫。

莉莉同意他的说法，只是叹了一口气。他们蹓跶了一会儿，过了好长时间，莉莉不自在地笑着说："我问您一点儿私事，行吗？说实话，我倒挺关心这个问题。"列奥耸了耸肩，可她还是用为难的口吻说下去："你怎么会干你这一行的？我说是不是灵感的突然冲动。"

列奥隔了一会儿慢慢地说道，"我对法典一直有兴趣。"

"你在法典里面见到上帝显身？"

列奥点点头，转换一个话题："我听说你在巴黎住过一段时间，是吗，海斯康恩小姐？"

"噢。是沙兹曼先生告诉您的吧，芬克尔拉比？"列奥微微一怔，她继续说道："那是好久以前的事，都快忘了。我只记得是姐姐结婚我才回来的。"莉莉还是不肯放松，哆嗦着嗓子问道："您是什么时候倾心上帝的？"

列奥目不转睛地盯着她。他渐渐明白过来，原来她说的不是列奥·芬克尔，而是个完全不相识的人，一个神秘人物，说不定是沙兹曼为她胡编出来的什么热情的先知，既不是活人，也不是死人。列奥浑身哆嗦，又气又怯。这骗子显然是耍了花招，哄她上当，也哄了他。他原想结识一位29岁的年轻妇女，谁知这张脸又紧张又急切，一眼就看出过了35，眼看快要衰老。亏得他涵养工夫好，才同她谈得这么久。

他严肃地说道："我不是个有天赋的虔诚信徒，"他搜索着词儿往下说，心里觉得又惭愧又害怕。他紧张地说："我看我皈依上帝，不是因为我爱他，而是因为我不爱他。"

这份招供说得很刺耳，因为它来得突然，使他很激动。

莉莉吓得往后缩，列奥看见许多面包像鸭子似的在他头上高高飞过，就像他昨天晚上数着才睡着的带翅膀的面包。接着，上天开恩，下起雪来，列奥相信这也许是沙兹曼的又一计谋。

列奥对媒人大为恼火，发誓他一进门就把他撵出

He courteously replied, "I am. "

"I mean, "she said with a little laugh—and it was all in good taste, to at least gave the effect of being not in bad—"do you mind that we came together so?"

He was not displeased with her honesty, recognizing that she meant to set the relationship aright, and understanding that it took a certain amount of experience in life, and courage, to want to do it quite that way. One had to have some sort of past to make that kind of beginning.

He said that he did not mind. Salzman's function was traditional and honorable—valuable for what it might achieve, which, he pointed out, was frequently nothing.

Lily agreed with a sigh. They walked on for a while and she said after a long silence, again with a nervous laugh, "Would you mind if I asked you something a little bit personal? Frankly, I find the subject fascinating. "Although Leo shrugged, she went on half embarrassedly, "How was it that you came to your calling? I mean was it a sudden passionate inspiration?"

Leo, after a time, slowly replied. "I was always interested in the Law. "

"You saw revealed in it the presence of the Highest?"

He nodded and changed the subject. "I understand that you spent a little time in Paris, Miss Hirschorn?"

"Oh, did Mr. Salzman tell you, Rabbi Finkle?"Leo winced but she went on, "It was ages ago and almost forgotten. I remember I had to return for my sister's wedding. "

And Lily would not be put off. "When, "she asked in a trembly voice, "did you become enamored of God?"

He stared at her. Then it came to him that she was talking not about Leo Finkle, but of a total stranger, some mystical figure, perhaps even passionate prophet that Salzman had dreamed up for her—no relation to the living or dead. Leo trembled with rage and weakness. The trickster had obviously sold her a bill of goods, just as he had him, who'd expected to become acquainted with a young lady of twenty-nine, only to behold, the moment he laid eyes upon her strained and anxious face, a woman past thirty-five and aging rapidly. Only his self control had kept him this long in her presence.

"I am not, "he said gravely, "a talented religious person, "and in seeking words to go on, found himself possessed by shame and fear. "I think, "he said in a strained manner, "that I came to God not because I loved Him, but because I did not. "

This confession he spoke harshly because its

去。可是沙兹曼那天晚上没有来。列奥气消了以后，又感到莫名的绝望。开头他只道是莉莉不称他的心，但是不久就弄清楚了，原来他当初找沙兹曼的时候，究竟怎么打算，自己心里没个谱。他心里像有一阵6只手正拽的那种空虚感，慢慢地领悟到，他请媒人上门，原来是自己没本事。他同莉莉·海斯康恩见了面、谈了话之后才悟出这一点，吓得他不轻。她追根究底，问个没完，惹得他没好气，结果倒是给他而不是给她弄清了自己同上帝究竟是什么关系，他从这一点得到启发，恍然大悟，原来他除了父母亲，谁也不爱。也许情况正好倒过来，正因为他不爱人类，所以也不能全力爱上帝。在列奥看来，他整个一生都显了原形，头一回见到自己的本相——没人爱他，他也不爱人。这番认识虽然不完全出乎意料，却很痛心，害得他惊惶失措，靠了极大的努力才控制住。他双手捂住脸，哭了起来。

打这以后的一个星期是他一生中最难熬的日子。他吃不下饭，体重减轻，胡子黑蓬蓬、乱糟糟的。课堂讨论他不去参加，书几乎没有打开过。他严肃考虑要不要退出雅西哇大学，只是学了多年，弃于一旦，想起来特别难受，好比眼睁睁瞧着一本书撕成一页一页，往街上撒，而且这么一来，他两位老人家要受不了。可是，他活到现在，没有认识自己，只怪自己不好，读了五书①，加上所有的评注本，都没有领悟到这个真理。他不知道上哪儿求教，在这片孤寂凄凉之中，又有谁可以依靠。他虽然常常想到莉莉，却总鼓不起劲儿下楼给她打电话。他动不动就发脾气，尤其是对女房东，因为她老喜欢打听他各种私人的事儿。有时候反过来，他明明意识到自己惹人厌，就在楼梯上拦住她，低三下四地向她赔不是，弄得她受不了，只好跑掉。然而，他从中也得到点儿自我安慰，觉得自己是犹太人，而犹太人生来就得受苦。漫长而又难过的一周过去了，他慢慢恢复了平静，也恢复了生活的目标，一切照常行事。他的人虽不完美，理想却是完美的。至于找老婆这件事，一想到还得找，就急得他心口灼热，不过他现在对自己有了新的了解，说不定找起来会比从前顺利些。说不定他会产生爱情，有了爱情自会有老婆。这是神圣的寻求，要沙兹曼干什么？

---

① 即摩西五书：《创世记》《出埃及记》《利未记》《民数记》和《申命记》。

unexpectedness shook him.

Lily wilted. Leo saw a profusion of loaves of bread go flying like ducks high over his head, not unlike the winged loaves by which he had counted himself to sleep last night. Mercifully, then, it snowed, which he would not put past Salzman's machinations.

He was infuriated with the marriage broker and swore he would throw him out of the room the minute he reappeared. But Salzman did not come that night, and when Leo's anger had subsided, an unaccountable despair grew in its place. At first he thought this was caused by his disappointment in Lily, but before long it became evident that he had involved himself with Salzman without a true knowledge of his own intent. He gradually realized—with an emptiness that seized him with six hands—that he had called in the broker to find him a bride because he was incapable of doing it himself. This terrifying insight he had derived as a result of his meeting and conversation with Lily Hirschorn. Her probing questions had somehow irritated him into revealing—to himself more than her—the true nature of his relationship to God, and from that it had come upon him, with shocking force, that apart from his parents, he had never loved anyone. Or perhaps it went the other way, that he did not love God so well as he might, because he had not loved man. It seemed to Leo that his whole life stood starkly revealed and he saw himself for the first time as he truly was—unloved and loveless. This bitter but somehow not fully unexpected revelation brought him to a point of panic, controlled only by extraordinary effort. He covered his face with his hands and cried.

The week that followed was the worst of his life. He did not eat and lost weight. His beard darkened and grew ragged. He stopped attending seminars and almost never opened a book. He seriously considered leaving the Yeshivah, although he was deeply troubled at the thought of the loss of all his years of study—saw them like pages torn from a book, strewn over the city—and at the devastating effect of this decision upon his parents. But he had lived without knowledge of himself, and never in the Five Books① and all the Commentaries—mea culpa—had the truth been revealed to him. He did not know where to turn, and in all this desolating loneliness there was no *to whom*, although he often thought of Lily but not once could bring himself to go downstairs and make the call. He became touchy and irritable, especially with his landlady, who asked him all manner of personal questions; on the other hand sensing his own disagreeableness, he

---

① The Torah, or five books of Moses (the Pentateuch): Genesis, Exodus, Leviticus, Numbers, Deuteronomy.

骨瘦如柴、两眼惊恐的媒人，那天晚上来了。他一副空等一场而灰心丧气的样子，好像他在莉莉·海斯康恩小姐身边等了一个星期电话，可电话一直没打来。

沙兹曼漫不经心地咳嗽了一声，开门见山，说到正题："你觉得她怎么样？"

列奥火气上来，禁不住训斥道："沙兹曼，你为什么哄我？"

沙兹曼脸色由苍白变成死白，这世界像雪崩似的压在他身上。

列奥追问："你不是说29岁吗？"

"我担保……"

"她肯定35岁。起码35岁。"

"这你可别说死了。她爸爸跟我说……"

"甭管她爸爸。最糟糕的是你也骗了她。"

"你怎么骗她来着，你说？"

"你跟她说的关于我的事，不是那么一回事儿。你把我说得高，结果呢，我反而低。她把我当成一个完全不同的人，当成半神秘的神仙拉比。"

"我只说你是虔诚的信徒。"

"我可以料想得到。"

沙兹曼叹了一口气。"这是我的毛病，"他承认，"我老婆说我不该把婚事当买卖做，可是我见了两个好人儿能天生地配对儿，心里一高兴，话就多了起来。"他苦笑了一声，"就因为这个缘故，沙兹曼才落得个穷光蛋啊。"

列奥气消了。"好吧，沙兹曼，我看这事儿就算完了吧。"

媒人眼神急切，盯着他。

"你不想讨老婆？"

列奥回答："想讨，不过我决计另想办法。托媒人这种办法，我没兴趣了。说真话，我现在认为，结婚之前先得有爱情，就是说，我爱上谁就跟谁结婚。"

沙兹曼大吃一惊："爱情？"他过了一会儿说道："我们这些人，爱情就是生活，不是女人。犹太区的人……"

列奥说："我知道，我知道。这事儿我常想。我跟自个儿说，爱情应当随着生活和信仰而来，不是为爱情而爱情。不过，在我这个处境，我有我的需要，应当满足这个需要。"

沙兹曼耸了耸肩，回答道："拉比，你听我说，你要

waylaid her on the stairs and apologized abjectly, until mortified, she ran from him. Out of this, however, he drew the consolation that he was a Jew and that a Jew suffered. But gradually, as the long and terrible week drew to a close, he regained his composure and some idea of purpose in life to go on as planned. Although he was imperfect, the ideal was not. As for his quest of a bride, the thought of continuing afflicted him with anxiety and heartburn, yet perhaps with this new knowledge of himself he would be more successful than in the past. Perhaps love would now come to him and a bride to that love. And for this sanctified seeking who needed a Salzman?

The marriage broker, a skeleton with haunted eyes, returned that very night. He looked, withal, the picture of frustrated expectancy—as if he had steadfastly waited the week at Miss Lily Hirschorn's side for a telephone call that never came.

Casually coughing, Salzman came immediately to the point: "So how did you like her?"

Leo's anger rose and he could not refrain from chiding the matchmaker: "Why did you lie to me, Salzman?"

Salzman's pale face went dead white, the world had snowed on him.

"Did you not state that she was twenty-nine?" Leo insisted.

"I give you my word—"

"She was thirty-five, if a day. *At least* thirty-five."

"Of this don't be too sure. Her father told me—"

"Never mind. The worst of it was that you lied to her."

"How did I lie to her, tell me?"

"You told her things about me that weren't true. You made out to be more, consequently less than I am. She had in mind a totally different person, a sort of semi-mystical Wonder Rabbi."

"All I said, you was a religious man."

"I can imagine."

Salzman sighed. "This is my weakness that I have," he confessed. "My wife says to me I shouldn't be a salesman, but when I have. two fine people that they would be wonderful to be married, I am so happy that I talk too much." He smiled wanly. "This is why Salzman is a poor man."

Leo's anger left him. "Well, Salzman, I'm afraid that's all."

The marriage broker fastened hungry eyes on him.

"You don't want any more a bride?"

"I do," said Leo, "but I have decided to seek her in a different way. I am no longer interested in an arranged marriage. To be frank, I now admit the necessity

爱情，我也可以替你找。我有这么漂亮的顾客，包管你一见钟情。"

列奥苦笑着说："恐怕你不明白我的意思。"

但是沙兹曼急急忙忙松开公事包的皮带，从里面抽出一个吕宋纸袋来。

"照片。"说着，他很快把信套放在桌上。

列奥叫他拿回去，可是沙兹曼好似乘风而去，早没影儿了。

3月来临。列奥回到原来正常的生活。他虽然没全复原，打不起精神来，却在安排更活跃的社交活动。这当然难免要付出代价，不过列奥善于精打细算，临到细无可细之时，还能精益求精。这些日子，沙兹曼拿来的照片一直放在桌上吃灰尘。列奥坐在那里学习或者喝茶，偶尔也朝信套瞟上一眼，可从来没打开看过。

日子一天天过去，他在社交活动中，却与任何女性没有值得一提的发展——以他的处境而论，事情自有难处。一天早晨，列奥使劲儿地爬上楼梯，进了屋，望着窗外的街市。天气虽好，他看去却是昏暗。他看了一会儿街上熙来攘往的人流，转身返回小屋，心中闷闷不乐。那包照片还是在桌上。他突然狠下心来，把信套撕开。他在桌子边上站了半个钟头，心情激动，仔细察看沙兹曼放在里面的照片。末了，他叹了口长气，放回桌子上。一共6张，各有动人之处，可是看得久了，一个个都成了莉莉·海斯康恩，都消失了青春。动人的笑容隐藏着饥渴，没有一个具有真实的个性。生活没有理会她们的拼命叫喊，还是在她们身旁流了过去，这些都是放在有鱼腥味的文件包里的照片。可是，过了一会儿，列奥想把照片装回去的时候，发现里面还有一张，是花两毛五分钱照的那种快照。列奥定神看了一会儿。不由得叫出声来。

这张脸把他迷住了，为什么呢，他开头说不清。她给人一种青春的印象，好比春天的花朵，然而，她岁月销蚀，又留下了风尘的痕迹。这从她分外熟悉而又完全陌生的眼神里看得出来。他印象鲜明，像在哪儿见过她，他几乎叫得出她的名字来，似乎见过她亲笔写下的名字，可是怎么也想不起来。不，这怎么可能呢，他该想得起来。她这脸蛋儿是够动人的，却不能说漂亮出众，不能这样说，这一点他心里明白，只是她脸上有一种什么东西，使他心摇神驰。把她的五官分别开来看，其他几张照片上面的妇女比她还强些。

of premarital love. That is, I want to be in love with the one I marry."

"Love?" said Salzman, astounded. After a moment he remarked "For us, our love is our life, not for the ladies. In the ghetto they—"

"I know, I know," said Leo. "I've thought of it often. Love, I have said to myself, should be a by-product of living and worship rather than its own end. Yet for myself I find it necessary to establish the level of my need and fulfill it."

Salzman shrugged but answered, "Listen, rabbi, if you want love, this I can find for you also. I have such beautiful clients that you will love them the minute your eyes will see them."

Leo smiled unhappily. "I'm afraid you don't understand."

But Salzman hastily unstrapped his portfolio and withdrew a manila packet from it.

"Pictures," he said, quickly laying the envelope on the table.

Leo called after him to take the pictures away, but as if on the wings of the wind, Salzman had disappeared.

March came. Leo had returned to his regular routine. Although he felt not quite himself yet—lacked energy—he was making plans for a more active social life. Of course it would cost something, but he was an expert in cutting corners; and when there were no corners left he would make circles rounder. All the while Salzman's pictures had lain on the table, gathering dust. Occasionally as Leo sat studying, or enjoying a cup of tea, his eyes fell on the manila envelope, but he never opened it.

The days went by and no social life to speak of developed with a member of the opposite sex—it was difficult, given the circumstances of his situation. One morning Leo toiled up the stairs to his room and stared out the window at the city. Although the day was bright his view of it was dark. For some time he watched the people in the street below hurrying along and then turned with a heavy heart to his little room. On the table was the packet. With a sudden relentless gesture he tore it open. For a half-hour he stood by the table in a state of excitement, examining the photographs of the ladies Salzman had included. Finally, with a deep sigh he put them down. There were six, of varying degree of attractiveness, but look at them long enough and they all became Lily Hirschorn: all past their prime, all starved behind bright smiles, not a true personality in the lot. Life, despite their frantic yoohooings, had passed them by; they were pictures in a beief case that stank of fish. After a while, however, as Leo attempted to return the photographs into the envelope, he found in it another, a snapshot of the type taken by a machine for a quarter. He gazed at it a moment and let out a cry.

但是她一下子跳到他的心上——她享受过生活,起码是想享受,还不止这个,也许悔不该当初过那种生活——心灵上似乎受过很深的创伤,这从她那对含恨的眼睛深处、从她灵魂所蕴藏和闪发出来的光彩之中看得出来。她打开了未来的境界,她有自己的个性。列奥要的就是她这样的人。他集中眼力凝视着照片,头都看痛了,眼睛眯成缝,于是,好像有一团迷雾突然在他脑子里膨胀开来,他感到对她害怕起来,省悟到他得到的可是一种邪恶的印象。他哆嗦了一下,轻轻地说,这个,我们都不能幸免。列奥冲了一小缸子茶,没放糖,坐下来呷茶,让心情平静一下。但是,茶还没有喝完,他又兴奋起来,细细端详这张脸,发现她确实美丽,在列奥·芬克尔眼里是美丽的。只有这样的姑娘才能了解他,才能帮助他寻求他一直在寻求的东西。说不定她会爱上他。她怎么会成了废牌,扔进沙兹曼的桶里,他怎么也猜不透,但是他明白他得赶紧去找她。

列奥冲下楼去,一手抓起勃朗克斯电话簿,找沙兹曼家的地址。电话簿上没有他家的地址,也没有办事处的地址。曼哈顿电话簿上也没有他。可是列奥记得,他在《前锋日报》"私人事务"栏上见过沙兹曼登的广告,当场就把地址记在一张小纸条上。他上楼进了屋,在纸堆里翻啊,找啊,就是没有。这真要命。他需要媒人的时候,却哪儿都找不见。幸好,列奥想起在皮夹子里找了找,发现一张卡片上记着沙兹曼在勃朗克斯街的地址。没有电话号码,原因是……他想起来了,他原先就是写信同沙兹曼联系的。他披上衣服,没脱睡帽就戴上帽子,急急忙忙赶到地铁车站。地点是在勃朗克斯街到底,他一路上坐也坐不住,不止一次想掏出照片来,看看这位姑娘的脸蛋儿是不是他印象中的模样,可是他终究克制住了,还是让照片放在上衣里边的口袋里,她贴得这么近,他心里高兴。火车刚到站,他早就等在车门口,一个箭步冲了出去,不一会儿就找到了沙兹曼在广告上说的那条街。

他要找的那幢楼离地铁不到一条街的路程,不过这不是一幢办公楼,不像统楼,也不像出租办事处的商店。这是一幢非常破旧的公寓。列奥在电铃下这一块脏布片上发现用铅笔写的沙兹曼的名字,他爬过三层黑洞洞的楼梯,到了他的房门口。列奥敲敲门,开门的是一个患着气喘病、头发灰白的瘦小女人,穿着毡做的拖鞋。

Her face deeply moved him. Why, he could at first not say. It gave him the impression of youth—spring flowers, yet age—a sense of having been used to the bone, wasted; this came from the eyes, which were hauntingly familiar, yet absolutely strange. He had a vivid impression that he had met her before, but try as he might he could not place her although he could almost recall her name, as if he had read it in her own handwriting. No, this couldn't be; he would have remembered her. It was not, he affirmed, that she had an extraordinary beauty—no, though her face was attractive enough; it was that *something* about her moved him. Feature for feature, even some of the ladies of the photographs could do better; but she leaped forth to his heart—had *lived*, or wanted to—more than just wanted, perhaps regretted how she had lived—had somehow deeply suffered: it could be seen in the depths of those reluctant eyes, and from the way the light enclosed and shone from her, and within her, opening realms of possibility: this was her own. Her he desired. His head ached and eyes narrowed with the intensity of his gazing, then as if an obscure fog had blown up in the mind, he experienced fear of her and was aware that he had received an impression, somehow, of evil. He shuddered, saying softly, it is thus with us all. Leo brewed some tea in a small pot and sat sipping it without sugar, to calm himself. But before he had finished drinking, again with excitement he examined the face and found it good: good for Leo Finkle. Only such a one could understand him and help him seek whatever he was seeking. She might, perhaps, love him. How she had happened to be among the discards in Salzman's barrel he could never guess, but he knew he must urgently go find her.

Leo rushed downstairs, grabbed up the Bronx telephone book, and searched for Salzman's home address. He was not listed, nor was his office. Neither was he in the Manhattan book. But Leo remembered having written down the address on a slip of paper after he had read Salzman's advertisement in the "personals" column of the *Forward*. He ran up to his room and tore through his papers, without luck. It was exasperating. Just when he needed the matchmaker he was nowhere to be found. Fortunately Leo remembered to look in his wallet. There on a card he found his name written and a Bronx address. No phone number was listed, the reason—Leo now recalled—he had originally communicated with Salzman by letter. He got on his coat, put a hat on over his skull cap and hurried to the subway station. All the way to the far end of the Bronx he sat on the edge of his seat. He was more than once tempted to take out the picture and see if the girl's face was as he remembered it, but he refrained, allowing the snapshot to remain in his inside coat pocket, content to have her so close. When the

"什么事?"她问,那口气是料到不会有什么事,一副爱听不听的样子。列奥敢说以前也见过她,不过明白这只是他的幻觉。

"沙兹曼……在这里住吗?宾尼·沙兹曼,"他问道,"那个做媒的?"

她打量他好一会儿才回答:"在这里住。"

他觉得很窘。"他在家吗?"

"不在。"她虽张着嘴,却没有第二句话。

"事情很急。能告诉我他在哪儿办公吗?"

"在天上。"她朝上指了一指。

"你说他没有办事处?"列奥问。

"在他袜子里。"

他偷偷朝屋里瞟一眼。里面又暗又脏,一间大屋子,用半拉开的帘子隔成两半,靠里面,只见一张中间下陷的铁床。近门的地方挤满了东倒西歪的椅子、旧柜子、一张三条腿的桌子,架上尽是锅碗瓢盆,还有一大堆厨房用具。没见沙兹曼和他那只魔桶的影子,说不定那也是虚幻的想象。一股炸鱼味儿憋得列奥腿都软了。

"他在哪儿呢?"列奥不罢休,"我得见你丈夫。"

临了,她回答说:"谁知道他上哪儿去了?他一想起个什么新主意,就窜出去了。你回家吧,他会去找你的。"

"跟他说列奥·芬克尔来过。"

她像没听见的样子。

他下了楼梯,闷闷不乐。

可是,沙兹曼正气喘吁吁地等在列奥的房门口。

列奥又惊又喜:"你怎么比我早到?"

"我赶来的。"

"进屋吧。"

他们进了屋。列奥弄茶,给了沙兹曼一块沙丁鱼夹馅面包。他们正喝着茶,列奥转过身去,拿起那包照片,递给沙兹曼。

沙兹曼放下杯子,殷切地问道:"有你喜欢的吗?"

"这里面没有。"

媒人转过脸去。

"我要的是这一位。"列奥递过照片去。

沙兹曼戴上眼镜,哆哆嗦嗦地拿起照片。他脸色大变,叫唤了一声。

"怎么啦?"列奥喊道。

"对不起,这张照片我弄错了。她不是介绍给

train pulled into the station he was waiting at the door and bolted out. He quickly located the street Salzman had advertised.

The building he sought was less than a block from the subway, but it was not an office building, nor even a loft, nor a store in which one could rent office space. It was a very old tenement house. Leo found Salzman's name in pencil on a soiled tag under the bell and climbed three dark flights to his apartment. When he knocked, the door was opened by a thin, asthmatic, gray-haired woman in felt slippers.

"Yes?" she said, expecting nothing. She listened without listening. He could have sworn he had seen her, too, before but knew it was an illusion.

"Salzman—does he live here? Pinye Salzman," he said, "the matchmaker?"

She stared at him a long minute. "Of course."

He felt embarrassed. "Is he in?"

"No." Her mouth, though left open, offered nothing more.

"The matter is urgent. Can you tell me where his office is?"

"In the air." She pointed upward.

"You mean he has no office?" Leo asked.

"In his socks."

He peered into the apartment. It was sunless and dingy, one large room divided by a half-open curtain, beyond which he could see a sagging metal bed. The near side of the room was crowded with rickety chairs, old bureaus, a three-legged table, racks of cooking utensils, and all the apparatus of a kitchen. But there was no sign of Salzman or his magic barrel, probably also a figment of the imagination. An odor of frying fish made Leo weak to the knees.

"Where is he?" he insistd. "I've got to see your husband."

At length she answered, "So who knows where he is? Every time he thinks a new thought he runs to a different place. Go home, he will find you."

"Tell him Leo Finkle."

She gave no sign she had heard.

He walked downstairs, depressed.

But Salzman, breathless, stood waiting at his door.

Leo was astounded and overjoyed. "How did you get here before me?"

"I rushed."

"Come inside."

They entered. Leo fixed tea, and a sardine sandwich for Salzman. As they were drinking he reached behind him for the packet of pictures and handed them to the marriage broker.

Salzman put down his glass and said expectantly, "You found somebody you like?"

"Not among these."

您的。"

沙兹曼激动地把吕宋信套往包里胡乱一塞,又把照片揣在口袋里,飞快地奔下楼去。

列奥愣了一会儿,赶紧追出去,在门口堵住了媒人。女房东尖叫起来,可这两个人全不理会。

"把照片还给我,沙兹曼。"

"不行。"眼睛里神色痛苦得可怕。

"那你告诉我,她是谁。"

"我不能告诉您,对不起。"

他想走。可是列奥气极了,一把拽住沙兹曼紧小的上衣,发疯似的摇着他。

"请别这样,"沙兹曼叹口气,"别这样。"

列奥不好意思地放了手,央求他:"你告诉我她是谁,我非常非常想知道。"

"她配不上您。她是个野姑娘,野,不要脸。不配给拉比做老婆。"

"野是什么意思?"

"像一头畜生。像一只狗。在她眼里,贫穷就是罪孽。所以,我现在只当她是死了。"

"天啊,你这是什么意思?"

"她,我不能介绍给您。"沙兹曼喊道。

"你干吗这么激动?"

"您问干吗,"沙兹曼边说边哭了起来,"她是我的孩子,我的斯妲拉,她应当入地狱,烧死。"

列奥上了楼,往床上一躺,一头埋进被窝里,把自己的一生寻思了一番。他虽然一会儿就睡着了,可是心里没法排遣掉她。他醒过来,捶着胸。他祷告上帝,别让自己想她,可是,祷告一点儿不灵。他这几天日子过得很痛苦,心里不断挣扎,可别让自己爱上她,但是怕真的不爱她了,所以又不敢这样。临了,他想出一个办法,规劝她改邪归正。自己呢,皈依上帝。这个想法一会儿使他厌恶,一会儿又叫他兴奋。

他在百老汇一家咖啡馆撞见沙兹曼。这时候,他才明白自己最后打定了主意。沙兹曼独自一人坐在靠后面的一张桌子边,吮着一根鱼骨头。媒人面容憔悴,瘦得快剩一个影子了。

沙兹曼抬起头,开头没认出他。列奥蓄起一撮尖胡子,眼里尽是智慧。

他说:"沙兹曼,爱情终于来到我的心上。"

媒人挖苦地说:"一张照片能产生爱情?"

The marriage broker turned away.

"Here is the one I want." Leo held forth the snapshot.

Salzman slipped on his glasses and took the picture into his trembling hand. He turned ghastly and let out a groan.

"What's the matter?"cried Leo.

"Excuse me. Was an accident this picture. She isn't for you. "

Salzman frantically shoved the manila packet into his portfolio. He thrust the snapshot into his pocket and fled down the stairs.

Leo, after momentary paralysis, gave chase and cornered the marriage broker in the vestibule. The landlady made hysterical outcries but neither of them listened.

"Give me back the picture, Salzman. "

"No. "The pain in his eyes was terrible.

"Tell me who she is then. "

"This I can't tell you. Excuse me. "

He made to depart, but Leo, forgetting himself, seized the matchmaker by his tight coat and shook him frenziedly.

"Please,"sighed Salzman. *Please.*

Leo ashamedly let him go. "Tell me who she is," he begged. "It's very important for me to know. "

"She is not for you. She is a wild one—wild, without shame. This is not a bride for a rabbi. "

"What do you mean wild?"

"Like an animal. Like a dog. For her to be poor was a sin. This is why to me she is dead now. "

"In God's name, what do you mean? "

"Her I can't introduce to you,"Salzman cried.

"Why are you so excited?"

"Why, he asks," Salzman said, bursting into tears. "This is my baby, my Stella, she should burn in hell. "

Leo hurried up to bed and hid under the covers. Under the covers he thought his life through. Although he soon fell asleep he could not sleep her out of his mind. He woke, beating his breast. Though he prayed to be rid of her, his prayers went unanswered. Through days of torment he endlessly struggled not to love her; fearing success, he escaped it. He then concluded to convert her to goodness, himself to God. The idea alternately nauseated and exalted him.

He perhaps did not know that he had come to a final decision until he encountered Salzman in a Broadway cafeteria. He was sitting alone at a rear table, sucking the bony remains of a fish. The marriage broker appeared haggard, and transparent to the point of vanishing.

Salzman looked up at first without recognizing him. Leo had grown a pointed beard and his eyes were weighted with wisdom.

"这不是不可能的。"

"你如果能爱她,就能爱别人。有些新顾客才寄来一些照片。我给你看看吧。有一位真是个小宝贝儿。"

列奥咕哝道:"我就是要她。"

"你别傻了,博士。别操心她了。"

"帮我同她联系吧,沙兹曼,"列奥谦卑地说,"也许我能帮着做点儿什么。"

沙兹曼停下不吃了,列奥心情激动,知道事情已经停当。

然而,列奥离开咖啡馆的时候,却生了一阵绞心的疑虑,事情朝这个路子发展,是不是沙兹曼一手策划的。

列奥接到来信,说她在某个拐角同他见面。一个春天的夜晚,她在路灯底下等着他。列奥来了,手里拿着一束紫罗兰和玫瑰花蕾。斯妲拉站在路灯柱子旁边,吸着烟。她一身白的装束,配上红色的鞋子,正合他的心意,只是他心慌意乱,看花了眼,以为身上穿红的,脚上穿白的。斯妲拉不安地、腼腆地等着。列奥老远就看到,她的眼睛分明是她父亲的眼睛,流露出无比的纯洁。他在心中描绘:他怎么从她的身上获得新生。空中回荡着提琴的声音,闪烁着烛光。列奥奔向前去,花儿冲着斯妲拉。

沙兹曼靠在拐角的墙边,为死者唱着祷文。

"Salzman," he said, "love has at last come to my heart."

"Who can love from a picture?" mocked the marriage broker.

"It is not impossible."

"If you can love her, then you can love anybody. Let me show you some new clients that they just sent me their photographs. One is a little doll."

"Just her I want," Leo murmured.

"Don't be a fool, doctor. Don't bother with her."

"Put me in touch with her, Salzman," Leo said humbly. "Perhaps I can be of service."

Salzman had stopped eating and Leo understood with emotion that it was now arranged.

Leaving the cafeteria, he was, however, afflicted by a tormenting suspicion that Salzman had planned it all to happen this way.

Leo was informed by letter that she would meet him on a certain corner, and she was there one spring night, waiting under a street lamp. He appeared carrying a small bouquet of violets and rosebuds. Stella stood by the lamp post, smoking. She wore white with red shoes, which fitted his expectations, although in a troubled moment he had imagined the dress red, and only the shoes white. She waited uneasily and shyly. From afar he saw that her eyes—clearly her father's—were filled with desperate innocence. He pictured, in her, his own redemption. Violins and lit candles revolved in the sky. Leo ran forward with flowers outthrust.

Around the corner, Salzman, leaning against a wall, chanted prayers for the dead.

045. 戴米舍

（法）马瑟尔·埃梅 著　　万　紫 译

045. Dermuche

by *Marcel Aymé*

为了把一张觊觎多年的唱片据为己有，他杀死了一家三口人。原告律师不必激烈辩论，被告律师激烈辩论也是徒劳。毫无异议地要杀头，法庭内外没有人对他表示丝毫同情。他的肩膀厚实，脖子粗壮，有一张颚骨凸出、显不出额角的扁平大脸和一双半开半闭、目光迟钝的小眼睛。即使他的罪还有疑点，他那粗野的外貌也会使任何敏感的陪审团把他定罪的。在整个审判过程中，他一动不动地待着，显出一副麻木不仁、困惑不解的模样。

"戴米舍，"首席法官问道，"你对犯下的罪行有悔过之意吗？"

"呵，法官先生，有点儿，但也没有，"戴米舍说，"我懊悔，可我又并不懊悔。"

"说清楚些。你感到悔恨吗？"

"什么啊，法官先生？"

"你不懂'悔恨'一词的意思吗？你想起被你杀死的人时，没有痛苦的感觉吗？"

"我感到蛮好，法官先生，我还得谢谢你呢。"

审判过程中只有一回，也就是起诉进行到出示那张唱片的时候，戴米舍才表示出一点兴趣来。他斜靠在被告席的栅栏边上，牢牢地盯着那张唱片，当书记官开动唱机，奏出乐曲来时，他那呆板迟钝的脸上掠过一抹十分温柔的笑容。

他在死牢里静候着执行死刑的那一日，似乎对自己的结局毫不担忧，他对走进牢房来的看守们也从不提到他的结局。他的确不想跟他们搭腔，回答别人的提问也仅仅是出于礼貌。他唯一的消遣就是哼哼那支驱使他去干杀人勾当的魔曲，可他又不很记得。他的记忆力非常之差，或许由于不能重新夺回在 9 月之

HE had murdered a family of three in order to get possession of a gramophone record which he had coveted for several years. The fiery eloquence of counsel for the prosecution was unnecessary, and that of the defending counsel unavailing. He was unanimously condemned to have his head cut off, and not a voice was raised in sympathy, in the courtroom or elsewhere. Heavy-shouldered and bull-necked, he had a huge, flat face, all jaw and no forehead, with small, half-closed, dull-staring eyes. Even had there been a doubt as to his guilt, his brutish aspect would have caused any sensitive jury to condemn him. Throughout the trial he stayed motionless, seemingly indifferent and uncomprehending.

"Dermuche," asked the presiding judge, "are you sorry for what you did?"

"Well, yes and no, your Honor," said Dermuche. "I am, and then again, I'm not."

"Try to make yourself more clear. Do you feel any remorse?"

"Pardon, your Honor?"

"Don't you know what the word 'remorse' means? Have you no feeling of distress when you think of your victims?"

"I feel all right, your Honor, thanking you all the same."

Only at one moment during the trial did Dermuche display any interest, and this was when the prosecution produced the gramophone record. Leaning over the edge of the dock he gazed at it steadfastly, and when the gramophone, set in motion by the clerk, ground out the refrain, a smile of great gentleness passed over his dull, heavy face.

In the condemned cell he waited calmly for the day of execution, seemingly untroubled by the prospect. He never spoke of it to the warders entering the cell. Indeed, he had no desire to talk to them, and merely replied politely to the questions put to him. His sole occupation was to hum the magical refrain that had driven him to murder, and he knew it badly. His

作者简介：**马瑟尔·埃梅**（**Marcel Aymé**，1902—1967），法国小说家、散文家和剧作家。1902 年 3 月 29 日生于琼尼，1967 年 10 月 14 日卒于巴黎。他的长篇小说包括《空地》（*The Hollow Field*，1929）、《寓言与现实》（*The Fable and the Flesh*，1943）和《短暂的时间》（*The Transient Hour*，1946）。农场动物的故事（反映他在农场长大的经历）受到大众的欢迎，其中部分以英文出版，收录在《神奇的农场》（*The Wonderful Farm*，1951）中。虽然他混淆幻想与现实的丰富创造力长期不被看重，但是他后来还是被公认为讽刺和故事大师。

夜引他到马恩河畔诺让的一幢朴素的别墅里去的那张唱片，使他感到愤怒。那幢别墅里住着三个小有资财的人，两个老小姐和一个挂着退伍军人荣誉勋章的怕冷的老人。每个礼拜天午饭过后，两个姊妹中的姐姐就摇起唱机来。碰到好天气，他们就让餐厅的窗户开着。3 年来戴米舍体验到了夏天迷人的魅力。他蜷缩在别墅的墙脚下，倾听着礼拜天奏放的乐曲，想在下一周里把那支曲子全部保存在记忆中，而他却从未能完全记住。但是秋天来临，怕冷的老人关了窗，于是那音乐也只好由几个有钱的人去欣赏了。连续 3 年，戴米舍想听听那曲子的一点儿享受被剥夺了，长年累月地过着没有音乐也没有快乐的日子。那曲子逐渐离他远去，一天天地从他心中消失了，到冬末，除了一片渴望已一无所有。到了第 4 年，他忍受不了这么长时期的等待，就闯进了那幢别墅。第二天早晨，警察找到他时，他正在听唱片，身旁躺着三具尸体。

那支曲子他只记牢了一个月，到审判的日子，他又忘记了。在死牢里，他把审判时听到唱片所记住的曲子的片断集拢起来，但是那支曲子还是一天天地变得更模糊了。咚咚的咚，那死囚从早到晚就这么哼哼着。

监狱牧师来看望戴米舍，发现他怀着一股小善意。要是那个可怜的人显得更能领会他的意思，让安慰的话深入他的心坎，牧师就会更喜欢那股子善意了。戴米舍像一株树木一样驯顺地听着，但是无论他的简短的答话或者毫无表情的脸都没有表明他对拯救灵魂，甚至对他有个灵魂那样的事儿发生兴趣。然而，在 12 月的某一天，当牧师讲到圣母和天使的时候，在戴米舍那双迟钝的眼睛里看到了一丝亮光，然而那亮光稍纵即逝，牧师也不能断定他真的看见了没有。谈话结束时，戴米舍突然发问："那么这个小耶稣，他还活着吗？"牧师没有犹豫。他无疑应该回答说圣婴耶稣曾经是活着的，但是自从他在 33 岁上钉死在十字架上以来，谈起他就不可能使用现在时态了。不过戴米舍的脑袋太笨了，要他理解是十分困难的。圣婴耶稣的故事对他来说较易理解，可以因此打开他的心扉，让他沐浴到神圣真理的光辉。于是牧师就讲起了上帝之子怎样选择诞生在一个牛棚里。诞生在牛和驴之间的故事。

"要知道，戴米舍，这说明耶稣是热爱穷人的，是为了穷人的缘故而来到人世间的。他同样可能选择

was a very slow memory, and perhaps it was his exasperation at being unable to recapture it which had taken him, on a September evening, to the modest villa in Nogent-sur-Mare. Three persons of small independent means lived in the villa, two old maids and an uncle, decorated with the Legion of Honor, who felt the cold. Every Sunday, at the end of the midday meal, the elder of the two sisters wound up the gramophone. In fine weather they kept the dining-room window open, and for three years Dermuche had known enchanted summers. Crouched at the foot of the villa wall he listened to that Sunday melody which during the ensuing week he sought to fix wholly in his memory, without ever being completely successful in doing so. But with the onset of autumn the uncle who felt the cold caused the window to be shut, and thereafter the music sounded only for persons of independent means. For three years in succession Dermuche had lived through the long months of deprivation, without music and without rapture. Little by little the refrain escaped him, diminishing day by day, until by the end of winter nothing was left of it but the longing. The fourth year he could not endure the thought of that long period of waiting, and so he broke into the villa. The police found him there next morning, listening to the song of the gramophone record in company with the three dead bodies.

For a month he had it by heart, but by the time the trial came on he had forgotten it again. Now, in the condemned cell, he gathered together the fragments restored to him by the playing of the record during the trial, but which every day became more uncertain. *Tum-tum-ti-tum*, hummed the condemned man from morning till night.

The prison chaplain visited Dermuche and found him filled with good will. He would have liked it better, however, if the poor wretch had shown himself more receptive, so that the words of consolation entered his heart. Dermuche listened with the docility of a tree, but neither his brief replies nor his expressionless face afforded any evidence that he was interested in his soul's salvation, or even that he possessed a soul. Nevertheless, one day in December, when he was talking of the Holy Virgin and the angels, the chaplain thought he caught a little gleam of light in those dull eyes—so fugitive, however, that he was not sure if he had really seen it. At the end of the interview Dermuche asked abruptly: "And the little Jesus, is he still alive?" The chaplain did not hesitate. No doubt he should have replied that the infant Jesus had once lived, but that, since he had died on the cross at the age of thirty-three, it was not possible to speak of him in the present tense. But Dermuche was so thick-headed that it was difficult to get him to understand. The fable of the infant Jesus was more within his range and might open his heart to the light of the sacred truths. The chaplain told the story of how the Son of God had elected to be born in a stable, between the ox and the ass.

"You see, Dermuche, it was to show that he loved the poor and had come for their sake. He might equally well have chosen to be born in a prison, among the most

在监狱中,在许多悲苦的人中间诞生。"

"先生,我懂了。耶稣真的可能会生在我现在住的牢房里,而不愿生在一个别墅里。"

牧师点点头表示满意。戴米舍的逻辑无懈可击,不过,与他那桩特殊的案子联系起来过于勉强,因而不易引导他走上悔悟之路。牧师不置可否地点了点头之后,继续对他讲起了向初生耶稣朝圣的三大博士,无辜者遭杀戮,逃亡等等圣经故事。最后讲到圣婴长大,生了胡须,他怎样在两个窃贼当中被钉死在十字架上,从而为人类打开了天堂的大门。

"戴米舍,你只要想一想,善良窃贼的灵魂一定会首先进入天堂,这并非偶然,而是因为上帝想启示我们,每一个罪人都可祈望得到上帝的宽赦。对上帝说来,即使是最大的罪也不过是生活中的偶然事故……"

但是戴米舍早就不再听牧师的啰唆了,善良窃贼的故事对他来说似乎与《圣经》上现世利益的奇迹一样模糊。

"那么后来小耶稣回到他的牛棚里去了吗?"

他只想到圣婴耶稣。牧师离开了牢房,他认为这凶犯的智力不过像个孩子。他甚至怀疑戴米舍是否能为自己的罪行承担责任。他祈祷上帝宽恕他。

"工人的身体,小孩的灵魂……杀死了三个老人,并不是蓄意犯罪。正像一个孩子剪开自己的玩偶,或者扯断玩偶的腿一样。真是一个不知道自己的力气的孩子。一个不幸的孩子,如此而已。他相信圣婴耶稣,就是明证。"

几天后,牧师又去探望戴米舍,他问打开牢门的看守:

"他在唱些什么?"

他们听到戴米舍的男子噪音,像一口声音低沉的钟,重复不停地唱着咚咚的咚。

"他咚咚咚地哼个没完,"看守说,"虽然听起来倒不怎么令人讨厌,就是不成个调子。"

一个尚未向上帝靠拢的囚犯,竟有这般明显的轻松心情,真使牧师感到迷惑。他发觉戴米舍比往常快活了。粗野的脸上有了少许灵活的表情,半开半闭的眼睑闪露一丝笑意。而且他的话也多了。

"先生,今天外面天气怎么样?"

"正下雪呢,我的孩子。"

"啊,那不打紧,雪阻挡不了他,他对雪可不在乎呢。"

牧师又一次谈及上帝的仁慈,谈及忏悔带来的光

unhappy of men."

"Yes, sir, I see. In fact, Jesus might have been born in this cell I'm in, but he wouldn't have wanted to be born in a villa."

The chaplain contented himself with a wag of the head. Dermuche's logic was unassailable, but it was related rather too narrowly to his own particular case, and seemed unlikely to lead him into the way of repentance. Having thus nodded non-committally, the chaplain went on to tell him about the magi, the slaughter of innocents, the flight, and finally how the infant Jesus, when his beard was grown, had died crucified between two thieves to open the gates of heaven to mankind.

"Only think, Dermuche. The soul of the good thief must have been the first of all human souls to enter Paradise, and that was not due to accident, it was because God wished to show us what every sinner may expect of His mercy. For Him even the greatest crimes are no more than the accidents of life. . . ."

But for some time past Dermuche had not been following the chaplain's narrative, and the story of the good thief seemed to him as obscure as the miracle of the loaves and fishes.

"And so then little Jesus went back to his manger?"

He could think only of the infant Jesus. The chaplain left the cell reflecting that this murderer possessed no more understanding than a child. He even questioned whether Dermuche could be held responsible for his crime, and he prayed God to have mercy on him.

"A child's soul in a laborer's body. . . . He killed those three old people without malice, just as a child cuts open its doll, or pulls off its legs. A child that doesn't know its own strength. An unhappy child and nothing more. And the proof is that he believes in the infant Jesus."

A few days later, paying Dermuche another visit, the chaplain asked the warder who opened the cell door:

"What's that he's singing?"

The male voice of Dermuche, like a deep-toned bell, could be heard incessantly repeating, *tum-tum-ti-tum*.

"He never stops that *tum-tum-tum* of his," said the warder. "If only it sounded like something it wouldn't be so bad, but it isn't even a tune."

This apparent lightness of heart, on the part of a condemned man who had not yet come to terms with Heaven, was disturbing to the chaplain. He found Dermuche livelier than usual. His brutish face had an expression of gentle alertness, and through the half-closed lids there shone a gleam of laughter. Moreover, he was almost talkative.

"What's the weather like outside today, sir?"

"It's snowing, my son."

"Well, that doesn't matter. The snow won't stop him. A fat lot he cares about the snow."

明,但是犯人频频打断他的话,问他关于圣婴耶稣的事,他的这一番规劝。丝毫起不了作用。

"小耶稣认识每个人吗?小耶稣在天堂里是个头儿吗?先生你说说,小耶稣喜欢音乐吗?"

最后牧师感到自己插不上嘴。当他转身朝门口走去时,戴米舍把一张折成四折的纸片塞到他的手上。

"这是我给小耶稣的信。"他笑着说。

牧师收下了,几分钟过后他把信拿来读了。

"亲爱的小耶稣,"信中写道,"请你帮个忙。我叫戴米舍。圣诞节快到了。我知道你对我弄死诺让地方三个老家伙一事并不在意。你不会愿意出生在像他们那样的房子里的。我不会在人间向你要求什么东西的,因为我不久就要死了。我要求的只有一桩事情,就是我进天堂时,能不能得到我的唱片?预先谢谢你并祝你好运气。——戴米舍。"

牧师读完信惊恐不已,这封信已再清楚不过,表明那凶犯对忏悔一事是多么无动于衷。

"真是的,"他想,"这个无知的人,比初生的婴儿还不懂事理。他在圣婴耶稣身上寄托的真诚,足以证明他孩童般的天真单纯。但是当他良心上带着三个被害者而又毫无忏悔之意地来接受上帝的最后审判时,即使上帝对他也无可奈何。他小小的灵魂仍然像泉水一般纯净。"

晚上,他去监狱教堂,为戴米舍祈祷后,把他的信放在圣婴耶稣的石膏摇篮里。

圣诞节前夕,12 月 24 日凌晨,一群衣着考究的绅士在看守们的陪同下走进了死牢。他们一个个还是睡眼惺忪,饥肠辘辘,嘴巴紧闭着,忍住呵欠,在离牢床不远处停了下来。透过朦胧的晨光,他们想辨认一个盖着床毯的身形。毯子微微地动着,从床上传出微弱的呜呜声。检察官感到一阵寒战,凉气直透脊梁骨。典狱官把黑色领带拉拉直,离开了人群。他双手一甩,企图摆出一副适合时宜的姿势,然后俯身屈臂十指交叉紧握,按在衣服的暗纽前,用一种演戏似的声音说道:

"戴米舍,你得放勇敢些,你的上诉失败了。"

回答他的又是一阵呜呜声,比前一次更响更明显了。戴米舍一动也不动,似乎连头发也盖住了,身子一点儿也没露到毯子外面来。

Once again the chaplain talked of God's mercy and the light of repentance, but the condemned man constantly interrupted him with questions about the infant Jesus, so that his exhortations were without effect.

"Does little Jesus know everybody? Is little Jesus the boss in Paradise? Would you say, sir, that little Jesus likes music?"

The chaplain finally found himself unable to get a word in edgeways. As he turned towards the door Dermuche thrust into his hand a sheet of paper folded in four.

"It's my letter to little Jesus," he said with a smile.

The chaplain took it and read it a few minutes later.

"Dear little Jesus," the letter ran. "This is asking you a favor. My name is Dermuche. It will soon be Christmas. I know you don't mind about me doing those three old geezers in Nogent. You wouldn't have wanted to be born in the house of people like that. I'm not asking for anything here on earth, seeing it won't be long before I have my chips. All I ask is, when I get to Heaven can I have my gramophone record? Thanking you in advance, and good luck to you—Dermuche."

The priest was horrified by the letter, which revealed all too clearly how impervious the murderer was to the idea of repentance.

"It is true," he reflected, "that the man is an innocent possessing no more discernment than a newborn babe. The trust he places in the infant Jesus bears sufficient witness to his childlike simplicity. But when he appears at the Seat of Judgment with three murders on his conscience, and no vestige of repentance, even God will be able to do nothing for him. Yet his small soul is as pure as the waters of a spring."

That evening he went to the prison chapel, and after having prayed for Dermuche, placed his letter in the plaster cradle of the infant Jesus.

At dawn on the 24th December, Christmas Eve, a party of welldressed gentlemen accompanied the warders into the condemned cell. Their eyes still heavy with sleep, stomachs rumbling and mouths suppressing yawns, they paused at a short distance from the bed, seeking in the pallid early light to make out the shape of a body stretched beneath the coverings. The blankets moved feebly and a faint wail came from the bed. The Public Prosecutor felt a shiver pass down his spine. The Governor of the prison straightened his black tie and moved apart from the group. Shooting his cuffs he sought a posture appropriate to the occasion, and with his head inclined forward, shoulders rounded and hands clasped in front of his fly-buttons, he said in a theatrical voice:

"You must be brave, Dermuche. Your appeal has failed."

Another wail answered him, louder and more

"起来吧,戴米舍,不要让我们再等了,"典狱官说,"表示一点儿合作吧,就此一遭了!"

一个看守走上前去摇动那犯人。他对着床弯下身子,立即又挺直了,神色慌张地转身看着典狱官。

"喂,你怎么啦?"

"我不知道,先生,床毯在动,不过……"

毯子下面发出长长的一声令人心碎的尖厉的悲号。看守突然把毯子掀开,尖叫起来。其余的人拥上前去,他们也傻了。惊叫起来。掀开床毯的铺上,躺着的不是戴米舍,而是一个几个月的婴孩。他见到亮光似乎很高兴,安静地微笑着看着来访者。

"这是什么意思?"典狱官转身对着看守大喊,"你把犯人放跑了么?"

"那不可能,先生。三刻钟前我值最后一班岗,我确实看到戴米舍躺在床上。"

典狱长气得脸色发紫,辱骂他的僚属,用最严厉的制裁威胁他们。与此同时,牧师正在朝着上帝、圣母、圣父、天公、圣子跪下去谢恩。但是并没有人注意到他。

"万能的上帝,"典狱官俯身对着孩子喊道,"你看见了吗?婴儿胸口也刺着与戴米舍身上一样的花纹呢!"

轮到其他的人上来俯视了。孩子胸口两边各刺着一个花纹,一边是女人头,一边是只狗头。与戴米舍身上的花纹一模一样,甚至大小也恰成比例。看守人都来证实此事。接着是一阵长时间的沉默。

"或许我错了,"检察官莱勃欧夫先生说,"不过我看这孩子跟戴米舍非常相像,正如一个那样年龄的孩子可以跟一个 33 岁的男子相像一样。瞧他那大脑袋,扁脸盘,低额角,还有眯缝着的小眼睛,甚至那鼻子的样子也长得很像。你不同意吗?"他转身对辩护律师布里顿先生说。

"这些看来真是一模一样。"布里顿先生说。

"戴米舍一条大腿的后部有一块棕色的胎记。"看守长说。

他们查看了孩子的腿,果然发现同样的胎记。

"给我把犯人的指印拿来,"典狱官说,"我们来比较一下。"

看守长拔腿跑了出去。其他人一面等他回来,一面企图找一找关于戴米舍变形的合乎情理的解释,已经没有人对他的变形持怀疑态度了。典狱官没有参

insistent than the first, but Dermuche did not move. He seemed to be buried even to his hair, and nothing of him emerged from the blankets.

"Come, Dermuche, you mustn't keep us waiting," said the Governor. "Do show a little co-operation, just for once."

A warder moved forward to shake the condemned man. He bent over the bed, then straightened himself and turned to the Governor with an air of astonishment.

"Why, what's the matter?"

"I don't know, sir. The bedclothes are moving, and yet. . ."

A long wail of heart-rending poignancy came from the blankets. With an abrupt movement the warder stripped them off the bed and then uttered a sharp exclamation. The others, who had pressed forward, in their turn uttered a cry of stupefaction. In place of Dermuche, on the uncovered bed, lay an infant a few months old. It seemed pleased to find itself in the light, and gazed placidly smiling at the visitors.

"What does this mean?" shouted the Governor, turning to the chief warder. "Have you let the prisoner escape?"

"It's impossible, sir. I made my last round three-quarters of an hour ago, and I'm positive I saw Dermuche in his bed."

Purple with fury, the Governor abused his subordinates, threatening them with the direst sanctions. The chaplain, meanwhile, had sunk to his knees and was offering thanks to God, the Holy Virgin, St. Joseph, Providence and the infant Jesus. But no one paid any attention to him.

"God almighty," cried the Governor, bending over the child, "will you look at that? It's got the same tattoo-marks as Dermuche on its chest!"

The others leaned over in their turn. The child had two pictures tattooed on either side of his chest, a woman's head on one side and a dog's head on the other. Dermuche had had exactly the same, even to their relative size. The warders all confirmed it. There was a long silence.

"I am perhaps mistaken," said M. Leboeuf, the Public Prosecutor, "but the child seems to me to be as much like Dermuche as a child that age can be like a man of thirty-three. Look at the big head, the flat face, the low forehead, the small, slit-eyes and even the shape of the nose. Don't you agree?" And he turned to M. Bridon, counsel for the defense.

"There does certainly seem to be a resemblance," said M. Bridon.

"Dermuche had a brown birthmark on the back of one thigh," the chief warder said.

They examined the child's leg and found the same thing.

"Fetch me the condemned man's finger-prints," said the Governor. "We'll see how those compare."

The chief warder went off at the double. While

加别人的谈话,独自神经质地在牢房里走来走去。婴孩被乱哄哄的声音吵醒,开始号哭,典狱官便走到床边,用威胁的声音说:

"等着,小鬼头。我会叫你哭个畅快的。"

莱勃欧夫坐在孩子旁边,神情诡秘地抬头看着典狱官。

"你真的还以为这是你手中的杀人犯吗?"他问。

"我想是的。不管怎样,我们马上会弄明白的。"

而对这微妙的奇迹,牧师不住地感谢上帝。他注视着这个实质上的神之婴孩躺在莱勃欧夫和典狱官之间,他的温情脉脉的眼睛湿润了。他有几分焦虑,不知道即将发生什么情况,但是他仍满怀信心地断定:"事情定会像圣婴耶稣裁决的那样进行下去的。"

当指纹的比较已证实了这离奇的变形时,典狱官宽慰地舒出一口气,搓了搓双手。

"好了,现在让我们进行下去吧!"他说,"我们简直是在浪费时间。去吧,戴米舍,去吧。"

牢房里嘟嘟嚷嚷地发出一阵抗议的声音,布里顿先生愤愤不平地嚷道:

"你可决不能打算去处死一个襁褓中的婴孩!这样做太可怕了,真是荒谬绝伦。即便我们承认戴米舍罪行属实,该判死刑,我们也绝无必要为一个新生婴孩的清白无辜做任何辩护。"

"不能在这些枝节问题上再纠缠不休了。'典狱官回答,"这是戴米舍,或者不是? 是他杀死了诺让地方的三个人? 他是否被判了死刑? 法律面前人人平等,我不想再找麻烦。断头台早已搭好,铡刀也装好不止一个小时了。再来空谈新生婴孩的无辜实在令人生厌。如果那样的话,任何人只要把自己缩成个婴孩就可逃避法律审判,这未免太便当了。"

辩护律师用一种母亲的姿势把毯子拉过来盖在他的委托人微微蠕动的身子上。婴孩暖和了,开心得又笑又叫,而典狱官则冷冰冰地瞧着他,认为这种快活的表现是不对头的。

"你们注意这玩世不恭的态度,"他说,"他似乎想这么老着脸皮混到底了。"

"亲爱的典狱宫,"牧师说,"你可能没有看出来,这事儿有上帝插手其中吗?"

"或许有上帝插手,又怎么样呢? 与我毫不相干嘛。授予我职位,负责给我晋升的并不是上帝。我有

they awaited his return the others sought to find some rational explanation for the metamorphosis of Dermuche, which none could any longer doubt. The Governor alone took no part in the conversation but paced nervously up and down the cell. When the infant, alarmed by the sound of voices, began to cry, he advanced to the bedside and said in a threatening voice:

"You wait, my lad. I'll give you something to cry about!"

M. Leboeuf, who had seated himself beside the child, looked up at him with an intrigued expression.

"Do you really think this is your murderer?" he asked.

"I hope so. In any case, we shall soon know."

Confronted by this exquisite miracle, the chaplain continued to give thanks to God, his eyes damp with tenderness as he gazed at the virtually divine infant lying between Leboeuf and the Governor. He wondered a little anxiously what was to happen now, but concluded with confidence, "It will be as if the infant Jesus decides."

When the comparison of finger-prints had confirmed the extraordinary metamorphosis the Governor gave a sigh of relief and rubbed his hands.

"Well, now let's get on with it," he said. "We've simply been wasting time. Come along, Dermuche. Come along."

A murmur of protest arose in the cell, and M. Bridon cried indignantly:

"You surely can't intend to execute a babe in arms! It would be a hideous thing to do, utterly monstrous. Even if we admit the fact of Dermuche's guilt, and that he deserved the death sentence, we have surely no need to plead the innocence of a newly born infant."

"I can't go into those details," answered the Governor. "Is this Dermuche, or isn't it? Did he murder three people in Nogent-sur-Marne? Was he condemned to death? The law applies to everyone and I don't want any trouble. The scaffold has been erected and the guillotine was set up more than an hour ago. This talk about the innocence of the newly born is merely tiresome. At that rate anyone could escape justice simply by turning themselves into an infant. It would be a bit too easy!"

The defending counsel, with a maternal gesture, had drawn the covers back over the dimpled body of his client. The infant, responding to the warmth, laughed and crowed with pleasure, and the Governor looked coldly at it, finding this manifestation of gaiety out of place.

"You note the cynicism," he said. "He means to brazen it out to the end."

"My dear Governor," said the chaplain, "is it possible that you cannot see in this episode the hand of God?"

"Perhaps, but that makes no difference. It's certainly nothing to do with me. It isn't God who gave me

上级的指令,我得执行。"典狱官转身对检察官说,"你不同意我是完全正确的吗?"

莱勃欧夫思忖了一会儿才发表他的意见。

"你的主张听起来无疑是合乎逻辑的。对一个杀人犯的罪行不给以应受的惩罚,而赦免他,让他重新开始生活,将是极其不公正的。另一方面,处决一个婴孩也是桩棘手的事。我想你最好还是请示一下上级。"

"我了解他们,"典狱官说,"他们会因为我使他们处于难堪的地位而生我气的。不过,我还是给他们挂个电话吧。"

有关的高级官员尚未到部上班,典狱官只好打电话到他们家里去。他们还是半睡半醒的,脾气不顶好。戴米舍的变形在他们看来是直接针对他们的奸诈的诡计。他们都勃然大怒。不过那犯人现在成了一个褓褓中的婴孩仍然是个事实。但是,时势很难,要是有人怀疑他们宽赦了犯人,就可能影响他们的前程。于是他们彼此取得了一致意见,做出决定:"鉴于犯人的身体在悔恨的重压之下,或者无论别的什么原因而有些缩小,不允许改变审判的规定。"

犯人按规定进行临刑前的梳妆,也就是将他裹在一条床毯里,把颈后面的一绺柔软的毛发剃光。接着牧师小心翼翼地给他行了洗礼。把婴孩抱在手中朝矗立在监狱院子里的杀人机器走去的也正是那位牧师。

当他们从行刑场回来时,他将戴米舍写信给圣婴耶稣的事告知了辩护律师。

"上帝不允许一个杀人犯丝毫不做忏悔而进入天堂。但是戴米舍在这方面是有希望的,他笃爱圣婴耶稣。因此,上帝把他有罪孽的生命消除了,使他回复到了清白无辜的婴孩的年龄。"

"如果戴米舍罪孽深重的生命被消除了,那么他并未犯过罪,而那几个住在诺让的人也根本没有被人杀害。"

律师想证明他的这一观点,立刻去到诺让。一到那儿他要人带他去那犯罪的房子,可是没有人听说有过任何犯罪行为。不过他还是毫无困难地找到了两位老小姐和他们怕冷的叔叔住的那幢房子。三位老人接待他时起先疑虑重重,待疑虑消除后,他们便告诉他,就在那天晚上,有人偷走了一张放在餐桌上的唱片。

my job or who is responsible for my advancement. I've had my instructions, and I intend to carry them out."　The Governor turned to the Public Prosecutor. "Don't you agree that I'm entirely right?"

M. Leboeuf took time for thought before giving his opinion.

"Undoubtedly your position is logically sound. It would be profoundly unjust for a murderer to be privileged to begin his life again instead of paying the just penalty of his crime. On the other hand, the execution of an infant is a rather ticklish matter. I think you would be wise to consult your superiors."

"I know them," said the Governor. "They'll be annoyed with me for putting them in an embarrassing position. However, I'll ring them up."

The high officials concerned had not yet arrived at the Ministry. The Governor had to ring up their homes. Being still only half awake they were not in the best of tempers. The metamorphosis of Dermuche seemed to them a treacherous stratagem aimed directly at themselves, and they were highly indignant. The fact remained, none the less, that the condemned man was now a babe in arms. But the times were harsh, and they feared for their advancement if they should be suspected of lenience. Having agreed among themselves they resolved that—"the fact that the murderer has somewhat shrunk beneath the burden of remorse, or from no, matter what cause, can in no way be allowed to divert the course of Justice."

Accordingly the condemned man's toilet was proceeded with—that is to say, he was wrapped in one of the bed coverings and the soft down on the back of his neck was shaved off. The chaplain then took the precaution of baptising him. It was he who carried him in his arms to the machine erected in the prison courtyard.

As they returned from the place of execution he told counsel for the defense of Dermuche's letter to the infant Jesus.

"God could not allow a murderer entirely untouched by remorse to enter Paradise. But Dermuche had hope on his side, and his love of the infant Jesus. So God effaced his life as a sinner and restored him to the age of innocence."

"But if his life as a sinner was effaced, then Dermuche committed no crime and those people in Nogent were never murdered."

Wanting to be quite sure on this point, the Counsel immediately went to Nogent-sur-Marne. Upon arriving there he asked to be directed to the house where the crime had been committed, but no one had heard of any crime. He had no difficulty, however, in finding the house where the two Mademoiselles Bridaine lived with their uncle who suffered from the cold. The three old people received him at first with mistrust, and after being reassured, complained to him that that very night someone had stolen a gramophone record lying on the dining-room table.

046. 黑圣母

（英）多丽丝·莱辛 著　　万 紫 译

046. The Black Madonna

by Doris Lessing

人文学科在某些国家是谈不上繁荣的，更不用说艺术了。尽管我们对此都有自己的一套理论，但是艺术上为何有此遭遇，倒也很难说明。因为有时正是最贫瘠的土壤上会出现盛开那种鲜花的花园，那些花朵会被我们一致认定是人生的荣耀和正直，由于有这么一个事实，使得我们最后很难断言：为什么赞比西亚①的土壤会长出如此难以培养的植物来。

赞比西亚这片土地，终日骄阳似火，百姓精力充沛，能吃苦耐劳，实事求是，不很敏感，也瞧不起精致的玩意儿。不过有几个这般情况的州也产生过艺术，虽然有点笨拙。赞比西亚对于在世界其他地方早已被人接受的那些观念，如自由、博爱等，说得婉转一点儿吧，也是不表同感的。有那么一些人，他们之中不乏优秀人物，坚持说，要是没有劳苦大众所保障的少数人的闲逸，就不可能有艺术。不管生活舒适的少数赞比西亚人可能缺少些什么，可并不缺少闲逸。

够了，别再对赞比西亚发议论了。出于自尊和对科学严密性的尊重，我们不应该匆促地做出结论。特别是当有人回忆起一位艺术家真的出现在他们之中的时候，赞比西亚人表现出求贤若渴的尊敬。

举个例，且来看看米开尔的事迹吧。

二次大战期间，当意大利成了道义上的同盟国时，米开尔从战俘营出来了。当局在这段时间里，极其紧张忙碌，因为一方面要对数千名必须以某种公认的标准对待的战俘负责，另一方面，日复一日地面临着把这数千人用某种国际上的手法转变为战友。这几千人中有一些留在原来的营房里，在那儿，他们至

---

① 赞比西亚现为莫桑比克的一个州。

THERE are some countries in which the arts, let alone Art, cannot be said to flourish. Why this should be so it is hard to say, although of course we all have our theories about it. For sometimes it is the most barren soil that sends up gardens of those flowers which we all agree are the crown and justification of life, and it is this fact which makes it hard to say, finally, why the soil of Zambesia should produce such reluctant plants.

Zambesia is a tough, sunburnt, virile, positive country contemptuous of subtleties and sensibility: yet there have been States with these qualities which have produced art, though perhaps with the left hand. Zambesia is, to put it mildly, unsympathetic to those ideas so long taken for granted in other parts of the world, to do with liberty, fraternity and the rest. Yet there are those, and some of the finest souls among them, who maintain that art is impossible without a minority whose leisure is guaranteed by a hard-working majority. And whatever Zambesia's comfortable minority may lack, it is not leisure.

Zambesia—but enough; out of respect for ourselves and for scientific accuracy, we should refrain from jumping to conclusions. Particularly when one remembers the almost wistful respect Zambesians show when an artist does appear in their midst.

Consider, for instance, the case of Michele.

He came out of the internment camp at the time when Italy was made a sort of honorary ally, during the Second World War. It was a time of strain for the authorities, because it is one thing to be responsible for thousands of prisoners of war whom one must treat according to certain recognized standards; it is another to be faced, and from one day to the next, with these same thousands transformed by some international legerdemain into comrades in arms. Some of the thousands stayed where they were in the camps; they were fed and housed there at least. Others went as farm

作者简介：多丽丝·莱辛（Doris Lessing，1919—），英国小说家。1919 年 10 月 22 日生于伊朗克尔曼沙。她定居英国后开始她的写作生涯。她的作品往往反映左翼政治激进主义，大部分是与社会和政治剧变中的人相关的。《暴力的孩子》（*Children of Violence*，1952—1969）是半自传体系列小说，描写了主人公玛撒·奎斯特在非洲的经历，被公认为是她最有潜力的作品。《金色笔记》（*The Golden Notebook*，1962）是女性主义的杰作。她的短篇小说分别收录在几部作品集中。其他作品包括一部科幻小说、两部以简·萨默斯为笔名出版的长篇小说和自传体作品《我的外壳之下》（*Under My Skin*，1994）等。

少有饭吃,有房子住。其余的,虽然人数不多,去农场当劳工。当时农民们一直缺乏劳力,但他们不知道如何管理这批和他们肤色相同的白种劳工,赞比西亚以前可从未碰到过这种情况。有些人走市镇,干临活,他们得时刻提防当地工会,因为当地工会既不接纳他们入会,也不同意他们做工。

这伙人真是命途多舛啊。不过幸而时间不长,不久,战争结束了,他们也就能回家了。

正如上文所说的,政府当局的日子也不好过。由于这个缘故,他们极想从这样的形势里捞取点儿好处。米开尔无疑就是一个能给当局带来好处的人。

当他还是一名战俘时,他的才能就已被人发现了。当时战俘营造了一座教堂,米开尔装饰教堂的内部。战俘营中的铁皮顶子教堂变成了展览馆。白粉墙上,画满了壁画:黝黑皮肤的农民在采摘葡萄酿酒,漂亮的意大利姑娘在跳舞,以及胖乎乎的黑眼珠孩童。在熙熙攘攘的意大利风俗画里,出现了圣母和圣子,圣母慈祥地微笑着,愉快地在她的子民中间随便走动。

贿赂了当局、被允许进战俘营来参观的爱好艺术的女士们会说:"可怜的人啊,他多么想家啊。"她们还会恳请给艺术家留下半个克朗。有些人则满腔义愤。他毕竟是一名囚犯,一名在反抗正义和民主的战争中被俘的囚犯,他有什么权利表示抗议?因为他们觉得这些画就是一种抗议。意大利有的东西,难道我们这儿,赞比西亚的首都和中心韦斯顿维尔没有吗?这儿难道没有阳光、高山、胖娃娃和漂亮姑娘吗?即使我们没有栽培葡萄,我们不是至少也栽培了许多柠檬、橘子和鲜花吗?

人们的思想混乱了——简陋教堂的白粉墙上的壁画表现了一种绝望的恋乡之情,按照各人的气质,而有不同的感受。

但是米开尔一获自由,他的才能又被人想起来了。人们称他为"意大利艺术家"。而事实上,他只是个砖瓦匠。那些壁画的优点被人们大大地夸张了。若是在一个壁画相当普遍的国家可能就一点儿也不起眼。

有一位来访的太太,从自己汽车里跳下来,径直冲进营房,要求他给她的孩子们画像。他起先说干不了,最后还是同意了。他在镇上弄了间房子,画了好几张孩子们的漂亮肖像。接着他又给最先来访的太太的许多朋友们的小孩画像,每次收费 10 先令。后来有位太太要画一张她自己的肖像,他要价 10 镑。

labourers, though not many; for while the farmers were as always short of labour, they did not know how to handle farm labourers who were also white men: such a phenomenon had never happened in Zambesia before. Some did odd jobs around the towns, keeping a sharp eye out for the trade unions, who would neither admit them as members nor agree to their working.

Hard, hard, the lot of these men, but fortunately not for long, for soon the war ended and they were able to go home.

Hard, too, the lot of the authorities, as has been pointed out; and for that reason they were doubly willing to take what advantages they could from the situation; and that Michele was such an advantage there could be no doubt.

His talents were first discovered when he was still a prisoner of war. A church was built in the camp, and Michele decorated its interior. it became a show-place, that little tin-roofed church in the prisoners' camp, with its whitewashed walls covered all over with frescoes depicting swarthy peasants gathering grapes for the vintage, beautiful Italian girls dancing, plump dark-eyed children. Amid crowded scenes of Italian life, appeared the Virgin and her Child, smiling and beneficent, happy to move familiarly among her people.

Culture-loving ladies who had bribed the authorities to be taken inside the camp would say, "Poor thing, how homesick he must be." And they would beg to be allowed to leave half a crown for the artist. Some were indignant. He was a prisoner, after all, captured in the very act of fighting against justice and democracy, and what right had he to protest? —for they felt these paintings as a sort of protest. What was there in Italy that we did not have right here in Westonville, which was the capital and hub of Zambesia? Were there not sunshine and mountains and fat babies and pretty girls here? Did we not grow—if not grapes, at least lemons and oranges and flowers in plenty?

People were upset—the desperation of nostalgia came from the painted white walls of that simple church, and affected everyone according to his temperament.

But when Michele was free, his talent was remembered. He was spoken of as "that Italian artist." As a matter of fact, he was a bricklayer. And the virtues of those frescoes might very well have been exaggerated. It is possible they would have been overlooked altogether in a country where picture-covered walls were more common.

When one of the visiting ladies came rushing out to the camp in her own car, to ask him to paint her children, he said he was not qualified to do so. But at last he agreed. He took a room in the town and made some nice likenesses of the children. Then he painted

他用了一个月时间画了那张像,太太很不高兴,不过还是付了钱。

米开尔带了一个朋友回到自己房里,他们待在那儿饮着好望角的红酒,谈着家乡的事。只要他手头上有钱花,谁也不能说服他再去给人画像了。

太太们大谈劳动的尊严,这题目她们可烂熟了。一位女士觉得她们讲得太多了,几乎说到把白种人和非洲卡菲尔黑人做比较,而卡菲尔人并不懂什么劳动的尊严。

人们觉得米开尔缺乏感恩戴德之心。有位太太跟踪他,看到他拿着一瓶酒躺在树下的一张行军床上,便一本正经跟他讲起墨索里尼的暴行以及意大利人不中用的气质来。接着她要求他立刻为她画一幅身穿簇新晚礼服的画像。他一口拒绝。太太十分气愤地回了家。

碰巧她是一位顶重要的公民的妻子,这位公民是位将军或者诸如此类的大人物。那时他正为公众利益筹备一次军事演习或军事展览。几周来整个韦斯顿维尔一直在谈论这件事。我们对跳舞啊,化装舞会啊,集市啊,有奖彩券啊,以及其他种种慈善性质的娱乐活动都厌烦已极。一些人在为自由献躯,而另一些人却在为自由跳舞,这话说得并不过分。一切事物都有个极限。自然啰,当战争真的结束时,驻扎在这个国家的几千名军人都得解甲归田。总之,当快乐生活不再是一桩义务时,会听到许多人感叹生活将不再是同样的了。

这时候,军事演习可以让我们大家换换口味。对这项计划负责的搞军事的先生们并没有想到这一层。他们想让我们了解一下真正的战争是个什么样子的,以此来振奋一下士气。报纸上用通栏标题进行宣传还不够,为了使之家喻户晓,他们计划让我们看见炮火摧毁一座村庄。

要毁掉一座村庄,首先得建造一座村庄。

将军和他的僚属,头顶烈日,在阅兵场的红色尘埃中站了一整天。他们的周围堆满建筑材料,一群群非洲劳工拿着木板和钉子跑来跑去,正在设法造一座看上去像村庄那样的东西。显然,为了摧毁一座村庄他们将不得不先造一座适当的村庄,而这样做的费用将会超过整个表演所允许的开支。将军回家时心情很不好,他太太说他们需要一名艺术家,他们需要米开尔。这倒并不因为她想给米开尔一个好机会,她一

the children of a great number of the first lady's friends. He charged ten shillings a time. Then one of the ladies wanted a portrait of herself. He asked ten pounds for it; it had taken him a month to do. She was annoyed, but paid.

And Michele went off to his room with a friend and stayed there drinking red wine from the Cape and talking about home. While the money lasted he could not be persuaded to do any more portraits.

There was a good deal of talk among the ladies about the dignity of labour, a subject in which they were well versed; and one felt they might almost go so far as to compare a white man with a kaffir, who did not understand the dignity of labour either.

He was felt to lack gratitude. One of the ladies tracked him down, found him lying on a camp-bed under a tree with a bottle of wine, and spoke to him severely about the barbarity of Mussolini and the fecklessness of the Italian temperament. Then she demanded that he should instantly paint a picture of herself in her new evening dress. He refused and she went home very angry.

It happened that she was the wife of one of our most important citizens, a General or something of that kind, who was at that time engaged in planning a military tattoo or show for the benefit of the civilian population. The whole of Westonville had been discussing this show for weeks. We were all bored to extinction by dances, fancy-dress balls, fairs, lotteries and other charitable entertainments. It is not too much to say that while some were dying for freedom, others were dancing for it. There comes a limit to everything. Though, of course, when the end of the war actually came and the thousands of troops stationed in the country had to go home—in short, when enjoying ourselves would no longer be a duty, many were heard to exclaim that life would never be the same again.

In the meantime, the Tattoo would make a nice change for us all. The military gentlemen responsible for the idea did not think of it in these terms. They thought to improve morale by giving us some idea of what war was really like. Headlines in the newspaper were not enough. And in order to bring it all home to us, they planned to destroy a village by shell-fire before our very eyes.

First, the village had to be built.

It appears that the General and his subordinates stood around in the red dust of the parade-ground under a burning sun for the whole of one day, surrounded by building materials, while hordes of African labourers ran around with boards and nails, trying to make something that looked like a village. It became evident that they would have to build a proper village in order to destroy it; and this would cost more than was allowed for the whole entertainment. The General went

想到他有事情不干而躺在那里唱歌，就受不了。将军说他如果去求一个意大利小子，那就不算人了，而太太又拒绝担任任何微妙的外交使命。她用她自己的办法帮丈夫解决了这个问题，派一名叫斯托克的上尉去接米开尔。

上尉仍然在那株树下的那张行军床上找到了他。他身穿无领衬衫，裤腿卷起，没有刮胡子，微露醉态，在他身边的地上放着一瓶酒。他正哼着一支粗野而悲凉的小曲，上尉听了很不舒服。他在离这个肮脏落拓的家伙十步远的地方站住了，感到自己的地位受了侮辱。一年以前，这人还是一个一见就要开枪的不共戴天的仇敌。6个月前，也还是一个战俘。而此刻却穿着一件邋遢的军用衬衫，竖起膝盖躺着。依上尉的意思，米开尔遇到这种情况，应该向他致敬。

"喂！"他厉声说。

米开尔转过头，从地平线望着上尉，和蔼地说了声"早安"。

"有人叫你去。"上尉说。

"谁啊？"米开尔说着坐了起来。他是个胖胖的、橄榄色皮肤的小个子，眼睛里露出愤怒的神色。

"政府当局。"

"仗不是打完了吗？"

上尉穿着烫过的黄卡其军装，腰板笔挺，容光焕发。他把头一仰，下巴一翘，皱紧了眉头。上尉个子高大，金黄头发，身上露出来的肌肉呈砖红色，蓝色的小眼睛满含怒气，布满漂亮的黄色汗毛的通红的双手，握成拳头摆在身旁。他在米开尔眼中看到了沮丧的神情，两只拳头就松开了。"仗没打完，"他说，"需要你来出力。"

"为战争出力？"

"为战争出力。我想你对击败德寇会感兴趣的。"

米开尔望着上尉，黑眼珠的小个子手艺人看着魁伟的白人军官，看着他那冷淡的眼睛，狭小的嘴，那双像布满毫毛的牛排一样的手，他看着他说："我对战争结束最感兴趣。"

"是吗？"上尉从牙缝里说。

"那么有报酬吗？"米开尔说。

"会给报酬的。"

米开尔站起来，对着太阳举起酒瓶喝了口酒，用酒漱漱口又吐掉。接着他把剩酒倒在红土上，地上泛起一摊起泡的紫色酒迹。

home in a bad temper, and his wife said what they needed was an artist, they needed Michele. This was not because she wanted to do Michele a good turn; she could not endure the thought of him lying around singing while there was work to be done. She refused to undertake any delicate diplomatic missions when her husband said he would be damned if he would ask favours of any little Wop. She solved the problem for him in her own way: a certain Captain Stocker was sent out to fetch him.

The Captain found him on the same camp-bed under the same tree, in rolled-up trousers, and an uncollared shirt; unshaven, mildly drunk, with a bottle of wine standing beside him on the earth. He was singing an air so wild, so sad, that the Captain was uneasy. He stood at ten paces from the disreputable fellow and felt the indignities of his position. A year ago, this man had been a mortal enemy to be shot at sight. Six months ago, he had been an enemy prisoner. Now he lay with his knees up, in an untidy shirt that had certainly once been military. For the Captain, the situation crystallised in a desire that Michele should salute him.

"Piselli!" he said sharply.

Michele turned his head and looked at the Captain from the horizontal. "Good morning," he said affably.

"You are wanted," said the Captain.

"Who?" said Michele. He sat up, a fattish, olive-skinned little man. His eyes were resentful.

"The authorities. "

"The war is over?"

The Captain, who was already stiff and shiny enough in his laundered khaki, jerked his head back frowning, chin out. He was a large man, blond, and wherever his flesh showed, it was brick-red. His eyes were small and blue and angry. His red hands, covered all over with fine yellow bristles, clenched by his side. Then he saw the disappointment in Michele's eyes, and the hands unclenched. "No it is not over," he said. "Your assistance is required. "

"For the war?"

"For the war effort. I take it you are interested in defeating the Germans?"

Michele looked at the Captain. The little dark-eyed artisan looked at the great blond officer with his cold eyes, his narrow mouth, his hands like bristle-covered steaks. He looked and said: "I am very interested in the end of the war. "

"*Well*?" said the Captain between his teeth.

"The pay?" said Michele.

"You will be paid. "

Michele stood up. He lifted the bottle against the sun, then took a gulp. He rinsed his mouth out with wine and spat. Then he poured what was left on to the red earth, where it made a bubbling purple stain.

"I am ready," he said. He went with the Captain

"这就走吧。"他说着与上尉一起朝停在那里的卡车走去。他爬上车坐在司机座的旁边,没有按上尉所希望,坐在卡车后部。他们到达阅兵场时,军官们已经留下口信,要上尉亲自对米开尔和那村庄负责,也对一百名左右工人负责,他们坐在周围草地上等候命令。

上尉说明了他们所要的东西。米开尔点点头,接着他对那伙非洲人挥挥手说:"我不要这些人。"

"你独个儿干这事儿——造一座村庄?"

"是的。"

"不要人帮忙?"

米开尔第一次露出笑容:"不要人帮忙。"

上尉犹豫不决。他原则上是不赞成白人干重活的。他说:"我留下6个人干重活。"

米开尔耸耸肩。上尉走过去把非洲人解散了,只留下其中6个人。他领着他们回到米开尔站的地方。

"天真热。"米开尔说。

"真热。"上尉说。他们正站在阅兵场中央,场地周围有树木、草地、片片阴影。而阅兵场上,只有热风低吹,红土飞扬。

"好渴啊。"米开尔咧着嘴说。上尉回答时,绷紧的嘴唇也不知不觉地松开了。两人的目光一相遇,双方的思想沟通了。上尉觉得这个意大利小子突然变成一个通情达理的人了。"我去安排。"他说完就离开米开尔,到城里去了。等到他向有关的人谈了情况,填写了表格,做好安排后,天色已晚。他带着一箱好望角牌的白兰地酒回到阅兵场,看见米开尔和那6名黑人正一块儿坐在树下。米开尔给他们唱一支意大利歌曲,他们和着唱。上尉看到这情景不由得感到一阵恶心。他走上前去,非洲人都站起身立正。米开尔还是坐着。

"你不是说你自己来干那活儿?"

"我说过。"

上尉解散了非洲人。他们友好地和米开尔分手,米开尔也向他们挥手告别。上尉气得满脸通红。"你还没有动手吗?"

"给我多少时间?"

"三个星期。"

"时间够多了。"米开尔盯着上尉手中的那瓶白兰地说。上尉另一只手拿着两只玻璃杯。"天晚了。"他提醒说。上尉皱着眉头站了一会儿,然后在草地上坐

to the waiting lorry, where he climbed in beside the driver's seat and not, as the Captain had expected, into the back of the lorry. When they had arrived at the parade-ground the officers had left a message that the Captain would be personally responsible for Michele and for the village. Also for the hundred or so labourers who were sitting around on the grass verges waiting for orders.

The Captain explained what was wanted. Michele nodded. Then he waved his hand at the Africans. "I do not want these," he said.

"You will do it yourself—a village?"

"Yes."

"With no help?"

Michele smiled for the first time. "I will do it."

The Captain hesitated. He disapproved on principle of white men doing heavy manual labour. He said: "I will keep six to do the heavy work."

Michele shrugged; and the Captain went over and dismissed all but six of the Africans. He came back with them to Michele.

"It is hot," said Michele.

"Very," said the Captain. They were standing in the middle of the parade-ground. Around its edge trees, grass, gulfs of shadow. Here, nothing but reddish dust, drifting and lifting in a low hot breeze.

"I am thirsty," said Michele. He grinned. The Captain felt his stiff lips loosen unwillingly in reply. The two pairs of eyes met. It was a moment of understanding. For the Captain, the little Italian had suddenly become human. "I will arrange it," he said, and went off down-town. By the time he had explained the position to the right people, filled in forms and made arrangements, it was late afternoon. He returned to the parade-ground with a case of Cape brandy, to find Michele and the six black men seated together under a tree. Michele was singing an Italian song to them, and they were harmonizing with him. The sight affected the Captain like an attack of nausea. He came up, and the Africans stood to attention. Michele continued to sit.

"You said you would do the work yourself?"

"Yes, I said so."

The Captain then dismissed the Africans. They departed with friendly looks towards Michele, who waved at them. The Captain was beef-red with anger. "You have not started yet?"

"How long have I?"

"Three weeks."

"Then there is plenty of time," said Michele, looking at the bottle of brandy in the Captain's hand. In the other were two glasses. "It is evening," he pointed out. The Captain stood frowning for a moment. Then he sat down on the grass, and poured out two brandies.

"Ciao," said Michele.

"Cheers," said the Captain. Three weeks, he was

下来,斟满两杯白兰地。

"干杯。"米开尔说。

"干杯。"上尉说。三个星期,他思忖着,要和这该死的意大利小子挨过三个星期! 他喝干一杯,又斟上一杯,放在草地上。草地凉爽而柔软。近旁有株树正在开花,微风送来伴随着花香的阵阵热浪。

"这儿美极了,"米开尔说,"我们一起过得挺愉快。即使在战争期间也有快活的时光,也有友谊。为战争结束干杯。"

第二天,上尉直到午饭后才到阅兵场上来。他看到米开尔拿着一瓶酒待在树下,阅兵场的那一头竖起了许多薄板筑成的两垛墙以及另外半垛墙,几根柱子支撑着一座尖尖的屋顶。

"那是什么东西?"上尉大发雷霆。

"教堂。"米开尔说。

"什——么?"

"以后你会明白的。天气真热啊。"他瞧着横放在地上的白兰地酒瓶说。上尉朝卡车走去,把那箱白兰地提了来。他们喝酒,时间就这么过去了。上尉在树下草地上坐了好久,也就是说,他大喝其酒消磨了好长时间。他时常喝大量的酒,不过他喝酒能够受情势和时令的节制。他是一个守纪律的人。此刻,他坐在草地上,坐在那个他仍然不得不认为是敌人的小个子旁边,并不是丧失了自我约束,而是感到自己有点异样,感到自己的行为一时有些不大正常。米开尔满不在乎。他听米开尔讲意大利,似乎在听一些原始野蛮的故事,类似南海诸岛神秘的传说,像他那样的人最好一生中能到那儿去一趟。他觉得他说过很想在战后去意大利旅行。实际上,他只是被北方和北方人吸引住了。他游览过希特勒统治下的德国,虽然此刻不宜这么说,他还是认为那地方令人十分满意。接着米开尔对他唱了几支意大利歌曲,上尉也唱了几支英国歌曲。后来米开尔拿出他妻儿的照片来,他们住在意大利北部山区的一个村庄里。他问上尉结过婚没有。上尉从来不谈自己的私生活。

在他一生中,他在一两个非洲殖民地担任过警察、文官、地方官员或别的相当的职务。打仗了,他很习惯军旅生活,但是他厌恶城市生活。希望战争结束,有他自己的理由。他经常和一两名白人,或者独自一人住在远离严格的文明世界的丛林驻地里。他和本地妇女有来往。他有时去妻子住的城市逗留一

thinking, Three weeks with this damned little Itie! He drained his glass and refilled it, and set it in the grass. The grass was cool and soft. A tree was flowering somewhere close—hot waves of perfume came on the breeze.

"It is nice here," said Michele. "We will have a good time together. Even in a war, there are times of happiness. And of friendship. I drink to the end of the war."

Next day, the Captain did not arrive at the parade-ground until after lunch. He found Michele under the trees with a bottle. Sheets of ceiling board had been erected at one end of the parade-ground in such a way that they formed two walls and a part of a third, and a slant of steep roof supported on struts.

"What's that?" said the Captain, furious.

"The church," said Michele.

"Wha-at?"

"You will see. Later. It is very hot." He looked at the brandy bottle that lay on its side on the ground. The Captain went to the lorry and returned with the case of brandy. They drank. Time passed. It was a long time since the Captain had sat on grass under a tree. It was a long time, for that matter, since he had drunk so much. He always drank a great deal, but it was regulated to the times and seasons. He was a disciplined man. Here, sitting on the grass beside this little man whom he still could not help thinking of as an enemy, it was not that he let his selfdiscipline go, but that he felt himself to be something different: he was temporarily set outside his normal behaviour. Michele did not count. He listened to Michele talking about Italy, and it seemed to him he was listening to a savage speaking: as if he heard tales from the mythical South Sea islands where a man like himself might very well go just once in his life. He found himself saying he would like to make a trip to Italy after the war. Actually, he was attracted only by the North and by Northern people. He had visited Germany, under Hitler, and though it was not the time to say so, had found it very satisfactory. Then Michele sang him some Italian songs. He sang Michele some English songs. Then Michele took out photographs of his wife and children, who lived in a village in the mountains of North Italy. He asked the Captain if he were married. The Captain never spoke about his private affairs.

He had spent all his life in one or other of the African colonies as a policeman, magistrate, native commissioner, or in some other useful capacity. When the war started, military life came easy to him. But he hated city life, and had his own reasons for wishing the war over. Mostly, he had been in bush-stations with one or two other white men, or by himself, far from the rigours of civilisation. He had relations with native women; and from time to time visited the city where his wife lived with her parents and the children. He

段时间。他妻子和她自己的父母以及孩子住在一起。他老是为妻子对他不贞这种想法而苦恼。近来他甚至委托了一名私家侦探去监视她,他认为那侦探十分无能。从他妻子住的 L 城来的部队朋友说起她在舞会上玩得很快活。如果战争结束了,她就会发觉不能那么轻易寻欢作乐了。那么为什么他不干脆和她一同生活呢?事实上他不能够。他长期离家远居丛林驻地就是为了要找个借口不和妻子住在一起。对妻子的事情考虑久了,他便忍受不了。可以这么说,她是他永远不能使之就范的生活的一部分。

然而现在他跟米开尔谈起妻子来了。他还谈到他心爱的丛林太太娜迪娅。他坐在树下给米开尔讲他生活的经历,直到他发觉那树影已从阅兵场延伸到了看台,他才摇摇晃晃地站起来说道:"还有事干呢,你干活是给报酬的。"

"天色一暗,我就给你看我造的教堂。"

太阳落山,夜幕降临,米开尔便叫上尉把卡车开到离阅兵场 200 码的地方,把灯开亮。立刻,一座白色的教堂从一堆堆木板的奇形怪状的阴影中涌现出来。

"明天,咱们再造几幢房子。"米开尔快活地说。

到了周末,阅兵场一端的空地上,筑起了一堆木板和板条钉成的歪歪斜斜、粗糙拙劣的建筑物,在阳光下看起来什么也不像。私下里,上尉感到迷惑,这堆骨架一样的东西,在灯光和黑暗的幻象下,竟能使他相信是一座村庄,这简直像一场梦魇。夜间,上尉驾驶卡车前来,开亮电灯,那儿就出现一座村庄,一座在绿树浓荫衬托下的坚固真实的村庄。然后,在早晨的阳光照耀下,就什么都不见了,只剩下矗立在沙地上的一些木板。

"完工了,"米开尔说。

"给了你三周的时间哪。"上尉说。这段假期是他自己弄来的,他不愿让它就此结束。

米开尔耸耸肩说:"军队就是有钱。"现在,他们为了避开人们好奇的目光,就带上那箱白兰地,坐到那座教堂的影子里去了。上尉没完没了地提老婆,谈着女人,一个劲儿地谈个不停。

米开尔听着,有一回他说:"等我一回到家里,我一回到家里,我就要张开双臂……"他大大地张开双臂,闭上眼睛,眼泪从面颊上流下来。"我要把妻子抱在怀里,我什么也不问,问。我不在乎。能生活在

was always tormented by the idea that she was unfaithful to him. Recently he had even appointed a private detective to watch her; he was convinced the detective was inefficient. Army friends coming from L——where his wife was, spoke of her at parties, enjoying herself. When the war ended, she would not find it so easy to have a good time. And why did he not simply live with her and be done with it? The fact was, he could not. And his long exile to remote bush-stations was because he needed the excuse not to. He could not bear to think of his wife for too long; she was that part of his life he had never been able, so to speak, to bring to heel.

Yet he spoke of her now to Michele, and of his favourite bush-wife, Nadya. He told Michele the story of his life, until he realized that the shadows from the trees they sat under had stretched right across the parade-ground to the grandstand. He got unsteadily to his feet, and said: "There is work to be done. You are being paid to work. "

"I will show you my church when the light goes. "

The sun dropped, darkness fell, and Michele made the Captain drive his lorry on to the parade-ground a couple of hundred yards away and switch on his lights. Instantly, a white church sprang up from the shapes and shadows of the bits of board.

"Tomorrow, some houses, "said Michele cheerfully.

At the end of a week, the space at the end of the parade-ground had crazy gawky constructions of lath and board over it, that looked in the sunlight like nothing on this earth. Privately, it upset the Captain; it was like a nightmare that these skeleton-like shapes should be able to persuade him, with the illusions of light and dark, that they were a village. At night, the Captain drove up his lorry, switched on the lights, and there it was, the village, solid and real against a background of full green trees. Then, in the morning sunlight, there was nothing there, just bits of board stuck in the sand.

"It is finished, "said Michele.

"You were engaged for three weeks, "said the Captain. He did not want it to end, this holiday from himself.

Michele shrugged. "The army is rich, "he said. Now, to avoid curious eyes, they sat inside the shade of the church, with the case of brandy between them. The Captain talked, talked endlessly, about his wife, about women. He could not stop talking.

Michele listened. Once he said: "When I go home—when I go home—I shall open my arms... "He opened them, wide. He closed his eyes. Tears ran down his cheeks. "I shall take my wife in my arms, and I shall ask nothing, nothing. I do not care. It is enough

一起就够了,这是战争教我的。够了,够了,我什么也不问,我会很幸福。"

上尉在他面前痛苦地瞪着眼睛。他想他自己是多么惧怕老婆啊。她是个厚颜无耻的东西,阴郁,冷酷,对他冷嘲热讽。结婚后便一直嘲笑他。打仗了,就叫他小希特勒,叫冲锋队员。"滚吧,小希特勒,"他们上次见面时她大喊道,"滚吧,冲锋队员。如果你要把钱花在私家侦探身上,那么就滚吧。但是别以为我不知道你在丛林里的所作所为,你干什么我都不在乎,不过你要记住,我是知道的……"

上尉想起了她说过的话。米开尔坐在木板箱上,说道:"我的朋友,侦探和法律对有钱人是桩乐事,甚至嫉妒也是乐事,我可不要那玩意儿。啊,我的朋友,我只要和妻儿重逢,这就是我对生活的全部要求。我们生活在一起,喝酒,吃饭,到了晚上就唱唱歌。"他的泪水沾湿了面颊,落到衬衣上。

男人这样流泪哭泣,我的天哪!上尉想,真是不知害臊!他抓起酒瓶痛饮起来。

在伟大的时刻到来之前三天,几名高级军官穿过尘埃走来,看到米开尔和上尉正坐在板箱上唱歌。上尉的衬衫敞开前襟,上面全是酒迹。

上尉起身立正,手中拿着酒瓶,米开尔出自对朋友的同情也站了起来立正。军官们都是上尉的老朋友,他们把他拉到一边,对他说,他是否明白他到底在干什么?为什么村庄还没有造好?

他们说完就走了。

"告诉他们村庄已经造好了,"米开尔说,"告诉他们我要走了。"

"别走,"上尉说,"别走。喂,米开尔,你会怎么样,如果你老婆……"

"这世界不错,我们会幸福的,那就是一切。"

"米开尔……"

"我要走了,没事可干了。他们昨天给了我工钱。"

"坐下,米开尔。还有三天呢,然后才结束。"

"那我就来画教堂内部,就像给战俘营教堂搞的那样。"

上尉在木板上躺下睡着了。待他一觉醒来,米开尔已给一罐罐颜料团团围住,这些颜料都是他在画村庄外部时用过的。上尉面前有一幅黑人姑娘的画,年轻而丰满,身穿蓝色绣花衣裳,柔滑的肩膀袒露在上

to be together. That is what the war has taught me. It is enough, it is enough. I shall ask no questions and I shall be happy."

The Captain stared before him, suffering. He thought how he dreaded his wife. She was a scornful creature, gray and hard, who laughed at him. She had been laughing at him ever since they married. Since the war, she had taken to calling him names like Little Hitler, and Storm-trooper. "Go ahead, my little Hitler," she had cried last time they met. "Go ahead, my Storm-trooper. If you want to waste your money on private detectives, go ahead. But don't think I don't know what *you* do when you're in the bush. I don't care what you do, but remember that I know it. . ."

The Captain remembered her saying it. And there sat Michele on his packing-case, saying: "It's a pleasure for the rich, my friend, detectives and the law. Even jealousy is a pleasure I don't want any more. Ah, my friend, to be together with my wife again, and the children, that is all I ask of life. That and wine and food and singing in the evenings." And the tears wetted his cheeks and splashed on to his shirt.

That a man should cry, good lord! thought the Captain. And without shame! He seized the bottle and drank.

Three days before the great occasion, some high-ranking officers came strolling through the dust, and found Michele and the Captain sitting together on the packing-case, singing. The Captain's shirt was open down the front, and there were stains on it.

The Captain stood to attention with the bottle in his hand, and Michele stood to attention too, out of sympathy with his friend. Then the officers drew the Captain aside—they were all cronies of his—and said, what the hell did he think he was doing? And why wasn't the village finished?

Then they went away.

"Tell them it is finished," said Michele. "Tell them I want to go."

"No," said the Captain, "no. Michele, what would you do if your wife. . ."

"This world is a good place. We should be happy—that is all."

"Michele. . ."

"I want to go. There is nothing to do. They paid me yesterday."

"Sit down, Michele. Three more days, and then it's finished."

"Then I shall paint the inside of the church as I painted the one in the camp."

The Captain laid himself down on some boards and went to sleep. When he woke, Michele was surrounded by the pots of paint he had used on the outside of the village. Just in front of the Captain was a picture of a black girl. She was young and plump. She

衣外面，背上背着一个系着红呢带子的婴孩。她的脸转向上尉微笑着。

"是娜迪娅，"上尉说，"娜迪娅……"他大声哼着。他瞧一眼黑孩子，闭起了眼睛。一会儿睁眼一看，那母子俩仍在那儿。米开尔小心翼翼地在黑姑娘和孩子的头上画着细细的黄色光圈。

"上帝啊，"上尉说，"你别那样画啊。"

"为什么不能画？"

"你不能有一个黑圣母。"

"她是农民，我画的是农民，黑人国家里黑人农民的圣母。"

"可这是一座德国人的村庄。"上尉说。

"但她是我的圣母。"米开尔发怒了，"德国村庄是你们的，圣母是我的。我把这幅画贡献给圣母，她会高兴的，我知道。"

上尉又躺下了，他感到周身不适，又睡着了。他第二次醒来，天色已暗。米开尔拿来一盏灯光闪烁的煤油灯，就着这灯光在长长的板壁上绘画，身边放着一瓶白兰地。他一直画到深夜。上尉就躺在一边看着，神态迟钝，像是给梦魇住了。后来他俩在木板上睡着了。第二天，米开尔一整天钻在那儿画着黑圣母，黑圣人，黑天使。外头太阳底下，军队在操练，乐队在奏乐，摩托车轰鸣着来回奔驰。米开尔继续画画喝酒，什么都不在意。上尉仰面躺着，喝着酒，咕咕哝哝地抱怨妻子。后来，他好像叫着"娜迪娅，娜迪娅"，呜呜地哭了。

傍晚，军队开走了。军官们回转来，上尉领着他们走过去。他要给军官们看看，阅兵场那头的电灯一亮，那座村庄是怎样显现的。他们都静静地注视着村庄。电灯一关，那儿只有一些搭成尖顶的木板，在月光下像墓碑一样高高矗立着。灯一亮——又成了一座村庄。他们满腹狐疑，沉默不语，似乎和上尉一样觉得不太对头。说这事儿怪诞不经吧，又不好这么说。反正是不对头——就是这句话。这是欺骗，是彻头彻尾的捣鬼。

"你那个意大利小子真是个机灵鬼。"将军说。

到那时为止一直呆板端正的上尉，突然间摇摇摆摆向将军走去，用手扶着将军尊严的肩膀让自己站稳了，口中嚷道："该死的意大利人，该死的卡菲尔人，该死的……不过让我告诉你，有个意大利人还算不错，是不错，我正要告诉你，他实际上是我的朋友。"

wore a patterned blue dress and her shoulders came soft and bare out of it. On her back was a baby slung in a band of red stuff. Her face was turned towards the Captain and she was smiling.

"That's Nadya," said the Captain. Nadya. . ." He groaned loudly. He looked at the black child and shut his eyes. He opened them, and mother and child were still there. Michele was very carefully drawing thin yellow circles around the heads of the black girl and her child.

"Good God," said the Captain, "you can't do that."

"Why not?"

"You can't have a black Madonna."

"She was a peasant. This is a peasant. Black peasant Madonna for black country."

"This is a German village," said the Captain.

"This is my madonna," said Michele angrily. "Your German village and my Madonna. I paint this picture as an offering to the Madonna. She is pleased—I feel it."

The Captain lay down again. He was feeling ill. He went back to sleep. When he woke for the second time it was dark. Michele had brought in a flaring paraffin lamp, and by its light was working on the long wall. A bottle of brandy stood beside him. He painted until long after midnight, and the Captain lay on his side and watched, as passive as a man suffering a dream. Then they both went to sleep on the boards. The whole of the next day Michele stood painting black Madonnas, black saints, black angels. Outside, troops were practising in the sunlight, bands were blaring and motorcyclists roared up and down. But Michele painted on, drunk and oblivious. The Captain lay on his back, drinking and muttering about his wife. Then he would say "Nadya, Nadya," and burst into sobs.

Towards nightfall the troops went away. The officers came back, and the Captain went off with them to show how the village sprang into being when the great lights at the end of the parade-ground were switched on. They all looked at the village in silence. They switched the lights off and there were only the tall angular boards leaning like gravestones in the moonlight. On went the lights—and there was the village. They were silent, as if suspicious. Like the Captain, they seemed to feel it was not right. Uncanny it certainly was, but *that* was not it. Unfair—that was the word. It was cheating. And profoundly disturbing.

"Clever chap, that Italian of yours," said the General.

The Captain, who had been woodenly correct until this moment, suddenly came rocking up to the General, and steadied himself by laying his hand on the august shoulder. "Bloody Wops," he said. "Bloody

将军看了他一眼,然后向部下点头示意。上尉因触犯纪律而被带走了。不过,他病了,这是可以肯定的,否则就无法解释这样荒唐的行为。他被安顿在自己房内的床上,由一位护士照看他。

24 小时以后他才醒来,几周来他第一次清醒。他慢慢回想起所发生的事儿,从床上跃起,匆匆套上衣服。他跑上小路,跨进卡车,护士才看见他。

他高速度地朝阅兵场驶去,场地上一片灯光,村庄仿佛融化在灯光之中不存在了。一切都在轰轰烈烈地进行。广场周围停了三重汽车,跑道上,甚至屋顶上都有人。看台也挤得满满的。妇女们打扮成吉卜赛女郎,乡村姑娘,伊丽莎白王朝的宫廷仕女等等,手拿托盘走来走去。托盘里装着姜汁啤酒,香肠面包以及节目单,每份 5 个先令。为战争募捐。广场上,军队调动着,士兵们把老式机关枪拖来拖去,军乐队在奏乐,摩托车隆隆地穿过火焰。

上尉刚把卡车停放好,所有的活动突然停止了,灯光也随之熄灭。上尉开始沿着广场外围奔跑,想跑到隐蔽在大堆网和树枝下的枪炮工事里去。他费劲儿地喘着气。他是个大块头,不惯于运动,又被白兰地灌得昏头昏脑的。他心中只有一个念头——阻止枪炮发射,不惜任何代价阻止枪炮发射。

幸亏出了点故障,电灯仍然不亮,广场那头神秘的墓地在一片月光下白花花地闪烁。接着电灯忽然亮了一下,村庄又出现了,足以使人们看到教堂旁边的一片白色建筑物上有几个巨大的红十字架。电灯又熄灭了。月光重又普盖大地,十字架又消失了。"咳,这该死的傻瓜!"上尉喘着气继续奔跑,他似乎在为自己的性命而奔跑。他不再想跑到枪炮跟前去了。他抄近路穿过广场一角,径直往教堂奔去。他听到背后一些军官在咒骂:"是谁把红十字架放在那儿了?是谁? 我们可不能朝红十字架开火。"

上尉跑到教堂时,探照灯突然大放光明。教堂里,米开尔跪在地上凝视着他画的头一幅圣母像。"他们要杀死我的圣母了。"他悲哀地说。

"快离开,米开尔,快离开。"

"他们要杀死……"

上尉抓住他的手臂拖着他走。可是他扭脱了上尉,拿起一把锯子乱锯起板壁来。外面是死一般的寂静。他们听到扩音器里一个声音在吼叫着:"将遭炮击的村庄是座英国村庄,不是节目单上所写的德国村

kaffirs. Bloody... Tell you what, though, there's one Itie that's some good. Yes, there is. I'm telling you. He's a friend of mine, actually."

The General looked at him. Then he nodded at his underlings. The Captain was taken away for disciplinary purposes. It was decided, however, that he must be ill, nothing else could account for such behaviour. He was put to bed in his own room with a nurse to watch him.

He woke twenty-four hours later, sober for the first time in weeks. He slowly remembered what had happened. Then he sprang out of bed and rushed into his clothes. The nurse was just in time to see him run down the path and leap into his lorry.

He drove at top speed to the parade-ground, which was flooded with light in such a way that the village did not exist. Everything was in full swing. The cars were three deep around the square, with people on the running-boards and even the roofs. The grandstand was packed. Women dressed up as gipsies, country girls, Elizabethan court dames, and so on, wandered about with trays of ginger beer and sausage-rolls and programmes at five shillings each in aid of the war effort. On the square, troops deployed, obsolete machine-guns were being dragged up and down, bands played, and motorcyclists roared through flames.

As the Captain parked the lorry, all this activity ceased, and the lights went out. The Captain began running around the outside of the square to reach the place where the guns were hidden in a mess of net and branches. He was sobbing with the effort. He was a big man, and unused to exercise, and sodden with brandy. He had only one idea in his mind—to stop the guns firing, to stop them at all costs.

Luckily, there seemed to be a hitch. The lights were still out. The unearthly graveyard at the end of the square glittered white in the moonlight. Then the lights briefly switched on, and the village sprang into existence for just long enough to show large red crosses all over a white building beside the church. Then moonlight flooded everything again, and the crosses vanished. "Oh, the bloody fool!" sobbed the Captain, running, running as if for his life. He was no longer trying to reach the guns. He was cutting across a corner of the square direct to the church. He could hear some officers cursing behind him: "Who put those red crosses there? Who? We can't fire on the Red Cross."

The Captain reached the church as the searchlights burst on. Inside, Michele was kneeling on the earth looking at his first Madonna. "They are going to kill my Madonna," he said miserably.

"Come away, Michele, come away."

"They're going to..."

The Captain grabbed his arm and pulled. Michele

庄。重复一遍,将遭炮击的村庄是座……"

米开尔已经把一方块画着圣母像的板壁锯成两半。

"米开尔!"上尉喘息着说,"快离开这儿。"

米开尔手中的锯子掉落在地,他抓住板壁的毛边,拼命地扳,这样一来,教堂开始摇晃、倾斜。一块破板折断了,米开尔一个趔趄跌入上尉怀中。轰隆一声巨响,教堂似乎绕过他们投入火焰之中。上尉紧拉着米开尔的手臂往外冲。"趴下。"他突然叫道,把米开尔扔到地上,自己也扑倒在米开尔身边。上尉从弯曲的手臂下向外望着,一声爆炸,他瞥见一股巨大的火焰柱子,村庄在一堆飞扬的碎片中完蛋了。米开尔跪着凝视火光中的圣母,圣母像蒙上了尘土,已经面目全非。米开尔脸色苍白,看上去可怕极了。一缕鲜血从他头发里渗了出来,流满半边面颊。

"他们炮轰我的圣母。"他说。

"咳,真该死,你可以再画一张嘛。"上尉说,他的声音自己听来也觉得异常陌生,像是梦呓一般。他一定发疯了,和米开尔一样发疯了……他站起身,把米开尔也拉了起来,推着他朝场地边上跑去。在那儿他们遇上了救护人员。米开尔被送进医院,上尉也被送回床上去了。

一个星期过去了,上尉住在一间昏暗的房间里,他显然得了某种精神衰竭症,有两个护士照看他。他有时睡得很安稳,有时喃喃自语,有时候用粗重的嗓音唱着几段歌剧,唱着意大利歌曲的片断,还一遍一遍地唱:"有一条漫长的小路。"他简直什么都不想。也竭力不去想米开尔,似乎想想也是危险的。因此,当他听到一个悦耳的女人的声音说,有位朋友来,会使他高兴起来的,有个人做伴对他有好处,而且朦胧中他看到白色绷带向他过来,他赶紧转过身面对墙壁。

"走开,"他说,"走开,米开尔。"

"我来看望你,"米开尔说,"带给你一件礼物。"

上尉慢慢地转过身来。那是米开尔,站在昏暗的房间里,像个快活的幽灵。"你这个傻瓜,"他说,"把什么都弄糟了。你画那些十字架干吗?"

"那是座医院,"米开尔说,"村子里有医院,医院上面有红十字,美丽的红十字,不是吗?"

"我差点儿受到军法审判。"

"这是我的错,"米开尔说,"我喝醉了。"

wrenched himself free and grabbed a saw. He began hacking at the ceiling board. There was a dead silence outside. They heard a voice booming through the loud-speakers: "The village that is about to be shelled is an English village, not as represented on the programme, a German village. Repeat, the village that is about to be shelled is..."

Michele had cut through two sides of a square around the Madonna.

"Michele," sobbed the Captain, "*get out of here.*"

Michele dropped the saw, took hold of the raw edges of the board and tugged. As he did so, the church began to quiver and lean. An irregular patch of board ripped out and Michele staggered back into the Captain's arms. There was a roar. The church seemed to dissolve around them into flame. Then they were running away from it, the Captain holding Michele tight by the arm. "Get down," he shouted suddenly, and threw Michele to the earth. He flung himself down beside him. Looking from under the crook of his arm, he heard the explosion, saw a great pillar of smoke and flame, and the village disintegrated in a flying mass of debris. Michele was on his knees gazing at his Madonna in the light from the flames. She was unrecognizable, blotted out with dust. He looked horrible, quite white, and a trickle of blood soaked from his hair down one cheek.

"They shelled my Madonna," he said.

"Oh, damn it, you can paint another one," said the Captain. His own voice seemed to him strange, like a dream voice. He was certainly crazy, as mad as Michele himself... He got up, pulled Michele to his feet, and marched him towards the edge of the field. There they were met by the ambulance people. Michele was taken off to hospital, and the Captain was sent back to bed.

A week passed. The Captain was in a darkened room. That he was having some kind of a breakdown was clear, and two nurses stood guard over him. Sometimes he lay quiet. Sometimes he muttered to himself. Sometimes he sang in a thick clumsy voice bits out of opera, fragments from Italian songs, and—over and over again—"There's a Long Long Trail." He was not thinking of anything at all. He shied away from the thought of Michele as if it were dangerous. When, therefore, a cheerful female voice announced that a friend had come to cheer him up, and it would do him good to have some company, and he saw a white bandage moving towards him in the gloom, he turned sharp over on to his side, face to the wall.

"Go away," he said. "Go away, Michele."

"I have come to see you," said Michele. "I have brought you a present."

The Captain slowly turned over. There was

"我得负责。"

"我做的事怎么让你担当责任？不过一切都过去了。你身体好点儿了吗？"

"嗯，我猜想是那些十字架救了你的性命。"

"我倒不这么想，"米开尔说，"是那些好心的红十字会人员。"

"啊，你给我住口，住口，住口。"

"我给你带来一件礼物。"

上尉在黑暗中看见米开尔拿着一幅画。一个背婴孩的黑人妇女，似乎在斜对着画框外微笑。

米开尔说："你不喜欢光圈，这回不画光圈。这是专为上尉画的，不是圣母。"他笑了起来，"你喜欢么？这是给你的，为你画的。"

"该死的！"上尉说。

"你不喜欢吗？"米开尔说，他伤心极了。

上尉闭上了眼睛。"那么你接下来准备干些什么呢？"他厌倦地问。

米开尔又笑了起来。"将军太太潘纳赫斯特夫人要画一幅穿白色礼服的画像，我画了。"

"你该为此感到荣幸啰。"

"那个蠢货，她以为我挺高兴。他们什么都不懂——原始人，野蛮人。上尉，你不是的，你是我的朋友。不过那伙人什么也不懂。"

上尉安静地躺着，胸中积聚着一团怒火。他想起将军的妻子。他不喜欢她，但对她十分了解。

"这些人，"米开尔说，"他们不识好画和坏画。我画啊，画啊，随意涂抹。有一张画，我看着心中直发笑。"米开尔笑出声来，"他们说，他是米开朗琪罗①。就是这个，他们杀我的价，米开尔——米开朗琪罗——真可笑，不是吗？"

上尉一声不吭。

"不过我为你画这幅画是要让你记得我们造那村庄时度过的好时光。你是我的朋友，我会永远记得你的。"

上尉斜着眼睛凝视画中的黑姑娘。她对他微笑着，一半天真，一半怨恨。

"滚！"他突然说。

米开尔走近一点儿，俯身看上尉的脸。"你要我

---

① 米开朗琪罗(1475—1564)，意大利雕刻家、画家、建筑家和诗人。米开尔这名字和米开朗琪罗同一个词头。

Michele, a cheerful ghost in the dark room. "You fool," he said. "You messed everything up. What did you paint those crosses for?"

"It was a hospital," said Michele. "In a village there is a hospital, and on the hospital the Red Cross, the beautiful Red Cross—no?"

"I was nearly court-martialled."

"It was my fault," said Michele. "I was drunk."

"I was responsible."

"How could you be responsible when I did it? But it is all over. Are you better?"

"Well, I suppose those crosses saved your life."

"I did not think," said Michele. "I was remembering the kindness of the Red Cross people when we were prisoners."

"Oh shut up, shut up, shut up."

"I have brought you a present."

The Captain peered through the dark. Michele was holding up a picture. It was of a native woman with a baby on her back smiling sideways out of the frame.

Michele said: "You did not like the haloes. So this time, no haloes. For the Captain—no Madonna." He laughed. "You like it? It is for you. I painted it for you."

"God damn you!" said the Captain.

"You do not like it?" said Michele, very hurt.

The Captain closed his eyes. "What are you going to do next?" he asked tiredly.

Michele laughed again. "Mrs. Pannerhurst, the lady of the General, she wants me to paint her picture in her white dress. So I paint it."

"You should be proud to."

"Silly bitch. She thinks I am good. They know nothing—savages. Barbarians. Not you, Captain, you are my friend. But these people they know nothing."

The Captain lay quiet. Fury was gathering in him. He thought of the General's wife. He disliked her, but he had known her well enough.

"These people," said Michele. "They do not know a good picture from a bad picture. I paint, I paint, this way, that way. There is the picture—I look at it and laugh inside myself." Michele laughed out loud. "They say, he is a Michelangelo, this one, and try to cheat me out of my price. Michele—Michelangelo—that is a joke, no?"

The Captain said nothing.

"But for you I painted this picture to remind you of our good times with the village. You are my friend. I will always remember you."

The Captain turned his eyes sideways in his head and stared at the black girl. Her smile at him was half innocence, half malice.

"Get out," he said suddenly.

Michele came closer and bent to see the Captain's

走？"他难过地说，"你救了我的命。那天晚上我真是个傻瓜。我在想着对圣母的奉献——我是个傻瓜，我自己也这么说。我醉了，我们喝醉时都成了傻瓜。"

"从这儿滚出去！"上尉又说。

白色绷带依然一动不动地待了一会儿，然后突然向下一鞠躬。

米开尔转身向门口走去。

"把那幅该死的画也拿走。"

一阵沉默。接着，在幽暗之中，上尉看见米开尔朝那幅画走去，白色的脑袋十分恭敬地鞠躬。米开尔挺直身子立正，一手拿着画，一手僵直地垂在一边，向上尉敬礼。

"是的，先生。"他说完就转身带着画走出门去。

上尉静静地躺着。他感到——他感到什么呢？他肋骨下面有些疼痛，呼吸起来很难受。他明白他十分痛苦，是的，一种可怕的痛苦感正慢慢地充塞胸间。他感到痛苦是因为米开尔走了。在上尉一生中，从来没有像那声嘲弄似的"是的，先生"使他更痛心的了。从来没有。他默默地转身面对墙壁流泪，但是悄悄的。没有发出一点儿声音，怕护士们听见。

face. "You wish me to go?" He sounded unhappy. "You saved my life. I was a fool that night. But I was thinking of my offering to the Madonna—I was a fool, I say it myself. I was drunk, we are fools when we are drunk. "

"Get out of here,"said the Captain again.

For a moment the white bandage remained motionless. Then it swept downwards in a bow.

Michele turned towards the door.

"And take that bloody picture with you. "

Silence. Then, in the dim light, the Captain saw Michele reach out for the picture, his white head bowed in profound obeisance. He straightened himself and stood to attention, holding the picture with one hand, and keeping the other stiff down his side. Then he saluted the Captain.

"Yes, sir,"he said, and he turned and went out of the door with the picture.

The Captain lay still. He felt—what did he feel? There was a pain under his ribs. It hurt to breathe. He realized he was unhappy. Yes, a terrible unhappiness was filling him, slowly, slowly. He was unhappy because Michele had gone. Nothing had ever hurt the Captain in all his life as much as that mocking *Yes, sir*. Nothing. He turned his face to the wall and wept. But silently. Not a sound escaped him, for the fear the nurses might hear.

047. A 和 P①

（美）约翰·厄普代克 著　　雨 宁 译

047. A & P
by John Updike

走进来了三位姑娘，穿的是游泳衣，没有其他衣服。我正在查货收款的第三个道口，背朝着门，直到她们靠近了面包柜台，我才看见她们。头一个吸引住我眼睛的是穿绿格子两件头的那个。她是一个矮胖姑娘，肥大得够意思的屁股软绵绵的，正好在屁股下面有两个白色的月牙，因为阳光似乎从来也照不到她大腿后面这两块最高的地方。我站在那儿，手放在一盒"嗨嗬"牌饼干上，正在想我有没有在现金出纳机上记下这一笔，我又按了按键钮，那位顾客就申斥了我一顿。她是那种盯住现金出纳机不放的人，一个在颧骨上涂了胭脂，没有眉毛，大约 50 岁的老妖精，我知道她抓住了我这个错会得意一天的。她盯住现金出纳机不放有 50 年了，大概以前从来没见到出过一次错。

等到我把她的羽毛捋顺了，把她买的东西都装在一个袋子里的时候，她顺便对我轻轻哼了一声，要是她生的是那个时候，他们大概会在萨勒姆把她活活烧死的②。等到我把她打发走了，那三个姑娘已经围着面包柜台转了一圈回来，并没有推着小推车，她们是在出纳口和特价品之间的过道，顺着柜台向我这里走过来的。她们连鞋子也没穿。那个矮胖姑娘穿的两件头游泳衣是鲜绿色的，奶罩的边缝仍然线脚分明，她的肚皮仍然相当苍白，所以我估计她是刚买来这套游泳衣的——拿她来说吧，胖脸蛋像个浆果，嘴唇在

---

① A 和 P 是"大西洋和太平洋茶叶总公司"的简称，这里讲的是该公司开办的超级市场。

② 萨勒姆是美国马萨诸塞州北部的一个城市，在殖民初期有烧死女巫的刑法。这里是用来咒骂那个女顾客的一句话。

IN walks these three girls in nothing but bathing suits. I'm in the third checkout slot, with my back to the door, so I don't see them until they're over by the bread. The one that caught my eye first was the one in the plaid green two-piece. She was a chunky kid, with a good tan and a sweet broad soft-looking can with those two crescents of white just under it, where the sun never seems to hit at the top of the backs of her legs. I stood there with my hand on a box of HiHo crackers trying to remember if I rang it up or not. I ring it up again and the customer starts giving me hell. She's one of these cash-register-watchers, a witch about fifty with rouge on her cheekbones and no eyebrows, and I know it made her day to trip me up. She'd been watching cash registers for fifty years and probably never seen a mistake before.

By the time I got her feathers smoothed and her goodies into a bag—she gives me a little snort in passing, if she'd been born at the right time they would have burned her over in Salem—by the time I get her on her way the girls had circled around the bread and were coming back, without a pushcart, back my way along the counters, in the aisle between the checkouts and the Special bins. They didn't even have shoes on. There was this chunky one, with the two-piece—it was bright green and the seams on the bra were still sharp and her belly was still pretty pale so I guessed she just got it (the suit)—there was this one, with one of those chubby berry-faces, the lips all bunched together under her nose, this one, and a tall one, with black hair that hadn't quite frizzed right, and one of these sunburns right across under the eyes, and a chin that was too long—you know, the kind of girl other girls

作者简介：约翰·厄普代克（**John Updike**，1932—），美国作家。1932 年 3 月 18 日生于宾夕法尼亚州希灵顿。他的作品以精致的技巧和对美国中层社会的细微描写而闻名。他著名的"兔子四部曲"包括《兔子，跑吧》（*Rabbit，Run*，1960）、《兔子回家》（*Rabbit Redux*，1971）、获普利策奖的《兔子富了》（*Rabbit Is Rich*，1981）和《兔子安息》（*Rabbit at Rest*，1990），讲述了 20 世纪晚期一个普通美国人几十年的生活。厄普代克其他的小说包括《马人》（*The Centaur*，1963）、《农场》（*Of the Farm*，1965）、《成双成对》（*Couples*，1968）、《伊斯威克的女巫》（*The Witches of Eastwick*，1984）和《圣洁百合》（*In the Beauty of the Lilies*）。

鼻子下面蜷缩成一团，这是她。还有一个高身材的，黑头发鬈曲得实在不大像样，紧贴着眼睛下面有一块晒脱了皮的痕迹，下巴太长，你明白，别的姑娘都认为她这种类型"触目"、"动人"，可就是永远赶不上趟儿，这一层，她们也都很清楚，也正是因为有这一层，她们才那么喜欢她。那第三个姑娘身材不太高。她是皇后。她大概是她们的带头人，那两个都是胁肩曲背，向四面窥探。这位皇后不下里张望，她只是慢慢地笔直向前走，移动着两条又白又长，自命不凡的腿。她的脚跟落地有点儿重，好像她并不是全靠两只赤脚走路，而是脚跟先下来，然后让身体的重量沿着脚掌移到脚趾的，好像她每一步都是在试探地板，都要故意添加一点儿小动作。谁也说不清女人的头脑是怎么活动的（你真认为那是头脑吗？还是以为那不过是一点儿嗡嗡的响声，像关在玻璃罐里的一只蜜蜂呢），不过你会想到是她说服了另外两个跟她到这里来的，她正在教她们怎么办，要慢慢地走，把身体挺直。

她穿的游泳衣是泛黄的粉红色的，也许是米色的，我说不清，那上面尽是小皱结，肩带是荡下来的，这可难倒了我。两根肩带都溜到肩外，松垮垮地系在手臂顶端的清凉皮肤上，我估计，这件游泳衣也因此在她身上松脱了一点，所以衣料上端的四周都是这种亮闪闪的边缝。要是没有这条边，你就不会知道还能有什么比这两个肩膀更白的东西了。既然肩带溜到了外面，在游泳衣的上端和她的头顶之间，除了她的身体就一无所有了。从肩胛骨到她胸部上方的那片清凉裸露的表面，像一块在灯光里倾斜的有凹痕的金属板，我的意思是说，不单单是漂亮。

她的头发是那种给太阳和海水弄得褪了色的栎木色，卷成了一个松散的面包卷，脸上一本正经。我想，肩带荡下来走进 A 和 P 超级市场的人，大概也只能是这副面孔。她的头扬得很高，她的头颈挺立在白肩膀上面，好像伸长了，不过我不在乎。她的头颈越长，也更能显出她的本色。

她一定从眼角里看到了我，而且掠过我的肩头，看出斯托克西在第二个出纳口注视着，可是她不露声色。这位皇后可不会。她的眼光继续掠过货架，停住，再慢慢地转动，慢得使我的肚子摩擦着我的围裙的里子，对另外那两个嗡嗡叫。她们都挤在她身边来寻求安慰，然后她们三个就向猫狗食品，早餐食品，谷类食品，通心粉，米，葡萄干，调味品，黄油果酱，意大

think is very "striking" and "attractive" but never quite makes it, as they very well know, which is why they like her so much—and then the third one, that wasn't quite so tall. She was the queen. She kind of led them, the other two peeking around and making their shoulders round. She didn't look around, not this queen, she just walked straight on slowly, on these long white prima-donna legs. She came down a little hard on her heels, as if she didn't walk in her bare feet that much, putting down her heels and then letting the weight move along to her toes as if she was testing the floor with every step, putting a little deliberate extra action into it. You never know for sure how girls' minds work (do you really think it's a mind in there or just a little buzz like a bee in a glass jar?) but you got the idea she had talked the other two into coming in here with her, and now she was showing them how to do it, walk slow and hold yourself straight.

She had on a kind of dirty-pink—beige maybe, I don't know—bathing suit with a little nubble all over it and, what got me, the straps were down. They were off her shoulders looped loose around the cool tops of her arms, and I guess as a result the suit had slipped a little on her, so all around the top of the cloth there was this shining rim. If it hadn't been there you wouldn't have known there could have been anything whiter than those shoulders. With the straps pushed off, there was nothing between the top of the suit and the top of her head except just *her*, this clean bare plane of the top of her chest down from the shoulder bones like a dented sheet of metal tilted in the light. I mean, it was more than pretty.

She had sort of oaky hair that the sun and salt had bleached, done up in a bun that was unravelling, and a kind of prim face. Walking into the A & P with your straps down, I suppose it's the only kind of face you *can* have. She held her head so high her neck, coming up out of those white shoulders, looked kind of stretched, but I didn't mind. The longer her neck was, the more of her there was.

She must have felt in the corner of her eye me and over my shoulder Stokesie in the second slot watching, but she didn't tip. Not this queen. She kept her eyes moving across the racks, and stopped, and turned so slow it made my stomach rub the inside of my apron, and buzzed to the other two, who kind of huddled against her for relief, and then they all three

利面条,不含酒精的饮料,饼干糕点那条过道走去。我从第三个出纳口向通往肉柜台的这个过道一直望过去,一路望着她们。那个皮肤晒成黄褐色的胖姑娘摸弄了一下成包的糕点,可是再一想,又把它们放回原处。驯服的人推着他们的小推车沿着过道走下去,这三个姑娘走的方向与寻常的人相反(这并不是说我们有单行道的标志或者什么的),她们说笑得挺热闹。你也看得出来,在小皇后用白肩膀对她们示意的时候,她们会突然停住,或者用一条腿跳起来,或者打个嗝,可是她们的眼睛会马上回过来又瞧着她们自己的篮子,继续推车前进。我敢说,要是你在 A 和 P 公司的一家超级市场引起爆炸性的事件,人们大半都会不断伸出手,把燕麦片从他们的单子上划掉,咕哝着,"让我想一想,还有第三件东西,是 A 字打头的,芦笋,不对,哦,对啦,苹果酱①!"他们也许咕哝的是什么别的东西。不过毫无疑问,这种事会使他们轻轻地跳一下。有几个头上戴着卷发圈的家庭主妇甚至在把她们的推车推过去之后,还要向周围瞧瞧来弄清楚她们所看到的东西是不是没有错。

　　你明白,一个穿游泳衣的女人在海滨走动是一回事,那儿的光线太强,反正没有人会去彼此多看几眼,可是在日光灯下面,在 A 和 P 公司清凉的超级市场里,那又是一回事,这地方堆满了成色的货物,她是光着脚在绿色和奶油色相间的花格子橡皮地板上走动的。

　　"哦,爹呀,"斯托克西在我旁边说,"我觉得晕得慌。"

　　"宝贝儿,"我说,"把我搂紧点。"斯托克西结过婚了,有两个小娃娃,都用粉笔在他的飞机机身上画了记号②,不过对我来说,也只有这么点区别。他今年 22 岁,我在 4 月里就满了 19 岁。

　　"都过去了吗。"他问道,这个责任心强的已婚男人又能说出声来。我忘了说一下,他认为有朝一日运气好,他会成为经理的,也许是在 1990 年,到了那时候,这里就成了亚历山德洛夫和彼得洛斯基茶叶总公司③或者什么别的公司。

---

　　①　芦笋(asparagus)和苹果酱(applesauce)都是以 a 字开头的。

　　②　美国飞行员在打下每一架敌机之后都要在他驾驶的飞机机身上画一个记号,这里是指婚后生子女的记录。

　　③　这两个姓氏的为首字母也是 A 和 P,与大西洋和太平洋茶叶总公司相同,这里是暗示斯托克西可能将来成为公司的所有人。

of them went up the cat-and-dog-food-breakfast-cereal-mac-aroni-rice-raisins-seasonings-spreads-spaghetti-soft-drinks-crackers-and-cookies aisle. From the third slot I look stright up this aisle to the meat counter, and I watched them all the way. The fat one with the tan sort of fumbled with the cookies, but on second thought she put the package back. The sheep pushing their carts down the aisle—the girls were walking against the usual traffic (not that we have one-way signs or anything)—were pretty hilarious. You could see them, when Queenie's white shoulders dawned on them, kind of jerk, or hop, or hiccup, but their eyes snapped back to their own baskets and on they pushed. I bet you could set off dynamite in an A & P and the people would by and large keep reaching and checking oatmeal off their lists and muttering "Let me see, there was a third thing, began with A, asparagus, no, ah, yes, applesauce!" or whatever it is they do mutter. But there was no doubt, this jiggled them. A few houseslaves in pin curlers even looked around after pushing their carts past to make sure what they had seen was correct.

　　You know, it's one thing to have a girl in a bathing suit down on the beach, where what with the glare nobody can look at each other much anyway, and another thing in the cool of the A & P, under the fluorescent lights, against all those stacked packages, with her feet paddling along naked over our checkerboard green-and-cream rubber-tile floor.

　　"Oh Daddy," Stokesie said beside me. "I feel so faint."

　　"Darling," I said. "Hold me tight." Stokesie's married, with two babies chalked up on his fuselage already, but as far as I can tell that's the only difference. He's twenty-two, and I was nineteen this April.

　　"Is it done?" he asks, the responsible married man finding his voice. I forgot to say he thinks he's going to be manager some sunny day, maybe in 1990 when it's called the Great Alexandrov and Petrooshki Tea Company① or something.

　　What he meant was, our town is five miles from a beach, with a big summer colony out on the Point, but we're right in the middle of town, and the women generally put on a shirt or shorts or something before

---

　　①　"A & P" is actually an abbreviation of Great Atlantic and Pacific Tea Company.

他的意思是说，我们这个镇市离海滨有 5 英里，在海滨尖地有一大片度夏的地方，可是我们这里正好处在镇市的中心，妇女们在走下汽车来到街上之前，一般都要穿上一件衬衫，一条短裤，或者什么其他的衣服。而且不论怎么说，这些妇女通常都是有了 6 个孩子，腿上露出曲张的静脉，连她们包括在内，谁也不能连这一点儿体面都不顾。我说过，我们这里正好是镇市的中心，如果你站在我们的大门口，你能看到两家银行，公理会教堂，报刊商店，三家房地产经理处，还有大约 27 名老资格吃白食的人在挖开中央大街的路面，因为下水道又坏了。谁也不能以为我们是在海角，我们这地方在波士顿北面，镇上的人有的已经有 20 年没见到海洋了。

这些姑娘去到肉食柜台，正在向麦克马洪问这问那。他指了指，她们也指了指，于是她们拖着踟步走到一堆像金字塔一般的乐口牌桃子后面不见。我们所能看到的只是用手帕擦嘴的老麦克马洪，他的眼光尾随着她们。正在打量她们的关节。可怜的姑娘们。我开始为她们感到惋惜，她们也都是没有办法。

现在到了这个故事里令人沮丧的那一段，至少我家里的人认为那是令人沮丧的，我自己倒不认为怎么令人沮丧。这时候是星期四下午，店里相当空闲，因此也没有什么事好做，我就靠在出纳机上，等那些姑娘重新露面。整个店面就像一台弹球机，我不知道她们会从哪一条过道里出来。过了一会儿，她们从老远的那个过道里出来了，那儿陈列的有电灯泡，廉价唱片，例如加勒比海六人合唱曲，东尼·马丁歌曲，还有你以为他们是在浪费材料灌唱片的那一类垃圾，六色一袋的棒糖，还有用玻璃纸包装的塑料玩具，这种东西只要让小孩子看到了就会分崩离析。于是她们过来了，小皇后仍然领头带路，手里拿着一个灰色的小罐子。第三到第七个出纳口都没有出纳员，我看得出她正在斯托克西和我之间犹疑不定，可是斯托克西的运气跟平常一样，招来了一个穿松垮垮的灰裤子的老年人，他蹒跚地走过来，带着四只巨大的菠萝汁罐头（我常常问我自己，这些闲着没事的人买这么多菠萝汁来干什么呢），于是那些姑娘就到我这里来了。小皇后放下罐子，我用指头把它拿起来，冰凉。鱼王牌什锦鲱鱼小吃，用纯酸奶油浸制的，四角九分。现在她两手空空，既没有戴戒指，也没有戴镯子，像上帝造物的时候那样光溜溜，我觉得奇怪，她的钱放在哪里

they get out of the car into the street. And anyway these are usually women with six children and varicose veins mapping their legs and nobody, including them, could care less. As I say, we're right in the middle of town, and if you stand at our front doors you can see two banks and the Congregational church and the newspaper store and three real estate offices and about twenty-seven old freeloaders tearing up Central Street because the sewer broke again. It's not as if we're on the Cape; we're north of Boston and there's people in this town haven't seen the ocean for twenty years.

The girls had reached the meat counter and were asking McMahon something. He pointed, they pointed, and they shuffled out of sight behind a pyramid of Diet Delight peaches. All that was left for us to see was old McMahon patting his mouth and looking after them sizing up their joints. Poor kids, I began to feel sorry for them, they couldn't help it.

Now here comes the sad part of the story, at least my family says it's sad, but I don't think it's so sad myself. The store's pretty empty, it being Thursday afternoon, so there was nothing much to do except lean on the register and wait for the girls to show up again. The whole store was like a pinball machine and I didn't know which tunnel they'd come out of. After a while they come around out of the far aisle, around the light bulbs, records at discount of the Caribbean Six or Tony Martin Sings or some such gunk you wonder they waste the wax on, sixpacks of candy bars, and plastic toys done up in cellophane that fall apart when a kid looks at them anyway. Around they come, Queenie still leading the way, and holding a little gray jar in her hand. Slots Three through Seven are unmanned and I could see her wondering between Stokes and me, but Stokesie with his usual luck draws an old party in baggy gray pants who stumbles up with four giant cans of pineapple juice (what do these bums *do* with all that pineapple juice? I've often asked myself) so the girls come to me. Queenie puts down the jar and I take it into my fingers icy cold. Kingfish Fancy Herring Snacks in Pure Sour Cream; 49 ¢. Now her hands are empty, not a ring or a bracelet, bare as God made them, and I wonder where the money's coming from. Still with that prim look she lifts a folded dollar bill out of the hollow at the center of her nubbled pink top. The jar went heavy in my hand. Really, I thought that was so cute.

呢。她仍旧一脸正经，从她那件有皱结的粉红色游泳衣上端，从正中凹进去的地方，取出了一张折叠起来的一元钞票。我手里的那个罐头变得沉重了。真的，我觉得这个办法太巧妙了。

接下来，人人都开始倒霉了。棱格尔为了把满满一卡车卷心菜全买下来争论了一番，后来他进来了，正要连忙走进写着"经理室"的那个房间，他眼睛里一看见有女人，就会在那里躲一整天。棱格尔这个人相当阴沉，他在主日学校教书，还有其他等等，不过他并不是一点儿事都看不到。他过来就说："姑娘们，这里可不是海滩。"

小皇后脸红了，现在她离我很近，也许我才注意到那不过是晒红了的。"我母亲叫我捎一罐鲱鱼小吃。"她的口音有点儿使我吃惊，大概初次跟人见面，听到的口音都有这种作用，都是一出口平平稳稳，闷声闷气，可是也有点花腔，她叽叽咕咕说到"捎"和"小吃"的时候，口气就有点儿花哨。突然间，我顺着她的口音一下子溜进了她家里的起居室。她的父亲和其他的男人都站在那儿，身穿冰淇淋色的上衣，打着领结，妇女们都穿着凉鞋，用牙签从一个大玻璃盘子里挑起鲱鱼小吃，他们都拿着饮料，颜色像水，里面有橄榄和薄荷枝。我的父母在家里有客人的时候，他们都喝柠檬汽水，如果是一次真正讲究的聚会，那就要用印有"乐此不疲"漫画的高大环箍杯喝史立滋牌啤酒。

"这当然没错。"棱格尔说，"不过这里可不是海滩。"他重说了一遍，我觉得奇怪，仿佛他刚想到这句话似的，这么多年，他一直认为 A 和 P 超级市场是个老大老大的海边沙丘，他就是救生员的队长。他不喜欢我笑的样子，我说过，他不是没有看出来，不过他正在集中精神，用主日学校校长的眼光瞪着这些姑娘。

现在，小皇后脸红可不是太阳晒出来的了，那个穿方格子游泳衣的胖姑娘（我觉得她的后影比前影好，屁股真动人）插嘴了："我们不是来逛商店的。我们是单单为这罐东西来的。"

"那也没有什么两样。"棱格尔对她说，我从他转动眼光的样子看得出来，先前他并没有注意到她穿的是两件头游泳衣。"我们要求你们在进来的时候穿得规矩一点儿。"

"我们都是规规矩矩的。"小皇后突然间说道，她伸出了下嘴唇，生气了，因为她想起了她是在什么地方，大概经营 A 和 P 超级市场的那伙人的神气都够差

Then everybody's luck begins to run out. Lengel comes in from haggling with a truck full of cabbages on the lot and is about to scuttle into that door marked MANAGER behind which he hides all day when the girls touch his eye. Lengel's pretty dreary, teaches Sunday school and the rest, but he doesn't miss that much. He comes over and says, "Girls, this isn't the beach."

Queenie blushes, though maybe it's just a brush of sunburn I was noticing for the first time, now that she was so close. "My mother asked me to pick up a jar of herring snacks." Her voice kind of startled me, the way voices do when you see the people first, coming out so flat and dumb yet kind of tony, too, the way it ticked over "pick up" and "snacks." All of a sudden I slid right down her voice into her living room. Her father and the other men were standing around in ice-cream coats and bow ties and the women were in sandals picking up herring snacks on toothpicks off a big glass plate and they were all holding drinks the color of water with olives and sprigs of mint in them. When my parents have somebody over they get lemonade and if it's a real racy affair Schlitz in tall glasses with "They'll Do It Every Time" cartoons stenciled on.

"That's all right," Lengel said. "But this isn't the beach." His repeating this struck me as funny, as if it had just occurred to him, and he had been thinking all these years that A & P was a great big dune and he was the head lifeguard. He didn't like my smiling—as I say he doesn't miss much—but he concentrates on giving the girls that sad Sunday-school-superintendent stare.

Queenie's blush is no sunburn now, and the plump one in plaid, that I liked better from the back—a really sweet can—pipes up, "We weren't doing any shopping. We just came in for the one thing."

"That makes no difference," Lengel tells her, and I could see from the way his eyes went that he hadn't noticed she was wearing a two-piece before. "We want you decently dressed when you come in here."

"We *are* decent," Queenie says suddenly, her lower lip pushing, getting sore now that she remembers her place, a place from which the crowd that runs the A & P must look pretty crummy. Fancy Herring Snacks flashed in her very blue eyes.

劲的。什锦鲱鱼小吃在她碧蓝的眼睛里闪烁了一下。

"姑娘们,我不想跟你们斗嘴。以后要穿上一点能遮住肩膀的东西再进来。这是我们的章程。"他背转了身体。那是管你们的章程。章程就是头儿脑儿要的东西。别人要的就是少年犯罪。

经过这一阵,顾客们都推着他们的车子出来了,不过,你知道,都是驯良的人,看到有一场争执,他们都向斯托克西那儿挤过去,斯托克西却像给桃子削皮那样轻轻地抖开一个纸口袋,他不愿意听漏一个字。我感觉得到,在这种无声无息的气氛里,人人都变得神经紧张,最紧张的是棱格尔,他问我:"萨米,你把她们这笔账登记了没有?"

我想了想,说:"没有。"不过我想的不是那个,我按下了那些键钮,4,9,副食,总价——这比你想的要复杂得多,在你做的次数多到一定程度之后,它就开始变成了一支歌,拿我来说,还听得见歌词。"喂(乒),怎么样,你这个(咕咚)走运的伙——计(哗啦)!"哗啦是出纳机的抽屉冲出来的声音。我把那张钞票摊平,你也许能想象得出我是多么温柔体贴地把它摊平的,它是刚才从我见所未见的两勺最匀净的香草冰淇淋中间取出来的,我把一枚五角的银币和一枚一分的铜币放在她的狭长泛红的手掌里,把鲱鱼装在一个袋子里,把袋子的上端拧好,递给她,在这一段过程里,我一直在想。

那些姑娘,谁也难怪她们,都急急忙忙要走出去,于是我对棱格尔说:"我不干了。"我说得很快,让她们能听到,希望她们能停下来瞧着我,她们猜也没猜到的英雄。她们继续向前走,到了电眼的范围内,门自动闪开,她们在停车场上一闪就进了汽车。小皇后,花格子和傻大高个儿(这不是说她的原料也不好)撇下了我跟棱格尔在一起,他皱起了眉毛。

"你刚才说什么,萨米?"

"我说我不干了。"

"我也觉得你是这么说的。"

"你不该弄得她们这么难堪。"

"是她们闹得我们难堪的。"

我要说什么,说出来的却是"嘀嘀咕咕"。这是我祖母的口头语。我知道她会高兴的。

"我看你连自己说的是什么话都不明白。"棱格尔说。

"我知道你不明白,"我说,"可是我明白。"我拉开

"Girls, I don't want to argue with you. After this come in here with your shoulders covered. It's our policy. " He turns his back. That's policy for you. Policy is what the kingpins want. What the others want is juvenile delinquency.

All this while, the customers had been showing up with their carts but, you know, sheep, seeing a scene, they had all bunched up on Stokesie, who shook open a paper bag as gently as peeling a peach, not wanting to miss a word. I could feel in the silence everybody getting nervous, most of all Lengel, who asks me, "Sammy, have you rung up their purchase?"

I thought and said "No" but it wasn't about that I was thinking. I go through the punches, 4, 9, GROC, TOT—it's more complicated than you think, and after you do it often enough, it begins to make a little song, that you hear words to, in my case "Hello(*bing*) there, you (*gung*) hap-py *pee*-pul(*splat*)!"—the *splat* being the drawer flying out. I uncrease the bill, tenderly as you may imagine, it just having come from between the two smoothest scoops of vanilla I had ever known were there, and pass a half and a penny into her narrow pink palm, and nestle the herrings in a bag and twist its neck and hand it over, all the time thinking.

The girls, and who'd blame them, are in a hurry to get out, so I say "I quit" to Lengel quick enough for them to hear, hoping they'll stop and watch me, their unsuspected hero. They keep right on going, into the electric eye; the door flies open and they flicker across the lot to their car, Queenie and Plaid and Big Tall Goony-Goony(not that as raw material she was so bad), leaving me with Lengel and a kink in his eyebrow.

"Did you say something, Sammy?"

"I said I quit. "

"I thought you did. "

"You didn't have to embarrass them. "

"It was they who were embarrassing us. "

I started to say something that came out "Fiddle-de-doo. " It's a saying of my grandmother's, and I know she would have been pleased.

"I don't think you know what you're saying, " Lengel said.

"I know you don't, " I said. "But I do. " I pull the bow at the back of my apron and start shrugging it off my shoulders. A couple customers that had been heading for my slot begin to knock against each other, like

围裙后面的活结，从我肩膀上把它脱下来。有两个本来向我这个出纳口走过来的顾客不由得相互碰撞起来，好像圈里受了惊的猪一样。

棱格尔叹了口气，开始露出很有耐心而且很苍老的神色。他是我父母的一位多年老友。"萨米，你总不愿意这样来对待你爹妈吧？"他对我说。这是实话，我不愿意。不过，我似乎觉得，一旦你开始表态了，如果你不能坚持到底，那可要命了。我把在口袋上绣有"萨米"字样的这件围裙卷起来，放在柜台上，把领结丢到它上面。如果你觉得奇怪的话，这个领结也是他们的。"你今后一辈子都要感觉到这句话的分量的。"棱格尔说，我也知道这是实话，可是想到他弄得那个漂亮姑娘脸红就使我十分揪心，我按下"无销售"的键钮，出纳机咕噜了两声，抽屉就哗啦一下冲出来了。夏天里闹出这种事有一个好处，我可以接下来干干脆脆一走了之，用不着到处摸索去找上衣和胶皮套鞋，我只不过穿着我母亲前一天晚上给我烫平了的白衬衫，逍遥自在地走到电眼范围内，门自动地闪开了，外面的阳光正在掠过柏油路面。

我向周围张望，想看到我那些姑娘，可是，当然，她们都走了。街上空空荡荡，只有个年轻的已婚妇女站在一辆粉蓝色猎鹰牌旅行汽车门前，因为没有买到糖果跟她的儿女叫嚷。人行道上堆着许多袋泥炭沼和一些铝制的户外乘凉家具，我从这些东西上面向那个大窗户望去，看见棱格尔接替我的位置站在出纳口，正在检查通过那里的驯良的人。他的脸色阴沉沉的，背挺得笔直，好像刚才注射过铁水，从今以后这个世界会对我多么严酷无情啊，想到这里，我的胃口就有点儿垮了。

scared pigs in a chute.

Lengel sighs and begins to look very patient and old and gray. He's been a friend of my parents for years. "Sammy, you don't want to do this to your Mom and Dad," he tells me. It's true, I don't. But it seems to me that once you begin a gesture it's fatal not to go through with it. I fold the apron, "Sammy" stitched in red on the pocket, and put it on the counter, and drop the bow tie on top of it. The bow tie is theirs, if you've ever wondered. "You'll feel this for the rest of your life," Lengel says, and I know that's true, too, but remembering how he made that pretty girl blush makes me so scrunchy inside I punch the No Sale tab and the machine whirs "pee-pul" and the drawer splats out. One advantage to this scene taking place in summer, I can follow this up with a clean exit, there's no fumbling around getting your coat and galoshes, I just saunter into the electric eye in my white shirt that my mother ironed the night before, and the door heaves itself open, and outside the sunshine is skating around on the asphalt.

I looked around for my girls, but they're gone, of course. There wasn't anybody but some young married screaming with her children about some candy they didn't get by the door of a powder-blue Falcon station wagon. Looking back in the big windows, over the bags of peat moss and aluminum lawn furniture stacked on the pavement, I could see Lengel in my place in the slot, checking the sheep through. His face was dark gray and his back stiff, as if he'd just had an injection of iron, and my stomach kind of fell as I felt how hard the world was going to be to me hereafter.

048.伊凡·伊里奇之死①

（俄）列夫·托尔斯泰 著　　草　婴 译

048.The Death of Ivan Ilych

by Leo Tolstoi

一

在法院大厦里，当梅尔文斯基案审讯暂停时，法官和检察官都聚集在伊凡·叶果罗维奇·谢贝克办公室里，谈论着闹得满城风雨的克拉索夫案件。费多尔·瓦西里耶维奇情绪激动，认为此案不属本院审理范围。伊凡·叶果罗维奇坚持相反意见。彼得·伊凡内奇一开始就没加入争论，始终不过问此事，而翻阅着刚送来的《公报》。

"诸位！"他说，"伊凡·伊里奇死了。"

"真的吗？"

"喏，您看吧，"他对费多尔·瓦西里耶维奇说，同时把那份散发出油墨味的刚出版的《公报》递给他。

在《公报》上印着一则带有黑框的讣告：普拉斯柯菲雅·费多罗夫娜·高洛文娜沉痛哀告亲友，先夫伊凡·伊里奇·高洛文法官于1882年2月4日逝世。兹订于礼拜五下午一时出殡。"

伊凡·伊里奇是在座几位先生的同事，大家都喜欢他。他病了几个礼拜，据说患的是不治之症。他生病以来职位还给他保留着，但大家早就推测过，他死后将由阿历克谢耶夫接替，而阿历克谢耶夫的位置则将由文尼科夫或施塔别尔接替。因此，一听到伊凡·伊里奇的死讯，办公室里在座的人首先想到的就是，他一死对他们本人和亲友在职位调动和升迁上会有什么影响。

"这下子我很可能弄到施塔别尔或文尼科夫的位

---

① 本文根据俄文原著翻译。

I

DURING an interval in the Melvinski trial in the large building or the Law Courte the members and public prosecutor met in Ivan Egorovich Shebek's private room where the conversation turned on the celebrated Krasovski case. Fedor Vasilievich warmly maintained that it was not subject to their jurisdiction, Ivan Egorovich maintained the contrary, while Peter Ivanovich, not having entered into the discussion at the start, took no part in it but looked through the *Gazette* which had just been handed in.

"Gentlemen,"he said,"Ivan Ilych has died!"

"You don't say so!"

"Here, read it yourself,"replied Peter Ivanovich, handing Fedor Vasilievich the paper still damp from the press. Surrounded by a black border were the words:"Praskovya Fedorovna Golovina, with profound sorrow, informs relatives and friends of the demise of her beloved husband Ivan Ilych Golovin, Member of the Court of Justice, which occurred on February the 4th of this year l882. The funeral will take place on Friday at one o'clock in the afternoon."

Ivan Ilych had been a colleague of the gentlemen present and was liked by them all. He had been ill for some weeks with an illness said to be incurable. His post had been kept open for him, but there had been conjectures that in case of his death Alexeev might receive his appointment, and that either Vinnikov or Shtabel would succeed Alexeev. So on receiving the news of Ivan Ilych's death the first thought of each of the gentlemen in that private room was of the changes and promotions it might occasion among themselves or their acquaintances.

"I shall be sure to get Shtabel's place or Vinnikov's,"thought Fedor Vasilievich. "I was promised that long ago, and the promotion means an extra eight hundred rubles a year for me besides the allowance."

"Now I must apply for my brother-in-law's transfer from Kaluga," thought Peter Ivanovich. "My wife

作者简介：列夫·托尔斯泰（Leo Tolstoi，1828—1910），俄国作家。1828年9月9日生于亚斯纳亚波利亚纳，1910年11月20日卒于阿斯塔波伍。他是显赫贵族的后代。短篇小说作品《塞瓦斯托堡纪事》（*Sevastopol Sketches*，1855—1856）和长篇小说如《哥萨克》（*The Cossacks*，1863）让他成名，《战争与和平》（*War and Peace*，1865—1869）让他跻身俄罗斯最卓越的小说家行列。《安娜·卡列尼娜》（*Anna Karenina*，1875—1877）出版后，他陷入了精神危机，转向基督教无政府主义。他全身心投入到社会改革中，提倡朴素和无暴力。他的后期作品包括公认为最伟大的俄罗斯中篇小说《伊凡·伊里奇之死》（*The Death of Ivan Ilych*，1886）和谴责时髦的唯美主义的《艺术是什么？》（*What Is Art?* 1898）等。

置，"费多尔·瓦西里耶维奇想，"这个位置早就说好给我了，而这样一提升，我就可以在车马费之外每年净增加800卢布收入。"

"这下子我就可以申请把内弟从卡卢加调来，"彼得·伊尼内奇想，"妻子一定会很高兴的。如今她可再不能说我不关心她家的人了。"

"我早就想到，他这一病恐怕起不来了，"彼得·伊凡内奇说，"真可怜！"

"他究竟害的什么病啊？"

"几个医生都说不准。或者说，各有各的说法。我最后一次看见他，还以为他会好起来呢。"

"自从过节以来我就没有去看过他。去是一直想去的。"

"那么，他有财产吗？"

"他妻子手里大概有一点儿，但很有限。"

"是啊，应该去看看她。他们住得实在太远。"

"从您那儿去是很远。您到什么地方去都很远。"

"嘿，我住在河对岸，他总是有意见。"彼得·伊凡内奇笑眯眯地瞧着谢贝克说。大家又说了一通城市太大，市内各区距离太远之类的话，然后回到法庭上。

伊凡·伊里奇的死讯使每个人都不由得推测，人事上会因此发生什么更动，同时照例使认识他的人都暗自庆幸："还好，死的是他，不是我。"

"嘿，他死了，可我没有死。"人人都这样想，或者有这样的感觉。伊凡·伊里奇的知交，他的所谓朋友。都同时不由自主地想到，这下子他们得遵循习俗，参加丧礼，慰问遗孀了。

费多尔·瓦西里耶维奇和彼得·伊凡内奇是伊凡·伊里奇最知己的朋友。

彼得·伊凡内奇跟伊凡·伊里奇在法学院同过学，自认为受过伊凡·伊里奇的恩惠。

午饭时，彼得·伊凡内奇把伊凡·伊里奇的死讯告诉了妻子，同时讲了争取把内弟调到本区的想法。饭后他不休息，就穿上礼服，乘车到伊凡·伊里奇家去了。

伊凡·伊里奇家门口停着一辆自备轿车和两辆出租马车。在前厅衣帽架旁的墙上，靠着带穗子和擦得闪闪发亮的金银饰带的棺盖。两位穿黑衣的太太在这里脱去皮外套，其中一位是伊凡·伊里奇的姐姐，彼得·伊凡内奇认识她，另一位却没有见过面。彼得·伊凡内奇的同事施瓦尔茨从楼上下来，一看见

will be very glad, and then she won't be able to say that I never do anything for her relations. "

"I thought he would never leave his bed again," said Peter Ivanovich aloud. "It's very sad. "

"But what really was the matter with him?"

"The doctors couldn't say—at least they could, but each of them said something different. When last I saw him I thought he was getting better. "

"And I haven't been to see him since the holidays. I always meant to go. "

"Had he any property?"

"I think his wife had a little—but something quite trifling. "

"We shall have to go to see her, but they live so terribly far away. "

"Far away from you, you mean. Everything's far away from your place. "

"You see, he never can forgive my living on the other side of the river," said Peter lvanovich, smiling at Shebek. Then, still talking of the distances between different parts of the city, they returned to the Court.

Besides considerations as to the possible transfers and promotions likely to result from Ivan Ilych's death, the mere fact of the death of a near acquaintance aroused, as usual, in all who heard of it the complacent feeling that, "it is he who is dead and not I. "

Each one thought or felt, "Well, he's dead but I'm alive!" But the more intimate of Ivan Ilych's acquaintances, his so-called friends, could not help thinking also that they would now have to fulfil the very tiresome demands of propriety by attending the funeral service and paying a visit of condolence to the widow.

Fedor Vasilievich and Peter Ivanovich had been his nearest acquaintances. Peter Ivanovich had studied law with Ivan Ilych and had considered himself to be under obligations to him.

Having told his wife at dinner-time of Ivan Ilych's death, and of his conjecture that it might be possible to get her brother transferred to their circuit, Peter Ivanovich sacrificed his usual nap, put on his evening clothes, and drove to Ivan Ilych's house.

At the entrance stood a carriage and two cabs. Leaning against the wall in the hall downstairs near the cloak-stand was a coffin lid covered with cloth of gold, ornamented with gold cord and tassels, that had been polished up with metal powder. Two ladies in black were taking off their fur cloaks. Peter Ivanovich recognized one of them as Ivan Ilych's sister, but the other was a stranger to him. His colleague Schwartz was just coming downstairs, but on seeing Peter Ivanovich enter he stopped and winked at him, as if to say: "Ivan Ilych has made a mess of things—not like you and me. "

Schwartz's face with his Piccadilly whiskers, and his slim figure in evening dress, had as usual an air of elegant solemnity which contrasted with the playfulness of his character and had a special piquancy here, or so it seemed to Peter Ivanovich.

Peter Ivanovich allowed the ladies to precede him and slowly followed them upstairs. Schwartz did not come down but remained where he was, and Peter

他进门,就站住向他使了个眼色,仿佛说:"伊凡·伊里奇真没出息,咱们可不至于如此。"

施瓦尔茨脸上留着英国式络腮胡子,瘦长的身体穿着礼服,照例表现出一种典雅庄重的气派,但这同他天生的顽皮性格不协调,因此显得很滑稽。彼得·伊凡内奇心里有这样的感觉。

彼得·伊尼内奇让太太们先走,自己慢吞吞地跟着她们上楼。施瓦尔茨在楼梯顶上站住,没有下来。彼得·伊凡内奇懂得施瓦尔茨的用意:他想跟他约定,今晚到什么地方去打桥牌。太太们上楼向孀妇屋里走去。施瓦尔茨却一本正经地抿着厚实的嘴唇,眼睛里露出戏谑的神气。挤挤眉向彼得·伊凡内奇示意,死人在右边房间。

彼得·伊凡内奇进去时照例有点困惑,不知做什么好,但有一点他很清楚,逢到这种场合,画十字总是不会错的。至于要不要同时鞠躬,他可没有把握,因此选择了个折中办法,他走进屋里,动手画十字,同时微微点头,好像在鞠躬。在画十字和点头时,他向屋子里偷偷环顾了一下。有两个青年和一个中学生,大概是伊凡·伊里奇的侄儿,一面画十字,一面从屋子里出来。一个老妇人一动不动地站在那里。一个眉毛弯得出奇的女人在对她低声说话。诵经士身穿法衣,精神饱满,神态严峻,大声念着什么,脸上现出神圣不可侵犯的样子。充当餐室侍仆的庄稼汉盖拉西姆蹑手蹑脚地从彼得·伊凡内奇面前走过,把什么东西撒在地板上。彼得·伊凡内奇一看见这情景,立刻闻到淡淡的腐尸臭。他上次探望伊凡·伊里奇时,在书房里看到过这个庄稼汉。当时他在护理伊凡·伊里奇,伊凡·伊里奇特别喜爱他。彼得·伊尼内奇一直画着十字,向棺材、诵经士和屋角桌上的圣像微微鞠躬。后来,他觉得十字已画得够了,就停下来打量死人。

死人躺在那里,也像一般死人那样,显得特别沉重,僵硬的四肢陷在棺材衬垫里,脑袋高高地靠在枕头上,蜡黄的前额高高隆起,半秃的两鬓凹陷过去,高耸的鼻子仿佛压迫着上唇。同彼得·伊凡内奇上次看见他时相比,他的模样大变了,身体更瘦了,但他的脸也像一般死人那样,比生前好看,显得很端庄。脸上的神态似乎表示,他已尽了责任,而且尽得很周到。此外,那神态还在责备活人或者提醒他们什么事。彼

Ivanovich understood that he wanted to arrange where they should play bridge that evening. The ladies went upstairs to the widow's room, and Schwartz with seriously compressed lips but a playful look in his eyes, indicated by a twist of his eyebrows the room to the right where the body lay.

Peter Ivanovich, like everyone else on such occasions, entered feeling uncertain what he would have to do. All he knew was that at such times it is always safe to cross oneself. But he was not quite sure whether one should make obeisances while doing so. He therefore adopted a middle course. On entering the room he began crossing himself and made a slight movement resembling a bow. At the same time, as far as the motion of his head and arm allowed, he surveyed the room. Two young men—apparently nephews, one of whom was a high-school pupil—were leaving the room, crossing themselves as they did so. An old woman was standing motionless, and a lady with strangely arched eyebrows was saying something to her in a whisper. A vigorous, resolute Church Reader, in a frock-coat, was reading something in a loud voice with an expression that precluded any contradiction. The butler's assistant, Gerasim, stepping lightly in front of Peter Ivanovich, was strewing something on the floor. Noticing this, Peter Ivanovich was immediately aware of a faint odour of a decomposing body.

The last time he had called on Ivan Ilych, Peter Ivanovich had seen Gerasim in the study. Ivan Ilych had been particularly fond of him and he was performing the duty of a sick nurse.

Peter Ivanovich continued to make the sign of the cross slightly inclining his head in an intermediate direction between the coffin, the Reader, and the icons on the table in a corner of the room. Afterwards, when it seemed to him that this movement of his arm in crossing himself had gone on too long, he stopped and began to look at the corpse.

The dead man lay, as dead men always lie, in a specially heavy way, his rigid limbs sunk in the soft cushions of the coffin, with his head forever bowed on the pillow. His yellow waxen brow with bald patches over his sunken temples was thrust up in the way peculiar to the dead, the protruding nose seeming to press on the upper lip. He was much changed and had grown even thinner since Peter Ivanovich had last seen him, but, as is always the case with the dead, his face was handsomer and above all more dignified than when he was alive. The expression on the face said that what was necessary had been accomplished, and accomplished rightly. Besides this there was in that expression a reproach and a warning to the living. This warning seemed to Peter Ivanovich out of place, or at least not applicable to him. He felt a certain discomfort and so he hurriedly crossed himself once more and turned and went out of the door—too hurriedly and too regardless of propriety, as he himself was aware.

Schwartz was waiting for him in the adjoining room with legs spread wide apart and both hands toying with his top-hat behind his back. The mere sight of that playful, well-groomed, and elegant figure

得·伊凡内奇却觉得没有什么事需要提醒他,至少没有事跟他有关系。他心里有点不快,就又匆匆画了个十字——他自己也觉得这个十字画得太快,未免有点失礼——转身往门口走去。施瓦尔茨宽宽地叉开两腿站在穿堂里等他,双手在背后玩弄着大礼帽。彼得·伊凡内奇瞧了瞧服饰整洁雅致、模样顽皮可笑的施瓦尔茨,顿时精神振作起来。他知道施瓦尔茨性格开朗,不会受这里哀伤气氛的影响。他那副神气仿佛表示,伊凡·伊里奇的丧事绝没有理由破坏他们的例会,也就是说不能妨碍他们今天晚上就拆开一副新牌,在仆人点亮的四支新蜡烛照耀下打牌。总之,这次丧事不能影响他们今晚快乐的聚会。他就把这个想法低声告诉从旁边走过的彼得·伊凡内奇,并建议今晚到费多尔·瓦西里耶维奇家打牌。不过彼得·伊凡内奇今天显然没有打牌的运气。普拉斯柯菲雅·费多罗夫娜同几位太太从内室出来了。她个儿矮胖,尽管她千方百计要自己消瘦,可是肩膀以下的部分却一个劲儿向横里发展。她穿一身黑衣,头上包一块花边头巾,眉毛像站在棺材旁的那个女人一样弯得出奇。她把她们送到灵堂门口,说:

"马上要做丧事礼拜了,你们请进。"

施瓦尔茨微微点头站住,显然犹豫不决,是不是接受这个邀请。普拉斯柯菲雅·费多罗夫娜认出彼得·伊凡内奇,叹了一口气,走到他紧跟前,握住他的手说:

"我知道您是伊凡·伊里奇的知心朋友……"她说到这里时对他瞧瞧,等待他听了这话后做出相应的反应。

彼得·伊凡内奇知道,既然刚才应该画十字,那么这会儿就得握手,叹气,说一句:"真是想不到!"他就这样做了。做了以后,他发觉达到了预期的效果,他感动了,她也感动了。

"现在那边还没有开始,您来一下,我有话要跟您说,"孀妇说,"您扶着我。"

彼得·伊凡内奇伸出手臂挽住她,他们向内室走去。经过施瓦尔茨身边时,施瓦尔茨失望地向彼得·伊尼内奇使了个眼色。"唉,牌打不成了!要是我们另外找到搭档,您可别怪我们。要是您能脱身,5人一起玩也行。"他那淘气的目光仿佛在这么说。

彼得·伊尼内奇更深沉更悲伤地叹了口气,普拉斯柯菲雅·费多罗夫娜便感激地捏了捏他的手臂。

refreshed Peter Ivanovich. He felt that Schwartz was above all these happenings and would not surrender to any depressing influences. His very look said that this incident of a church service for Ivan Ilych could not be a sufficient reason for infringing the order of the session--in other words, that it would certainly not prevent his unwrapping a new pack of cards and shuffling them that evening while a footman placed four fresh candles on the table; in fact, that there was no reason for supposing that this incident would hinder their spending the evening agreeably. Indeed he said this in a whisper as Peter Ivanovich passed him, proposing that they should meet for a game at Fedor Vasilievich's. But apparently Peter Ivanovich was not destined to play bridge that evening. Praskovya Fedorovna(a short, fat woman who despite all efforts to the contrary had continued to broaden steadily from her shoulders downwards and who had the same extraordinarily arched eyebrows as the lady who had been standing by the coffin), dressed all in black, her head covered with lace, came out of her own room with some other ladies, conducted them to the room where the dead body lay, and said: "The service will begin immediately. Please go in."

Schwartz, making an indefinite bow, stood still, evidently neither accepting nor declining this invitation. Praskovya Fedorovna recognizing Peter Ivanovich, sighed, went close up to him, took his hand, and said: "I know you were a true friend to Ivan Ilych..." and looked at him awaiting some suitable response. And Peter Ivanovich knew that, just as it had been the right thing to cross himself in that room, so what he had to do here was to press her hand, sigh, and say, "Believe me...." So he did all this and as he did it felt that the desired result had been achieved: that both he and she were touched.

"Come with me. I want to speak to you before it begins," said the widow. "Give me your arm."

Peter Ivanovich gave her his arm and they went to the inner rooms, passing Schwartz who winked at Peter Ivanovich compassionately.

"That does for our bridge! Don't object if we find another player. Perhaps you can cut in when you do escape," said his playful look.

Peter Ivanovich sighed still more deeply and despondently, and Praskovya Fedorovna pressed his arm gratefully. When they reached the drawing-room, upholstered in pink cretonne and lighted by a dim lamp, they sat down at the table—she on a sofa and Peter Ivanovich on a low pouffe, the springs of which yielded spasmodically under his weight. Praskovya Fedorovna had been on the point of warning him to take another seat, but felt that such a warning was out of keeping with her present condition and so changed her mind. As he sat down on the pouffe Peter Ivanovich recalled how Ivan Ilych had arranged this room and had consulted him regarding this pink cretonne with green leaves. The whole room was full of furniture and knick-knacks, and on her way to the sofa the lace of the widow's black shawl caught on the carved edge of

他们走进灯光暗淡、挂着玫瑰红花布窗帘的客厅，在桌旁坐下来。她坐在沙发上，彼得·伊凡内奇坐在弹簧损坏、凳面凹陷的矮沙发凳上。普拉斯柯菲雅·费多罗夫娜想叫他换一把椅子坐，可是觉得此刻说这话不得体，就作罢了。彼得·伊尼内奇坐到沙发凳上时，想起伊凡·伊里奇当年装饰这客厅时曾同他商量过，最后决定用这带绿叶的玫瑰红花布做窗帘和沙发套。客厅里摆满家具杂物，孀妇走过时，她那件黑斗篷的黑花边在雕花桌上挂住了。彼得·伊凡为奇欠起身想帮她解开斗篷，沙发凳一摆脱负担，里面的弹簧立刻蹦起来，往他身上弹。孀妇自己解开斗篷，彼得·伊尼内奇又坐下来，把跳动的弹簧重新压下去。但孀妇没有把斗篷完全解开，彼得·伊尼内奇又欠起身，弹簧又往上蹦，还噔地响了一声。等这一切都过去了，她拿出一块洁净的麻纱手绢，哭起来。斗篷钩住和沙发凳的弹簧蹦跳这些插曲使彼得·伊凡内奇冷静下来，他皱紧眉头坐着。这当儿，伊凡·尹里奇的男仆索科洛夫走进来，把这种尴尬局面打破了。他报告普拉斯柯菲雅·费多罗夫娜，她指定的那块坟地要价 200 卢布。普拉斯柯雅难·费多罗夫娜止住哭，可怜巴巴地瞟了一眼彼得·伊尼内奇，用法语说她的日子很难过。彼得·伊尼内奇默默地做了个手势，表示他深信她说的是实话。

"您请抽烟。"她用宽宏大量而又极其悲痛的语气说，然后同索科洛夫谈坟地的价钱。彼得·伊凡内奇一面吸烟，一面听她怎样详细询问坟地的价格，最后决定买哪一块。谈完坟地，她又吩咐索科洛夫去请唱诗班。索科洛夫走了。

"什么事都是我自己料理。"她对彼得·伊凡内奇说，把桌上的照相簿挪到一边。接着发现烟灰快掉到桌上，连忙把烟灰碟推到彼得·伊凡内奇面前，嘴里说："要是说我悲伤得不能做事，那未免有点做作。相反，现在只有为他的后事多操点儿心，我才感到安慰……至少可以排遣点儿悲伤。"她掏出手绢又要哭，但突然勉强忍住，打起精神，镇静地说：

"我有点儿事要跟您谈谈。"

彼得·伊凡内奇点点头，不让他身下蠢蠢欲动的沙发弹簧再蹦起来。

"最后几天他真是难受。"

"非常难受吗？"彼得·伊凡内奇问。

"唉，太可怕了！他不停地叫嚷，不是一连几分

the table. Peter Ivanovich rose to detach it, and the springs of the pouffe, relieved of his weight, rose also and gave him a push. The widow began detaching her shawl herself, and Peter Ivanovich again sat down, suppressing the rebellious springs of the pouffe under him. But the widow had not quite freed herself and Peter Ivanovich got up again, and again the pouffe rebelled and even creaked. When this was all over she took out a clean cambric handkerchief and began to weep. The episode with the shawl and the struggle with the pouffe had cooled Peter Ivanovich's emotions and he sat there with a sullen look on his face. This awkward situation was interrupted by Sokolov, Ivan Ilych's butler, who came to report that the plot in the cemetery that Praskovya Fedorovna had chosen would cost two hundred rubles. She stopped weeping and, looking at Peter Ivanovich with the air of a victim, remarked in French that it was very hard for her. Peter Ivanovich made a silent gesture signifying his full conviction that it must indeed be so.

"Please smoke," she said in a magnanimous yet crushed voice, and turned to discuss with Sokolov the price of the plot for the grave.

Peter Ivanovich while lighting his cigarette heard her inquiring very circumstantially into the prices of different plots in the cemetery and finally decide which she would take. When that was done she gave instructions about engaging the choir. Sokolov then left the room.

"I look after everything myself," she told Peter Ivanovich, shifting the albums that lay on the table; and noticing that the table was endangered by his cigarette-ash, she immediately passed him an ashtray, saying as she did so: "I consider it an affectation to say that my grief prevents my attending to practical affairs. On the contrary, if anything can—I won't say console me, but—distract me, it is seeing to everything concerning him." She again took out her handkerchief as if preparing to cry, but suddenly, as if mastering her feeling, she shook herself and began to speak calmly. "But there is something I want to talk to you about."

Peter Ivanovich bowed, keeping control of the springs of the pouffe, which immediately began quivering under him.

"He suffered terribly the last few days."

"Did he?" said Peter Ivanovich.

"Oh, terribly! He screamed unceasingly, not for minutes but for hours. For the last three days he screamed incessantly. It was unendurable. I cannot understand how I bore it; you could hear him three rooms off Oh, what I have suffered!"

"Is it possible that he was conscious all that time?" asked Peter Ivanovich.

"Yes," she whispered. "To the last moment. He took leave of us a quarter of an hour before he died, and asked us to take Volodya away."

The thought of the sufferings of this man he had known so intimately, first as a merry little boy, then as a school-mate, and later as a grown-up colleague, suddenly struck Peter Ivanovich with horror, despite an

钟,而是一连几个钟头。三天三夜嚷个不停。实在叫人受不了。我真不懂我这是怎么熬过来的。隔着三道门都听得见他的叫声。唉,我这是怎么熬过来的哟!"

"当时他神志清醒吗?"彼得·伊凡内奇问。

"清醒,"她喃喃地说,"直到最后一分钟都清醒。他在临终前一刻跟我们告了别,还叫我们把伏洛嘉带开。"

彼得·伊凡内奇想到,他多么熟识的这个人,原先是个快乐的孩子,小学生,后来成了他的同事,最后竟受到这样的折磨。尽管他觉得自己和这个女人都有点做作,但想到这一点,心里却十分恐惧。他又看见那个前额和那个压住嘴唇的鼻子,不禁感到不寒而栗。

"三天三夜极度的痛苦,然后死去。这种情况也可能随时落到我的头上。"他想,刹那间感到毛骨悚然。但是,他自己也不知怎的,一种常有的想法很快就使他镇静下来:"这种事只有伊凡·伊里奇会碰上,我可绝不会碰上。这种事不应该也不可能落到我的头上。"他想到这些,心情忧郁,但施瓦尔茨分明向他做过暗示,他不应该有这种心情。彼得·伊凡内奇思考了一下,镇静下来,详细询问伊凡·伊里奇临终前的情况,仿佛这种事故只会发生在伊凡·伊里奇身上,可绝不会发生在他身上。

在谈了一通伊凡·伊里奇肉体上所受非人痛苦的情况以后(这种痛苦,彼得·伊凡内奇是从普拉斯柯菲雅·费多罗夫娜神经所受的影响上领会的),孀妇显然认为该转到正题上了。

"唉,彼得·伊凡内奇,真是难受,真是太难受了,太难受了。"她又哭起来。

彼得·伊凡内奇叹着气,等她擦去鼻涕眼泪,才说:"真是想不到……"

接着她又说起来,说到了显然是她找他来的主要问题。她问他丈夫去世后怎样向政府申请抚恤金。她装着向彼得·伊凡内奇请教,怎样领取赡养费,不过他看出,因丈夫去世她可以向政府弄到多少钱,这事她已了解得清清楚楚,比他知道得还清楚。她不过是想知道,可不可以用什么办法弄到更多的钱。彼得·伊凡内奇竭力思索,想到几种办法,但最后只是出于礼节骂了一通政府的吝啬,说不可能弄到更多的钱了。于是她叹了一口气,显然要摆脱这位来客。他

unpleasant consciousness of his own and the woman's dissimulation. He again saw that brow, and that nose pressing down on the lip, and felt afraid for himself.

"Three days of frightful suffering and then death! Why, that might suddenly, at any time, happen to me," he thought, and for a moment felt terrified. But—he did not himself know how—the customary reflection at once occurred to him that this had happened to Ivan Ilych and not to him, and that it should not and could not happen to him, and that to think that it could would be yielding to depression which he ought not to do, as Schwartz's expression plainly showed. After which reflection Peter Ivanovich felt reassured, and began to ask with interest about the details of Ivan Ilych's death, as though death was an accident natural to Ivan Ilych but certainly not to himself.

After many details of the really dreadful physical sufferings Ivan Ilych had endured (which details he learnt only from the effect those sufferings had produced on Praskovya Fedorovna's nerves) the widow apparently found it necessary to get to business.

"Oh, Peter Ivanovich, how hard it is! How terribly, terribly hard!" and she again began to weep.

Peter Ivanovich sighed and waited for her to finish blowing her nose. When she had done so he said, "Believe me...." and she again began talking and brought out what was evidently her chief concern with him—namely, to question him as to how she could obtain a grant of money from the government on the occasion of her husband's death. She made it appear that she was asking Peter Ivanovich's advice about her pension, but he soon saw that she already knew about that to the minutest detail, more even than he did himself. She knew how much could be got out of the government in consequence of her husband's death, but wanted to find out whether she could not possibly extract something more. Peter Ivanovich tried to think of some means of doing so, but after reflecting for a while and, out of propriety, condemning the government for its niggardliness, he said he thought that nothing more could be got. Then she sighed and evidently began to devise means of getting rid of her visitor. Noticing this, he put out his cigarette, rose, pressed her hand, and went out into the anteroom.

In the dining-room where the clock stood that Ivan Ilych had liked so much and had bought at an antique shop, Peter Ivanovich met a priest and a few acquaintances who had come to attend the service, and he recognized Ivan Ilych's daughter, a handsome young woman. She was in black and her slim figure appeared slimmer than ever. She had a gloomy, determined, almost angry expression, and bowed to Peter Ivanovich as though he were in some way to blame. Behind her, with the same offended look, stood a wealthy young man, an examining magistrate, whom Peter Ivanovich also knew and who was her fiancé, as he had heard. He bowed mournfully to them and was about to pass into the death-chamber, when from under the stairs appeared the figure of Ivan Ilych's schoolboy son, who

理会了,就按灭香烟,站起身,同嫠妇握了握手,走到前厅。

餐厅里摆着伊凡·伊里奇十分得意地从旧货店买来的大钟。彼得·伊凡内奇在那里遇见神父和几个来参加丧事礼拜的客人,还看见一位熟识的美丽小姐,就是伊凡·伊里奇的女儿。她穿一身黑衣,腰身本来很苗条,如今似乎变得更苗条了。她的神态忧郁,冷淡,甚至还有点愤慨。她向彼得·伊凡内奇鞠躬,但那副神气显出仿佛他有什么过错似的。女儿后面站着一个同样面带愠色的青年。彼得·伊凡内奇认识他是法院侦讯官,家里很有几个钱,而且听说是她的未婚夫。彼得·伊凡内奇沮丧地向他们点点头,正要往死人房间走去,这时楼梯下出现了伊凡·伊里奇在中学念书的儿子。这孩子活脱就是年轻时的伊凡·伊里奇。彼得·伊凡内奇记得伊凡·伊里奇在法学院念书时就是这个模样。这孩子眼睛里含着泪水,神态也颇像那些十三四岁的愣小子。他一看见彼得·伊凡内奇,就忧郁而害臊地皱起眉头。彼得·伊凡内奇向他点点头,走进灵堂。丧事礼拜开始了,又是蜡烛,又是呻吟,又是神香,又是眼泪,又是啜泣。彼得·伊凡内奇皱紧眉头站着,眼睛瞅着自己的双脚。他一眼也不看死人,直到礼拜结束他的心情都没有受悲伤气氛的影响,并且第一个走出灵堂。前厅里一个人也没有。充任餐厅传仆的庄稼汉盖拉西姆从灵堂奔出来,用他那双强壮的手臂努力在一排外套中间翻寻着,终于把彼得·伊凡内奇的外套找出来,递给他。

"嗯,盖拉西姆老弟,你说呢?"彼得·伊凡内奇想说句话应酬一下,"可怜不可怜哪?"

"这是上帝的意思!我们都要到那里去的。"盖拉西姆露出一排洁白整齐的庄稼汉的牙齿说,接着就像在紧张地干活那样猛地推开门,大声呼喊马车夫,把彼得·伊凡内奇送上车,又奔回台阶上,仿佛在考虑还有些什么事要做。

在闻过神香、尸体和石碳酸的臭味以后,彼得·伊凡内奇特别爽快地吸了一大口新鲜空气。

"上哪儿,老爷?"马车夫问。

"不晚。还可以到费多尔·瓦西里耶维奇家去一下。"

彼得·伊凡内奇就去了。果然,他到的时候,第一局牌刚结束,因此他就顺当地成了第五名赌客。

was extremely like his father. He seemed a little Ivan Ilych, such as Peter Ivanovich remembered when they studied law together. His tear-stained eyes had in them the look that is seen in the eyes of boys of thirteen or fourteen who are not pure-minded. When he saw Peter Ivanovich he scowled morosely and shamefacedly. Peter Ivanovich nodded to him and entered the death-chamber. The service began: candles, groans, incense, tears, and sobs. Peter Ivanovich stood looking gloomily down at his feet. He did not look once at the dead man, did not yield to any depressing influence, and was one of the first to leave the room. There was no one in the anteroom, but Gerasim darted out of the dead man's room, rummaged with his strong hands among the fur coats to find Peter Ivanovich's and helped him on with it.

"Well, friend Gerasim," said Peter Ivanovich, so as to say something. "It's a sad affair, isn't it?"

"It's God's will. We shall all come to it some day," said Gerasim, displaying his teeth—the even, white teeth of a healthy peasant—and, like a man in the thick of urgent work, he briskly opened the front door, called the coachman, helped Peter Ivanovich into the sledge, and sprang back to the porch as if in readiness for what he had to do next.

Peter Ivanovich found the fresh air particularly pleasant after the smell of incense, the dead body, and carbolic acid.

"Where to, sir?" asked the coachman.

"It's not too late even now. . . . I'll call round on Fedor Vasilievich."

He accordingly drove there and found them just finishing the first rubber, so that it was quite convenient for him to cut in.

II

Ivan Ilych's life had been most simple and most ordinary and therefore most terrible.

He had been a member of the Court of Justice, and died at the age of forty-five. His father had been an official who after serving in various ministries and departments in Petersburg had made the sort of career which brings men to positions from which by reason of their long service they cannot be dismissed, though they are obviously unfit to hold any responsible position, and for whom therefore posts are specially created, which though fictitious carry salaries of from six to ten thousand rubles that are not fictitious, and in receipt of which they live on to a great age.

Such was the Privy Councillor and superfluous member of various superfluous institutions, Ilya Epimovich Golovin.

He had three sons, of whom Ivan Ilych was the second. The eldest son was following in his father's footsteps only in another department, and was already approaching that stage in the service at which a similar sinecure would be reached. The third son was a

二

伊凡·伊里奇的身世极其普通,极其简单,而又极其可怕。

伊凡·伊里奇是个法官,去世时才 45 岁。他父亲是彼得堡一名官员,曾在好几个政府机关供职,虽不能胜任某些要职,但凭着他的资格和身份,从没被逐出官场,因此总能弄到一些有名无实的官职和 6000 到 10000 卢布的有名有实的年俸,并一直享受到晚年。

伊里亚·叶斐莫维奇·高洛文就是这样一个多余机关里的多余的三级文官。

他有 3 个儿子。伊凡·伊里奇排行第二。老大像他父亲一样官运亨通,不过在另一个机关,也快到领干薪的年龄。老三没有出息。他在几个地方都败坏了名声,眼下在铁路上供职。父亲也好,两位哥哥也好,特别是两位嫂子,不仅不愿同他见面,而且非万不得已从不想到有他这样一个兄弟。姐姐嫁给了格列夫男爵,他同他岳父一样是彼得堡的官员。伊凡·伊里奇是所谓家里的佼佼者①。他不像老大那样冷淡古板,也不像老三那样放荡不羁。他介于他们之间,聪明,活泼,乐观,文雅。他跟弟弟一起在法学院念过书。老三没有毕业,念到五年级就被学校开除了,伊凡·伊里奇则毕了业,而且成绩优良。他在法学院里就显示了后来终身具备的特点,能干,乐观,厚道,随和,但又能严格履行自认为应尽的责任,而他心目中的责任就是达官贵人所公认的职责。他从小不会巴结拍马,成年后还是不善于阿谀奉承,但从青年时代起就像飞蛾扑火那样追随上层人士,模仿他们的一举一动,接受他们的人生观,并同他们交朋友。童年时代和少年时代的热情在他身上消失得干干净净。他开始迷恋声色,追逐功名,最后发展到自由放纵的地步。不过,他的本性还能使他保持一定分寸,不至于过分逾越常规。

在法学院里,他认为自己的有些行为很卑劣,因此很嫌恶自己。但后来看到地位比他高的人都在那样干,而且并不认为卑劣,他也就不以为意,不再把它

———————
① 原文是法语。

failure. He had ruined his prospects in a number of positions and was now serving in the railway department. His father and brothers, and still more their wives, not merely disliked meeting him, but avoided remembering his existence unless compelled to do so. His sister had married Baron Greff, a Petersburg official of her father's type. Ivan Ilych was *le phénix de la famille* as people said. He was neither as cold and formal as his elder brother nor as wild as the younger, but was a happy mean between them—an intelligent, polished, lively and agreeable man. He had studied with his younger brother at the School of Law, but the latter had failed to complete the course and was expelled when he was in the fifth class. Ivan Ilych finished the course well. Even when he was at the School of Law he was just what he remained for the rest of his life: a capable, cheerful, goodnatured, and sociable man, though strict in the fulfilment of what he considered to be his duty: and he considered his duty to be what was so considered by those in authority. Neither as a boy nor as a man was he a toady, but from early youth was by nature attracted to people of high station as a fly is drawn to the light, assimilating their ways and views of life and establishing friendly relations with them. All the enthusiasms of childhood and youth passed without leaving much trace on him; he succumbed to sensuality, to vanity, and latterly among the highest classes to liberalism, but always within limits which his instinct unfailingly indicated to him as correct.

At school he had done things which had formerly seemed to him very horrid and made him feel disgusted with himself when he did them; but when later on he saw that such actions were done by people of good position and that they did not regard them as wrong, he was able not exactly to regard them as right, but to forget about them entirely or not be at all troubled at remembering them.

Having graduated from the School of Law and qualified for the tenth rank of the civil service, and having received money from his father for his equipment, Ivan Ilych ordered himself clothes at Scharmer's, the fashionable tailor, hung a medallion inscribed *respice finem* on his watch-chain, took leave of his professor and the prince who was patron of the school, had a farewell dinner with his comrades at Donon's firs-class restaurant, and with his new and fashionable portmanteu, linen, clothes, shaving and other toilet appliances, and a travelling rug, all purchased at the best shops, he set off for one of the provinces, where, through his father's influence, he had been attached to the Governor as an official for special service.

In the province Ivan Ilych soon arranged as easy and agreeable a position for himself as he had had at the School of Law. He performed his official tasks, made his career, and at the same time amused himself pleasantly and decorously. Occasionally he paid official visits to country districts, where he behaved with dignity both to his superiors and inferiors, and performed

们放在心上，即使想到也无动于衷。

伊凡·伊里奇在法学院毕业，获得十等文官官衔，从父亲手里领到治装费，在著名的沙尔玛裁缝铺里定制了服装，表坠上挂一块"高瞻远瞩"①的纪念章，向导师和任校董的亲王辞了行，跟同学们在唐农大饭店欢宴话别，带着从最高级商店买来的时式手提箱、衬衣、西服、剃刀、梳妆用品和旅行毛毯，走马上任，当了省长特派员。这个官职是他父亲替他谋得的。

伊凡·伊里奇到了外省，很快就像在法学院那样过得称心如意。他奉公守法，兢兢业业，生活得欢快而又不失体统。他有时奉命到各县视察，待人接物，稳重得体，对上对下恰如其分，不贪赃枉法，而且总能圆满完成上司交下的差事，主要是处理好分裂派教徒事件。

他虽然年轻放荡，但处理公务却异常审慎，甚至可以说是铁面无私。在社交场中，他活泼风趣而又和蔼有礼，正像他的上司和上司太太——他是他们家的常客——称赞他的那样，是个好小子。

他同省里一位死缠住他这个风流法学家的太太有暧昧关系，还同一个女裁缝私通；有时同巡察的副官们狂饮欢宴，饭后还去花街柳巷寻欢作乐。他奉承上级长官，甚至长官夫人，但手法高明，无懈可击，从未引起非议，人家至多说一句法国谚语——年轻时放荡在所难免。这一切他都干得体体面面，嘴里说的又是法国话，主要则是因为他跻身最上层，容易博得达官显贵的青睐。

伊凡·伊里奇就这样干了5年。接着他的工作调动了，因为成立了新的司法机关，需要新的官员。

于是伊凡·伊里奇就调任这样的新职。

伊凡·伊里奇被推荐任法院侦讯官的职务，他接受了，虽然这位置在另一个省里，他得放弃原有的各种关系，另起炉灶，重新结交新朋友。朋友们给伊凡·伊里奇饯行，同他一起摄影，还赠给他一个银烟盒留念。他就走马上任去了。

伊凡·伊里奇当法院侦讯官同样循规蹈矩，公私分明，并且像做特派员一样受到普遍尊敬。对伊凡·伊里奇来说，侦讯官的工作比原来的工作有趣得多，迷人得多。以前他感到扬扬得意的是，身穿精工缝制

---

① 原文是拉丁语。

the duties entrusted to him, which related chiefly to the sectarians, with exactness and incorruptible honesty of which he could not but feel proud.

In official matters, despite his youth and taste for frivolous gaiety, he was exceedingly reserved, punctilious, and even severe; but in society he was often amusing and witty, and always good-natured, correct in his manner, and *bon enfant*, as the governor and his wife—with whom he was like one of the family—used to say of him.

In the province he had an affair with a lady who made advances to the elegant young lawyer, and there was also a milliner; and there were carousals with aides-de-camp who visited the district, and after-supper visits to a certain outlying street of doubtful reputation; and there was too some obsequiousness to his chief and even to his chief's wife, but all this was done with such a tone of good breeding that no hard names could be applied to it. It all came under the heading of the French saying: '*Il faut que jeunesse se passe*.'①It was all done with clean hands, in clean linen, with French phrases, and above all among people of the best society and consequently with the approval of people of rank.

So Ivan Ilych served for five years and then came a change in his official life. The new and reformed judicial institutions were introduced, and new men were needed. Ivan Ilych became such a new man. He was offered the post of Examining Magistrate, and he accepted it though the post was in another province and obliged him to give up the connexions he had formed and to make new ones. His friends met to give him a send-off; they had a group-photograph taken and presented him with a silver cigarette-case, and he set off to his new post.

As examining magistrate Ivan Ilych was just as *comme il faut* and decorous a man, inspiring general respect and capable of separating his official duties from his private life, as he had been when acting as an official on special service. His duties now as examining magistrate were far more interesting and attractive than before. In his former position it had been pleasant to wear an undress uniform made by Scharmer, and to pass through the crowd of petitioners and officials who were timorously awaiting an audience with the governor, and who envied him as with free and easy gait he went straight into his chief's private room to have a cup of tea and a cigarette with him. But not many people had then been directly dependent on him—only police officials and the sectarians when he went on special missions—and he liked to treat them politely, almost as comrades, as if he were letting them feel that he who had the power to crush them was treating them in this simple, friendly way. There were then but few such people. But now, as an examining magistrate, Ivan Ilych felt that everyone without exception, even the most important and self-satisfied,

---

① Youth must have its fling.

的文官制服,昂首阔步地经过战战兢兢等待接见的来访者和对他羡慕不止的官员们的面前,一直走进长官办公室,并且跟长官一起喝茶吸烟。但那时直接听命于他的人只有县警察局长和分裂派教徒,而且要在他奉命出差的时候。他对待他们总是客客气气,使他们感到,他尽管操着生杀大权,却平易近人,毫无架子。那个时候,这样直接听命于他的人不多。如今伊凡·伊里奇当上法院侦讯官,他懂得就连达官贵人的命运也都操在他手里,他只要在公文上批几句,不论哪个要人都将成为被告或证人来到他面前,并且得站着回答他的问题,如果他不请他坐下的话。伊凡·伊里奇从不滥用权力,相反总是不露锋芒,而这种权力意识和适当用权的技术,就成了他担任新职后最感兴趣的事。从事这项新职,也就是说审查工作,伊凡·伊里奇很快就掌握一种本领,能排除一切与本案无关的情节,使各种错综复杂的案情在公文上表现得简单明了,不带丝毫个人意见,完全符合公文要求。这是一项新的工作,而伊凡·伊里奇则属于第一批执行 1864 年新法典的人。

自从在新地方就任法院侦讯官以来,伊凡·伊里奇结交了一批新朋友,建立了一些新关系,获得了新的社会地位,并多少采取了新作风。他在省里同政府保持一定距离,却周旋于司法界头面人物和豪门巨富之间,对当局稍表不满,发表温和的自由主义言论和开明观点。此外,伊凡·伊里奇就任新职后仍旧讲究服饰,注意仪表,只是不再刮去下巴颏儿上的胡子而听其自然生长。

伊凡·伊里奇在新地方过得很愉快。他跟一批反对省长的人关系很好,薪俸比以前优厚,他逢场作戏,打打纸牌,以增添乐趣。他头脑聪敏,很会打牌,因此常常赢钱。

伊凡·伊里奇在新地方任职两年后遇见了后来成为他妻子的普拉斯柯菲雅·费多罗夫娜·米海尔。她是伊凡·伊里奇出入的圈子里最迷人最伶俐最出色的姑娘。伊凡·伊里奇在公余之暇,找点儿消遣,其中包括同普拉斯柯菲雅·费多罗夫娜戏谑调情。

伊凡·伊里奇任特派员时常常跳舞,但当上侦讯官后就难得跳了。如今他跳舞只是为了要显示,尽管他身为侦讯官和五等文官,跳舞水平可决不比别人差。这样,有时晚会将近结束,他就请普拉斯柯菲雅·费多罗夫娜一起跳舞,主要借这种机会征服普拉

was in his power, and that he need only write a few words on a sheet of paper with a certain heading, and this or that important, self-satisfied person would be brought before him in the role of an accused person or a witness, and if he did not choose to allow him to sit down, would have to stand before him and answer his questions. Ivan Ilych never abused his power; he tried on the contrary to soften its expression, but the consciousness of it and of the possibility of softening its effect, supplied the chief interest and attraction of his office. In his work itself, especially in his examinations, he very soon acquired a method of eliminating all considerations irrelevant to the legal aspect of the case, and reducing even the most complicated case to a form in which it would be presented on paper only in its externals, completely excluding his personal opinion of the matter, while above all observing every prescribed formality. The work was new and Ivan Ilych was one of the first men to apply the new Code of 1864. ①

On taking up the post of examining magistrate in a new town, he made new acquaintances and connexions, placed himself on a new footing, and assumed a somewhat different tone. He took up an attitude of rather dignified aloofness towards the provincial authorities, but picked out the best circle of legal gentlemen and wealthy gentry living in the town and assumed a tone of slight dissatisfaction with the government, of moderate liberalism, and of enlightened citizenship. At the same time, without at all altering the elegance of his toilet, he ceased shaving his chin and allowed his beard to grow as it pleased.

Ivan Ilych settled down very pleasantly in this new town. The society there, which inclined towards opposition to the Governor, was friendly, his salary was larger, and he began to play *vint* [a form of bridge], which he found added not a little to the pleasure of life, for he had a capacity for cards, played good-humouredly, and calculated rapidly and astutely, so that he usually won.

After living there for two years he met his future wife, Praskovya Fedorovna, and as relaxations from his labours as examining magistrate, Ivan Ilych established light and playful relations with her.

While he had been an official on special service he had been accustomed to dance, but now as an examining magistrate it was exceptional for him to do so. If he danced now, he did it as if to show that though he served under the reformed order of things, and had reached the fifth official rank, yet when it came to dancing he could do it better than most people. So at the end of an evening he sometimes danced with Praskovya Fedorovna, and it was chiefly during these dances that he captivated her. She fell in love with him. Ivan Ilych had at first no definite intention of marrying, but when the girl fell in love with him he

---

① After the emancipation of the serfs in 1861, judicial proceedings were reformed.

斯柯菲雅·费多罗夫娜的心。她爱上了他。伊凡·伊里奇并没有明确想到要结婚，但既然人家姑娘真的爱上了他，他就问自己："是啊，那么何不就结婚呢？"

普拉斯柯菲雅·费多罗夫娜出身望族，长得不算难看，而且有家产。伊凡·伊里奇可以指望找到一个更出色的配偶，但这个配偶也算不错。伊凡·伊里奇自己有薪俸收入，他希望她也有同样多的进项。她出身名门，生得又温柔美丽，很有教养。说伊凡·伊里奇同她结婚，是因为爱上这位小姐，并且发现她的人生观同他一致，那不符合事实。说他结婚，是因为在他的圈子里大家都赞成这门婚事，那同样不符合事实。伊凡·伊里奇结婚是出于双重考虑：娶这样一位妻子是幸福的，而达官贵人们又都赞成这门亲事。

伊凡·伊里奇就这样结了婚。

在准备结婚和婚后初期，夫妻恩爱，妻子尚未怀孕，再加上崭新的家具，崭新的餐具，崭新的衣服，日子过得很美满。伊凡·伊里奇认为他原来的生活轻松愉快而又高尚体面，并且受到上流社会的赞许，如今结婚不仅不会损害这种生活，而且使它更加美满。但在妻子怀孕几个月后，出现了一种痛苦难堪而有失体统的新局面，那是他万万没有料到的，而且怎么也无法摆脱。

伊凡·伊里奇认为妻子完全出于任性破坏快乐体面的生活，莫名其妙地动辄猜疑，要求他更加体贴她。不论什么事她都横加挑剔，动不动就对他大吵大闹。

起初伊凡·伊里奇想继续用快乐体面的人生态度来排除烦恼。他不管妻子的情绪，照旧高高兴兴地过日子，请朋友到家里来打牌，自己上俱乐部或者到朋友家串门子。可是，有一次妻子气势汹汹地对他破口大骂。这以后只要他稍不顺她的意，她就把他臭骂一顿，显然非要把他制服不可，也就是说，要他安守在家里，并且像她一样唉声叹气，无病呻吟。这使伊凡·伊里奇感到心惊胆战。他懂得了，夫妇生活，至少是他同妻子的生活，并不能始终维持快乐体面，相反，常常会损害这样的气氛，因此必须设法防范。伊凡·伊里奇借口公务繁忙来对付普拉斯柯菲雅·费多罗夫娜。他发现这种办法很有效，因此常用它来保卫自己的独立天地。

孩子生下后，喂养很费事，常常发生这样那样的麻烦，不是婴儿害病就是做母亲的害病，有时是真病

said to himself: "Really, why shouldn't I marry?"

Praskovya Fedorovna came of a good family, was not bad looking, and had some little property. Ivan Ilych might have aspired to a more brilliant match, but even this was good. He had his salary, and she, he hoped, would have an equal income. She was well connected, and was a sweet, pretty, and thoroughly correct young woman. To say that Ivan Ilych married because he fell in love with Praskovya Fedorovna and found that she sympathized with his views of life would be as incorrect as to say that he married because his social circle approved of the match. He was swayed by both these considerations: the marriage gave him personal satisfaction, and at the same time it was considered the right thing by the most highly placed of his associates.

So Ivan Ilych got married.

The preparations for marriage and the beginning of married life, with its conjugal caresses, the new furniture, new crockery, and new linen, were very pleasant until his wife became pregnant—so that Ivan Ilych had begun to think that marriage would not impair the easy, agreeable, gay and always decorous character of his life, approved of by society and regarded by himself as natural, but would even improve it. But from the first months of his wife's pregnancy, something new, unpleasant, depressing, and unseemly, and from which there was no way of escape, unexpectedly showed itself.

His wife, without any reason—de gaieté de coeur as Ivan Ilych expressed it to himself—began to disturb the pleasure and propriety of their life. She began to be jealous without any cause, expected him to devote his whole attention to her, found fault with everything, and made coarse and ill-mannered scenes.

At first Ivan Ilych hoped to escape from the unpleasantness of this state of affairs by the same easy and decorous relation to life that had served him heretofore: he tried to ignore his wife's disagreeable moods, continued to live in his usual easy and pleasant way, invited friends to his house for a game of cards, and also tried going out to his club or spending his evenings with friends. But one day his wife began upbraiding him so vigorously, using such coarse words, and continued to abuse him every time he did not fulfill her demands, so resolutely and with such evident determination not to give way till he submitted—that is, till he stayed at home and was bored just as she was—that he became alarmed. He now realized that matrimony—at any rate with Praskovya Fedorovna—was not always conducive to the pleasures and amenities of life but on the contrary often infringed both comfort and propriety, and that he must therefore entrench himself against such infringement. And Ivan Ilych began to seek for means of doing so. His official duties were the one thing that imposed upon Praskovya Fedorovna, and by means of his official work and the duties attached to it he began struggling with his wife to secure his own independence.

With the birth of their child, the attempts to feed it and the various failures in doing so, and with the

有时是假病。不管怎样,伊凡·伊里奇都得照顾,尽管他对这些事一窍不通。而伊凡·伊里奇保卫自己独立天地、不受家庭干扰的欲望却越来越强烈。

妻子的脾气越来越暴躁,要求越来越苛刻,伊凡·伊里奇也越来越把生活的重心转移到公务上。他更加喜爱官职,醉心功名。

不久,在结婚一年后,伊凡·伊里奇懂得了,夫妇生活虽然也有一些好处,但却是一种很复杂很痛苦的事,而要尽到自己的责任,过一种受社会赞许的体面生活,必须像做官一样建立适当的关系。

伊凡·伊里奇就给自己建立了这样的夫妇关系。他对家庭生活的要求,只是能吃到家常便饭,生活上有照料和过床第生活,而这些都是她能向他提供的。他主要的要求是维持社会所公认的体面的夫妇关系。此外,他就自寻欢乐,获得欢乐也就心满意足。要是家里遇到不愉快,他就立刻逃到公务活动的独立天地里去,并在那里自得其乐。

伊凡·伊里奇当侦讯官,声誉显赫,3年后就升任副检察官。新的官职、重要的地位、控诉和拘捕任何人的权力、当众的演说、辉煌的功绩——这一切使伊凡·伊里奇更加官迷心窍。

孩子一个个生下来。妻子变得越来越乖戾,越来越易怒,但伊凡·伊里奇所确立的家庭关系,几乎不受妻子脾气的影响。

伊凡·伊里奇在这个城市里任职7年,接着被调到另一个省里当检察官。他们搬了家,手头的钱不多,妻子又不喜欢那新地方。薪俸尽管比原来多,但生活水平高,再说又死了两个孩子,因此伊凡·伊里奇就感到家庭生活比以前更乏味了。

普拉斯柯菲雅·费多罗夫娜搬到新地方后,不论遇到什么麻烦,总要责怪丈夫。夫妇间不论谈什么事,尤其是谈教育孩子问题。总会联想到以前的不和,引起新的争吵。夫妇俩如今难得有恩爱的时刻,即使有,也是很短暂的。他们在爱情的小岛上临时停泊一下,不久又会掉进互相敌视的汪洋大海,彼此冷若冰霜。要是伊凡·伊里奇认为家庭生活不该如此,他准会对这种冷漠感到伤心,不过他不仅认为这样的局面是正常的,而且正是他所企求的。他的目标就是要尽量摆脱家庭生活的烦恼,而表面上又要装得若无其事,保持体面。为了达到这一目的,他尽量少同家人待在一起,如果不得已必须这样做,也总是竭力找

real and imaginary illnesses of mother and child, in which Ivan Ilych's sympathy was demanded but about which he understood nothing, the need of securing for himself an existence outside his family life became still more imperative.

As his wife grew more irritable and exacting and Ivan Ilych transferred the centre of gravity of his life more and more to his official work, so did he grow to like his work better and became more ambitious than before.

Very soon, within a year of his wedding, Ivan Ilych had realized that marriage, though it may add some comforts to life, is in fact a very intricate and difficult affair towards which in order to perform one's duty, that is, to lead a decorous life approved of by society, one must adopt a definite attitude just as towards one's official duties.

And Ivan Ilych evolved such an attitude toward married life. He only required of it those conveniences—dinner at home, housewife, and bed—which it could give him, and above all that propriety of external forms required by public opinion. For the rest he looked for lighthearted pleasure and propriety, and was very thankful when he found them, but if he met with antagonism and querulousness he at once retired into his separate fenced-off world of official duties, where he found satisfaction.

Ivan Ilych was esteemed a good official, and after three years was made Assistant Public Prosecutor. His new duties, their importance, the possibility of indicting and imprisoning anyone he chose, the publicity his speeches received, and the success he had in all these things, made his work still more attractive.

More children came. His wife became more and more querulous and ill-tempered, but the attitude Ivan Ilych had adopted towards his home life rendered him almost impervious to her grumbling.

After seven years' service in that town he was transferred to another province as Public Prosecutor. They moved, but were short of money and his wife did not like the place they moved to. Though the salary was higher the cost of living was greater, besides which two of their children died and family life became still more unpleasant for him.

Praskovya Fedorovna blamed her husband for every inconvenience they encountered in their new home. Most of the conversations between husband and wife, especially as to the children's education, led to topics which recalled former disputes, and those disputes were apt to flare up again at any moment. There remained only those rare periods of amorousness which still came to them at times but did not last long. These were islets at which they anchored for a while and then again set out upon that ocean of veiled hostility which showed itself in their aloofness from one another. This aloofness might have grieved Ivan Ilych had he considered that it ought not to exist, but he now regarded the position as normal, and even made it the goal at which he aimed in family life. His aim was to free himself more and more from those unpleasantnesses and to give them a semblance of

有旁人在场的机会。不过伊凡·伊里奇这样过日子，主要靠的是他有公务。他把全部生活乐趣都集中在官场的天地里。而这种乐趣支配了他的整个身心。意识到自己的权力，对任何人都操有生杀大权，每次走进法庭和遇到下属时那种威风凛凛的气派（即使只是表面的），在上司与下属之间周旋的本领，尤其是自觉高明的办事能力——这一切都使他扬扬得意，再加上跟同事们谈天、宴会和打牌，他的生活就显得很充实。总之，伊凡·伊里奇的生活过得合乎他的愿望，快乐而体面。

就这样他又过了 7 年。大女儿已经 16 岁，另外又死了一个孩子，只剩下一个男孩在中学念书。这个孩子是引起夫妇争吵的一大因素。伊凡·伊里奇要送他读法学院，而普拉斯柯菲雅·费多罗夫娜却偏把他送进普通中学。女儿在家里学习，成绩良好，儿子也学得不错。

三

伊凡·伊里奇婚后就这样过了 17 年的光阴。现在他已是一个老检察官了。他推辞了几次工作上的调动，一心想找个更称心的职务，不料出了一件不愉快的事，把他生活的安宁给破坏了。伊凡·伊里奇想谋取大学城首席法官的位置，但被戈佩捷足先得。伊凡·伊里奇十分生气，提出责问，同戈佩吵嘴，又冒犯了顶头上司，他从此受冷遇，下一次任命也没有他的份儿。

这是 1880 年，也是伊凡·伊里奇一生中最倒霉的年头。他一方面入不敷出，另一方面又被人家遗忘。他觉得人家待他极不公平，人家却认为对他已仁至义尽。就连父亲都认为无须再帮助他了。他觉得大家都把他抛弃了，并认为他有 3500 卢布年奉已很不错，甚至可说是十分幸福了。人家待他这么不公平，妻子经常责骂他，家里入不敷出，开始负债。这种情况当然谈不上正常，而且只有他一个人知道。

今年夏天，伊凡·伊里奇为了节省开支，司妻子一起到内弟乡下度假。

在乡下不做事，伊凡·伊里奇第一次不仅感到无聊，而且觉得十分愁闷。他认定无法这样生活，必须采取断然措施。

harmlessness and propriety. He attained this by spending less and less time with his family, and when obliged to be at home he tried to safeguard his position by the presence of outsiders. The chief thing however was that he had his official duties. The whole interest of his life now centred in the official world and that interest absorbed him. The consciousness of his power, being able to ruin anybody he wished to ruin, the importance, even the external dignity of his entry into court, or meetings with his subordinates, his success with superiors and inferiors, and above all his masterly handling of cases, of which he was conscious—all this gave him pleasure and filled his life, together with chats with his colleagues, dinners, and bridge. So that on the whole Ivan Ilych's life continued to flow as he considered it should do—pleasantly and properly.

So things continued for another seven years. His eldest daughter was already sixteen, another child had died, and only one son was left, a schoolboy and a subject of dissension. Ivan Ilych wanted to put him in the School of Law, but to spite him Praskovya Fedorovna entered him at the High School. The daughter had been educated at home and had turned out well: the boy did not learn badly either.

III

So Ivan Ilych lived for seventeen years after his marriage. He was already a Public Prosecutor of long standing, and had declined several proposed transfers while awaiting a more desirable post, when an unanticipated and unpleasant occurrence quite upset the peaceful course of his life. He was expecting to be offered the post of presiding judge in a University town, but Happe somehow came to the front and obtained the appointment instead. Ivan Ilych became irritable, reproached Happe, and quarrelled both with him and with his immediate superiors—who became colder to him and again passed him over when other appointments were made.

This was in 1880, the hardest year of Ivan Ilych's life. It was then that it became evident on the one hand that his salary was insufficient for them to live on, and on the other that he had been forgotten, and not only this, but that what was for him the greatest and most cruel injustice appeared to others a quite ordinary occurrence. Even his father did not consider it was his duty to help him. Ivan Ilych felt himself abandoned by everyone, and that they regarded his position with a salary of 3,500 rubles as quite normal and even fortunate. He alone knew that with the consciousness of the injustices done him, with his wife's incessant nagging, and with the debts he had contracted by living beyond his means, his position was far from normal.

In order to save money that summer he obtained leave of absence and went with his wife to live in the country at her brother's place.

In the country, without his work, he experienced

伊凡·伊里奇不能入睡，在露台上踱了个通宵，决定上彼得堡奔走一番，争取调到其他部门工作，以惩罚他们，惩罚那些不会赏识他才能的人。

第二天早晨，他不顾妻子和内弟的劝阻，乘车上彼得堡。

他唯一的目的就是弄到一个年俸 5000 卢布的位置。他不再计较是哪个机关，是哪个派别和哪种工作。他只要一个位置，年俸 5000 卢布的位置，不论政府机关、银行、铁路、玛丽皇后御用机关，甚至海关都行，但一定要有 5000 卢布收入，一定要离开那个不会赏识他才能的机关。

伊凡·伊里奇此行取得了意外的收获。在库尔斯克火车站，头等车厢里上来一个熟人，名叫伊林。伊林告诉他库尔斯克省刚接到电报，部里最近人事上有重大变动，彼得·伊凡内奇的位置将由伊凡·谢苗内奇接任。

这次调动，除了对国家有一定影响外，对伊凡·伊里奇具有特殊意义。因为起用了新人彼得·彼得罗维奇和他的朋友扎哈尔·伊凡内奇。这对他伊凡·伊里奇极其有利，因为扎哈尔·伊凡内奇是伊凡·伊里奇的同学，又是他的好朋友。

在莫斯科，这个消息得到了证实。伊凡·伊里奇来到彼得堡，找到了扎哈尔·伊凡内奇，后者答应给他在原来的司法部里谋一个好差事。

一星期后，他给妻子发了一份电报：

"扎哈尔接替米勒，我申请后即可提升。"

伊凡·伊里奇通过这次人事调动在他的旧部里获得意外任命，比同事高两级，年俸 5000 卢布，再加调差费 3500 卢布。伊凡·伊里奇消除了对原来对头和整个机关的怨气，感到十分得意。

伊凡·伊里奇回到乡下，兴高采烈。他好久没有这样快活了。普拉斯柯菲雅·费多罗夫娜也很高兴，夫妇俩变得和好了。伊凡·伊里奇讲到他在彼得堡怎样受祝贺，原来的对头怎样厚着脸皮巴结他，怎样羡慕他的地位，特别讲到他在彼得堡怎样受人尊敬。

普拉斯柯菲雅·费多罗夫娜听着他讲，装出相信的样子，也不打岔，心里却盘算着怎样到新地方去重新安排生活。伊凡·伊里奇高兴地看到，他的想法跟她的想法不谋而合，他们一度坎坷的生活又变得快乐而体面了。

伊凡·伊里奇只回家几天。9 月 10 日他就得走

ennui for the first time in his life, and not only *ennui* but intolerable depression, and he decided that it was impossible to go on living like that, and that it was necessary to take energetic measures.

Having passed a sleepless night pacing up and down the veranda, he decided to go to Petersburg and bestir himself, in order to punish those who had failed to appreciate him and to get transferred to another ministry.

Next day, despite many protests from his wife and her brother, he started for Petersburg with the sole object of obtaining a post with a salary of five thousand rubles a year. He was no longer bent on any particular department, or tendency, or kind of activity. All he now wanted was an appointment to another post with a salary of five thousand rubles, either in the administration, in the banks, with the railways, in one of the Empress Marya's Institutions, or even in the customs—but it had to carry with it a salary of five thousand rubles and be in a ministry other than that in which they had failed to appreciate him.

And this quest of Ivan Ilyich's was crowned with remarkable and unexpected success. At Kursk an acquaintance of his, F. I. Ilyin, got into the first-class carriage, sat down beside Ivan Ilych, and told him of a telegram just received by the Governor of Kursk announcing that a change was about to take place in the ministry: Peter Ivanovich was to be superseded by Ivan Semenovich.

The proposed change, apart from its significance for Russia, had a special significance for lvan Ilych, because by bringing forward a new man, Peter Petrovich, and consequently his friend Zachar Ivanovich, it was highly favourable for Ivan Ilych, since Zachar Ivanovich was a friend and colleague of his.

In Moscow this news was confirmed, and on reaching Petersburg Ivan Ilych found Zachar Ivanovich and received a definite promise of an appointment in his former department of Justice.

A week later he telegraphed to his wife: "Zachar in Miller's place. I shall receive appointment on presentation of report."

Thanks to this change of personnel, Ivan Ilych had unexpectedly obtained an appointment in his former ministry which placed him two stages above his former colleagues besides giving him five thousand rubles salary and three thousand five hundred rubles for expenses connected with his removal. All his ill humour towards his former enemies and the whole department vanished, and Ivan Ilych was completely happy.

He returned to the country more cheerful and contented than he had been for a long time. Praskovya Fedorovna also cheered up and a truce was arranged between them. Ivan Ilych told of how he had been feted by everybody in Petersburg, how all those who had been his enemies were put to shame and now fawned on him, how envious they were of his appointment, and how much everybody in Petersburg had liked him.

Praskovya Fedorovna listened to all this and

马上任。此外,他还得在新地方安顿下来,把家具杂物从省里运去,再要添置和定做许多东西。总之,要根据他同普拉斯柯菲雅·费多罗夫娜几乎一致的想法把新居布置好。

现在,一切都进行得称心如意,他同妻子又意气相投。他们俩一起生活的时间很少,像现在这样投契,除了婚后头几年,还不曾有过。伊凡·伊里奇想把家眷随身带走,可是姐姐和姐夫①对伊凡·伊里奇一家忽然十分亲热,弄得伊凡·伊里奇只好独自先走。

伊凡·伊里奇走了。事业上一帆风顺,同妻子言归于好,这两件事互为因果,使他心情愉快。也找到一座精美的住宅,恰合夫妇俩的心意。高大宽敞的老式客厅、豪华舒适的书房、妻子的房间、女儿的房间、儿子的书房,一切像是特意为他们设计的。伊凡·伊里奇亲自布置房间,选择墙纸,添置家具——从旧货店买来的,式样特别古雅——定制了沙发套和窗帘。房子布置得越来越漂亮,符合他的理想。他布置到一半,发觉比他希望的更美。他相信等全部完工,将更加富丽堂皇,而决不会流于庸俗。临睡前,他想象他的前厅将是什么样子。他瞧着没有布置好的客厅,仿佛看到壁炉、屏风、古董架、散放着的小椅子、墙上的挂盘和铜器都已安放得井井有条。他想妻子和女儿在这方面跟他有同样的爱好,看到这种排场,准会大吃一惊,不禁暗暗高兴。她们一定想不到会有这样的气派。他特别得意的是买到一些价廉物美的古董,使整座房子显得格外豪华。他在信里故意把情况说得差一些,这样她们一看到就会更加惊讶。他热衷于装饰新居,就连心爱的公务都不那么感兴趣了。有时法庭开庭,他也心不在焉,他在考虑究竟用什么样的窗帘顶檐,直的还是拱的。他对这事兴致勃勃,亲自动手安放家具,重新挂上窗帘。有一次他爬到梯子上,指点愚笨的沙发裁缝怎样挂窗帘,一不留神失足掉下来,但他是个强壮而灵活的汉子,立刻站住了,只是腰部撞在窗框上。伤处痛了一阵子不久就好了。这一时期,伊凡·伊里奇觉得自己特别快乐和健康。他写信说:"我感到自己仿佛年轻了15岁。"他原想到9月底把房子布置好,结果拖到10月半。不过,房子布置

① 从上下文看,这里似应作内弟和内弟媳妇。毛德英译本加以改译,看来是有道理的。

appeared to believe it. She did not contradict anything, but only made plans for their life in the town to which they were going. Ivan Ilych saw with delight that these plans were his plans, that he and his wife agreed, and that, after a stumble, his life was regaining its due and natural character of pleasant lightheartedness and decorum.

Ivan Ilych had come back for a short time only, for he had to take up his new duties on the 10th of September. Moreover, he needed time to settle into the new place, to move all his belongings from the province, and to buy and order many additional things: in a word, to make such arrangements as he had resolved on, which were almost exactly what Praskovya Fedorovna too had decided on.

Now that everything had happened so fortunately, and that he and his wife were at one in their aims and moreover saw so little of one another, they got on together better than they had done since the first years of marriage. Ivan Ilych had thought of taking his family away with him at once, but the insistence of his wife's brother and her sister-in-law, who had suddenly become particularly amiable and friendly to him and his family, induced him to depart alone.

So he departed, and the cheerful state of mind induced by his success and by the harmony between his wife and himself, the one intensifying the other, did not leave him. He found a delightful house, just the thing both he and his wife had dreamt of. Spacious, lofty reception rooms in the old style, a convenient and dignified study, rooms for his wife and daughter, a study for his son—it might have been specially built for them. Ivan Ilych himself superintended the arrangements, chose the wallpapers, supplemented the furniture (preferably with antiques which he considered particularly *comme il faut*), and supervised the upholstering. Everything progressed and progressed and approached the ideal he had set himself: even when things were only half completed they exceeded his expectations. He saw what a refined and elegant character, free from vulgarity, it would all have when it was ready. On falling asleep he pictured to himself how the reception-room would look. Looking at the yet unfinished drawing-room he could see the fireplace, the screen, the what-not, the little chairs dotted here and there, the dishes and plates on the walls, and the bronzes, as they would be when everything was in place. He was pleased by the thought of how his wife and daughter, who shared his taste in this matter, would be impressed by it. They were certainly not expecting as much. He had been particularly successful in finding, and buying cheaply, antiques which gave a particularly aristocratic character to the whole place. But in his letters he intentionally understated everything in order to be able to surprise them. All this so absorbed him that his new duties—though he liked his official work—interested him less than he expected. Sometimes he even had moments of absent-mindedness during the Court Sessions, and would consider whether he should have straight or curved cornices for his

得十分雅致——不仅他自己这么认为,凡是看到的人都这么说。

其实,房子里的摆设无非是那种不太富裕,却一味模仿富裕人家的小康之家的气派。千篇一律地尽是花缎、红木家具、盆花、地毯、古铜器、发亮铜器等等。一定阶级的人总是拿这些东西来表示他们一定的身份。伊凡·伊里奇家里的摆设同人家没有什么两样,因此引不起人家的注意,但他却洋洋自得,以为与众不同。他到车站去接家眷,把她们带到装修一新的寓所里,系白领带的男仆打开摆满鲜花的前厅,她们走进客厅、书房,高兴得欢呼起来。他领她们到处观看,得意洋洋地听着她们的称赞,容光焕发,感到十分幸福。当天晚上喝茶的时候,普拉斯柯菲雅·费多罗夫娜随便问到他是怎么摔跤的,他就笑着做给她们看,他怎样从梯子上掉下来,把沙发裁缝吓坏了。

"幸亏我练过体操。要是换了别人,准会摔坏的,可我只在这儿撞了一下,摸摸有点疼,但已经好多了,只是有点青肿。"

就这样他们在新居开始生活,并且也像一般人移居到新地方那样,觉得还少一个房间,收入虽然增加,但还嫌钱少——少这么 500 卢布。不过总的来说,他们感到称心如意了。最初他们过得特别愉快,房子还没有完全布置好,需要再买些什么,定制些什么,有些东西需要搬动,有些东西需要调整。尽管夫妇之间有时意见分歧,但两人对新的生活都很满意,而且有许多事要做,因此没有发生大的争吵。等一切都安排齐整。他们就开始感到有点空虚,但当时还需要去结交一批新朋友,培养新习惯,因此生活还是很充实。

伊凡·伊里奇上午在法院办公,下午回家吃饭,开头一个时期情绪很好,虽然为房子的事有时也有点儿烦恼(例如,他发现桌布或沙发面子上有污点,窗帘系带断了,就会发脾气,因为看到他煞费苦心置办的东西被损坏,心里难过)。不过,伊凡·伊里奇的生活还是过得合乎他的理想,轻松、愉快而体面。他每天早晨 9 时起床,喝咖啡,看报,然后穿上制服去法院。那儿已为他准备好"轭",让他一到就套到身上:接见来访者,处理诉讼有关的问题,主持诉讼案件,出席公开庭和预备庭。他必须排除各种外来干预,免得妨碍诉讼程序,同时严禁徇私枉法,严格依法办事。要是有人想探听什么事,而这事不属伊凡·伊里奇主管,他就不能同这人发生任何关系,但要是这人有正式公

curtains. He was so interested in it all that he often did things himself, rearranging the furniture, or rehanging the curtains. Once when mounting a stepladder to show the upholsterer, who did not understand, how he wanted the hangings draped, he made a false step and slipped, but being a strong and agile man he clung on and only knocked his side against the knob of the window frame. The bruised place was painful but the pain soon passed, and he felt particularly bright and well just then. He wrote: "I feel fifteen years younger. "He thought he would have everything ready by September, but it dragged on till mid-October. But the result was charming not only in his eyes but to everyone who saw it.

In reality it was just what is usually seen in the houses of people of moderate means who want to appear rich, and therefore succeed only in resembling others like themselves: there were damasks, dark wood, plants, rugs, and dull and polished bronzes—all the things people of a certain class have in order to resemble other people of that class. His house was so like the others that it would never have been noticed, but to him it all seemed to be quite exceptional. He was very happy when he met his family at the station and brought them to the newly furnished house all lit up, where a footman in a white tie opened the door into the hall decorated with plants, and when they went on into the drawingroom and the study uttering exclamations of delight. He conducted them everywhere, drank in their praises eagerly, and beamed with pleasure. At tea that evening, when Praskovya Fedorovna among other things asked him about his fall, he laughed, and showed them how he had gone flying and had frightened the upholsterer.

"It's a good thing I'm a bit of an athlete. Another man might have been killed, but I merely knocked myself, just here; it hurts When it's touched, but it's passing off already—it's only a bruise. "

So they began living in their new home—in which, as always happens, when they got thoroughly settled in they found they were just one room short—and with the increased income, which as always was just a little (some five hundred rubles) too little, but it was all very nice.

Things went particularly well at first, before everything was finally arranged and while something had still to be done: this thing bought, that thing ordered, another thing moved, and something else adjusted. Though there were some disputes between husband and wife, they were both so well satisfied and had so much to do that it all passed off without any serious quarrels. When nothing was left to arrange it became rather dull and something seemed to be lacking, but they were then making acquaintances, forming habits, and life was growing fuller.

Ivan Ilych spent his mornings at the law court and came home to dinner, and at first he was generally in a good humour, though he occasionally became irritable just on account of his house. (Every spot on the tablecloth or the upholstery, and every broken window-

文,上面写明事由,那么伊凡·伊里奇就会根据法律许可的范围尽力去办,并且办得不违反人情,也就是说面子上过得去。但只要公事一结束,其他关系也就结束了。分清法律和人情,这种本领伊凡·伊里奇已达到登峰造极的地步,而且凭着天赋的才能和长期的经验,他有时故意把法律和人情混淆起来。他之所以敢于这样做,那是因为他自信总有能力划清两者的界限,如果需要的话。伊凡·伊里奇办这种事不仅轻松、愉快和体面,简直可以说是得心应手。在休庭时,他吸烟,喝茶,随便谈谈政治、社会新闻和纸牌,而谈得最多的还是官场中的任命。然后,他像第一小提琴手,出色地演奏完毕,疲劳地乘车回家。回到家里,发现母女俩出去了,有时在家接待客人,儿子上学了,有时在跟补课教师复习功课。一切都井井有条。饭后要是没有客来,伊凡·伊里奇就看些当时流行的书籍。晚上,他坐下来处理公事:批阅文件,查看法典,核对证词。他干这些既不感到无聊,也不觉得有趣。要是有机会打牌,那么处理公事就感到无聊;要是没有机会打牌,那么处理公事总比独自闲坐或者跟妻子面面相对要好得多。伊凡·伊里奇喜欢举行便宴,邀请有钱有势的先生夫人参加。这种消遣跟其他同样身份的人没有差别,犹如他的客厅跟人家的客厅没有差别一样。

他们家里还举行过一次舞会。舞会办得很好,伊凡·伊里奇心情愉快,可惜最后为蛋糕的事同妻子大闹了一场。普拉斯柯菲雅·费多罗夫娜有她的打算,但伊凡·伊里奇坚持要到最高级糖果铺去买糕点,结果买了许多蛋糕。争吵就是由蛋糕太多吃不完,而糖果铺的账却高达 45 卢布引起的。争吵很激烈,闹得很不愉快。普拉斯柯菲雅·费多罗夫娜骂他:“傻瓜,低能。”伊凡·伊里奇气得双手抱住脑袋,恨恨地说出离婚之类的话来。不过,晚会本身还是很快活的,前来参加的都是社会名流。伊凡·伊里奇同特鲁峰诺娃公爵夫人跳舞。特鲁峰诺娃的姐姐就是著名的“消灭苦难会”的创办人。身居要职的乐趣在于满足自尊心,社会活动的乐趣在于满足虚荣心,但伊凡·伊里奇的真正乐趣却在于打牌。他认为,不管生活上遇到什么烦恼,那像蜡烛一样驱除黑暗的最大乐趣,就是同几个规规矩矩的好搭档坐下来一起打牌,而且一定要 4 人一起(5 人一起打就很难有结果,虽然得装出很感兴趣的样子),认认真真地打(要是顺手的话),然后

blind string, irritated him. He had devoted so much trouble to arranging it all that every disturbance of it distressed him.) But on the whole his life ran its course as he believed life should do: easily, pleasantly, and decorously.

He got up at nine, drank his coffee, read the paper, and then put on his undress uniform and went to the law courts. There the harness in which he worked had already been stretched to fit him and he donned it without a hitch: petitioners, inquiries at the chancery, the chancery itself, and the sittings public and administrative. In all this the thing was to exclude everything fresh and vital, which always disturbs the regular course of official business, and to admit only official relations with people, and then only on official grounds. A man would come, for instance, wanting some information. Ivan Ilych, as one in whose sphere the matter did not lie, would have nothing to do with him: but if the man had some business with him in his official capacity, something that could be expressed on officially stamped paper, he would do everything, positively everything he could within the limits of such relations, and in doing so would maintain the semblance of friendly human relations, that is, would observe the courtesies of life. As soon as the official relations ended, so did everything else. Ivan Ilych possessed this capacity to separate his real life from the official side of affairs and not mix the two, in the highest degree, and by long practice and natural aptitude had brought it to such a pitch that sometimes, in the manner of a virtuoso, he would even allow himself to let the human and official relations mingle. He let himself do this just because he felt that he could at any time he chose resume the strictly official attitude again and drop the human relation. And he did it all easily, pleasantly, correctly, and even artistically. In the intervals between the sessions he smoked, drank tea, chatted a little about politics, a little about general topics, a little about cards, but most of all about official appointments. Tired, but with the feelings of a virtuoso—one of the first violins who has played his part in an orchestra with precision—he would return home to find that his wife and daughter had been out paying calls, or had a visitor, and that his son had been to school, had done his homework with his tutor, and was duly learning what is taught at High Schools. Everything was as it should be. After dinner, if they had no visitors, Ivan Ilych sometimes read a book that was being much discussed at the time, and in the evening settled down to work, that is, read official papers, compared the depositions of witnesses, and noted paragraphs of the Code applying to them. This was neither dull nor amusing. It was dull when he might have been playing bridge, but if no bridge was available it was at any rate better than doing nothing or sitting with his wife. Ivan Ilych's chief pleasure was giving little dinners to which he invited men and women of good social position, and just as his drawing-room resembled all other drawing-rooms so did his enjoyable little parties resemble all other such parties.

吃点儿夜宵,喝一大杯葡萄酒。打过牌以后睡觉,尤其是稍微赢一点儿钱(赢得太多也不好),他觉得特别愉快。

　　他们就这样过着日子。他们家的来客都是达官贵人,有的地位显赫,有的年少英俊。夫妻和女儿待人的态度完全一致。凡是满脸堆笑,投奔到他们那间墙上装饰着日本盘子的客厅来的潦倒亲友,他们都加以排斥。不久,这些寒酸的亲友不再上门,高洛文家的来客就限于达官贵人。

　　年轻人纷纷追求丽莎,其中包括彼特利谢夫。那是德米特里·伊凡内奇·彼特利谢夫的儿子。又是他财产的唯一继承人,现任法院侦讯官。他也在热烈地追求丽莎,弄得伊凡·伊里奇已在跟普拉斯柯菲雅·费多罗夫娜商量,要不要让他们一起坐三驾马车,或者举办一次堂会看看表演。

　　他们就这样过着日子,一切都称心如意,没有任何变化。

四

　　家里人个个身体健康。只有伊凡·伊里奇有时说,他嘴里有一种怪味,左腹有点儿不舒服,但不能说有病。

　　这种不舒服的感觉逐渐增长,虽还没有转变为疼痛,但他经常感到腰部发胀,情绪恶劣。他的心情越来越坏,影响了全家快乐而体面的生活。夫妇吵嘴的事越来越多,轻松愉快的气氛消失了,体面也很难维持。争吵更加频繁,夫妇之间相安无事的日子少得就像汪洋大海里的小岛。

　　如今普拉斯柯菲雅·费多罗夫娜说丈夫脾气难弄,那倒不是没有道理的。她说话喜欢夸张,往往夸张地说,他的脾气一直很坏,要不是她心地善良,这20年可真没法子忍受。的确,现在争吵总是由伊凡·伊里奇引起的。他吃饭总要发脾气,往往从吃汤开始。他一会儿发现碗碟有裂纹,一会儿批评饭菜烧得不好吃,一会儿责备儿子吃饭把臂肘搁在桌上,一会儿批评女儿发式不正派。而罪魁祸首总是普拉斯柯菲雅·费多罗夫娜。普拉斯柯菲雅·费多罗夫娜起初向他回敬,也对他说了一些难听的话,但有两三次他一开始吃饭就勃然大怒。她明白了,这是一种由进食而引起的病态,就克制自己,不再还嘴,只是催他快

Once they even gave a dance. Ivan Ilych enjoyed it and everything went off well, except that it led to a violent quarrel with his wife about the cakes and sweets. Praskovya Fedorovna had made her own plans, but Ivan Ilych insisted on getting everything from an expensive confectioner and ordered too many cakes, and the quarrel occurred because some of those cakes were left over and the confectioner's bill came to forty-five rubles. It was a great and disagreeable quarrel. Praskovya Fedorovna called him "a fool and an imbecile," and he clutched at his head and made angry allusions to divorce.

But the dance itself had been enjoyable. The best people were there, and Ivan Ilych had danced with Princess Trufonova, a sister of the distinguished founder of the Society "Bear my Burden."

The pleasures connected with his work were pleasures of ambition; his social pleasures were those of vanity; but Ivan Ilych's greatest pleasure was playing bridge. He acknowledged that whatever disagreeable incident happened in his life, the pleasure that beamed like a ray of light above everything else was to sit down to bridge with good players, not noisy partners, and of course to four-handed bridge (with five players it was annoying to have to stand out, though one pretended not to mind), to play a clever and serious game (when the cards allowed it) and then to have supper and drink a glass of wine. After a game of bridge, especially if he had won a little (to win a large sum was unpleasant), Ivan Ilych went to bed in specially good humour.

So they lived. They formed a circle of acquaintances among the best people and were visited by people of importance and by young folk. In their views as to their acquaintances, husband and wife and daughter were entirely agreed, and tacitly and unanimously kept at arm's length and shook off the various shabby friends and relations who, with much show of affection, gushed into the drawing-room with its Japanese plates on the walls. Soon these shabby friends ceased to obtrude themselves and only the best people remained in the Golovins' set.

Young men made up to Lisa, and Petrishchev, an examining magistrate and Dmitri Ivanovich Petrishchev's son and sole heir, began to be so attentive to her that Ivan Ilych had already spoken to Praskovya Fedorovna about it, and considered whether they should not arrange a party for them, or get up some private theatricals.

So they lived, and all went well, without change, and life flowed pleasantly.

IV

They were all in good health. It could not be called ill health if Ivan Ilych sometimes said that he had a queer taste in his mouth and felt some discomfort in his left side.

吃。普拉斯柯菲雅·费多罗夫娜认为自己的忍让是
一种值得称道的美德。她认定丈夫脾气极坏，给她的
生活带来不幸，她开始可怜自己。她越是可怜自己，
就越是憎恨丈夫。她巴不得他早点儿死，但又觉得不
能这样想，因为他一死就没有薪俸了。而这一点却使
她更加恨他。她认为自己不幸极了，因为就连他的死
都不能拯救她。她变得很容易发脾气，但又强忍着，
而她这样勉强忍住脾气，却使他的脾气变得更坏。

有一次夫妻争吵，伊凡·伊里奇特别不讲理。事
后他解释说，他确实脾气暴躁，但这是由于病的缘故。
普拉斯柯菲雅·费多罗夫娜就对他说，既然有病，就
得治疗，要他去请教一位名医。

他乘车去了。一切都不出他所料，一切都照章办
理。又是等待，又是医生装出一副煞有介事的样
子——这种样子他是很熟悉的，就跟他自己在法庭上
一样——又是叩诊，又是听诊，又是各种不问也会知
道的多余问题，又是那种威风凛凛的神气，仿佛在说：
"你一旦落到我手里，就得听我摆布。我知道该怎么
办，对付每个病人都是这样的。"一切都同法庭上一
样。医生对待他的神气，就如他在法庭上对待被告
那样。

医生说，如此这般的症状表明你有如此这般的
病，但要是化验不能证明如此这般的病，那就得假定
您有如此这般的病，要是假定有如此这般的病，那么
……等等。对伊凡·伊里奇来说，只有一个问题是重
要的，他的病有没有危险？但医生对这个不合时宜的
问题置之不理。从医生的观点来说，这问题没有意
思，不值得讨论。存在的问题只是估计一下可能性，
是游走肾，还是慢性盲肠炎。这里不存在伊凡·伊里
奇的生死问题，只存在游走肾和盲肠炎之间的争执。
在伊凡·伊里奇看来，医生已明确认定是盲肠炎，但
又保留说，等小便化验后可以得到新的资料，到那时
再做进一步诊断。这一切，就跟伊凡·伊里奇二千次
振振有词地对被告宣布罪状一模一样，医生也是那么
得意洋洋，甚至从眼镜上方瞟了被告一眼，振振有词
地做了结论。从医生的结论中伊凡·伊里奇断定，情
况严重，对医生或其他人都无所谓，可是对他却非同
小可。这结论对伊凡·伊里奇是个沉重的打击，使他
十分怜悯自己，同时十分憎恨那遇到如此严重问题却
无动于衷的医生。

不过他什么也没有说，就站起来，把钱往桌上一

But this discomfort increased and, though not exactly painful, grew into a sense of pressure in his side accompanied by ill humour. And his irritability became worse and worse and began to mar the agreeable, easy, and correct life that had established itself in the Golovin family. Quarrels between husband and wife became more and more frequent, and soon the ease and amenity disappeared and even the decorum was barely maintained. Scenes again became frequent, and very few of those islets remained on which husband and wife could meet without an explosion. Praskovya Fedorovna now had good reason to say that her husband's temper was trying. With characteristic exaggeration she said he had always had a dreadful temper, and that it had needed all her good nature to put up with it for twenty years. It was true that now the quarrels were started by him. His bursts of temper always came just before dinner, often just as he began to eat his soup. Sometimes he noticed that a plate or dish was chipped, or the food was not right, or his son put his elbow on the table, or his daughter's hair was not done as he liked it, and for all this he blamed Praskovya Fedorovna. At first she retorted and said disagreeable things to him, but once or twice he fell into such a rage at the beginning of dinner that she realized it was due to some physical derangement brought on by taking food, and so she restrained herself and did not answer, but only hurried to get the dinner over. She regarded this self-restraint as highly praiseworthy. Having come to the conclusion that her husband had a dreadful temper and made her life miserable, she began to feel sorry for herself, and the more she pitied herself the more she hated her husband. She began to wish he would die; yet she did not want him to die because then his salary would cease. And this irritated her against him still more. She considered herself dreadfully unhappy just because not even his death could save her, and though she concealed her exasperation, that hidden exasperation of hers increased his irritation also.

After one scene in which Ivan Ilych had been particularly unfair and after which he had said in explanation that he certainly was irritable but that it was due to his not being well, she said that if he was ill it should be attended to, and insisted on his going to see a celebrated doctor.

He went. Everything took place as he had expected and as it always does. There was the usual waiting and the important air assumed by the doctor, with which he was so familiar (resembling that which he himself assumed in court), and the sounding and listening, and the questions which called for answers that were foregone conclusions and were evidently unnecessary, and the look of importance which implied that "if only you put yourself in our hands we will arrange everything—we know indubitably how it has to be done, always in the same way for everybody alike." It was all just as it was in the law courts. The doctor put on just the same air towards him as he himself put on towards an accused person.

放,叹了一口气说:

"也许我们病人常向您提些不该问的问题,"他说,"一般说来,这病是不是有危险?……"

医生用一只眼睛从眼镜上方狠狠地瞪了他一下,仿佛在说:"被告,你说话要是越出规定的范围,我将不得不命令把你带出法庭。"

"我已把该说的话都对你说了,"医生说,"别的,等化验结果出来了再说。"医生结束道。

伊凡·伊里奇慢吞吞地走出诊所,垂头丧气地坐上雪橇回家。一路上他反复分析医生的话,竭力把难懂的医学用语翻译成普通的话,想从中找出问题的答案:"我的病严重? 十分严重? 或者还不要紧?"他觉得医生所有的话都表示病情严重。伊凡·伊里奇觉得街上的一切都是阴郁的。车夫是阴郁的,房子是阴郁的,路上行人是阴郁的,小铺子是阴郁的。他身上的疼痛一秒钟也没有停止,听了医生模棱两可的话后就觉得越发厉害。伊凡·伊里奇如今更加心情沉重地忍受着身上的疼痛。

他回到家里,给妻子讲了看病的经过。妻子听着。他讲到一半,女儿戴着帽子进来,准备同母亲一起出去。女儿勉强坐下来听他讲这无聊的事,但她听得不耐烦了,母亲也没有听完他的话。

"哦,我很高兴,"妻子说,"今后你一定要准时吃药。把药方给我,我叫盖拉西姆到药房去抓。"说完她就去换衣服。妻子在屋子里时,他不敢大声喘气,等她走了,才深深地叹了一口气。

"好吧,"伊凡·伊里奇说,"也许真的还不要紧……"

他听医生的话,服药,养病。验过小便后,医生又改了药方。不过,小便化验结果和临床症状之间有矛盾。不知怎的,医生说的与实际情况不符。也许是医生疏忽了,也许是撒谎,也许有什么事瞒着他。

不过伊凡·伊里奇还是照医生的话养病,最初心里感到安慰。

伊凡·伊里奇看过病后,努力执行医生的指示,讲卫生,服药,注意疼痛和大小便。现在他最关心的是疾病和健康。人家一谈到病人、死亡、复元,特别是谈到跟他相似的病,他表面上装作镇定,其实全神贯注地听着,有时提些问题,把听到的情况同自己的病做着比较。

疼痛没有减轻,但伊凡·伊里奇强迫自己认为好

The doctor said that so-and-so indicated that there was so-and-so inside the patient, but if the investigation of so-and-so did not confirm this, then he must assume that and that. If he assumed that and that, then. . . and so on. To Ivan Ilych only one question was important: was his case serious or not? But the doctor ignored that inappropriate question. From his point of view it was not the one under consideration, the real question was to decide between a floating kidney, chronic catarrh, or appendicitis. It was not a question of Ivan Ilych's life or death, but one between a floating kidney and appendicitis. And that question the doctor solved brilliantly, as it seemed to Ivan Ilych, in favour of the appendix, with the reservation that should an examination of the urine give fresh indications the matter would be reconsidered. All this was just what Ivan Ilych had himself brilliantly accomplished a thousand times in dealing with men on trial. The doctor summed up just as brilliantly, looking over his spectacles triumphantly and even gaily at the accused. From the doctor's summing up Ivan Ilych concluded that things were bad, but that for the doctor, and perhaps for everybody else, it was a matter of indifference, though for him it was bad. And this conclusion struck him painfully, arousing in him a great feeling of pity for himself and of bitterness towards the doctor's indifference to a matter of such importance.

He said nothing of this, but rose, placed the doctor's fee on the table, and remarked with a sigh: "We sick people probably often put inappropriate questions. But tell me, in general, is this complaint dangerous, or not?. . . "

The doctor looked at him sternly over his spectacles with one eye, as if to say: "Prisoner, if you will not keep to the questions put to you, I shall be obliged to have you removed from the court."

"I have already told you what I consider necessary and proper. The analysis may show something more." And the doctor bowed.

Ivan Ilych went out slowly, seated himself disconsolately in his sledge, and drove home. All the way home he was going over what the doctor had said, trying to translate those complicated, obscure, scientific phrases into plain language and find in them an answer to the question: "Is my condition bad? Is it very bad? Or is there as yet nothing much wrong?" And it seemed to him that the meaning of what the doctor had said was that it was very bad. Everything in the streets seemed depressing. The cabmen, the houses, the passers-by, and the shops, were dismal. His ache, this dull gnawing ache that never ceased for a moment, seemed to have acquired a new and more serious significance from the doctor's dubious remarks. Ivan Ilych now watched it with a new and oppressive feeling.

He reached home and began to tell his wife about it. She listened, but in the middle of his account his daughter came in with her hat on, ready to go out with her mother. She sat down reluctantly to listen to this tedious story, but could not stand it long, and her

一点儿了。没有事惹他生气,他还能欺骗自己。要是同妻子发生争吵,公务上不顺利,打牌输钱,他立刻就感到病情严重。以前遇到挫折,他总是希望时来运转,打牌顺手,获得大满贯,因此还能忍受。可是现在每次遇到挫折,他都会悲观绝望,丧失信心。也对自己说:"唉,我刚刚有点好转,药物刚刚见效,就遇到这倒霉事……"于是他恨那种倒霉事,恨给他带来不幸并要置他于死命的人。他明白这种愤怒在危害他的生命,但他无法自制。照理他应该明白,他这样怨天尤人,只会使病情加重,因此遇到不愉快的事不应该放在心上,可是他的行为正好相反。他说,他需要安宁,并且特别警惕破坏安宁的事。只要他的安宁稍稍遭到破坏,他就大发雷霆。他读医书,向医生请教,结果有害无益。情况是逐渐恶化的,因此拿今天和昨天比较,差别似乎并不大,他还能聊以自慰,但同医生一商量,就觉得病情在不断恶化,而且发展得很快。尽管如此,他还是经常请教医生。

这个月里他又找了一位名医。这位名医的话,简直同原来的那位一模一样,但问题的提法不同。请教这位名医,只增加伊凡·伊里奇的疑虑和恐惧。另外有位医生,是他朋友的朋友,也很出名。这位医生对他的病做了完全不同的诊断。尽管他保证他能康复,但提出的问题和假设却使伊凡·伊里奇更加疑虑。一个提倡顺势疗法的医生又做了另一种诊断,给了不同的药,伊凡·伊里奇偷偷地服了一个礼拜。可是一礼拜后并没有见效,伊凡·伊里奇对原来的疗法丧失了信心,对这种新疗法也丧失了信心,于是越发沮丧了。有一次,一位熟识的太太给他介绍圣像疗法。伊凡·伊里奇勉强听着,并相信她的话。但这事使他不寒而栗。"难道我真的那样神经衰弱吗?"他自言自语,"废话! 真是荒唐,这样神经过敏要不得,应该选定一个医生,听他的话好好疗养。就这么办。这下子主意定了。我不再胡思乱想,我要严格遵照这种疗法,坚持到夏天。到那时会见效的。别再犹豫不决了! ……"这话说说容易,实行起来可难了。腰痛在折磨他,越来越厉害,一刻也不停。他觉得嘴里的味道越来越难受,还有一股恶臭从嘴里出来,胃口越来越差,体力越来越弱。他不能欺骗自己,他身上出现了一种空前严重的情况。这一点只有他自己明白,周围的人谁也不知道,或者不想知道。他们总以为天下太平,一切如旧。这一点使伊凡·伊里奇觉得格外难

mother too did not hear him to the end.

"Well, I am very glad," she said. "Mind now to take your medicine regularly. Give me the prescription and I'll send Gerasim to the chemist's." And she went to get ready to go out.

While she was in the room Ivan Ilych had hardly taken time to breathe, but he sighed deeply when she left it.

"Well," he thought, "perhaps it isn't so bad after all."

He began taking his medicine and following the doctor's directions, which had been altered after the examination of the urine. But then it happened that there was a contradiction between the indications drawn from the examination of the urine and the symptoms that showed themselves. It turned out that what was happening differed from what the doctor had told him, and that he had either forgotten, or blundered, or hidden something from him. He could not, however, be blamed for that, and Ivan Ilych still obeyed his orders implicitly and at first derived some comfort from doing so.

From the time of his visit to the doctor, Ivan Ilych's chief occupation was the exact fulfilment of the doctor's instructions regarding hygiene and the taking of medicine, and the observation of his pain and his excretions. His chief interests came to be people's ailments and people's health. When sickness, deaths, or recoveries, were mentioned in his presence, especially when the illness resembled his own, he listened with agitation which he tried to hide, asked questions, and applied what he heard to his own case.

The pain did not grow less, but Ivan Ilych made efforts to force himself to think that he was better. And he could do this so long as nothing agitated him. But as soon as he had any unpleasantness with his wife, any lack of success in his official work, or held bad cards at bridge, he was at once acutely sensible of his disease. He had formerly borne such mischances, hoping soon to adjust what was wrong, to master it and attain success, or make a grand slam. But now every mischance upset him and plunged him into despair. He would say to himself: "There now, just as I was beginning to get better and the medicine had begun to take effect, comes this accursed misfortune, or unpleasantness..." And he was furious with the mishap, or with the people who were causing the unpleasantness and killing him, for he felt that this fury was killing him but could not restrain it. One would have thought that it should have been clear to him that this exasperation with circumstances and people aggravated his illness, and that he ought therefore to ignore unpleasant occurrences. But he drew the very opposite conclusion: he said that he needed peace, and he watched for everything that might disturb it and became irritable at the slightest infringement of it. His condition was rendered worse by the fact that he read medical books and consulted doctors. The progress of his disease was so gradual that he could deceive himself when comparing one day with another—the

受。家里的人,尤其是妻子和女儿,都热衷于社交活动。他看到,他们什么也不明白,还埋怨他情绪不好,难以伺候,仿佛还是他不对似的。他看出,尽管他们嘴里不说,他已成了他们的累赘,妻子对他的病已有成见,不管他说什么或者做什么,她的态度都不会变。

"不瞒您说,"她对熟人说,"伊凡·伊里奇也像一切老实人那样,不能认真遵照医生的话养病。今天他听医生的话服药,吃东西,明天我一疏忽,他就忘记吃药,还吃鳇鱼(那是医生禁止的),而且坐下来打牌,一打就打到深夜一点钟。"

"哼,几时有过这种事?"伊凡·伊里奇恼怒地说,"总共在彼得·伊凡内奇家打过一次。"

"昨天不是跟谢贝克一起打过吗?"

"反正我疼得睡不着……"

"不管怎么说,这样你就永远好不了,还要折磨我们。"普拉斯柯菲雅·费多罗夫娜向人家也向伊凡·伊里奇本人说,他生病主要是他自己不好,给她这个做妻子的带来痛苦。伊凡·伊里奇觉得她有这样的看法是很自然的,但心里总感到难受。

在法院里,伊凡·伊里奇发现或者自己感到人家对他抱着奇怪的态度。一会儿,人家把他看作一个不久将把位置空出来的人;一会儿,朋友们不怀恶意地嘲笑他神经过敏,因为他自己认为有一种神秘可怕的东西,在不断吮吸他的精神,硬把他往哪儿拉。朋友们觉得这事挺好玩儿,就拿来取笑他。尤其是施瓦尔茨说话诙谐生动而又装得彬彬有礼,使伊凡·伊里奇想起10年前他自己的模样,因而格外生气。

来了几个朋友,坐下来打牌。他拿出一副新牌,洗了洗,发了牌。他把红方块跟红方块叠在一起,总共7张。他的搭档说没有王牌,给了他2张红方块。还指望什么呢?快乐,兴奋,得了大满贯。伊凡·伊里奇突然又感到那种抽痛,嘴里又有那股味道。他在这种情况下还能因得大满贯而高兴,未免太荒唐了。

他瞧着他的搭档米哈伊尔·米哈伊洛维奇,看他怎样用厚实的手掌拍着桌子,客客气气地不去抓一墩牌,却把它推给伊凡·伊里奇,使他一举手就能享受赢牌的乐趣。"他是不是以为我身子虚得手都伸不出去了?"伊凡·伊里奇想,忘记了王牌,却用更大的王牌去压搭档的牌,结果少了三墩牌,失去了大满贯。最可怕的是他看见米哈伊尔·米哈伊洛维奇脸色十分痛苦,却表现得若无其事。他怎么能若无其事,这

difference was so slight. But when he consulted the doctors it seemed to him that he was getting worse, and even very rapidly. Yet despite this he was continually consulting them.

That month he went to see another celebrity, who told him almost the same as the first had done but put his questions rather differently, and the interview with this celebrity only increased Ivan Ilych's doubts and fears. A friend of a friend of his, a very good doctor, diagnosed his illness again quite differently from the others, and though he predicted recovery, his questions and suppositions bewildered Ivan Ilych still more and increased his doubts. A homoeopathist diagnosed the disease in yet another way, and prescribed medicine which Ivan Ilych took secretly for a week. But after a week, not feeling any improvement and having lost confidence both in the former doctor's treatment and in this one's, he became still more despondent. One day a lady acquaintance mentioned a cure effected by a wonder-working icon. Ivan Ilych caught himself listening attentively and beginning to believe that it had occurred. This incident alarmed him. "Has my mind really weakened to such an extent?" he asked himself. "Nonsense! It's all rubbish; I mustn't give way to nervous fears but having chosen a doctor must keep strictly to his treatment. That is what I will do. Now it's all settled. I won't think about it, but will follow the treatment seriously till summer, and then we shall see. From now there must be no more of this wavering!" This was easy to say but impossible to carry out. The pain in his side oppressed him and seemed to grow worse and more incessant, while the taste in his mouth grew stranger and stranger. It seemed to him that his breath had a disgusting smell, and he was conscious of a loss of appetite and strength. There was no deceiving himself: something terrible, new, and more important than anything before in his life, was taking place within him of which he alone was aware. Those about him did not understand or would not understand it, but thought everything in the world was going on as usual. That tormented Ivan Ilych more than anything. He saw that his household, especially his wife and daughter who were in a perfect whirl of visiting, did not understand anything of it and were annoyed that he was so depressed and exacting, as if he were to blame for it. Though they tried to disguise it he saw that he was an obstacle in their path, and that his wife had adopted a definite line in regard to his illness and kept to it regardless of anything he said or did. Her attitude was this: "You know," she would say to her friends, "Ivan Ilych can't do as other people do, and keep to the treatment prescribed for him. One day he'll take his drops and keep strictly to his diet and go to bed in good time, but the next day unless I watch him he'll suddenly forget his medicine, eat sturgeon—which is forbidden—and sit up playing cards until one o'clock in the morning."

"Oh, come, when was that?" Ivan Ilych would ask in vexation. "Only once at Peter Ivanovich's."

"And yesterday with Shebek."

一点想想也可怕。

　　大家看出他很痛苦,对他说:"要是您累了,我们就不打了。您休息一会儿吧。"休息?不,他一点儿也不累,可以把一圈牌打完。大家闷闷不乐,谁也不开口。伊凡·伊里奇觉得是他害得大家这样闷闷不乐,但又无法改变这种气氛。客人们吃过晚饭,各自回家了。伊凡·伊里奇独自留在家里。意识到他的生命遭到毒害,还毒害了别人的生命,这种毒不仅没有减轻,而且越来越深地渗透到他的全身。

　　他常常带着这样的思想,再加上肉体上的疼痛和恐惧,躺到床上,疼得大半夜不能合眼。可是天一亮又得起来,穿好衣服,乘车上法院,说话,批公文。要是不上班待在家里,那么一天 24 小时,每个小时都得活受罪。而且,在这样的生死边缘上,他只能独自默默地忍受,没有一个人了解他,也没有一个人可怜他。

五

　　就这样过了两个月光景。新年前夕,他的内弟来到他们城里,住在他们家。那天,伊凡·伊里奇上法院尚未回家。普拉斯柯菲雅·费多罗夫娜上街买东西去了。伊凡·伊里奇回到家里,走进书房,看见内弟体格强壮,脸色红润,正在打开手提箱。他听见伊凡·伊里奇的脚步声,抬起头,默默地对他瞧了一会儿。他的眼神向伊凡·伊里奇说明了问题。内弟张大嘴,正要喔唷一声叫出来,但立刻忍住了。这个动作证实了一切。

　　"怎么,我的样子变了吗?"

　　"是的……有点儿变。"

　　接着,不管伊凡·伊里奇怎样想使内弟再谈谈他的模样,内弟却绝口不提。普拉斯柯菲雅·费多罗夫娜一回来,内弟就到她屋里去了。伊凡·伊里奇锁上房门,去照镜子,先照正面,再照侧面。他拿起同妻子合拍的照片,拿它同镜子里的自己做着比较。变化很大。然后他把双臂露到肘部,打量了一番,才放下袖子,在软榻上坐下来,脸色变得漆黑。

　　"别这样,别这样。"他对自己说,霍地站起来,走到写字台边,打开卷宗,开始披阅公文,可是脑子里进不去。他打开门,走到前厅。客厅的门关着。他踮着脚走到门边,侧着耳朵听。

"Well, even if I hadn't stayed up, this pain would have kept me awake. "

"Be that as it may you'll never get well like that, but will always make us wretched. "

Praskovya Fedorovna's attitude to Ivan Ilych's illness, as she expressed it both to others and to him, was that it was his own fault and was another of the annoyances he caused her. Ivan Ilych felt that this opinion escaped her involuntarily—but that did not make it easier for him.

At the law courts too, Ivan Ilych noticed, or thought he noticed, a strange attitude towards himself It sometimes seemed to him that people were watching him inquisitively as a man whose place might soon be vacant. Then again, his friends would suddenly begin to chaff him in a friendly way about his low spirits, as if the awful, horrible, and unheard-of thing that was going on within him, incessantly gnawing at him and irresistably drawing him away, was a very agreeable subject for jests. Schwartz in particular irritated him by his jocularity, vivacity, and *savoir-faire*, which reminded him of what he himself had been ten years ago.

Friends came to make up a set and they sat down to cards. They dealt, bending the new cards to soften them, and he sorted the diamonds in his hand and found he had seven. His partner said "No trumps" and supported him with two diamonds. What more could be wished for? It ought to be jolly and lively. They would make a grand slam. But suddenly Ivan Ilych was conscious of that gnawing pain, that taste in his mouth, and it seemed ridiculous that in such circumstances he should be pleased to make a grand slam.

He looked at his partner Mikhail Mikhaylovich, who rapped the table with his strong hand and instead of snatching up the tricks pushed the cards courteously and indulgently towards Ivan Ilych that he might have the pleasure of gathering them up without the trouble of stretching out his hand for them. "Does he think I am too weak to stretch out my arm?" thought Ivan Ilych, and forgetting what he was doing he overtrumped his partner, missing the grand slam by three tricks. And what was most awful of all was that he saw how upset Mikhail Mikhaylovich was about it but did not himself care. And it was dreadful to realize why he did not care.

They all saw that he was suffering, and said: "We can stop if you are tired. Take a rest. "Lie down? No, he was not at all tired, and he finished the rubber. All were gloomy and silent. Ivan Ilych felt that he had diffused this gloom over them and could not dispel it. They had supper and went away, and Ivan Ilych was left alone with the consciousness that his life was poisoned and was poisoning the lives of others, and that this poison did not weaken but penetrated more and more deeply into his whole being.

With this consciousness, and with physical pain besides the terror, he must go to bed, often to lie awake the greater part of the night. Next morning he had to get up again, dress, go to the law courts, speak,

"不,你说得过分了。"普拉斯柯菲雅·费多罗夫娜说。

"怎么过分? 你没发觉,他已经像个死人了。你看看他的眼睛,没有一点儿光。他这是怎么搞的?"

"谁也不知道。尼古拉耶夫(一位医生)说如此这般,可我不知道。列谢季茨基(就是名医)说的正好相反……"

伊凡·伊里奇回到自己屋里,躺下来想:"肾,游走肾。"他回忆起医生们对他说过的话,肾脏怎样离开原位而游走。他竭力在想象中捕捉这个肾脏,不让它游走,把它固定下来。这事看上去轻而易举。"不,我还是去找找彼得·伊凡内奇(那个有医生朋友的朋友)。"他打了铃,吩咐套车,准备出去。

"你上哪儿去,约翰?"妻子露出非常忧愁和矫揉造作的贤惠神情问。

这种矫揉造作的贤惠使他生气。他阴沉着脸对她瞅了一眼。

"我去找彼得·伊凡内奇。"

他去找这个有医生朋友的朋友,然后跟他一起到医生家去。他遇见医生,跟他谈了好半天。

医生根据解剖学和生理学对他的病做了分析,他全听懂了。

盲肠里有点儿毛病,有点儿小毛病,全会好的。只要加强一个器官的功能,减少另一个器官的活动,多吸收一点儿,就会好的。吃饭时他晚到了一点儿。吃过饭,他兴致勃勃地谈了一通,但好一阵不能定下心来做事。最后他回到书房,立刻动手工作。他披阅公文,处理公事,但心里念念不忘有一件要事被耽误了。等公事完毕,他才记起那件事就是盲肠的毛病。但他故作镇定,走到客厅喝茶。那里有几个客人,正在说话,弹琴,唱歌。他得意的未来女婿,法院侦讯官也在座。据普拉斯柯菲雅·费多罗夫娜说,伊凡·伊里奇那天晚上过得比谁都快活,其实他一分钟也没忘记盲肠的毛病被耽误了。11点钟他向大家告辞,回自己屋里去。自从生病以来,他就独自睡在书房里。他走进屋里,脱去衣服,拿起一本左拉的小说,但没有看,却想着心事。他想象盲肠被治愈了。通过吸收,排泄,功能恢复正常。"对了,就是那么一回事,"他自言自语,"只要补养补养身体就好了。"他想到了药,支起身来,服了药,又仰天躺下,仔细体味药物怎样在治病,怎样在制止疼痛。"只要按时服药,避免不良影响

and write; or if he did not go out, spend at home those twenty-four hours a day each of which was a torture. And he had to live thus all alone on the brink of an abyss, with no one who understood or pitied him.

V

So one month passed and then another. Just before the New Year his brother-in-law came to town and stayed at their house. Ivan Ilych was at the law courts and Praskovya Fedorovna had gone shopping. When Ivan Ilych came home and entered his study he found his brother-in-law there—a healthy, florid man—unpacking his portmanteau himself. He raised his head on hearing Ivan Ilych's footsteps and looked up at him for a moment without a word. That stare told Ivan Ilych everything. His brother-in-law opened his mouth to utter an exclamation of surprise but checked himself, and that action confirmed all.

"I have changed, eh?"

"Yes, there is a change."

And after that, try as he would to get his brother-in-law to return to the subject of his looks, the latter would say nothing about it. Praskoyva Fedorovna came home and her brother went to her. Ivan Ilych locked the door and began to examine himself in the glass, first full face, then in profile. He took up a portrait of himself taken with his wife, and compared it with what he saw in the glass. The change in him was immense. Then he bared his arms to the elbow, looked at them, drew the sleeves down again, sat down on an ottoman, and grew blacker than night.

"No, no, this won't do!" he said to himself, and jumped up, went to the table, took up some law papers and began to read them, but could not continue. He unlocked the door and went into the reception-room. The door leading to the drawing-room was shut. He approached it on tiptoe and listened.

"No, you are exaggerating!" Praskovya Fedorovna was saying.

"Exaggerating! Don't you see it? Why, he's a dead man! Look at his eyes—there's no light in them. But what is it that is wrong with him?"

"No one knows. Nikolaevich (that was another doctor) said something, but I don't know what. And Leschetitsky (this was the celebrated specialist) said quite the contrary. . . "

Ivan Ilych walked away, went to his own room, lay down, and began musing: "The kidney, a floating kidney." He recalled all the doctors had told him of how it detached itself and swayed about. And by an effort of imagination he tried to catch that kidney and arrest it and support it. So little was needed for this, it seemed to him. "No, I'll go to see Peter Ivanovich again." (That was the friend whose friend was a doctor.) He rang, ordered the carriage, and got ready to go.

"Where are you going, Jean?" asked his wife, with

就行。我现在已觉得好一点儿了,好多了。"他按按腰部,按上去不疼了。"是的,不疼了,真的好多了。"他熄了蜡烛,侧身躺下……盲肠在逐渐恢复,逐渐吸收。突然他又感觉到那种熟悉的隐痛,痛得一刻不停,而且很厉害。嘴里又是那种恶臭。他顿时心头发凉,头脑发晕。"天哪!天哪!"他喃喃地说,"又来了,又来了,再也好不了啦!"突然他觉得完全不是那么一回事。"哼,盲肠!肾脏!"他自言自语,"问题根本不在盲肠,不在肾脏,而在生和……死。是啊,有过生命,可现在它在溜走,而我又留不住它。是啊!何必欺骗自己呢?除了我自己,不是人人都很清楚我快死了吗?问题只在于还有几个礼拜,几天,还是现在就死。原来有过光明,现在却变成一片黑暗。我此刻在这个世界,但不久就要离开!到哪儿去?"他觉得浑身发凉,呼吸停止,只听见心脏在扑扑跳动。

"等我没有了,那还有什么呢?什么也没有了。等我没有了,我将在哪儿?难道真的要死了吗?不,我不愿死。"他霍地跳起来,想点燃蜡烛,用颤动的双手摸索着。蜡烛和烛台被碰翻,落到地上。他又仰天倒在枕头上。"何必呢?反正都一样,"他在黑暗中瞪着一双眼睛,自言自语,"死。是的,死。他们谁也不知道,谁也不想知道,谁也不可怜我。他们玩得可乐了(他听见远处传来喧闹和伴奏声)。他们若无其事,可他们有朝一日也要死的。都是傻瓜!我先死,他们后死,他们也免不了一死。可他们还乐呢。畜生!"他愤怒得喘不过气来。他痛苦得受不了。难道谁都要受这样的罪吗!他坐起来。

"总有什么地方不对头,我得定下心,从头至尾好好想一想。"他开始思索,"对了,病是这样开始的。先是腰部撞了一下,但过了一两天我还是好好的。稍微有点儿疼,后来疼得厉害了,后来请医生,后来泄气了,发愁了,后来又请医生,但越来越接近深渊。体力越来越差,越来越接近……越来越接近……我的身子虚透了,我的眼睛没有光。我要死了,可我还以为是盲肠有病。我想治好盲肠,其实是死神临头了。难道真的要死吗?"他又感到魂飞魄散,呼吸急促。他侧身摸索火柴,用臂肘撑住床几。臂肘撑得发痛,他恼火了,撑得更加使劲儿,结果把床几推倒了。他绝望得喘不过气来,又仰天倒下,恨不得立刻死去。

这当儿,客人们纷纷走散。普拉斯柯菲雅·费多罗夫娜送他们走。她听见什么东西倒下,走进来。

a specially sad and exceptionally kind look.

This exceptionally kind look irritated him. He looked morosely at her.

"I must go to see Peter Ivanovich."

He went to see Peter Ivanovich, and together they went to see his friend, the doctor. He was in, and Ivan Ilych had a long talk with him.

Reviewing the anatomical and psychological details of what in the doctor's opinion was going on inside him, he understood it all.

There was something, a small thing, in the vermiform appendix. It might all come right. Only stimulate the energy of one organ and check the activity of another, then absorption would take place and everything would come right. He got home rather late for dinner, ate his dinner, and conversed cheerfully, but could not for a long time bring himself to go back to work in his room. At last, however, he went to his study and did what was necessary, but the consciousness that he had put something aside—an important, intimate matter which he would revert to when his work was done—never left him. When he had finished his work he remembered that this intimate matter was the thought of his vermiform appendix. But he did not give himself up to it, and went to the drawing room for tea. There were callers there, including the examining magistrate who was a desirable match for his daughter, and they were conversing, playing the piano and singing. Ivan Ilych, as Praskovya Fedorovna remarked, spent that evening more cheerfully than usual, but he never for a moment forgot that he had postponed the important matter of the appendix. At eleven o'clock he said good-night and went to his bedroom. Since his illness he had slept in a small room next to his study. He undressed and took up a novel by Zola, but instead of reading it he fell into thought, and in his imagination that desired improvement in the vermiform appendix occurred. There was the absorption and evacuation and the re-establishment of normal activity. "Yes, that's it!" he said to himself "One need only assist nature, that's all." He remembered his medicine, rose, took it, and lay down on his back watching for the beneficient action of the medicine and for it to lessen the pain. "I need only take it regularly and avoid all injurious influences. I am already feeling better, much better." He began touching his side: it was not painful to the touch. "There, I really don't feel it. It's much better already." He put out the light and turned on his side... "The appendix is getting better, absorption is occurring." Suddenly he felt the old, familiar, dull, gnawing pain, stubborn and serious. There was the same familiar loathsome taste in his mouth. His heart sank and he felt dazed. "My God! My God!" he muttered. "Again, again! And it will never cease." And suddenly the matter presented itself in a quite different aspect. "Vermiform appendix! Kidney!" he said to himself "It's not a question of appendix or kidney, but of life and... death. Yes, life was there and now it is going, going and I cannot stop it. Yes. Why deceive myself? Isn't it obvious to everyone but me that I'm dying, and

"你怎么了?"

"没什么。不留神把它撞倒了。"

她走出去,拿着一枝蜡烛进来。他躺着,喘息得又重又急,好像刚跑完了几里路,眼睛停滞地瞧着她。

"你怎么了,约翰?"

"没……什么。撞……倒了。"他回答,心里却想:"有什么可说的。她不会明白的。"

她确实不明白。她扶起床几,给他点上蜡烛,又匆匆走掉了,她还得送客。

等她回来,他仍旧仰天躺着,眼睛瞪着天花板。

"你怎么了,更加不舒服吗?"

"是的。"

她摇摇头,坐下来。

"我说,约翰,我们把列谢季茨基请到家里来好吗?"

这就是说,不惜金钱,请那位名医来出诊。他冷笑了一声说:"不用了。"她坐了一会儿,走到他旁边,吻了吻他的前额。

她吻他的时候,他从心底里憎恨她,好容易才忍住不把她推开。

"再见。上帝保佑你好好睡一觉。"

"嗯。"

六

伊凡·伊里奇看到自己快要死了。经常处于绝望中。

他心里明白,他快要死了,但他对这个念头很不习惯,他实在不理解,怎么也不能理解。

他在基捷韦帖尔的逻辑学里读到这样一种三段论法:盖尤斯是人,凡人都要死,因此盖尤斯也要死。他始终认为这个例子只适用于盖尤斯,绝对不适用于他。盖尤斯是人,是个普通人,这个道理完全正确,但他不是盖尤斯,不是个普通人,他永远是个与众不同的特殊人物。他原来是小伊凡,有妈妈,有爸爸,有两个兄弟——米嘉和伏洛嘉,有许多玩具,有马车夫,有保姆,后来又有了妹妹卡嘉,还有儿童时代、少年时代和青年时代的喜怒哀乐。难道盖尤斯也闻到过他小伊凡所喜爱的那种花皮球的气味吗?难道盖尤斯也那么吻过妈妈的手,听到过妈妈绸衣褶裥的窸窣声

that it's only a question of weeks, days. . . it may happen this moment. There was light and now there is darkness. I was here and now I'm going there! Where?" A chill came over him, his breathing ceased, and he felt only the throbbing of his heart.

"When I am not, what will there be? There will be nothing. Then where shall I be when I am no more? Can this be dying? No, I don't want to!" He jumped up and tried to light the candle, felt for it with trembling hands, dropped candle and candlestick on the floor, and fell back on his pillow.

"What's the use? It makes no difference," he said to himself staring with wide-open eyes into the darkness. "Death. Yes, death. And none of them know or wish to know it, and they have no pity for me. Now they are playing. (He heard through the door the distant sound of a song and its accompaniment.) "It's all the same to them, but they will die too! Fools! I first, and they later, but it will be the same for them. And now they are merry. . . the beasts!"

Anger choked him and he was agonizingly, unbearably miserable. "It is impossible that all men have been doomed to suffer this awful horror!" He raised himself.

"Something must be wrong. I must calm myself— must think it all over from the beginning." And he again began thinking. "Yes, the beginning of my illness: I knocked my side, but I was still quite well that day and the next. It hurt a little, then rather more. I saw the doctors, then followed despondency and anguish, more doctors, and I drew nearer to the abyss. My strength grew less and I kept coming nearer and nearer, and now I have wasted away and there is no light in my eyes. I think of the appendix—but this is death! I think of mending the appendix, and all the while here is death! Can it really be death?" Again terror seized him and he gasped for breath. He leant down and began feeling for the matches, pressing with his elbow on the stand beside the bed. It was in his way and hurt him, he grew furious with it, pressed on it still harder, and upset it. Breathless and in despair he fell on his back, expecting death to come immediately.

Meanwhile the visitors were leaving. Praskovya Fedorovna was seeing them off. She heard something fall and came in.

"What has happened?"

"Nothing. I knocked it over accidentally."

She went out and returned with a candle. He lay there panting heavily, like a man who has run a thousand yards, and stared upwards at her with a fixed look.

"What is it, Jean?"

"No. . . o. . . thing. I upset it." ("Why speak of it? She won't understand," he thought.)

And in truth she did not understand. She picked up the stand, lit the candle, and hurried away to see another visitor off When she came back he still lay on his back, looking upwards.

"What is it? Do you feel worse?"

吗？难道盖尤斯也曾在法学院里因点心不好吃而闹过事吗？难道盖尤斯也那样谈过恋爱吗？难道盖尤斯能像他那样主持审讯吗？

盖尤斯的确是要死的，他要死是正常的，但我是小伊凡，是伊凡·伊里奇，我有我的思想感情，跟他截然不同。我不该死，要不真是太可怕了。

这就是他的心情。

"我要是像盖尤斯那样也要死，那我一定会知道，一定会听到内心的声音，可是我心里没有这样的声音。我和我的朋友们都明白，我跟盖尤斯完全不同。可是如今呢！"他自言自语，"这是不可能的。不可能发生的，可是偏偏发生了。这是怎么搞的？这事该怎么理解？"

他无法理解，就竭力驱除这个想法，把这个想法看做虚假、错误和病态的，并且用正确健康的想法来挤掉它。但这不只是思想，而是现实，它出现了，摆在他面前。

他故意想想别的事来排挤这个想法，希望从中找到精神上的支持。他试图用原来的一套思路来对抗死的念头。但奇怪得很，以前用这种办法可以抵挡和驱除死的念头。如今却不行。近来，伊凡·伊里奇常常想恢复原来的思绪，以驱除死的念头。有时他对自己说："我还是去办公吧，我一向靠工作过活。"他摆脱心头的种种疑虑，到法院去。他跟同事们谈天。在法庭上坐下来，照例漫不经心地扫一眼人群，两条干瘦的胳膊搁在麻栎椅扶手上，照例侧身凑近旁边的法官。挪过卷宗，同他耳语几句，然后猛地抬起眼睛，挺直身子，说几句老套，宣布开庭。但审讯到一半，腰部不顾正在开庭，突然又抽痛起来。伊凡·伊里奇定下神，竭力不去想它，可是没有用。它又来了，站在他面前，打量着他。他吓得呆若木鸡，眼睛里的光也熄灭了。他又自言自语："难道只有它是真的吗？"同事和下属惊奇而痛心地看到，像他这样一位精明能干的法官竟然说话颠三倒四，在审讯中出差错。他竭力振作精神，定下心来，勉强坚持到庭审结束，闷闷不乐地回家去。他明白，法院开庭也不再能回避他想回避的事，他在审讯时也不能摆脱它。最最糟糕的是，它吸引了他。并非要他有什么行动，而只是要他瞧着它，什么事也不做，难堪地忍受着折磨。

为了摆脱这种痛苦，伊凡·伊里奇寻找另一种屏风来自卫，但另一种屏风也只能暂时保护他，不久又

"Yes."

She shook her head and sat down.

"Do you know, Jean, I think we must ask Leshchetitsky to come and see you here."

This meant calling in the famous specialist, regardless of expense. He smiled malignantly and said "No." She remained a little longer and then went up to him and kissed his forehead.

While she was kissing him he hated her from the bottom of his soul and with difficulty refrained from pushing her away.

"Good-night. Please God you'll sleep."

"Yes."

VI

Ivan Ilych saw that he was dying, and he was in continual despair.

In the depth of his heart he knew he was dying, but not only was he not accustomed to the thought, he simply did not and could not grasp it.

The syllogism he had learnt from Kiezewetter's Logic: "Caius is a man, men are mortal, therefore Caius is mortal," had always seemed to him correct as applied to Caius, but certainly not as applied to himself. That Caius—man in the abstract—was mortal, was perfectly correct, but he was not Caius, not an abstract man, but a creature quite quite separate from all others. He had been little Vanya, with a mamma and a papa, with Mitya and Volodya, with the toys, a coachman and a nurse, afterwards with Katenka and with all the joys, griefs, and delights of childhood, boyhood, and youth. What did Caius know of the smell of that striped leather ball Vanya had been so fond of? Had Caius kissed his mother's hand like that, and did the silk of her dress rustle so for Caius? Had he rioted like that at school when the pastry was bad? Had Caius been in love like that? Could Caius preside at a session as he did? "Caius really was mortal, and it was right for him to die; but for me, little Vanya, Ivan Ilych, with all my thoughts and emotions, it's altogether a different matter. It cannot be that I ought to die. That would be too terrible."

Such was his feeling.

"If I had to die like Caius I should have known it was so. An inner voice would have told me so, but there was nothing of the sort in me and I and all my friends felt that our case was quite different from that of Caius. And now here it is!" he said to himself. "It can't be. It's impossible! But here it is. How is this? How is one to understand it?"

He could not understand it, and tried to drive this false, incorrect, morbid thought away and to replace it by other proper and healthy thoughts. But that thought, and not the thought only but the reality itself, seemed to come and confront him.

And to replace that thought he called up a succession of others, hoping to find in them some support. He tried to get back into the former current of

破裂了,或者变得透明了,仿佛它能穿透一切,什么东西也挡不住它。

最近有一次他走进精心布置的客厅——他摔跤的地方,他嘲弄地想,正是为了布置它而献出了生命,因为他知道他的病是由跌伤引起的——他发现油漆一新的桌上有被什么东西划过的痕迹。他研究原因,发现那是被照相簿上弯卷的青铜饰边划破的。他拿起他深情地贴上照片的照相簿,对女儿和她那些朋友的粗野很恼火——有的地方撕破了,有的照片被颠倒了。他把照片仔细整理好,把照相簿饰边扳平。

然后他想重新布置,把照相簿改放到盆花旁的角落里。他吩咐仆人请女儿或者妻子来帮忙,可是她们不同意他的想法,反对搬动。他同她们争吵,生气。但这样倒好。因为他可以不再想到它,不再看见它。

不过,当他亲自动手挪东西的时候,妻子对他说:"啊,让仆人搬吧,你又要糟蹋自己了。"这当儿,它突然又从屏风后面出现,他又看见了它。它的影子一闪,他还希望它能再消失,可是他又注意到自己的腰。腰还是在抽痛。他再也无法把它忘记,它明明在盆花后面瞧着他:"这是干什么呀?"

"真的,我为了这窗帘就像冲锋陷阵一样送了命。难道真是这样吗? 多么可怕而又多么愚蠢哪! 这不可能! 不可能! 但这是事实。"

他回到书房里躺下,又同它单独相处。他同它又面面相对,但对它束手无策。他只能瞧着它,浑身发抖。

七

伊凡·伊里奇生病第三个月的情况怎样,很难说,因为病情是逐步发展的,不易察觉。但妻子也好,女儿也好,儿子也好,佣人也好,朋友也好,医生也好,主要是他自己,都知道,大家唯一关心的事是,他的位置是不是快空出来,活着的人能不能解除由于他存在而招惹的麻烦,他自己是不是快摆脱痛苦。

他的睡眠越来越少。医生给他服鸦片,注射吗啡,但都不能减轻他的痛苦。他在昏昏沉沉中所感到的麻木,起初使他稍微好过些,但不久又感到同样痛苦,甚至比清醒时更不好受。

家里人遵照医生的指示给他做了特殊的饭菜,但

thoughts that had once screened the thought of death from him. But strange to say, all that had formerly shut off, hidden, and destroyed, his consciousness of death, no longer had that effect. Ivan Ilych now spent most of his time in attempting to re-establish that old current. He would say to himself: "I will take up my duties again—after all I used to live by them." And banishing all doubts he would go to the law courts, enter into conversation with his colleagues, and sit carelessly as was his wont, scanning the crowd with a thoughtful look and leaning both his emaciated arms on the arms of his oak chair; bending over as usual to a colleague and drawing his papers nearer he would interchange whispers with him, and then suddenly raising his eyes and sitting erect would pronounce certain words and open the proceedings. But suddenly in the midst of those proceedings the pain in his side, regardless of the stage the proceedings had reached, would begin its own gnawing work. Ivan Ilych would turn his attention to it and try to drive the thought of it away, but without success. It would come and stand before him and look at him, and he would be petrified and the light would die out of his eyes, and he would again begin asking himself whether It alone was true. And his colleagues and subordinates would see with surprise and distress that he, the brilliant and subtle judge, was becoming confused and making mistakes. He would shake himself, try to pull himself together, manage somehow to bring the sitting to a close, and return home with the sorrowful consciousness that his judicial labours could not as formerly hide from him what he wanted them to hide, and could not deliver him from It. And what was worst of all was that It drew his attention to itself not in order to make him take some action but only that he should look at It, look it straight in the face: look at it and without doing anything, suffer inexpressibly.

And to save himself from this condition Ivan Ilych looked for consolations—new screens—and new screens were found and for a while seemed to save him, but then they immediately fell to pieces or rather became transparent, as if It penetrated them and nothing could veil It.

In these latter days he would go into the drawing-room he had arranged—that drawing-room where he had fallen and for the sake of which (how bitterly ridiculous it seemed) he had sacrificed his life—for he knew that his illness originated with that knock. He would enter and see that something had scratched the polished table. He would look for the cause of this and find that it was the bronze ornamentation of an album, that had got bent. He would take up the expensive album which he had lovingly arranged, and feel vexed with his daughter and her friends for their untidiness—for the album was torn here and there and some of the photographs turned upside down. He would put it carefully in order and bend the ornamentation back into position. Then it would occur to him to place all those things in another corner of the room, near the plants. He would call the footman, but his daughter or wife would come to help him. They would not agree,

他觉得这种饭菜越来越没有滋味,越来越倒胃口。

为他大便也做了特殊安排。每次大便他都觉得很痛苦,因为不清洁,不体面,有臭味,还得麻烦别人帮忙。

不过,在这件不愉快的事上,伊凡·伊里奇倒也得到一种安慰。每次大便总是由男仆盖拉西姆伺候。

盖拉西姆是个年轻的庄稼汉,衣着整洁,容光焕发,因为长期吃城里伙食长得格外强壮。他性格开朗,总是乐呵呵的。开头,这个整洁的小伙子身穿俄罗斯民族服,做着这种不体面的事,总使伊凡·伊里奇感到困窘。

有一次,他从便盆上起来,无力拉上裤子,就倒在沙发上。他看见自己皮包骨头的大腿,不禁心惊胆战。

盖拉西姆脚登散发着柏油味的大皮靴,身上系着干净的麻布围裙,穿着干净的印花布衬衫,卷起袖子,露出年轻强壮的胳膊,带着清新的冬天空气走进来。他目光避开伊凡·伊里奇,竭力抑制着从焕发的容光中表现出来的生的欢乐,免得病人见了不高兴,走到便盆旁。

“盖拉西姆。”伊凡·伊里奇有气无力地叫道。

盖拉西姆打了个哆嗦,显然害怕自己什么地方做得不对,慌忙把他那张刚开始长胡子的淳朴善良而又青春洋溢的脸转过来对着病人。

“老爷,您有什么吩咐?”

“我想,你做这事一定很不好受。你要原谅我,我是没有办法。”

“哦,老爷,好说。”盖拉西姆闪亮眼睛,露出一排洁白健康的牙齿,“那算得了什么?您有病嘛,老爷。”

他用他那双强壮的手熟练地做着做惯的事,轻悄地走了出去。过了5分钟,又那么轻悄地走回来。

伊凡·伊里奇一直那么坐在沙发上。

“盖拉西姆,”当盖拉西姆把洗干净的便盆放回原处时,伊凡·伊里奇说,“请你帮帮我,你过来。”盖拉西姆走过去。“你搀我一把。我自己爬不起来,德米特里被我派出去了。”

盖拉西姆走过去。他用他那双强壮的手,也像走路一样轻松、利索而温柔地把主人抱起来,一只手扶住他,另一只手给他拉上裤子,想让他坐下来。但伊凡·伊里奇要求把他扶到长沙发上。盖拉西姆一点儿也不费劲儿,稳稳当当地把他抱到长沙发上坐下。

and his wife would contradict him, and she would dispute and grow angry. But that was all right, for then he did not think about *It*. *It* was invisible.

But then, when he was moving something himself, his wife would say: "Let the servants do it. You will hurt yourself again." And suddenly *It* would flash through the screen and he would see it. It was just a flash, and he hoped it would disappear, but he would involuntarily pay attention to his side. "It sits there as before, gnawing just the same." And he could no longer forget *It*, but could distinctly see it looking at him from behind the flowers. "What is it all for?"

"It really is so! I lost my life over that curtain as I might have done when storming a fort. Is that possible? How terrible and how stupid. It can't be true! It can't, but it is."

He would go to his study, lie down, and again be alone with *It*: face to face with *It*. And nothing could be done with *It* except to look at it and shudder.

VII

How it happened it is impossible to say because it came about step by step, unnoticed, but in the third month of Ivan Ilych's illness, his wife his daughter, his son, his acquaintances, the doctors, the servants, and above all he himself, were aware that the whole interest he had for other people was whether he would soon vacate his place, and at least release the living from the discomfort caused by his presence and be himself released from his sufferings.

He slept less and less. He was given opium and hypodermic injections or morphine, but this did not relieve him. The dull depression he experienced in a somnolent condition at first gave him a little relief, but only as something new, afterwards it became as distressing as the pain itself or even more so.

Special foods were prepared for him by the doctor's orders, but all those foods became increasingly distasteful and disgusting to him.

For his excretions also special arrangements had to be made, and this was a torment to him every time—a torment from the uncleanliness, the unseemliness, and the smell, and from knowing that another person had to take part in it.

But just through this most unpleasant matter Ivan Ilych obtained comfort. Gerasim, the butler's young assistant, always came in to carry the things out. Gerasim was a clean, fresh peasant lad, grown stout on town food and always cheerful and bright. At first the sight of him, in his clean Russian peasant costume, engaged on that disgusting task embarrassed Ivan Ilych.

Once when he got up from the commode too weak to draw up his trousers, he dropped into a soft armchair and looked with horror at his bare, enfeebled thighs with the muscles so sharply marked on them.

Gerasim with a firm light tread, his heavy boots emitting a pleasant smell of tar and fresh winter air, came in wearing a clean Hessian apron, the sleeves of

"谢谢。你真行,干得真轻巧。"

盖拉西姆微微一笑,想走。可是伊凡·伊里奇同他一起觉得很愉快,不肯放他走。

"还有,请你把那把椅子给我推过来。不,是那一把,让我搁腿。腿搁得高,好过些。"

盖拉西姆端过椅子,轻轻地把它放在长沙发前,然后抬起伊凡·伊里奇的双腿放在上面。当盖拉西姆把他的腿高高抬起时,他觉得舒服些。

"腿抬得高,我觉得好过些,"伊凡·伊里奇说,"你把这个枕头给我垫在下面。"

盖拉西姆照他的吩咐做了。他又把他的腿抬起来放好。盖拉西姆抬起他的双腿,他感到确实好过些。双腿一放下,他又觉得不舒服。

"盖拉西姆,"伊凡·伊里奇对他说,"你现在有事吗?"

"没有,老爷。"盖拉西姆说,他已学会像城里仆人那样同老爷说话。

"你还有什么活儿要干?"

"我还有什么活儿要干? 什么都干好了,只要再劈点儿木柴留着明天用。"

"那你把我的腿这么高高抬着,行吗?"

"有什么不行的? 行!"盖拉西姆把主人的腿抬起来,伊凡·伊里奇觉得这样一点也不疼了。

"那么劈柴怎么办?"

"不用您老爷操心,这我们来得及的。"

伊凡·伊里奇叫盖拉西姆坐下抬着他的腿,并同他聊话。真奇怪,盖拉西姆抬着他的腿,他觉得好过多了。

从此以后伊凡·伊里奇就常常把盖拉西姆唤来,要他用肩膀扛着他的腿,并喜欢同他谈天。盖拉西姆做这事轻松愉快、态度诚恳,使伊凡·伊里奇很感动。别人身上的健康、力量和生气往往使伊凡·伊里奇感到屈辱,只有盖拉西姆的力量和生气不仅没有使他觉得伤心,反而使他感到安慰。

伊凡·伊里奇觉得最痛苦的事就是听谎言,听大家出于某种原因都相信的那个谎言:他只是病了,并不会死,只要安心治疗,一定会好的。可是他知道,不论采取什么办法,他都不会好了,痛苦只会越来越厉害,直到死去。这个谎言折磨着他。他感到痛苦的是,大家都知道,他自己也知道他的病很严重,但大家都讳言真相而撒谎,还要迫使他自己一起撒谎。谎

his print shirt tucked up over his strong bare young arms and refraining from looking at his sick master out of consideration for his feelings, and restraining the joy of life that beamed from his face, he went up to the commode.

"Gerasim!"said Ivan Ilych in a weak voice.

Gerasim started, evidently afraid he might have committed some blunder, and with a rapid movement turned his fresh, kind, simple young face which just showed the first downy signs of a beard.

"Yes,sir?"

"That must be very unpleasant for you. You must forgive me. I am helpless. "

"Oh, why, sir," and Gerasim's eyes beamed and he showed his glistening white teeth, "what's a little trouble? It's a case of illness with you, sir. "

And his deft strong hands did their accustomed task, and he went out of the room stepping lightly. Five minutes later he as lightly returned.

Ivan Ilych was still sitting in the same position in the armchair.

"Gerasim,"he said when the latter had replaced the freshly-washed utensil. "Please come here and help me. "Gerasim went up to him. "Lift me up. It is hard for me to get up, and I have sent Dmitri away. "

Gerasim went up to him, grasped his master with his strong arms deftly but gently, in the same way that he stepped—lifted him, supported him with one hand, and with the other drew up his trousers and would have set him down again, but Ivan Ilych asked to be led to the sofa. Gerasim, without an effort and without apparent pressure, led him, almost lifting him, to the sofa and placed him on it.

"Thank you. How easily and well you do it all!"

Gerasim smiled again and turned to leave the room. But Ivan Ilych felt his presence such a comfort that he did not want to let him go.

"One thing more, please move up that chair. No, the other one—under my feet. It is easier for me when my feet are raised. "

Gerasim brought the chair, set it down gently in place, and raised Ivan Ilych's legs on to it. It seemed to Ivan Ilych that he felt better while Gerasim was holding up his legs.

"It's better when my legs are higher," he said. "Place that cushion under them. "

Gerasim did so. He again lifted the legs and placed them, and again Ivan Ilych felt better while Gerasim held his legs. When he set them down Ivan Ilych fancied he felt worse.

"Gerasim,"he said. "Are you busy now?"

"Not at all, sir," said Gerasim, who had learnt from the townfolk how to speak to gentlefolk.

"What have you still to do?"

"What have I to do? I've done everything except chopping the logs for tomorrow. "

"Then hold my legs up a bit higher, can you?"

"Of course I can. Why not?"And Gerasim raised his master's legs higher and Ivan Ilych thought that in that position he did not feel any pain at all.

"And how about the logs?"

言,在他临死前夕散布的谎言,把他不久于人世这样严肃可怕的大事,缩小到访问、挂窗帘和晚餐吃鳇鱼等小事的程度,这使他感到极其痛苦。说也奇怪,好多次当他们就他的情况编造谎言时,他差一点儿大声叫出来:"别再撒谎了,我快要死了。这事儿你们知道,我也知道,所以别再撒谎了。"但他从来没有勇气这样做。他看到,他不久于人世这样严肃可怕的事(就像一个人走进会客室从身上散发出臭气一样),还要勉强维持他一辈子苦苦撑住的"体面"。他看到,谁也不可怜他,谁也不想了解他的真实情况。只有盖拉西姆一人了解他,并且可怜他。因此只有同盖拉西姆在一起他才觉得好过些。盖拉西姆有时通宵扛着他的腿,不去睡觉,嘴里还说:"您可不用操心,伊凡·伊里奇,我回头会睡个够的。"这时他感到安慰。或者当盖拉西姆脱口而出亲热地说:"要是你没病就好了,我这样伺候伺候你算得了什么?"他也感到安慰。只有盖拉西姆一人不撒谎,显然也只有他一人明白真实情况,并且认为无须隐讳,但他怜悯日益清瘦虚弱的老爷。有一次伊凡·伊里奇打发他走,他直截了当地说:"我们大家都要死的。我为什么不能伺候您呢?"他说这话的意思就是,现在他不辞辛劳,因为伺候的是个垂死的人,希望将来轮到他的时候也有人伺候他。

除了这个谎言,或者正是由于这个谎言,伊凡·伊里奇觉得特别痛苦的是,没有一个人像他所希望的那样可怜他。伊凡·伊里奇长时期受尽折磨,有时特别希望——尽管他不好意思承认——有人像疼爱有病的孩子那样疼爱他。他真希望有人疼他,吻他,对着他哭,就像人家疼爱孩子那样。他知道,他是个显赫的大官,已经胡子花白,因此这是不可能的,但他还是抱着这样的希望。他同盖拉西姆的关系近似这种关系,因此跟盖拉西姆在一起,他感到安慰。伊凡·伊里奇想哭,要人家疼他,对着他哭。不料这时他的法院同事谢贝克来了,伊凡·伊里奇不仅没有哭,没有表示亲热,反而板起脸,现出严肃和沉思的神气,习惯成自然地说了他对复审的意见,并且坚持自己的看法。他周围的这种谎言和他自己所说的谎言,比什么都厉害地毒害了他生命的最后日子。

八

有一天早晨。伊凡·伊里奇知道这是早晨,因为

"Don't trouble about that, sir. There's plenty of time."

Ivan Ilych told Gerasim to sit down and hold his legs, and began to talk to him. And strange to say it seemed to him that he felt better while Gerasim held his legs up.

After that Ivan Ilych would sometimes call Gerasim and get him to hold his legs on his shoulders, and he liked talking to him. Gerasim did it all easily, willingly, simply, and with a good nature that touched Ivan Ilych. Health, strength, and vitality in other people were offensive to him, but Gerasim's strength and vitality did not mortify but soothed him.

What tormented Ivan Ilych most was the deception, the lie, which for some reason they all accepted, that he was not dying but was simply ill, and that he only need keep quiet and undergo a treatment and then something very good would result. He however knew that do what they would nothing would come of it, only still more agonizing suffering and death. This deception tortured him—their not wishing to admit what they all knew and what he knew, but wanting to lie to him concerning his terrible condition, and wishing and forcing him to participate in that lie. Those lies—lies enacted over him on the eve of his death and destined to degrade this awful, solemn act to the level of their visitings, their curtains, their sturgeon for dinner—were a terrible agony for Ivan Ilych. And strangely enough, many times when they were going through their antics over him he had been within a hairbreadth of calling out to them: "Stop lying! You know and I know that I am dying. Then at least stop lying about it." But he had never had the spirit to do it. The awful terrible act of his dying was, he could see, reduced by those about him to the level of a casual, unpleasant, and almost indecorous incident (as if someone entered a drawing-room diffusing an unpleasant odor) and this was done by that very decorum which he had served all his life long. He saw that no one felt for him, because no one even wished to grasp his position. Only Gerasim recognized it and pitied him. And so Ivan Ilych felt at ease only with him. He felt comforted when Gerasim supported his legs (sometimes all night long) and refused to go to bed, saying: "Don't you worry, Ivan Ilych. I'll get sleep enough later on," or when he suddenly became familiar and exclaimed: "If you weren't sick it would be another matter, but as it is, why should I grudge a little trouble?" Gerasim alone did not lie; everything showed that he alone understood the facts of the case and did not consider it necessary to disguise them, but simply felt sorry for his emaciated and enfeebled master. Once when Ivan Ilych was sending him away he even said straight out: "We shall all of us die, so why should I grudge a little trouble?"—expressing the fact that he did not think his work burdensome, because he was doing it for a dying man and hoped someone would do the same for him when his time came.

Apart from this lying, or because of it, what most tormented Ivan Ilych was that no one pitied him as he wished to be pitied. At certain moments after

每天早晨都是盖拉西姆从书房里出去,男仆彼得进来吹灭蜡烛,拉开一扇窗帘,悄悄地收拾房间。早晨也好,晚上也好,礼拜五也好,礼拜天也好,反正都一样,反正没有区别,永远是一刻不停的难堪的疼痛,意识到生命正在无可奈何地消逝,但还没有完全消逝,那愈益逼近的可怕而又可恨的死,只有它才是真实的,其他一切都是谎言。在这种情况下,几天、几个礼拜和几个小时有什么区别?

"老爷,您要不要用茶?"

"他还是老一套,知道老爷太太每天早晨都要喝茶。"他想,接着回答说:"不用了。"

"您要不要坐到沙发上去?"

"他得把屋子收拾干净,可我在这里碍事。我太邋遢,太不整齐了,"他想了想,回答说:

"不,不用管我。"

男仆继续收拾屋子。伊凡·伊里奇伸出一只手。彼得殷勤地走过去。

"老爷,您要什么?"

"我的表。"

彼得拿起手边的表,递给他。

"八点半了。她们还没有起来吗?"

"还没有,老爷。瓦西里·伊凡内奇(这是儿子)上学去了,普拉斯柯菲雅·费多罗夫娜关照过,要是您问起,就去叫醒她。要去叫醒她吗?"

"不,不用了。"他回答,接着想:"要不要喝点儿茶呢?"于是就对彼得说:"对了,你拿点儿茶来吧。"

彼得走到门口。伊凡·伊里奇独自留着觉得害怕。"怎么把他留住呢?有了,吃药。"他想了想,说:"彼得,给我拿药来。"接着又想:"是啊,说不定吃药还有用呢。"他拿起匙子,把药吃下去。"不,没有用。一切都是胡闹,都是欺骗,"他一尝到那种熟悉的甜腻腻的怪味,就想,"不,我再也不能相信了。可是那个疼,那个疼,要是能停止一会儿就好了。"他呻吟起来。彼得向他回过头来。"不,你去吧,拿茶来。"

彼得走了,剩下伊凡·伊里奇一个人。他又呻吟起来。他疼得很厉害,可呻吟主要不是由于疼痛,而是由于悲伤。"老是那个样子,老是那样的白天和黑夜。但愿快一点儿。什么快一点儿?死,黑暗。不,不!好死不如赖活!"

彼得托着茶盘进来。伊凡·伊里奇茫然看了他好一阵,认不出他是谁,不知道他是来干什么的。他

prolonged suffering he wished most of all (though he would have been ashamed to confess it) for someone to pity him as a sick child is pitied. He longed to be petted and comforted. He knew he was an important functionary, that he had a beard turning grey, and that therefore what he longed for was impossible, but still he longed for it. And in Gerasim's attitude toward him there was something akin to what he wished for, and so that attitude comforted him. Ivan Ilych wanted to be petted and cried over, and then his colleague Shebek would come, and instead of weeping and being petted, Ivan Ilych would assume a serious, severe, and profound air, and by force of habit would express his opinion on a decision of the Court of Cassation and would stubbornly insist on that view. This falsity around him and within him did more than anything else to poison his last days.

VIII

It was morning. He knew it was morning because Gerasim had gone, and Peter the footman had come and put out the candles, drawn back one of the curtains, and began quietly to tidy up. Whether it was morning or evening, Friday or Sunday, made no difference, it was all just the same: the gnawing, unmitigated, agonizing pain, never ceasing for an instant, the consciousness of life inexorably waning but not yet extinguished, the approach of that ever dreaded and hateful Death which was the only reality, and always the same falsity. What were days, weeks, hours, in such a case?

"Will you have some tea, sir?"

"He wants things to be regular, and wishes the gentlefolk to drink tea in the morning," thought Ivan Ilych, and only said "No. "

"Wouldn't you like to move onto the sofa, sir?"

"He wants to tidy up the room, and I'm in the way. I am uncleanliness and disorder," he thought, and said only:

"No leave me alone. "

The man went on bustling about. Ivan Ilych stretched out his hand. Peter came up, ready to help.

"What is it, sir?"

"My watch. "

Peter took the watch which was close at hand and gave it to his master.

"Half-past eight. Are they up?"

"No sir, except Vladimir Ivanich"(the son) "who has gone to school. Praskovya Fedorovna ordered me to wake her if you asked for her. Shall I do so?"

"No, there's no need to. ""Perhaps I'd better have some tea,"he thought and added aloud: "Yes, bring me some tea. "

Peter went out. Left alone Ivan Ilych dreaded being left alone. "How can I keep him here? Oh yes, my medicine. ""Peter, give me my medicine. ""Why not? Perhaps it may still do me some good. " He took a spoonful and swallowed it. "No, it won't help. It's all

这种目光弄得彼得很狼狈。彼得现出尴尬的神色，伊凡·伊里奇才醒悟过来。

"噢，茶……"他说，"好的，放着。你帮我洗洗脸，拿一件干净衬衫来。"

伊凡·伊里奇开始梳洗。他断断续续地洗手，洗脸，刷牙，梳头，然后照照镜子。他感到害怕，特别是看到他的头发怎样贴着苍白的前额。

彼得给他换衬衫。他知道他要是看到自己的身体，一定会更加吃惊，因此不往自己身上看。梳洗完毕，他穿上晨衣，身上盖了一条方格毛毯，坐到扶手椅上喝茶。有那么一会儿他觉得神清气爽，但一喝茶，立刻又感到那种味道，那种疼痛。他勉强喝完茶，伸直腿躺下来。他躺下，让彼得走。

还是那个样子。一会儿出现了一线希望，一会儿又掉进绝望的海洋。老是疼，老是疼，老是悲怆凄凉，一切都是老样子。独个儿待着格外悲伤，想叫个人来，但他知道同人家待在一起更难受。"最好再来点儿吗啡，把什么都忘记。我要请求医生，叫他想点儿别的办法。这样可真受不了，真受不了！"

一小时，两小时就这样过去了。忽然前厅里响起了铃声。会不会是医生？果然是医生。他走进来，精神饱满，容光焕发，喜气洋洋。那副神气仿佛表示：你们何必这样大惊小怪，我这就来给你们解决问题。医生知道，这样的表情是不得体的，但他已经习惯了，改不掉，好像一个人一早穿上大礼服，就这样穿着一家家去拜客，没有办法改变了。

医生生气勃勃而又使人宽慰地搓搓手。

"啊，真冷，可把我冷坏了。让我暖和暖和身子。"他说这话时的神气仿佛表示，只要稍微等一下。等他身子一暖和，就什么问题都解决了。

"嗯，怎么样？"

伊凡·伊里奇觉得，医生想说："情况怎么样？"但他觉得不该那么问，就说："晚上睡得怎么样？"

伊凡·伊里奇望着医生的那副神气表示："您老是撒谎，怎么不害臊？"但医生不理会他的表情。

伊凡·伊里奇就说："还是那么糟。疼痛没有消除，也没有减轻。您能不能想点儿办法……"

"啊，你们病人总是这样。嗯，这会儿我可暖和了，就连普拉斯柯菲雅·费多罗夫娜那么仔细，也不会对我的体温有意见了。嗯，您好。"医生说着握了握病人的手。

tomfoolery, all deception, "he decided as soon as he became aware of the familiar, sickly, hopeless taste. "No, I can't believe in it any longer. But the pain, why this pain? If it would only cease just for a moment!" And he moaned. Peter turned towards him. "It's all right. Go and fetch me some tea."

Peter went out. Left alone Ivan Ilych groaned not so much with pain, terrible though that was, as from mental anguish. Always and for ever the same, always these endless days and nights. If only it would come quicker! If only *what* would come quicker? Death, darkness?. . . No, no! Anything rather than death!

When Peter returned with the tea on a tray, Ivan Ilych stared at him for a time in perplexity, not realizing who and what he was. Peter was disconcerted by that look and his embarrassment brought Ivan Ilych to himself.

"Oh, tea! All right, put it down. Only help me to wash and put on a clean shirt."

And Ivan Ilych began to wash. With pauses for rest, he washed his hands and then his face, cleaned his teeth, brushed his hair, and looked in the glass. He was terrified by what he saw, especially by the limp way in which his hair clung to his pallid forehead.

While his shirt was being changed he knew that he would be still more frightened at the sight of his body, so he avoided looking at it. Finally he was ready. He drew on a dressing-gown, wrapped himself in a plaid, and sat down in the armchair to take his tea. For a moment he felt refreshed, but as soon as he began to drink the tea he was again aware of the same taste, and the pain also returned. He finished it with an effort, and then lay down stretching out his legs, and dismissed Peter.

Always the same. Now a spark of hope flashes up, then a sea of despair rages, and always pain; always pain, always despair, and always the same. When alone he had a dreadful and distressing desire to call someone, but he knew beforehand that with others present it would be still worse. "Another dose of morphine—to lose consciousness. I will tell him, the doctor, that he must think of something else. It's impossible, impossible, to go on like this."

An hour and another pass like that. But now there is a ring at the door bell. Perhaps it's the doctor? It is. He comes in fresh, hearty, plump, and cheerful, with that look on his face that seems to say: "There now, you're in a panic about something, but we'll arrange it all for you directly!" The doctor knows this expression is out of place here, but he has put it on once for all and can't take it off—like a man who has put on a frock-coat in the morning to pay a round of calls.

The doctor rubs his hands vigorously and reassuringly.

"Brr! How cold it is! There's such a sharp frost; just let me warm myself!" he says, as if it were only a matter of waiting till he was warm, and then he would put everything right.

"Well now, how are you?"

Ivan Ilych feels that the doctor would like to say: "Well, how are our affairs?" but that even he feels that

接着医生收起戏谑的口吻,现出严肃的神色给病人看病,把脉,量体温,叩诊,听诊。

伊凡·伊里奇清清楚楚地知道,这一切都毫无意义,全是骗人的,但医生跪在他面前,身子凑近他,用一只耳朵忽上忽下地细听,脸上现出极其认真的神气,像体操一般做着各种姿势。伊凡·伊里奇面对这种场面,屈服了,就像他在法庭上听辩护律师发言一样,尽管明明知道他们都在撒谎以及为什么撒谎。

医生跪在沙发上,还在他身上敲着。这当儿门口传来普拉斯柯菲雅·费多罗夫娜绸衣裳的窸窣,还听见她在责备彼得没有及时向她报告医生的来到。

她走进来,吻吻丈夫,立刻振振有词地说,她早就起来了,只是不知道医生来了才没有及时出来迎接。

伊凡·伊里奇对她望望,打量她的全身,对她那白净浮肿的双手和脖子、光泽的头发和充满活力的明亮眼睛感到嫌恶。他从心底里憎恨她。她的亲吻更激起他对她难以克制的憎恨。

她对待他和他的病还是老样子。正像医生对病人的态度都已定型不变那样,她对丈夫的态度也已定型不变。她总是亲昵地责备他没有照规定服药休息,总是怪他自己不好。

"嗳,他这人就是不听话!不肯按时吃药。尤其是他睡的姿势不对,两腿搁得太高,这样睡对他不好。"

她告诉医生他怎样叫盖拉西姆扛着腿睡。

医生鄙夷不屑而又和蔼可亲地微微一笑,仿佛说:"有什么办法呢?病人总会做出这样的蠢事来,但情有可原。"

检查完毕,医生看了看表。这时普拉斯柯菲雅·费多罗夫娜向伊凡·伊里奇宣布,不管他是不是愿意,她今天就去请那位名医来,让他同米哈伊尔·达尼洛维奇(平时看病的医生)会诊一下,商量商量。

"请你不要反对。我是为我自己才这样做的。"她嘲讽地说,让他感到这一切都是为他而做的,因此他不该拒绝。他不作声,皱起眉头。他觉得周围是一片谎言,很难判断是非曲直。

她为他做的一切都是为了她自己。她对他说这样做是为了她自己,那倒是真的,不过她的行为叫人很难相信,因此必须从反面来理解。

11点半,那位名医果然来了。又是听诊,又是当着他的面一本正经地交谈,而到了隔壁房间又是谈肾

this would not do and says instead: "What sort of a night have you had?"

Ivan Ilych looks at him as much as to say: "Are you really never ashamed of lying?" But the doctor does not wish to understand this question, and Ivan Ilych says: "Just as terrible as ever. The pain never leaves me and never subsides. If only something..."

"Yes, you sick people are always like that.... There, now I think I am warm enough. Even Praskovya Fedorovna, who is so particular, could find no fault with my temperature. Well, now I can say good-morning," and the doctor presses his patient's hand.

Then, dropping his former playfulness, he begins with a most serious face to examine the patient, feeling his pulse and taking his temperature, and then begins the sounding and auscultation.

Ivan llych knows quite well and definitely that all this is nonsense and pure deception, but when the doctor, getting down on his knee, leans over him, putting his ear first higher then lower, and performs various gymnastic movements over him with a significant expression on his face, Ivan Ilych submits to it all as he used to submit to the speeches of the lawyers, though he knew very well that they were all lying and why they were lying.

The doctor, kneeling on the sofa, is still sounding him when Praskovya Fedorovna's silk dress rustles at the door and she is heard scolding Peter for not having let her know of the doctor's arrival.

She comes in, kisses her husband, and at once proceeds to prove that she has been up a long time already, and only owing to a misunderstanding failed to be there when the doctor arrived.

Ivan Ilych looks at her, scans her all over, sets against her the whiteness and plumpness and cleanness of her hands and neck, the gloss of her hair, and the sparkle of her vivacious eyes. He hates her with his whole soul. And the thrill of hatred he feels for her makes him suffer from her touch.

Her attitude towards him and his disease is still the same. Just as the doctor had adopted a certain relation to his patient which he could not abandon, so had she formed one towards him—that he was not doing something he ought to do and was himself to blame, and that she reproached him lovingly for this—and she could not now change that attitude.

"You see he doesn't listen to me and doesn't take his medicine at the proper time. And above all he lies in a position that is no doubt bad for him—with his legs up."

She described how he made Gerasim hold his legs up.

The doctor smiled with a contemptuous affability that said: "What's to be done? These sick people do have foolish fancies of that kind, but we must forgive them."

When the examination was over the doctor looked at his watch, and then Praskovya Fedorovna announced to Ivan Ilych that it was of course as he pleased, but she had sent to-day for a celebrated specialist who would examine him and have a consultation

脏,谈盲肠,又是一本正经地回答,又是避开他现在面临的生死问题,大谈什么肾脏和盲肠有毛病,ﾒ哈伊尔·达尼洛维奇和名医又都主张对肾脏和盲肠进行治疗。

名医临别时神态十分严肃,但并没有绝望。伊凡·伊里奇眼睛里露出恐惧和希望的光芒仰望着名医,怯生生地问他是不是还能恢复健康。名医回答说,不能保证,但可能性还是有的。伊凡·伊里奇用满怀希望的目光送别医生,他的样子显得很可怜。普拉斯柯菲雅·费多罗夫娜走出书房付给医生出诊费时都忍不住哭了。

被医生鼓舞起来的希望并没有持续多久。还是那个房间,还是那些图画,还是那些窗帘,还是那种墙纸,还是那些药瓶,还是他那个疼痛的身子。伊凡·伊里奇呻吟起来。给他注射了吗啡,他便迷迷糊糊地睡着了。

他醒来时,天色已开始发黑。仆人给他送来晚餐,他勉强吃了一点儿肉汤。于是一切如旧,黑夜又来临了。

饭后7点钟,普拉斯柯菲雅·费多罗夫娜走进他的房间。她穿着晚礼服,丰满的胸部被衣服绷得隆起,脸上有扑过粉的痕迹。早晨她就提起,今晚她们要去看戏。萨拉·贝娜到这个城里访问演出,她们订了一个包厢。那也是他的主意。这会儿,他把这事儿忘记了,她那副打扮使他生气。不过,当他记起是他要她们订包厢去看戏的,认为孩子们看这戏可以获得美的享受,他就把自己的愤怒掩饰起来。

普拉斯柯菲雅·费多罗夫娜进来的时候得意洋洋,但仿佛又有点负疚。她坐下来,问他身体怎么样,不过他看出,她只是为了应酬几句才问的,并非真的想了解什么,而且知道也问不出什么来。接着她就讲她要讲的话。她本来说什么也不愿去,可是包厢已经订了,爱仑和女儿,还有彼特利谢夫(法院侦讯官,未来的女婿)都要去,总不能让他们自己去,她其实是宁可待在家里陪他的。现在她只希望她不在家时,他能照医生的嘱咐休息。

"对了,费多尔·彼得罗维奇(未来的女婿)想进来看看你,行吗?还有丽莎。"

"让他们来好了。"

女儿走进来。她打扮得漂漂亮亮,露出部分年轻的身体。对比之下,他觉得更加难受。她却公然显示

with Michael Danilovich (their regular doctor).

"Please don't raise any objections. I am doing this for my own sake," she said ironically, letting it be felt that she was doing it all for his sake and only said this to leave him no right to refuse. He remained silent, knitting his brows. He felt that he was so surrounded and involved in a mesh of falsity that it was hard to unravel anything.

Everything she did for him was entirely fot her own sake, and she told him she was doing for herself what she actually was doing for herself, as if that was so incredible that he must understand the opposite.

At half-past eleven the celebrated specialist arrived. Again the sounding began and the significant conversations in his presence and in another room, about the kidneys and the appendix, and the questions and answers, with such an air of importance that again, instead of the real question of life and death which now alone confronted him, the question arose of the kidney and appendix which were not behaving as they ought to and would now be attacked by Michael Danilovich and the specialist and forced to amend their ways.

The celebrated specialist took leave of him with a serious though not hopeless look, and in reply to the timid question Ivan Ilych, with eyes glistening with fear and hope, put to him as to whether there was a chance of recovery, said that he could not vouch for it but there was a possibility. The look of hope with which Ivan Ilych watched the doctor out was so pathetic that Praskovya Fedorovna, seeing it, even wept as she left the room to hand the doctor his fee.

The gleam of hope kindled by the doctor's encouragement did not last long. The same room, the same pictures, curtains, wall-paper, medicine bottles, were all there, and the same aching suffering body, and Ivan Ilych began to moan. They gave him a subcutaneous injection and he sank into oblivion.

It was twilight when he came to. They brought his dinner and he swallowed some beef tea with difficulty, and then everything was the same again and night was coming on.

After dinner, at seven o'clock, Praskovya Fedorovna came into the room in evening dress, her full bosom pushed up by her corset, and with traces of powder on her face. She had reminded him in the morning that they were going to the theatre. Sarah Bernhardt was visiting the town and they had a box, which he had insisted on their taking. Now he had forgotten about it and her toilet offended him, but he concealed his vexation when he remembered that he had himself insisted on their securing a box and going because it would be an instructive and aesthetic pleasure for the children.

Praskovya Fedorovna came in, self-satisfied but yet with a rather guilty air. She sat down and asked how he was but, as he saw, only for the sake of asking and not in order to learn about it, knowing that there was nothing to learn—and then went on to what she really wanted to say: that she would not on any account have gone but that the box had been taken and Helen and their daughter were going, as well as

她健美的身体。显然她正在谈恋爱，对妨碍她幸福的疾病、痛苦和死亡感到嫌恶。

费多尔·彼得罗维奇也进来了。他身穿燕尾服，头发烫出波纹，雪白的硬领夹着青筋毕露的细长脖子，胸前露出一大块白硬衬，瘦长的黑裤紧裹着两条强壮的大腿，手上戴着雪白的手套，拿着大礼帽。

一个中学生在他后面悄悄走进来。这个可怜的孩子穿一身崭新的学生装，戴着手套，眼圈发黑——伊凡·伊里奇知道怎么会这样。

他总是很怜悯儿子。儿子那种满怀同情的怯生生的目光使他心惊胆战。伊凡·伊里奇觉得除了盖拉西姆以外，只有儿子一人了解他，同情他。

大家都坐下来，又问了一下病情。接下来是一片沉默。丽莎问母亲要望远镜。母女俩争吵起来，不知是谁拿了，放在什么地方。这事儿弄得大家很不高兴。

费多尔·彼得罗维奇问伊凡·伊里奇有没有看过萨拉·贝娜。伊凡·伊里奇起初没听懂他问什么，后来才说："没有。您看过吗？"

"看过了，她演《阿德里安娜·莱科芙露尔》①。"

普拉斯柯菲雅·费多罗夫娜说，她演那种角色特别好。女儿不同意她的看法。大家谈起她的演技又典雅又真挚——那题目已谈过不知多少次了。

谈话中间，费多尔·彼得罗维奇对伊凡·伊里奇瞧了一眼，不作声了。其他人跟着瞧了一眼，也不做声了。伊凡·伊里奇睁大眼睛向前望望，显然对他们很生气。这种尴尬的局面必须改变，可是怎么也无法改变。必须设法打破这种沉默。谁也不敢这样做，大家都害怕，惟恐这种礼貌周到的虚伪做法一旦被揭穿，真相就会大白。丽莎第一个鼓起勇气，打破了沉默。她想掩饰大家心里都有的感觉，却脱口而出：

"嗯，要是去的话，那么是时候了。"她瞧了瞧父亲送给她的表，说道。接着对未婚夫会意地微微一笑，衣服窸窣地响着站起来。

大家都站起来，告辞走了。

等他们一走，伊凡·伊里奇觉得好过些，因为虚伪的局面结束了，随着他们一起消失了，但疼痛如旧。依旧是那种疼痛，依旧是那种恐惧，一点儿也没有缓和，而是每况愈下。

时间还是一分钟又一分钟，一小时又一小时地过

---

① 法国戏剧家斯克里布(1791—1861)作的剧本。

Petrishchev （the examining magistrate, their daughter's fiancée) and that it was out of the question to let them go alone; but that she would have much preferred to sit with him for a while; and he must be sure to follow the doctor's orders while she was away.

"Oh, and Fedor Petrovich" (the fiancé) "would like to come in. May he? And Lisa?"

"All right."

Their daughter came in in full evening dress, her fresh young flesh exposed (making a show of that very flesh which in his own case caused so much suffering), strong, healthy, evidently in love, and impatient with illness, suffering, and death, because they interfered with her happiness.

Fedor Petrovich came in too, in evening dress, his hair curled *à la Capoul*, a tight stiff collar round his long sinewy neck, an enormous white shirt-front and narrow black trousers tightly stretched over his strong thighs. He had one white glove tightly drawn on, and was holding his opera hat in his hand.

Following him the schoolboy crept in unnoticed, in a new uniform, poor little fellow, and wearing gloves. Terribly dark shadows showed under his eyes, the meaning of which Ivan Ilych knew well.

His son had always seemed pathetic to him, and now it was dreadful to see the boy's frightened look of pity. It seemed to Ivan Ilych that Vasya was the only one besides Gerasim who understood and pitied him.

They all sat down and again asked how he was. A silence followed. Lisa asked her mother about the opera-glasses, and there was an altercation between mother and daughter as to who had taken them and where they had been put. This occasioned some unpleasantness.

Fedor Petrovich inquired of Ivan Ilych whether he had ever seen Sarah Bernhardt. Ivan Ilych did not at first catch the question, but then replied: "No, have you seen her before?

"Yes, in *Adrienne Lecouvreur*."

Praskovya Fedorovna mentioned some roles in which Sarah Bernhardt was particularly good. Her daughter disagreed. Conversation sprang up as to the elegance and realism of her acting—the sort of conversation that is always repeated and is always the same.

In the midst of the conversation Fedor Petrovich glanced at Ivan Ilych and became silent. The others also looked at him and grew silent. Ivan Ilych was staring with glittering eyes straight before him, evidently indignant with them. This had to be rectified, but it was impossible to do so. The silence had to be broken, but for a time no one dared to break it and they all became afraid that the conventional deception would suddenly become obvious and the truth become plain to all. Lisa was the first to pluck up courage and break that silence, but by trying to hide what everybody was feeling, she betrayed it.

"Well, if we are going it's time to start," she said, looking at her watch, a present from her father, and with a faint and significant smile at Fedor Petrovich relating to something known only to them. She got up with a rustle of her dress.

去,一切如旧,没完没了,而无法避免的结局却越来越使人不寒而栗。

"好的,你去叫盖拉西姆来。"他回答彼得说。

九

妻子深夜才回家。她踮着脚悄悄进来,但他还是听见她的脚步声。他睁开眼睛,连忙又闭上。她想打发盖拉西姆走开,自己也陪他坐一会儿。他却睁开眼睛,说:

"不,你去吧。"

"你很难受吗?"

"老样子。"

"服点儿鸦片吧。"

他同意了,服了点儿鸦片。她走了。

直到清晨3点,他一直处在痛苦的迷糊状态中。他仿佛觉得人家硬把他这个病痛的身子往一个又窄又黑又深的口袋里塞,一个劲地往下塞,却怎么也塞不到袋底。这件可怕的事把他折磨得好苦。他又害怕,又想往下沉,不断挣扎,越挣扎越往下沉。他突然跌了下去,随即惊醒过来。依旧是那个盖拉西姆坐在床脚跟,平静而耐心地打着瞌睡。他却躺在那里,把那双穿着袜子的瘦腿搁在盖拉西姆的肩上。依旧是那支有罩的蜡烛,依旧是那种一刻不停的疼痛。

"你去吧,盖拉西姆。"他喃喃地说。

"不要紧,老爷,我坐坐。"

"不,你去吧。"

他放下腿,侧过身子躺着。他开始可怜自己。他等盖拉西姆走到隔壁屋里,再也忍不住,就像孩子般痛哭起来。他哭自己的无依无靠,哭自己的孤独寂寞,哭人们的残酷,哭上帝的残酷和冷漠。

"你为什么要这样做?为什么把我带到这儿来?为什么,为什么这么狠心地折磨我?……"

他知道不会有回答,但又因得不到也不可能得到回答而痛苦。疼痛又发作了,但他一动不动,也不呼号。他自言自语:"痛吧,再痛吧!可是为了什么呀?我对你做了什么啦?这是为了什么呀?"

后来他安静了,不仅停止哭泣,而且屏住呼吸,提起精神来。他仿佛不是在倾听说话声,而是在倾听灵魂的呼声,倾听自己思潮的翻腾。

They all rose, said good-night, and went away.

When they had gone it seemed to Ivan Ilych that he felt better; the falsity had gone with them. But the pain remained—that same pain and that same fear that made everything monotonously alike, nothing harder and nothing easier. Everything was worse.

Again minute followed minute and hour followed hour. Everything remained the same and there was no cessation. And the inevitable end of it all became more and more terrible.

"Yes, send Gerasim here," he replied to a question Peter asked.

IX

His wife returned late at night. She came in on tiptoe, but he heard her, opened his eyes, and made haste to close them again. She wished to send Gerasim away and to sit with him herself, but he opened his eyes and said: "No, go away."

"Are you in great pain?"

"Always the same."

"Take some opium."

He agreed and took some. She went away.

Till about three in the morning he was in a state of stupified misery. It seemed to him that he and his pain were being thrust into a narrow, deep black sack, but though they were pushed further and further in they could not be pushed to the bottom. And this, terrible enough in itself, was accompanied by suffering. He was frightened yet wanted to fall through the sack, he struggled but yet co-operated. And suddenly he broke through, fell, and regained consciousness. Gerasim was sitting at the foot of the bed dozing quietly and patiently, while he himself lay with his emaciated stockinged legs resting on Gerasim's shoulders; the same shaded candle was there and the same unceasing pain.

"Go away, Gerasim," he whispered.

"It's all right, sir. I'll stay a while."

"No. Go away."

He removed his legs from Gerasim's shoulders, turned sideways onto his arm, and felt sorry for himself. He only waited till Gerasim had gone into the next room and then restrained himself no longer but wept like a child. He wept on account of his helplessness, his terrible loneliness, the cruelty of man, the cruelty of God, and the absence of God.

"Why hast Thou done all this? Why hast Thou brought me here? Why, why dost Thou torment me so terribly?"

He did not expect an answer and yet wept because there was no answer and could be none. The pain again grew more acute, but he did not stir and did not call. He said to himself: "Go on! Strike me! But what is it for? What have I done to Thee? What is it for?"

Then he grew quiet and not only ceased weeping but even held his breath and became all attention. It

"你要什么呀?"这是他听出来的第一句明确的话。"你要什么呀? 你要什么呀,"他一再问自己。"要什么?"——"摆脱痛苦,活下去。"他自己回答。

他又全神贯注地倾听,连疼痛都忘记了。

"活下去? 怎么活?"心灵里有个声音问他。

"是的,活下去,像我从前那样活得舒畅而快乐。"

"像你以前那样,活得舒畅而快乐吗?"心灵里的声音问。于是他开始回忆自己一生中美好的日子。奇怪的是,所有那些美好的日子现在看来一点儿也不美好,只有童年的回忆是例外。童年时代确实有过欢乐的日子,要是时光能倒流,那是值得重温的。但享受过当年欢乐的人已经不存在了,存在的似乎只有对别人的回忆。

自从伊凡·伊里奇变成现在这个样子以来,过去的欢乐都在他眼里消失了,或者说,变得不足道了,变得令人讨厌了。

离童年越远,离现在越近,那些欢乐就显得越不足道,越加可疑。这是从法学院开始的。在那里还有点儿真正美好的事,还有欢乐,还有友谊,还有希望。但读到高年级,美好的时光就越来越少。后来开始在官府供职,又出现了美好的时光,那是对一个女人的倾慕。后来生活又浑浑噩噩,美好的时光更少了,越来越少,越来越少。

结婚……是那么意外,那么叫人失望。妻子嘴里的臭味,放纵情欲,装腔作势! 死气沉沉地办公,不择手段地追求金钱,就这样过了一年,两年,十年,二十年——始终是那么一套。而且越往后,就越是死气沉沉。我在走下坡路,却还以为在上山。就是这么一回事。大家都说我官运亨通,步步高升,其实生命在我脚下溜掉……如今瞧吧,末日到了!

这究竟是怎么一回事? 为什么会这样? 生活不该那么无聊,那么讨厌。不该! 即使生活确是那么讨厌,那么无聊,那又为什么要死,而且死得那么痛苦? 总有点儿不对头。

"是不是我的生活有些什么地方不对头?"他忽然想到,"但我不论做什么都是循规蹈矩的,怎么会不对头?"他自言自语,顿时找到了唯一的答案:生死之谜是无法解答的。

"如今你到底要什么呢? 要活命? 怎么活? 像法庭上听到民事执行吏高呼'开庭了……'时那样活。'开庭了,开庭了,'"他一再对自己说。"喏,现在要开

was as though he were listening not to an audible voice but to the voice of his soul, to the current of thoughts arising within him.

"What is it you want?"was the first clear conception capable of expression in words, that he heard.

"What do you want? What do you want?"he repeated to himself

"What do I want? To live and not to suffer,"he answered.

And again he listened with such concentrated attention that even his pain did not distract him.

"To live? How?"asked his inner voice.

"Why, to live as I used to—well and pleasantly. "

"As you lived before, well and pleasantly?" the voice repeated.

And in imagination he began to recall the best moments of his pleasant life. But strange to say none of those best moments of his pleasant life now seemed at all what they had then seemed—none of them except the first recollections of childhood. There, in childhood, there had been something really pleasant with which it would be possible to live if it could return. But the child who had experienced that happiness existed no longer, it was like a reminiscence of somebody else.

As soon as the period began which had produced the present Ivan Ilych, all that had then seemed joys now melted before his sight and turned into something trivial and often nasty.

And the further he departed from childhood and the nearer he came to the present the more worthless and doubtful were the joys. This began with the School of Law. A little that was really good was still found there—there was light-heartedness, friendship, and hope. But in the upper classes there had already been fewer of such good moments. Then during the first years of his official career, when he was in the service of the Governor, some pleasant moments again occurred: they were the memories of love for a woman. Then all became confused and there was still less of what was good; later on again there was still less that was good, and the further he went the less there was. His marriage, a mere accident, then the disenchantment that followed it, his wife's bad breath and the sensuality and hypocrisy: then that deadly official life and those preoccupations about money, a year of it, and two, and ten, and twenty, and always the same thing. And the longer it lasted the more deadly it became. "It is as if I had been going downhill while I imagined I was going up. And that is really what it was. I was going up in public opinion, but to the same extent life was ebbing away from me. And now it is all done and there is only death. "

"Then what does it mean? Why? It can't be that life is so senseless and horrible. But if it really has been so horrible and senseless, why must I die and die in agony? There is something wrong!"

"Maybe I did not live as I ought to have done,"it suddenly occurred to him. "But how could that be, when I did everything properly?"he replied, and immediately dismissed from his mind this, the sole solution

庭了！可我又没有罪！"他恨恨地叫道。"为了什么呀？"他停止哭泣，转过脸来对着墙壁，一直思考着那个问题，为什么要忍受这样的恐怖？为什么？

然而，不管他怎样苦苦思索，都找不到答案。他头脑里又出现了那个常常出现的想法：这一切都是由于他生活过得不对头。他重新回顾自己规规矩矩的一生，立刻又把这个古怪的想法驱除掉。

十

又过了两个礼拜。伊凡·伊里奇躺在沙发上已经起不来了。他不愿躺在床上，就躺在长沙发上。他几乎一直面对墙壁躺着，孤独地忍受着那难以摆脱的痛苦，孤独地思索着那难以解答的问题："这是怎么回事？难道真的要死吗？"心灵里有个声音回答说："是的，要死的。""为什么要受这样的罪？"那声音回答说："不为什么，就是这样。"除此以外就什么也没有了。

自从伊凡·伊里奇开始生病，自从他第一次看医生以来，他的心情就分裂成两种对立的状态，两种状态交替出现着。一会儿是绝望和等待着神秘而恐怖的死亡，一会儿是希望和紧张地观察自己身上的器官。一会儿眼前出现了功能暂时停止的肾脏和盲肠，一会儿又出现了无可避免的神秘而恐怖的死亡。

这两种心情从一开始就生病就交替出现，但随着病情的发展，他就觉得肾脏的功能越来越可疑，越来越虚幻，而日益逼近的死亡却越来越现实。

他只要想想 3 个月前的身体，再看看现在的情况，看看他怎样一步步不停地走着下坡路，任何侥幸的心情就自然而然地土崩瓦解了。

近来，他面向沙发背躺着，感到异常孤寂，那是一种处身在闹市和许多亲友中间却没有人理睬他而感到的孤寂，即使跑到天涯海角都找不到的孤寂。处身在这种可怕的孤寂中，他只能靠回忆往事度日。一幕幕往事像图画般浮现在他眼前。他总是从近期的事开始，一直回忆到遥远的过去，回忆到童年时代，然后停留在那些往事上。譬如他从今天给他端来的李子酱，就会想到童年吃过的干瘪法国李子，觉得别有风味，吃到果核，还满口生津。同时他又会想到当年的种种情景，保姆、兄弟、玩具。"那些事别去想了……太痛苦了。"伊凡·伊里奇对自己说，思想又回到现实

of all the riddles of life and death, as something quite impossible.

"Then what do you want now? To live? Live how? Live as you lived in the law courts when the usher proclaimed 'The judge is coming. The judge is coming, the judge!'" he repeated to himself "Here he is the judge. But I am not guilty!" he exclaimed angrily. "What is it for?" And he ceased crying, but turning his face to the wall continued to ponder on the same question: Why, and for what purpose, is there all this horror? But however much he pondered he found no answer. And whenever the thought occurred to him, as it often did, that it all resulted from his not having lived as he ought to have done, he at once recalled the correctness of his whole life and dismissed so strange an idea.

X

Another fortnight passed. Ivan Ilych now no longer left his sofa. He would not lie in bed but lay on the sofa, facing the wall nearly all the time. He suffered ever the same unceasing agonies and in his loneliness pondered always on the same insoluble question: "What is this? Can it be that it is Death?" And the inner voice answered: "Yes, it is Death."

"Why these sufferings?" And the voice answered, "For no reason—they just are so." Beyond and besides this there was nothing.

From the very beginning of his illness, ever since he had first been to see the doctor, Ivan Ilych's life had been divided between two contrary and alternating moods: now it was despair and the expectation of his uncomprehended and terrible death, and now hope and an intensely interested observation of the functioning of his organs. Now before his eyes there was only a kidney or an intestine that temporarily evaded its duty, and now only that incomprehensible and dreadful death from which it was impossible to escape.

These two states of mind had alternated from the very beginning of his illness, but the further it progressed the more doubtful and fantastic became the conception of the kidney, and the more real the sense of impending death.

He had but to call to mind what he had been three months before and what he was now, to call to mind with what regularity he had been going downhill, for every possibility of hope to be shattered.

Latterly during that loneliness in which he found himself as he lay facing the back of the sofa, a loneliness in the midst of a populous town and surrounded by numerous acquaintances and relations but that yet could not have been more complete anywhere—either at the bottom of the sea or under the earth—during that terrible loneliness Ivan Ilych had lived only in memories of the past. Pictures of his past rose before him one after another. They always began with what was nearest in time and then went back to what was most remote—to his childhood—and rested there. If

上来。他瞧着羊皮沙发上的皱纹和沙发背上的纽扣。"山羊皮很贵，又不牢。有一次就为这事争吵过。还记得当年我们撕坏父亲的皮包，因此受罚，但那是另一种山羊皮，是另一次争吵……妈妈还送包子来给我们吃。"他的思想又停留在童年时代，他又感到很难过。他竭力驱散这种回忆，想些别的事。

在一系列往事的回忆中，他又想到了那件事，他怎样生病和病情怎样恶化。他想到年纪越小，越是充满生气。生命里善的因素越多，生命力也就越充沛。两者互为因果。"病痛越来越厉害，整个生命也就越来越糟，"他想，"生命开始还有一点儿光明，后来却越来越黯淡，消逝得越来越快，离死越来越近。"他忽然想到，一块石子落下总是不断地增加速度。生命也是这样，带着不断增加的痛苦，越来越快地掉落下去，掉进痛苦的深渊。"我在飞逝……"他浑身打了个哆嗦，试图抗拒，但知道这是无法抗拒的。他的眼睛虽已疲劳，却依旧瞪着前面，瞪着沙发背。他等待着，等待着那可怕的坠落、震动和灭亡。"无法抗拒，"他自言自语，"真想知道，为什么会这样？可是无法知道。要是说我生活得不对头，那还有理由解释。可是不能这么说。"他对自己说，想到自己一辈子奉公守法，过着正派而体面的生活。"不能这么说，"他嘴上露出冷笑，仿佛人家会看到他这个样子，并且会因此受骗似的，"可是找不到解释！折磨，死亡……为了什么呀？"

十一

这样过了两个礼拜。在这期间发生了伊凡·伊里奇夫妇所希望的那件事，彼特利谢夫正式来求婚。这事发生在一个晚上。第二天，普拉斯柯菲雅·费多罗夫娜走进丈夫房间，考虑着怎样向他宣布彼特利谢夫求婚的事，但就在那天夜里，伊凡·伊里奇的病情又有新的发展。普拉斯柯菲雅·费多罗夫娜发现他又躺在长沙发上，但姿势跟以前不同。他仰天躺着，呻吟着，眼睛呆滞地瞪着前方。

她谈起吃药的事。他把目光转到她身上。她没有把话说完，因为发现他的目光里充满对她的愤恨。

"看在基督份儿上，让我安安静静地死吧！"他说。

她正想出去，但这当儿女儿进来向他请安。他也像对妻子那样对女儿望望，面对女儿问候病情的话只

he thought of the stewed prunes that had been offered him that day, his mind went back to the raw shrivelled French plums of his childhood, their peculiar flavour and the flow of saliva when he sucked their stones, and along with the memory of that taste came a whole series of memories of those day: his nurse, his brother, and their toys. "No, I musn't think of that. . . . It is too painful," Ivan Ilych said to himself, and brought himself back to the present—to the button on the back of the sofa and the creases in its morocco. "Morocco is expensive, but it does not wear well: there had been a quarrel about it. It was a different kind of quarrel and a different kind of morocco that time when we tore father's portfolio and were punished, and mamma brought us some tarts. . . . " And again his thoughts dwelt on his childhood, and again it was painful and he tried to banish them and fix his mind on something else.

Then again together with that chain of memories another series passed through his mind—of how his illness had progressed and grown worse. There also the further back he looked the more life there had been. There had been more of what was good in life and more of life itself The two merged together. "Just as the pain went on getting worse and worse so my life grew worse and worse," he thought. "There is one bright spot there at the back, at the beginning of life, and afterwards all becomes blacker and blacker and proceeds more and more rapidly—in inverse ratio to the square of the distance from death," thought Ivan Ilych. And the example of a stone falling downwards with increasing velocity entered his mind. Life, a series of increasing sufferings, flies further and further towards its end—the most terrible suffering. "I am flying. . . . " He shuddered, shifted himself, and tried to resist, but was already aware that resistance was impossible, and again with eyes weary of gazing but unable to cease seeing what was before them, he stared at the back of the sofa and waited—awaiting that dreadful fall and shock and destruction.

"Resistance is impossible!" he said to himself "If I could only understand what it is all for! But that too is impossible. An explanation would be possible if it could be said that I have not lived as I ought to. But it is impossible to say that," and he remembered all the legality, correctitude, and propriety of his life. "That at any rate can certainly not be admitted," he thought, and his lips smiled ironically as if someone could see that smile and be taken in by it. "There is no explanation! Agony, death. . . . What for?"

XI

Another two weeks went by in this way and during that fortnight an event occurred that Ivan Ilych and his wife had desired. Petrishchev formally proposed. It happened in the evening. The next day Praskovya Fedorovna came into her husband's room considering how best to inform him of it, but that very night

冷冷地说,他不久就会让她们解脱的。母女俩默不作声,坐了一会儿走了。

"我们究竟有什么过错呀?"丽莎对母亲说,"仿佛都是我们弄得他这样似的!我可怜爸爸。可他为什么要折磨我们?"

医生按时来给他看病。伊凡·伊里奇对他的问题只回答"是"或者"不是",并愤怒地盯住医生,最后说:

"您明明知道毫无办法,那就让我去吧!"

"我们可以减轻您的痛苦。"医生说。

"这点您也办不到,让我去吧!"

医生走到客厅,告诉普拉斯柯菲雅·费多罗夫娜情况很严重,只有一样东西可以减轻他的痛苦,就是鸦片。

医生说,他肉体上的痛苦很厉害,这是事实,但精神上的痛苦比肉体上的痛苦更厉害。而这也是他最难受的事。

他精神上的痛苦就是,那天夜里他瞧着盖拉西姆睡眼惺忪、颧骨凸出的善良的脸,忽然想到,我这辈子说不定真的过得不对头。

他忽然想,以前说他这辈子生活过得不对头,他是绝对不同意的,但现在看来可能是真的。他忽然想,以前他有过轻微的冲动,反对豪门权贵肯定的好事,这种冲动虽然很快就被他自己克制住,但说不定倒是正确的,而其他一切可能都不对头。他的职务,他所安排的生活,他的家庭,他所献身的公益事业和本职工作,这一切可能都不对头。他试图为这一切辩护,但忽然发现这一切都有问题,没有什么可辩护的。

"既然如此,那么现在在我即将离开世界的时候,发觉我把天赋予我的一切都糟蹋了,但又无法挽救,那可怎么办?"他自言自语。他仰天躺着,重新回顾自己的一生。早晨他看到仆人,后来看到妻子,后来看到女儿,后来看到医生,他们的一举一动,一言一语,都证实他夜间所发现的可怕真理。他从他们身上看到了自己,看到了他赖以生活的一切,并且明白这一切都不对头。这一切都是掩盖着生死问题的可怕的大骗局。这种思想增加了他肉体上的痛苦。比以前增加了十倍。他不断呻吟,辗转反侧,扯着身上的衣服。他觉得衣服束缚着他,使他喘不过气来。他为此憎恨他们。

医生给了他大剂量鸦片,他昏睡过去,但到吃晚

there had been a fresh change for the worse in his condition. She found him still lying on the sofa but in a different position. He lay on his back, groaning and staring fixedly straight in front of him.

She began to remind him of his medicines, but he turned his eyes towards her with such a look that she did not finish what she was saying; so great an animosity, to her in particular, did that look express.

"For Christ's sake let me die in peace!" he said.

She would have gone away, but just then their daughter came in and went up to say good morning. He looked at her as he had done at his wife, and in reply to her inquiry about his health said dryly that he would soon free them all of himself. They were both silent and after sitting with him for a while went away.

"Is it our fault?" Lisa said to her mother. "It's as if we were to blame! I am sorry for papa, but why should we be tortured?"

The doctor came at his usual time. Ivan Ilych answered "Yes" and "No," never taking his angry eyes from him, and at last said: "You know you can do nothing for me, so leave me alone."

"We can ease your sufferings."

"You can't even do that. Let me be."

The doctor went into the drawing-room and told Praskovya Fedorovna that the case was very serious and that the only resource left was opium to allay her husband's sufferings, which must be terrible.

It was true, as the doctor said, that Ivan Ilych's physical sufferings were terrible, but worse than the physical sufferings were his mental sufferings which were his chief torture.

His mental sufferings were due to the fact that that night, as he looked at Gerasim's sleepy, good-natured face with its prominent cheek-bones, the question suddenly occurred to him: "What if my whole life has really been wrong?"

It occurred to him that what had appeared perfectly impossible before, namely that he had not spent his life as he should have done, might after all be true. It occurred to him that his scarcely perceptible attempts to struggle against what was considered good by the most highly placed people, those scarcely noticeable impulses which he had immediately suppressed, might have been the real thing, and all the rest false. And his professional duties and the whole arrangement of his life and of his family, and all his social and official interests, might all have been false. He tried to defend all those things to himself and suddenly felt the weakness of what he was defending. There was nothing to defend.

"But if that is so," he said to himself, "and I am leaving this life with the consciousness that I have lost all that was given me and it is impossible to rectify it—what then?"

He lay on his back and began to pass his life in review in quite a new way. In the morning when he saw first his footman, then his wife, then his daughter, and then the doctor, their every word and movement confirmed to him the awful truth that had been

饭时又开始折腾。他把所有的人都赶开,不断地翻来覆去。

妻子走过来对他说:

"约翰,心肝儿。你就为了我这么办吧。这没有什么害处,常常还有点儿用。真的,这没什么。健康的人也常常……"

他睁大眼睛,问:

"什么事? 进圣餐吗? 干什么呀? 不用了! 不过……"

她哭了。

"好吗,我的亲人? 我去叫我们的神父来,他这人挺好。"

"好,太好了。"他说。

神父来了,听了他的忏悔,他觉得好些,疑虑似乎减少些,痛苦也减轻了。刹那间心里看到了希望。他又想到了盲肠,觉得还可以治愈。他含着眼泪进了圣餐。

他进了圣餐,又被放到床上,刹那间觉得好过些,并且又出现了生的希望。他想到他们曾经建议他动手术。"活下去,我要活下去。"他自言自语。妻子走来祝贺,她敷衍了几句,又问:

"你是不是感到好些?"

他眼睛不看她,嘴里说:"是。"

她的服装,她的体态,她的神情,她的腔调,全都向他说明一个意思:"不对头。你过去和现在赖以生活的一切,都是谎言,都是对你掩盖生死大事的骗局。"他一想到这点,心头就冒起一阵愤恨,随着愤恨又感到肉体上的痛苦,同时意识到不可避免的临近的死亡。接着又增加了一种新的感觉,抽痛、刺痛和窒息。

当他说"是"的时候,他的脸色是可怕的。他说了一声"是",眼睛直盯住她的脸,接着使出全身的力气异常迅速地把脸转过去,伏在床上嚷道:

"都给我走,都给我走,让我一个人待着。"

十二

从那时起,他连续三天一刻不停地惨叫,叫得那么可怕。就是隔着两道门听了也觉得毛骨悚然。当他回答妻子的时候,他明白他完了,无法挽救了,末日

revealed to him during the night. In them he saw himself—all that for which he had lived—and saw clearly that it was not real at all, but a terrible and huge deception which had hidden both life and death. This consciousness intensified his physical suffering tenfold. He groaned and tossed about, and pulled at his clothing which choked and stifled him. And he hated them on that account.

He was given a large dose of opium and became unconscious, but at noon his sufferings began again. He drove everybody away and tossed from side to side.

His wife came to him and said:

"Jean, my dear, do this for me. It can't do any harm and often helps. Healthy people often do it."

He opened his eyes wide.

"What? Take communion? Why? It's unnecessary! However...."

She began to cry.

"Yes, do, my dear. I'll send for our priest. He is such a nice man."

"All right. Very well," he muttered.

When the priest came and heard his confession, Ivan Ilych was softened and seemed to feel a relief from his doubts and consequently from his sufferings, and for a moment there came a ray of hope. He again began to think of the vermiform appendix and the possibility of correcting it. He received the sacrament with tears in his eyes.

When they laid him down again afterwards he felt a moment's ease, and the hope that he might live awoke in him again. He began to think of the operation that had been suggested to him. "To live! I want to live!" he said to himself.

His wife came in to congratulate him after his communion, and when uttering the usual conventional words she added:

"You feel better, don't you?"

Without looking at her he said "Yes."

Her dress, her figure, the expression of her face, the tone of her voice, all revealed the same thing. "This is wrong, it is not as it should be. All you have lived for and still live for is falsehood and deception, hiding life and death from you." And as soon as he admitted that thought, his hatred and his agonizing physical suffering again sprang up, and with that suffering a consciousness of the unavoidable, approaching end. And to this was added a new sensation of grinding shooting pain and a feeling of suffocation.

The expression of his face when he uttered that "yes" was dreadful. Having uttered it, he looked her straight in the eyes, turned on his face with a rapidity extraordinary in his weak state and shouted:

"Go away! Go away and leave me alone!"

XII

From that moment the screaming began that continued for three days, and was so terrible that one could not hear it through two closed doors without

到了,生命的末日到了,可是生死之谜始终没有解决,永远是个谜。

"哎哟!哎哟!哎哟!"他用不同的音调惨叫着。他开始嚷道:"我不要!"接下去又是哎哟、哎哟地惨叫。

整整三天,他一刻不停地在那个黑口袋里拼命挣扎,而一个肉眼看不见的力量却无可抗拒地把他往口袋里塞。他好像一个死刑犯,落在刽子手手里,知道没有生路了。他每分钟都感觉到,不管他怎样挣扎,他是越来越接近那恐怖的末日了。他觉得他的痛苦在于他正在被塞到那个黑窟窿里去,而更痛苦的是他不能爽爽快快地落进去。他所以不能爽爽快快地落进去,是因为他认为他的生命是有价值的。这种对自己生命的肯定,阻碍了他,不让他走,使他特别痛苦。

突然,他的胸部和腰部受到猛烈的打击,呼吸更加困难,他掉到了窟窿里。在窟窿底里有一道亮光。他觉得自己仿佛处身在火车车厢里,你以为火车在前进,其实却在后退。这时他突然辨出了方向。

"是的,一切都不对头,"他自言自语,"但没有关系,可以纠正的。可怎样才算'对头'呢?"他问自己,接着突然沉默了。

第三天傍晚,他临终前两小时,念中学的儿子悄悄地进来,走到父亲床跟前。垂死的人一直在惨叫,挥动双臂。他的一只手落在儿子的头上。儿子捉住他的手,把它贴在嘴唇上,哭了起来。

就在这时候,伊凡·伊里奇掉了下去,看见了光。他领悟到他的生活过得不对头,但还可以纠正。他问自己:怎样才"对头",接着一动不动地留神听着。他感到有人在吻他的手。他睁开眼睛,对儿子瞧了一眼。他可怜起儿子来。妻子走到他跟前。他对她瞧了一眼。她张开嘴,鼻子上和面颊上挂着眼泪,露出绝望的神情瞧着他。他为她难过。

"是的,我把他们害苦了,"他想,"他们真可怜,但等我一死,他们就会好过些。"他想把这话说出来,可是没有力气说。"不过,何必说呢,应该行动。"他想。他对着儿子用目光示意妻子说:

"带他走……可怜……你也……"他还想说"原谅我",但却说了"原来我"。他已经没有力气去纠正,只摆了摆手,知道谁需要听懂自然会懂的。

他恍然大悟,原来折磨他的东西消失了,从四面八方消失了,从一切方面消失了。他可怜他们,应该

horror. At the moment he answered his wife he realized that he was lost, that there was no return, that the end had come, the very end, and his doubts were still unsolved and remained doubts.

"Oh! Oh! Oh!" he cried in various intonations. He had begun by screaming "I won't!" and continued screaming on the letter "o".

For three whole days, during which time did not exist for him, he struggled in that black sack into which he was being thrust by an invisible, resistless force. He struggled as a man condemned to death struggles in the hands of the executioner, knowing that he cannot save himself. And every moment he felt that despite all his efforts he was drawing nearer and nearer to what terrified him. He felt that his agony was due to his being thrust into that black hole and still more to his not being able to get right into it. He was hindered from getting into it by his conviction that his life had been a good one. That very justification of his life held him fast and prevented his moving forward, and it caused him most torment of all.

Suddenly some force struck him in the chest and side, making it still harder to breathe, and he fell through the hole and there at the bottom was a light. What had happened to him was like the sensation one sometimes experiences in a railway carriage when one thinks one is going backwards while one is really going forwards and suddenly becomes aware of the real direction.

"Yes, it was all not the right thing," he said to himself, "but that's no matter. It can be done. But what *is* the right thing?" he asked himself, and suddenly grew quiet.

This occurred at the end of the third day, two hours before his death. Just then his schoolboy son had crept softly in and gone up to the bedside. The dying man was still screaming desperately and waving his arms. His hand fell on the boy's head, and the boy caught it, pressed it to his lips, and began to cry.

At that very moment Ivan Ilych fell through and caught sight of the light, and it was revealed to him that though his life had not been what it should have been, this could still be rectified. He asked himself. "What *is* the right thing?" and grew still, listening. Then he felt that someone was kissing his hand. He opened his eyes, looked at his son, and felt sorry for him. His wife came up to him and he glanced at her. She was gazing at him open-mouthed, with undried tears on her nose and cheek and a despairing look on her face. He felt sorry for her too.

"Yes, I am making them wretched," he thought. "They are sorry, but it will be better for them when I die." He wished to say this but had not the strength to utter it. "Besides, why speak? I must act," he thought. With a look at his wife he indicated his son and said: "Take him away... sorry for him... sorry for you too..." He tried to add, "forgive me," but said "forego" and waved his hand, knowing that He whose understanding mattered would understand.

And suddenly it grew clear to him that what had been oppressing him and would not leave him was all dropping away at once from two sides, from ten sides,

使他们不再受罪。应该使他们，也使自己摆脱种种痛苦。"多么简单，多么快乐，"他想。"疼痛呢?"他问自己，"在哪儿去了? 嗳疼痛，你在哪儿啊?"

他留神倾听。

"噢，它在这里。好吧，疼就疼吧。"

"那么死呢? 它在哪里?"

他找寻着往常折磨他的死的恐惧，可是没有找到。它在哪里? 什么样的死啊? 他一点儿也不觉得恐惧，因为根本没有死。

没有死，只有光。

"原来如此!"他突然说出声来，"多么快乐呀!"

对于他，这一切都只是一刹那的事，这一刹那的含义再没有变。但旁人看到，临死前他又折腾了两小时。他的胸膛里咯咯发响，皮包骨头的身体不断地抽搐。接着咯咯声越来越少，喘息也越来越微弱。

"过去了!"有人在他旁边说。

他听见这话，心里重复了一遍。"死过去了，"他对自己说，"再也不会有死了。"

他吸了一口气，吸到一半停住，两腿一伸就死了。

and from all sides. He was sorry for them, he must act so as not to hurt them: release them and free himself from these sufferings. "How good and how simple!" he thought. "And the pain?" he asked himself. "What has become of it? Where are you, pain?"

He turned his attention to it.

"Yes, here it is. Well, what of it? Let the pain be."

"And death... where is it?"

He sought his former accustomed fear of death and did not find it. "Where is it? What death?" There was no fear because there was no death.

In place of death there was light.

"So that's what it is!" he suddenly exclaimed aloud. "What joy!"

To him all this happened in a single instant, and the meaning of that instant did not change. For those present his agony continued for another two hours. Something rattled in his throat, his emaciated body twitched, then the gasping and rattle became less and less frequent.

"It is finished!" said someone near him.

He heard these words and repeated them in his soul.

"Death is finished," he said to himself. "It is no more!"

He drew in a breath, stopped in the midst of a sigh, stretched out, and died.

049. 新娘来到黄天镇

(美)斯蒂芬·克莱恩 著　万 紫 译

一

　　豪华的普尔门式列车像一阵旋风,威风凛凛地向前驶去。你只要向窗外一瞥,就可以证明得克萨斯平原向东倾泻而去。广阔的绿野,长着牧豆树和仙人掌的色彩单调的空地,一簇簇木屋,明亮嫩绿的对林,一齐朝着东方掠去,掠过地平线,一片悬崖。

　　一对新婚夫妇在圣安东尼奥上了车,新郎多日来日晒风吹,皮肤红红的。一身崭新的黑衣服,使得那双砖红色的双手总是显得非常窘困的样儿。他不时小心地低头打量自己的一身打扮,双手放在膝头上坐着,好像在理发店里等待理发。他用诡秘而羞涩的目光瞟着别的旅客。

　　新娘并不漂亮,也不很年轻。她穿一件有许多钢纽扣的蓝色开司米外衣,缀着几小块天鹅绒。她老是扭头看看自己的胖袖,又硬又高又直,使她很不舒服。很明显,她是上过厨房的,此后,也准备尽责烧菜做饭。她的外貌,平静而冷漠。当她走进车厢时,有几个旅客无意中看了她几眼,使那平凡的、下等人的脸庞上泛起了少见的红晕。

　　他俩显然十分幸福。"从前你乘过这样阔气的客车吗?"他快活地笑着问她。

　　"没有,"她回答,"我没有乘过。这车子真好,是不是?"

　　"太好了! 过一会儿我们到前边去吃饭。好好花上一笔。叫一份儿世上最好的菜,花它一块钱。"

　　"啊,真的?"新娘喊出声来,"要花一决钱? 我们……花得太多了吧,嗯,杰克?"

I

THE great Pullman was whirling onward with such dignity of motion that a glance from the window seemed simply to prove that the plains of Texas were pouring eastward. Vast flats of green grass, dull-hued spaces of mesquit and cactus, little groups of frame houses, woods of light and tender trees, all were sweeping into the east, sweeping over the horizon, a precipice.

A newly married pair had boarded this coach at San Antonio. The man's face was reddened from many days in the wind and sun, and a direct result of his new black clothes was that his brick-coloured hands were constantly performing in a most conscious fashion. From time to time he looked down respectfully at his attire. He sat with a hand on each knee, like a man waiting in a barber's shop. The glances he devoted to other passengers were furtive and shy.

The bride was not pretty, nor was she very young. She wore a dress of blue cashmere, with small reservations of velvet here and there, and with steel buttons abounding. She continually twisted her head to regard her puff sleeves, very stiff straight, and high. They embarrassed her. It was quite apparent that she had cooked, and that she expected to cook, dutifully. The blushes caused by the careless scrutiny of some passengers as she had entered the car were strange to see upon this plain, underclass countenance, which was drawn in placid, almost emotionless lines.

They were evidently very happy. "Ever been in a parlor-car before?"he asked, smiling with delight.

"No," she answered; "I never was. It's fine, ain't it?"

"Great! And then after a while we'll go forward to the diner, and get a big lay-out. Finest meal in the world. Charge a dollar."

作者简介: 斯蒂芬·克莱恩(**Stephen Crane**,1871—1900),美国小说家。1871 年 11 月 1 日生于新泽西州纽瓦克,1900 年 6 月 5 日卒于德国巴登维勒。克莱恩上了大学后,迁居到纽约。他的《街头女郎玛吉》(*Maggie, A Girl of the Streets*,1893)描写了一位贫民窟女孩堕落的故事,是自然主义流派的里程碑。描述内战中一名年轻战士混乱心理的《红色英勇勋章》(*The Red Badge of Courage*,1895)和他的第一本诗集《黑骑士》(*The Black Riders*,1895)让他蜚声国际。在担任战地记者期间,他的船沉没了,几乎被淹死,后来就写下了《海上扁舟》(*The Open Boat*,1898)。他的短篇小说文集包括《小军团》(*The Little Regiment*,1896)和《怪物》(*The Monster*,1899)等。

"这次旅行怎么花都不算太多，"他理直气壮地回答，"我们全得尝试尝试。"

后来，他向她谈起这列火车来。"告诉你，从得克萨斯这一头到那一头，有1000英里。这列火车，正好通过得克萨斯，全线只停4个站。"他怀着主人般的自豪，把车厢里令人眼花缭乱的设备指点给她看。真的。她眼睛睁得大大的，凝视着织有图案的海蓝色天鹅绒、耀眼的黄铜、白银和玻璃的装饰与器具，以及像油池表面一样乌亮的木制品。车厢的一头，立着一具作为单人卧室支柱的青铜像。在车厢天花板的合适的地方，绘着橄榄色和银白色的壁画。

在这对新人的心目中，这周围的事物，反映了他们早晨在圣安东尼奥的婚姻的光辉。这是他们的新生活环境。特别是新郎的脸上，露出自鸣得意的微笑，在列车的黑人侍者眼中，显得十分滑稽可笑。那侍者远远地瞧着他们，时时高傲地咧嘴而笑逗乐。有机会，他就用刁钻的方法欺侮他们，而不使他们十分明显地感到受了欺侮。他狡猾地表现了各种十分难堪的势利态度。他欺凌他们。但他们对此漠然无知。不少旅客用嘲弄的眼光瞧着他们，他们也全然不顾。他们所处的地位，真的，处于他们的环境，实在有不少可笑的地方。

"我们3:42分就要到黄天镇了。"新郎温柔地看着新娘的眼睛说。

"啊，是吗？"她说着，好像一点儿也不知道似的。她对丈夫的话感到吃惊，一部分也是她做妻子的一种亲热的表示。她从口袋里掏出一块小银表来。当她把表拿到眼前皱着眉头注视时，新郎的脸上露出了光彩。

"这是我在圣安东尼奥一个朋友那里买来的。"他兴奋地告诉她。

"现在是12:17分。"她带着怯生生的笨拙的媚态抬头看着丈夫说。一个旅客看到这一幕，对着一面镜子（车厢里装着许多镜子），眨巴着眼睛，尽量嘲笑他们。

他俩终于去餐车了。两排穿着白得发亮的制服的黑人侍者，他们得到预告，兴趣十足而又泰然自若地看着他俩走进餐车。这一对儿正好碰到一个很高兴照料他们的侍者。他像父辈般的向导一样招待他们，他像做了一件善事似的显得容光焕发。这种并未超逾一般敬意的照拂，对他们说来已很不寻常了。当他们回到自己的车厢时，脸上显露出逃避的表情。

"Oh, do they?" cried the bride. "Charge a dollar? Why, that's too much—for—us—ain't it, Jack?"

"Not this trip, anyhow," he answered bravely. "We're going to go the whole thing."

Later he explained to her about the trains. "You see, it's a thousand miles from one end of Texas to the other; and this train runs right across it, and never stops but four times." He had the pride of an owner. He pointed out to her the dazzling fittings of the coach; and in truth her eyes opened wider as she contemplated the sea-green figured velvet, the shining brass, silver, and glass, the wood that gleamed as darkly brilliant as the surface of a pool of oil. At one end a bronze figure sturdily held a support for a separated chamber, and at convenient places on the ceiling were frescos in olive and silver.

To the minds of the pair, their surroundings reflected the glory of their marriage that morning in San Antonio; this was the environment of their new estate; and the man's face in particular beamed with an elation that made him appear ridiculous to the Negro porter. This individual at times surveyed them afar with an amused and superior grin. On other occasions he bullied them with skill in ways that did not make it exactly plain to them that they were being bullied. He subtly used all the manners of the most unconquerable kind of snobbery. He oppressed them; but on this oppression they had small knowledge, and they speedily forgot that infrequently a number of travellers covered them. with stares of derisive enjoyment. Historically there was supposed to be something infinitely humorous in their situation.

"We are due in Yellow Sky at 3:42," he said, looking tenderly into her eyes.

"Oh, are we?" she said, as if she had not been aware of it. To evince surprise at her husband's statement was part of her wifely amiability. She took from a pocket a little silver watch; as she held it before her, and stared at it with a frown of attention, the new husband's face shone.

"I bought it in San Anton' from a friend of mine," he told her gleefully.

"It's seventeen minutes past twelve," she said, looking up at him with a kind of shy and clumsy coquetry. A passenger, noting this play, grew excessively sardonic, and winked at himself in one of the numerous mirrors.

At last they went to the dining-car. Two rows of Negro waiters, in glowing white suits, surveyed their entrance with the interest, and also the equanimity, of men who had been forewarned. The pair fell to the lot of a waiter who happened to feel pleasure in steering them through their meal. He viewed them with the manner of a fatherly pilot, his countenance radiant with benevolence. The patronage, entwined with the ordinary deference, was not plain to them. And yet, as they turned to their coach, they showed in their faces a sense of escape.

左边,顺着一条长长的紫色的斜坡往下几英里,有一条缎带样的薄雾,那是水声潺潺的里奥格兰河。火车向河边斜坡驶去。铁路与河流的交叉点就是黄天镇。不久,黄天镇越来越近了,显然那位丈夫变得非常不安起来。他那双砖红色的手也更加惹人注目了。有时新娘俯身同他说话,他甚至有些心不在焉,神情恍惚。

说实话,杰克·波特开始感觉到一个阴影象一块铅板似的压在他身上。他是黄天镇的警长,一个在他那角落受人爱戴也叫人害怕的有名人物。在圣安东尼奥与一位他所爱的姑娘相会,经过照例的求婚,竟然劝说她嫁给了他。关于这件事他什么也没有和黄天镇的人商量。现在他就要带着自己的新娘来到这个天真的、毫不猜疑的社会上来。

当然,黄天镇的人们按照一般的风俗习惯也可以凭自己喜欢和人结婚。但是波特想到他对朋友们的义务,或者是尊重朋友们的意见的义务,或者想到在这些事情上虽不能控制人们的一种无形的约束,他深感内疚。他好似犯了大罪。他和那姑娘在圣安东尼奥面对面地相处,一时冲动,就轻率地逾越了社会上所有的障碍。在圣安东尼奥,他好像是个隐身在黑暗中的人。在这遥远的城市里,他可以轻易地斩断对朋友的任何义务,任何约束。但是黄天镇的时刻到了——也就是天亮的时刻到了。

他很清楚,这桩婚姻对他那个小镇来说是件重要的事情。这一消息只有像新旅馆起火那样的事才能相比。他的朋友是不会原谅他的。他屡次想.最合适还是打电报告诉他们,但每次都因胆怯而作罢。他怕这样做,现在,火车在载着他向那惊奇、欢乐而又要指责他的地方驰去。他向窗外看去,一带烟雾正慢慢地朝着火车弥漫而来。

黄天镇有一支为老百姓的喜庆事儿吹吹打打的钢管乐队,吹奏起来令人十分讨厌。他一想到这个乐队,不由笑了起来。如果镇上的居民们梦想到他可能携同新娘归来,他们会在车站上摆开乐队,在一片欢笑和庆贺声中把他们簇拥着送回他那土墙围筑的家中。

他决定要尽快抄近路走完从车站到家中的一段路。一旦到了安全的堡垒里,他就可以放出消息来,然后等居民们的热情随着时间推移稍稍消退下去时再到他们中间去。

To the left, miles down a long purple slope, was a little ribbon of mist where moved the keening Rio Grande. The train was approaching it at an angle, and the apex was Yellow Sky. Presently it was apparent that, as the distance from Yellow Sky grew shorter, the husband became commensurately restless. His brick-red hands were more insistent in their prominence. Occasionally he was even rather absent-minded and far-away when the bride leaned forward and addressed him.

As a matter of truth, Jack Potter was beginning to find the shadow of a deed weigh upon him like a leaden slab. He, the town marshal of Yellow Sky, a man known, liked, and feared in his corner, a prominent person, had gone to San Antonio to meet a girl he believed he loved, and there, after the usual prayers, had actually induced her to marry him, without consulting Yellow Sky for any part of the transaction. He was now bringing his bride before an innocent and unsuspecting community.

Of course people in Yellow Sky married as it pleased them, in accordance with a general custom; but such was Potter's thought of his duty to his friends, or of their idea of his duty, or of an unspoken form which does not control men in these matters, that he felt he was heinous. He had committed an extraordinary crime. Face to face with this girl in San Antonio, and spurred by his sharp impulse, he had gone headlong over all the social hedges. At San Antonio he was like a man hidden in the dark. A knife to sever any friendly duty, any form, was easy to his hand in that remote city. But the hour of Yellow Sky—the hour of daylight—was approaching.

He knew full well that this marriage was an important thing to his town. It could only be exceeded by the burning of the new hotel. His friends could not forgive him. Frequently he had reflected on the advisability of telling them by telegraph, but a new cowardice had been upon him. He feared to do it. And now the train was hurrying him toward a scene of amazement, glee, and reproach. He glanced out of the window at the line of haze swinging slowly in toward the train.

Yellow Sky had a kind of brass band, which played painfully, to the delight of the populace. He laughed without heart as he thought of it. If the citizens could dream of his prospective arrival with his bride, they would parade the band at the station and escort them, amid cheers and laughing congratulations to his adobe home.

He resolved that he would use all the devices of speed and plainscraft in making the journey from the station to his house. Once within that safe citadel, he could issue some sort of vocal bulletin, and then not go among the citizens until they had time to wear off a little of their enthusiasm.

The bride looked anxiously at him. "What's worrying you, jack?"

新娘焦虑地望着他:"你在担心什么,杰克?"

他又笑了一下:"我没担心什么,姑娘,我只是在想黄天镇。"

她领会他的意思,脸红了起来。

他俩心中产生了一种共有的内疚,因而他俩更加情意绵绵了。他们互相用温柔发亮的眼光对视着。但是波特老是神经质地笑着,因而新娘脸上的红晕似乎永远不会退了。

这个背叛黄天镇感情的人凝视着窗外飞速闪过的景色。"我们快到了。"他说。

这时,侍者过来告诉波特快到家了。他手里拿着一把刷子,一脸的傲气完全不见了。他刷着波特的衣服,波特缓慢地将身子转过来转过去。波特学着别人的做法,摸出一枚硬币递给侍者。这事儿波特做来又困难又僵硬,好像一个人第一次给马钉蹄铁一样。

侍者提起他们的行李包,当火车放慢速度时,他们就向车厢一头的平台走去。这时,两台机车拖着长长的列车驶进了黄天镇车站。

"他们要在这里加水。"波特压低嗓子用一种哀痛的声调说着,好像一个人在说他快要死了一样。在火车靠站前,他扫视了一下整个站台,使他感到又高兴又惊讶的是站台上除了一个站长外,什么人也没有。站长正向水塔匆匆走去,神态略显焦虑。火车停了,那侍者首先跳下车,摆好一个小小的踏脚。

"下车吧,姑娘。"波特嗓门嘶哑地说。他扶她下车时,两人都尴尬地笑了笑。他从黑人手上接过行李包,叫妻子挽住他的手臂。当他们快步溜走时,他偷偷地瞥见人们正在卸下两只箱子,还远远看到在行李车前的站长,已经转过身来打着手势向他奔来。他看到他的婚事对黄天镇第一次产生影响时,他笑了起来,笑的时候又发出叹息。他紧挽着妻子的手臂飞快地溜去。在他们背后,站着那侍者,咯咯地傻笑着。

二

南方铁路上的加利福尼亚特快车再过 21 分钟就要到达黄天镇了。黄天镇的"倦绅士"酒吧间里坐着 6 个人。一个是行商,他的话又多又快。三个是得克萨斯州人,他们不喜欢在那样的时候讲话。还有两个是墨西哥羊倌,他们没有在"倦绅士"酒吧间里攀谈的习

He laughed again, "I'm not worrying, girl; I'm only thinking of Yellow Sky."

She flushed in comprehension.

A sense of mutual guilt invaded their minds and developed a finer tenderness. They looked at each other with eyes softly aglow. But Potter often laughed the same nervous laugh; the flush upon the bride's face seemed quite permanent.

The traitor to the feelings of Yellow Sky narrowly watched the speeding landscape. "We're nearly there," he said.

Presently the porter came and announced the proximity of Potter's home. He held a brush in his hand, and, with all his airy superiority gone, he brushed Potter's new clothes as the latter slowly turned this way and that way. Potter fumbled out a coin and gave it to the porter, as he had seen others do. It was a heavy and muscle-bound business, as that of a man shoeing his first horse.

The porter took their bag, and as the train began to slow they moved forward to the hooded platform of the car. Presently the two engines and their long string of coaches rushed into the station of Yellow Sky.

"They have to take water here," said Potter, from a constricted throat and in mournful cadence, as one announcing death. Before the train stopped his eyes had swept the length of the platform, and he was glad and astonished to see there was none upon it but the station-agent, who, with a slightly hurried and anxious air, was walking toward the water-tanks. When the train had halted, the porter alighted first, and placed in position a little temporary step.

"Come on, girl," said Potter, hoarsely. As he helped her down they each laughed on a false note. He took the bag from the Negro, and bade his wife cling to his arm. As they slunk rapidly away, his hang-dog glance perceived that they were unloading the two trunks, and also that the station-agent, far ahead near the baggage-car, had turned and was running toward him, making gestures. He laughed, and groaned as he laughed, when he noted the first effect of his marital bliss upon Yellow Sky. He gripped his wife's arm firmly to his side, and they fled. Behind them the porter stood, chuckling fatuously.

II

The California express on the Southern Railway was due at Yellow Sky in twenty-one minutes. There were six men at the bar of the Weary Gentleman saloon. One was a drummer who talked a great deal and rapidly; three were Texans who did not care to talk at that time; and two were Mexican sheepherders, who did not talk as a general practice in the Weary Gentleman saloon. The barkeeper's dog lay on the board walk that crossed in front of the door. His head was

惯。酒吧老板的狗躺在横贯门前的木板路上。它用脚爪支着脑袋。带着常要被人踢而养成的永久的警惕性，懒洋洋地东张张西望望。沙砾路对面骄阳暴晒下的沙地中，有几块嫩绿的草坪。看到这些青草奇妙地长在这里，真使人不敢相信。这些草坪真像铺在舞台上用来代表草地的草垫一样。在火车站比较凉快的那一头，一个没穿上衣的男子坐在一张歪歪斜斜的椅子上，抽着烟斗。格兰德河新开的河岸绕镇而过。河那边可以看到一大片长着牧豆树的梅子色的平原。

除了酒吧间里那个喋喋不休的行商和他的同伴，整个黄天镇已昏昏欲睡。这个初来的行商姿态优美地倚着酒柜，怀着开拓新区的行吟诗人的自信，讲着许多故事。

"……正在那个当儿，老头儿双手抱着衣柜跌下楼来，老太婆正提着两筐煤上去，当然啰……"

行商的故事被突然出现在门口的一个青年打断了。青年大喊道："斯克拉奇·威尔逊喝醉了，又要无法无天了。"两个墨西哥人一听此话立刻放下酒杯，从酒吧间后门溜走了。

行商还漠然无知地打趣说："好啊，老朋友，管他怎么样，进来喝上一杯！"

但这个消息显然在酒吧间那些人们中间引起了很大震动。行商也不得不承认它的严重性。大家立刻变得严肃起来。"喂，"他迷惑不解地问，"怎么回事呀？"他的三个同伴做出富于表情的手势正准备说话。门口那个青年已抢在他们前头了。

"我的朋友，"他一面走进酒吧间一面回答，"这就是说，在两小时里，这个小镇已经不是个疗养胜地了。"

酒吧老板走到门口，锁了门，上了闩，又把手伸出窗外，拉下沉重的窗板，也上了闩。这地方马上就像蒙上了一种严肃的教堂似的气氛。行商看看这个，又望望那个。

"你们说啊，"他喊了起来，"到底是怎么回事啦？你们是不是说就要发生一场枪战啦？"

"不知道是不是真会发生枪斗，"有个人冷冷地回答，"不过一定会打枪，狠狠地打枪。"

跑来告警的青年挥了挥手："呵，如果有人想打，马上会打起来的，谁都可以在马路上打上一仗。有人正等着开仗呢。"

行商似乎因初来乍到对此既感兴趣，又感到个人的危险。

on his paws, and he glanced drowsily here and there with the constant vigilance of a dog that is kicked on occasion. Across the sandy street were some vivid green grass-plots, so wonderful in appearance, amid the sands that burned near them in a blazing sun, that they caused a doubt in the mind. They exactly resembled the grass mats used to represent lawns on the stage. At the cooler end of the railway station, a man without a coat sat in a tilted chair and smoked his pipe. The fresh-cut bank of the Rio Grande circled near the town, and there could be seen beyond it a great plum-coloured plain of mesquit.

Save for the busy drummer and his companions in the saloon, Yellow Sky was dozing. The new-comer leaned gracefully upon the bar, and recited many tales with the confidence of a bard who has come upon a new field.

"—and at the moment that the old man fell downstairs with the bureau in his arms, the old woman was coming up with two scuttles of coal, and of course—"

The drummer's tale was interrupted by a young man who suddenly appeared in the open door. He cried: "Scratchy Wilson's drunk, and has turned loose with both hands." The two Mexicans at once set down their glasses and faded out of the rear entrance of the saloon.

The drummer, innocent and jocular, answered: "All right, old man. S'pose he has? Come in and have a drink, anyhow."

But the information had made such an obvious cleft in every skull in the room that the drummer was obliged to see its importance. All had become instantly solemn. "Say," said he, mystified, "what is this?" His three companions made the introductory gesture of eloquent speech; but the young man at the door forestalled them.

"It means, my friend," he answered, as he came into the saloon, "that for the next two hours this town won't be a health resort."

The barkeeper went to the door, and locked and barred it; reaching out of the window, he pulled in heavy wooden shutters, and barred them. Immediately a solemn, chapel-like gloom was upon the place. The drummer was looking from one to another.

"But say," he cried, "what is this, anyhow? You don't mean there is going to be a gun-fight?"

"Don't know whether there'll be a fight or not," answered one man, grimly; "but there'll be some shootin'—some good shootin'."

The young man who had warned them waved his hand. "Oh, there'll be a fight fast enough, if any one wants it. Anybody can get a fight out there in the street. There's a fight just waiting."

The drummer seemed to be swayed between the interest of a foreigner and a perception of personal danger.

"你刚才说他叫什么名字?"他问。

"斯克拉奇·威尔逊。"他们异口同声地回答。

"那么他会杀人吗? 你们准备怎么办? 这种事常常发生吗? 他每个礼拜都要这样横冲直撞吗? 他会打破那扇门吗?"

"不,那扇门他是打不破的,"酒吧老板回答,"他已打过三次了。不过他进来的时候,你这个外乡人最好还是躺在地上! 他肯定要开枪射门,子弹会穿进来的。"

于是行商把眼睛牢牢盯着那扇门,虽说还没有到要他睡地板的时候,他为了稍作提防,把身子斜倚着墙壁。"他会杀人吗?"他又问道。

对这个问题,那个青年轻蔑地低声笑笑。

"他出来开枪,出来闹事,和他打交道没有好处。"

"但是碰到这种事你们怎样对付? 你们怎样对付?"

有人回答:"嗯,他和杰克·波特……"

"但是杰克·波特在圣安东尼奥。"别的人齐声打断他的话。

"噢,他是谁? 他来管这些事干吗?"

"哦,他是镇上的警长。斯克拉奇喝醉酒大吵大闹时,他就出来了。"

"啊!"行商擦擦眉毛说,"他干的真是好事。"

说话声渐渐低下来变成了耳语。行商更加焦急迷惑,想再问些问题,但是当他刚要发问时,人们就怒目向他,示意他别再出声。他们在沉默中紧张地等待着。他们倾听着街上传来的声音,眼睛在屋内幽暗的阴影里闪闪发光。有人向酒吧老板做了三次手势,老板像个鬼魂似的移动着,递给那人一只玻璃杯和一瓶酒。那人倒满一杯威士忌,悄悄地放下酒瓶。他一口喝下威士忌,又默默地转过身来对着门口。行商看到老板没有一点声响地从酒柜下面取出一枝猎枪,接着又看到他向自己招手,于是他就踮着脚走了过去。

"你最好跟我一起待在酒柜后面。"

"不,谢谢你,"行商说着,汗也出来了,"我还是待在可从后门逃出去的地方。"

老板做了个亲切而又带命令式的手势,行商听从了,坐到一只箱子上,脑袋低低地埋在酒柜后面。他看到周围有好多锌铜器皿仿佛装甲板一样保护着他,就像服下了一颗定心丸。老板也在他旁边的箱子上舒舒服服地坐了下来。

"What did you say his name was?"he asked.

"Scratchy Wilson,"they answered in chorus.

"And will he kill anybody? What are you going to do? Does this happen often? Does he rampage around like this once a week or so? Can he break in that door?"

"No; he can't break down that door,"replied the barkeeper. "He's tried it three times. But when he comes you'd better lay down on the floor, stranger. He's dead sure to shoot at it, and a bullet may come through. "

Thereafter the drummer kept a strict eye upon the door. The time had not yet been called for him to hug the floor, but, as a minor precaution, he sidled near to the wall. "Will he kill anybody?"he said again.

The man laughed low and scornfully at the question.

"He's out to shoot, and he's out for trouble. Don't see any good in experimentin' with him. "

"But what do you do in a case like this? What do you do?"

A man responded: "Why, he and Jack Potter—"

"But,"in chorus the other men interrupted, "Jack Potter's in San Anton'. "

"Well, who is he? What's he got to do with it?"

"Oh, he's the town marshal. He goes out and fights Scratchy when he gets on one of these tears. "

"Wow!"said the drummer, mopping his brow. "Nice job he's got. "

The voices had toned away to mere whisperings. The drummer wished to ask further questions, which were born of an increasing anxiety and bewilderment; but when he attempted them, the men merely looked at him in irritation and motioned him to remain silent. A tense waiting hush was upon them. In the deep shadows of the room their eyes shone as they listened for sounds from the street. One man made three gestures at the barkeeper; and the latter, moving like a ghost, handed him a glass and a bottle. The man poured a full glass of whisky, and set down the bottle noiselessly. He gulped the whisky in a swallow, and turned again toward the door in immovable silence. The drummer saw that the barkeeper, without a sound, had taken a Winchester from beneath the bar. Later he saw this individual beckoning to him, so he tiptoed across the room.

"You better come with me back of the bar. "

"No, thanks,"said the drummer, perspiring; "I'd rather be where I can make a break for the back door. "

Whereupon the man of bottles made a kindly but peremptory gesture. The drummer obeyed it, and, finding himself seated on a box with his head below the level of the bar, balm was laid upon his soul at sight of various zinc and copper fittings that bore a resemblance to armour-plate. The barkeeper took a seat comfortably upon an adjacent box.

"你知道，"老板悄声说，"我们这儿，斯克拉奇·威尔逊是个带枪的怪物，一个真正的怪物。他出来打架闹事，我们只好躲起来，毫无办法。他是沿河一带游荡的老流氓中最后一个了。他喝醉了酒，可怕极了。他不喝醉，可就没事。头脑简单，连只苍蝇也不会去伤害，是我们镇上最好的人。可是一旦他喝醉了酒……嘿！"

一阵长时间的沉默。"我真希望杰克·波特已从圣安东尼奥回来了，"酒吧老板说，"有一次，他干枪打威尔逊，打中了他的腿。他会威风凛凛地赶来，解决问题的。"

正在这时，他们听到远处一声枪响，接着是三声粗野的号叫。立刻，待在幽暗的酒吧间里的人们如释重负，他们挪动一下脚，互相望望。他们说："他来了。"

三

一个男子，身穿纽约东区犹太妇女缝制的作为装饰品的栗色法兰绒衬衫，转弯走到黄天镇大街当中，两手各握一支长而沉重的墨蓝色左轮手枪。他不时地狂叫着。那叫声仿佛穿过一个荒村，尖厉的声音飘过屋顶，这种音量似乎不是一般人嗓子所能发出来的，仿佛四周的寂静造成一个拱形的坟墓笼罩着他。这种凶猛的挑衅性的叫声在周围寂静的墙壁间回响着。他脚上穿的是新英格兰山坡上滑雪少年在冬季爱穿的那种烫金的红头靴子。

那人喝多了威士忌，满脸怒气。一双眼睛转来转去，警惕着埋伏的人，搜索着毫无动静的门窗，他蹑手蹑脚地走着，像只深夜出行的猫，他一想起什么，就吓人地咆哮几声。那长长的左轮枪在他手中轻如稻草，转动起来像闪电那样快。有时，他双手小小的指头像奏乐似的拨弄着枪支。他的衬衫领口开得很低，可以清楚地看到他脖子上的青筋由于狂怒而一张一弛地起伏着。唯一的声音就是那可怕的挑战声。当这小东西在街心中经过时，两旁寂静的土墙泰然屹立着。

没有人接受他的挑战——没有人接受他的挑战。那人向天大喊，也没有反应，他到处咆哮着，怒叫着，不停地舞动手中的双枪。

"倦绅士"酒吧老板的那条狗没有意识到事态的

"You see," he whispered, "This here Scratchy Wilson is a wonder with a gun—a perfect wonder; and when he goes on the war-trail, we hunt our holes—naturally. He's about the last one of the old gang that used to hang out along the river here. He's a terror when he's drunk. When he's sober he's all right—kind of simple—wouldn't hurt a fly—nicest fellow in town. But when he's drunk—whoo!"

There were periods of stillness. "I wish Jack Potter was back from San Anton'," said the barkeeper. "He shot Wilson up once—in the leg—and he would sail in and pull out the kinks in this thing."

Presently they heard from a distance the sound of a shot, followed by three wild yowls. It instantly removed a bond from the men in the darkened saloon. There was a shuffling of feet. They looked at each other. "Here he comes," they said.

III

A man in a maroon-colored flannel shirt, which had been purchased for purposes of decoration, and made principally by some Jewish women on the East Side of New York, rounded a corner and walked into the middle of the main street of Yellow Sky. In either hand the man held a long, heavy, blue-black revolver. Often he yelled, and these cries rang through a semblance of a deserted village, shrilly flying over the roofs in a volume that seemed to have no relation to the ordinary vocal strength of a man. It was as if the surrounding stillness formed the arch of a tomb over him. These cries of ferocious challenge rang against walls of silence. And his boots had red tops with gilded imprints, of the kind beloved in winter by little sledding boys on the hillsides of New England.

The man's face flamed in a rage begot of whisky. His eyes, rolling, and yet keen for ambush, hunted the still doorways and windows. He walked with the creeping movement of the midnight cat. As it occurred to him, he roared menacing information. The long revolvers in his hands were as easy as straws; they were moved with an electric swiftness. The little fingers of each hand played sometimes in a musician's way. Plain from the low collar of the shirt, the cords of his neck straightened and sank, straightened and sank, as passion moved him. The only sounds were his terrible invitations. The calm adobes preserved their demeanour at the passing of this small thing in the middle of the street.

There was no offer of fight—no offer of fight. The man called to the sky. There were no attractions. He bellowed and fumed and swayed his revolvers here and everywhere.

The dog of the barkeeper of the Weary Gentleman saloon had not appreciated the advance of events.

发展,仍躺在主人的门口打瞌睡。那人一看到狗就停住脚步,好玩地举起左轮枪。狗一看到人就跳起来,愠怒地嗥叫着,向斜刺里跑去。那人一声号叫,狗惊得飞跑起来。它正要跑进一条小巷,忽然一声吆喝,一声口哨,还有一个什么东西打在它前面的地上。狗尖叫起来,恐惧地转身朝另一个方向奔去。又有一声吆喝,一声口哨,沙子在狗的前面猛烈地弹起来。狗被吓昏了,像一只关在笼子里的野兽,慌张地转来转去。那人站在那里笑,手枪捶在屁股袋里。

终于那"倦绅士"酒吧的关着的大门引起了他的注意。他走过去,用手枪捶着门,讨酒吃。

门依然安稳不动,他从木板路上拣起一片纸,用一把小刀钉在门框上,然后他傲慢地转身离开这个公共场所,朝大街对面走去。到了街对面,他敏捷灵活地一转脚跟,返身就朝那片纸开了火。他打偏了半英寸,他咒骂了自己几声,走开了。后来他竟毫不客气地朝着他最亲密的朋友家的窗户发出一连串的猛烈射击。他在镇上胡作非为,像要自己的玩具一样。

但是仍旧没有人出来应战,他想起了他的宿敌杰克·波特的名字。他认为要是上波特家去攻击,引他出来应战,会是一件大快事。他哼着阿柏支印第安胜利乐曲,朝着他想去的方向走去。

他到了波特家,波特家外表别家一样,毫无动静。他选好一个有利的位置,就号叫着要决斗。那房子可能把他当作一尊大石像,一点儿反应也没有。等了好一会儿,他又喊着要决斗,并夹杂着许多不可思议的语句。

这时人们可以看到一个盛怒的人对着一间毫无动静的房屋暴跳如雷的场面,他发疯地大骂那房子,好像寒冬的烈风在袭击北方平原上的小屋。从远处听来,这种喧嚣之声,真像有 200 个墨西哥人在打仗。必要时,他停下来歇歇气,或者给手枪重新装上子弹。

四

波特和新娘胆怯地快步走着,有时他们还一同害羞似的低声笑笑。

"再拐个弯就到了,亲爱的。"他终于说道。

他俩低头顶着强烈的风往前走着。他们拐过一个街角,波特正要举手指给妻子看刚出现的新房时,

He yet lay dozing in front of his master's door. At sight of the dog, the man paused and raised his revolver humorously. At sight of the man, the dog sprang up and walked diagonally away, with a sullen head and growling. The man yelled, and the dog broke into a gallop. As it was about to enter an alley, there was a loud noise, a whistling, and something spat the ground directly before it. The dog screamed, and, wheeling in terror, galloped headlong in a new direction. Again there was a noise, a whistling, and sand was kicked viciously before it. Fear-stricken, the dog turned and flurried like an animal in a pen. The man stood laughing, his weapons at his hips.

Ultimately the man was attracted by the closed door of the Weary Gentleman saloon. He went to it and, hammering with a revolver, demanded drink.

The door remained imperturbable, he picked a bit of paper from the walk, and nailed it to the framework with a knife. He then turned his back contemptuously upon this popular resort and, walking to the opposite side of the street and spinning there on his heel quickly and lithely, fired at the bit of paper. He missed it by a half-inch. He swore at himself, and went away. Later he comfortably fusilladed the windows of his most intimate friend. The man was playing with this town; it was a toy for him.

But still there was no offer of fight. The name of Jack Potter, his ancient antagonist, entered his mind, and he concluded that it would be a glad thing if he should go to Potter's house, and by bombardment induce him to come out and fight. He moved in the direction of his desire, chanting Apache scalp-music.

When he arrived at it, Potter's house presented the same still front as had the other adobes. Taking up a strategic position, the man howled a challenge. But this house regarded him as might a great stone god. It gave no sign. After a decent wait, the man howled further challenges, mingling with them wonderful epithets.

Presently there came the spectacle of a man churning himself into deepest rage over the immobility of a house. He fumed at it as the winter wind attacks a prairie cabin in the North. To the distance there should have gone the sound of a tumult like the fighting of two hundred Mexicans. As necessity bade him, he paused for breath or to reload his revolvers.

IV

Potter and his bride walked sheepishly and with speed. Sometimes they laughed together shamefacedly and low.

"Next corner, dear," he said finally.

They put forth the efforts of a pair walking bowed against a strong wind. Potter was about to raise

迎面碰到一个身穿栗色衬衫的人。那人狂热地往一支大左轮枪中装子弹,刹时间,他的左轮枪落在地上,他像闪电一样地把另一支手枪从枪套中拔出来,对准了新郎的胸膛。

一阵子沉默。波特张口结舌,一句话也说不出来。他本能地立刻甩脱被女人紧紧挽住的手臂,把行李放在沙地上。新娘吓得面如死灰,像是在可怕的仪式中作祭品的奴隶,盯着那条幽灵似的毒蛇。

两个男子面对面的相距只有三步。持枪的那个脸上露出从未有过的镇静的凶恶样子。

"想偷袭我,"他说,"想偷袭我!"他的眼睛变得凶狠起来。波特略为挪动一下,那男子就把手枪恶狠狠向前一伸。"不,你别动,杰克·波特!对着手枪你别想动一动你的手指,眼睫毛也不许动一动。跟你算账的时候到了,我要用我的办法来了结。浪费时间,没有用。你要我不用手枪对付你,你就记住我的话。"

波特望着他的敌人,"我没有带枪,斯克拉奇,"他说,"真的,我没有带枪。"他的态度变得坚定强硬起来。但是在他的脑海里,浮现出普尔门式卧车的景象来:海蓝色的织有图案的天鹅绒、耀眼的黄铜、白银、玻璃的器具和装饰,像油池表面一样乌亮的木制品……所有结婚的光彩和新的生活环境。"斯克拉奇·威尔逊,"他说,"你知道,我到应该决斗时我会决斗的。但这回我没带枪。你要开枪就开枪吧!"

他的敌人脸色铁青,走上前来,在波特胸前来回晃动着手枪。"你别说你没有带枪,你这狗崽子。你别在我面前撒谎了。在得克萨斯还没有人看到过你出门不带枪的呢。别把我当孩子了。"他的目光炯炯,喉咙像只气筒喘着气。

"我不骗你。"波特说,他的脚跟分毫没有往后移动,"我说你这该死的傻瓜,我跟你说我没带枪就没带枪。你想开枪,现在就开吧。你以后可再也得不到这样好的机会了。"

他对狂怒的威尔逊说了那么多,后者比较镇静一些了。"你没带枪,那你为什么不带枪呢?"他嘲讽地说,"上主日学校去了?"

"我没有带枪,因为我刚和老婆从圣安东尼奥回来。我结婚了。"波特说,"要是我想到我带老婆回家时会有你这样的笨蛋暗中算计的话,我是会带枪的。这一点你可不会忘记吧!"

"结婚了!"斯克拉奇说。他一点儿也想不到。

a finger to point the first appearance of the new home when, as they circled the corner, they came face to face with a man in a maroon-colored shirt, who was feverishly pushing cartridges into a large revolver. Upon the instant the man dropped his revolver to the ground and, like lightning, whipped another from its holster. The second weapon was aimed at the bridegroom's chest.

There was a silence. Potter's mouth seemed to be merely a grave for his tongue. He exhibited an instinct to at once loosen his arm from the woman's grip, and he dropped the bag to the sand. As for the bride, her face had gone as yellow as old cloth. She was a slave to hideous rites, gazing at the apparitional snake.

The two men faced each other at a distance of three paces. He of the revolver smiled with a new and quiet ferocity.

"Tried to sneak up on me," he said. "Tried to sneak up on me!" His eyes grew more baleful. As Potter made a slight movement, the man thrust his revolver venomously forward. "No; don't you do it, Jack Potter. Don't you move a finger toward a gun just yet. Don't you move an eyelash. The time has come for me to settle with you, and I'm goin' to do it my own way, and loaf along with no interferin'. So if you don't want a gun bent on you, just mind what I tell you."

Potter looked at his enemy. "I ain't got a gun on me, Scratchy," he said. "Honest, I ain't." He was stiffening and steadying, but yet somewhere at the back of his mind was a vision of the Pullman floated: the seagreen figured velvet, the shining brass, silver, and glass, the wood that gleamed as darkly brilliant as the surface of a pool of oil—all the glory of the marriage, the environment of the new estate. "You know I fight when it comes to fighting, Scratchy Wilson; but I ain't got a gun on me. You'll have to do all the shootin' yourself."

His enemy's face went livid. He stepped forward, and lashed his weapon to and fro before Potter's chest. "Don't you tell me you ain't got no gun on you, you whelp. Don't tell me no lie like that. There ain't a man in Texas ever seen you without no gun. Don't take me for no kid." His eyes blazed with light, and his throat worked like a pump.

"I ain't takin' you for no kid," answered Potter. His heels had not moved an inch backward. "I'm takin' you for a damn fool. I tell you I ain't got a gun, and I ain't. If you're goin' to shoot me up, you better begin now; you'll never get a chance like this again."

So much enforced reasoning had told on Wilson's rage; he was calmer. "If you ain't got a gun, why ain't you got a gun?" he sneered. "Been to Sunday-school?"

"I ain't got a gun because I've just come from San Anton' with my wife. I'm married," said Potter. "And if I'd thought there was going to be any galoots like you prowling around when I brought my wife home, I'd had a gun, and don't you forget it."

"是的,结婚了,我结婚了。"波特清楚地说。

"结婚了?"斯克拉奇说。他似乎才看到对方身边还有一个萎靡颓丧的女人。"不!"他说,好像一个人看到了另一个世界。他后退了一步,持枪的手垂了下来。"是这位女士吗?"他问。

"是的,就是这位女士。"波特回答。又是一阵沉默。

"好吧,"威尔逊缓慢地说,"我想,现在一切都算了吧!"

"你这样说,那就一切算了吧。斯克拉奇,你知道我可没有来找麻烦。"波特提起他的行李包。

"好吧,就此一切算了吧,杰克。"威尔逊眼睛看着地面说,"结婚了!"他不是一个会向女士献殷勤的大学生,在这种外国风气的场合里,他只是一个早期平原上思想单纯的小子。他拾起右边那把枪,把两支手枪插进枪套,走了。他的脚在厚厚的沙地上留下两行喇叭形的脚印。

"Married!" said Scratchy, not at all comprehending.

"Yes, married. I'm married," said Potter, distinctly.

"Married?" said Scratchy. Seemingly for the first time, he saw the drooping, drowning woman at the other man's side. "No!" he said. He was like a creature allowed a glimpse of another world. He moved a pace backward, and his arm, with the revolver, dropped to his side. "Is this the lady?" he asked.

"Yes; this is the lady," answered Potter.

There was another period of silence.

"Well," said Wilson at last, slowly, "I s'pose it's all off now."

"It's all off if you say so, Scratchy. You know I didn't make the trouble," Potter lifted his valise.

"Well, I 'low it's off Jack," said Wilson. He was looking at the ground. "Married!" He was not a student of chivalry; it was merely that in the presence of this foreign condition he was a simple child of the earlier plains. He picked up his starboard revolver, and, placing both weapons in their holsters, he went away. His feet made funnel-shaped tracks in the heavy sand.

050. 冬 梦

（美）弗·司各特·菲兹杰拉德 著

雨 宁 译

050. Winter Dreams

by F. Scott Fitzgerald

一

高尔夫球场的球童，有的穷得罪过，住在只有一单间的房子里，在前院养着一头神经衰弱的母牛。可是迪克斯特·格林的父亲是黑熊镇最好的第二家食品杂货店的业主（最好的那家叫做"轮毂"，顾客都是从雪利岛来的阔人），迪克斯特当球童只是为了赚几个零用钱。

秋季里．天气变得多霜而沉闷，漫长的明尼苏达州冬季仿佛给一只匣子扣上了一个白盖子，高尔夫球场的整齐草地覆上了白雪，迪克斯特于是套上雪橇在雪上活动。遇到这类季节，这地方会使他觉得十分消沉，他感到恼火的是，在漫长的冬季里，这片高尔夫球场竟然硬给撂荒了，任凭嘈杂的麻雀常来常往。他感到沉闷的还有，那些在夏天里飘动着鲜艳旗帜的小沙堆，如今都成了埋在齐膝盖深的冰雪下的荒凉沙堆。当他滑过那些小山坡时，寒风凛冽，使他难受，如果太阳出来了，他会迈开沉重的脚步，乜斜眼睛瞟着那耀眼的无从衡量的强烈光芒。

4 月里，冬季突然结束了。冒着冬寒来得早的高尔夫球爱好者还没有试试他们的红球和黑球，当雪已经毫不流连地流进了黑熊湖。既没有自鸣得意的春寒，也没有引以为荣的那一段潮湿期间，寒气就溜失了。

迪克斯特知道北方的春天有些时候是沉闷无趣的，这正像他知道秋天也自有其绚丽姿采一样。秋天会使他握紧双手，颤抖，自言自语，翻来覆去说些蠢话，面对着想象中的观众和军队，做出一些突如其来的轻快手势。10 月使他充满了希望，在 11 月里，这种

I

SOME of the caddies were poor as sin and lived in one-room houses with a neurasthenic cow in the front yard, but Dexter Green's father owned the second best grocery-store in Black Bear—the best one was "The Hub," patronized by the wealthy people from Sherry Island—and Dexter caddied only for pocket-money.

In the fall when the days became crisp and gray, and the long Minnesota winter shut down like the white lid of a box, Dexter's skis moved over the snow that hid the fairways of the gulf course. At these times the country gave him a feeling of profound melancholy—it offended him that the links should lie in enforced fallowness, haunted by ragged sparrows for the long season. It was dreary, too, that on the tees where the gay colors fluttered in summer there were now only the desolate sandboxes knee-deep in crusted ice. When he crossed the hills the wind blew cold as misery, and if the sun was out he tramped with his eyes squinted up against the hard dimensionless glare.

In April the winter ceased abruptly. The snow ran down into Black Bear Lake scarcely tarrying for the early golfers to brave the season with red and black balls. Without elation, without an interval of moist glory, the cold was gone.

Dexter knew that there was something dismal about this Northern spring, just as he knew there was something gorgeous about the fall. Fall made him clinch his hands and tremble and repeat idiotic sentences to himself, and make brisk abrupt gestures of command to imaginary audiences and armies. October filled him with hope which November raised to a sort

作者简介：司各特·菲兹杰拉德（**Scott Fitzgerald**，1896—1940），美国小说家。1896 年 9 月 24 日生于明尼苏达州圣保罗，1940 年 12 月 21 日卒于加利福尼亚州好莱坞。他的作品抓住爵士乐时代的粗俗的行为和缭乱的承诺，包括《尘世乐园》（*This Side of Paradise*，1920），《美丽与毁灭》（*The Beautiful and Damned*，1922），还有短篇小说集《爵士时代的故事》（*Tales of the Jazz Age*，1922）和《所有悲伤的年轻人》（*All the Sad Young Men*，1926）。《了不起的盖茨比》（*The Great Gatsby*，1925）讲述了美国的财富与腐败，被称赞为 20 世纪最好的小说之一。

希望会上升到使他欣喜如狂的胜利,在这种心情下,夏天里在雪利岛上得到的辉煌印象会一幕一幕地闪过,成了供他遐思的现成材料。他变成了一位高尔夫球锦标选手,在一次妙不可言的比赛中打败了T·A·赫德里克先生,这场比赛在他想象中的草地上打了一百次,他不厌其烦地变幻着这场比赛中每一个细节。有时他胜得那么容易,简直有些可笑,有时他又很精彩地反败为胜。有一次,他像莫提默尔·琼斯先生一样,从一辆皮尔斯-埃罗牌汽车里走出来,摆出一副冷面孔,信步走进雪利岛高尔夫球俱乐部的休息室里——也许是这样,在一群羡慕他的人们的簇拥下,他从俱乐部木筏的跳板上表演了一次花式跳水……在那些惊讶得张开嘴望着他的人群中间,还有莫提默尔·琼斯先生。

有一天发生了这么一件事,琼斯先生(这是他本人,不是他的鬼影子)两眼含泪走到迪克斯特跟前,说迪克斯特……是俱乐部里最好的球童,如果琼斯先生能使他感到再工作一段时间也是值得的,他是否可以决定不辞职了,因为每一个……俱乐部里其他的每一个球童都要在他向每一个球穴进攻时丢掉一个球。

“不行,先生,”迪克斯特下定决心地说,“我再不要当球童了。”然后,停了一会儿,“我的岁数太大了。”

“你还不到14呐。真见鬼,为什么你偏偏在今天早晨决定不干了呢,你答应过,下星期你愿意跟我去参加全州的比赛嘛。”

“我下定了决心,我的年龄太大了。”

迪克斯特交出了他的“甲级”证章,从球童管理员那里领回了他份内应得的钱,徒步走回黑熊村。

“他是我所见到的最好的……球童,”当天下午莫提默尔先生在一次饮酒时喊叫道,“从来没丢过一个球!主动!有头脑!不声不响!诚实!感恩知情!”

真正做出这件事的是个小女孩,才11岁——丑中有美,小女孩常常是这样,几年之后,她们准会变成难以形容的美人,给一大群男人带来无穷的痛苦。不过,这点儿火星还是看得出的。她在微笑时嘴唇会向两个嘴角下面撇一下,还有她那双眼睛(老天保佑!)……那几乎是一片热情,仿佛把上帝也一概不放在心上。在这种女人身上,生命力出现得很早。这完全是有真凭实据的,她的瘦小身体当时正焕发着生命力的光辉。

她急不可耐地在早晨9点钟到了高尔夫球场,随

of ecstatic triumph, and in this mood the fleeting brilliant impressions of the summer at Sherry Island were ready grist to his mill. He became a golf champion and defeated Mr. T. A. Hedrick in a marvellous match played a hundred times over the fairways of his imagination, a match each detail of which he changed about untiringly—sometimes he won with almost laughable ease, sometimes he came up magnificently from behind. Again, stepping from a Pierce-Arrow automobile, like Mr. Mortimer Jones, he strolled frigidly into the lounge of the Sherry Island Golf Club—or perhaps, surrounded by an admiring crowd, he gave an exhibition of fancy diving from the spring-board of the club raft. . . . Among those who watched him in open-mouthed wonder was Mr. Mortimer Jones.

And one day it came to pass that Mr. Jones—himself and not his ghost—came up to Dexter with tears in his eyes and said that Dexter was the——best caddy in the club, and wouldn't he decide not to quit if Mr. Jones made it worth his while, because every other—— caddy in the club lost one ball a hole for him—regularly—

"No, sir," said Dexter decisively. "I don't want to caddy any more." Then, after a pause: "I'm too old."

"You're not more than fourteen. Why the devil did you decide just this morning that you wanted to quit? You promised that next week you'd go over to the state tournament with me."

"I decided I was too old."

Dexter handed in his "A Class" badge, collected what money was due him from the caddy master, and walked home to Black Bear Village.

"The best——caddy I ever saw," shouted Mr. Mortimer Jones over a drink that afternoon. "Never lost a ball! Willing! Intelligent! Quiet! Honest! Grateful!"

The little girl who had done this was eleven—beautifully ugly as little girls are apt to be who are destined after a few years to be inexpressibly lovely and bring no end of misery to a great number of men. The spark, however, was perceptible. There was a general ungodliness in the way her lips twisted down at the corners when she smiled, and in the——Heaven help us! —in the almost passionate quality of her eyes. Vitality is born early in such women. It was utterly in evidence now, shining through her thin frame in a sort of glow.

She had come eagerly out on to the course at nine o'clock with a white linen nurse and five small new golf-clubs in a white canvas bag which the nurse was

身带来一位穿白布衣服的保姆,还有 5 根崭新的小高尔夫球棍,装在一个白帆布袋里,由保姆背着。迪克斯特首先看到她的时候,她正在球童房旁边站着,好像很烦躁,为了掩盖这种心情,她正在缠着她的保姆,分明是硬要找些话谈谈,她还故意做出一些神色惊讶和其他不相干的鬼脸。

"嗯,天气可真好呀,希尔达。"迪克斯特听到了她说的这句话。她抿着嘴角微笑,一面偷偷瞟着周围,暗送秋波,她的眼光一霎时落到了迪克斯特身上。

接着她又对保姆说:

"嗯,我看今天早晨没有多少人要到这儿来的,是不是?"

她又微笑了,喜盈盈地,分明是做作——倒也令人信服。

"现在我也不知道我们该怎么办。"保姆说,她并没有望着什么特别的地方。

"哦,那没有关系。我有办法。"

迪克斯特一动不动地站着,微微张着嘴。他知道如果他前进一步,他那凝视的目光必然会落到她的视线里,如果他向后退,他又会看不见她的全部面孔。一时间,他也没有想到她的年龄多么小。现在他记起来了,去年他见过她几次,她穿的是短裙子和灯笼裤。

突然间,他不由自主地大笑起来,短暂地突然一笑——他的笑声使他自己吃了一惊,于是他扭转身,迅速地拔腿走开了。

"小伙计——"

迪克斯特停住了。

"小伙计——"

毫无疑问,这是招呼他的。不仅如此,也还博得了那莫名其妙的嫣然一笑,几近荒唐的微笑——至少有一打男人活到中年还会记这嫣然一笑的。

"小伙计,你知道高尔夫球教练在什么地方吗?"

"他正在指导练球。"

"嗯,你知道球童管理员在哪儿吗?"

"今天早晨他还没来哩。"

"哦。"一时间,她不知道该怎么办了。她一会儿跷起左脚,一会儿跷起右脚站着。

"我们想找一个球童,"保姆说,"莫提默尔·琼斯太太吩咐我们来打高尔夫球。要是找不到球童,我们可不知道该怎么办了。"

说到这里,她停住了,因为琼斯小姐向她递了个

carrying. When Dexter first saw her she was standing by the caddy house, rather ill at ease and trying to conceal the fact by engaging her nurse in an obviously unnatural conversation graced by startling and irrelevant grimaces from herself.

"Well, it's certainly a nice day, Hilda," Dexter heard her say. She drew down the corners of her mouth, smiled, and glanced furtively around, her eyes in transit falling for an instant on Dexter.

Then to the nurse:

"Well, I guess there aren't very many people out here this morning, are there?"

The smile again—radiant, blatantly artificial—convincing.

"I don't know what we're supposed to do now," said the nurse, looking nowhere in particular.

"Oh, that's all right. I'll fix it up."

Dexter stood perfectly still, his mouth slightly ajar. He knew that if he moved forward a step his stare would be in her line of vision—if he moved backward he would lose his full view of her face. For a moment he had not realized how young she was. Now he remembered having seen her several times the year before—in bloomers.

Suddenly, involuntarily, he laughed, a short abrupt laugh—then, startled by himself, he turned and began to walk quickly away.

"Boy—"

Dexter stopped.

"Boy—"

Beyond question he was addressed. Not only that, but he was treated to that absurd smile, that preposterous smile—the memory of which at least a dozen men were to carry into middle age.

"Boy, do you know where the golf teacher is?"

"He's giving a lesson."

"Well, do you know where the caddy-master is?"

"He isn't here yet this morning."

"Oh." For a moment this baffled her. She stood alternately on her right and left foot.

"We'd like to get a caddy," said the nurse. "Mrs. Mortimer Jones sent us out to play golf, and we don't know how without we get a caddy."

Here she was stopped by an ominous glance from Miss Jones, followed immediately by the smile.

"There aren't any caddies here except me," said Dexter to the nurse, "and I got to stay here in charge until the caddy-master gets here."

"Oh."

眼色,马上又嫣然一笑。

"除了我之外,这儿没有别的球童,"迪克斯特对保姆说,"可是管理员还没来,我得留在这儿照管。"

"哦。"

琼斯小姐和她的随从退出了这个场面,在跟迪克斯特隔开一段适当距离之后,她们卷进了一番激烈的交谈,结果,琼斯小姐拿起一根球棍,狠狠向地上摔打。为了进一步加强气氛,她又举起球棍,准备向保姆的胸部狠狠打下去,可是被保姆一手抓住,从她手里夺过了球棍。

"你这个小坏老东西!"琼斯小姐发狂似的大哭起来。

她们又争论了一番。迪克斯特看出了这场戏的喜剧成分,有好几次都要大笑,可是每一次都忍住了,没有笑出声来。他禁不住大逆不道地认为那个小女孩打保姆倒也有点道理。

这时候,幸而球童管理员来了,这场纠纷也解决了,保姆立刻来向管理员申诉。

"琼斯小姐要找一个小球童,可是这个小孩说他走不开。"

"麦克肯纳先生说过,在你来之前,要我在这儿等着。"迪克斯特连忙说。

"好啦,现在他来啦。"琼斯小姐喜盈盈地对球童管理员嫣然一笑。于是她扔下球棍袋,倨傲地扭扭捏捏地向她的第一个发球沙堆走过去。

"唔?"球童管理员转过脸对迪克斯特说道,"你还像个木头人站在这儿干什么?过去把小姐的球棍拾掇起来。"

"我今天不想去了。"迪克斯特说。

"你不去……"

"我想不干了。"

他的决定之重大使他自己也吓了一跳。他是一个最讨人欢喜的球童。他能在这一夏天赚 30 元,这是在湖周围的任何其他地方都做不到的。可是他的感情受到了一次强烈冲击,他的心情紊乱,需要马上猛烈地发泄一通。

可是事情也并没有这样简单。迪克斯特不知不觉地受到了他那些冬梦的支配,而且将来的情况也往往是这样。

Miss Jones and her retinue now withdrew, and at a proper distance from Dexter became involved in a heated conversation, which was concluded by Miss Jones taking one of the clubs and hitting it on the ground with violence. For further emphasis she raised it again and was about to bring it down smartly upon the nurse's bosom, when the nurse seized the club and twisted it from her hands.

"You damn little mean old *thing*!" cried Miss Jones wildly.

Another argument ensued. Realizing that the elements of the comedy were implied in the scene, Dexter several times began to laugh, but each time restrained the laugh before it reached audibility. He could not resist the monstrous conviction that the little girl was justified in beating the nurse.

The situation was resolved by the fortuitous appearance of the caddy-master, who was appealed to immediately by the nurse.

"Miss Jones is to have a little caddy, and this one says he can't go."

"Mr. McKenna said I was to wait here till you came," said Dexter quickly.

"Well, he's here now." Miss Jones smiled cheerfully at the caddymaster. Then she dropped her bag and set off at a haughty mince toward the first tee.

"Well?" The caddy-master turned to Dexter. "What you standing there like a dummy for? Go pick up the young lady's clubs."

"I don't think I'll go out to-day," said Dexter.

"You don't—"

"I think I'll quit."

The enormity of his decision frightened him. He was a favorite caddy, and the thirty dollars a month he earned through the summer were not to be made elsewhere around the lake. But he had received a strong e-motional shock, and his perturbation required a violent and immediate outlet.

It is not so simple as that, either. As so frequently would be the case in the future, Dexter was unconsciously dictated to by his winter dreams.

II

Now, of course, the quality and the seasonability of these winter dreams varied, but the stuff of them remained. They persuaded Dexter several years later to

二

　　如今，当然啰，这些冬梦的性质和时令机遇都变了，但冬梦的实质依然如故。几年之后他们劝他放弃在州立大学学习商业的机会（他父亲现在富裕了，大概会供给他费用），为了那种靠不住的好处，到东部的什么历史比较悠久、比较著名的大学去读书，而且他正在为自己的钱有限感到为难。但是不要得出错误的印象，以为他那些冬梦既然首先同他对有钱人的向往有关，这个孩子内心里想的总不外是什么趋炎附势的念头。他可不是要同那些闪闪发光的东西和闪闪发光的人们有什么联系，他要的是那些闪闪发光的东西本身。他时常会伸手去拿那个最好的东西而不知道为什么他要这种东西。有时候，他也会碰上在生活中往往难免的那些神秘地使他望洋兴叹的事情和许多禁律。这个故事要讲的不是他的全部生涯，而是这些使他望洋兴叹的事情之一。

　　他赚了钱。这可真令人惊奇。在读完大学之后他进了城，黑熊湖的阔绰顾客就是从这座城市里吸引来的。当时他只有 23 岁，他在城里住了不满两年，已经有人喜欢说："这可是个好样的小伙子。"在他周围，有钱人的子弟都在冒冒失失忙于经营债券，或者冒冒失失拿祖产来投资，或者苦苦钻研 25 大卷的《乔治·华盛顿商业教程》，可是迪克斯特凭着他的大学学位和他那自信的口吻借到 1000 元，买下了一家洗衣店的股权。

　　在迪克斯特入股的时候，这是一家小洗衣店。他专心研究，学会了英国人怎么洗细羊毛高尔夫球袜而使它不缩水的窍门，不到一年就使那些穿灯笼裤的顾客感到中意。男人们都一定要把他们的谢特兰牌袜子和毛衣送到他的洗衣店里，正像他们一定要有个能找到高尔夫球的球童一样。过了不久，他还照样收洗了他们的妻子的内衣，并且在这个城市的不同地区开了 5 家分店。他还不到 27 岁已经在他家乡一带拥有为数最多的一连串分支洗衣店。就在这时候，他卖掉他的全部产业，到纽约去了。不过，我们要讲的他那一段经历却要回溯到他初次获得巨大成就的那个时期。

　　当时他 23 岁，哈特先生（一位头发斑白的人，他喜欢说"这可是个好样的小伙子"）给了他一份到雪利岛高尔夫球俱乐部度周末的请帖。于是有一天，他在

pass up a business course at the state university—his father, prospering now, would have paid his way—for the precarious advantage of attending an older and more famous university in the East, where he was bothered by his scanty funds. But do not get the impression, because his winter dreams happened to be concerned at first with musings on the rich, that there was anything merely snobbish in the boy. He wanted not association with glittering things and glittering people—he wanted the glittering things themselves. Often he reached out for the best without knowing why he wanted it—and sometimes he ran up against the mysterious denials and prohibitions in which life indulges. It is with one of those denials and not with his career as a whole that this story deals.

He made money. It was rather amazing. After college he went to the city from which Black Bear Lake draws its wealthy patrons. When he was only twenty-three and had been there not quite two years, there were already people who liked to say: "Now *there's* a boy—" All about him rich men's sons were peddling bonds precariously, or investing patrimonies precariously, or plodding through the two dozen volumes of the "George Washington Commercial Course," but Dexter borrowed a thousand dollars on his college degree and his confident mouth, and bought a partnership in a laundry.

It was a small laundry when he went into it, but Dexter made a speciality of learning how the English washed fine woolen golf-stockings without shrinking them, and within a year he was catering to the trade that wore knickerbockers. Men were insisting that their Shetland hose and sweaters go to his laundry, just as they had insisted on a caddy who could find golf-balls. A little later he was doing their wives' lingerie as well—and running five branches in different parts of the city. Before he was twenty-seven he owned the largest string of laundries in his section of the country. It was then that he sold out and went to New York. But the part of his story that concerns us goes back to the days when he was making his first big success.

When he was twenty-three Mr. Hart—one of the gray-haired menwho like to say "Now there's a boy"—gave him a guest card to the Sherry Island Golf Club for a week-end. So he signed his name one day on the register, and that afternoon played golf in a foursome with Mr. Hart and Mr. Sandwood and Mr. T. A. Hedrick. He did not consider it necessary to remark that he had once carried Mr. Hart's bag over this same

登记簿上签上了他的姓名,并且在当天下午跟哈特先生,山德伍德先生和T·A·赫德里克先生一行4人去打高尔夫球。他并不认为有必要来谈起当初正是在这些草坡上,他曾经一度为哈特先生背过球棍袋,他闭上眼睛也认得出每一个陷阱和每一条水沟……可是他发现自己正在瞅着跟在他们后面的那4个球童,他想捕捉到一点迹象或者一个手势,使他会回想到他自己,缩短他的现在和他的过去之间的差距。

这一天很奇怪,出人意外地劈面闪过了多次转瞬即逝的熟悉印象。在这一分钟里,他会产生一种他闯进了私人园地的感觉,在下一分钟里,他得到的印象是,他觉得他比T·A·赫德里克先生高超得太多了,赫德里克不仅讨人厌,甚至也不再是优秀的高尔夫球运动员了。

后来,由于哈特先生在第15片草坪附近丢了一个球,发生了一次重大事件。当时,他们正在障碍区域寂静的草丛中找球,从后方的小山坡后面传来了嘹亮的喊声:"让开!"他们不顾找球,全猛地转过身来。这时,突然有一只鲜明的新球越过山坡曲向一侧,正好打中T·A·赫德里克先生的肚皮。

"天哪!"T·A·赫德里克先生喊道,"他们真应当把有些疯疯颠颠的女人赶出这个球场。这可是胡闹得叫人受不了啦。"

从山坡上露出了一个人头,同时传来了人声。

"要是我们把球继续打下去,你们有意见吗?"

"你打中了我的肚子。"赫德里克先生怒冲冲地声明。

"真的吗?"那位女郎朝这群男人走过来了。"对不起。我喊过'让开'的。"

她漫不经心地朝这些男人一个一个地瞟了一眼,然后把眼光扫过草坪来寻找她的球。

"我是不是把它打到障碍区域里去了?"

谁也不可能确定这个问题究竟是别出心裁,还是恶意中伤。不过,停了一会儿,她消除了一切疑团,因为她的伙伴从山坡那面过来了,她高兴地叫道:

"我在这儿! 我本来会在草坪上继续打下去的,没想到我打中什么东西了。"

她摆好姿势,准备用铁头球棍攻球入穴,这时候,迪克斯特仔细眺着她。她穿的是一件蓝格子花布连衫裙,领口和肩头衩口都镶着白边,更加衬托出她那晒得棕褐的肤色。夸张,瘦削,这些曾经使她那双热情的眼睛和向下撇的嘴在11岁时显得荒谬可笑的特

links, and that he knew every trap and gully with his eyes shut—but he found himself glancing at the four caddies who trailed them, trying to catch a gleam or gesture that would remind him of himself, that would lessen the gap which lay between his present and his past.

It was a curious day, slashed abruptly with fleeting, familiar impressions. One minute he had the sense of being a trespasser—in the next he was impressed by the tremendous superiority he felt toward Mr. T. A. Hedrick, who was a bore and not even a good golfer any more.

Then, because of a ball Mr. Hart lost near the fifteenth green, an enormous thing happened. While they were searching the stiff grasses of the rough there was a clear call of "Fore!" from behind a hill in their rear. And as they all turned abruptly from their search a bright new ball sliced abruptly over the hill and caught Mr. T. A. Hendrick in the abdomen.

"By God!" cried Mr. T. A. Hedrick, "They ought to put some of these crazy women off the course. It's getting to be outrageous. "

A head and a voice came up together over the hill:

"Do you mind if we go through?"

"You hit me in the stomach!" declared Mr. Hedrick wildly.

"Did I?" The girl approached the group of men. "I'm sorry. I yelled 'Fore!'"

Her glance fell casually on each of the men—then scanned the fairway for her ball.

"Did I bounce into the rough?"

It was impossible to determine whether this question was ingenuous or malicious. In a moment, however, she left no doubt, for as her partner came up over the hill she called cheerfully:

"Here I am! I'd have gone on the green except that I hit something. "

As she took her stance for a short mashie shot, Dexter looked at her closely. She wore a blue gingham dress, rimmed at throat and shoulders with a white edging that accentuated her tan. The quality of exaggeration, of thinness, which had made her passionate eyes and down-turning mouth absurd at eleven, was gone now. She was arrestingly beautiful. The color in her cheeks was centred like the color in a picture—it was not a "high" color, but a sort of fluctuating and feverish warmth, so shaded that it seemed at any moment it would recede and disappear. This color and the mobility of her mouth gave a continual impression of flux, of intense life, of passionate vitality—balanced

点,现在都消失了。她美得引人注目。她双颊的红晕
像图画上的胭脂那样点得适中,然而不"艳",时浓时
淡,兴奋时热乎乎的,可又像随时都会收敛而消失。
这样的红晕和她那么灵活的嘴唇使人得到一种印象,
觉得她心潮起伏不停,生活紧张,洋溢着生命力,那双
眼睛里悲哀的豪华气概只不过抵消了上述特点的一
部分而已。

　　她烦躁地、不感兴趣地挥动铁头球棍,把球打到草
坪对面的一个沙堆上,连忙假意微笑了一下,漫不经心
地说了一声:"谢谢你!"便追随她的球继续向前走去。

　　"裘迪·琼斯这个人哪!"赫德里克先生在接下去
的那个发球沙堆上说,因为他们要等一等,过那么一
会儿,让她在前面打球。"要制伏她只需要把她翻过
来打一顿屁股,照这样整她 6 个月,然后让她嫁给一
位老式的骑兵上尉就行了。"

　　"天哪,她真长得漂亮!"山德伍德先生说,他才过
30 岁。

　　"长得漂亮!"赫德里克先生用鄙视的口气说,"她
总是装出她要人跟她接吻的神气! 那双大母牛眼睛
总是滴溜溜向城里的每一头小公牛转来转去!"

　　至于赫德里克先生是不是在有意暗示母性的本
能,那也靠不住。

　　"只要她认真,她的高尔夫球也能打得挺好的。"
山德伍德先生说。

　　"她没有礼貌。"赫德里克先生一本正经地说。

　　"她的身材很好。"山德伍德先生说。

　　"还是谢谢天主吧,她打出的球总算飞得还不够
快。"哈特先生说着,对迪克斯特挤了一眼。

　　到了傍晚,日落时彩色缤纷,金霞和各种蓝色红
色的云霞变幻着,于是剩下了西部夏季干燥而沙沙有
声的夜晚。迪克斯特从高尔夫球俱乐部游廊里望出
去,望着微风中水浪均匀地交迭,望着收获季节里满
月泻出的银浆。然后月亮把一根手指放在唇边,于是
湖面变成了一泓清泉,暗淡,寂静。迪克斯特穿上他
的游泳衣,游到最远的那个木筏,水淋淋地躺在跳板
的潮湿帆布上。

　　有一条鱼在跳跃,一颗星在照耀,湖周围的灯光
正在闪烁。远处黑沉沉的半岛上,一台钢琴奏起了去
年夏天和往昔若干个夏天的歌曲——《请请》《卢林
堡伯爵》和《巧克力小兵》里的歌曲,因为对迪克斯特
来说,从一泓清泉上传来的钢琴声总是仿佛优美之极,

only partially by the sad luxury of her eyes.

　　She swung her mashie impatiently and without
interest, pitching the ball into a sand-pit on the other
side of the green. With a quick, insincere smile and a
careless "Thank you!"she went on after it.

　　"That Judy Jones!"remarked Mr. Hedrick on the
next tee, as they waited—some moments—for her to
play on ahead. "All she needs is to be turned up and
spanked for six months and then to be married off to
an old-fashioned cavalry captain. "

　　"My God, she's good-looking!" said Mr. Sandwood, who was just over thirty.

　　"Good-looking!" cried Mr. Hedrick contemptuously, "she always looks as if she wanted to be kissed!
Turning those big cow-eyes on every calf in town!"

　　It was doubtful if Mr. Hedrick intended a reference to the maternal instinct.

　　"She'd play pretty good golf if she'd try," said
Mr. Sandwood.

　　"She has no form,"said Mr. Hedrick solemnly.

　　"She has a nice figure,"said Mr. Sandwood.

　　"Better thank the Lord she doesn't drive a swifter
ball,"said Mr. Hart, winking at Dexter.

　　Later in the afternoon the sun went down with a ri-
otous swirl of gold and varying blues and scarlets, and left
the dry, rustling night of Western summer. Dexter
watched from the veranda of the Golf Club, watched the
even overlap of the waters in the little wind, silver molasses under the harvest-moon. Then the moon held a finger
to her lips and the lake became a clear pool, pale and quiet. Dexter put on his bathingsuit and swam out to the farthest raft, where he stretched dripping on the wet canvas
of the springboard.

　　There was a fish jumping and a star shining and
the lights around the lake were gleaming. Over on a
dark peninsula a piano was playing the songs of last
summer and of summers before that—songs from
"Chin-Chin"and "The Count of Luxemburg"and "The
Chocolate Soldier"—and because the sound of a piano
over a stretch of water had always seemed beautiful to
Dexter he lay perfectly quiet and listened.

　　The tune the piano was playing at that moment
had been gay and new five years before when Dexter
was a sophomore at college. They had played it at a
prom once when he could not afford the luxury of
proms, and he had stood outside the gymnasium and
listened. The sound of the tune precipitated in him a
sort of ecstasy and it was with that ecstasy he viewed
what happened to him now. It was a mood of intense

于是他静悄悄地躺着，静悄悄地听着。

这时钢琴演奏的曲调，都是 5 年前迪克斯特还是大学二年级学生时欢快的新曲。在大学生舞会上曾经演奏过一次，当时他没有力量享受这种舞会，只好站在体育馆外面听着。曲调的声音使他心醉神迷，现在他正是以心醉神迷的感情来看待身旁的境遇。这是一种全神贯注来欣赏的心情，他感到，总算有了这么一次，他同生活精彩地协调了，他周围的一切都在散射着光辉和他也许今后再也不会感知的魅力。

一个低矮、苍白、狭长的东西突然脱离了黑暗的岛屿，迸发出摩托赛艇回荡的响声。艇后有两道分叉的白浪随着它滚滚而来，几乎顷刻之间小船就到了他身旁，它那浪花四溅的突突声淹没了热烈的钢琴铿锵声。迪克斯特用手臂把身体撑起来，依稀觉得在驾驶盘旁边有一个站着的人影，两只黑眼正在越过长长的水面瞧着他，然后小艇开走了，在湖中央无目的地绕来绕去。卷起一大圈浪花。同样奇怪的是，有一圈浪花平伸出一道浪，直奔木筏这边来了。

“那是谁呀？”她关闭了马达，叫道。这时，她来得很近了，迪克斯特可以看到她的游泳衣，显而易见，这是一件粉红色连裤游泳衣。

船头撞上了木筏，木筏歪斜着翘起一头，把他摔到了她那面。他们彼此认出了，都觉得有趣，但在程度上各不相同。

“你跟今天下午打球的那些人都是一伙的吧？”她质问道。

他就是其中之一。

“嗯，你会驾驶摩托艇吗？因为要是你会的话，我想请你来驾船，让我能在船后面踏着滑水橇。我叫裘迪·琼斯。”她为了对他表示好感，不近情理地向他自鸣得意地微微一笑——说得更确切一些，这本来是做作的傻笑，尽管她故意扭动着嘴，样子却并不离奇古怪，而且笑得真美——“我住在这座岛上，就是那儿的一栋房子。有一个男人在那栋房子里等着我。他把小艇开到门口，我就从码头上把船开出来了，因为他说我是他理想的人。”

有一条鱼在跳跃，一颗星在照耀，湖周围的灯光正在闪烁。迪克斯特坐在裘迪·琼斯身旁，她说明了一下要怎样来驾驶她这条船。于是她下到水里，用动作柔软的自由式游向漂浮着的滑水橇。观察她的动作，眼睛不需要费力，这就仿佛望着一根树枝在飘动

appreciation, a sense that, for once, he was magnificently attune to life and that everything about him was radiating a brightness and a glamour he might never know again.

A low, pale oblong detached itself suddenly from the darkness of the Island, spitting forth the reverberate sound of a racing motorboat. Two white streamers of cleft water rolled themselves out behind it and almost immediately the boat was beside him, drowning out the hot tinkle of the piano in the drone of its spray. Dexter raising himself on his arms was aware of a figure standing at the wheel, of two dark eyes regarding him over the lengthening space of water—then the boat had gone by and was sweeping in an immense and purposeless circle of spray round and round in the middle of the lake. With equal eccentricity one of the circles flattened out and headed back toward the raft.

"Who's that?" she called, shutting off her motor. She was so near now that Dexter could see her bathing-suit, which consisted apparently of pink rompers.

The nose of the boat bumped the raft, and as the latter tilted rakishly he was precipitated toward her. With different degrees of interest they recognized each other.

"Aren't you one of those men we played through this afternoon?" she demanded.

He was.

"Well, do you know how to drive a motor-boat? Because if you do I wish you'd drive this one so I can ride on the surf-board behind. My name is Judy Jones"—she favored him with an absurd smirk—rather, what tried to be a smirk, for, twist her mouth as she might, it was not grotesque, it was merely beautiful—"and I live in a house over there on the Island, and in that house there is a man waiting for me. When he drove up at the door I drove out of the dock because he says I'm his ideal."

There was a fish jumping and a star shining and the lights around the lake were gleaming. Dexter sat beside Judy Jones and she explained how her boat was driven. Then she was in the water, swimming to the floating surfboard with a sinuous crawl. Watching her was without effort to the eye, watching a branch waving or a sea-gull flying. Her arms, burned to butternut, moved sinuously among the dull platinum ripples, elbow appearing first, casting the forearm back with a cadence of falling water, then reaching out and down, stabbing a path ahead.

They moved out into the lake; turning, Dexter saw that she was kneeling on the low rear of the now

或者一只海鸥在飞翔。她的双臂晒成了灰胡桃色,在暗淡的白金色涟漪里柔软地运动,先露出肘部,继而随着水泼下落的节拍把前臂向后甩去,然后伸出手臂向下划动,冲刺前进。

他们开到了湖里,在转弯的时候,迪克斯特看见她跪在这时已翘起头来的滑水橇向下垂的后半截上。

"开得快一点儿,"她招呼道,"越快越好。"

他惟命是听,把操纵杆推向前,船头起了白沫飞溅的浪花。他又回过头瞧了一下,这时她正在从急速前进的滑水橇上站起来,双臂完全张开,两眼向上望着皓月。

"真冷啊,"她叫喊着,"你叫什么名字?"

他告诉了她。

"嗯,明天晚上你来吃晚餐好不好?"

他的心像赛艇的飞轮那样翻腾起来,他偶尔的一时之兴第二次把他的生活引到了一个新的方向。

三

第二天晚上,迪克斯特在避暑别墅里等她从楼上下来,他设想在这个柔和深邃的房间里,以及与它相通的日光浴游廊上,有若干早先爱上了裘迪·凉斯的人。他了解这种人。在他刚进大学的时候,他们都是从那些大名鼎鼎的预科学校毕业后入学的,服装优雅,都有着夏天健康的深棕褐肤色。他看得出来,在某种意义上,他比他们都好。他发家比较新,他胜过别人一筹。可是他自己承认,他希望他的子女都要像他们那样,这无异于承认了他不过是那种粗糙强劲的材料,他们永远都是从这种材料里出生的。

到了他要穿讲究服装的时候,他已经知道谁是美国最好的裁缝,今天晚上他穿的这套衣服是美国最好的裁缝做的。他养成了他那所大学独有的,使它与其他大学有所不同的审慎有节制的特殊作风。他认识到这种作风对他的价值,并且采取了这种作风。他知道他需要有更强的自信心,才能在服装仪表上粗心大意,倒不如慎重为妥。不过他的子女可以粗心大意。他母亲姓克里麦里契。她是波希米亚农民阶级的人,她一口蹩脚的英语,直到她去世都是这样。她的儿子必须保持老样子。

7点稍过,裘迪·琼斯从楼上下来了。她穿约是一

uptilted surfboard.

"Go faster,"she called,"fast as it'll go. "

Obediently he jammed the lever forward and the white spray mounted at the bow. When he looked around again the girl was standing up on the rushing board, her arms spread wide, her eyes lifted toward the moon.

"It's awful cold,"she shouted. "What's your name?"

He told her.

"Well, why don't you come to dinner to-morrow night?"His heart turned over like the fly-wheel of the boat, and, for the second time, her casual whim gave a new direction to his life.

III

Next evening while he waited for her to come downstairs, Dexter peopled the soft deep summer room and the sun-porch that opened from it with the men who had already loved Judy Jones. He knew the sort of men they were—the men who when he first went to college had entered from the great prep schools with graceful clothes and the deep tan of healthy summers. He had seen that, in one sense, he was better than these men. He was newer and stronger. Yet in acknowledging to himself that he wished his children to be like them he was admitting that he was but the rough, strong stuff from which they eternally sprang.

When the time had come for him to wear good clothes, he had known who were the best tailors in America, and the best tailors in America had made him the suit he wore this evening. He had acquired that particular reserve peculiar to his university, that set it off from other universities. He recognized the value to him of such a mannerism and he had adopted it: he knew that to be careless in dress and manner required more confidence than to be careful. But carelessness was for his children. His mother's name had been Krimelich. She was a Bohemian of the peasant class and she had talked broken English to the end of her days. Her son must keep to the set patterns.

At a little after seven Judy Jones came downstairs. She wore a blue silk afternoon dress, and he was disappointed at first that she had not put on something more elaborate. This feeling was accentuated when, after a brief greeting, she went to the door of a butler's pantry and pushing it open called:"You can serve dinner, Martha. "He had rather expected

身适合于下午的蓝绸子衣服。起先，他感到失望，觉得她应当穿得更讲究一些。接着，他更失望了，在短暂的问候之后，她走到配膳室门口，推开门招呼道："可以上菜了，玛莎。"他本来指望会由一位男管家来宣布开餐，还会有鸡尾酒。可是当他们在一张长沙发上并排坐下来，面对面瞧着的时候，他把这些思想撇开了。

"父亲和母亲都不会来了。"她若有所思地说。

他记得上一次他看到她父亲的情形，他感到高兴，今天晚上她父母都不在场——他们也许要猜想他是谁。他出生在奇布尔朝北去 50 英里的一个明尼苏达村庄。他一向都说他家在奇布尔，不是黑熊村。农村镇市本来是挺好的父母之乡，只要不是诸多不便地处在湖区的视野之内，不被时髦的湖区利用来作为它的踏脚凳就好。

他们谈到了他的大学，过去两年里常常到那儿去。他们谈起了附近的那座向雪利岛提供顾客的城市，以及迪克斯特是不是要在明天回到他那些生意兴隆的洗衣店去。

进餐的时候，她渐渐变得心绪抑郁，使迪克斯特感到不安。无论她用沙哑的噪音说什么使性子的话，他都感到心烦意乱。无论她对什么东西微微一笑，无论是对他，对鸡肝，或者无缘无故，他都感到不自在，觉得她的微笑不会是出于高兴，甚至也不是因为有什么好笑。当她的鲜红嘴唇两角向下弯曲的时候，与其说这是微笑，倒不如说她想要接吻。

晚餐之后，她引他到外面黑暗的日光浴游廊上，故意改变了当时的气氛。

"我想哭一会儿，你不嫌我吗？"她说。

"大概是我惹得你心烦了吧。"他的反应很迅速。

"你没有。我喜欢你。不过我今天下午过得很不痛快。有一个我关心的人，今天下午他青天白日里跟我说什么他穷得像教堂里的耗子似的。以前他甚至从来没吭过一声。这种话多俗气呀，你说是不是？"

"也许他从前不敢对你说。"

"就算他以前不敢吧，"她回答道，"他一开头就不对碴儿。你要知道，假使我认为他这么穷——咳，我原先也像着了迷似的爱上过好些好些穷汉子，真心诚意地觉得跟他们都可以结婚。可是拿这件事来说，我对他没有那种心思，我对他没有那么大的意思，经不起这样大吃一惊。好比一个女人平心静气地告诉她的未婚夫她是个寡妇。他也许不反对寡妇，可是……"

that a butler would announce dinner, that there would be a cocktail. Then he put these thoughts behind him as they sat down side by side on a lounge and looked at each other.

"Father and mother won't be here," she said thoughtfully.

He remembered the last time he had seen her father, and he was glad the parents were not to be here tonight—they might wonder who he was. He had been born in Keeble, a Minnesota village fifty miles farther north, and he always gave Kebble as his home instead of Black Bear Village. Country towns were well enough to come from if they weren't inconveniently in sight and used as footstools by fashionable lakes.

They talked of his university, which she had visited frequently during the past two years, and of the near-by city which supplied Sherry Island with its patrons, and whether Dexter would return next day to his prospering laundries.

During dinner she slipped into a moody depression which gave Dexter a feeling of uneasiness. Whatever petulance she uttered in her throaty voice worried him. Whatever she smiled at—at him, at a chicken liver, at nothing—it disturbed him that her smile could have no root in mirth, or even in amusement. When the scarlet corners of her lips curved down, it was less a smile than an invitation to a kill.

Then, after dinner, she led him out on the dark sun-porch and deliberately changed the atmosphere.

"Do you mind if I weep a little?" she said.

"I'm afraid I'm boring you," he responded quickly.

"You're not. I like you. But I've just had a terrible afternoon. There was a man I cared about, and this afternoon he told me out of a clear sky that he was poor as a church-mouse. He'd never even hinted it before. Does this sound horribly mundane?"

"Perhaps he was afraid to tell you."

"Suppose he was," she answered. "He didn't start right. You see, if I'd thought of him as poor—well, I've been mad about loads of poor men, and fully intended to marry them all. But in this case, I hadn't thought of him that way, and my interest in him wasn't strong enough to survive the shock. As if a girl calmly informed her fiancé that she was a widow. He might not object to widows, but—"

"Let's start right," she interrupted herself suddenly. "Who are you, anyhow?"

For a moment Dexter hesitated. Then:

"I'm nobody," he announced. "My career is largely

"让我们一开始就对碴儿吧,"她突然打断了她自己的话头,"不管怎么说,你是个什么样的人?"

一时间,迪克斯特迟疑不决。然后:

"我是个无名小卒,"他声明道,"我的事业主要得看将来的变化。"

"你穷吗?"

"不穷,"他坦率地说,"在西北部我这个岁数的人里面,我大概比任何人赚的钱都多。我知道说这种话会引起反感的,可是你劝我一开头就要对碴儿。"

到此停顿了一会儿。然后她嫣然一笑,低垂着嘴角。几乎令人觉察不出便微微一歪,靠得他更紧了,还望着他的眼睛。迪克斯特觉得喉管给什么东西堵住了,他屏住呼吸等待着这次试验,面临着那种未可预测的,由他们嘴唇的各种成分不可思议地构成的结合。然后他理会了,她的亲吻,把她的激动情绪深深地传给他了,毫不吝惜,这种接吻不是许愿,而是一种满足,它并没有勾起他那压不住的饥饿,却引起了贪得无厌的食欲……这样的接吻好像施舍赈济品,虽则毫无保留,反而落了个供不应求。

他用不了几个小时便断定了,从他还是个骄傲的、憧憬着未来的小孩子时候起,他所需要的一直是裘迪·琼斯。

四

这件事就是这样开头的,而且照这个调子时冷时热地继续下去,直到故事收场。迪克斯特从来没有接触过这样极其直截了当、极不讲道德的人品,他的一部分向它投降了。裘迪无论要什么,都施展出她的妖媚全力以赴。方法一成不变,既不排挤别人来取得有利地位,也不事先考虑后果——她在情场上做任何事情都不假思索。她只不过让男人们意识到她的体形可爱到了极点。迪克斯特并没有要使她改变作风的愿望。她的种种缺点,都由她满腔热情的能量弥补过来了,而且胜过她的缺点,起到了为它们辩护的作用。

在那第一个夜晚,裘迪头靠在他肩上,轻轻地说:"我不知道我出了什么毛病。昨天夜里我以为我爱上了一个男人,可是今天夜里我觉得我爱上了你……"当时,他似乎认为这种话说得很美,很风流。他感到极其兴奋,他承认这一点,可是当时他也控制住了这种情绪。不过,一个

a matter of futures."

"Are you poor?"

"No," he said frankly, "I'm probably making more money than any man my age in the Northwest. I know that's an obnoxious remark, but you advised me to start right."

There was a pause. Then she smiled and the corners of her mouth drooped and an almost imperceptible sway brought her closer to him, looking up into his eyes. A lump rose in Dexter's throat, and he waited breathless for the experiment, facing the unpredictable compound that would form mysteriously from the elements of their lips. Then he saw—she communicated her excitement to him, lavishly, deeply, with kisses that were not a promise but a fulfillment. They aroused in him not hunger demanding renewal but surfeit that would demand more surfeit... kisses that were like charity, creating want by holding back nothing at all.

It did not take him many hours to decide that he had wanted Judy Jones ever since he was a proud, desirous little boy.

IV

It began like that—and continued, with varying shades of intensity, on such a note right up to the denouement. Dexter surrendered a part of himself to the most direct and unprincipled personality with which he had ever come in contact. Whatever Judy wanted, she went after with the full pressure of her charm. There was no divergence of method, no jockeying for position or premeditation of effects—there was a very little mental side to any of her affairs. She simply made men conscious to the highest degree of her physical loveliness. Dexter had no desire to change her. Her deficiencies were knit up with a passionate energy that transcended and justified them.

When, as Judy's head lay against his shoulder that first night, she whispered, "I don't know what's the matter with me. Last night I thought I was in love with a man and to-night I think I'm in love with you—"—it seemed to him a beautiful and romantic thing to say. It was the exquisite excitability that for the moment he controlled and owned. But a week later he was compelled to view this same quality in a different light. She took him in her roadster to a picnic supper, and after supper she disappeared, likewise in her roadster, with another man. Dexter

星期之后，他不得不用另一种眼光来看待这种情绪了。她用她的双座敞篷汽车带他去参加一个郊外晚餐会，晚餐之后，她不见了，也乘的是她那辆敞篷汽车，但带走了另外一个男人。迪克斯特变得十分心烦意乱，几乎都不能对在场的其他人保持正当的礼貌。事后她向他保证她没有和那个人接吻，他知道她在撒谎——可是他也高兴，她居然会不嫌麻烦来向他撒谎。

在夏季结束之前，他发现，他是她周围的十多个男人之一。他们之中的每一个人都在一段时间内受到比其他任何人都高的恩宠——大约有一半仍然享受着偶尔可以重叙旧情的恩泽。每逢有人由于长期受到冷遇而露出掉队的迹象的时候，她就会甜甜蜜蜜地跟他谈上短短的一小时，鼓励他再尾随着她一年或者再多一点儿时间。裘迪向无能的败军之将进行这一类的袭击并无恶意，她确实只有一半意识到她的所作所为带有一点儿恶作剧的性质。

每逢镇上来了一位新人，其他的每一个人都要中途退出——那些约会都自动勾销了。

要是有人想办法来挽回局面，那也无能为力，因为她事必躬亲。她不是从动力学意义上来讲可以"赢得"的那种女人。聪明手段对她不起作用，引诱也对她不起作用，如果他们之中的任何人过分强烈地向她进攻，她会立刻从身体的基础上来解决这件事，她的多姿多彩的体态的魔力，使那些刚强和高明的人都来给她帮腔助势，而不能施展他们自己那一套。只有满足了她的愿望，或者直接由她来施展她自己的魅力，才能博得她的欢心。也许由于她有过那么多青春之恋，又有那么多青春恋人，她出于自卫，才采取了完全从内心里来滋育她自己的方式。

在迪克斯特初次的兴奋情绪过后，接下来便是感到烦躁不安和没有满足。他如痴如狂地迷上了她，且不能自拔，这种感觉是麻醉性的，没有滋补强身的作用。幸而对他冬天的工作来说，使他心醉神迷的时刻并不时常出现。在他们相交之初，有一阵似乎有一种深挚而自发的相互吸引力，例如8月初的那一阵，有三天，他在她家里昏暗的游廊上度过漫长的夜晚，还有那些奇特的似倦似愁的轻吻，有时是在接近傍晚的时候，在阴暗的凉亭里，或者在花园里葡萄架的屏障棚后面，有时是早晨，她像梦一样新鲜，她在日色初升的清澈光辉里会见他的时候，她几乎有点羞怯。他定情的心醉神迷之乐也只有这些，但由于他后来认识到

became enormously upset and was scarcely able to be decently civil to the other people present. When she assured him that she had not kissed the other man, he knew she was lying—yet he was glad that she had taken the trouble to lie to him.

He was, as he found before the summer ended, one of a varying dozen who circulated about her. Each of them had at one time been favored above all others—about half of them still basked in the solace of occasional sentimental revivals. Whenever one showed signs of dropping out through long neglect, she granted him a brief honeyed hour, which encouraged him to tag along for a year or so longer. Judy made these forays upon the helpless and defeated without malice, indeed half unconscious that there was anything mischievous in what she did.

When a new man came to town every one dropped out—dates were automatically cancelled.

The helpless part of trying to do anything about it was that she did it all herself. She was not a girl who could be "won" in the kinetic sense—she was proof against cleverness, she was proof against charm; if any of these assailed her too strongly she would immediately resolve the affair to a physical basis, and under the magic of her physical splendor the strong as well as the brilliant played her game and not their own. She was entertained only by the gratification of her desires and by the direct exercise of her own charm. Perhaps from so much youthful love, so many youthful lovers, she had come, in self-defense, to nourish herself wholly from within.

Succeeding Dexter's first exhilaration came restlessness and dissatisfaction. The helpless ecstasy of losing himself in her was opiate rather than tonic. It was fortunate for his work during the winter that those moments of ecstasy came infrequently. Early in their acquaintance it had seemed for a while that there was a deep and spontaneous mutual attraction—that first August, for example—three days of long evenings on her dusky veranda, of strange wan kisses through the late afternoon, in shadowy alcoves or behind the protecting trellises of the garden arbors, of mornings when she was fresh as a dream and almost shy at meeting him in the clarity of the rising day. There was all the ecstasy of an engagement about it, sharpened by his realization that there was no engagement. It was during those three days that, for the first time, he had asked her to marry him. She said "maybe some day," she said "kiss me," she said "I'd like to marry you,"

他们并没有定情,这些情景更显得历历在目。也就是在这三天里他第一次对她说,要她嫁给他。她说:"也许有那么一天吧。"她说:"亲亲我。"她说:"我倒也是愿意嫁给你的。"她说:"我爱你。"……好说……其实什么也没说。

这三天给从纽约来的一个人打断了,9月里这个人在她家里做客有半个月。迪克斯特感到痛苦的是,关于他们的流言蜚语很多。这个人是一家大信托公司董事长的儿子。到了月底,据说裘迪在打呵欠了。有一天夜里开舞会,她整个晚上都和当地的一位情郎坐在一只摩托艇里,而那个纽约客却激动发狂似的在俱乐部里到处找她。后来她告诉那个当地的情郎,她对她的客人感到厌烦了,两天之后,他走了。有人看到她在车站上送他,据说他的确是看起来十分悲伤。

夏天就按照这个调子结束了。迪克斯特已经有24岁,他发现他自己处在一天比一天更加称心如意的地位。他参加了城里的两个俱乐部,并且住在其中的一个俱乐部里。虽然他绝不是到俱乐部里找舞伴的单身汉之中的一个固定成员,但是他总要设法来参加裘迪·琼斯可能到场的那些舞会。他能够随意到体面的社交场合。他现在是一个有资格的青年,在城里的父辈当中很得人心。他向裘迪·琼斯表白了他的一片衷肠,这件事反倒巩固了他的地位。不过他在社交上并没有什么抱负,而且很瞧不起那些跳舞的男人。他们一向是星期四或星期六舞会上的常客,有时还会和较年轻的已婚夫妇一起在宴会上补缺。他已经动了要到东部纽约去的念头。他要带着裘迪·琼斯一起走。即使他对她生长成人的那个世界,感到泡影已经破灭,那也治不好他这种只有她才称心如意的幻想。

记住这一点,因为只有用这种眼光才能了解他为她做出的那些事。

在他和裘迪·琼斯初次见面过了18个月之后,他同另一位女郎订了婚。她的姓名是艾琳·席勒尔,她的父亲是一向信任迪克斯特的那些人之一。艾琳发色浅,甜蜜可人,品德高尚,稍胖一点儿。她原来有两个向她求婚的人,当迪克斯特正式向她求婚的时候,她和颜悦色地把这两个人都放弃了。

夏尽秋至,冬去春来,又过了一夏,又是秋天了。在一年半的时间里,他把他的忙碌生活都献给了裘迪·琼斯不可救药的双唇。她对他有时兴致勃勃,有时加以鼓励,有时怀有恶意,有时冷淡,有时轻蔑。她曾

she said "I love you"—she said—nothing.

The three days were interrupted by the arrival of a New York man who visited at her house for half September. To Dexter's agony, rumor engaged them. The man was the son of the president of a great trust company. But at the end of a month it was reported that Judy was yawning. At a dance one night she sat all evening in a motor-boat with a local beau, while the New Yorker searched the club for her frantically. She told the local beau that she was bored with her visitor, and two days later he left. She was seen with him at the station, and it was reported that he looked very mournful indeed.

On this note the summer ended. Dexter was twenty-four, and he found himself increasingly in a position to do as he wished. He joined two clubs in the city and lived at one of them. Though he was by no means an integral part of the stag-lines at these clubs, he managed to be on hand at dances where Judy Jones was likely to appear. He could have gone out socially as much as he liked—he was an eligible young man, now, and popular with down-town fathers. His confessed devotion to Judy Jones had rather solidified his position. But he had no social aspirations and rather despised the dancing men who were always on tap for the Thursday or Saturday parties and who filled in at dinners with the younger married set. Already he was playing with the idea of going East to New York. He wanted to take Judy Jones with him. No disillusion as to the world in which she had grown up could cure his illusion as to her desirability.

Remember that—for only in the light of it can what he did for her be understood.

Eighteen months after he first met Judy Jones he became engaged to another girl. Her name was Irene Scheerer, and her father was one of the men who had always believed in Dexter. Irene was light-haired and sweet and honorable, and a little stout, and she had two suitors whom she pleasantly relinquished when Dexter formally asked her to marry him.

Summer, fall, winter, spring, another summer, another fall—so much he had given of his active life to the incorrigible lips of Judy Jones. She had treated him with interest, with encouragement, with malice, with indifference, with contempt. She had inflicted on him the innumerable little slights and indignities possible in such a case—as if in revenge for having ever cared for him at all. She had beckoned him and yawned at him and beckoned him again and he had responded often with bitterness and narrowed eyes. She had brought

经使出在这种情形下做得到的无数次稍稍怠慢无礼的手段来折磨他,仿佛这是为了她居然会对他有意而进行的报复。她曾经把他招呼来,对他打呵欠,以后又把他再招呼来。他往往以深切的怨恨和眯缝的两眼来回报。她给他带来过使他心醉神迷的幸福和不能忍受的精神痛苦。她弄得他为难的次数说也说不清,还给他造成了非同小可的麻烦。她曾经侮辱他,欺负他,利用他对她的情意来捉弄他对工作的兴趣,以此取乐。她对他什么事都做过,就是没有批评过他,她没有做过这种事,在他看来,仿佛仅仅因为她要是这样做了使她对他的漠不关心就会掺进了杂质,她曾经明确表示她对他漠不关心.这是她的由衷之言。

秋天来了,又过去了,他想过,他不能跟裘迪·琼斯结合。他勉强把这个想法塞进他的头脑里,但他终于说服了他自己。晚上他一时睡不着,反复地思索。他对自己诉说她给他造成的麻烦和痛苦。他数说着她作为妻子的那些彰明较著的缺点。然后他又对自己说他爱她,过了一会儿,他睡着了。有一个星期,因为生怕自己会想象到她在电话里沙哑的口音,或者在午餐时跟她面对面的那双眼睛,他辛勤地工作得很晚,夜晚还到他的办公室里去制订他今后多年的计划。

有一个周末,他去参加一次舞会,一度要求她的舞伴让位给他。自从他们相交以来,这几乎是第一次他没有要求她跟他到外面坐一会儿,没有对她说她长得可爱。不料她并没有惦记着这些事,使他伤了自尊心,如此而已。这天晚上,他看到她有了一位新欢,他并不妒忌。他在很久以前就硬下心肠不妒忌了。

他在舞会上待得很晚。他跟艾琳·席勒尔一块儿坐了一小时,谈论书籍,又谈论音乐。他对这两方面都不过略知一二。可是现在他开始成了他自己时间的主人,他有一个相当自负的想法——既然迪克斯特·格林年轻有为,成就出众,他应当对这些方面了解得多一些。

这是 10 月里的事,当时他 25 岁。在 1 月里,迪克斯特跟艾琳订婚了。这要到 6 月里才宣布,他们准备在 3 个月之后结婚。

明尼苏达州的冬季拖拖拉拉,没完没了,几乎到了 5 月里风才变得柔和,雪才终于流进了黑熊湖。在这一年时间里,迪克斯特第一次享受到精神上的某种安宁。裘迪·琼斯到佛罗里达州去了,后来又到了温泉。她曾经在什么地方订婚,又在什么地方解除了婚

him ecstatic happiness and intolerable agony of spirit. She had caused him untold inconvenience and not a little trouble. She had insulted him, and she had ridden over him, and she had played his interest in her against his interest in his work—for fun. She had done everything to him except to criticise him—this she had not done—it seemed to him only because it might have sullied the utter indifference she manifested and sincerely felt toward him.

When autumn had come and gone again it occurred to him that he could not have Judy Jones. He had to beat this into his mind but he convinced himself at last. He lay awake at night for a while and argued it over. He told himself the trouble and the pain she had caused him, he enumerated her glaring deficiencies as a wife. Then he said to himself that he loved her, and after a while he fell asleep. For a week, lest he imagine her husky voice over the telephone or her eyes opposite him at lunch, he worked hard and late, and at night he went to his office and plotted out his years.

At the end of a week he went to a dance and cut in on her once. For almost the first time since they had met he did not ask her to sit out with him or tell her that she was lovely. It hurt him that she did not miss these things—that was all. He was not jealous when he saw that there was a new man to-night. He had been hardened against jealousy long before.

He stayed late at the dance. He sat for an hour with Irene Scheerer and talked about books and about music. He knew very little about either. But he was beginning to be master of his own time now, and he had a rather priggish notion that he—the young and already fabulously successful Dexter Green—should know more about such things.

That was in October, when he was twenty-five. In January, Dexter and Irene became engaged. It was to be announced in June, and they were to be married three months later.

The Minnesota winter prolonged itself interminably, and it was almost May when the winds came soft and the snow ran down into Black Bear Lake at last. For the first time in over a year Dexter was enjoying a certain tranquillity of spirit. Judy Jones had been in Florida, and afterward in Hot Springs, and somewhere she had been engaged, and somewhere she had broken it off. At first, when Dexter had definitely given her up, it had made him sad that people still linked them together and asked for news of her, but when he began to be placed at dinner next to Irene Scheerer people

约。起初，迪克斯特分明是对她不抱希望了，可是人们仍然把他们俩联系在一起，向他打听她的消息，使他感到悲伤，等到在宴会上他的席位开始被安排在艾琳·席勒尔旁边的时候，人们就不再向他打听她的情况了，他们反而把和她有关的事情告诉他。他不再是一位了解她的权威人士了。

终于到了 5 月里。晚上，迪克斯特在街上行走，黑夜犹如令人沮丧的苦雨，他心里纳罕，时间这么短，也没有搞出什么名堂，他却失去了那么多使他心醉的欢情。一年前的 5 月里，裘迪掀起的波澜强烈得令人难以忍受，既不可原谅却又得到了原谅，这些都历历在目。这段时间是他幻想着她渐渐变得对他有了情意的那些罕有的时光之一。他用往日值一便士的幸福换来这一蒲式耳的内容。他知道艾琳至多不过是在他身后展开的幕布，在几盏光亮的茶杯之间活动的一只手，呼儿唤女的声音……热情和妩媚都已消失，夜色的魔力，变换的时刻和四季的奇观……一双秀唇，下曲成弧形，落到他唇边，使他仰望着那明眸，如登天堂……这种感受很深。他的性格过于坚强，精力过于旺盛，不会让这种感受轻易消逝的。

5 月中旬，有几天的天气在过渡到盛夏的平衡木上摇摆，有一天晚上他来到艾琳家里。他们的婚约就要在一星期内宣布，谁也不会为这件事感到诧异。他们要在今天夜里到大学俱乐部的休息室里坐在一块儿，观看一小时的舞蹈。跟她出去使他感到稳稳当当，她真是深得人心，真是极其"了不起"。

他登上那幢褐色沙石房屋的台阶，走到里面。

"艾琳。"他叫喊道。

席勒尔太太从起居室里出来迎接他。

"迪克斯特，"她说，"艾琳头疼得厉害，到楼上去了。她本来要跟你出去。可是我让她上床睡觉了。"

"不要紧吧，我……"

"哦，没什么。明天早晨她还要跟你去打高尔夫球哩。你让她就歇一晚上吧，行吗，迪克斯特？"

她的笑容可亲。她跟迪克斯特彼此间的感情很好。他在起居室里谈了一会儿才说晚安告辞。

他回到大学俱乐部里，那儿有他住的房间，他在门廊里站了一会儿，瞧着那些跳舞的人。他靠在一根门柱上，向一两个人点点头，便打起了呵欠。

"喂，亲爱的。"

他身边响起的这种熟悉的声音使他吃了一惊。裘

didn't ask him about her any more—they told him about her. He ceased to be an authority on her.

May at last. Dexter walked the streets at night when the darkness was damp as rain, wondering that so soon, with so little done, so much of ecstasy had gone from him. May one year back had been marked by Judy's poignant, unforgivable, yet forgiven turbulence—it had been one of those rare times when he fancied she had grown to care for him. That old penny's worth of happiness he had spent for this bushel of content. He knew that Irene would be no more than a curtain spread behind him, a hand moving among gleaming teacups, a voice calling to children... fire and loveliness were gone, the magic of nights and the wonder of the varying hours and seasons... slender lips, down-turning, dropping to his lips and bearing him up into a heaven of eyes.... The thing was deep in him. He was too strong and alive for it to die lightly.

In the middle of May when the weather balanced for a few days on the thin bridge that led to deep summer he turned in one night at Irene's house. Their engagement was to be announced in a week now—no one would be surprised at it. And to-night they would sit together on the lounge at the University Club and look on for an hour at the dancers. It gave him a sense of solidity to go with her—she was so sturdily popular, so intensely "great."

He mounted the steps of the brownstone house and stepped inside.

"Irene," he called.

Mrs. Scheerer came out of the living-room to meet him.

"Dexter," she said, "Irene's gone up-stairs with a splitting headache. She wanted to go with you but I made her go to bed."

"Nothing serious, I—"

"Oh, no. She's going to play golf with you in the morning. You can spare her for just one night, can't you, Dexter?"

Her smile was kind. She and Dexter liked each other. In the livingroom he talked for a moment before he said good-night.

Returning to the University Club, where he had rooms, he stood in the doorway for a moment and watched the dancers. He leaned against the door-post, nodded at a man or two—yawned.

"Hello, darling."

The familiar voice at his elbow startled him. Judy

迪·琼斯离开了一个男人,从室内出来走到他身旁——正是裴迪·琼斯,像一个苗条的用金色服装打扮的瓷娃娃,头上的带子是金色的,长裙之下露出两个鞋尖也是金色的。在她向他微笑的时候,她脸上虚弱的红润似乎变得含芬吐艳。一片温暖发光的微风吹彻室内。他插在小礼服口袋里的两手像痉挛似的握紧了。他突然感到十分激动。

"你是什么时候回来的?"他漫不经心地问道。

"到这儿来,我会告诉你的。"

她转过身去,他跟着她。她在外面远游了一次——他本来会为她还乡的奇迹哭一场。她走过很多迷人的街道,做过一些像耐人寻味的音乐的事。那种种不可思议的往事,一切新生的和复苏的希望,都随着她的远离而逝去,现在又随着她的还乡而回来了。

她在门廊里转过身来。

"你有车停在这儿吗?要是你没有的话,我有。"

"我有一辆两扇门的小轿车。"

于是,金衣窸窣,她上了车。他砰地关上了车门,她曾经跨进许多辆汽车,有这样的,也有那样的,她倚着皮靠背,胳膊肘儿搁在车门上,就这样等着。要是除她自己以外,有什么东西能玷污她,那她早已被玷污了,可是这是她的自我倾诉。

他勉为其难,一发狠开动了汽车,倒车来到街上。他一定记得,这算不了什么。以前她也做过这种事,他也曾把她放在脑后,仿佛从他的账簿上勾销了一笔倒账。

他慢慢向城区开去,装作心不在焉,在商业区荒凉的街道上行驶,经过了电影散场时人群出来的地方,还经过了患肺病的青年或者以拳击为业的青年在弹子房前面闲逛的地方。从酒店里,从装配着玻璃的游廊和污秽的黄色灯光里传出了玻璃杯相碰和用手猛击的声音。

她紧紧地盯着他,沉默无言是很尴尬的,可是在这个紧急关头,他说不出什么不打紧的话来亵渎这种时刻。到了一个便于转变的地方,他左一转右一转把车子向大学俱乐部开回去。

"你想念过我吗?"她突然问道。

"人人都想念你。"

他疑惑她是不是知道关于艾琳·席勒尔的事。她才回来一天,她的远游和他的订婚几乎是同时发生的。

"这是什么话!"裴迪黯然大笑起来,但并没有感到黯然。她左思右想地打量着他。他反倒心不在焉

Jones had left a man and crossed the room to him—Judy Jones, a slender enamelled doll in cloth of gold; gold in a band at her head, gold in two slipper points at her dress's hem. The fragile glow of her face seemed to blossom as she smiled at him. A breeze of warmth and light blew through the room. His hands in the pockets of his dinner-jacket tightened spasmodically. He was filled with a sudden excitement.

"When did you get back?" he asked casually.

"Come here and I'll tell you about it. "

She turned and he followed her. She had been away—he could have wept at the wonder of her return. She had passed through enchanted streets, doing things that were like provocative music. All mysterious happenings, all fresh and quickening hopes, had gone away with her, come back with her now.

She turned in the doorway.

"Have you a car here? If you haven't, I have. "

"I have a coupé. "

In then, with a rustle of golden cloth. He slammed the door. Into so many cars she had stepped—like this—like that—her back against the leather, so—her elbow resting on the door—waiting. She would have been soiled long since had there been anything to soil her—except herself—but this was her own self outpouring.

With an effort he forced himself to start the car and back into the street. This was nothing, he must remember. She had done this before, and he had put her behind him, as he would have crossed a bad account from his books.

He drove slowly down-town and, affecting abstraction, traversed the deserted streets of the business section, peopled here and there where a movie was giving out its crowd or where consumptive or pugilistic youth lounged in front of pool halls. The clink of glassesand the slap of hands on the bars issued from saloons, cloisters of glazed glass and dirty yellow light.

She was watching him closely and the silence was embarrassing, yet in this crisis he could find no casual word with which to profane the hour. At a convenient turning he began to zigzag back toward the University Club.

"Have you missed me?" she asked suddenly.

"Everybody missed you. "

He wondered if she knew of Irene Scheerer. She had been back only a day—her absence had been almost contemporaneous with his engagement.

"What a remark!" Judy laughed sadly—without sadness. She looked at him searchingly. He became

地凝视着仪表板。

"你比原来更英俊了，"她满腹心事地说，"迪克斯特，你有一双最叫人难忘的眼睛。"

他本来可以一笑了之，但他并没有笑。这种话是只好对大学二年级学生说的。可是这句话刺伤了他。

"我样样都觉得腻烦透了，亲爱的。"她把人人都称做亲爱的，用不经心的个把朋友之情来馈赠亲爱的称呼。"要是你能和我结婚就好了。"

她说得这么直截了当，倒使他不知所措了。他本来应当告诉她现在他正要跟另一个女人结婚，可是他不能告诉她。他也可以轻而易举地向她发誓，说他从来没有爱过她。

"我觉得我们俩会合得来的，"她用同样的调子继续说道，"要不，也许你把我忘了，爱上了别的女人。"

她的自信显然是心比天高。她的话实际上等于说，她认为这种事是不可能相信的，即使这件事是真的，他不过是做了一件幼稚的有失检点的事。她会原谅他的，因为这不是什么了不起的事，而是可以轻描淡写地置之度外的。

"当然，除了我，你绝不会爱上别人的，"她继续说道，"我喜欢你爱我的那种模样。喂，迪克斯特，你没忘了去年吧？"

"没有，我没有忘。"

"我也没有忘记！"

她究竟是真心实意地有感于衷，还是在她自己一浪接一浪地表演下去的时候不由自主地随波逐流呢？

"要是我们能再像那样就好了。"她说，于是他硬着头皮回答：

"我看我们都不会再像那样了。"

"我看也不会了……我听说你正在拼命向艾琳·席勒尔献殷勤呢。"

她这样指名道姓，丝毫也没有加重语气，可是迪克斯特突然感到很难为情。

"唔，送我回家吧，"裘迪突然叫了起来。"我不要回到那个无聊的舞会去跟那些小孩子跳舞。"

他把车子开到通往住宅区的街上，这时，裘迪开始轻轻地哭了起来。以前，他从来没见她哭过。

黑暗的街道亮起来了，在他们周围隐隐现出了富人的宅第，他把汽车停在莫提默尔·琼斯一家的白色大厦面前，大厦睡意正浓，豪华壮观，受到潮润月色的光辉的浸染。它的构造之坚固使迪克斯特感到惊讶。

absorbed in the dashboard.

"You're handsomer than you used to be,"she said thoughtfully. "Dexter, you have the most rememberable eyes. "

He could have laughed at this, but he did not laugh. It was the sort of thing that was said to sophomores. Yet it stabbed at him.

"I'm awfully tired of everything, darling. " She called everyone darling, endowing the endearment with careless, individual camaraderie. I wish you'd marry me. "

The directness of this confused him. He should have told her now that he was going to marry another girl, but he could not tell her. He could as easily have sworn that he had never loved her.

"I think we'd get along," she continued, on the same note, "unless probably you've forgotten me and fallen in love with another girl. "

Her confidence was obviously enormous. She had said, in effect, that she found such a thing impossible to believe, that if it were true he had merely committed a childish indiscretion—and probably to show off. She would forgive him, because it was not a matter of any moment but rather something to be brushed aside lightly.

"Of course you could never love anybody but me,"she continued, "I like the way you love me. Oh, Dexter, have you forgotten last year?"

"No, I haven't forgotten. "

"Neither have I!"

Was she sincerely moved—or was she carried along by the wave of her own acting?

"I wish we could be like that again,"she said, and he forced himself to answer:

"I don't think we can. "

"I suppose not.... I hear you're giving Irene Scheerer a violent rush. "

There was not the faintest emphasis on the name, yet Dexter was suddenly ashamed.

"Oh, take me home," cried Judy suddenly; "I don't want to go back to that idiotic dance—with those children. "

Then, as he turned up the street that led to the residence district, Judy began to cry quietly to herself. He had never seen her cry before.

The dark street lightened, the dwellings of the rich loomed up around them, he stopped his coupé in front of the great white bulk of the Mortimer Joneses' house, somnolent, gorgeous, drenched with the splendor of the damp moonlight. Its solidity startled him. The strong walls, the

墙壁牢固，钢铁般的大梁，它的宽度、桁条和堂皇气派，这一切只是为了同他身旁年轻的美女形成鲜明的对比。大厦之坚实更加显得她脆弱，仿佛这是为了显示一只蝶翼能产生怎样的微风。

他不吭一声地坐着，神经却在猛烈呼号。生怕动一动就会发现她已经不容推却而在他怀抱里了。两滴眼泪从她湿漉漉的脸上滚下来，在她唇上颤抖着。

"我比别人都长得美，"她断断续续地说，"为什么我偏偏得不到幸福？"她那泪汪汪的两眼撕碎了他不动摇的心旌——她的嘴慢慢向下弯曲，含着微妙的哀愁。"我多么愿意嫁给你啊，迪克斯特，假使你肯要我的话。我觉得你大概认为我不值得你要，不过，跟你相配，我会显得多么美啊，迪克斯特。"

恼怒、骄傲、情欲、忿恨、柔情，汇成了百万言语在他唇上斗争起来。然后，一片纯粹出于感情的浪潮淹没了他，冲刷掉了沉积的智慧、习俗、怀疑和恐惧。这是他的佳人在说话，是他自己的美貌佳人，他引以自豪的佳人。

"你要进来吗？"他听见她在猛力吸气。

等待。

"好吧，"他的声音颤抖，"我进来。"

<h1 style="text-align:center">五</h1>

奇怪的是，无论在事毕之初或者过了很久之后。他并不为那天夜里的事感到后悔。以 10 年为期的角度来看，裘迪为他而迸发热情仅仅持续了一个月，这件事似乎无足轻重。至于他因为一时迁就而使自己受了很深的痛苦，并且使艾琳·席勒尔和对他友好的艾琳父母受到严重的创伤，那也无关紧要。艾琳的悲伤并没有什么生动的形象足以在他头脑里留下印痕。

迪克斯特是个本质上硬心肠的人。在他看来，全城的人对他的态度都无关紧要，这并不是因为他就要离开这座城市，而是因为外人对这种事情的态度都嫌肤浅。他对大众的舆论完全漠不关心。这也不是说，当他知道这都没有用的时候，他自己没有那种采取根本行动或者管得住裘迪·琼斯的能力，如果他对她怀有恶意的话。他爱她，他会一直爱她，要爱到他年纪太老了，不能产生爱情的那天。因此，他尝到了只留给强者来感受的深重痛苦，正像他也有一小段时间尝到了深挚的幸福那样。

steel of the girders, the breadth and beam and pomp of it were there only to bring out the contrast with the young beauty beside him. It was sturdy to accentuate her slightness—as if to show what a breeze could be generated by a butterfly's wing.

He sat perfectly quiet, his nerves in wild clamor, afraid that if he moved he would find her irresistibly in his arms. Two tears had rolled down her wet face and trembled on her upper lip.

"I'm more beautiful than anybody else," she said brokenly, "why can't I be happy?" Her moist eyes tore at his stability—her mouth turned slowly downward with an exquisite sadness: "I'd like to marry you if you'll have me, Dexter. I suppose you think I'm not worth having, but I'll be so beautiful for you, Dexter."

A million phrases of anger, pride, passion, hatred, tenderness fought on his lips. Then a perfect wave of emotion washed over him, carrying off with it a sediment of wisdom, of convention, of doubt, of honor. This was his girl who was speaking, his own, his beautiful, his pride.

"Won't you come in?" He heard her draw in her breath sharply.

Waiting.

"All right," his voice was trembling, "I'll come in."

<h1 style="text-align:center">V</h1>

It was strange that neither when it was over nor a long time afterward did he regret that night. Looking at it from the perspective of ten years, the fact that Judy's flare for him endured just one month seemed of little importance. Nor did it matter that by his yielding he subjected himself to a deeper agony in the end and gave serious hurt to Irene Scheerer and to Irene's parents, who had befriended him. There was nothing sufficiently pictorial about Irene's grief to stamp itself on his mind.

Dexter was at bottom hard-minded. The attitude of the city on his action was of no importance to him, not because he was going to leave the city, but because any outside attitude on the situation seemed superficial. He was completely indifferent to popular opinion. Nor, when he had seen that it was no use, that he did not possess in himself the power to move fundamentally or to hold Judy Jones, did he bear any malice toward

裘迪解除婚约的理由是,她并不想从艾琳那里"把他夺走"(其实,裘迪正是要拆散他们),这种话虽然虚伪之极,却并没有引起他的反感。对于任何厌恶他或者试图引起乐趣的手段,他都无动于衷。

他在 2 月里到东部去,打算卖掉他的洗衣店,在纽约定居,可是 3 月里战争来到美国,改变了他的计划。他于是回到西部,把生意交给他的合伙人来管理,在 4 月下旬来到了第一个军官训练营地。他是以多少有些如释重负的心情来迎接战争的成千青年人之一,觉得从纠缠不清的情网里得到解放是件好事。

六

这个故事不是他的传记,请读者记住,不过其中也掺和了一些与他青年时代的梦想毫无牵连的情节。关于这些梦想和关于他的情节,现在我们差不多讲完了。只有一件小事还需要再讲一讲,那是在又过了 7 年之后发生的。

这件事发生在纽约,他在那里干得很好,几乎没有不能克服的困难。这时,他有 32 岁了,除云战后他曾经立即乘飞机回去一次之外,在这 7 年里他一直没有到西部去过。有一个从底特律来的人,名叫德夫林,到他的办公室里来洽商业务,这件事就是在此时此地发生的,同时也可以说,从此结束了他生活中的这一特殊方面。

"原来你是中西部人,"这个名叫德夫林的人不假思索地出于好奇心说道,"这真是怪事,我以为像你这样的人大概都是在华尔街出生,在华尔街长大的。你知道吗,我在底特律有一个最好的朋友,他的妻子就是你那个城市的人。我在他们举行婚礼的时候是招待来宾的人员之一。"

迪克斯特等他说下去,并没有警觉到会有什么下文。

"裘迪·西姆斯,"德夫林不在意地说,"她以前叫做裘迪·琼斯。"

"哦,我认识她。"一种乏味的不耐烦的感觉传遍了他全身。他当然听人说过她已经结婚了,也许是经过深思熟虑,他才没有再听到别人说起的。

"非常好的一个人,"德夫林毫无目的地沉思起来,"我有点为她感到惋惜。"

her. He loved her, and he would love her until the day he was too old for loving—but he could not have her. So he tasted the deep pain that is reserved only for the strong, just as he had tasted for a little while the deep happiness.

Even the ultimate falsity of the grounds upon which Judy terminated the engagement that she did not want to "take him away" from Irene—Judy who had wanted nothing else—did not revolt him. He was beyond any revulsion or any amusement.

He went East in February with the intention of selling out his laundries and settling in New York—but the war came to America in March and changed his plans. He returned to the West, handed over the management of the business to his partner, and went into the first officers' training-camp in late April. He was one of those young thousands who greeted the war with a certain amount of relief, welcoming the liberation from webs of tangled emotion.

VI

This story is not his biography, remember, although things creep into it which have nothing to do with those dreams he had when he was young. We are almost done with them and with him now. There is only one more incident to be related here, and it happens seven years farther on.

It took place in New York, where he had done well—so well that there were no barriers too high for him. He was thirty-two years old, and except for one flying trip immediately after the war, he had not been West in seven years. A man named Devlin from Detriot came into his office to see him in a business way, and then and there this incident occurred, and closed out, so to speak, this particular side of his life.

"So you're from the Middle West," said the man Devlin with careless curiosity. "That's funny—I thought men like you were probably born and raised on Wall Street. You know—wife of one of my best friends in Detroit came from your city. I was an usher at the wedding."

Dexter waited with no apprehension of what was coming.

"Judy Simms," said Devlin with no particular interest; "Judy Jones she was once."

"Yes, I knew her." A dull impatience spread over

"为什么?"迪克斯特立刻警觉起来,也立刻听得入耳了。

"啊,路德·西姆斯可以说是在精神上垮台了。我的意思不是说他虐待她,可是他酗酒,而且有了外遇……"

"她没有外遇吗?"

"没有。她待在家里抚养她的儿女。"

"哦。"

"她年龄太大了,跟他不相称。"德夫林说。

"太大了!"迪克斯特叫了起来,"喂,老兄,她才27岁呀。"

一个疯狂的念头缠住了他,他想奔到大街上,乘火车到底特律去。他像痉挛似的站起身来。

"我看你大概很忙,"德夫林连忙道歉,"我没有想到……"

"不忙,我没有什么事,"迪克斯特说,他稳定了话音,"我一点儿也不忙。根本不忙。你说过她是……27岁吗? 不对,是我说她有27岁的。"

"是这样,是你说的。"德夫林冷冰冰地表示同意。

"说下去吧。那么说下去吧。"

"你要我说什么?"

"关于裘迪·琼斯的事情。"

德夫林无可奈何地望着他。

"唔。这件事,我已经通通讲给你听了。他待她很不好。啊,他们也不是要离婚或者怎么的。遇到他实在无礼取闹的时候,她就原谅他。其实,我倒认为她爱他。她刚到底特律来的时候还是个漂亮姑娘呐。"

漂亮姑娘,这种措词使迪克斯特觉得荒唐可笑。

"她已经不再是个……漂亮姑娘了吗?"

"哦,她还可以。"

"喂,请你注意,"迪克斯特说,他突然坐下了,"我不明白。你说她是个'漂亮姑娘',现在你又说她'还可以'。我不明白你的意思是怎么回事——裘迪·琼斯根本不是个什么'漂亮姑娘'。她的相貌之美是无双的。咳,我认识她。我认识她。她是……"

德夫林和颜悦色地大笑起来。

"我不是要来跟你斗嘴的,"他说,"我认为裘迪是个挺好的女人。我不明白像路德·西姆斯那样的人怎么会不要命地爱上了她,可是他就爱上了她。"然后他又说,"大多数的女人都喜欢她。"

迪克斯特紧瞅着德夫林,胡乱思索起来,认为这

him. He had heard, of course, that she was married—perhaps deliberately he had heard no more.

"Awfully nice girl," brooded Devlin meaninglessly, "I'm sort of sorry for her."

"Why?" Something in Dexter was alert, receptive, at once.

"Oh, Lud Simms has gone to pieces in a way. I don't mean he ill-uses her, but he drinks and runs around—"

"Doesn't she run around?"

"No. Stays at home with her kids."

"Oh."

"She's a little too old for him," said Devlin.

"Too old!" cried Dexter. "Why, man, she's only twenty-seven."

He was possessed with a wild notion of rushing out into the streets and taking a train to Detroit. He rose to his feet spasmodically.

"I guess you're busy," Devlin apologized quickly. "I didn't realize—"

"No, I'm not busy," said Dexter, steading his voice. "I'm not busy at all. Not busy at all. Did you say she was—twenty-seven? No, I said she was twenty-seven."

"Yes, you did," agreed Devlin dryly.

"Go on, then. Go on."

"What do you mean?"

"About Judy Jones."

Devlin looked at him helplessly.

"Well, that's—I told you all there is to it. He treats her like the devil. Oh, they're not going to get divorced or anything. When he's particularly outrageous she forgives him. In fact, I'm inclined to think she loves him. She was a pretty girl when she first came to Detroit."

A pretty girl! The phrase struck Dexter as ludicrous.

"Isn't she—a pretty girl any more?"

"Oh, she's all right."

"Look here," said Dexter, sitting down suddenly. "I don't understand. You say she was a 'pretty girl' and now you say she's 'all right.' I don't understand what you mean—Judy Jones wasn't a pretty girl, at all. She was a great beauty. Why, I knew her, I knew her. She was—"

Devlin laughed pleasantly.

"I'm not trying to start a row," he said. "I think Judy's a nice girl and I like her. I can't understand how a man like Lud Simms could fall madly in love with her but he did." Then he added: "Most of the women

番话必然有些道理,那个男人大概有些麻木不仁,或者这里面有些私人怨恨。

"许多女人,"德夫林弹指示意,"就像这样一下子枯萎了。你一定也见过这种事情。也许我忘记了她在举行婚礼的时候有多么漂亮,可是你知道,打那以后我时常见到她。她的眼睛挺漂亮。"

一种木然的沉闷罩住了迪克斯特。有生以来第一次,他觉得好像他正在醉得昏昏沉沉。他知道因为德夫林说了什么话他不由放声大笑起来,可是他不知道那是怎么一句话,也不知道为什么那句话这么可笑。几分钟之后,德夫林走了,他躺在大沙发上,望着窗外纽约市高楼林立的天际,太阳正在这些高楼之间西沉,落照浸没在暗淡的粉红色和金色的美妙暮霭之中。

他曾经想过,既然他没有什么可以失去的别的东西了,他也终于不会受到创伤了——可是他知道他刚才又失去了一些东西,确实是这样,仿佛他跟裘迪·琼斯结了婚,又看到她在他眼前枯萎凋零了一般。

梦消失了。他是有所失的。他一时惊慌,用手掌揉了揉眼睛,想回忆起那些画面。湖水拍打着雪利岛,月光照亮着游廊,高尔夫球场上的格子花衣,干巴巴的太阳,她头颈上金色的细软汗毛,还有他亲吻时她那湿润的嘴,她那双流露出凄楚的哀怨的眼睛,她的清新犹如早晨细白的新床单。咳,这些东西都已经不在人世间了!原先这些都是真情实景,如今它们都不会再发生了。

多年以来第一次,他脸上流下了泪水。不过现在他是为自己落泪的。他并不关心什么嘴呀,眼睛呀,移动着的双手呀。他要关心,然而他不能关心。因为他远游在外,永远也不能再回去了。那些门都关闭了,太阳西沉了,无美可寻,除非是那耐得住永久的灰色钢铁之美。甚至连他可能产生的哀伤也都遗留在幻景之乡、青春之乡和多姿多彩的生活之乡了!原先,他的冬梦也正是在这里滋长起来的。

"好久以前,"他说,"好久以前,我还有一股子什么东西,可是现在那种东西消失了。现在那种东西消失了,那种东西消失了。我哭不出来。我也无从放在心上。那种东西再也不会回来了。"

like her. "

Dexter looked closely at Devlin, thinking wildly that there must be a reason for this, some insensitivity in the man or some private malice.

"Lots of women fade just like *that*," Devlin snapped his fingers. "You must have seen it happen. Perhaps I've forgotten how pretty she was at her wedding. I've seen her so much since then, you see. She has nice eyes. "

A sort of dullness settled down upon Dexter. For the first time in his life he felt like getting very drunk. He knew that he was laughing loudly at something Devlin had said, but he did not know what it was or why it was funny. When, in a few minutes, Devlin went he lay down on his lounge and looked out the window at the New York sky-line into which the sun was sinking in dull lovely shades of pink and gold.

He had thought that having nothing else to lose he was invulnerable at last—but he knew that he had just lost something more, as surely as if he had married Judy Jones and seen her fade away before his eyes.

The dream was gone. Something had been taken from him. In a sort of panic he pushed the palms of his hands into his eyes and tried to bring up a picture of the waters lapping on Sherry Island and the moonlit veranda, and gingham on the golf-links and the dry sun and the gold color of her neck's soft down. And her mouth damp to his kisses and her eyes plaintive with melancholy and her freshness like new fine linen in the morning. Why, these things were no longer in the world! They had existed and they existed no longer.

For the first time in years the tears were streaming down his face. But they were for himself now. He did not care about mouth and eyes and moving hands. He wanted to care, and he could not care. For he had gone away and he could never go back any more. The gates were closed, the sun was gone down, and there was no beauty but the gray beauty of steel that withstands all time. Even the grief he could have borne was left behind in the country of illusion, of youth, of the richness of life, where his winter dreams had flourished.

"Long ago," he said, "long ago, there was something in me, but now that thing is gone. Now that thing is gone, that thing is gone. I cannot cry. I cannot care. That thing will come back no more. "

051. 岩 石

（美）詹姆斯·鲍德温 著　　万　紫 译

051. The Rockpile

by James Baldwin

在他们房屋的马路对面，两座房屋中间的空地上，有一块大岩石。这是一块罕见的突出在地面上的大岩石。有人，可能是弗洛伦姑姑对他们说，这岩石不可以把它弄走。否则地下铁道的列车会飞出来，乘客全部丧生。这个有关地球表面和地心的自然界的秘密，过于迷人了，使人不能置之不理。并且由于它赋予岩石这种神奇的重要性，使罗伊感到在那里玩要是他的权利，而不是他的义务。

每天下午放学以后，以及整个星期六和星期天，都可以看到其他孩子也都在那儿。他们在岩石上打架，他们彼此追逐，或在高处扭打，有的脚步平稳，有的危险百出，有的粗心大意。有时他们躲到岩石的另一面去大喊大闹，双脚倒立着。他们的母亲有时从太平梯看到他们时，就说："真奇怪，他们不会摔死！""你们这班小鬼，听我的话！快离开这里！"她嘴上说的是"你们"，眼睛看的却是和约翰一起坐在太平梯上的罗伊。"上帝知道，"她继续说，"我不愿你每天回家来像只上帝送来的血淋淋的小猪。"罗伊不耐烦地转过身，继续向大街望着，好像这样看着会长出翅膀来似的。约翰不说什么，他的确没说什么，他在为岩石担心，为那些在岩石上玩要的孩子们担心。

每个星期六上午，约翰和罗伊坐在太平梯上看那下面被禁止下去的大街。有时，他们的母亲坐在他们后面的房间里缝衣服，或者给他们的妹妹穿戴，或者给婴儿保罗喂奶。太阳带着傲慢而仁慈的淡漠神气经过他们，经过太平梯落下去。在他们下面，男人女人，男孩女孩，芸芸众生，踯躅街头。有时路过一个教

ACROSS the street from their house, in an empty lot between two houses, stood the rockpile. It was a strange place to find a mass of natural rock jutting out of the ground; and someone, probably Aunt Florence, had once told them that the rock was there and could not be taken away because without it the subway cars underground would fly apart, killing all the people. This, touching on some natural mystery concerning the surface and the center of the earth, was far too intriguing an explanation to be challenged, and it invested the rockpile, moreover, with such mysterious importance that Roy felt it to be his right, not to say his duty, to play there.

Other boys were to be seen there each afternoon after school and all day Saturday and Sunday. They fought on the rockpile. Sure footed, dangerous, and reckless, they rushed each other and grappled on the heights, sometimes disappearing down the other side in a confusion of dust and screams and upended flying feet. "It's a wonder they don't kill themselves," their mother said, watching sometimes from the fire escape. "You children stay away from there, you hear me?" Though she said "children," she was looking at Roy, where he sat beside John on the fire escape. "The good Lord knows," she continued, "I don't want you to come home bleeding like a hog every day the Lord sends. "Roy shifted impatiently, and continued to stare at the street, as though in this gazing he might somehow acquire wings. John said nothing. He had not really been spoken to: he was afraid of the rockpile and of the boys who played there.

Each Saturday morning John and Roy sat on the fire escape and watched the forbidden street below. Sometimes their mother sat in the room behind them, sewing, or dressing their younger sister, or nursing the baby, Paul. The sun fell across them and across the

---

作者简介：詹姆斯·鲍德温（James Baldwin，1924—1987），美国评论家、小说家和剧作家。1924 年 8 月 2 日生于美国纽约，1987 年 12 月 1 日卒于法国圣保罗。他在纽约黑人住宅区长大，十几岁时成了传教士。他首篇半自传体的小说，《向苍天呼吁》（Go Tell It on the Mountain，1953）被看做他最好的作品。他的作品还有文集《土生子的札记》（Notes of a Native Son，1940）和《没人知道我名字》（Nobody Knows My Name，1961），长篇小说《乔万尼的房间》（Giovanni's Room，1956）和《另一个国度》（Another Country，1962），长篇辩论文章《下一次将是烈火》（The Fire Next Time，1963）和《查理先生》（Mister Charlie，1964）。他多年来对种族问题的雄辩和热情使他成为美国最富有感染力的黑人作家。

徒,看到他们,向他们招手,他们虽害怕,但仍有礼貌地向他回礼。他们看着男的或女的圣徒,直到看不见他或她为止。一个救世者的路过,使他们不免茫然地考虑那大街上的邪恶,他们自己坐在那儿的潜伏的邪恶,并使他们想到他们的父亲,他在星期六很早回家,他会马上转过眼前的拐角,走进他们下面阴暗的门厅。

但是他们仍一直在大街的上方坐着,注视着,渴望着,直到他们的父亲来结束他们的自由。靠近他们房屋的大街一端是一座横跨哈莱姆河的桥。直通弗洛伦姑姑所住的布朗克斯城。但是他们看到她不是从桥那儿来,而是从大街的那一端来的。这个,在他们脑海里感到没有说服力,虽然她解释说她不愿走路,是乘地铁来的。此外,她并非住在布朗克斯市区里。他们知道布朗克斯在河对面,他们始终不相信这个,而是按照父亲对她的态度,假定她正好离开某个她不敢讲的坏地方,譬如电影院。

在夏天,孩子们从木船坞上跳到河里去游泳,或从倒满垃圾的河岸涉水而行。有一次,一个名叫理查德的男孩淹死在河里。他母亲不知道他在哪里,甚至到他们家里来问她儿子在不在。后来,傍晚6点钟,他们听到一个妇人在街上又哭又喊,他们就跑到窗口去探望,理查德的母亲从街上走来,头仰着天,满脸流泪地大声啼哭。另一个妇人在她身旁走着安慰她,要她平静下来。她们后面跟着一个男人,就是理查德的父亲,抱着理查德的尸体,还有两个穿白制服的警察在排水沟上走着,他们似乎不知道该怎么办。理查德父子俩都湿透了。理查德的尸体在他父亲手中像个布娃娃。妇人的哭声闹得满街都听到了,所有的车子都慢下来,里面的人都伸出头来探看。人们都开窗张望,并跑出门口站在排水沟上注视着。然后,小小的队伍消失在岩石旁的屋里。"上帝!上帝!上帝!"他们的母亲伊丽莎白喊着。后来,窗户砰的一声关上了。

有一个星期六,罗伊在他父亲回家前一小时在岩石上受了伤,他尖叫着被人扶上楼梯。他和约翰本来坐在太平梯上,他们的母亲在厨房里和修女麦肯德莱斯喝茶。渐渐罗伊厌烦起来。他坐在约翰身边,虽不出声,却很不耐烦。约翰把报纸上电动火车头的广告画到他的笔记本上去。罗伊的几个朋友从太平梯下走过,喊他。他坐立不安,从栏栅里向下喊他们。然

fire escape with a high, benevolent indifference; below them, men and women, and boys and girls, sinners all, loitered; scmetimes one of the church-members passed and saw them and waved. Then, for the moment that they waved decorously back, they were intimidated. They watched the saint, man or woman, until he or she had disappeared from sight. The passage of one of the redeemed made them consider, however vacantly, the wickedness of the street, their own latent wickedness in sitting where they sat; and made them think of their father, who came home early on Saturdays and who would soon be turning this corner and entering the dark hall below them.

But until he came to end their freedom, they sat, watching and longing above the street. At the end of the street nearest their house was the bridge which spanned the Harlem River and led to a city called the Bronx; which was where Aunt Florence lived. Nevertheless, when they saw her coming, she did not come from the bridge, but from the opposite end of the street. This, weakly, to their minds, she explained by saying that she had taken the subway, not wishing to walk, and that, besides, she did not live in *that* section of the Bronx. Knowing that the Bronx was across the river, they did not believe this story ever, but, adopting toward her their father's attitude, assumed that she had just left some sinful place which she dared not name, as, for example, a movie palace.

In the summertime boys swam in the river diving off the wooden dock, or wading in from the garbage-heavy bank. Once a boy, whose name was Richard, drowned in the river. His mother had not known where he was; she had even come to their house, to ask if he was there. Then, in the evening, at six o'clock, they had heard from the street a woman screaming and wailing; and they ran to the windows and looked out. Down the street came the woman, Richard's mother, screaming, her face raised to the sky and tears running down her face. A woman walked beside her, trying to make her quiet and trying to hold her up. Behind them walked a man, Richard's father, with Richard's body in his arms. There were two white policemen walking in the gutter, who did not seem to know what should be done. Richard's father and Richard were wet, and Richard's body lay across his father's arms like a cotton baby. The woman's screaming filled all the street; cars slowed down and the people in the cars stared; people opened their windows and looked out and came rushing out of doors to stand in the gutter, watching. Then the small procession disappeared within the house which stood beside the rockpile. Then, "*Lord, Lord, Lord!*" cried Elizabeth, their mother, and slammed the window down.

One Saturday, an hour before his father would be coming home, Roy was wounded on the rockpile and

后，一阵沉默。约翰向前看着，罗伊则站起来望着他们。

"我要下楼去。"他说。

"你最好还是留在你原来的地方，孩子。你晓得妈妈不愿意你下楼去。"

"我会马上回来的。她不会晓得我走开过，除非你去告诉她。"

"我才不会去告诉她哩。可是怎么能不让她到这儿来，从窗口看出来呢？"

"她在讲话。"罗伊说时向房间里看了一看。

"但爸爸快要回家了！"

"我会在他回家前回来的。你为什么老是害怕？"他已进了屋子，并转身靠在窗台上不耐烦地发誓说，"5分钟我就回来。"

约翰愠怒地看着罗伊小心翼翼地开门走了。一会儿，他就看到罗伊和他的朋友们在人行道上。他不敢把罗伊离开太平梯的事去告诉他的母亲，因为他确已答应过不去告诉的。他正想大喊："记住，你说过 5 分钟！"但罗伊的一个朋友正在向上看着太平梯，约翰低头看他的笔记本，他又为那火车头而出神了。

当他重新抬头时，已不知过了多久。他看到那岩石上正在打群架。几十个孩子在烈日下互相搏斗。他们爬在岩石上，挥拳相向，拖着鞋子在光滑的石头上溜来溜去，明亮的阳光下充满着各种咒骂和欢呼声。空中还舞着各种武器：石子、棒头、空听子、垃圾，拣到什么就丢什么。约翰看得出神了——直到他想起罗伊还在楼下，并且是岩石上孩子们中的一员，他害怕了。他在阳光下的人群中看不到他弟弟的影子，他站起来俯身在太平梯的栏杆外探视着。罗伊在岩石的那一边出现了。约翰看到他的衬衫已经撕破，他在大笑，他一直爬到岩石的顶上。忽然，有个什么东西——一个空听子飞来打在他额头上，刚刚在一只眼睛上面，立刻，罗伊的半边脸上流下血来。他跌倒了，他的脸滚在石头上。这时，所有的动作、声音都停下来了。太阳也停止在街上、人行道上一动也不动的孩子们身上。后来，有人叫喊起来，孩子们跑开了，沿着街，向桥上跑去。地上那个屏息流血的人开始尖叫起来。约翰喊着"妈妈，妈妈"跑进屋去。

"别发愁，别发愁，"当她们从狭小的摇摇摆摆的楼梯冲下去时修女麦肯德莱斯气喘吁吁地说，"别发愁。养了孩子，难免常常要碰伤，我的上帝！"她们急

brought screaming upstairs. He and John had been sitting on the fire escape and their mother had gone into the kitchen to sip tea with Sister McCandless. By and by Roy became bored and sat beside John in restless silence, and John began drawing into his schoolbook a newspaper advertisement which featured a new electric locomotive. Some friends of Roy passed beneath the fire escape and called him. Roy began to fidget, yelling down to them through the bars. Then a silence fell. John looked up. Roy stood looking at him.

"I'm going downstairs," he said.

"You better stay where you is, boy. You know Mama don't want you going downstairs."

"I be right *back*. She won't even know I'm gone, less you run and tell her."

"I ain't *got* to tell her. What's going to stop her from coming in here and looking out the window?"

"She's talking," Roy said. He started into the house.

"But Daddy's going to be home soon!"

"I be back before *that*. What you all the time got to be so *scared* for?" He was already in the house and he now turned, leaning on the windowsill, to swear impatiently, "I be back in *five* minutes."

John watched him sourly as he carefully unlocked the door and disappeared. In a moment he saw him on the sidewalk with his friends. He did not dare to go and tell his mother that Roy had left the fire escape because he had practically promised not to. He started to shout, *Remember, you said five minutes!* but one of Roy's friends was looking up at the fire escape. John looked down at his schoolbook: he became engrossed again in the problem of the locomotive.

When he looked up again he did not know how much time had passed, but now there was a gang fight on the rockpile. Dozens of boys fought each other in the harsh sun: clambering up the rocks and battling hand to hand, scuffed shoes sliding on the slippery rock; filling the bright air with curses and jubilant cries. They filled the air, too, with flying weapons: stones, sticks, tin cans, garbage, whatever could be picked up and thrown. John watched in a kind of absent amazement—until he remembered that Roy was still downstairs, and that he was one of the boys on the rockpile. Then he was afraid; he could not see his brother among the figures in the sun; and he stood up, leaning over the fire-escape railing. Then Roy appeared from the other side of the rocks; John saw that his shirt was torn; he was laughing. He moved until he stood at the very top of the rockpile. Then, something, an empty tin can, flew out of the air and hit him on the forehead, just above the eye. Immediately, one side of Roy's face ran with blood, he fell and rolled on his face down the rocks. Then for a moment there was no movement at all, no sound, the sun, arrested, lay on the

急走到阳光下去了。一个男人已经把罗伊扶起来,慢慢向她们走来。一两个孩子静静地坐在他们的门阶上。街的两头都有一群孩子张望着。"他伤得不厉害,"那男人说,"如果他真的伤得厉害,大家也别这样吵吵闹闹。"

伊丽莎白发着抖走过去抱罗伊,但比她高大而镇静的修女麦肯德莱斯从那男人手中接过罗伊,像抱过一包棉花那样,把他甩在肩头上。"上帝保佑你,"她对那男人说,"上帝保佑你,老弟。"罗伊仍在尖叫。伊丽莎白站在麦肯德莱斯修女后面仔细察看他流血的面孔。

"这不过是一点儿皮伤,"那人继续说,"不过伤了皮肤,就是这些。"她们经过人行道往屋里走去。约翰现在已不再害怕那些盯着看的孩子们了,他往下看着街角他父亲是不是来了。

在楼上,她们止住了罗伊的喊叫,洗掉了血迹,发现正好在眉上有一个锯齿形表皮上的伤口。"上帝保佑,"伊丽莎白喃喃地说,"再低一英寸,他的眼睛就完蛋了。"她忧心忡忡地看着时钟。"幸而没有真的伤在眼睛上。"麦肯德莱斯修女说着,急忙给他擦碘酒,系绷带。

"他是什么时候下楼的?"他母亲终于问了。

在罗伊躺着的沙发一头,麦肯德莱斯修女正坐在安乐椅里扇扇子。罗伊头上扎着绷带,静静地躺着。她停下来,严厉地朝约翰看了好一会儿。约翰站在窗口,手里拿着报纸上的广告和自己画的东西。

"我们坐在太平梯上,"约翰说,"他几个熟识的孩子叫了他。"

"什么时候?"

"他说他5分钟就回来的。"

"为什么你不来告诉我他下楼去了?"

他看看他的手,合上笔记簿,没有回答。

"孩子,"麦肯德莱斯修女说,"你听到你母亲在对你说话吗?"

他看看他的母亲,重复说:

"他说他5分钟后就回来的。"

"他说他5分钟后就回来的,"麦肯德莱斯修女嘲弄地说,"别指望我喜欢这样不合适的回答。你是这屋里的大人了。你该照顾好你的弟弟妹妹……你不该让他们出去,摔个半死。不过我想,"她从安乐椅上起来,放下纸板做的扇子继续说,"你爸爸会让你说真

street and the sidewalk and the arrested boys. Then someone screamed or shouted; boys began to run away, down the street, toward the bridge. The figure on the ground, having caught its breath and felt its own blood, began to shout. John cried, "Mama! Mama!" and ran inside.

"Don't fret, don't fret," panted Sister McCandless as they rushed down the dark, narrow, swaying stairs, "don't fret. Ain't a boy been born don't get his knocks every now and again. *Lord*!" they hurried into the sun. A man had picked Roy up and now walked slowly toward them. One or two boys sat silent on their stoops; at either end of the street there was a group of boys watching. "He ain't hurt bad," the man said, "Wouldn't be making this kind of noise if he was hurt real bad."

Elizabeth, trembling, reached out to take Roy, but Sister McCandless, bigger, calmer, took him from the man and threw him over her shoulder as she once might have handled a sack of cotton. "God bless you," she said to the man, "God bless you son," Roy was still screaming. Elizabeth stood behind Sister McCandless to stare at his bloody face.

"It's just a flesh wound," the man kept saying "just broke the skin, that's all." They were moving across the sidewalk, toward the house. John, not now afraid of the staring boys, looked toward the corner to see if his father was yet in sight.

Upstairs, they hushed Roy's crying. They bathed the blood away, to find, just above the left eyebrow, the jagged, superficial scar. "Lord, have mercy," murmured Elizabeth, "another inch and it would've been his eye." And she looked with apprehension toward the clock. "Ain't it the truth," said Sister McCandless, busy with bandages and iodine.

"When did he go downstairs?" his mother asked at last.

Sister McCandless now sat fanning herself in the easy chair at the head of the sofa where Roy lay, bound and silent. She paused for a moment to look sharply at John. John stood near the window, holding the newspaper advertisement and the drawing he had done.

"We was sitting on the fire escape," he said. "Some boys he knew called him."

"When?"

"He said he'd be back in five minutes."

"Why didn't you tell me he was downstairs?"

He looked at his hands, clasping his notebook, and did not answer.

"Boy," said Sister McCandless, "you hear your mother a-talking to you?"

He looked at his mother. He repeated:

"He said he'd be back in five minutes."

"He said he'd be back in five minutes," said Sister

话的。你妈妈对你太好了。"他没有看她，而看那放在她坐过的暗红色的低陷的座位上的扇子。扇子上印着润发油的广告，一个棕色女人和她的婴孩，头发闪闪发光，幸福地相视而笑。

"亲爱的，"麦肯德莱斯修女说，"我要走了，今晚晚些时候可能我会再来。我想你今晚大概不会去做泰利礼拜了吧？"

泰利礼拜是每星期六晚上在教堂里举行的祈祷会，用以团结教徒，并为礼拜天到来的圣灵节做准备。

"我不打算去了。"伊丽莎白说着站起来。她和麦肯德莱斯修女互相吻了一下面颊。"你一定要在祈祷时记着我。"

"我一定这样做。"她歇了一会儿，把手放在门钮上看着罗伊笑着说，"可怜的小伙子，他现在会知道应该安心坐在太平梯上了。"

伊丽莎白和她一同笑着说："这对他真是一个教训，你以为，"她不安地问，依然带着笑容，"他会留下疤痕吗？你说呢？"

"老天，不会，"麦肯德莱斯修女说，"那不过是一点儿擦伤。我说克兰姆斯姐姐，你还不如一个孩子，不消半个月，你就会看不到伤疤了。不，你去忙你的家务吧，亲爱的。谢谢上帝，事情并不那么糟。"她们听到楼梯上有脚步声，她就去开门。"我想，这是牧师先生，"麦肯德莱斯修女安静地说，"我打赌，他是来引起骚乱的。"

"可能是弗洛伦，"伊丽莎白说，"有时她在这时来。"她们站在房门口注视着，听那脚步声到了下面的平台上。然后又爬上她们这一层来。"不，"于是伊丽莎白说，"这不是她的脚步声，这是加布里埃尔。"

"好啦，我要走啦！"麦肯德莱斯修女说，"多少当心他的情绪。"说时她按按伊丽莎白的手，走进门厅，让门半开着出去了。伊丽莎白慢慢地转身走进房间。罗伊没有张开眼睛，动也不动。她知道他没有睡着，他要等他父亲回来，最后可能对他发作的时刻。约翰把报纸和笔记本放在桌上，靠在桌旁看着她。

"这不是我的错，"他说，"我不能制止他下楼去。"

"不，"她说，"你不是毫不相干的。你一定要对你爸爸说实话。"

他径直地望着她。她转身到窗口向街头望着，麦肯德莱斯修女说的话是什么意思？她听到德莉拉在她卧室里小声啼哭，她转身皱着眉头看看卧室，向依

McCandless with scorn, "don't look to me like that's no right answer. You's the man of the house, you supposed to look after your baby brothers and sisters—you ain't supposed to let them run off and get half-killed. But I expect," she added, rising from the chair, dropping the cardboard fan, "your Daddy'll make you tell the truth. Your Ma's way too soft with you."

He did not look at her, but at the fan where it lay in the dark red, depressed seat where she had been. The fan advertised a pomade for the hair and showed a brown woman and her baby, both with glistening hair, smiling happily at each other.

"Honey," said Sister McCandless, "I got to be moving along. Maybe I drop in later tonight. I don't reckon you going to be at Tarry Service tonight?"

Tarry Service was the prayer meeting held every Saturday night at church to strengthen believers and prepare the church for the coming of the Holy Ghost on Sunday.

"I don't reckon," said Elizabeth. She stood up; she and Sister McCandless kissed each other on the cheek. "But you be sure to remember me in your prayers."

"I surely will do that." She paused, with her hand on the door knob, and looked down at Roy and laughed. "Poor little man," she said, "reckon he'll be content to sit on the fire escape *now*."

Elizabeth laughed with her. "It sure ought to be a lesson to him. You don't reckon," she asked nervously, still smiling, "he going to keep that scar, do you?"

"Lord, no," said Sister McCandless, "ain't nothing but a scratch. I declare, Sister Grimes, you worse than a child. Another couple of weeks and you won't be able to *see* no scar. No, you go on about your housework honey, and thank the Lord it weren't no worse." She opened the door; they heard the sound of feet on the stairs. "I expect that's the Reverend," said Sister McCandless, placidly, I *bet* he's going to raise cain."

"Maybe it's Florence," Elizabeth said. "Sometimes she get here about this time." They stood in the doorway, staring, while the steps reached the landing below and began again climbing to their floor. "No," said Elizabeth then, "that ain't her walk. That's Gabriel."

"Well, I'll just go on," said Sister McCandless, "and kind of prepare his mind." She pressed Elizabeth's hand as she spoke and started into the hall, leaving the door behind her slightly ajar. Elizabeth turned slowly back into the room. Roy did not open his eyes, or move; but she knew that he was not sleeping; he wished to delay until the last possible moment any contact with his father. John put his newspaper and his notebook on the table and stood, leaning on the table, staring at her.

"It wasn't my fault," he said, "I couldn't stop him from going downstairs."

"No," she said, "you ain't got nothing to worry

然开着的门走去。她知道约翰注视着她。德莉拉还在哭,她想这女孩那么大了还要啼哭,不免有些恼怒。但是她怕德莉拉哭醒保罗,就急急跑进卧室,哄她再睡一回。她听到前门一开一关,声音太响了。德莉拉哭声高了起来。伊丽莎白愤怒地叹了一口气,抱起了她。她和加布里埃尔的孩子是罗伊、德莉拉和保罗。约翰是没有姓的,是一个局外人,他的生存成为他母亲犯罪时刻的铁证。

"发生了什么事?"加布里埃尔开始查问了。他身材高大魁梧,站在房间当中,黑色的饭盒子挂在手上,他往罗伊躺着的沙发探视。约翰正站在他面前。这在她看来真是一个可怕的景象,他在他的下面,在他沉重的拳脚之下。孩子吓得魂不附体地朝他望着——好像一个姑娘回家来,看见兔子在狂吠的狗面前吓得呆立在那里一样。她急急经过加布里埃尔跑到沙发前面,感到她手中的德莉拉重得像盾牌一样。她站在罗伊面前说:

"现在,没有什么要办了。加布里埃尔,这孩子在我转身时溜下楼去受了一点儿伤。现在他已没事了。"

罗伊好像要证实妈妈的话,张开了眼睛,严肃地望着他父亲。加布里埃尔喀哒一声丢掉他的饭盒,跪在沙发旁。

"儿子,你感到怎么样? 告诉你爸爸,出了什么事?"

罗伊张嘴要想说话,然后重又感到恐慌而哭了起来。他父亲抱住了他的肩膀。

"你别哭,你是爸爸的小儿子,告诉你爸爸出了什么事?"

"他下楼去了,"伊丽莎白说,"他没有事干,他和那些在岩石上玩的坏孩子打架。就是这点事儿,幸而没有什么不好。"

他向她看看:"你不能让孩子自己回答我么?"

她不理这个,更加温和地继续说:"他的额上弄破了,不过没有什么可担心的。"

"你请了医生么? 你怎么知道没有什么可担心的?"

"你有钱去丢给医生么? 不,我没去请医生。我的眼睛又没坏到看不出他伤得厉害不厉害。他不过吃了一惊。该感谢上帝教训了他一顿。"

"你有那么多话要讲,"他说,"还有我,我还得讲一分钟。我要知道是什么时候发生的。那时你的眼

about. You just tell your Daddy the truth. "

He looked directly at her, and she turned to the window, staring into the street. What was Sister Mc-Candless saying? Then from her bedroom she heard Delilah's thin wail and she turned, frowning, looking toward the bedroom and toward the still open door. She knew that John was watching her. Delilah continued to wail, she thought, angrily, *Now that girl's getting too big for that*, but she feared that Delilah would awaken Paul and she hurried into the bedroom. She tried to soothe Delilah back to sleep. Then she heard the front door open and close—too loud, Delilah raised her voice, with an exasperated sigh Elizabeth picked the child up. Her child and Gabriel's, her children and Gabriel's: Roy, Delilah, Paul. Only John was nameless and a stranger, living, unalterable testimony to his mother's days in sin.

"What happened?" Gabriel demanded. He stood, enormous, in the center of the room, his black lunch-box dangling from his hand, staring at the sofa where Roy lay. John stood just before him, it seemed to her astonished vision just below him, beneath his fist, his heavy shoe. The child stared at the man in fascination and terror—when a girl down home she had seen rabbits stand so paralyzed before the barking dog. She hurried past Gabriel to the sofa, feeling the weight of Delilah in her arms like the weight of a shield, and stood over Roy, saying:

"Now, ain't a thing to get upset about, Gabriel. This boy sneaked downstairs while I had my back turned and got hisself hurt a little. He's alright now. "

Roy, as though in confirmation, now opened his eyes and looked gravely at his father. Gabriel dropped his lunchbox with a clatter and knelt by the sofa.

"How you feel, son? Tell your Daddy what happened?"

Roy opened his mouth to speak and then, relapsing into panic, began to cry. His father held him by the shoulder.

"You don't want to cry. You's Daddy's little man. Tell your Daddy what happened. "

"He went downstairs," said Elizabeth, "where he didn't have no business to be, and got to fighting with them bad boys playing on that rockpile. That's what happened and it's a mercy it weren't nothing worse. "

He looked up at her. "Can't you let this boy answer me for hisself?"

Ignoring this, she went on, more gently: "He got cut on the forehead, but it ain't nothing to worry about. "

"You call a doctor? How you know it ain't nothing to worry about?"

"Is you got money to be throwing away on doctors? No, I ain't called no doctor. Ain't nothing wrong with my eyes that I can't tell whether he's hurt bad or

睛在干什么?"他返身向着罗伊。他本来安静地躺着在呜咽,眼睛张得老大,身体挺得笔直。现在,在他父亲的安慰下,想起了他脚下那高地,那又尖又滑的石头,那太阳,那炙热的太阳,想起他突然眼前漆黑,他的咸的血。当他父亲碰他的额角时,他退缩着尖叫起来。"别动,别动,"他父亲摇手低声说,"别动,别哭,爸爸不会弄痛你,他只要看一看绷带,看一看他们怎样弄他的小儿子。"可是罗伊仍尖叫着不肯停下来。加布里埃尔不敢再碰那绷带,怕更把他弄伤了。他怒气冲冲地望着伊丽莎白说:"你不能放下那孩子帮我弄一弄这个? 约翰,去给你妈抱妹妹——别光看着,好像你们两个都神志不清似的。"

约翰抱了德莉拉坐在安乐椅上。他母亲俯身按住了罗伊,他父亲小心地松开绷带——罗伊仍不停地尖叫着——观察那伤口。罗伊的哭声轻一些了。加布里埃尔重新扎好绷带。"你看,"伊丽莎白终于说,"他死不了。"

"这确不是你的错,他还没死。"他和伊丽莎白悄悄地商量了一回,"他真差一点儿就会瞎掉一只眼睛。当然,他的眼睛没有你的大,所以我断定你认为这没有多大关系。"听了这话,她的脸沉了下来。他笑着说,"上帝保佑。你以为你总是干得对的吗? 这事发生时你在哪里? 谁让他下楼去的?"

"没人让他下楼去,他自己去的。他的脑袋和他父亲的一样,要他低头,宁可把头打破的,我在厨房里。"

"约翰在哪里?"

"他在这里。"

"哪里?"

"在太平梯上。"

"他知道罗伊在楼下么?"

"我认为他知道。"

"你认为,这是什么意思? 他长了你一样的大眼睛,什么也没有看吗?"他望着约翰,"孩子,你看到你弟弟下楼去吗?"

"加里布埃尔,责备约翰有什么意思。你十分清楚,如果你不能把罗伊教好,他不会听他哥哥的话。我的话他也不大肯听哩。"

"罗伊下楼去,你为什么不去告诉你妈?"

约翰不说什么,眼睛盯着盖在德莉拉身上的毛毯。

not. He got a fright more'n anything else, and you ought to pray God it teaches him a lesson."

"You got a lot to say *now*," he said, "but I'll have *me* something to say in a minute. I'll be wanting to know when all this happened, what you was doing with your eyes *then*." He turned back to Roy, who had lain quietly sobbing eyes wide open and body held rigid; and who now, at his father's touch, remembered the height, the sharp, sliding rock beneath his feet, the sun, the explosion of the sun, his plunge into darkness and his salty blood; and recoiled, beginning to scream, as his father touched his forehead. "Hold still, hold still," crooned his father, shaking, "hold still. Don't cry. Daddy ain't going to hurt you, he just wants to see this bandage, see what they've done to his little man." But Roy continued to scream and would not be still and Gabriel dared not lift the bandage for fear of hurting him more. And he looked at Elizabeth in fury: "Can't you put that child down and help me with this boy? John, take your baby sister from your mother—don't look like neither of you got good sense."

John took Delilah and sat down with her in the easy chair. His mother bent over Roy, and held him still, while his father, carefully—but still Roy screamed—lifted the bandage and stared at the wound. Roy's sobs began to lessen. Gabriel readjusted the bandage. "You see," said Elizabeth, finally, "he ain't nowhere near dead."

"It sure ain't your fault that he ain't dead." He and Elizabeth considered each other for a moment in silence. "He came mightly close to losing an eye. Course, his eyes ain't as big as your'n, so I reckon you don't think it matters so much." At this her face hardened; he smiled. "Lord, have mercy," he said, "you think you ever going to learn to do right? Where was you when all this happened? Who let him go downstairs?"

"Ain't nobody let him go downstairs, he just went. He got a head just like his father, it got to be broken before it'll bow. I was in the kitchen."

"Where was Johnnie?"

"He was in here?"

"Where?"

"He was on the fire escape."

"Didn't he know Roy was downstairs?"

"I reckon."

"What you mean, you reckon? He ain't got your big eyes for nothing, does he?" He looked over at John. "Boy, you see your brother go downstairs?"

"Gabriel, ain't no sense in trying to blame Johnnie. You know right well if you have trouble making Roy behave, he ain't going to listen to his brother. He don't hardly listen to me."

"How come you didn't tell your mother Roy was downstairs?"

John said nothing, staring at the blanket which

"孩子,你听见我说的话吗?你要我揍你一顿吗?"

"不,不要,"她说,"你不要揍这孩子,今天你不要揍他。罗伊现在躺在这里,你若要怪人的话,只要怪你自己——因为你宠坏了他。他想干啥就干啥,而且逃避惩罚。现在我告诉你,没有方法是教不好孩子的。你不用祈祷上帝帮你干得比过去好些,上帝今天不接受你的灵魂,你将活着流你的苦泪。"她颤抖着,她看也不看地走向约翰,从他手里抱过德莉拉来。她转身瞧着加布里埃尔,他已站起来走近沙发向她看看。她看到他脸上不仅仅是愤怒——她对此已不感惊奇——而是深深的仇恨,这种仇恨由于他缺少品德而深沉得叫人难以忍受。他的眼睛像是活活地受了打击,一动也不动,毒瞎了似的——真像天崩地裂一样,她感觉到他渴望她的毁灭。于是,她摇勾她怀中的孩子,好像能得到慰藉似的。看到这,他的眼睛有了变化,看着伊丽莎白,他孩子们的母亲,上帝赐予的终身伴侣。于是她泪眼模糊地离开房间,她勾脚碰到了地上的饭盒。

"约翰,"她说,"把你父亲的饭盒拣起来,像个好孩子。"

她听到在她后面他离开椅子时的走动声,他拣起饭盒时刺耳的摩擦声。他把他的黑色脑袋伏在他父亲沉重的靴子尖上。

covered Delilah.

"Boy, you hear me? You want me to take a strap to you?"

"No, you ain't," she said. "You ain't going to take no strap to this boy, not today you ain't. Ain't a soul to blame for Roy's lying up there now but you—you because you done spoiled him so that he thinks he can do just anthing and get away with it. I'm here to tell you that ain't no way to raise no child. You don't pray to the Lord to help you do better than you been doing, you going to live to shed bitter tears that the Lord didn't take his soul today." And she was trembling. She moved, unseeing, toward John and took Delilah from his arms. She looked back at Gabriel, who had risen, who stood near the sofa, staring at her. And she found in his face not fury alone, which would not have surprised her; but hatred so deep as to become insupportable in its lack of personality. His eyes were struck alive, unmoving, blind with malevolence—she felt, like the pull of the earth at her feet, his longing to witness her perdition. Again, as though it might be propitiation, she moved the child in her arms. And at this his eyes changed, he looked at Elizabeth, the mother of his children, the helpmeet given by the Lord. Then her eyes clouded; she moved to leave the room; her foot struck the lunchbox lying on the floor.

"John," she said, "pick up your father's lunchbox like a good boy."

She heard, behind her, his scrambling movement as he left the chair, the scrape and jangle of the lunchbox as he picked it up, bending his dark head near the toe of his father's heavy shoe.

重要词汇
Glossary

A

Abstract 抽象　抽象是作为纯粹的概念独立出来的性质或特征。一粒糖是具体的实物，有自己的性质，但是我们可以把它的白色、质硬、味甜等性质抽象出来（形象地说是剥离出来）。文学作品从其特点来看更多的是具体而非抽象，是个别而非普遍。所有这些并非意味着文学作品不涉及那些能够抽象地表达出来的概念，比如爱情、勇气、公平，在文学作品中，这些概念很少以抽象出来的形式出现，它们总是和具体的元素结合在一起，在小说中，就是和特定的角色、情境和事件结合在一起。从故事的特定因素中抽象出来的总体观点，对于人类本性或生活的观点，与故事是不相等同的。抽象和概括不是故事自身具体特定因素的全部，仅仅是其间的一部分。

Action 动作　一系列有意义的连贯的事件。

Action story 动作小说　着重情节悬念的故事，比如历险小说或侦探小说。

Allegory 寓言体故事　寓言体故事是指一个故事，其中的角色、物体和事件都不被看作是真实存在的，而是象征着一套成体系的思想。也就是说这个故事中的每个细节都等同于那套思想中的某个细节。比如，班扬的《天路历程》，离开自己的家、登上去往"天国之城"旅途的基督徒代表着所有这类希望过基督徒生活的人，旅途上发生的每件事都代表着人们在精神世界中遇到的问题。

Alliteration 头韵　指重复相同的辅音，特别是重复单词开头的辅音，比如 lullaby 或 "levels of the lake"。

Anecdote 轶事　对于某个事件的简短记述。

Anticlimax 反高潮　打破事件或结果整体的发展趋

A

ABSTRACT　Abstractions are qualities and characteristics isolated as pure ideas. A piece of *sugar* is a concrete substance with its own qualities but we may *abstract*(literally *draw away*) from it *whiteness*, *hardness*, *sweetness*. Literature characteristically deals with the concrete rather than the abstract, and also the specific rather than the general. All of which is not to say that ideas, which are capable of being stated abstractly—love, courage, justice—are not involved in literature, but such ideas rarely emerge as abstractions, rather, they are incorporated in the concrete elements—in the case of fiction, in the particular characters and situations and events. The general observations that one may abstract from the particulars of a story—observations about human nature or about life—are not to be taken as the equivalent of the story. The abstraction—and the generalization—are something less than—merely a part of—the concrete particularity of the story itself.

ACTION　A series of events having unity and significance.

ACTION STORY　A story in which the principal interest lies in plot suspense, such as adventure or detective fiction.

ALLEGORY　An allegory is a kind of narrative in which the characters, objects, and events are to be taken, not as real but as standing for some set of ideas. That is, each item in the narrative is equated with some item among the ideas. For example, in Bunyan's *The Pilgrim's Progress*, the character Christian, who leaves his home to journey to the Celestial City, is to be taken as the type of all people who try to lead the Christian life, and each event that takes place on the journey stands for some problem in the spiritual life.

ALLITERATION　Repetition of consonants, particularly of initial consonants as in *lullaby* or"*l*evels of the *l*ake. "

ANECDOTE　A brief narrative account of some incident or event.

ANTICLIMAX　A break in the climactic order of

势，没有出现人们所期待的事件发展到高潮的激化效果。

Atmosphere 氛围 一篇小说中笼罩各个要素的总体感觉，比如背景、人物、主题及其他，是对整个作品进行把握的结果。要与"背景"和"语调"区分开。可以结合氛围和语调这两个词的比喻意义的本体来理解其含义。语调指作者对要呈现的事物的态度（讲话者声音的语调对他所说的话有修饰限定作用），氛围指来自素材本身的总体条件（阳光、欢快的氛围，阴郁的氛围，等等）。但是，在一般的讨论中，这些词的使用经常会有交叉，没有明确的界线。在针对某篇具体的小说时，学生应该问问自己是想强调作者的态度还是仅仅强调素材的效果。

C

Cliché 套话 指由于使用频繁，失去其原有效力的短语，比如，"坠入梦乡"(in the arms of Morpheus)和"沉重的一击"(a dull sickening thud)。这个词偶尔会用到成为某种范式的老调重弹的虚构的场景和事件中。套话一般代表读者的一种习惯反应。但是，它也能够被作者合理地应用，表达讽刺效果，或者因为某类人物在他的语言中通常会用到套话，或者因为其他的一些原因。总体来说，想要制造生动、令人难忘的效果时，套话是起不到作用的，因为它不能表现出新的看法和感悟。

Climax 高潮 一个上升的序列的最高点。比如，在小说中，是指矛盾中的各个力量到达最激化的一点。

Coherence 连贯性 一篇小说的各个部分结合在一起，互相连接。连贯的真实性与一篇文学作品的内在连贯性相关。

Coincidence 巧合 某些事件凑巧地发生（见"意外结局"）。一方面来说，巧合在小说中的运用是不可避免的，任何故事的原始状况就可能定义为一个巧合。但是一般来说，在解决小说虚构的问题时，巧合的运用是不合逻辑的，也就是说，某个情节的结局，与之前叙述的事件之间没有逻辑联系。

Complication 开展 人物和事件之间的相互影响，为故事原始状况制造出张力，提出问题。

Concrete 具体 见"抽象"。

events or effects, a falling off from the expected intensification of effect. See **CLIMAX** and **IRONY**.

ATMOSPHERE The general pervasive feeling aroused by the various factors in a piece of fiction, such as setting, character, theme, and the like; the general effect of the handling of the total work. To be distinguished from SETTING and from TONE. Considerations of the metaphorical origin of the two terms, *atmosphere* and *tone*, may be helpful here. *Tone* is to be referred ultimately to the author's attitude (the tone of voice of a speaker as qualifying what he says) toward what is being presented, whereas *atmosphere* is to be referred to the general qualification provided by the materials themselves (an atmosphere of sunshine, of cheerfulness, an atmosphere of gloom, and the like). There is, however, a good deal of overlapping and vagueness about the use of these terms in ordinary discussion. The student, in referring to a particular case in fiction, should ask himself whether he wishes to emphasize the author's attitude or the mere effect of the materials as such.

C

CLICHÉ Usually used in reference to a phrase which has lost its force because of continual use; for example, "in the arms of Morpheus," or "a dull, sickening thud." But the term is also applied occasionally to fictional situations or events which have become hackneyed and stereotyped. The cliché represents one kind of appeal to a STOCK RESPONSE on the part of the reader. But, of course, clichés may be used justifiably by the author, for ironical effect, or because a certain kind of character would normally use clichés in his speech, or for other reasons. In general, it may be said that a cliché is bad when used with the intention of creating a vivid and memorable effect; it fails in such cases because it does not represent a fresh perception.

CLIMAX The highest point in an ascending series; in fiction, for example, the point at which the forces in conflict reach the highest intensification.

COHERENCE The hanging together—the interconnectedness—of the parts of a piece of fiction. TRUTH OF COHERENCE has to do with the internal consistency of a piece of literature.

COINCIDENCE An accidental coming together of certain events. (See SURPRISEENDING.) The use of coincidence is, in one sense, unavoidable in fiction, for the original situation in any story may be defined as a coincidence. But the use of coincidence is, generally speaking, illegitimate when it functions to solve the fictional problem; that is, when the events which bring about the resolution of a plot have no logical connection with preceding events.

COMPLICATION The interplay between character and event which builds up a tension and develops a problem out of the original situation given in the story.

CONCRETE See **ABSTRACT**.

Conflict 矛盾　所有的小说都在不同层面上涉及到矛盾的问题。人物与环境抗争或者人物之间相互斗争（外部矛盾），抑或人物自身斗争（内部矛盾）。理解小说的一个重要途径就是确定其中矛盾的性质以及各股对立力量的格局。

Connotation 引申义　见"本义"。

Convention 惯例　所有明晰默认的方法、手段或者规则。比如，字母 t 带有辅音性质，橄榄球赛持球触地可得 6 分，这些不是由其本质决定的，而是源于惯例。所有艺术形式，包括小说，都会运用惯例。比如，运用全知视角叙事的小说中，作者可以深入小说人物的内心，这就是惯例。作者不断地运用沿袭下来的传统惯例。但是，他在作品中不能创新运用传统惯例的成分解决新问题，那么他的作品会被界定为"俗套"，这显然是贬义的。

Conventional 俗套　见"惯例"。

Cutback 倒叙　叙述中间的一段，打破了叙事的时间顺序，讲述这之前发生的事情。

D

Denotation 本义　文字所指的具体事物或思想。本义不仅仅指基本含义，还指具体和抽象的含义。科学文章只需要用文字的本义，试图构造一种科学的技术性的语言。但是一个词的引伸义是指这个词暗示的或者与之相关的东西。尽管引申义肯定是含混、不确切的（与本义相比），但是引申义仍然很有效力，而且很重要。熟练的作者，如果他的写作目的是文学性的而非科学性的，他会充分运用引申义。

Denouement 结局　情节的最后结果。有时与高潮一致。

Distance 距离感　指在对小说人物的进行观察过程中与其的疏离程度。

Dramatic 戏剧性　严格地讲，作者对素材进行纯粹的客观展现，不加主观评论、主观概括或者对人物情感和思想的分析，这种创作手法就是戏剧性手法。本书中最明显的例子就是《杀手》。对使用戏剧性手法的小说，读者必须根据外部动作和对话推断内在情境。但是在更宽泛的定义下，这个词仅仅用来指小说中强大的张力和尖锐的冲突，或者用来指与抽象陈述相对的具体叙述。

CONFLICT　All fiction involves, at one level or another, conflict. The characters struggle against environment or with each other (external conflict) or are engaged in struggles with themselves (internal conflict). One important approach to the understanding of any story is to determine the nature of the conflict involved and the pattern that the opposing forces assume.

CONNOTATJON　See **DENOTATION**.

CONVENTION　Any method, device, or rule that is accepted by explicit or tacit agreement. For example, the fact that the letter *t* shall have a certain consonantal value, or that a touchdown shall count for six points depends upon nothing intrinsic but is determined by convention. All the arts, including that of fiction, make use of *conventions*. For example, the omniscient author's ability to enter into the innermost thoughts of several of his characters depends upon a convention. The author continually makes use of traditional conventions handed down to him from the past. His work, however, is termed CONVENTIONAL in a bad sense when it fails to justify the conventional items it employs by relating them freshly to the new problem.

CONVENTIONAL　See **CONVENTION**.

CUTBACK　A passage in a narrative which breaks the chronological sequence to deal with earlier events.

D

DENOTATION　The exact thing or idea indicated by word. The denotation is not only the primary meaning, but it is the specific and abstract meaning. Scientific prose needs no more than the denotations of words, and the attempt to build up a scientific and technical language is in harmony with this situation. But the CONNOTATIONS of a word are the things suggested by or associated with the word. These connotations, though necessarily vague and inexact (as compared with denotations) are nevertheless powerful and important, and the skillful writer whose intention is literary rather than scientific makes full use of them.

DENOUEMENT　The final resolution or untying of the plot. It sometimes, but not always, coincides with the climax.

DISTANCE　The term is used to mean the degree of detachment with which the characters in a story are viewed.

DRAMATIC　Strictly speaking, fictional method is said to be dramatic when the author gives a purely OBJECTIVE rendering of his material, without indulging either in editorial comment and generalization of his own or in the analysis of the either in editorial comment and generalization of his own or in the analysis of the feelings and thoughts of his characters. The clearest case of such a method in this book is "The Killers". Where a dramatic method is used the reader must infer the inner situation from the external action and dialogue. But the term is used more loosely to indicate merely the presence of strong tension and sharp conflict in a story or novel; and it is used more loosely still to indicate concrete presentation as opposed to abstract statement.

E

Episode 片断　较大的动作过程中单独的事件。

Episodic 片断式的　如果一篇小说没有强调片断之间的连续性,那么它就被称为片断式的。从逻辑上讲,片断式结构就情节而言是一种松散结构。

Exposition 破题　给予读者关于故事的"动作"开始之前的人物和事件的必要信息。

F

Fable 寓言　通常是一个十分简练的故事,用来阐述有关人性的普遍真理。

Fiction 小说　对于一个事件或多个事件的叙述,不一定是要真实发生的事件,是虚构出来的故事,其真实性不是来自于实际发生的事实。本书的第一章介绍了小说的基本要素。

First-person narration 第一人称叙事　见"叙事焦点"。

Focus 焦点　虚构作品所有素材围绕的中心。在一篇小说中,焦点可以时时转换,也可以保持一致。例如,焦点可以是人物、思想、场景或者其他元素。

Focus of character 人物焦点　一篇小说不仅仅是一连串的事件,这些事件会关注某个人,或者某群人,他们参与到事件当中,从一方面看,叙事结构取决于小说主要关注的这个人或这群人的相关情况。

Focus of narration(point of view)叙事焦点(视角)　叙事焦点是指如何讲故事。我们可以将其分为四类:(1)人物以第一人称讲述自己的故事;(2)人物以第一人称讲述他看到的故事;(3)作者从纯客观的角度讲述发生的故事——行为、语言、姿势——不进入人物的思想,不加自己的评论;(4)作者自由地讲述发生的故事,进入人物的思想,加以自己的评论。这四类叙事视角分别被称为:(1)第一人称;(2)第一人称旁观;(3)作者旁观;(4)作者全知。当然可以将这些方法进行组合运用。

Foreshadowing 伏笔　给读者留下下文即将发生的事件的暗示。

Form 形式　文学作品中各种元素的安排方式,各类素材(思想、图像、人物、场景和其他)的组织,以达到

E

EPISODE　A separate incident in a larger piece of action.

EPISODIC　A piece of fiction is said to be *episodic* when there is not a strongly emphasized causal continuity between one episode and the next. Episodic structure is, logically, loose structure, in so far as plot is concerned.

EXPOSITION　The process of giving the reader necessary information concerning characters and events existing before the action proper of a story begins.

F

FABLE　A tale, usually rather simple and often illustrating some maxim about human nature.

FICTION　A narrative of an event or events that did not necessarily actually occur; a story produced by the imagination, the truth of which does not rest upon fact. The first 31 pages of this book attempt to suggest what the basic elements of fiction are.

FIRST-PERSON NARRATION　See FOCUS OF NARRATION.

FOCUS　The center around which the material of an imaginative work is concentrated. The focus may shift from moment to moment in a piece of fiction or it may remain constant. For example, the focus may be primarily upon character, upon an idea, upon a setting, or the like.

FOCUS OF CHARACTER　A piece of fiction is not merely a sequence of events. The events are of special concern to some person, or group of persons, involved in them, and the structure of the narrative depends, in one sense, upon the reference to the person or persons, most fundamentally concerned.

FOCUS OF NARRATION(POINT OF VIEW)　The focus of narration has to do with who tells the story. We may make four basic distinctions:(1) a character may tell his own story in the first person;(2) a character may tell, in the first person, a story which he has observed;(3) the author may tell what happens in the purely objective sense—deeds, words, gestures—without going into the minds of the characters and without giving his own comment;(4) the author may tell what happens with full liberty to go into the minds of characters and to give his own comment. These four types of narration may be called:(1) first-person,(2) first-person observer,(3) author-observer, and(4) omniscient author. Combinations of these methods are, of course, possible.

FORESHADOWINC　The process of giving the reader an intimation of some event which is to follow later in the action.

FORM　The arrangement of various elements in a work of literature; the organization of various materials

一个单一的效果。可以说，一个作品采取了某种形式，它的所有元素互相有机地连接，每个部分都达到其预期的效果，那么这个作品就是成功的。形式并不仅仅是故事的一种载体，它是总的组织原则，影响作品构成的各个方面。"结构"和"风格"也被用来形容作者为了达到希望的效果对素材的组织形式。但是，结构通常用来指较大的元素的排序，如片断、情境、动作细节，而风格通常用来指文字的组织。大体上看，这两个词都是形式的同义词，但是在本书中，风格仅用来指语言的选择和顺序。

Functional 功能性的　与一篇小说的整体效果形成相关。在本书中，这个词用来表示小说当中组成小说复杂性和完整性的元素，与之相对的是由于流行时髦使用的元素，或者为了满足某种外部兴趣使用的元素，或者只是为了起到轰动效果、起装饰效果或吸引人使用的元素。

Imagery 意象　一切感知经验的表现。意象不仅仅包括"脑海中的画面"，而且与一切感知相关。所有文学作品，由于要保持其各自的具体性和特殊性，都会大量运用意象，不仅用于描述性语言当中，而且用于修辞语言当中。最常用的修辞形式是明喻和暗喻。明喻是直接将那两种事物进行比较，这种比较通常由"好像"或"比如"引出。暗喻并不突出比较，而是间接地指出两种事物的相似性。尽管这些细节在小说中看起来微不足道，它们的效果确实很微妙而且显著的。有时，作者的基本态度（见"语调"）以及小说的要义可以很大程度上通过这些细节传达出来。见"氛围"。

Imagination 想象力　各类虚构文学作品创作中展现出来的创造力——充分的描写，有冲击力的暗喻和明喻，活灵活现的人物，真实可信的剧情和叙述。应该区分"想象的"和"有想象力的"这两个形容词。前者强调"虚构的"性质。后者指成功的文学创作者的成果。尽管这些创作者并不是对真实的事件进行逐字逐句的报道，但是他们的作品里却都具备其自身的真实性。小说作者们试图展现人生的真意，本书就是他们想象力的成果（有时也不乏失败）的集中展现。

(ideas, images, characters, setting, and the like) to give a single effect. It may be said that a story is successful—that it has achieved form—when all of the elements are functionally related to each other, when each part contributes to the intended effect. Form is not to be thought of merely as a sort of container for the story; it is, rather, the total principle of organization and affects every aspect of the composition. STRUCTURE and STYLE are also used to indicate the author's arrangement of his materials to give his effect. *Structure*, however, is usually used with more special reference to the ordering of the larger elements such as episodes, scenes, and details of action, in contrast to the arrangement of words, for which the term *style* is ordinarily employed. In the fullest sense, both the terms become synonymous with form, but in this book *style* is used merely to refer to the selection and ordering of language.

FUNCTTONAL　Having to do with the development of the total effect of a piece of fiction. The term is used in this book to denote those elements of a story which actually play a part in building up the complex and rich unity of a story in contrast to those used merely because they are fashionable, or feed some external interest, or are merely sensational or decorative or engaging.

IMACERY　The representation of any sense experience. Imagery does not consist merely of "mental pictures," but may make an appeal to any of the senses. In keeping with its insistence upon the concrete and the particular, all literature, including fiction, makes much use of imagery, not only in obvious descriptive fashion but also in figurative language. The most common forms of figurative language are SIMILES and METAPHORS. A *simile* is a direct comparison between two things, and such a comparison is introduced by *like* or *as*. A *metaphor* does not announce the comparison and proceeds indirectly to indicate an identification of the two items involved. Although such details of style may seem trivial in fiction, their effects are subtle and important. Sometimes the fundamental attitude of an author (see **TONE**), and hence the fundamental meaning of a piece of fiction, may be largely conveyed in terms of such details. See also **ATMOSPHERE**.

IMAGINATION　The creative power that manifests itself in the making of literary fictions of all kinds—rich descriptions, striking metaphors and similes, life-like characters, and credible dramas and narratives. One must distinguish between the adjectives *imaginary* and *imaginative*. The former stresses the quality of *unreality*. The latter refers to the accomplishment of the great literary artist. His fictions possess their own kind of truth in spite of the fact that they make no claim to give a verbatim report of actual events. This whole textbook is devoted to the accomplishments (and occasional failures) of the fiction writer's imagination as he at tempts to present the truth about human life.

Inevitability 必然性　所呈现的结果是之前给予的情境下唯一可能发生的结果。如果按照现实标准评判，小说中的必然性并不能严格保证是绝对的。人们生活中的偶然事件或者那些表现为偶然事件的情况太多了，所以不可能存在这里严格定义的必然性。这个词只是用来指对情节或者人物发展按照最符合逻辑的方向进行处理。

Ironical 反衬的　见"反衬"。

Irony 反衬　反衬通常是指一种反差，是预期情况和真实情况之间、表面情况和真实情况之间存在的差异。这种反差以多种形式出现。例如，一个演说者故意在说到某事物的时候不是指这个事物，而根据他的语调我们可以判断他的所指，那么他就是在使用反衬。克制叙述，对事情叙述产生的效果不如事情自身发展所能达到的效果。悖论，某事物看上去是不真实的，但是经过验证证明是真实的或者是部分真实的。这两种手法都属于反衬。除了这种叙述性反语，还有各类情境性反衬。情境性反衬指对某动作的预期结果或者看似合理的结果与真实结果之间存在的差异。在碰到反衬时，学生应该记住反衬在程度上有上千微妙的差别，比如明显的讽刺，因此，不能一成不变的看待。

Logic 逻辑性　小说中，人物和人物之间或者人物和背景之间的关系。见"必然性"。

Melodramatic 情节剧式的　纯粹表现暴力或者夸张的情节，与故事中人物的动机或者其他因素没有充分联系，这种效果被称为情节剧式的效果。但是应该指出纯粹的暴力并不能构成情节剧情节。如果暴力是有逻辑性、有意义的，那就不属于情节剧式的表现手法了。

Metaphor 暗喻　见"意象"。

Motivation 动机　决定人物行为的目的或多个目的的组合，甚或无意识的冲动。

INEVITABILITY　The sense that the result presented is the only possible result of the situation previously given. It cannot be strictly maintained that inevitability in fiction is absolute, if one is to judge by realistic standards. The element of chance, or what appears as chance, in human affairs is too great to admit of such an interpretation. The term is simply used in most discussions to indicate a high degree of logic in the handling of the development of plot or character.

IRONICAL　See **IRONY**.

IRONY　Irony always involves contrast, a discrepancy between the expected and the actual, between the apparent and the real. Such contrast may appear in many forms. A speaker uses irony, for example, when he deliberately says something which he does not mean, but indicates by his tone what he does mean. UNDERSTATEMENT—the saying of less than what one feels the occasion would warrant—and PARADOX—the saying of something, which is apparently untrue but which on examination proves to be true, or partially true—both of these are forms of irony. In addition to such forms of IRONY OF STATEMENT, there are also various forms of IRONY OF SITUATION. The irony of situation involves a discrepancy between what we expect the outcome of an action to be, or what would seem to be the fitting outcome, and the actual outcome. In dealing with this term, the student should always remember that there are a thousand subtle shadings of irony, and must, therefore, not take it in too restricted a sense, for example, in the sense of obvious sarcasm.

LOGIC　In fiction, the relation that exists between character and character, or character and setting. See also **INEVITABILITY**.

MELODRAMATIC　An effect is said to be melodramatic when the violent or the sensational seems to be used for its own sake without adequate reference to the motivation of the characters or to other elements in the story. But the mere fact of violence, it should be pointed out, does not constitute melodrama. If the violence is logical and meaningful, it is not melodramatic.

METAPHOR　See **IMAGERY**.

MOTIVATION　The purpose, or mixture of purposes, or even the more or less unconscious impulses that determine the behavior of a character.

O

Objective 客观　从小说角度讲,客观和主观这两个词存在两种联系。首先与作者相关,其次与作品中的某个人物或若干人物相关。在第一种情况中,作者客观的处理意味着与所表现的素材的一种疏离的态度(见"距离感"、"戏剧性"、"比例")。另一方面,主观的处理指带有作者高度的个人感情色彩和信仰色彩。当然,主观性和客观性的分量多少通常是个程度的问题。既然所有的小说从根本上说都涉及作者的解读、感情、判断和其他因素,因此不存在严格意义上的客观叙述,但是我们可以从手法上对两者进行区分。对于小说中的一个人物或若干人物,倒是可以更加绝对地使用这两个词。如果没有对人物思想或感情的直接叙述,这种处理手法就是客观的;如果有对人物思想或感情的直接叙述,这种处理手法就是主观的。但是大部分小说都会混合使用这两种手法,一些事件是客观表现,一些人物是客观处理,而另外一些则是主观处理。

P

Pace 节奏　故事各个部分进展的速率,从概括描述到充分描写。

Parable 寓言故事　通常是一个十分简练的故事,用来表达一个显而易见的观点或者象征意义。这种手法与寓言体故事关系密切,但是寓言体故事是指更加成体系的复杂的故事结构。

Paradox 悖论　见"反衬"。

Pathos 感伤　怜悯的感觉。作者一定要自圆其说,让故事中的感伤情绪能够从所给出的情境当中合理的生发出来。如果感伤情绪没有合理的人物和情境基础,就会产生"多愁善感"的效果。要区分"感伤"和"悲剧性"这两种性质。在悲剧情境中,怜悯的感觉与斗争和冲突的效果相交织。对由弱者所受苦难的展现能够制造感伤效果。而要达到悲剧性效果,受难者必须有足够的力量与他的环境进行抗争。

Personification 拟人　给物体或思想赋予人的特性。

O

OBJECTIVE　In relation to fiction, the pair of terms OBJECTIVE and SUBJECTIVE, is used in two connections. In the first, they are used with reference to the author, and in the second they are used with reference to a character, or characters, in the work of fiction. In the first connection, an *objective* treatment by the author implies an attitude of detachment toward the material which is being presented, a refusal to comment and interpret directly. (See DISTANCE, DRAMATIC, and SCALE.) A *subjective* treatment, on the other hand, is one which is highly colored by the author's own feelings and beliefs. Of course, the amount of subjectivity or objectivity is always a matter of degree. Since all fiction involves, ultimately, the author's interpretations, feelings, judgments, and the like, there is strictly speaking no absolutely objective presentation, but we can say that, in terms of method the distinction can be made. In reference to the character, or characters, in a work of fiction, the terms can be applied more absolutely. When there is no direct presentation of the thoughts or feelings of a character, the treatment is said to be objective; when such presentation is made the treatment is said to be subjective. But most pieces of fiction tend to mix the two methods, some events being rendered objectively, some characters being treated objectively, and some subjectively.

P

PACE　The rate of speed with which the various parts of the story are made to move, ranging from summary to fully reported scene.

PARABLE　A story, usually simple, which makes an obvious point or has a rather obvious symbolic meaning. The method of parable is closely related to that of ALLEGORY, but the tendency is to use the term *allegory* to indicate a more systematic and complicated structure of equivalents.

PARADOX　See IRONY.

PATHOS　The sense of pity. The author, however, must be on his guard to make sure that the pathos in a story emerges legitimately from the situation given. When there is no reasonable basis in character and situation for the pathos, one has an effect of SENTIMENTALITY. The quality of being *pathetic* is to be distinguished from that of being *tragic*. In a tragic situation the sense of pity is complicated by an effect of struggle and conflict. The pathetic effect may be given by the spectacle of a weak person suffering; the tragic effect requires that the sufferer have strength enough to struggle vigorously against his situation.

PERSONIFICATION　The attribution of the qualities of a person to an inanimate object or idea.

Plot 情节 小说或戏剧中展现的有组织的动作。情节,作为情节模式来讲,是故事整体构思的一个方面。

Point of view 视角 广义上讲,这个词指作者的基本态度和思想,例如,一个人可以用疏离的视角叙述,用同情的视角叙述,或者用基督教的视角叙述。狭义上讲,这个词指表现故事素材的故事讲述者或者思想。故事可以用第一人称或者第三人称叙述,讲述者可以只是旁观者或者更多参与进故事里的人。见"叙事焦点"。

Propaganda 布道 布道文学是指抽象地陈述其主题,不惜牺牲其他元素,坚持传达其"教义"的文学作品。通常这种文学作品过分简化其素材以达到强调特定观点的效果。

PLOT   The structure of action *as presented* in fiction or drama. Plot, as PLOT PATTERN, is one aspect of the total design of a story.

POINT OF VIEW   This term is loosely used to refer to the author's basic attitudes and ideas; for example, one may speak of a detached point of view, a sympathetic point of view, a Christian point of view. More strictly, the term is used to refer to the teller of the story—to the mind through which the material of the story is presented. The story may be told in the first or in the third person, and the teller may be the mere observer or much more than that. See also FOCUS OF *NARRATION*.

PROPAGANDA   Propaganda literature is literature which tends to state its theme abstractly and tends to insist upon its "message" at the expense of other elements. Usually it can be said that such literature oversimplifies its material in order to emphasize a particular interpretation.

R

Realism 现实主义 见"现实"。

Realistic 现实 具有强烈的事实和真实感。在这里这个词指对于普通的、易于观察的细节的表现,给人以忠实于现实经验的印象。现实与传奇相对,传奇含有遥远的、异国情调的、夸张的意思(本书不会对"现实"和"经典"之间的区分加以定义)。

Rhythm 韵律 反复出现的节拍或重音。诗歌多数是以韵文的形式创作的,尽管散文的韵律不像诗歌的韵律那么明显,散文的韵律还是很重要的,而且确实很有表现力。

REALLSM   See REALISTIC.

REALISTIC   Having a strong sense of fact or actuality. The term is used in this text to refer to the presentation of ordinary, easily observable details which give an impression of fidelity to experience. *Realistic* is to be contrasted with ROMANTIC, which implies the remote, the exotic, the exaggerated. (There is no attempt in this book to go into the distinction between *romantic* and *classic*.)

RHYTHM   Movement with a recurrent beat or stress. Though prose rhythms are not so marked as those in poetry, most of which is written in *verse*, the rhythms in a piece of prose are frequently important and may indeed be highly expressive.

S

Scale 比例 对故事各部分处理的相对分量。

Selection 选材 小说创作都要经过对众多事件、形象、色调等因素的选择过程。作者对结构原则和细节的选择取决于他想展现的主题,取决于他想探索的人类困境的方方面面。见"形式"和"风格"。

Selectivity 选择性 见"选材"。

Sentimentality 感伤情调 对某事件产生过多的情感反应,这种情感反应不是故事中预期产生的。

Setting 背景 故事的物质背景,地点要素。

Simile 明喻 见"意象"。

Stock response 习惯反应 读者对文学作品中某个词、短语、情境、人物或主体的自动的、习惯性的、没有疑义的反应。见"套话"。

SCALE   The relative amount of detail of treatment allowed to the various parts in a story.

SELECTION   The creation of a piece of fiction involves a constant process of selection from a multitude of possible events, images, tonalities, etc. The writer's choice of principles of structure and matters of detail will obviously depend upon what theme he is concerned to dramatize and on what aspects of the human predicament he wishes to explore. See also FORM and STYLE.

SELECTIVITY   See SELECTION.

SENTIMENTALITY   Emotional response in excess of the occasion; emotional response that has not been prepared for in the story in question. See also TONE.

SETTINC   The physical background, the element of place, in a story.

SIMILE   See IMACERY.

STOCK RESPONSE   The automatic or conventional or generally uncritical response of a reader to some word, phrase, situation, character, or subject in literature. See also CLICHÉ.

Structure 结构　见"形式"。

Style 风格　见"形式"。

Subjective 主观　见"客观"。

Surprise ending 意外结局　故事的结局给读者带来震撼之感(区分"合理意外结局"和"不合理意外结局")。见"巧合"。

Symbol 象征符号　物体、人物或事件用来代表或暗示其他的物体、人物或事件,这些就是象征符号。不过我们要区分两种象征符号。皇冠和十字或旗帜一样,都是约定俗成的象征符号。也就是说人们认同十字象征基督教,带有特定图案的旗帜象征美国,金质的环形饰物象征皇权。这种约定俗成的象征符号在文学作品中的使用和它们在我们日常话语中的使用是一样的。但是我们读诗或小说时特有的象征就不是约定俗成的了,它们是特定的,与具体的上下文相关。因此,《国王迷》中德雷沃特的金皇冠最终象征的是更令人钦佩的更具真正帝王气质的东西,而不仅仅是他统治卡菲里斯坦(Kafiristan)部落的权力。而《项链》中,故事结尾闪亮的项链所具有的意义已不仅仅是一件首饰了,它已经成为人类虚荣心的象征符号,人们愿意为了这种虚荣心牺牲生命。在文学作品中,物体和事件常常会带有象征意义,拥有更多的意义,表达作者的意图。小说总是会进行具体、戏剧性的叙述,在某种层面上讲,作者必须利用一些象征符号,因为他不可能"直陈"他的意图,只能利用一些具体的细节来表现。

T

Theme 主题　故事或小说的主旨或意图。

Tone 语调　语调是小说中反映出来的作者对素材和读者的态度(与"氛围"区分开)。见"感伤情调"。

Tragedy 悲剧　见"感伤"。

U

Understatement 克制叙述　见"反衬"。

Unity 统一性　整体或统一的感觉。

STRUCTURE　See **FORM**.

STYLE　See **FORM**.

SUBJECTIVE　See **OBJECTIVE**.

SURPRISE ENDINC　An ending in a story that comes with some sense of shock to the reader. (For the grounds for distinguishing between legitimate and illegitimate surprise endings.) See also **COINCIDENCE**.

SYMBOL　An object, character, or incident that stands for something else, or suggests something else, is a *symbol* of that thing. But we need to distinguish between two kinds of symbols. The crown, like the cross or flag, is a *conventional* symbol. That is, men *have agreed* that the figure of the cross should stand for Christianity, that a flag of a certain design should stand for the United States of America, or that a circlet of gold should stand for the authority of kingship. Such conventional symbols occur in literature just as they occur in our daily speech, but the symbolism with which we are characteristically concerned as we read poems and stories is not conventional. It is special, and it is related to a particular context. Thus, in"The Man Who Would be King", Dravot's crown of gold comes in the end to stand for something more admirable and more truly kingly than his power over the barbarous tribesmen of Kafiristan. Or consider"The Necklace". The sparkling circlet has, at the end of the story, become in meaning more than just another piece of jewelry. It has become a symbol of the vanity for which human beings may sacrifice their lives. In literature, objects and events often become symbolic, possessing a wider significance and thus becoming expressive of the author's meaning. Since fiction is concrete and dramatic in its presentation, the author must necessarily make use of symbols at some level, for he does not "state" his meanings abstractly but renders them through the presentation of concrete particulars.

T

THEME　The"point"or"meaning"of a story or novel.

TONE　The tone is the reflection in the story of the author's attitude toward his material and toward his audience. (It is to be distinguished from ATMOSPHERE, which see.) See also **SENTIMENTALITY**.

TRAGEDY　See **PATHOS**.

U

UNDERSTATEMENT　See **IRONY**.

UNITY　The sense of wholeness or oneness.

出版后记

什么是小说？什么是成功的小说？什么是成功小说的真谛？这些就是《小说鉴赏》要给读者解答的问题。

本书是新批评派"细读"（close reading）式批评和理论阐述的名著，与《诗歌鉴赏》共同推动了新批评的观念和批评方法在美国大学里的普及，对文学教学与批评实践影响深远。新批评（New Criticism）是在20世纪20年代开始出现、三四十年代蓬勃发展、四五十年代在美国文坛和大学占据霸主地位、50年代末开始衰败的一个批评流派，其批评特色是以作品为中心，以作品细读为基本方法，以维护作品的独立的审美价值为原点。

新批评提倡细读式的文本分析，把对文学作品本体的研究当作文学研究的主要任务，认为文学研究可以不考虑文学自身之外的其他一切因素，而应通过语言分析、通过细读法去寻绎作品的本意。它摒弃了前人观点的不足，将文学看成是一个以文本为中心的独立自足的世界，为推进文学本质研究起到了重要作用，摆脱了过去着重探讨作家思想、背景以及作品思想、历史、社会政治意义的传统批评方式。他们认为，一部真正好的文学作品应具有连贯性和完整性的语言结构，其各个组成部分是相互作用，有机统一的。"有机论"的观点使新批评家拒绝了对作品做"形式"和"内容"这样传统的二分法。在他们看来，所谓"形式"正是作品的生命所在，形式就是意味，形式和内容是不可分的。与"有机论"紧密相连的，是新批评对文学作品"真实性"、"合理性"的要求。从这样的文学观念出发，新批评家们对作品展开了"细读"，考察词语的细微差别、修辞手段以及意义的微小差异，追踪这些不同的成分如何相互作用以实现作品的意图。新批评的"细读法"常常能够帮助读者即使在对作者所知甚少的情况下，也能成功地解读其作品（哪怕是晦涩难解的作品），发掘其深刻的内涵。

本书在美国与世界其他地方是一本供大学教学使用的文学教科书，其特殊之处在于，所选小说是按照理论研究的概念或范畴来分类的。全书共七个章节，每个章节摘选若干篇小说，前五章的每篇小说后还附有讨论和思考题，具体分析每章的论题在这篇小说里是怎样体现的，有何特色或者不足，并对读者提出若干问题以引发读者的思考。于是，抽象、枯燥的理论概念便通过小说的具体叙述，化为容易理解的感性对象了。第六章则在每一篇小说之后接有该作家关于那篇小说的创作过程和体会的文章。第七章的12篇小说则是供读者自己独立阅读思考用的。全书所收录的51篇短篇小说，题材广泛，风格多样，都是名家的短篇小说佳作，很有代表性。因此，在阅读过小说以及文后的讨论之后，读者不仅能够领略小说创作的真谛，学会鉴别好小说的原则，而且更能够品尝到英美著名作家的作品风采。

其实在中国很多读者早就听过本书的大名，国内的一些大学已经将本书列为教材或者教学参考读物。1986年，由海外著名女作家、耶鲁大学教授聂华苓推荐，中国青年出版社出版了中文译本，受到读者的热烈欢迎。但因为时隔已久，致使读者难觅踪迹。外研社于2004出版过本书的英文影印版，但对于普通读者来说，还是有很多障碍与不便。

这次我们的新版是在《小说鉴赏》英文版第3版基础上采用中英文对照出版的形式，中文译文则采用1986年版主万等人翻译的中文译本，这个中文译本多为名家译作，读者可以从本书前面的译者简介看出。在新版当中，我们邀请曹文轩和李文俊先生对译文进行了审阅并作序，对中文译本进行了重新修订，让译文更为精准。翻译家李文俊先生在译者序言中说："即使光从学习英语的角度来说，这些作品可以说都是值得细读的范文。作者们（包括英译者们）的语言都是既准确而又优美的。所附的中译文，据我判断，我自己译的姑且不论，也都译得严谨而又相当流畅。我相信，原来就有一定英语水平的朋友，在参照中译读过这部集子后，再阅读一般的英语小说原著，应该不会有太大的问题。"中英文双语设计，既可以让专业读者看到作品的英文原貌，也方便普通的英美文学爱好者阅读这些小说精品，更能够让读者在阅读小说的过程中提高英文水平。

另外在新版中，我们在每篇小说之前加入了对小说作者的简短介绍，对每位作家的生平、代表作品及其写作特色加以概括性的介绍，方便读者对作家有更清晰的了解，而且也为读者进一步阅读作者的其他作品起到引介作用。此部分由吴兴培编写，马昕校订。并由马昕译出了1986年版未译的术语表，这里叫"重要词汇"，对一些常用的小说术语做了清楚的解释，便于读者的查找和理解。精选世界版画名作并配文为每一章做了辑封，以便于读者对各章节的主题有形象而清晰的认识。

希望我们在这些细节上所下的功夫，能有助于读者朋友们更好地理解和阅读；也希望这个中英双语版本能够让读者在欣赏名家名作的同时，更加了解小说，更加接近成功小说的真谛。

另外，我们希望凡是我们未联系上的译者或译者的著作权继承人见到本书后能主动跟我们联系，以便奉上稿酬；同时请你们谅解我们未能与你们取得联系，虽然我们努力过。

此次增订版较之前的版本，又有新的变化。在此次增订版中，除了小说正文部分的中英对照以外，我们还为书前的原序，每一章开头的前言，前五章每一篇小说之后的讨论和思考题，以及最后的重要词汇表添加了对应的英文原文。这一版成为了真正意义上的中英文对照版。我们希望新添加的内容能让各位读者更全面地领略这本国外优秀文学教科书的风貌，也能为各个层次的英美文学爱好者提供更多阅读和研习的空间。

欢迎采用本书做教材的老师与我们或培生教育出版集团北京办事处联系，以便得到我们为您提供的教学资料和相关服务。

服务热线：133-6631-2326 188-1142-1266
读者服务：reader@hinabook.com

后浪出版公司
2019年8月

图书在版编目（CIP）数据

小说鉴赏：双语修订第 3 版 /（美）布鲁克斯
(C. Brooks)，（美）沃伦 (R. P. Warren) 编著；主万
等译 . -- 成都：四川人民出版社，2019.9（2021.1 重印）
ISBN 978-7-220-11549-3

Ⅰ . ①小… Ⅱ . ①布… ②沃… ③主… Ⅲ . ①短篇小
说—文学欣赏—美国—现代 Ⅳ . ① I712.074

中国版本图书馆 CIP 数据核字 (2019) 第 233408 号

四川省版权局
著作权合同登记号
图字：21-2019-594

XIAOSHUOJIANSHANG
小说鉴赏

著　　者	［美］克林斯·布鲁克斯　罗伯特·潘·沃伦
译　　者	主　万　冯亦代　草　婴　丰子恺　汝　龙　等
选题策划	后浪出版公司
出版统筹	吴兴元
编辑统筹	朱　岳　梅天明
特约编辑	王华伟　杨　宁　周　格　赵　波
责任编辑	熊　韵
装帧制造	墨白空间·黄　海
营销推广	ONEBOOK
出版发行	四川人民出版社（成都槐树街 2 号）
网　　址	http://www.scpph.com
E - mail	scrmcbs@sina.com
印　　刷	北京盛通印刷股份有限公司
成品尺寸	190mm×260mm
印　　张	45.5　插页 4
字　　数	1317 千
版　　次	2019 年 12 月第 1 版
印　　次	2021 年 1 月第 2 次
书　　号	978-7-220-11549-3
定　　价	128.00 元

.